MAEVE
BINCHY

MAEVE BINCHY

Firefly Summer

Echoes

Published in 1994 by Index
by arrangements with Cresset Editions
an imprint of the Random House Group
20 Vauxhall Bridge Road
London SW1V 2SA

ISBN 1 8759 8021 0

Jacket illustration by John Paul Tibbles

Typeset in 9.5 on 10.5 pt Baskerville by
Pure Tech Corporation, Pondicherry, India
Printed and bound by
Griffin Paperbacks, Australia

CONTENTS

FIREFLY SUMMER

ECHOES

Firefly Summer

I want to thank all my friends for their support and encouragement, particularly Rosie Cheetham and Chris Green.
And to Gordon Snell, who has made my life so good and so happy, I would like to dedicate Firefly Summer *with all my gratitude and all my love.*
London and Dublin: Summer 1987

Part One

CHAPTER ONE

The sun came in at a slant and hit all the rings and marks on the bar counter. Kate Ryan managed to take a cloth to them at the same time as she was kicking off her house shoes and pulling on her wellington boots. She tucked her handbag under the counter and in almost the same movement opened the kitchen door to make sure that Eddie and Declan weren't torturing the new girl. The new girl had red eyes and a sad face and was missing her farm home. She might run back to it if Eddie and Declan were at their worst. But mercifully the appeal of the tortoise was still very strong even after three weeks. They lay on their stomachs and fed it stalks of cabbage, screaming with delight when it accepted them.

'John,' she shouted, 'will you come down to the bar, I have to go across the river and see what's keeping the twins. They have to be polished and smartened up for the concert and there isn't a sign of them.'

John Ryan groaned. His train of thought was gone again. He had thought he would manage an hour or two on his own, struggling with his poetry. 'Give me a minute,' he called, hoping to catch the idea before it was gone.

'No, they'll be late as it is. Listen, bring your paper and pencil down, there's likely to be no one in, but there has to be someone behind the counter.'

The door banged behind her and John Ryan saw, through the bedroom window, his wife run across the small footbridge opposite the pub. She climbed over the gate like a girl instead of a woman in her thirties. She looked altogether like a girl in her summer dress and her boots as she ran lightly across to the ruined house, Fernscourt, to find the twins.

He sighed and went down to the pub. He knew there were poet publicans, he knew there were men who wrote the poetry of angels in the middle of the stinking trenches of war. But he wasn't like that.

John Ryan moved slowly, a big man with a beer belly that had grown on him sneakily during the years standing behind a bar, jowls that had become flabby at the same trade. His wedding picture showed a different person, a thinner more eager-looking figure, yet the boyish looks hadn't completely gone. He had a head of sandy brown hair only flecked with grey and big eyebrows that never managed to look ferocious even when he willed them to, like at closing time or when he was trying to deal with some outrage that the children were reported to have committed.

Kate had hardly changed at all since their wedding day, he often said, which pleased her, but she said it was just a bit of old plamas to get out of having to stand at the bar. It was true, though; he looked at the girl with the long, curly dark hair tied back in a cream ribbon that matched her cream dress and coat. She looked very smart on that wet day in Dublin, he could hardly believe she was going to come and live with him in Mountfern. Kate hadn't developed a pot belly from serving drinks to others, as she often told him sharply. She said that there was no law saying you must have a drink with everyone who offered you one or pull a half pint for yourself to correspond with every half-dozen pints you pulled for others.

3

But then it was different for women.

John was the youngest of the seven Ryan children and the indulged pet of a mother who had been amazed and delighted at his arrival when she had been sure that her family was complete. He had been overfed and given fizzy drinks with sweet cake as long as he could remember. As a lad the running and leaping and cycling miles to a dance had kept him trimmer. Now, between sessions of writing his poetry and serving in his bar, it was a sedentary life.

He didn't know if he wanted it for his sons; he had such hopes for them – that they might see the world a bit, study maybe and go on for the university. That had been beyond the dreams of his parents' generation. Their main concern had been to see their children well settled into emigration; the church had helped of course, educating two nuns and two priests out of the Ryan family. John didn't see any vocation amongst his own offspring. Michael was dreamy and thoughtful: maybe a hermit? Or Dara a resourceful Reverend Mother somewhere? Eddie was a practical child, possibly a missionary brother teaching pagan tribes to build huts and dig canals. Declan the baby. Maybe they could make a curate out of him near home where they could keep an eye on him.

This was all nonsense, of course. None of them would end up within an ass's roar of a religious life. Still, John Ryan never saw the future standing surrounded by three sons and possibly his daughter all in the trade.

There would never be enough business, for one thing. Like many Irish towns Mountfern had the appearance of having far too many pubs already. If you went down the main street, Bridge Street, there were no less than three public houses. Foley's at the top of the town, but that was hardly a pub at all these days, just a counter really and a few friends of old Matt Foley drinking at night, they'd hardly know how to serve a real customer. Then there was Conway's which was more a grocery but it had the bar at the back. Conway's had a clientele of secret drinkers, people who didn't admit to any kind of drinking, who were always going out for a packet of cornflakes or a pound of flour and would toss back a brandy for their health. Often too, it had a funeral business since old Barry Conway was the undertaker as well. It seemed only right to come back to his place to drink when someone had been buried up on the hill. And Dunne's was always on the verge of closing. Paddy Dunne never knew whether to reorder supplies, he always said that it would hardly be worth it since any day now he'd be going to join his brother who ran a pub in Liverpool. But then either there would be a downturn in the fortunes of the Liverpool pub or an upswing in the drinking patterns of Mountfern. There was an unsettled air about his place and constant speculation about how much he would get if he were to sell his licence.

John Ryan's pub had its rivals then, three of them in a small place like Mountfern. Yet he had all the business that came from the River Road side of the place. He had the farmers on this side of the town. It was a bigger and better bar than any of the other three, it had not only more space but it had more stock. And there were many who liked the walk out along the river bank.

John Ryan knew that he was a man who had been given a great deal by fate. Nobody had gathered *him* up to swoop him off to a religious order when he was a young impressionable boy. Neither had he been sponsored out to a life of hard graft in America like two of his elder brothers. By all their standards he had a life of ease and peace where he should well have been able to run his business and write his poetry.

But he was a man who did one thing at a time, almost overmethodically, too predictable sometimes for his wife who felt that people should be able to fire on several cylinders at the same time.

John wanted time to write or time to serve drink, he couldn't switch from one mode to another like lightning. Like Kate. He couldn't switch towards the children like she could as well. Either they were good or they weren't. He wasn't able to see the swift changes of mood like Kate was. He would not be cross and then smile minutes later. If he was cross he was very cross indeed. It was rare but it was all-embracing when it happened. One of Daddy's great angers was remembered long, whereas Mammy had a dozen quick and easily forgotten angers in a week.

John sighed again at his wife's swiftness and the annoyance at having to leave his work, his real work, just at that time. He knew that in this pub fate had handed him something that many a man in Ireland would envy mightily. It didn't bring in enough money for them to employ another pair of hands, but it wasn't so slack that a man could sit at the counter and write undisturbed. John Ryan hadn't brought his paper and pencils with him, any more than his thoughts. If customers saw you with paper and pencil they thought you were doing the accounts and making a small fortune. Anyway what would have been the point? There was Jack Coyne from the garage who had just sold a heap of rusty metal to some unsuspecting farmer and they were in to seal the bargain with a pint.

Jack Coyne had a face like a ferret and two sharp eyes looking round him for a bargain or a business deal. He was a small wiry man equally at home underneath a car, covered in grease and shouting out about the extent of the repairs, or in a suit showing off his newly acquired vehicles which was what he called his second-hand stock. Everything about him seemed to be moving, he never stood still, even now at the bar he was shifting, moving from foot to foot.

'Great day, John,' said Jack Coyne.

'It's been a great day all the time,' said John, preparing to pull the pints.

'Bad for the crops,' the farmer said.

'When were you lot ever pleased with the weather?' Jack Coyne laughed, the happy sound of a man who could sell second-hand cars no matter what the weather did.

The children of Mountfern had a place to play like no other children in the land. It was Fernscourt, the ruined house on the bank of the River Fern. It had been burned down one day forty years ago in 1922 during the Troubles. The Fern family had not been there on the day of the fire, they had been gone for many months before.

The children often asked their grandfathers about the fire but found a strange lapse of memory. The passions that had run so high in those years had settled down as time went by. The Ferns and all they symbolized had been forgotten. Their house stood as a beautiful ruin, where once it had stood as a beautiful big empty shell anyway. Now as a place to spend the long summer days it was quite simply perfect.

5

The orchards that the Ferns had asked their gardeners to plant all those years ago still grew wild and plentiful. The apple trees didn't know that the Ferns had gone. Their old gnarled branches bent to the ground, sometimes making even more places for the children to play.

There was thick trailing ivy everywhere over the walls that remained of the house. The outhouses which had once been the stableyard had survived better than the main house. Here there were still rooms with roofs to run through, here there were limestone arches and well-made stone walls. In the days when Fernscourt had been built people saw the stables as being very important; guests would expect them to be of the same high standard as the rest of the house.

As Kate Ryan marched through the laurels that grew wild now on each side of the path up from the river she could hear the cries and the laughter. She thought back on her own childhood in a small silent house in Dublin, her mother always an invalid. She had not had brothers and sisters to play with; friends were frowned on and kept well away from the home.

These children had a wild, free life by comparison.

Fernscourt belonged to the group that were here today. Those who were the right age for it. It had always been like that. You were too young if you were Eddie and Declan's age, you were hunted away and sent about your business, which was anywhere but here. Then the older boys and girls went to the bridge and showed off to each other. Where boys dived from the ledge to oohs and ahhs, where girls were sometimes pushed in horseplay and had to climb up the bank with wet dresses clinging.

But if you were in Fernscourt, no other world existed. It had been a fine summer and as soon as any work that had to be done in the various homes in Mountfern was finished they gathered, coming in dribs and drabs across the fields, up the River Road and across the footbridge in front of Ryan's, or some of them braving the brambles and briars on the towpath at the other side of the river, a disused way that saw no traffic these days.

Fernscourt belonged to all the children but it was Dara and Michael's special home. The twins had their own place, a pretend-house. They played there even when none of the others came up to join them. They had an old table and two broken stools from the bar. There was cutlery too, a twisted fork and a rusty knife, and some chipped plates. These were for private feasts. Ever since they had been old enough to go across to Fernscourt alone the twins had said that this is where they would live when they were grown up.

It would be nice and near home, they said reassuringly, but it would be theirs. They would buy the whole place and have a boat and go everywhere by river instead of by road.

It would be their palace, their castle, their home.

It was because they lived so close to the place, because they could see it from their windows over the pub, and they could go there every day winter and summer, that they felt it was their own.

But of course they didn't want to own it exclusively. Fernscourt was also for everyone, particularly during the long summer holidays when no day was long enough for the games they all played there.

There was no form to the games, but the huge mossy stones, the crumbling walls, the great fronts of ivy hanging down like curtains, and the window and doorway gaps in half-standing walls meant there were plenty of places to climb, to perch, to jump, to sit and giggle.

The girls had made a makeshift home in the old clock tower which still stood in the stableyard, though the clock and dome were long gone. The boys would use the long shallow steps that were now almost indistinguishable as steps, so overgrown with weeds and moss had they become, and arrange a jumping competition that was a cross between a longjump and a chicken run. They would all gather to see who could jump down the greatest number of steps; it was the sissy who would opt out of the jump that seemed likely to break a limb.

Yet they had ways out of being a softy. It was always time to go home or to milk the cows or to go for a swim. The boys of Mountfern had no death wish as they played in their own magnificent ruined house.

Kate saw that some of the children were already heading for home where they would be ill-received because of the need to smarten up for the concert. She saw Tommy Leonard racing down to the towpath – it would be a bit quicker that way for him. Leonard's paper shop was near the big bridge, he would do the distance faster than by crossing over to the River Road where there was a proper surface to walk on. At Tommy's age children didn't mind having half their clothes and even bits of their arms torn and scratched by the thorny branches, Kate thought in wonder. Little Maggie Daly, who was Dara's great friend, was heading towards the laurels and Kate.

'Just running, Mrs Ryan,' Maggie said, knowing well that the twins' mother was not coming to pay a social call. 'I think Dara and Michael are just finishing up now.'

'I'm sure they are.' Kate was grim. Maggie Daly had big anxious eyes, she always looked startled by the most ordinary things. She was terrified of Leopold, the pub's big harmless dog. When poor Leopold stretched his misshapen body in the sun, little Maggie Daly would look at him fearfully as if he were about to go for her throat.

And Maggie's older sister Kitty, who was nearly grown up enough for the crowd on the bridge, was sauntering down the laurel path too. Kitty was too mature to scuttle, she was being bored this summer, bored by Fernscourt and the games they played, bored by having to go home and dress up for the concert. Bored by being neither one thing nor the other. Neither a real person of fifteen who could have a smart red bathing costume and be able to sit on the raft having a crowd laughing and admiring; too old to find fun every day climbing up to an old room in a ruined clock tower, or squeezing through the chinks in the mossy walls. Kitty Daly sighed heavily as she passed Kate Ryan.

'I suppose you're coming to beat their heads in,' she said as if this was the usual practice of elderly parents when they arrived in Fernscourt.

'Not at all,' Kate said brightly, 'I came to wonder was there anything they'd like, afternoon tea on a tray maybe, I'd be delighted to . . . my beloved twins . . .'

Kitty moved on hastily.

Dara and Michael had taken after their mother. No sandy brows like John Ryan – those only seemed to come out in Eddie. They were thin and wiry too, but of

7

course their father had been as a boy. But Kate realized that in their strong dark good looks they didn't have the Ryan laugh lines either, the face that always seemed to smile even when nobody was watching. All the Ryans looked like that – even the disapproving old mother-in-law who hadn't thought Kate a suitable wife for her favourite son, she had had a face that seemed to smile. Dara and Michael often looked solemn, their eyes big, dark and too concentrated. Like her own. Whenever Kate saw a photograph of herself she would scream and say she looked like the hag of Bearra or an avenging angel. She always seemed to be burning with intensity rather than smiling at the camera.

Nobody else noticed it at all.

And everyone always said the twins were a handsome pair, particularly in the summertime when, tanned and eager in their shorts and coloured shirts, they roamed the countryside far and wide and explored every corner of Mountfern and its environs.

Kate wondered briskly how they would accept the blame today. They should have been home a good half hour ago to get smartened up for the school concert. She was annoyed but she would try not to show it, otherwise they would be mutinous about the washing and brushing and maybe less sure in their party pieces. Dara had a poem in Irish to recite and Michael with the boys from the brothers would be singing Moore's melodies.

Young Miss Lynch up at the school had been so enthusiastic and given so much of her free time to organizing it that everyone in Mountfern had been drawn into the whole thing unwillingly. Normally the convent and the brothers had few joint undertakings but old Canon Moran thought it seemed a much better notion to have one concert rather than two, and everyone agreed with them so Nora Lynch had won the day; it was being held in the church hall and all participants had to be there in their finery at five o'clock. The concert began at six o'clock sharp and promised to be finished by eight.

Kate was nearly at the house now. In the old days it must have been an impressive place: three storeys tall but with high, high ceilings, big rooms and tall windows. The Fern family who had lived here, different generations of them for over a century, surely loved this home. Kate wondered if any of them had ever paused in their gracious way of life to imagine that one day it would be a ruin played in by all the children of the village who would never have got inside the walls except to carry scuttles of coal or great jugs of water in the old days.

The children had all scattered. Only her own two were inside. What could they be doing that made them stay when all the others had gone? A wave of annoyance came over Kate at their disregard for any kind of order in life. She pushed through the hanging wall of ivy and saw them: sitting on a great fallen pillar and looking ahead of them through the gaps in the wall.

They looked at something in the distance with a caution that was more like fear than anything else.

Below them two men with instruments mounted on tripods peered and wrote notes in their pads. Then they would replace the tripods and start again.

Kate came up behind the twins.

'What are they?' Michael asked in a whisper.

'They're called theodolites,' Kate said. 'I know that word, it's always very useful in crosswords.'

'What do they do?' Dara wanted to know.

'It's a sort of survey, you know, getting levels. I'm not totally sure, to be honest.'

'They shouldn't be here, the theodalists,' Michael said, face red with upset. 'Tell them it's private land. Go on Mam, tell them to go away.'

'No, the things are called theodolites, not the people. The men are surveyors, I suppose. Anyway it isn't private land. If it was we couldn't be here.'

'Could you ask them . . . like will they be coming back again or is it only today that they're doing their photographing or whatever. You could ask them, Mam,' Dara pleaded. 'You're good at asking people awkward things. Please.'

'I have one awkward thing to ask at the moment and it's this: why when I gave you my good alarm clock, and the strictest instructions to be back home at four o'clock, why is it half-past four and we're all here? That's the awkward question I'm asking today, and I want an answer to it.'

The twins seemed not to hear the rising impatience in her tone, they barely heeded her.

'We didn't really play at all, we've been wondering what . . .' Dara said.

'And hoping that they'd go away . . .' Michael finished for her. They often finished each other's sentences.

'And not understanding it one bit . . .'

'And not liking it one bit . . .'

Kate took them by the shoulders and marched them back for the alarm clock and their uneaten lunches, then headed for the footbridge. There seemed to be a commotion on the other side. Eddie and Declan were lying on the edge of the water trying to reach something that was floating downstream on a piece of plywood.

Carrie, the new maid, was standing twisting her hands helplessly as the boys screamed, and Kate realized that Maurice the tortoise was heading off into the unknown.

'Get the garden rake, and the big sweeping brush,' she shouted. Michael and Dara raced across to find them, delighted to be released from the pinching grip and abuse. Eddie, who was eight, was scarlet with the knowledge that he would get the blame; Declan was only six and the baby – he got off with everything.

Kate manoeuvred the tortoise ashore and with a face like thunder brought it back to its original home in the turf room. Watched by the four children and the terrified Carrie, she dried the animal with a clean towel and put it in a bed of hay. With a voice that was going to take no argument she said that she would very much like to see Carrie at the kitchen sink washing the faces and hands of Eddie and Declan. She would like to see Michael and Dara in the bathroom and emerging in five minutes with necks, ears and knees all shining. She mentioned knees, ears and necks only because *particular* attention would be paid to those parts but the rest was to be spotless too. A great deal of heavy scrubbing took place, and after inspection Dara and Michael were allowed to head off towards the hall. An unusually silent Eddie and Declan sat waiting sentence from their mother. They didn't know whether they were going to be barred from the concert . . . which mightn't be a bad thing. Or if there might be a slapping of the legs administered. The slapping wasn't too likely; if it was coming at all it would have been done at the time.

They were unprepared for the severity of it.

'That is no longer your tortoise, Edward and Declan. That is now my tortoise. Do you understand?'

Things were bad when Eddie was called Edward.

'But do you mean . . .'

'Yes, he's mine now. And I can do what I like with him. I can bring him back to the pet shop where I so stupidly bought him, thinking you were the kind of children who could love a pet. Or I could eat him. I could ask Carrie to serve him for lunch tomorrow.'

They were aghast.

'Well, why not?' she continued airily. 'You tried to drown Maurice, why don't I try to roast him? It's a hard old life being a tortoise.'

Eddie's eyes filled with tears. 'Ma, we weren't trying to drown him. It was to see if he could swim, and when he didn't seem to be managing it too well we got him a raft, then it floated off.'

'Thank you, Edward. You are telling me it was just a careless accident, is that it?'

'Well, yes?' Eddie thought salvation lay this way but he wasn't totally sure.

'Right, well now that he's mine other careless accidents could happen. I could let him fall into the oven or something. Still, that is none of your business now. You are forbidden to go near him in the turf room or the rayburn or wherever else he happens to be.'

Declan let out a roar. 'Mammy, you wouldn't burn Maurice. Please don't burn my tortoise.'

'It's mine,' Kate said.

'You're not allowed to kill things,' Eddie raged. 'I'll tell the guards. I'll tell Sergeant Sheehan.'

'Certainly do, and I'll tell him about the drowning.'

There was a silence.

'Don't be stupid,' Kate said. 'I'm not going to hurt Maurice, but he *is* mine, you know, so you can't play with him any more. And no ice creams in Daly's tonight after the concert.'

It was bad but it was better than what might have been. They accepted it.

'Come on, Carrie,' Kate said, suddenly pitying the seventeen-year-old spending her first Saturday night away from home. 'Tidy up your hair a bit and we're off.'

'Am I to come with you?' Carrie's face lit up.

'Of course you are, did you think we'd leave you here on your own?' Kate had only just thought of it, looking at the stricken face of the girl as she had listened to the possible future of the tortoise.

'You're a real gentleman, Mam,' said Carrie and ran to put on a clean blouse and fix two new slides in her hair.

Canon Moran was small and fussy, a kind man with pale blue eyes that didn't see very far or very much. He believed that basically most people were very good. This made him a nice change from many other parish priests in the country who believed that most people were intrinsically evil. The word went round for young curates that Mountfern would be a great posting altogether. And the young priest Father Hogan knew he was indeed a lucky man. Once Canon Moran had a nice big chair for the concert and a little footstool because he sometimes got a cramp, then he would be happy. He would clap every item enthusiastically, he would praise all the brothers and the nuns by name, he would know that old Mr Slattery the solicitor had made a contribution so that they could have proper curtains instead of the desperate old screens they used to make do with before. The canon would thank him briefly because that was all the Slatterys would need, but he would dwell longer on the generosity of Daly's Dairy in providing the cakes for the tea at eight o'clock, and the excellence of the programmes printed free thanks to Leonard's the stationers. The canon began confessions on a Saturday at five, and he would make sure that they were all well completed in time for the concert. Father Hogan knew that Canon Moran believed a kind word of encouragement and a pious hope that things would be better soon helped a lot of his parishioners. And they felt sure, because of his pale dreamy blue eyes, that he was also somehow deaf and wouldn't recognize the voices that whispered their sins.

Father Hogan thought Mountfern was a warm, kind place to live, and though it didn't perhaps offer as much of a challenge as he had dreamed about in the seminary, he followed his canon's belief that there were souls to be saved everywhere, and that running a concert for the people of this place might have equal value in the great scheme of things to working in the missions or running a boys' club for delinquents in a tough city parish.

Miss Lynch was more or less walking out with young Mr Slattery so he had to come to the concert as moral support. He sat beside Kate Ryan and the two chastened small boys, and the girl with reddened eyes called Carrie.

'And how does the master of your house escape this great cultural event?' Fergus Slattery asked with envy.

'Someone has to run the bar. I know it looks as if half the county is here, but you'd be surprised how many men find the excuse for a drink when their children are up here on the stage,' Kate said.

'Well for him, then.' Fergus was genuinely admiring. 'I can't say that I have to work on a Saturday evening, they don't think solicitors work at all, but my office is too near. I'd actually have to be in the window in my shirt sleeves before they'd believe me.'

Fergus grinned boyishly. He was very like a tall gangly boy, Kate thought, though he must be in his mid or late twenties now. She had always thought of him as a kind of irrepressible student home for the holidays. Even though he ran his father's office almost entirely on his own now, it was hard for her to think of him as a grown-up. Maybe it was because he looked untidy; his hair was sort of jutting out at an angle no matter whether he had been to the barber or not. His shirts were perfectly and lovingly ironed by the Slatterys' faithful housekeeper, Miss Purcell, yet the collars sometimes stood at an angle away from his neck. Kate wouldn't be at all surprised if he bought the wrong size or had the button in the wrong place. He had dark eyes and if he had held himself differently and worn long smooth dark coats he might have been thought very handsome and elegant indeed.

11

But part of his charm was that he would never be elegant; he was totally unaware of his tall, dark and almost handsome looks, and that he had caused many a flutter and several specific hopes around Mountfern.

'You mean you wouldn't want to come – what with that Nora Lynch killing herself to impress you?' Kate was disbelieving.

'Impress *me*!'

'Of course. Why else would that young girl kill herself and show herself to be part of a small backwater like this unless it was to prove to you that she could fit in and be part of it?'

'But why would she prove that to me?'

'Aren't you and she going out?' Kate wondered about men a lot. They couldn't all be as dim as they often seemed.

'Yes, sure, we go out to the pictures and we go to a dance, but there's nothing in it.' Fergus looked baffled and honest.

'What do you mean there's nothing in it, aren't you a right beast to be leading her on and then tell me there's nothing in it? You know, the older I get the more I believe the nuns were right, men are basically wild animals at heart.'

'But there *is* nothing in it,' Fergus pleaded. 'I mean we don't love each other or anything, or have the same plans or the same hopes. Nothing's been said or agreed. Truly.'

'I believe you.' Kate was cynical. 'O Lord, protect me or mine from ever falling for a lawyer. You'll have yourself covered from every angle.'

'But she doesn't think . . .' Fergus began, but at that moment Nora Lynch, resplendent in a new hair-do from the Rosemarie salon, in a new yellow dress short enough to be fashionable but not so short as to cause adverse comment from the canon, the nuns and the brothers, appeared on stage. She said she hoped everyone would enjoy this show, the first combined effort; she thanked the canon, the brothers, the convent and the sponsors, the children and the parents, and knew that everyone would have a wonderful evening. She said that as an outsider she felt very privileged to be allowed to get involved in something as much a part of the community as this was. But then in many ways she felt that she had always been part of this place and always would.

'How old are you, Fergus Slattery?' Kate whispered suddenly.

'I'm twenty-seven,' he replied, confused.

'Twenty-seven years in the world and you try to tell me that young woman has no hopes of you. May God forgive you, I mean it Fergus, may he forgive you and send you some kind of sense.'

'Thanks, Kate,' said Fergus, not knowing whether he was being attacked or pitied, and not liking it whichever it was.

Dara Ryan felt as if she had swallowed an ice cream whole; her stomach was cold and heavy and she wondered if she might be sick.

'I'll never be able to say it,' she told Maggie Daly.

Maggie believed Dara could do anything. 'You're great, Dara, you never minded saying it at school in front of everyone there.'

'That's different.' Dara hopped around on one leg and looked through the door that they were meant to keep firmly closed, to see how big the audience was.

'Lord, it's full of people,' she said theatrically.

'They'll love it.' Maggie was loyal.

Dara would have fought with her shadow at this stage. 'No, they'll hate it, it's in Irish, they won't understand a word of it.'

'But it will *sound* terrific.'

'Why don't I just go and make sounds then, nice sounds, or better still take up a gong and just bang it for three minutes and bow to the applause?'

Maggie giggled. Things were all right once Dara started making up outlandish things.

Maggie was not doing any solo piece. She was in the girls' choir which would sing Gounod's 'Ave Maria', and later on come back and sing 'I think that I shall never see, a poem lovely as a tree'. But Dara would stand in front of the whole of Mountfern and recite 'Cill Cais' which Miss Lynch had told them was a lament for an old house, a ruin like Fernscourt, except that it had been a different kind of household who had lived there, an Old Catholic family who used to have mass said in the stately home and everyone would come from far and near to attend it.

'Dara, you're on.'

Crossing her fingers and giving Dara a squeeze for luck, Maggie Daly stood and watched her friend walk up on the stage.

Miss Lynch, knowing very well that hardly anyone would get even the vaguest glimmer of what the poem was about without some kind of translation, said that of course everyone knew the story of 'Cill Cais', and told it without appearing to. The audience, flattered to be thought of as people who would know this, nodded at each other sagely and waited for the young Ryan girl to tell it to them again in Irish. Dara's voice sounded confident and she fixed her eyes on the back of the hall as Miss Lynch had told her to do. There was a storm of clapping and people told each other that she made a very good fist of it, then she was off and it was time for the choir from the brothers'.

Brother Keane had chosen three of Moore's finest Irish melodies. He announced that the boys would sing them in the same magnificent spirit that Thomas Moore had brought to bear when he was writing them. Brother Keane had calculated without the enormously humorous content that the songs seemed to hold for his choir of twelve-year-olds, depleted as it was by six whose voices chose the time of the concert to break.

'Silent, O Moyle, be the roar of thy water,
Break not, ye breezes, your chain of repose.'

Brother Keane loved this above all other of Moore's melodies. He could see none of the allusions to breaking wind, pulling chains and passing water that the entire group in front of him seemed to see written in letters of fire on their song sheets. He glared at them ferociously as with the most enormous difficulty the forty boys tried to stifle their mirth, and led them into the next song called, unhappily, 'The Meeting of the Waters'. The entire choir seemed to choke with the daring double entendre of the name and Brother Keane resolved to deal with them very sternly in a less public place.

The admission price had included tea, sandwiches and cakes. The sandwiches had been supervised by Mrs Whelan who ran the Post Office and was generally accepted to be the nicest person in Mountfern. A small wiry woman with a skin that seemed to have been tanned by whatever sun shone intermittently in the Irish midlands or beaten by the winds that blew more regularly from one coast across to the other, Sheila Whelan had three cameo brooches she had bought from a tinker: a pink one, a green one and a beige. She wore them at the neck of her white blouses and had done for as long as anyone could remember. She owned about three skirts which she must have worn for ever and a series of soft knitted cardigans which she must have made herself. Usually she was knitting for someone else, for the new babies that were arriving with great regularity around Mountfern, or shawls for the old, even school jumpers for the children who might need them. She always managed to have an extra bit of wool which she said it would be a pity to waste. She had a kind, dreamy face and far-away pale blue eyes that were never known to concentrate inquisitively on anything that might not bear too much scrutiny.

She seemed to have no interest in the private lives of the rest of the parish: she never appeared to notice, let alone comment on the emigrants' remittances that came home or didn't come home; nor did she seem to notice the disability pensions for people who were perfectly well, or the dole for those who were obviously working. She was able to discuss the most direct questioning about the whereabouts of Mr Whelan with calm and even with interest, but without ever revealing that he had left her for a married woman in Dublin, and that the two of them now had four children. If anyone asked whether he was coming back, Mrs Whelan was always able to get into the same interrogative mood and say it was very hard to know, wasn't it? She found that some things were almost impossible to work out, weren't they? And somehow the questioner found himself or herself enmeshed in the Meaning of Life instead of the specific whereabouts of Mrs Whelan's husband.

She was the kind of woman you'd go to if you had committed a murder, Fergus Slattery had always said. And oddly, there was one killing near Mountfern. A farmer's son had attacked his father in a drunken fight and killed him. It was to the post office, not the presbytery or the Garda station that he had come, carrying the murder weapon, a pitchfork.

Mrs Whelan had involved the presbytery and the Garda station, but gently and in her own time. Nobody had thought it even remotely unusual that the demented man had come to Mrs Whelan nor had she made anything of the incident; she said she supposed he was on his way to the canon and her light had been on.

Nobody knew, either, that it was Mrs Whelan who had encouraged the sandwich makers to cut the crusts off and to do just one plate each. That way she was sure of getting what everyone had promised, though it meant much more work for her. Fergus knew, because Miss Purcell had been fussing about whether to have chicken paste or egg and mayonnaise in her offering and this had meant at least three calls to Mrs Whelan for discussion.

'You are the only sensible woman in this town, Mrs Whelan,' he began.

'What can I do for you, Fergus?' she asked simply.

'You mean I wouldn't say it unless I wanted something?'

'Not at all.' But she waited.

'Is my name up with Nora Lynch?' he asked.

'Why do you ask?' she said.

'Because Kate Ryan, a woman I like and respect, told me it was, and as true as the day is long I didn't mean it to be.'

'Well if there's any misunderstanding I'm sure you'll sort it out.'

'But *is* there any misunderstanding, Mrs Whelan? That's what I'm asking you. I don't want to go sorting things out if there's nothing to sort out.'

'Ah, nobody tells me anything, Fergus.'

'But I'm only asking you about *me*, not about other people.'

'As I said, I've not got an idea in the wide world, but I know if you think that there's some confusion you'd be the man to clear it up. One way or another.'

'By saying something out straight, you mean? Like "I don't want to marry you"?'

Mrs Whelan's eyes were shuttered. Open but closed at the same time. They told him he had gone too far in his revelations. That she expected a solicitor to be even more discreet than a postmistress.

'Other people go to you with their business, Fergus, you're as much in demand now as your father, and that's your job after all. If there's a need for the right words you'll find them.'

'You'd have been great as a prisoner of war, Mrs Whelan,' said Fergus. 'The secrets would have been safe with you all right.'

Fergus and Nora went for a drive after the concert. The last thank yous and congratulations had been said; people walked home in the sunny early summer evening. The older children had gone to sit on the bridge. The cinema had a special late start, so many of them headed to the pictures. Fergus had the car out ready and waiting. Nora Lynch came running over to join him.

Small and slightly plump, she had the perfect skin and apple cheeks of a picture poster. Her fair hair was curled carefully, and she wore a little lipstick but not enough to do any damage.

'I thought we might go up on the hill,' he said as Nora put on her white jacket with the little yellow trim which matched her dress so well.

'The hill?' She was surprised.

'It's a nice quiet place to talk, and I have something I want to say to you.'

Nora's eyes lit up with pleasure and her face was pink. 'I'd love that,' she said in a sort of husky way, not in her usual voice at all.

With a sickening lurch of his stomach Fergus realized that this pleasant, empty-headed, chirruping little teacher whom he had kissed a dozen times thought that he was about to propose marriage to her.

Slowly he started the car and headed for the hills.

CHAPTER TWO

Ryan's Licensed Premises, like any other pub in Ireland in 1962, had a steady clientele that would never desert it. There never seemed to be any need to do renovations to attract new trade. The trade was there, like it had been in John's father's time; the people who lived on that side of Mountfern found it handy to call in rather than walk all the way down to the centre. Ryan's had the great advantage, some thought, of being on the outskirts. The whole place didn't see you going in and coming out as they would if you visited Foley's, Conway's or Dunne's.

When John's father was alive the place still sold groceries but though the big old chest of tea drawers still stood there they held no stock now. There was a little huckster's shop run by Loretto Quinn, whose husband had been killed in a terrible accident. It wouldn't have been right for the Ryans to take the bread from her mouth even if they wanted to get back into the grocery business. And anyway most people liked going into Mountfern proper and walking along Bridge Street to see what was going on. Ryan's was a bit out of the way in terms of doing your weekly shopping.

John Ryan was glad that Kate agreed with him on this. For a Dublin woman she had adapted extraordinarily well to Mountfern; she knew better than he did all that went on, who was speaking and who not. It was Kate who helped the children with their homework, found and trained the girls from the country who would leave for brighter lights and noisier towns once they knew the way to run a house. Kate served behind the bar as if she had been born to do it. She knew when to join in the conversation and when to stay far from it.

She polished glasses and cleaned the big ashtrays with Gold Flake printed around the rim. She loved the words Whiskey Bonder on the sign over the door, even though it wasn't true any more. John's father, like many a publican, used to buy whiskey in a cask from the distiller, lodge it in a bonded warehouse and pay the excise duty when he took it from the warehouse for bottling and sale. In those days the name James Ryan was on the bottle, but nowadays distillers discouraged such fancy and old-fashioned notions. They preferred to sell whiskey already bottled. But Kate would still polish the sign lovingly, getting up on a ladder early in the morning with a soapy cloth, a wet cloth and a dry cloth.

She was the same behind the bar, she shone up the bar decorations as if they were precious ornaments. A lot of pubs had the mock Staffordshire figures of a hurler and a footballer standing on a plinth, dressed in the colours of the particular county. Underneath it said, 'On all grounds, Players Please'. Kate had explained the puns to the twins as John had marvelled. He had looked at the thing a thousand times and never even noticed the words and what they meant. Fine that, for a man who thought himself a poet.

And Kate had been great about that too. She never came up with any talk about what did a fat, country pub owner think he was doing rawmeishing away in verse. Far from it, she would sit at his knee and ask him to read what he had written. Sometimes her head rested on his lap, and she would sigh in appreciation or else

16

she might question it and ask what image was in his mind. She had long dark curly hair and very dark brown eyes, almost black. She never grudged the time he spent up in their bedroom trying to write – and trying it often was. She minded the bar happily, only suggesting that John should be there at set times like for the lunchtime trade and for the time when they had the half-past-six news on Radio Eireann, and the customers would expect the man of the house to be present to serve their pints and comment on the day's events.

John Ryan was not a great man for formal prayers. Mass time was spent as near the back of the church as possible; in summertime right out in the open air and in thoughts not connected with the actual liturgy taking place. But he did offer prayers of thanks to somewhere, that he had met Kate. He could so easily have not met her. Suppose Jack Coyne's had not been closed that time when she came in with the puncture, suppose the puncture had happened eleven miles on down the road – they'd have gone to the big town instead. Suppose she had been travelling with a girl who could mend a puncture instead of that giggling friend of hers, who could hardly ride a bike.

All these things were too much to think about. Like the really black bit after John had seized his chance and arranged to meet Kate again and again, and his mother had said that he was to bring no flighty Dublin girl into this pub, the business belonged to the whole family. John had nearly upped and off at that stage, but Kate had begged him to be understanding. What did the poor old mother mean except that she was afraid of losing him like she had lost her husband and all the rest of her family, two sons priests and far away, two daughters nuns and even farther away in Australia, and the other two sons in America without a notion of coming back.

Kate said he should be patient, sit it out. Old Mrs Ryan would come round in time: in the meantime Kate would learn the bar trade in Dublin. And learn it she did, dropping her good salary as a secretary in a firm of solicitors and becoming a maid of all work in a small hotel so that she could become accustomed to working the bar.

By the time Mrs Ryan had mellowed, Kate knew all she would need to know about serving a ball of malt, a half one, a black and tan, and a half. She knew when a customer had too much and when to cash a cheque or start a slate. They had been married quietly. It was 1948, there wasn't much money about and not many relations either. John's mother was there, face sour, clothes black, but at least she was there.

Kate had no family at all. Her mother had died after a life of martyrdom and self-pity. Her father had married again and believed that his new wife had been slighted by everyone, so went nowhere. No amount of persuasion would make them come to her wedding, so Kate O'Connell stood with four friends including Lucy, the girl who couldn't mend punctures either, and married John Francis Ryan, sandy-haired, plump poet who had to run his family pub to please his mother and then to continue running it after his mother's time to keep his wife and four children.

Kate told him that she thanked God for him too. Yes, seriously, when she prayed at night as she always did on her knees for three or four minutes no matter how great his need and desire for her.

'You can say your prayers afterwards,' he used to beg.

'Not at all, I'll fall asleep in your arms afterwards,' she would reply.

But she assured him she thanked God for his honesty and his kindness and the marvellous way he had of looking at things, and for the four marvellous children. She, who had nobody for so long, had everybody who mattered now. Outsiders said they were well matched but they had no idea how well.

Nobody watching the quick Kate and the slower John as they smiled at each other across their busy public house would know how much they needed each other and relied one on the other for the qualities that they each lacked. Probably the men might have thought that the youngest of old Ryan's sons did well for himself getting this handsome city girl to liven up his business. Possibly the women in Mountfern might have said that Kate O'Connell, who came in one day on a bicycle and seemed to have no people to speak of, fell on her feet marrying into Ryan's pub. But this was to miss the point.

Kate, uncertain of herself in so many ways, unsure that she had a place anywhere, was more aware than anyone would suspect of how she had found a home and a base and an anchor in the reliable John Ryan. She knew he would never change and cease to love her, as her father had. She knew she didn't have to act out a role to please and entertain him as she had done to everyone else in the world since she was fourteen. She had got by through being brisk – and sometimes she knew that she was too brisk, she left the children bewildered and bothered, and only John could make the world seem sensible to them again.

Kate marvelled at the time and patience John had with their children, how he could sit for what seemed like for ever on the bank of the river with them, making them as still as he was himself to lure the fish out of the water. Only the other day he had them all – even Declan, who never stopped moving around – transfixed over the workings of the old clock which he had taken to bits and put back together. He told them stories of the Fern family who lived over the river, tales of long ago, since John Ryan never knew the house when it stood. The twins would listen for ever to how the provisions might come up the river by boat.

'How would they get them up to the house?' Dara had asked and her father had led the children out to the footbridge and they had all stood speculating what way the great boxes would have been carried up to the mansion. All this when he should have been seeing to the barrels and getting the pub ready for opening.

But Kate loved him for it, and sometimes she wanted to go over and put her arms around his neck and kiss him full on the lips to tell him how much she loved him and how good he was. Not only to his children and to her, but to the old farmer who would tell the same story twice a day. John could nod and polish a glass and hear it again and again. Kate sometimes got a lump in her throat as she watched his patience and his respect for people, for all kinds of people.

She felt a tenderness and love for him that was just as strong as any love you saw in the pictures where she sometimes went on a little outing with Sheila Whelan as a treat. But she didn't show that love too openly. Mountfern wasn't a place where endearments were used openly. There were no darlings or loves or dears used in Ryan's pub. They accused each other good-humouredly of all kinds of failings . . .

'My wife would spend the takings of the year if you didn't watch her . . . all women are exactly the same.'

'John, would you ask Mrs Connolly there would she like a drop more lemonade in her port? A man wouldn't notice your drink, Mrs Connolly. If it wasn't a pint or a glass of whiskey he wouldn't know how to handle it.'

But together, alone together, they knew they had something that a lot of people didn't have. That their own parents certainly didn't come anywhere near having. And they determined on the day that the twins were born that no child of this new family would grow up in a house of uncertainty and loneliness like the young John and the young Kate in the dark days. Money was not important to either of them but recently they had realized that four children did not live off the air and neither were shoes, schoolbags, dentists' bills, copy books, winter coats, more shoes, textbooks, to be found growing in the rushes along the river bank.

One of the reasons they had got the young country girl to come in was because Kate was going to get a job. She had discussed it with Fergus Slattery last night after the concert and he had said there was no reason she couldn't start right away. With office experience in Dublin, with day-to-day experience of balancing the books in a business, she would be perfectly qualified to help in the solicitor's office. Kate Ryan was known not to be a teller of other people's business. This was most important of all.

She was looking forward to the whole business of going out to work. The children did not share her enthusiasm.

'Does this mean we're poor?' Dara wanted to know.

'Of course, we're not poor,' Kate snapped. It was hard enough to find something that would look smart for going out to an office from all her shabby clothes in the bedroom cupboard without having to answer questions like this.

'Well why are you going out to work for a living then?'

'In order to keep you and your brothers in leather shoes which you will kick to bits, to buy nice schoolbags that you'll lose and a few things like that.' Kate looked without any pleasure at what she had always thought of as a smart green two-piece and which now turned out to be a crumpled, faded rag.

'Will we have to sell the pub?' Michael was behind her, always the more anxious of the two. His eyes seemed troubled.

'Lord, not at all, what has the pair of you so worried?' Kate softened her tone.

'You look very upset, you keep frowning,' Michael said.

'Oh that's only because my clothes look like a lot of jumble.'

The other two children had come to join in. It wasn't usual to find a council of war upstairs on a summer evening; Eddie and Declan had come to investigate.

'Are you afraid of looking like Miss Barry?' Eddie asked. Kate looked at him. Miss Barry was the elderly alcoholic who lived in the presbytery and passed by the dignified title of Priest's Housekeeper. In fact she was there because of the goodness of the canon, who couldn't bear to turn her out on the roads. For long periods of time Miss Barry didn't touch a drop and was a sober if rather erratic worker, cooking and cleaning for the two priests. When she did go on a tear it was an almighty one. At no stage did she ever look like anyone Kate would wish to be compared to.

'Thank you, Edward,' she said.

'What have I said?' Eddie wailed.

The twins felt the conversation was degenerating, as it usually did when Eddie came into it.

'We'll be off now.' Dara was lofty.

'We'll leave Eddie with you, Mam,' Michael said. He could see an awful clinging look in Eddie's face that meant he wanted to come with them.

'The last thing I want is any of you with me.' Kate rummaged deeper. She had to have something that looked like what a person wore in an office.

'It's a free country,' Eddie said, his face red with fury. 'I can go anywhere I like in Mountfern, anywhere. You can't stop me.'

'It shouldn't be a free country,' Dara said, 'not if it means Eddie's free to go wherever he likes.'

'Go away from me,' Kate cried. 'And Declan, if you set one foot outside this door you are not going to like what happens to you.'

'Why isn't it a free country for me?' Declan asked. Not very hopefully.

'Because you're the baby,' Dara said.

'Not that so much. It's because you're six. Six-year-olds, in places with rivers in them, stay at home at night.' Kate smiled at his round cross face.

'Will we have another baby?' he suggested.

'We will not, thank you,' Kate said firmly.

Dara and Michael giggled at this, and Eddie was put out because he felt there was something else he was being kept out of.

'What am I going to do? It's ages before it gets dark,' Declan complained.

Kate was going to give in over the tortoise and let him have visiting rights to the turf room where the tortoise was going to live under her sole control. But it was too soon, they wouldn't realize the seriousness of the near drowning if she weakened so quickly.

'Why don't you go and teach Leopold some tricks?' she suggested, not very hopefully. You couldn't teach Leopold any tricks. He had joined the household when he was found with a broken leg and a poor bark by Jack Coyne in the back of a truck, and when nobody had claimed him, the Ryans saved him from being put in a sack by Jack Coyne and meeting a watery death.

Leopold's bark had never improved significantly, he did have a plaintive yowl, but Jaffa, the huge orange cat who had a purr like thunder, would have been a greater source of alarm to any burglar than the lame and silent Leopold. But there weren't burglaries or crimes like that in Mountfern. Sergeant Sheehan was always proud to say that people in his place didn't have to lock their doors at night.

Leopold was more of an indulgence than a watchdog.

'Teach him some tricks?' Declan was astounded.

'You couldn't even teach Leopold to walk straight, Mam.' This was undeniable.

'You could exercise Jaffa in the garden,' she offered.

'We don't have a garden.'

'We do. I call it a garden, you call it a yard. Go on, Jaffa would love a bit of exercise.'

'Will I make her do handstands?' Declan was interested now. Kate realized this had been a wrong road to travel down. She would never find anything to wear, she would spend the rest of the evening wondering if the big orange cat's back would be broken.

'Sit in the garden until it's dark . . . tell Jaffa to come towards you and then go to the other end of the garden and ask her to come back,' she told Declan.

'That's a very dull thing to do. There's no point in spending the evening doing that,' Declan complained.

'You'll find as you grow older there's a lot of things you'll spend morning, noon and night doing that there's no point in,' Kate said, holding a blue houndstooth skirt up to the light. It looked so respectable there must be a reason why it was not to the fore in her meagre selection.

'When I'm old I'll have a great time,' Declan said wistfully. 'I'll have bags of crisps for every meal and I'll stay out all night until even eleven o'clock if I feel like it.'

His small round face looked sadly out the window at Dara and Michael racing off down River Road, and at Eddie, hands in pockets, striding across the footbridge.

Kate Ryan had discovered the fatal flaw, a broken zip and a triangular rip where she had caught it on a door handle.

'Maybe half-past eleven,' Declan said, looking at her sideways to show that he was a person of no half measures when it came to long-term plans for the future.

It was a bright warm evening. Eddie looked at the men with the clipboards and instruments.

'What are you doing?' he asked them.

'A survey.'

'What's that?'

'Making a measurement of the land.'

'Why haven't you got a ruler then?'

They looked at each other. Eddie was small and sandy and tousled-looking. He was like a caricature of a Troublesome Boy.

'We managed without one,' one of the men said.

'Is it a game, like guessing the weight of a cake?'

'A bit more scientific I hope.'

'Who wants to know how wide it is?'

'The fellow who's going to buy it.'

'There's someone going to live in there?' Eddie looked up at the ruined Fernscourt in amazement.

'That would appear to be what it's about all right.'

'God, isn't he lucky,' Eddie said with feeling. 'I'd love to live in a place like that with no roof, and no floors and no wiping your feet.'

Dara and Michael went first to Loretto Quinn's for sweets. Mam had always said to give Loretto the turn, toffees were the same price there as everywhere, but Loretto would appreciate it.

The twins thought they must be her only customers for Scots Clan. The jar showed no signs of any other takers. She weighed out the two ounces and gave them an apple each free.

'We couldn't,' Dara said. A polite and meaningless protest since Michael had already sunk his teeth in his.

'Ah go on, don't I get them for nothing,' Loretto said.

This was not strictly true; she got them from an old man, Papers Flynn, a tramp of sorts who had encircled Mountfern all his life. He lived by picking fruit from low-hanging boughs or feeling gently into the soft nesting places that contrary hens used to find for themselves far from their rightful quarters. Sometimes he offered these as gifts to shopkeepers, who gave him a cheese sandwich or a mug of tea in return.

'Fierce activity across the river: fellows with cameras on long stilts,' Loretto said conversationally.

She liked the twins, full of chat without being cheeky. Their young brother Eddie was a different kettle of fish.

'They're theologists,' Dara said confidently.

'Or something a bit like that.' Michael was a stickler for getting things right.

'Maybe they're going to make a film.' Loretto was hopeful. 'Like *Quiet Man* all over again, wouldn't it be great?'

Dara didn't smile. 'I think it's something to do with changing it all over there, someone buying it and making it different.'

'We'll let you know if we find out anything,' Michael said.

Loretto stood at the doorway of her shabby little shop and watched the twins as they headed for the bridge and the heart of Mountfern.

People used to say that if you bent your head to light a cigarette on the main road you'd miss the two signs to Mountfern and that even if you did see one of the signs and drive off the road through the semi-circle that led down Bridge Street to the River Fern and then back up River Road to the main road again you would wonder what kind of a place it was that you had been through.

One street, Bridge Street, more or less petered out at the bridge where the church was. The road got narrow across the bridge, and went off meandering to the various townlands and small farms. Bridge Street looked well when the sun shone on the different pastel colours of the houses and shops that fronted right on to the road. Some of them were whitewashed still like Judy Byrne's house and Conway's, the place that was both undertaker and pub. Others were pink like Leonard's the stationers and paper shop, like Meagher's the small jewellery shop where watches and clocks were mended and gifts were displayed in boxes with cellophane fronts. Daly's Dairy was a very bright lime green. Mrs Daly had been very pleased with the colour, and was flattered when Fergus Slattery said they would all have to wear sunglasses now to cope with the sudden brightness that radiated from its walls.

There were some houses that didn't have coats of paint or coloured distemper on them. Like old Mr Slattery's tall house with the steps going up to it, which was covered with ivy. And the Garda barracks was just stone, as was the presbytery. The Classic Cinema had once been a smart beige colour but it had got very shabby-looking, with paint peeling off. Mr Williams, who was the rector-in-charge of the small Protestant church, had a cottage that was all covered with climbing roses – his wife spent from dawn to dusk gardening. To the outsider Mountfern looked a slow sleepy place, badly planned, straggling towards a river, but not having any real purpose.

It had been an estate village of course, a collection of smallholdings which all depended on the big house. The days of a community depending on one family seat for livelihood and living quarters were long gone. But Mountfern had not died with the house.

The farmers would always need somewhere to send their children to school, and shops where their wives could sell vegetables, eggs and poultry, where they could buy the essentials without having to travel to the big town, sixteen miles down the main road.

The visitor might have thought Mountfern a backwater but there were few visitors to have such thoughts. It hadn't anything to offer to the sightseer; you had to have some reason to come to Mountfern, otherwise you would think it was a place where nothing happened at all.

Dara and Michael Ryan never thought of Mountfern like that. It was the centre of their world and always had been. They hardly ever left it except to go to the town maybe four times a year. They had been to Dublin of course with the school on educational tours, and once with Dad and Mam when they were very young and there had been an excursion to see Santa Claus in the various Dublin shops. Eddie always resented hearing about this excursion and wanted to know why it hadn't been repeated for the rest of the family.

'Because Santa Claus would vomit if he saw you,' Dara had explained.

This evening, however, they had forgotten what a thorn in the flesh their younger brother Eddie was. They were setting out with a purpose. To find out what was happening to Fernscourt. They had seen the men with the measuring instruments but had not wanted to ask them straight out – it was almost too direct. They felt without actually saying it to each other that they would find out what was the collective view first. Then armed with this knowledge they would face the people that Loretto thought were making a version of *The Quiet Man* (a tamer version, the scenery in this part of the Irish midlands wasn't spectacular and there were very few Maureen O'Haras around the place).

They passed Coyne's motor works before they got to the bridge. Jack was working as he always seemed to be, day and night, a cigarette hanging out of his mouth.

The twins had heard their father say that it was the mercy of God that Jack Coyne hadn't set himself alight with all the petrol and oil around the place, and that one day he could well blow the whole of Mountfern sky high with his dangerous practices. Dara and Michael didn't like Mr Coyne much, he always looked as if he were about to have a fight with someone. He was old of course, nearly as old as Mam and Dad, small and pointed looking. He wasn't married, and he always said that a man who voluntarily took on a wife to nag the life out of him, and spend all he earned, was a man on whom no sympathy should be wasted. Dara had once said to him that if everyone had felt the way he did, the world would have come to an end long ago. Jack Coyne said that everyone might have been better off if it had,

23

and let Dara remember that when she grew up and her head got full of nonsense about love and the like.

'Good evening Mr Coyne.' It didn't matter that he might be an old grouch, they still had to be polite and salute him.

'Out gallivanting,' he said disapprovingly. 'Still I hear that they've big plans for Fernscourt. That'll put a halt to your gallop, the lot of you.'

'What plans?' The twins ignored the gratuitous offence; they had never done anything to irritate Jack Coyne.

To his own immense annoyance Jack Coyne didn't know what plans were afoot. Those fellows doing a survey had been far from forthcoming. But he had his own views.

'A big religious house I hear, so that's the end of all the trick-acting by the children of this parish, I'm glad to say. You'll have to start to do a day's work for a change and be like we were at your age.'

'Is it brothers or nuns would you say?'

'That would be telling,' said Jack Coyne, who didn't know.

'Isn't he a pig?' Dara said cheerfully when they had left him. 'A small dark offensive-looking pig.'

'Imagine him young,' Michael said, as they passed the bag of toffees between them. It was a feat of imagination too difficult for either of them.

'An offensive piglet,' Michael said, and they were in a fit of giggles by the time they reached the bridge and turned left up the main street.

There would be no place for Dara and Michael on the bridge, even Kitty Daly was a bit too young for the small group that met there in the evenings. They saw fellows sitting up on the stone parapet clowning, and a group of girls laughing. There was Teresa Meagher whose mother and father were always fighting. If you went past Meagher's any night when the shop was closed you always heard voices raised. Teresa was going to get a job in Dublin it was always being said, but then her parents would cry and cling on to her so she had to relent and stay. Nobody on the bridge was courting. If you were courting you were down the river bank, or in Coyne's wood, or at the pictures.

Devotions were over and Father Hogan was closing up the church. He waved at Michael.

'Any hope you'd be able to sing *Panis Angelicus*?' he said without much confidence.

'No Father, sorry Father, I haven't a note in my head,' Michael said.

'Come on out of that, you were in the choir at the concert. Why don't you . . .'

'No Father, I can't sing, and anyway you'd never know what might happen to my voice.' Michael had been dying for his voice to break like Tommy Leonard's had. Every morning he tried it out and was disappointed that it still sounded the same.

Dara was no help. 'You should hear him singing from the bathroom, Father, he'd have the tears in your eyes.'

'I'll kill you,' Michael said.

'Well I'm certainly not going to beg and cajole you.' Father Hogan was huffy now. 'I didn't think a Catholic boy would have to be flattered and pleaded with to sing in the House of God.'

Dara realized she had gone too far.

'I was only saying that to tease him, Father. Really and truly he'd be no good, he'd embarrass you, it's like an old tin can. I know he would sing if he could, but he's just in the choir to make up the numbers for Brother Keane, to sort of fill the stage up a bit.'

Father Hogan said that was all right then.

'Now.' Dara was triumphant. 'Didn't I rescue you?'

'You needn't have gone on so much.' Michael hadn't enjoyed being described as an old tin can that would embarrass you. There were times when Dara felt the need to give far too many explanations. They had reached Tommy Leonard's house. The stationery shop was closed for business so the twins knocked at the door beside the shop. Tommy was there to greet them, his finger on his lips. Behind him a voice called.

'Where are you going, Thomas?'

'Just out for a bit of a walk.'

'All right, but be back at nine o'clock, and no skitting and playing with all that crowd of hooligans.'

'Right oh.' Tommy was good-natured. It was easier not to bring the whole thing down round your ears with a catechism of questions. That was Tommy Leonard's view. Just say yes and no, don't get involved in long explanations. Michael thought he was dead right; if he had desperate parents like Tommy's he would be exactly the same. Dara thought that this was entirely the wrong way to handle things, and if she were Tommy she would make it all clear from the word go, instead of giving in to all the cracked notions. That only made them come up with more cracked notions still.

Maggie Daly said they were to wait until she showed Dara the gorgeous yellow dress that had arrived in the parcel from America. There were often parcels from America for all of them. Not as many as years back, when Mountfern was poorer maybe, and American uncles and aunts more generous, or postage cheaper. An American parcel was a rarity nowadays. Mrs Daly probably would say nothing about it and its contents, but Maggie was so excited by the yellow net that she couldn't wait to show it off.

The bad thing was that Kitty was in the bedroom.

Kitty yawned when Dara came in. 'Going to try on the yellow are you?'

'Well look at it anyway,' Dara said. Kitty was a pain.

'Not at all, you're coming to try it on. Half of Mountfern will pass through here trying it on, I can see that. The room will be full of people in vests and knickers bursting into the yellow dress.'

'Are you going to wear it?' Dara asked Maggie, deliberately ignoring the elder girl.

'I don't think so.' Maggie was pleased to be consulted.

'You see it's a bit low-necked, and it's a bit big, I'm kind of lost in it. And it's so gorgeous it would be a pity to cut it down for me. Wasting so much material, you see.' Her face showed her longing for the yellow satin with an overskirt of yellow net, and with yellow embroidery and sequins on the bodice. It was like something you'd see in the pictures; it was far too old for them in one way, and yet it was a girlish-looking dress with big puff sleeves. Dara was dying to put it on but she wouldn't give Kitty the satisfaction of watching her.

'You wouldn't have to get much taken out of it, Maggie, wouldn't Miss Hayes do a great job on it?' Miss Hayes did some dressmaking in Mountfern but had never been let loose on exotic fabric like this, to their knowledge.

Kitty was lying on her bed reading the life story of Helen Shapiro who had managed to escape from childhood by having a voice that took her into the hit parade. She'd never have escaped if she had been born in Mountfern, Kitty Daly thought darkly.

'It would look ridiculous on Maggie, no matter what Miss Hayes did to it. That's a dress that needs a chest. Maggie hasn't got a chest to put into it.'

'None of us has a chest to put into it yet,' Dara cried with spirit. 'While we're waiting we could put a rolled-up pair of socks. Like you often do, Kitty Daly.'

'You told her!' Kitty's face was dark red with rage, and she looked menacingly at Maggie.

'I didn't know!' Maggie was transparently honest and terrified.

'Come on, Maggie, let's leave Kitty the room to herself, we're only in the way.' Dara felt it was time to escape. They hung up the yellow dress carefully and pulled back the transparent plastic cover that came with it. It was the most beautiful thing they had ever seen. They envied the cousin of the Dalys somewhere in America who had worn it to her Junior Prom. Whatever a Junior Prom might be.

They were going to the Protestant graveyard at the top of the town. Nobody would disturb them there. Mr Williams the vicar had realized that the children didn't tear around playing hide and seek among the headstones, there was no disrespect to the graves of the various members of the Fern family and the rest of the small Protestant community hereabouts.

It was a peaceful place for the children to come and talk. Mr and Mrs Williams had no children of their own, they were indulgent with the children of others.

Up Bridge Street the little band walked slowly. They looked wistfully at the Classic which was showing *The Glass Mountain*. Imagine having the money and freedom just to drop in to the pictures whenever you wanted to.

'We'll be able to do that when we're old,' Dara said.

Tommy Leonard didn't think so; he thought being old was going to be more of the same.

They looked into Conway's grocery and pub. At the back, hidden away, they saw the feet of three drinkers in the discreet bar area. They often had a game guessing whose feet they were.

They never tried to play this game in any other pub since anyone who drank in Foley's or Dunne's, or indeed in Ryan's itself, did so openly. It was only in Conway's that they pretended not to be there.

Beyond Conway's was Doctor White's and they called there for Liam and Jacinta. That was it for tonight; some of the other children they played with lived out in the countryside, and others weren't allowed out to wander in the evenings. There were some boys who were up at the brothers' in the football field and there were some girls who had to help in their houses, or who had been bad and therefore denied the night's outing.

The six went to the graveyard and sat on a tombstone which they particularly liked.

It was the memorial for a William James Fern who had died in 1881 at Majuba Hill in the Transvaal, aged eighteen. It was during the Boer War they knew that, and he had been fighting for the British against the Dutch in South Africa.

'It was a long way to go,' Maggie Daly often said.

'I suppose he wanted to get away.' Tommy Leonard could understand it only too well.

Dara had never understood it.

'What did he want to go off and fight in other people's wars for? If he was a Mountfern man then, why wasn't he here having a great time? And if he was eighteen he could have done what he liked. Think of it, he could have gone to the Classic every night.' She looked at their faces. 'That is if the Classic was there in the 1880s, which I don't think it was.'

But tonight they didn't talk long about the dead William James who fell at Majuba Hill. Tonight they talked about what was going to happen to William James's old home. What was happening in Fernscourt.

They were not alone, this little group, in their speculations. If they could have seen into every house down Bridge Street and along River Road they would have come across conversations on the same theme.

Over in Foley's Bar at the top of the town old Matt Foley and his friends said that there was oil sighted there. Some fellow had pulled a pike from the fern and his gills were full of oil. So the drilling would start any day now.

Next door to Foley's, in her neat little house, Judy Byrne the physiotherapist sat with Marian Johnson whose family owned the Grange, a country house which took guests of a superior type and even arranged hunting for them. They were women of around the same age, one side or the other of forty, not married and not likely to find any husbands at this stage of their lives in this part of the country. Neither ever admitted that to the other.

They had heard that Fernscourt was going to be an agricultural college, which would be very good news indeed as it would mean lectures and all kinds of talent not seen in these parts before. While saying that the people would probably be quite unspeakable they were having a small sherry to celebrate.

Seamus Sheehan in the Garda barracks was taking a lot of abuse from his wife. Why had he heard nothing about Fernscourt? Everyone else in the place had some view on what was happening. There was no point in being married to the sergeant if he was the one man in the whole country who seemed to be too remote as to inquire what was going on in his own back yard.

Next to the barracks Jimbo Doyle lived with his mother. Jimbo's mother had heard that the new place had been bought by an order of contemplative nuns. They would have a grille on the window and pull it back so that one nun, the Reverend Mother, would be able to address the outside world. When it was necessary, which would not be often.

Jimbo's mother told him that they would need a reliable man around the place, and that he should get in quick before someone else did.

Jimbo, whose idea of opportunities in life did not include being a reliable handyman to an order of contemplative nuns, asked what his mother expected him to do. Write to the pope, or just the bishop saying he was the man? His mother said he should be glad that someone in the family was looking to the practical side of things instead of singing raucous songs and laughing loud laughs.

In Paddy Dunne's pub all talk of emigration to Liverpool to the brother's pub had stopped. This was now the hub of the universe. Paddy Dunne had it from one of the travelling salesmen who came in trying to get him to take biscuits. Biscuits in a pub! Anyway this man knew all about Fernscourt: it was an agricultural research place. Foreigners were going to come and test soil and plants and the place was going to be a boom town as a result of it. The smart man would expand now or expand a little and then sell when prices were going up. It provided hours of speculation.

Sheila Whelan sat in the comfortable sitting room behind the post office and listened to a concert on Radio Eireann. She loved all that Strauss music and it didn't sweep her into a world of people waltzing in Vienna; instead it reminded her for some reason of the first time she had come to Mountfern with Joe Whelan. He had taken her to Coyne's wood which was full of bluebells. Literally carpeted with them. They had picked armfuls of them and Joe had told her that he loved music and that he would take her to concerts. He told her lots of things. Sheila lay back in her chair, tired. She knew a bit more about Fernscourt than the others because the telegrams all came through her post office. But she didn't know it all. She sighed and wondered what the changes would mean.

Across the road in the Whites', the doctor was telling his wife all the theories he had heard. It was mainly nuns, he reported, but there was a considerable weight of opinion behind a college, and a strong vocal minority thought it was going to be a development of twelve luxury bungalows each with a quarter acre of garden and a river view.

'What would be the best?' Mrs White wondered.

'It depends where you stand.' Dr White was philosophical. 'If Jacinta were going to join the Poor Clares or whatever, it would be nice to have her down the road; on the other hand if she were to land a millionaire let's hope she might buy one of the new bungalows.'

'It's going to make everyone look out for themselves,' said Mrs White suddenly, as if the thought had just hit her.

Close to Dr White's house, in Conway's, Miss Barry was having a small port for her stomach. She sat fearfully on a high stool. The Conways wished she would buy a bottle of port and take it home with her, she made everyone uneasy by looking around nervously and protesting that she had a cramp which meant that her body was crying out to be warmed.

Miss Barry had heard that there was definitely oil in the ground, that a research organization was going to come and test it, but they were going to install an order of silent enclosed nuns there as a disguise to keep people away – three theories rolled comfortably into one. She found a ready and unexpected audience in Conway's. They looked at her as if there might be some truth in it; they had all heard elements of this story and this explanation would at last tie it all together.

In the Classic Cinema twenty-three people sat and watched the romantic tale

28

of *The Glass Mountain* unfold itself on the screen, while Declan Morrissey who ran the place sat in the projection room and read an article he had cut out of a Sunday newspaper. Are the days of the cinema numbered? He wondered should he get out now or wait and see if these daft rumours about half the civil service being transplanted from Dublin to the midlands were true. Wouldn't it be a very stupid thing to sell the Classic just as the horde of possible cinema viewers were about to arrive?

In Meagher's, the watch-menders and small jewellers, Teresa's parents fought on bitterly. Mrs Meagher said it didn't matter if the Prince of Wales had left and that Mrs Simpson was coming to live in Mountfern and give parties, life still wouldn't be any way good for her. It had been a vale of tears since she had married Mr Meagher.

Mr Meagher tired suddenly of the arguments; he had a pain in his chest and down his arm. He said he would call a halt to the barney and go to bed. He might feel better in the morning. He said that his wife was probably right. Life was a vale of tears and perhaps he had contributed to it. In the morning he would try to consider what could be done about it.

Next morning Teresa Meagher was sent running for Dr White but it was too late. Mr Meagher had not recovered from his heart attack. Dr White knew that he was dead but still arranged for him to be taken to the hospital in the town. It would be less distressing for the family. That's what a lot of his work was about. Minimizing the distress. There was little he could have done to prevent Frank Meagher's heart attack. The man ate like a fat man in a circus, smoked four packets of cigarettes a day and existed on a level of tension that should have finished him off years ago. Dr White left Mrs Meagher weeping to the canon, whose faded blue eyes clouded further with the memory of the happy family life the two Meaghers had led, and before long Mrs Meagher began to believe it herself.

The news of Frank Meagher's death did not take long to travel around Mountfern. In Leonard's stationers, Tommy's mother and father discreetly moved the Deepest Sympathy cards to the front of the stand. They hunted in the drawers for the black-edged Mass cards and flowery Spiritual Bouquet cards as well. People would want to pay their respects.

In Conway's they realized that a coffin would be needed. Discreetly they set about getting one ready. Frank Meagher was a big man. It would be a big coffin. His wife would be as guilty as hell about the life she had led him, it could be an expensive one. But they probably didn't have much insurance, maybe standard was the right thing to suggest.

At seven o'clock mass that morning he was prayed for. The religious bent their heads. Miss Purcell, Miss Hayes and Jimbo Doyle's mother exchanged glances. They could have said a lot about the Meaghers, but they would say no more now, not after a bereavement like this.

Miss Purcell looked after the Slattery household with an unsmiling face and unstinting effort. Old Mr Slattery's clothes were clean, ironed and mended, his shoes were polished and his newspaper laid in front of his well-served breakfast at eight-thirty every morning. Miss Purcell would already have been to seven o'clock mass, she was a daily communicant; she would have collected fresh milk at Daly's and the newspaper at Leonard's. His son Fergus was equally well looked after. His shirts were ironed for him, and left hanging on the big heavy wardrobe in his room. Miss Slattery always took the one he was going to wear next day to give it a little warm in the hot press. She had a horror of the damp.

Fergus had a series of sleeveless vee-necked knitted pullovers, almost all of them in a grey to blue shade. In the long evenings when others went out looking for diversion Miss Purcell knitted fresh supplies and darned the existing force. Though old-fashioned and obviously home-made, they gave him an even more boyish charm than he had already. Many a girl's heart turned over to see him sitting at his desk in his shirt sleeves with the light on of an evening, reading through papers with hair tousled and glasses often pushed back into his thick dark hair.

If someone had offered Fergus a thousand pounds to strike attitudes or adopt a pose he wouldn't have been able to do it. Like his father he was a pleasure to work for, Miss Purcell told her few cronies, a courteous and considerate man, always opening doors, carrying buckets of coal for her, and saying how much he liked whatever she put on the table. It would be hard to find his equal in three counties or more. Miss Purcell never understood any of his jokes but Fergus seemed to be very witty and make clients laugh. Often when they were leaving she heard them say that he was too human to be a lawyer. She had been worried about this and made two novenas that he should become less human in case he endangered the practice. Sometimes Fergus cleaned his own shoes – he didn't think it was right to let a woman polish the black laced shoes that had been on his feet all day – but Miss Purcell didn't like any changes in routine. She sniffed disapprovingly at his efforts and said she would prefer if he wouldn't disgrace her in the town by going about with such ill-kept feet.

It was said that Canon Moran had often looked with envy at the Slatterys and wished they would give him their housekeeper. The purse-faced Miss Purcell who kept such a good house would be indeed a delight compared to poor Miss Barry, but she had been there so long and had no other home to go to, so in Christian kindness Canon Moran couldn't, and made no efforts to replace her.

Miss Purcell was tall, thin and had a small face with two deceptively cheery-looking spots of red on her cheeks. These were not jolly ruddy cheeks, they were in fact two spots of colour whose redness increased according to how disapproving she was. At breakfast that morning they were very red indeed: a sure sign that something was about to blow up. Father and son avoided recognizing this for as long as they could.

'Do you want a bit of the *Independent*?' Fergus's father offered him the middle pages.

'I wish we'd get the *Times*, it's a better paper altogether,' Fergus said. They were both avoiding the eye of Miss Purcell who stood ready to sound off.

'Well it is and it isn't, but nobody dies in the *Irish Times*. You don't get the list of deaths in it like the *Independent*. A country solicitor needs to know who has died.'

'Couldn't we go into Leonard's and sort of race down the deaths without buying the paper at all?' Fergus suggested.

'Fine thing that would be to do in a small town, depriving the Leonards of their income. Couldn't the whole town do that? Couldn't they come in here and look at our law books? Where's the sense in that?' Mr Slattery rattled his half of the paper in annoyance.

Miss Purcell cleared her throat.

'Miss Ryan is here. A bit early I said to her but she seemed to think that you expected her before nine.'

'Is that Marian Ryan come to make her will again?' Old Mr Slattery looked over his glasses.

'No, it's Kate, Kate Ryan from the pub up the River Road,' said Fergus. 'Isn't it, Miss Purcell?'

'Oh yes, Mr Fergus, that's the Mrs Ryan it is, all right. And if I might say ...'

'Yes, Miss Purcell?' Fergus decided to take it manfully, whatever it was.

'Mrs Ryan arrived five minutes ago with the information that she is going to be working here.'

'That's right,' Fergus said cheerfully. 'She's going to start this morning. Well she's nice and punctual, that makes a change from the rest of Mountfern.'

'I can't recall any occasion anything was late in this house ...' Miss Purcell began to bristle ...

'Oh not you, Miss Purcell, for heaven's sake, everyone else.'

'And what work will Kate Ryan from the pub be doing here, and why wasn't I consulted?' The spots on the cheeks were dangerously red now. Even old Mr Slattery had put down his paper and was looking anxiously like an old bird from one to the other.

'Well, lots of things, I hope.' Fergus was still bewildered by this storm, and the sudden dropping of the Mrs Ryan, and changing it to Kate from the pub.

'In nineteen years working in this house I have never had such treatment.' Miss Purcell looked ten feet tall; she had drawn herself up into a long thin stick quivering with rage. 'If my work was not to your satisfaction, the very least I would have expected was to be told. Instead of allowing me to be humiliated by seeing that Kate Ryan from the pub, come along with her apron and things in a basket prepared to do my work for me.'

The eyes were very bright. Old Mr Slattery's glasses had fallen off his nose with shock.

Fergus was on his feet. 'Miss Purcell, Miss Purcell! What an idea, what a thought that we would dream of improving on your housework! Don't you keep the best house in the town? Aren't we the envy of the whole of Mountfern, including I might say the canon himself? You can't have thought for a moment that we'd as much as contemplate getting anyone else, let alone doing it without telling you ...'

'But Kate from the pub out there with her basket?'

'I don't know what she has in the basket but Mrs Ryan is going to work in the office. She was trained in a solicitor's office in Dublin, you know. She'll be doing the files and typing letters.'

'Oh,' Miss Purcell had to spend a moment doing some social adjustment.

'So you see you were quite wrong to think we have anything except the highest regard for you, isn't that right, Dad?'

'Heavens yes. Oh Miss Purcell, the house would fall down without you,' said Mr Slattery anxiously.

'But that would mean Kate ... that Mrs Ryan and her family would know all your business, confidential business of the town.' Miss Purcell wasn't going to give in.

'We wouldn't take her on if we didn't know she could be trusted. It's not easy to find the kind of discretion and loyalty that you have, Miss Purcell. You are, as my father has said, the mainstay of this house, but we think we have found someone who will be able to keep our business private, as you do. It's very good of you to be worried about it.'

There was no more to be said. Miss Purcell had to go back to the hall where she had left Kate standing, and usher her into the office, asking the while whether she took sugar in her tea and if she would like a plain biscuit, a sweet biscuit or a slice of home-made currant bread. Kate wisely chose the home-made bread and disclosed four punnets of raspberries which she had brought as a gift because she had heard it said that Miss Purcell made the best jam in the county. The pink spots began to lose their ferocity and the 'Mrs Ryan' was pronounced without the sarcastic overtones. Kate was in, she was starting a new career. There was hardly any trade in the pub in the mornings, and John was in agreement with her that the few pounds the Slatterys paid would be helpful. Young Declan was off at school, so they were all out of the house, and Carrie knew how to put a lunch on the table at the stroke of one. It would be nice to be behind a typewriter again for a change rather than behind a bar. Mr Slattery was such a gentleman, a real old-fashioned man who was spending more and more time fishing; and Fergus was the best company in the world, self-mocking and droll, full of compassion for some of the people who came to see him, slow to send a bill where it would be a hardship to pay it, but also quick with his tongue to abuse anyone who wanted to work a fiddle or hide an income.

Fergus had told her that it wasn't a big practice and that normally he was well able to deal with the clerical side. He could type like the wind with two fingers and he had a fairly reasonable filing system but he wanted his father to take more time off, now people really did trust him with their affairs rather than thinking of him as a boy in short trousers. So Kate would be a godsend. And indeed she was. It took her about three days to see that his reasonable filing system was hopeless, and to set up a better one.

'Come here till I show you what we do with these papers now,' she ordered him.

'No, no, that's your work, that's what we pay you inordinate sums of money for, so that I don't have to look at things like that.'

'Wrong,' Kate cried. 'You have to understand it, otherwise it's useless to any of us. You won't know where to put back a letter, find a counsel's brief, where the deeds are, anything. Suppose I get flu or you sack me, or you're working late at night. Come on now, it will only take ten minutes a day.'

'Do you run the pub like this too?' Fergus asked.

'Of course not, but I do the accounts, and I've insisted that John does them with me otherwise he'd have to leave them till the wife gets back and it would just double the work.'

'I'm surprised the place isn't a gold mine with your organizational skills.'

'Come out our way one evening and have a pint in it and you'll see what a gold mine it is. Would I be in here setting up filling systems for beautiful idle professional men too lazy to look at them if it was a gold mine? Now suppose you had this query from the town agent's clerk about the fee in that workman's compensation case which was appealed, where would you look first?'

'In the bad old days I'd look on the table at the window.'

'But in the good days that have now come?'

'I've forgotten, young Mrs Ryan, show me, show me.'

'Oh thank God I'm happily married. You'd break my heart.'

'You're sure you're happily married?'

'Very sure. And isn't it time you had a romance yourself? Now that Nora Lynch has gone off to fresh fields and better chances we hear nothing about your activities.'

'Listen to me, after that business with Nora I'm afraid to lay my hand or eye on anyone. There's no activities to hear about. It was all a terrible misunderstanding.'

'You lost us a fine schoolteacher over it all. My Dara loved her. She hates the new woman, about a hundred she says, and a habit of hitting them accidentally on the knuckles with a ruler.'

'Poor Dara, maybe I should have given Miss Lynch an engagement ring to keep her in the town, and keep all the little girls like Dara happy.'

'I don't think anything's going to make my Dara happy for a long time, but no stories about children. This workman was called Burke, Fergus, in the name of God where are you going to look for this file?'

'Under the Bs, Miss?'

'We have a child prodigy,' said Kate Ryan and went back to her typewriter.

'What are you doing, Daddy?' John jumped guiltily at Dara's voice.

What he should have been doing was writing. This was the time that Kate stood minding the bar, tired already from her morning in the office. But there was just so long you could look at blank paper without it beginning to drive you mad. John Ryan had nothing to say and no way of saying it. He had come out to what Kate called the garden and everyone else called the yard to do a little experiment. Ryan's licensed premises was flush on the road. Its front door opened straight on to River Road. It would have been unheard of to have a pub with a garden in front. The supplies came to the back yard and the barrels took up most of it . . . a place of half-used outhouses and sheds. That was where the back door of the house was, that was the only way the children were ever allowed to enter their home. But beside the house there was what they called the side yard. Here the hens wandered, and Jaffa sat like a buddha in calm control, purring and lazily washing her big orange face. Leopold didn't sit much in the yard, there wasn't an audience sufficiently sympathetic to his whimperings and cringings. He liked to cower in the pub. Maurice was still in the turf room after the ugly river-bank incident. John had devised a marvellous way to avoid working on his poems: he was going to build a large hen coop, a wired-off area for the hens to live in, so that they could scratch and wander but be away from the few pathetic attempts that Kate had started in the line of making a real garden. Once the hens were corralled life would be easier. But John Ryan had wanted to do it quietly and undisturbed by his family. He didn't want to admit, even to himself, that he was shirking his writing work, and mitching from his desk. Dara stood with a mutinous look on her face. Her eyes were dark and cross under her fringe of black hair . . . her hands thrust into the pockets of her shorts.

'Are you changing things, is that it?' she said in the tones of someone looking for a fight and determined to find one.

'I have a bit of a plan. I was working it out, that's all,' her father said, looking guilty and shifty.

'I bet it's something new and desperate,' Dara said.

'It was just a plan to gather the hens all together in a run, that's all it was,' John said mildly.

'They're perfectly all right the way they are, they don't want to be gathered, they don't want to be changed, they love things just as they are.' Her eyes were suspiciously bright as if she could start to cry any minute. Dara had never expressed any view about the hens up to this. The hens were like the river bank and the crates in the yard, they were just part of the background.

John Ryan sat back on his hunkers and put an arm round his daughter's knees. 'Come here and give your old father a hug.'

'There's no point in hugs,' Dara said.

'Right.' He stood up. 'I know exactly. It's the same with me. I don't feel like writing now so I came down to play with the chickens.'

Dara couldn't help laughing at the thought of her father playing with chickens. She managed a snort but John Ryan wisely didn't build on it. He knew she was upset and it would all come out. He supposed it was a row with Kate. But he was wrong.

'Daddy, are we poor?'

'No we're not poor. You know that.'

'But we're not rich are we?'

'You don't have to be one or the other, you can be in between, like most of us are round here.'

'Will we ever be rich?'

'We'll be all right. What's this worry about money?'

'We're going to need it to buy our house.' Her face was very determined.

'But we have our house, silly old thing, this is our house,' he indicated the pub and the whitewashed walls of the house with a wave of his hand.

'Not here, our house across in Fernscourt. You know where they have the diggers. They're clearing it for someone to live there, some American, he'll live there unless we can buy it.'

'Now, now, Dara,' John began soothingly.

But she was on her feet full of anger and wouldn't be soothed.

'It's our house, Michael's and mine, and everyone's.'

John sighed.

'Will you come for a bit of a walk with me?'

'I don't feel like a walk.'

'I don't feel like a walk with such a disagreeable weasel as you, but it might help.'

'Where will we go?'

'We could go to Fernscourt.'

'All right then.'

Kate Ryan was in the bar talking to Jimbo Doyle and Jack Coyne, who were not her idea of the best of company, when she saw through the window the two figures crossing the footbridge. Her husband who was meant to be working on his poetry and her daughter who had been like a bag of hedgehogs all week. Her knuckles ached to rap on the window, but she wouldn't give that sharp-faced Jack Coyne the satisfaction of seeing her act the bossy wife.

Kate had always spoken impetuously, and not long ago in confession had told Canon Moran that she was quick-tempered. Canon Moran had suggested that she think of Our Lord's Blessed Mother whenever she was tempted to say something sharp. She should think what Our Lady might have said. She needn't actually say what Our Lady would have said, but thinking it might delay the caustic response or the hurtful crack.

Looking at the man and girl hand in hand walking across the footbridge Kate Ryan thought that the Mother of God might have blessed them and wished them well and happiness and thanked God for her good fortune. Right, Kate Ryan would think similar noble thoughts. She turned round and faced Jack Coyne and Jimbo Doyle with what she thought was a saintly smile.

'Jaysus, Kate, have you a toothache?' asked Jimbo Doyle in alarm.

'And Michael and I planned to live here when we grew up. Everyone knew that we'd get a proper roof made over this bit, and probably build windows and a door.' Dara was pointing out the extent of the house.

'But it was only a dream.' John was gentle.

'No it wasn't.'

'Yes, of course it was . . . and is. Like going to see the man in the moon. Do you remember when you were very young we used to take you out to have a look at the man in the moon before you went to bed? Now you don't think it's a man up there, you're quite happy to look at the moon for itself, as something beautiful lighting up the sky over Mountfern.'

'Yes but . . .'

'And when you were very young altogether you and Michael used to be staring up the chimney in the kitchen, didn't you, at Christmas time, the way Declan did last Christmas? You thought that if the chimney was too old and too awkward you wouldn't get any presents. But they came all the same, didn't they, and you don't mind now where they come from?'

'That's not the same . . .'

'I know it's not the same . . . but I was just saying that the way we look at things changes as life goes on, it couldn't always stay the same, otherwise we'd all be still living in caves with clubs or if we didn't grow up in some kind of way wouldn't we all be in nappies waddling round the place in playpens . . .'

'You don't understand . . .' she wailed.

'I don't understand completely, but I understand a bit. Don't I?' She looked up at him, her face softening.

'I know, Dara, it'll always be here in some way for you, not the same way, remember the man in the moon. The moon didn't go, and it still looks beautiful, doesn't it, when you can see all the cattle over on the hills, and the spire of the church and the woods and . . . and Fernscourt . . .'

'Will it be the same when this awful man comes, him with all his American money?'

'He's not going to be awful. He has children, we hear, you'll love them as sure as anything.'

'I won't, I won't.'

'Well you'll meet them anyway, and you *might* like them. Would that be reasonable?'

'And we'd never be able to afford to buy it ourselves.'

'No, that isn't a thing you should think about, that's not a possible thing, that's like imagining a square circle, or imagining that Jaffa grew a long neck like a giraffe in the picture books. Cats don't grow long necks, this isn't a *real* home for you and Michael, it was a home for last summer and before that.'

'And now?' Her lip had stopped trembling.

'It's still special but it isn't anything you start getting all het up about and start saving your pocket money to buy. That's like the days when you used to want to know if the man in the moon had to wash his neck.'

'Will you explain that to Michael, Daddy? I'm not great at explaining.'

'I'm not great at it either.'

'Well, you're better than me,' Dara said in the matter-of-fact voice which meant that he had sorted this one out anyway.

John Ryan hadn't written a poem or built a hen run, but he had convinced his angry little daughter that the world wasn't going to come to an end. Now all he had to do was to get into the house without his wife knowing he had played hookey from his poetry writing.

It was a busy night in the bar, they had hardly time for a word of any kind let alone the attack that John feared was brewing. Kate moved so quickly around the place, she had glasses swept up, and washed or refilled quicker than he would have decided whether to move the glass in the first place. Yet she didn't give the customers the impression that they were being rushed, only that there was an urgency in getting their pint in front of them.

Kate had decided to say nothing until everyone was gone, then she was going to force her voice to stay low, not to get high and excited, and she would not allow herself to speak too quickly until it became a gabble. She was going to point out – in tones that no one could find offence in – that she got up every morning and saw the children off to school, then she went and did what amounted to a day's work in an office, and not that she was complaining but she spent the afternoon listening to almighty bores rawmeishing out of them instead of getting on with her own work of which she had plenty, but she had stood in the bar to let her husband work . . . She would keep her voice very calm as she told him how she would like to take a cleaver to him and split him in two.

Her humour was not helped by the behaviour of Eddie and Declan who had come into the pub, despite all the strictures against this, to know could they take possession of the tortoise again. They had burst into the pub, mouths stained with the jam which Carrie had been making a very poor fist of setting. They looked like the children of tinkers both of them in the most torn clothes that they could have found. In front of the drinking population of Mountfern – who probably had looked at her askance because she was an outsider from the first day and had now committed the crime of going outside the family home to work – she had been guilty of the worst sin of all . . . neglecting her children. And had John supported her, had he removed them with an authoritative wave and a thunderous warning? He had *like hell*!

John Ryan had put an arm around the shoulder of each small furious son and he chose with a slow deliberation for each of them a chocolate biscuit from the shelf behind the bar and he had walked them out as if they had been honoured guests instead of his own children who had broken his own most strict rule of coming into the family pub.

But Kate would not let her tone betray her rage, otherwise he would just walk away from it saying that the last thing on earth he wanted was a fight. It was infuriating. The only way she could convince him of how badly he was behaving was to speak in a reasonable tone as if she were the most contented woman on earth.

For a wild moment she wondered how the Mother of God would have coped, and then realized that Mary wouldn't have had nearly as many problems in Nazareth. There was never any mention of her running Joseph's carpentry business almost single-handed and doing another job for a local lawyer as well. Kate's resentment knew no bounds.

The last straggler finally went home. The glasses were washed, the windows opened to air the place, two clean dishcloths lay out to dry on the counter. Kate felt sweaty and weary, not in the mood to list her wrongs.

Her husband smiled at her across the counter. 'Will I pour you a port wine?' he asked.

'Oh Jesus, Mary and Joseph isn't that all I'd need tomorrow, a roaring port hangover.'

'Just one glass each, we'll bring it out to the side garden and I'll tell you my plans for it.'

She bit her lip. He was like a big child.

'Well?' He had the glass and the port bottle ready.

She was too tired.

'Hold on till I rinse this blouse out,' she said, and took off the blue and white cotton blouse that was sticking to her back. Standing in her slip top and dark blue skirt, she looked flushed and very beautiful, John thought. He touched her neck where the long dark curly hair was loosely tied with a narrow blue ribbon.

'That's lovely for them to see that kind of carry on if they pass the window,' she said shaking his hand away.

'Well you're the one who's half-dressed, I'm quite respectable,' he laughed.

The blouse was left to hang on the back of a chair, it would be dry in the morning. Kate gave herself a quick sluice with the water in the sink that was meant to wash only glasses.

'If we're going to go to the side garden, let's go then,' she said more ungraciously than she felt; she was glad at any rate that he was calling it a garden rather than a yard. That was an advance.

The moonlight made it look a great deal better than it seemed by day. Jaffa sat still as a statue on the wall. Leopold was dreaming of beatings and his hard life. He gave a gentle whimper now and then in his sleep. From the hen house there was a soft cluck.

John folded a sack and left it on an upturned barrel. 'I was to ask you about the tortoise.'

'No, no.' Her eyes flashed with rage. 'It's not fair, John, really it isn't. You're always the lovey dovey one, ask poor old Daddy, he's so soft, he'd melt as soon as he looks at you. Mammy's the nagging old shrew . . . It's not fair to let them grow up thinking that.'

'They do not think that.'

'They do, and they will more if you say they can have the tortoise back. Do you think I want the smelly old thing in the turf room looking at me like something out of one of those horror pictures they have in the picture house? I've wished a hundred times it would die one day and we could have a funeral and it would all be over, and all the fighting.'

'They live for years, you know, you're on a loser there,' he grinned.

She wouldn't give in. 'No, they can't have it back, they broke all the rules coming into the pub like pictures of children you'd see when they're collecting for charity. They're worse than Leopold, they pretend they never got a meal or a bath in their lives.'

Kate Ryan was very aggrieved.

'Did I ever try to countermand any of your decisions?' John asked.

'No, but you try to get round me. We've got to be consistent, John, otherwise how do they know where they are?'

'I couldn't agree more.'

'But?'

'But nothing. I couldn't agree more.'

'So what about the bloody tortoise? What were you going to suggest?'

'Come here, I want to show you something . . .' He took her by the hand and pointed out where they should build a long hen run, with netting over it. The hens would have freedom, but within frontiers. The rest was going to be a garden. He showed where they could have a rockery. And how they would build a raised flower bed maybe and she could grow the flowers she had always said she would like.

'You should have been writing your poetry.'

'It's not like making things in a factory, Kate, you can't sit down in front of a conveyor belt and turn out bits of writing and in the end a poem emerges.' He spoke quietly and with dignity.

'I know, I know.' She was contrite.

'So when it didn't seem to come, I thought I'd do something for you and plan you a garden.'

'That's lovely.'

'I'll have a word with Jimbo Doyle and he could do a couple of days and build up a few beds. Now wouldn't that be nice?'

'It would.' She was touched, she couldn't deliver her attack now. It would be ingratitude, flying in the face of God, to attack a husband who was so kind.

'I was over in Fernscourt today, there's heaps of stones lying round the place. We could get some nice big rocks, Jimbo could wheel them across the footbridge.'

'I don't suppose they belong to anyone.' Kate didn't want her voice to sound grudging . . . 'That would be grand,' she added.

'And this thing about the tortoise, I wouldn't countermand your orders. God, what would be the point? What I was wondering was now that the hens have a place of their own someone will have to feed them properly you know, mix up the scraps with the bran . . .'

'Yes.'

'So suppose we made those two scallywaggers do that? They'd be well able for it, and they'd give the hens a feed twice a day . . . and to encourage them maybe they could have some kind of access to that tortoise, maybe take him out of your way in the turf room, not have him looking up at you like a prehistoric monster. What do you think?'

Kate tried to hide her smile. Unsuccessfully.

'What do I think?' she said, laughing in spite of herself. 'I think I might be persuaded . . . but . . .'

'But it would have to come from you. If you think it would be a good idea, then you should suggest it.' He was adamant about this.

'I suppose you sorted Dara out too,' Kate said gently and with admiration. 'They should have you up on the platform in Geneva sorting things out for everyone.'

'Ah, the poor child was very upset, it's giving up a bit of fairyland. None of us like doing that.'

'People like you didn't have to, it's still all there in your heads,' Kate said, but she said it with a hint of envy in her voice, and she kissed his lips softly so that he tasted the port wine.

CHAPTER THREE

That night Michael sat on the landing window seat and looked across at Fernscourt in the moonlight.

. The curtains of ivy waved over the hummocks of moss. It was easier than ever to see the ruins since some of the big straggly trees and bushes had been cut down.

Eddie and Declan were long asleep in their bunk beds. Michael had been reading with a torch, but his mind had strayed from the knight who had rescued the Lady Araminta with the golden tresses. He wanted to look at real life, which was Fernscourt. For a long time he looked at the shadows over the moon and the patterns they made on the soft green banks up from the river towards the house.

Then he saw a figure moving in the moonlight. Nobody *ever* walked there at night. Michael knelt up and opened the window to have a better view. It was a man, an old man even older than Daddy. He was wandering around with his hands in his pockets looking up at the walls. Sometimes he touched the moss, sometimes he pushed aside the ivy. Michael was kneeling on the window seat now, peering and straining to see as the figure disappeared and emerged again behind the ruined walls. He felt a hand on his shoulder, and there was his father in his pyjamas.

'Dad, I think he's come. I think he's here.'

'Who?'

'The American. I think that's him in our house.' The boy's face was white even on the shadowy landing with moonlight coming in irregular darts through the window.

John Ryan looked out and saw a figure walking round touching walls and almost patting the bits of building that still stood. John felt he was spying somehow. The man was as if naked over there, in that he didn't know he was being observed.

Michael was wriggling off the seat. 'I'll have to wake Dara,' he said, his face working anxiously.

'Wait, Michael.'

'But it's our house, he's here, he came after all. People said he might not be going to live here. But look at him, he *is* going to live in it, isn't he? Isn't he?'

John sat down on the window seat, and lifted his feet a little off the cold lino floor covering. 'Michael, don't wake the child up.'

'She's not a child, she's twenty minutes older than I am.'

'That's true. She's not a child any more than you are.'

Michael's face was troubled. 'She'll need to know, Dad.'

'Nobody needs to know.'

'It's partly her house.'

'It's *his* house Michael.' John indicated the man across the river.

'I know, I know.' The boy's thin shoulders were raised, tense. He was troubled and unsure what to do.

'Give me something to put my feet on so they're not like two big blocks of ice when I get back into the bed with your mother.'

Michael rooted round under the comics and books that were on the window seat and found a raggedy cushion.

'Will this do?'

'That's fine, thank you son.'

Some of the quivering tension had left the boy. He sat down, still looking out of the window, but prepared to talk rather than wake his sister and the whole house in his grief.

'Do you know, when I was a lad your age we used to go over there and play too. Your Uncle Barry, now, he was a great climber, there was nothing he couldn't get right up on, and there were more bits of wall then than now.'

Michael was interested.

'And then your Aunt Nuala; my heavens wouldn't those little Australian boys and girls be surprised to know that their Mother Superior used to climb trees like a boy? She used to tie her skirts up around her waist and climb with Barry.'

'What did you do, Daddy?'

'Sure I was only like poor Eddie, looking at them,' John sighed. 'They usually wanted me to go away, if I remember rightly.'

Michael took this as a criticism of the twins' own attitude to their younger brother.

'I'm sure you were fine when you were young, Dad. But God, you couldn't have Eddie hanging round with you, I mean really and truly.'

'Oh I know that, I'm not disputing it, Eddie would have your heart scalded. But I was only talking about the old days across there . . . and the kind of things we used to do . . .'

He talked on gently, his voice low enough that it wouldn't wake Kate and have her storming out on to the landing. Yet raised enough for Michael to think it was a normal conversation and that these were normal times.

John dug deep into his memory of games played, and accidents averted, of guards on bicycles, of two young bullocks that ran wild, away from someone's secure field up the hill. He talked until he saw the lids begin to droop on his son's thin white face, and knew that sleep was going to come at last, that Michael wouldn't wake Dara and sit all night watching in helpless despair as this stranger walked through what they still wanted to think their home.

That night old Mr Slattery couldn't sleep and he came down to get himself some warm milk. He dozed off at the kitchen table as the milk boiled and didn't smell the burning until Fergus appeared, wild-eyed with shock.

'Don't put me away, don't put me in the county home,' wept the old man. 'I'll take milk to bed in a flask. I'll never try to boil it again. Please.'

Fergus had been filling the blackened saucepan with water and opening the windows.

'Are you going mad altogether, Father? Would I put you in the county home? Would I?'

'If I were mad altogether you'd have to,' Mr Slattery said reasonably.

'Yes, but you're not, and even if you were I don't think I would.'

'Why not? It would be the right thing to do, we've often advised clients ourselves.'

'You're not a client. You're my father.'

'You've got to get on with your own life.'

'But I *do* get on with my own life, for God's sake. I was out getting on with it this evening and I'd only just got to bed. That's why it was my nose that caught the milk, not Miss Purcell's.'

'I'm a burden, I don't do much work in the office.'

'You're not a burden, we don't *have* much work in the office.'

'I've let the place run down, why else didn't we get the business for Fernscourt?'

'Oh is *that* what's worrying you? I'll tell you why. Your man O'Neill is in business in a big way over there, really big, owns at least half a dozen restaurants or bars or whatever they are. He has other business too, he pays accountants and lawyers big fees. Now he's opening here, the big lawyers look up a map . . . Ireland they say, Ireland, where's that? Then they find it. What's the capital they say, what's the capital? Then someone tells them and they get Dublin solicitors. That's all.'

'You make it sound so simple. I suppose it will be good when he arrives, this American. He's given work in the place already.'

'Here's some fresh milk.' Fergus had boiled another saucepan. 'We'll tell Miss Purcell that I was drunk and burned the arse out of the saucepan. The American? It has to be good for the place. I suppose the poor devil will be full of nonsense and trying to hunt and shoot and fish. We'll have great sport with him. Imagine worrying about the American! It'll be the best sport we ever had. I can't wait for him to arrive.'

That night Sergeant Sheehan found somebody lying in a very awkward position, legs splayed, head lolling, and stretched right across the footbridge at the end of the town. Sergeant Sheehan was a thickset man who used to be a great hurler in his day, a man with ferocious eyebrows which made him look very frightening when he had to. But he was running to fat now, with slow and undemanding life in a country town. He felt his uniform was constantly tight around his neck, and rolls of fat gathered when he buttoned his top collar.

He loosened the collar now by opening several buttons, and looked at the sleeping woman. It was Miss Barry, the canon's housekeeper. A fine place for her to have passed out and to be snoring at 1 a.m. Sergeant Sheehan went back to the station to think the matter over, having tidied her legs into a more respectable position. He wasn't quite sure what his next move would be. To wake the canon with such bad news would be unwise. To allow Miss Barry to be found by someone else, asleep and obviously the worse for wear, would hardly be wise either. To wake Miss Barry might be the least wise course of all. What a pity Mrs Whelan wasn't around. He walked up Bridge Street. There was still a light on.

He tapped gently. She came to the door fully dressed.

'Do you ever sleep, Sheila?' he asked, full of relief to see her.

'Not so much these days. Telegrams come in at funny times too. They don't know what time we wake or sleep,' she said.

He told her; she pondered. She decided it was best left; even another three or four hours would mean she had slept the worst off. Had she anything to support her head? No, but the sergeant would arrange it.

'I get up early,' Mrs Whelan said. 'I could throw some water over her at around six, and then we could pretend she had been out early to pick mushrooms for His Reverence's breakfast and fallen into the river.'

This way face was saved. He couldn't thank her enough. Mrs Whelan said they would speak no more of it; she was flattered to be asked for her advice. She would sleep now for a couple of hours.

It was years since Patrick O'Neill had stayed up all night. He tried to think back. In the 1930s during the Depression often, very often, hardly a week went by when nights were not spent hauling boxes and crates, doing favours here, moving goods that had to be out of warehouses there. Counting, taking note, proving himself reliable. Telling Italians and fellows with long Polish names that they could always rely on Patrick O'Neill. He used to say his own name with pride to these men, roll it around as if it were an incantation. He spoke of himself in the third person to these business associates in the early days: 'Patrick O'Neill won't let you down. You can always rely on Patrick O'Neill.'

They could rely on him and his truck at first, and then on his fleet of truck drivers who didn't ask questions but just shifted what had to be shifted.

And then Patrick O'Neill's name was over neighbourhood bars. He was one of the first to welcome the end of Prohibition, just as he had enjoyed the income and lifestyle which Prohibition had created for him, and those Italians and Poles who had given him early jobs were not forgotten. When life became less risky Patrick O'Neill invited them and their wives to his bar-restaurants and treated them with respect. Flowers for the wives, discreet smiles when they brought girlfriends instead. They appreciated it; they sent him custom. But it had meant a lot of staying up all night. There had been the night when he had gone through the books over and over again. It was dawn when he had to admit that it was a fellow Irishman who had been cheating him. He called to Tom Brady's house at seven, shirt open and eyes red.

Tom Brady realized what had happened and tried to run.

'Mrs Brady,' Patrick O'Neill had said quietly, 'take the children out, maybe for the day. To family perhaps? Don't let them come back before nightfall. Oh and move any really good ornaments and pieces from your front parlour.'

'This isn't a movie, Patrick,' Tom started to bluster.

'Sure it isn't, otherwise you'd be dead on your floor for what you've done to me.'

Tom Brady's wife gasped.

'Take the children,' Tom had said, 'and do what he says. He's not going to kill me.'

Patrick beat him with a violence he didn't even know he possessed. With every blow he grunted and spat out more rage. *This* was for the false smiles and the drinks after a day spent cheating. *This* was for letting Patrick fire an innocent Italian two months back. *This* was for the sleazy shabby way the goods were stolen, taking them out in trash cans and coming back later to root amongst the garbage and remove the good bottles of liquor. *This* was for taking a bonus last Christmas, and *this*, the hardest blow of all, had been for being an Irishman and doing it all to another

43

Irishman. He had been up all that night all right. And on the night he had met Kathleen.

He had never intended to marry, or fall in love. There wouldn't be time. Work was scarce first and then it was too plentiful, and then came responsibility and long hours. There wouldn't be time for a wife and family. But Kathleen had looked so lovely and she was so lively then, eyes dancing, long fair hair swept up into a top knot of some sort. She had been so excited about his bars and restaurants, and so enthusiastic. She said over and over that America was so alive and so full of hope she pitied anyone who lived anywhere else.

'Except Ireland, of course,' Patrick had said.

'Particularly Ireland.' She had tossed her curls.

It was the one thing they differed on. Huge in ways, and yet it never mattered all that much, because he knew that when he was ready to go back – 'to go back' was how he put it, though he himself had never seen Ireland – Kathleen would come too. He wasn't to know that as her health deteriorated she would become less and less interested in any scheme, be it in New York or in Ireland. Kathleen, who used to sit on the tables in a new bar holding swathes of material up to the light at the window to see which would make the classiest curtains, lost her involvement in anything except the big white house in New Jersey, and in the latter years even that couldn't hold her frail attention.

He hadn't spent any night awake over Kathleen's illness; there was not one night when he knew she wouldn't get better. He was never given any bad diagnosis, or expectation or time when her illness would run its course. Possibly, the last time he had stayed up all night without going to bed or lying down was the night Kerry was born. In 1947. The child had been born at home and the doctors told Patrick it was going to be long and hard, even though Kathleen was still young and strong in those days. He had spent all night pacing, trying to read, doing anything to distract himself from the cries upstairs. It had been a clear bright dawn when he held his son in his arms and rocked him. Kerry's tiny, scrunched-up face was so touching, Patrick had swallowed hard and swore that no harm would come to this boy, and that he would go back and walk in his rightful place in Ireland with head held high.

As he clutched the little bundle to him he felt tears in his eyes and wondered how his own father, Michael O'Neill – amiable, drunken, good-for-nothing Michael O'Neill – felt when he had held Patrick in his arms. Did he not wish too that he could take his son back to Mountfern? No, Patrick's father must have felt no such thing. At the age of twenty Michael O'Neill, his parents, brothers and sisters, had left Mountfern because there was no work and his father had been thrown out on the road. He never went back, nor had he ever thought it possible. He had sung songs about Ireland, and told tales, and filled young Patrick with a hatred of this Fern family whom he had never met.

Patrick was eight when he heard that the Ferns' house had been burned down. The news came by letter. It was too late to be any good to any of the O'Neills then. There was no O'Neill around to watch the flames lick through the windows of this house, the house which had held the family that did them down.

Patrick O'Neill touched the moss-covered stones almost religiously; he leaned against the ivy-covered walls and walked by the moonlight into a room which still had its walls. To his surprise there were orange boxes as furniture, and toy tea-sets. Some local children had obviously been playing there. He smiled at the jam jars full of wild flowers. He wondered who the children were. Certainly they wouldn't have been allowed in the door during the Ferns' time. He would love to see their faces when they heard his plans for the old ruin.

Mrs Whelan was the first to see him. She had just delivered a dripping Miss Barry back to the presbytery while Father Hogan and Canon Moran clucked sympathetically at the mishap that caused their housekeeper to fall into the river. Mrs Whelan had even provided some mushrooms as a kind of proof that the bewildered woman had been on an errand for her employers. Just as she was walking back to her post office, she saw a man in a crumpled suit, tie loosened, walk up Bridge Street towards a hired car. It could be no one else.

Patrick O'Neill stood handsome and pale in his unaccustomed dark suit. Big and broad-shouldered with a head of dark brown curly hair, he was a man who normally wore tan or beige jackets. Few people in the States ever remembered seeing him in dark colours. Even if there had been a formal occasion he had worn a green tuxedo in deference to his national origins.

His enemies in business had often said that he had the thickset looks of an Irish paddy who should still be shovelling dirt. This pleased Patrick rather than otherwise; he said he was glad to wear the signs of his forefathers so openly, and to be living proof that they had to work hard and that they survived. But he didn't have the pugilistic face of a man who would like to have a fight, he had no boxer's scowl, nor the low forehead of a man who found it hard to cope with whatever life dealt him. His face was broad and open, his eyes blue and twinkling. From his eyes lines came out like a star, meaning that they often looked as if he was smiling even when he was far from it.

He was more attractive and younger than Sheila had expected. But then, what should she have expected, just seeing telegrams and telex messages pile up for him? He looked as if he could do with a welcome.

She crossed the street. 'And you're very welcome to these parts, Mr O'Neill,' she said warmly.

Patrick looked at her gratefully. 'How did you know it was me, did you know my people?'

'Who else would it be, Mr O'Neill? And I have a foot of telegrams and messages for you up at the post office. Would you like a cup of tea and I'll give them to you?'

'Now that's what I call efficiency.' He threw back his head and laughed.

Mrs Whelan led him through the post office to her room behind. She put him sitting down beside a pile of communications and put on the kettle. She said no more till she placed a cup of tea beside each of them, and some buttered soda bread. Yes, a very handsome man, she thought, he was going to cause a bit of a stir. Mrs Whelan smiled to herself, thinking of all the excitement there would be.

Patrick read the telegrams from Gerry Power, the man who had replaced Tom Brady as his second in command all those years ago. He read the telegrams from Rachel too quickly, and put them into a different pocket. He felt the heat coming back into his body with the strong tea and the thick buttered bread. She was a gracious woman, this Mrs Whelan. No curiosity about him, no need to talk and chatter like so many women, telling you their business and wanting to know yours. If they were all going to be like this in Mountfern, he had made the best move in his life.

Despite the hard, silent disapproving face of Gerry Power.

Despite the hurt, bewildered eyes of Rachel Fine.

Despite the confused chirrupings of little Grace.

And the stern scornful look of Kerry, the tall golden-haired son. The boy he had promised to take back home. The boy who said so little to him these days that Patrick had no idea what he was thinking about, at all.

Fergus wondered what it would be like to be a solicitor in a big place where you had no idea what the day would bring. In other places he supposed he could stand on his own doorstep and stretch without four passers-by asking him had he a bad back like his father, and sending messages in to Miss Purcell or advising him on the rather glum-looking window boxes. Still he wouldn't change it. And he could escape and get on with his life a bit, as he had told his father last night, if he went twenty-five miles to a dance organized by a rugby club. There were grand girls there who wouldn't expect to be taken to Meagher's jewellery shop next morning if a kiss and a cuddle had been part of the night's entertainment.

He saw Kate Ryan walking up River Road and turning into Bridge Street. She waved.

'Are you out with your stopwatch in case I'm a second late?'

'Just waiting for the bells to ring for mass. If there had been one peal you'd have been fired. No, I was having a good stretch actually.'

'Don't you look like a young Greek god. Did you have a good time in Ballykane last night?'

His arms dropped to his sides mid-stretch. 'How did you know where I was . . .?'

'I was there myself dancing away beside you. You never saw me?'

'No you weren't, don't be ridiculous, who said it to you?'

'Jack Coyne. Some fellow couldn't start his car and rang Jack at all hours in the morning to go and pick him up.'

'God, you can't do much in this place, can you? And there was I thinking it wasn't such a bad place. No surprises.'

'It isn't a bad place. Do you want surprises?'

They were walking companionably in to start the day's work as the church bells began to peal at ten to nine to let the devout know it was time to put on the hats and pick up the missals for daily mass. The early devout would already have attended seven o'clock mass, said this morning by a perplexed Father Hogan, whose mind was as much on the dripping and drunken housekeeper as it was on the liturgy.

'No I don't want surprises,' Fergus said. 'In the last few hours I've found my father nearly burning the house down, and now you tell me Jack Coyne has the entire details of my little escapade last night.'

Kate was at her desk opening post. It was a job they did together since the invention of the filing system. Kate wanted to check that the young master knew not only where to find everything but where to file it as well. She had arranged a bowl of flowers, a blotter and pens on his famous table by the window where every document used to end up in the old days.

'I think I'll lay off surprises for a while,' Fergus said, throwing a heap of papers on the floor beside him out of habit, and picking them up sheepishly to place them in the pending tray on the desk.

'You know they say they come in threes,' said Kate absently, as she began to read a letter which had been delivered by hand. It was a request from Patrick J. O'Neill that Slattery and Slattery should act for him in his application to build a hotel and apply for a pub licence as well. He thought that since he was going to live in the area he would very much like the local man to act on his behalf.

'God Almighty, he's going to build a hotel,' Kate said, standing up.

Fergus had come to read the letter over her shoulder. 'I won't act for him – he can find his own attorney and counsellors and whatever they call them over there,' he said after a long silence.

She looked at him blankly. 'Why won't you act for him?'

'Because if his application is granted and he gets his licence, then he'll open a pub . . .'

'You have to take his business . . .' Kate was pale.

'I do not have to take his business, thank you. I can accept or refuse any work I like. I am not going to accept anything which is going to take the bread and butter out of your mouth.' He looked angry and upset as he stood beside her and she found herself weeping on his shoulder. 'Do you want to go home, and tell John?'

'No, not yet.' Kate shook her head and sat down purposefully at her desk. 'Not for a while. If our bread and butter's going to disappear in the pub I'd better make sure I don't lose the job in the office as well.' She gave a smile to show that the emotional bit was over.

'You'd never lose a job here,' Fergus said gently. 'I just wish it paid better. Maybe you should tell John now, before someone else does.'

'Nobody else will. It's silly but last night he was saying, when we were sitting out in the side garden bit . . . he was saying that nothing bad was ever going to happen to us. Maybe this isn't very bad. I want to have a think before I tell him. That's all.' There were no words to say. It was about as bad as it could be. Fergus didn't say anything. He took off his glasses and polished them. He saw Kate looking at him gratefully.

'All right. All right, I know I have a weak face without them, I'm putting them back on. Let's open more mail, shall we? Who knows what other little surprises may be lurking in these nice brown envelopes?'

Patrick O'Neill drove to the Grange, some three miles from Mountfern. It was a big, gracious house that had always been in the Johnson family. It had known good days and bad, and just now was going through a fairly prosperous phase. Marian Johnson had discovered that there was a business in offering riding holidays. City people and English visitors liked to come and stay in the vaguely country house atmosphere. The Johnsons always left a decanter of sherry out instead of charging people by the glass, it gave them the feeling that they were guests on a country weekend. Last summer Marian had quite a few Americans, who usually came in groups. This big, handsome O'Neill man was different.

He said he would like to ride, but since he had not sat on a horse's back for years he wondered if it was foolish to begin again at the age of forty-eight.

Marian Johnson aged thirty-nine looked into his blue eyes with the crinkly laugh lines coming away from them at the sides. No, she thought that was the perfect age to start again. She would take him riding herself.

Marian was fair-haired, but no one would ever have called her a blonde; her hair was wispy and flyaway, and no style ever seemed to tame it. She had a big soft bosom and often wore twinsets, mauves or pale green light jumpers with a matching cardigan. She looked her best when her hair was tidied into a net and under a bowler hat, and her soft drooping bosom gathered into the mannish coat of the hunt. The Johnsons were people who considered themselves of importance in the neighbourhood; normally Marian would never have shown the slightest interest in any American visitor. A man passing through, a man with no family, no background or stake in the area. Marian would have little time to waste. Yet there was something about Patrick O'Neill that attracted her.

'Does your wife like the idea of riding?' Marian asked.

'My wife passed away this year,' Patrick said.

'Oh, I am most awfully sorry.'

'She had been in poor health for a long time,' murmured Patrick.

Marian said no more; she arranged for the horses and assured Patrick that there would be no broken bones.

Companionably they walked the horses over to a stile where she advised Patrick to mount his animal.

'Go on,' she laughed. 'It's more dignified than all this getting a leg up by putting your foot in someone's hand. It's like stepping on.'

'It's too easy,' Patrick complained. 'I don't mind the undignified way.'

Astride their horses, they rode down the quiet lane with the fuchsia-filled hedges. Marian pointed out landmarks, towers on small hills and when they came to the corner she said, 'And that's Fernscourt . . . they say it's going to be . . .'

'I bought it. It's mine,' he said quickly.

'Of *course*, they said you'd be here soon. How stupid of me not to recognize it must have been you, I thought you were another tourist. Well, well, what a beautiful place you've got for yourself, Mr O'Neill, and will you be making a home of it, or what?'

'I'm going to be the opposition, Miss Johnson,' he said simply. 'I'm going to build a hotel. I don't know whether we will be exactly in competition or not; I feel sure that we will be going for different markets. But what I was hoping was that we might be able to cooperate . . . If you wanted to expand your riding school say, and incorporate some of the guests from Fernscourt . . .?' He looked at her openly and eagerly.

It was very honest of him to come right out and say it straight, she thought. Another man might have sniffed around her hotel to steal a few ideas before declaring his hand.

'Do you know anything about the hotel business?' she asked.

'I have one small motel in New Jersey. I bought it really for tax purposes, so I'm not what you'd call experienced. But I have bars and restaurants, so I guess you could say I know something about what the public wants. Only the New York public mind you, but New York is pretty cosmopolitan, and it might be a good sample of what all kinds of people want.' He wasn't only after the American package-tour business, he explained, he wanted local people to feel involved. It was to be their place too. Too long the walls of Fernscourt had kept them out. For nearly a hundred and fifty years the real Irish people of the parish had been refused access to places that rightly belonged to them. That wouldn't be the way any more.

'I don't think people were refused access,' Marian said. 'It's been a ruin for years. It belonged to the Land Commission, didn't it? We used to go there on picnics when I was a girl.'

'No, I mean before that, when the Ferns were there, barring everyone from their door.'

Marian was cheerfully vague about that side of things. 'Did they? How stupid of them. They were gone long before my time, of course, but I think my father remembers them. He used to play bridge with someone called Fern. But it mightn't have been them, the people from the house. It could have been a cousin or something.'

Patrick was slightly irritated by this affectionate view. He thought that perhaps Marian had been overprotected and didn't really know the story of the big house. After all, the Johnsons were Catholics, Patrick had seen the Infant of Prague in the hall and there was a picture of Our Lady of Perpetual Succour in the bedroom where he had laid his case. Suddenly the tiredness of last night began to reach him. His eyes felt heavy.

'Do you think it's a possibility . . . our getting together over some aspects of the tourist trade?' he asked Marian.

'I see unlimited possibilities,' said Marian, running her tongue lightly across her lower lip and thinking that life was looking up.

CHAPTER FOUR

Now that he was here they all claimed to have been the first to meet him and the one who knew him best. Those who had been telling stories only hours ago about the certainty of the nuns or the agricultural research institute were now eager to tell how they had known all along that it was going to be a hotel. The possibilities of a big tourist undertaking were legion. Patrick O'Neill was said to have told people that this was going to be his home, and his home would be open three hundred and sixty-five days a year, no closing down in the winter leaving the boys and girls to find some other jobs for the long harsh wet months from September to Easter.

Judy Byrne was peeved to note that he had been spotted riding horses with Marian Johnson in the morning light. That was fast moving of a spectacular nature. Kate Ryan had heard that he was seen in Conway's and Dunne's, and she was sure he must have been in Foley's too. Rita Walsh, who ran the Rosemarie hair salon, had seen what she thought must have been him in the moonlight over at the ruin. Hard to see at that distance but he had looked a fine cut of a man.

Tommy Leonard's mother said that Tommy was under no circumstances to be seen running wild with that gang of young criminals he called his friends. This was a chance sent from heaven for him to better himself. Maybe his whole future could be assured if he were seen by the new owner of Fernscourt to be a sensible boy. Tommy wondered how could he sort out his future if he turned his back on his friends? But Mrs Leonard said there were a million ways if Tommy would put his mind to it. That hotel was going to need a shop on the very premises to sell things to its visitors who mightn't want to walk the whole way to Mountfern. What more sensible than to offer the concession to the local existing stationers and booksellers? Tommy must be ready to seize the chance.

'But I'm only twelve,' Tommy wailed. 'How could I seize a shop in a hotel?' He saw his whole youth and adolescence trickling away standing behind counters of one sort or another.

'By the time that hotel is up and ready to have a shop you'll be well old enough to work in it,' his mother said firmly.

Maggie Daly's mother couldn't understand how it was that they hadn't seen him. He was meant to have been in Sheila Whelan's, and in all three pubs on Bridge Street; he had been seen standing looking at the Stations of the Cross in the church, but Canon Moran hadn't focused on him properly and didn't want to interrupt a man at prayer, so he was no use as an informant.

Then he had been observed driving up past Coyne's wood. Could he have been going to the convent maybe? The whole thing might still have something to do with an order of enclosed nuns. The only people who knew for sure were Sheila Whelan, because he had been in the post office for an age, but of course it was hopeless trying to get anything out of Sheila. And Marian Johnson, she didn't talk to everyone easily in Mountfern, so there would be no news from that quarter.

Jack Coyne was very anxious for a description of the American who had bought Fernscourt and was going to turn it into a hotel. Very anxious indeed. Yesterday he had got a call from the railway station in the big town: an American wanting to hire a car. Jack had driven in to him.

'Why did a well-heeled person like yourself not hire a car from Avis or Hertz?' Jack inquired.

'Always believe in supporting the local industry,' the Yank had said.

'Here for the fishing?'

'Yup,' the man said.

Jack Coyne had too much on his mind to make conversation with a taciturn foreign visitor whom he would never see again. He charged the American two and a half times the normal price and gave him a poor rate for his dollar. Jack was ashen-faced trying to get a proper account of the Patrick O'Neill who had bought Fernscourt. He had an uneasy feeling that he might have cheated the man who was going to live across the river from him. The man who could have brought him the kind of wealth he never dreamed of.

Miss Barry was quite unaware that she had met Mr O'Neill. She had been struggling under the weight of two heavy shopping bags when a man stopped to give her a lift. She had climbed clumsily into the car, opening the window with that native cunning she had when she smelled of drink. Fresh air was an ally, closed spaces were a giveaway. She told this man about the saintly Canon Moran, the angelic young Father Hogan and even sang a few bars of a song.

'Tell me does your poor wife take a drink?' she asked him suddenly. She got the reply that the late Mrs O'Neill had not in fact been partial to liquor.

'Best way to be,' Miss Barry said approvingly. 'She'll live to be a hundred, God spare her.'

She rattled her plastic bags which contained bottles and smiled at him beatifically.

But none of this remained in any part of her consciousness.

Patrick had indeed gone to the convent when he had been sighted driving towards Coyne's wood. He left the car at Coyne's garage and walked up the shabby ill-kept avenue to the school. Sister Laura greeted him, a small shrew-like woman, eyes dark and bright in her round face, like two currants in a bun. She saw within minutes why he was there. He was trying to work out whether this country school would in any way approach his hopes and plans for his only daughter's education.

Sister Laura was a sensible woman. She knew that it would be counterproductive to encourage this American to believe that hers was the finest educational establishment in Ireland. She spoke praisingly of the Sacred Heart Convent, the Loretto nuns, the Holy Child Order, the FCJ (Faithful Companions of Jesus), all of them excellent sisters running very highly thought of boarding schools for girls. But that was just the point. They would be boarding schools. And if Mr O'Neill wanted his child with him, then this was the only game in town.

She didn't put it as racily as that, but Patrick realized that if she had known the phrase she would have.

She listed the disadvantages. Grace would be much more sophisticated than the simple girls who came from smallholdings over the fields to this school each day. Grace would have to learn Irish: it was compulsory in schools, and they wouldn't have any facility for her to study something else at the time Irish-language lessons were taking place. It would be fairly rough and ready; sports would not be as she had known them in the United States, the girls played camogie, a form of hockey. Sister Laura said it was the female equivalent of hurling for boys.

But on the plus side Grace would grow up with the children amongst whom her father intended her to live. She would be at his side, she would make friends of all kinds, which was essential if a family were to live in a small community. She would avoid the princess-in-the-castle role. Patrick had looked with dismay at the shabby building, and particularly what Sister Laura described with pride as the new extension: classrooms thrown together, without thought or design. The finish was shoddy, obviously a local builder doing it for half nothing and knowing that the nuns weren't going to complain. The library where the small nun lingered so lovingly was a big barren room lined with jerry-built shelves. Soon to contain a couple of hundred books, most of them the lives of the saints. But the nun was right, he could see all this. He knew that he would send his child to the convent. What Grace Mary O'Neill might lose on polish and a broader approach to education, she would surely gain in a sense of belonging. And that was what this journey was all about.

Sister Laura had pursed her lips over the thought of Mr O'Neill's son being educated in Mountfern. Of course the brothers were the best in the world. But . . .

And of course one had to take into consideration that a boy, a young man would have to be prepared to make his way in the world. Especially a young man who would inherit a huge property. So, she didn't actually say that he should forget the brothers, nor was there a mention of any inadequacies. But there was a veiled hint that only a madman might entrust the son and heir to Brother Keane and his colleagues in the big red-brick school behind the church. Mention was made of Jesuits, of Benedictines and of Holy Ghost Fathers. All known to Mr O'Neill, certainly,. in the United States, she was sure, and all running exceptionally good boys' boarding schools in Ireland, for the sons of gentlemen and people who were going to get on in life. After all, with a boy it was much more important. And with a boy there wouldn't be the same sense of loss seeing the child go to boarding school.

For courtesy and diplomacy Patrick O'Neil called on Brother Keane too. He went with no sense of apology. Instead he asked the man for advice. He had to send his son as a boarder. He would be most grateful if Brother Keane could mark his card. Would he favour the Jesuits in County Kildare, the Benedictines in Limerick, the Holy Ghost or Vincentians in Dublin?

Brother Keane had never been so flattered in his life. He gave great care to his deliberations and between them the two men came up with the ideal school for Kerry O'Neill.

Patrick O'Neill felt that slowly things were placing themselves together.

He was back in Mountfern, the sale of the land was going through. He had been assured there would be no problems with the licences. The grants towards building a hotel would be even greater than he had thought. The people were friendly from what he could judge; usual sprinkling of rogues and drunks but basically a solid place. The place his people had come from. He let his mind rest lightly on the images of his children. Grace with the beautiful curls and dimples, Grace almost twelve now, the prettiest girl in her year, the apple of his eye. And Kerry. Handsome distant Kerry. Fifteen and as tall as Patrick. No paddy features in Kerry, his face was chiselled and had classic good looks. Even as a small child.

What would his two striking children make of Mountfern? They had never really believed that he would change their lives so totally. Part of them thought it was a huge adventure, another – perhaps the greater – part would find it a wrench to leave their surroundings, their friends, the memory of the way things had always been when their mother was alive. Patrick squared his shoulders. There was to be no wallowing in the past. This had been his dream, to take his family back to the place they had come from.

This town would be their home now. It had its shortcomings. He was not so blinded with the yearning to return that he couldn't see that. The untidiness of it irritated him. An Irish village, his Irish village shouldn't have yards full of rusting, broken machinery, there should be bright paint on all the doors. There should be a fountain or something at the end of Bridge Street instead of just letting it peter out and wind away.

He had called into the local public houses, each one in turn. None of them would be any opposition to him, of course, but even more importantly he didn't think his hotel would be a threat to any of them. Dunne's looked as if it were about to do a moonlight flit, Conway's had three serious drinkers sitting on high stools behind its grocery. You'd need radar to find out that there was a bar there at all. And in Foley's he had the distinct impression he had wandered into a private house. Matt Foley had eyed him beadily but the chat died down while he was there. No, there was only that place with the nice old sign, Ryan's, which was right opposite his new estate. He would need to handle them with tact. If anyone was going to lose by his plans for Fernscourt it would be this little place. While still incognito he had inquired about the family. He heard that the mother went out to work, a rare thing in Irish country towns, and that the business was steady. The rest of the brothers and sisters who owned the place had all emigrated, so John Ryan had only his own family to support out of it.

Patrick had looked at it often when he had been visiting the site. He had even looked at it by moonlight last night when he was walking around his land. It had been very still with everyone asleep, and nobody knowing that he watched it from across the river.

He walked from the brothers past the church and along in front of the bridge, and looked up Bridge Street. It could be a fine town. He would make so many changes here, give people a bit of pride in their surroundings again. He would walk to Fernscourt now. This was not New York, home of the automobile, this was his place, to walk around, to stop and talk, or just to watch the river if he wanted to. Past Jack Coyne's, past a shabby little store with the name Quinn in faded lettering, then across a rickety footbridge. He would walk his land before going to introduce himself to the Ryans in that attractive little shebeen.

He heard the sound of children's voices as he walked through the laurel bushes on the path from the footbridge to the house.

Then he saw them.

A boy and girl obviously twins, dark-eyed, dark-haired and moving in exactly the same way, gestures and smiles utterly identical.

Patrick looked at them fondly.

'Hey, is it moving day?' he asked good-naturedly.

They hadn't seen him arrive. They looked at him, startled. There was no doubt in their eyes. They knew who he was, the man who had come to take away their place for playing in.

He knew he would have to walk warily. His smile was broad but it got nothing in response.

'You're packing up. Is that right?'

The dark-eyed twins talked to him alternately, one beginning a sentence and the other finishing it, as if they had always done this.

'People always come here . . .' the girl said defensively.

'Always as far as anyone can remember,' supported the boy.

'So it's not as if it was trespassing . . .'

'Or being on private property . . .'

Patrick gave a big infectious laugh.

'But I know that, I *know*. I saw your home last night, it was mighty impressive. I came up to see the place by moonlight. Have you lot ever been here in the moonlight?' They shook their heads.

'It's very strange. It has a life of its own, all the shadows seem to mean something. You'd really like it.' He spoke as if he were their own age, suggesting they do something as out of their world as going off on midnight treks across the river. Mammy and Daddy would kill them.

'Come some evening with me, I'll square it with your folks, and I'll go off for a walk by myself and leave you in your . . . in your house?' He sought for the right word to describe the dismantled room.

'It's not going to be knocked down, is it?'

He answered the girl indirectly. 'Changed a bit,' he said. 'You know, roofs and good firm walls.'

'You mean it *is* to be knocked down.'

He decided not to talk baby talk to the girl with the big dark eyes under her bangs of black hair.

'That's it, knocked down to be rebuilt. They tell me a lot of these old walls are dangerous, you could tip them over with your little finger. Not the things to build on, unfortunately.'

She nodded silently. The boy nodded too. It was as though they had both accepted what he said in exactly the same way and were thinking about it.

'Still, it won't be for a while. No need to move all your things.' He indicated with his head their box of possessions.

'If it's coming down anyway . . .' Michael began.

'There's really not any point . . .' Dara took up.

'In leaving things here . . .'

'That'll have to come out anyway.'

'Sure, everyone's got to do what they've got to do. All I'm saying is that there's no great rush. It will be weeks before anyone gets as far as this room. What do you call it, by the way?' He smiled at them, looking from one to the other. They were not to be won over.

'What do you call what?' the girl asked.

'This . . . this room . . . do you have a special name for it or anything?'

'No. No special name,' she said.

'It used to be the morning room,' the boy said. The first offer.

'Not by us. We didn't call it the morning room. Or any name.' The dark girl was giving nothing away.

'I guess it was the morning room because it got the morning sun. It faces east, south-east. That's right, would you say?'

But the boy felt he had been too friendly, and his sister was suggesting they leave.

'We've really got to go now.'

'Come back again, any time; you're welcome here always,' he said. Somehow he knew it was the wrong thing to have said.

'Well, like you always were. When a place is special you don't need anyone to welcome you to it. That's right, isn't it?'

They nodded at him, shoulders slightly less tense, their stance not so hostile.

'So we have to be off,' the boy said, picking up one side of the box that contained their life in this room.

'So goodbye,' said the girl, picking up the other side. They walked away from him, two little figures probably the same age as his Grace. Reasonably well cared for, grubby knees and dirty hands from playing . . . or indeed packing all their house things – they must have been covered in clay and dust. He watched them through the open walls of the house. They headed not for the town and the big bridge across into Bridge Street itself, but they went the other way towards River Road. Going to cross that little footbridge . . . maybe they belonged to that crook Jack Coyne?

Patrick was glad he hadn't asked them if they were twins. It was obvious they were and yet people always had a habit of asking the obvious. He found it very irritating even when it was well meant, like when people said to him 'You're an American!' with an air of discovery. They were fine kids, a little prickly, especially the girl. He'd catch up with them again, give them some job maybe, make them a few pounds. Or maybe they might resent that. He'd see. And when Grace came over, she'd charm them to bits anyway.

Now to see the Ryans in the poky little pub and then back to the dark room with the heavy mahogany furniture which had been in the Johnson family for generations, and the picture of Our Lady of Perpetual Succour which had helped them through some of the bad times. And a long, long sleep.

Kate had come back early. Fergus was right. She couldn't really concentrate and John would have to be told before anyone else came with the news.

The angelus was ringing as she walked down River Road. She looked across the banks and tried to imagine what it would be like with a huge hotel, a car park, with signs for a pub, with music maybe . . . Americans did things in style. She called into Loretto Quinn's little shop for a bag of sugar and a dozen candles. She always tried to give Loretto the turn; the small white face behind the counter moved Kate to pity. Loretto and Barney Quinn had saved and saved for a business, any business. They had done any work to get the deposit on the tumbledown place. They could be seen night and day working to make it right. They knew they were no competition to the shops on Bridge Street, so Barney Quinn had bought a van in which to do deliveries.

A week after the van was delivered, Barney threw it into reverse and went into the river. It happened so quickly that Loretto never even knew. She was still out in the back filling bags of potatoes when the alarm was raised and she realized half the town was outside her front door with ropes and pulleys trying to get her husband, dead now in his van, out of the River Fern. There had never been any colour or much life in her face after that. The child she had been expecting was stillborn, and she kept the shabby little shop as a memory of her young husband and in honour of the way things might have been.

Jack Coyne had been helpful about the unpaid-for van and the insurance and everything. People had been kind at the time. Not everyone continued to be helpful like Mrs Ryan. Loretto knew it would be very easy for her to get things cheaper in Bridge Street where she went to work, or to get them delivered, but nearly every day she called in for something. Today she was early.

'You're not taken sick coming home early?' she asked, concerned.

'Ah, not at all Loretto, nothing would make me feel badly, thank God. No, it's light there this morning and I thought I'd come on back to John to give him a hand. Not that there's likely to be any custom much for another hour.'

'Will the place across make any difference to you? Jack Coyne was in earlier. He wondered would it take any of your custom. I said it would be a different class of person entirely . . .'

'Thanks, Loretto.' Kate should have left earlier. John Ryan must know by now that his livelihood was threatened and that the days of Ryan's, Whiskey Bonder, were numbered.

John was sitting on a high stool reading the paper. He put down the newspaper automatically as the door opened.

'That's never the time!' he said, amazed, looking up at the old clock and back at his watch trying to work it out.

'No. I came home a bit early.' Kate put down her parcels and sat up as if she were a customer.

'Couldn't wait for a ball of malt?' he teased her.

'John.'

'What is it?' His face showed that he knew something was wrong. 'Are you all right, do you feel all right?'

'I'm fine.' Suddenly she was weary; she knew it would be an uphill struggle trying to make him realize how serious things were going to be.

'What *is* it then?'

'Did you hear what's happening to Fernscourt? They're going to make it into a hotel, have a bar. Americans are going to stay there, and there'll be a bar the size of a football pitch. He's put in for planning permission.'

'I heard that it was going to be a hotel all right. Tommy was round with the mineral water deliveries. Oh, he left the invoice there on the shelf by the way, it's behind the . . .'

'Will you stop bleating on about invoices? It's mighty few of those we'll be seeing in the future. Did you hear what I said?'

'I heard you, Kate. There's no need to shout like a fishwife.'

'Like a what?'

'A fishwife, look at you; you have your hands on your hips even. Stop being so impatient, and let's discuss this thing properly.'

'I'm the one who ran the whole way back from Fergus as soon as I heard about it. Don't you think I want to discuss it properly?'

'I'm the one who ran the whole way back from Fergus as soon as I heard about it. Don't you think I want to discuss it properly?'

'Yes, Kate. But not in public. Not in the middle of the bar.'

Kate looked around at the empty room.

'God Almighty, have you lost your mind? Who's here except Leopold, are you afraid the dog's going to start gossiping about us and our business round the town?'

'Don't let's start something that we'll have to cut off as soon as someone comes in that door.'

'All right, all right.' She made a gesture with her hands as if calming things down. 'Very well, but in the meantime do you mind if we talk about what's going to become of us, or would you rather read me Curly Wee out of the paper, or have a discussion about the weather?'

'We can't know what to think, until we know what's going to happen. How many times do I tell you not to go off at half cock about every single thing? We'll hear in good time what he's going to do. It might be the making of us for all we know. A whole lot of new people coming to the place, a lot of business we never had before. How many times have we wished that we were a tourist area where the people came on holidays? Now we will be, if what Tommy said is true.'

'The making of us; the making of us. How could it be anything except the end of us? For as many times as we said we'd like tourists, haven't we been thanking the stars that they're all so dozy in there in Foley's and Conway's and half packed to leave in Dunne's? We never had any competition, and even then we barely make a living. How can you be so blind?'

A flash of annoyance crossed John's big, good-natured face.

'Listen to me, I know you work hard, I know you put in all the hours that God gives you making a life for us, but answer me this, why am I being blind? What should I have done? Should I have bought the place myself? Or killed the fellow who did? Come on now, tell me. I'm standing here minding what I agree is at the moment a very slow business, some would say non-existent . . . and hoping that there's going to be some kind of good spin-off instead of doom and disaster for us, and you come rushing in the door shouting at me like a tinker's woman and saying I'm blind. That's a lot of help, Kate, thank you very much.'

Before she could reply the door opened and in came Marian Johnson, face flushed and wispy hair blowing all directions. Rita Walsh of the Rosemarie hair salon said that she had often known people with two crowns in their head of hair, but Marian Johnson had three. The woman couldn't be blamed for looking like a refined haystack. Marian was anxious to know if John Ryan could oblige her with a bottle of Jack Daniels.

John Ryan couldn't. He had Scotch all right, but nothing else except Irish whiskey. They might have it in the town, he supposed.

'Very fancy tastes you're getting above at the Grange,' he said companionably. He couldn't have said anything more welcome. Marian was dying to release the news. It was for the American, the man who was going to buy Fernscourt, or who had bought it in fact, but was going to open a hotel there. She went on and on, words falling over each other in excitement. There were going to be fishermen, not people like from here, not just the visitors from England who stayed in guest houses, but rich Americans with their own rods going to come and fish the Fern for pike and rudd, for bream and perch. And there were going to be Americans who would want to ride horses, they would even come in winter so they could hunt. They'd be here the whole year round. She was unaware of the silence that she spoke to. But eventually even Marian ran out of wind.

'Isn't it great?' she said, looking from one to the other.

'I'd have thought you'd be very put out. Isn't that all your kind of business that he's going to be taking?' Kate said, avoiding the look of caution that her husband was trying to beam at her.

Marian tossed her head. 'Heavens no, isn't it all to the good, isn't it going to build the whole thing up for all of us? They're going to want horses. Apparently I'll be expanding all that side of our business. It's going to change the whole place.' Marian hugged herself almost girlishly at the thought of it.

'That's what I'm afraid of,' Kate said. 'That it's going to change the whole place.'

'Oh Kate Ryan, you're as young as I am,' tinkled Marian, who was most definitely the older of the two. 'Don't be an old stick in the mud. It's going to transform your lives. Think of all the people that'll come tripping across that footbridge there to have a drink in your place. It will be just what you need.'

John seized her words as if they were a lifeline. 'That's just what I was saying to Kate when you came in the door. It could be the making of us. It could be the bit of luck we were always hoping for.' His face was bright with enthusiasm.

Kate watched, wordless, as her husband and Marian Johnson made plans for the future. They never talked about all the people who would like to go and have a drink in the big hotel, who would trip across the footbridge in the other direction. She looked at John and tried to work out whether he really believed this optimistic line of chat, or if he was only trying to buoy up the Ryan family. She decided that he really believed it; he wanted so much for things to turn out well that he refused to look at any other possibility. She felt a mixture of annoyance that he should be so naïve, and a protective, almost maternal anxiety because she had this cold fear that things were indeed going to change, and that something very bad was about to happen.

The twins crept in through the back door. They were filthy and carrying a big battered box between them. They looked like small dark criminals. They both put their fingers on their lips, warning Carrie not to cry out.

'Oh God, you'll get killed,' Carrie said, half pleased and half worried on their behalf. They'd been up to no good whatever they'd been doing.

'We'll be clean by the time Mammy gets back,' Michael said to reassure her.

'She's back already,' Carrie cried triumphantly. 'She'll take you apart so she will.'

Carrie, who greatly feared Mrs Ryan's hurricane-like visits to the kitchen, and her great ability to see things that were not done right, was always guiltily pleased when the wrath fell elsewhere. Carrie had long straight hair that fell into her frightened eyes – except when she saw Mrs Ryan looking, then she took a hair slide from her apron pocket. She was a mousy little thing who could look very nice when she tidied herself up. Mrs Ryan was always finding a blouse or a brooch or some little thing for her. Carrie only wore this finery on her day off when she walked four miles back to the farm from which she had been glad to escape.

She was fine unless she was fussed, and this was fussing her, the twins having skipped school and dragging this big box guiltily upstairs. Nobody ever came to Carrie's kitchen during the mornings except young Declan. And now here were Dara and Michael home way in advance. And the mistress was home early too. Really it was very troublesome. Carrie always arranged to have the kitchen looking well when Mrs Ryan came back at one o'clock; the pots were washed and put away. Now it looked a mess, and she was bound to be criticized. She sighed heavily and started to clear up the things that were most likely to offend.

Gently Michael and Dara eased themselves into the bathroom to shake out their crumpled school clothes and wipe off most of the grime. What was Mammy doing home so early, on this of all days? They had banked on at least an hour to get themselves to rights. This was the very first time they had ever mitched from school. Dara had told Sister Laura that she had a pain in her tummy, and Michael had told Brother Kevin that he had eaten too many potato crisps. Sister Laura had been understanding in case it might be Dara's first period, Brother Kevin had been dismissive and said what could you expect of a boy brought up in a pub but to eat like a pig all the rubbish in packets that was put in front of him? But it was too dangerous for them to go to school that day. If the man had been wandering around Fernscourt in the middle of the night they had to go and take their things away. Somehow they both knew that at the same time and realized it had to be done. They never dreamed they'd meet the man himself.

The Ryans never ate lunch together as a family since John was always in the bar. And the first rule of the house was that the children never appeared in the bar at all. John said that most of his customers came there to escape from households of screaming children racing round the place, and they mustn't be allowed to see a hint of the same thing in Ryan's. So Dara and Michael would have had no idea who was in the bar as they sat down to lunch.

Eddie and Declan had come in at the normal time.

'You were quick,' Eddie said to Michael. Normally they all raced together from the brothers, beyond the bridge down River Road. Dara's convent was up the other way, past the Rosemarie hair salon and Jack Coyne's. Nobody could tell whether or not she had come home. It was only Michael who might have been missed.

'Yes, we got out a bit early.' Michael looked from under his lashes to see if Mammy had made anything of this exchange, but her mind seemed to be miles away. She hadn't even noticed how crushed their clothes were from being bundled in a bag.

The twins hadn't decided what to do for the afternoon. They would have to walk towards school of course, and then they could meet somewhere else. Eddie and

Declan had no afternoon school so there would be no need for Michael to go all the way to the brothers. There were a host of possibilities. But before any were settled, the door of the pub opened and Daddy came through.

'Kate, Kate, come out and meet Mr O'Neill who's bought Fernscourt. He's called to pay his respects. And bring the children too, he says he'd like to meet them.'

Leopold, who was the most antisocial dog in the world, decided for once that he was included in the invitation too. Looking exactly like an advertisement from a Cruelty to Animals brochure, he walked ahead of them, sidling and cringeing as if expecting a blow at every turn.

Kate smoothed her skirt and shepherded the children in front of her. There was time only to wipe the excess of food from Declan's mouth; to pause and titivate them would have been a weakness with the door open and the great O'Neill waiting for them. Declan and Eddie hung back and had to be pushed forward. Dara and Michael were equally unwilling. In fact they both looked as if they had been caught out in some crime. Kate supposed they felt awkward meeting the man whose arrival they had hated so much. She didn't realize how deadly accurate her first thought was. They had been caught out. He was going to say he had met them this very morning. They would be discovered.

Kate was surprised at his looks. Like a handsome Irishman on a fair day with a drove of young bullocks to sell. Not like an American tycoon. He had a tweed jacket in a pepper and salt colour. It was very well cut. It would suit John, she thought, hide some of his stomach. This man was big, with bright blue eyes and a million laugh lines. His big hand was stretched to her.

'Mrs Kathleen Ryan. My own wife, the Lord have mercy on her, was Kathleen too. I'm glad to know you.'

He *seemed* glad to know her.

She had never got such a shock in her life.

All morning she had been thinking of him as the enemy, and here he was standing in their own pub, all smiles. No man could do that if he was going to take all your business. Even in America, where you had to be shrewd and tough to get on, they wouldn't do that. There were half a dozen customers all eager and interested to see the introductions. They, too, would be introduced, they knew. But first the children.

'These are the twins, Dara and Michael, and here's Eddie. Take your arm from over your face, Eddie and Declan. Declan, come out from behind me.'

He repeated their names slowly. *That's* why Americans were so good at remembering people. They didn't just say how do you do, or hello. They actually repeated the name.

'Dara . . . there's a name. Is it short for something?'

'It means oak tree. You know Kildare. That's Cill Dara, the churchyard of the oak tree.'

'Oak tree . . . Isn't that something? And Michael. That's the archangel, I guess?'

'And my grandfather,' Michael said more prosaically.

'And you'll come back and spend more mornings in Fernscourt, I hope,' he said.

The twins were glum. Here it was. The discovery.

'They will on their holidays, if they aren't in the way,' Kate said, filling the silence. 'But these days it's all schoolwork, I'm afraid. No idle mornings playing in Fernscourt until they get their holidays.'

Dara closed her eyes.

Michael looked at him in desperation.

'Sure,' said Patrick O'Neill. 'Sure, I know that, but after school or at weekends or any time. The place is always there and I'm sure you must love it, what with living so near and everything.' He wasn't going to say anything.

They looked at him in amazement.

John and Kate Ryan also exchanged glances of relief. Whatever else was going to happen, at least this big man understood somehow that the place was important to the twins. What a relief that they would not be getting into trouble over trespass or being a nuisance. The man in full view of the whole bar had literally invited the children to continue playing in the house.

'That's very kind of Mr O'Neill; thank him, children,' Kate said.

'Thank you,' said Dara.

'Very much,' finished Michael.

It was time for them to go back to school. They were hooshed out back through the house again. The children had never been known to go out on to River Road through the pub entrance. Kate went silent behind the bar and helped to serve. Nobody would move until the introductions had been properly made. Jimbo Doyle, the man who did a bit of everything in Mountfern, was particularly pleased. If he could be present as a friend of the establishment it might mean work on the new place across the river. He was a big fair man with hair like straw and a healthy red face. He often wore a check shirt and looked about to break into a square dance at any moment.

Charlie, who worked in Daly's, would be sure to be a frequent visitor there anyway, with milk and cream. Unless, of course, the man was going to have his own cow, his own dairy. Maybe Charlie could ask him now.

Patrick O'Neill was open with all of them. He wasn't at all sure if they would have their own cows. Some day possibly. But not for a good bit. He'd be needing all the milk, butter and cream that Daly's Dairy would provide. Charlie felt very important to be the bearer of this news and specially so when Mr O'Neill remembered his name.

'See you again then, Charlie,' and a cheerful wave as he was leaving to ride down River Road and back to Bridge Street to Mrs Daly with the good tidings.

Jimbo Doyle's red face was positively scarlet after the encounter. Mr O'Neill said that the work on the site was all in the hands of an overseer, a Brian Doyle who came from the big town sixteen miles away. Possibly Jimbo and Brian were related? It could be, couldn't it? Jimbo shook his head ruefully. Ah no, there were lots of Doyles and if this man was a building contractor and in a big way over in the town then it wasn't likely that he would be any family to Jimbo. But still, maybe it was an omen. If the man's name was Doyle, he might find it hard to refuse another Doyle.

'He won't refuse you, Jim,' Patrick O'Neill said. 'I'll tell him I met you and that your work has been highly spoken of.'

Kate polished glasses with a snow-white cloth and watched the big, handsome American speaking easily with them all. One by one they left, secure in the knowledge that they would be remembered, and somehow warmed by his interest. Kate felt admiring and then a little fearful. It wasn't that she feared he would forget these men in their working clothes, with their humble hopes. No, she was afraid more that he *would* remember them. And this all meant that he was very determined to come back to some kind of roots. Roots which he was finding it increasingly hard to establish, as he'd just told them in the bar. Nobody, not even the older men, could remember any O'Neills around the place, not living on the demesne in Fernscourt anyway. There were O'Neills up the other side of the town, the far end of Bridge Street. But Patrick's kith nobody could recall. 'It was all a long time ago,' they said, as if to forgive themselves and each other.

Yet the man who had come back to build here remembered it all. As if he had been present.

Kate made the glasses shine as she puzzled over it. A man like that must have another wife in mind, someone in America, an Irish-American widow perhaps. Would she be coming over too? He must be worth a fortune. Look at what he must have paid out already for site investigation, and that was before he started work on the house. He must be very determined to make this a success. And if he did, what would happen to them?

They were alone in the bar now, the three of them. Patrick had let them buy him a drink to welcome him to these parts; now they let him buy one for them. Kate's small port felt as if it were choking her, but she drank it and smiled at the handsome man with the open face, the open shirt and the well-cut tweed jacket.

'To the dream.' He raised his glass. 'John, Kate . . . I want you to be part of the dream as well. I want us all to share in it.'

'Well sure, we'll be glad to share anything there is to share,' John said, a bit at a loss.

'I'll drink to the dream,' Kate said. 'And to your happiness and success across the river. You won't find it too tame for you after New York?'

'All my life I wanted to come back here,' he said simply. 'In the middle of big deals and buying more neighbourhood bars I always said to myself . . . Patrick, this is one step nearer coming home.'

'Imagine that, and you weren't born and brought up here at all.' John shook his head in wonderment.

Kate hoped her voice didn't sound tinny. 'And what exactly do you plan, or have you worked it out yet?'

She tried to listen to the words as they came out, and wondered, did they betray her anxiety. If they had, the big man didn't seem to notice. He leaned over the bar eagerly, and like a boy told his plans. The house was going to rise again, like it had been before. There were old pictures and drawings, and he had people working on those country homes built all over the land in the 1780s; it would all be in keeping and in the right period. It was going to be a hotel for the kind of Irish-American who wanted to feel welcome, and as if he had come home. Limo services would be arranged to take them to their own part of the country so that they could find their own roots. There would be fishing and horse riding, and in the correct seasons there would be shooting and hunting. Very few of the Irish who had emigrated to America had any of the gentlemanly sports like these in their background. They had gone to the States because other gentlemen, gentlemen of a different race and religion, had ousted them from their homes. It would be a real homecoming in every sense of the word for any American of Irish stock.

And there would be names on the rooms instead of numbers. Like the O'Brien room, or the Lynch room, or the Kennedy room, or whatever. Kate listened to the list and gave her little oohs and aahs to coincide with the genuine ones of her husband. Her lower lip was almost flattened with the effort of staying calm until he came to the bit about the bar.

Oh, there would be a cocktail lounge certainly, for pre-dinner drinks where orders could be taken before guests went into the dining room. And then there would be the Thatch Bar. A thatched cottage on the grounds in what Patrick thought must be the exact spot his own ancestors lived before they were thrown out on the road. There was a lot of talk about ancestors being forced to workhouses before Kate could get him silkily back to the Thatch Bar. A real traditional Irish Bar, with fiddlers playing and every night some little entertainment, like Irish dancing or a singer, or some old storyteller telling a tale.

And there would be ordinary prices in it too, not fancy ones. Patrick O'Neill wanted his own to come to his bar, not just the gentry. The pint would cost the same in the Thatch Bar as it would anywhere else. It would attract the local people in and the visitors would really and genuinely get to know them.

Kate looked at the boyish face in astonishment. What kind of a mind did you need to get on in America if this was the proof of it sitting opposite her? What did he *mean*, he didn't want just the gentry? What gentry would go to a flash place like this anyway? Could he see the Walters, or the Harrises, or the Johnsons from the Grange even, spending an evening in the Thatch Bar? The man must be mad. But what was he thinking about, telling them these plans? He must know that he would ruin their trade if this all came to pass. He must know they would try to oppose his licence on the ground that the area was well covered with licensed premises already. What was he talking about, telling them that he wanted to share a dream with them?

Kate looked at John for some support, and found that she couldn't read his face. It was just as it had been when he was talking to Marian Johnson earlier on, smiling and thoughtful. Was he really taken in by all this patter, or had his heart missed a beat when he heard of the Thatch Bar and all the dangers it looked like bringing on top of them? She could find no words to speak, everything she wanted to say would sound harsh and hysterical. She wanted to take this O'Neill man by the lapels and look straight into his smiling blue eyes. Burrow into them until she could see the truth. She would like to beg him not to ruin their business. She wanted to tell him that, as he had so much money, and so many chances, could he not just have Fernscourt as a home, to entertain his American friends. Surely he didn't *need* a bar business there. Then that mood vanished, and she wanted to tell him there would be no further pretence at amicable conversation. She and her husband would oppose his getting a licence, and they would raise everyone in the neighbourhood to support them in their case.

But Kate Ryan knew with heavy heart that she could do nothing of the sort.

Had she not seen the gratified delight already on everyone's face? There would be a very slender army to raise against Patrick O'Neill.

John was asking all kinds of questions, idiotic questions, Kate thought, as if he were delighted to see such opposition arriving on his doorstep.

Would the guests go round in buses? What part of America would they come from mainly?

Kate could have killed him for his eager interest in the unimportant side of things. What did it matter if these visitors travelled by bus or by wheelbarrow? Who could care less if they came from one part of America or another? They didn't know *any* parts of America, for God's sake. And yet little by little John was learning more about the whole undertaking across the river than anyone else would have learned from this clever American. There could be a purpose to his questions. She looked hard at John, fighting the lump in her throat which made her want to burst into tears. He looked so good and patient; he had worked for so many years at a job that he would never have chosen. It would be cruel to see it swept away by this successful man who could have had power and riches anywhere else on the earth.

Kate knew she should join in the conversation. She had been conspicuously silent. In fact she saw John glance at her, his face still cheerful and his smile all-embracing.

'Well I can't tell you, Patrick, what an excitement all this will be.' He looked at his wife as if he were leaving the way open for her to add her words of delight and welcome. Kate was still too full to trust herself to conversation.

'The excitement is mainly mine,' Patrick said. 'If you knew how many times I dreamed of this, and often I had to say it aloud to myself, you know like a chant or a prayer. It will happen; it will happen.' He looked at them both with an engaging smile.

'Now I almost have to tell myself it *has* happened, it *has* happened.' He looked so boyish and delighted it was hard not to like him.

Kate decided to speak. 'And how would we come into all this? How can we . . . um . . . help you in it all?' she asked. Her voice was definitely faltering and she wasn't far from tears.

'But that's what good neighbours will always do,' he cried triumphantly. 'I'll get my guests to come to you, send them over to you before lunch or in the early afternoon . . . when maybe you could do with an injection.' He looked around the empty bar and left a short significant pause. 'I guess this would be a good time to send a group over for an Irish coffee or something. And you can tell your regulars when there's entertainment on in the Thatch that they might like to come and see. Or better, any of them who are talented, if they want to come and perform. Play for people. It's their place now.' He smiled from one to another.

'I guess you know that it's a principle of business that one successful establishment leads to another. Business grows out of custom to an area. Mark my words, there's going to be new places starting up out on River Road before we know it. By the end of the sixties they'll be asking where Bridge Street is . . . they'll all think that River Road is the centre of the universe, and the Ryans and O'Neills will have been here from the outset.'

John was smiling back at him. Was John Ryan under the net? Had the web of companionship and complicity caught him up? Kate realized that there were going to be very few people who would not be caught in that net. Even her own Dara and Michael, who had vowed never to speak to the new owner of Fernscourt, were flashing him grateful smiles and friendly glances when he said that they could continue playing there.

So far only Fergus Slattery had managed to remain aloof, and he hadn't met the American yet; perhaps he would be bowled over like the others had all been. Kate smiled on, though she felt there was a distant ache in her face. If John could smile so could she. Anyway there was nothing to be gained by showing her hand now. She must remember that if she came straight out with all her worries and hostilities, it would do nothing but harm. Living all these years with the solid John Ryan had taught her that much anyway.

So she accepted with a dimpling smile when the laughing American begged to be allowed to buy them one more drink so that they could toast the success of River Road and especially those who were in at the very start.

Fergus Slattery heard that the American was doing the rounds. He didn't want to be in. His father had gone fishing; he put a closed sign on the door and headed out.

'Where will I say you've gone?' Miss Purcell asked, not because she thought anyone would call, but because she wanted to know what was taking him away from his business in the middle of the afternoon.

'Go out on the doorstep every hour and say to the crowds that Sergeant Sheehan and I have raised a posse of men and we've gone out to see if we can bring in any poachers. Dead or alive. That should satisfy them,' he said.

'You have a very strange way of going on, Master Fergus. It's not every woman that could stay in this house and put up with it.'

'Haven't we always said you are a woman in a million, a woman different to all others?' Fergus said, and he was gone before she could put another question to him.

He took the car not because he had any idea where he was going, but at least in the car he wouldn't have to answer half a dozen questions about where he was going in the middle of the afternoon. He waved and nodded as he drove up Bridge Street to the main road. He saw the signpost to Dublin and parked for a while. Suppose he was in Dublin, he wouldn't be even slightly affected by a licensing application. He would do it; there was no chance that he would know the people it would hurt, there was no way in Dublin that he might already feel slighted by this applicant. Without meeting Patrick O'Neill, Fergus was somehow prejudiced against him. He had heard about the way he had bought the fishing rights and it was perfectly legal, the way he had organized the searches on the land, and dealt with the Land Commission, was all above board. If in the future he was seen to have had drinks with this politician and with that local councillor nobody was going to cast an aspersion. This was how things were done. The planning permissions and the licence would go through and he would build his monstrosity. After a few years it might be a white elephant and it could be written off as a tax loss. Patrick O'Neill was of the breed who would start again. Somewhere else, different scheme.

Fergus was old-fashioned, he wanted things to remain the same. The same kind of quiet practice, the same kind of food. He didn't like moving on, cutting losses.

He didn't at all like the notion of a stage-Irish bar across the Fern, and taking all the trade from Kate Ryan. It took a lot to upset that woman, and today she had left early, saying truthfully that she couldn't concentrate. Perhaps he would call in and see had they any news. A half of Guinness would go down very well on a warm summer afternoon.

He decided to leave the car parked where it was near the main road to the big town in one direction and Dublin in the other. He could walk down that lane which came out through Jack Coyne's wood, right on to River Road, not far from Ryan's. He whistled as he walked. Partly from the sheer freedom of being out among the trees, and partly because he wanted to cheer himself up over this Yank business. The rhododendrons were out in a great purple show, and darker red ones too. In other countries, Fergus thought, this place would be a public park with manicured grass and seats and litter bins. As he was debating to himself whether this would be good or bad he came across four frightened dark eyes.

Kate Ryan's twins Dara and Michael who were quite obviously meant to be at school, and had no business, any more than himself, wandering the woods on a working afternoon.

'You see, Mr Slattery . . .'

'We didn't exactly say at home . . .'

'Just we weren't going back to school . . .'

'If you see what I mean . . .'

Fergus pretended neither to hear nor see them. He began to talk to himself.

'Ho hum, what a lovely thing it is to walk in a wood, and see nobody at all. That's what I like best: a walk where you don't see another human being. That's the kind of thing that does me good when I'm on my way to Ryan's Bar to have a drink. A walk where I don't meet another sinner.'

He began whistling.

Dara and Michael looked at each other in amazement.

'Grown-ups are extraordinary,' said Michael.

'They seem to be improving all the time.'

That was twice in one day they had been rescued. Dara wondered if it would be possible to leave school entirely. There seemed to be a great conspiracy working for them at the moment.

Patrick O'Neill declined the invitation of Marian Johnson to dine with her that night. He pleaded great fatigue, and said he would be no company. A glass of milk and a sandwich and bed in the elegant room were what he wanted. He noticed the disappointment on Marian's face and the fact that she had had her hair fixed since they had been out riding; maybe she had gone to a beauty parlour specially.

'You look very nice,' he said tiredly.

Marian's face lit up. That was compliment enough.

He said that if she were free he would love another ride on that nice mild-mannered horse tomorrow. That brought on further smiles. He could go to bed now without being thought boorish.

He wished there were phones in the bedrooms. He wanted to call Grace back home. It would be great to dial direct and hear the reassurance of Bella and Andy that Grace was at home. It was eight-thirty here in Mountfern: it would be three-thirty in New Jersey, just the time that Andy was driving Grace up the avenue. Patrick's sister, a fussy woman called Philomena, was in residence as chaperon. Kerry was away at school. Rachel was in her apartment. He really should call her. But not from the hall of the Grange. Not with Marian Johnson listening to every word. There were obviously some calls which were going to be made through that pleasant woman who ran the post office, who had made tea for him this morning. Was it only *this* morning? Lord, why had he stayed up all night in Fernscourt? His bones ached with tiredness.

He took a hot bath and felt much better. Better still after the milk and sandwiches. He lay on his bed and looked out at the green fields leading off to clumps of trees. Behind those trees was the winding River Fern, and his own place. It had been some day. Still he had done almost everything he set out to do. The lawyer chap hadn't been in, which was rather lackadaisical. Even in a sleepy hollow like this, someone should have been looking after the shop. And Kate Ryan hadn't been convinced. She was the only real opposition – not that she had said it, of course. That made her smart. A handsome woman too, probably the brains of that business. The dreamy pleasant husband was not a man with much drive. Bright smart children too. Lucky he had been able to get them on his side by shielding them. Little rascals, skipping school.

Canon Moran had been so helpful about looking up records, and the young curate had promised to inquire about burial grounds and possible tombstones. Strangely, that old wino bag lady he had picked up in the car was their housekeeper. She looked extremely ropey today, as if she had just had another night on the tiles.

And the Dalys had been magnificent, and the Leonards, and Jack Coyne – knowing now too late that he had blown it by overcharging Patrick for the car – said that he hoped they would be able to talk man to man about business one day. Patrick had smiled and said of course, but he and Jack Coyne knew that not one cent's worth of business was ever going to cross the River Fern from Fernscourt to Coyne's Garage. He talked to Sergeant Sheehan casually, to Dr White who happened to be in Daly's, to assorted others whose names would come back to him when he was less tired. He had an excellent memory and never had to write down the names of the people he met through work. To some people today might seem like a leisure day, wandering round talking to folk. But to Patrick O'Neill it was work. His life's work. And really and truly it had gone very well today. It wouldn't take long to convince that fine tall Kate Ryan that he didn't mean her and hers any harm. It was true he did not. And it was always a bit easier convincing people if the thing was actually true.

Rachel Fine applied her throat cream exactly as the label had advised with short upward strokes. She then applied her eye cream in the recommended manner with a feather-light fingertip so as not to damage the delicate tissue around the eye. She sat in her cotton nightdress looking without pleasure at the reflection that stared from the mirror. She looked like any sad Jewish mamma left on her own this night. There must be a thousand of them in this area alone. But she hadn't even the satisfaction of being a mamma. And her husband Herbert had been in California for eight years. She and he had ended their relationship long before hers with Patrick had begun. Herbert had given her the apartment and a car. The divorce had been genuinely amicable. They sent each other postcards even; they remained casual friends, bewildered that they had ever thought they knew each other well enough to marry and to remain married for so long.

But however lonely, Rachel would not ring Herbert for company. And she had very few friends left. When you devote your life to a man, his business, and his limited free time as Rachel had done, it didn't leave much time for friends. She still had work to do for O'Neill Enterprises even while he was in Ireland, but she did it in a mechanical way. When there was no Patrick to discuss her ideas with the fire went out of them.

Sure she was a designer. Sure, sure, everyone realized that she was worth her salary, her ideas had been praised in the newspapers and magazines, and her style had lifted the O'Neill chain way out of the commonplace. Rachel had never wanted to see her own name over the smart corner-bistro-type restaurants, it was quite satisfying enough to know that her choosing of colours and fabrics, her layout and her selection of decor, waitresses' uniforms and lighting techniques contributed to the O'Neill empire. When Patrick had eight pub-restaurants and the motel in New Jersey he said he had enough. He bought no more until this huge bottomless pit that was Fernscourt, bleeding away his profits in a way that nobody would believe.

Gerry Power, Patrick's second in command, knew this. He was tight-lipped and disapproving, but not even to Rachel, whose position he knew very well, would he hint that he took anything less than delight in all of Patrick's schemes.

Rachel looked again at the telephone. It was ten p.m. here. It was three o'clock tomorrow morning in that godforsaken place. Perhaps he would call tomorrow. Perhaps he might even call at his lunchtime, which would be getting up time here. Yes, surely that's what he would do.

Rachel laid a towel over her pillowcase. The only advantage of not having your man living with you all the time was that you could do your beauty routines adequately. On the nights when Patrick stayed, there was a satin nightgown, not a cheap cotton one, there was no throat cream or eye cream. There were certainly no exercises.

But what was Patrick's great phrase? 'It's always either a feast or a famine.' Rachel Fine sighed deeply. It had been a famine for her for a very long time, and the worst bit was that she could see long lean years of famine still ahead.

Mrs Whelan understood without being told and without the need for comment that Patrick would need to make calls in privacy. She settled him next day in her own sitting room, two closed doors away from anyone who might be standing in the post office with their ears flapping.

She gave him a table for his papers and said she would add up the charges each time and he could pay at the end. Another cup of strong tea, a cushion to cure his saddle sores.

'You're a wonderful woman. Did the late Mr Whelan appreciate you?'

'He's not late, he just went off,' she said simply.

Patrick knew how hard it was for a woman in a small community to admit something like this, she would say it to him once because her common sense would tell her that he would hear it elsewhere, then it would never be mentioned again. He too would acknowledge it once and then forget it.

'A foolish man. Did he find the happiness he thought he was going to find? Most people who run away don't.'

She thought about it.

'At first he did, I'd say. But times aren't great now, I hear. When I do hear, which isn't often.' That mean the subject was closed. 'I'd better leave you and start to get through to the operator for you.'

Patrick hadn't been thinking of phoning Kerry in his big school. But why not? They would certainly get him to the phone. As he settled himself into the chair and cushions provided by Sheila Whelan, Patrick realized that in ways she was a little like Rachel. She knew how to make a man feel welcome and comfortable and important. How strange that Rachel was sitting alone in Brooklyn just as Sheila lived alone in Mountfern. Did it prove that it was a bad thing to make a man comfortable?

Patrick had never been able to understand people who could use the telephone for long chatty conversations. For too many years now he had used it for work to be able to think of it as a way of talking unselfconsciously. Grace could talk for hours on the telephone to friends whom she had just left at school. People told Patrick that it was the same with their daughters, and indeed their wives.

He put the first call through to Gerry Power. At least Gerry felt the same way about telephones. A necessary but unappealing part of business life. He wouldn't complain that Patrick was not being sufficiently warm or forthcoming over three thousand miles on a piece of machinery.

Gerry Power wasted no time congratulating him or expressing any surprise. If Mr O'Neill had said he was going to go and throw away his fortune on this heap of old stones, then this is what he was going to do. He listened to instructions, and nodded and grunted. At the end of the catalogue he read them back. Patrick smiled; he could almost see Gerry Power in his shirt sleeves, writing with a stubby pencil.

'And that's three air tickets you want. Three not four?'

'You're very numerate Gerry, three. One each for Kerry, Grace and me.'

'Just checking.' Gerry Power was in no way put out. He hated grey areas and wanted to make sure that his boss hadn't expected him to book a seat for Mrs Fine, without asking him directly to do so.

Grace was always excited to hear from him. When was he arriving? Good, good. And how long was he staying home? Only a few days, but that was awful! He had been gone so long. He was *what*? Was this true? He was really and truly going to take Kerry and Grace with him to Ireland? And she could go to school there? Grace's voice disappeared into squeaks of excitement.

Patrick spoke to his sister Philomena. She shared neither Grace's excitement nor Patrick's enthusiasm. She listened to the facts in a disapproving silence. Yes she would have clothes organized; and she would explain to the nuns here that Grace would not return in the fall.

'Well, what do you think of my getting back to the old country in the end?'

Patrick hated having to ask her, despised himself for fishing for the praise and congratulation that he felt were his due.

He was getting none of them from Philomena anyway.

'You've always done whatever you wanted to do, Patrick, and to be fair, the rest of us have done well out of your endeavours. But it is quite beyond us to know why you want to go and undo the work of the very people who got us here. Our grandfather as sure as hell didn't come over here on the deck of a ship so that his grandson and his great-grandchildren should end up going back to the godforsaken bog that he left behind him. But it was never any use talking to you and it won't be any use now.'

They got Kerry out of class to talk to him. It was the first time he had ever called his son at school; he could not credit the time it took to find the boy. Kerry could not believe that his father had called just for a conversation. Especially as he learned he would see his father within a few days.

'I wanted to share the good news with you.' Patrick felt a trace of tears come into his voice, and fought it desperately. Kerry hated emotion. More than once he had accused his father of being what he called Italian. In flatter tones than he intended he told his son that the dream was now a reality. He said that the land had been bought, the plans were under way. And that he had heard of a good school where Kerry would start in the fall. There was a silence at the other end of the telephone which chilled him.

In business Patrick had never pleaded on the telephone, and he knew it was pathetic to ask if someone was still there when there was a silence. Sitting in Sheila Whelan's floral armchair, he steeled himself and waited. But Kerry waited longer.

Eventually Patrick spoke. 'So we'll talk about all that when I see you. Right?'

'What do we talk about?'

'About how great it will all be. So many people have something that they always want to do, all their lives they talk about it and so often it never happens. Your mother and I talked about this for so long . . .'

This time Kerry spoke. 'Mother never talked about it to me,' he said.

'But you know it was what she wanted?'

'Maybe.'

With difficulty Patrick controlled himself. His hands were shaking when he put down the telephone. He had one more call to make, and he needed something stronger than tea to steady him for this one.

Sheila Whelan wouldn't hear of his going to buy a brandy. She would slip into Conway's for it. No point in his getting a reputation in the first couple of days. She was back in minutes and the half bottle of brandy, glass and jug of water were beside his elbow on a round tray advertising Craven A cigarettes. Patrick O'Neill took a long swallow and made a person to person call to Mrs Rachel Fine.

Afterwards he walked out into Bridge Street; he looked down to the river as his grandfather must have done, and up the town. It would all have changed so much since those days. There would have been no calling the States. And no calling home once he had arrived on the other side of the world. Patrick crossed the street, nodding at Mr Conway, the man who unbelievably ran twin trades of publican and mortician without anyone thinking it was slightly odd. He waved at the two young White children going into their house and he gave a glance to see what ancient movie the Classic was offering tonight.

His grandfather would have had no contact at all with the family. Going to America was like going to the next world. No wonder the Irish held American wakes for the man who was leaving for America and would be out of touch with his kith and kin from now on. Maybe it might have been sensible, Patrick thought gloomily. His sister, his son, his manager and Rachel Fine had hardly been overjoyed to hear from him.

'He's only staying a few more days,' John said. 'He was in here earlier with some plans, showing me an artist's impression. You never saw the like of it.'

'No permission or no licence granted yet,' Kate remarked coolly.

'A formality,' Fergus Slattery said. Fergus had called again. It was a restful place, Ryan's. You could read your paper, or you could join in the chat. It made a nice stretch to his legs after his supper. And anyway he felt an overwhelming loyalty to the shabby little place.

'You shouldn't have refused good money,' John Ryan said in a low voice so that the others wouldn't hear. 'Kate told me you won't handle his business in case it might be in conflict with us . . . No, no . . . let me finish. Fergus, you're a decent man as your father before you is, but there's no conflict. There's nothing but cooperation with that man. The best man you could meet; he'll put new life in the place.'

'I did meet him,' Fergus said.

'Well. Didn't you like him?'

'Of course I liked him,' Fergus growled. 'You couldn't not like him. I told him that I'd feel it more sensible not to get involved in his application just in case there was the unlikely event of one of my fellow parishioners wanting to get involved on the other side.'

'And what did he say?' John and Kate were both eager. This was new; this had happened this afternoon.

'Oh, he was charm itself. Said he quite understood, said it was very ethical of me, showed I was a man with a community spirit, hoped he'd be able to prove that he felt the same community spirit himself.'

'That's just it.'

'I know, John. I'm not disputing it. I'm just saying that he's a mixture, we're always one thing or the other here; he's more than one thing.'

'How do you mean?'

'Well at the same time he was telling me how much he wanted to feel part of the place and a member of the local community, he also made sure I realized that he had extinguished a licence. Ahearne's pub, way beyond. Now that's sharp legal talk for an innocent Yank who's building his own place. He not only knows that you have to buy up and extinguish one pub licence before you get another, but he's done it. That's a bit quick for me.'

John Ryan smiled as he polished the bar counter. 'Well by God you're a very impatient young fellow, Fergus, for all your great education and studies at the universities.'

'Stop making fun of me. Wouldn't I need to be impatient with all that's going on round here?'

'No,' said John slowly. 'That's the last thing you'd need to be. There's all the time in the world. Look at all that could happen before any of this comes into being.'

'What do you mean?'

'Your father would understand better than you. He has a feeling for the river, and how things go on and on. That river was there just the way it is now when your man's grandfather left Mountfern, and it will be here for ever.'

'John, you sound like some old soothsayer, will you stop it?' Kate laughed at him good-naturedly.

'No, I mean it. Patrick O'Neill has great plans like fireworks but they may never materialize.'

'He's hardly bought Ahearne's licence just for fun,' Fergus said.

'No, but look at what could happen. I remember that place that was going to be built about ten miles out on the Galway road. *That* never materialized, did it?'

'They ran out of money,' Fergus said.

'Exactly,' said John.

'But that fellow O'Neill has a fortune.'

'So had the other crowd. Or maybe he'd lose interest, or something else would distract him, or it wouldn't turn out right for him.'

'But aren't you only helping him to install himself instead of praying that it will turn out wrong for him?' Kate was mystified.

'None of us would pray that things would turn out wrong for people, Kate, that would be only asking for trouble to come on ourselves. All I mean is that there's no point in getting hot and bothered until things do happen.'

'That's not the American way,' Fergus said, doing a poor imitation of Patrick's accent. 'That's not your up-and-attem-boy.'

'That's not my way,' John said quietly.

'We're two of a kind then, John. Give me another pint, if you will. I can't see myself practising law for ten minutes in New York without having a very bad nervous breakdown.'

Kate smiled at them affectionately as they toasted each other on the notion of savouring life, rather than racing through it. She would prefer to race a bit faster herself, but not as fast nor in the same direction as the smiling American, who had seemed to read her mistrust of him and smile yet more warmly on the two occasions in two days that she had met him. She was glad he was going back soon.

A few nights later Dara crept from her room to the window just at the very moment Michael left his bed. They were never surprised that their timing was so exact, they took it for granted that they would turn up at the same time. In Fernscourt they could see him walking, touching this wall and that.

'If he loves it so much why is he tearing it down?' Dara asked yet again.

'Well he keeps saying he tried to think of ways of keeping the old ruin like it was,' Michael said, always his defender.

'He didn't try very hard. He's so rich, all he has to do is to say let it stay and it stays,' Dara grumbled. 'Look, he's leaving now. I wonder where did he park his car?'

'He leaves it up a bit when he comes at night, so as not to wake people when he leaves. Look, look he's coming over the bridge.'

They watched as Patrick O'Neill paused on the little footbridge opposite their pub and stared across at Fernscourt in the same way that they had done so often, a hand on each railing of the narrow bridge.

'He's saying goodbye before he goes home,' Michael breathed.

'Will you ever realize that to him this is his home?' said Dara.

The moonlight wasn't bright enough for them to see the tears on Patrick's face as he said goodbye to Fernscourt.

CHAPTER FIVE

It took a little time to get things organized, but compared to the speed that most people would have moved at, Patrick was a human tornado. The finance had been organized already. The big white house in New Jersey, the symbol of his success, would be put on the market. Not at once, because that way he would have to take any price from any bidder. But it would be rented for a year first.

Bella and Andy, the couple who had looked after him, had to be paid off, thanked, found new positions. Aunts and cousins had to be placated and reassured that it wasn't the act of a madman. He saw to passports, visas for the children, had endless discussions with numerous priests and nuns in the two schools, all of whom were sorry to see Mr O'Neill, the number one benefactor, disappear off to Ireland with his two handsome children.

There were never quite enough hours in the day for all the form-filling, document-signing, telephoning, crating, packing, sorting and deciding what had to be done.

But in a far swifter time than anyone would have believed possible, Patrick had everything done. He was ready to come home to Ireland.

Patrick was so proud of his children when they stepped from the plane at Shannon Airport that he wanted to cry aloud to anyone who would listen that these two shining golden people belonged to him. Even after the night flight when others were blinking sleepily into the dawn, Kerry and Grace O'Neill looked untouched and stared around them with interest at the land that was going to be their home.

Patrick had noticed the looks of admiration that the brother and sister had got from onlookers both in Idlewild Airport, New York, and here in Shannon. They had clean-cut looks and they both seemed in such high good humour. They had always got along well together, no rivalry, no resentment ever. They had spent long hours together during their mother's illness, and since he had been away from home before, after and even during that time, they had been thrown together a lot. They always enjoyed each other's company. In the plane they had chattered together happily. He had never been close with Philomena or Catherine or Maureen like that. Nor with his brothers. There had been too much hardship in their family. The fight to exist had taken all their time. Friendship was a luxury they didn't have when they were growing up.

He had hired a car from one of the big companies that had a desk at Shannon Airport. Jack Coyne had had only one chance. One chance to be in car rental in a bigger way than he had ever dreamed, but he had lost it for ever. To have cheated Patrick O'Neill was the most foolish act of his life.

'Come on, kids,' Patrick called as he held the door of the car open. 'Come on, climb in, I'm going to take you home.' Their faces showed the excitement they felt.

Patrick looked at them with a lump in his throat. They were extraordinarily beautiful, he thought, both of them. It was not just the pride of a father who has worked his guts out so that his children would have everything he never had. Surely he was being objective as he looked at them standing close together in the early morning sun.

Grace had a head of hair that looked like an advertisement for a shampoo, her curls seemed to be shiny and bouncy and there was no way they could be kept down. Two minutes after she came from her shower, or even running out of the waves when they went to the ocean, it was the same. She had big blue eyes and a dimpled smile. Her father called her his little princess, and her brother had called her a baby doll. Her mother said she was like an angel in human form.

It was just as well for Grace O'Neill that she went to a school where the nuns did not believe in praising the girls and that she had an aunt who regarded all good looks as a personal calling from the devil leading to sin and possibly damnation.

Grace was a cheerful child, not nearly as spoiled as she could have been, the idolized baby in that big house. She had realized early in life that you got your way much more easily by smiling and thanking rather than sulking and crying. Nobody told her this; she had always known, or else she had seen it work with her brother and picked it up from him. It was unusually nice to be the centre of attention, with people admiring and patting her on the head.

Kerry O'Neill was tall and blond; he looked like a Swede, not as if he came from Irish stock. His hair curled softly around his neck; on another boy it could have looked sissy, but not on Kerry. His skin was always lightly tanned, summer or winter. His eyes were a bright and unsettling blue. They were rarely still, but moved here and there almost as if they were looking for something. It didn't matter, though, because they looked back at whoever he was talking to often enough to show he hadn't lost interest. You got the notion that Kerry's restless eyes moved even when he was asleep.

His smile was wide and all-embracing. Nobody could smile like Kerry; all those white teeth seemed to crack his face in half. The smile never got to his eyes but that's because his eyes moved very fast. They hadn't time to smile. Grace had once seen a picture of the Blue Grotto in Capri, and said that it reminded her of nothing as much as Kerry's eyes.

Kerry never said much, but people didn't realize this. They usually thought he was very interesting because he agreed with them or listened or seemed to be taking part in conversations all the time. It was only with Mother that Kerry had talked a lot. When he came back from school or college he would sit and talk for ages in Mother's room. Mother had been in bed for so long it was hard to remember when she had been up and around.

They drove across the countryside in the early morning sunshine, pointing things out to each other. Patrick told them that this was a city, Limerick, and that Nenagh was a big town. City? Big town? They couldn't believe it. It was like seeing one of those model villages he had taken them to once, where ordinary mortals seemed like giants.

'We don't go on too much about how much bigger things are back in the States,' he began carefully.

'Of course not,' Kerry said. 'They'd think we were boasting about home.'

'And it would be bad-mannered,' Grace agreed.

They couldn't believe when they saw signs for Killarney. Please could they go there. It was in the wrong direction, their father said. People in Mountfern thought Killarney was the other end of the country nearly, but one day he'd take them there. And there were signs to Galway. Yes, he had seen Galway Bay on his last visit. Then the roads became narrower, they left the main routes and headed into the midlands. Soon the signs for the town came up. 'Not far now,' Patrick said. His heart was beating faster at the thought of taking these golden children to the spot they had come from. Back to their home.

They wanted to know why were there no signs for Mountfern.

'It's too small for a road sign. It's only when you're on the road going past it that there are directions. It's only a little place.' He hoped he had explained this sufficiently to them.

'It's only little now,' Kerry said. 'One day everyone will know it.'

Patrick flashed him a grateful look and then said no more. They came to the first of the two signs saying Mountfern half a mile.

'Hey, have you passed it?' Kerry called out.

Patrick explained that this was one way which brought you along River Road, he wanted to come in by Bridge Street so that they could get an impression of the place.

'Will they have a band on Main Street?' Grace giggled.

'Nothing would surprise me,' Patrick said as they came to the turn and approached the place that had always been a name on his father's birth certificate.

Everyone knew they were coming. From their garden the vicar and Mrs Williams waved at the car.

Judy Byrne was parking her small car outside her house; she peered out of the window to get a good look at the handsome American and his family.

Mrs Sheehan was looking out of the top window of the barracks. There were two or three people standing outside Conway's, who held their hands to their eyes to shield them from the light and get a good view. It was too early even by Conway's peculiar opening hours to have gathered drinkers; these must be people talking on their way back from mass.

Patrick explained that some people in the parish went to mass every day.

'Do we have to?' Grace asked anxiously.

'No way.' Her father patted her reassuringly.

Daly's was opening for business, so was Leonard's. Sheila Whelan's blinds were up long ago, but normally it was a sleepy, slow-moving place.

On the bridge a group of children had gathered; they bent forward to glimpse the passengers in the car, then they hung back again, lacking in confidence. It annoyed Patrick to see the Irish children so uncertain when his own two were so sure, so easy.

Quickly he turned the wheel and manoeuvred them into River Road. Loretto Quinn waved enthusiastically from the shop, young Father Hogan striding along in his soutane waved his breviary cheerfully. Then they were passing Ryan's licensed premises.

'Is that a real place where they sell liquor?' Grace asked.

'Yes, why?' Her father was interested.

'It looks like a kind of toy shop, you know, in a board game. It just needs a thatched roof and it's a typical Irish cottage.'

'Ah, we'll be having the thatched cottage bit ourselves,' Patrick said.

'Why are we stopping?' Kerry asked.

'Let's get out for a moment.' Patrick held the doors of the car open for them.

They scampered out, stretching their legs after the drive. With an arm around each shoulder he walked them to the footbridge and pointed out the ruins of Fernscourt.

'That will be our home,' he said. He was glad that they were looking at the old house which stood magical in the morning mists and sunshine, its ivy walls and odd shapes looking more picturesque than anything Hollywood could have dreamed up as a beautiful ruined castle. He was glad that they couldn't see the tears in his eyes. The effect couldn't have been more satisfying. His son and daughter looked in amazement at the sight in front of them.

Across the river from the little wooden bridge where they stood was a great path of laurel bushes. On either side cattle grazed among old rocks and boulders, some covered with moss. The ruins of a great house stood open to the skies. Ivy tumbled from the highest walls, and old portals stood open: doorways leading nowhere except into further open-roofed space. There were gorse bushes and heather dotted around the place, splashes of bright yellow and deep purple.

'You're going to build all this up, make it like it was?' Kerry was unbelieving.

He had seen the artist's impressions certainly, but nothing had prepared him for seeing the place as it was . . . a magnificent ruin.

'That's what we're going to do,' Patrick said proudly.

'It's going to look like a castle,' Grace breathed.

'That's the idea,' Patrick said.

'And how much land, Father?' Kerry was shielding his eyes with his hand and looking around the landscape of a dozen different shades of green.

'Not as much as I'd have liked. You see a lot of people were granted their land back, you know they were tenants but they were able to buy it outright, so naturally that's theirs now and they don't want to sell. It was only the house and the immediate surrounds we got from the Land Commission. I got a couple of acres from fellows who were anxious to sell . . . but you see the problem . . .' He was about to explain, but Kerry saw it too.

'You don't want to be seen to be buying up the land, taking it away from the peasants again, in case you are seen to be the bad guy wearing the black shirt, instead of the good cowboy.'

'Right son, got it in one.' Patrick was pleased mainly that Kerry was so interested.

'And will this all be gardens . . .?' Grace gave a sweep of her hand.

'Yes, coming down to the river . . . there's going to be a landing stage for boats there, and footpaths.'

'And where will the entrance be?' Kerry looked left and right.

'Funny, that's one thing still in dispute. The original one went off that way. There's a big overgrown path, that's the way vehicles will be coming on site. I'll take you round and show you. The Dublin architects want to keep it that way. They say it follows the original plan, even though nothing else will be like the original. The American architects say it would be better to open up that overgrown path over there and have the entrance coming from the town, from the big bridge.'

Kerry said nothing for a while, just looked at each side and then straight ahead. 'Why couldn't it be here?' he asked.

'Here?'

'Yes. Just here, where we are. This is the best view you'll get of the place with the river in front, and you say it's going to be facing the river, so why not here?'

'But there isn't room. People would have to get out of their cars and coaches and haul all their bags way up there. It's only a footbridge, Kerry.'

'No, make it into a proper bridge and have that part of the drive. Hey, why *don't* you do that? It would be very impressive.'

His handsome face lit up thinking of it.

'It's a great idea but there isn't room. Look how sharp the turning would be. The buses would back into the unfortunate pub, go through the front window.'

'Knock it down,' Kerry said simply.

'I can't knock it down.'

'You're going to knock Fernscourt down,' Kerry said, indicating the ruins.

'Yes, but it's falling down and anyway it's mine.'

'That pub's practically falling down, and you could buy it, then it would be yours to do what you wanted with it.'

It was so simple when you were fifteen.

'Where would they go? Kerry, suppose we were to do it, where would the family who live there go?'

'If they're publicans then they could work for us, just moving across the river from their home, *and* they'd have a nice lump sum.'

'I'll think about it,' Patrick said. 'But as I was going to suggest we have a drink there now, maybe we should sit on this possibility for a while, don't you think? No point in alarming people or telling them too much.'

'You're so right,' Kerry said. 'Then they'd know we're interested and they'd raise the price to the roof and stick, knowing they had us over a barrel.'

Patrick looked at his son with a mixture of dismay and pride. It wasn't hard to know where he had got his business sense. But did it always have to be as cold as that? Transplanting a family who had hopes and dreams of their own. He looked back at his site. The boy was quite right, the only possible place to have an entrance was here at this little footbridge. A big wide entrance with lanterns maybe, and should there be old gates or not? It was something he would discuss with Rachel when she arrived. Later on.

Kate and John had seen them coming and she had run in to change her blouse. She put on her best one, the one with the high neck, and fixed on the cameo brooch. This way she felt she looked more like the lady of the house than someone helping behind the bar. She dusted on a little face powder and added a dab of lipstick.

Carrie saw them as she was slipping out to give the hens a cake of bread that she had burned. The poor hens weren't at all particular, but Mrs Ryan was. Very recently she had been rather sharp with Carrie about the late hours spent with Jimbo Doyle and had reminded her tartly that she was responsible for Carrie's welfare while she lived in the house. When she heard the voices and recognized Mr O'Neill's, her heart skipped a beat. Jimbo had taken a four-day job helping a roofer in the big town. Mr O'Neill thought he was working for him. Oh God, there would be trouble in store.

Eddie and Declan saw them coming and sighed. It meant they would have to wash their faces; they went glumly to the kitchen and took up the facecloth like robots. They had the worst grime removed by the time their mother arrived to do the very same thing for them.

The twins saw them coming and stopped dead in what they were doing, which was playing chess on the landing window seat. Never in their lives had they seen anyone like Mr O'Neill's family as they stood in the sun on the footbridge pointing and waving and making a sort of diagram with their hands.

Dara looked at the face of the young man in the grey sweater and white flannels. His head was thrown back and he was laughing. He was the most magnificent boy she had ever seen in her life. And this wasn't in a magazine, or at the cinema. This was here on their own bridge in Mountfern. She was about to say to Michael that he was gorgeous, but she saw her brother staring at the blonde girl. She wore a short tartan pleated skirt and a lemon-coloured sweater. Her curls had a tartan ribbon in them, holding them up in what wasn't really a pony tail because it wasn't all tied in but could have been one if she had managed to squeeze in the curls. Michael was looking at her as if he had been blind from birth and had suddenly been given his sight.

Judy Byrne was furious when she realized that she had not been quick enough. Mr O'Neill had asked her about what he called her fine cottage. Had she thought of letting it and moving to some smaller place even temporarily? Judy had not seen the drift of his conversation. She had been anxious to make it clear to this handsome and charming American, the first serious bachelor to come their way for a long time, that her roots were firmly planted in Mountfern, that she was a woman of this place who would not be moved.

In fact the little house would have been ideal for the O'Neills. Every time Judy thought of it she raged again at her own blindness. It would have been central; it was just the right size. He would have paid most generously anything she had asked. But the real benefit would have been that Patrick O'Neill and his children would have been living there in her house. There were a million places Judy could have gone for the months that were involved. Sheila Whelan had a spare room. Poor Mrs Meagher of the jewellery shop was thinking of letting a room. Oh why had she been so foolish as not to see that of course the man would want a place to live while he was building his hotel? She would have had every right to call, to be a family friend. What more natural than that she should return to her own house from time to time?

Judy worked three afternoons in the physiotherapy department of the hospital in the town. But there was plenty of work for her in Mountfern and around. She had come home when her mother was bedridden, and even after her mother's death she saw no reason to leave the small quiet country practice. Dr White made sure she had plenty of work. He always said that she was indispensable with patients who were recovering from a stroke or who had broken an arm or a leg. It was a satisfying life in many ways. But she was lonely, and there were so few chances to meet anyone at all suitable in these parts, at her age. And now that she had met one, and he had been very charming, she had sent him right into the arms of that foolish Marian Johnson.

Marian Johnson had nearly died of delight when she realized why Patrick O'Neill was asking about the gate lodge. In the beginning she had been about to apologize for the place, saying that it was so run down there was hardly anything that could be done with it. In fact it was a perfectly serviceable house where Joe Whelan's people had once lived. That was long ago; they used to open the gates and take the messages, and lived rent free for years, but the family had all scattered. Even before Joe Whelan hightailed it for Dublin after some peroxide blonde, he had been living in Bridge Street with Sheila in the post office.

There had been vaguely unsatisfactory people in it since then, but the Johnsons had never stirred themselves to arrange a better let. Suddenly she saw unlimited possibilities.

'I was hoping to do it up so that people, nice people, could live there. I can't think who would like it, though.' She smiled an arch smile, but let it fade suddenly when she got the feeling that Patrick might have seen through it. He spoke quite directly.

'I had been thinking of asking you about it myself. I was wondering, though, if it might be a little too far from town.'

'Not at all,' Marian cried. 'Don't you have a car? Won't the girl have a bicycle, and won't the boy be off with the Jesuits or the Benedictines or wherever?'

Patrick had smiled.

'If you're sure it won't be too much trouble?' he said.

Marian Johnson said it would be no trouble at all. It would be a pleasure for her.

And indeed it was. Jimbo Doyle was in and instructions were given in crisp barks by Marian. No expense was spared, chimneys were swept, baskets of logs were cut, the best bedding from the Grange Hotel was brought to the Lodge. Some of the antiques that Patrick had admired in the house were also given a new home. Windows were stripped clear of the overhanging ivy; the little garden was dug, a space cleared for Patrick's car, and he was assured that all would be ready when he came back from America with his children. He would also need someone to look after them.

This, Marian found a bit of a poser. No young skit of a girl would be any use, it had to be someone responsible. A local widow, perhaps, Patrick had suggested, someone who might be glad of the chance to live with a family for some months. Marian thought deeply. Not Mrs Meagher in the jeweller's. She was too recently widowed to think of making any plans, Marian said. She was also a handsome if neurotic red-haired woman who would most certainly cause trouble of some kind. Not poor Loretto Quinn with her little huckster's shop on River Road. She could hardly cope with her own establishment. Certainly not Mrs Rita Walsh of the Rosemarie hair salon, whose reputation was widely known.

Marian decided to consult Sheila Whelan, who of course knew exactly the person. Miss Hayes. She was sixty if she was a day; she was efficient. She could cook, she could mend, and she would stand no nonsense if the children were troublesome.

Miss Hayes was an inspired idea. Marian Johnson took all the praise and the thanks.

'And what shall I call you, Miss Hayes?' Patrick said to her on the first evening.

'Miss Hayes would do very well,' she said.

'It's just that everyone is so friendly around here. I didn't want to do the wrong thing.'

'Oh I'm sure you would never do that, Mr O'Neill.'

'I hope the children will settle in well here.' Patrick was not a man who was ever at a loss for a word, but Miss Hayes was proving that his charm was not as irresistible as he had hoped.

'I'm sure they will, Mr O'Neill. It would be strange children that wouldn't love a house like this, a room each, their own wireless and a bathroom for themselves and no one else.' Miss Hayes shook her head in awe of the second bathroom.

Grace and Kerry giggled behind Miss Hayes's back after their first evening meal. But not too loudly; she had an air of authority about her, and also she had just fixed them a truly great meal.

Grace fell asleep almost at once. The door of her room was open and Patrick went in to kiss her forehead with the curls damp from her bath. She looked babyish, younger than her twelve years as she lay asleep there. He stood and looked at her for a long, long moment.

Kerry was not sleepy, he said.

'Do you want to drive over with me and walk in Fernscourt by night?' he asked.

Kerry shrugged. It was as if he had gone back to his old self – the Kerry who had nothing much to say to his father.

'Not really,' he said.

'Sure.' Patrick was easy. He wouldn't rush the boy. 'Go in your own time; see it your own way.'

'Yes, that's what I'll do, Father,' Kerry had said. His face, in spite of his golden tan and his piercing blue eyes, looked curiously empty.

They were the talk of the town. Tommy Leonard said that he had asked Kerry how old he was. He had asked him straight out.

'You spoke to him?' Maggie Daly was over-excited by it all.

'Yeah, that's the way people ask questions,' Tommy said. 'With speech. Words and all.'

'What did he say?' Michael rescued poor Maggie.

'Didn't you ask him yourself? Wasn't he inside in your place for ages?' Tommy Leonard was jealous of the time that the two star-like Americans had spent in Ryan's.

'I couldn't ask much. Mam asked us to show them the animals. God, imagine asking *anyone* to look at our animals let alone people like that.'

Tommy Leonard was mollified. He was actually in the poor position of not knowing *what* age Kerry O'Neill actually was. He had asked, it was true, but Kerry had just smiled at him knowingly and asked him to guess.

Tommy Leonard had guessed fifteen, and Kerry had just smiled again. As an encounter it hadn't pleased Tommy, he got no glory in recalling it.

'Wasn't she beautiful?' Maggie said, in what was almost a whisper.

'She was more than beautiful,' Dara said firmly. 'She had classic good looks.'

Dara didn't know exactly what that meant, but she had heard it said once about some actress. It seemed the highest praise there could be to have good looks that were classic. It gave them a virtue somehow, took them out of the ordinary variety.

'Imagine, she's going to be at school like the rest of us.' Maggie could hardly take it in.

'I'm sure she'll hate it.' Dara was sympathetic to Grace and outraged that school wouldn't live up to her hopes.

'Everyone hates school,' said Jacinta White, who hadn't met Grace and Kerry personally. She had only waved to them as they passed in the car with Mr O'Neill. Jacinta and her brother Liam were peeved not to have met the new arrivals; it left them at a disadvantage somehow.

They had planned to go fishing that day; often the six of them waded up the river with their simple fishing rods. They had all been catching fish for as long as they could remember, and they used to laugh at the fishermen who came from Dublin and far-off places with all their expensive tackle. Young Mr Slattery had once told them that the whole principle of fishing for thousands of years had been some sort of an old hook, some sort of an old stick and a length of thread to connect the two. Only fancy folk who wouldn't know a pike from a perch, or either of them from a brown trout, went to all this ungodly fuss about rods and tackle. Sometimes young Mr Slattery came and sat with them and told them things about the river. He always sounded as if he were making some kind of joke about it, or as if he didn't really believe what he was saying himself. He said that the Fern wasn't cold enough or fast enough for game fish. You wouldn't find any salmon leaping around it or refined sort of trout. These were classier fish that needed a load of oxygen. The Fern was a coarse fish for a coarser fisherman. It was low in oxygen, and full of slow ponderous fish like the tench that could live with no oxygen at all. Like the people of Mountfern themselves. Young Mr Slattery puzzled the children, he was neither one thing nor the other.

Today, somehow, the fishing had lost its appeal. And they didn't play in Fernscourt any more. It was not the same now that they knew the bulldozers were coming to take it down. They were all restless and unsettled. They wanted Grace O'Neill and her big brother Kerry to be there again. Like they had been yesterday. But nobody said it. Jacinta White said it in a sort of way.

'Will we go up to the lodge and ask them if they want to come fishing?' she suggested.

They all looked at each other doubtfully.

The mood was against it. Grace and Kerry O'Neill were the kind of people who made the running. You didn't go knocking on their door. They came to join you when they were ready.

Jack Coyne made one attempt to regain the lost business. He called to the lodge formally. He was met by Miss Hayes, a quiet woman who did dressmaking and who lived in a couple of rooms in Bridge Street.

'What has you ending up here?' he asked ungraciously.

'Did you wish to see Mr O'Neill?'

'Yes, I wished that, please.' He was mocking her now.

'Would you like to come in to the sitting room? The family are at breakfast at the moment.'

'Who's that, Miss Hayes?' Patrick's voice called out good-naturedly.

'It's Mr Coyne, a car dealer.' Miss Hayes was disapproving.

'Oh, Mr Coyne, I had the pleasure of doing business with you once. Do come in and join us for coffee. Another cup if you'd be so kind please, Miss Hayes?'

Jack Coyne was distinctly wrong-footed now. He came into a sunny alcove where two smartly dressed children were having breakfast, at a table by a big window. The children stood up politely at his approach. Jack Coyne wished he had dressed more smartly for the occasion. He had thought he would find them unpacking and confused.

'I didn't want to disturb you but I was going to inquire if you wanted a car.' Jack decided to come straight to the point. He nodded at the two children who sat down again, realizing that there would be no further greeting. Patrick made a great play out of pouring the coffee and was extremely anxious that Jack Coyne had the right amount of sugar and cream. Then he turned his blue eyes and his crinkly smile directly on Jack.

'A car?' he said, interested and amused, as if he had been offered a flying saucer.

'Yes, you won't want to be hiring that car-rental job outside for any longer than you have to.'

'No indeed.' Patrick still looked amused.

'And since I'm the local man, a businessman too, in my own small way, I thought I'd put it on the line for you, Mr O'Neill, ask you to come down to Coyne's Motor Works and tell me what you had in mind, and I could go and look for it for you.'

Patrick looked at him blankly. As if he didn't understand. 'You mean *you* would go and get *me* a car from a third party? Is this what you are proposing?'

'Yes, well that's what getting a car for someone is.' Jack was confused now.

'But why would you do that, Mr Coyne?'

'Why? Well so that you would get a good deal, a proper car from someone you could trust.'

'Who would that be, this person I could trust?' Patrick's eyes were innocent and blue.

Jack Coyne shuffled and stumbled over his words. 'Like I'm here, I'd know the people, I'd be in the way of knowing who would give you a fair price and who would . . . well . . . who would be the kind of fellow who would see you coming as it were.'

Patrick looked at him directly. 'I'd have to avoid those, wouldn't you say?'

'You would too, and sometimes it's hard to tell one from another; the man who would look to your interests and serve you well, and the man who would just try to make a quick few quid out of you.'

'Yes.' Patrick was grave.

'And we're all in business, as I say, Mr O'Neill, and there are those of us who might make a quick few quid always from passing trade as it were, people who had more money than sense, but when it comes down to a good working relationship . . .'

Patrick O'Neill beamed all over his face.

'I think that's very neighbourly of you, Mr Coyne, and I will take your point about the kind of sharks who would fleece the passing trade for a few quick bucks . . . It's that kind of thing that can destroy a place. One visitor leaving with one story like that could kill tourism stone dead. I agree with you so much. So thanks again for marking my card. I'll be on the look-out.'

Jack Coyne heard the goodbye in the tone. He stood up.

'So you might call in to Coyne's Motor Works?'

'I'll sure as anything see you round these parts, Mr Coyne.'

In the hall Jack Coyne got the feeling that the wordless Miss Hayes had heard everything, and realized he was getting the bum's rush.

'Haven't you a good enough living below in the town making clothes for people without cleaning up after this lot?' he said to her.

'Like yourself, Jack Coyne, I'm always willing to see a business opportunity,' she said with a smile.

Olive Hayes had no relations left except a sister who was a nun in New Zealand. She had always dreamed of going out to spend a winter in the South Island. If she worked for Mr O'Neill, if she let her little place behind Meagher's jewellery to this building fellow who needed a place in Mountfern, if she continued her making of curtains and any other dressmaking she could manage, then she would have the fare in a year.

Mr O'Neill thought he would be out of the lodge and into his new castle in a year but he didn't understand about the way things were done here. It would be several years. And in that time Olive Hayes could gather a small fortune, enough to take her to New Zealand, and to give her sister's order a financial contribution which would make her a welcome visitor for as long as she wanted to stay. Indeed she thought sometimes that if the weather was as good as her sister wrote it was, and if she liked it there, she might stay altogether. But these were only half-formed plans. And nobody except Sheila Whelan in the post office had any inkling of them. She hadn't told that bossy Marian Johnson who hired her, and she certainly wouldn't tell that crook Jack Coyne. She closed the door after him and went to refill the coffee pot.

The girl was a lovely little thing; the boy looked as if he could be a great deal of trouble.

Judy Byrne rang the Grange. She said it was about old Mr Johnson's arthritis.

'You said yourself there was nothing more you could do for him,' Marian said.

'Yes, I know, but in this fine weather he should be feeling a lot better. I was wondering did he want to go over the exercises I tried with him before.'

'He said they weren't worth a curse. You can neither lead him nor drive him. It's always been the same.'

'Oh I don't know, sometimes the right word at the right time . . . I have to be over that way, will I call in and have a chat with him?'

'No point, Judy, he's gone fishing.'

'Well tell him to take care of himself and not to get damp out on that river bank.'

'You're very nice to be so concerned,' Marian said.

'Not at all, how are things?'

'Things are frightfully busy, what with the lodge and everything . . .'

'Oh, are you getting involved there? I thought they wanted to be left on their own.'

'I wouldn't dream of interfering, but there are some things of course that simply have to be done, and poor Miss Hayes is splendid but she does have her limitations.' Marian gave a little tinkle.

Judy Byrne banged down the receiver and told herself aloud yet again that she was possibly the most stupid woman on earth. It would serve her right if she were to be invited by that Marian Johnson, whose face was like a meringue, to the wedding of the century at the Grange, with a honeymoon to be spent across the river in the elegant Fernscourt, new home of the bride and groom.

The children of Mountfern could talk of nothing but the O'Neills but they didn't know how or when they would meet them again. It was solved on the day that Grace was driven by her father to Fernscourt. And left there.

Patrick was engrossed in conversations with surveyors and engineers. Grace wandered around touching the long strands of ivy and holding them up so that they trailed in different directions.

With solemn dark eyes Dara and Michael watched her. After an eternity, Dara made the first move.

'We'll ask her would she like an ice cream in Daly's,' she said firmly.

'We don't have enough money,' Michael protested.

'We have enough for two.'

'But we'd have to buy three.'

'You can suddenly decide at the last minute you don't want one.'

'All right.'

They walked hesitantly up to Grace, who was standing on tiptoe to examine what she thought might be a bird's nesting place.

'Would you like to come for an ice cream or something?' Michael asked gruffly.

Grace's face broke into a dazzling smile. 'Can I?' she asked.

Michael was wordless again.

Dara took over. 'We'd love you to come down to Daly's, and show you the rest of the town.'

'I was longing to see everything, but I didn't want to . . .' Grace looked doubtful. 'You're all friends already, I didn't want to get in the way.'

'Nonsense.' Dara was brisk. 'You're just as much entitled to have an ice cream and walk round Mountfern as anyone else.'

She linked Grace O'Neill's arm and walked purposefully across the footbridge. Michael followed happily, and Patrick O'Neill watched from a distance with a pleased smile.

Eddie Ryan was escorted home to the family business by an irate Declan Morrissey, the manager of the Classic Cinema. Eddie had drawn moustaches on Audrey Hepburn, and on Doris Day. He had drawn them not with a pencil, nor even a ballpoint pen, but with creosote which could not be removed and which meant that no new poster could be affixed on top of the mutilated ones. Declan Morrissey said he did not want the child to be disembowelled but as near to it as could be done within the law.

'You are a thorn in my flesh,' Kate Ryan told her son as she marched him upstairs to where John was working with papers and notebooks scattered around him.

'John, I know that Wordsworth and the lads never had this kind of distraction, but I'm going to have to interrupt you and ask you to beat Eddie within an inch of his life.'

'What has he done now?' John was weary.

'According to Declan Morrissey, he has defaced the Classic Cinema in a manner from which it will never recover.'

'Didn't Declan do that himself with his rows of coloured lights around it?'

'*John!*'

'I know, that has nothing to do with it. Right, Eddie, before I take my belt to you . . .'

'Ah no, Dad, please no.'

'Before I take the belt, have you *any* reason or explanation? I am a reasonable man. I will listen.'

There was silence.

'Pure badness, I'm afraid,' Kate said.

'There's nothing else to do. If there was anything at all to do I'd do it, but there isn't.' Eddie looked very sad.

Kate and John looked at each other, weakening momentarily.

'But the others don't put creosote on Morrissey's walls,' Kate said.

'And have us heart-scalded every day of our lives,' John said.

'They've got a life of their own,' Eddie said. 'A life with people in it.'

For some reason that he never understood the strap was not raised.

He was ordered to go and apologize to Mr Morrissey, to take a scrubbing brush and Vim and do his best. To tell Mr Morrissey that his parents would pay Jimbo Doyle to have a go at it if all else failed.

'A life of their own with people in it,' Kate said wonderingly to John. 'Imagine, that's all he wants, poor little clown.'

'I suppose it's what everyone wants,' John said and went back to his writing, delighted that he didn't have to beat his small and very difficult son.

Nineteen sixty-two was the summer of the bicycle.

Mr O'Neill had done an extraordinary deal in the big town. It all happened the time he went to buy a car. Apparently he got friendly with the man who sold it to him, and had gone to have a drink with him. The man's brother had been trying to emigrate to America, but he had no one to stand for him at the other side, no one to give him a job and to be responsible for him. This was a great pity because the poor fellow had just been crossed in love. A woman he had his eye on for many years had upped and married another man entirely. So the brother had only one hope and that was to start a new life in the New World. He wasn't a man who was afraid of hard work.

It all evolved in the conversation that Mr O'Neill could get his manager back in the States, a Mr Gerry Power, to sponsor him in, and the thing was arranged in a matter of days. All the man had to do now was to have his medical and get his visa. Nobody could believe the speed at which it was done. How could this benefactor be thanked? Mr O'Neill had seen a load of old bicycles. What about a job lot of those at a knockdown price. A price? Not at all, they were a gift. Thirty-odd bicycles were delivered to Jack Coyne's for nothing. Jack was to test the brakes and do any re-fitting that was necessary. The bikes were available for all who wanted them. Dara and Michael cycled round in circles on theirs; they were the first to get them. The Whites had bikes already, and so had Tommy Leonard, but Maggie didn't, so a small one was found for her. Grace and Kerry had theirs and there had been some cans of paint thrown in with the deal. The bicycles were all the colours of the rainbow.

Jack Coyne scratched his head many times as children came to choose their free bicycles and to paint them on his premises. He had a suspicion that Patrick O'Neill had in fact pulled a fast one on him. The man had not bought his car through Jack, that was all right, that was his privilege to go where he wanted to. But this business of unloading all these broken bicycles on him. In theory it looked as if Coyne's were being given the turn. But in fact it was different. There was no money anyway in fiddly jobs like that, and then added to it was the problem that Jack would have to charge half nothing to Patrick O'Neill anyway to try to show that he had mended his wicked ways. And half the kids in the town painting their bicycles on the premises.

He felt sure that Patrick O'Neill wasn't so stupid as to think that this was doing him a favour.

'Who can have bikes? Is it only people of eleven?' Patrick looked down at the small furious boy with hair sticking out in all directions.

'Who are you?' he asked.

'That doesn't matter,' the child said. 'I just wanted to know if it was worthwhile or if I'd be belted out of there.' He jerked his head at Jack Coyne's.

'What do people say?'

'Mr Coyne says he can't get them out of his sight quick enough. Father Hogan said we should give them to those in need first.'

'But aren't we all in need?' Patrick asked him.

'That's what I said, but you couldn't argue with a priest.'

'I know it.' Patrick was sympathetic.

The small boy wasn't prepared to let the conversation wander into philosophical waters.

'So what are the rules, Mr O'Neill?'

Patrick liked him, he was a little toughie.

'You know my name, why can't I know yours?'

'Because then you'd say there were too many bicycles gone to our family because of the twins,' Eddie said.

'Oh it's young Mr Ryan, I see.'

'Well it's no use now.' Eddie's hands were deep in his pockets.

'Are you able to ride a bike?'

'Everyone is.' Eddie was scornful.

'No they're not. Come on, pick one out. If you can ride it straight up and down here for me without wobbling, you can have it.'

Eddie was back like a flash with a bike and a following of half a dozen children. Patrick watched him attempt a few false starts and then get going. He came back triumphantly.

'Well?' he cried.

'No,' Patrick said.

'What do you mean no. I stayed on, didn't I?'

'Yes, but you rode on the wrong side of the road, you young fool. You'd have been killed if anyone was coming towards you.'

'You didn't *say* you were counting things like that.'

'Sorry, friend. Try again next week, same time, same place, new test.'

Eddie grinned back at him. This was the kind of deal he understood.

Grace O'Neill said she thought that Mountfern was the most beautiful place she had ever been. She said that they were all so lucky to have grown up here, it was like a magic place. The children preened themselves when they heard this. Grace didn't boast about all the places she had been. She didn't say that New York was better than Mountfern, and she had been to all kinds of things and places they had only seen in the films. She had been up the Empire State Building, and on Broadway. She had been up the Statue of Liberty and she had been across the Brooklyn Bridge. But this was only revealed when they questioned her. Normally she said little about what had been her home up to now. Her chat was all of the future. They knew that her mother had died. They asked her was it awful. Grace said that the worst part had been knowing somehow for ages that she was never going to be really well. They had stopped making plans for the things they would do when mother got cured. She didn't know when it began but that was the worst part. The time she had died was hard to remember, there were so many people coming in and out of the house.

She had looked so sad when she talked about that, they changed the subject. Maggie Daly had asked could they see some of her American clothes and all the girls had got on their bicycles and cycled off to the lodge just like that. Of course Tommy Leonard and Michael Ryan and Liam White were far too grown up and male to want to do anything stupid like cycling nearly three miles to see clothes. But they felt a bit empty sitting there by the river when all the girls had gone. It wasn't that they would have gone if they had been asked. But they would like to have been asked. They would have preferred if the girls hadn't gone at all.

Kerry didn't come and join in the games. He was far too old for them. He was nearly old enough to be on the bridge with the fellows and girls who were almost grown up. But he didn't hang around there either.

Grace said he cycled a lot on his own; he had found some ruined abbey he liked. And he used to read too, and he was catching up on some work he had to do before he went to his boarding school, and he had some Latin lessons from Mr Williams the vicar, who had said that life was very droll when you had the Protestant parson teaching the Roman Catholics Latin, even though it was never used in Mr Williams's church and nothing else was used in Canon Moran's establishment down the road.

'O'Neill's children seem to have taken over the place like the Lords of the Soil,' Fergus said to Kate.

'I'm quick to find fault, quicker than you are, and I can't see anything against them,' Kate said.

'Oh, cocky little pair of swaggerers,' Fergus grunted. 'Sailing round on their bicycles as if they owned the place. Which they do of course. Own the place.'

'Ah, come on, Fergus, at least half the place is on wheels now, that can't be bad.'

'That's what the people of Hamelin said to each other about the Pied Piper. At least they're all dancing, that can't be bad.'

'God, Fergus, nothing would please you about that unfortunate family. Seriously, the children smile and they're being patronizing, they don't smile and they're being standoffish. What could they do to please you?'

'Go back to America,' he said.

'You're worse than Eddie when you have that puss on you. What have you so much against them?'

Kate was bright and fresh-looking in a pink blouse and a red pinafore dress. She had bought the blouse in a sale and the pinafore dress was something she had worn years ago, before Declan was born. With a smart black belt to take the maternity look off it she felt as smart as paint. Fergus looked at her, a long admiring look.

'The main thing I have against them is that they are going to take your business away.'

'Oh Fergus.' She was touched to the heart.

'Don't "Oh Fergus" me, go on being nice to them, silly little over-dressed vipers in your bosom.' He blew his nose loudly. 'Just wait until those children have taken away your children's inheritance. See how you'll feel then.'

Kate was totally at a loss.

'It's not the children's fault,' she began.

He put away his handkerchief. 'You're quite right. They make me feel old and grubby and silly. Your children make me feel . . . I don't know, splendid, fascinating.'

'Which is what you are,' Kate said, and then went back to work.

CHAPTER SIX

Everyone asked Miss Hayes what they were like at home, the Americans. Was there a ton of money spent in the place? What did they talk about? Olive Hayes was never sufficiently forthcoming. They were very nice people, she reported, thoughtful and considerate. She had never worked in a house before, it was all a very new experience for her. People thought Miss Hayes was a poor informant. Soon they didn't bother to ask her any more. She was a woman with no stories to tell.

Olive Hayes was a woman saving her fare to New Zealand. She was going to keep her position in this small comfortable house with the American family. There would be no tales about the arrogant resentful Kerry, the impatient father who could find nothing to say to his son, but who idolized his beautiful daughter. Nor would Miss Hayes talk about Grace outside the house even though there was nothing but good to report. She was a delightful child, anxious to help, willing to learn. She made her bed and kept her room in perfect order. She always asked permission if she were to invite the other children into the house. She had a ready smile and she soldiered on bravely to keep the peace between her father and brother. Miss Hayes had never felt any yearning to marry and rear a family. But sometimes when she looked at Grace O'Neill in the kitchen, helping her to wipe dishes and tumbling out stories of how the day had been spent, she sighed and a soft look came to her long angular features. It would have been good to have had a daughter like Grace O'Neill.

Kitty Daly had thought that the summer would never end, long endless boring summers with that crowd on the bridge being so dismissive and all Maggie's friends being so loud and awful. But it all changed when Kerry O'Neill came to town. He came in to Daly's Dairy from time to time. Kitty hated working in the shop during the summer and was normally so sulky and unhelpful that her parents thought it was counter-productive to have her behind the counter. They had a girl from out the country, and Charlie who hauled and dragged things in and out and did deliveries.

Kerry held out his hand the first time he called.

'Hi, I'm Kerry O'Neill,' he had said, as if Kitty didn't know. As if everyone for miles around didn't know.

She shook his hand and mumbled.

'What's your name?' he asked, as if he had expected her to give it.

'Kitty. Kitty Daly.'

'Oh this is your place?' He looked around the clean bright shop in admiration. Its cakes and bread in one section, milk, butter and bacon at another counter and the main body of groceries all together behind the main counter.

'Yes, it is.' Kitty wished she could think of something else to say, but she couldn't. She gave a big shrug to let this gorgeous fellow know that she thought it was all terrible. So that he wouldn't think of her as a poor country hick. But he didn't seem to think it was dreadful.

'It's a very handsome store,' he said. 'You must like working in it, you must feel proud of it.'

Kitty was about to change her stance completely and express great pride in the dairy.

But her mother spoke first. 'Oh there'd be white blackbirds before Miss Kitty here would do a hand's turn in the shop.'

A dark red stain came into Kitty's face, but Kerry seemed to understand at once.

'I'm just the same,' he said, looking straight at her, though he spoke lightly. 'I'm very interested in my father's hotel but he thinks I'm only fooling around. It's not just, is it?'

'No it isn't.' Kitty Daly was hoarse with excitement as the bright blue eyes of Kerry O'Neill rested on her for a little longer. Then he had bought a bar of chocolate and was gone. She watched him walk easily down Bridge Street and go into Leonard's. She resisted the urge to run after him and talk more. She would see him again. He was here for ever. And he liked her. He had made it obvious. Kitty saw her mother looking at her and immediately put on a face.

'I suppose you'll go getting notions about him now, that's the next cross we'll have to bear,' Mrs Daly said in tones of great weariness.

'It's a pity that older people have such sad, sick minds,' said Kitty, and resolved to be very nice to Mrs Walsh from the Rosemarie hair salon in case there was a chance she might give her a cheap hair-do.

Grace O'Neill said that she would love to catch a fish. A real fish herself, and then she would cook it and eat it. Nobody she ever knew before had done anything like this. She made life seem much more exciting than it was for the children of Mountfern. She loved everything. She thought it was wonderful that they had a river all for them, not in a park or anything, but in their own town. And she thought it was great to know everyone's names. Grace made a point of saying, 'Good morning Mrs Williams; Hi, Mr Slattery; Good day Father Hogan.' She said that in the United States you never met anyone you knew or who knew you. Reluctantly the others agreed that it was all right. Before Grace's arrival they had always thought it tiresome to be under the ever-watchful eyes of the whole town no matter what you did or where you were going. It was hard to see it as a positive asset.

But fishing. That was something the girls hadn't been involved in.

'You won't like it, the fish look terrible when you do get them out of the water,' said Maggie Daly.

'They have all blood by the side of their mouths,' Jacinta White said.

'And their eyes look terrified,' said Maggie, maybe with fellow feeling. Her own eyes often looked big and frightened.

'And they wriggle and twitch and you'd be dying to throw them back in,' Jacinta said.

'Except that the poor mouth is tore off them.' Maggie was perplexed by the enormity of the decision. 'So you wouldn't know what would be for the best, to kill them quickly and get it over with or let them back with half their jaw gone.'

Dara hadn't joined in, which was unusual.

Then she spoke.

'I think that's a lot of sentimental rubbish. If Grace says she would like to fish then we should. After all we've lived beside the river for all our lives and we've never objected before . . .'

Grace flashed her a grateful and admiring look.

'But we never did it ourselves . . .' Maggie began.

'Because we've no guts,' Dara said firmly, and with that female fishing was on. They were going to get rods and hooks. Michael was terrific, he'd show them.

'Michael won't want us hanging along with them,' Jacinta said.

'I'm sure he won't mind showing us how it's done,' Grace said, with a sunny confident smile.

Michael didn't mind showing Grace how it was done, and he was pleased that his twin had suddenly developed an interest in fishing. Tommy Leonard was helpful too, and Liam White. They bent over hooks and bait. Maggie Daly forced herself to look into jars of maggots, even though it made her stomach heave. Michael explained that you had to just nick the edge of the maggot with the hook so that the maggot still wriggled about in the water and the fish would believe it was a live grub and snap at it. There was other bait too: bread made into a paste, or bits of crust. Maggie wondered could they stick to this, but Michael and Tommy and Liam said you had to use maggots and worms as well.

Jacinta said she felt sick watching the hook going through the worm. But Grace and Dara looked on steadfastly. Taking a deep breath, Maggie looked on too and said nothing about the nausea rising in her, together with the feeling that this was all a silly phase. They would get over it soon, and go back to being as they were. She hoped Grace would like looking at the tombstones in the Protestant graveyard, but it was probably wiser not to suggest it too soon.

Grace wanted to know could she try out some of the rods which Michael said they had back at the pub. It was nearly teatime. There was indecision. Suddenly the twins looked at each other in the way they often did, as an idea seemed to come to them at exactly the same time.

'We'll ask can you come to tea,' Dara said.

'Just what I was thinking.'

'Oh no,' Grace protested.

'Yes, then we can look at the rods.'

Grace was firm. 'Miss Hayes will have my tea ready. No, I can't call her, that would be very high-handed. But maybe I could ask Father if I can cycle back again tonight.'

That was agreed, and they scattered to go back to their houses as the six o'clock bell pealing out the angelus was heard all over Mountfern.

Maggie walked along River Road with her hands in her pockets. Dara hadn't asked her to come back after tea. Michael hadn't been keen to show her any rods. Tommy Leonard and the Whites were chatting on cheerfully. They didn't notice that Maggie hung behind and was very quiet.

But next day Maggie was called by her mother.

'Come down quickly, Maggie, your friend is here.'

Something about the way she said friend was unusual. Usually Mrs Daly said that Jacinta or Dara was there, in a way that you knew she was casting her eyes up to heaven. Maggie ran down the stairs of Daly's and into the shop.

There was Grace, full of chat to everyone, asking questions about what kind of pastry this was on the cream cakes, and what kind of filling was in the eclairs.

'Would you like to taste one?' Mrs Daly asked her.

'Heavens no, thank you Mrs Daly, thank you so much; I was only interested, that's all. I ask too many questions, I'm afraid.'

'Nice to see someone awake and not half dozy all the time.' Maggie's father was full of approval.

Maggie stood there, feeling very shabby in her beige shirt and brown shorts. Grace was in a yellow and white dress with a big white collar, she had little yellow shoes. She must have a dozen pairs of shoes, Maggie thought enviously, always something to go with her outfit.

Grace took her arm. 'Is it all right if we go off now?' she asked to nobody in particular but to everybody at the same time. Grace forced other people to be charming too. Mrs Daly was nodding and smiling, Mr Daly was wishing them good weather, Charlie looked up from the boxes he was collecting, to grin at them.

Out on Bridge Street Grace looked at Maggie anxiously. 'It was all right to come, wasn't it? I wanted you to show me the tombstones you were talking about.'

'Yes, but . . .?' Maggie was bewildered. Surely Grace wouldn't want to go off with her, with just Maggie when there was so much else to do, so many other people to meet and such an amount of revolting wriggling maggots to be threaded on to those hooks.

But apparently that was what Grace did want.

'Please, Maggie,' she said. 'I'd love to see the names and the things people said.'

Maggie was still hesitant.

'The fishing . . .' she began.

'Oh we can join them later, I met Liam on my way here. I said we'd be along in about an hour or more.'

'What did he say?'

'He said "fine" or something.' Grace was unconcerned.

She left her bicycle parked at the back of Daly's, and arm in arm, they went up Bridge Street to the top of the town. Grace peeped into the Garda barracks just to see what it looked like, she said.

Sergeant Sheehan told her to come in and have a look around.

'Do you have prison cells here?' Grace asked with interest.

'Not here, child.' He looked at her affectionately.

Seamus Sheehan had only sons; this was a beautiful sunny girl. The little one of the Dalys seemed dazzled by her almost.

'What do you do with criminals?'

'They go to gaol in the big town. I've a room back there with a big padlock on it if you'd like to be kept in detention.'

Grace giggled. 'No, I was only getting to know the place.'

'Quite right too.' Sergeant Sheehan seemed much more cheerful today, Maggie thought, like her father was, and her mother, and like Miss Byrne the physiotherapist who made it her business to come over and ask Grace how they were settling into the lodge, and hoping it wasn't too damp for them.

Grace was fascinated with the graves and the tombstones. She said she would bring a notebook the next time so that she could write them all down.

'We won't be buried here, of course,' Grace said conversationally.

'No, we'll be in the Catholic graveyard. Well *we* will, anyway,' Maggie explained. 'If you stay then I suppose you will too.'

'Of course we'll stay, why would we not stay?' Grace sat on the edge of an old untended grave. 'Hey, we should do something for this poor James Edward Gray, nobody's weeded round him for years. Of course, we're going to stay.'

Maggie was helping to remove some of the bigger dandelions from James Edward Gray's resting place.

'People were wondering would you not find it all too dull for you here,' she said in a small voice.

'Heavens no, it's fantastic. You want us to stay, Maggie? You don't want us to go away, do you?' Grace's beautiful face was troubled. She looked really anxious.

Maggie couldn't remember why she had felt so upset yesterday evening as she had walked home along by the Fern, and how she had wished that the O'Neills had never come here.

She looked at the worried blue eyes of Grace O'Neill, and with a great big smile that went all over her face, Maggie Daly said, 'Of course we don't want you to go away; it's great that you're here.' And she meant it.

She meant it not just at that moment but for a long time. Like when they joined the fishing party which was waiting for them at the footbridge.

'Sorry,' Grace said casually, 'I dragged Maggie off to show me the graves. You're right, they're fabulous. We're going to try and smarten up James Edward Gray a bit.'

'Where's he? In the corner near the wall is it?' Dara asked.

Maggie breathed a sigh of relief. Dara wasn't a bit annoyed that Maggie had taken Grace away. People like Dara didn't get annoyed, Maggie told herself. Only mean-spirited people like herself got jealous and possessive and annoyed. Grace was telling Michael that on consideration she wondered could he bait their lines with those lumps of bread they had been talking about yesterday; she said she thought it would be easier to learn on bait made from crusts and then she could progress to maggots later.

Dara was disappointed. She had a jar of maggots ready for threading on to hooks. But Michael said Grace was right, better get used to this kind first, because it was always easier to hand.

Grace flashed Maggie Daly a smile. Things were much easier than they seemed, the smile said.

Kitty Daly thought that Mrs Ryan wasn't bad for a grown-up; at least she wasn't a religious maniac like her own mother was. She was a woman you could talk to a bit.

'Do you think I could work for a bit in the bar, Mrs Ryan?'

'No, Kitty, I'm sorry.'

'Why not?'

'You're too young. That's one reason. We don't need anyone. That's another.'

'I'm almost fifteen. That's not young.'

'I know it's not.' Kate sighed. All this terrible sulking and mulish behaviour probably lay ahead with her own Dara. 'But it is too young for bar work. I suppose this is a silly question, but why couldn't you work in your own shop?'

She took one look at Kitty's face and decided that it was a silly question. The girl looked distressed.

'Did you want the money for something in particular?'

'Yes.'

'Well, maybe you could try to see if there is any other way of getting what you want. Like if it's clothes, could you make them?'

'It's hair, Mrs Ryan.'

'Hair?' Kitty had the Daly curls, frizz really. There was nothing startlingly bad about the child's hair. It was clean and neat, and a brownish reddish colour.

'Yes, a good cut would make all the difference, and no matter what else Mrs Walsh is she does know how to cut hair.'

Kate let the comment pass. No point in drawing an argument on herself with this difficult girl.

'Could you do a deal with her? Sweep up the hair from the floor, make people cups of tea, put the towels out to dry for two weeks, say, and then she might give you a haircut free?'

Kitty considered it without much pleasure.

'It wouldn't be much fun.'

'No, but if she agreed it would get you the haircut.'

'Two weeks is an awfully long time.'

'True. I suppose you'd have to work out whether it's worth it or not.'

Kitty thought a bit. Mrs Ryan was a lot better than most people's mothers. She didn't say things like, your hair was fine the way it was, or, at your age I didn't have the chance to go to hairdressers. She put her mind to the question properly.

'Yes, well I'll give it a go,' she said ungraciously.

'Kitty.'

'Yes, Mrs Ryan?'

'Do you want a hint?'

'All right.'

'If I were you, I'd tell Mrs Walsh how much you admire her own hair, and the way she cuts other people's, and you were wondering if you could make her a proposition. I'd be over-polite if I were you, because Mrs Walsh is a very busy person with a lot on her mind, and she'd be quick to dismiss an idea unless it was put to her nicely.' Kate Ryan saw the defensive look on Kitty's face, and hastened to say, 'I mean, Kitty, I couldn't care less if you shaved your head bald and painted the Irish flag on it. I think your hair is fine as it is, but I know what you mean about a good cut giving it a better shape. So you can take my hint if you like, or ignore it if you like. Now I must get along with my work.'

Kitty thanked her, less grumpily than she had been going to. And in fact it was a good idea. She would ask Mrs Walsh straight away. Imagine Mrs Walsh going to bed with men for money. It was unbelievable, but that is what she did. Everyone knew, but no one talked about it much. Imagine men paying to go to bed with anyone as old as Mrs Walsh.

Kerry O'Neill had no great hopes about his new school. He had gone there with his father for an unsatisfactory visit, and Father Minehan had marked out a certain amount of work that would have to be done. He had agreed that since Kerry was fifteen it would not be practical for him to learn the Irish language at this stage, but he would be expected to master enough of it to get the general sense of things Irish.

He was a forbidding-looking man, white, ascetic, with a nervous smile. He had managed to suggest more than once to Kerry's father that the school, which was a very illustrious one, had fallen on hard times due to a massive and expensive rebuilding programme. There was a building fund that would cripple the community eventually; they couldn't raise the fees yet again this year, so they often had to rely on the generosity of those parents who were lucky enough to be financially secure to help in some of the extreme times of need.

Kerry had been quiet and respectful through most of the interview. At an early stage in the proceedings he realized that Father Minehan didn't respond to charm. He walked admiringly around the old buildings and asked bright questions about the original building and the time that the order had first set it up.

'It's only been here a hundred years. It's not one of our older foundations,' Father Minehan had said a little testily.

'Don't forget, I'm from the United States. That seems very old to me,' Kerry said with a smile.

Father Minehan softened then. Kerry had said the right thing.

Coming home in the car his father looked at Kerry.

'You handled that one well, son. Our sort of cleric, wasn't he?'

Kerry didn't join in what he considered his father's all-men-together mode. 'I think he was all right, he has a job to do.'

Patrick was annoyed. 'What do you mean, he has a job to do?'

'Well, just that. He has to keep me in my place, arrogant young American know-all, trample me down a bit. He has to try to fleece you for his building fund. Irish-American: more money than sense, get him to sign a cheque.'

Patrick gave a genuine shout of laughter.

'It didn't take you long to sum him up. Still, it's got a great reputation. It's one of the finest schools in Ireland.'

Kerry turned away to look out of the window; he knew what his father would say next, and he knew the tone he would say it in. Patrick was about to say that he got the poorest of educations in grade school and had to go back when he was twenty to learn more than reading and writing. He often said this. But he never got the response he was hoping for. Kerry O'Neill never once said that it certainly hadn't made any difference, as Father had done so well. He never said anything at all.

Grace, on the other hand, was looking forward to starting school. It was different for her, she told Kerry, she knew all her friends already, she would be in the same class as Dara and Maggie and Jacinta. They had told her all about the worst things, and how to get round Sister Laura. Grace was going to have to learn Irish, and Sister Laura had suggested she become familiar with the alphabet and a small amount of vocabulary before term began.

The others had been very helpful, although the boys had taught her a really rude phrase which she might easily have said unless Dara had told her what it meant. She had got her navy uniform in the big town, and even the plain skirt and jumper and the pale blue shirt which looked so dull, and drained the colour out of the other girls, could not take from Grace O'Neill's healthy good looks. She bought a navy hair ribbon and tied up her golden curls.

She paraded with her school bag for her brother.

'How do I look?'

'Great.' His mind was elsewhere.

'Thanks a lot.'

'No, seriously, you do look great. You look older than you are.'

'Older in this?' Grace was disbelieving.

'Yes, you look much more grown up than all the other puddings here. Don't let these fellows make any more rude remarks. You hear?'

'Oh Kerry, it wasn't fellows telling rude remarks. It was Tommy and Liam and . . .'

'Just not any more.'

Grace wished now she hadn't told him. He didn't understand how funny it had been.

'Sure, sure,' she said to placate him.

'You've no mother, Grace, and Father lives in his own world. Somebody has to look after you. That's why I sound like an old bear, an old hen . . . whichever it is that does the clucking and fussing.'

'I think it's a hen,' she laughed, and ran towards him to give him a hug. 'It's hens that fuss. It's the bears that hug. You're very good to me, Kerry.'

The door opened and Patrick came in.

'Is that your new uniform? You look fantastic; a real scholar,' he said admiringly.

Grace still had her arms around her brother's waist.

'Kerry's been setting me right, and giving me all kinds of good advice about going to school.'

Patrick looked pleased. He often wondered what the children talked about when they were on their own. They seemed quite content.

'I just thought someone should mark her card,' Kerry said with a note of insolence that Grace noticed too. She looked up at him anxiously, and let her arms drop.

'Good.' Patrick was easy and relaxed. 'I'm glad you're doing it. I'm afraid that I have too much faith in you pair; I think you were born knowing everything, being able to do everything. I don't mark your cards enough, I suppose.'

'That's a good complaint to have, Father.' Grace was hasty in her attempts to avert this scene, whatever it was.

She spoke quickly. 'I hear so many people complaining about their parents who tell them this and order them to do that. You just stay as you are. Tommy Leonard says his father is at him night and day.'

'Not enough to get him to keep a clean tongue in his head,' Kerry said.

Suddenly Grace felt weary. 'Look, fight if you want to, I'm not going to keep chatting. I think I'll go to bed.'

The light had gone from her face. Both her father and brother looked stricken. 'I wasn't fighting, Gracie, really,' Kerry said.

'Listen to me, honey, I couldn't fight with anyone, not tonight, now that I see you all dressed up to go to your Irish convent school. My heart is so full, Grace. I wish, I wish so much . . .'

They knew what he wished. They knew that Father wished their mother were alive. But he didn't say it. He just said that he wished things were different.

Grace had met most of the girls who would be in her class and who lived in Mountfern. But there were quite a few from out the country. When they saw the newcomer they were dazzled. At first they giggled a bit at the beautiful girl with the golden curls tumbling down from a top knot tied with a shiny navy ribbon. And they nudged each other at her American accent.

Sister Laura made a small speech of welcome at assembly and said that she knew the girls of Mountfern convent would be, as they always were, welcoming to a stranger in their midst and help her to feel at home. Dara whispered to Grace that this was all nonsense. There never had been a stranger in their midst before. Grace was the first one. Maggie saw Grace and Dara laughing together at assembly, and tried to stop this feeling that she was being left out of things.

Sister Laura was speaking about the school year that lay ahead. She had every hope that 1962–1963 would be a year that they would all remember for the amount of hard work they put into their studies. Even those who had no formal examinations this year would, it was hoped, show a diligence that would be long remembered in the establishing of the convent in Mountfern as a legend in the houses of the order. Sister Laura said that sister houses had been achieving a reputation for scholarship which had so far evaded Mountfern. Let 1962–1963 be the year that all changed, the year they emptied their minds of silliness and let the sun of learning shine in.

They stood there in the navy uniforms. Kitty Daly splendid with the new hairstyle which had caused Kerry O'Neill to say 'You look nice. Did you change something about yourself?' and sang the hymn to Our Lady to mark the beginning of the new term. Kitty had put all silliness out of her mind and was concentrating heavily on the information that Kerry did not go to his boarding school for another week. Grace would be out of the way at school. If Kitty were to feign a terrible sickness and go home, they would never suspect her of malingering, not on the very first day of term. Then she could walk up as far as the Grange, and if that old bag Miss Hayes didn't get suspicious, she should surely find a chance to run into Kerry. Sister Laura was right, start the year as you mean to go on.

Dara sang lustily as well. It had been a great summer holiday after all, in spite of all the changes at Fernscourt. She and Michael had said last night, as they sat on the window seat, that they wished they had somewhere to go, some special place still like that room they had in Fernscourt that was theirs. But wasn't it funny that none of them ever wanted to go back and play in the ruins now? They had only been once with Grace and it was like going back somewhere that belonged to another part of their life. Mr O'Neill had urged them to continue playing there, but things had changed, there were bicycles for one thing, and the fishing for another. And it was great to have someone as lively as Grace around. Maggie was a great friend, but she was very mousy, and always afraid of what would happen, and of someone objecting or getting annoyed. Grace hadn't a fear in the world. She was magnificent.

Sister Laura sang to Our Lady, Queen of the Angels and Star of the Sea, and wondered why she felt Grace O'Neill was unsuitably dressed for school. The child wore her navy school uniform; she had no hint of make-up. She did not have pierced ears and great loops of earrings. She had no bosom apparent beneath her navy jumper. She was singing the hymn as assiduously as the others. What was it about her that made her seem not a twelve-year-old, but something much more precocious? Sister Laura liked to consider herself a fair woman. She hoped that she was not taking an unreasonable dislike to the child just because she had a beautiful face, tanned skin and golden hair.

Jacinta White nudged Maggie Daly to ask her why she wasn't singing.

'Sorry,' whispered Maggie, and joined in the hymn.

Jacinta was relieved. She thought Maggie's face looked very worried, as if she had something that was upsetting her. But of course Maggie often looked like that.

Fergus Slattery called to the Grange to see old Mr Johnson about a sale. It appeared that Patrick O'Neill had made an offer, a most generous offer for a small paddock owned by the Johnsons, and the right of way to bring horses to and fro from this field from the main road across the Johnsons' land.

'I can't see a thing wrong with it myself, but the American said to be sure, and do it through a solicitor; so here we are, Fergus. I'm sorry for bringing you all the way up here, I thought maybe your father might come, and we'd have a bit of a chat.'

'He has a cold on his chest, and Miss Purcell won't let him out of the house. He says he's going to look for a writ of habeas corpus if she keeps him there much longer.' Fergus spoke absent-mindedly. He was looking at the papers. 'What does this fellow want the land for up here?'

'I can't tell you, that's for certain. Marian says he's doing it out of the generosity of his heart, because he knows we're a bit strapped for cash. We wanted to get a bit of a paint job done but it costs the earth these days.'

'Is that field useful to you?'

'Not at all, it's only a nuisance to us. The hedges and walls are all broken anyway, but it says somewhere there, doesn't it, that he's going to build them up?'

Fergus had been reading this. 'Yes, he can build walls and low constructions for the maintenance of cattle, livestock or horses. I suppose that's what he wants, to set up a rival stables, take the one bit of business you have left.'

'I don't think so.' Mr Johnson was mild. 'He's signed an agreement with us about using our horses, paying a retainer even, in case he doesn't have sufficient guests for them. He's going to be the making of us, Fergus. Paying a great big rent for that falling-down Gate Lodge too, and a year in advance because we had to do a bit of smartening it up.'

'Smartening it up! From what I hear, you practically built a new house,' Fergus snapped.

'What have you against him, boy?'

'It's a good question, Mr Johnson, and a timely one. I'll look at this document now, and stop all this sounding off.'

Fergus read the totally straightforward deed of sale drafted by a perfectly honest solicitor. Reluctantly he agreed that if Mr Johnson wanted to sell, then there was nothing here that was out of the way, and that the price offered was well higher than the normal rate per acre hereabouts.

As a last, and almost petty gesture, Fergus asked whether Mr Johnson could see *any* reason, apart from the goodness of Patrick O'Neill's heart and his wish to give them decorating money, why a businessman should suddenly make an offer for that particular field.

Mr Johnson's mild old eyes looked surprised.

'Well of course there's a reason, Fergus. He needs a place where he can keep horses himself. And suppose he and Marian fall out, suppose Marian sets her cap at him too obviously and he isn't willing, well he'd need to have a fall-back position if he's offering his guests riding lessons, pony trekking, hunting and all. It's to cover himself.'

Fergus was astonished at such clarity of vision.

'And does Marian see it like this?' he gasped.

'Now, now, now Fergus, do women ever see things the way they are? Have you known a woman who could see further than romance and yards of veil and wedding days? Let them go on like that, it doesn't do anyone any harm.'

Fergus felt a chill. It was like playing God with people's future, he thought, as he arranged the signature of the deed of sale.

Olive Hayes wrote a long letter to her sister in New Zealand every month. She kept a carbon copy of it, and knew her sister probably did the same. They could refer back easily to small incidents that each had described over the years and they never forgot anything, no matter how trivial. Miss Hayes knew of the health of the elderly Reverend Mother who was always expected to die and then rallied, just when a successor had been more or less agreed for the community. Over on the other side of the earth in a convent on a cliff in South Island, Sister Bernadette knew about the O'Neill family, and how little Grace continued sunnily her life in Mountfern. Grace had even asked Miss Hayes if she would like to come to the sale of work up at the convent which was usually for the children's parents.

'You helped me make all the jam and cakes. You're more entitled than anyone,' Grace had said.

Miss Hayes had been very pleased, but she wondered was she stepping out of place.

'Perhaps Miss Johnson?' she had said tentatively.

'Ugh, ugh, no thank you very much,' Grace had giggled. 'We don't want to be giving her ideas, Miss Hayes.'

Olive had found that very endearing. She told her sister that Patrick O'Neill had gone to the States again. He travelled the whole way there as easily as some people took a train from the big town to Dublin. Miss Hayes felt that he had waited until Kerry was safely installed at his boarding school before he went. It was no trouble to look after Grace, but Kerry might have been a handful.

Miss Hayes looked back at the carbons of her previous letters and noticed with satisfaction that she had made this very same pronouncement in July when the O'Neills had arrived. Now, five letters later, she was interested to know that she had been right.

Kate Ryan decorated the Slatterys' office with holly at Christmas time. She thought how strangely unfestive it all was compared to everywhere else in Mountfern. The church had its huge crib and in the window of the presbytery there was a Christmas candle and another smaller crib, lovingly tended by Miss Barry who hadn't touched a drop since the summer.

Leonard's stationery and paper shop was all done up with the paper chains and streamers it sold. Mrs Meagher was still in mourning for her husband, but she had sprigs of tinsel and glitter around the Christmas-wrapped brooches and earrings in the window of the shop. The cinema had two large Christmas trees with lights that flashed on and off. Declan Morrissey said it gave him a headache to look at them, and every single year he managed to fuse the lights in the cinema when he was putting up these ridiculous Christmas decorations. Daly's Dairy had very smart plaited rings of ivy and holly twisted around each other and tied with a red ribbon. They had been made by Kitty apparently, who was a changed girl according to all accounts, and had seen how to do this home-made decoration in one of those American magazines she was always reading.

In the post office there were some coloured paper chains, a big silver banner saying Peace on Earth, and a collection box discreetly placed in case anyone might interpret the season of good will as a time to give a few pennies towards gifts for a children's orphanage. Dunne's pub had a big plastic Santa Claus in the window. There was hardly any point in their putting up any further decoration since they were yet again on the verge of packing up and going to Liverpool. Jimbo Doyle had put a Christmas tree for his mother in the window of their small house, and had agreed after much nagging to get proper fairy lights that worked. His mother had said that she was sick of hearing all the work Jimbo was doing in other people's houses while their own looked like a very good imitation of a rubbish tip.

In the Garda barracks Seamus Sheehan looked in some doubt at the decorations Mary had bought on her last visit to Dublin. He wondered whether they were appropriate to the walls of a Garda Siochana station. Arty-looking cut-out robins and reindeer with little holes where you inserted mistletoe or holly. But Mrs Sheehan had been adamant. She had read about them in a magazine which said that all the best people in Dublin had these in their homes now, and she wanted to drag a bit of style into Mountfern no matter how much they all resisted it.

Judy Byrne had planted two neat window boxes of her small house with holly bushes and miniature Christmas trees. They looked very festive and elegant at the same time, people told her. Patrick O'Neill had made a point of coming in to congratulate her on them. He had stayed for a drink at Judy's insistence because of the season. She ran next door to Foley's with a tray and came back with a large whiskey for Patrick and a small sherry for herself.

She told Patrick that she didn't keep drink in the house. She thought it was a pity for single ladies to start opening the bottle at a regular hour each evening. Single women had to be so careful. Not that she was saying a word against Marian Johnson of course, and in a hotel poor Marian had to be sociable. Still it *was* a danger, and it could run away with you all too easily.

Across the road Mr and Mrs Williams had their house neatly draped in holly and ivy. The Protestant church had been decorated by their few parishioners. Dr White and his wife had threatened to have no decorations this year if this ridiculous row about mistletoe wasn't solved. Jacinta wanted a big bunch of it on the door just as you came in; Liam wanted none of it in or near the house. Never had a battle been fought so long and bitterly. Tommy Leonard said it was better than being at the pictures listening to the two of them. Dr White decided eventually that a small discreet sprig of mistletoe be placed over the kitchen door, that it should not be publicly referred to, and that if this row began again, both Jacinta and Liam would remember Christmas 1962 as the year they not only had no decorations but no presents and no turkey either.

Miss Purcell wasn't best pleased when she saw Kate Ryan on a chair with a sprig of holly and a packet of thumb tacks.

'It was never the way here; Mr Slattery never requested it,' said Miss Purcell, lips in a hard line and the two red spots coming up magnificently on her cheeks.

'I know, Miss Purcell.' Kate was falsely apologetic. 'It's quite ridiculous really, but the children went up to Coyne's wood and they picked lovely bits full of berries, so I thought the least I could do . . . you know Mr Slattery wouldn't want to offend . . . and in the spirit of Christmas . . .'

She finished no sentence and did not explain that she had asked Michael and Dara to collect a big box and deliver it to the office for her. A Christmas card from Fergus's sister Rosemary in England and then old Mr Slattery, Fergus and Miss Purcell in paper hats sitting round a small turkey dinner. It didn't seem nearly celebratory enough for someone as warm and funny as Fergus.

He was pleased and surprised. He had been at the district court in the town, his father had gone to talk to an old crony on the grounds of a will that might be changed, but really in the knowledge that a bottle would be opened. Fergus looked at the holly with pleasure.

'We never had that; it's lovely,' he said simply.

'Not even when your mother was alive?'

'Not really. She was never strong, you know. She didn't have all that energy like you have.'

To herself Kate thought that it didn't really take much energy to stick a few bits of holly on a wall behind pictures, or round a doorway for a man and a boy. But she said nothing. She didn't mention that Grace O'Neill had said the very same thing; her mother had been unwell always. They didn't have Christmas decorations, it would have been tiring for her.

'I got you a present, Kate,' Fergus said. 'You're a hard person to buy for; you have everything.'

'I felt the same about you.' She produced a big wrapped parcel.

'Isn't that great, to be the two people who have everything,' Fergus said, and waited for her to open hers first. It was a day excursion ticket to Dublin, two gift vouchers – one for Switzer's and one for Brown Thomas – and a note saying: 'On presentation of this paper to her employer, Mrs Kate Ryan will be granted one day's leave from her lawful employment during the working week.'

Kate stared at it in delight.

'I thought you could go to the January sales, and those vouchers are to make sure you go to Grafton Street and see nice things. You're not to be buying up household goods in Clery's, mind.' He spoke gruffly to hide his pleasure in her delight.

'I'll enjoy every minute of the day.' She hugged him. 'Fergus, you are a darling. Thank you very much.'

'Well now, let's see what you gave me.' He opened the box. It was a beautiful edition of *Moore's Melodies* with huge over-flowery illustrations by Daniel Maclise.

'I remembered you said you like Thomas Moore – that day at the concert, when Michael's class was murdering some of the melodies. I thought you'd like this.' She beamed at him and saw to her consternation that his eyes were far too bright. She spoke quickly until he had recovered a calm voice himself. 'I got it inside in the town. You know, Gorman's bookshop, I asked them to look out for an old edition and they came up with this. John and I have been looking at it ourselves. I hope you like it.'

Fergus had recovered his voice.

'I love it. Miss Purcell and my father won't know what's ahead of them this Christmas day. They're going to get a blast of the lot here . . . I might come over to your place and sing them through for you as well.'

Kate said that was a promise and she was holding him to it. At some stage over Christmas Fergus Slattery was to walk up River Road with his Moore book in a plastic bag in case it rained on it, and he would sing the entire repertoire for whoever was in Ryan's Licensed Premises.

'That should empty the place for you and lose you your trade before O'Neill takes it away,' Fergus said.

'Now Fergus, it's Christmas time. Stop giving out about him. And wasn't John Ryan right, as he is in so many things? For all his great chat and plans there isn't a sod turned on that site yet. It's going to take longer than he thinks to get his hotel going in a place that moves as slowly as Mountfern.'

Kerry came home from school on a day when Patrick had to be in Dublin for further talks with the Tourist Board. The train would need to be met. Marian Johnson was only too happy to oblige. She had heard that Patrick was trying to arrange that Brian Doyle the builder see to it, and Brian had replied with spirit that he was a building contractor, not a chauffeur. He would be quite happy to do anyone a favour, but would not be asked to do a driving job as if it were part of his terms in getting the Fernscourt contract.

Patrick had admired this viewpoint and apologized. Many another man would have had less pride and courage than Brian Doyle, and would not have jeopardized their chance of the biggest building job in these parts in years. But Brian was not one to sit back and allow anyone to assume he was what he was not. He did himself more good by his truculent attitude with Patrick than he ever knew.

Marian was pleased too, although she thought Brian Doyle was insane. She stood on the platform raking the crowd of passengers who got off, looking for Kerry.

He seemed to have got taller or thinner somehow at school. Very handsome in his school blazer, and carrying his sports bag as well as his suitcase. He smiled pleasantly at Marian, and looked around for Grace.

'She's busy decorating the lodge for Christmas,' said Marian, who had told the child there was no room in the car. 'She'll see you back at home. Your father has to be in Dublin. He said to tell you he's very sorry.'

'I'm sure he is,' Kerry was polite and cold.

'So I thought we might have a little lunch, you and I in the hotel . . . to get to know each other.' She twinkled at him, but Kerry didn't twinkle back.

'We do know each other don't we . . . ?' he said, bewildered. 'You're Miss Johnson . . . from the Grange.'

'Marian,' she said.

'Yes, well.'

It was most unsatisfactory. Marian had wanted to lean her elbows on the table of the Grand or the Central and have a lunch with this handsome blond son of Patrick's. Now it was all falling to pieces.

Kerry looked at her carefully and long. It was as if he were deciding what to do. And then it was as if he had decided to turn on the electric light of his charm.

'Well Marian . . . if you're sure I may call you that, I'd love to have lunch with you even though we do know each other already. That would be very nice.'

They went to the Central. Marian waved at the people she knew whose heads went close together to discuss what she could possibly be doing with this teenage boy. They had tomato soup, boiled bacon and cabbage followed by apple pie and ice cream. Kerry told her little about school, less about his father and nothing about their life as it used to be in America. However he did learn about what had been going on in Mountfern, and that Grace seemed to love her school, had plenty of nice little girls as friends. Grace and his father had been taking riding lessons and both were progressing very well. There had been endless delays about clearing the title for the final land purchase in Fernscourt.

Marian prattled on in what she had hoped would be their lunch of getting to know each other, and she managed to present herself to Kerry as three different ages during the space of half an hour. She was getting younger as the lunch continued. She said that she was quite demented trying to get the O'Neills to give up this ridiculous idea of having Christmas lunch on their own, as a family. They should join her and her father, and there would be four other guests, charming people whom they would like, one of them was actually the Honourable and was terribly natural and unassuming, as if she were like everyone else.

On the journey back Marian had the vague feeling that she had got to know Kerry O'Neill not at all, but he had got to know almost all there was to be known about her.

'I'll call in later when your father gets back from Dublin,' she said as she dropped him at the lodge and he was thanking her courteously.

'Why will you do that?' He was perfectly polite.

'Well. Gosh. Well, to see if he got back all right and to tell him that I met you safely.'

Kerry looked at her, a clear unflinching look.

'Or maybe I'll drop in tomorrow . . . or some time,' Marian said foolishly.

She saw Grace racing out of the lodge to throw her arms around Kerry.

'Where *were* you? Miss Johnson said I couldn't come. I've been looking out for you for ages. Come in and tell me all about it, I've been dying for you to get here . . .'

The door of the lodge closed behind them. Marian saw the long stern face of Olive Hayes who was washing up at the kitchen sink. Marian told herself, as she had done many times before, that she mustn't rush it. Patrick O'Neill was a man not long a widower, a busy man with a million things on his mind. He had a tight self-sufficient little family. It would be foolish to try to break into it until they were ready.

That was the silly mistake Judy Byrne was making all the time, with her little invitations to a drink, and then fluttering in and out of Foley's instead of realizing that any man likes a woman with a good Waterford glass decanter on the sideboard.

They had a tradition in Mountfern that there was only one mass on Christmas Day. It meant that one priest was then free to go around and take holy communion to the people who weren't able to leave home. The mass was at nine o'clock. And the whole parish was there.

Judy Byrne wore a mantilla to communion, which looked very well on her. Miss Purcell, who really would have preferred a seven-thirty mass but would never criticize the clergy, wore a nice blue scarf that Kate Ryan had knitted for her, because she knew Miss Purcell had a blue coat.

Sheila Whelan had had a tiring night: young Teresa Meagher had had yet another row with her mother and wanted to leave home. There were no buses on Christmas Eve. Sheila had spent a great deal of time making cups of drinking chocolate, and taking further bars of Kit Kat out of the shelves. She cajoled and soothed. She told Teresa that if somebody left home at Christmas it had a terrible effect because it didn't just destroy *that* Christmas, but every other Christmas afterwards for both sides. She knew this, she told Teresa, very very well. She didn't go into details about how Joe Whelan had left her at Christmas, and how the big row over the road many years ago with Rosemary Slattery had been at Christmas time also. There was something about the season and all its expectations. Sheila talked long and gently about Teresa's mother feeling sad and lonely this Christmas, the first since her husband died; she must be given some little extra understanding; no of course, not over things that were totally unfair, but just an overall understanding.

Eventually the troubled child went to sleep on the sofa. Sheila put a rug over her, and a cushion under her head. Then she crossed the road and heard the whole story again from Teresa's mother, the insolence, the selfishness . . . Again she tried to talk of a daughter who had lost her father, and eventually Mrs Meagher's red puffy eyes began to close, so Sheila left her.

She had urged them for form's sake to dress properly and go to mass as if nothing had happened. They were all going to Christmas lunch with the Whites. Judy Byrne was going too. Sheila would have preferred to have spent the day stock-taking, or sitting and listening to Radio Eireann. They had lovely programmes on Christmas Day for people at home. It would be a real treat not to have to leave the house at all.

Patrick O'Neill walked his son and daughter up the church for their first Christmas Day in Mountfern. They had given Miss Hayes a lift from the lodge, but she didn't sit with them. She said she had friends to meet, and Christmas greetings to exchange. Everyone looked at the trio. Patrick in his camel-haired overcoat, stocky and handsome, smiling at this one, at that. Kerry taller definitely, he must have grown another two inches during his first term at boarding school. He wore a belted tweed coat, the kind many a youth of his age might wear, but it looked impossibly stylish because of the way the collar was turned up. Grace had a new outfit brought back from New York. It was a soft pale pink, a dusty pink coat with big velvet cuffs and collar in a darker pink. She had a velvet beret, a sort of tam o'shanter perched on top of all those golden curls as well. People turned to each other to smile at the beautiful child. Grace saw Dara and Michael and gave a little wave; they both stared at her open-mouthed.

Her father must have given this to her this morning already. She hadn't mentioned it yesterday. Maggie Daly sat in her brown coat which used to belong to Kitty. She felt like a colourless blob. Canon Moran was blessing everyone and wishing that the spirit of the Holy Child be with them now and always, and all Maggie Daly could think of was her own awful coat. No wonder Our Lord wasn't kinder to her, if she couldn't even drag her mind to think of him on his birthday of all days. Maggie gloomily accepted that she didn't deserve golden hair and a pink coat, or to be Dara Ryan's best friend.

The children all went for a walk in Coyne's wood on Christmas afternoon. It was a lovely clear, crisp day, and they wrapped up well and set out.

Kerry O'Neill came too. He told them about his school and spoke as if he were exactly the same age as everyone else, instead of being fifteen. Grace hung on to his arm a lot, and encouraged him to tell more tales, like the night the boy in the dormitory was listening to a transistor radio on an earphone and forgot where he was, and kept singing along with the Beatles. Yeah, Yeah, Yeah . . . and all the time Father Minehan was standing at the end of the bed watching him.

Kerry O'Neill remembered everyone's names. He was interested in everything they did. Tommy Leonard did one of his great imitations of Miss Barry the priest's housekeeper when she was on a tear. Michael explained to Kerry the best parts of the river, and told him a great hint about always noting a place where the cattle went to drink from. The cows stirred up mud, and also disturbed the water plants as they came to drink, so this meant fish would find it a good area for feeding, and you should position yourself about ten or twenty yards downstream and wait for them there. Kerry took all this in gravely and agreed with Jacinta White that Christmas wasn't Christmas without mistletoe, and at the same time agreed with her brother Liam that too much palaver could go on about it, just let it be there was the best solution. He asked Maggie Daly if all their family had that nice auburn hair. Did her sisters who were away nursing in Wales have it too? And Maggie pinked up happily and said that nobody had ever called it auburn before. Kerry said he heard that Dara was a demon fisherwoman, great at threading the maggots on the hooks and had caught a huge pike that struggled and fought. He said he thought Mountfern was the greatest place in the world, and as dark fell and they all went back to their homes, there wasn't one of the children who had come to Coyne's wood that would have remembered the day six months ago when they thought it was the end of the world because somebody had bought Fernscourt.

Part Two

CHAPTER SEVEN

Old Mr Slattery died in the spring. He died exactly as he would have liked, sitting on his fishing stool and leaning back against a tree. Many people must have passed him by that afternoon thinking he was asleep. Miss Purcell's back was like a ramrod at the funeral mass. Her little wine-coloured hat was replaced by a precisely similar one in black, and her disapproving face was set in harder lines than ever.

Fergus had felt achingly sorry for her.

She had mothered and bossed and bullied the old man for years. In return she had received a courteous fearful attention from him. What would she find as a replacement? He was very swift to tell her that he wanted no change in the situation.

'Oh indeed, and then when you up and marry, Master Fergus, when I'm an old woman, what will happen to me then?'

'I don't think I'll up and marry, I'm nearly thirty, and anyway if I do, won't she be a lucky woman to get the both of us?' He didn't say that Miss Purcell was an old woman already.

Fergus had one sister, Rosemary, married and living in Manchester. She came home for the funeral but she and he were like strangers. Rosemary was ten years older, she had been headstrong, he believed, and impatient. There had been rows, he remembered, when he was only six or seven and then she had left home. It had been made up of course but only in a fashion. Not properly. Letters at Christmas and cards on birthdays. No visits, no phone calls. There had been no rows with her little brother, but somehow Fergus hadn't expected his sister to come home. She came without her husband James, and without her sons. There was little mention of her family during the preparations for the funeral. She wore smart black and smoked the moment they were outside the church. Miss Purcell, who had been with the family at the time she left, hated her and barely disguised it.

'Back for the money,' she hissed at Fergus, who only laughed. There was very little money, he had read his father's will. A legacy for Miss Purcell, a couple of hundred pounds to the church for masses, a small insurance policy whose small proceeds went to his grandsons in Manchester. There was nothing for the long-gone Rosemary. She would know that too. The business and the house were for Fergus. There was a touching personal note of gratitude that the young man had come back to Mountfern to keep the business going. Fergus had blinked a bit over that, he hadn't known how much his father had appreciated it. Rosemary sat and drank a whiskey with him; the conversation was brittle. He had the feeling that this was the last time he would ever see her, and he was determined for both their sakes that he would be pleasant and allow no recriminations to come into the conversation.

'Does it seem strange to be back home again?' he asked her.

She shrugged. 'It's not home to me, never was really.'

He hid his irritation. 'I know. I forget. Well, people were glad to see you again.'

'Did you think so? I think most of them had forgotten I ever existed. Real country bumpkins most of them.'

'I suppose they must seem that way to you.'

111

'And to you?'

'Oh I'm jes' an ole country bumpkin myself . . . like to sit in me ole rockin' chair and talk about the times gone by.' He smiled at her, expecting some kind of an answering laugh.

Rosemary frowned at him. 'You're turning into an old man, Fergus. It's a fact. You walk in small steps as if you were wearing slippers, and a cardy . . .'

Fergus felt the smile die on his face. He had been play-acting to entertain her.

'Good Lord, I must watch that,' he said, deliberately taking giant steps across the room. 'Is that any better?' He took her glass to refill it and strode across the room as if he were playing grandmother's footsteps. This time it worked. She laughed at him affectionately.

'You're much too smart for here, Fergus. This is a dead-end town. Quit while you can, get to Dublin, even if you haven't the guts to sell up entirely. Drop it before it's too late and you turn into a vegetable or an alcoholic, or both.'

He didn't comment on the fact that it was she who had had three whiskies while he had not finished his first.

'And what would I do that would be so exciting in . . . say Manchester?' he asked, hoping he kept the sarcasm out of his voice.

'You'd meet real people, not just the butcher, the baker, the candlestick maker. You'd find someone for yourself, instead of having to be like a eunuch here.'

'Is that what they say I am?' He was very angry indeed. But there must be no more screaming matches with Rosemary in this house. History must not repeat itself.

'It's what I can see you are,' she said, her eyes too bright, her hair slipping from the coil at the back of her neck. 'What else could you be in a place like this, making sheep's eyes at that woman from the pub who does your typing? And never doing a thing about it.'

'Sorry, Rosemary, hold on a minute, I've got to get us more water,' he said.

He went into the kitchen and filled the jug, which he gripped with both hands to the sink until his knuckles were thin and white. How *dare* she speak of Kate like that? He would like to have hit her across the side of her silly drunken head. But it was a matter of hours. They would talk for another short while, then tomorrow she would have breakfast and he would drive her to the train in the big town. He would offer her something from the house as a souvenir. He had been going to suggest an old Victorian sewing box that had belonged to their mother. But, God damn it, no. It was too good for her, and Rosemary didn't look like anyone who would ever sew. Just keep the peace for a few more hours. That wasn't a weak thing to do, surely; it was a strong thing. He came back in smiling.

'Sorry, I was waiting for it to run cold. Where were we? I was making sheep's eyes at Kate Ryan. Who would I be making sheep's eyes at in Manchester?'

'I didn't say you were to come to Manchester.' She sounded sulky now.

'But I will some day, surely. Not to work but to visit. I'd love to see my nephews. They must be nearly left school by now. Tell me about them.'

He settled himself in his chair, his smile of interest and concern masking his rage.

'They've left,' she said gruffly.

'Surely not? Hugh can only be barely sixteen?'

'Headstrong, impatient, won't wait, won't get an education.' She looked into the fire.

'And what does James say about it?'

'He's hardly ever there to say anything. He's not around much.'

Rosemary still looked into the fire.

Fergus poured them both a last drink, and moved to less troubled waters. He suggested that Rosemary take a silver cigarette box back with her as a memento. Awkwardly she accepted it, and before she went to bed she gave him what passed for a kiss on the cheek. A sort of lunge.

'You're not the worst, Fergus, even though you're a bit of an eejit,' she said, and her tones were those of love and praise, inasmuch as she could give either.

He lay awake for a long time and wondered about sheep's eyes. What way did one sheep look at another that the world regarded as foolish?

Eddie Ryan asked Mr Williams the vicar if he could become a Protestant and be accepted into the Church of Ireland faith. Mr Williams listened to him gravely and said it was a very big step and perhaps he should think more about it, maybe even discuss it with his priest or his parents. Mr Williams was a kind man; never for a moment did he betray his knowledge of Eddie's latest deed, which involved breaking the little shutter in the confessional, something that had never been done since the church was built and had hardly ever been done in Christendom according to Canon Moran and Father Hogan. Eddie explained that the church was empty at the time, and he wondered what it felt like to sit where the priest did, pushing the shutters back and forth to listen to the penitents. He got a bit excited and kept whizzing them to see which one would close quickest, and that was when one came away from its moorings entirely.

Jimbo Doyle had to be summoned, and it was all very serious and high level. Canon Moran said he couldn't believe that the child would say the church was empty. Wasn't our Blessed Lord in the church in the tabernacle, watching Eddie Ryan desecrate church property and disassemble the place where the holy sacrament of penance took place?

Father Hogan kept saying, 'What Cromwell left undone Eddie Ryan will finish,' and pretending to panic when he saw him coming near the church.

It would be easier for him to be a Protestant.

'I have thought about it,' he assured Mr Williams. 'I'm dead certain. Would I need an admission card to start coming here on Sunday?'

'Of course not, Eddie, but . . .'

'And if there's any questions, trouble like, you'll tell them I asked to join. That it's all above board. If they come hounding me?'

'Who would come hounding you, Eddie?'

'Almost everyone in the place, Mr Williams, you wouldn't credit it. My mother said if she set eyes on me again today she wouldn't be responsible for what she'd do. Sergeant Sheehan said he has a room in the barracks with a lock on it and he's thinking of putting my name on it because it's where I'll end up. I couldn't tell you what the priests are like, because we're all meant to be . . . whatever it's called these days, you know loving all other religions . . . so it wouldn't do you any good to know what they're like down at the presbytery just now.'

'Life can be very difficult.' Mr Williams was trying hard not to smile.

'You wouldn't know the half of it up here, with no flock so to speak of, and pots of money.'

The impoverished Mr Williams listened to this wryly.

'I don't have all that much, Eddie.'

'I bet you have four pounds though,' Eddie said.

'Well I do, but I need it. I can't give it to you, no matter how great your need.'

'No, my need isn't great. If I join your church I won't have to pay it.'

'How, exactly?'

'I can say I'm a different faith, a different crowd altogether. I can't be responsible for some sum of money they say I owe in the last faith. For repairs. I'd never make four pounds. Never.'

Mr Williams was very kind. He could see that Eddie Ryan was not trying to put a touch on him; the sum was too huge to be possible even for the wildly optimistic.

'Why don't you weed a few graves for me, Eddie, tidy up the graveyard. I could pay you say, five shillings. If you did a good job, then after several five-shilling days you could return to your old faith and pay your debts, and everyone would be happier.'

'I thought you were supposed to be looking for converts, and snatching people away from the true faith.'

'Oh no, we don't do much snatching here, more patting people down; that's what it seems to be about these days. Will I give you a sack for the grass and the weeds?'

Dara and Grace were in the graveyard looking after James Edward Gray. They had brought cowslips and primroses and had made an unsuccessful attempt to remove some of the moss and lichen from his stone with Vim. It had looked much better before their efforts, they realized. Maggie had been a bit funny about James Edward Gray, claiming that she found him and *she* was the one to look after him. Grace and Dara had agreed and gone to look for someone else who was pretty neglected. But Maggie had come after them in tears and said they could have James Edward Gray and keep him, she didn't care. Then she had stormed off home. She had been a bit like that lately, maybe it was trouble at home.

Maggie's elder sister Kitty was a bit bossy, and she had two sisters who were nursing in Wales. They could have lost their religion or not written home, or something. Mrs Daly was an awful one for doing the right thing and the trimmings on the Dalys' rosary at night were as long as the rosary itself. Maggie must be getting some kind of trouble from her mother. That could be the only explanation of why she was so touchy these days.

Tommy Leonard came to collect Michael.

'There's no fish. What's the point?' Michael said.

'There's often no fish. As far as I'm concerned there's nearly always no fish. What are you after, some kind of record catch?'

Tommy was indignant. He had spent half an hour explaining to his father why a boy of thirteen should be allowed to go and fish with his friend, and now Michael didn't want to come.

'It's pointless, can't see any reason to drag all that stuff miles up the bank and miles back,' Michael said.

'Lovely! When did this happen, this road to Damascus? Just when I was assuring my father that there was no better, healthier way of spending the afternoon.'

'I don't know,' Michael said.

'Listen Michael, you are a pain, and a big pain. What *is* it? Why was fishing what we did yesterday, and suddenly today it's what we don't do? I don't mind, I just want to know.'

Michael punched Tommy to show that there was no personal ill-will involved.

'You know the way it is sometimes. There seems no point in anything. Anything at all,' Michael said.

'Do I know how it is? Of course I know how it is. I feel that way most of the time. But why today? Now I'll have to go on my own or go back to the shop and say to my father he was right, I am a selfish pleasure-seeking lout . . .'

'Oh all right, I'll come with you.'

'What about Dara and Grace and the others? Where are they? Did they all give up fishing too, suddenly? Did everybody except me?' Tommy wondered.

'Oh, who knows where they are? The Whites have gone to Dublin with their mother for the day; Dara and Grace are giggling somewhere, you can be sure of that.'

'Where's Maggie?'

'I don't know. I think she's as browned off with all this giggling as we are. Come on then Tommy, if we're going to spend the day getting pneumonia for no fish, let's go and catch it.'

'The sun is shining, you clown,' Tommy said.

The sun had come out and Miss Hayes was planting some pansies that Kate Ryan had given her. Mrs Ryan was very good about all kinds of flowers and Miss Hayes had heard some disparaging remarks that Judy Byrne had made about the appearance of the gate lodge of the Grange. Miss Hayes was feeling personally slighted. She had called at Ryan's merely for advice. Mrs Ryan had given her the pansies and got her a lift back too from a passing customer. It was too far to walk in the sun, she had said.

Olive Hayes watered them well in, just as she had been advised. She would make a macaroni cheese for the tea, that little Ryan girl was coming this evening. She and Grace O'Neill were very thick with each other. They never stopped talking and laughing. It would do your heart good to see them.

Grace and Dara left the graveyard hastily when they saw Eddie being instructed in the details of grave-tending.

'It's more than flesh and blood could bear, we'll have to leave,' Dara said as soon as she saw her small brother.

'He's not that bad,' Grace laughed.

'You don't know how bad he is, he'll probably dig up half the bodies in the graveyard. We're well out of it before he gets at it.'

They scrambled to the wall where they had left their bicycles.

'We'll walk home through Coyne's wood. That way we won't get drawn into the fishing,' Dara said.

'Yes, sure. Or else we could just say that we're not going fishing today.' Everything was simple to Grace.

They wheeled their bikes through the woods which looked beautiful in the Easter sunshine. They heard pigeons and cuckoos, and small rabbits ran across their path as they walked.

'It's like fairyland here,' Grace said happily.

'Is your father glad he came?' Dara asked.

'Oh yes, of course he is. Why?'

'He was in our pub the other night. I thought he looked kind of tired and upset.'

'He gets upset over Kerry. Remember at Christmas I was telling you; and there's been something on his mind at the moment. I don't know what it is, he won't tell me. That means it's either about Kerry or about women.'

'Women?' Dara's eyes were round.

'Yes, women falling in love with him. You know, I told you yucky Marian Johnson has.'

'Oh yes, but you wouldn't mind that,' Dara dismissed Marian.

'And I think Miss Byrne, you know, the chiropractor.'

'Physio.'

'Yes, whatever. And there's this woman in America.' Grace looked troubled.

'Lord he *does* collect them,' Dara said in mystification.

'I know, he's very old and everything, but he's very nice,' Grace said defensively. 'And rich of course,' she added, in order to be strictly fair.

'Who's the woman in America?'

'A Mrs Fine.'

'Do you think it's serious? Isn't she married to someone else, if she's a missus?'

'No, he's dead or separated. There's no Mister Fine around.'

'Do you like her?'

'She's OK. I don't want Father to marry anyone else. That's all.'

'I know, but maybe he's not going to. Wouldn't she be here or he be over there if they were getting married? After all they're pretty old. They wouldn't want to be wasting time.'

'He calls her a lot. He called her twice on Christmas Day.'

'Oh that means nothing. Mrs Whelan says people are always telephoning each other on Christmas Day and putting the heart across everyone else.'

'I don't know.' Grace was doubtful. 'I had this friend in the States, Brigid Anne Moriarty. Well, she told me that her mother said Father was going to marry again, that everybody knew it, that he had a lady friend he worked with, and that they were going to get married quietly in New York.'

'How did Brigid Anne know all this, and you and Kerry didn't?'

'Who would tell us? Anyway I told Kerry this on the day of mother's funeral.'

'You mean Brigid Anne knew your father had a lady friend *before* your mother died?' Dara's face was horrified.

'But you see it wasn't true; obviously it wasn't. It was only a tale people told because Father was so well known amongst all these people, and because Mother was an invalid for so long.'

Grace looked wretched as she went over this. Impulsively Dara threw her arm around her friend's shoulder.

'Don't worry about it, Grace, *please*. It's not happened. It's not going to happen. We can head off the awful Marians and awful Judys, and Mrs Fine can't be any threat, otherwise she'd be here.'

'Yes, I'm sure that's right.'

'So why are you still sad?'

'Because I'm thinking about the day of the funeral and how upset Kerry was when I told him about what people were saying. But you're right. It's not going to happen: I won't think about it any more.'

They came out of the wood and cycled to the lodge. Miss Hayes said that Mr O'Neill had been on the telephone to say he would not be back for tea. He had gone to Kerry's school. The boys had spent some of the Easter holidays there to take part in the Easter vigil and church services. They were meant to be getting holidays in a week. But Kerry was coming back tonight.

All through their macaroni cheese they chattered excitedly about Kerry coming home. They cleared the table and washed the dishes with Miss Hayes. Dara marvelled at the peace and quiet in this house, no Carrie clattering pans in the kitchen, no bar on the other side of the green door, no Leopold howling, no Declan complaining that he was going to be the baby in this family until he was an old-age-pensioner, no Eddie bringing some new doom and destruction down on them. No bustle. It must be lonely for Grace sometimes too, of course, so far from everyone.

They sat in Grace's room, and Dara tried on all her clothes. The shoes were a little too small, which was a pity since Grace had so many she could have given Dara any amount without missing them.

'Does your father ever fight with Michael?' Grace asked.

'No, no he doesn't.'

Grace sighed heavily. 'No, I think it's just my father and Kerry. It's something in them that doesn't mix.'

'Of course Daddy gets very irate with Eddie, almost every day of our lives,' Dara offered, in the hope of reassuring her friend.

'Eddie's different, as you said yourself.'

'Yes,' Dara agreed. 'Eddie's very different, nobody could mix with him.'

Dara cycled home and saw a man slipping into the Rosemarie hair salon, having looked up and down River Road nervously first. Could the unlikely rumour they had heard at school *possibly* be true? She must tell Grace tomorrow morning. She hoped Grace wouldn't be lonely as she waited for Kerry and her father to come home.

Grace wished she had never told Kerry about that stupid thing that Brigid Anne had said, about the gossip that Father had some other lady in mind to marry.

117

Obviously it hadn't been true. It was nearly two years since Mother had died, and Father had no intention of marrying again. Father Devine had introduced him to several likely people, awful women from the parish, widows and terrible people. But Father used to laugh about them with her so Grace had no worries.

Kerry had a picture of Mother in his billfold, and also in the plastic folder at the back of his assignment book. Grace had seen him taking it out to look at it one day when he thought nobody was watching. And the picture of Mother that stood on the piano . . . Kerry was always adjusting it and making sure it stood right where it was best lit.

There was a portrait of Mother hanging in the hall. Mother had never liked it, she thought it made her look as if she had been dressed up to play the part of a fine lady. Father had laughed and told her that she *was* a fine lady. Kerry didn't like that picture, he never stopped to look at it. Once Grace asked him why he didn't like it, and he had said that Father had only dressed Mother up in jewellery and silks, and paid a society painter to do the portrait, to show what a big man *he* was. It had nothing to do with Mother herself.

Kerry had said that when things were his to do what he liked with, he would take the picture outside and burn it. Then Mother would know how well he had understood her. Kerry said some very odd things from time to time.

Grace wished she knew why her father had driven all the way up to his school to collect him. Perhaps it was a sign that Father was going to be warmer to Kerry, but somehow she didn't think so.

Father Minehan was a fussy man. Anything that could be said directly and simply, he managed to dress up and obscure. Patrick had been fifteen minutes in the dean's study and still didn't know why he was being asked to take Kerry away. That very day.

'So, when all aspects are considered, and taking everything into account, very often, the greater good is achieved by the simpler option,' Father Minehan said.

Patrick looked at the priest with disgust. His blue eyes were hard and unsmiling.

'Briefly, what did he do?' he asked again, but his tone was more curt.

'There are so many explanations and ways of looking at what we do and why we do it . . .' Father Minehan was beginning again.

'In two or three sentences, Father.' Patrick had never been so ill-mannered to a man of the cloth. His old training made him feel a thrill of wrongdoing because he was interrupting a priest with a bark of command.

'If it were as easy as that . . .'

'It is as easy as that. I have driven for two hours to a school where I thought you were educating my son, a school to which I have given generous contributions I may add, and I hear, or think I hear that you want him to leave. Now. Why?'

Father Minehan was at a loss to answer a question so directly put. He remained silent.

'Come on, Father, I can't stay all week playing guessing games. What did he do?'

'Let's take it slowly, Mr O'Neill.'

'Let's take it at a nice brisk pace, Father Minehan. Did he bugger one of the other boys?'

'Mr O'Neill, *please!*'

Now, for the first time, the priest was shaken into a direct response.

'He's a fifteen-year-old boy, Father, almost sixteen. Eventually, I suppose, if I ask enough questions we might get an answer. Was he drunk? Did he hit one of the masters? Did he miss mass? What in God's name prompted all these letters and phone calls that the FBI couldn't work out?'

'I'm trying to explain.'

'God damn it, you are not trying to explain. Did he screw one of the maids? Did he deny the infallibility of the pope? If I drive here and take him away with me leaving behind buildings I'm goddamn paying to erect, I would like to know why.'

'He took a great deal of money.'

Patrick felt an ice-cold pool in the base of his stomach.

'That's not possible.'

'I assure you . . .'

'How much?'

'Two hundred pounds.'

'Have you any proof of this?'

'Oh yes.'

'Perhaps you would be good enough to let me have it.'

'Do you want your son here?'

'Not immediately. Let me hear it from you first, then we'll ask Kerry his side of things. Right?'

The old Patrick had returned on the outside. A brisk smile, the kind he used in his business deals . . . a charm not fulsome, just there. He composed his face to listen.

It was a tale of a charity football match in aid of deprived children. Patrick held his mask face with difficulty. The priest was so unctuous. He spoke of deprived children as if they were another species of life. The rugby match had attracted a lot of attention. People came from all over to attend it. There were three Irish internationals playing on each side. It wasn't often that you saw such talent gathered on one afternoon on the playing fields of an Irish school. The entrance fee had been two shillings.

The boys in the school all attended, of course, people from the neighbourhood and rugby fans from all over Ireland, as well as some people from the newspapers. Father Minehan's voice lowered again, in case someone from the newspaper might be in the room with them. It was all highly unfortunate. Over fourteen hundred people attended the match, many of them being men of property and generosity who gave much more than the two-shilling entrance fee.

Over two hundred pounds had been collected at the small tables placed near the school gate. It was taken into the school in leather bags, each with the amount it contained neatly written on a label attached to it. The money was in Father Bursar's office ready to be checked into a bank account next day. It disappeared. There was a search. The search revealed among other things that some of the senior boys were not in their dormitory; they came in later over the wall. They were met by a reception committee.

Kerry O'Neill had an envelope with fifty-seven pounds of the collection still in his pocket.

'Balls,' snapped Patrick. 'Nobody could spend all that in a night. What did he do? Buy a couple of properties down town?'

'He has not said what he did with it,' Father Minehan said simply.

'But he hasn't said he took it, surely?'

'He cannot say otherwise. He is not a fool.'

Again Patrick felt ice water moving in his stomach.

Kerry had packed. They had told him that morning that he was to have everything ready; he would be leaving with his father. When he came to the dean's study he had his fawn overcoat thrown casually over his shoulders.

Patrick was annoyed by this, and by seeing the boy's luggage outside the door. It was showing they were beaten before they began.

'Can you throw any light on this, Kerry?' He was firm, not accusatory, but wasting no time in pleas or expostulations.

'I'm sorry you had to drive up here, Father.' Kerry was perfectly calm.

'Tell us what you have to tell.' Patrick didn't look at Father Minehan, who stood there in classic thoughtful pose with one arm across his waist, supporting the elbow of the other arm. A hand with long white fingers spread discreetly over his face.

'I'm afraid there's nothing to tell, Father.'

'You deny you took this money.'

'No, I can't deny that, I'm very sorry.'

'You don't mean you took it?'

'Yes, I did.'

There wasn't a sound from the priest.

'In the name of God why did you do that? I could have given you money, I give you a bloody allowance every month, for Christ's sake.'

Kerry stood still; regret was the only emotion Patrick could see on his face. Mild regret. No shame, no sorrow.

'So what did you want it for?'

An inclination of the head towards the priest, that was all.

'Could you leave us alone, Father Minehan?'

'No, Mr O'Neill, this is my study. I do not choose to leave it.'

Patrick made a decision.

'Yes, that's your privilege. Now you asked me to take my son away. I shall do that. Thank you for the part your community has played in his education so far.'

Father Minehan had been prepared for a day of recriminations and explanations, and bringing in bigger guns like the Father Superior. He couldn't believe it was over already.

'Well, I have to say . . .' he began.

'I hope you have to say very little. We will not discuss any fees that might be owing by me to you, since I think we will agree that donations already given would make the pursual of those fees a grotesque impertinence on your part . . .'

'I assure you that . . .'

'I accept all your assurances. If I am owed any balance why not add that to the already significant sum I have given to the college? And I expect full and favourable reports and references on my son's progress and achievements in this school. I have fulfilled to the letter your request to me, once I understood it. I am taking him away with me in the next five minutes. Within the next five days I expect a detailed report which I can give to the principal of the next college he will attend. *And,* Father Minehan, I shall expect the most glowing of verbal references, should any school call you to inquire about Kerry.'

'Well, there will have to be . . .'

'You are quite right, there *will* have to be arrangements made to that effect immediately, otherwise I will create such a stink and a scandal that the smell will remain over these college walls for three generations to come. I will talk of the blackmail in order to get subscriptions, the extortion of further money from the children by making them pay to see rugby matches in your own premises. I will speak to the newspapers about the lax security and discipline that allows children in your care to scale walls and disappear in the evenings.' He lowered his voice suddenly. 'But all this would be very unpleasant, and I am sure quite unnecessary.'

He walked with Kerry from the school to his car. He looked at the creeper on the walls and remembered the day he had driven here to start Kerry off as a pupil.

Kerry sat in silence as they drove.

Patrick waited five minutes for an apology, an explanation.

He looked at his son's arrogant profile: he remembered his dead wife's hopes. He drew into a petrol station. Beyond the pumps where there was some waste ground.

He got out, and with deliberate steps went around to Kerry's side of the car and opened the door. Kerry got out, a look of polite mystification on his face. Patrick hit him.

As Kerry reeled from the blow, Patrick hit him again on the jaw and rained blows into his body. Winded, Kerry made no real effort to defend himself, except to cry out . . .

'You big ape, you bog man . . . you're nothing but a bloody Irish bog man, that's why you wanted to come back to the bogs, you never left them.'

Patrick had stopped punching anyway. He indicated a gents' toilet. 'Be back here in five minutes. We're going home,' he said, and he got into his car, wearily watching Kerry stagger away, bruised and bloodstained, to try and repair the damage to his face and clothes.

CHAPTER EIGHT

They knew that something had happened in the O'Neill family. And whatever it was, Grace was not going to talk about it.

Tommy Leonard thought that it was because Mr O'Neill was being bad-tempered. He had heard stories of him shouting at people about delays and messing and inefficiency. And to Tommy Leonard all fathers were bad-tempered, because his own was a demon altogether.

Jacinta and Liam White thought that it might have something to do with someone being sick. Their father had been called up to the lodge one evening. So maybe it was an illness. Dr White wouldn't tell them; he never talked about his patients. But if it was something simple like measles or mumps he would have said, so it could be a fatal disease.

Maggie Daly had heard that they were going away, people had said that Mr O'Neill was so fed up with not getting the hotel built straight away he was going to pull out and forget the whole thing. Maggie half hoped they would, but in another way she wanted them to stay. She didn't hate Grace; she wanted to be her friend. The best that could possibly happen was that Grace would want the three of them – Dara, Maggie and her – to be friends, to be a proper gang with nobody left out.

Kitty Daly kept asking Maggie why Grace didn't come to play any more, and whether Kerry had come back from boarding school. She was not at all satisfied when her little sister didn't seem to know.

Dara knew that Kerry had come back from school because she had been there the evening that Mr O'Neill had gone to collect him. But the next day she had a telephone call from Grace asking her not to say anything to anyone about anything.

'What do you mean?' Dara was totally confused. 'If someone says hallo, am I not to say hallo back?'

'This is serious,' Grace said.

'I know it is. I'm serious too. Why can't you *tell* me what I'm not to say anything about? Why aren't you here anyway?'

'Is anyone listening to you?'

'No, I mean Dad's in the pub. Mam's at work, Carrie's in the kitchen, Michael's in the yard, Eddie is probably eavesdropping somewhere. What *is* it?'

'There's been a bad row, and I can't come out for a few days. Not till we're back at school, we might even be going away.'

'Where, where are you going?'

'I don't know, *please* Dara, don't tell anyone what I told you.'

'You didn't tell me anything. I don't understand any of this.'

'About my father and Kerry not getting on. You know?'

'Oh that. No, I won't tell anyone. I wouldn't have anyway.'

'And could you try to take the drama out of it all?'

'I didn't know it was a drama . . .'

'I've got to go now.' Grace hung up.

They didn't see Grace until the first day of term, a whole week. She looked very pale.

Jacinta was triumphant. 'I told you it was a disease,' she said proudly. 'It could be TB.'

'Why don't you ask her?' Maggie said.

'You don't ask people who are riddled with TB if they're riddled with it; you pretend everything is normal,' Jacinta replied, the doctor's daughter.

Maggie noticed that Dara wasn't racing up to Grace as usual. Dara was on her own.

Good, Maggie thought. Now she knows how it feels to be left out of things.

But if anyone looked left out of things it was Grace. She was like someone recovering from a bad bout of flu.

Even Sister Laura warmed to the girl.

'Did you get any time to do those Irish lessons I set you?' she asked, in a kinder tone than she usually used when checking on homework.

'Yes, Sister, I have them here.' The girl produced pages of sentences:

'I am going to town. Was he going to the town? We were not going to the town.' All neatly written in the slopy writing and purple ink that the nun objected to, and was annoyed with herself for the unreasonable objection.

'That's very good,' she said, impressed. 'You must have spent a lot of time working.'

'I spent all last week. I sat in my room all day, Sister.' She looked downcast.

'Well, you're an example to them all, I must say. How is your brother getting on at his school, tell me?'

It was a courtesy, a little personal remark to show that Sister Laura cared about Grace and her family. The girl's face flushed a bit.

'He liked it very much, but the place was a bit damp so they decided because he has a weak chest . . . they thought . . . they said it would be better if he went to another school. Which isn't damp. More modern. So he's going there.'

'Very wise, you can't be too careful with chests,' Sister Laura said.

It was an odd thing to move the boy at the beginning of the summer term, very upsetting to child and school to have changes in the middle of the academic year. And surely the place couldn't be all that damp in the summer.

Still it was no business of hers. Sister Laura put her mind to the business of keeping the children's minds on school when everything outside was tempting them out of the classroom and on to the river bank, into the woods and over the springy green fields around Mountfern.

Patrick and Kerry sat at the breakfast table in the lodge. Miss Hayes left the refilled coffee pot on the table and explained that she was about to cycle into Mountfern for the messages. She wished Kerry good luck at his new school and said she hoped it wouldn't be damp like the last place. There was nothing as bad as a chill that settled on the chest. And she was gone.

She knew of course that there had been hell to pay between father and son.

Mr O'Neill had said to her on that evening when he came back with the boy, looking as if he'd been in a fight with a crowd of thugs, that there were a few things the family wanted to discuss in confidence and they would probably go away for some days to do so in privacy. Olive Hayes had given it a little thought and said that it would be much better if *she* were to go away and let them have the house on their own. She had stocked up the larder and gone to a cousin in Galway without either giving or getting any further explanations. She knew that she had done the right thing; Mr O'Neill had gripped her hand firmly when she returned and said that they had been greatly blessed to have found someone like her. He had also added that there would always be a place and role for her when the new hotel was built. *If* it was *ever* built. Life was full of obstacles, he had said with his engaging smile.

And so now she left them alone once more so that the father and son could say goodbye in whatever way they wanted to without having to lower their voices for fear of her overhearing them.

In fact they sat in silence for some minutes after they heard her bicycle creak out through the big iron gates of the Grange.

'I've done a lot of thinking, Kerry.'

Kerry looked at him politely.

'We seem to have discovered that it wasn't for drugs, or for alcohol. It was not for anyone else . . . you do not appear to have made any friends. It was hardly for a woman, and at your age you are unlikely to have done anything for which you could be blackmailed. There was no race meeting where you could have lost it, and you aren't known in the bookies near the school, so it couldn't have been that. If you bought anything with it then that item was not delivered. You will not tell me and I have not been able to find out.'

Kerry said nothing.

'Is that a summary of what has happened?'

'Yes, you left out a bit here and there.' Kerry rubbed his bruised jaw.

'I wish that I hadn't beaten you. I've said that.'

'I don't mind. It makes us quits.'

'It *does* not make us quits. In no way does it make us anything like quits.'

Patrick stood up and walked towards the window.

'It leaves me knowing that I can't control my temper; that's a weak position to be in. I am also left with the knowledge that you stole an enormous sum of money for a purpose which you cannot or will not explain, which leaves me in an even weaker position. How am I to continue in this way of life that I am trying to build for us if I cannot trust you? You may take money from Miss Hayes's purse; you may reach over the counter in Daly's and put your hand in the till. I may have to drive to this new school and hear a similar story.

'All that's happened to you is that you got beaten. Your life goes on exactly the same – new school, clean slate, reputation totally unsullied even to your little sister.'

Kerry remained very still.

'In five minutes Marian is coming to drive you into the town, and you are getting the train to a school I have not seen. The principal has had a lying letter from that death's head Minehan. I've seen a copy of it. He will *not* have gone behind my back, so you start here with nothing on your record. This is your last chance, Kerry, your only chance.'

'Yes, Father.'

'No, I mean it. We've done a cosmetic job on it; we've papered it over. The last school was damp, you had a wheeze in your chest, medical advice ... even Grace more or less believes it now. You've been given a new start. I'd like to embrace you and come with you to the school, and tell this new head priest, whoever he is, that I'm proud of my son and I want him to do well, like I did last time, but I don't have the stomach for it. So Marian is taking you to the train. And we agreed that in front of anyone round here we act as normal, as if we were the best of friends.'

'Sure.'

They heard the wheels of Marian's car.

'And maybe we can be the best of friends again some day.'

'I hope so, Father.'

He looked so handsome and straightforward standing there. Patrick really did believe that it was going to be all right. He had gripped Kerry's hand and put his other hand on the boy's shoulder when Marian came in.

'Yoo hoo! I'm not too early am I? I always think it's best to leave plenty of time, that way nobody's rushing too much.' She glanced eagerly, like a bright fluffy bird, from one to the other. Patrick felt a sense of shame at using her like this. She was an honourable if boring and fussy woman. It was not fair to keep involving her like this when he had no intention of involving her more permanently. Marian would be useless in a crisis. She was perfect for domestic trivia. But she would have no idea what to do in any important area of life. Unlike Rachel Fine.

Patrick had telephoned her immediately after he had got his son cleaned up, seen by the doctor and sedated. After he had reassured Grace with bland words, he had asked Rachel what to do. Rachel said that since he hadn't beaten it out of the boy, he was unlikely to discover it by any further force. She said that if she might draw on a metaphor taken from her own trade, the design and decor business ... he should paper over the cracks. Pretend that everything underneath was as elegant as the surface, and make sure he created a believable surface. He had waited long enough to get back to his roots and realize his dream. Surely he wasn't going to let it all disintegrate into a public dog fight that would entertain the locals and people for miles around. Dignity had to be kept, position maintained. Give Kerry one more chance.

For a week Patrick had worked on her advice; it seemed the natural thing to do. He had almost forgotten how practical Rachel was, and how well she knew the right thing for him.

He wished Rachel were here in Mountfern.

He wished he had encouraged her to come with him.

After the first day of term Grace seemed to be all right again. Not as cheerful as last term but still more like her old self.

'Do you mind if we don't talk about it?' she asked Dara.

'That's all right.' Dara was a bit huffy.

'It would be the same if there was a problem in your family, you wouldn't want to tell an outsider ...'

Dara agreed grudgingly.

Maggie was much more understanding.

'I'm sorry I've been a bit . . . I don't know . . . recently, Maggie. I was just worried about something, do you know the way it is?'

Maggie knew. She said so clearly. Grace was pleased.

Arm in arm with Maggie she went off to the graveyard, and they finished the tomb of James Edward Gray to everyone's satisfaction.

Mr Williams said it was wonderful to see young people be so helpful. Not far away Eddie Ryan gloomily chopped nettles and gathered up sacks of grass and groundsel and dandelions. Grace discovered that Maggie took the same-size shoes and said she must come along to the lodge some evening and see if she wanted any that were there. Maggie never asked Grace what it was she had worried about. From time to time she wondered but still didn't ask.

Dara made a few pronouncements that if you were a true friend you could tell *everything* and any holding back meant that it wasn't friendship at all. But Dara bore her no ill-will, and organized Irish classes for Grace which worked so well that soon Grace O'Neill was getting better marks in class than the rest of them. Maggie's wish had come true, they were a gang, with Jacinta on the fringes of it.

They were all very disappointed when the summer holidays were approaching and Grace announced out of the blue that she was going to go on a trip with her father and brother. It was meant to be a familiarization tour of Ireland, she confided, but really it was a spying mission. They were going to spend a night in lots of different hotels and see what they were doing right or doing wrong. They would get ideas for their own hotel. A friend of Grace's father, who used to work with him back in the States, had suggested this would be a good thing to do. They were off as soon as term ended, just after Kerry came back from his boarding school.

Kerry had liked his new school very well, he said. No, he didn't want to ask anyone back during the holiday; it wasn't a place like that. You got to know everyone a bit, rather than a few people a lot. He was very enthusiastic about the voyage of inspection.

Once more Patrick O'Neill marvelled at the wisdom of Rachel Fine. Even at three thousand miles she seemed to know what was best both for him and his troubled son. He would call her and say that she must come to Ireland this summer. After all, if John Fitzgerald Kennedy, the President of the United States, was coming to Ireland, why shouldn't Rachel Fine do the same?

It wasn't only the O'Neills who went away. Suddenly their whole gang started to disintegrate. The twins looked at each other in dismay.

Tommy Leonard was told that he was a grown man now, thirteen and a half going on fourteen, no less. He could stand in the paper shop this summer and work to build up the business that was going to be his one day. And he would like it. There would be a smile on his face, and none of his scruffy friends trick-acting in and out of the shop.

The Whites were sent to Irish College. Their father said it was pointless half learning a language, and they were both packed off to learn Irish dancing, to a place where they fined you if you were heard to speak in English and the man who ran it, An Fear Mor, was a person of great power and authority.

Maggie Daly had to work in Daly's Dairy, just like Tommy had to be in Leonard's. They both envied Dara and Michael for living in a business that didn't allow them to be behind a counter.

The twins were on their own again. They never actually admitted that they had grown apart in the last year or so. But they knew it. They missed golden-haired Grace with her plans and her excitement; they missed Tommy with his good humour, and the two Whites who argued with each other about everything and had outlandish views on almost every subject. They missed Maggie, who never dreamed anything up, but who always, after a little hanging back, would join in whatever they suggested.

The only problem was getting rid of Eddie.

Eddie wrongly thought that because Dara and Michael were now without their usual group, they would be delighted to have his company. More than once he got ready to go out with them and was bitterly disappointed when he was not allowed to go.

'I'd be better than no one,' he said.

'No you wouldn't,' Dara replied.

'You'd be much worse than no one, actually,' Michael said.

'Why can't I come?'

'Because you're not our generation. You're a different generation to us. We are going to be thirteen in September, teenagers. You are only a very juvenile person.'

'How will I ever grow up, unless I am with older people?'

Eddie was stung by the lack of avenues.

'Listen Eddie, enough is enough; it doesn't matter if you ever grow up, it couldn't matter less. You begin all nice and please this and please that, but by the time we'd have gone twenty paces with you, there'd be some row.'

'No Dara, there wouldn't.'

'Look at the past,' Michael said mildly. 'It's always happened.'

'Now we must be off.' And they were gone. Eddie kicked the stones round the back yard in disappointment.

'I can find you plenty to do if you like,' Kate said. 'And stop kicking. You're taking the top off your new shoes.'

'They're not new,' Eddie said mulishly. 'Nothing is new, they're only Michael's shoes.'

'And we'd like to have them for your brother Declan too, please, so kindly stop kicking with them or you'll have them taken away for the day, and you won't go far in your bare feet.'

John had watched sympathetically. He waited till Kate had gone, and then called Eddie into the bar.

'Come here, I want to show you something.'

'I don't want to do any work,' Eddie said.

'Not at all, why should you, haven't you done the crates?'

'Yes.'

'Well come on then. I'll show you something funny.'

This was better than anything that had been offered so far. Eddie went suspiciously into the bar, his hair standing up in spikes that no amount of combing, brushing or even dampening would ever change. His father had an old, faded chocolate box out on the counter. Eddie scrambled on to a high stool to see.

'Look at this, Eddie, come on, it's funny.'

'What is it? It's only an old picture.'

'It's me years ago.'

'Why are you wearing women's knickers?'

'Those aren't knickers; that was trousers.'

'Go on.'

'Yes, that was the day your Auntie Nuala went to Australia with the nuns, there was a picture taken here outside the door. That's your Aunt Nuala all dressed in black.'

'She's very young-looking to be a nun.'

'Ah she was too; they gave them a school education you see, and then in turn she became a nun and educated children out there.'

'It seems daft to me,' said Eddie, who was not a great scholar.

'There's a bit of daftness in it, certainly,' his father agreed. 'Wouldn't she be better up with Sister Laura in her own home town? Still, what I was going to tell you was this: look at my feet.'

'You've no shoes on.'

'Didn't I kick the front of my shoes out just like you were . . . No, no, not giving out to you. Shoes are your mother's province. I wanted to tell you the whole front came away, and I couldn't go with them all to see her off in the town. That was the last I ever saw of her, that day in 1930. Imagine. And I was so put out that I didn't get the trip to the town, I went for a walk up to Coyne's wood, and in my poor bare feet I spent the whole day building myself a house in a tree. I was covered in scratches and cuts, and when they all came back sobbing and crying from seeing Nuala off, they nearly murdered me, but the house was there. It's still there. I went past it the other day.'

'It couldn't be.'

'It is, bits of it, thirty-three years in the wood where it's very hard to find. Anyone could have a house that's easy to find. I thought having a secret one was better.'

'You never told anyone?'

'No, not until now.'

Eddie believed his father absolutely, but he was suspicious.

'So why are you telling me?'

'I've been having all kinds of old rheumaticky aches; I don't think I'll climb into it again. I thought you might go and keep an eye on it for me.'

'How would I find it?'

'Good question. When you go into Coyne's wood from this side, you go up the path; you know, the one that has all the rowan trees.'

'The red ones, is it?'

'Yes, the mountain ash trees. Anyway where they end you go in to the right, you'll have to bend down a bit and then it's in there. You'll find it. Maybe you could even build it up a bit.'

Eddie was looking enthusiastic at last. 'It'd be better than having a place of my own,' he said eventually.

'Much better.'

'You won't tell Dara and Michael, and have them spoiling it? They'd come and take it over and turn me out of it.'

'Not at all. Not a word.'

'Right.' Eddie gave a last look at the box of photographs. 'Were we desperately poor in those days that they couldn't get you a new pair of shoes?'

'We'd be hard pushed to get *you* a new pair of shoes these days, so will you wear your old wellies when you go up to Coyne's wood?' his father said. 'And for the love of God will you make sure you've done your jobs before you go.'

They all had jobs to do each day before they were free to play. Michael had to polish the brasses and shine up the counter in the pub. The ashtrays would have been emptied, and the glasses washed the night before, but he had to air the place and see that there were no grease stains or dust where the customers would sit.

Dara had to feed the hens, now moved to the back yard as their coop had become very smelly and messy in the side garden, and completely spoiled the classy look of the place.

The hens clucked enthusiastically over household scraps mixed with bran. She also collected the eggs they laid in their nesting boxes; she gave Jaffa her breakfast; took Leopold for a run up as far as the Rosemarie hair salon and back; and inspected the whereabouts of Maurice the tortoise, in case he had got stuck under a stone, or in case Eddie and Declan had broken their vow and started to play with him again.

Of all these jobs, Dara hated most being seen out with Leopold. Whenever another human being approached, Leopold would cower and shiver and whine piteously, rolling his eyes as if expecting a further beating. Never had a dog been lavished with such love, never did a dog give the impression of being whipped by his masters to within an inch of his life every evening.

Rita Walsh in the Rosemarie hair salon, who sometimes had an overnight guest leaving in the morning, didn't like the regular appearance of the Ryan girl with that awful dog racing up to her doorstep and turning round again every morning.

'Why don't you take him down towards the bridge?'

'I'm too ashamed to be seen with him, Mrs Walsh,' Dara said truthfully. 'Up this way I don't ever meet anyone except you, or maybe Mr Coyne, so I don't have to explain him.'

The child probably never noticed anyone leaving at an early hour. That was a relief.

Eddie and Declan had to stack boxes neatly for the distributors and collectors who picked them up when they brought new supplies. All four young Ryans had to bring in vegetables from the back field: potatoes which had to be washed at the yard sink, cabbages or cauliflowers, carrots or turnips. Then they were free for the day, lunch sharp at one.

Patrick wanted a history of Fernscourt written, and who better to ask, he had said, than the local scribe literally on the very doorstep. Of course there were people in Dublin who would do it, and do a professional job on it. Later indeed some aspects of their expertise might be used in editing and layout and even some of their hints in how to express parts of it. But there could be nobody who would do the job with such local knowledge and in such personal terms as John Ryan.

'You're never going to do it for him?' Kate was astounded.

'Why on earth not? It's a job, a writing job, there'll be something at the end of it, not just a few pages of a child's copybook scribbled on. That's what *you've* always looked for, something to show for it.'

'But not this. Not glorifying him and what he's doing.'

'It's not glorifying, and he's doing it whether I write the history of Fernscourt or some PhD up in Dublin writes it. It's a professional job, there's a fee, whoever does it.'

'I don't know.' Kate was troubled.

'Well I do. My only problem is, will I do it right? Maybe he has too much faith in me; I could have sold myself too well.'

Kate changed immediately.

'I don't know what you're talking about. Won't you do it as well as anyone? Better, because you're from these parts. You're the obvious one to do it.'

John smiled quietly. The battle had been won. First it meant he had to do a lot of reading and research. His head was ever now in books about Georgian houses, antiquarian journals and the records of archaeological and historical societies. He became a familiar figure in the library in the big town where he went once a week, and they bent the rules in order to let him take some of the reference books back to his pub. It was different when a man was writing a book. He wasn't an ordinary borrower.

He discovered that Fernscourt was only one of many houses built at the time and all over the country. That year 1780 seemed to have been a great year altogether. He told that to Brian Doyle one day, and Brian said that it was always a feast or a famine in the building trade. You either sat on your backside for three years eating crusts or you had them screaming at you to dig the foundations for almighty jobs in three counties. It was interesting to know that the lads in 1780 had the same kind of aggravation.

Of course it was the time when Grattan's Parliament was sitting; it was the eighteen years when there was an Irish Parliament in College Green in Dublin, before it was snuffed out and the Act of Union was passed. Those parliamentarians needed big houses all over the place. But the Ferns didn't sit in Parliament, they were farmers with estates in the north of England. They had bought the land here in the 1770s for one of their sons. The house itself had been built in the same style as many others.

John Ryan was affronted to read in one journal that Fernscourt was considered a minor and rather inferior example of the art. He had shown it to Kate in disbelief.

'The wise man would forget that piece of information,' Kate advised. 'Patrick O'Neill is not paying for any reference to minor and inferior houses: you should pretend you didn't uncover that particular bit of lore.'

'I'm meant to be doing serious research.' John's face was very red.

'Of course, and you are, but that's only one person's opinion. You don't have to give some crackpot's view, do you? I mean if I met someone up in Bridge Street who said that you were no good to man or beast would I believe them?'

'What?'

'Of course I wouldn't any more than you have to believe that fellow. Just get on to the facts, the things that can't be challenged, how many windows there were, what kind of people worked on it. Oh, Fergus said to tell you that he'll help you get documents from the land registry if you want; he says that once you translate legal documents into English instead of fusty old law you get great information out of them. I don't agree with him myself, typing them as I do all day. But Fergus would understand anything you put in front of him. He could make sense of the Dead Sea Scrolls at a glance.'

'He's got a very quick mind, Fergus,' said John admiringly. 'You must find it a great change working with him.' He smiled quietly.

Kate thought for a moment.

'Yes, he is great to work for. He's a real schoolboy though, a tall thin overgrown schoolboy, he's not a fellow you'd fall in love with like you are.'

'Okay, that's all right, then,' John Ryan said in mock relief.

It was a great relief to get rid of Eddie. The twins knew they were harsh to him, but Eddie wasn't like other people, He didn't understand hints. You had to be fairly brutal. They didn't have any money for ice creams, so there was no point in going to Daly's. It would only embarrass Maggie, and make Mrs Daly cast her eyes up to heaven and mouth silent prayers. Mrs Daly's mouth was moving the whole time. Maggie said she got through dozens of memorares that she was saying for special intentions, while she was serving in the shop.

The twins knew that they mustn't be seen in Leonard's unless they were doing a brisk message like buying the paper or getting a writing pad. Grown-ups were allowed to leaf through the magazines, but there was no similar facility for children with the comics. And Tommy would hate them there.

There weren't many people on the bridge. Those who were there had organized a jumping competition. Usually you jumped from the big rock at the side. But today they were raising it and making it higher in stages. First by an old box, then by a stone on top of the box. Then by a plank on top of the stone. Dara and Michael watched for a bit. It was mainly boys that were jumping, shivering in their underpants. But there were a few girls too. Teresa Meagher in a black bathing costume much admired by all, and laughing over-excitedly as she jumped with the best.

The twins tired of it after a while. They walked across the bridge away from the town and back down the river bank on the other side. This was the road which would soon change. Instead of being a path with reeds on one side and a hedge on the other, it would be a road to the huge hotel. They didn't talk about things like that, it had been long accepted. The hedge was full of fuchsia growing wild as anything. Mam had told them that in city places this was a very rare flower, and people paid big sums of money to buy little bushes of it to put in their gardens; sometimes it didn't even grow properly. Dara stopped beside a huge tree of it.

'Isn't it like something in the South Sea Island picture book?' she said.

'Here, I'll climb it and be like a native,' Michael said, leaving their picnic bag on the path.

As he went to the back of the tree to find a good starting-off place, he gave a great shout . . .

'Dara, look, careful, careful mind you don't fall.'

In front of them, totally hidden by the trees and bushes, was an opening. A cave, or better still, a tunnel. They couldn't believe it. They had found their new home at last. They hardly dared go in beyond the entrance in case it was already somebody else's home. Those colourful tinkers who came by once a year and annoyed everyone old, by stealing chickens and leaving all their mess and rubbish behind them. They might be in there. Mad Marty who disappeared for months on end and then turned up again, wilder than ever. It could be his home. It was too good a place to be nobody's.

'Halloo . . .' they called as they went round the corner. It was pitch dark.

They paused and shouted again.

'Do you mind if we come in?' Dara called.

'Just for a moment,' Michael added.

There was no reply. Surely if anyone was there they would have said *something*.

The twins looked at each other in delight and pealed with laughter at their over-caution and politeness.

'There's nobody here at all,' Dara said.

Michael ran to Mrs Quinn's for candles; he was back in no time and they went in together. They each held two of the half-dozen candles that Loretto Quinn had parted with so willingly, as well as a box of matches. It wasn't like a cave or a tunnel in books or comics. There were no dripping rocks, just earth and stone, and it was quite high. Even grown-ups could have walked without bending.

The twins stepped forward, each with a tight feeling of anxiety about what might be ahead.

'It doesn't smell like coffins or anything,' Michael said.

'We don't know what coffins smell like.'

'No,' Michael agreed. 'But it doesn't smell frightening.'

Dara wanted to show she hadn't been superior. 'It doesn't look as if it's going to fall and block our way back, either,' she said, more to reassure herself than her brother.

'No indeed, it's very sound.'

'And it might be coming out somewhere soon?' Dara's voice was thin.

'Bound to, we must be up at the house now.'

And then, round the next turn, they saw the urns and the long shallow steps at the back of Fernscourt. They saw them through the branches of thorns and brambles. Beyond those were huge big beds of nettles. That's why they had never seen the opening. Who would want to wade through feet of nettles, big high stinging ones, when there were so many other things to explore?

They realized it couldn't belong to them if they told anybody. So they told nobody at all.

But they thought about it all the time, and they brought back their belongings, slowly and little by little, so as not to create any suspicion. The old orange box, the tableware, the so-called curtains and rugs, the broken cutlery. Once more it was home. This time by candlelight. When they were older and could do what they liked they would ask Brian Doyle, if he wasn't dead, if they could make a skylight in the tunnel, because sometimes it was a bit hot and dark, and they would have liked the sunlight.

The roof looked sound enough. Surely Brian Doyle and his workers would be able to put in a window for them. There was a scaffolding: a very rough and ready kind of arrangement of wooden poles and boards keeping the ceiling up. It looked very firm and steady. The twins tested it gingerly, and then more firmly. It was rock solid. They wondered who had built it and why it was there. But they were afraid to ask anyone about it now in case it might all be taken away.

At home they tried to find out what an underground tunnel might be doing in these parts.

'Would there have been other ways in to big houses in the old days?' Michael asked one suppertime. Dara frowned. It was too obvious.

Their mother had noticed nothing out of the ordinary.

'Like back doors, do you mean?' she asked absently. 'Carrie, don't leave the saucepan on the table, there's a good girl. It just means it harder for you washing the cloth.' Mammy was very good at giving out to Carrie; it didn't seem like giving out at all.

'I don't know. I suppose there were, and in those kinds of places people probably didn't bring in a ton and a half of mud with them. Eddie, do you have to bring half of Coyne's wood home with you every day?'

Mam obviously didn't have any idea of a tunnel. But then she hadn't been brought up here. Maybe Dad knew. Dad had been here for ever.

But they'd have to be even more careful approaching him.

'You're very interested in old houses, aren't you, Dad?' Dara had a prissy kind of face on, not her normal look at all.

'Well, I suppose I am a bit,' John Ryan agreed.

'Would you remember what Fernscourt looked like before it was burned down?'

'No, child, I wouldn't. I was only two when it was burned. Tommy Leonard's father would remember, and Maggie Daly's dad, but don't go asking them too much about it. They were there at the burning of it. In those days it seemed the right way to go. My own father stood looking at the flames from our front doorstep. He said to me often. But there's pictures of it of course, you'd be able to see what it was like in those.'

'Yes well, but . . .' Dara didn't want to be sidetracked by old pictures and the possibility of a history lesson.

'Would they have had secret rooms in it do you think? You wouldn't be able to see those in photographs.'

'I don't *think* so. Why, did you think they might?'

Michael came in hastily. 'We were just wondering, you know, taking an interest in everything round us, like you're always saying to do.'

'Oh that's great,' John said approvingly. 'Yes, I love to see you doing that.'

'So we take an interest in all kinds of things you see,' Dara added. 'Like, would they have had tunnels out of a house like Fernscourt, you know, underground tunnels?'

'All tunnels are underground,' Michael said quickly, not to put her down, but to warn her not to be too explicit.

If John saw the way the wind was blowing he gave no sign.

'I never heard of any underground tunnels around here,' he said absently, brushing the earth and dust off the thin shoulders of his son. 'But as I say, the place was well gone by the time I was old enough to play in it, so there could have been. I'm sure it would be quite possible to find one if you looked hard enough.'

He caught the look of alarm, and went on, 'But it would be so well covered over, that sort of thing, that I don't think anyone would ever find the entrance.'

There was a hint of relief in their faces.

'What would they have been for, if there were tunnels? That is from houses like Fernscourt, say?'

'Do you mean, say, possibly going from the house to the river? That is if there was a river?'

They nodded eagerly.

John Ryan paused; they waited for an explanation. He seemed to know the kind of thing they were talking about, but then his face became puzzled again.

'It's very hard to say, it would have been exciting, whatever the reason was. Of course if you found one of those things you'd have to be very careful. I mean a person would have to take great care that the roof wouldn't fall in, or that it wasn't all crumbling before they went and explored it.'

'Oh there's no danger, it's quite safe,' said Michael. 'I mean I'd say they'd be quite safe.'

'No parts where it's supported with props or anything?'

The twins looked at each other. *How* could he know?

'Like scaffolding,' their father said helpfully.

'Well . . .'

'Um . . .'

'That'd be the bit to stay well away from if you ever found one,' John Ryan said firmly. 'It's like in old mines, those would be the parts where it would all cave in.'

'I suppose you could test it by pushing and pulling at bits near the entrance if you ever found one,' he went on.

They went away in case they let anything slip.

'He said it would have to be an exciting reason for it,' Michael said.

'We knew that,' Dara said. 'But what could it have been?'

It provided hours of happy speculation for them.

Dara decided it was built by a young Miss Fern to meet her lover in a boat.

Michael decided it was built by a cousin of the Ferns who had an intent of storming Fernscourt one night and claiming it as his own. But they told no one. Without actual lies they managed to suggest they spent the time hanging around the bridge in the town. Kate was glad to think that they were making other friends.

'Am I beautiful, Carrie?' Dara asked. She was sitting on Carrie's bed, watching the preparations for the day off.

'I don't know.' Carrie giggled at the question, but mainly concentrated on her own appearance in the speckled mirror over the dressing table. The table was covered with powder and hairpins and nearly finished pots of make-up that had been castoffs of other people.

'I think I might be beautiful, if only I had curly hair,' Dara persisted.

'You might be.' Carrie was doubtful. 'Isn't it sickening that we don't have curly hair. Your Mam has a rake of it and she doesn't need it at all.'

'Why doesn't she need it?'

'Well she's old and she's got her fellow. It's the likes of yourself and myself that need curls.' Carrie looked at her reflection without pleasure.

'Why do you want to get all dressed up just for going home?' Dara asked with interest.

Carrie looked at her suspiciously. 'Well, why do *you* want to be beautiful?' she countered.

'I want to be beautiful so that Kerry O'Neill will admire me,' Dara said simply.

Carrie looked at her and softened. 'You're grand as you are,' she said. 'And listen, I'll tell you a secret; I'm not going home to my people at all today, I'm going on an outing, with a fellow. With Jimbo Doyle.'

'Not Jimbo Doyle,' Dara screeched.

'Why not? He's very nice, Jimbo is, and he said he'd take me for a walk up to Coyne's wood on my day off.' Carrie looked annoyed now, and a little uncertain.

Dara bit her lip. She had offended Carrie greatly, she must make it up somehow.

'I know he's nice, and he's a great singer. I heard him singing "The Yellow Rose of Texas" when he was building the rockery. You could ask him to sing to you up in Coyne's wood.'

'Yes, I suppose I could.' Carrie was doubtful. She felt that Jimbo Doyle hadn't planned on an afternoon of singing among the quiet trees and on the springy moss of Coyne's wood.

They held their resolve, to tell no one about the tunnel. No one at all.

'Not even Grace?' Michael said.

Dara paused. She thought about it.

'Not even Grace,' she said.

'If we told Grace, we'd have to tell Maggie and Tommy and everyone else,' Michael said.

'Yes.' Dara frowned. 'And that would change it. Do you think we're being a bit childish about all this?'

'Not at all,' Michael reassured her. 'I think we're doing the right thing.'

They grinned at each other. The twins were back where they had always been. Best friends against the world.

There was a postcard from Grace from Donegal where the waves were huge and they had been swimming. They were having a great time, she said, and whenever she thought they were coming back to Mountfern, father thought of somewhere else to visit. But they would be home soon, she missed everybody and longed to see them again. She sent cards to Tommy and Maggie too, and sent her love to Jacinta and Liam, but didn't dare to write to them in case they would be punished for having communications in English rather than Irish.

Ryan's pub filled up with all the men who were working on the site. Every lunchtime there was a good crowd round the bar. Kate found herself rushing back from Slattery's office and straight in behind the bar. Sometimes she looked at John with a smile of triumph. At least some of their fears about the new hotel were proving groundless. There was a bit of business coming their way. For the moment anyway.

Judy Byrne ran into Marian Johnson in Meagher's jewellers. Mrs Meagher had to send out the repairs and she was most apologetic that the clock wasn't ready.

'I did want it for the lodge by the time they came back,' Marian was saying.

'Oh, when will that be?' Judy Byrne had come in to buy a brooch for her niece's birthday. She was looking without much pleasure at Mrs Meagher's selection.

'Hard to say. Any day now, I imagine,' Marian said airily.

'He doesn't keep in touch, then?'

Marian was furious.

'Heavens, Judy, it's their house to come and go as they please. I'm not a boarding house landlady type, you know, Judy. They've just rented our gate lodge, that's all.'

'So he doesn't write. Well, I expect we'll know they're back when we see them.' Judy thanked Mrs Meagher for letting her see the brooches, and said she would think about them and come back later.

Sheila Whelan knew exactly where the O'Neills were, and when they would be back. She had telegrams from America and messages that didn't go through to Brian Doyle the builder. Patrick rang her every second day.

Brian Doyle had the demolition men ready; he was surprised that O'Neill said they could go ahead and make the arrangements to take down the walls without him. He thought the man would have been on the crane that swung the great ball himself.

Brian Doyle didn't know that Patrick O'Neill and Rachel Fine had discussed this lengthily on the phone. They agreed that it would be wiser for him to stay away from the tearing down. Be there for the building up, not the pulling down.

CHAPTER NINE

Patrick O'Neill had discovered that few Irish hoteliers stayed open in the winter time. Very few of them. They said that nobody would come to Ireland in the bad weather, and it cost a fortune heating a place up and paying staff all through the lean months when there would be no business.

Patrick thought that this was short-sighted. Nobody ever came to Ireland for the weather anyway. When you thought of sunshine, you didn't immediately think of Ireland. It was the people who brought visitors to Ireland, the people and the scenery and the activities. Those things were there in the winter too, and cheaper to get to.

Charter flights in winter from the United States would be very reasonably priced. But there was no point in telling that to these hoteliers. They saw their season as beginning in May and ending in September. Some of the more adventurous opened as early as the Easter weekend.

Patrick O'Neill sighed at the waste of it all. But then he sighed a lot these days. It had been much harder than he would have believed possible to get this far in his attempts to rebuild Fernscourt. It had been a year since he had bought the place. Twelve months of delays and impediments, and only now was he able to get the ruins knocked down so that the building proper could begin.

It was the biggest test of Patrick O'Neill's character that he had ever known. A vein began to jut out on his forehead with anger and frustration. He found himself standing up, sitting down, taking long deep breaths in the middle of ruinously expensive transatlantic phone calls.

Twice he decided to abandon it, but slept on the decision, and the following morning decided that he would go ahead. Three times he was on the point of firing Brian Doyle and shouting that any builder in the goddamn Western world would be on his knees for a lifetime, begging for such a job. Three times he restrained himself. He did bawl out an architect, a mild man who said that it was always the same with Americans. They came over here like God Almighty and expected the people to change their ways for them. Patrick didn't see himself in that role; he liked to think of the O'Neills as the sons of the soil coming back, not the overlords giving orders. He apologized to the architect, who told him not to think of it again. Everyone knew that the pressure in New York drove most people mad most of the time.

He had been back to America twice. At the end of that time not one stone had been laid on another. But he kept his smile.

And he convinced the conservationists that he wasn't destroying anything valuable. That had been a stroke of luck, sighing over it in Ryan's pub one day, and then John Ryan discovering a quote from some archaeological journal to back up his claim that the house was of minor importance architecturally.

He found himself telling genial lies in two continents. Standing on the bridge with Fergus Slattery: Was he disappointed at the length of time things took? No, no, this was the pace, this was the way it had to be done. He would not have the town

137

typecast him as a rushing, bustling Yank. And then back in the other home, in his New York headquarters talking to Gerry Power: Sure, sure, things didn't get done at the same speed. They hadn't the technology; no of course he didn't have second thoughts. No, he wasn't mad with them.

And to Rachel Fine, sipping a brandy in her red-gold apartment, which always looked so soft and restful compared with the rest of New York, he told more truth than to anyone. He told her that at times he thought he would blow up into a million pieces with frustration over it all. He could see now why his countrymen back home had achieved nothing, *nothing*. No wonder their economy was so pathetic, so shabby. He knew now why they stood toothless and laughing with their hats on back to front, because they had never bloody learned to work. They knew nothing of the actual ache that work brings, and they didn't want to know it. No goal was high enough to force them to do more than the very minimum. He could rail like this to Rachel because he knew she would never agree with him. She would smooth his forehead and tell him that Irish people rose in every walk of life . . . they had their own country . . . well almost . . . Look at her people, the Latvians . . . they had let the Soviets take over and Latvia would never rise again. All the Latvian Jews who could escape had come to America, but there would be no going back and building castles there nowadays.

Rachel would encourage him softly, remind him of all he had achieved so far, tell him that no other grandson of a cottage-dweller had gone back to buy the big house and make it into a great business that would employ his own far and wide. He liked to hear that, it gave some reason to all the work and the endless delays and complications. One evening he asked Rachel why she encouraged him. She had been against it at the start, and wanted him to make his life in New York.

'Only a very foolish woman wouldn't encourage a dream. What would you be if your dream were to be taken away, or people talked you out of it? You would lose your fire and enthusiasm. You would only be a shell.'

He held her closely to him. She was a wonderful woman. What a shame, what a bloody great shame that she was who she was, a divorced Jewess. Even if everyone else would let him, he could never marry her. It just wasn't possible.

But the day came, and the machinery moved in, huge cranes and a great ball that swung backwards and forwards, and the stone walls of Fernscourt came down. Rachel Fine had advised at long distance that the stones should be kept to form any walls or rockeries. There must be a place to store them and surely big stones dating from the days when America was still a fledgling must be attractive and beautiful in themselves. Brian Doyle had said it was a cracked idea, but then he had been hoping to use the stones himself in other building work if they had been thrown out, so he secretly admired the cop-on of the Yank with the big notions and the belief that everything could be done in five minutes.

Grace linked Kerry happily as they walked in the Irish countryside. This was the first real holiday they had taken together. She chattered on about the convent in Mountfern and told him tales of the girls and the tricks they played on the nuns. She begged him for stories of his school. Did he like being away at boarding school?

Was he lonely? Was he glad it was holidays now? Grace wanted Kerry to be glad about everything. Like she was.

'It's a shame we can't be there,' Grace said for the tenth time, as the O'Neills walked along a cliff path in Donegal. 'I'd love to see it.'

'Yes.' Patrick was absent-minded. He looked out at the ocean. Had his father seen these hills when he was leaving Ireland, or were they too far north? He could never discover whether it had been from Galway or way down in Cork from the harbour at Cobh that those earlier O'Neills had taken a ship for the United States. None of the family knew or ever wanted to find out. John Ryan said it might have been Galway. It would have been a likelier place to have started from rather than all the way down in Cobh. Ships used to go from Galway all the time in those long-ago days.

'It wouldn't take us all that long to go back. Why didn't we leave last night?' Grace was insistent.

'Oh, I don't know, Gracie. We'll see it in a few days when we get back there. Aren't you having a good time?'

'Oh yes, but . . .' It was such a big thing, why were they missing it? She wished he would explain.

'Father doesn't want us to be there for the demolition, it would be better not to associate ourselves with destroying . . . with knocking down what's there.' Kerry spoke without blame or praise, just as if he were giving directions from a map.

Patrick looked at him sharply. 'Hey, what makes you say that?' He half laughed.

'Well it's true, isn't it? That's the way I'd feel.'

'Yes, it *is* true in a way.' Patrick was very surprised.

'We're the good guys, the ones who ride into town when all the shooting's over. Right?'

'Right in a sort of a way.'

'I think it's ridiculous,' Grace argued. 'Everyone's delighted we're building a new hotel; they love us for being there. Why all this running away and hiding for the best bit, the big machine going boom boom? I'd *love* to see that.'

'So would I,' Patrick said simply.

He was going to call Brian Doyle and find out how it all went. He wished that Brian had the gift of explaining things in style, with some description, a little colour. Doyle would be likely to tell him about the overtime, the breakages, the need to revise this figure and that, and leave out completely any of the symbolism about the old order changing.

'I wonder what they're doing at this very moment?' he said as he led his son and daughter down a sandy path on to a magnificent beach and they ran along beside the waves like any ordinary family.

Not like a man who watched his son nervously, wondering what could have made the boy step so out of character and remain so adamant about not discussing it again. Not like a man who had arranged the demolition of a huge house and planned to build his own monument on the spot where his father and grandfather had been turned out on to the roads.

Half the town came by and watched the demolition machinery getting into action.

The best view was from Ryan's pub on River Road and many of them watched with a glass in their hands.

Jack Coyne stood with a look of false cheer. He cursed that day long back when he had short-changed Patrick O'Neill. The man had always been perfectly courteous to him since, but not one bit of business had he thrown his way. Jack Coyne's small pointed face glanced from one to another. Everyone else had benefited from the Yank. Look at the trade that John Ryan had, and it was the same in the town, there wasn't a business that hadn't been promised or already received some profit. Why on that day of all bloody days in the world had he taken the quiet American for a fool who didn't understand the rate he would get for a dollar? Why had he not seen that those blue eyes were the sharp eyes of a businessman?

Jack Coyne stood, hands in pockets, looking across the river at all the machinery which could all have been hired through him. Coyne's could have got the demolition people in and taken a legitimate ten per cent. He shook his head and told himself that in this life you never knew. You never bloody knew.

'Big day this,' Jack Leonard said to no one in particular.

'Nearly as big as the day we burned it down,' said Tom Daly, and there was an uneasy laugh. Nobody talked much about those times now, the days and nights when big houses all over the country were burned as a symbol of all they represented.

It was forty-one years since Tom Daly, Jack Leonard and a dozen more had joined hastily organized groups from the big town to go out on their mission. Old Mr Leonard and old Mr Daly were so respectable now, such pillars of Mountfern with their dairy and their newsagent businesses, it was quite impossible to imagine them as twenty-year-old firebrands. It was a different time, a different culture. Neither Tom Daly nor Jack Leonard had a good word to say for those young fellows who had been going up north on the border campaign blowing up electrical installations, taking pot shots at sentry posts and considering themselves national heroes. No, the 1920s had been a proper war.

John and Kate pulled pints, filled small glasses of whiskey, and even dragged a few chairs out into the sunshine. Leopold stood shivering with terror at the noise across the river and recoiled from every attempt to stroke or reassure him.

'You're such a kind woman, Kate, why don't you have that animal put to sleep?' Fergus asked as Leopold turned two anguished eyes on him and bayed to the skies.

'That animal is healthier than most people here, and much better looked after,' snapped Kate. 'I can't bear people who make superficial judgements about things they know nothing about.'

'Don't bite the nose off the man,' John laughed. 'Leopold's a great actor, Fergus, he plays to the gallery. He goes and lies outside Reidy's the butchers every day after he's had a good meal here and they give him a bone, every single day. And he howls at Loretto Quinn until she gives him half a pound of biscuits. Wherever the unfortunate cat sits he goes and wails at it, until Jaffa has to get up and let him sit there.'

'He's just making up for having had a desperate childhood,' Dara said. She was nearly thirteen now, tall and strong. Her thick dark hair went in slightly underneath as a result of heavy hair-grip work at night. She would have loved a perm in the Rosemarie salon, and Mrs Walsh said she would do a light natural perm, but Dara's mother wouldn't hear of it. A perm at twelve? Who would permit such extravagance? It was all very well for her mother, who had curly hair anyway, to speak like that. Dara was full of resentment. To make matters worse Michael, who didn't need curls, had a great sort of wavy bit in his hair. *And* he had longer eyelashes. Much. It was so unfair, like almost everything.

'Tell me about Leopold's childhood.' Fergus liked the leggy girl who was so like her mother in looks, and in that independent streak.

'He was found in one of Jack Coyne's trucks.'

'That's a poor start,' agreed Fergus.

'And someone had squeezed his throat, and hurt his hind leg,' Michael finished for her.

Fergus often thought they could make a good double act on stage.

'And for ages after we got his poor back leg mended, he used to hold it out to people to shake hands with them,' Dara said.

'Oh all right, you've convinced me, he had a rotten childhood, puppydom wasn't the best time of his life. Let him live, let him grow older and madder like the rest of us.'

The twins giggled.

'I thought you two would be very upset to see it all come down.' He indicated across the river.

'No, one time maybe . . .' Michael said.

'But not now, not now . . .'

'Not now that we're more grown up . . .'

'And have our own life. It used to be a bit of pretend life there, you see.'

'Oh well, it's different now that you've grown up, I see what you mean.' He could have been laughing at them, but they didn't think so. 'And have you found somewhere else to live when you grow old, really old like me? Now that you won't be living across there?'

'We have our plans . . .' said Dara.

'Nothing definite of course . . .'

'That could be spelled out . . .'

Fergus hastened to agree. 'No, no, much better not. Spell out as little as possible, I always say.'

'There is one thing, Mr Slattery . . .' Dara said.

'Yes . . .'

'It's sort of advice we might need . . .'

Michael flashed her a warning look.

'No, it's all right, I'm only going to speak sort of generally.'

'Best way to start,' Fergus agreed encouragingly.

'Yes, well, it's like this. Does every bit of land have to be owned by someone?'

'I beg your pardon?' They had never taught him how to answer questions like this when he was up in Dublin at the Incorporated Law Society.

'I mean, is the whole of Ireland all divided up and parcelled up? You own your house, we own this place, Mr O'Neill owns Fernscourt now. Are there bits nobody owns?'

'That's a bit difficult to answer in general terms. There *are* bits, I suppose, that nobody really owns, like say the Curragh. You know, in Kildare. If you have land near it you can graze your sheep there, and it's the same with some bogs. A lot of people can cut turf there without actually owning it. Is that what you mean?'

'Not quite. You know, would all fields and ditches and boreens be owned by some one person? You couldn't say suddenly, I own this ditch because I found it.'

Fergus scratched his head.

'But you couldn't really *find* a ditch, could you? It would be there all the time. You couldn't look at it one day and claim it?'

'But suppose you couldn't see it?' Dara persisted.

Michael didn't want her to say any more.

'God, Dara, you have me foxed,' Fergus said. 'But as your mother will tell you, I'm no good at all as a solicitor. I ask stupid questions like how in the name of the Lord could you try to own something you can't see? I only irritate clients, I'll be struck off the rolls any day and be left wandering round with straws in my hair.'

Dara looked alarmed. 'No, please, it's our fault. You see, it's that we have to ask these questions so that you won't actually know what we're talking about . . . No, shut up, Michael. It's all *right*. Mr Slattery's not going to tell anyone, he's like Canon Moran.'

'The image of him,' Fergus said ruefully.

'No, you can't tell people's business, like he can't tell their sins,' Dara insisted.

'That's a fact. They'd strike me off the rolls.'

'Would they hit you?' Michael asked interested.

'I think it might mean rolls, like the rolls at school. You know, for roll call,' Dara said helpfully. 'But anyway, it won't happen, because you won't tell anybody what we've been discussing.'

'I most certainly will not,' he said solemnly, not that he had any idea of what they *had* been discussing.

'Wouldn't you think Patrick would have been here to see his day of triumph?' John Ryan said as a great cheer went up when the last bit of wall fell down.

Kate neatly scooped the froth off the top of five pints of stout with a wooden spatula.

'He knows all about it, you can be sure. He'll be on the phone to Brian Doyle in ten minutes' time.'

'I was sure he'd have been here. He hates that house and all it stood for. He doesn't want me to say a good word about the Ferns, he hates the bit about them being fairly decent in the Famine. He would be delighted to see the stones going down.'

'No, Patrick O'Neill is more interested in what's going up there instead,' Kate said, putting the pints on a tray and coming round the counter to take them outside. 'He's forward-looking like all the Americans.'

'Would we have been better if we had gone to America, do you think?' John asked, half seriously.

'I don't know, maybe now isn't the time to debate it.' Kate laughed good-naturedly as she swept out with the tray of pints to the people outside.

Rita Walsh wondered if the arrival of the hotel might mean that there would be a proper living out of hairdressing after all. It would make a nice change. She had heard a great deal about the plans for Fernscourt from Marian Johnson who now had her hair done regularly and had even sought advice about skin creams and manicures. Rita thought it unlikely that a man like Patrick O'Neill would think seriously about Marian Johnson, whose dry scalp and flyaway hair were getting so much attention these days. Yet it was hard to know. A man like that might be keen to ally himself with old money, and the quality. The Johnsons knew everyone in the hunting set.

Rita surveyed her little salon without much pleasure. American women or rich Dublin women might not find it to their liking, but it would be madness to spend good money on new equipment. Rita had a fair bit saved for the days when she would no longer be able to stand on her feet and give perms. And indeed earn money from a position that didn't at all involve standing on her feet. Both of these sources would end eventually. She kept all her savings in Sheila Whelan's discreet post office. There was no bank in Mountfern and Sheila often acted as an unofficial adviser on people's finances.

Rita decided to be swayed by the advice of the postmistress. Sheila was not one to inquire why the earnings were large sometimes, and irregular. She would answer only the questions that were asked, never raising any others.

Sheila Whelan said that her advice would be to hold on a while until the building of the hotel got under way, then when it really did look as if Fernscourt were rising from the ground and about to bring new life into the town, that was the time to buy new hairdressing equipment. And chairs and anything else that would make the Rosemarie hair salon attractive to visitors. There was no sense of irony in any of this, no hint of what might be the present attractions of the establishment. Just wait until the hotel got under way, then everyone could make their plans.

In Rachel Fine's New York apartment the small travelling clock on the table beside her bed said that it was six-thirty in the morning. In Mountfern it would be lunchtime and the ruins might well be down by now. Rachel had not slept well. All night she had dreamed that there had been some terrible incident at this demolition ceremony.

That a body had risen from the ruins calling out, 'I am the spirit who will not be mocked . . . you shall not build here in peace.'

She had got up twice in the night and sat beside the window, looking out on the moonlit city to reassure herself that everything was normal. She wished this part was all over. Perhaps when this part was finished, then things might go well. He might send for her and she would come to Ireland and make herself part of the place, so that he would never send her away.

Patrick found the afternoon went very slowly. He didn't want to call until he was absolutely certain that it had actually happened. Later that evening he would talk to the States, tell Gerry Power that it had been done, and tell Rachel. Already it was a picture in his mind . . .

He could imagine it. Even before he called Brian Doyle, he could see knots of children coming on to the bank to watch. He hadn't realized that the rest of the town would come too and that they would drink pints in John and Kate Ryan's during the day, and cheer when the walls fell. He made Brian tell him every detail. At first Doyle thought he wanted proof that the job had been done properly, and had been full of huffs and shruggings, but when he realized that the man only wanted a description of the day, he became most lyrical.

Patrick couldn't believe it when he heard that the people had cheered the walls coming down.

'What did they say . . . did they call for three cheers or what?'

'Well, it was just a big cheer went up,' Brian said.

'Like what? Did they say "Hurrah", or "More, more", or what?'

Brian was beginning to wish he had never mentioned the cheer. 'You know, a big shout. No words, just a shout.'

'There *have* to be words in a shout.'

'No there don't, Mr O'Neill. It was like, let me say a great *Waaah*! Now do you know what I mean?'

Patrick said he did. He was very pleased.

'Do you know they gave a great cheer when the last walls of Fernscourt went down?' he said when he called Gerry Power.

'Is that a fact?' Gerry was a man who was quite happy to go back to Ireland some time in the future for St Patrick's Day and maybe ten days there. He thought Patrick was insane to plough all his fortune into this venture.

'I wonder why they cheered,' Patrick said.

'So shocked to see a proper day's work done for once, they couldn't help cheering, I guess,' said Gerry.

He told Rachel that evening. 'A big cheer, Brian Doyle said. Like a great *Waaahh*! sound. Oh God, I *wish* I had been there. I would have given anything to be there, to have heard it.'

'I think you were quite right not to go,' Rachel said. 'Your instinct is always right for that sort of thing. Don't associate yourself with the knocking down, only with the building up. You've always done it here.'

Rachel knew why they had let out a cheer. It was something to do, something to see on a dull morning in a one-horse town. It all meant a bit of work here and there and the promise of more work for the people who stood around, apparently, if the story was to be believed, with great double glasses of beer in their hands in the middle of the morning. No wonder they cheered.

'They cheered because the dream is coming true,' she said. 'Because the old house is gone and the new life is about to start.'

The site had been excavated, the foundations were ready to start. Brian Doyle had already had four major rows with the architects. The Irish architects had refused to work with the American architects unless guarantees were received that there would be no more last minute interference. The Irish Tourist Board had revised its grant, the situation on charter groups was still not clear from Aer Lingus. Two farmers whose land had not been bought up by Patrick O'Neill tried to get Fergus Slattery to claim they had been victimized. Two small tenant farmers, who had willingly sold him half an acre each a year ago, now felt they hadn't got enough for it, and wanted Fergus to represent them. Fergus refused to have anything to do with any of them.

'Greed. That's what this man has brought to Mountfern, inordinate greed. Those men never thought of profits on their miserable bits of land before, they were bloody glad to have it.'

'I don't think you can go round preaching to them like that, Fergus,' Kate Ryan said disapprovingly. 'You should shrug and say that it's a pity but there isn't really a case. Pretend to be on their side, be clever.'

'Like Hereford bullock O'Neill,' Fergus growled.

Kate laughed. 'He *has* got curls but that's no nickname for him. Yes, like him. He's great at being tactful. That's what's got him so far, I suppose.'

'Or telling downright lies,' Fergus said.

'He hasn't really, has he? I know you don't trust him, and neither do I. I don't trust him because I think he knows he'll ruin us if his business ever gets off the ground. I don't know why you care about him.'

'Because he's hurting you . . . all of you,' Fergus said.

Kate looked up, startled, and Fergus remembered his sister's drunken slurred accusation . . . he was good for nothing except making sheep's eyes at the local publican's wife. Was that so?

No, in truth, hand on heart, it wasn't just Kate, it was the whole household. That stupid dog with the terrified eyes trying to shake hands with you by raising its twisted back paw. That John Ryan scribbling his poetry in a child's exercise book and thinking that Patrick O'Neill was a great fellow. Those two small lads with a face on each of them that spelled out divilment. Those dark handsome twins, entirely self-contained, speaking half a sentence each, suntanned and energetic as wild monkeys; he used to see them scrambling in those brambled hills on the other side of the Fern . . . There was something about the whole family that touched him in a way it was hard to understand. Truthfully, it was not the handsome mother with her quick wit. No, eunuch or no eunuch, he was making no sheep's eyes at her.

Fergus made a series of promises to himself there and then. He resolved that he would go off for a long weekend to a seaside town and have a sexual adventure of great passion with a young attractive woman. That he would close the office when President Kennedy arrived and drive as many of the Ryans as wanted to come with him to Dublin to see the parade. He would speak in less eccentric tones to local farmers who were, after all, only anxious to get a bit of whatever was going. And lastly, he would watch Patrick O'Neill like a hawk. Never in his life had he known a feeling so strong and convincing as this one. That O'Neill and his family were going to destroy the Ryans.

The O'Neills were back. Everyone knew it half an hour after they had driven down Bridge Street. Judy Byrne knew because she was polishing her brasses. She hated being caught doing anything so domestic. She preferred Patrick to think of her as a woman in an important medical role.

Sheila knew because she heard someone in the post office calling out that their car was parking. Sheila gathered her telegrams and messages quietly, and put them in a big anonymous-looking envelope to have them ready.

Maggie Daly knew and was delighted.

Grace and Kerry came into the shop. They were buying cream cakes and bacon and eggs for their tea. Miss Hayes hadn't expected them, so they were getting supplies. Maggie's smile nearly split her face in half when Grace raced over to hug her. Kitty, who was filling the shelves in a very bad humour, was equally delighted when Kerry came over to her without any prompting at all.

'Hi,' he said, 'did you miss me?'

'Were you away?' Kitty asked with spirit.

Kerry liked it. He had his elbow leaning on the shelf.

'Yes, we *were*, and I bet you knew it,' he said.

'Sorry.' Kitty was triumphant now. 'I don't really keep up with all the comings and goings of people I hardly know. I'm much too busy.'

'Then I'll have to get to know you better, so that you *will* notice when I'm not around,' Kerry said, with a smile that would melt all the ice in the deep freeze.

Tommy Leonard knew they were back because he saw their car, and his father said he hoped there would be no racing out on the road and abandoning his post. Tommy fumed behind the counter, but the O'Neills came in to buy papers and postcards. They were going to send a card to all the hotels where they had stayed, to say thank you. To show them what Mountfern looked like. In a few years they would all know only too well where it was and what it looked like.

Kerry asked Tommy about the fishing, and wondered had they been swimming in the river. He said that, after all the beaches they had seen around the country, he was dying to go for a swim.

'Not until after the shop closes,' Tommy's father said firmly.

Tommy wished his father wouldn't. Not in front of Kerry O'Neill, who was a grown person, and who seemed to be treating Tommy as equally grown.

'Workers of the world,' Kerry said sympathetically.

'We close at six,' Tommy said rapidly. 'It would be lovely then.'

'Tea at six,' said Mr Leonard.

'Seven then?' Kerry suggested.

'Right oh.' Tommy was thrilled.

'At the bridge?'

'It's a bit crowded and noisy there.' What Tommy meant was that he and his friends were considered too young for the gang on the bridge.

'The footbridge, then?'

'That's it.' Tommy started patting the papers and magazines, proudly happy.

'See you then, Tommy.'

Grace looked gorgeous. Very suntanned, in a blue and white stripy dress.

'See you, Grace,' Tommy beamed.

'My God, when I think of the time you children have today,' said Tommy's father, a sour displeasure coming over his face.

The twins didn't know they were home because the twins were in the tunnel. Kate Ryan said they were out. She didn't know where. Hadn't they been down on the bridge? No? Well, they'd be back for their tea at six. Had Kerry and Grace enjoyed the tour? Were they impressed with Ireland? What did they think of the land over the river there without the ruins? It took a bit of getting used to. Wasn't it a pity they had missed it all? Kate chattered on cheerfully to the two blond children who stood in the crowded bar as easily and confidently as they stood in any other place in Mountfern. Their father was getting a drink for a group that was busy describing in detail the moment when the old ivy-covered masonry toppled down.

The twins would be very sorry to miss Grace. No, she had no idea where they were; they always came back at teatime covered in dust and dirt. Like they did every day.

Going swimming at seven o'clock, yes that was a great idea. Not right in front of the pub, if they didn't mind. People liked the idea of a quiet stroll down River Road in the evenings, not to get into the middle of a screaming mob of children splashing. A bit further along. No, not exactly opposite the Rosemarie hair salon either, that mightn't be such a great idea; just on the bend. Sure, she would send any stragglers up that way, and tell Dara and Michael.

'Aren't you marvellous the way you can talk and work, Mrs Ryan,' Grace said admiringly. Kate was pleased.

'Ah, it's a knack, like riding a bicycle. You find yourself pulling pints and washing glasses almost automatically. I don't even notice myself doing it, like those people who can knit and look at television. You'll find it yourself if you work in the bar over beyond. Or will you work in the hotel, do you think?'

'I don't know, Mrs Ryan. Isn't that funny? We never seem to talk about what it's going to be like when it's a working hotel. Just getting it built seems to be as far as we go.'

She smiled almost apologetically, and Kate realized, with a sudden stab, the power of such beauty. A man would do anything for a face like Grace O'Neill's, anything to keep those blue eyes laughing and happy.

Patrick asked the children to telephone Miss Hayes and let her know they were on their way. Brian Doyle had a litany of complaints that had to be heard. Jimbo Doyle had backed a lorry-load of tree branches into the presbytery and broken the front windows, and had to spend two days replacing them with new glass.

Father Hogan had been very droll about it, and said that the canon and himself had been very relieved that it was only Jimbo and a lorry-load of timber. They had been afraid it was something serious like Eddie Ryan about to dismantle the place on them.

Teresa Meagher had hitch-hiked to Dublin and sent a message through the post office that she was never going to come back to Mountfern as long as she lived. Mrs Meagher was going to sell the jeweller's. Brian Doyle wondered did Mr O'Neill want to buy it.

'What do I want with a souvenir shop like that?'

'It might be useful as property on Bridge Street. She'd be glad of a few thousand now; you'll always need an office or some kind of base in the town.' Brian was a businessman.

'That's the kind of thing I'd expect from Jack Coyne, not from you, Doyle. I have no intention of buying a woman's only property when she's in a state of distress. What will she feel in six months? Conned and resentful.'

'You're a smart man, all right,' Brian said grudgingly.

Papers Flynn was at the back door asking to speak to the lady of the house; he had some lovely little bantam eggs for her.

Declan asked, could he bring a ladder round to the front of the house. Eddie was stuck in the chimney.

'Mother of God! What is Eddie doing in the chimney? Is he all right?' Kate was very alarmed.

'He's all right, it's just that he can't get out.'

'Which chimney did he go up?' Kate's eyes were wild.

'He didn't go up any. He went down one.'

'He *couldn't* have! He wouldn't fit.'

'Only his arm,' Declan said.

'Oh God, *what* are we going to do with him?' She ran out and was relieved to see Eddie perfectly safe but with his arm wedged in a chimney pot.

'Don't move,' she shouted up at him. 'I'll send someone up to you, though by rights I should leave you there for the night.'

'I'll explain it all when I get down.'

'Indeed you will,' said Kate.

She turned to Declan. 'I don't suppose you could throw any light on what possessed him to start climbing into the chimney, could you?'

'It was going to be his new career, I think.' Declan sounded doubtful.

'Terrific,' Kate said. She went back into the pub and looked around to see who might go and rescue him. Who would be the best person to disturb? Her eye lit on the tall figure of Kerry. She explained the problem and told him where the ladder was kept. Kerry said he had always fancied himself as a knight doing brave deeds for beautiful ladies.

Even though she thought it was far too flowery, it pleased Kate.

'It's all great fun,' Grace said wistfully. 'It's so quiet at home. It's like a three-ring circus here.'

'You can say that again,' said Kate resignedly.

Eddie's sweeping brush had fallen down the chimney. He had bent down to try to retrieve it, and in the effort his foot had slipped. He was well and truly stuck now, no way of getting his footing on the slippery roof from which three slates had already been dislodged and many more were beginning to shift.

Kerry climbed up easily and, watched by an admiring Grace and an anxious Declan, walked lithely over to the struggling boy.

'Relax friend, Superman is here,' said Kerry.

'This is not as easy as it looks,' Eddie said firmly.

'It doesn't even *look* easy,' Kerry said. 'It looks very dangerous indeed.'

That was the right thing to say. Eddie didn't have to worry about his dignity any more.

Kerry manoeuvred Eddie's feet on to a sure base, then he was able to withdraw his arm from the chimney himself.

'Something very wrong with the flue,' he said.

'You could be right,' Kerry said.

'Should have a cowl, in my view.'

'Very possibly.'

Kerry had no idea what the child was talking about; possibly he was even mentally deficient. He always looked fairly sinister, and was reported to be in constant trouble.

'I'll be off now,' Eddie said, sliding down the roof. 'It was handy you happened to be passing.'

'Yes, one of those coincidences.'

Eddie slid to the drainpipes and nipped down the ladder, which he was about to take with him.

'Leave the ladder, you bonehead,' Kerry shouted.

'I need it for my trade,' Eddie shouted back. Then thought better of it. 'But I don't mind leaving it here for a bit.'

Shamefacedly he went round the side of the bar and in the back door. Nothing, not even his rescue from the jaws of death in the chimney, would excuse his walking through the pub during opening hours.

'Were you frightened, Eddie?' Declan asked.

'Oh shut up, Declan, you're a stupid pudding,' Eddie said ungratefully to the agent of his rescue.

Kerry sat on the roof of Ryan's and looked over the river at the site where the new hotel would rise. How much better it would be to approach it from here, turn the footbridge into a magnificent wide bridge with big lanterns on each end. On the other side of the river he saw Dara and Michael walking along the towpath.

They were startled to see him sitting on their roof. When they got near enough to shout, they saw Grace. She ran across the footbridge to meet them, and they all stood in a little semi-circle looking up at him.

'What can you be doing up there?' Dara called.

'If I told you, you'd never believe it, so let's say I came early for Christmas,' Kerry laughed.

He looked so handsome up there with the sun shining on his hair, a white open-necked shirt and a dark suntan. Dara shielded her eyes as if she were looking at an angel.

'Will we all go up there?' she asked.

'I don't mind, but your folks might object,' Kerry called.

'It's six o'clock,' Michael said. 'Time for tea anyway.'

'Typical male, thinking of what to eat,' Dara said scornfully.

She ran to the ladder and climbed easily up. Kerry reached his hand down from the rooftop to haul her up over the slates. He made room beside himself.

'It's *great* up here,' Dara said excitedly. 'Look at all you can see.' River Road below them wound slowly to the bridge. They could see the cars inside Coyne's Motor Works. Usually you only saw the outer walls. They saw all the empty boxes and crates in the back of Loretto Quinn's, and further over they could see into the small back gardens of Mr Slattery's house and of the other houses in his terrace, the

149

back of the Classic Cinema and as far up Bridge Street as into Dr White's. Companionably they pointed out places to each other. Behind them Coyne's wood stretched away up towards the Grange and down the river to the other side they could see the banks getting greener and more country-like as they were further from Mountfern and leading on towards the ruined abbey. From here Dara could see very clearly the big bushes of thorn and bramble that hid the entrance to their tunnel at the Fernscourt end. The fairy fort had remained untouched. Her eyes followed what must be the path of the tunnel – a slow incline, easy for rolling barrels or shifting crates or whatever they used to do in years gone by.

She felt Kerry looking at her and following her glance.

'Where do you go during the day?' he asked.

She wondered was he psychic.

'Here and there, different places,' she shrugged. A bit too casually, maybe.

His arm was touching hers as they sat side by side. He picked up her hand.

'Well, wherever you go, you sure get scratched,' he said, looking at a great scrape from a coarse blackberry bush at the mouth of their tunnel.

'It's nothing.' She was about to take her hand away.

His fingers traced the length of the scratch from the inside of her wrist up her arm.

'Looks painful,' he said sympathetically.

'No, no it's okay.' She found her voice was suddenly hoarse.

'You should take more care,' he said.

'Why?' Her voice was quiet. He was still holding her arm and lightly tracing the long red mark.

'We're all going swimming later. You don't want to have cuts like this that will sting when we go swimming.'

She looked up at him in alarm. His words were innocent, casual. She felt suddenly that he was saying something else.

It was like a lot of little electric shocks prickling all over her.

CHAPTER TEN

Kerry came home for a long half term.

Without the others knowing exactly why, this seemed to change things for everybody. Having him join in made things different, more grown up somehow.

Sometimes Kerry came along when they went swimming up at the bend of the river. And sometimes he didn't. They never knew if he was going to be there or not. Grace never knew either.

Sometimes he would cycle along with her, other days he would head off in a different direction. Or he would lie in his room and read.

Kerry got on much better with Father these days, Grace thought. There had never been anything like those awful days at Easter when she had to go to her room and work all day on those Irish exercises, while her father and brother had this war that involved Kerry refusing to explain something, and Father alternately wheedling or shouting threats.

Grace didn't believe that Kerry had left his first boarding school because the walls were damp. But Father had said he would greatly appreciate it if Grace did not interfere and ask questions. Kerry had only shrugged when she asked him. They had both said she should put it out of her mind, and that was what Grace had tried to do.

Sometimes it was easier than others. When the three of them were running along the beach up in Donegal and laughing. Then it was easy. Sometimes when they were there in the lodge, all three of them, Father's eyes would leave his papers and look at Kerry long and thoughtfully. Then Grace knew that whatever it was had not been forgotten.

She loved it when Kerry joined them. She was so proud of him, and he was such fun to be with. It was Kerry who said that it had to be simple to make a raft. After all, people had been doing it to explore the world or escape from desert islands for years now. It had to be only a matter of binding bits of wood all the same length together, didn't it? Suddenly they were all looking for wood – Tommy Leonard in the back of his shop, Maggie trying to break up the packing cases behind the dairy, or beg bits of wood off Charlie, who worked there. Michael found old poles in a shed in the back yard. Liam White sent a postcard from the Irish College which he said was diabolical, with awful girls giggling and terrible dances that four-year-olds would be ashamed to do at night, and nobody being able to speak any longer in any language. He had been driven mad with jealousy by Grace's letter telling him about the raft.

'You wrote to Liam?' Michael asked.

'Sure,' Grace said. 'Didn't you?'

Michael felt mean, somehow, that he hadn't. Grace was so nice to everyone. First she had made certain that it wouldn't cause dreadful punishments for Liam to get a letter in a language like English, and then she sat down and wrote. Michael wished he was away somewhere so that Grace would write to him. He could imagine her going in to Mrs Whelan to get a stamp and licking it carefully to put on the envelope. He could imagine her sitting at the desk in the sitting room of the lodge, looking out the window and thinking of more things to say.

The raft looked great and Kerry had been quite right, of course it floated. They wondered why they had never made one before.

'I hope it's not dangerous,' Kate said when she heard about it. 'Kerry's much older than you lot. Make sure you don't do anything foolish.'

The twins were annoyed. It was like a criticism of Kerry. And some days when they expected him, he never turned up.

On Wednesdays it was early-closing day, and so Tommy and Maggie could escape from their shops. Kitty came along too, unexpectedly. She was much more pleasant than usual, and admired the raft greatly.

'Can it go on long journeys?' she asked.

'Yes, to the sea, if you like,' Kerry offered.

Dara didn't like Kitty coming along, with her waist and her chest. She looked around for support but didn't get any. Maggie was Kitty's sister after all; she had to be nice to her, and Grace was literally nice to everyone. Nobody seemed to be shooing Kitty away.

'I expect you could take the raft all the way down to the old abbey, if you wanted to,' Kitty said.

Kerry was interested in the abbey; it didn't sound too bad, but there'd be a lot of paddling the raft, coming back upstream from that far. Wouldn't it be easier by bicycle?

'Much,' Kitty said, and they exchanged a long look.

That had been a lovely day. Kitty had drifted off and Dara was glad she hadn't sulked over her having joined them. In a way it was a compliment, older people wanting to be with them.

They climbed on and off the raft all day. Tommy had said it was a great pity that they couldn't get empty barrels, or oil drums, then it would float magnificently. But who would give them anything like that?

'They'd have them in Coyne's Motor Works,' Kerry said.

'Mr Coyne wouldn't give you the time of day,' Michael said.

'I'll ask him nicely.' And Kerry had raced down to Jack Coyne's yard.

Jack Coyne thought there might be a belated chance to get back in O'Neill's good books if he were nice to the lad. He carried up two empty oil drums and even gave them a couple of lengths of rope.

It bobbed up and down like a dream then, and they all jumped on and off it. Dara's long hair got into her eyes, she envied Grace's springy curls which seemed to dry in seconds. Even Maggie's frizz looked great when it was wet. Only drippy, dopy Dara looked awful. She sniffed and pulled at the damp, straight locks in disappointment.

'Here, I know, we'll gather it up with a rubber band,' Kerry said.

'It would look worse than ever then.' Dara hated him looking at her, suddenly. She felt cold and ugly in her navy swim suit and all this lank wet hair. But Kerry was full of practical ideas. Just as he had insisted it was easy to make the raft, he knew what to do with Dara's hair. Unselfconsciously he got his own comb and combed the long wet strands. It felt lovely sitting there on a tree trunk while he

combed. She never wanted him to stop. The others were manoeuvring a complicated way of climbing on to the raft straight from the bank; nobody noticed Kerry
combing Dara's hair.

He went to where his trousers were folded on the bank and found a rubber
band; he tied the wet hair neatly into a pony tail, having pulled out the dark fringe
first.

'Now,' he said triumphantly, 'now that's better. It won't get in your eyes. And
it looks great too. Truly grown up.'

Dara saw the admiration in his eyes and she yearned for a mirror, but of course
there wasn't one.

'Look in the river,' he said, reading her thoughts.

She looked and she could see the reflection of the clouds racing across the sky
and she could see herself. A bit stern, she thought, and severe. But she saw the
reflection of Kerry behind her and he was smiling.

'Thanks,' said Dara in a shaky voice. 'I think it's much better like that. Tidier,
you know.'

'And prettier, you know.' He smiled.

Dara felt an ugly red flush like a rash starting on her neck and going down her
chest. She was terrified he would notice.

'Race you into the river,' she said suddenly.

He had dropped the comb and was there before her. A clean dive far out into
the centre of the river. Dara flopped in at the edge and swam out towards the raft.

'Your hair is smashing like that,' Maggie said admiringly.

'Kerry always says that Dara looks like Pharaoh's daughter,' Grace said.

'Is that good or bad?' Dara had seen a picture of Pharaoh's daughter in a book
of stories from the Bible; she looked terrific.

'Oh good, of course,' Grace said.

'But old, definitely ancient,' Tommy added.

'Not in *her* time, she wasn't, Tommy.' Michael was defensive.

Kerry was sitting on the raft.

'Don't forget what she found down by the river, Dara, a baby in a basket. I
don't think they'd believe you here in Mountfern if you came home with that
story.'

'I don't know. Canon Moran might, he'd believe anything.'

'He's about the only one who would,' Maggie said seriously. 'I think we'd better
look away from the weeds and the rushes in case we find anything like that. It would
only lead to endless trouble.'

They all laughed at Maggie; Grace put her arm around her, and Kerry said
that she was magnificent. Maggie was never so pleased in her life, and quite glad
that Kitty had gone away. She would have felt foolish being the centre of all this
praise and laughter in front of Kitty.

Her mother thought her hair looked better like that, which gave Dara grave doubts
about it.

'It would look great if I had pierced ears,' she said without very much hope.

'Out of the question,' Kate said.

'I *knew* you'd say that, no debate, no discussion, just out of the question. It's always the same.'

'No, it's not. I'm a magnificent mother,' Kate said.

'Huh.'

'I was just telling Fergus the other day how good I was. How I didn't murder you and Grace when you wrote Maurice's name on his shell with nail polish.'

'We took it off with polish remover,' Dara protested.

'But it might have hurt him.'

'It's a *shell*, Mammy. Next you'll be saying it hurts the potatoes to dig them up, or the cabbages, and we'll all die off like flies because you'll be afraid of hurting things.'

'I am endlessly patient. Fergus agreed.'

'He must be bored to death, listening to you telling this litany of how great you are.' Dara was full of scorn.

'No, he was fascinated. And so was Grace when I was telling her about what it was like when I was young. She thought it was very interesting. Not like you, my Dara, who would run a mile rather than hear my views on anything.'

Kate spoke lightly, but Dara felt that her mother was being serious.

And it was true, Grace *did* love to hear tales of the old days. She wasn't just pretending in order to be polite, she would sit and ask all kinds of questions. She told Dara and Michael that their parents were far nicer than anyone else's, which was true, but it was nice to be told. Dara wondered what would Grace do if she wanted to have pierced ears. She would ask nicely and she would get what she wanted. That's what happened every time.

'Do you know, Mammy, I was just sitting here thinking.'

'And what were you thinking, Dara?' Kate looked at her and smiled. 'You know, pet, you really do look very nice with your hair pulled away from your face like that. I think you've inherited my excellent bone structure, instead of the puddingy, sandy looks of the Ryans.'

'I was just thinking that a fine-looking woman like yourself would want to be proud of her only daughter. Glad that her one girl would be a credit to her, with a smart appearance . . . and possibly to complete the look, pierced ears.'

'No, Dara.'

'Why?'

'Because you'd look like a gypsy, like a tramp. *No*.'

Dara looked crestfallen. She could read the tones, and this was a very definite no.

'Listen, I know it's not the same thing, but I'll get you a nice ribbon for your pony tail, you know the way Grace wears those ribbons.'

'Oh Mam, Grace could wear anything in her hair and it would look great. I'd look like a jack-in-the-box with ribbon.'

'You've no idea how lovely you are,' said her mother. 'And we will discuss your ears when you're sixteen. Not a day before then, not an hour.'

'That's over three years. I can't believe it's going to be as long as that,' wailed Dara. 'I'll be so old then, nobody will want to look at my ears, or any part of me.'

'Yes, well that's possible, but just to get value out of these days when everyone *is* looking at you, I'll get a ribbon. Would you like a stripy ribbon or spots?'

Dara spent a long time curling her pony tail with pipe cleaners. It looked great next morning, tied up with an old blue ribbon she had found in Carrie's room.

Dara was first at the raft, but Kerry O'Neill didn't turn up. Dara thought the day was very long. No Maggie, no Tommy, no Whites, and mainly no Kerry. Three times Dara asked Grace where he might be. Three times Grace shrugged; you knew what Kerry was like. He turned up or he didn't.

Grace and Michael lay on the raft for ages, just talking. Dara felt very discontented, and dangled her feet in the water from the bank as she looked back up at Coyne's wood in case she would see Kerry O'Neill approaching on his bicycle.

The twins sat on the window seat and looked at the moon shining on the river.

'Can we take Grace to the tunnel, do you think?' Michael asked.

'We *said* it was going to be ours,' Dara complained.

'Yes, well it is, of course.'

'So why take Grace?'

'She's your best friend.'

'I know. That's not the point; we'd have to take Maggie and Tommy. It would stop being special.'

'We wouldn't, we could have it as a secret, the three of us.'

'You can't keep secrets in threes.'

'How do we know? I bet you and Grace have secrets. Things you don't tell me.'

'So, if we do, what is the point?'

'The point is that if you do, then it means she *is* able to keep a secret. It would be great to bring Grace to the tunnel.'

'No,' said Dara.

'Okay.'

'What do you mean, okay?'

'Just that. If you say no, then we don't. If you'd wanted someone to come and I'd said no it would be the same.'

'No sulks, Michael?'

'No sulks, Dara.'

Fergus Slattery left his invitation to Dublin too late. The O'Neills had got in before him. Just two hours before him. He called formally to the pub and told John that he was going to hire a station wagon to take the Ryan family to Dublin to see President Kennedy. He had friends with a solicitor's office on the very route of the cavalcade and they could sit at the window there above the crowd and see the whole thing.

John's good-natured face had a look of sorrow to refuse such generosity. But hadn't Patrick O'Neill been in that very morning with a similar suggestion? Imagine the Ryans being asked twice in the one day to go to see the President of America! Patrick was taking his own big car, Marian Johnson was taking her station wagon, and between them they were inviting the Ryans – John had decided to close the pub – and Sheila Whelan, whose nephew was going to be at the post office to deal with emergencies.

'Well, well, that's a pity,' Fergus said between clenched teeth. 'And what a chance to pass up. A seat on the very route itself.'

But it appeared that Patrick had some American friends with three hotel rooms overlooking the route so they would miss nothing.

Fergus had a whiskey, which burned his throat. Would he even bother to go now? The whole outing had gone as sour on him as the drink. He could hardly swallow. And to think that O'Neill had the decency to ask Sheila Whelan. That was something Fergus should have thought of himself, but hadn't. Why did the bloody man make all the right moves, *and* make them first?

Fergus walked back down River Road and back home.

'Miss Purcell,' he shouted. 'Miss Purcell, would you like to go to Dublin next week and see John Fitzgerald Kennedy with me?'

'Are you drunk, Mr Fergus?'

'No, Miss Purcell, I am sober. I am, however, inviting you to watch the President of the United States visit Ireland.'

'There's no need to shout, Mr Fergus. I'll think about it.' Miss Purcell was flustered – the red spots were beginning to burn brightly, like bicycle tail-lamps.

'Good, while you think about it I am going across the road to invite Father Hogan if he'd like to come too. I think the canon's a bit too frail for the journey, and anyway some cleric had better mind the shop in case there's call for spiritual assistance.'

'You're inviting Father Hogan?' Miss Purcell was now in seventh heaven. To travel to and from Dublin with the curate!

'Yes, I hope he'll have the graciousness to say thank you Fergus, I'd love to come, rather than deciding he's going to *think* about it.'

'I'd love to come, Mr Fergus, thank you very much,' said Miss Purcell. 'You see, I didn't really believe it was true. I didn't want to say yes too quickly.'

Fergus found a strange stinging behind his eyes, and wondered was he going soft in the head, or had the whiskey in Ryan's been drugged.

Dara dreamed that Kerry could drive and that he had invited her to go to Dublin in his car, and it had broken down, and they had to stay in a wood. They built two beds out of bracken and moss and slept beside each other holding hands.

None of them would ever forget the day that John Fitzgerald Kennedy came to Ireland. He was so boyish and young, they all said. Imagine him having that huge responsibility, and being in charge of half the earth, in a manner of speaking.

Fergus met Jimbo Doyle, who said that a van had been arranged on loan from Jack Coyne for a few pals, and he was taking Carrie out of Ryan's with him. He told Fergus that he had asked her only just in time, because there was a question of Mr O'Neill himself including her in his party as part of the household.

'Would you believe that?' Jimbo said wonderingly. 'And Carrie just a maid in the house.'

'She's not just a maid, she's your girlfriend. Hasn't she as much right to go and see Kennedy as anyone?' Fergus snapped.

'I know she's my girlfriend, Mr Slattery, but she *is* the maid in their house too. I mean, that's her job.' Jimbo spoke in some bewilderment.

'I'm sorry. I'm an ignorant bosthoon.'

'You are not,' Jimbo said. 'You're one of the most educated men for miles round these parts.'

The solicitor who had invited Fergus to bring some friends with him may have been startled at the young priest and the elderly housekeeper. But then he was a city man to begin with, he probably expected country people to be eccentric.

The crowds were shouting and cheering long before the cavalcade even came in view. Two newspaper photographers perched from nearby windows and they could even see a television camera team on the corner. Father Hogan and Miss Purcell waved the Irish and American flags they had been given, and as he saw their great excitement and pleasure, a lump came in Fergus's throat, and he made himself a promise that he would try to be less selfish. All right, so he didn't walk over people like that O'Neill did, but on the other hand he didn't have the same genuine feeling for what would make people happy. Once or twice he had wondered how the Ryans were faring in the unfamiliar posh hotel. But soon the momentum had gathered and taken over, and like everyone else he was leaning out of the window waving, certain that there was a special wave and smile up at them.

Marian talked a lot about the trip to Dublin. She told everyone in the Rosemarie hair salon that Patrick O'Neill was a simply superb host.

'Has he done much entertaining in that cottage of yours?' Judy Byrne asked as she waited, thumbing through Rita Walsh's rather old magazines.

'No, they keep very much to themselves in the lodge, just family, you know.' Marian sounded much more knowing than she was. She could not believe it possible that a family could live in her grounds and she would know so little of their everyday life. They were perfectly pleasant if mildly startled when she came to call; they refused all offers of hospitality that she and her father showered on them. Marian had heard that a woman was coming across from New York, a Mrs Fine. There had already been two phone calls to the Grange for her. It was a mystery. Patrick had made no booking; usually he was assiduous about booking well in advance and paying a full rate.

Who was Mrs Fine?

She longed to ask did anyone in the salon know, but she hated to reveal her hand.

She would call at Ryan's perhaps, and inquire there.

Marian didn't even need to do that. She met Grace and Dara as soon as she left Rita Walsh's door.

'Your hair looks lovely.' Grace was always so enthusiastic, so willing to praise.

'Thank you, dear. Grace, who is Mrs Fine?'

'I don't know what you mean.'

157

'I mean is she somebody who is a family friend?'

'No, she's not a family friend.'

'Is she coming over here to Ireland?'

'Not that I know of, Miss Johnson.'

'It's just that there have been two calls for her, and I hadn't heard anything. Your father is usually so good about booking people in; I was wondering whether it had slipped his mind . . .'

'No, it wouldn't have slipped his mind. She can't be intended to stay in the Grange. They must have got it wrong back in the States.'

'So who *is* she then, dear?'

'A sort of designer, I think; someone rather old who works with Father.'

'And she and Mr Fine aren't friends of yours back home?'

'No, I think it's all a work thing.'

'I see.' Marian was satisfied.

Grace linked Dara on towards their raft on the bend of the river.

'I'll tell you something, because I tell you all my secrets.'

'You don't have to.' Dara still felt guilty about the tunnel.

'Well, I will. The woman that Marian's rabbiting on about, she's the woman I was telling you about. The one that was meant to be interested in Father. You know, the things people said.'

'Oh heavens.' Dara was worried for her friend.

'No, it couldn't be anything. I know that now. Father isn't interested in women and all that sort of thing. It's too late, and he's only interested in being part of things here.'

'Well, that's all right then.' Dara was relieved that there were no more storm clouds on the horizon.

'Kerry, Mrs Fine's coming.'

'She's not. He wouldn't dare.'

'I thought I'd tell you now, so that you wouldn't make a scene.'

'He can't mean to bring her *here*.' Kerry looked round the lodge in dismay.

'No, not here, I mean to Mountfern.'

'Is she staying in the Grange?'

'No, or Marian knows nothing about it, if she is.'

'It's revolting.' Kerry was walking around, agitated.

'Please don't make a scene. We've been over this a hundred times. We've said it *can't* be true. Not all this time, not at their age.'

'Look at what we hear about the people going to the Rosemarie hair salon, they must be about a hundred.'

'But not Father!'

'Whyever not? He's just the same.'

'I'll ask him if you like. Let me ask him.' Grace was anxious to avoid what would happen if Kerry asked.

'No, don't ask him. Don't sink to asking him. If she comes to this place then he'll have to explain her, let him explain her himself without us asking.' Kerry's lip was curled in disapproval.

Papers Flynn called to Dr White's surgery, as if he were the most regular visitor there, coming for prescriptions and patent medicines. Mrs White was surprised to see him at the surgery door; his usual approach was to the kitchen door in search of cardboard, when he would not be averse to a cup of tea.

Then she saw he had a gigantic bump on his forehead and a cut all round it.

'Oh Papers, have you been in the wars?' she asked, concerned for the gentle old man whose wits were long gone.

'I don't know what happened, Mam, but I was sitting there minding my own business in the dump near the brothers' school and I saw Miss Barry from the presbytery, who often gives me a cup of tea. Anyway she threw this bag of bottles in, and she didn't look at all to see if there was anyone there, and it's opened my head. I can't imagine what came into her.'

Mrs White sighed. It was about time for one of Miss Barry's batters. But really and truly she was getting quite dangerous, if she had nearly laid out Papers. Still she could hardly be faulted for thinking that a rubbish dump might be free of people sitting on the debris having their tea. Mountfern was a very mad place, Mrs White often told her husband, on the frequent occasions when she was trying to encourage him to find a practice somewhere with a bit more life in it.

Jimbo Doyle put his head round the door of Leonard's paper shop.

'Tommy, do us a favour.'

'What is it, Jimbo?' Tommy looked round to see if his father was watching. His father had accused Jimbo of reading every paper in the shop and buying none of them; it had been highly embarrassing.

'Look up the paper and tell me what's on in the Slieve Sunset tonight.'

'What's on there? Is it turned into a cinema?'

'No, smartie, they have different kinds of talent contests. I wanted to know about the Country and Western one. If it's tonight I might have a go, get Carrie out there, have a real night.'

'I'll look it up for you.' Tommy was good-natured. It wouldn't cross his mind that Jimbo should be buying a paper.

'Ah there you are, Jimbo,' his father cried suddenly. 'Come to mend your ways and buy a paper at last, have you?'

Jimbo was very hard to insult.

'Not a chance of it Mr Leonard, just called in to say hallo to your fine son here. We were having a bit of a chat about matters musical.'

Tommy loved this; his eye had been racing down the advertisements in the local paper and found the appropriate listing.

'Yes, Dad, Jimbo and I were just talking about these talent contests. There's a very interesting one on tonight out in the Slieve Sunset, tonight at eight o'clock sharp, it says Jimbo, and it's Special Nashville Nite, spelled N-I-T-E, with fun for one 'n' all.'

'Isn't it terrible to think that it was for the likes of this the republic was born,' sighed Mr Leonard. 'For people who spell night, NITE. For halfwits who name their hotels half in one language and half in another and who encourage louts to get notions, togging themselves up in fancy dress as cowboys.'

Jimbo thought Mr Leonard must be talking about some loutish element which he imagined patronized the Slieve Sunset.

'No, it's a very nice crowd you'd get out there,' he explained. 'They have all kinds of restrictions, and there's no bad language of any kind allowed near the tables. The bar is different, but once you get near the tables where the ladies sit, it's out you go if a curse word is heard. You'd be impressed by it, Mr Leonard, I tell you.'

'I would,' said Jack Leonard. 'Oh I know I would.'

'I'm taking Grace into town, she wants to get a couple of things to wear. Would you like to come for the trip?' Marian asked Kerry.

She loved this motherly role with Grace and thought she could extend it to the whole family.

'No thank you, Miss Johnson, I'm off for a cycle.'

'Will you be back for lunch, did you tell Miss Hayes?' Grace asked him.

'Oh, I've explained to her, I'll be gone all day. I'm going to look at that ruined abbey down the river. She's making me some sandwiches.'

Grace knew that Kitty Daly was taking a picnic off on her bike too that day. She knew also that Kerry was keeping well out of Father's way. He was very annoyed to hear that Mrs Fine might be coming to Mountfern.

Rachel Fine looked at the Slieve Sunset hotel in disbelief. It was quite bad enough of Patrick to say they couldn't stay in the same hotel for discretion . . . but to put her up in this dump was inexcusable. The Grange was a country house, covered in virginia creeper, the Grange had horses in stables. It had a decanter of sherry to which the guests helped themselves before dinner. It had a lady with a plummy voice called Marian Johnson who was the daughter of the house and who ran the place very well. So what was Rachel doing in this fleapit? It was such a low-grade motel, it was definitely an insult.

She pulled off her long cream gloves and sat on the bed to inspect the room. There was no chair to sit on. Hideous drapes in huge sunbursts clashing with a carpet of equally hideous, but non-toning, shades. The light switch was not even beside the bed. There was no bathroom, you could share a tub or shower room with Lord knew how many people. A handbasin with a dripping faucet, a small uneven-looking wardrobe as an excuse for a closet. Four rattling wire coat hangers inside.

Rachel's head was aching. She had flown from New York to Shannon. She had rented a car on Patrick's suggestion. He had been hard to pin down on the telephone, but it was something to do with wanting her to see a bit of the country. Big clown. She could still see the countryside if he had come to meet her.

And what was all this need for discretion, here of all places? Here nobody knew them. It could be like that one week they had spent in Mexico where they could check into any hotel as man and wife, where they could hold hands at dinner. Who in Ireland would know or care that they stayed in the same hotel? Why, there was even his daughter as chaperon.

Tired and angry, Rachel began to unpack. She smoothed out her best silk suit; she had expected to hang it over a tub of steaming, scented water when she arrived, but *that* was not on. She looked at her face in the mirror. She looked every day of forty-eight and a few more days as well. She could *kill* him. But she wouldn't. She hadn't waited this long, and put up with so much already, to blow the whole thing in a dump in a one-horse town in a second-rate country.

Patrick was locked in a never-ending argument with architects and structural engineers all morning. He had said goodbye to Kerry the previous night, glad that the boy would be gone before Rachel arrived. He hadn't even said anything about her coming. With Grace there was no problem; the child had no idea of any relationship, and anyway she was so taken up with the Ryan twins she had no time for anyone else.

It was a warm day and the architects were being excessively stubborn; the whole planning could be negated even at this stage, they insisted, if he wouldn't tell them where he had finally decided to place the entrance.

'I'll tell you any goddamn place to get the show on the road, but we can change it again later, that's the deal,' Patrick said.

That was not the deal, apparently. It was very wearing. Brian Doyle had been no help either.

'There's only two places you can put the entrance, in the name of God, Mr O'Neill,' he shouted, exasperated. 'Where it is, where it was always meant to be. Or where the Yank architects say, which is along that sort of overgrown towpath, which will cost you another thousand pounds just to cut back the brambles. All you've got to say is one or the other.'

None of them had seen what his son had seen, that the best and indeed the only place to have an imposing entrance, was from the small piece of ground where Ryan's Licensed Premises stood at this very moment.

Patrick decided to end the meeting. Kerry had left. Rachel was arriving, Marian was billing and cooing about dinner for the two of them that evening, when he most certainly would not be free. But most important of all, he realized, he had to talk to the Ryans. He had always despised other businessmen who pussyfooted about. He was going to ask those people straight away if there was any chance that they would consider selling. It was tempting to let other people do the dirty work, ask the questions that were almost impossible to ask. But Patrick O'Neill knew that in almost every aspect of life, if you want to do something it's best to do it yourself. If he did it quickly he might even have the conversation finished one way or another before lunch. Then he'd hightail it up to the Slieve Sunset and pray that Rachel wasn't spitting blood once she had seen the style he had relegated her to for her visit.

Miss Purcell had been in a very good humour since the trip to Dublin. She had been treated as the highest in the land with a window seat at which the young president looked up and waved directly. There had been tea and sandwiches, and Father Hogan had been a delightful companion for the day. Mr Fergus was so odd of course, and put people off by his funny manner, but there was no doubt he had a heart of gold. She had ironed his shirts lovingly for him; she hoped he would look very well in this nice hotel he was going to, and people would admire him. She hoped he would meet a nice class of person, and have a good social life. He refused to play bridge, and he was on his own far too much. Miss Purcell didn't really want to see a wife for Mr Fergus – that would mean too many changes – but she would like him to have more people of his own class and education to talk to in the evenings. He had taken to long walks, and heavy pints in Ryan's Licensed Premises with farm labourers.

She was glad of the thought of two weeks on her own. She could spring clean the house properly. It would be very quiet, of course, without Mr Fergus and Kate Ryan and the clients trooping in and out. But the Lord knew the man was entitled to his two weeks off, and she went out on the doorstep to examine the skies, hoping for good weather for the young master on his holidays.

At that very moment a small car drew up and a very well-dressed woman jumped out.

'Pardon me, but seeing that you live here, can I ask you where I should go to find Mr Patrick O'Neill who is doing major building works in these parts?'

Miss Purcell was delighted, an American lady just arrived in town. What a chance to meet her at once, just because she had gone to look at the weather.

'Of course I can tell you,' she said. 'You turn right at the big bridge you see here before you, then go along River Road. Park your car outside the public house called Ryan's and cross a footbridge. It's a bit of a walk but that's the site.'

'That's where the old Fernscourt was . . .' the American lady said.

'The very place,' Miss Purcell said. 'Mr O'Neill's building a fine new hotel there, they tell me.'

'So I walk over the footbridge and it's a fair way?' The woman looked down at her very elegant high-heeled shoes. 'Well, I guess I'm going to have to get used to different ways.'

Miss Purcell was bursting with assistance.

'Seeing you have the motor car with you, you could always go back the way you came up to the main road, along a bit and then you'd see a rough sort of entrance, and a boreen where there are lorries and JCBs and the like. They have all kinds of signs telling people to beware of this and beware of that, so you should blow your horn at them all the time to let them know you're coming.'

The woman thanked her. 'No, I'll risk the little walk. And if I can't make it the whole way, I'll just holler.'

Miss Purcell looked after her with interest. Now, who could she be? She looked a bit . . . overdressed, a bit foreign to be any kind of lady friend. Maybe someone he had met on an aeroplane or somesuch. Time would tell. They'd soon know.

Fergus Slattery had been out in the country making a will for a dying farmer. It was the last thing he had to do before he went back to pack. The old man clutched at him and thanked him for his patience.

'But then you wouldn't be your father's son if you were any other way,' he wheezed.

'Was my father patient?' Fergus had worked beside the older man for years and realized that he was certainly well read and certainly slow.

'He had all the time in the world for you. It's the hallmark of the busy man; they never look rushed.'

That was true of Patrick O'Neill, Fergus thought ruefully; he seemed to have time for chats and pints and strolls along the river bank. He had time to come and talk to the angling club and show them new flies he had brought from somewhere on his travels, chatting in a leisurely way, while all the time there were huge deals being done in New York to move money here and there, to finance even huger investments for his Fernscourt project. Already the walls were in evidence – only feet above the ground, but within a few months of levelling of the ruin the new order was beginning to appear.

Fergus shook himself back into the present.

'Well, I do have all the time in the world, so now if there's any little thing here that isn't clear to you, I can read it over again with you, Danny.'

'No, it seems fair enough, fair enough.'

'And sure, you've all the time in the world yourself, if you want to change anything,' Fergus lied into the man's eyes. 'When I come back from my holidays you can ask me to come up here again, if you've anything you want to add or take away.'

'When you come back from your holidays, boy, I'll be in the churchyard, and we both know that. I'll tell your father that you're doing a good job.'

'If you see him, will you ask him to send me a message about what in God's name he did with the papers in the Scanlan case? They're irretrievably lost and I have someone on to me about them every month.'

The old man laughed, the thought of death pushed further away.

Fergus felt better himself. He thought he might call into Ryan's for a lunchtime pint. Since he had closed his own office he was childishly light-hearted, he felt his holiday had begun. He said goodbye to the old man he would never see again, and drove off towards Ryan's.

That funny thin woman with the dutch-doll colouring hadn't lied, Rachel thought, when she saw what a fair step it was to walk towards the busy site. She looked again at her shoes and said this was madness. Even squinting into the sunlight she couldn't see Patrick amongst the diggers, the earthmovers and the men going in and out of a prefab hut which must be the site office.

She stood for a while looking at the scene which was the heart's desire of the man she loved. It was as incomprehensible to her, now that she was four hundred yards from it, as when she had been three thousand miles away from it. Perhaps she had been foolish to come here on her own. Maybe she should have waited. But that hotel was beginning to make her flesh crawl. She had lain without closing her eyes on that uncomfortable bed in the garish room. Sleep would not come. But it had benefited her nothing to come this far. Unless, of course, he was in the habit of calling at this public house for his lunch. She went up to the front door and into Ryan's.

She had assumed it would be a simple place; it certainly didn't look much from the outside but at least they had the good sense not to change the front and destroy the whole feel of the place like so many others, notably the dreaded Slieve Sunset, had done. She had thought it might be dark, and there might be men who would resent a woman calling in for a morning drink.

163

What she had not expected was a totally empty saloon with a husband and wife embracing each other behind the bar. The woman was dark-haired and good-looking, with tears running down her face. The man was sandy and plump, and looked as if someone had just told him that he had won the Irish Sweepstake.

But it was far better than that. John Ryan was holding the *Irish Press* newspaper of that day, in which his first poem had been published.

It was a poem called 'Sleep in Peace', and it was telling the Fern family to sleep peacefully in their graves because the old order had changed. They must rest on and never come back because everything was so changed that they wouldn't be able to walk as Lords of the Soil, as they once had. It was both gentle and savage. John had written it to put in the book that he was doing for Patrick, then his confidence had failed and he thought that perhaps Patrick wouldn't like it. Kate had urged him to show it to someone who might know. She had typed it out and posted it to the *Irish Press*, which sometimes published poetry.

There it was, in black and white in the paper. He had only turned to the page five minutes before, and had come in shouting and roaring like a bull from the garden. Leopold, genuinely frightened for once, was whimpering under a table.

Rachel Fine had never seen such intense excitement and pleasure. She felt utterly out of place, as if she had intruded into a marriage bed.

'I guess I'm a little early for bar hours,' she said.

They disentangled themselves and Kate wiped her eyes.

'You must excuse us, Ma'am,' said John. 'But you arrived at a big moment for us. Can we ask you to share it . . . whatever you like to drink. Anything at all. This is a big celebration.'

Kate was composed. 'My husband has just had his first literary work published. Here it is in the newspaper. We're so pleased. It's been *so* long.'

'And Kate never lost faith in me; she never thought for a minute that I wouldn't succeed.' The man's face gave off rays like the sun.

Rachel looked politely at the paper. 'Oh, it's about the Ferns,' she cried.

'They used to own that house . . . well the house that *was* over there.' John was so excited he could hardly talk.

'John, give the lady the promised drink and give me one too,' Kate said.

Rachel looked from one to another. 'I'm useless; I'm an orange-juice lady. I have no business being in a bar at all. I'm sorry not to be more festive on your great occasion.'

'I'm often an orange-juice lady myself,' Kate confided. 'But I daren't say it in a public house. It's bad for business. You are most welcome to a nice glass of Club Orange if you're sure that's what you'd like.'

John was staring at the paper as if it might vanish before his eyes.

'I'm Rachel Fine,' Rachel said, stretching out her hand. 'I work for Patrick O'Neill, I'm his designer and adviser.'

Kate thrilled with sudden recognition. My God, he's got a fancy woman, she said to herself as she shook hands with the well-groomed woman and poured her a Club Orange to celebrate the success of the poem.

Rachel suggested that John go and buy up several copies of the paper, which he thought was a great idea. If Leonard's didn't have any more copies left, they could telephone somebody in the big town to keep some copies, or even the paper itself. They could get them copied too on a photocopier. He would inquire about that too when he was in Bridge Street.

'Don't be gone all day,' Kate said. 'There's bound to be a bit of a crowd in at lunchtime.'

'I'll be back. Won't I want to show them?' Like an excited child he headed off down River Road. Kate knew he would stop first to tell Loretto Quinn, and could see her clapping her hands with pleasure for him.

'You must think we're quite mad,' Kate said to Rachel. 'Any other day of the year, you'd come in here and find us the most quiet respectable pub in the country. In fact I'd be up in the solicitor's office where I work in the mornings. But today is such a red-letter day, you have no idea, you really don't.'

'I do, I can see only too clearly how pleased you are for him,' Rachel said.

It wasn't the words, which were ordinary enough, but it was the way she said them that made Kate more expansive than usual. Normally she never told anyone what she felt about John.

'You see I wouldn't mind if he never wrote a poem that was published. I wouldn't want any fame or money or anything for me or for us out of his writing. But it's him. Often he says he's only a fool to be scribbling and writing, and maybe he's half-cracked to have such notions. Now he'll never think that again. His dream is official, as it were.' She gave a little laugh at this definition of John's dream.

'That's a wonderful way of putting it,' Rachel said. 'His dream is official. Like Patrick's dream. I suppose now that he sees brick going on brick, he knows it's official.' The two women looked across the river at the huge building site up the slope.

In a gentle voice Kate said, 'Patrick will be over shortly, he nearly always comes in at lunchtime.'

In a couple of sentences they had exchanged a great deal of information. And without saying very much at all they knew they were going to be great friends.

It was indeed busy at lunchtime as Kate had predicted, and with all kinds of unexpected people. Miss Barry had decided to begin what looked like a spectacular breakout by sitting on a bar stool and ordering a brandy and port. She had rarely been seen in a public house before; all her drinking had been done from surreptitious paper bags bought in off-sales in the big town.

Kate managed to get her out by saying that they had neither brandy nor port for sale in the pub, but if Miss Barry liked, she could give her a half bottle of each in a private transaction since she was sure that Miss Barry wanted them for medicinal purposes at home. This brought Miss Barry to her limited senses and she slipped away with two small brown-paper parcels towards a three-day binge and a spectacular hangover.

Fergus Slattery came in to say goodbye and said the place was like Portsmouth on pay night, with all the activity. When Kate told him about the poem, his pleasure was so genuine it touched her heart. He went straight to John and congratulated him loudly. He promised to tell everyone at the hotel he was going to that he knew the poet himself, and John Ryan's ears pinked up with the pleasure of it all.

165

Jimbo Doyle, who wouldn't have read a poem in a million years normally, said that all the children above with the brothers and the nuns should be made to learn it off by heart, and that it should be recited at the next concert.

In the middle of it all Patrick O'Neill came in. He didn't see Rachel, now on her third orange juice and happily settled in. He looked preoccupied and somehow annoyed to see so many people.

'Any chance of a word with yourself and John today?' he asked.

'Fire ahead,' Kate said. 'I may have to interrupt you, John's buying drinks for everybody, he had a poem published.'

'That's good,' Patrick said mechanically. 'It's just that . . .'

'Oh Patrick,' Kate's face was stricken. 'Don't say "That's good", it's much more than good. For God's sake the man has had his first poem published and you just say "That's good". It's magnificent, that's what it is.' Her eyes had begun to blaze at the inadequacy of his remark.

Patrick realized he had been crass. 'I'm sorry, I had something on my mind . . . I beg your pardon . . . where is he . . . must tell him how pleased I am.'

'That's more like it.'

'I am sorry, I know it sounds mean-spirited of me, I genuinely am pleased, it's just that there's something I'm anxious about . . .'

'Oh, she's here . . .' Kate cried triumphantly. 'I'm sorry, I should have said it before . . . she's over there behind the snug. Rachel, Rachel, Patrick's here.'

Patrick's face was in a tight line where his mouth had been. How had it happened that Kate Ryan seemed to have guessed immediately that Rachel was more than a member of his staff, and why did she feel able to call this fact out familiarly across the pub?

He had been mad to let Rachel come here in the first place. He saw her then, surrounded by local people and laughing. But she looked wrong, she could never be part of this place. He must make that clear soon. Sweet Lord, how had it all turned into this, making things clear to people, speaking his mind?

Rachel looked up and waved at him nice and casually, as she would have done back home.

'Well Mr O'Neill, I made it to Ireland. Isn't it a great place?' she said, and his heart softened towards her again.

Things were getting very complicated indeed.

By three o'clock the bar was empty. John and Kate were exhausted. The glasses were washed; two clean cloths, washed through after the polishing, lay across the beer and stout pumps. The place was ready for any afternoon visitor who might stray in, and for the teatime trade.

'God, if we were to have a crowd like that again we'd have to hire a young lad,' John said.

'There speaks the man with the second income,' Kate teased.

'Wasn't it great when Patrick read it out?' John said.

Kate had thought Patrick's mind was miles away but she didn't say that.

'I'm very, very proud of you,' she said.

'Would we risk it and go up to bed for a while?' he said.

'Are you mad?'

'Ah go on, we could ask Carrie to step in here.'

'And what would she think?'

'Does it matter what she thinks?'

'Don't be ridiculous, John, the children could come home.'

The twins had gone for a picnic with Grace, Eddie was out with his gang of toughs, Declan could be anywhere.

'Let them, the door would be locked.'

'We'll lock it tonight instead,' she said.

'And what am I going to do here, mad with desire for you?'

'Why don't you look through your other poems, the ones we liked, and you could maybe give me some of them. I'll type them and you can always say I have had work published already, I enclose an example . . .'

'But there's only one example . . .'

'You don't have to tell them that,' Kate said.

'God, you're a fox, Kate. Between yourself and Patrick O'Neill you could rule the world. There's a pair of you in it.'

'I hope not,' Kate said, shivering slightly.

'And what are you going to do if you're not going to fulfil your marital duties?' John asked sulkily.

'I'm going to have a little walk. I'm restless and over-excited . . . but *no* I do *not* see a way to cure all that. I'm not going to let us become the talk of the neighbourhood by abandoning our pub and going off to bed in the middle of the afternoon.' She skipped out of his way and took her cardigan off the back of a chair.

'Go on, John, get your poems down, truly now . . . I love the one about the nun looking into the river, the nun with the very sad face.'

She walked out and stretched in the sunshine. She had said the truth, she *was* restless and over-excited. She was happy for John in a way she had never expected to be, but everywhere around her, like a big black cloud, she felt a sense of danger. Even when Patrick had said he wanted to talk to them she had thought it was going to be something bad, and was glad that the crowds and the circumstances had meant he couldn't bring up whatever it was. It was like a reprieve. .

She felt there was something odd about Kerry. It wasn't that he never smiled – his face was one big smile, for God's sake, with those perfect white teeth. And he couldn't be more polite. It wasn't anything to do with Grace. The twins seemed to love her, and she was a warm little thing, all smiles too.

She really couldn't say that the work on Fernscourt had harmed their business. When else had they been full on a Tuesday at lunchtime? And perhaps these people would keep coming back even when the building works were over. So why then was she restless? Was it the holidays and knowing that young Fergus was off to find himself a woman? Surely not. She *wanted* Fergus to find himself a woman.

She crossed the footbridge and looked up at the site. Patrick would not be there now, he had told Rachel that he would drive out to the Slieve Sunset with her and see if they could make any improvements. Kate wondered why on earth she hadn't been allowed to go to the Grange and then remembered that Grace was at the lodge and might suspect something. Could that be it?

It would be very hard to be in love with Patrick O'Neill, hard to come first in his life. There would always be business, or the children, or travel or long-distance telephone calls. Kate sighed thinking of it all, and wished Rachel Fine luck in her uphill struggle. She remembered how warm and nice Patrick had been that day last week when they had gone to see President Kennedy arrive in Dublin. He had been so anxious to please them all with drinks and sandwiches in the big Dublin hotel. He had hardly ever stopped smiling and laughing. It would be easy to fall in love with him. She walked up the slope that the twins used to think of as their own private boreen at one time, now more open and exposed with a lot of the brambles and briars cut away. She hadn't been in to look at the site since the foundations were dug and already the walls were showing, so that you could see the shape it would be.

Kate felt she must know what it was going to be like, no point in being like an ostrich any more. She was going to go right up there and look, and ask Brian Doyle which room was which, and talk about it to Patrick O'Neill, and ask Rachel Fine what kind of colours it was going to be. She quickened her step and threw back her head with confidence. There's a time for everything, she thought. I wasn't ready to know about it before, but I'm ready now.

She saw Brian Doyle waving at her frantically as she approached the site. He had both hands in the air and was shouting something. But she hadn't heard what it was by the time she felt the terrifying sharp pain. It was so sudden and worse than anything she had ever known, like the terror in a dream or a nightmare. And it only lasted seconds, because that was all it took for Kate Ryan to be hit sideways by the huge digger, flung up in the air and crashed to the ground. It only took a few seconds to break her spine.

John knew only when the third person rushing away from the site to get help refused to look him in the eye and tell him what had happened. Roaring like a bull, he ran across the footbridge and had to be held back from the scene by three men. White-faced Brian Doyle begged him not to go near her.

'Jesus, the only thing we *do* know, John, is not to move her. For God's sake believe that. Stand back from her, don't touch her. You could make it worse.'

John sat down like a child and put his big face into his hands. Strong men who had known him and had drunk pints in his pub for twenty years couldn't find the words or the gestures to touch him. They stood awkwardly around, eyes averted from the crumpled body on the ground.

Patrick O'Neill knew when there was a great hammering on the door of Rachel Fine's room in the Slieve Sunset hotel.

'No, of course Mr O'Neill is not here,' Rachel called through the door. 'What on earth makes you think he is?'

'Sorry ma'am,' the young girl called. 'We've had a message from Brian Doyle, he said he's trying everywhere in the country to find Mr O'Neill, there's been a terrible accident . . . a terrible accident and Mr O'Neill's got to come at once.'

Patrick was out of bed and had pulled his trousers on.

'What kind of an accident?' He shouted through the door.

'On the site of the new hotel in Mountfern.'

'What happened?' Patrick had opened the door now; Rachel was cowering behind it. Patrick had pulled his shirt on at the same electrifying speed.

'Someone's been killed, I think. Some woman.'

'A woman, killed on the site?' Patrick's shoes were on and he had picked up his car keys.

'Did he say what woman? What was a woman doing there? Did he say how it happened?'

'No, he said if we found you to get you over there as quick as possible.'

Patrick was down the corridor by this stage and the girl was round-eyed at the thought of the American millionaire who was building the big hotel five miles away being in bed in the middle of the afternoon with a strange American woman and not being a bit ashamed of it. Weren't things going to liven up a bit here when the Yanks started coming over in force?

Mrs Whelan in the post office knew fairly early on because Dr White stopped his car outside her door and ran in to collect her.

'Put some kind of sign on the door, do anything but come with me, Sheila. They're going to need someone sensible at the pub to look after them.'

She didn't question whether she was the right person or not, she just closed the door behind her and stepped quietly into his car.

'Have you told the canon?'

'Someone has. Father Hogan will be there in a minute, he's got his own car.'

'Do you know is she bad?' Mrs Whelan's voice was calm.

'No, all I know is that they've had the sense not to move her. I've got the ambulance coming anyway. I didn't wait to see her, we can always send it back if it's not needed.' His face was set hard as he headed for the accident.

The twins were the last to know. They had been in their tunnel all afternoon. Grace had gone to the big town with Marian Johnson to get some more summer clothes. The invitation had not included Dara and Michael, pleasant but scruffy children from that pub. Anyway Marian wanted to get to know Grace, make an ally of her.

So for the first time in days they had a chance to play again in their home. They had been happy to note from the Fernscourt end of the tunnel that there seemed to be no intention of clearing the undergrowth and bramble which disguised the tunnel's mouth. The new gardens would end well over two hundred yards further on. The string had already been stretched over the part where the high hedges were going to be planted and the stone walls were to be built.

All they had to worry about now was whether the entrance would be down by the towpath.

They had torches with batteries, and an old bicycle lamp up high on a ledge. They had rescued a torn tablecloth that Mammy had said was beyond mending. There were two boxes filled with hay which were sofas, and would double up as beds when they came to live here permanently. The day's play had seemed long for the first time. The kind of games they used to invent in the ruins seemed suddenly rather childish. But neither wanted to admit it to the other. Nor even to admit it in the heart. If the game was over, what was there?

In the hot tunnel, which for the first time seemed a bit close and smelly today, they played and hoped it was soon going to be evening.

They came out and pulled across the fuchsia bush as they always had done. Not twenty yards down the towpath they heard the people calling them. There must have been a search party out for them.

It was Loretto Quinn who saw them from across the river. She waved and shouted. 'Where on earth have you been?' she cried.

Dara and Michael looked at each other in dismay.

'Nowhere.'

'Just playing.'

But by this time the children from the bridge had come towards them in a group, and then suddenly hung back as if not wanting to be the first to say the words.

'You've got to go home now,' Tommy Leonard said eventually. 'They've been looking for you for hours.'

'We've only been just around . . .'

'Just around here and there . . .'

Tommy's face was serious. 'Something very bad's happened.'

The other children held back.

Loretto Quinn was there by now, she was kneeling down on the ground in front of them to be nearer to their height, but that made her much too low and then they had to bend to hear what she was saying.

'You have to be as brave as two little lions now. Do you hear me? They all need you to be brave.'

'What happened?' They spoke together, faces calm, timing precise.

'Your Mammy got hit by a machine up in the site, she hurt herself very badly. They've taken her to the hospital in an ambulance.'

The children crowded closer to hear. Now that someone else was telling the twins, now that a grown-up had taken the burden off them, they wanted to be part of it.

'Is she dead?' Dara asked.

'No, she's not dead,' said Loretto Quinn.

'Is she going to die?' Michael asked, equally calmly.

Loretto remembered the people who had given her false hope and told her that her Barney might recover when they took his lifeless body from the River Fern all those years ago. They had meant well, but they had been no help.

'They think she might die, yes,' she said. The group of children drew back suddenly and Loretto held the twins in her arms and supported them from the towpath, across the bridge in the eyes of dozens of people, and back to the pub.

Mrs Whelan took them into the kitchen. 'Your daddy's in hospital now. Do you think your place is in there with him, or is it here with me looking after the children?'

Eddie and Declan's faces were swollen from crying. They sat in unaccustomed stillness on kitchen chairs while Carrie made bread at Mrs Whelan's suggestion.

Dara thought for a minute. 'I suppose she'd want us to keep an eye on Dad in case he'd get too upset at the hospital.'

'Right,' said Mrs Whelan and she sent someone in the bar for Jack Coyne who would drive them into the town.

Part Three

Part Three

CHAPTER ELEVEN

The church was crowded at eleven o'clock mass on Sunday. The two priests, who were faced with getting their own lunch due to the non appearance of Miss Barry, had answered many requests to say masses for Mrs Ryan. Young Father Hogan became impatient when a poor old tramp called Papers Flynn came with half a crown to have a mass said for the poor woman in the pub.

'No need to give an offering, Papers,' Father Hogan had said gruffly. 'We'll be saying mass for her anyway.'

'I want my mass said for her,' Papers insisted. She had been very good to him always, he said, given him a yellow blanket to wrap round him under all the newspapers he normally wore when sleeping in a ditch. She had never given him a lecture about sleeping out. It was as if she understood somehow.

The young American girl had come with five dollars.

'I guess this might not be the way to do it, but when my Mother was alive she used to give an offering for a mass. Could you write Mrs Ryan's name in your book, Father? And could you say a mass for her?'

Tramps and children. Father Hogan had never thought it was going to be like this. Tramps, children, drunken housekeepers, kind if doddering parish priests. And trying to explain why it was God's will that a young woman, mother of a family, should be struck by a huge earthmover as she walked unheeding on a summer's day. They never told you in the seminary that it was going to be like this. But maybe, of course, they didn't know.

It was Canon Moran who would say eleven o'clock mass; Father Hogan would go and struggle with the range. He sighed as he folded his own vestments from the earlier mass in the vestry and watched Canon Moran take tottering steps out towards the altar. He had arranged sensible altar boys like Tommy Leonard and Liam White. With the canon you couldn't have any possible troublemakers.

The canon turned to face the congregation and in his thin reedy voice he said, 'Your prayers are asked for the happy death or speedy recovery of Katherine Mary Ryan of River Road.'

Fergus put a finger in his collar to loosen it. He wondered what he was doing sitting here listening to this mumbo jumbo. Happy death! Should it not be speedy death rather than lying there paralysed, in traction, so heavily sedated because of the pain that she didn't even know her own family or where she was? What did this old fool mean? Praying for happy deaths and speedy recoveries, that's what you said about old people lingering on and on, it was a way of announcing to the parish that old Jimmy this or Michael that was on the way out. Like the old fellow he had made the will for a few days back. It wasn't for Kate Ryan, a young woman. A young woman who had been killed – or almost killed – by a machine on that man's land.

Fergus felt himself getting a hot flush of anger and loosened his collar and tie still further.

He thanked God for the wisdom of Sheila Whelan who had phoned him the night it had happened. She had simply said that she knew he would want to know, rather than come back a week or two later from his holiday and find out what had happened in his absence.

Miss Purcell had sniffed, of course, and said that Mrs Whelan had a deal of impertinence interrupting the man on his holiday. But Miss Purcell knew nothing, and Sheila Whelan knew everything. She knew that he would have come back from the ends of the earth.

Loretto Quinn was not following the mass; she was saying the thirty days' prayer. She had promised Our Lady that she would start the prayer immediately. She knew that Our Lady would realize how important Kate Ryan was to her family, and spare her. She prayed determinedly, trying to mean the words, and never once thinking that Our Lady might also have known how important Barney Quinn had been.

Sheila Whelan wasn't following the mass either. She was trying to work out a plan in her head. The Ryans hadn't thought a day ahead of the day they were living. Someone had to think for them. They couldn't live on the way they were. They needed a woman into the house, someone who could serve in the bar, someone who could keep an eye on the children, and see to it that Carrie did what she was meant to do. She had a cousin.

She wondered would it work. The cousin had been disappointed. A man had given her an engagement ring and there were plans for the wedding. Mary Donnelly had given up her fine job teaching and drew out her savings to put a deposit on a house. The man had disappeared, with the savings.

In fact Sheila Whelan was the only member of the family to know anything. Mary Donnelly felt that Sheila, having been abandoned by her own husband, might understand. She had told her everything only six weeks ago.

Mrs Whelan decided to ring her and suggest it anyway. No harm could come from suggesting something and for poor Mary, bruised and betrayed, anything would be better than staying where she was and enduring the pitying glances of friends and relations.

John Ryan was not at mass, he was at his wife's bedside. Kate's face was very white, her breathing was troubled and she gave little snores and half-choking sounds. Kate had never snored although she claimed that John would raise the roof unless she nudged him and pinched him to change his position in bed.

There was a tube attached to her arm and another to her bladder. She didn't look like Kate, she looked like a picture of Kate that had been given to medical students to experiment on.

Once or twice she seemed to know him.

'John,' she said once.

'I'm here, love.'

'I'm sorry, John.'

Then nothing more for a long time.

'The children?' she asked quite clearly.

'Fine, not a worry about them, in great form.'

'Who . . . who?'

'Carrie's coping very well, Loretto's in and out, Sheila Whelan came in all three days. We're fine, they're fine.'

'Three days?' She seemed mystified.

'Since it happened,' John said.

'My God, three days.'

'Don't think about it, you're getting better, they say you're on the mend.' His face was red with exertion.

Kate had slipped away into unconsciousness again.

Dara had washed Eddie's neck and Declan's ears before they went to mass. She had refused their protestations.

'Mammy says she could plant rows of potatoes in your neck, Eddie. Stand still and let me scrub it.'

'Put some soap and water on the facecloth,' roared Eddie.

'There's plenty on it. It's just that you're so filthy.'

Declan stood waiting for his turn. 'Maybe I'd do my own ears to save you the trouble,' he offered.

'No,' Dara said. 'I'll do them.'

Michael sat saying nothing. Carrie had come back from early mass and was standing unhappily wondering about the lunch.

'Are you clean, Michael?' Dara asked.

He shrugged.

'Ah, come on, Michael, it's the only thing we can do for Mammy, not to be like tinkers. That's what she'd say.'

'We don't know what she'd say.' He was mutinous.

'What do you mean?'

'You have half of Mountfern saying "Your mother would say this", and the other half saying "She'd say that" . . . When will she be able to say something for herself, not have us all listening to other people saying it for her?'

'When she *is* able to say something I'm sure she'd prefer you to stop moping and *do* something.'

'All right.' Michael went at Declan's ears with such savagery that the boy roared for mercy.

'Isn't it disgusting to think that our mother has to look at such awful things as necks and ears,' Michael said.

'I bet yours were just as bad and maybe still are, for all we know.'

'Stay *still*, Declan. It hurts less if you don't move, you clown.'

Michael thought he'd like to skip mass; he felt sure that God would understand that he could pray better for Mam if he were to walk up the bank a bit. He remembered a great day he had walked off for miles up the Fern and met old Mr Slattery who was deep in conversation with a Dutchman. The Dutchman was telling him all the names they would call the fish if they were in Holland. A perch was a *baars*, and a pike was a *snoek*. Old Mr Slattery had been delighted with that word and had said that if ever Michael went to foreign places like Amsterdam or The Hague he could talk about *snoek* with the best of them.

Michael had often thought that he and Dara might take trips to foreign parts when they lived in Fernscourt. They would travel once or twice a year. How stupid and babyish they had been. He should have known that good things never happened really. Everyone said that Mam was going to get better, and they said she'd be running in the door again like she always did in no time. But Michael didn't believe it. People were saying it the way they said that it was going to be a great summer or that they were going to beat Offaly in the match. Just a hope. Not something real. Michael wished he could tell God about this on the river bank, and explain without being all mopey and dismal-sounding that it couldn't help anyone to keep Mam sick in hospital, but it would help everyone to make her better. He was sure that God would listen better on the banks of the Fern than in the church with everyone coughing and fidgeting. But there was no way you could explain that to anyone.

Only a madman or a heretic would suggest not going to mass on a Sunday when his mother was lying with a broken back.

Mrs Daly caught sight of Maggie leaving the house. 'Where are you going, Maggie? It's too early for mass.'

'I was going down to collect Dara and Michael to walk them to the church,' Maggie said.

'Don't be going in there on top of them all, they'll have the house filled with people.'

'No, their Dad's gone in to the town, they'll have nobody,' Maggie said.

'You can see them in the church. Don't be dragging up there and living in their pockets at a time like this.'

'But isn't this the time they *would* like people round?' Maggie asked simply.

'Stop contradicting me at every hand's turn. Comb that mop of hair of yours, will you, Maggie, and wait till the bell rings before going to mass.'

Mrs Daly's mouth was in a thin disapproving line.

In the lodge Olive Hayes was sitting at the kitchen table writing a long letter to Sister Bernadette on the other side of the world. Miss Hayes had put a breakfast on the table but none of the O'Neills had been able to eat. There had been yet another row between Mr O'Neill and his son. And Grace had wanted to go and stay in the Ryans' pub after the terrible accident. But her father had said no. You could have cut the atmosphere at breakfast with a knife. As Olive Hayes wrote page after page she paused now and then to think how true it was that riches did not automatically bring happiness. This very morning she had seen the O'Neills sit white-faced around their table leaving the scrambled eggs, crispy bacon and home-made bread untouched. She had seen Marian Johnson go by in a ridiculous hat that must have cost a fortune and looked like a bird's nest. Marian's face was tense and anxious.

And now Mr O'Neill and his daughter had driven off to eleven o'clock mass but Kerry had not gone with them. He had gone to his room. That meant he would miss mass entirely this Sunday. Olive Hayes wrote on in wonder to her sister about how changed the world had become. Could either of them ever imagine a situation where a boy of sixteen would refuse to go to mass on a Sunday because of some row with his father? It was outside their comprehension.

Tommy Leonard came up River Road and called to collect the Ryans for mass.

'I thought I'd walk with you,' he said to Dara. 'It's the only thing I can think of that might help.'

Dara was grateful.

'And Dara, I did something else. I went up to Miss Byrne and asked her did backs ever mend, and she was full of information. She said that after a bit when they know how bad the injuries are they will decide on what programme to follow. It's programmes, you see, one kind for one kind of a back one kind for another. She said they do marvellous things now.'

Tommy's face shone with the good news. Dara managed a watery smile.

Michael looked very white, Tommy thought, as if he had been sick.

'I'd say you could have a dispensation not to go to mass,' Tommy said after some reflection.

'Did you get that straight from the pope?' Michael asked with a sort of a grin.

Tommy was pleased. At least he had made both of them smile a bit. They walked down River Road, the four Ryan children and Tommy.

'Will I have to walk ahead of you or behind you?' Eddie asked.

'Of course not,' Dara said.

'You're all right with us,' said Michael.

Eddie's face registered great alarm. Things must be worse than he thought if he was allowed to walk with the twins and Tommy Leonard. Mam must be in a very bad way altogether.

Kitty Daly wheeled her bicycle out quietly.

If anyone asked her why she needed a bike to go the few yards to mass she would say that she was going out to her best friend's house afterwards. This was a girl who lived on a farm three miles out beyond the bridge.

But nobody asked her, so Kitty looked up and down Bridge Street and set off at a great pace towards Coyne's wood. While the mass bell was ringing over Mountfern she pedalled on and got to the old stile at the same time as Kerry O'Neill.

Hand in hand they walked through the paths that had hardly changed since their grandparents and great-grandparents had been young and had visited Coyne's wood all those years ago.

Patrick O'Neill could have done without this parade. But he knew that not to have come to mass would have caused more comment still. His face was grim as he walked into the church. A year ago he would have known nobody here, now there wasn't a face that he didn't recognize nor a person who didn't know him.

He knelt beside Grace and wondered to himself how the church had survived so long with ineffectual old men like Canon Moran in charge of parishes. Possibly because there were no thrusting young men anxious to topple them as there were in ordinary business.

Or if the thrusting young men *did* feel like that then they were not in the right calling. Thrusting young men reminded him of his son, and the great wave of annoyance came over him again. As it had when he had spoken to Kerry and told him about the accident.

'We're insured aren't we?' Kerry had said.

Patrick had remained silent.

'Well we are, Father, hey?' Kerry's voice had sounded impatient.

'Yes we're insured,' Patrick had said.

'And Father, the whole place is hung with notices. Christ, they can't even expect *our* insurance to pay.'

Patrick hadn't trusted himself to speak. He realized that if Kerry O'Neill reacted this way he had inherited it from his father.

Patrick saw Fergus Slattery loosening his collar and tie and looking around him a bit wildly. He wondered was the lawyer coming adrift in some way. There had been that very unpleasant and unexpected scene in the hospital where Fergus had shouted at him, not caring who heard.

'Don't think you can buy your way out of this, O'Neill, as you bought everything else.'

The man had been almost deranged.

Patrick had put out a hand to calm him and Fergus had flung it away.

'Your tactics won't work with me, O'Neill, you can't glad-hand me like you do everyone in the county. Kate Ryan was injured – possibly fatally injured – on your premises by a machine in your ownership by a man in your employ. Making a few grand gestures about American surgeons, friends of yours no doubt who'll say that her spine was broken always . . . that's not going to change the mind of the courts of law.'

'Ah Fergus, will you stop and think? Who's talking about courts of law? We're talking about making Kate better.'

'*I'm* talking about courts of law, district courts, circuit courts, the High Court, the Supreme Court. Don't worry, O'Neill, this time you're not getting away with it. This time you won't smile your way out of ruining people's lives.'

They had calmed him, other people had. Patrick had walked away knowing that his presence was inflaming Fergus Slattery more every second.

Patrick wondered if Slattery was sweet on Mrs Ryan. There was something very passionate and personal in the way he talked. But he realized that in fact it didn't matter whether Fergus Slattery was in love with Kate Ryan or not, what mattered was that he held Patrick totally responsible for the accident. And so might a lot of other people.

Marian Johnson was at eleven o'clock mass. She had tried on her three hats and examined herself with distaste in all of them. They were ageing, every single one of them. She looked like a middle-aged frump.

But then she didn't want to wear a headscarf. People like Marian Johnson always wore hats, it said something about who you were to wear a hat at mass.

She had driven quickly to the church and looked in the mirror of her car without pleasure. She saw Patrick and Grace, and thank heavens there was no sign of that foreign-looking American woman who had arrived a few days ago. She had heard some very unsettling stories about Patrick being discovered in the same room as this Mrs Fine when they were searching for him after the accident.

But that couldn't be so. Anyway she would be here at mass with him if she were a close friend of any kind.

She had hardly spoken to Patrick since Kate Ryan's accident. He was so preoccupied and either on the phone to America or over in the hospital as if it were his fault..

Heavens, everyone was saying that he hadn't a thing to blame himself for. It wasn't his fault if that woman didn't know what dangers and hazards there were there. Living right across the river from them. It was terrible for her of course, and all those children.

Marian's eye fell on them in a row: the solemn dark-eyed twins who were such friends of Grace O'Neill, and two scruffy little boys with spiky hair.

She heard Canon Moran's reed-thin voice pipe on about happy death or speedy recovery. The man must be getting senile. How could you recover from a broken spine speedily, for heaven's sake? Then she saw Dara taking the smaller scruffy boy by the hand and leading him out of the church.

With his other hand rolled into a fist and stuck into his eye, the child was roaring.

'He said happy death, Mammy's not going to have a happy death, they said she was all right. They *said* she was all right.'

Kate struggled during the night. She was very agitated and wouldn't be comforted.

'Shush shush now. I'm here, there's nothing to worry about,' the night nurse soothed.

'There's everything to worry about.' Kate was suddenly clear and rational. 'I can't stay here, I have to go home. They'll never manage.'

'Of course they'll manage, they're managing fine, isn't that what your husband has been saying to you every day for a week?'

'A *week*? I don't believe it.'

'Don't think about it now, try to rest.'

'It can't be a week,' Kate Ryan said, and her over-bright eyes closed heavily as she went back to something that was neither sleep nor complete unconsciousness. She had been there for a time that she couldn't work out. Every time things cleared people told her some different time scale.

Her breathing was heavy and jerky.

The night nurse took her pulse and marvelled at the resilience of the human body. To be able to survive those injuries. To be able to lie still while people worked out just how bad those injuries were.

They were managing in a sort of a way. Often it was the well-meant curiosity and concern that was the hardest to take. People came with stories of bone setters who had made the crippled walk, with details of saints who had interceded with God in startling ways and with herbal cures which had been known in these parts for years and never once known to fail.

People came with kind worried faces saying that Kate should be kept still for six months or that she should be on her feet now before the paralysis had time to set in, or that she should have hot seaweed baths.

The support of a small community had its good side and its wearying side. Nobody could be offended, nobody could be ignored. And it didn't have the advantage of taking their minds off things. Everyone was talking about the same thing. How to get Kate Ryan cured and back in their midst.

Jack Coyne was the last person John wanted to see come into the pub.

'It's all right, don't stand up. I'm not here socializing.'

'Sorry, Jack, what can I get you? It *is* a public house; I have to try and keep things normal for everyone's sake.'

'No you don't, things are *not* normal. You've been on to solicitors, I suppose.'

'Ah Jack, stop will you . . .'

'Someone has to keep you straight, John. You'll need a big firm of solicitors, Fergus will be the first to tell you that. Don't just go to someone in the town, go right to Dublin. You'll have to in the end.'

'It's doctors she needs and a run of luck, not lawyers for Christ's sake.'

'She's the businesswoman in this family, she'd be the first to agree with me.'

'Please, Jack. I know you mean well. You're not helping.'

'I can give you the name of a big firm. I let one of the partners have a car last year, he came down here fishing. Jesus Mary and Joseph, John, O'Neill has to be stopped. He has to be stopped, I tell you, and you'll need the big guns on him. He can't come in here to this parish throwing his weight around, favouring one, ignoring another and in the end getting Kate into this terrible mess.'

'It's not the time . . . I beg you.'

'If you don't act now it'll be too late, he'll outfox you. There's a lot of people in this place standing up for you, John, don't let them down.'

'Mr Ryan?'

'What is it, Carrie?'

'Mr Ryan, Jimbo asked me to find out kind of if you were going to be taking Mr O'Neill to the law for all that's happened to Mrs Ryan.'

'And what on earth business is it of Jimbo's, can I ask?'

'I know, Mr Ryan. I didn't want to ask you at all, but he said a lot of the fellows who work for Mr O'Neill were wondering and that I was in a grand position to know, working here and all.'

She looked wretched, her long lank hair falling into her eyes. John knew that if Kate were standing here she would hand Carrie a hair clip so that she wouldn't blind herself.

He looked at her helplessly without saying anything.

'I'm very sorry, Mr Ryan.' Her face was scarlet. 'It's just that he said it would be easy, but I didn't know what else to do but ask. There'd be no point in my listening at doors.'

'No point, Carrie.' He was weary. 'Tell Jimbo that you think suing Patrick O'Neill is the last thing on my mind. There's no plans to stop him in his building, their jobs will be all right. That's what it's about.'

'I suppose it is,' Carrie said miserably.

'Was that Miss Johnson from the Grange leaving in such a hurry?' Mrs Daly from the Dairy wanted to know.

'It was indeed.' Rita Walsh tossed her head. She had just had words with Marian Johnson. Unpleasant words. Rita had said like any human would have said that it was a tragedy about Kate Ryan, wasn't it appalling to think she had been so badly injured only yards from her own home, in a place that used to be green fields and wild brambles.

Marian Johnson had taken this as some kind of criticism of Patrick O'Neill; she had answered hotly that the Ryan woman should have been able to read the dozen notices around the building site.

It had all been very unfortunate; the hair-do had not been a success. Every attempt to organize a parting in Marian's many-crowned head had been interrupted by further defence of the American. Rita had been foolish enough to pass some remark about Patrick being well able to look after himself and if he wasn't, hadn't he that foreign-looking woman, the one he had installed over in the Slieve Sunset, to look after him? This had caused an unexpected reaction, and Marian had left before her hair was finished.

'It's pathetic at her age,' Mrs Daly said disapprovingly. 'She's well into her forties, what does she think is going to happen? A big white wedding up in the church with Canon Moran blessing the happy couple? She should have sense.'

Mrs Leonard from the stationer's was coming out from under one of the big heavy chrome hairdryers. She didn't want to miss anything that was going on.

'I was in Conway's this morning – you know, the shop part, not the pub of course.' She gave a tinkle of a laugh. 'They were saying in there that they hoped there'd be no bad feeling over this. An act of God is all it was.'

'Well yes,' Rita said unthinkingly. 'But an act of God that happened because of that man's machinery and diggers. If he hadn't come back and filled the place up with things you'd never expect in the heart of the country . . .'

She felt Mrs Daly's shoulders tense slightly under the pink cotton cape. She knew that for a second time that morning she was going to find herself in disagreement with a client.

'That's all very well, Rita,' Mrs Daly said, 'but it doesn't do to forget what benefits that man is bringing to this place. It would be a pity if people were to go round saying things carelessly that might drive him out of it. He's in a terrible way, I hear, near to tears over the whole thing, and he's like a child about Mountfern and wanting to be part of it. The smallest thing could blow him away from here like a puff of wind. We'll have to watch what we say.'

Rita looked in the mirror and her eyes met Mrs Daly's eyes, small and round like Mrs Daly's face, satisfied with life the way it now was since the American had come to breathe hope into the town and to give Daly's Dairy the chance of supplying a large hotel.

'I know what you mean,' Rita Walsh said. 'It doesn't do to give the wrong impression.'

'Exactly.' Mrs Daly wriggled her plump little shoulders and waited for Rita's expert fingers to arrange the finger wave to the best advantage on her forehead.

Dr White came into the post office with relief. Here at least nobody would expect him to know the ins and outs of Kate Ryan's injuries, the likely chance of her ever being able to walk again.

The door to the back room was open and the doctor saw the big stocky figure of the American at the telephone.

'Well, Sheila,' Dr White said mildly, 'I didn't know this was going on. Is it a serious romance or are you just setting up an opposition to the Rosemarie hair salon?'

'Ah, leave poor Rita alone.' Sheila Whelan didn't bother denying the reputation of Mrs Walsh's establishment. Neither did she offer any explanation for the presence of Patrick O'Neill in her sitting room, but she had quietly closed the through door with her foot.

'Can I get you stamps, or are you eligible for the old-age pension suddenly?' she asked.

'God, I feel I could do with the pension. Be like old man Slattery used to be, take my little stool and bag and spend my days eyeball to eyeball with lovely eight-pound – ten-pound, even – pike. Dangle a few little herrings in front of them, that's what a man should do with his days on this earth.'

'Never saw the sense of it myself,' Sheila Whelan said. 'Taking one kind of fish to attract another kind of fish, and not even eating the ones you take out of the river. Still.'

'That's it. Still, let people do what they want to. I came in for one thing and one thing only, to avoid running into the canon. I saw him coming up the road, and I fled in here. I can't take another dose of the Lord's will, and the goodness of Our Blessed Lady.'

Sheila Whelan smiled. 'Come on out of that, you're a very saintly man.'

'Yes I am, but it's not the kind of saintly that sees the hand of God and his mother in paralysing Kate Ryan all in the cause of building a flashy hotel.'

'She'd have been paralysed whether the hotel was going to be flashy or whether they were building a library for enclosed orders over there.'

'You always stand up for him.' Dr White jerked his head towards the door.

'No, that's not so. I don't always stand up for him or always stand up for anyone, but Lord God it's not his fault, is it?'

'I suppose like the rest of the town you're terrified he'll go, and take his money with him.'

Sheila was mild. 'What do I see of his money? I'm hardly making a fortune from his being here. A lot more work, and certainly revenue for the Department of Posts and Telegraphs. I'm hardly benefiting myself.'

'Of course not.' Dr White was ashamed.

'I know what you mean though, Martin. And it's very hard to look at it. The way people look out for themselves. But it's not a thriving place, this. I suppose you'd have to expect it.'

'You're too tolerant.'

'I'm not. I can't sleep at night thinking of Kate Ryan's injuries, but that doesn't mean I blame that poor man in there. He can't even make a call without a circle of people round him waiting to hear what he's at.'

'And hasn't he a phone above in the lodge?'

'A lot of these are calls to the States, it's easier on him to be here. I've shown him how to get through.'

'Oh well, that's all right. Business as usual then, or maybe he's on to some smart lawyers over there, fellows that will come over here and say he isn't even in the remotest way responsible for what happened.'

'That is very unjust and very unlike you, Martin White.'

The doctor looked at her, startled. Perhaps he had gone too far. He waited to see if she would explain why it was so unfair. But Sheila Whelan said nothing. It wasn't up to her to explain that Patrick O'Neill was on the phone to America trying to get a particular specialist to come over from America and examine Kate Ryan.

He had been on the telephone all day trying to get the right people. His phone bill would be staggering.

Patrick said he didn't care how offended anyone was, he was flying the specialist from New York and he would be here on Monday. No, he didn't care whose toes were being stepped on, in a case of life or death, in a case of paralysis he would presume that medical men and women would be large enough and sufficiently generous-spirited to realize that the patient came first. No aspersions were being cast, no offence should be taken.

He knew that the New York man would probably confirm everything that was being done here, so where was the harm, where was the insult?

The hospital, which had been horrified to hear of outsiders, succumbed as Patrick had known they would.

He couldn't bear to think they might bungle it, move her when she shouldn't be moved, or leave her in a country hospital when she should be at the remedial centre in Dublin. Only when he heard an independent and expert view from a man he had chosen and paid would Patrick believe that everything possible was being done.

The whole thing had an air of unreality to it. He thanked God that he hadn't broached the matter of the entrance to them; if he had spoken of it then he would always have felt sure that Kate's accident was in some way connected.

One night John found the twins asleep on the window seat.

Before he woke them he made three mugs of drinking chocolate and they drank them together as the summer moon shone down on the river and the building site.

'You're very good the way you manage, but you'll have to get some proper sleep, not with crooked necks and cramps here on the window.' His voice was gentle.

'Everything's different,' Michael said.

'I know, son.'

There was a long silence.

'Do you think . . .' Dara began.

'I don't know. I hope so, but I really don't know.'

A little later he took their empty mugs and left them on the chest of drawers under the Sacred Heart lamp and saw the twins off to bed.

Dara had wanted to have Grace O'Neill to stay. She said it would be lovely to have someone to talk to at night.

John Ryan had hated saying no, but he felt it would be wrong in some way. He felt that until things were sorted out, O'Neill's child shouldn't really sleep under their roof.

CHAPTER TWELVE

Kate stirred in the hospital.

'Mrs Ryan, you're fine. Fine. Don't move too much.'

'Nurse, is my husband here?'

'He's been here all morning, he stepped out for a smoke. Will I get him?'

'No, send him home.'

'He doesn't want to go home, he wants to be here with you.'

'He has no business wanting that, he's got a business to run. How will he keep it if he's here?'

Kate was fretful and worried. Sometimes it was clear to her that she had cracked her spine and broken several vertebrae, sometimes nothing was clear. There were bits when she wanted to cry and cry it all out of her and then she knew she would feel fine, she could get off this ridiculous table she was on and tear out these tubes and go home. There were other bits when she thought she would never move again. It wasn't clear to her what happened.

Sometimes she would ask. But she would drift off before the explanation.

John had peeped through the circle of glass in the door and seen that Kate was awake. He had stubbed out his cigarette and come in eagerly.

'What time is it?' she asked.

'It's midday, love, I just heard the angelus.'

'Then what are you doing here?'

'What?'

'The pub opens in half an hour, John, who's going to open it?'

'Not today, love, they all know I'm here with you.'

'They won't know that till they get to the door and find the place closed. John, have sense. Please. Please don't leave me to make all the decisions, even though I'm lying here with a broken back. For God's sake do something on your own initiative. Just once.'

The nurse had called for assistance and the houseman came in. Kate was thrashing around and the injection was swift in coming.

John stood rooted to the spot.

Kate's face was calm again as if in a normal peaceful sleep.

'I don't know what to do,' he said to the young nurse pitifully.

'I think you should go home, Mr Ryan, she's had a very strong sedative now, she won't be able to talk for a while.'

'But what would I do at home?'

'I don't know, maybe you could open the pub as she said.'

John Ryan turned and went out with a heavy tread.

Sitting outside in a hired car was Paudie Doyle, the younger brother of Brian. He was eighteen and had a driving licence. Patrick O'Neill had hired him with the car and said that he was to drive the Ryan family backwards and forwards from the hospital to Mountfern – a hundred times a day if needs be. And to be there always at their beck and call.

187

He was a kind young fellow and he couldn't bear to see the look of pain on John's face.

'In about twenty-five minutes the pubs will be open, or maybe you might know someone who'd open early for you. Would that be nice? A drop of brandy maybe?'

'Thanks, Paudie. Drive me home to my own place like a good lad. I've got to open up, got a business to run, you know.'

'Of course you do, I thought you'd have someone else doing that. They would you know, people are very willing to do anything to help. You know they are.'

'I know,' said John dully. 'I just don't seem to be able to think of anything they could do.'

Kate had been right of course, there were plenty of people anxious to know how she was and to give the Ryans their custom.

Grace wanted to know was it all right if she stayed to lunch.

'Certainly.' John was pleased that the twins would have company. He sent her on into the kitchen behind and concentrated on serving. Patrick sat on a stool and asked about everything, and when Fergus came in, he sat on the stool beside the American.

'And what did the injection do, did she go out at once or did it take time?' Patrick asked.

'Why don't you ask him to put a bulletin up on the door as they do in Buckingham Palace?' Fergus asked suddenly.

Patrick looked at him, startled.

'There are fourteen people in this public house needing pints, half ones, glasses of whiskey, bottles of minerals opened for them. Would you not have the common sense to let the man get on with it instead of interrogating him about every twist and turn of his unfortunate wife.'

'Fergus.' John was shocked.

'I mean it, John, you get on with serving while you still have a pub to serve in.' Fergus had a voice very near tears.

'He's right, of course.' Patrick stood up. 'I'll call back to ask about Kate when you're not busy, John.' In four steps he was out the door.

John Ryan was very upset.

'Ah, Fergus, what did you have to go and do that for? Now I'll have to go after him. He's been so good to us, Fergus, you have no idea. He has cars for us everywhere, we'd never be able to get in and out to the hospital, and he's paying for a specialist to come from America, someone who actually treated the Kennedys coming the whole way to look at Kate. What did you have to go and insult him for? He was only being interested and asking.'

'*I'm* interested but I want you to keep your business,' Fergus hissed, indicating a small group at the other end of the counter needing refills. 'And I could drive you in to see Kate, I could give you my car, for God's sake. He's not the only one who wants to help.'

'But that's it. He *does* want to help. Don't be on at him like you were up in the hospital. It only makes things harder.' John was still looking at the door wondering if he should run after Patrick.

'No, you're right.' And Fergus swung off the stool to stride out also – leaving John Ryan without two customers he realized as he walked sadly along River Road and saw the figure of Patrick O'Neill walking sadly amongst the machinery and small walls of his building site on the other side of the river.

Kerry O'Neill had bought a get-well card in Leonard's. He had chosen it carefully. Not a funny one, and not a mournful one either, full of flowers and verses about Good Friendship and Health.

Tommy Leonard thought that Kerry was very considerate to put so much thought into it. A lot of people just bought the first thing or the cheapest thing they saw.

Kerry's father didn't share this view. He thought Kerry was cold and distant about the accident, he felt there was something a little calculating about finding a meaningless printed card and signing it '. . . from all your friends in Mountfern, and Kerry O'Neill.' But then very little that Kerry did or said pleased Patrick these days. The boy seemed to be entirely wrapped up in himself. There was no room for anyone else in his life.

The chicken was boiled a long time now. Carrie looked at it anxiously – it was beginning to break up in the pot. Usually the mistress came out and made a white sauce at this stage; she used to come like a whirlwind into the kitchen. Up to the Rayburn and pound pound pound in a small saucepan, flinging in the milk, the butter and the flour at random, it seemed. The instructions were given to Carrie like a series of short and rapid machine guns being fired. Kate Ryan used to speak firmly but kindly:

'Potatoes drained and into the dish, now. Thanks, Carrie, and plates warming, there's a good girl. Thanks, Carrie. Pass me the carving knife and fork. Right, call Michael, it's his turn to serve today.' It used to go like clockwork. But today nothing was right. Carrie didn't have enough hands. The children were all sitting inside like lords and ladies waiting to be served, the master was in the pub where it seemed half the parish had come up to drink like pigs at a trough.

Carrie was flustered and confused. When she put the chicken down it started to go cold out of the pot so she put it back in again while she got out the potatoes, then the chicken seemed to have broken into fragments with all the shifting it about.

Since the mistress wasn't here to criticize her, she thought she'd risk taking the potatoes to the table in the big black pot. She ran with it because it was so heavy. She hadn't known that the young O'Neill child was sitting at the table inside. She began to run out again but the pot slipped. She banged it on the table and there was a noise, a sizzling noise. The pot had burned a huge weal into the table.

Carrie looked at it, her face as aghast as the five children's faces that looked first at the burning table and then at her.

She couldn't bear it any more. There was nobody to advise her. Carrie ran from the room in tears.

John heard a commotion and excused himself from the bar.

In the breakfast room the children were trying to scrape the burn marks from the table. They looked up guiltily.

'Well God, that's a nice way to behave,' he said, looking from one to another to see who was the culprit.

'Nobody here was responsible, Mr Ryan.' The clear voice of the little American Grace was coupled with a dimpling smile

She was like a little blonde angel interceding for frailer folk. But he knew without her having to tell tales that poor Carrie had done it again.

In the kitchen things were worse than he had expected. The chicken looked more like chicken soup than any kind of boiled fowl. The cabbage was overcooked and smelling badly in its saucepan. A pot of something else that might have been a milk pudding had burned dry. Wearily he took the burning saucepan from the Rayburn and looked glumly at the scene.

There was no sign of Carrie but he thought he saw a figure in the back yard near the old pump, sobbing into her apron.

Dara was beside him. 'Try to pick the best bits out of the chicken, Dara, and give everybody two potatoes. Leave the table, we'll see to it later.'

'What about the cabbage?'

'Give it to the hens when it cools down.'

'And the rest of the chicken, all these stringy bits?'

'It would hardly be tactful to give that to the hens, if you see what I mean.'

Dara giggled. 'You're very funny, Daddy,' she said approvingly.

'Wouldn't I need to be?' said John Ryan.

'It's all hopeless, Father,' Grace said. 'There's this maid and she brought the pot of potatoes to the table and burned the table top and then she ran out and cried, and it's all just hopeless.'

'What do they need?' Patrick asked.

Grace was thoughtful. 'I think they just need proper help, you know, someone efficient like Miss Hayes.'

'Yes, yes.'

'Well, will you get them someone?'

'I think not, Grace. I think we might do more harm than good. We wouldn't know who to send in, we could pick the wrong person.'

'Marian should know, she runs a hotel.'

'I don't want to get Marian involved.'

'She fancies you,' Grace said.

'Don't be silly.'

'You know it too. Don't you like her?'

'She's fine, but don't give me this silly talk about fancying. That's teenage stuff, not old men and old ladies.'

'So we won't get them a maid? The Ryans I mean.'

'No, there are times when I think you have to stand back a bit.'

Grace said she wanted to help. Please, she didn't *mind* things being untidy, or whatever they were trying to keep from her because she was a guest. Couldn't she just join in like the family?

Michael and Dara found things for her to do. She took Leopold for his walk, she picked vegetables, she brought the washing in from the line.

She encouraged them to go out to play. They hadn't been allowed to visit their mother in the intensive-care ward but Grace said she was sure Mrs Ryan wouldn't want them sitting around the house being gloomy. She'd want to think of them swimming and doing normal things. Little by little they agreed, but there was always such confusion at home it was easier not to go out at all.

'I never knew running a house was like this,' Dara wailed.

'I don't know what anyone gets married for,' Michael said with feeling.

'But it needn't be like this, I suppose.' Grace meant if you had enough money to pay someone to do it properly.

Like Miss Hayes was being paid to keep things right in the lodge. There was always bread in the bread bin, cake in the cake tin. There were clean towels and sheets. Why were things so confused in the Ryans' household?

'We used to think that we'd live in Fernscourt once,' Michael said unexpectedly. 'Dara and I had a section of it all planned. And we'd have no proper mealtimes or bedtimes, or sheets or cleaning shoes . . . I think it would have worked.'

He sounded very wistful.

Grace patted his hand. 'It's terrible for you being the eldest,' she said.

'Yes, well, joint eldest,' Michael said, struggling to be fair.

'But it's harder on boys, I remember . . .' She stopped suddenly.

'What?' The twins spoke together.

'Nothing.'

'Go on, Grace, what do you remember?' Dara was insistent.

'I don't want to remember it, I can't remember it.'

'Please, Grace.' Michael had a better way with him, obviously.

'Okay, the reason I didn't want to finish it was because . . . well, I remember when my mother was ill, Kerry said it was harder being a boy because you wanted to cry just as much as a girl wanted to cry but the world didn't let you cry, you had to pretend somehow that it didn't matter so much to you. Kerry said that was the hardest bit because he couldn't show Mother how much he loved her by crying with her.'

The twins were silent.

Grace looked apologetic. 'So now, so you see why I didn't want to finish it, I didn't want to talk about my mother who *did* die in the same breath as talking about your mother who is *not* going to die. Do you see?'

Dara gave her a great hug and Michael squeezed her hand.

Grace lost her troubled look and smiled with them both. 'Let's finish these goddamned apples and then we'll go for a swim.'

They peeled and cored the apples in the gloomy knowledge that somehow Carrie would make a brown unappetizing mess from all their hard work.

Mrs Whelan was quiet and to the point, it would be doing everyone a great favour if John could see his way to providing a busy life and home for her cousin Mary

Donnelly. There was no need to go into details but the girl had a bit of a crisis in her private life and the last thing she needed was to be left alone brooding. She was extremely capable, she would not want a large salary – just a change for the few weeks, months, whatever it was until Kate was home.

John was never so relieved. He had been shattered by the events of the day: Kate wrestling with her pain and shouting at him that he couldn't take the initiative, ever; Fergus and Patrick almost coming to blows and then both walking out of the pub; Carrie having retired to bed in hysterics and the kitchen looking as if a bomb had hit it. Opening time in another half an hour. He was never so relieved as to hear of this efficient Mary Donnelly who could come on the bus in two days if called for. Where would she sleep?

Mrs Whelan had thought of that too. There was an outhouse at the back and it didn't need a great deal of work. They could get a couple of men off the site to fix it up, run an electric wire through it, a coat of paint.

There would be plenty of beds up in the Grange and Marian Johnson had offered any kind of help, a small second-hand bed would be great.

John didn't know if he could accept all this. Sheila was adamant that he should. 'When something awful happens people feel helpless, the one thing they want to do is to be of assistance. Let them help, John, it will make them feel much better if nothing else.'

John held her hand gratefully. Only this morning he had been thinking, when young Paudie Doyle had said that people wanted to help, that he didn't know what to ask them. And now Mrs Whelan was making it possible.

Once she got the green light from John, Sheila went to Brian Doyle.

'You said you wondered what you could do,' she began.

And it was done in a trice. Men and materials were arranged. The old outhouse was stripped of its rubble, broken wood and boxes were carted away. Other things which most certainly were rubbish but should not be thrown out without reference to Kate were transferred into an even older outhouse which was round at one side of the pub. They were stacked neatly there waiting the verdict of the mistress on her return.

The whitewash on the walls was done three times to make sure it looked presentable.

The new house became the focal point for all the children.

Jacinta and Liam White were back from their Irish College, even more at loggerheads with each other than usual and according to themselves still unable to speak a word of Irish.

Liam said that Jacinta had been tiresome and in love with the boy who taught dancing. Jacinta said that Liam had been embarrassing and was caught smoking first and then caught being sick later as a result of the earlier smoking. They told the twins that their father had said Mrs Ryan was most definitely not going to die, but he said that nobody knew when she'd be home. They had asked him would it be days or months or years and he still couldn't say.

'I suppose it must be months anyway; this is why we're doing the place up,' Dara said gloomily.

Maggie Daly wanted a more cheerful view. 'Listen, it could be tomorrow for all we know, but she'll still need someone to help her. Didn't you say yourself it's non stop?'

Dara brightened. 'That's what it is, non stop. As soon as one meal's finished and washed up it's time for the next. People eat far too much, you know.'

Maggie burst out laughing.

Brian Doyle who had come to supervise, gave them a shout. 'If you two girls have come to be entertained by all this and to giggle would you think of putting on a kettle and getting some tea for these men here? All right?'

This reduced Maggie and Dara to further hysterics.

'Non stop, a woman's work, non bloody stop,' Dara said as they headed for the kitchen.

'Dara, you'd better mind your language, your mother'd make a swipe at you if she heard you saying bloody,' said Carrie, shocked.

Dara paused a moment thinking how great it would be to have Mam running around the place like she used to and able to make a swipe at anyone instead of lying on her back in the hospital.

Grace told Marian Johnson about the new room and she sent down a bed from the Grange. Fergus Slattery brought a wardrobe he said he didn't need. He drove it up in his car and carried it in himself. Maggie's mother sent Charlie with a small table, a blue cloth and a statue of Our Lady with a little blue glass that held a night light which you could put in front of the statue. The Leonards sent a rug for the floor and a brand-new unopened pad of writing paper and envelopes, in case the new lady wanted to write home. Loretto Quinn gave a chair. The Williamses said they had a roll of lino which they had bought by mistake and the shop wouldn't take it back; they had been hoping to hear of a place that might need it.

John looked in from time to time and said that as far as he could see it was better by far than any other room in Ryan's Licensed Premises and private house.

When Mary Donnelly got off the bus on Tuesday her new home was ready for her.

She was given a short briefing by Mrs Whelan in the post office and then she walked purposefully down River Road carrying her small grip bag. She had left her big case with Sheila Whelan so that the family would not realize how long she was coming to stay.

She knew the most important place to head for, and went straight to the kitchen.

'I'm Mary,' she said to Carrie. 'It must have been an awful shock for you and nobody telling you what's expected and what's not.'

Carrie looked at her gratefully. 'That's just it, Miss,' she said. 'If only I knew what they all want . . .'

'We'll have to sort it out,' Mary Donnelly said, hanging up her coat on the back of the door.

'Why didn't you come to me, Sheila? I'd have got a better job done, anything you wanted,' Patrick said.

'I thought it was better not to deal with you directly.' Her voice was bland.

'Whyever not?' But he knew. He knew exactly why.

'Better let others do it, I thought.'

'I feel responsible, yes, that Kate hurt herself on my property, but I don't feel guilty about it, for Christ's sake.'

'Of course not.'

'And everyone else must feel the same. They do, don't they?'

'Not really. People take sides easily in a thing like this. For one reason or another.'

'I thought it was that crackpot attorney that was the only one, and that he was upset because he's got the hots for her.'

'Really!'

'No, sorry, I shouldn't have said that, but you know . . .'

'I don't know, and you should not have said it, and it is *not* true.'

'Sheila, don't turn against me, you were the first person who welcomed me to this place, don't turn on me.'

She patted his hand. 'Don't be so dramatic,' she said. 'I'm just marking your card a little like I did at the start, and you were glad then. Maybe I've stepped over the limit.'

'Do they really think it's my fault?'

'Some of them do.'

'But it's so unfair,' he cried out.

'Who said life was fair?'

He remembered her own personal circumstances and nodded in silence.

'You see . . .' she began.

'Yes?'

'You see, logical or illogical, this is what they think. If you had never come here, there would have been no machines and no earthmover on that site. None of this would ever have happened.'

'If I hadn't come here, everything would have been all right?' he asked quietly.

'Well, for the Ryans it would,' Sheila said simply.

Dr White didn't like the American. It had nothing to do with his importing a Yank specialist. That rather pleased White because it got up the noses of the hospital consultants, always an arrogant bunch.

But the American felt that money or business was the universal answer.

Once he had commented that Dr White's practice would expand considerably when the hotel was built.

'I hope that your guests will have scant need of my professional services. It would spoil their holidays,' Dr White had said politely.

'Yes, but when they do get the belly ache they'll be people of substance, you can charge them properly.'

'I'll charge them what I charge everyone, I won't fleece sick people just because they happen to be rich and American,' Dr White had said haughtily.

He knew Patrick called him a stuffed shirt.

The doctor was surprised to see him calling at the surgery.

'Can you give me something to make me sleep, knock me out for eight hours at a time?' Patrick asked.

'No. Not just like that I can't.'

'What do you want, my life story?'

'Why didn't you ask that Yank doctor who treated the entire Kennedy family? He could have given you something.'

'Goddammit man, he's an orthopaedic surgeon.' Patrick's annoyance was so great that Dr White smiled, and the American smiled too.

'Sorry, I'm very edgy, a proof of lack of sleep.'

'Tension, I suppose. Strain. Do you have a prescription already?'

'Never needed them in my life, thought they were the tool of a weak man. But if you're lame you use a walking stick. I guess I'm lame as regards sleep.'

'Fine, whatever you say.'

'You'll give them to me?'

'Mr O'Neill, you are a grown-up man, you could buy and sell everyone in this town and probably will. Who am I to deny you a prescription for two weeks of non-addictive sleeping pills?'

'What do you mean, buy and sell?'

'It's an expression, Mr O'Neill. If you meet a bright child, you say, "That boy would buy and sell you." It's a term of high praise.'

'Why are you mocking me, Doctor?'

'I beg you not to think that. Will two weeks be sufficient? One a night, warm milk. Keep warm, don't try to go to sleep. It will come, I assure you, with these.'

He signed his name with a flourish and handed Patrick the small piece of paper.

'Do you think I'm responsible for Kate Ryan's accident?'

'No, of course not.'

'You don't?'

'No, how could you be? Weren't you miles away, they say, at the time?'

'But morally responsible?'

'I suppose we could argue that since no man is an island we are all involved in everyone's life and death and success or injury. No more than that.'

'I'm so sorry it happened, if you knew.'

'I know. Most people do know. Aren't you moving heaven and earth to get her better?' The doctor's voice sounded kind.

'But she's not going to get better, that's what they say.'

'They say it will be long.'

'They say she'll never walk again. Your doctors say that, my doctor says that.'

'They say long useful life.'

'In a fucking wheelchair.'

'Alive not dead.'

'It's like talking to the priests talking to you, Dr White.'

'I hope you use better language talking to the priests.'

'I hope so, I'm sure I forget sometimes.'

'Listen, it was great that your man from Cape Cod or wherever said they were doing things right in the hospital. Now everyone's happy.'

'Up to a point,' Patrick said.

'Sure, I know, but if you see as much difficult birth, hard life and rotten death as I do you'd realize that a wheelchair isn't the end of the world.'

'No,' said Patick. 'It's not. Thank you, Doctor. Your bill?'

'Forget it.'

'I can't do that.'

'I don't see why not. I only wrote my name.'

'It has a price, your years of training, remember?'

'No, it has no price if I wish it to have none. Believe me, there are things without a price on them.'

'And you believe me too, Doctor White.' Patrick's eyes blazed with anger. 'I know there are things that have no price. If I was out for a return on my money do you think I would be building this folly here? That's what my manager back in the States calls it, O'Neill's Folly. There's no price on this that anyone could recognize. It's an act of love. Of faith. It's not the act of a businessman who wants to make a quick buck, or indeed any bucks for a very long time.'

Dr White shook his head sadly and said nothing.

'Well, go on, say it whatever it is'

'But of *course* there's a price. The price is your wish to be home, and to be a person of importance in these parts where your grandfather came from, not just one of a few million Irish in America. That's what you want – isn't it? – much more than money. I was just saying there are some people who want nothing or very little.'

'Like the Ryans,' Patrick said sadly. 'They wanted very little indeed, and look at what they have now.'

'It will be better for you now that you've got someone to look after things,' Grace said.

'She looks a bit fierce,' Dara complained.

'It doesn't matter, she's going to run things, that's what it's about.'

Grace was always so sunny. Dara wondered did she ever have great times of doubt and worry? Was it only Dara? Maybe if you were as beautiful as Grace was, there was no need to worry about things. Everyone loved you.

'Are things okay at your home now? You remember you asked me not to talk about that row ages ago between your father and Kerry, so I didn't, I didn't even think about it until now . . .'

Grace was full of understanding. 'I know you didn't tell anyone. You're a great friend.'

They were sitting in Dara's bedroom. Grace got up to walk about; she seemed restless.

'No, things are not great at home. But I don't know whether that's because of Kerry and Father, or because of Father being so worried about everything, your mother and all that.'

She looked terribly young somehow. Those curls could make her look like a toddler sometimes, otherwise they made her like a film star.

'Do they fight?'

'No, that's just it, they hardly talk at all. They sort of talk through me, if I weren't there I think not a word would be said.'

'It's hard to believe that with Kerry, he's so nice and such fun.'

Dara was wistful for those carefree days which seemed so long ago now. Kerry was one of the few people within miles who had not come to the pub to say how sorry he was, but perhaps he had not been able to think of anything to say.

'He's as sure as anything no fun with Father,' Grace said. Then she deliberately forced herself into a good humour again. 'But I think it will all blow over, you know, this Mrs Fine. I think Kerry was very uptight that she came to Ireland. You know, in case she and Father . . . Well, I told you.'

'Yes, but it's not true, is it?'

'No, not true at all.' Grace was her sunny self again. 'No, she's staying miles away and she doesn't see Father at all, it was all a false alarm. Kerry must realize that now, and things will be back to normal again.'

Maggie Daly wished that her mother wouldn't see things in such black and white ways. Her mother had this fear now that if everyone made too much of Mrs Ryan's accident it would look as if they were criticizing all the progress Mr O'Neill brought to Mountfern. This was the biggest and best thing that had ever happened to their town and they must be sure that no foolish sentimentality was allowed to intrude.

Whenever Maggie said she was going up to Ryan's, her mother said that she should watch her step and not make herself into a camp follower on one side or the other. Yet when Grace asked Maggie to come to the lodge Mrs Daly was delighted. She spent ages hunting for a nice white collar to sew on Maggie's dress and gave her a cream cake free to present to Miss Hayes with her compliments.

Mrs Daly had not said anything about it being camp following to go to tea at the lodge.

Judy Byrne was delighted to see Patrick O'Neill at her door.

'This is a professional call, and I must ask you to keep it very much to yourself,' he said.

'Certainly.' Judy's eyes sparkled with interest and anticipation.

'We don't have the same medical schemes in the States as here. Can you tell me how you work? Are you attached to the hospital?'

'Only in a locum capacity. Sometimes I do a day here and there when some of their staff are away. And I cover for people's holidays.'

'But mainly you are in private practice, is that it?'

'Yes.' Judy wondered where this was leading.

'But you don't have a clinic, a surgery here. Is your work mainly domiciliary?'

'I do go to people's homes, or I can go to Dr White's surgery if I am needed. If it's a matter of teaching people exercises or movements they can come here.' She looked defensively round her small sitting room with its desk and her shelf of text books. She didn't like him dismissing it so casually.

'And who pays you?'

'I beg your pardon?'

Judy's eyes were round in disbelief.

'I am sorry. I did say it was a business call. I must learn to speak less crassly.' The famous O'Neill smile was there now. Lines radiating out from his eyes, head on one side, half contrite, half mischievous. It was the little-boy look that Patrick O'Neill had been wearing for so many years he did not even realize when it was on his face. Not until he saw Judy smiling back. Then he pressed on.

'You see, I'm just a poor hick from the States, I don't understand the way things work here. The hospital is free . . . for one thing. I didn't know that.'

'Well, the county hospital is free if you go through the dispensary doctor, certainly,' Judy said. 'If you are a person of means then of course you would go to the nuns in the nursing home, or perhaps to one of the private rooms that the consultants have for their patients in the hospital.' She thought she was explaining what he wanted to know clearly but she couldn't see the drift of his conversation.

'Yes, I see that now.' Patrick had endless patience.

He knew the system now. Kate was in intensive care, when she left it she would go to a ward. Unless he got her a private room. This he had arranged to do. But she would also need physiotherapy both in the hospital and when she returned home. This was the knotty problem he had come to discuss with Judy and had wrongly thought that it could be done crisply and quickly if he designated it a business call. He must learn, he would learn eventually that in Mountfern the dividing line between business and socializing was a minefield.

'And in your own case?' he tried delicately. 'Are you reimbursed by hospital, patient, or is there someone else like the doctor that one goes through?'

He thought that if he said 'reimbursed' she might find it less offensive than using the word 'paid'.

Finally, like drawing teeth, Patrick O'Neill extracted the information he needed.

Judy Byrne was indeed a private physiotherapist. She did not make what anyone could call a living wage by her work. She had come back to live in Mountfern when her mother was elderly. Her mother had died leaving her this small attractive house, a car and a small undisclosed sum of money in the bank.

It was possible for Judy Byrne to live comfortably on the fairly limited amount of work that came her way through Doctor White, through locum work in the hospital, and anything else that consultants recommended her for.

She was fully qualified; she would be ideally placed to give Kate Ryan the physiotherapy she would need. Her rates were, to Patrick, very reasonable, and he thought that others would think so too. But he reminded himself yet again how different were his circumstances from anyone else's in Mountfern.

If he were to book Judy Byrne to come three times a week to Kate Ryan on her return, surely it would suit everyone? Kate, Judy and himself. But perhaps it would humiliate everyone and be the worst thing to do.

'You're doing very well, Mrs Ryan,' the nurse said.

'Did they tell you it was going to be like this?' Kate asked wearily.

'Like what, Mrs Ryan?'

'Like wiping bottoms and pulling soiled sheets out from under people?' Kate said.

'That's only a small part of it, the main part of it is people getting better.'

'It's not much better if I can't decide when to go to the lavatory. It's not better if I'm going to relieve myself over anyone and everyone who comes near me.'

'Tut tut, it's not like that.'

'It *is* like that, Nurse, for God's sake, that's the second time this morning. If I had ten seconds' warning I'd shout for you, but it just comes out.'

'It doesn't matter to anyone but you.'

'I hope it will *always* matter to me; I don't want to get to a stage where I expect people to wipe up after me.'

'I've told you it won't always be like this.'

'But when? When will it get better? Last week you said it would be better this week. The week before you said it would be better last week.'

'If you knew how well you're doing, Mrs Ryan, you'd be pleased instead of worrying about things that honestly don't worry us. You'd be rejoicing like we are that you've made so much progress.'

'That's a load of nonsense and you know it, Nurse.'

'Now Mrs Ryan, please.'

'What's your name, Nurse?'

'Geraldine.'

'Right, Geraldine, and you call me Kate. We're obviously going to be together for years and years, let's not have any formalities.'

'It's not going to be years and years, Mrs . . . er, Kate.'

'Will I be home by Christmas? Answer me that.'

'I can't. I don't know.'

'It's only July and you don't know if I'll be home by Christmas. Oh God, oh God, what am I going to do?' Kate began a low moan.

'I only said I don't know. I'm only a nurse, I'm not a doctor or a surgeon.'

'Stop apologizing for yourself. What do you mean *only* a nurse?'

Geraldine grinned.

'Stop laughing at me,' Kate snapped.

'You're marvellous, no wonder they're all mad about you back there in Mountfern,' the girl said.

'They're not mad about me, they've forgotten me.'

'Well they don't sound as if they have, we get a ton of requests from people wanting to see you, but we say only the family.'

'Requests. Who in the name of God would want to come and see someone who might have diarrhoea all over the bed in front of them?'

'There's a Mr Slattery rings two or three times a day, a Mr O'Neill rings every day over and over, and others – Coynes, Walshes, Quinns, Dalys – and there's a foreign woman called twice to see you, she was the one who left the plant.'

'I don't know anyone foreign, she can't have been for me.'

'Mrs Fine.'

'No.'

'Well I'll check again, she thinks she knows you – small dark American but foreign at the same time.'

Something stirred. But the events of the day she had met Rachel Fine were still blurred. It was the day John had his poem published, so he had told her. And the day that Patrick O'Neill had come into the bar urgently saying he wanted a consultation with the pair of them. John had told her that too but she couldn't remember it. Was there a Mrs Fine? It seemed familiar and the memory was good rather than bad.

'If she comes back I'll see that Mrs Fine,' Kate said.

'And what about these other men – the Slattery man and the O'Neill man?'

'No. Not yet. I'd cry with one and I might fight with the other.'

'Right. That's understood. Now.'

'Oh God,' Kate said. 'I know what "Now" means.'

Now meant more of the same. The endless round. Changing her position in the bed every four hours to avoid the bed sores that she felt sure were going to come anyway, so great was the pressure where she touched the bedclothes under her. Now meant the physiotherapy. So far she only had to lie there but they told her that soon she would be taking part herself and strengthening her own muscles.

There were the hopeless attempts to make her control her bladder and her bowels. It was useless trying to go at certain times, the body didn't work like that. It betrayed you. There was the painful business of putting in the catheter and taking it out. Lord, had she ever valued the whole business of being able to run into a bathroom and close the door behind you with no agony and pulling of flesh?

Had she ever given one minute of thought or sympathy to all the people she heard having records played for them on Hospital Requests? People having catheters and bedsores and drips all the time. Did they ever learn to accept it as normal? Would Kate ever learn?

CHAPTER THIRTEEN

On the day that Mary Donnelly arrived in Ryan's, Leopold got ready to give her one of his traditional welcomes. He cowered against the wall shivering from his large misshapen head to his long awkward-looking tail. Then he rolled his eyes, flinched and gave a whimper of terror.

'Oh for goodness' sake dog, will you stop that?' Mary Donnelly said to him firmly.

Leopold looked at her doubtfully. Usually he got a different reaction: people said, 'Poor dog', 'Nice dog', or 'What has him so frightened?' There was nothing of this in the new woman's tone.

'I saw you, dog, not half an hour ago up in the main street of this town and you had a bone the size of a hurling stick.'

Leopold hung his head as if he had been discovered.

'Now I'm not against that, it's good that a butcher gives a bone to a dog instead of burning it, but all I want is you to quit putting on the poor mouth, there's no call for that.'

The children stood open-mouthed as Leopold almost nodded in agreement.

'We'll get on fine once we realize that there is no point in either of us feeling sorry for ourselves,' she said.

Her eyes moved around the watching group.

'What is this fine animal called?' she asked.

Eddie was the only one with enough breath to deliver the dog's name.

Mary pronounced it several times, rolling it around to see if she liked it. She decided she did.

'Leopold,' she said loudly. Just hearing his name was usually enough to set Leopold baying to the moon as if he were being tortured. He began, but stopped in mid yowl.

Mary smiled. 'That's better,' she said. 'Any other animals?'

'Jaffa and Maurice,' said Eddie, an unaccustomed spokesman for the family.

'Can I see them?'

Gravely she inspected Maurice in the turf room and Jaffa on the wall.

On her first day she toured the house, asking the role of this and that.

Everywhere she nodded with instant understanding and convinced them that she knew the place had been run magnificently before the accident. This way they didn't feel they had to keep explaining or apologizing.

When the pub closed the first night she asked John to give her a quick instruction in her pub duties.

'It's not a thing that can be done quickly,' John smiled. 'A pint must be poured lovingly, slowly. No, a lot of bar work is the complete reverse of speed.'

'You may or may not be right,' Mary said, 'and in the matter of the slowly poured pint, I have to believe you because there can be no other reason why men would sit in a bar and wait interminable lengths for froth to settle. But there are other aspects of the pub business which must be swift. Can you explain the measures to me, and what people call them, naggins and noggins and jorums and the like.'

'There'd be a month of explaining in that,' John said.

He saw a frown of impatience cross her face. 'But we can make a start on it anyway,' he added hastily.

Mary Donnelly seemed to settle in immediately. She introduced herself to the local women Loretto and Rita Walsh as the cousin of Mrs Whelan who had come to help out until Mrs Ryan was home. Nobody felt threatened by her. She was a small woman in her thirties, with curly brown hair and freckles. She might have been attractive with a little effort, but she wore brown jumpers and skirts and brown laced shoes. Around her neck she wore a gold chain with a cross on it, and she never put on any make-up.

Because she had been a teacher she was able to make everyone listen to her without even raising her voice. The house became much more quiet with Mary Donnelly's arrival. If anyone shrieked for each other as they had been accustomed to do she would walk purposefully over to them and say, 'I wonder why you had to raise your voice like that?' It was very effective.

Because she had been a teacher she knew exactly what they should all be doing at school, and prepared a small amount of holiday work for them. This was badly received, and the children appealed to their father for a judgement against it. However, Mary had presented her case so well that they found him firmly on her side.

'She says it's only a matter of half an hour a day. It will keep you well up with your books, she'll correct it like a teacher above in the school. It'll distract you a bit in the mornings not to be thinking about your mother, and best of all your mother will be delighted with you for it.'

Mary Donnelly gave most of her attention to Dara. 'You'll need it in this world,' she said gloomily.

'Why will I need it more than anyone else?' Dara was alarmed.

'What life is there for a woman unless she equips herself and trains herself and gets on? Women have to fight in this world. Better believe it and know it now, and don't let any soft soap about love and marriage get into your soul and start to rot it.'

It seemed a bit far fetched as a reason for doing fractions and parsing sentences.

At the start she hadn't wanted Mary Donnelly at all. They could manage, she had said, she was nearly thirteen. It was grown up. In some countries you could be married at that age. But everyone had insisted and it was true that Mary did make things easier.

After the homework, she gave them their jobs like Mam used to. The hen feeding, the box stacking and the pub sweeping went on, and she was just as adamant as Mam was about being home in time for lunch. Then there was the journey in to see Mam in the hospital and the instructions to bring all the news and information. And there were books provided for them to read as they sat in the waiting room while Dad was in with Mam alone.

Mary served the bar for the afternoon. She fixed all the clients with a baleful glare, filled their pints and gave their change, but would be drawn into no conversation. If any of them dared to pass her a compliment she would say that she had no time for fancy talk, which came cheaply to an Irishman. She would ask them cuttingly if they gave such praise to their wives and indeed if they ever favoured their wives with an invitation out to share a drink with them. No. No indeed. And they really thought the wives would not want to join them? How very interesting. How fascinating a mind which thought that a wife *liked* being at home sweeping floors, cleaning boots, minding children, cooking, serving and washing up meals. How hysterically funny to think that men assumed women *liked* that sort of thing.

The men in Ryan's took no more notice of her than they did of Leopold cringing and whining by the wall. Mary Donnelly was obviously cracked in the head over some imagined slight or wrong that some man must have done to her in the past. But she poured a pint properly and she was a great help to poor John Ryan and his family in their time of need.

At night Mary Donnelly helped in the bar by washing glasses, joining not at all in the conversation. John gave up trying to make her feel part of the place. Without being actually rude she made it clear that she thought his clientele were the scum of humanity. She would withdraw to the kitchen and tell Carrie that she was setting up a store of trouble by painting and preening herself for the weekly dance, or else attempt to teach Declan and Eddie to darn.

'Why are you teaching the little fellows?' Carrie asked, mystified.

'Because there might be some hope for these as the young men of the next decade if we teach them to be normal and share in women's work,' Mary said.

Eddie was quite good at darning as it happened and said he regarded it as a puzzle where you had to fit all the pieces in. He threatened to knock Declan's head off his neck if he ever told anyone at the brothers that they were being taught darning at home.

Mary had no time for Michael. At first Michael was very pleased about this. He considered himself well off to be away from this bossy woman. But as the days went by and she had become part of their lives it was somewhat galling to be dismissed so summarily. He was never asked to clear or serve as he used to do, his role as a shoe polisher was laughed out of the way. Mary said she would prefer to be in charge of the shoes herself so that she would know for certain that they would be done. She didn't like leaving things to a young man to do.

She said the words 'young man' as others might say 'village drunk' or 'known criminal'. Sometimes Michael felt that there was no need for him in the home – everyone else had their little jobs to do, only he stood there useless and idle.

He offered to help Dara and Carrie clean some candlesticks. They seemed to be enjoying the Brasso, it got all over their hands and they were laughing companionably. But Mary Donnelly refused him. She was courteous but firm. Thank you, but she would really prefer the job to be done properly without any trick-acting or distraction.

Moodily Michael left the kitchen. Kicking a stone all round the back yard, he was spotted by his father.

'Would you have a moment, son?'

Michael was pleased. His father had a great box of papers out on the table in the breakfast room. Since the accident he hadn't opened any of the research he was meant to be doing on the book for Mr O'Neill.

'Michael, I have to do something about this, even if it's only tidy it up and let Patrick give it to someone else to finish. He must have his book, that's only fair.'

'I suppose he'd wait a bit, with everything.' Michael sounded very down.

'Oh of course he'd wait, but that's not the point. I must leave it in some kind of state that another writer – well, that a real writer – could see what I've done. Could you help me here for a minute?'

'What am I to do?'

'Suppose I were to fill this folder with what has already been written . . . not very much of it, I'm afraid. Then this one for under way, and that one we could call "still to look at".'

Michael separated the three piles on the table and his father called out which category the pages and the scribbled notes were to go to. In spite of his low form Michael became interested.

'Look at those drawings. Is *that* what it looked like?'

'No, that was a much grander house. It's in the style, though, so we could point out the features that would have been the same.'

'Is that what his hotel is going to look like?'

'No no, it's going to have the middle bit the same. He's building up the old house more or less like it would have been, then there's going to be a wing back on each side from the main house, that's where the bedrooms will be.'

'I wish he hadn't come here.'

'Michael.'

'I know. I'm sorry. It's so hard, you see.'

'Ah, don't I know myself,' John sighed. 'Look, that's an old engraving of what the river used to look like years and years ago.' He was deliberately changing the subject, trying to steer them both away from the fruitless wishing for the impossible. 'Isn't it extraordinary to think that's the same river, that's our Fern, all those years ago. Lord, George the third was still the king of England then. Do you know anything about him?'

'Was he the one who was always half-cracked, in and out of mental homes most of the time?' Michael asked.

'I don't think there was a question of mental homes, but he was certainly wandering in mind. Not that the Ferns of Fernscourt probably ever knew anything about that, they'd have been snug there in their grand house and no news of the royal goings-on would get to them for months and by that time it would all be changed . . .'

Michael wasn't listening to him . . . he was looking at one of the line engravings that had come from an old journal.

His father followed his gaze. It was a drawing that showed a barge delivering goods to what looked like a flat landing place behind which there was the mouth of a cave.

It was just like their tunnel even though it was a picture of some other county entirely. Michael studied it intensely, turning it round and drinking in every detail. He raked through the text to see if there was any mention of it.

John Ryan broke in on his thoughts. 'Oh, I see you're getting interested in it now! That's the whole problem I find, anyway. You start reading little bits and they make you interested and you read more little bits and you travel far from what you were meant to be writing in the first place. What's that you're looking at?'

His voice was deliberately casual – he had seen the boy find a prosaic explanation for the magic tunnel.

Michael's face was red and white alternately.

'Nothing. I mean it's not anything.'

'Oh, that's one of those ways they had of getting deliveries up to the grand houses without offending the eyes of the quality. You know, like a tradesman's entrance.' John was light but not dismissive.

'Oh, is that all they are?' The disappointment was huge.

'Well, that's one use for them of course, those kind of tunnels, but like anything they could have a million other uses.'

'Like what?'

'Well, like whatever was needed, I mean a tunnel's a tunnel isn't it? It could be used for anything – smuggling, for lovers' meeting, for secret societies, kidnappings, escapes . . . Come on, Michael, it doesn't matter what it was built for, it's what happens to it that's important.'

The boy was greatly cheered. 'Do you think there might be one across there?' He nodded towards the river.

'There might well be.' John was mild. 'Kind of thing that could be left unearthed for years and years. Even with all the big hotel coming.'

'I don't mind helping you whenever you need a bit of a hand,' Michael offered. 'I have a bit of time on my hands these days, Mary doesn't think I can do anything.'

'Ah, be tolerant of her, will you, she has a mad figario in her head about men, that's all.'

'But it's very unfair. I'd do as much as anyone to make things a bit better, or keep things going . . .' His lip trembled.

'Listen to me, Michael, I'll tell you a secret. Not for anyone else – is that all right?'

'Dara?'

'Yes, if you tell it properly, but not to be talked about outside of you two. Poor Mary was all ready to get married, she had saved all her money and given up her job, she was making her wedding dress, even sewing things on it so as to look lovely on the day . . .'

'Mary Donnelly married? Looking lovely on her wedding day, you must be joking.' Michael interrupted.

'No, shush or I won't finish it.'

'All right . . .'

'So anyway this fellow was a rat, he didn't love Mary Donnelly at all, he only loved her money, and she had given him everything she saved for to put a deposit on a house . . .'

'And he ran off with it?' Michael's eyes were bright and he was rushing ahead in the story.

'It's easy known you're so young you can see anything in it except black treachery. Think of it, every week – or every month I suppose, teachers get paid by the month – she put so much away for the great day, and this boyo took the lot . . .' John Ryan's kind face was misty at the thought of it.

'Yeah, well it wasn't fair.'

'It was worse than just taking her money, you see, he took everything else, he took away any pride she had, and made a fool of her in front of everyone in her place . . . Like she'd always be remembering how she had talked of her plans, saying we're doing this and we're doing that, and all the time he had no plans for anything except to separate her from her bit of money.'

'Maybe he didn't always intend to steal her money, he could have loved her and then went off her,' Michael said as if it were only too possible to go off Mary Donnelly.

'I don't know whether that would be better for her to believe or worse.' John spoke thoughtfully.

'Anyway she's sure taking it out on the rest of us,' Michael grumbled.

'But big strong men like yourself and myself can cope with it surely?'

'We've a lot to cope with these days.'

'Indeed we have, son.' The sigh was very deep.

'Dad? I don't ask you this in front of people, but . . .'

'Ask away.'

'Will Mam ever be able to walk again? Nobody ever says.'

'That's the problem, they don't ever say. Not to me either.'

'But what do you *think*, Dad?'

'I think there's a possibility that she may not. And that it's going to be very hard for her, Michael. The hardest thing in the world.'

Fergus invited Mary Donnelly to the pictures.

'Why?' she asked him.

The real reason was because Fergus, hearing how good she was in the Ryan household, feared that Mary Donnelly might leave unless some little diversion was planned for her.

He could hardly say that.

'Because I like you and would like to get to know you more,' he said.

'How would you get to know me at the pictures?' she asked.

Fergus felt sorry he had started on this course.

'Well it's a way to go out, isn't it? Perhaps you would prefer just to go for a drive if you don't like the cinema.'

'I never said I didn't like the cinema. I just wondered what way two people would get to know each other if they sat in silence watching a film.'

'I suppose it would be a matter of talking about it afterwards,' Fergus said desperately.

Mary thought about this.

'Usually it's a matter of taking liberties during the film, that's what I've noticed,' she said.

Fergus had never got such a shock in his life.

'I assure you nothing would be further from my mind,' he began, horrified. 'I am a solicitor, a grown man.'

'What a pompous thing to say, Mr Slattery, as if desire were confined only to the lower orders. It is there in men of every class and breeding.'

'Yes, well,' Fergus said, totally at a loss. 'If there's ever anything.'

'I doubt if there will be, but thank you for raising the matter,' Mary said.

'How in the name of God do you get on with that one?' Fergus asked John when they had some privacy.

'She's a godsend, that's what she is. It's the one thing that keeps Kate any way calm in there, the thought that we've got a cousin of Mrs Whelan looking after us. It's the next best thing to having Sheila.'

'But Sheila's normal, John, she's not a nutcase like this one.'

'Ah, she has her ways like everyone has their ways. She's a bit off men, that's all.'

'That's a bit steep, to be off half the human race, and isn't she living in a family of four men and a girl, for God's sake?'

'I think she prays for us.' John was tolerant.

'I'm surprised she hasn't taken a pike to you, and the day might well come when she does.' Fergus was still smarting.

'She's certainly taking no chances, she got Jimbo to fit a lock to her door. I suppose she was afraid I'd lose the run of myself and come in and savage her.'

'Do you tell that to Kate?' Fergus asked wistfully.

'I do, she doesn't believe me.'

'I'd love to go and see her,' Fergus said.

'She'll tell you when. You know Kate, she's very proud. She hates people seeing her the way she is, with all the tubes and the bags.'

'As if I'd mind.'

'She minds.'

'Tell her . . . well, just tell her.'

'Sure, Fergus, I'll tell her.'

Dara and Michael had finished their work. Mary had made them sandwiches and a flask of soup. They weren't normally given a flask. This was an honour.

'I understand that you can go off on your own.'

It had been cleared with their father. The twins nodded. They were nervous. This was their first day going back to the tunnel since the day of the accident. They were almost afraid it would be bad luck to go back there again. They might come out and find the whole of Mountfern waiting to tell them more bad news.

Without saying it they both remembered that it hadn't even been much fun in the tunnel that day, even before they learned of Mam's accident.

They had almost forgotten how much earth and rubble there was around the place and how dirty it made everything. Still, in the new system that Mary Donnelly had set up they all had to steep their own clothes in a big zinc bath of detergent. Twice a week all the shorts and shirts and underwear and pyjamas went in. That way extra grime wasn't really noticed.

They pushed forward and there it was, with the tables and chairs they had been arranging at the very time that Mam was having her accident overhead. It was strange and almost frightening to think about.

They went round the tunnel as they had often done before, stroking its sides and marvelling at how well made it was and how long it had lasted.

'They must have been desperate in those days to keep their groceries hidden from the public if they went to all this trouble to hide them, building a whole tunnel just so the neighbours wouldn't see,' Dara said in wonder.

'They didn't *have* neighbours,' Michael was more authoritative. 'It was so that they wouldn't have to look at them themselves.'

'What was so bad about groceries?'

'I don't think it was just a few brown-paper bags like we'd get in Loretto Quinn's, it was barrels and boxes.'

'Well that's even more posh, they must have been half cracked, the Ferns,' Dara said.

'Apparently it's all over the country, I read it in all that research Daddy's doing. Mr O'Neill says that the book will be on display at the hotel with Dad's name on it.'

'Do you think the hotel will ever get built?' Dara asked suddenly.

'I don't know, I suppose it will. Why?'

'It doesn't seem real any more.'

'Nothing does.'

The twins sat there for a long moment. Neither wanted to say anything falsely cheering.

As usual they spoke at the same time when they did speak.

'Do you think Lourdes would work . . .' Dara began.

'I wonder if there really are miracles . . .' Michael began.

They burst out laughing.

'Maybe our minds got divided,' Dara said. 'We didn't get a full one each but between us we have a fantastic Super mind.'

'Which is why we can only work out things when there are the two of us,' Michael agreed.

'So what do we think about Lourdes?' Dara said.

'There must have been some miracles there, some of them have to be real.' Michael's face was full of hope.

'Yes, Sister Laura said that if it was all a fraud the enemies of the Church would have found it out.' Dara was eager also.

'So maybe if we could get her there. It could work, couldn't it?'

'And it would be better than just sitting round waiting.'

Dara and Michael were much revived. It was like old times, having some kind of project. Something important to do.

The twins didn't know that the village of Mountfern was already planning to send Kate to Lourdes. Money had been collected, people had been in touch with the travel agencies in Dublin and had received details from the Joe Walsh Travel Agency and the Michael Walsh Travel Agency.

The collection had begun. Sheila Whelan was approached to put the money in the post office. She thought it should be a proper fund administered through a solicitor's office.

At first Fergus didn't want anything to do with it. It was grotesque to build up people's hopes, Kate's hopes too. Why let simple people believe that there was a way that a place would mend a broken spine? Perhaps John Ryan would feel patronized, he might not like the idea that the people of Mountfern should pay for his wife to go to Lourdes instead of waiting for him to send her himself.

'If you don't start it for us then as sure as anything Patrick O'Neill will organize it,' Sheila said.

'I'll open a bank deposit account tomorrow,' said Fergus.

'Father, did you know that there's a collection being organized to take Dara and Michael's mother to Lourdes?' Grace asked.

'Yes, people are very generous, they're digging very deep in their pockets.'

'Who's organizing it?' Kerry asked.

'I don't know, I don't think anyone is. You can give your money at the church to either of the priests, or at the post office or to Mr Slattery, you know – the lawyer.'

'Slattery. That figures,' Kerry said.

'Why?' Grace asked.

Kerry smiled knowingly. His hair was longer than he usually wore it, it clustered around his neck. His father thought it made him look like a girl. Kerry said that there wasn't a barber within miles and that he might be misjudged if he went to the Rosemarie hair salon. He was tanned and relaxed looking, like a boy who had been on a holiday in a resort, Patrick thought with some annoyance. He had seen the young Ryan boy and Tommy Leonard today; both of them looked peaked and as if they had not seen a ray of sun all year.

'Well, your sister asked you a question. Why does it figure that Slattery is taking up the money? Sure he is. He's a lawyer, as Grace said.'

'And he's the leader of the other side.'

'Yes, but when the time comes for litigation the Ryans will have other lawyers.'

'I mean the other side here in Mountfern. He's the head of the pack that wants to run us out of town. So naturally he collects money to send the injured Mrs Ryan to Lourdes.'

'He doesn't want to run us out of town. Does he?' Grace looked alarmed.

'Of course not, your brother is playing games.'

'Not so, Father. He hardly welcomed us here with open arms, did he? And now we are blacker still; one of the great and good has been injured on our property. Of course he wants us out, like a lot of them do.'

'Where do you get these kinds of ideas?' Patrick's tone sounded a lot milder than he felt.

'Because I'm not stupid.' It was very arrogant the way Kerry said it. The direct implication was that Patrick was stupid. Very.

'Neither am I, Kerry. I'm not at all stupid no matter what you might believe.'

Kerry shrugged as if it were a matter of indifference to him what his father thought or was.

'I do know all about the collection, Grace.' His remarks were now addressed to his daughter. Patrick didn't trust himself to speak to Kerry.

'I think it's a great idea. I don't believe it will cure her but they do say, and I've heard all kinds of people say this, even people who would scorn the whole idea of miracles . . . They say that nobody ever comes back from Lourdes the worse for having been there, they all come back better in some way. Happier, more resigned, feeling that compared to what they saw there then they aren't too badly off.'

Kerry smiled. 'That's well put,' he said admiringly. 'Send people off there so they see what terrible things other people have, they come home quietened . . . I never heard that line.'

Patrick ignored him. 'I could have given Kate Ryan a cheque to take her to Lourdes, Gracie, but I didn't, I felt it had to come from her own people here. Not from us.'

'Like Mary Donnelly?'

'Exactly. So of course I've contributed to the fund, but nothing excessive.'

'You know, I misjudged you, Father.' Kerry seemed genuinely admiring now. But with Kerry it was often hard to know.

There was no time to discuss it. A shadow passed the window.

'Oh Jesus,' Patrick said, 'it's Marian.'

Marian was full of chat. She had come to invite them all to be her guests at an upcoming angling festival.

Patrick would simply love it, she said, it was tailor-made for him, he would get the entire atmosphere of one of these occasions at first hand, he would know how to describe it to those Americans who were keen fishermen. There would be an excellent buffet lunch in a marquee to which they would be invited.

It would be frightfully boring for the young people of course, lots of standing round talking and drinking. But possibly they would love it too. Or it might even be that they would prefer to be with their own friends that day. They must do whichever they pleased, come with her to the lake or stay here in Mountfern and have a great time. Their decision entirely.

Covering the snuffles and giggles of his children, Patrick said graciously and firmly that he would let her know tomorrow. He hadn't yet been able to work out their plans next week.

Patrick thought that it was no mean achievement that he had managed to conduct the entire conversation extremely courteously but without allowing Marian to sit down. In what was after all her own house.

Brian Doyle telephoned Patrick to say that it was probably unimportant but there was some paint daubed on the wooden hoarding around some of the digging on the site. They'd have it removed but he thought Patrick should know.

'What does it say?'

'It says Yanks Go Home, but I wouldn't take a blind bit of notice of that,' said Brian Doyle.

Marian Johnson was extremely put out when her offer to show Patrick the lake and introduce him to the people who ran angling in the country was so suddenly and almost curtly refused.

Patrick had been apologetic but had given no real explanation. Marian had the bad luck to run into Jack Coyne who had said that it was devoutly to be hoped that Patrick O'Neill hadn't any plans to build a monstrosity like the Slieve Sunset, because that was the place he was seen hurrying in and out of at all hours of the day and night, and that he was there at this moment with that foreign-looking woman, the one with the beautiful hair.

Marian Johnson patted her own sparse hair, newly arranged in the Rosemarie hair salon for an outing which was not now going to take place.

It was impossible to make sense of Patrick O'Neill. He had spent his entire life getting ready to come home, to mix with the best in the land. She had been ready to introduce him to people from Prosperous and Belturbet, from Boyle and Ballinasloe. She knew the families who owned the fishing rights from Lough Ree to Lough Allen, from the Erne to the Lee. She had already made sure he had met the Master socially so that he would not be considered an outsider when it came to foxhunting. And what was the thanks she got, his sneaking away to see that woman in the Slieve Sunset. But there couldn't be anything in it. Not after all his hopes of coming home and being Irish, properly Irish. He could never get involved with a foreign woman, not at this stage.

Kate didn't remember meeting Rachel Fine before. She was dark and exotic-looking, with a beautiful suit that must have cost a fortune. She wore a scarf in such an elegant way too. Usually you only saw people in photographs wearing scarves like that; when they moved it would go into a rag.

She came towards the bed. 'Your husband says you have a very sketchy memory of the day.'

'Very.' Kate felt at a loss with this elegant woman.

'Perhaps that's good, it means you won't remember too much about the shock and the pain.'

'No, I can't remember that at all. I can only remember waking up here and someone telling me it was three days before.' Kate's face closed up in pain at the memory.

'I believe there are some wonderful surgeons here, Patrick tells me that his hotshot from New York was highly impressed.'

Patrick. She called him Patrick. Nobody else who worked with him did. It was coming back to her. John had told her that Rachel Fine was some kind of decorator or designer, she had been staying out in the Slieve Sunset, and then she went on a tour to see about ordering Irish fabrics and things. John had been very vague.

'You're very good to come and see me. Especially as I've been a bit like a madam and saying I didn't want people to come.'

'No way should you have people gaping at you if you don't feel like it.'

Rachel was gentle and easy, she was no effort to talk to. She explained that she had brought glossy magazines, the kind of thing you wouldn't dream of buying for yourself or reading when you were well. Kate, who had read nothing in the weeks she lay here, was pleased. Those magazines she could just about manage, she felt.

'Why *did* you come?' she asked suddenly.

'Because . . . when I had just arrived in Mountfern you made me welcome. I was sitting in that pub waiting for Patrick to come in, I was anxious and tense and you were kind to me. I liked you.'

It was a flowery speech. Kate paused for a moment. Then it came back to her the way it had before. She was Patrick O'Neill's woman!

Perhaps the woman saw the recognition in her eyes. Anyway she went on to speak of it.

'I thought you were someone I could talk to. I can't tell you how distressed I was. How unreal it seemed when you were so lively and laughing . . .' Her eyes filled with tears.

Something in Kate responded to her warmly. Here was someone who was not afraid to say it was a bloody tragedy. For the first time since it happened, she looked into the face of another human being who was prepared to admit that Kate was very very unlucky, someone to be pitied rather than jollied along. It was a huge relief.

'Thank you,' Kate began, and found to her horror that she was beginning to sob. 'Thank you. I *was* lively and laughing, wasn't I? I wasn't always like this. I *was* able to run and move and grab things up rather than lie here while people rub oil and powder on me like a giant baby. I used to decide what to do and where to go myself. I did, I did.'

'Yes, that's the way you were.' She was matter of fact.

Kate waited for the cheery sentence saying that she'd be like that again some day. But it didn't come.

'It's so unfair,' Rachel said instead. 'I'd be able to cope with life if it wasn't so terribly unjust. All you were doing is looking. Standing looking and thinking about what the place was going to be like, and you end up with your back broken, lying here.'

Such warmth and sympathy meant that Kate didn't have to put on any act in return, she didn't have to bite her lip and be stoic like she did for John, nor pretend a jolly getting-better-every-day role as she did with the children.

She cried and cried and Rachel held her face to her and didn't mind about the tears all over her good suit, and didn't call the nurse. After a while the crying stopped as unexpectedly as it had begun. Kate looked tired.

'Can I come and see you again?' Rachel asked.

'Please. Please.'

Patrick wasn't pleased.

'Why didn't you tell me you were going to see her?

'I don't have to tell you everything.'

'It was sneaky and underhand.'

'I honestly think you can't be well to say something like that. What on earth could be underhand about going to see someone in hospital?'

'You didn't ask me should you go.'

'I am not your servant, nor your ten-year-old child. You have told me often enough that you want us to lead separate lives here. I am trying to do that, and now that doesn't seem to please you either.' Rachel's eyes flashed in an unaccustomed display of anger.

'No, but you wouldn't have mentioned it, I would never have known if Grace hadn't told me.'

'Grace. Yes.'

'Oh, don't take that tone, Grace was full of how much Mrs Ryan loved you and how nice you were, she got it all from the twins. She told me in innocence, not full of tittle-tattle as you are trying to imply.'

'This conversation is getting nowhere. Shall we talk about something else? Work perhaps. I have some samples to discuss with you for wall hangings.'

'To hell with wall hangings . . . What did she say?'

'Kate Ryan? Not much really. She cried a lot. But that was between us.' Rachel stood up and walked restlessly around the plastic and Formica lobby of Slieve Sunset. Since the incident of their discovery in Rachel's bedroom on the day of the accident Patrick had been most anxious that all meetings should take place in the public eye and that they be known as colleagues.

'It's just that it wouldn't be a good idea to say anything,' Patrick began. He looked troubled and not like his usual decisive self.

'Say anything?' Rachel was nonplussed.

'Yeah, well I know this sounds a bit odd, but the lawyers said not to say anything, anything that might admit liability.'

'You can't be serious.'

'I know, that's what I said, but they say you're not dealing with decent people like the Ryans, there's always a load of gangsters waiting to get on the bandwagon if they can. Urging people on to litigation.'

'But what litigation? You said you'd pay?'

'Yes I did and I will, but there's a danger that people could take you for all you had if you admit too much, that's all.'

'I don't understand you at all. You told me that you had made several attempts to see her. So why are *you* going? Isn't it much more likely that *you* would commit yourself or whatever?'

'No, because I'm a careful man. I guess I was just afraid you might have said something like Patrick will look after everything.'

'I didn't say it because I assume she knows it, and so does everyone.'

'Let's stop this, Rachel,' he said wearily.

'Yes, let's.' She was back in her passive role of pleasing him now. She didn't remind him that it was he who had started the conversation and refused to let it go.

He looked old and worried.

'Wouldn't it be great if Mary Donnelly would smile sometimes?' Fergus said confidentially to Sheila Whelan. 'She's not a bad-looking woman, but there's a terrible ferocity about her.'

'She puts that on. Underneath she's as nice as anything.'

'Well, life is short. You wouldn't have the energy to dig down for it,' Fergus said.

'She's doing well enough above in the pub, I think?' Mrs Whelan's voice was anxious. 'She's not putting people off by glowering at them, is she?'

'It would take more than a glower to put a thirsty man off his drink. Not at all, she's part of the furniture there now, and John is delighted with her. He says she's the most efficient person he ever had working in a bar in his life.'

'She's grand if she has plenty to do.'

'There's plenty in that house all right. How poor Kate ever managed *and* did my work as well I'll never know.'

'You speak of her as if she were dead, Fergus. She'll be home in a matter of weeks.'

'She might as well be dead for all her life can give her now.'

'Lord Almighty, I hope you don't go saying that to her.'

'I haven't been allowed near her to say anything.' He sounded bitter.

'Well, she just wanted the family for a while.'

'Oh, but I think I'll be allowed to go next week. After all, O'Neill's tart has been in so that should open the floodgates.'

'That is not only unlike you, it's disgusting.'

Fergus said nothing.

'We're all upset by what happened, you're not the only one to feel it. You'd be a very unwise man to talk like that. I mean it.'

He had never known her so sharp.

He nodded. 'Right.'

'If you know how much I mean it. We need people like you of good sense, people who are right about things and know what to do. Half the people have gone mad in Mountfern since Patrick O'Neill came, and Kate's accident is only one of the big changes we'll have to see here. Fergus, let you not change too, I beg you.'

'It was a cheap, vulgar thing to say. I'm glad I have a good friend like you to put me right from time to time.'

'That's the only time I ever tried to put you right in my life,' Sheila said simply. She patted his hand. They were indeed friends.

The traction was over. They were moving her into a chair. Everyone spoke about it as if it were a huge breakthrough, as if she were going to be able to fly.

Kate felt leaden. She'd had a low feeling since she woke but she tried to take part in all the enthusiasm around her. After all it would be ungracious and mulish not to show pleasure at a step forward.

It didn't hurt, the moving, they were able to lift her and anticipate what would give a stab of pain and what would be fine, and really there was a lot of her that didn't ache at all.

There was a little team around her, the nice young nurse Geraldine and the staff nurse, there was Sister Winston, and two of the hospital porters who seemed to be on call for everything that involved movement, from ambulance stretchers to windows that were stuck with paint. The great Mr Brown the surgeon was there, and so were two physiotherapists.

She got her first shock when she saw the chair. It was a wheelchair.

'I didn't think . . .' Her hand was at her throat.

Sister Winston was quick. She must have been used to this reaction. 'Why be in a chair that can just face one way when you can face any way in this?'

'But an ordinary chair would do . . .'

'It would *do*, certainly, but you wouldn't be able to go to the window and back to your bed or to the handbasin.'

'I don't *want* to go to any of those places, I just want to sit in a chair like an ordinary person.'

'This one's been prepared for you; tomorrow we can discuss an ordinary chair.'

There were so many people looking and hoping for her to be well and upright in the chair, Kate could say no more.

'Of course,' she said in a small voice. 'I'm sorry.'

The lifting was surprisingly easy, just a gradual movement. After those weeks of lying down and thinking it was normal to wake looking at the ceiling and that people always talked bending over you slightly, it was going to be hard to readjust to sitting up again.

They had eased her into the chair, her legs wrapped well in a rug. The family would be so pleased to see her sitting up, the nurses said. The porters who had brought the chair smiled their pleasure. Mr Brown said she was making great progress, the two physiotherapists moved here and there to settle her. And that was it. She sat and tried to smile back at all the good humour around. But the smile wouldn't come.

She felt faint, and a roaring in her ears.

They saw it at once, and her head was pushed down. A glass of water, medication was discussed and waved away. It often happened. Sister Winston had seen it all before. That's why she never let the friends and relatives in until much later.

Kate Ryan's mouth was in an O of horror, her hands gripped the sides of the chair.

'I can't feel . . .' she cried. 'I can't feel it.'

'What can't you feel?' Geraldine was on her knees beside the chair, holding Kate's hand. 'Shush now, you're grand altogether, everyone's delighted with you . . .'

'I can't feel my bottom, I have no bottom, no legs, nothing. There's only emptiness where I'm sitting in the chair.'

Mr Brown was gentle. 'You've known always . . . you've known about the paralysis. The realization comes and goes. You've adapted so well in traction, now it's just a new adapting.'

'It's like air, it's not real. I can't be going to live like this till I die, can I?' Kate looked around piteously at the semi-circle.

'No no,' said Geraldine soothingly.

'I couldn't stand years of this, I couldn't stand it. There's nothing *there*,' Kate cried.

The silence of sympathy broken by clucks of encouragement frightened her even more. Perhaps there weren't going to *be* years ahead. Perhaps her life might be nearly over already.

They put the family off. It seemed the wisest thing. They said there was no cause for alarm but she needed sedation and it would be tiring for Mrs Ryan rather than comforting to have to cope with visitors.

They didn't tell John that his wife sat for her first day in a wheelchair staring ahead of her and thinking of a life of dependency on others. Thinking of the fears she would have . . . or they all would have if she got any infection and she might not have the strength to fight it.

She thought about the children having to push an old mother around in a wheelchair; because she would be an old mother, she might as well be their grandmother for all the say she was going to have in things, for all the fun and companionship she could give them.

She thought about the bar and what would happen if Patrick's hotel took away all their business from them as she had been afraid it would. They couldn't go on living on his charity as they already were, a private room, a car at John's beck and call, and anything she said she'd like she knew he would give her.

It wasn't his fault that she had walked past those notices saying danger, and men at work. It wasn't Patrick's fault that she had walked across the line of a man with a digger who had not expected there to be another human on that part of the site.

But Kate wept as she had never wept lying flat on her bed. This was the best she could hope for. This terrible dependent sitting posture worse altogether than lying down, which everyone knew was only temporary.

And when she had learned how to propel the bloody thing with her weak arms and learned how to lift her wasted legs out of it and on to some hideous-looking lavatory bowl, they would say she was cured and send her home. Cured! Cured to go home a cripple and watch this Mary Donnelly, whoever she was, taking Kate's place.

Mary Donnelly didn't want to speak to the men from the brewery or the men from the distillery who called to the pub.

'I've had quite enough huggermugger with men since I came to this establishment,' she said to John. 'And in any event you are the man of the house, whatever that expression means. You should talk to them yourself.'

John sighed. Every day he realized more how much of the running of the household Kate had done. Had he been properly grateful? No of course he had not. He had taken it for granted. Now there was no time to go and write his poems, there was no time to take a walk to clear his head after the smoke and noise in the bar. The days fell into a pattern.

As August became September and Mary got the children ready to go back to school, John began to think he had known no other life than the one where he was picked up at two o'clock in the afternoon and driven in to see his invalid wife in a hospital bed. Like any life, some days were better than others. Sometimes Kate was tired and impatient after long sessions trying to use the wheelchair and manoeuvre herself from bed to chair, with failure all the way. Some days she was elated. There were times when he was tired and depressed and picked a row, there were good afternoons where he sat and talked to her easily without either of them thinking how the situation had changed and would still be changed when he got her home.

He was glad that she seemed friendly with Rachel. He couldn't quite see what they had to talk about and giggle at, but it was undoubtedly good for her.

She didn't want too many visitors, she said, it tired her, so it was rationed to one a day apart from the family and Rachel. John was pleased that she now saw Fergus Slattery, the poor fellow seemed to be most upset about her and very black about apportioning blame and responsibility. He even kept trying to make appointments with John to talk about the case, and the compensation.

'What case?' John had wanted to know. 'There's no case, surely. It was a terrible accident.'

Fergus had become more impatient than ever about it. And finally Kate said that John should agree to talk about it. Just to calm Fergus down.

'You don't know the way he is, John. I worked for him, remember? He's up to his eyes in the letter of the law, not what things people are really involved in. You should see the small prints, and the clauses about this and about that, and the whereases. It's a different world. Just do me a favour and go to see him in his office, tell him how good Patrick has been, tell him we're not the kind of people who sue over things, it would be flying in the face of God.'

'The office? But that would be like as if I'd gone in order to take him on.'

'You're not going to get much talked about in the pub, are you? The door opening every time you're getting somewhere?'

He agreed. Unwillingly. And went to Fergus on a bright September morning.

Miss Purcell had told him of a novena that was being done for Kate and a bouquet of masses which would be offered on the first Tuesday of the month. She wondered when would poor Mrs Ryan be able to travel to Lourdes, the fund had been generously subscribed. Eventually John got away from her and sat down in the room where his wife used to work every morning.

'Haven't you got anyone yet?' he asked kindly, knowing that Fergus Slattery had put off getting any permanent help out of loyalty to Kate and to the belief that she might work again.

'Your wife told me off about that too. I'll have to, I will. Soon.'

'Right.' John didn't nag him, he knew how irritating it was to be told to do something if you didn't want to. Jack Coyne was always urging him to get a new roof or a light-up sign over the pub. Things that sounded sensible things that he might do one day, but not immediately.

'I'll speak as simply and quickly as I can, John. I know you don't want to be here in case it looks as if you're going to take Patrick O'Neill to court, so I'll try to put you in the picture as best I can.'

'I know you will, Fergus.' John nodded politely like an obedient child.

Fergus felt his collar a bit tight around his neck, and loosened it with his finger. He seemed almost reluctant to begin now that he had the undivided attention of the man who was usually moving away to pull pints or to greet those who came in the door.

'Well, it's a matter of just spelling it out,' he said.

John looked at him and waited.

'And if there's anything you don't agree with you'll say . . . of course.'

'Of course,' John agreed.

'Well, obviously it *wasn't* the time before, with everything being so upset and on top of us, but now we have to think in terms of practicalities. Like what happens when Kate comes home.'

John was silent. He was looking around the room thoughtfully as if imagining Kate working here, moving quickly from typewriter to cupboard, from big scales where she would have weighed the long narrow envelopes of documents before they were taken to Sheila Whelan's to post.

'John,' Fergus said.

'Yes, I know, practicalities. Well, those are being thought of in most ways. Judy Byrne will come in three times a week at first to keep Kate doing the exercises. And Patrick's getting his builders to even out the floor levels so that she can come into the pub on the chair without anyone having to lift it. He's been very generous, Patrick has, generous and thoughtful.' John's glance went round the lawyer's office again, slowly and deliberately.

Fergus could barely conceal his irritation.

'I don't doubt that. *No*, look at me, John, I know you've heard me giving out about the man, I don't doubt that he has been generosity itself, but can I beg you to listen? Now two years ago there was this act passed, the Civil Liability Act of 1961, and up to this there were just three kinds of person who were deemed to exist on your land: an invitee, a licensee and a trespasser. There were no other people. So if anyone got injured the decision was, which kind of person were they? If they were an invitee they got one kind of compensation, a licensee got another – a licensee would be somebody, say, who had permission to be there in some category or other – and the trespasser got another.'

He saw John fidgeting.

'Please listen John, I'm making it very short and you'll see why it is important in a minute. There used to be lots of innocent trespassers, people who weren't intending trespass . . .'

'But Kate wasn't . . .'

'*Listen*, will you, like children or like Kate, say, who was a neighbour and friend . . . So the law was changed making the landowner more liable than he used to be in the old days. So Patrick or his insurance company has a legal liability to pay compensation . . .'

'But he has, I tell you, we don't want to be blackmailing him . . .'

'The law; God Almighty, the law of the land we live in says he has to pay it, he knows he has to pay it, he doesn't live in some cloud-bloody-cuckoo-land like you do.'

'Why are you shouting at me, Fergus?'

'I don't know. I don't know. I think it's because I'm being so long winded and you won't wait till I get to the point.'

'All right.'

'So the system is you have to sue Patrick. Kate has to sue him. That's the machinery, that's the way it's done. His insurance company won't pay, can't pay until there's a case set up, until the proper requirements of the law are complied with.'

'We don't want to sue him.'

'He knows that, you know that, I know that, his lawyers know that. Even his insurance company knows that. Jesus, Mary and Joseph, people are suing each other day in and day out who are the best of friends.'

218

'I don't believe you!'

'But it's the way, it's the system. You know Marian Johnson up at the Grange. When she was about eighteen she drove her father home from some place out the country and they had an accident, he was badly injured, he sued her. The insurance company gave him compensation. He didn't sue her because he was her enemy, he sued her because that's how it's done. That's the way you unlock the money.'

'It seems very hypocritical and devious to me.'

Fergus was weary. 'It's not really, John, it's sensible, it's the only way to keep control, otherwise insurance companies would have to be paying out huge awards and they couldn't afford it and the premiums would be enormous. This way at least they know it's a genuine case when the parties are prepared to go to court about it. It gives them a sort of authenticity, if you see what I mean.'

'You're very good at explaining the law, and you obviously understand it too, which is more than a lot of lawyers . . . but Fergus, do you have any understanding at all about what it is to be a neighbour? I mean, you're here in this house in the middle of the street, nothing changes for you no matter who comes to live here. You don't depend on good will and rubbing along with people like we do in a pub. It doesn't make sense to go into a court of law and say things about a neighbour, things that cannot be unsaid.' John was calm but he seemed very resolute.

Fergus tried again.

'There'll be very little said, and you and Patrick won't have to do any of the saying. The question is, would you like a different solicitor?'

'Not you?'

'I'm very close to you, to all of you. Perhaps it might be easier with someone from the town. It often is.'

'If we want to have anyone, Fergus, then Kate and I would want to have you.'

'Right.'

'Do we need to do anything immediately?'

'No, not for a while, leave it with me.'

'Oh and Fergus, could you explain to Patrick O'Neill about it all being friendly when it starts? You know, tell him about Marian Johnson in the Grange and her father and all. It would make it a bit less formal.'

'I don't need to tell him that, he's a businessman, John, he knows.'

'I'd like you to tell him all the same.'

'If it comes up easily I will,' Fergus said.

CHAPTER FOURTEEN

Patrick was pleased to get a message from Rachel that Kate would like to see him on Friday afternoon.

'She must be getting better, is she?' he asked.

'She says she is,' Rachel said doubtfully. 'I think she looked a bit feverish, excited. Still, it's better than all that terribly depressed way she was last week.'

'What would she like? She has a radio, you say?'

'Yes, she hardly listens to it. She might like a game – Scrabble, say. She could play it with the little guys when they go in.'

'That's a great idea, Rachel,' he beamed. 'Where in the world will I get Scrabble? I may have to go to Dublin for it, or Shannon.'

'Don't be silly. I'll get it for you.'

She had already got a set, and many other things. She wanted Kate to think that Patrick was thoughtful and concerned.

John sat on the edge of the bed and told Kate everything.

'He seems dead set that there's going to be a case,' she said, biting at her lower lip.

'I'm just reporting everything that he said, and trying to give you the sort of tone he said it in.'

'You're doing very well.' She grinned ruefully. 'I can practically hear him speaking.'

'He's so out for our good, he wants the best for you.'

'The best for me is not to have to lock horns with Patrick O'Neill in public. The best would be not having to lie here worrying myself sick what he'll think, what he'll do when we turn on him like an ungrateful dog. That's what it's going to be like, John, no matter how many fine words Fergus says about the law . . .'

She was distressed, her eyes full of tears and her face red with exertion.

John took her hand. 'You're not going to spend any time lying here worrying, not even five minutes. I'll tell you what we'll do . . . and you're the one who can do it.'

Soothing and shushing down her protests he explained to her that she could sort everything out if she happened by accident to arrange that Patrick O'Neill and Fergus Slattery should both turn up at the same time in her hospital bedroom.

Then it could all be said out in the open.

Fergus was told by the hospital that Friday would be a good day to come in and see Mrs Ryan. He drove glumly to the hospital. She had been so low the last time, it had been an effort to keep up any kind of conversation at all.

He had brought the application forms of the four young women who had applied for jobs as his secretary. He knew two of them, daughters of local farmers who had done secretarial courses. He thought they would be very unlikely candidates, he wanted Kate's advice badly. Wouldn't it be great if she was in good sparkling form? Dr White said that some days she was the old Kate, laughing and joking, and you would think she was just lying down for a rest. Other times she had been awake all night, convinced she had not very much longer to live, and was railing at the injustice of it.

Please may it be a good day. For all their sakes.

She was as flushed as a girl, he hoped it was a good sign. She was delighted that he had brought the confidential files, and urged strongly in favour of Deirdre Dunne, a girl who lived about three miles away.

'Look, she's given you all kinds of detail, like how it will be no trouble to get a lift in and out. That's sensible. And I know Deirdre, her father comes into Ryan's. A tighter-mouthed man you never met. He wouldn't tell you what day it was let alone anyone else's business.'

She was indeed like the old Kate, teasing him, sending him up, full of plans. Rachel Fine had said that her room should be moved downstairs; soon builders would go in and flatten out all the steps in the downstairs so she could come into the pub and the kitchen. The parlour was going to be made into a big bed-sitting room for her, with a special bathroom beside it. There would be a rail all round it, and garden doors – you know those French windows with glass in them down to the floor – out to the side yard, which would be made posh, and she could wheel herself out there.

Fergus took off his glasses and wiped them because they had misted up with delight that she was able to think of a life after this white hospital room, and with pity that it would be limited by wheelchairs and rails round walls.

John Ryan came in then, told him to sit where he was, no need to go, he'd been in and out a dozen times during the afternoon and would be again. Just then there was a tap, and Patrick stood there.

He looked shy in his country tweeds and his crisp shirt, and his curly hair combed just outside the door. In his arms he held a big gift-wrapped parcel and a glass bowl with fruit in it. Nothing very dramatic, just healthy-looking apples and thick-skin oranges and two yellow pears.

Fergus wished he had brought something like that instead of the box of sweets which lay on the cabinet beside the bed.

'They tell me that I'd find you better today than any day.' Patrick was lit up with pleasure. You could see it.

Kate stretched out her arms in greeting from the bed.

'Thank you for all you've done. I can never thank you enough. The room, the car for everyone to come in and out. You've been too good.'

'I couldn't do enough, Kate, to tell you how sorry I am that it had to happen. And if it did have to happen why did it have to be on my land, with diggers working for me?'

There was no mistaking his sincerity.

'Don't I know that. I've every proof of it,' Kate said.

Patrick seemed to notice for the first time that John and Fergus were in the room. He went to John first and shook him by the hand.

'My, doesn't she look well, after all she's been through.'

It was just the right touch, Fergus thought miserably. He in no way minimized her agonies, yet he concentrated on the hopeful side. Then it was Fergus's turn.

'Slattery, you must be as pleased as all of us. It's a good time to meet.'

'Yup.' Fergus got this urge to behave like a taciturn cowboy every time he met Patrick O'Neill nowadays. The fact that he was somehow ungracious made him even more annoyed with himself.

'And I'm very glad you both happen to be here at the same time,' Kate said, looking at them eagerly from her bed, her cheeks pink, her hair tied with a yellow ribbon matching the ribbon in her lacy bedjacket, both given to her by Rachel Fine.

'Why is that?' Fergus was suspicous: Kate was too bright, John was looking at the floor.

Patrick knew nothing about it, whatever it was. He smiled to know what Kate was going to say.

'Because I am determined to get out of here and live a proper life again, and I'm tired of people coming to my bed and talking about formalities. All I want to know now, and it will help me to get better, is that there will never be any animosity between us no matter what formalities there are.'

'How could there be animosity?' Patrick cried.

'Kate, why don't you leave this until later? Until you're better,' Fergus said levelly.

'One of the things stopping me getting better is this,' she said. 'Honestly it is, I swear it, at night I wake up and think my life is over, it's so unfair; and other nights I wake up and think of the things people tell me down in physiotherapy – that I should claim this and I should claim that, and it would make life more bearable, and it's all from faceless insurance companies anyway so nobody gets hurt. Then I think of Patrick living beside us and what it's going to be like, and of Grace and Kerry and the twins and how I'd hate a fight more than anything . . . So that's why I'm asking you, my friends, will it be done without animosity?'

Fergus opened his mouth and closed it again like a fish.

John said nothing, but laid his hand supportively on Kate's arm.

Patrick O'Neill smiled more broadly than ever as if he could have heard no better news than this current subject Kate wanted to discuss. 'But of course we'll talk about it, from now until you feel too tired. Kate, John, I assure you I was only waiting until you felt *able* to talk about it. And obviously since you have Mr Slattery here too I feel he would be glad it was brought up as soon as . . .'

'I assure you, Mr O'Neill,' Fergus began a trifle pompously.

'No, I know it just happened to come up, but let me say something, hand on heart, for weeks now I've been wanting to say to someone of you three and never finding the right moment. I *know* the law, I am so well insured it would make your head swim. The courts will decide a compensation and they will pay it.

'Kate, you can never get your spine back, but you can get *some* comforts, goddamn it. I'll see to it that you do.'

'But we don't want to go to court against *you*, Patrick,' John said, avoiding Fergus's eye.

'Nobody wants to go to court and maybe we mightn't even have to go inside the door,' said Patrick. 'It could all be settled at the last moment. That's what always happens. But that's the machinery, that's the formula . . . the same way as there's a process for getting a licence for a pub or permission to hold a raffle . . . That's right, isn't it, Attorney?'

Fergus nodded, not trusting himself to speak. The man was making himself clear in a way that Fergus hadn't been able to do. John and Kate hadn't trusted him. He felt his mouth full of acid. 'That's right,' he said.

'So, let's get the insurance guys, hey? God, if you know how much they get me for every year. It will be a pleasure to get them to give you as much as we can squeeze from them. All I say, though, is that it's a shame crying out to heaven that it has to be over something like this.'

He was so full of generosity, no mention of the no-claim bonus he would lose, no mention of the pressure that giant insurance companies who handled his business both here and in America would put on him. Fergus felt moved by the man's warmth. But in his heart he felt sure that Patrick was right. Some settlement would be reached on the steps of a courthouse, and at this moment Patrick knew exactly how much it was.

Fergus felt an urge so strong that it was almost overpowering to take him on and fight him in every court of the land, refusing offers, settlements and recommendations until he got for Kate Ryan something that would even in a paltry way compensate for the life that Patrick O'Neill and his mechanical diggers had taken away from her.

Later he remembered, with his mouth in a thin line, that the cute fox O'Neill had said nothing about the private room in the hospital being a gift from Patrick to Kate or the use of a car for the Ryan family being a gift from Patrick to Kate. Oh, no. These would be included in the settlement when the time came.

He remembered how pleased Kate had been with the game of Scrabble. He wished he had thought of it, with a pain that almost tore him in two.

He felt that there was great truth in Mrs Whelan's words that everyone had gone a little mad since O'Neill came to Mountfern. He hoped he hadn't gone madder than most. Fergus knew that he must do something practical rather than sit and rage against what had been done and couldn't be undone.

He decided to teach John Ryan to drive and get them a second-hand car somewhere so that O'Neill couldn't claim months more of transport when the day of reckoning arrived.

It was so strange going back to school without their mother to harass them and organize the huge hunt for satchels, textbooks and clean shirts, and shoes being taken to the mender's. This is what the end of the summer holidays meant before.

Mary Donnelly had it all in order. The Ryans' house had never worked in such a streamlined way before. There was no fuss about going back to school. All the clothes were ready mended and ironed anyway. The children had almost forgotten a time when they didn't strip and air their beds every day, and when there wasn't a weekly examination of shoes and clothes, so that the one could be brought to old Mr Foley's odd wordless brother who stitched away silently at the soles of Mountfern in the back of Foley's bar. Clothes were all darned or mended at that weekly session too.

Kate Ryan in her hospital bed looked in amazement at neat patches and false hems to be told that Dara and Eddie were a dab hand at any kind of dressmaking now. Michael and Declan had resisted it and were responsible for shoe polishing instead.

A cupboard had been cleared in the dining room and all schoolbooks and bags were stored there. The four children had a shelf each. The summer exercises had continued, and even Eddie was able to approach an exercise book now without scribbling all over it. Mary had always shown such surprise and horror at any doodling it was easier to leave the book clean.

And when school did begin Mary seemed to regard it with a reverence that the children found disconcerting. She almost spoke of school in hushed tones. She managed to inquire about their progress and particularly about what homework they had to do with an air of such interest that they did not realize how much they were giving themselves away and putting their lives into her hands.

'Now, Dara, let me help you clear away, you've got all those geography questions to do tonight, you said. And Michael has that big long poem to learn. Eddie, you aren't too badly off – only ten sums, was it?'

They would look at each other glumly. Why had they been so specific? Now there was no escape.

The breakfast room became a study both before and after tea. There was always a dictionary, an atlas, rulers, pencils and spare paper. The wireless was turned down respectfully. Callers were discouraged and if their father ever came looking for them for anything, the children heard Mary speaking to him in low urgent tones explaining that they were doing their homework. It was said in the voice that someone might have used about the College of cardinals being in conclave to elect a pope. And after a few false starts it worked. The homework did get finished, and almost in silence. It was easier to learn the poem, Michael would decide, rather than have Mary offer to hear it to him at breakfast and expose his ignorance. Dara would find that Mary, when approached about homework that had been completed, was always cooperative and helped to get her better marks, but Mary would not even discuss work that had been left undone.

Eddie felt life was too short to have to put up with Mary mentioning that she must ask Brother Keane why the children in Eddie's class got no homework. It really was simpler to admit to the homework and do it. Then at least he would be free.

Declan at seven didn't have very much homework, but he liked the scene around the table. Mary had drawn him a map of Ireland and he spent each evening colouring in the different counties and labelling them. He had asked Mary was this the kind of thing a person could do in a circus as a trick. Mary had said that to be truthful it hadn't been done much, but there was no reason why there couldn't be a first time. And she could say hand on heart that to know the thirty-two counties of Ireland, how to spell them and where they all were would be something that would advance you in *any* career. So Declan sat happily mastering difficult spellings like Monaghan and Laoghais.

Sometimes John looked in at the industry and gave a deep sigh of relief.

By the time he got Kate home, some kind of order would reign in the house, and all the time Kate's new domain was being built. With huge financial help from

Patrick O'Neill, and great advice and care from Patrick's lady friend Rachel Fine. Even Leopold was better behaved these days, John noticed, and slept outside Mary's door on a sack which he dragged out to the yard each evening. It was as if he lay there protecting her from the world.

'What does Kerry do all the time? He's never around and his school doesn't open for another week.' Dara and Grace were sitting in Dara's room. Sometimes Grace came to do her homework too; Mary Donnelly looked in and out casually to make sure that the time was not being wasted around the table, but the little O'Neill girl seemed industrious enough.

'Kerry never says. I think he studies quite a lot. This is his last year, he wants to get a good Leaving Cert.'

'And will he?' Dara loved to hear news of the handsome Kerry. 'Will he get a lot of Honours do you think?'

'He thinks he'll get four. Or so he says, I don't know.' Grace seemed doubtful.

'Why don't you know?'

Grace wondered whether to speak and then decided she would.

'Well, I just said I think he studies a lot, I'm not sure. You see, he goes to these extra lessons.'

'The Latin, with Mr Williams?'

'No, as well as those. He goes into the town twice a week, there's a schoolmaster there and Kerry's meant to be going for math.'

'Maths,' corrected Dara automatically.

'Yes, well, whichever, he's not going to it. He takes the money from Father and he gets a lift with Paudie Doyle or Brian or someone, but the teacher called last week to say he was sorry that Kerry hadn't taken up the lessons.' Grace shook her head.

'Where was he?'

'That's it, I have no idea; and as it happened, I answered the telephone. Not Miss Hayes, and not Father. So I just said that I'd pass on the message and the man said he just wanted to clear things up because Father had sent him some kind of letter thanking him for his time.'

'Oh dear,' Dara said.

'So it looks as if Kerry wasn't going at all. But saying that he was.'

The girls sat in silence to contemplate the enormity of this.

'What *could* he have been doing instead?' Dara hoped he didn't have a girlfriend or anything awful like that.

'I asked him, but he just laughed, he said it was great I had headed the guy off at the pass, that was the way he said it. And you know Kerry, Dara, he didn't say any more and he will not say any more.'

'Does your father know?'

'No, he does not know.'

'And Miss Hayes, she wouldn't . . .'

'No, I have a feeling that even if she did know she wouldn't . . .'

'Well then, it's all right.' Dara was always optimistic.

'I suppose so.' Grace was less sure.

Tommy Leonard told Michael that the Lourdes fund for Mrs Ryan was getting huge now. There was going to be enough for someone else to go with her. People were wondering who it would be. Would it be Mr Ryan? Or would one of the children get to go? Imagine Lourdes, in France. Imagine being there.

'Do you really think Our Lady came there? She did, didn't she?' Michael was very anxious to have it confirmed. If Our Lady hadn't, if it had all been some kind of misunderstanding, then there would be no chance for Mam.

'I suppose she must have,' Tommy said. 'I mean, it would be the kind of place you'd go, France.'

Michael agreed.

Tommy said that Maggie Daly was often afraid that Our Lady might come to Mountfern, like she came to Fatima. Maggie didn't look up into trees in case she saw her.

'Why doesn't she want to see her?' Michael was interested. 'I mean, if she came here you'd want to *see* her.'

'Maggie thinks that you'd be martyred if you saw her, it's what always happens,' Tommy said.

'Poor Maggie, she's always worrying,' said Michael sympathetically.

'Not like Kitty. Kitty was off on the back of a motorbike with Kerry O'Neill.' Tommy loved a bit of excitement.

'Kerry's not old enough to have a motorbike, is he?'

'Oh, Kerry's old enough for anything, he took it out of Jack Coyne's yard and brought it back secretly, and he and Kitty went off miles on it.'

'How do you know?'

'Maggie told me. Did she not tell you?'

'No. I wonder why?' Michael said.

'Why didn't you tell me all about Kerry and the motorbike and everything?' Dara was furious with Maggie.

'I don't know. It was a secret,' Maggie stammered.

'If it was a secret, Maggie Daly, why did you tell Tommy Leonard?'

'I don't know.'

'Oh, you don't know, you don't know,' Dara blazed. 'You're so boring, Maggie. You don't know anything, you have nothing to say.'

'I know,' Maggie said wretchedly.

There were Halloween games in Ryan's kitchen. Snap apple with everyone's hands tied behind their backs and the apple hanging from a string in the middle of the room. And bobbing for apples in the sink of water, and trying to pick up the sixpence in your teeth from the floor.

Carrie loved the fun of it, and John Ryan came in from the pub occasionally.

Rachel Fine looked on; she had been seeing to Kate's new room and was in and out of the house a lot. The Whites were there, bitterly disputing whose turn it was to play, and Tommy Leonard was there.

'Where's Maggie?' Tommy asked at one point.

'I didn't ask her,' said Dara. 'I forgot. Like she forgets sometimes.'

226

Dara's face was set and cross. She was very annoyed that Maggie had not told her about her sister's carry-on. And she was even more annoyed to hear about Kerry O'Neill off galivanting on a borrowed motorbike.

'I'll run down for her,' Michael said. 'She'd be upset. I'll just go to Daly's now.'

'I'll come with you,' Grace offered.

Dara felt that she had been too mean. She would go herself for Maggie. But it was too late. Michael and Grace had run off.

They came back later without her.

'Her mother said she had a cold, she was in bed.'

'Oh well then, it wouldn't have mattered anyway,' Dara said airily. But in her heart she felt ashamed of herself. And she felt that Maggie didn't really have a cold.

Grace was very nice to Maggie. She insisted too that Maggie come with them on the day that Patrick O'Neill drove some of the children in on what he called an official visit to Mrs Ryan in hospital.

The twins were delighted to show their mother off to Liam, Jacinta, Tommy and Maggie, and Kate was touched to see the small crowd around the bed.

'There's a small fortune in the Lourdes fund, Mrs Ryan, you'll be able to take the whole family with you,' Tommy said enthusiastically.

'My goodness, isn't that generous? But if anyone's going it should be other invalids, don't you think?' Kate said.

'Mrs Williams has a broken arm,' Jacinta suggested.

'You don't go to Lourdes with a broken arm, eejit, you have to have much worse.' Liam looked half fearfully at Kate.

'Oh, I think you can go with anything, really,' Kate said, trying to make light of it.

'Now.' Jacinta was triumphant. 'And Mrs Williams is always very nice, giving us things out of her grden. She should be one of the first to go.'

'She is a Protestant of course,' Tommy said doubtfully.

'Not to mention a vicar's wife,' Kate said, trying to keep her face straight.

'It might convert her to the real faith, though, if she was taken there,' Maggie suggested.

'Particularly if her arm was cured,' Patrick O'Neill laughed.

He shooed the children out of the hospital room and told them there would be lemonade and biscuits.

'You're marvellous to bring them all in to see me,' Kate said. She felt easy and relaxed talking to the big American.

'I love playing the big guy,' he mocked himself.

'No you don't, not at all. You're very fatherly to them all. My twins tell me how kind you've been up at the lodge, teaching them chess and Scrabble and spending the time playing with them, a busy man like you.'

She smiled at him warmly.

'They're very easy to like, your children,' he sighed.

'Well, aren't yours also?' She was genuinely surprised.

'Grace is.'

'Fathers and sons always have friction. It's a known thing.'

'John doesn't.'

'You should hear him with Eddie.'

'Kate, I know you'll forgive my saying this, but most of the Western world has some kind of friction with Eddie at some time or another. No, my case is a bit different.'

He looked very strained somehow.

'Would it help to tell me about it?'

'Some day, maybe. Yes, it might help a lot. But not just now. I have a gang of people who were promised refreshments, I can't welsh on that. And you'll be back home to us soon, isn't that great?' He seemed genuinely delighted.

'In a couple of weeks,' Kate said. 'Then it will be as before.'

His eyes rested on her for a moment. 'It will not be as before, Kate. But please God it will be a good life.' He had so much concern in his voice that it quivered a little.

Kate swallowed and gave him a smile.

They didn't say any more because there wasn't any need.

Dara got a postcard from Kerry O'Neill from the town near his school.

'We are here for a half day, they took us to see a castle on a river. The river is brown and muddy, I think it's nothing compared to the Fern. Glad to hear your mother is coming home soon. Hope to see you all in Mountfern during the Christmas holidays. Kind wishes to all, Kerry.'

Dara hugged it to her and knew every word, not only every word but how every letter of each word was formed.

'Just tell me straight out, Maggie, no dithering, did Kitty get a card from Kerry O'Neill too? Just a yes or a no would do.'

'No. There was no card from Kerry for Kitty. I can tell you that.'

Maggie spoke firmly. Because what she said was true. There had been no postcard for her sister. But Kitty had been looking very cheerful, and there were letters from time to time, which were not discussed. And they did have a postmark of the county where Kerry's school was. But it would be foolish to enter into that kind of speculation. Maggie never wanted to draw things on them. And she had been asked specifically about postcards, nothing else.

Maggie was glad when Dara took her arm. It would have been stupid to upset Dara over something that might not even be true. Kitty could have been getting letters from anyone.

'I hope Mrs Ryan will like the way I run things,' Mary Donnelly said doubtfully.

'Why wouldn't she?' John was unused to Mary in an insecure role.

'She's the mistress of this house, it will be hard for her coming back after five months and seeing another woman in her place.'

'But hasn't she told you over and over how delighted she is with you, and all you've done for us?' John was bewildered. Mary had been a visitor several times to Kate in the hospital. They had got on very well.

'But her coming home, and to that grand room, it will be hard for her not being in total charge again. If you'd like me to go I'd quite understand.'

'Mary, we'd die if you went.' John was alarmed. 'You couldn't go, not now that she's coming back at last. Please don't think of leaving. Is it that you think she'd be giving you orders? Because Kate's not like that. She'll be only too glad for things to go on the way they are. You'll be happy here. Please don't go.'

'I'm very happy here, Mr Ryan. It's very nice, it's the first place I ever thought of as home, and it's a place where people don't make your life a torture for you.'

'But who would make your life a torture for you. Ever?'

'My mother did, my colleagues at the school. The other women round where I lived.'

John was at a loss for words.

'Well,' he said eventually, aware that it wasn't enough.

'So what I say is that Mrs Kate Ryan, if she had to be married and evidently she had, could have done far worse for herself with the husband and three sons that she found.'

John knew he would never hear such praise again.

'Thank you,' he said very seriously. 'I hope we will always be able to have your trust, my sons and I.'

Fergus had found Mary a surprising ally when he was trying to teach John to drive. She had urged the two of them to go out as often as possible, saying that she could well keep an eye on the bar. It never occurred to her that Fergus might have any work to do himself, so she was always putting forward unlikely hours like 11 a.m. as good for a quick lesson.

As it happened the little girl Deirdre he had got for the office was every bit as reliable as Kate said she would be. She was always able to tell a caller that Mr Slattery had gone out on urgent business with a client, and she would take all the details. Somehow, like her father, she gave off a look of utter secrecy. You felt that she would survive well under torture, rather than reveal the most trivial of business.

And she wasn't telling lies, she explained to Fergus. After all, Mr Ryan was a client, and teaching him to drive was important business.

It took twenty lessons, and then John felt confident enough to drive all on his own into the hospital. This too was a secret and a surprise for Kate. Several times he nearly blurted it out, and Rachel Fine nearly let it slip as well.

Then together Fergus and John went to Jack Coyne and put it to him squarely: he was to supply the soundest second-hand car in the world. Not just the country, but the world.

It was to be ready and roadworthy and shining clean on the morning of Friday 23 November, for that was the day it would be driven into the town by John Ryan and he was going to pick up his wife and bring her home to Mountfern.

They all wanted to go, all the children. John said there would be no room in the car. But they wanted to see her face when she saw him driving, that was part of the fun.

Very well, they went with Paudie Doyle as usual, they drove in convoy. Fergus first with Sheila Whelan, then John in the Vauxhall, and then the four Ryan children speechless with excitement in Paudie Doyle's Austin.

There were a lot of tears in the hospital, and Geraldine the nurse said she would miss Kate more than any other patient.

People in wheelchairs came out to say goodbye, and in her own wheelchair she went to say a word to people who weren't even able to move.

She said she'd be in and out of the hospital for treatment.

All the time she thought she was going to be in Paudie Doyle's Austin.

'Where will all the children fit?' she asked Rachel.

'Hush, wait wait.'

Kate knew something was up but she could never have believed anything as splendid as the sight of her husband drawing up in the big black Vauxhall.

Both her hands went up to her mouth as she saw him at the wheel. 'Glory be to God, he'll kill himself,' she said, and then they all cheered.

John Ryan got out with a flourish. 'Here's your coach, Katy Ryan, and your coachman come to take you home and anywhere in the world you want to go.'

In a blur she saw the children's faces in front of her. The twins were struggling with what looked like a banner and Kate saw it had a welcome-home message on it. Eddie and Declan looked faintly mutinous as if they had wanted to share in the banner but had not been allowed to have any part of it.

John had learned to drive, this was their car, he kept saying it. In the confusion it was hard to take in, they had a family car now. The children were racing round it in excitement, Rachel Fine was trying to line them up so that she could take a picture.

John had learned how to drive a car! They could maybe go off for a day without having to ask Jack Coyne or Fergus or Paudie Doyle. *How* had he learned to do that? Were there any more surprises and could she cope with them?

'I'm only crying because I'm so happy,' she said into Declan's tousled head. He had run to throw his arms around her when he saw the tears.

'*I* wanted to have a welcome home,' he snuffled.

'But you have a welcome home for me,' she protested. 'Isn't all this lovely? It's the best welcome I could have.'

'I wanted to put *my* name,' he said, fists digging into his eyes still. 'They wouldn't let me' – a hate-filled glance at the twins.

'But you can do your own when we get back, when we're back in Mountfern. Tell me, Declan, Eddie, am I really going back or is it a dream?'

Eddie took it on himself to explain the realities of the situation. 'It's real enough,' he said grudgingly, pleased to have been singled out to define things.

Kate put her hands out to the twins and their banner. 'Let you both hold it high up there so that Rachel can get it into the picture,' she said.

Her eyes told the twins that the banner was something that had touched her so much she hardly dared speak. She sat with her hands holding theirs tightly as the picture was taken.

And then they moved her to the car. She was near to hysteria as they lifted her into the front seat.

'Don't tell me you can really drive this, John Ryan,' she gasped. And then out the window to the nurses: 'Listen, don't give my room away, I'll be back with more injuries in half an hour.'

But the pride as she sat beside her husband in their own car was shining out like a beacon.

The entourage would follow them, Fergus with Sheila as his passenger, Rachel in her own car, and the Ryan children travelling for the last time in Paudie Doyle's car.

A rug had been placed over Kate's knees, and she sat straight and proud like a queen in the front of the second-hand Vauxhall that Jack Coyne had found as the bargain of the century.

When Rachel turned aside so that nobody would see her brushing away the tears, she saw that the nice nurse and the lawyer were doing the very same thing, wiping their eyes at the sight of so much delight.

Mountfern never forgot the day that Kate Ryan came home from hospital. Years later they could remember every detail of that evening.

It had been arranged that the bar remain open as usual, with Mary Donnelly serving. Sheila Whelan was brought in as well in case there would be extra people there pretending to be having a drink but in reality waiting to see the return of the invalid.

There was a great cry that they were coming when the car was reported to have come in view of the Rosemarie hair salon, and Rita Walsh was out waving from the salon doorstep. Loretto Quinn ran up from her shop, and Brian Doyle ran over the bridge to be there too.

The procession went through the bar, where old men got off stools and shook hands, unable to say the words. They were relieved she was back, and stricken to see her still so pale and sitting awkwardly in a wheelchair.

Carrie was excited, in a new navy dress with a white collar, and she ran in and out of the kitchen a dozen times asking Mary when would she serve the tea. A dozen times Mary replied that she should ask Mrs Ryan.

But Kate was beyond listening to any subtleties like this. There was so much to admire.

Why had nobody told her that the whole place had been repainted? And the steps, all those steps – one down here and one up there – had gone. That must have been huge work, levelling everything.

It *was* a big undertaking, John Ryan agreed, as if he had done it himself. All they had done was stand back and use the back doors while Patrick's men were withdrawn from work on the hotel to do a job on it.

Then there was the room. Kate couldn't believe it. Walls of light green, huge glass doors framed by green flowery curtains. The big bed was white, with a green and white cover. All around the room there was a broad white shelf like a counter, almost. The wheelchair would fit under it, and there were magazines, sewing things, books, files laid out at intervals to suggest activities for Kate. One section of the shelf was a dressing table. It had a mirror and lights around it like a film star would have in a dressing room.

The bathroom was huge. Rachel called it the dressing room. It had huge presses for Kate's clothes, on rails that could be lowered so that she could reach them and choose what to wear. There were drawers that moved in and out silently, effortlessly.

Not like the drawers that stuck and had to be pushed and pulled. The bath had a seat, and a shower, the lavatory had rails. But it wasn't like the hospital bathroom, all white and clinical. It was soft green colours, with big fluffy green towels and bath salts in a big green glass jar.

In her life Kate had never seen anything so elegant. And it was hers. It wasn't something she was looking idly at in a magazine.

They crowded round, Fergus and Brian Doyle, Rachel and Loretto, John in the middle and the children on the edges pushing in and out to see her face.

And that's how they all remembered it because that was when the news came in from the bar where the wireless was on. The news that President Kennedy had been shot in Dallas.

They all went slowly towards the bar to wait for more news. The phone kept ringing, people wanted to tell other people. There was television up in the Grange and some of those with cars said they would drive there and see if they could find out any more. Anything was better than not knowing what had happened to him – the president who had waved at them all in Dublin only five months ago.

'It'd be better for him if he died, poor bastard,' Brian Doyle said in the middle of a silence. 'Young man like that stuck in a wheelchair for the rest of his life. He couldn't take it, he'd go off his head.'

It was a long minute before anyone realized what he had said. They were all thinking of John F. Kennedy, not about Mrs Ryan, a younger woman stuck in a wheelchair for the rest of her life.

Then Brian Doyle noticed a couple of faces crumpling up and remembered.

'But of course they can do great things now,' he said desperately. Nobody helped him out.

'Great things altogether,' said Brian, wishing he was dead and six feet under the clay.

CHAPTER FIFTEEN

The spring of 1964 was a wet one in Mountfern. The river flooded its banks twice, and there were even photographers sent from Dublin to take a picture of the Fern in flood. The trees hung heavy over River Road and let loose what felt like waterfalls when anyone shook them.

The children's raft broke loose from its moorings and bobbed down to the big bridge in the town, where it remained battering itself against the side.

The schools smelled of wet clothes and everyone had colds.

People still managed to go out for a drink, however, and often the wet weather meant that there was more custom than ever in Ryan's bar.

In her light room with its soft green colours Kate Ryan sat and spent the first spring in a wheelchair.

She would have gone mad, she realized, if she had not got the side garden to look out on through the big glass doors. She was the first to know when snowdrops came, when crocuses started to open and when the primroses and cowslips began in a yellow corner that she had never noticed before.

Jaffa the big orange cat looked out longingly, waiting for the days to come when the sun would shine and she could sit and sleep on the old stone walls. Sitting still in her chair, Kate Ryan scratched the cat's ears and told Jaffa that for her the day would come. She sighed a lot and wondered had it rained like this always but because she had been so busy she had never noticed it?

Little by little the people of Mountfern came to accept that this would be Kate Ryan's life. They ceased to shake their heads over the sudden accident, the one quick blow that would leave her for ever paralysed. Once people had seen the bright attractive room and the handsome dark woman in her chair, laughing and cheerful for their visit . . . then that was how she remained in their minds. They didn't tell each other any more about how swift she had been, and how light running up and down the steps of Mr Slattery's office. They talked no longer of the way she ran down River Road like a young girl.

Rachel had found a great roll of green rush matting. She said they should cut it off in lengths and spread it out to make a path over Kate's new carpet. Otherwise people would be afraid to visit her in the room for fear of walking in the mud with them.

Rachel came every day; she had become adept at helping to lift the two white, wasted-looking legs out of the bed and on to the wheelchair. Then she would bend while Kate pulled herself out of bed by putting her arms round Rachel's neck.

She wasn't able to do it with Carrie; the girl was too nervous and might move away. She didn't want to ask Mary Donnelly to help her. It would place too much of an emotional burden on Dara. And she didn't want John to see her like that *every* day. On the mornings when he came in and found her dressed and sitting at some part of the giant desk that went three sides of the room, he could almost believe that things were normal.

233

The two women had tea and a chat, as if they had been neighbours for many years, as if they had been young married women together and shared all the years of childbirth and watching toddlers. Neither of them ever felt it was odd that they had only met on one day before they were in the roles of hospital patient and visitor. It was as if they had always known the easy companionship and the undemanding shorthand of friendship.

Kate could tell of her unreasonable dislike of Mary Donnelly, Rachel of her irritation with Marian Johnson.

'He has no interest in Marian Johnson,' Kate assured her friend.

'She's much more suitable for this life . . . the life he wants.'

'Oh but no, you mustn't think that. Can you imagine him loving her? Even loving her a little bit?' Kate shook her head at the idea of it.

'He can't love *me* much, either. One day I'll accept that I'm not part of his plan. Then I'll be free.'

'But you'd be very lonely,' Kate said.

Rachel smiled, relieved. This was the counsel she had wanted to hear.

'Will Mrs Fine be here for long?' Dara asked.

She had got into the habit of sitting with her mother as soon as she came back from school, and the others agreed without ever saying it that this was Dara's time.

'I don't know, my love, I don't ask her. Do you mind if we ask her for meals now and then? It's terrible for her up in that awful hotel all the time.'

Dara agreed immediately. 'Oh we must ask her as much as possible, she'd start talking to herself if she had to stay in the Slieve Sunset all the time.'

Kate laughed. Dara had become so grown up, she was able to talk to her much more freely than before. The months must have made a huge difference to the girl, living here in the pub without her mother, unsure of what was going to happen and if Kate would ever come home. It was a very noticeable change. Before the accident Dara had been a tomboy, dying to get away from the house, to escape any kind of involvement or conversation, sighing at grown-up conversation, and flinching away from any confidences. And now, that was all gone. She seemed older than Michael too, while once she had waited for his every move before she decided what to do herself. She was technically a woman, and Dara already felt the stirrings of . . . well if not love . . . at least hero worship. Kate had noticed how her face changed when she spoke of Kerry. That little crush must have developed since the previous summer.

Kate felt she could tell Dara things that sometimes might seem a bit petty when she told them to John. Maybe it was a conspiracy kind of thing between women . . . she hoped she didn't overdo it. Dara seemed to approve of Rachel coming to the house. Her connection with Patrick O'Neill was never mentioned; Kate was far too loyal to bring up the matter herself, but she felt that Dara instinctively had some understanding of it.

'Will Mary Donnelly be here for much longer?'

Kate tried to look concerned and kind. 'I've no idea, she must suit herself.' A sharp note had come into her voice.

234

'Why don't you like her, Mam? She's very helpful.'

'I know, I know. What do you mean I don't like her? Don't be silly, Dara.'

'But you don't. Why? It's not as if she's after Dad or anything. She hates men, she even hates them when they're only Michael's age.'

'She's so childish to be going on with all that kind of rawmaishing out of her,' Kate snapped.

'Is that why you don't like her, because she's against men?'

'No, I'll tell you the truth, I don't like her because she's doing what I should be doing, she's standing there serving people in the bar and not talking to them when I would be talking to them pleasantly, she's going down to Loretto Quinn and beating her down over the price of this and that instead of paying her. She has the kitchen clean and tidy, better maybe than I'd keep it. She has Leopold changed beyond recognition. But she has Carrie terrified of her, and crying if she breaks a saucer. She has the sheets clean on the beds but she has a smell of boiling in the house from Monday to Saturday.'

Dara looked at her mother open-mouthed.

'And mostly I don't like her because she has two good legs that start at the top and go down to her feet and she can put one of them in front of the other and walk. If she's in a hurry she can put one in front of the other quickly and she can run. She doesn't have to drag herself by her arms and strain and stretch and pull and at the end of it be just a few inches towards the edge of the bed. I suppose *that's* why I don't like her.'

Dara still couldn't speak.

'Because I'm a mean old pig,' Kate added as an explanation.

Dara flew into her arms, literally hurled herself at Kate.

'You're *not* a mean old pig, it's the unfairest thing in the world that you should be like this. I told Sister Laura that God must have a very cruel streak in him to let you be just in the path of that machine.'

Dara sobbed into her mother's shoulder as Kate patted the dark hair and the heaving slender body.

'What did Sister Laura say about God's mean streak?' she asked gently.

Dara drew away from her for a moment and looked at her with a tear-stained face.

'She said that Almighty God had a purpose in everything, and that we couldn't see it now. In years to come we'll see it. Do you think we will?'

Kate held the hands of her daughter and spoke slowly. 'I don't know. That's the truth. I don't know. If it was something that might be cured, *then* perhaps all these months and even a couple of years in a wheelchair might have a purpose.'

'But . . .' Dara waited anxiously.

'But because it's *not* going to be cured, and I will never walk again, I find it hard to believe that God has a purpose. God *can't* believe that I'm a better citizen, a better Christian to him stuck in this chair. Maybe it's just that he knew I might be a desperate sinner if I was out of the chair so he keeps me in it. That could be his purpose, I suppose.' She half smiled.

'But you wouldn't have any sins would you, Mam, in or out of the wheelchair?'

Dara could never imagine that grown-ups committed sin anyway, they were allowed to do everything just because they were grown up, it seemed impossible to know what was left except murder and worshipping idols which Mam wouldn't be likely to be at.

'I suppose the biggest sin I have is not accepting what God has sent me. That is a sin, you know, Dara. I'm going to have to confess it to Father Hogan when he comes today, and I'm going to tell him also that I don't want to go to Lourdes. That's going to be even harder.'

Dara's eyes were filled with tears again. 'You *must* go to Lourdes, Mam, you must, it's the only hope. That's what Michael and I say all the time. There have been miracles and you could be one of them.'

'No, darling Dara, I'm not going, there's no miracle for me there. If Our Lady wants to cure my spine she can do it in Mountfern, I am not going to spend all those people's money going there, and have all their hopes disappointed. That's it. I didn't mean to tell you so suddenly, I was going to put it gently, maybe even differently. But you're such a joy to me and such a comfort, I treat you like a grown-up daughter instead of a child.'

The tears had dried and Dara was as pleased as anything. 'Well, I'm going to have to look after you properly if I'm a grown-up. If you get your way about Lourdes can we have your word that you'll be sensible about Mary Donnelly and be civil to her in case she packs her bags and leaves?'

Kate burst into peals of laughter. Dara's voice was such a good imitation of her own when she was being bossy. Even her face had the same look.

'I'll be so civil, it will frighten you,' she laughed.

'There's no need to over-do it, Mam,' Dara said disapprovingly.

John was taking a stroll with his daughter along the river bank.

'I'm glad that Rachel is here,' he said. 'Your mam likes her a lot. It will take her mind off things.'

'Do you think her mind's on things a lot?' Dara wanted to know.

'It's so hard to know. She says she's almost forgotten her life before the wheelchair. She doesn't even dream of herself as being able to walk any more.' He sounded sad.

'Don't get all depressed, Daddy, she hates that more than anything.'

'I wouldn't be depressed in front of her, Dara. But Lord, on my own or with you, can't I let the mask drop a bit?'

They walked on companionably past the people fishing, careful not to disturb them by idle chatter. They were both remembering some of the scenes when a red-faced and furious Kate would shout and cry that she wanted no sympathy, no sad faces around her. She had even thrown a jug of milk and had broken plates and saucers, flinging them at John when he was in what he considered a gentle and concerned mood. Kate had taken it as defeatist and said it made her worse.

'I can't even bloody walk, you can all do everything, so for Christ's sake stop moaning and saying, "Poor Mam, Poor Kate". What is the point of that? I'd prefer to be dead. Dead, dead and buried long ago than to be poor Kate, poor Mam.'

She had frightened them so much they had rung for Doctor White. He came to

236

see her, and the family waiting outside got little consolation from him as he came out.

'Nothing wrong with Mrs Ryan except that she is paralysed,' he said bluntly. 'And that she is surrounded by people who don't give her any reason or point in living. They call the doctor if she shows any bit of fire and life, and their way of supporting her is to offer her pity. Good evening.'

They never forgot it. Even Declan and Eddie knew that the mood was to be optimistic. Mam wanted to believe that things were getting better all the time. That's what gave her the energy to drag herself from bed to chair, from chair to lavatory or bath stool, and to push herself to the garden or the kitchen or the pub. If she didn't believe that things were getting better all the time, she wouldn't even sit up in the mornings.

Dara linked her father as they turned to come back along the road. 'What do you think *really* Dad, about the hotel? Is it going to take away all our business? Mary Donnelly says it could be the ruination of us.'

'Mary, for all that we are blessed to have her, is wrong about almost everything.'

Dara looked at her father affectionately. 'It would be a terrible thing to hate men, not to see them as friends.'

'I think it would be a pity all right,' John agreed. 'I think you'd lose out on it in the long run. And on the same subject, what's a beautiful girl like you doing on a summer evening walking the river bank with her old father? Why aren't the Tommy Leonards and the Liam Whites and the others of Mountfern beating me out of the way? Tell me that.'

'Because they're all eejits, Daddy, and you're not.'

'That's nice to hear. But isn't there anybody who isn't an eejit? Anybody at all?'

'Not a one.' Dara was airy about it. It was just a fact. 'I might be hard to please, like Mary Donnelly, or just a bit slow in seeing my chances. I keep dreaming of course, that something marvellous would happen, like that beautiful Kerry O'Neill would notice me.'

'Would you like that?'

'I'd *love* it, but I'd have to fight the whole town for him. Grace says he and his father don't get on.'

'Nobody gets on with their father,' said John, patting Dara's arm.

'Stop fishing, Daddy,' she said.

'I think Declan's turning into a proper hooligan,' John said to Kate.

'God, he must be really bad if you say a word against him.' Kate was surprised to hear such criticism. 'What has he done now?'

'He hasn't *done* anything, it's just that he has the instincts of a gangster. He goes round punching things for no reason.'

'What kind of things?' Kate was alarmed.

'I don't know, the hen house for one thing, he nearly knocked it down.'

'I could knock that down myself even in this thing.' Kate gave a disgusted wave at her wheelchair.

'You could knock the house down in that chair, you look so terrifying when you head for us,' John laughed. 'No, he just seems to tear things apart automatically without even knowing he's doing it.'

'He's upset.'

'We're all upset,' her husband said.

'No we're not, we're fine. He's just a baby. Send him in to me when he gets back. I'll play with him for a bit.'

'He'll probably have you on the floor.'

'It's just being the youngest . . . poor little fellow.'

'I was the youngest, I'll have you remember, and look at how well I turned out.'

'You did, too.' She looked at him admiringly. John Ryan had lost some of his beer belly, he stood more erect and, despite new lines on his face, he looked a younger man than he had been at the beginning of the summer.

Kate found herself turning to him for a lot more than just physical assistance. He had been able to manage in some kind of fashion without her for almost half a year. There were a lot of areas where she had to look to him now for advice.

'Do you think it's going to affect them all?' She spoke in a small voice. 'You know, will it change their lives altogether . . . all this?' Again she waved in exasperation at her legs and the chair.

'No, I think they'll be less affected by it than we expect. You know how adaptable children are, they get used to any old thing after a while.' He spoke gently and lovingly to take the possible hint of indifference out of his words. 'I think that now you're home they'll all get on with their lives. Normally – almost embarrassingly normally.'

'I hope so.' She closed her eyes.

'Kate, we've been through all this before. What makes you start worrying now?'

'I expect hearing that Declan's going round kicking things, and I think maybe I treat Dara as too much of a grown-up. I've taken her childhood away from her.'

'No, no.' He was soothing. 'She's flattered that you talk to her as an equal. No, don't worry about that.'

'And Eddie?'

'He's with a gang of toughies, he hasn't time to think about anything except walls to be climbed, orchards to be robbed, jam jars to be discovered in far places so that he'll collect enough to go to the pictures.'

'So that leaves Michael. He's too quiet these days, isn't he?'

'He is, and I was going to say that if you don't think it's the act of a madman I was going to ask him to go off fishing for a day with me. We keep telling people the Fern is full of pike. Why don't we go and see is it true?'

She reached over and touched his hand. 'Do, of course, and tell Michael I love him.'

'I won't tell him anything of the sort, he'd knock me into the river.'

'No, I mean say it without saying it.'

'He knows, but I'll say it without saying it anyway.'

'Will you come out fishing with me on Saturday?'

'*Fishing!* In this weather? We'd be frozen, and what would we catch?'

'We spend our time telling people that the Fern is alive with pike all year round. Shouldn't we see are we right?'

'God, Dad, it'd be miserable out there. Why would you never ask me a thing like that in the summer, I'd love it in the summer.'

'I'd love it in the summer, too, son, but the pub wouldn't be half empty like it is this weather.'

'But why, why now?'

'I wanted us to have a day out, a chat even.'

'What have I done?'

'Oh Jesus God, you haven't done anything. It's great when your son thinks the only reason you're going to ask him out for a treat is to attack him, punish him.'

'But you never ask me out,' Michael complained with what John had to admit was some justification.

'And I don't seem to make too good a fist of it when I do. All right, if it's not fishing what would you like to do on Saturday after lunch?'

'I suppose the pictures are out?'

'You suppose correctly.'

'Could we do the book?' His eyes lit up.

John genuinely didn't know what he meant.

'The book, Dad, Mr O'Neill's book, you haven't done it for ages. I mean, take out the boxes of papers and things . . .' His voice trailed away. John was just standing there with a blank expression. 'I mean, you *are* going to do it . . . to finish it?'

'What? Oh yes. Yes.'

Michael looked relieved. 'Well then, could we look at some of the research and I could help you like I did before?'

'Yes. Certainly.'

'Is anything wrong, would you prefer to go fishing? I suppose if we wrapped up . . .'

'No. No, you're a very good fellow . . . no.'

'So have you been thinking about doing the book . . . or maybe after everything . . . you sort of didn't want to?'

'I think you're a genius, that's the very thing we'll do on Saturday. We'll take the boxes upstairs out of everyone's way and you can indeed help me. What with everything that happened I never found a moment to get down to it again, and it's been there at the back of my mind . . .'

He beamed at Michael, but the boy had the feeling that there was some sort of struggle taking place. His father had been deciding there in front of him whether to go on writing the story of Fernscourt for Grace's father.

'It's not as if it would make Mam any better by not doing it,' he said suddenly, and his father gripped him on the shoulder.

'That's the truth, Michael. We must never forget that.'

'Well, how much purgatory did he give you?' Rachel asked when Father Hogan had left and she was allowed to come in to see Kate.

'It's not purgatory he gives me, you heathen, it's penance, it's to keep me out of purgatory.'

'It's all nonsense, you're a saint already. Did you tell him about Lourdes?'

'Yes, he hated it, poor man, but he's going to help me. He said to put it a different way, say that I'd like it to go to a parish fund to send others there, get even more money, and not to dwell too much on the fact that I'm not going to take it up myself. It might hurt people or offend them.'

Rachel nodded.

'You look restless. Is anything wrong?'

'Hard to hide anything from you Kate. I've been thinking, I should go back. Back to the States.'

'You don't call it home, you don't say back home.'

'It doesn't feel like home, not this year.'

'Maybe because you are in the middle of moving . . . all these plans about the hotel, and what it will look like and what will be here. No wonder the office in New York doesn't seem real. But your flat – think of that. It's going to be like paradise compared to the Slieve Sunset.'

'Yes.'

'You don't have to go, you could stay here with us.'

'No, I have to go. I'm only inventing work here . . . and . . .'

'But isn't he glad that you like the place so much, feel so at home here in Mountfern? I'd have thought he'd have been delighted with you.'

'I thought that too.'

'Whyever not? What did he say?'

'He just wondered why I was spending so long here. I stupidly said something about getting the feel of the place. He was very short with me. Very short indeed.'

Kate reached for Rachel's hand. It was hardly credible that this elegant woman with the wine suit trimmed with suede, with a silk blouse which must have cost a fortune – a cream silk with a floppy bow – should be as awkward as a child when it came to the great Patrick O'Neill. No sixteen-year-old could have been more distraught.

'You'll come back here again, it's not just a job.' Kate soothed her as she had soothed her daughter earlier in the day.

'But the message is loud and clear. It will never be my home.'

Rachel had never been so careless of her make-up, her silk blouse or the fine wool rug that lay on Kate's lap. She cried as she had cried in Yiddish to her mother years and years ago when the children on the block had called her a little Jew girl.

Each time Kate got a letter from Rachel she wrote back that very day. That way their letters stayed in order. They weren't crossing in the post, they could ask and reply.

Rachel must have written just as quickly.

They learned to depend on each other in a way they would never have believed possible. Rachel wrote about working for O'Neill Enterprises in New York, though finding that the heart had gone from the business since Patrick O'Neill was many miles away in an Irish village.

Kate found it a great ease to be able to tell someone how boringly well Mary Donnelly ran the house, and how irritating it was to be told a dozen times a day, perfectly accurately, that they were blessed to have found her. It was true, which made it worse! Kate said it was a sneaky relief to be able to tell Rachel that if she heard one more Mountfern person say that Mary Donnelly was a genius she would go berserk and race round the pub in her wheelchair knocking over tables and pouring drinks on to the floor.

Rachel wrote that she had to put up with the insults and veiled triumph of Gerry Power, who had said in one hundred different ways that he was sorry it didn't work out for Rachel in Ireland. In one hundred different ways she had deliberately misunderstood him and said with a broad smile that it had all worked out magnificently and he *must* go over some day himself and see the wonderful place that Patrick had bought for himself.

Kate could admit that her new-found all-girls-together relationship with Dara was becoming very rocky, and Rachel could admit that sometimes weeks went by without Patrick telephoning her, even though she stayed in to wait for his calls.

Week after week the two women wrote of their lives, month after month they told of the changes that were happening. Neither really noticed things changing, it was only by looking back over the old letters that each realized how the other's life was moving from one direction to another.

Kate wrote of John more and more as the man who made the decisions, not as the man who was trying to cope. She never said it in so many words but Rachel could read it like a thread in the letters. There was the tale about John and the rough crowd of tinkers who came into the pub. Everyone had feared a fight if he were to throw them out, and a worse one if he were to let them stay. But there had been no fight in Ryan's, the tinkers were served as pleasantly as they could have wished. It was just the number of times that John said how heart-scalded he was from Sergeant Sheehan dropping in that sent the band on their way. John had leaned conspiratorially over the counter and said that a man wasn't free to breathe in this day and age without that sergeant coming and poking his nose into what people had in the boots of their cars or on the crossbars of their bicycles. The tinkers, who were practically festooned with pheasants they had taken illegally from Coyne's wood, were on their way, with grateful glances at John and vaguely dispiriting promises that they would return.

Rachel read how John Ryan now had poems published by two newspapers, to a total of seven published works, and there was the distinct possibility of an anthology. The history of Fernscourt and its surroundings was proving long and complicated, but there were no pleas to hasten it from the man who had commissioned it, so it was taking its time.

There was the story of John and the man trying to sell him an insurance policy: John had refused it and the man had turned ugly. He had said that John must be expecting to come into a big windfall from the Fernscourt insurance people. John had been icy in his dismissal, but the man had retorted that he was only saying what half of Mountfern was saying behind his back. Kate had been upset but John had shrugged and said that a village had to have something to talk about, and since they hadn't had a two-headed calf born recently, nor a cure at the may bush, nor even a visit from a politician, they had to fill in the long winter evenings somehow.

Kate read about art galleries that Rachel had visited, and a course of ten lectures that she had been attending. She heard of trips taken by train to cities in the United States which were further apart than the whole width of Ireland.

She knew that Rachel had seen a lot of movies and heard too little from Patrick, and that she was now considered a world authority on Ireland by the people in her circle.

Without Rachel having to write it, Kate knew there were a lot of empty nights.

Without Kate having to put it down on paper, Rachel knew that Kate sometimes found the imprisonment in her chair almost more than she could bear. The frustration seeped across the Atlantic in spite of herself. The days when it seemed to rain and rain and her lovely side garden with all the plants that she was meant to admire from her green room had turned into a mire of mud.

There were the times when it was obvious that Kate Ryan might in fact explode if she hadn't this safety valve, this marvellous friend she could write to and explain everything as it was.

Like how irritating Dara could be, how downright maddening her own lovely daughter had become.

Dara had lost her unruly look, Kate said in these letters, she had become graceful in a way that was very hard to describe. She had also become almost impossible again. Everything was a shrug, a sulk and a sigh.

The record player that had been a gift from Grace played high and loud in her room, then the sounds of that dreadful Radio Luxembourg and its awful music replaced the record player.

Kate wrote in a matter-of-fact way about Patrick. She told how he was working night and day, and had little time for socializing. She knew this would please Rachel on the other side of the Atlantic Ocean. It was also totally true.

Judy Byrne, who came twice a week to do the exercises that were meant to strengthen Kate's arms, and improve the muscles that would pull her from chair to bed to bath and back, often let slip how she had invited Mr O'Neill to this concert, or that exhibit, but never had he been able to accept. Judy shook her head sadly as she pummelled Kate, and made her repeat again and again the tiresome and stressful movements, saying that there hardly seemed to be any point in having all that money and power if you were never able to enjoy yourself.

Marian Johnson had said more or less the same thing: How sad it was that Patrick O'Neill didn't get more cooperation from everyone so that he would have some leisure time, poor man. Marian would tinkle in that *unwise* little-girl laugh and say that he had been simply desolate not to have been able to go to the hunt ball, or the charity dinner or whatever social ruse she had tried yet again in vain.

Life went on as before in the lodge, Kate wrote, or so she thought. Grace was utterly charming, and the more loathsome Dara became the more sweet and endearing did Grace appear to be. She would sit for any length of time talking to Kate, asking her advice, begging to hear stories about Kate's own teenage years. Dara couldn't bear to be in the same room as her mother these days.

Kate had heard some disturbing things about Kerry. That he had been in a game of poker up in Foley's bar, that he had been playing for high stakes with men who should have known better than to play cards with the son of the man who was going to change the face of the town and make their fortunes for them. She didn't tell that to Rachel, since it was only a rumour, no point in worrying her over something that might not be at all likely.

Several times she apologized for the trivia and small-town gossip, and she said she was sure Rachel thought of her as a poor country cousin who was to be pitied for the narrowness of her life.

But as the months went on Kate apologized less. She realized that Rachel did indeed love to hear of the small town where she had felt so much at home. Rachel wrote about how she had glorified Mountfern in her memory now. She had forgotten that there was any rain, any mud or any bad temper. She had begun to think of the terrible Slieve Sunset as a place of worth. As she spent Christmas in the Catskills the notion of her ever sitting down at a table and having turkey with the Ryans seemed so remote that she wondered how she could ever have considered it as part of her lifestyle.

John realized that without the trade from the site they would be in a poor way. The foremen, the surveyors, the visiting experts of one sort or another came for drinks at all hours of the day. They didn't necessarily drink a great deal but they sat and discussed plans . . . opened out big grey bits of paper, argued over lists of supplies.

It was all much more comfortable for them than the prefab site offices that Brian Doyle had put beside the actual Fernscourt, which was rising very slowly from its foundations. It was Mary who noticed that they bought packets of crisps and this was often their only lunch.

'Do you think there'd be a future in sandwiches at all?' she asked Kate.

Kate was annoyed she hadn't thought of it first. Grudgingly she agreed that there might be a small profit in providing something to eat. She arranged to make a dozen sandwiches a day – ham and salad, cheese and home-made chutney. Anything that wasn't eaten would be devoured by the family in the evening.

John was against them at first. Turning the place into some kind of café, he sniffed, not what ordinary men wanted. But when he saw Brian Doyle and the two engineers eating two rounds each the very second day, he changed his tune.

Kate and Mary smiled their first genuine smile of friendship. And Kate said that they might even think of serving soup later on if there seemed to be any demand for it.

Mary nodded her head approvingly. 'You're absolutely right,' she said. 'I think you should get the soup going as soon as possible. Better do something before the Yank takes all the business off you with a smile.'

'That's what's going to happen, isn't it?' Kate said.

'Unless we try to fight back,' said Mary gruffly. 'And we'll have to fight the way he does. Like a man, of all things. Like a dirty, rotten man.'

In fact there seemed to be delay after delay in building the hotel. Patrick O'Neill said that if he were a superstitious man he would think that he wasn't really *meant* to build it.

First there was an earth subsidence. Not too serious, but serious enough to mean a re-think. And then, expensively, a re-doing of a whole wall.

There was the time that all the cattle had got in through a hole in a fence and done unimaginable damage to wood that had been stored in an open shed. The hole in the fence was never explained, but was said to be the work of a crowd of kids after school one day. Patrick tried to find out if it had been malicious but Brian Doyle told him that children were the devil incarnate. There was no use looking for malice or virtue in them, they were just bestial by nature.

There was the time that no vehicle seemed able to start or move on the site, and it was discovered that those which didn't have bags of sugar poured into them had water mixed with the petrol. Jack Coyne couldn't be blamed because he was away at Shannon Airport on the day it was all discovered. But there were definitely tales that he had been telling youngsters how to immobilize cars should they ever need to know, and further tales that he had said it would be a real laugh if none of the cars up on the site could move. Nothing could be proved. Those who were most protective of Patrick were those who most wanted to ensure that he stayed. They would never confirm any of his suspicions that there was vandalism and that much of it was directed at him.

Then there was a problem about a farmer who had said he would sell his acre of land and it turned out when the title was investigated that he didn't own the land at all, it had been signed over to his son years ago. The son being a cunning man realized there was capital to be gained and the deliberations delayed the work that should have been under way long back in that particular area.

Patrick wondered whether the bad-tempered attorney Fergus Slattery had anything to do with it, but was reliably informed by Sheila Whelan that the reverse was true. Fergus had refused to act for the mean-minded son on the ground that opportunism was something best left to wily Americans, and that since a fair price had been offered, the normal man should accept a fair price.

Each time Patrick visited Kate Ryan he felt better in his heart. The frailty, the wan look seemed to be less. Or maybe he was only telling himself this.

He liked to sit in her airy green room and talk. Here he was far from the problems that seemed to beset him everywhere else. It was a peaceful room even though it was only yards from a noisy bar. It reminded him of Rachel's apartment, an oasis of calm right in the middle of the mad Manhattan noise. Then he remembered suddenly that it was the same woman who had created both places. He never discussed Rachel although he knew how friendly the two women had become; he spoke no words of his increasing despair over ever finishing his project, his life's dream. Nor of the anonymous letters he had got telling him that Irish businessmen could well have developed that site, or even more upsettingly that he was responsible before God and man for Mrs Ryan being in a wheelchair.

He smiled as he talked. The crinkly lines were still there around his eyes, but Kate thought they had etched a little deeper and there were other lines too. His voice was still cheery and his laugh hearty but some of the evenings they sat and talked she wondered was he forcing his humour and begging his laugh to echo a little more.

Kate suspected that he was a man who had a lot of doubts about the way his life had taken him. She never brought the subject up.

He had accepted her paralysis when she was in hospital. But it seemed totally out of place in Ryan's pub. He kept looking up expecting her to swing in as she used to behind the counter. It seemed to come as a repeated shock each time he heard the high slow whine the wheelchair made on its approach.

Sometimes she did serve there, if there were friends in. A ramp had been made to a corner wing of the bar where Kate could position herself.

But usually it was that appalling virago Mary Donnelly who looked at him as if he were the devil made into flesh each time he appeared. He had been told that she felt some similar distaste for all men, but he felt singled out for her particular dislike.

Leopold had a new collar. Mary had been at a carnival where they made dog collars with names on them. In a fit of generosity she had bought one with the words Leopold Ryan. The dog had been suitably grateful and seemed pleased with it. He would approach people and arch his neck pathetically, looking like a whipped hound showing off his wounds, but in fact wanting his collar admired.

'We have to have you looking well for Princess Grace,' Mary whispered to him.

Dara heard her. 'Why don't you like Grace?' she had asked straight out.

'I couldn't like the seed or breed of anyone who would do such harm to your poor mother.'

'But it wasn't their fault . . . the accident,' Dara cried.

'I don't just mean the accident. I mean the living, taking the living away from her.'

'But Mam has a very good life,' Dara said, not understanding. 'She always says that she hates us not to think of it as a real way of living.'

Mary had opened her mouth and closed it again. 'That's a fact,' she said unexpectedly. 'She's a great deal happier than most.'

In the hope that it might soothe some of Dara's outbursts Kate suggested that she invite Grace to spend the night with them. They might enjoy chatting together and it would save Grace the long journey back to the Grange.

'Oh, so I *am* allowed to have her to stay now. There was a time when it wasn't suitable.'

'I never said that,' Kate said.

'No, but Daddy did when you went to hospital first. It wasn't suitable, he said, because of . . . oh, I don't know why.'

Kate sighed. 'That was a long time ago, Dara, all those kinds of worries are long behind us now.'

'I don't think she'd really want to stay here anyway.'

'Whyever not? She always seems happy when she comes to visit.'

'Oh, that's just being polite.' Dara was lofty.

'The offer is there, if she'd like to come.' Kate kept her temper with difficulty.

'She might come, of course,' Dara said as if it were all a favour to her mother.

Rachel had written that although she didn't know from personal experience, every other mother of every other thirteen- and fourteen-year-old girl in the entire world told her the same story. And the story had a happy ending. They grew out of it. Kate hoped with all of her heart that Rachel was right.

It's hard to change the habits of a lifetime, and when Deirdre Dunne came across the two young Ryan boys as part of a gang that wrote silly things on the walls of

Fernscourt, she said nothing. She just walked past with her eyes ahead of her as if she were slightly wandering in her mind.

The kids, who had hidden when they saw her, breathed with relief and told each other that Deirdre Dunne was as mad as Papers Flynn and Miss Barry and would be no threat to them. Happily they carved out 'Yank Go Home' and 'This is Ireland not America' with big nails, scratching away.

Deirdre Dunne had grown up on a smallholding where the great philosophy had been to say nothing. She had been warned not to say anything since she was a child, and even when the neighbouring farmer was known to come back drunk from a market and beat his wife senseless, the same rules had held.

It would sort itself out, she was told, and indeed it had. One day the farmer fell into a ditch on the way home. It was a cold night and he had a weak chest anyway. Deirdre had seen his wife pass the ditch where he lay, and throw more brambles and briars over it in order to make sure that there was even greater delay in finding the body.

Or had she pieced together afterwards that this is what the woman had been doing. But like a true Dunne, and the daughter of her taciturn father, she said nothing.

She was almost designed to work in the office of a law firm which dealt in the human everyday business of the community. Sometimes she wondered whether she stood too far back. People like Mr Slattery and Mrs Whelan did get involved when they saw things as a matter of right or wrong. Perhaps it was more honourable.

Fergus Slattery was very pleased with Deirdre. A pale girl with sandy hair, she was quiet as a mouse and efficient as one of those huge new computers people were always talking about. She was as discreet as he could have hoped and when a rich farmer left a totally untoward sum to Mrs Rita Walsh of the Rosemarie hair salon you would never have known from Deirdre's impassive face that it was anything except the norm.

She had high praise for Kate's filing system and was just as adamant that he kept in touch with how it worked. It had fallen into great chaos in the months after Kate's accident and it was a measure of Deirdre's intelligence that she had brought a notebook to the hospital to Kate to ask for confirmation of new decisions she had made.

One of the files that Deirdre had to open was called Katherine Mary Ryan versus O'Neill Enterprises and the International Insurance Society.

Part Four

CHAPTER SIXTEEN

The twins were to have a fifteenth birthday party in September. The excitement was intense, there weren't many parties in Mountfern. To be honest none of them had been to a party since they were children. But Kate Ryan had insisted. By letter she and Rachel had decided that something which would concentrate and channel all Dara's energies would be a good idea. Kate didn't suggest the party herself, of course, that way Dara would reject it as some plot. The wish had to come from the twins themselves.

So Kate spoke of the party to everyone else in a sort of sighing voice, saying she supposed now that Dara and Michael were so grown up they would want a party when they were fifteen.

It didn't take long. Carrie wanted to know what they would do at the party, would there be dancing? Loretto Quinn said she'd love to be fifteen again and she thought it was the best age of all.

Grace was asked by Miss Hayes what she was going to wear to the twins' fifteenth birthday party. And Tommy Leonard's father told him that he would have thought that poor John and Kate Ryan would have had more sense than to lash out money entertaining hulking young folk who wouldn't give them a word of thanks for it.

And so Michael and Dara realized that a party was a possibility.

'Where could we be?' Dara wailed. 'We can't be in the pub, or in Mam's room, and the kitchen is a mess and the breakfast room is tiny.'

'There's no point in asking for a party unless there was somewhere to have it,' Michael agreed.

But Kate had that planned too. The big outhouse attached to the pub looked fine from the outside. It was whitewashed and as its only entrance was from the side garden nobody knew what a mess it was inside.

If it were to be cleaned out . . .

They could always use it for something . . .

And it would be ideal for the party.

So John suggested that as a way of earning more pocket money they should all work on it. Even involve their friends if they wanted to. It involved a few days of dragging rubbish off to the dump. There were broken beds, old bits of wood with nails sticking out of them. There was a box of jam jars with spiders in them, and a load of things that had been taken from the other outhouse in the other yard to make room for Mary Donnelly.

On the afternoon that the boys had whitewashed the big room, Jacinta looked round it in admiration.

'It's fabulous looking, it's good enough to have a party in.'

And that was it.

They wheedled and begged and cajoled. And pretending an unwillingness, Kate and John gave in. The music was not to be too loud. Everyone was to be well gone home by midnight, the children had to organize the food themselves. There was to be no trick-acting, over-excitement nor people jumping into the river. They agreed to everything and began the preparations.

Kate wrote to Rachel saying that she felt as guilty as anything pulling all these strings but it did seem to be working like a dream. Dara had even hugged her in excitement one day.

She wrote that the invitation list had been assembled and discarded and readjusted more often than anyone could believe; there had never been such a magnificent way of keeping them all totally content.

Grace had all the Beatles records, and Gerry and the Pacemakers and Freddie and the Dreamers, so she would bring those.

Tommy Leonard wondered about the lighting, they would need some kind of power brought out into the place.

John Ryan said he wasn't made of money, installing electrical lighting into a place that would be used once. But he would be able to get them one extension lead which meant they could plug in one lamp, and the record player as well if they had an adaptor.

Maggie said you could make marvellous lights with old turnips and pumpkins and marrows like people did at Halloween.

There was endless scooping and hollowing, and Loretto Quinn provided a box of night lights that would be put inside.

Kitty Daly said it all sounded terrific, which alarmed Maggie greatly. She had hoped that Kitty would think it was childish and beneath her and not want to come. Maggie knew that Dara had set her heart on Kerry O'Neill being on his own and maybe taking an interest in Dara herself. It would be very complicated if Kitty was there too. But before Maggie had to discuss it with anyone a letter arrived in Daly's with the good news that Kitty had been accepted for nursing in Dublin. It was a good hospital and the Dalys were pleased; their elder girls had gone to Wales where there was a shortage of any kind of nurses, so Dublin seemed like a step up to the Dalys.

Dara asked Rita Walsh was there anything in the world that made hair look shiny like all these advertisements, or was it all a cod? Mrs Walsh told her that it was all a cod really, but gave her some sample bottles of conditioner and said to comb it through and leave it on for as long as possible.

Carrie said that if Dara was really badly stuck she could use the new hair lacquer she had bought, but to go sparingly on it.

Eddie said that Dara was trying on lipstick in the bathroom and rubbing it off on bits of toilet paper. They all said that Eddie was a boring sneak to have announced this for no reason except getting Dara into trouble because Mam said she looked like a tart with that white-coloured lipstick on. Eddie said he didn't care what people thought of him because he'd be grown up soon and out of this place and he would never write to anyone not even at Christmas. And when he got rich he'd send a telegram saying 'Yah Boo' and Mrs Whelan would have to take it down and have it delivered.

Eddie's mother said that he was going to end on the gallows, and that if she had her legs she would get up and catch him and paste him into the wall.

Eddie's father took him aside and said that life was all about rubbing along with other people and not making fights out of nothing.

250

'But if I do *anything* I'm murdered,' Eddie complained. 'Dara can do anything she likes and people think it's grand.'

'To be fair,' said John, 'you do things like daubing the walls of Fernscourt with white paint. Dara only puts white paint on her own mouth in the privacy of the bathroom.'

That startled Eddie, who didn't know that his father was up to date on the last little activity.

'Yes, well. Yes,' he said, at a loss.

'And another thing, Eddie. You don't really want the O'Neills to clear out, do you?'

'Well, you know. It's not right him coming in here and changing everything.' He was a small parrot of Jack Coyne's whining tone.

'So no more of it. If you're going to write on walls and get caught for it, then for God's sake get yourself caught for writing something you mean, not something a fellow with a grudge told you to write.'

'A fellow. What fellow?' Eddie was too innocent.

'Do you know why Jack Coyne does all this? He doesn't give a damn about Mountfern and whether it's changing or not. He doesn't give a damn about your mother having the accident there, for all that he claims he does.'

'He says it was all that man's fault.'

'That's balls, Eddie, and if you think about it you'll realize it is. Patrick O'Neill doesn't send any business to Jack Coyne because he was cheated by Jack years back, and he knows what a chancer he is. Jack can't bear that, and it makes him look a fool.'

Eddie's eyes were round.

'I'm telling you this *not* so that you'll tell all those other beauties you hang around with, but just so that you'll know. When you're sent to a reformatory or whatever you should know *why* you're going.'

'I wouldn't be sent to a reformatory?'

This was much more frightening than his mother's belief he would end on the gallows. What made him sure that he was in real danger of a reformatory was this plain speaking. His father was treating him as a grown-up and telling him that Mr Coyne was a cheat. And he had said 'balls'. As far as Eddie was concerned that clinched it. Things must be in a bad state if his own father would use words like that to him instead of belting the ear of anyone else who might be heard to say it.

Eddie was allowed to help at the party, he was told, but under no circumstances was he to join in. And when asked to leave he must leave at once with no arguments. It seemed a poor sort of deal. But it was the only way he would be let near the place at all.

'Will I empty ashtrays?' Eddie asked helpfully.

Dara and Michael looked at each other in despair. Wouldn't you know that Eddie would manage to bring up the subject of smoking somehow.

'There will be no need for that, thank you,' Dara said in a glacial voice.

'Just be generally helpful,' Michael said.

'Doing what?' Eddie asked.

It was unanswerable.

He couldn't take their coats, they wouldn't have any. He couldn't pass round the bottles of orange and lemon because they would all be on a table. He wouldn't be allowed near the record player and it was probably better to keep him well away from the food too. The thought of Eddie presenting a plate of sausages or serving a trifle was not one that gave any pleasure.

'Maybe you needn't help at all,' Dara said after some thought. 'Maybe you would like an early night.'

Michael was more sensitive, he knew that an early night was something Eddie Ryan would never like, now or any time in the future.

Eddie's face was bitterly disappointed. 'I can't go to bed on the night of the *party*,' he said, hurt disbelief all over his round freckled face.

Even in her wish to have him one hundred miles away from the scene Dara saw that this would be too harsh.

'Perhaps you could control the animals,' she said.

'What animals?'

'Our animals, curb them, sort of.'

'Do you mean Leopold and Jaffa?' Eddie was totally bewildered.

'Well yes, and Maurice.'

'God, Dara, what could a cat and a tortoise do at the party?' Eddie asked.

'Aha, you put your finger on it. Not much, but Leopold might break the place up. Perhaps you could be in charge of Leopold.'

'Like how? Not take him on a walk now, that wouldn't be fair.' Eddie was cunning.

'No, but . . . um . . . put him on a lead and sort of patrol with him. They do that at parties in America, I saw it at the pictures, somebody patrols the grounds with a dog. You know, you must have seen them, they wear sunglasses and uniforms.'

Dara was thinking of a security guard she had seen in a film.

It worked like a dream.

'All right, I'll borrow some sunglasses and get Leopold's lead and patrol a bit.' Eddie sounded pleased with this role.

'Not inside, of course,' Michael said hastily.

'Of course not.' Eddie was superior. 'Leopold mightn't know it was all posh now, he might think it was the old shed still and squat down and have a scutter.'

'Yes, that's what we don't need,' Dara said, feeling faint.

They spent ages on the invitations. Nothing in the Leonards' shop was right for them. Either they were teddy bears holding balloons asking people to come to a jolly party or they were heavy silver lettering saying 'You are invited.' One was too babyish, one was too formal.

In the end they bought plain white cards and wrote them out individually. They knew that these invitations would be kept for a long time in the different homes of Mountfern. Written invitations didn't often arrive in the post.

There had been long debates about the food. Dara had wanted food on a plate, like a real supper. Michael said that sausages and rolls would be better, food on a plate would be messy, people might let bits of gravy fall off.

Carrie was looking out big dishes that could cook lots of sausages at the same time. Mary got one of the beer companies to give them brightly coloured trays which they could use for serving the rolls. There would be sandwiches too on the ground that everyone loved tomato sandwiches at moments of high excitement, and there would be tons of crisps and nuts.

The pudding was a trifle which Kate would make herself. She loved putting on the hundreds and thousands, she said, and she explained to Grace that it was because she never had jelly and cream or trifle herself when she was young that she got so excited over party food. Her parents had not been festive people, birthdays were low priority.

Grace told Mrs Ryan that her own mother had often been too ill for any real birthday, but she did remember years back when Kerry was twelve and Grace was nine, Mother had put on paper hats and they had all had a birthday tea in the garden. The three of them.

Father had been out at work. Like he always was.

Kate patted the golden curls and wished that Dara would be eager and confiding like this.

Still, it had to be said that since the party was planned Dara was a much easier soul to live with. Kate was forgiving, it was hard being fifteen whether you had a family that loved you or not. Dara did, Kate hadn't, but at fifteen nobody was too clear about that sort of thing.

The cake was to have thirty candles, and it was a surprise. Kate had asked Marian Johnson, who knew all kinds of people, to recommend a firm that would deliver a cake already iced.

Marian had been very cooperative and even got something off the price because she knew the people who owned the firm.

Kate thought it was sad to see Marian boasting of all the connections she had and the people she knew socially. It was not at all the way to make Patrick O'Neill think more warmly of her. Patrick needed someone like Rachel. How blind and stupid he was not to realize it. How insensitive he was to write her a note every three months or so just at the exact moment when she was making a resolve to forget him and get on with her own life.

Rachel had sent the twins magnificent shirts for their birthday. Michael's was black and red, Dara's was silver and white.

Kate had encouraged Dara to buy a white pleated skirt. But not directly. She had just left a magazine about, and let enough hints fall without saying she thought it was nice. Grace as usual did the persuading. She said she thought the skirt looked fabulous and when Dara got her birthday money in advance of the day she went into the big town and bought it.

They were dressed and nervous, ages before people came. Michael was handsome in the unusual colours, Dara dazzling, Kate thought, in the shimmering silver and white. Her eyes were huge and dark, her hair shone like satin. Kate looked at them proudly.

'I hope it will be a night you'll always remember,' she said, trying to keep the choking emotion out of her voice.

'I wish you were able . . .' Michael began.

'To be able to run in and out a bit,' Dara finished.

Kate brushed the tear away quickly and decided to be very non sentimental. 'Not at all, that's the last thing you'd wish. If I had to come in and upset the proceedings you'd hear this old chair a mile away. It will be great altogether, the place outside looks like a palace. Your father will go in from time to time to make sure you have enough of everything.'

The twins nodded. That was understood. Their father would be calling in to make sure there wasn't too much of everything, that's what was really meant.

It was awkward in the beginning, because these were people they saw every day. The girls were at school together in the convent, the boys in the brothers, they knew each other from Fernscourt in the old days, some of them from the bridge, and some from the raft, Coyne's wood or just around the town. They saw each other a dozen times a week, in the cinema, on their bicycles. They were suddenly ill at ease in their finery in a room hung with hollowed-out shells holding lights.

The conversations began and died.

Apart from Grace O'Neill: she seemed not to notice any little silences any shyness, her laughter pealed, she begged for crisps, and more fizzy orange. She praised the room over and over, she admired the girls' dresses, and said that she was just dying to dance. Could they get some music started? And arm in arm with Maggie, who looked nervous in a pink dress with a thousand polka dots on it, she rummaged through the records, exclaiming over them even though they were her own. In no time the party had started.

Eddie, patrolling, would stop wistfully and lift his sunglasses to watch the dancing inside what used to be the old shed. It was full of mystery and enchantment tonight, but Eddie could never pause too long. Leopold would look up thoughtfully at the sky and Eddie knew that an unmerciful baying was about to begin, so the dog had to be hastened away to the river bank until the wish to howl at the stars had passed.

Tommy Leonard told Dara that she looked beautiful.

'That's the only word for it,' he said, anxious that there should be no misunderstandings. 'It's not just pretty, or nice, it's beautiful.'

'Thank you Tommy, you look great yourself,' Dara said, pleased.

'No, it's not just a question of looking well or not looking well. This is a description of what you *are*. Beautiful.'

Poor Tommy was bursting with eagerness to make it clear that this was no ordinary exchange of pleasantries. But Dara wasn't really listening. She was looking at the door.

Kerry O'Neill had sent a note saying that if he was able to make it he would very much like to attend the party.

The note had been addressed to both of them.

Grace had said that Kerry was very unpredictable. He had left school, had got six Honours in his Leaving Certificate, and he was about to start work in a hotel in Donegal. Father had thought the best way for Kerry to learn the business of running a hotel was to start in someone else's. Nobody knew when he would be off.

Grace hoped it wouldn't be before the party, but with Kerry she said you never knew.

Dara hadn't wanted to keep asking. It looked so babyish.

Maggie wondered if her dress clashed with her hair. Pink and polka dots would not have been her choice but this was a dress which had never fitted Kitty properly and was therefore pronounced almost new in the Daly family. Maggie had brought it to Miss Hayes over in the lodge and Miss Hayes had trimmed it with a red ribbon and assured Maggie that all girls with red in their hair wore this colour now.

Maggie danced with Liam White a lot at the party. Liam said that Maggie was easier to dance with than the others because she was smaller than normal girls and there wasn't the same danger of being knocked down by her doing rock and roll. Maggie thought this was a mixed compliment, but at least it did mean she was being asked out into the centre of the floor a lot.

Jacinta White asked Tommy Leonard did he intend to dance with the hostess all night, because there was a good variety of other partners around.

Michael realized that as host he must dance with everyone, but his head turned from time to time to watch Grace as she whirled with her golden curls tied in a huge black velvet bow, and her head thrown back laughing. Grace was so alive and so beautiful. He would love to have danced with her all night, but he knew he couldn't. He went over to Maggie Daly who looked very nice. Maggie was talking to Liam by the record player.

'Will you dance?' he asked her.

'Who, me? Are you sure?' Maggie looked startled.

Michael was annoyed. He was only asking her to dance, for heaven's sake, why did she have to look as if it were some huge thing and she wasn't worthy of it?

John looked in on the pretence that they might need more minerals from the bar. He sneaked back and reported to Kate that all seemed to be under control.

'Nobody smoking, no one with a bottle of brandy under the table, and they all have their clothes on,' he said.

'My God what a terribly dull party!' Kate exclaimed jokingly, and the two of them smiled at each other in the bar. He touched her face suddenly and she held his hand to her cheek.

Brian Doyle at the counter saw it and wondered if all that sort of thing had gone by the board for the Ryans. He presumed it had. You couldn't get up on an unfortunate woman who had all those injuries, could you. It was a terrible thing to happen to them. But still, Brian brightened, they were in their forties after all, they'd probably given all that sort of thing up long ago. Brian was thirty-four with a girlfriend in the town who was going to pack her bags and move off to another town if he didn't make a move one way or another. He put the idea out of his mind and ordered another pint.

Carrie wanted to know should she serve the sausages and Mary said give them a bit more time yet.

Mary kept a weather eye out for Leopold and Eddie. She could see why the twins had resisted having their brother around, but she wanted to make sure that Eddie didn't tie Leopold to some far-off tree and forget him. The animal wasn't used to being taken on such heavy walks with the lead.

When Mary saw them pass again, she made signs and invited Eddie to join her in the kitchen.

'What's it about?' Eddie was suspicious.

'I thought you and Leopold and I might have a sausage or two ourselves before the rush starts, what do you think?'

Eddie thought it was great. Carrie served them all and brought a big bottle of tomato ketchup as well, which was more than the people outside at the party would have.

Jimbo joined them for a few moments and gave Carrie's ear a nuzzle.

'Enough of that, Jimbo,' Mary said firmly.

'It's only a bit of affection,' Jimbo said.

'It's roguery and trickery and what's more it's unhygienic in a place where food's being prepared,' Mary said.

'All right.' Jimbo was good-natured.

Eddie was given another sausage to reward him for his hard work patrolling.

'What are you patrolling?' Jimbo asked.

Eddie was at a loss. He didn't rightly know.

'What is it exactly?' he asked Mary.

'Anyone knows you have to patrol at a function,' Mary said.

'Will there be patrolling across the river when the hotel starts?' Jimbo asked.

'Bound to be,' said Mary.

'Maybe I should get in quick and apply for it.'

Eddie smiled to himself. It *was* a real job, he had been afraid it might have been Dara and Michael making something up to keep him out of the way.

Kerry was the last to arrive. Dara was the first to see him; she tried to stop herself running to the door, but she got there very speedily all the same.

Kerry looked wonderful. He wore a pale blue shirt with dark blue stitching all over it, it was like the kind of thing a cowboy might wear. He carried two packages, one he left by the record player, one he gave straight to Dara.

'Happy birthday, Princess,' he said.

'Why do you call me that?' It was what Mary Donnelly called Grace when she was speaking disparagingly.

'All beautiful girls are princesses on their birthdays, and you more than most.' He smiled at her warmly.

Dara got that breathless feeling as if she had been running.

'Will I open it?'

'If you like.'

She was almost afraid to lose him by struggling with the wrapping paper too long, and yet it would be terrible to rip it off.

She managed to open it, and he was still standing there. It was a beautiful hair clip with a big red rose attached. If you wore it, it would look as if there was a rose in your hair. Dara looked at it in delight.

'I must put it on, I'll go to a mirror and see what I'm doing.'

'Don't run away. Here, I'll put it on for you.' He lifted the thick dark hair and slid the grip with its big silk rose into place. He had drawn the hair right back from her face on that one side, it gave her a faintly gypsyish look.

'Is it nice?' Dara asked eagerly.

'It's quite lovely,' Kerry said.

At that moment the record player began to play a slower number, 'Michelle'. Without asking her or breaking the mood, Kerry's arms went straight around Dara and they were dancing.

Dara looked around her and sighed with pure pleasure. The lights from the lanterns were twinkling on the white walls, the paper garlands hung artistically around, the tables looked festive with all the bottles of fizz and plates of snacks. Outside the night air was warm and the flowers in Mammy's side garden looked romantic and like something in a calendar picture. She and Michael were fifteen, almost grown up, all their friends were here. But mainly Kerry O'Neill, who was eighteen and the most handsome man in Ireland, had come in the door, given her a magnificent rose for her hair, told her she looked beautiful, and was holding her in his arms as they danced to Paul McCartney. Dara hadn't known it was possible to be so happy.

Maggie Daly said to Michael that she thought this party was like something you'd dream about.

Michael didn't really listen, he was wondering if as host he could reasonably change the music. He wanted to put on something more lively, like the Rolling Stones. And it was particularly silly to have Grace dancing with that good-looking but basically thick fellow John Joe Conway. Grace was so nice to everyone, she shouldn't be so polite to stupid John Joe Conway, letting him hold her close like that.

The sausages were passed round, the trifle was eaten, every bit of it. The parents and a few people from the pub, plus Declan and Eddie in his dark glasses clutching Leopold for dear life, gathered for the Birthday cake. Mary Donnelly, Carrie, Jimbo, and by chance Papers Flynn who was passing by, all gathered at the door for the blowing out of the candles. There were no speeches but a lot of clapping and cheering which made Leopold over-excited and Eddie had to clench his mouth closed for fear of rousing the neighbourhood.

Then the grown-ups, relieved that the party was going so well, retired, and someone had taken out the bulb of the only real light so now the place was lit entirely by the lanterns on the walls.

It smelled of the end of the summer, of Nivea Cream and Blue Grass perfume, of cheese and onion potato crisps, of sausages and of the September flowers in the garden.

The music was almost all slow now. It was as if the energy for jumping around to the noisier tunes before supper was no longer there.

Michael didn't mind if there were girls he hadn't danced with yet, they probably didn't want to dance with him, they all seemed happy. He stood and talked to Grace or they moved out to dance. All the time she laughed and listened to him and told him things, and many times she said 'Michael you are wonderful', and he knew she meant it.

Liam White danced a lot with Maggie.

Tommy Leonard looked wistfully for an opportunity to dance with Dara again, but he never got one because Dara had never left Kerry O'Neill's arms from the moment he had come into the room and given her the beautiful rose for her hair.

'It's a quarter to twelve, I suppose we should start making some noises,' Kate said.

'You don't know the whole principle of drinking-up time,' John said.

'Jesus, Mary and Joseph, you have the heart across me, tell me they have no drink in there.'

'No, I was speaking figuratively,' John said.

'Don't said Kate.

'I meant we told them twelve, so just after twelve we go in making noises, that's the way things are done.'

'How right you are,' Kate said. She felt a yearning to hold John close to her tonight. And she knew he felt the same.

She had always thought that people in wheelchairs didn't feel like that any more, that the feeling just sort of disappeared when so much else had gone.

There were so many things she hadn't known.

'I hope this isn't all very babyish for you,' Dara said to Kerry.

'How do you mean? It's lovely!' He looked at her fondly.

'No, this party, lemonade, no real drink, no band, it must be a bit . . .'

'I don't want real drink, we'd never get a band as good as the Beatles to come to Mountfern so we have their records instead . . . What are you worried about?'

'Nothing,' she said.

'That's good,' said Kerry, 'because you're very beautiful when you are not worried. I don't want to see you frown again. Is that a deal?'

'It's a deal.'

Tommy Leonard asked Jacinta White to dance.

Jacinta was pleased.

'It's been very successful, I suppose,' Tommy said.

'Yes, it's terrific.' Jacinta liked Tommy a lot.

'But the O'Neills took over a bit, didn't they?'

'Did they?' Jacinta was genuinely surprised.

'Maybe they didn't.' Tommy struggled to be fair. 'I just thought they did, for a bit. Like as if they were the only ones that mattered.'

John Ryan came in and collected the empty bottles rather noisily.

'It can't be time yet, Daddy,' Michael hissed at him.

'No, not at all, only about ten past twelve. I was just clearing a few of these away.' John was pleasant.

He noted that the light bulb was laid neatly beside the record player. He put it back in its socket and the place became suddenly very bright. John continued collecting the bottles as if he were unaware how the appearance of the place had changed.

In ten minutes, without his having to call out any message or threat, the party ended.

The youngsters of Mountfern walked home by River Road or up towards the main road or in some cases with their bicycles they headed off to the smallholdings around Mountfern.

The river rippled and rustled in the dark, the moorhens and ducks clucked gently in their resting places as children's feet swished by. The moonlight shone on the nearly completed buildings in Fernscourt, where a new Georgian mansion had risen from the ruins, and where the two great bedroom blocks swept away behind it looking like half-folded wings. For most of them it had been the first night like that they had ever known, and they were filled with thoughts of a future where there would be many more.

The twins sat on the window seat and talked for ages about the party. They talked about how funny Liam was and rude without meaning to be, and how pretty Maggie had looked, and what a clown that big John Joe Conway was, and wasn't Eddie a scream with the dark glasses, and how nice Carrie had been and wasn't it great that Declan had been shy and hung back, and how Mam hadn't come near them and how funny Dad was at the end.

Dara didn't tell Michael about the end of the party.

Michael didn't tell Dara about how much he loved Grace. Yes, love. That wasn't too strong a word for it.

Dara ran her tongue across her lips again and tried to remember Kerry's kiss. It had been so soft.

His mouth had pressed on hers gently at first, and then a little more firmly. That was the first time, that was when they were in the darkest corner of the room, where nobody would see.

She had closed her eyes. She didn't know why but it seemed to come naturally, and he had said again that she was beautiful, so it must have been a normal thing to do.

Then when the party was over and they were all going through the side yard and filing out, he had pulled her back suddenly and behind that archway with the climbing rose, he had held her face between both his hands and kissed her again for a long long time.

'Happy birthday lovely Dara,' he had said.

During all the goodbyes, he had said he would see her soon. She stopped herself from asking when.

The next day and the day after she stopped herself asking Grace had he gone away to Donegal. She knew he wouldn't go without saying goodbye. Not after that kissing.

Dara hugged herself and wanted to cry out to the night skies about it all. But she didn't, she told nobody. Not Michael. Not Grace. Not Maggie.

And certainly not Tommy Leonard, who had said he loved the party himself personally of course, but he would have thought that Dara might have found it a bit dull, what with only dancing with the same person all night.

'No,' Dara had said airily. 'Funny that. I didn't find it dull at all.'

Rachel was responsible for the entire design and decor of Fernscourt. She knew she would come to Ireland again, since this could not be done at long distance. For a while she had hoped she could cut Patrick and his hotel from her life totally. Then she would hand over her meticulous files to her successor, or to whatever firm of interior decorators Patrick could employ.

But this was not to be.

Too much of her life had been spent too deeply enmeshed. She was not going to leave before she saw his dream castle built and built right.

Patrick would not allow himself to be convinced by the unscrupulous in any other field, but when it came to the design of this hotel he had several very blank spots. He had been going to build a phony castle with turrets and Disneyland looks because someone had suggested that this would be suitable for a conquering O'Neill. Rachel had been the one to insist that the original house be built again and the bedroom wings tucked away at an angle.

He would have had it filled with shamrocks, shillelaghs and leprechauns if her watchful eye had not been through every stage with him. Now that the building was complete, and the decorating about to start, it was time for Rachel to return.

She was stronger now, and harder. She was a more lonely woman than the Rachel who had left here eighteen months ago hoping every moment that he would beg her to stay. Now when she came back it would be with fewer illusions.

And with fewer millstones around her neck.

Like she knew she would not set foot in the Slieve Sunset.

She asked Kate to put her mind to thinking about this, and within hours of getting the letter Kate was on the phone.

'I've found you the perfect place,' she said overjoyed that her great friend was coming back to Mountfern and coming to be beside her. It had taken a little persuasion. But she had found exactly the right place for Rachel to stay.

Loretto Quinn was appalled.

'A smart American woman with all those grand clothes like Mrs Fine. No Kate, honestly, I couldn't cope with that. I only agreed to do all this because you said there'd be a few shillings in it once the hotel was built. No, I don't want the fright and the worry of trying to please people that are way beyond me like that.'

'Shush, Loretto, listen. This is the best thing you could have. Rachel will be coming back and forward all the time, she will want her own place, she might even take them permanently.'

'Won't she be staying in the hotel yonder when it's finished?'

'It won't be finished for ages and the Grange is too far away. Your place would be just ideal. I only thought of it this morning when she was on the phone. I am a sort of genius so I am.'

'You might be and all, Kate, but you have the heart across me. There's only beds and chairs in those rooms, there's no proper furniture, only the plainest of white curtains on them that you'd see in a lunatic asylum . . .'

'Leave it just as it is, I beg you. That's Rachel's job, that's what she gets paid a fortune for, knowing what to put on this and what not to put. You and I couldn't see it in a million years. She'll give you great advice altogether. I mean it. Look at what she did for me. She'll have your bedrooms the talk of the town. Marian Johnson will be green with envy, she'll be climbing the drainpipes to get a peep at them.'

The thought of Marian Johnson being envious of poor little Loretto Quinn was such a happy one that the women laughed imagining it.

'What'll she put her clothes on till it's all done up though?' Loretto was practical.

'I know, we'll get one of those coat rails they have in shops, a big long one. Jimbo could get you one from one of the bigger shops away in the town. I'll ring a few places for you.'

'It wouldn't be too bare?'

'Nothing can be too bare, apparently. That's what having style is all about.'

Rachel brought them all gifts. For Dara a red dress with white tassels, bright and showy and ready to transform her into the colourful girl that Kate always knew she could be. For Michael a huge book about fish and fishing all over the world, for Eddie a bicycle lamp that looked like something from outer space, for Declan a box of horrible joke items including a cushion that made a sound like a fart when you sat on it.

Rachel had remembered that John had lost weight – there was clearly nothing she had forgotten from Kate's letters – so she had brought him two smart linen jackets: one in navy, one in a daring gold-tan colour. He looked bashful trying it on but delighted with the inspection in the mirror.

Kate was right, John Ryan had slimmed down and looked somehow taller. He was so pleased with the tan jacket he planned an entire outfit based on the colour and said Rachel would have to come to the big town with him one day to advise him.

For Kate there were magnificent green, blue and gold silk scarves, each one more elegant than the next. Rachel had magic in her fingers when it came to draping them and arranging them. Everyone gasped as Kate spun her wheel-chair around for admiration in the blue and silver scarf. Leopold, who had been watching through the glass door, set up a howl of approval and chased his tail happily.

It was lovely to be back in this place, and better to be back on her own terms. Rachel didn't have to worry about Patrick, about what mood he would be in, or what time he got back from Dublin. She didn't have to feel alarmed when Marian Johnson put her ludicrous oar in trying to drag up remembered incidents and share jokes. No indeed, she didn't miss Patrick here, and as Kate had said, it *did* make her feel more independent. More her own woman.

She was touched at how welcome they made her and specially by the nervousness of Loretto Quinn, who was up at Ryan's apologizing for the bedrooms before Rachel had even seen them. She hastened to inspect them and put the nervous woman at her ease.

'This is magnificent, Loretto,' Rachel had said. 'And if you wouldn't take it amiss I'll have plenty of spare samples of fabrics and little extras and if you like we could do these rooms up for next to nothing while I'm here.'

Loretto thought that she was in heaven. In days beautiful lilac-coloured curtains had arrived – and by an extraordinary coincidence they were just the right size – together with the heather carpet and the cream fabric with lilac flowers for bedspread and cushions. In front of her eyes and with no fuss Loretto saw her rooms transformed. She would walk upstairs and look at her tasteful guest rooms and clasp her hands with pleasure.

There had also been an offcut in some big heavy red for a bedspread for Loretto's own room, and red and white curtains. Rachel for all her glamour was as nice as anything, she had even found a very bright colourful lino offcut that was just the right size for Loretto's shop, and since it looked so smart in that nice green and red, why not paint the counter red and the shelves green? Those young lads of Kate Ryan's would only be delighted to help out. People began to praise Loretto in terms that they never had before. Wasn't she the smart little thing now to brighten up her huckster's shop in readiness for all the visitors? Who would ever have thought that she had so much sense?

When Patrick called on Loretto Quinn he couldn't believe the transformation. Her pathetic little place looked smart and cheerful. Even the woman herself looked as if she had been made over by some women's magazine for a before and after feature.

'Mrs Fine about, is she?' he said casually.

Loretto had been given her instructions very clearly.

'She's away on business, Mr O'Neill.'

'What business?'

'Mrs Fine didn't tell me, sir.'

'When's she coming back?'

'She didn't say that either, Mr O'Neill.'

'She's being mighty secretive about her movements, I must say.'

'Oh no, nothing like that, she's full of chat, Mrs Fine, such a nice person. I was nervous of her coming here in the first place, but now I can't think why. She couldn't have been more help to me.'

Patrick had suspected he saw Rachel's hand in the transformed shop.

'Yes, I'm sure that's true, Mrs Quinn, it's just that I expected her here to give me a report on everything.'

'Did she know you were coming here, Mr O'Neill? She couldn't have surely?'

'No, well it was a last-minute thing.'

'There you are.' Loretto was triumphant that her new friend Mrs Fine hadn't been at fault.

'I'll take a look at her rooms while I'm here,' Patrick said grumpily.

Loretto looked embarrassed. 'I don't think . . . I mean . . .'

'Oh, Mrs Fine wouldn't mind, Rachel would like me to see that she had a nice place to stay.'

'It's just that . . . you see. If I let rooms to one person I can't be responsible to let other people in. You do see that, Mr O'Neill, I can't be letting people traipse through.'

'I'm not other people, I'm not traipsing through . . .' Patrick was very annoyed now.

'But you do see. Perhaps when Mrs Fine gets back, if *she* would like to show you her rooms, it would be different.'

Patrick banged out of the shop.

The woman was right, of course, but for God's sake the last time he had been here she was like a bag lady shovelling potatoes out of dirty old bags. Now she was all dressed up, the potatoes were in big clean containers, Loretto was taking attitudes and striking poses about showing the rooms upstairs. It was too much.

Patrick didn't risk going into Ryan's Licensed Premises. He had managed to fight with everyone he met since getting back, so he decided to put off the possibility of taking John by the lapels or entering into a screaming match with Kate in her wheelchair. He parked his car out of sight of them, and walked across the footbridge. The mansion gave him scant pleasure this morning. All he could see were the faults – the ugly angle of the drive for one thing. How much better it would have been to have come straight down in one long tree-lined sweep to the river. But how could he have suggested that when, the very day he was going to propose buying their property, Kate was crippled for life on his own building site? Then he didn't like the huge forecourt, either. It was too bare, too like a parking lot. Which was what it was. Rachel had urged him to leave three trees there but he had thought they would hide the house too much and they would be just further objects to negotiate for buses and cars. He had been wrong and Rachel had been right.

Where *was* she for God's sake?

Brian Doyle was glad to see him anyway. That made a nice change, Patrick thought grimly. He took off his jacket and sat down in Brian's site office.

'Tell me why you're glad to see me, Brian, is it because I am such a good kind employer responsible for the livelihood of at least two hundred people give or take, responsible for your own inflated lifestyle and yet another new car which I see parked outside? Is that why my presence makes you glad? Or is it because I'm the first peasant within five hundred miles who bought the Big House and made it live the way we want it to live? Or is it because of my curly brown hair and twinkling blue eyes?'

Brian looked at Patrick in alarm. He supposed the man must have been drinking, it could be the only explanation.

'Would you like a cup of coffee?' he began.

'This may come as a shock to you, Brian, but I would not like a cup of coffee. I have never, since all this began, liked any cup of coffee I have had here. It has become an interesting guessing game to know whether it *is* coffee, or tea or Bovril or the water that all these things have been washed up in.'

'Oh well then, forget it.' Brian wasn't at all offended at the insult to the coffee made on site, he took it that Mr O'Neill was beyond coffee, and wanted a drink fast.

'Will we go down to Ryan's and talk then?' he said agreeably.

'We will *not* go down to Ryan's, we will talk here. It may have escaped your notice that it is ten-fifty in the morning, not a time for adjourning to a pub even by your standards.'

'Jesus Christ, nothing would please you today.'

'You may be right. Why were you glad to see me?'

'There's been a lot of messages for one thing, people wanting to get in touch with you. The phone's not stopped all morning.'

'Right,' Patrick grunted. 'Where's Rachel?'

'Who?'

'Rachel Fine. Has it escaped your notice that she has been working with me since 1963 in the design and interior decoration of this hotel which has made you a millionaire ten times over?'

You couldn't insult Brian Doyle, which was one of his great strengths.

'Oh, Mrs Fine? I've no idea where she is, she's been in and out, but you know what she's like, a very helpful lady – never gets in the way, does her work, leaves a note about it and is gone.'

'Yes, well what note did she leave?'

'It was measurements, someone here gave her the wrong figures for the dining room, they'd got it all wrong, the shop was going to send twice too much material, Mrs Fine headed them off. She's saving you a packet that lady, I tell you. A packet.'

'I'm glad somebody's saving me a packet, with the way that other people lash it all out.'

'Maybe when you feel more yourself,' said Brian in the tone that you'd use to talk to a drunk about to fall off a bar stool.

'I *am* myself, you idiot,' said Patrick. 'I just want you to *ring* these guys as you call it. *Ring* them on that phone, as you call it, and tell them I'm not here.'

'Everyone calls it *ring*, it's not a word I made up,' cried Brian, stung at last to some kind of response. 'And you told me yourself that you always grasped the nettle, Mr O'Neill, you always took the bull by the horns, you said that was the one sure road to success. I've been following your example, I've been doing it myself, and it does seem to work. I've been doing much better.'

'You've been doing much better because I handed you the job of a lifetime on a plate and you are taking a lifetime to complete it!' Patrick was aware that his bad temper was doing him no good but he wasn't ready to stop yet.

'Now Brian, listen to me. You do what I say, and do it now. I'm getting the hell out of here before I have a heart attack and the litigation about the hotel becomes legal history and with any luck you'd never get paid the last bit.'

'And when do I say you're going to be here?'

'You don't know. You haven't a goddamn clue.'

Patrick grabbed his jacket and got up to head for the footbridge.

'But Mr O'Neill, can't I show you what we've done . . .'

'I see what you've done, the front is like a tarmac in an airport.'

'Shit, Mr O'Neill, everything was in the plans . . .'

'Don't you say shit to me . . .'

'But don't you want a tour of the site as usual?'

'How can I if I'm not here?'

Patrick was half way down to the footbridge when he saw Dara Ryan running towards him excitedly.

'Hallo, Mr O'Neill,' she called, pleased to see him.

'Well Dara, good to see you.' He noticed that she was becoming a striking-looking girl, tall, dark, in a white tee shirt, jeans and a red flower tucked behind her ear – or maybe it was a bit of jewellery.

'When did you get back?' she asked.

'A little while ago. Everyone I've met has fought with me so far. You're not going to have a punch-up are you?'

'Lord, no.' She seemed eager to talk. 'Did you have a good time?'

'In Dublin. No, not really, not at all in fact. Nothing but meetings and more meetings and nothing much at the end of it. Despite what you may think I actually don't enjoy fighting.'

'I never thought you enjoyed fighting,' Dara said. She was anxious to ask him something. He wondered what it was.

'Well, you're right.' He smiled warmly at her. It was true, he didn't enjoy a fight. He had not enjoyed the scenes some weeks back after a demarcation dispute between two sets of workers. In front of fifty men he had told Brian Doyle that they had three hours in which to decide which men did what work. If it were not agreed then every single man would be paid off that afternoon. There had been something in his face that sorted out the dispute in far less than the three hours he had given them.

It was a victory but he hadn't enjoyed it.

'And what are you doing here on the footbridge? Were you lying in wait for me?' he asked.

'Not really, I was wondering when you'd be back, there's a folk concert up in the grounds of the ruined abbey, lots of quite well-known singers, and I was wondering . . .'

'I think I'm a bit old for it, Dara,' he teased.

'No, I meant if Kerry was interested in going. I wasn't sure when you were both coming back so I kept an eye out.'

He looked at her and sighed. 'Kerry won't be back for the concert,' he said.

'He's not with you?'

'No, he wasn't in Dublin, he went straight to Donegal, did he not tell you?'

'I must have got it wrong,' said Dara Ryan. The light had gone out of her big dark eyes.

'Can we go out for a walk?' Rachel said. It was a very sunny afternoon but with a nice breeze.

'Sure, hold on a moment until I get some gum and stick my spine together, then I'll leap up and come with you,' Kate said without rancour.

'I meant me going for a walk, you going for a push.'

'It's boring,' Kate said. 'You have to shout over my shoulder, I have to crane my neck. I wish I had a pram, people can talk *to* babies, not over their heads.'

'We can talk when we get there,' Rachel said.

'Get where?'

'Mystery tour.'

'Why not? Let me drape one of your scarves elegantly around me so that I'll knock the eyes out of anyone we meet.'

They went first to Loretto Quinn's. Kate couldn't believe the changes that had been made. Normally Loretto was so indecisive she couldn't decide whether to wrap your potatoes in newspaper, put them into a paper bag or feed them straight into your shopping bag. Now it appeared that in under two weeks her entire shop had been refurbished. There was even a man re-doing the sign over the door.

Two men in the shop lifted Kate's wheelchair inside so that she could see. She propelled herself around touching this and stroking that. There was so much room here now. The place looked an entirely different *class* of a shop. Much more upper-class or something. Yet her prices were the same. Kate was full of praise.

'But it's all Mrs Fine, Kate, she's a walking saint – a bit like yourself. I don't know why she did all this for me, I really don't. I'd never in a month of Sundays have been able to think of it all myself, or if I thought of it, I'd never have been able to do it.'

Loretto looked taller, Kate thought, suddenly, which was nonsense. But maybe she was standing up more straight now, and she had tidied herself up. It wouldn't do to be the old wishy-washy Loretto with pale hair falling into her eyes and a grubby pink overall. She wore a smart brown shopcoat, with a white blouse underneath. Her hair was clipped back with a smart red slide, undoubtedly a gift from Rachel.

Kate sighed. 'You're a sort of magician, you know, you've changed Loretto's life,' she said to Rachel as they went back along River Road.

'It's easy to change other people's lives, it's your own that's the problem,' Rachel laughed.

'Hey, is the tour over? That was very short as a mystery tour – up to Loretto's and back.'

'No no, it hasn't begun. I thought we'd go across the footbridge and look at the hotel.'

It was said lightly, but they both knew it wasn't light. Kate hadn't been across the Fern for more than two years. Not since the day she had walked across the footbridge herself and been carried out of the site unconscious in an ambulance.

'Oh I don't think so, Rachel.'

They were at the footbridge. Rachel came round to the front of the wheelchair and squatted down in front of Kate. Her perfectly arranged hair in its short natural looking curls that took her thirty minutes to arrange every morning hadn't been disturbed. Her make-up made her look like a young girl. Her big dark eyes were troubled and fixed on Kate.

She spoke very seriously.

'I'm not some kind of psychologist trying to get you over the shock of where you had your accident. Lord, Kate, why would I want to do that? You could live for the rest of your life without going back to the spot where your back was broken. What good on earth would it do you to see the place? Not that you *will* be able to see the place now anyway.'

'So why do you want me to go over there?'

'I want to talk to you.'

'Can't we talk here or go back to my green room and talk?'

Kate sounded upset but Rachel pretended not to notice.

'Please, Kate, I want to talk to you about the hotel. We might as well talk about it in Brooklyn if you don't come with me and see what I mean.'

'I know what it's like, I've heard.'

'Please.'

'You're the one with the legs, I might as well give in graciously.'

'This is giving in graciously?' Rachel laughed.

The little path that Rachel hadn't been able to walk on that summer day because of her high heels and flimsy shoes was now a tarmacadamed all-weather pathway. With little seats placed here and there, often set into rocks or under trees. It wasn't neat and orderly like a public park, it was more as if someone had decided here would be a good place to sit and talk. The ground had been turned and dug and planted, with evergreen bushes here and lawns there. The steep slopes were planted in terraces.

'I had no idea there was so much work done here,' Kate breathed as they paused to look at shrubs and rock gardens.

'It cost a fine penny I can tell you, fleets of gardeners still working on it, but it's destined not to need too much maintenance once it's finished.'

On and up they went towards the house.

Although she had seen it many times from her own home across the river, Kate was unprepared for the sheer size of it. This was a huge place. She looked at the big sweep up to the front door. A dozen tour buses could come in and turn here, and perhaps fifty cars park as well, but this wasn't the real car park, that was round the side. The three-storey house faced across the river. It was a reproduction of a classic Georgian house, with its high windows, its fanlight over the door. Plain and clean-lined and already, Kate noticed, at least twenty well-watered plants of virginia creeper. In five years the place would look as if it had always stood there. Patrick had been given very good advice.

Kate noticed the broken urns that she had heard about, the expensive ornaments that had been dashed to the ground one night. There had been talk about it in the pub, children some said.

There had been much more than the usual run of vandalism and hooliganism around the place. Sergeant Sheehan had confided that it looked as if it were orchestrated, which seemed hard to believe. After all, who would have a grudge against Patrick O'Neill setting up a business that would bring prosperity to everyone, the Sergeant had asked.

Kate looked up at the house in wonder. It was so like those old pictures that John had unearthed in journals and lithographs of the time. It was like the sepia pictures that he had also shown her. A big house with its two bedroom wings folded away neatly behind, not spoiling the impression of the main house. She could hardly wait to see inside.

There was a ramp into the hotel at one side, where Rachel pushed the wheelchair easily.

'What made you think of this?' Kate asked in self-mockery. 'Was it so as I could come to call?'

Inside there were men working still, putting in light fitments. Others were working on the huge staircase going up from the hall. Some of the men knew Kate to see and came over to welcome her. Others remembered her from the day of the accident. Everyone knew Mrs Fine and everyone could have given their view on her relationship with the big man Mr O'Neill, if pressed.

'The elevators are installed but they haven't been passed as safe yet, so all things considered I don't think we will . . .'

'Too right,' Kate agreed enthusiastically. 'To be carried unconscious from here a second time would be overdoing it.'

Brian Doyle, who was surprised to see her there in the first place, scratched his head in wonder.

Kate decided she had been very stupid. Rachel had taken her on a tour of the Thatch Bar, a huge place with seating for two hundred and a stage for the entertainment. Four thatchers had been working on it for months and the roof looked like velvet. Not at all like the real thatch around here, often neglected and full of weeds, but perfect and what was more the perfect American idea of a dream Irish cottage.

They had been round the back and seen the terrace where little stone tables had been installed. The plan was to serve drinks out here in the summer.

Then inside the house one of the panelled rooms was called the Study Bar. Here, from a bar surrounded by old books in glass cases, further drinks would be served. Of course there would be a cocktail lounge too, just before going into the dining room.

Slowly it sank in.

'I see why you took me on the mystery tour, Rachel, dear Rachel,' Kate said.

'Can you wheel me to one of those nice stone seats we passed, somewhere where no machinery can fall on us? And we can have our little talk.'

In silence Rachel found them a quiet place. Looking downhill and over the footbridge they could see Ryan's Licensed Premises nestling where it always had nestled.

'I didn't realize. I really didn't realize,' Kate said simply. 'Nothing was hidden from me, no lies were told, but I just couldn't see.'

'That's why I wanted you to come here,' Rachel said.

'We might as well close down now, rather than wait until the opening.'

'No, that's not what I was trying to tell you,' said Rachel.

'Well what then?'

'I'm not sure yet, something different.'

'What's different than closing down when you've no business?'

'No, I mean could you do something different, could you change things a bit?'

'Dancing girls maybe?' Kate was bitter-sounding now. 'That's about the only thing he hasn't thought of . . . a big neon sign, Ryan's Raunchy Roadhouse . . . see the ladies in corsets flinging their legs around. Maybe Canon Moran could come and take the money at the door.'

'What would make them come down a path, cross a bridge to go somewhere else?'

'Somewhere much duller.'

'What would make them?'

'If I knew that would my heart be pounding inside me?'

'Think, Kate, think what do visitors want, what do you want when you go somewhere?'

'I don't ever go anywhere. I go to mass, and what do I want then, I want it to be Father Hogan because he's quicker, I want there not to be two collections, I want not to be parked in a draught.'

'Kate. I'm trying to help you.'

'I *know* you are, but why ask me what do I want when I go somewhere? I swear I don't go anywhere, I've only been on three holidays in my life, the first one down here when I met John, the second our honeymoon in Killarney and the third when we went to Dublin to see President Kennedy. How do I know what I'd want or what anyone would want?'

Rachel gave up trying to draw things out of her. She leaned over. She counted on the well-manicured fingers of her hands.

'Listen, one, they might want fishing gear, you could specialize in bait and hooks.'

'*Bait?*' screamed Kate. '*Bait* in a public house where people are supposed to be drinking, a nice smelly jar of worms and a glass of Guinness!'

'No, I meant around the side. Two, they might want stationery to write home, postcards. You could sell those.'

'How could I tell Jack Leonard I was going to sell writing pads and envelopes? Have sense, Rachel, you've been here long enough to know that we wouldn't *do* that sort of thing to each other.'

'What else do people need?' Rachel went on remorselessly. 'Three, they'll need their hair fixed, and I can tell you that Rita Walsh is getting ready for that in the Rosemarie hair salon. She has offered me a free permanent in return for a little advice about how to have the place right.'

'And did you help her?'

'Sure I did, I got her a bit of this and that, suggested she rent a few new dryers – hers would frighten you just to look at them. Then I told her the truth, that Patrick had been planning a beauty salon in the hotel itself and I had said give the Rosemarie a year to see if it can cater for the guests. Rita has no time for her other activities these nights, she's too busy getting the place to rights before the grand opening.'

Kate was impressed. 'That's Rita and Loretto fixed up, and I suppose Jack Coyne might get a bit of business now. Is the feud over?'

'Not really, but Patrick must see that it is handier to have someone across the road in case the guests want to rent a car. He'll have to watch him like a hawk, and all accounts direct to the hotel, not to the client.'

'So that only leaves the poor Ryans, and we won't sell bait or stationery. What had you planned for us?'

Rachel took Kate's hand. 'Please Kate, don't be like that with me.'

269

'It's unforgivable, you're quite right. Here, lean over and give me a kiss, I'm afraid to lean over at you in case I upset the wheelchair and roll down into the river.'

They held on to each other for a long minute.

'Right. Seriously, I've got over it now, that rotten spiteful temper of mine. Please help me, Rachel.'

'I was wondering would you consider doing traditional Irish teas, and selling souvenirs. Potato cakes maybe, toasted brack, Irish soda bread.'

'We couldn't. Not in a pub. Rachel, you don't understand pubs and drinking people. They would go stark staring mad if there was a hint of a leprechaun for sale or a cup of tea being served.'

'Not in the pub. Beside it.'

'Where we had the twins' party?' Kate asked in disbelief.

'It wouldn't be a big job,' Rachel was saying thoughtfully.

'It would be way beyond us even if we'd consider it, which we would not in a million years.'

'No, it wouldn't be expensive, a couple of the men could come from here, they're paid by the week anyway and sometimes there just isn't any work *for* them, and Patrick is never anxious to pay people to stand about, he prefers to have something for them to do . . .'

'And I know,' Kate broke in, 'there's going to be a few offcuts of lino, and on-cuts of carpet and end rolls of tablecloths and starts of rolls for curtains, and you'll furnish the whole place for us and we'll think we did it ourselves. And one day when Dara is dressed as an Irish colleen and the boys are all doing step dancing between tables of soda bread, we'll say to each other, "*Whatever* was it like in the old days?" '

Rachel looked at her and saw the tears were pouring down Kate's face. 'I'm so sorry, Kate. Oh God, I'm sorry.'

Kate sat alone in her room for a long time. She told herself that she hadn't learned much since her accident, she was still impatient and quick to judge what was right and what was wrong. But at least she had learned something about thinking before you speak. She wouldn't burden John with all she had discovered today, no more blurting out everything. She would definitely think before she spoke. In the old days she used to say it was the hallmark of a knave and a con man, someone who would have weighed up the pros and cons before venturing an opinion. But that was the old days.

She tried out some of her notions.

You need to test market ideas, she had read somewhere.

'Dara do you think we should run a guest house? You know, have people to stay and charge them. For staying like?'

'I know what a guest house is, Mammy,' Dara said.

'Well, should we?'

'Here? There's hardly room enough for us in this house let alone other people. Where would they sleep?'

'I suppose we could build rooms for them?'

270

'But why? Why on earth would we do that?'
'I don't know. I just thought we might. Everyone else seems to be – Loretto, and I believe Rita Walsh is thinking of it too.'
'What would we want to get in to it for with all that competition?'
'We have a licence, they don't. We could have a bar trade. Maybe keep commercial travellers.'
'Are you feeling all right, Mammy?'
'Perfectly. Why do you ask?'
'Only a very unwell person would think up such an idea. And *now* of all times, where's all this business going to come from suddenly? Nobs across the river by the busload, ordinary people on this side, and now you want a guest house full of drunks.'
'I didn't say that.'
'Yes you did, you said there'd be a whole lot of commercial travellers who'd want to get blind drunk at night and stay in rooms that we'd have to build on for them.'
'I never heard of anything so mad,' Kate said, exasperated.
'That's what I thought, Mam, that's why I asked you were you feeling all right. If there were all these drunken commercial travellers roaming the land looking for places to stay we'd have heard of them surely?'

'Loretto, where do you buy your eggs?'
'From about four farmers' wives, I spread it round a bit to give them all a turn, and then I have four families who come and deal with me as a result.'
'Are they very dear?'
Loretto was puzzled. 'No of course they're not, they're whatever the cost, you know.'
Kate felt that Loretto should really be able to explain things a bit more clearly. 'I meant it must be hard on you having to depend on farmers' wives.'
'It's not a bit hard, aren't they dying to sell the eggs and make a few shillings? What made you think of that?'
'I was thinking of how much handier it would be if you had someone near you with a lot of hens, someone you could rely on.'
'Oh, I'd hate that,' Loretto said airily. 'I'd have to pay them whatever they said, it wouldn't be the same at all. I like the women coming in and chatting. Everyone likes that, that's the way they buy eggs above in Bridge Street too.'
'I see.' So there was no point in thinking of a small poultry farm.
Loretto's face suddenly took on a new expression.
'Oh Kate, I'm very thoughtless, I forgot you had a few hens. Did *you* want to sell me the odd half-dozen or anything?'
'No, we've only five hens and we eat all they produce and more. No, I was just thinking about the economy, that's all. I do sometimes but it's always a mistake.'

'Sheila, did you ever wonder why nobody ever started a launderette in this place?'
Mrs Whelan said the thought had never crossed her mind.
'It has to be something that nobody thought of, that's all. You can rent the

271

machines, you know, you don't have to have any great outlay. Then all you do is watch the people coming and filling them up with coins.'

'It wouldn't ever take off here, of course,' Mrs Whelan said simply.

'I don't know, the place is getting bigger, what with the hotel and everything, it's going to be a much bigger place than we thought.'

'It is and it isn't, Kate. But the hotel will have its own laundry, you won't see the guests taking a pillow case of dirty washing down to Bridge Street...'

'Or...'

'Or to wherever someone would put it.' Mrs Whelan seemed anxious for Kate to divulge no mad little hopes.

'A laundermat or whatever they're called would need a place where there'd be young people living on their own, there isn't even a bank here employing a dozen youngsters. No, nobody would be seen going to a laundermat. Can you see Miss Purcell taking Fergus Slattery's smalls to a public washing place? The humiliation of it!'

'You don't think it would work?'

'No, Kate, I think it would be foolish.'

'I see.'

'Times will get better.'

'Times are fine now. It's later I worry about.'

'You'll manage, you always have.'

'I don't know, I really don't.'

'Fergus, it's Kate Ryan.'

'Well now.' The warmth and delight in his voice were obvious.

'I wanted to talk to you, about a worry. Would you be able to come out here at lunchtime?'

'I'll come right away.' He took a file from the cabinet. Deirdre paused in her work to notice that it was Kate Ryan's compensation file.

'Is she going to talk about it?' she asked.

'I think so,' Fergus said.

Mary Donnelly looked at him suspiciously.

'She's been a bit flushed and feverish. You won't upset her?'

'I never upset any woman, Mary,' said Fergus. 'That has been my weakness and sorrow in life.'

'Don't make a mock out of something very serious.' Mary banged into the kitchen but she was back in twenty seconds.

'I forgot, Mrs Ryan, you said you'd look after the bar for an hour...'

'I forgot too,' Kate said agreeably. 'Still, I can do it. No one comes in this early, we'll have the place to ourselves. You go on about your business, Mary.'

Fergus marvelled at the easy graceful way Kate manoeuvred the wheelchair into the bar. Up the ramp behind the counter.

He went to his accustomed place on a high stool.

'Would you like a drink since you're in the right place for it?' She smiled.

'No, even mad country solicitors don't start this early.' He looked at her. Mary was right, her eyes were very bright, her colour high.

'What is it?' He was gentle.

'I hate saying this to you of all people, because I always shut you up about it, but I'm worried. I think that we're going to be in big trouble when Fernscourt opens.'

'You're in big trouble already.' He looked at the wheelchair.

'No, we are not going to go over that again. I can't fight a man on the grounds that I went in despite all those notices and got hurt. I'm talking about something else, about the trade. I think he and the hotel are going to take all our trade.'

Fergus was silent.

'So I just wanted your advice. I was thinking of all kinds of things we might do. I mean I could do anything. *Anything.*'

'Oh Kate.'

'Don't "Oh Kate" me . . . I can and will do anything to keep this place in the black, I really will. It's just that I got a bit frightened. I seem to be the last person in Mountfern to realize how changed everything is going to be.'

'But I tell you.'

'No, don't go on about how terrible he is and how he should have stayed in America, that's useless. It's practical advice I want. Look at everyone else: Loretto is all smartened up, and have you seen Rita Walsh's place, it's like something in Grafton Street.'

Fergus smiled bitterly. 'I've looked at everyone all right. Oh, they were all able to jump at the smell of money. Simple country town, how are you? This lot have their eye to the main chance, they'd be a fair match for the shysters on Broadway or the Bowery or the Bronx wherever it was your man made his money.'

'Don't make people out to be grasping, they're not, they're just . . .'

'No, not all of them are, I give you that. There are a few who have their loyalty. Not a lot, but a few.'

'But what loyalty?' Kate was puzzled. 'Who are they being loyal to if they don't want to make a bit of money out of all the changes?'

'To you for one,' Fergus said simply.

'Oh, don't be ridiculous.' She was really annoyed now. 'What has it to do with me? I don't want to be the cause of any fighting. I was talking about the changes and how we should all be ready for them. Yes, us too. I've been thinking about nothing else. How it's going to change our lives. How everything's going to be different.'

'It will be different all right.' Fergus was grim. 'You were up there yourself, Jimbo told me that Rachel brought you up for a gander at the place. How many bars did you see? Not counting the ones they'll have in the function rooms whenever there's a do on. I counted them. I counted four, didn't you? That's a fair amount of drinks for a guy to get through before dinner, if he wants a hightail or a screwball.'

'Highball, screwdriver,' she corrected him automatically, as she would Michael.

'I know, I wondered if *you* did.'

Her eyes flashed at him angrily. 'All right, Mr Know-all, if you know so much can you tell me what to do?'

'Yes, certainly I can.' He took the file from its big brown envelope and laid it on the bar.

273

She flinched away from it. '*No*, that is *not* what I want. I don't want his charity, I don't want it all to be in court. That's not what I want at all, a future based on money I got from him by a trick of law. I want to earn a living, be his equal that way.' She was both troubled and annoyed.

So was Fergus. 'Stop being a Christian martyr, Kate, it's too late for all that.'

'I will *not* have this place divided over my accident, I will not have them taking sides, I don't want the whole of Mountfern getting upset about this and fighting over it . . .'

'If I have to tell you this once more I will lose what marbles I have left, and I assure you they are not many. It is *not* his charity it is his insurance, and the whole of Mountfern is not fighting about you. Can you get that into your thick skull?'

'Fergus!'

'I mean it. I really have lost patience with you. You pay insurance here, if a man falls off this stool and breaks his head, it's your insurance that pays for it, Einstein, not you and John. That's why you pay the bloody thing.'

She laughed and relented. 'I suppose you're right. I'll talk to John about it tonight. We must stop behaving like ostriches.'

He looked a little mollified.

She reached across and took both his hands in hers. 'You are a good true friend to us, I mean that.'

As they sat holding hands the pub door opened silently and in the way nuns have of moving without appearing to take steps Sister Laura rolled silently into the bar.

Kate cursed the greater freedoms that allowed nuns to enter public houses instead of denouncing them.

Fergus wondered was there a law of timing like a law of gravity. Something that almost made people arrive in places at the wrong time.

'I hope I haven't come at a wrong time, Mrs Ryan.'

Sister Laura had a great devotion to St Francis of Assisi which was unfortunate because Leopold sensed an animal lover and opened his great jaws, closed his sad eyes and gave a treble wail drowning any possible explanation that Mrs Ryan and Mr Slattery might have been about to make about their untoward conduct.

'There's no doubt about it, Sister, but your lot are everywhere now,' Fergus said admiringly. 'I'll be off.'

'Well, if you're sure you've finished.' Sister Laura's eyes were innocent.

'It's very hard ever to be finished in a pub, Sister, but of course your lifestyle hasn't as yet led you to explore that side of the human condition.'

He waved from the door. 'Kate, I'll come up with some ideas and when you've talked to John I'll come and discuss them.'

'Thanks.' Kate waved back.

'Very nice young man,' Sister Laura said, sitting down as if she had been used to going into pubs all her life. 'Does the most marvellous work for the community for minimal cost. Of course it's really time he got married and settled down. Bachelors don't seem to fit into today's world like they did in previous generations. Steady him down, don't you think?'

'Well yes . . .' Kate was at a great disadvantage now. Anything she said would be bound to be taken the wrong way.

'I won't stay long, Mrs Ryan, it would turn away trade seeing a nun in here. What I wanted to say was that we've had a letter from a convent in France and there are a lot of families there who are very anxious to make contact with Irish Catholic families and have Irish Catholic girls come out there.'

Kate sighed. 'You know, that was something I had really hoped for Dara, to do an exchange with a French girl, but we didn't have the money this year when I was working it out. The cost of having a girl here would not be great, I know, but we'd have to entertain her, take her places. That would cost money.'

'No, this is au pair. You know, doing a little light domestic duties and speaking English to the children.'

'When would that be, Sister?' Kate was interested.

'It was summer they were really thinking about. Two families in particular. We have the highest references. It's in the Loire country where the châteaux are. It would be a great opportunity.'

'I'll have to talk to Dara's father, Sister Laura. There are a lot of things to take into account. The fare, and that. And if she'll go! She's very thick with the Americans, she may not want to go off to France in the middle of her summer.'

'She'll learn no French and very little else from an American girl.' Sister Laura had fairly trenchant views about everything. 'I'll be off anyway and if you do decide, let me know.'

'I will indeed, Sister. Thank you for your interest.'

'She's a nice bright girl that Dara,' Sister Laura said. 'She's a very bright girl. She lost a lot of ground the year you had your accident, poor child, she was grieving for you a lot.'

'I don't know how she managed at all,' Kate said.

'Of course she's probably like a lighting devil nowadays, they all *are* at home.' Sister Laura spoke in a matter-of-fact way that made Kate giggle.

'I don't seem to be able to do much right, that's true,' she admitted.

'I think you'd find her a lot more appreciative after a spell in France, they learn to be grateful for home comforts.'

The nun had bright laughing eyes. Kate wondered what life would have been like for Sister Laura if she hadn't entered the convent. Would she have been an all-wise all-knowing mother of a fifteen-year-old? Very possibly.

'John?'

'Hold on a minute, I'll come in to you.' He came in and perched on the edge of the long table that went round the walls. He looked at the pages of notes and files strewn around Kate but didn't ask her what they were.

'Wasn't that a great idea, that long table? In a million years I'd never have thought of anything so useful.' He patted the furniture admiringly.

'Is there nobody in the bar?' Kate didn't want business neglected.

'Divil a one.' He was hamming at her. It annoyed her suddenly, there would be enough call for all that stage Irishry later.

'Well listen, if you have a minute I want to tell you . . . well to ask you really. To discuss . . .' She shuffled all the papers with her writing on them together.

'Yes?' He was mild and encouraging. Could he really be so blind to his surroundings, and to the fact that his business was going to the wall?

'We'll have to change a lot, I was thinking.'

'I know. I know.'

She didn't want to hear a soothing voice, she wanted some fire, she wanted him to take the initiative.

'I think we've been fools sitting here believing that it's all going to be sunshine and laughter when the place beyond opens . . .' She paused for a moment, half expecting him to say something in defence of Patrick, but he said nothing.

'I think we'll have to start up something else, it would be mad to think they'll leave all the bars they have over in that place to drink in ours.'

'Particularly on a bad day,' John agreed. 'And our own crowd will want to be where there's all the activity. So we'd better offer them something else apart from drink.'

Kate looked at him surprised. 'What would you think about a café, you know, traditional sort of teas? I know it's not what you're used to, what you expected things would be like.'

John didn't look at all taken aback by the idea, she realized. He must have come to the same conclusion himself.

'Nothing's what we were used to,' he said, touching the wheelchair. 'Nothing was what we expected things to be like. But we've survived, and we'll go on surviving.'

CHAPTER SEVENTEEN

Fergus Slattery told Kate that the case was in the Lists for next September. That it would now have to be heard, no further delays would be tolerated. Fergus hoped that the case would coincide with the hotel opening. He would love the thought of the great O'Neill missing his party because he was in court hearing a huge award for compensation being given against him. The thought of it made Fergus almost dizzy with delight. He felt his life had become grey and tired; only the thought of Kate's compensation gave it any fire at all.

Sometimes Deirdre saw Fergus finger the slim pile of documents as he took out a letter or added one to the pile. It was moving very slowly, and even when Counsel had been briefed and it should have gone much further ahead, all kinds of things intervened. There was the delay caused by the courthouse in the big town being declared unfit for use, and so cases were adjourned. Then there was a backlog occasioned by that delay. Then the insurance company changed by merging with another insurance company and all the documents had to be reissued.

Fergus had never failed to refer briskly and efficiently to the delays and adjournments, he was always up to date on the last letter that had been sent backwards and forwards and you would believe that he had no other case on his files.

Patrick was invariably polite and equally informed; he made it his business to be equally up to date in case he might be accused of not caring what happened.

He had offered on more than one occasion to pay some money on account. It had always been coldly refused. Barely within the bounds of civility, Fergus would hint that by paying any sum now Patrick would be getting himself in well as a philanthropist with the courts later when the assessment came.

'Any sum I paid now would be without prejudice and would be to alleviate hardship.'

'They don't live in hardship, they don't need handouts and American food parcels to alleviate poverty,' Fergus had snapped.

'Do you dislike all Americans, or is it only me?' Patrick had asked one day, exasperated.

'I'm interested to note you describe yourself as American, O'Neill. Any time I've heard you speak you always call yourself an Irishman . . .'

It was never announced that the Ryan compensation case had been listed for hearing, but still everybody knew. Kate and John realized to their alarm that people had begun to take sides. There were those who wished the Ryans to take O'Neill and all belonging to him for as much as they could win in the Irish Sweepstakes. There were, it seemed, as many who said that the whole thing was flying in the face of all the generosity that Patrick O'Neill had shown to this parish. That they hoped the compensation would be insignificant and that somehow by this he would know that nobody in Mountfern or anywhere in the environs wished him anything but good.

'We'll have to pretend we don't know what they're saying; after all they never say it in front of us,' John said.

'But that's very hard, why don't we tell people that we have no fight with him, and try to explain all that business about insurance companies and how it's all a formula?'

'We can't start explaining our business like that, you'd be the last to want us to air it all.'

'But it's so unfair,' wailed Kate. 'Why should we spend our lives pretending that things are fine.'

'A lot of people do,' John said mildly.

'Not the *whole* time,' she stormed.

'A fair bit of the time.' He spoke so quietly she stopped in her tracks. She picked up his hand and laid it to her face.

Perhaps John was pretending things were fine for a fair bit of the time. And she had never noticed.

Michael couldn't see any difficulty ahead about the court case. Several times Jack Coyne had said that the twins shouldn't be too friendly with Grace O'Neill since one day they were all going to have to face each other across the bar of the court. But that was nonsense. Everyone knew that it was all a matter of what insurance the companies would pay, nothing to do with Mr O'Neill himself who had been so good to them all.

When Michael talked to Grace they never felt there was any problem between their families. That's what made it so galling to hear the fellows at school talking about the big battle ahead. And even more infuriating to have those two eejits of younger brothers joining in all the silly antics and writing 'Go home O'Neill' on the walls.

In the summery feeling of his first love Michael Ryan was able to brush all these annoyances aside. It was only Grace he thought of.

The lodge was three miles away. He could cycle two and a half miles and she could cycle half a mile and they could meet in that nice clump of trees on the hill which looked down on Mountfern. But it took so long, and then there were the explanations of where he had been. And Grace had to explain.

And all he wanted was to lie with her and stroke her and read her the poems he made up about her, about her eyes and her feet and her soft skin. And recently her beautiful breasts. Oh God, how he yearned for it to be like it had been just after the party, but there was *nowhere* they could see each other now without causing the most immense fuss.

Perhaps Mam understood more than he thought because occasionally she would ruffle his hair and say that it wouldn't be long now before the hotel was open and Grace would be living across the river from them all. But Mam said it with a shiver too, as if it were going to be somehow very frightening when the hotel opened. Michael was counting every day until his Grace could move from the lodge, which seemed a million miles away.

She had told him she loved him, she told him she had never dreamed it could be so lovely lying beside him as he stroked her from head to toe, and she trusted him and let him linger where he wanted to, she said she liked it too, and she knew he would never force her to do anything she didn't want to. Which of course he wouldn't. Never in a million years.

Kerry was learning a lot about the hotel business in Donegal; old Mr Hill who had been running a family hotel for years there was a good teacher. He was getting a sizeable fee to have O'Neill's son in his place for a type of apprenticeship, and he was determined to earn it.

The boy would learn the business from every angle. He would work in the kitchens and at the reception desk, he would groom the ponies for the day's trekking, he would stand by the trolley as the beef was being carved. Dennis Hill said that he could give a better training than the Shannon Hotel School if he was asked to.

'Why don't you?' Kerry asked him one day. 'You could easily set up a sort of training course here.'

'And build up a whole breed of rivals to myself?' Mr Hill shook his head.

'Well what about us, aren't we rivals?'

'Not at all, boy, aren't you down in the midlands there where no one in their right mind would want to spend a holiday, a big turf bog of a place miles from the sea. You're no rivals to anyone there.'

His eyes were laughing. Dennis Hill was no fool, he knew that O'Neill's Fernscourt would be no threat to him as it was so far away; he also knew that if he did a good job on this handsome troublesome playboy then O'Neill would send business his way for a long time.

Hills of Donegal was a famous hotel already, its name easily remembered, its clientele faithful, its food vastly superior to almost anything Ireland offered. Dennis Hill had a large family; he kept his hotel open at a loss all winter so that they could practise for the very busy summer season.

He had never taken a foolish step.

Sometimes he looked at Kerry O'Neill's striking face and cold eyes and wondered what would become of the boy. At the first sign of any trouble here Kerry would be packed off from the Hills of Donegal household back to his father, who seemed a grand fellow all set to make an outstanding success of his venture if reports could be believed.

Dara got postcards from Kerry, but they were inside envelopes so that anyone and everyone couldn't read what he wrote. There were things you wouldn't want anyone to read, like how he wanted to kiss her lovely lips again, and he wanted to smell her beautiful hair and hold her in his arms. And there were things you would want everyone to read, like how much he missed Mountfern and was looking forward to being back.

She wished he realized that he didn't *have* to write on a postcard, he could have got a writing pad and written pages and pages to her. Dara wrote pages and pages back.

Tommy Leonard said when she bought the writing pad that she must be going to get like St Paul and write epistles that nobody read.

'What do you mean, that nobody reads, aren't we demented with St Paul?' Dara said.

'Yes we are, but the Corinthians and the Ephesians and whoever didn't take a blind bit of notice of him.'

'They did too. He converted the lot of them.'

'No he did not. Most of them went on their own way.'

Tommy's father came over and asked through gritted teeth would it be possible for his son and young Miss Ryan to continue this interesting screaming match about the New Testament outside working hours.

Kitty Daly came home from Dublin for a weekend. She looked very much more grown up, they all thought. Her skirt was very short and she had a lot of make-up. Instead of taming her wild frizzy hair she let it all hang in a long curtain down her back. They nudged each other at mass when she went up to holy communion.

'I'd say she's up to no good in Dublin,' whispered Dara, who always feared that Kitty had her eye on Kerry O'Neill.

'She can't be up to that much if she's going to communion,' said Michael, which settled it.

Mrs Meagher told Kate Ryan in great confidence that her bold strap of a daughter Teresa was pregnant at last. It had only been a matter of time. Mrs Meagher wept. It was bound to happen. What in the name of the Lord was she to do? Kate soothed her, sent for more tea and spoke in low tones. Teresa could stay in Dublin, that was one thing, or she could have the child and they could bring it up in Mountfern together, that would be another. It would be a nine-day wonder and then Mountfern would let them settle down, mother and daughter living together, and then a new life to look after. It might be the making of them. Mrs Meagher didn't think so.

There was no question, apparently, of the father being forced to marry Teresa; the girl was vague to the point of confusion about who the father might be. Mrs Meagher wept again.

Kate said that they were living in 1966, not the dark ages, surely she wouldn't want to *force* some child to marry another child over this?

Mrs Meagher said if there was any chance of it that is exactly what she would like.

'Wait for a little while,' Kate begged. 'Don't go round telling everyone, just wait, something will turn up to make it seem clear to you.'

She was so calm, so confident sitting there in her chair, unruffled, and unshocked. Mrs Meagher really *did* feel better and was glad she had come to see her.

She would have been interested to know that five minutes after she left Kate Ryan had reached out of the wheelchair, and caught Carrie's arm in a hard grip.

'Listen to me, Carrie, listen to me good. Get some kind of organization into your life with Jimbo, do you hear? Fix a day whenever you like, and don't get yourself thrown aside.'

'What do you mean?' Carrie was frightened.

'I don't care if you have a baby, I'd like a baby for God's sake, I'd love to be playing with it, looking after it. I'm never going to have any more of my own, but it's going to be no good to *you*. It may well be 1966 but as far as Mountfern is concerned it's centuries ago and you'd be an outcast.'

'But there'd be no question of that . . .' Carrie began to stammer.

'Of course there would, Carrie. I'm not a fool. And you do like him, don't you?

So put it to him straight. Say you'd like to get married. Give yourself some kind of a chance.'

'But he wouldn't think I'm good enough. You know he's doing great as a singer, he'd want someone with a bit more class.'

'Then for Christ's sake develop a bit more class.'

'Why are you shouting at me, Mrs Ryan?'

'I don't know, Carrie, I really don't.'

'Will Kerry be home for a weekend soon?' Dara asked Grace.

She got the usual reply. 'Oh, you know Kerry.'

It was a very unsatisfactory reply indeed. Because she didn't really know Kerry. She would love to get to know him much much better. She wished he would say in these cards if he was ever coming back home.

Brother Keane said that the boys were to write a letter to Mr O'Neill that would try to put into words how grateful they were for the new pitch. It would have taken years and years to have got what they now had through the generosity of this good man. Their own sons would have barely been playing on a good field like this if it hadn't been for Mr O'Neill.

Tommy Leonard was the best at English; he was chosen to write the letter. Every boy in the school was to sign it. It would then be framed in carpentry class and presented to Mr O'Neill at a public ceremony.

Tommy's first three efforts were refused. Brother Keane said to him in a voice like thunder that it was hard to believe Tommy could be so insensitive as to begin by saying 'Despite the fact that you did not think this school good enough for your own son . . .' Really and truly, Brother Keane thought, all this jazz and the like had young boys half cracked these days.

Brian Doyle liked Rachel Fine. She had a very good way with people, he noticed, she spoke in a very low voice so that they strained to hear rather than shouting over them. Sometimes he felt she wanted to criticize something here and there but never did. Once or twice he actually asked her did she like something or if she could suggest an alternative. Very reluctantly she would give her views. Like the landing stage. Brian was going to paint it brightly. Rachel wondered would it be better in natural woods. It looked much better without the garish paint, but Rachel never claimed any of the credit, she joined in the general admiration and praise of Brian Doyle.

He wondered why O'Neill hadn't married her yet.

'Kerry's coming back this weekend,' Michael said.

'Never!' Dara felt something like a lump of coal in her throat.

'Yes, he rang last night, he's got a couple of days off. Grace's father was very surprised.'

'When does he arrive?'

'I think he's going by Dublin so it won't be till Saturday.'

'He never said.'

'Does he write much to you?'

'The odd card.' Dara was deliberately casual.

'It may have been a last-minute thing.' Michael was reassuring. 'He probably didn't tell any of the other girls either.'

'What other girls?'

'Oh, can't you be sure that Kerry would have girls everywhere?'

Michael looked at Dara's face and was sorry that he had said that.

Maggie Daly's mother had sent her in to inspect Loretto Quinn's and see was it true that the place had smartened up beyond all recognition since the Jewish lady had gone to live upstairs. The Dalys had heard disturbing rumours that it would nearly be a rival for their own place. Loretto of all people! God help her, she used to look like a poor tinker.

Loretto was kind to Maggie and spent ages helping her choose between one kind of sweet and another while poor Maggie did her best to spy on the lie of the land.

'Wouldn't you have these sweets for nothing in your own place?' Loretto asked innocently.

'Yes, but I'm not meant to be eating too many of them.' Maggie knew she was hopeless at this kind of subterfuge.

Mrs Fine came down the stairs just then; she had armfuls of materials with her.

'Heavens, haven't you the most beautiful auburn hair!' she said, standing in admiration.

'Who me?' Maggie looked around in case someone else had come into the shop.

'It's gorgeous, isn't it Loretto?'

Privately Loretto thought all the Dalys had terrible heads of frizz, but maybe Mrs Fine was just being kind.

'Lovely altogether,' she agreed.

'It's Maggie, isn't that right?'

Maggie was delighted. 'That's it, Mrs Fine.'

'Listen Maggie, I have something here which will look lovely with that hair.' She put down her materials and found a length of ribbon. It was in a copper satin.

'Shall I fix it in your hair for you, would you like that?'

Maggie was thrilled. This woman looked like something out of a magazine herself. She was very old of course, but her style was the talk of the place and here she was playing with ribbons in Maggie's hair.

'I'd love it,' she said.

Rachel took a strand of the hair and half plaited it in with the ribbon. She swept back some of the rest of the hair. Then she took a compact out of her handbag and showed Maggie the mirror.

'Look, aren't you lovely!' she said.

It was true. Maggie *did* look much nicer. Her face split into a huge smile.

'You must keep it, you're like a little Pre-Raphaelite,' Mrs Fine said.

Neither Loretto nor Maggie knew what it meant but it sounded good. Loretto's eyes held genuine admiration and Maggie could see it. She went home to abuse from her mother because she couldn't remember how or in what ways Loretto's shop had improved.

Liam White told her she wasn't looking as scraggy as usual, and Michael Ryan stopped on his bicycle for a chat.

'You look a bit different today,' he said in approval.

Mary Donnelly said that if they were going to make any kind of a fist of this café they were going to run in the hopes of getting a bit of custom, they should have a plan.

'We'll have to get into the minds of Americans, that's a hard thing to do,' Kate said.

'Aren't you best friends with an American woman, for heaven's sake?' Mary said as if she expected Rachel to help them every bit of the way.

And in many ways Rachel did. She told them of places that sold cheap but very authentically Irish pottery and even ordered it for them so that she could get a proper discount for them. She told them that American visitors would love to feel they were somewhere that was *really* Irish.

'Do you mean leprechauns and begorras?'

'No,' said Rachel, but she didn't say it with a great deal of conviction.

'Do you mean a hint of leprechauns and begorras?' Kate suggested again.

'That's exactly what I mean, a hint of it.'

'Jesus, Mary and Joseph,' Kate said. 'It's worse than I thought.'

Eddie had another breakage. This time it was the side mirror of Judy Byrne's car. It had been parked outside Ryan's while Judy was inside doing the exercises with Kate. Eddie had been seeing how far it would turn round. Not as pliable as he had thought.

It was there in his hand when Judy came out.

'I'll fix it.'

'You won't,' said Judy. 'You'll pay for it.'

Mary suggested a source of money to him. 'Your mam will pay you piece work for hemming the green napkins for the café.'

'Me hem table napkins? You must be mad,' Eddie stormed.

'Look at it this way: there aren't many jobs open to you, and you've done the Protestant graveyard already, so what else is there? You've a fine hand with a needle, I'm always telling you that.'

'Just as long as you don't tell anyone else . . .' Eddie warned.

'Do a dozen a night, up in your room if you don't want anyone to see you, or you can come out to my house if you like, and sit there with Leopold and the wireless.'

It wasn't the life Eddie Ryan had planned for himself. Sitting in a converted outhouse hemming green linen serviettes with a mad dog and Radio Eireann for company. Mary's wireless didn't seem to get Radio Luxembourg.

Still, it paid for Miss Byrne's old mirror, and Mam was very nice to him and sometimes said that he was an old dote despite everything.

Dara and Michael waited for Grace to collect them on Saturday to go to the pictures. They met Tommy and the Whites just outside – it was going to be very crowded. Declan Morrissey rubbed his hands happily. If he had his way he'd show musicals all the year round. This was the third or fourth time he had *Seven Brides for Seven Brothers* and it was always the same, you got the old and the young alike to come to it.

Michael was pleased to see the queue, it meant that they might all get separated. Then he and Grace could go to the back somewhere. There couldn't be any touching Grace if the others were all there.

Maggie was late. 'Sorry,' she apologized, even though it didn't matter, they were still in the line waiting to get in.

'Sorry, Kitty rang from Dublin, she wanted me to think up some story about why she's not coming home for the weekend.'

'She picked a poor one to invent a story for her,' Tommy Leonard said affectionately.

'I know, I get so flustered,' Maggie said.

'Why can't she tell them herself?' Dara said.

'She didn't want to talk to Mam, because Mam would worm it out of her, so she rang when Mam was at benediction.'

'Worm what?' Dara said.

'She's meeting Kerry in Dublin, that's why she's not coming home,' said Maggie excitedly, and looked around at the faces of her friends.

Kerry arrived on Sunday evening. He called into Ryan's at a slack time. Kate was behind the counter in her wheelchair.

'What can I serve you?' Her smile was pleasant.

'I don't drink alcohol at all, Mrs Ryan.'

'Very sensible of you, but then that's a little hypocritical of me. If everyone was to feel like you do where would our business be, I wonder?'

'Your business going okay, is it?' He looked pointedly around the almost empty pub.

'Usually a little more lively than this.' Kate felt annoyed somehow that this young fellow hadn't come in when they were doing a really good business. She wondered why she was trying to impress him.

'I just came to know if I could take your lovely daughter for a walk by the river on this beautiful evening,' he asked.

'My lovely daughter has homework to do.' Kate smiled.

'I'm sure she'll be able to do it later.' Kerry smiled.

'At just fifteen she's a little young to let walks with young men get between her and her studies.' Kate was still smiling a smile she didn't feel.

'Oh now, Mrs Ryan, she's not *just* fifteen. I had the pleasure of being at her fifteenth birthday, a long long time ago. Way back last September, if I remember rightly.'

'You remember rightly, Kerry.'

'So you are saying she can't come out with me. Is this what I hear?'

'No it is not what you hear, you must go and ask her herself.'

'Oh well, that's all right then. May I go into the house?'

'No, I'll call her.'

Dara had seen him coming from the window seat. She had combed her hair and rubbed a little lipstick on and off again.

'Hi,' she said.

'Lovely to see you again,' he said warmly. 'I was trying to persuade your mother here to let us go for a walk.'

Dara looked at him levelly. 'I'd love to, Kerry, but I have all this homework to do,' she said.

He was surprised. 'Can't you leave it till later?' He was sure he would convince her.

'No, at this stage there's so much to be done. I wish I'd worked harder earlier in the year but you know how it is, I'm afraid I've left it all to the end.'

'You're not doing your Leaving this year.' There was an edge to his voice.

'You've obviously never met Sister Laura, she thinks this is the most important year in our lives. We have exams nearly every week.'

Kerry was furious. 'Another time then,' he said, and walked out.

Kate looked at her stricken daughter.

Round One to Dara, she thought with a mixture of pride and anxiety.

Miss Hayes had never known a prayer to Saint Anthony to fail, but this time it had. Nowhere could she find the two silver salvers that had stood on the sideboard.

Marian had admired them often and said that they were magnificent silver. She had been startled to discover that Mrs Fine had bought them for Patrick at an auction, at his request.

Mrs Fine often bought old Irish silverware, and had said that the O'Neills should have the pleasure of looking at it before it went to the hotel eventually.

Every two weeks Olive Hayes cleaned the little collection. Mrs Fine had called once and praised her highly for the wonderful way it had been cared for. Now Miss Hayes was worried – what could have happened to them? It was unlikely that they had been robbed. There had been no break-in, and anyway there was always someone in the house.

Marian Johnson did drop in from time to time but she would never . . . of course not. And those little Ryan twins and Maggie Daly from the dairy. No, it was out of the question.

She would have to think again – was it possible that she had placed them somewhere else? Or perhaps Mr O'Neill had already taken them to the hotel, or to have them valued.

Olive Hayes was very troubled.

Americans would want entertainment. Kate knew that.

But what kind? It couldn't be amateurish in their café when it was professional and well organized across the river.

What would they expect in an Irish café? If it was to be truly authentic then of course there wouldn't be singing and dancing, nobody would be doing anything except getting stuck into their tea and scones. But this plan was for something that wasn't quite authentic but looked as if it might be.

MAEVE BINCHY

What a pity that none of them played the harp, and that they didn't have a big tuneful harp handy in one of their outhouses.

Carrie asked Jimbo would they get married some time.
'Sure, we'll get married some time,' Jimbo said.
Carried felt vaguely dissatisfied with this reply.

Jack Coyne asked Loretto did the great O'Neill spend the night above in the rooms with your woman.
Loretto said certainly he did not.
Jack said Loretto was right to keep her mouth shut. He would do the same in her place. Loretto was annoyed about that, since she was not being diplomatic. It was the truth. Patrick O'Neill came to call sometimes but he never stayed the night.

Dennis Hill rang to know whether Kerry's father had recovered from his illness.
Olive Hayes told him that there had been no illness.
'There has to have been an illness, why else did he go home?' Mr Hill wanted to know.
Miss Hayes decided to rescue the situation. 'There was a bit of trouble all right, it wasn't exactly an illness,' she said.
Mr Hill never pried. He had just been ringing out of courtesy, he said. When would they expect Kerry back?
'I'll ask him to ring you himself,' said Miss Hayes.
She told Kerry that he should call Donegal. She told him that Mr Hill was now under the impression that what he had thought was an illness was in fact a little trouble.
Kerry smiled a great charming smile at her. 'You are a great ally, Miss Hayes,' he said.
'I wouldn't rely on it, Kerry,' she said.
'I get the picture,' Kerry said.

Dara and Maggie were on the footbridge, when Kerry came along.
'Maggie, could you do something for me? Please.' His eyes were a piercing blue. They looked straight at little Maggie.
'Sure,' she said good-naturedly.
'Could you go up to the hotel and see is my father about? I want to go up and talk to Brian Doyle about something, but my father thinks I've gone back to Donegal so I want to make sure he isn't there. Can you look and see if his car is there? Do you mind?'
'Not at all, but am I the right one . . . ? I often get things wrong.'
'No, you're perfect, you look so innocent no one would know you were my spy.'
Maggie scampered up the path by the laurel bushes.
'Well,' Kerry said to Dara.
'Well what?'
'Well what was all this performance, you had homework to do? I came straight out and put myself on the line and asked your mother . . . and you turn me down.'

286

What was all that about?' He looked very angry. Dara's heart began to pound. It had been a very risky thing. She had wondered afterwards had she been mad.

'No reason,' she said, shrugging.

'Don't do that, it's so silly, it makes you so cheap, so common. I came to see you. I thought you liked me. Why are you playing silly games?' His handsome face looked hurt.

'Well . . .' She didn't know what to say.

'Because if you don't want to see me, that's fine, just say it straight out. But if you do, let's go up to Coyne's wood.'

'When?'

'What's wrong with now?'

'You can't mean now. You've just sent Maggie on a message.'

'That was so that I could talk to you. My father's in Shannon today.'

'You told her a lie . . .'!

'It was so that I could ask you what was wrong.'

'And you met Kitty in Dublin too!'

'Silly little Maggie, getting everything wrong. I *saw* Kitty in Dublin and she clung and clung. Kitty the clam I call her.'

'We can't go off and leave Maggie to come back and find us not here.'

'Yes we can if you want to.'

It was the longest moment of Dara's life.

'No, I'll wait for Maggie. You sent her on a fool's errand,' she said.

If Kate Ryan had been watching she would have said, 'Round Two, Dara.'

'John, will you read me some poetry?'

'Aren't you too tired, love?'

Kate sat in her green room, her eyes too bright, her face drawn.

'No, I have that feeling I'm not going to sleep.'

'Let me get you into bed first then I'll go and find something you might like. I haven't written anything for so long.'

'How could you?' She touched his hand in sympathy. 'But tonight I want you to read me other people's poetry, not just your own, and no, I won't go to bed yet.'

'Other people's poetry?' He was disappointed.

She was deliberately light and joky. 'Yes, isn't it very presumptuous of them, but other people did write poetry, like Yeats, or Oscar Wilde or James Clarence Mangan.'

'Will I read you the *Lays of Ancient Rome*? I love that . . .'

'No, something Irish.'

'Or *Hiawatha* . . . I've never read the whole of *Hiawatha* aloud. *That* will send you off to sleep all right.'

'No.' She gripped the sides of the wheelchair in impatience.

'All right, all right . . .' He went to the bookshelves, and ran his finger along the backs of books for what seemed a long time. Eventually he took out a book and began:

'Oh my dark Rosaleen

'Do not sigh do not weep . . .'

'Stand up over there so that I can see you,' Kate said. 'Now start again.'

He read the poem with gestures, putting a lot of emphasis into it and giving the repetition a fine sonorous sound.

'That was very good,' Kate said approvingly.

John's face was empty. 'That wasn't me reading poetry to you, that was an audition, wasn't it?'

'Yes,' Kate said in a small voice.

'Well?'

'It was very good. Could you bear it?'

'Of course, if we *have* to.'

'We have to.'

Rachel was adamant about not letting him stay the night. If Patrick wanted to preserve the fiction that he and Rachel were just good friends, then preserve it. She did not even countenance making love in her rooms. She was a respectable woman staying in Loretto's, she didn't want any reputation, thank you very much. And Patrick always had to leave early.

Once or twice they had managed it in Coyne's wood, and in the back of the car and in a far distant corner of the river bank on a rug. It had been exciting and uncomfortable at the same time.

'I may have to go back to New York for a week, come with me,' Patrick said suddenly one May evening, in Loretto's.

'What for?'

'Well, we could make love properly for one thing without risk of half the town discovering us or getting curvature of the spine.' He was grinning at her in the way she loved and hadn't seen a lot recently.

'No, I've a lot to do here.'

'You've nothing to do here, stop fooling yourself.'

A flash of anger. 'Shall I list the things I have to do here . . .'

'No, don't be tedious, Rachel, we both know why you're here, we both think it's a great idea, so what? Just quit pretending it's a real career and you can't be taken from it to come to New York for a week.'

Never had she been so angry. Never.

They both knew why she was here, it was so obvious was it?

She knew she must keep calm. Nothing must be thrown away for the very unimportant luxury of losing her temper.

'What had you in mind for us in New York?' she asked levelly.

'I don't know.' He put on a teasing smile. 'Maybe we could get ourselves to a justice of the peace and get hitched, that way I wouldn't have to be thrown out of here like a college boy at ten o'clock at night.'

'Would you like to get married?' Her voice was calm.

'No, what man *likes* to get married? Hell, of course I don't want to get married, Rachel, I'm too old, you're too old, we're fine as we are. Hey?'

No response.

'Hey? Rachel, you're not sulking now, are you? We're fine as we are. Why complicate it? Why think I love you more if you tie me down by some bit of paper?'

She looked at him levelly.

'Well, say something, woman, for God's sake, have I done the one unforgivable sin saying this? You did ask me would I *like* the idea of being married. I'm telling you. Straight up.'

'Sure,' she said.

'What does that mean?'

'Not much, I guess.'

'So what did I say that was so terrible?'

'I suppose what was terrible was that you thought a piece of paper would only tie *you* down, you never thought that it might also tie down whoever you married. It's a bargain you know, marriage, not just one person being lassooed by another. It's a sharing thing.'

'You didn't do very well during your attempt at it,' he lashed out.

'You weren't exactly faithful during *your* attempt at it,' she said straight back.

He was silent.

Rachel sat still in her chair. Her cream linen suit and her little sprig of purple heather worn at the lapel matched the room perfectly.

She didn't look at Patrick, she looked across at the sun setting over Fernscourt. Her face was not sad, she was calm and entirely in command. She was thinking that this was the end of the road. She had travelled so far, so many years and so many thousands of miles and it would end now, in recriminations like so many relationships.

'It's got nothing to do with you. With you as a person,' Patrick began.

Rachel said nothing, she didn't even listen, it was as if she had always known it was coming, this conversation, the goodbye.

'In fact I want your company and to be with you more than anybody. You know this.'

She looked across and saw men still working in the fading light. They were getting overtime now to finish the job in time.

'Shit Rachel, what do you have to go and suggest we got married for? Why couldn't you let things go on the way they were?'

Almost reluctantly Rachel lifted her eyes from the men who were finishing the stone wall around the forecourt, and brought her glance to Patrick.

'I did not bring up marriage, Patrick, *you* did. You said we would find a justice of the peace in New York and get hitched. Please be fair.'

He was wrongfooted over this. 'Yeah sure, but you said ...'

'Forget what I said. Don't let it end in a war of words – you said, I said. What does it matter? And as you said it has nothing to do with me as a person.'

She stood up, straightening her skirt. 'I'll show you out now.'

'Well ...'

'Goodnight, Patrick. I'll be going to Connemara in the next day or two, probably tomorrow. We'll consider we said goodbye now. Right?'

He put his hands on her shoulders. 'Listen ...'

'Yes?' Her eyes were large and dark, they looked into his very directly, they didn't dart about anxiously trying to read his face.

'Listen Rachel, I'm not worth it.'

She smiled patiently as she might have smiled at a child.

He was struggling for words.

'Even if I were, if I could . . . even if I did feel . . . there would be so many complications, there'd be all hell to pay. You have no idea how much trouble and everything . . .'

He looked at her, pleading, begging her to understand that their marriage would be opposed by Church and society even if he could bring himself to propose.

Rachel Fine had some dignity left. She chose not to understand what he was saying.

'Patrick, you've a lot of work tomorrow and so have I.' She kissed his cheek.

'But . . .'

She had closed the door behind him.

She leaned against the door as she had seen so many heroines do in movies. But no heroine had ever behaved as stupidly, she thought, no woman who ever leaned against a door like that had been such a downright idiot as Rachel Fine letting her man go like that.

Possibly to the arms of Marian Johnson. And even, when the hotel was built and he was lonely, possibly he might marry Marian Johnson. Church and society wouldn't oppose that, they'd be delighted with it, and the divorced Jewess could be moved from the scene. She didn't cry, she felt too empty to cry. She didn't go to the window to see him driving off.

She just stood motionless for a long time.

John Ryan sighed. Sometimes he wished he could discuss things with someone. Mary Donnelly was out, she hated Patrick O'Neill with a passion. He couldn't speak to Fergus because young Slattery seemed to hold the O'Neills personally responsible for Kate's accident and could only think of the day when the huge compensation would be paid over.

Dr White was not a good ally. Dr White seemed to think that John was a bit of an old misery. On more than one occasion the doctor had told him straight out that Kate's condition could be made much more bearable if her immediate family surrounded her with hope and optimism.

No point in talking to his son, the boy was like a moonstruck calf pining over the little American girl.

He felt unwilling to bring his worries to Dara. She was still a child and it made him seem weak to tell his own daughter that he couldn't communicate with her mother.

As he went ahead with the preparations for Ryan's Café, John's heart was heavy.

One afternoon when Mary was minding the bar, when Kate was busy hemming green table napkins for the café, when the children were at school and the menagerie reasonably peaceful – Leopold snoring in the garden, the cat purring like an engine on the window sill – John sat down to write a poem.

This time he didn't write about the land or the people who had once walked this land. This time he wrote about the cage he found himself in; the cage which he couldn't escape from because he himself had built the bars. They were bars of

. concern and love and good manners. They were rules he had made so that he would not hurt anyone else. He wrote how by forcing yourself to take one course of action and adopt one set of attitudes you can also be untrue to yourself and deny your real worth.

It was the cry of a strong man who found himself trapped and couldn't see an escape. He looked into Kate's room – she had fallen asleep over her sewing. Gently he took the needle and green linen from her hands and arranged the cushion behind her back in the chair. He left the poem beside her and went for a long walk. He walked up to Coyne's wood and beat at the undergrowth with a stick for a while. Then he found himself climbing that big mossy hill towards the Grange.

He went in and asked for a pint of beer.

Marian's place was slipping, he noticed, the bar was not clean and it was late afternoon, there were still ashtrays full and glasses uncollected. The stocks hadn't been checked, you could see some bottles had nearly run out and others had marks of liquid down their sides.

It had been years since he had come here and it used to be much smarter in the old days.

The youth serving had neither manner nor charm. He gave the wrong change and didn't apologize when it was pointed out.

Who would stay in the Grange when there was a luxury place like Fernscourt opening three miles away? John gave a little shiver. He had heard too of the way that Patrick had interviewed the staff, how he had told them that American guests liked to be made much of, to have their names remembered. They liked people to say 'You're welcome' when they said 'Thank you'. Patrick had searched Ireland for the right manager and, not being satisfied with any of the applicants, had gone to another hotel and offered Jim Costello twice his salary to leave at once and come to manage Fernscourt. Costello, an attractive go-getting young man, had given the matter five minutes' thought, which had raised his salary even higher, and then left the hotel after serving three weeks' notice and finding a successor for himself. Costello was the right man for Patrick O'Neill. A man who would not burn his bridges, he had left his old employers on good terms and he could always go back if Patrick and he had a falling out; on the other hand he had impressed his new boss with his quick thinking and decision. He was a man of great charm, he had drunk many a pint in Ryan's and delighted everyone with his easy ways.

Patrick O'Neill and Jim Costello wouldn't have employed a surly youth like this boy behind Marian Johnson's bar. John pondered on just how much the old order was changing.

He left, thanking the boy and getting no response, and walked down the hill. There was a scurry at one stage when he passed the big clump of trees, as if he had disturbed a courting couple. He smiled to himself, thinking how stony and uncomfortable the ground must be. .

For half a moment he wondered whether it was Michael and Grace he saw disappearing into the bushes. But he dismissed the notion. For heaven's sake, it was the middle of the afternoon.

What would they be doing up here? And anyway they were *far* too young for that sort of thing.

Mary Donnelly was glaring at an inoffensive couple of farmers who took no notice of her whatsoever.

'This is a great pub, Mary,' John said as he came in.

The farmers looked up, amused.

'If you can't say it who can?' one of them laughed.

'Have you been drinking?' Mary asked suspiciously.

'You're right, Mary. God, it would need to be a sharp man to fox you. I was up having a pint in the Grange, as it happens.'

'And it wasn't to your liking?'

'It was not. There was no warm service with a smile like you get when you come in this door. Oh boy no. There was only glares and surly shrugs. What human would want a pint in a place like that? People want to be made welcome in a place, that's what running a pub or a hotel is about, it's not just about pouring alcohol down their throats.'

The farmers looked at each other and grinned conspiratorially.

Mary flushed a dark red. 'If you're saying that I . . .'

'I'm saying that it's lovely to be back in a friendly atmosphere,' he said firmly. 'That's all, and if we're going to keep any custom from going over to O'Neill's Thatch Bar we'll have to let them know that they're welcome here, and really welcome too.'

He banged out of the bar and into the house.

Mary was open-mouthed. That was the first time John had ever admitted publicly that there was a threat from O'Neill, and imagine admitting it in front of two customers. He must be really upset.

Kate was sitting by the open French window, wearing her gardening gloves and tidying up one of those high urns that Rachel Fine had cleverly positioned, one on each side of the door. These were Kate's alone, she grew herbs and heathers in them, they were easy to reach and made her feel she was really gardening.

'I've been thinking,' John said.

He pulled off her gloves and held her hands.

'So have I. When I read your poem and realized what it's like for you, not wanting to upset me, and not knowing how to talk to me, I felt I could have put the power into my body and run after you. I woke up and read it and I could feel such energy surging through me, I was sure I'd have the strength to stand.'

Her eyes were wild with trying to explain, she was like a child straining to have more movement than she had.

'Gently, Kate. Gently,' he soothed her.

She would not be calmed. She thought as she had so often thought about that summer's day when he had wanted to make love and she said no, it was ridiculous in the middle of the afternoon, and that she had felt restless. Restless indeed! If she had stayed with him as he had wanted she would never have wandered into Fernscourt and into this life in a chair.

'You *do* have great strength,' he told her. 'Aren't you the strongest woman in this county? I mean it.'

'But tell me that you *know* I'd be nothing without you. The children will grow up and go away, and the pub may win or lose but the only thing I want is for us to be together. In so far as we can ever be together because of this bloody chair.' She hit the arms of the wheelchair in frustration.

'But you're only saying what I know. I know you love me.' He was smiling a huge smile of pleasure.

'I can give you nothing. Nothing a wife can give.'

'Stop, stop.'

'I've been so selfish, I never sort of helped you or anything.'

She was talking about some of her earlier attempts to give John pleasure. They had both been embarrassed and Kate had cried at not being able to do it properly. John had been embarrassed at something so obviously selfish that could not be shared. They had attempted it less and less.

'I'm all right, look at what you have to bear, for God's sake. It doesn't seem all that important to me that we can't make love as we used to.'

'But I was thinking we could.' Kate's eyes were definitely excited, her colour was high.

'How do you mean?'

'Draw the curtains,' she said.

He closed the glass doors and pulled the soft green and white curtains.

'Come here,' she whispered.

'Wait till I lock the door. It would be the one time we'd have Leopold, Mary, Carrie, the children and half the bar arriving in on top of us.'

She laughed like a teenager.

'Get me out of this bloody chair, John Ryan, and love me.'

He lifted her on to the bed. Her dress opened easily; she had all her clothes made front-fastening so that she could dress herself with the minimum of fuss.

'But we can't . . .' he stammered.

'Why not? It's my body. It won't hurt, I won't feel much but I can feel above the belt, if you know what I mean. That's nice.'

'But can I . . . inside you . . . wouldn't that be bad for you?'

'Why would it? It's just paralysed, it isn't out of bounds.' She was high with excitement and was stroking him encouragingly.

'Kate, I don't want to do anything that might damage you . . .'

'It won't. I checked.'

'You checked? When did you check?'

'This afternoon. I rang Dr White.'

'My God! What did he say?'

'He said fire ahead, and that he was delighted, he thought we'd never get round to it.'

Fergus Slattery called and was told that Mr and Mrs Ryan were in Mrs Ryan's room and weren't to be disturbed.

'Nothing wrong?' Fergus inquired.

'John is like a lighting devil today, perhaps they're having a row,' Mary Donnelly said. 'There isn't a man in this house that will speak straight to you, I'm afraid.'

She was still smarting from Michael's cross-questioning. He had been highly alarmed to find that his mother and father were closeted together, and felt sure that the only reason could be that Dad had actually seen him with Grace. The thought was too mortifying even to entertain for a moment.

What could Dad be telling Mam, and how soon would he be called in and *what* would he say? And why couldn't that awful Mary stop snarling at him and tell him what *kind* of a peculiar humour had his father been in when he came home?

Michael, white with anxiety, had gone to throw stones from the footbridge, and pray. If God arranged it so that Dad hadn't seen, then he would . . . what would he do? He couldn't offer to give up being with Grace because that was what he wanted most in the world. Suppose he offered God a rosary. Not enough. God was known to be particularly against Immodest Touches, and whatever he and Grace were up to it would certainly come into that category. Perhaps if he gave God a promise that he would go to confession soon, and fixed a firm date. Perhaps that might do.

'Was it important, your message?' Mary remembered belatedly John's startling instructions that she was to be high on charm.

'You could always write it down, Mr Slattery, and I'd see that they got it.'

'No, I'll phone them later,' he said.

'They've taken the phone off the hook,' Mary explained.

'God, it must be a terrible row altogether,' Fergus said.

Rachel looked into the window of Meagher's. As always she was looking out for the kind of thing that Kate might be able to display in a glass cabinet when they got the café going.

Meagher's window was not the most inspiring of places, and the woman who ran it seemed to know little or nothing about the odd selection of stock she carried. People had told Rachel that it was the late Mr Frank Meagher who was the one who knew something about the business. The window held the usual collection of musical boxes, travel clocks and some really appalling candlesticks, and there in a box with tissue paper were the two silver salvers that Rachel had bought for Fernscourt. Salvers that had been on Patrick's sideboard on the only occasion when Rachel had visited the lodge. She had been there once when she knew both children would be far away.

Rachel stared unbelievingly at the two pieces of silver. They were worth everything else in the window three times over. Patrick surely could not have sold them. Surely, surely not. Rachel went in and bought a brooch shaped like an L which she would give to Loretto. She spoke to Mrs Meagher, a sad-faced, worried-looking woman about the silver salvers, and with shaking hand managed to pay for the brooch. She needed to be in the open air quickly.

In the Lodge Olive Hayes had come to a decision. She was going to mention the salvers to Mr O'Neill.

The only question was the matter of approach. Should she ask whether he had in fact taken them elsewhere for safekeeping? Or should she say that she had not been able to find them?

There was nobody she could discuss it with. If only her sister Bernadette were not at the other end of the earth.

She could have talked about it with Sheila Whelan of course. Even if it had been Marian, Sheila would not have told the whole town.

She could even have approached Mrs Ryan in the pub. She would never have thought of it as a slight on her own twins.

Sergeant Sheehan was the kind of man she could speak to quietly, but it wouldn't have been fair. Once she spoke to him it would have to be official.

No, it would have to be Mr O'Neill himself, without the luxury of asking advice from others.

Patrick came in, his face weary.

She decided to give him a while to settle down.

But he had read her face. 'What is it, Miss Hayes?'

'How did you know there was anything, sir?'

'I haven't worked with people since I was fourteen years of age without learning something. What is it?'

'It's the silver salvers, sir, for the hotel, that used to be on the sideboard.'

'It's all right, Miss Hayes.' He looked very weary.

'I only noticed today they aren't there.'

'It was a misunderstanding. They'll be back.'

'Oh, that's all right then.' She moved away, about to go back to her kitchen.

Patrick realized that she was not going to launch into a line of questions or explanations.

'Miss Hayes.'

'Sir?'

'I value you more than you'll ever know.'

Her face became brick red with pleasure. 'Thank you very much indeed, Mr O'Neill. It's a pleasure working here. You are all very appreciative people.'

'I meant what I said about coming to the hotel with us. I think we'll need you.'

'Oh, we'll discuss that nearer the time, Mr O'Neill.'

'How sensible you are. I'm afraid those nuns in your sister's place will snap you into the convent and you'll never be heard of again.'

She went away smiling. But she looked back at him before she got to the kitchen and saw that the smile had fallen away and under the genial affable face that he presented to the world Patrick O'Neill was angrier than she had ever seen anyone in her life.

Brian Doyle had handed him a note. It was all sealed with sticky paper.

'Mrs Fine said you were to open this on your own over a desk or something. It's got something very fine in it that might fall out.' Brian was uncaring, but keen to deliver the message exactly as Rachel had instructed.

'All right.'

He had opened it in his car. Alone.

'Patrick.

I am writing this because there is no way you and I could discuss it usefully.

In Meagher's the jewellers on Bridge Street you will find the two silver salvers.

295

Mrs Meagher bought them from Kerry three days ago for a fraction of their worth. Mrs Meagher is not to be blamed for trying to cheat him, she is also selling them at an equally impossible price.

I have no idea, nor do I want to know what happened. For all I know you may be party to this, but I think not and I wanted to forewarn you. Naturally I said nothing at all to Mrs Meagher that would indicate I knew anything about the pieces.

For your own information Mrs Meagher is a gossipy, unstable person who is unhappy here in Mountfern and has been considering leaving. Her problem is that she has little capital and even less get up and go.

I leave it with you. Obviously I will be happy to do anything to help but I feel this is something you will want to handle on your own.

I told Brian Doyle a rigmarole about this letter needing to be opened carefully, I thought that way you would be sure to read it on your own. I feared if I said it was very urgent and private he would have had every kettle on the building site at work on it. But perhaps I misjudge him.

Love always, Rachel.'

'Mrs Meagher, how are you this fine day?'

'Dragging the divil by the tail as usual, Mr O'Neill. How is it that you are always so cheerful?'

'It's in my nature, I expect,' Patrick smiled broadly.

He pulled up the small rickety chair close to the counter. 'About those salvers that my son brought in, the ones that are in the window.'

'He said he had full authority . . .'

'Oh yes, no problem like that at all . . .'

'And if you want them back, Mr O'Neill . . . I did think that maybe it wasn't a good enough price but your lad seemed very pleased . . .'

'Not at all, nothing like that . . . no no.' Patrick's voice was soothing.

'So I hope I didn't do anything out of turn . . .'

'You know the way children are, Mrs Meagher, you do your best and then you wonder *what* was the right thing to do . . .'

Mrs Meagher sat down on the other side of the counter and leaned across to Patrick.

'Mr O'Neill, you don't know the truth you're saying . . .'

Patrick O'Neill drove himself slowly back to the lodge to wait for his son. In his briefcase he carried the two silver salvers.

'I'll give them a little polish, will I?' Olive Hayes had suggested.

'That would be lovely, Miss Hayes.'

The evening shadows lengthened, he sat alone looking in front of him. He had telephoned Loretto Quinn's. No, there was no sign of Rachel and she had not said where she would be.

He had telephoned Ryan's and she was not there. The ridiculous harridan who looked after the bar for them said that Mrs Ryan was not to be disturbed.

There was no sign of his daughter either.

The key turned in the lock.

Kerry came in.

He was surprised to find his father sitting alone and with no work in front of him.

Surprised but not alarmed.

'This is all very peaceful,' Kerry said slightly mockingly.

'I'd like to go out, Kerry.' Patrick's voice was very calm.

Kerry decided to be flip. 'Well then you *must* go out, Father, don't let me stop you,' he said.

'We'll go straight away.'

Something in his tone made Kerry follow his father's look, and on the sideboard he saw the two gleaming silver salvers.

His face did not change. 'I see,' he said.

'Good.' Patrick looked dangerously quiet.

They left the house without words.

Miss Hayes watched them from the kitchen window. They walked towards the woods.

'Why did you do it?' Patrick asked his son.

'I needed the money.'

'You are a fool as well as a thief. Do you have any idea how much they were worth?'

'A great deal more than that woman gave me, but that wasn't the point.'

'What was the point?'

'The point was that I needed this amount and she could give it to me, so it couldn't matter less what the real value of those trays was. They only represented to me enough to get what I needed.'

'So if you are going to steal from my house and make us a public exhibition in my town, my place, it doesn't even matter that you get a fraction of what these items were worth.'

'No. Their worth is not important.'

Patrick's hand went into a fist without his having any control over it.

Kerry saw. 'Don't forget all you spent on that orthodontal work, Father. I mean, if you're talking about value for money, why smash it all up? It cost you a fortune to get me all this bridge work.'

The spasm of white anger passed; it was replaced with something much deeper. Something, Patrick felt, that was going to be with him for a long time.

'Do you hate me, Kerry?'

'Of course I don't, Father.'

'Then why?'

'I told you, I needed money. Why do you have to be so Italian about everything? Love, hate – life isn't like that.'

'What is it like then? Tell me, I'd love to know what life *is* like.'

Kerry leaned against a tree. He looked impossibly beautiful in the evening light. He looked like a painting of a young hero, not a cheat and liar who had stolen from his own father and showed not an ounce of remorse.

'Life is about excitement, Father, it's not about the past and the old days and the old order and righting wrongs that were done centuries ago – if they were done at all.'

'Excitement?' Patrick said.

'Yes, that's about the best I can do to explain.' Kerry seemed bored.

'Is there not sufficient *excitement*, as you call it, in Donegal? Why did you have to come to that centre of excitement – Mountfern – and humiliate me in my own place?'

'You are not humiliated, Father, I'm sure you got out of it.'

'You're goddamn right I did. I bought Meagher's shop.'

'Hey,' Kerry laughed. He gave a natural, amused little laugh. The boy was not even remotely touched by what he had done.

'I told Mrs Meagher that there had been a misunderstanding, she told me that children were all the same. I listened to her woes, one of them being that she couldn't find a buyer. We need a place in Bridge Street. She's leaving almost at once. She will say nothing about your misunderstanding. I will say nothing about some of her circumstances.'

'Like her daughter being a teeny bit pregnant.' He laughed again.

'We don't have you to thank for that, do we?'

'Teresa Meagher, Father. Please. You must think I'm hard up!'

'Why did you need the money?'

'My business, Father.'

'No, Kerry. My business now.'

'Are you going to beat me again?'

'No, of course not.'

'There's no of course about it, you want to.'

'No, I want you to tell me. Tell me why.'

'You're such a man of the world, you have this sixth sense, you tell me, Father. You always say you have a feel for things.'

'Cards?' Patrick said.

Kerry paused. 'Yes,' he said.

'Was that it at school all that time ago?'

'Sort of. Betting, big talk.'

'Aren't you a fool.'

'No, sometimes I win.'

'I'm sure you do. At the start of every game in the sucker's build-up.'

Now it was Kerry's turn to look scornful. 'How would you know, Father? You're much too cagey, too cautious to play a hand of cards.'

'I did once. For long enough to know I hadn't the time to invest in it.'

'Very praiseworthy,' Kerry mocked.

'No. Very practical. That's what it was. If I wanted to play cards I'd have learned how to do it, not get taken by every half-assed two-bit man around, like seems to be happening to you.'

'I was unlucky one night, that's all.'

'Unlucky? Do you even know the odds?'

'It all depends, Father.'

'It does not depend. There are odds on filling a straight, there are odds, you fool, on getting a house if you have two pairs. Actual odds – you don't know them and you expect to steal my silver to pay for your idiocy.'

'Yes, I can see that from where you stand, it's hard.'

'No it's not hard. It's easy.'

'How do you mean?'

'You get taught, taught to play properly. If that's what you want.'

'It's not like that. You can't enrol in night classes.'

'You can if you want to.'

'How on earth?'

'Brian Doyle's brother is a card player, deals in a club somewhere out the Galway Road. One of the best, they tell me.'

'He can't be great if he's dealing cards in a club near Galway.'

'He liked the liquor as well. That's what slowed him down. Go to him next time you're home, bring him a bottle of Powers, say you'd like to learn a few fancy deals, waterfalls, that kind of thing. He'll set you right.'

Kerry's mouth was open.

'He doesn't deal from the bottom, he doesn't have marked cards. He'd be the first to tell you of people who have no fingers to play with if they do that sort of thing.'

'This is Ireland, Father, not Chicago in Prohibition.'

'This is card playing all over the world, Kerry.'

'Do you mean that I should go to this guy? You'll set it up?'

'I won't set it up, you set it up. You heard of him, turn up there. Meanwhile get your ass back to Dennis Hill. I suppose you told him some lie.'

'I had to. They were pushing me a bit for the money, these guys.'

'Are they in the hotel?'

'God no, the hotel's as dead as a dodo. They're over the border, in Derry.'

'That should be excitement enough for you.'

'They're good people, it's just that someone else was pushing them.'

Kerry got a feeling that his father wasn't interested.

'How did you find out, Father? About Meagher's?'

'My business.'

'And you don't seem to have . . . well, too many hard feelings.'

'I don't have any feelings. That's what is so strange. I have no feelings at all. Maybe you always felt that towards me so you know what it's like. But it's new to me. When I got up this morning I suppose if anyone asked me how I felt about you, I'd have said I loved you. When I saw those salvers in Meagher's and had to negotiate with that stupid woman, and saw you leaning against the tree there . . . I might have said I hated you. But now. Nothing. Nothing at all.' Patrick seemed mildly regretful.

Kerry knew that his father was speaking from the heart.

'What happens to me now, Father?'

'As I said, you go back to Dennis. After the opening you and I talk again, it could be you want to go to the Shannon school. You could go abroad to a hotel in France, Germany, Switzerland. We'll have visitors from there too, and that seems to be the way of the future.'

'Of course you might want to go to university. I don't know, Kerry, let's not look too far into the future.'

'And this . . . this business?'

'It's over now, isn't it? I mean there's nothing else gone in the house, I won't go into the church and see our candlesticks on the altar?'

'No, Father.'

'Well that's it. Twice. Anyone's allowed two mistakes. The third time is it.'

'How do you mean, it's it?'

'It's goodbye, it's notice in the paper time, I am not responsible for the debts of . . . That sort of thing.'

Kerry was silent.

Patrick rattled his car keys. 'I don't expect you to stop playing cards, that would be childish of me, and anyway if you're going to talk to Francis Doyle, you may get quite good and make a nice living. I don't expect you to stay clear of debt. If you do get into debt again come to me, come back and we'll discuss it. Within reason, and in return for work or whatever, I will try to help you, and you must come home here for the holidays and stand by my side at the opening and all of that. But if you steal from me or from anyone else, then it's over, it's as if you were never my son.'

No emotion in his voice. No pleas, no hate. No wishing for love.

For the first time in his life Kerry felt a chill of fear.

Rachel and Patrick missed each other by minutes. She went to walk along the towpath in the evening light. He went into Ryan's for a drink. There was always company there, he thought, always a welcome.

It was odd that the only people who should make him feel really welcome were the very people whose business would suffer most by his coming to Mountfern in the first place. He looked at John and Kate Ryan and how they seemed to sparkle so well at each other. As if they were still very much in love. After all these years. After all that terrible accident.

He wished that Rachel were at home. He had seen that there were no lights, and there was no car outside Loretto's.

He would have liked more than anything else to talk to her tonight and to have slept with her, to have laid his head on her breast while she stroked his hair and soothed away his worries. She knew him so well, and he had hurt her so badly.

Rachel walked alone on the towpath past bushes and brambles and briars. She couldn't understand why they hadn't been cut back to give the guests a better walk to the town. But there had been some story about a fairy ring which it would have been bad luck to cut down.

She met Maggie Daly walking along.

'All on your own?' she asked. A foolish question, she thought, just as she said it.

'Just like you, Mrs Fine,' the child said with no hint of insolence. She was only stating a fact.

'Where's everyone?' Rachel persisted.

'I think Grace went for a cycle ride with Michael, and Tommy's been playing

football with John Joe Conway and Liam White, and Jacinta's gone to get a new coat, and Dara's . . . I don't know where Dara is. So I came for a walk on my own.'
'I don't know whether it's a great idea or not, I do that sometimes.'
'What else is there to do?' Maggie asked simply.
'What would you like to do? Now, this minute.'
'I think I'd like a gorgeous new dress in just the right colour that would make everyone notice me and people say, "Would you look at Maggie Daly?" That's what I'd like.'
'Well come on home with me and we'll look through some books and magazines and we'll see what might suit you.'
Maggie hesitated for a moment. Her mother had been a bit disparaging about Mrs Fine, something to do with her not being baptized, and leading an immoral life. But her mother didn't know where she was, and wouldn't it be lovely to have Mrs Fine give her ideas like she had with that beautiful ribbon that everyone had admired?
'I'd love that,' she said, and they went across the footbridge, away from the sound of Ryan's and up to Rachel's rooms.

Mary Donnelly was glad the row had blown over. In fact it must have ended in some kind of reconciliation. They kept smiling at each other that evening in the bar. At one stage she even saw them holding hands.
It was probably about that business of John going to be reciting poetry in the bar. He had been dead against it at the time, but tonight he had books of old Irish poems out on the table and was busy marking some of them as if he were a boy back at school. And talking about boys back at school, Michael had recovered his good temper and even apologized to her for being short with her earlier. A misunderstanding, he had said humbly.
She saw John take his wife's hand and bring it to his lips when he thought nobody was looking. The way they smiled at each other gave her a lump in her throat. For the first time for a long while she thought of the man who had let her down and wondered what it would have been like to have him take her hand like that. Then she put the thought out of her mind and concentrated on being charming, which frightened the farmers more than anything she had done so far.

CHAPTER EIGHTEEN

'Wasn't it odd that the Meaghers left so quickly?' Loretto said.

'Oh I don't know, they got a chance of a place in Dublin, a small lock-up shop, and Patrick paid them a good price for the shop in Bridge Street. It was all for the best to go quickly. She's never been the same since poor Frank died.'

Kate had congratulated herself several times on the amazing foresight she had had in telling Mrs Meagher to hang on for a bit, something was bound to happen. And hadn't she been right! Imagine Patrick O'Neill wanting a small place in the centre of town. It had solved the Meaghers' problems at a stroke.

Loretto was still musing. 'She'll have the divil of trouble with that strap of Teresa in Dublin. If she was able to run wild in Mountfern, imagine what she'll get up to in Dublin.'

Kate didn't agree. 'She may have done all her running wild, she could be about to settle down for a bit now, have a quiet period for a change.'

Loretto looked at her in wonder. 'Isn't that extraordinary, Kate. Her mother said almost the very same thing to me herself.'

'Would Dara be insulted if I offered her some material to have a dress made?' Rachel asked Kate.

'Insulted? She'd grab it out of your hands. But you can't be giving them things. You're too generous as it is.'

'No truly, I have lovely bits of material, really nice pieces of fabric. They're samples, some of them are for drapes or wall hangings – furnishing fabrics. But they're quite elegant enough for a skirt or a dress.'

'Well wouldn't she love it!'

Kate was never without something in her hands these days – if it wasn't the table napkins it was tray cloths. They were sitting companionably in the green room. The summer was almost with them, and the weather was warm enough for the two glass doors to be left wide open.

Carrie served tea on a trolley, another gift from Rachel; she said she had ordered some for the hotel. Kate hoped she was telling the truth; sometimes she thought that Rachel disguised her generosity by pretending it was some cast-off from the hotel.

'Am I imagining it or is Carrie thickening around the waist?' Kate whispered.

'You *are* imagining it.' Rachel pealed with laughter. 'My goodness, what a suspicious mind you have. Perhaps Carrie and Jimbo just sit and talk when they're out together.'

'Not very likely,' Kate said dismissively. 'But you're right, I mustn't start fancying things.'

'Is anything worrying you? Anything apart from Carrie?'

'No.' It was not very convincing.

'I don't mean to pry,' said Rachel.

302

'I'd tell you if it was sensible.' Kate sounded as if she were ashamed of herself.
'Worries are rarely sensible,' Rachel smiled.
'I'll tell you. I worry a bit about Dara and Kerry. I get this feeling that Kerry
is a bit . . . well, a bit dangerous.'
'I worry about Kerry too,' Rachel said unexpectedly. 'And I think Kerry is very
dangerous.'
The two women sat, heads close together, sewing forgotten, and sighed over
the impossible situation. The more that Dara was warned against him the
more attractive he would be to her. And if Kate were to put difficulties in his
way about meeting her daughter, he would enjoy the challenge and come home
more often still from his Donegal posting to move heaven and earth in pursuit of
Dara.

Jacinta White told Dara that Mrs Fine was the mistress of Mr O'Neill. They had
been lovers for years in America. Jacinta knew this on the highest authority. She
said that Liam didn't believe it because he didn't really understand mistresses and
lovers. But it was true.
Dara, who thought it was indeed true from the days when Grace had told her
of their fears that Mrs Fine might become their stepmother, denied it utterly.
'You're full of drama, Jacinta,' she said, defending her own friend Grace from
having a wicked father and defending her mother from having a wicked friend.
'And you're full of airs, Dara, and you haven't a hope with Kerry O'Neill.'
Jacinta flounced off in a bad humour.
'What's wrong with Jacinta, why won't she come with us any more?' Grace's
eyes were big and innocent.
'Oh, Jacinta's an eejit, she's always taking notions over one thing or another.'
Dara gave no explanations.
'She's very jealous of you, of course,' Grace said.
'Of me?' Dara sounded like Maggie now.
'Yes, she fancied Tommy and Tommy has time for nobody but you.'
'Oh that's not true. Is it?' Dara was pleased.
'Michael tells me that Tommy writes your name all the time on his jotters at
school. Michael says he writes mine, but he says Dara is interleaved with all those
Celtic letters – you know, on the front of copy books.'
'Heavens.' Dara wasn't quite sure what to say. It was nice to be someone fêted
on the cover of exercise books, as Grace herself was. But it was not Tommy Leonard
that she wanted writing her name.
'I wish I was really really beautiful like you are, Grace,' Dara said suddenly.
Grace stared at her in amazement. 'But you are *much* more beautiful than I am.'
She seemed to be burningly sincere. 'I've only got a round chocolate-box face, I look
like that silly boy blowing bubbles in the picture up in the Grange. I have no looks,
you are the one with the gorgeous face . . . Dara you *must* know that. Kerry was
saying . . .'
'What was he saying?' Dara was eager.
'He was saying that,' Grace said.
'How did he say it, I mean what was it exactly . . .?'

303

'Just that.' Grace couldn't see any need to dawdle on what Kerry, who was only her brother, said. 'And you look terrific when you have a suntan, Dara you look great. I look as if I have a skin disease if I stay out in the sun.'

There was going to be no more about what Kerry had said and when he had said it. Dara hadn't much pride, but she had too much pride to ask again.

He was home the next weekend.

'Straight up. Permission and everything.' He grinned at his father, and to Grace's pleasure Father smiled back.

Things were definitely better these days.

'How do we spend Saturday?' Kerry asked his sister when Father had gone off to the hotel. Patrick O'Neill didn't work office hours, he worked a great deal too many hours for Brian Doyle's taste.

'Oh good, are you going to be around?'

'Well yes. I think so.'

'Michael and I are going fishing. I've got rather good at it lately.' Grace giggled a bit. 'We cycle off for miles and find really quiet places.' She looked down and up again and caught Kerry's eye.

He wasn't smiling.

'You *are* sensible aren't you, Grace?'

She pretended not to understand.

'Oh very. Anyway the places we go, the river isn't dangerous. It's narrow and shallow, usually.'

'That's not what I mean.'

'Oh.'

'Father's not going to look after you, as long as he has his folly . . .'

'Why do you call it that? You used to love Fernscourt.'

'Someone has to. You're very young, Grace, it would be terrible if you made any silly mistake.'

'No, Kerry, I wouldn't.'

'But it's different for boys. Does Michael respect you, or does he take advantage of you?'

'We just kiss a bit. That's all.' Grace looked down again.

'That had better be all, and don't go to far-away places to kiss. Listen to me, Grace, I know what I'm talking about. Michael's only a kid but he could make you do something . . . something foolish.'

'No, it's not like that . . .' She wished the conversation would end.

Just then there was a ring at the door. Miss Hayes didn't go immediately so Grace seized the opportunity.

It was Rachel Fine.

Kerry looked annoyed.

'I'm sorry, but Father has gone up to Fernscourt,' he said, barely politely, when Grace had ushered Mrs Fine into the room.

'I'm very sure he has.' Rachel smiled pleasantly. 'He was always an early worker, and all days of the week. No, I didn't come to see your father, Kerry. I came to visit with Miss Hayes.'

Kerry smiled at her as if this were the way things should be. Rachel Fine was welcome in the lodge if she had only come to talk to the help.

Olive Hayes had spoken once or twice before to Mrs Fine – a very pleasant woman, she had always thought. A Jewess they said, and a lady friend of Mr O'Neill, but there had never been any impropriety in this house and not in Loretto Quinn's either. She was surprised to see her come into the kitchen.

'Patrick has told me how well you run this household for him, Miss Hayes, and perhaps I am speaking out of turn when I ask you if you have enough free time to make a few simple summer dresses.'

'For you, Mrs Fine? I'd not be able to make anything good enough for you.'

Rachel smiled easily. 'No, I won't ask you to take on my complicated figure, Miss Hayes, you would have nightmares trying to get anything to hang straight on me. I meant for some of the girls, for Dara Ryan, Maggie Daly . . .'

'Make dresses for them . . .'

'Yes, I've been told that you're the dressmaking genius of Mountfern . . .'

Rachel took out two lengths of silky material – one copper-coloured, one in a clear aquamarine. They were beautiful fabrics.

Miss Hayes ran her hand lovingly under the folds. 'Oh, these are too good altogether for children, Mrs Fine.'

'Suppliers send me samples, Miss Hayes. There's two and a half yards there in each of them, they're no use to me and I was thinking that if you could make a dress each for the girls . . .'

She broke off. Grace was standing at the kitchen door.

'Aren't they *gorgeous*,' she said in admiration.

Rachel was pleasant. 'I have all these pieces, Grace, and I was asking Miss Hayes if I could persuade her to make dresses for Dara and Maggie. Miss Hayes is very gifted. She made a wedding dress last year that was the talk of the town, Loretto told me.'

Olive Hayes looked very pleased.

'I didn't know that.' Grace was interested.

'Oh, I do a bit now and then in the afternoons.' Miss Hayes was as pleased as punch.

'So if you and I could come to an agreement about a fee, do you think . . .'

'It would be a pleasure, Mrs Fine.'

Grace fingered the copper silk weave. 'Who's this for?'

'It's for Maggie, it's the exact colour of her hair.'

'Is it?'

'Yes, it will look quite lovely on her. This is for Dara.'

'Do they know, or is it a surprise?' Grace had heard nothing about it.

'They know that I was coming to see Miss Hayes, and they've seen the fabric.'

'Heavens,' Grace said.

'I've plenty more, Grace, if you . . .'

'I didn't mean to ask.'

'No, and I'm sure Miss Hayes . . .'

'I'd love to make something for Grace, but she has such expensive clothes already, I didn't like to . . .'

None of them were finishing their sentences but there was already an easy friendship between the three.

Kerry could see this when he came out to see what was happening. And his handsome face frowned slightly.

Sister Laura didn't know that there was such an interest in clothes, but she did realize that there wasn't sufficient interest in work. And she was disappointed that she couldn't drum up any greater enthusiasm about these exchanges with little French girls. All the families would have to find was the fare, and Lord knew they were well able to find money for other things like drink and television sets.

Sister Laura wished that she'd had such opportunities when she was young. Nobody ever went anywhere then. She had always wanted to see the great cathedral of Notre Dame in Paris, and go to Chartres. Girls had so many chances today. And an easy life too! No school on Saturdays now. Sister Laura's lips were pursed about that. It was better far when they had lessons right up to lunchtime, and this new way made the weekend far too long, they got up to all kinds of mischief.

Dr White had urged Sister Laura to take more exercise and get more fresh air. Dutifully she took a Saturday constitutional through Coyne's wood, down to River Road, along up Bridge Street and back to the convent by the Protestant church and graveyard.

In Coyne's wood she found Dara Ryan sitting on a stile watching eagerly to see who came through the trees. The child seemed disappointed – even dismayed – to see her teacher.

Down by the river bank she saw Grace O'Neill – holding hands, no less – with Dara's twin brother. They were much too young to be at that class of thing. Sister Laura barked a greeting at them that made them drop hands hastily.

When she called into Daly's for a cream cake – which Dr White had told her should form no further part of her diet – Sister Laura was met by a saga of complaints about little Maggie who, according to her mother, had taken up with the foreign woman and was spending all her waking hours admiring herself in the mirror. Across the road from Daly's was Dr White's. Sister Laura quickened her step and lowered her eyes in case she might catch the doctor's observant eye and he would read the cream cake written in her guilty face. Instead she saw Jacinta swinging on the gate and for once anxious for a chat.

Jacinta said that it was great to see nuns being normal now, and eating cream buns. Everything had got much better since the Vatican Council.

Sister Laura realized she had a moustache of cream on her face and pounded up Bridge Street in a very bad temper, thinking that fifteen-year-old girls in 1966 were a severe cross to have to bear.

She was glad she had not been called to the Married State. It was quite enough to have to deal with them in the classroom.

Kerry came through the wood and smiled easily.

'Well this *is* a lovely thing to discover in the woods on a summer day.'

'Hallo Kerry.'

'Is that all you have to say to me?' He slid his arms around her but she wriggled out of them.

'What is it? Don't you like me?'

'I like you well enough.'

'So what's with all the hard-to-get nonsense then?'

'I'm not being hard to get, it's just that I haven't seen you for a while, I thought it would be nice to talk, you know, rather than . . . straight away.'

'Sure, let's talk.' He sat down on the ground and stroked her foot. 'Could we talk about your ankles, for one thing? They're very beautiful . . .'

'Oh, please.' Dara was at a total loss.

'Why don't you like me to admire you?' He looked genuinely bewildered.

'Because . . . because it's like as if you're not admiring me as a person, it's only an ankle or a mouth or whatever.' She looked troubled.

'Oh Dara, that's not so, if you must know I like you as a person. You are totally special. I've told you that so many times.'

'No you haven't, we haven't talked much at all, you and I.'

'You're right!' he said, grinning broadly. 'We haven't talked nearly enough. I think about you so much, that's what makes me think we did talk much more than we have. Will you come and walk with me, we'll walk through here and down to the river, and honestly' − he held both his hands up in the air − 'no touching, promise.'

Dara felt very silly but it did look like a sort of a victory.

'That would be nice,' she said and leaped from the stile.

Kerry got up lithely from his sitting position without putting his hands on the ground.

'That was clever,' Dara admired.

'Oh come on, anyone can do that,' Kerry challenged.

'Maybe, but you had your legs crossed.'

'Go on, try it.'

Dara sat down on the mossy ground and crossed her legs. 'Let me see, what did you do?' She automatically kept trying to put her hands on the ground.

Kerry stood looking at her, laughing.

'It's not nearly as easy as you make it look.' Dara was cross.

'Here, I'll sit down beside you and show you.'

But when Kerry sat down beside her they were very close.

He looked at her flushed face.

He bent a little closer to her.

Dara bit her lip with indecision.

'It's very easy,' Kerry said. He put his head slightly to one side and smiled at her.

'I don't think I'm going to be able to do it . . .' Dara said.

'Oh, I think you are,' Kerry said. His face was closer still but he made no move to hold her.

She moved towards him. Their lips brushed lightly.

Kerry pulled back slightly. 'No hands,' he said triumphantly, showing both hands as he had done before.

But it didn't matter now. Their lips were together and nobody was working out technical details like that.

Kate was impatient that evening.

'Dara, where on earth were you? You look as if you rolled around on the ground, you're so full of leaves and dirt.'

It was so precisely what Dara had been doing that she got a shock, but she realized her mother was on a different track.

'Really and truly you twins are like tinkers. When you see how neat and clean Grace looks, and even Maggie has smartened herself up a lot. I don't know what we're all working our fingers to the bone earning money to dress you pair for, we might as well buy the clothes and just rub them in the ground.'

'I'm sorry,' Dara said automatically.

'No you're not. Where were you anyway?'

This was the question she had been trying to avoid.

'Oh, Michael will explain, I'd better go and have a wash,' she said, and ran off.

Minutes later Michael burst into her room. 'That was beautiful,' he said furiously. 'Why did you have to do that?'

Dara giggled. 'I'm sorry, I couldn't think of anything else. What did you say?'

'I said we were down playing on the towpath. Where all the brambles were. You should have warned me.'

Dara was sitting on her bed hugging her knees.

'I think that if we're going to spend this summer with the O'Neill family in different parts of the forest we should think up a story and stick to it,' she said.

'Were you with Kerry?' he asked.

'Of course.' She looked triumphant.

'Gosh, Dara. What were you doing?'

'Never mind!'

'You'd better be careful. Kerry's very old, and experienced.'

'I know.'

'You're awfully silly when you put on that face. You think you sound grown-up and clever, but in fact you sound silly. Like Jacinta when she's having one of her awful moods.'

'You should hear what *you* sound like sometimes – Grace says, Grace thinks, Grace always believes, Grace was wondering . . . Like a record stuck and going on over and over.'

'I don't,' Michael said. 'Do I?' he asked anxiously after a minute.

'A bit. Listen, let's not have a fight about it. Mam's on the warpath. The main thing is to keep the peace.'

'Sure.' Michael was distracted. 'Does everyone else notice, about my mentioning Grace I mean?'

'No.'

'Grace always says that I believe people too easily, I get taken in,' Michael said.

Miss Purcell had a problem. Old Mr Slattery had once said there was no problem that could not be solved by walking along by the river. Canon Moran said that God often spoke to the heart in peaceful riverside surroundings more clearly than he spoke in the midst of rush and bustle.

Miss Purcell took a riverside walk to try to work out her worry. Should she leave Fergus Slattery and go to work at the presbytery? To leave your post was an act of desertion. That was true. To work for the priests of God was a high calling. That too was true.

To forget the Slattery family who had been good to her for many years would be base ingratitude. To replace Miss Barry would mean that Miss Barry would definitely have to go for treatment to the county home. Would that be a good or a bad thing?

Miss Purcell walked on long and purposefully, hoping to hear some voice that would make things seem clear.

What she did hear among the reeds and rushes was some giggling and laughing. She craned her neck to see what was going on and stepped up to her ankles in water.

She saw two fleeing figures, children she thought. One of them was almost definitely that little O'Neill girl, she couldn't identify the boy. When she came back bad-tempered, with soaking feet and no decision made, she met Fergus in the hall.

'Really, Miss Purcell, if you go paddling the point is to take off your shoes and stockings,' he said in a mock-reproving voice.

Miss Purcell was in no mood for light-hearted banter. 'I don't know what this place is coming to,' she said. 'I saw that young O'Neill girl and she's only a child, up to no good at all, keeping company up in the reeds. She can only be fourteen or fifteen. It's disgraceful.' Two red spots burned in Miss Purcell's face.

'Oh a chip off the old block, her father's the greatest whoremaster for a hundred miles,' Fergus said casually.

'Mr SLATTERY please.' Miss Purcell had never listened to this kind of conversation before and she didn't intend to now. Unwittingly Fergus had made the decision that no voice had made for her on the river bank. Miss Purcell would spend the autumn of her life with the Clergy. Where she wouldn't hear words or sentiments like that.

Kerry had a long weekend, he didn't have to go back until Monday night he told Dara. He would be able to see her on Sunday AND on Monday.

'Don't call to the pub . . . I'll go out and meet you,' Dara said.

'I'm trying to be respectable,' Kerry said. 'Do the right thing, ask your parents' permission and everything. Is that not the way to go?'

'Of course it's not,' Dara said. 'They'd never give their permission for what we do.'

Kerry smiled. 'They wouldn't know.'

'They'd guess. I'll say I'm going up to the lodge.'

'Whatever you say.'

'And where will I meet you?'

'I'll come and find you in the wood.'

He did. But only late in the evening. Dara had been waiting, she was upset and annoyed.

'We didn't make a time,' Kerry said. 'We didn't fix a date and a place, you wouldn't let me come and pick you up. So what's all the drama?'

'There's no drama,' Dara said.

'Good, I hate girls that make a fuss over nothing,' Kerry said.

Dara heard two warnings in that.

One warning. There had been and probably still were plenty of other girls. And also the warning that fussy girls mightn't last long in the picture.

Dara gave a watery smile.

'Sure, anyway it was nice here. I love this wood, I always have.'

'It's beautiful in the evening,' Kerry said. 'I think it's one of the loveliest places ever. Imagine Jack Coyne having a wood called after him. I wish we had an O'Neill's wood.'

'It's not really Jack's wood, there have always been Coynes in this part.' Dara didn't want to give the ferret-faced man from the motor works any part of the mossy, flower-filled place.

Kerry seemed restless. Edgy almost.

'What did you do today?'

He looked at her in surprise. Dara swallowed. It hadn't been such a terrible question, had it?

'I beg your pardon?' he asked.

'I was just wondering what kind of things you did.' She bit her lip and wished she had let the silence be. It was so hard to talk to him today, yesterday he had been like an angel.

'If you must know I went to a bar way out on the Galway road.'

'A bar. But you don't drink?'

'No, Miss Curiosity 1966, you are right. I do not drink. But I do play cards and that's what they were doing there.'

'Cards in a pub on a Sunday?'

'In a back room. A brother of Brian Doyle works there – well, sort of deals cards there. It was great.'

'Did you play for money?'

He paused. As if he were debating something.

'No. Not this time.'

'Will you another time?'

'Yes, no point in it otherwise.'

'Why didn't you put money on the cards today then?'

'Francis said not to, just to watch, watch him dealing. It was great.'

'Could I come with you next time?'

'No way. I'm even a bit young for this place, they'd think you were a baby in a cradle.'

'I'm pretty grown up.'

'You are very pretty, and very grown up,' Kerry said, slipping an arm around Dara. 'So I won't let them clap eyes on you.'

Dara smiled happily. She wriggled out of his arm for a moment as Sheila Whelan walked past, greeting them both briefly.

'I hope she won't tell,' Dara said.

'What can she tell?' Kerry sounded bored.

She changed the subject. 'Did you have woods like this back in America?'

'Not like this. We had trees of course on our property . . . but it was different to here.'

'Did you walk under the trees?'

'Yes. With my mother, when she was well.'

Even Grace hardly talked about their mother. Dara held her breath a little.

'What was it like?' she asked tentatively.

'It was good. We used to walk in the evenings, and watch the fireflies. You don't have them here?'

'Fireflies?' asked Dara.

'I've never seen any. I wonder why that is.'

'What are they like?'

'Like little points of light, like a million tiny stars.'

'They must be lovely,' Dara breathed.

'It was lovely then, but it all changed. Anyway, it's silly wanting fireflies when we have so much else here.'

'What have we here?'

'We have some very beautiful girls for one thing.'

'Oh, lots of them is it?' Dara pretended a sense of outrage and started to run off down the slope.

'Yes thousands, but you're the most beautiful. By far.' He ran after her and caught her easily.

Because Dara wasn't running very fast.

Dara Ryan is too young for Kerry O'Neill, Sheila Whelan thought to herself. Far too young. She shouldn't be up in Coyne's wood alone with him at this time of the evening.

But Sheila had never told anyone anything about anyone else's business. And even though it was a fifteen-year-old girl, she felt this sense that she must not interfere.

She wondered, if she had a daughter of her own, what would she like a good friend to do? It was impossible to know.

Fergus Slattery had a distressing case to cope with. The parents of a fifteen-year-old boy came to him saying that their son had been named as the father of a girl's baby. It was a matter of a paternity order.

They were stern unblinking people who did not believe such a thing to be possible.

'It couldn't be done, a child of fifteen to father another child,' the farmer said in bewilderment.

'It could be done all right,' Fergus said. Even though he was twice the boy's age and had fathered nobody he knew it could indeed be done.

311

'The girl's a dirty tramp who lay with half the country,' said the farmer's wife. Fergus had already spoken to the terrified schoolboy.

'We'll get nowhere talking like that. Your son is too young to marry, it's a simple case of finance. We have to work out what can be fairly paid.'

'You're not saying that our child is responsible for this girl's bastard?'

'I'm saying that we'll save ourselves a heap of trouble if we try to bring it down to pounds, shillings and pence, and keep all the recriminations for your own kitchen around the fire, or even better not have them at all.'

'God knows what you can be thinking about Mr Slattery, you mustn't be of this world at all.'

'I'm probably not of this world,' Fergus agreed. His face was grim, what he had been thinking of was Michael Ryan. Suppose by some horrendous ill chance Michael were to father a child of Grace O'Neill's. What in God's earth would happen then?

He wondered should he warn Kate Ryan or was it the action of a mad maiden aunt?

Dr White called to see Kate as a matter of course and courtesy rather than because he could do anything for her.

He never referred again to her inquiry about whether sexual intercourse would be wise or indeed possible. He was a dour man without great charm but Kate liked him. She trusted him because he never gave her false hopes, and he had always been able to interpret the more flowery pronouncements of consultant doctors at the hospitals, and the specialists she had seen.

'Nothing wrong with you these days except a broken back,' Martin White said in a manner that some would have found offensively direct.

'No, not a thing. That and being the mother of teenagers. It's a hard old station, isn't it?'

'Ah, don't talk to me. We have Jacinta around the house day and night now, a fit of the sulks. Some awful slight or row or something, she has us demented.'

'Oh dear. Who with?' Kate hadn't heard any of this.

'Your lot I think, and that little one of the Daly's and Tommy Leonard. Never mind, it'll pass, that's what we keep telling ourselves. The only thing is will *we* survive it?'

'Oh, I hope Dara and Michael weren't out of turn with her . . .'

'You wouldn't know what it was all about. Jealousy I think, mainly. Jacinta complains that Dara and Michael have fallen in love with the O'Neill children and are wandering around starry-eyed hand in hand, and the old gang as they knew it isn't the same. Fat lot of time we had for that sort of thing or indeed talking about it, at their age.'

'I thought they all played together still.' Kate's voice was tinny.

'God, Kate, they may well do. Jacinta would remind you of one of those circular saws when she gets started, I don't listen half the time.'

Kate allowed him to change the subject.

At supper the children's father spoke sternly.

'There's going to be an end to all this rambling off on your own from now on, you're all to be where we can keep an eye on you.'

'That would mean being in the bar,' Eddie was quick to protest.

'Shut up, Eddie, not you for once.'

'Why not?' Eddie was outraged.

'I meant not only you, I meant all of you. Dara, Michael, are you listening to me?'

They exchanged glances.

'Where *do* you go anyway?' their father persisted.

'Here and there,' Michael said.

'Mainly the lodge,' Dara lied.

'That's odd, your mother had a message from Miss Hayes above in the lodge asking if you could favour her with your presence for a fitting for this dress she's making you. She hasn't seen hair nor hide of you up there all weekend, apparently.'

'She must have been in a different part,' Dara mumbled.

'Yes, it's a huge place all right, four rooms I believe, you'd easily lose a battalion up there.'

John's face was not amused. He hadn't liked what Kate had reported to him. The thought of anyone making free with Dara made him feel bile rise in his throat. The fact that Dara was so obviously lying made it quite sure that Dr White's information had been correct.

'Where do you want us to be?'

'Where I can call you, by the footbridge, or down by the real bridge at the end of the town.'

'We're not old enough for the bridge,' Eddie said.

'Get on with your tea, Eddie,' John Ryan said wearily.

'Why's nobody interested where *I'm* going to be?' Eddie wanted to know.

'Do you think he suspected?' Michael asked Grace that evening. They stood on the footbridge while Michael explained the new edict.

'No of course not.'

'I want to be with you, on your own. We're not doing anything *really* wrong.'

'We can still be together,' Grace was soothing.

'It's not together with awful people about.'

'They're not awful people, they're our friends.'

'People like John Joe Conway.' Michael was mutinous.

'Don't be ridiculous, Michael, you're always imagining that he has some interest in me.'

'Everyone's interested in you, Grace, we know that, it's just that John Joe is so coarse, I couldn't bear him looking at you, touching you . . .'

'He doesn't touch me.'

'Looking at you even.'

'That's crazy to talk like that.'

'I am crazy about you.' He put out his hand towards her.

'Watch it,' Grace said, 'we're in full view of the pub.'

'This is going to be great for the rest of the summer,' said Michael.

Olive Hayes asked Mrs Fine to be present for the fittings.

The dresses were all at the same stage – the aquamarine for Dara, a soft rosy pink for Grace and the unusual burnished copper for Maggie.

'Don't you have another friend, isn't it Dr White's daughter who goes about with you? I could get her some material too,' Rachel offered.

'Jacinta. Oh, she'd love that,' Maggie said.

'She doesn't deserve it,' Dara said sternly, remembering Jacinta's view of Mrs Fine as a mistress.

'Come on, Dara. Don't be mean. We're all having a dress, why not Jacinta?' Grace was always generous.

Rachel looked at the beautiful blonde daughter of frail Kathleen O'Neill and Patrick. She had always felt the child was withdrawn and hostile towards her until recently. Now Grace was looking at her delightedly as if she were her closest friend.

'Could *you* suggest it to her, Mrs Fine? We had a sort of falling out with Jacinta. Could you tell her about the dresses? It would mend things again.'

'Oh *please*, Mrs Fine,' Maggie asked.

'What do *you* think, Dara? I'd need to have everyone's views.'

'I think Jacinta's being silly. But Grace is right, and if *you* said it she couldn't snarl and take offence.'

'Right.' Rachel was pleasant about it. 'I'll call at the house, I have an excuse anyway.' It was true. Rachel wanted to ask Dr White if it would be too tiring for Kate to go on a shopping trip to Dublin with her. She felt her friend needed a break away from the pub and the worry about the new café.

'This needs to be lifted a little here, do you think, Mrs Fine?'

Miss Hayes didn't want to take any initiatives. She held the fabric in place where she was going to put the little dart that would shape it.

The others looked at Maggie Daly's small thin shoulders and her little pointed breasts seen to their best advantage.

'You look great, Maggie,' Dara said spontaneously. 'You look totally different to usual.'

Maggie saw only the compliment, she didn't want to believe it. 'You're only saying that,' she said.

'Why would I say it? Doesn't she?'

Grace was looking at her wordlessly. 'Honestly Maggie, it's extraordinary, you look like a painting.'

Maggie clasped her hands together and pulled them apart in delighted embarrassment. It was as if she were clapping.

'I'll never be able to thank you enough, Mrs Fine, imagine there being this bit of curtain just the right colour.'

'I know, isn't it extraordinary!' Rachel marvelled, thinking of the hours she had spent in the material departments of Brown Thomas and Switzer's looking for the exact shade.

'You're terrific, Mrs Fine,' Grace said, delighted that Maggie was getting the Cinderella treatment.

Rachel looked at the beautiful daughter of the man she loved and knew she must not say anything that would threaten this new friendship.

'It makes a very nice change for me to see three good-looking girls getting dressed up than to see yards and yards of wall coverings, and to work out why half the bedroom carpets are one shade and half are different when they were all meant to have come from the same batch. This is the fun bit here, I assure you.'

She mustn't give them any hint about how it was the only bit. This and her conversations with Kate Ryan.

Why else was she in this town? She felt that she and Patrick were miles apart. Further than they had ever been, even when they were on different sides of the ocean.

Jacinta White didn't want a dress.

'I don't have to follow everyone else, be a copycat,' she said.

'I think you're right. Anyway you look good in those pants.'

Jacinta looked down at her jeans and boots in surprise. 'What?' she said suspiciously.

'I was never able to wear anything like that – slacks, trousers, pants, whatever you call it. My bottom was too big. I always wanted to, though.'

Jacinta would not be won so easily.

'Oh, I haven't much time for clothes,' she said loftily.

'Sensible of you. Anyway, it's always there if you want it.'

'Thank you, but I haven't time for fittings and choosing and all that sort of stuff.'

Rachel saw the aching loneliness of a fifteen-year-old who had fallen out of the pack. She knew that any more persuasion would result in further refusals.

'Maggie and Grace were saying that they wanted you to have a dress too. But don't be dragged in if you don't want to.' Rachel prepared to leave.

'I bet Dara didn't want me to have a dress. Dara's a pain in the neck, she thinks Tommy Leonard is her little slave. It would sicken you.'

'I think Dara did want you to share in all these remnants, actually, and I definitely heard that she fancied Kerry O'Neill rather than Tommy Leonard.'

'Well, she's out of her mind fancying Kerry O'Neill, he's far too old for her and he has girlfriends all over the place. You don't have any material that would make jeans, do you?'

It was very ungracious.

'No, but what I do have that might be nice is a bit of leather fringe. We could put some on your shirt and some on your boots.'

'On the boots?'

'Yes, isn't there a man up in Foley's who does shoe repairs? If we asked him nicely he could stitch some of this fringe on to the top of the boots.'

'And you would give it to me, would you?'

'With pleasure,' Rachel smiled.

Fringes on her shirts and her boots, that would make Tommy Leonard sit up and wipe the smile out of Dara's eye, Jacinta thought.

'I'll come along with you now and get it,' she said in case Mrs Fine might change her mind.

315

Patrick was in Meagher's with Brian Doyle organizing the changes.

The place was going to be a small office and travel agency.

He would employ just one person, who would arrange tours for the guests and do any other business that Mountfern might need.

He saw Rachel coming down Bridge Street with that sulky child Jacinta, the daughter of the gloomy doctor fellow.

Patrick was about to go over to them but he stopped himself.

In front of this child they would have to behave as near-strangers. They would have to play a role.

Was it worth it? There were so many of these non conversations all day. What was the point of another? He stopped just on the doorway of the shop and turned back in again. Rachel saw him, and her heart felt cold. He had actually got to the stage of avoiding her now.

'Kerry?'

'Yes Mr Hill?'

'A word if I may?'

'Of course.'

'My own sons don't listen to my advice, you probably don't listen to your father. That's the way things are, always have been possibly.'

Kerry held his head politely on one side, waiting for the old man to come to the point. He was working in the bar this week, and liking it. The summer business was beginning to build up and Kerry was an easy conversationalist, people got on well with him.

Dennis Hill looked at him without speaking for a few seconds.

'That crowd who were in last night, McCann, Burns, those . . .'

'Yes Mr Hill?'

'They're not the class for this hotel. Too rough. They don't fit.'

'Are they barred?'

'Of course they're not barred. They were never here before, they came to see you. They're from Derry.'

Kerry's eyes narrowed slightly. The old man noticed more than he thought.

'Yes, I did meet them outside the hotel, I thought it was good to ask them to come in and swell the numbers. But if you think they're not the right kind of guests, I won't encourage them here. Is that what you'd like me to do?' The insolence was well hidden, you'd have to dig deep to find it. But it was there.

'No, I don't mind if they come in or not, we're well able to move people on if they're difficult, don't worry about that. It's you I'm thinking about.'

'Me?'

'You. They're a rough crowd. I don't mean their accents or the way they dress. I mean what they do.'

'What do they do?'

'A good question. A very good question. Nothing you could describe too well, or put down in the space on your passport where it wants to know your occupation.'

'I think they're in business.'

'Yes, that's what I think too. Mainly criminal business.'

316

'Oh Mr Hill . . .'

'Some of it's just on the right side of things, but only some of it and only just.'

'So?'

'So. I'm warning you about them. You need take no notice, you might appreciate having your card marked. You might just wish that I'd clear off and shut up.'

'No, Mr Hill, I appreciate your advice.'

'Which means to hell with your advice. All right Kerry, I've done my duty. Now about your holidays. Would you like to take off now before we get really busy in July and August?'

Kerry got the feeling that the old man was sending him away from his new friends. He was about to make an excuse and then he thought of Mountfern in the sunshine, and the sparkling river and the beautiful little Dara waiting like a fruit to be plucked.

'That's very nice of you, Mr Hill, and I'll think about what you said.'

'I'm sure you will Kerry,' Dennis Hill sighed.

Kerry went out with Tony McCann and Charlie Burns that night to play cards. He was luckier than he had been before. Or was the advice of Francis Doyle, Brian's pisspot brother, really working? Anyway he would be going back to Mountfern with a billfold full of pound notes and fivers.

Patrick told John and Kate that young people's lives were like a holiday camp nowadays. There was his Kerry being offered three weeks' holiday from Hill's hotel. Kerry was buying a car no less, imagine it. Not nineteen years of age, and he had everything he wanted.

'Isn't that why you killed yourself working, so that your children *could* have everything they wanted?' Kate asked him.

'I suppose so.' Patrick was doubtful.

'Well it certainly was,' John said. 'What else would any of us do anything for, if we didn't have the next lot coming after us to provide for?'

'What would you do if you hadn't a family of children?' Patrick asked with interest.

'I think I'd put a pack on my back and wander off round the world talking to people about this and that, as it took my fancy.'

'Like Papers Flynn,' Kate scoffed.

'I'd go further afield than Papers, but that's what I'd do.' John was adamant.

'You would not!' Kate flashed. 'Even if he had none of us trailing out of him, he'd still stand here looking at his river.'

She wanted to find out Kerry's plans for his holiday at home. She didn't like the sound of the car, she felt it might be used to spirit Dara to places well beyond the jurisdiction.

'Won't Kerry find it very quiet for him here? Playing with youngsters?' Her eyes were innocent. But she swore that Patrick saw what she was getting at.

'I'll keep an eye on him as much as I can,' he promised.

'Perhaps he'll go off to other parts of the country. Specially if he gets a car?' Kate was hopeful.

'No, I've a feeling that he sees a lot of attraction here. Still, as I said, we'll make sure that he doesn't get too carried away.'

He had said nothing, and he had said everything.

Kate gave a little shiver of fear.

'I wish there could be another party,' Maggie said.

'Why don't you ask your family if you could have one? There's plenty of room in your house,' Dara said.

Maggie rolled her eyes. 'Us have a party! It's on our knees saying the thirty days prayer tacked on to the rosary and ending up with a trip to devotions. That's my mother's idea of a good evening.'

The others giggled. Maggie seemed to have much more confidence these days. She apologized less, she was even joining in the swimming from the bridge. Maggie used to be shy to be seen down in the middle of town in her bathing costume; nowadays she would sit and laugh with the others, not self-conscious any more.

The old raft they had made way back, which had floated down to the bridge, became their centre of activities. They used it to dive from. Sometimes they piled boxes up on it to make a higher diving platform. Tommy Leonard could dive from the bridge itself. He was like a swallow, Dara said admiringly, he just seemed to swoop down. The rest of them bent their legs or belly flopped.

Only Tommy, John Joe Conway and Jacinta were any good diving from the bridge, they were the undoubted champions.

Gradually Jacinta had come back into things. She couldn't stay away any more, the fun had moved to the bridge at the end of the street where she lived. This was the summer they were old enough for the bridge, there was no way Jacinta would stay out of things.

And being so athletic was an advantage. It was no use when you were at the pictures or being watched parading up and down Bridge Street, but it was marvellous when you were the only girl who could dive from the wall of the bridge and when Tommy Leonard admired you.

'Do you mind if I buy a car from Jack Coyne? I know you and he don't get on,' Kerry said.

'How have you enough money to buy a car?'

'We said there would be no discussion about money, ever again.'

'No, we said there would be no discussion about stealing unless it happened again.'

'Well it hasn't.'

There was a silence.

'I won it in the north.'

Patrick nodded. 'Very well. Now about Coyne, he's a mean, dishonest little shit, but Rachel warned me against alienating locals, however unlikeable. Go ahead. Watch out that it's a real car, mind. Make sure he doesn't sell you a dummy.'

'No, he'll be so anxious to get into your good books he'll give me a fantastic bargain,' Kerry grinned.

Patrick smiled too. This was good thinking. That is exactly what Jack Coyne would do. How sensible his son was to capitalize on it.

'You might find that the pattern has changed a bit this summer,' he said.

'What way changed?'

'Not so much wandering off on your own, it looks like, everyone swimming by the bridge.'

'Well, I'll have a car, that should change the pattern a bit more.'

'You might find a bit of resistance along the way. Dara Ryan's mother for one.' Patrick spoke lightly.

Kerry was sunny. 'That's no problem, there are plenty of other girls to take for drives. And anyway I like swimming too.'

He smiled at his father as if there weren't a problem in the world.

Loretto Quinn told Rachel that Jack Coyne was like the cat that got the cream. The young O'Neill boy had said he would like to buy a second-hand car from him. Jack Coyne had sped off to the town in high excitement. He said he was going to find a little honey of a little car for the boy. Loretto hadn't known him as pleased for years.

'He calls in here a lot. Is he an admirer do you think?' Rachel asked.

Loretto pealed with laughter. 'Jack Coyne an admirer? Lord, all that man ever admired was a roll of fivers. But it's very flattering of you to think I might have a caller, Mrs Fine.'

'You're a fine woman, Loretto. Why wouldn't you have callers and admirers?'

'Ah, Mrs Fine, you've improved me but not that much. Not in a place like this. Anyway I wouldn't want them, I'm happy as I am. Much happier since you came.'

Rachel was pleased. Even if she had to resign herself that her coming to Mountfern had not achieved its aim, at least she could console herself that she had done a lot to help the women and girls of the place. Rachel was reading about the women's liberation that seemed to be sweeping the States at the moment. Not much of it had found its way to Mountfern. But she was definitely helping to improve the quality of life for a few of the female citizens of the place anyway.

Maggie Daly hung up her new dress all by itself on the back of her door. She didn't want to put it in the wardrobe in case it got crushed. And anyway she couldn't see it in the wardrobe.

She wondered what Kitty would say about it. Kitty was coming home for a weekend.

Kerry's car was red and had an open roof. It wasn't quite a sports car but it was almost.

He took Grace for a lap of honour up and down Bridge Street, turning neatly in front of the Classic Cinema, which nearly gave Declan Morrissey a heart attack as he thought the boy was through the cinema doors. Grace's hair, blown by the wind, stood like a halo around her head. Michael fixed a smile on his face and wished with such intensity that it hurt him physically that he was old enough to drive, that he had the money to buy a *white* sports car and that he and Grace could drive around Mountfern like that.

Dara fixed a smile on her face as she sat beside Maggie on the wall of the bridge.

She wished with an intensity that hurt her that she could be sitting where Grace was and that Kerry and she would do one more tour of the town and then drive off for miles in the beautiful car. She wished that her hair curled under and that she had her ears pierced. Then she would be truly happy.

Father Hogan and Canon Moran were taking a walk when they saw the red car. They were about to cluck at each other and say that Mr O'Neill really spoiled his children and gave a bad example when the car stopped.

'Do you want to test it out? I only have it an hour.' Kerry sounded excited.

'Test it out?'

'I'll take you for a test ride.'

The priests looked at each other in amazement. Nobody had ever offered them anything so racy.

'Us?' Canon Moran croaked in disbelief.

'Yes Canon, one at a time, it only seats two.'

'It's very nice of you, Kerry . . . but my old bones.'

There was naked longing on Father Hogan's face.

'What about you, Father, you'll risk it won't you?'

'Aren't you very good to be bothering with the clergy . . .' Grace had got out and was holding the door open, Father Hogan had gathered up the skirts of his soutane and settled himself in.

'But of course I bother with the clergy, Father Hogan, aren't they the most important people in town?' Kerry smiled and slipped through the gears to roar off with Father Hogan in the passenger seat.

It was a warm evening, warm enough to come back to the bridge and swim again after tea.

At seven o'clock they gathered there again.

Jacinta did some spectacular dives. This was the first time Kerry had seen them, he was full of praise. Jacinta was gruff and red with delight. She looked at Tommy Leonard to see whether he had noticed. But Tommy's eyes were wide. Maggie was approaching in her new dress. She looked quite different to the Maggie they all knew.

'I didn't know we were going to wear them now, I thought we'd wait till there was something special,' Dara grumbled.

'What will there be special?' Maggie asked.

'You look like a picture,' Michael said.

'That's exactly what I told her,' Grace said eagerly.

'Hey, you're even more dazzling than your big sister,' Kerry said.

Dara felt plain and foolish.

Mam had been watching her like a hawk – where are you going, what are you doing, will you be with Michael? It was maddening. Just as she was coming out Mam had told her not to be dressing up like as if she was going to a ball, so she wore her striped tee shirt and the plain blue skirt.

She felt like a deck chair in the outfit, canvas and stripes. Who would look at her? And here was Maggie with her hair all brushed and shimmering and reminding Kerry of Kitty up in Dublin.

The light went out of the evening for Dara. Hands in the pockets of her dull plain shirt, she turned away. The others were so busy admiring Maggie they hardly noticed.

Dara began to walk towards River Road. There was nothing here for her, every moment she stayed just pointed out how dull she was. She couldn't do dives like Jacinta, she wasn't lovely like Grace was or Maggie was turning out to be. She was boring old wooden Dara.

She had turned into River Road and was nearly at Jack Coyne's when she realized Maggie was running after her.

'Why won't you stay?'

'What do you care?'

'We were having fun, weren't we?' Maggie asked anxiously.

'Oh Maggie, can't you ever make up your mind about anything?' Dara snapped.

Maggie looked at her, dismayed.

'You're so weak. You don't even know whether we were having fun or not. You ask me were we? I don't know about you. I wasn't, so I came home. But at least I know. You never know.'

'What don't I know?'

'See!' Dara was triumphant. 'You don't know if you'd like an ice cream, you don't know if you'd like a trip in Kerry's car, you don't know if you want to swim or to wear a bathing cap. You don't know *anything*.'

'What did I do, Dara?' wailed poor Maggie after Dara's back.

Dara didn't even turn round, she just shouted over her shoulder. 'You did nothing. You never do anything. That's just the point.'

Maggie stood stricken on the river bank, Dara stormed home and threw herself on her bed to cry.

Mary came up and knocked on the door. 'Your mother would like you to go to her room and talk to her.'

'Tell her I'm in bed.'

'Dara. Please. Your mother sent me up specially.'

'I'm in bed, I'm not going down.'

'She can't come up.'

There was a silence.

'So please, Dara, will you come down?'

The door opened and Dara's tear-stained face appeared. 'That's the most cruel blackmail I ever heard. Reminding me that Mam can't ever get up the stairs. How mean and unfair.' She stormed past Mary and nearly took the hinges off the door of her mother's green room.

Mary sighed. It went against her principles to say that boys were easier round the house than girls at this age. But maybe it was because women were so much more sensitive.

'Yes?' Dara stood inside the door she had just banged.

'I was wondering if you could help me.'

'Do what?'

'To think of a name for our café. We will have to get it painted for one thing and then if we call it something we can start painting that on trays and perhaps even embroidering it on aprons.'

Dara looked at Kate as if her mother had gone mad.

'I don't care *what* you call it,' she said.

'You'll be looking at it for a long time.'

'Not necessarily,' Dara said.

'Well, even if you're going to leave home, you might want to have a say in what the café is called.'

'No, Mam, honestly I don't. I'm not being rude, I don't mind what name you choose.' She made as if to go.

'Ryan's Ridiculous Café, maybe?' Kate tried. 'Ryan's Rubbishy Café, Ryan's Wreck of a Café. Ryan's Roadhouse.' She pretended to be considering each of them. Dara couldn't raise a smile even.

'Could you sit down do you think?'

'No Mam, if you don't mind . . . I'd prefer to go to bed.'

'It's not eight o'clock, you're the one who told me not two hours ago that it was inhuman to ask people to be home by ten o'clock. Do you remember?'

'Yes.'

'Is there anything I can do? Anything at all.'

'No. No there isn't, really. Thanks all the same.'

'Dara?'

'Yes.'

'I asked you to come down because I love you, no other reason, I love you with all my heart and I don't want you to be unhappy. I know it's not much use just to have *me* loving you, but it might be a help some time, so just remember it will you?' Kate smiled at her and continued, 'No, of course you don't need to sit here any more. I got lonely too sitting by myself and I thought it might work if you came and sat with me, we might get less lonely. But it didn't work. Off you go to bed. Goodnight now, love.'

'You'll think of a name.'

'Yes I will, or you will or someone will.'

'Why does it have to have a name at all?'

'I'm not sure,' Kate said. 'Rachel thinks it would stick in people's minds more. You know the way they like things to be defined – Emerald Isle, Land of Shamrocks. I suppose we're the same with other places, we think of Spain and we think of castanets.'

'You *could* call it Shamrock Café,' Dara said.

'Ryan's Shamrock Café,' Kate said slowly. 'That might do.'

'Goodnight Mam.'

'Goodnight my love.'

Dara longed to rush back and throw herself into her mother's arms, but it would have meant too many tears and trying to explain what she was crying about. So she resisted it and went back upstairs to the window seat, where she sat and watched the sun set over the River Fern, and saw Michael walk disconsolately home at five minutes to ten.

Grace flashed by in Kerry's little red car.

'Were you swimming and all till now?' Dara asked Michael.

'Jacinta said you went off in a sulk. Did you?' he asked.

'Of course not,' Dara lied. 'What did everyone do?'

'If you'd stayed you'd have found out,' he said and went into the boys' room and closed the door.

Dara felt more alone than she had ever felt.

She thought about Mam saying that she loved her. It was a nice thing to say but Mam was right, it wasn't much use at the moment.

The next evening they had all made separate resolutions.

Dara was not going to sulk. She wore a red shirt over her black bathing suit, and the silk rose that Kerry had given her on her fifteenth birthday all those months ago behind her ear. She smiled at everyone.

Maggie had decided not to wear her good new dress. It had been overdoing it, they had all got annoyed with her somehow. She wore an old Viyella dress that used to belong to Kitty once, it was faded and shrunk now. It made Maggie look about ten.

Jacinta's father had told her that he was prescribing himself headache remedies because of the continuous whine tone in her voice, so she had resolved to speak more cheerfully.

Michael had decided that it was not the end of the world if John Joe Conway said 'Fine girl you are' every time he looked at Grace. And that it only made *him* look the stupid one if he reacted all the time.

Tommy Leonard had decided that Dara *did* like him, she wasn't sighing at him, she was sighing at everything around her.

Liam White thought that he might ask Maggie Daly to the pictures. She was so small he could even get her in for half price as an under twelve.

Grace made a vow to be much nicer to Michael. It was awful for him, his parents had turned into policemen and insisted that they all move in packs. Someone must have seen them. She shuddered to think what her own father would say if anything was reported to him. But then he was so busy and out so much he wouldn't notice.

They sat swinging their legs on the bridge, the four girls, Dara, Maggie, Grace and Jacinta. The boys perched on their bikes and chatted to them.

Half a dozen others came and went, John Joe Conway with his loutish laugh saying there was nothing to look at since the girls were all covered up.

There was no sign of Kerry.

Then they saw him walking down Bridge Street, the evening sun hitting his golden hair. He looked like a young god as he walked, in his open-necked blue shirt the exact colour of his eyes, and his white trousers gleaming. He looked like a cowboy in a Western, the good guy who had come in to save the town. Tonight he did not have the red car – he had left his bike slung casually against the railing of Slattery's house.

He was coming to join the gang on the bridge. The evening could begin.

They had never seen Kerry swim in this part of the river. Up beyond the footbridge yes, long ago. But here was more public somehow. Up in the old place with the raft it had never mattered whether you could swim or not, it was wallowing and flapping about in the water from the bank to the raft and back.

But here it was altogether more showy.

They watched as Kerry kicked off his canvas shoes and slipped off his trousers. He was wearing his swimming trunks underneath. He stood in the golden rays of the evening sun, blinking. Then he threw off his blue shirt, and laughed at them.

'It only gets worse thinking about it,' he said as if he were totally unaware that all their eyes were on him. Lean and tanned, golden and confident, he stood on the parapet of the bridge and did one long clean dive into the River Fern.

Tommy Leonard thought gloomily that that was that. There went his only chance of being good at something. Kerry O'Neill turned out to be much better at diving than Tommy. Wouldn't you know?

Dara looked at Kerry in wonder. He was perched on the raft, the drops of water clinging to his tanned shoulders and arms making him look shimmering. He was so very very handsome and he was smiling straight up at her.

'Come on, Dara, let's see you do it.'

Without thinking, Dara peeled off her red shirt, took the silk rose carefully from her hair and scrambled up on the wall of the bridge.

'Careful, Dara,' Michael said.

'Move more to the middle,' Tommy Leonard warned.

Dara dived in. She seemed surprised at herself when she surfaced, shaking the water from her face.

'Great stuff,' Kerry said, moving over on the raft to make room for her.

'Very good, keep your legs straight though,' Jacinta called.

'Is it very high?' Grace shouted.

'Not bad, don't stop and consider it,' Dara laughed.

In her smart stripy bathing suit Grace turned to Michael for advice. 'What do you think?'

'Why don't we go down the side? We can dive from the raft,' he said.

But Grace wanted to do the high dive.

Once up there it looked very far.

'Stop thinking about it!' Dara called.

This was good advice. In a splash Grace was beside them in the water. She looked back up at the bridge.

'I never thought I could dive that far,' she said in wonder.

And so it was that they all managed it. It was the only summer when they were all able to jump or dive from the bridge itself. They all remembered summers years ago when some people went from the high bridge, but there was never a summer surely where everyone was able to do it.

Little Maggie Daly realized that. It looked like a million miles.

'Try a jump first,' Liam White encouraged. 'Once you've done the jump it's easy to do the dive.'

'Is it deep enough?' Maggie asked fearfully.

'It's over twenty feet,' Liam laughed. 'That's enough water for you, Maggie.'

Quivering with determination that she would not be left out, Maggie clambered up on to the wall.

'Hey Maggie, it's too high for you,' Kerry called.

'Come down the side,' Grace shouted.

Maggie took no notice. She leaped out as far as she could and appeared from the huge splash she had made still quivering. She climbed on to the raft beside Dara and Kerry.

'It's not that cold,' Kerry said soothingly.

Maggie was shivering not from cold but from fright.

Now they had all done it, even Maggie, and in the evening light, pleased with themselves, they climbed back up again. Dara straightened her legs, Tommy Leonard did a back flip which Kerry said was terrific and insisted on getting Tommy to teach him.

Suddenly Tommy felt important again.

Grace told Michael that she thought he dived better than either Tommy or Kerry because he had more style and less showing off.

Jacinta said they could get a much better angle if only they could have a proper springboard attached to the bridge.

Maggie climbed up again. This time she was going to try a dive. Just as she was poised to go her foot slipped.

Maggie Daly fell at an awkward angle, not into the deep water that flowed under the bridge. But to the side where her head hit the corner of the raft with a sickening crack.

For years afterwards they remembered that sound. It was so sharp. It was like the crack of a rifle shot, or of a big twig snapping on the mossy earth up in Coyne's wood.

And they looked unbelievingly as Maggie lay splayed half in the water and half over the raft.

At a very awkward angle indeed.

It wasn't the blood coming from the corner of her eye that was so frightening. It was the way Maggie lay.

As if her neck was broken.

They didn't have to go for Jacinta and Liam's father. Dr White heard the screams himself.

He was coming out of the presbytery where he had been talking seriously about Miss Barry's limited life expectancy if she were allowed to continue in her present ways.

His heart lurched when the sound of panic and crisis reached him. He started to run. As he ran he knew the thought that was going through his head like a refrain was unworthy. Please God let it not be Liam or Jacinta, Please God not Liam or Jacinta. Please God.

Charlie who worked in Daly's was coming out of Conway's pub when he heard the commotion.

Charlie was a man who frightened easily. He ran back into Conway's and ordered himself a brandy.

'That's not like you, Charlie,' Mr Conway said.

'There's been an accident on the bridge,' Charlie said.

Mr Conway lifted the flap and ran out from behind the bar.

'Mother of God may it not be John Joe,' he cried, and ran down Bridge Street to see if he could find his big bostoon of a son John Joe, whom he had given three blows in the ear earlier on.

He saw John Joe running up towards him and his face flooded with relief.

John Joe was crying, fighting for words.

'It's Maggie Daly,' he cried. 'They think she's dead. She can't be dead, can she?'

Mr Daly was given a sedative. Dr White was able to get him on to a bed and to roll up his sleeve while it was injected into his arm.

Mrs Daly was different. Her face was white and still. But she was calm to the point of being unnatural.

'It was the will of Our Lord,' she said in a matter-of-fact way. 'He wanted Maggie this evening. Tonight she is with our Blessed Lord and his Holy Mother. She is in a better place by far than Mountfern.'

Martin White looked at her angrily. How could a mother be so philosophical? What kind of God would want Maggie by dashing her to her death from a bridge at fifteen years of age with the complete understanding and acquiescence of her mother? A vein started to throb in his forehead.

'It's all right, Martin.' Sheila Whelan was gentle at his side. 'Everyone has to mourn in their own way.'

'This is grotesque,' he whispered.

'No, isn't it great that she has this kind of faith?'

'It's not faith, it's hysteria. Her child is dead, she hasn't shed a tear.'

'You're always very good to people here in this place, don't start making judgements on them. Not now.'

It was a timely warning. Martin White looked gratefully at Sheila Whelan. He spoke now in his normal voice.

'I'll leave you with Mrs Daly, Sheila, and I'll try to sort out the children. They're almost all in shock.'

He left the Daly's house, walking through the little knot of people who had already gathered around the door to sympathize.

The children were in Fergus Slattery's house.

Miss Purcell had made cups of tea and opened a tin of biscuits.

Dr White had told them to get out of their wet things and put on their clothes.

He had asked Fergus and Miss Purcell to get them rugs and blankets. Fergus had turned on two electric fires. One at each end of the room.

He had been coming out of his house when he heard the screams. He was at the bridge in moments, at the same time as the doctor. His eyes had met Martin White's, and the doctor had shaken his head.

'Get them into your house, Fergus, and let someone tell Seamus Sheehan to come down.'

Fergus shepherded the children into his house and sent them off to various rooms to change.

Then he went to telephone the Ryans. John wasn't there. Kate said it was his only social engagement in the year, a meeting of the county Historical Association. As a published poet and a man finishing a book about Fernscourt, he was now highly regarded there.

Fergus cut across her pleasantries. 'I have your twins here in the house with me. They're fine, they're both here.'

She caught the tension in his voice at once. And knew something terrible had happened.

'What is it? Tell me immediately,' she said.

He did. Without frills. She would hear within minutes. He wanted her to know that what could be done was being done, and that he would look after Dara and Michael.

'God, why does it have to be the night that John is out, the one night in the whole year? Will I come up there? Eddie could push me.'

'No, there are too many people up at the bridge. There's nothing you can do. The children are all right here. I know it's hard, but stay where you are.'

She saw the reason in this.

'I'll ring Patrick,' she said firmly. 'Otherwise he's bound to get a garbled version too, above in the lodge. Are his two there?'

'They're here,' Fergus said grimly.

He looked at Grace and Michael clinging to each other wrapped in a blanket, Grace unable to stop shivering and refusing to be parted from Michael even to the point where she could remove her wet bathing suit under her dress.

Kerry was sitting on a chair, his handsome face drawn with shock. Tucked into his side, almost under his arm, was Dara Ryan, white and still disbelieving what had happened. Kerry absently stroked Dara's dark hair, which had a curiously inappropriate artificial rose stuck in the side.

Fergus didn't like to see the young Ryans so firmly enmeshed with the O'Neills. But this wasn't a time for such thoughts. He tried to put the haunting little face of Maggie Daly — those huge worried eyes and all that massive hair — way out of his mind. What could have possessed a frail nervy little thing like that to jump from a high bridge? And why didn't some of the others stop her? Looking around the stricken group in his house Fergus realized that this is what they must all be thinking too.

The night seemed to go on for ever.

John Joe Conway's father excused himself from the bar and went into his workshop at the back. There would be need of a small coffin.

John Joe followed him out and railed at him. Why did his father always have to think of business, and making money, when someone was dead, for God's sake? John Joe kept saying the word over and over because he couldn't believe it.

His father was short on explanations and excuses.

'What would you like us to do with Maggie? Leave her lying there looking at the sky? The only thing we *can* do for the dead is to give them a decent burial. If this is ever going to be your place John Joe, you'll have to learn that.'

'I don't want to run a business, I don't want to be grown up,' John Joe said.

His father gave him a long look. 'I know son, it's not the greatest thing in the world being grown up and being in business. But look at the alternative.'

For the first time in their lives John Joe Conway and his father looked at each other with something like understanding.

Rachel was in her room reading when she heard the commotion from the bridge. At first she thought it was just horseplay and high spirits. Then she became worried. She closed her book and came downstairs. Loretto was standing fearfully on the doorstep, her hand at her mouth.

'There's been an accident,' she said to Rachel. 'Jack Coyne's just run up to see what happened. I couldn't go myself.'

'Of course not.' Rachel knew the story of how Barney Quinn had been taken from the river in his new truck that he was so proud of. She put her arm around Loretto's shoulder.

'Come back in. Can you make us a cup of tea? Jack will come and tell us soon. We can't help by peering out here.'

Gratefully Loretto went back into the kitchen.

They were barely sitting at the table when Jack Coyne rushed in. He had tears in his eyes, something the women had never expected to see.

'Poor stupid little girl,' he said over and over before he could even manage to give them her name.

'Poor stupid little thing, she hadn't begun to live and now she's lying under the bridge with a broken neck.'

Even though Jacinta and Liam's mother had come down to collect them, they wanted to stay with the others. They wanted to stay in the unreal world of Mr Slattery's, where there were cups of tea and people pressed biscuits on them, where the night began to fall outside and the electric bars of the two fires began to glow red in the room where nobody turned on the light.

Fergus was in and out, reassuring without fussing them. Comforting them by the very fact that he didn't say it was all right, he said it was terrible.

Marian Johnson arrived to know whether she could take the O'Neill children back to the lodge. Fergus looked into the room and raised his eyebrows in a question. The children had heard her voice in the hall. Kerry shook his head. Grace said nothing, just huddled closer to Michael.

'I'm sorry, Marian, they think they should stay here for the moment. I'll get them home later, or their father will.'

Marian was disappointed not to be able to participate.

'One feels so helpless,' she said to Fergus. 'I just wish there was something I could do to help.'

He felt a wave of affection for Marian. She was ridiculous and snobby at times of course, but she was lonely, and what was so vile about regarding Patrick O'Neill as possible husband material? Marian was a decent honourable person for all her nonsenses. Fergus added to his list of things he disliked about Patrick O'Neill the way he made a fool of this woman. Leading her on to believe there was some interest, when everyone knew he had installed his mistress in rooms above Loretto Quinn's huckster's shop.

Sergeant Sheehan had seen a few sad things in the course of his work. And many accidents that were the result of thoughtlessness. He had no daughters, only sons, he would always have liked a little girl. He thought fondly that a daughter would have hung on his every word in a way that his wife did not. A daughter would not have been ambitious for him and wanted his promotion and preferment, and even for him to meet people of importance and be recognized by them. He knew it was a sentimental notion. People with daughters had just as many problems with them as he had with his sons.

Look at poor Mrs Mcagher and that Teresa for example. And Doctor White's little girl could be a bit of a madam, they said.

But poor Maggie Daly. Nobody had ever anything to say against her. Even her own disagreeable mother could only complain that the child was not constantly in the church at prayer.

Seamus Sheehan's hands were gentle as he lifted the broken body off the raft and laid it on the stretcher.

He and Martin White had been up to their waists in water pulling the raft towards them. The doctor had pronounced life extinct.

Seamus Sheehan had closed Maggie Daly's huge frightened eyes tenderly and arranged her thin body with the arms straight by her sides. He was watched by a crowd of about fifty people.

The child looked incongruous and unsuitable for death in her skimpy blue bathing suit. Young Grace O'Neill had lifted a shabby print dress in a faded colour and given it to him.

'That's what she was wearing.'

'You're meant to be back up in Mr Slattery's house.'

'I couldn't bear her to be without her clothes. You know Maggie,' the child said.

Then Michael Ryan had come running to take Grace away.

Sergeant Sheehan thought the shabby dress was even less suitable. But he laid it over her, before they drew the sheet over her head.

Quietly and with great dignity in front of the shocked and silent crowd Dr White and Sergeant Sheehan carried Maggie Daly back up to the stretcher. The ambulance had come from the town very quickly. But now that there would be no need to speed back the men stood waiting while Maggie's own people lifted her body from the river. She would be taken to the hospital, the post-mortem formalities would have to go ahead. The date for the inquest would be fixed and then the body would be released to come home to Mountfern, to lie surrounded by candles in her own house, and then the church and then the graveyard.

A great sense of heaviness came over Sergeant Sheehan. He wished he could stand in the water and cry all alone.

The sun was becoming a red ball of fire, and mocking them with its beauty and its sense of peace in the light it shed over the small town.

329

Fergus realized that when the O'Neills went home everyone else would.

Patrick's big car drew up outside his door and he came in with his quick light step.

Grace had somehow managed to disentangle herself from Michael, and was in her father's arms.

Then Fergus saw him put a hand on Kerry's shoulder.

'I've come to take you home,' he said firmly. 'None of us are going to help Maggie by sitting here in the dark. Maggie is at peace now.'

It was a good thing to say somehow. Fergus wished he had said something like that himself. It seemed to break the stranglehold.

The children began to move normally, not like puppets. They even got ready to go back to their homes.

Tommy Leonard said he'd walk up River Road with the Ryans.

Liam pulled Jacinta and said to come on, their mother would be annoyed and would come looking for them again.

'I can't believe it,' Dara said. 'It's not something you can believe, I keep looking round for Maggie, I feel she should be here, coming with us. She should be running to the door ahead of us.'

Dara had put into words what they all felt.

Their group was never together without Maggie, and running to the door is exactly what she would have been doing, hurrying people up, apologizing to Mr Slattery for having stayed so long, asking anxiously where they were going to meet next morning in case there was some change, and they were all going to meet without her.

There was a charged silence when Dara spoke. It was almost too true in its realizing the way they were all thinking.

Suddenly something in Jacinta snapped. 'Well, if it hadn't been for you, Dara, she'd never have done it,' she said. Taking no heed of the horrified looks she went on. 'Stop being all upset now that it's too late. You were horrible to her yesterday and had her crying and running after you, and even today you were just showing off and didn't throw a word to her.

'Maggie would never have done a dive like that unless she was trying to show that she was as good as the rest of us. Show Dara, please Dara. That's all Maggie ever wanted to do. It wasn't much, and now she's dead, she is dead from trying to please Dara . . .'

Jacinta began a laugh which veered from tears to laughing, and the sound got higher and higher.

Patrick O'Neill let go his daughter and strode over to Jacinta. The one quick crack across the face was all it took. Jacinta was silent.

'I want to go home,' she said eventually.

'Take her home, Liam. I suppose your father will dislike me more than ever now but try to tell him it had to be done, will you?'

Patrick took his children out of the door, down the stone steps and into the car. Fergus saw him lift Kerry's bicycle and fling it into the boot as lightly as if it had been a toy.

Tommy Leonard and Michael took one of Dara's arms each.

'She was hysterical,' Fergus said. 'It takes people different ways. She didn't mean a word of it. None of it is true.'

The little procession went silently to the door.

'It was a terrible accident, that's what it was. An accident,' he called after them into the night. And it stirred something in his mind, something about people telling *him* it was a terrible accident three years ago when Kate Ryan had gone into the town in an ambulance.

As expected the hospital released Maggie Daly's body within twenty-four hours.

Mr Conway had been in there to see to things.

Mrs Daly wanted her laid out in the house.

Dr White protested. This was a child, it would be too distressing for everyone. A child didn't have the tradition that a lot of the older people might know and want. Better to close the coffin and leave it overnight in the church.

Mrs Daly had said with that ominous calm that she thanked the doctor for all his services so far, but his words were useless. Friends and neighbours would come to pray for Maggie's soul by her body in the way it had been done for centuries.

Martin White went in a rage to the presbytery.

'Canon Moran, you have a duty, a duty I tell you to stop that madwoman talking about sins on Maggie Daly's soul. There are no sins, for God's sake. What kind of a mockery is this, getting people into a hysteria, coming and droning prayers for nonexistent sins?'

'Calm yourself, Dr White, I beg you.' The old canon's faded eyes looked at him kindly. 'You're not going to tell me that prayers to God and his Blessed Mother could ever be wasted, could ever go unheard?'

'Oh, forget it, Canon,' Dr White said and banged the presbytery door behind him.

'He's under great strain, poor man,' the canon said forgivingly to young Father Hogan, who was making a poor attempt at scrambling some eggs for the two of them.

Martin White had to admit that the American had done the right thing to his daughter. He had heard an account of the scene both from Fergus Slattery and from young Liam.

Jacinta was unwilling to speak about the incident.

Her father came and sat by her bed.

'We all lose our tempers, you know,' he began.

Nothing.

'I lost mine with the canon now, it's an easy thing to do. You must have inherited it from me.'

Silence.

'The only thing to do is to apologize for it as soon as possible. That neutralizes it a bit, like an acid and an alkali. You know?'

'*You* never apologize,' Jacinta said. It was true. He rarely did.

'Say something to Dara. She's very upset.'

'We're all upset,' Jacinta said.

'What *is* all this?' Dr White looked old and tired suddenly.

Jacinta bit her lip as she looked at him. 'You wouldn't understand, Daddy,' she began.

'I might,' he sighed. 'I just might if you told me.'

'It's just I got cross with Dara, she's got everything, she's gorgeous-looking and they're all mad about her, Kerry and Grace, and her brother Michael's lovely to her not like Liam, and Maggie sort of worshipped her, and Tommy Leonard can't stop talking about her.' Jacinta's face was red and her shoulders were heaving.

'Of course I shouldn't have said it but it's not all that terrible, people often say things in a hurry and don't mean the half of it.'

She looked at him to see if he had any glimmer of understanding. To her surprise he was patting her hand.

'I know,' he said. 'It's very hard.'

'Oh Daddy, I'm sorry,' she wept.

He held her while she cried and he patted her as if she were a baby.

Then when the storm had died down he said gently, 'I'll go and bring the car round, you get up out of this bed now and get dressed. I'll take you over to Ryan's, and you can tell Dara you didn't mean it. That it's not true.'

'Do I have to?'

'Yes, you have to.'

'Dara has been sitting there all day, apparently, and not taking in what's going on all round her. She's in a very bad way.'

'It's not due to me surely . . .'

'No, it's not all due to you. This time yesterday your little friend died. Died, Jacinta, that's a terrible thing to have seen. No wonder you are all upset. What we have to do is try to make it a bit easier on everyone, not harder.'

'Very well.' Jacinta swung her feet out of bed.

She stood in her pyjamas choosing which garments to wear. She looked for a moment at the shirt with the leather tassels on it. But she rejected it, it was too festive for these times.

Kate was surprised to see Dr White and Jacinta. She had heard various versions of the incident. But in view of everything else that had happened it seemed almost minor. Surely Dara would understand when the shock lessened that Jacinta had only been grumbling and complaining the way she always did.

'I'm afraid Dara's up in her room,' she said.

Dara had come down for meals and said nothing. She had eaten nothing either. She said that the food literally would not go down.

Kate had decided to leave her for one day.

John had been up to see her several times, maddened with his grief not to have been in Mountfern when it happened. Shocked still at the news that was waiting when he came back happily from his meeting and the beer and sandwiches that had followed it.

But Dara hadn't talked to him. He told Kate that she sat there white-faced twisting this false rose on a wire sten and clip backwards and forwards in her hands.

Sometimes tears came down her face. Strange tears without any sobs, they looked as if they were painted on.

'Can Jacinta go up and see her?' Dr White asked tentatively.

'She doesn't seem to want to talk to anyone. It's terrible times for all of them, all of you.' Kate gave Jacinta a slight pat on her arm as some kind of token that she wasn't siding against her.

Jacinta understood. 'I said something a bit stupid yesterday. I wanted to tell her I didn't mean it.'

'Well then, why don't you go up and tell her? I'm sure she'll be relieved,' Kate said.

She poured a whiskey for Martin White without asking him whether he wanted one or not, and he took it without asking himself the same question. They sat and waited for their daughters to make their peace.

'Dara?'

'Yes.'

'Can I come in?'

Jacinta stood at the door.

Dara looked up listlessly.

'I'm sorry for what I said.'

'What?'

'It had nothing to do with you. She just fell. She would have fallen anyway.'

'I know.'

'But I'm sorry I said it.'

'That's all right.'

Jacinta and Dara had never had the arm-in-arm friendship of any of the other girls. There would be no embracing, no tears, no emotional reconciliation.

'It's like a nightmare, isn't it?' Jacinta said.

'I wonder did she know,' Dara said.

'Did she know what?'

'That she was going to die.'

'She couldn't have. It was so quick.'

'But they say people do . . .'

'No, Dara, she couldn't have, it was too short. Try to think of a jump or a dive, it's over in a second, it would have been for her too.'

'Yes.'

'Will you . . . will you be all right?'

'Who, me?' Dara sounded like Maggie without realizing it. 'Yes, I'll be all right.'

Jacinta came back into the bar.

'That didn't take long,' Dr White said.

'She doesn't feel like talking. She said it was all right.'

'I'm sure it's all forgotten now,' Kate said. She didn't really feel that at all, but she had to say something to try to console this wretched child in front of her.

'She looks very lonely there, as if she could do with some company,' Jacinta said.

'I know. But what company? Even if I could get up the stairs I'm not what she wants. And she can't talk to her father, or even Michael.' Kate looked anxious.

Dr White stood up. 'Come on, Jacinta, we've done what we came to do, no point in wearing everyone out.'

'Will they have her in an open coffin?'

'Apparently.' Martin White was grim.

'The children shouldn't go.'

'Of course they shouldn't, it's not the goddamn middle ages, but that madwoman will probably go out to the highways and byways finding children to terrify them.'

'I wouldn't be afraid of seeing Maggie lying in a coffin,' Jacinta said suddenly. 'In fact I'd prefer to. Anything would be better than seeing her all broken on the raft.'

Martin White and Kate Ryan exchanged surprised glances. They hadn't thought of it like that.

They brought Maggie's body back that evening. Twenty-six hours after she had died Barry Conway's hearse drove down Bridge Street and parked almost opposite his own premises.

The front parlour in Daly's had been made ready. Candlesticks burned and holy water fonts hung on the wall.

Her father looked a broken man, her sisters from Wales looked unfamiliar and startled. Kitty, who had been going to come home from Dublin for the weekend, sat white-faced in a corner. Charlie brought more and more chairs into the parlour.

They were not going to sit there all night, it was not a wake in the old sense of the word. But between nine o'clock and midnight almost every single man and woman in Mountfern would call to tell the family how sorry they were about what had happened.

They would look at the face, and say a prayer. Then they would leave their mass card, a silver or black-edged card stating that the holy sacrifice of the mass had been offered for the repose of the soul of Maggie Daly. Most of them wrote Margaret Daly. Maggie seemed the wrong kind of name for a dead person.

'I'm not going to go,' Kate stormed to John.

'Of course you're not to go,' he soothed.

'No, I mean even if I had my own two good legs I wouldn't go.'

'Easy, Kate, easy.'

'The children? Do you think Jacinta was right? Would it be better for them to see her . . . ?'

'I think it might.' He was quiet but firm. 'Don't forget they have already seen her dead. This has to be better.'

'Will you tell Dara?'

'Yes.' His heart was heavy. 'I'll go up now.'

'If you like, Dara, I'll walk along to Daly's with you. Is that what you want to do, or would you prefer to remember her the way she was, laughing and running around?'

'Will her eyes be open, Daddy?'

'No, pet, they'll be closed.'

'I couldn't bear to see her eyes, but I would like to say goodbye to Maggie in some way.'

'You tell me when you want to go, I'll come with you.'

'Michael?' It was the first time she had mentioned him all day.

'He says he would like to say goodbye to her also. You always say the same you two, it never changes.' His smile was gentle.

'It must be the only thing that doesn't. Everything else has changed. For the worse.'

'Call me when you want to go, Dara.'

'Is Michael ready now?'

'Yes, he is, love.' ·

'Can we go straight away?'

They walked in complete silence by the river.

They didn't even look into Loretto Quinn's. They might have seen Rachel sitting by her window. And Loretto sitting downstairs with all the memories of the night that Barney died clear in her mind. They didn't look into Coyne's Motor Works. They might have seen Jack Coyne doing something he hadn't done for a long time. He was sitting at his table with his mug of tea in front of him as usual.

But Jack Coyne was not reading the newspaper, which is what he usually did at night, hunting bargains through the small ads. Jack was reading aloud to himself a verse of poetry.

He had been trying to remember it all day and in desperation had gone up to the brothers. Brother Keane had lent him an anthology.

And he had found it under Yeats.

Come away, O human child!
To the waters and the wild.
With a faery, hand in hand,
For the world's more full of weeping than you can understand.

He didn't read any more of the poem. He didn't even know what it was about, but it seemed to sum up what had happened in Mountfern.

Tommy Leonard stood at the door.

He knew that sooner or later Dara would come to Daly's.

He moved over to join the three Ryans. 'I wanted to wait so that we could go together.'

'Thank you,' Dara said simply.

John Ryan almost felt he should let them go in on their own.

Just as they got to the door of Daly's Dairy, Dara paused. The others stopped, thinking she didn't want to go in.

'We should ask Jacinta and Liam to come as well,' she said.

Michael ran up to Whites'; in minutes he was back with the two White children behind him.

'Grace's father didn't want her to come,' Dara explained. 'He doesn't understand that this is the best thing we can do.'

Just then a car drew up. Grace got out and she walked slowly, almost hesitantly over to the others.

'Father didn't want me to come, but Mrs Fine saw you all walking down the road so she called him, and he drove me here at once.'

Nobody asked where Kerry was. It was as if they had forgotten him.

Unaware of the sympathetic looks they were getting from the adults, the six children walked into the house. They went to the front room where the candles flickered and they heard the rise and fall of prayers.

Maggie looked like a wax doll. Her face was a clear almost transparent white. Because she had been injured so badly by the fall her hair was arranged to cover the sides of her face. The great cut over her eye wasn't visible.

She was dressed in a white gown with long sleeves, and had a rosary threaded through her hands.

She didn't look what they thought of as dead, she looked odd. Too still, and as if she were acting a part.

Mrs Daly sat by the coffin. 'Thank you for coming to pray for Maggie,' she said.

The children knelt down. They hadn't intended to, but that was what Mrs Daly seemed to expect.

They said a decade of the rosary together, then they stood and looked again, a last look.

It was as if they had forgotten the presence of her family and the other adults in the room. They talked to each other in low voices.

'It doesn't look *too* frightening,' Tommy said.

'She doesn't have that worried look she sometimes has,' Grace said.

'She won't have to worry about things any more,' said Michael.

'It can't be possible that she won't get up,' Jacinta said.

'She was very nice, you know, very very nice,' said Liam White.

'I'm terribly terribly sorry, Maggie,' said Dara.

Eddie Ryan arrived at the door of Daly's.

Sheila Whelan exchanged glances with Martin White and Judy Byrne who were standing in the corridor.

She was about to discourage him.

'It's all right,' said Eddie. 'I know nobody would want me here.'

'It's not that . . .' Sheila began.

'I'm too young to see anyone dead. But I brought some flowers.'

Sheila looked at the wilting collection in his hands. Some of them were wallflowers taken from Judy Byrne's windowboxes, some were the purple wild valerian that grew in the cracks of walls. There was a selection of cowslips and some dandelions.

There was little life or bloom in any of them since they had been squeezed in a hot hand.

They were almost entirely weeds. To Eddie Ryan they were flowers.

Sheila took them gently from the boy's hand. 'Thank you very much, Eddie. I'll see that these are put in a special place. Mrs Daly will be very grateful that you had such a kind thought.'

'They might need a bit of water if they're to go on the coffin,' Eddie said anxiously.

And Mrs Whelan said she'd see to it, never fear.

Everyone said that it would break your heart next day to see the children at mass. They sat so still near the front of the church. The nuns were all there from the convent, and all the brothers too. The men had come from the building site; many of them knew the Dalys in one way or another.

Rachel asked Kate if it would be out of place for her to attend the service. She didn't want to do anything that would be out of place.

'You'll be expected to be there,' Kate assured her. 'Weren't you one of her great friends?'

The small coffin covered in summer flowers stood at the steps of the altar. Father Hogan had asked Sister Laura if she could assemble some of the better singers in the school to act as a choir.

She found a dozen of the older girls whom she hoped would not cry. Girls who were two classes ahead of Maggie. She arranged they should sing 'Ave Maria' and 'Panis Angelicus', and at the end of the mass they would have 'The Lord's my Shepherd'.

There was no time for a rehearsal, Sister Laura said to them, it had to be right first time. She put all her sorrow and loss into conducting the hastily formed choir. It meant that she didn't have to think of why the Lord saw fit to take Maggie Daly so soon in such a strange way.

Rachel had been to one Catholic service in her life. A big Italian-American wedding where the church had been filled with mink coats and expensively decorated by a florist. She had particularly remembered the incense, it was a heady thing and went up your nose, making you slightly light-headed.

She got the same feeling in the church in Mountfern. Tommy Leonard and Michael Ryan were serving the mass; this meant they were attending the priests as assistants of some sort, Rachel noticed. They wore choirboy surplices, both of them were pale and they swung the thurible with the incense around the coffin that held the body of their friend. Rachel didn't see Patrick in the church, though she knew he was somewhere there. She hadn't told him she was coming nor asked his advice. This was nothing to do with Patrick or her wish to fit into his community. This was all to do with the death of Maggie Daly, her friend.

As the pure high voices of the girls from Mountfern Convent sang the words of the Twenty-third Psalm, the tears came down Rachel's face. It seemed curiously inappropriate to hear the children singing the words about 'He leadeth me the quiet waters by'. It was odd to be able to think of quiet waters as a kind of heaven when the child had ended her life in the water not two hundred yards from this church.

Rachel remembered the excitement on Maggie's face over the dress. The look of disbelief when she saw herself in the mirror that day up at the lodge, the way she had clapped her hands with pleasure.

Rachel thought about Maggie's anxious look and her unsureness 'Are you sure I'm not staying too long, Mrs Fine?'

'Is it really all right if I keep this ribbon all for myself?'

'I used to want all my hair to fall off and start again until I met you, Mrs Fine, now I think it's grand, I'm delighted with it.'

'Tell me what it was like for you growing up, was it all Jews and Jewesses where you lived or were there ordinary people there too?'

And on that last day: 'I did wear the dress once, Mrs Fine, but it wasn't really the right time to wear it. You know me, I'd get it wrong. But next time I'll make sure that it gets a proper showing.'

Rachel heard that Sheila Whelan had suggested Maggie should be buried in her new dress, it had meant so much to her.

Mrs Daly had not even considered it. The child would not go to Eternal Life in the trappings and vanities of this life. She would wear a white shroud.

The dress still hung on the back of Maggie's door.

Rachel felt an overwhelming urge to ask for it back, but she knew it would be misunderstood.

She couldn't bear to think of Kitty Daly wearing it some day. Or it being given away and worn by some other girl in some other town who had no idea how much it had meant in the short frightened life of a girl who was being buried before her sixteenth birthday.

Uncaring of the careful make-up and the streaks that must be all over her face, Rachel let the tears fall. She looked across the church and saw Kate Ryan, still in her wheelchair. There were tears falling on her face also.

They followed the small coffin to the grave. In the background the river sounds went on, familiar and almost unheard now by everyone who lived by its side. The June sunshine came down on the graveyard and marble headstones shimmered and shone as if they were lovely exciting things instead of the record of death.

The children stood almost huddled together for comfort. Kerry was a few paces behind.

As the last holy water was shaken and the last prayers said, the grave diggers began to fill the great dark hole in the ground, a space that looked far too big for Maggie.

The children waited motionless until the very last sod was in place. They gathered up the flowers and wreaths and laid them on top. Only then would they leave.

As they walked through the other headstones – the celtic crosses, the plain iron cross shapes, the marble slabs – they remembered all the times they had spent examining the words on the tombstones in the churchyard. Fingering the inscription to William James Fern who died young at Majuba Hill in the Transvaal. He had been young all right but not as young as Maggie. And the tombstone of James Edward Gray which had been so neglected and they had tried to smarten it up for him. They decided that they would go again and do something to James Edward Gray's resting place.

Maggie would have liked that.

'I suppose you think it's barbaric that people will come in here to spend hours drinking on account of the funeral,' Kate said to Rachel.

'No, I think it's very comforting somehow,' Rachel said. 'I'm becoming more and more assimilated you know. Not looking from the outside in any more.'

'I've always said they gave your mother the wrong baby in that hospital, you're more Irish than we are.' Kate said it as a high compliment.

'It was the last thing I expected when I came here,' Rachel said. 'I used to hope that he would find it a disappointment, and decide to go back, back home to New York. I never thought for one moment that I would feel it was home myself.'

Kate looked at her in concern. Despite her praise for Mountfern there was a very lonely note in Rachel's voice. As if she had been abandoned.

'You do know how much you mean to everybody here.'

Rachel smiled. 'Yes, I feel very much at home, very peaceful here. More so than Patrick does in ways. He expected so much, and I expected so little. That must be it.'

'What kind of things do you expect now?' Kate spoke gently.

'I've no long-term plans any more, no strategies, hardly any hope. I just go along one day at a time.'

Dara walked up to Coyne's wood with Leopold.

Mary Donnelly said you should never underestimate Leopold. There were times when no human being could give you the company and solidarity you needed and Leopold often rose to those times.

More to please her than from any great hopes of companionship Dara took Leopold to the wood.

To her surprise he was very well behaved, pausing considerately to inquire her intentions at every turn rather than racing off wildly on one direction or sitting down whimpering and refusing to follow.

Dara thought that secretly Mary must have been training Leopold. He actually *looked* much better too, as if somebody had been brushing him. Dara had never thought you could make any impression on that coat but in fact it looked quite shiny and his eyes were bright rather than alternately dulled with despair or rolling in a madness.

She sat on a tree trunk and Leopold went sniffing and snuffling but keeping a courteous eye on Dara in case she decided to move. She didn't move. She sat there with a long daisy, and threaded the heads of other daisies on its stem to make a flowery bracelet.

She hadn't wanted to spend any more time with the others. Tommy Leonard had been nice, he said it was bad at a time like this to go off on your own, you needed others around you whether you felt like it or not. Michael said he was going to go up the river and fish on his own. He hoped Dara didn't think that was rude.

She squeezed his arm. She understood completely, as people always said they seemed to feel the same about everything.

She didn't expect Kerry. This was a part of the wood she had never been with him. It was a place off the main path, a big bank of fuchsia hedge surrounded it. Kerry came in softly through the trees.

'If you like to be on your own I'll go away,' he said.

He was still in the dark grey suit he had worn at the funeral. He had opened the collar of his shirt and his black tie was loose around his neck. She had never seen him more handsome.

'No, no I'm glad to see you.' She spoke simply.

She sat playing with the daisies, her hair falling over her face as she bent in concentration. She wore a plain white tee shirt and a denim skirt, changed from the good navy dress with the white collar she had worn at the funeral. She looked very young and lost.

Kerry squatted down beside her. He picked a daisy and started to make a collection of daisy heads on one stem too. For a while they said nothing.

Leopold realized that this was somehow important. He stopped his burrowing and sniffing. He sat politely with his head on one side as if waiting for the conversation to begin.

'I wish I could do something to help you,' Kerry said.

'I'm all right. It's just so terrible for Maggie.'

'It's like being asleep,' Kerry said.

'And she wouldn't be in purgatory or anything. You know, waiting to get into heaven.'

'Oh Dara, of *course* she wouldn't!' Kerry laughed tenderly at the very idea.

'Well why were we all praying that she'd be forgiven her sins and soon see God? She can't be there yet can she?'

'Where?'

'Heaven. She'd not have gone straight to heaven unless she died coming out of confession.'

Kerry was confused. 'Dara sweetheart, it's like being asleep, I tell you. I saw my mother when she was dead, it was a big sleep. Grace said she saw Maggie's face last night, her eyes were closed. That's all it is.'

'And are you sure that she's not in the fires of purgatory?'

He reached out and held her close to him. 'I'm very sure. I know definitely.'

Dara sobbed into his chest. 'Oh, I'm so glad, I couldn't bear Maggie to be all by herself in purgatory, she'd be terrified.'

Sister Laura said that there would be a lot of delayed shock about the accident. The girls were taking it too calmly. They went up and tended a grave in the Protestant churchyard, they planted a tree near the footbridge. They had asked Mrs Daly without success if they could have her copper-coloured dress. They didn't know what they wanted to do with it but they wanted it anyway.

Sister Laura couldn't understand why Dara, Grace and Jacinta did not want to come up to the school to join in a special novena for the repose of Maggie Daly's soul.

'It's reposed already,' Dara had said, and the others had gone along with it.

Sister Laura was confused. Dara really meant this, as if she had been given a special message that Maggie was sleeping the sleep of the just. And the others all agreed with her.

Grace and Michael went fishing a lot. Or that's what they said they were doing. Michael left early and came back late.

Nobody expected any games or swimming to continue on the bridge. Tommy Leonard had to work in the shop almost all the time, Jacinta and Liam had a horrible cousin from Dublin staying with them and they had to entertain her. They were rightly too embarrassed to bring her anywhere near their friends so it was a matter of cycling energetically to the old ruined abbey by day and going to the pictures at night.

Dara was all alone.

This is what she wanted to be.

She wanted to walk by herself, she wanted to think.

Sometimes Kerry O'Neill come to find her, and when he did they walked, often without saying a word for a half hour or more. Then he might take her face in his hands and kiss her gently. Or he would lay his arm comfortingly around her shoulders as they walked.

'It will pass one day,' he said. 'One day you'll realize that it's a different sort of memory.' He looked very thoughtful.

'Did you feel that about your mother?'

'Yes. One day it didn't hurt as much thinking about her. I didn't believe people when they told me, I thought they were just being nice.'

'What did it feel like, after the day you changed?'

'I felt she was at peace and I must leave her there and not keep thinking of her all the time, and regretting, and wishing and getting angry . . .'

'Ah, but you loved your mother, you were good to her. Grace told me you used to sit by her bed and read to her.'

'That was hardly much consolation.' His face looked bitter.

The silence fell again, easy and companionable.

Dara didn't ask him why he thought his mother needed consolation. He didn't ask Dara why she sounded so guilty about her friend.

'Do you dream about Maggie?' Dara asked Grace.

'No, I haven't.' Grace seemed apologetic. 'I do think about her but I haven't dreamed of her at all.'

She looked at Dara anxiously. Dara's face was very white.

'I do,' Dara said simply. 'Every night.'

'Were you nice to your father?' Dara asked Fergus Slattery unexpectedly.

'No, I expect I was fairly unpleasant to him. I am to most people. Why do you ask?'

'I was wondering do you wish he was back here so that you could explain things to him?'

'No, Dara, he was old. His life was lived. It's different with Maggie, everyone wishes she was back so that they could explain things to her. And anyway you have nothing to explain, you were all very nice to her, she had a load of grand friends even if her mother was a bit of a trial.' He was trying to be light without being flippant.

'No, I don't think her friends were good to her,' Dara said. 'I think she was lonely and frightened all her life, and I didn't know it until now when it's too late.'

'Kerry, why do you like me? Seriously. I'm not joking.' Dara's big dark eyes were troubled.

'Because I like to be with you. You are beautiful and loving, you are bright and intelligent, and funny. And that's enough for a start, isn't it?'

'I'm not old enough for you,' Dara said.

'What's age got to do with it?'

'I don't know enough, I'm only a schoolgirl when all's said and done. You should have someone much brighter, who knows things.'

'You know enough things for me.'

'It's very mysterious.' Dara shook her head. 'If I were rich I'd say you were after my money, and you *know* I'm not going to sleep with you . . . So I can't see why.' She spoke in a very matter of fact tone.

'You might sleep with me some day,' Kerry said.

'I don't think so.'

'We can but hope,' he said lightly. 'But in the meantime we have to try to take you out of this melancholy. Maggie wouldn't have wanted you to be like this.'

'I'm sick of people telling me what she would or wouldn't have wanted,' Dara snapped. 'Her mother was telling me that Maggie's in heaven looking down on us all and very heartsore about the kind of films that Declan Morrissey is getting in the Classic Cinema.'

'Gently, Dara,' he said, reaching for her hand.

'I'm not mad or depressed, I just feel very confused,' she said.

He held her close and the confusion seemed to go further away. After that, he held her close all the time.

They didn't laugh and race away from each other as they once had. They didn't swim and splash and shout in the river. They lay together on the mossy ground of Coyne's wood and clung to each other.

The sunlight came flickering through the trees above and Kerry O'Neill peeled off the little blue shirt that Dara wore. He opened her simple cotton brassiere and took it gently away from her. He lay his head on her breasts and heard her heart beating.

At no stage did she stop him.

They lay like that and he stroked her so that it felt both exciting and peaceful at the same time.

At no time did she feel it was wrong.

Only when he made a move to take off his own clothes did Dara stir.

'I don't want to,' she said.

He sat up coldly. 'As you say.'

342

'Don't be cross. Don't change.'
'Don't be a tease then, don't promise and then go back on it.'
'I didn't mean to,' she said piteously.
'But you liked it. You like my holding you.'
'I don't know what to say.'
'Well, tell me when you do.' He had leaped to his feet and was walking angrily through the trees.

'I think Dara spends all her days with Kerry in Coyne's wood,' Kate said to John.
'Don't they all go out together? I thought they were never out of each other's sight,' John said.
'No. The Whites have this cousin, poor Tommy's stuck in the shop, Grace and Michael are off fishing.'
'How do you know all this?'
'When Rachel took me up to Bridge Street today I was in Leonard's. I was talking to Tommy. He looks very badly still.'
'Why do you think she's with Kerry?'
'She looks flushed and nervy but she doesn't have the look of a child who sat alone all day in a wood.'
'What will we do?' He was anxious.
'I don't know. What *can* we do? I mean even if she is with him, we can't upset her any more by hounding her,' Kate said resignedly.
'I don't suppose he . . .' John didn't finish the sentence.
'And I don't think if he wanted to that she would really . . .' Kate didn't finish the sentence either.

Olive Hayes was sitting at the kitchen table writing to Bernadette. The young Ryan girl knocked at the door.
'I'm afraid Grace has gone off out. I thought she was meeting you and your brother,' Miss Hayes said.
'Oh yes, they're all down at the river,' Dara said, covering up for Grace and Michael. 'I was just passing and I thought I'd call in just in case Kerry was here.'
'No, child, he went off in that car of his. Off to a place way out on the Galway road.'
'Oh I see.' Dara looked disappointed.
'Do you want a drink of milk or tea or anything before you go back down to the others?' Miss Hayes thought the child looked disturbed. It must have been harrowing for them all to have watched a violent death.
'The others?' Dara said vaguely.
'Down on the river. You said they were all on the bank . . .'
'Oh yes, I forgot. The others.' Her voice sounded dull.
'Are you all right, Dara?'
'Fine, Miss Hayes. I'll be off now.'
Olive looked out of the window. The child didn't take the road down towards the river. She headed out to the main road.

Dara had never hitch-hiked before. She would have to be very careful not to stop anyone she knew.

A big and unfamiliar van came into view. It wasn't anyone from Mountfern so she held out her hand.

It was a traveller looking for a bit of chat, even from a schoolgirl. He had a van of crisps, and peanuts.

'Do you know this place . . . it's a kind of a roadhouse?' Dara told him about the pub where Kerry said he had been playing cards.

The man knew it well, he'd be stopping there himself. A few other places on the way before they got there. Funny sort of a place for a girl to be going on her own.

Dara told him a story about looking for her brother. The commercial traveller thought this was perfectly reasonable. He chattered on, hardly noticing that the grave dark-eyed girl spoke little in return.

He talked about Mountfern.

'That place is going to get a rare shake-up, used to be the sleepiest town in the midlands,' he said.

He seemed to expect a reply. 'Is that right?' Dara asked.

'Well, seeing as how it's where you came from you'd know better than I would. I bet you're looking forward to the new hotel?'

'Yes, in a way.' She was looking out the window.

'It'll bring a fortune to the town, you might get a job in it yourself when you grow a bit older.' He was a good-natured man, he would like to think that this attractive girl could stay in her own place rather than be forced to emigrate.

'Of coure there's always going to be some who'll lose by it. You're not connected with the Grange there where I picked you up?'

'No, no, I was just visiting someone in the lodge.'

'Well the Grange will feel the pinch, I tell you. Who'd stay there when there's the new place? And who'd have a drink in Ryan's, come to think of it?'

'Why not?' She turned to look at him.

'Your man, the American's going to have a real bar, not a fancy lounge with uppity prices, but a normal bar across the bridge there from them, it will take all their trade. Very hard on them. Poor man's wife in a wheelchair already after an accident and now this on top of it all.'

Dara turned away and looked out the window.

'Tell me, did you know that unfortunate child who was killed there last week, wasn't it the saddest thing . . .?'

His voice trailed away as he saw the glint of tears on the girl's face. 'Of course you must have known the girl. I'm sorry,' he said, mad with himself.

Dara just kept looking out at the road taking them towards Galway.

'Will I wait and see that you meet your brother all right?'

'No thanks, I'm fine now. Really I am.'

'You must take no notice of me, Mikey the big mouth, that's what they call me.'

'No, you were very kind to give me a lift.'

'The little girl who died is in heaven of course.'
'Of course,' Dara said in an odd flat voice.

There didn't seem to be a back room when she went in first. Just a shabby-looking bar with a loud jukebox. There were cigarette butts on the floor and bits of litter everywhere.

It must be through the door that said toilets on a hand-scrawled sign.

She pushed through the door and saw ahead of her another one, she touched it and it opened a little. Kerry sat at a table with a drunk. Kerry was shuffling cards in a way that they seemed to make an arc. His face was clenched in concentration.

She stood looking at him for what felt like a long time before he looked up and saw her.

His face didn't change, he looked neither annoyed nor surprised.

'Hi,' he said and continued with the shuffle.

'Not that way, Kerry, get your thumb in there properly.' Francis Doyle's voice was slurred.

Dara sat down and watched. The drunken man helped himself to more whiskey from time to time. Neither of them even acknowledged her being there.

'I felt lonely so I thought I'd come out here,' she said eventually.

'Sure.' Kerry was pleasant but abstracted.

'To find you,' she said.

'And you did,' he said.

Francis Doyle took no more notice of her than if she had been a fly that had buzzed into this close, overpowering room. She felt slightly light-headed as if she might faint.

'Are you going to talk to me?' she asked Kerry.

'Not now, no.'

'When?'

'When I've learned the waterfall,' he said.

Dara's mind went blank as she sat in the airless room. She was unaware of her surroundings or how long she sat there. Then she felt Kerry touching her shoulder.

'I'll drive you home now,' he said in a light casual way as if it were the most normal thing in the world to find her in this strange place miles and miles from home.

He held open the door of the little red car. They drove back to Mountfern, fast through the twisty roads. Dara didn't speak. But she felt more at ease. She settled herself low in the car and once or twice she closed her eyes. On a hill a few miles from Mountfern the car stopped. Kerry looked at her.

'What are we going to do with you, Dara?' He said it with a mixture of affection and irritation.

She turned to him. 'I don't know. I felt so empty. The only thing that made any sense was to be with you.'

'But you don't *want* to be with me. You made that clear in the woods.'

'I don't want to sleep with you.'

'We were wide awake.'

'You know what I mean.'

'I know you keep pushing me away. Why should I think you want to be with me?' He looked puzzled.

Dara took Kerry's hand and held it to her lips. 'I've never loved anyone before. You see this is the first time and it's very confusing. It's all mixed up with everything else that's happened, and I feel strange and frightened.'

She looked terribly young. He took her hand and kissed it gently the way she had his. He said nothing.

'You mightn't even love me at all,' she continued. 'So I had nothing to lose by going to find you. I'm not playing any sort of game.'

'I don't know if I love anyone,' Kerry said. 'But if I do the nearest I'd come to it would be you. Come here to me.'

He took her in his arms and she stretched across the little red car to reach him.

He had ten more days' holiday.

Dara still looked pale and anxious. But she went to sit in the woods each day. Some days he came there, some he did not. She never knew whether he would be there or not.

Each time he held her close to him, he seemed to be more demanding and urgent. Dara felt her resistance changing in degree. What she had fought off a week previously seemed acceptable now.

'When is Kerry going back to Donegal?' Kate asked Rachel.

'Patrick says he still has a few days.'

'I wish he'd go now.'

'Don't worry so much, Kate.'

'I can't help it. She looks totally feverish and her mind is a thousand miles away when she's here, or to be more precise three miles away up at the lodge.'

'I asked her to come for a drive with me, but she said no.' Rachel had done her best.

'I know you did, you're very good. I suppose we can just hang on until he goes.'

'Do you have friends in Donegal?' Dara asked.

'Not really. It's mainly work, you know . . . I play cards sometimes, with a couple of guys I met, Tony McCann, Charlie Burns, they live in Derry across the border.'

'Don't they have red buses and red letter boxes there?'

'You've never been to the north?'

'No, how would I go to the north, Kerry?'

'They have red everything, and red, white and blue flags.'

'Well it's part of England.'

'It's part of the United Kingdom.'

'Same thing.'

'Don't you care about it not being part of Ireland?'

346

'Not very much. It will be eventually, I suppose.'

'McCann cares, and his friends care. They feel very strongly about it.' Kerry's voice sounded as if he were quoting rather than talking.

'That's all big talk because you're an American,' Dara said.

'What do you know about it?'

'Nothing,' she giggled.

'Will you miss me when I go back?' he asked.

'Very much. Do you have to go back?'

'Maybe I could stay . . . perhaps I could think of an excuse to stay . . .' he said teasingly.

'Really?'

'If I stay will you be nice to me?' He had reached his arms out for her.

'I'm always nice to you. How would you get off work?'

'I can get anything I want,' Kerry said.

'When's Kerry going back?' Kate asked with an innocent air.

'I don't think he is,' Dara said, eyes dancing.

'That's right, Grace said he was hoping to get some more time,' said Michael.

'Doesn't he have to work in Hill's?' Kate's voice was crisp.

'Oh, Kerry could talk his way out of anything,' Michael said.

Dara frowned: she didn't want Kerry presented as too much of a playboy. 'He'll be able to arrange more time, there's going to be no problem,' she said.

She looked excited and eager.

Kate's mouth was a hard narrow line.

'Would you like me to take Dara off on a skite somewhere?' Fergus asked Kate next day.

'Dara?'

'It would keep her out of Kerry O'Neill's clutches. At least you'd know she was safe with me. Everyone's safe with me,' Fergus added gloomily.

Kate didn't give the usual good-humoured riposte. She said nothing for a moment.

Then she said, 'No, I think it's time for Dara to go on a skite much further afield.'

'Where do you mean?'

'I don't know. I'll talk to John about it. We have to stop pretending it isn't happening.'

'Of course we don't know if anything *is* happening.' Fergus began to backtrack.

'We have an educated guess,' Kate said grimly.

They sat in the side yard. The whitewashed walls of the big outhouse which had been where the twins had their party now had clematis and honeysuckle growing up and winding round. The front of that building out on River Road looked well too, bright-coloured windowboxes getting ready for the day it would open as Ryan's Shamrock Café.

John and Kate often sat for a while in the side yard. After a night in a room that smelled of cigarette smoke and porter it was like a cool waterfall to sit here where the flowers took over. The night-scented stock and the jasmine were everywhere.

'What will we do with Dara?' Kate's voice was heavy and sad.

'I've been thinking,' John said slowly.

'I knew you would.' She looked at him hopefully.

'Do you remember what Sister Laura wanted us to do in the first place? Why don't we send her to France?'

CHAPTER NINETEEN

Madame Vartin looked like the Mother of Sorrows. She had a long white face and a thin mouth that trembled as if on the verge of tears constantly. She had pale blue eyes swimming in sadness. Monsieur Vartin was quite different – he was small and round and laughed like a machine gun firing in continuous rattles and blasts. Neither of them spoke a word of English. Mademoiselle Stephanie, who was a cousin of Madame Vartin, spoke enough to explain Dara's duties to her.

She was to prepare breakfast for the three small Vartin children, she was to take them for a walk and teach them five phrases in English each day. Then she was to play with them till their lunch; after that she was free to study. At dinner she was to help serve at table and to clear afterwards.

She got pocket money which worked out at about £3 a week and there was nothing to spend it on as they were miles from anywhere in the middle of the country. The children were horrible and Monsieur was inclined to touch her a lot, pressing up against her when he passed by. Madame's eyes brimmed with such sadness Dara felt almost afraid to talk to her at all. If it had not been for Stephanie, Dara felt she would have gone mad. It was hard to know what Stephanie did in the house. She was often to be seen folding linen or gathering flowers. She made curtains for one of the rooms, a job that took her almost all the summer. Sometimes she took the small car and drove off in the afternoons, sometimes she picked fruit. Dara couldn't make it out at all.

'Avez vous un vrai job, Mademoiselle Stephanie?' she asked one day. Stephanie laughed at her and quite unexpectedly gave Dara a kiss on each cheek.

'Je t'adore, mon petit chou,' she said, still pealing with laughter.

Dara was confused. Why did Stephanie adore her? Why didn't she say whether she had a job or not? Why did she use the familiar 'tu' form? Ever since she had arrived she had known that she must be formal and call everyone except the children 'vous'. It was a mystery. For a couple of days Stephanie would keep repeating un vrai job and shake her head with laughter each time.

Dara could hardly believe how quickly she had managed to find herself transported to France. She, Dara Ryan, who had never even been to London or Belfast had been through Paris in a car and had seen the Arc de Triomphe and the Eiffel Tower. Then she had been driven by Mademoiselle Stephanie to this far-away falling down house in the French countryside.

Mademoiselle Stephanie, blonde and curvy, said she liked the opportunity to practise her English; one day she would visit Ireland and meet all the great and famous people in Ireland. Dara wondered fearfully if Sister Laura had exaggerated the attractions of Mountfern or the connections of the Ryan household.

But mainly she wondered why she was here. It had been so sudden, the explanations all quite unsatisfactory.

Mam had been no help. She had been all excited and said it was wonderful, that Dad had found the money, and what a great, wonderful chance for Dara. Michael had said it was a pity they didn't take boy au pairs, Grace said it was the

349

most exciting thing she had heard of in her life. Tommy Leonard had said he would write to her every few days in case she was lonely. Mary Donnelly told her that of all men, Frenchmen were known to be the lowest.

Kerry had said nothing.

She had rushed to tell him in Coyne's wood and he had shrugged.

'Well if you *want* to go, that's great.'

'I don't want to go and leave you.'

'Why don't you do what you want to do, Dara?'

It was a frightening echo of the way she had spoken to Maggie. She remembered the way she had spoken to Maggie the night before the accident.

'You don't ever know what you want.' She had shouted that as an accusation, and Kerry was saying the same thing to her. She looked at him aghast.

He relented a little. 'Have a lovely summer,' he said, and kissed her on the nose.

'Will you write to me?' she asked.

'I'll send you a card.'

'Will you?'

'I said I would.' He sounded impatient.

'Will you stay here now that I'm going back or do you think you should go back to Donegal?'

'Who knows, little Dara? Who knows?' He had kissed her again on the nose.

She had gone to the lodge twice in the hope of seeing him. But he had been out both times.

Grace thought he might have gone to some place he liked miles out on the Galway road. Miss Hayes said that she hoped he had not. It was a place with a bad name, full of drunks and layabouts.

'No it's not, it's just shabby and dirty,' Dara had said and they looked at her with surprise.

She longed to ask Grace to write and tell her about Kerry. She longed to tell Grace how much she yearned to hear of him. But it would be useless, Grace had no idea how much Dara envied her the easy access, the nearness and the closeness to Kerry.

She nearly asked Michael, but she couldn't do that either.

'I'll miss you a lot,' Michael said the night before she left.

'No you won't, you have Grace.'

'That's different, I'll still miss you, Dara,' he said, surprised. 'You're my twin, for heaven's sake.'

'So I am,' she said emptily.

'Is anything wrong?'

'Everything's all changed.'

'We're just getting older.'

'Maggie didn't,' she said.

And suddenly here she was in the French countryside taking children for walks down strange kinds of country roads that had no character in them at all. The fields didn't have proper walls, they went on for miles and miles without any fences even. The farmhouse was terribly shabby on the outside, but very rich and full of huge furniture on the inside.

There was Maria, an Italian maid who had great tufts of long black hair at her armpits and who seemed almost as miserable as Madame. Only Madame, Maria and Dara went to mass on Sundays, which seemed to make nonsense of the nuns saying they were Catholic families looking for equally good Catholics to come and stay. Monsieur had been to the church five times he told her, for his christening, his first communion, his wedding, and the christening of two of his three children; the third managed without him. At least that's what Dara thought he was saying; he seemed to be counting out the occasions proudly on the fingers of one hand for her. She shuddered to think what Canon Moran, or anyone at school would think if she told them, and for some reason she didn't quite understand, she felt that she wouldn't tell them.

Madame's visit to Lourdes involved a lot of preparation. An open suitcase sat on the landing and there was a lot of folding and refolding of clothes, and placing and replacing of missals and small prayer books. There was never a smile or an eagerness, just a more determined business than ever. Dara wondered what the woman could be going so far to pray for.

'Desirez vous un miracle, Madame Vartin?' she asked boldly on the morning of the departure.

The thin dark woman stopped and looked at her as if she had never seen Dara before.

'Un miracle!' she repeated. 'Un miracle. Tiens!'

And suddenly and totally unexpectedly, she took Dara by the shoulders and kissed her on each cheek. There were tears in her eyes.

Dara felt terrible. Perhaps Madame Vartin was very sick. How stupid to ask her if she was seeking a miracle! Dara wished she could have bitten back the words, but strangely Madame's softness remained, and when she was being waved off by the entire family at the door she had a special pat for Dara. It was impossible to understand the French.

Dara went for her usual walk in the orchard to find apples that would stave off hunger until the impossibly late meal that evening. She decided to write a long letter to her mother and went upstairs to get her writing paper.

There was summer lightning out over the strange unwalled fields of France. She ate the green apples, and she wrote about Madame going to Lourdes and her own tactless remarks. Dara had got into the habit of writing to her mother just like she talked. She knew that the letters were not read out at home, but that her mother gave edited extracts.

'I wonder why she's so sad,' Dara wrote. 'I mean she doesn't have any awful things to put up with like you do, not being able to walk, and getting stuck behind the counter listening to old bores drinking and rawmaishing on for hours. I can't understand why Monsieur married her really, he must have known she would be a misery. She looks like a wet week even in their wedding picture. But I think you'd need to live here for a lifetime to know what any of them are at.'

Next morning she knocked on Mademoiselle Stephanie's door to ask for a stamp. They gave their letters to the postman when he arrived with the incoming mail.

Mademoiselle Stephanie was still in bed, which was odd. Beside her was Monsieur Vartin, which was so unexpected that the letter fell from Dara's hand.

'I'm terribly sorry . . .' she began.

Mademoiselle Stephanie didn't seem in the slightest put out. She indicated the middle drawer of the desk for the stamps, and asked Dara to remember to give the postman some other letters which were on the hall table.

Now that Dara had gone to France it was a little more difficult for Michael to meet Grace without calling attention to himself. Eddie and Declan were particularly revolting this summer; they made kissing sounds when he said he was going fishing with Grace. Admittedly Dad and Mam shushed them up, but it was very annoying.

Grace didn't seem to care, which was a relief. She came into the pub as regularly as when Dara had been around. She asked to see Dara's letters but Mam said that letters were only for the people they were sent to. If Grace wrote to Dara then she would get letters back, and so would Michael.

Dara felt tears of homesickness fall down her face. Madame Vartin found her reading her letter, and put her bony thin arm around the girl's shoulder. She said soothing things in French and Dara said cheerful things between noseblows, things like she wasn't really lonely, and she was just being silly.

Then she looked at Madame Vartin's long sad face and she became more weepy than ever.

She had tried to tell Madam Vartin about Maggie. It was so hard to explain, she had looked up words in the dictionary but even then it was too complicated. Sometimes she had to abandon the story in the middle. And anyway she was more sorry for Madame Vartin than she was for herself. It became almost unbearable when she saw Monsieur give Madame a little peck on the cheek as if nothing untoward had ever gone on in her absence.

Dara sighed. Perhaps men were by nature faithless. Sister Laura had more or less implied it, said that it came from nature where a male animal was used to servicing several female animals. Mary Donnelly never said anything else. Dara thought sadly of the world of men. Starting with Kerry.

There had been letters from everyone, even a card from nice Fergus Slattery. Pages from the Whites, and almost daily something from Tommy Leonard. But from Kerry nothing at all.

He couldn't have found somebody else already. He *couldn't* have. Why say all those things, and want to be so close to her if he could forget her so quickly?

But then Dara thought gloomily of Mrs Whelan's husband who had gone away, of Kerry's father who wouldn't make up his mind between Mrs Fine, Miss Johnson and quite possibly Miss Byrne the physiotherapist. And Brain Doyle had a girlfriend in the town that he hardly paid any attention to.

And those men who called on Rita Walsh in the Rosemarie hair salon. Dara knew now they hadn't come to fix hair dryers or to see to the hot water. No, now that she was a sophisticated woman who knew about the world. Now she realized only too well why they went there, and why they looked so secretive when they came out and scuttled off home.

Dara thought about all the men she knew and only her father and brother seemed blameless to her. Her father wouldn't look at another woman and Michael had put Grace on such a pedestal that he probably just kissed her chastely. She couldn't imagine Michael doing what Kerry had. She thought about Kerry for a bit and supposed she'd better tell in confession about all that stroking and kissing. Though how to describe it was a mystery.

It would be lovely to know enough French to confess to a French priest. By the looks of things you'd get away with murder here.

'How's Dara getting on minding the children by the Loire?' Fergus asked.

'It's the poor French children I worry about,' Kate laughed. 'I got a letter from her this morning and she said that she has taught them all to say *pogue mahone*. They think it's Irish for good morning.'

Fergus laughed. 'Knowing the French I'd say they'd be pleased to think their children were being taught anything as racy as kiss my arse. A very lavatorial sense of humour, I always found.'

'Don't be lofty, you always found. When did you always find? On your five-day trip to Paris ten years ago was it?'

'How many days did *you* spend in Paris, brain box?' he asked.

'No days. And now I'll never go.'

'Remember we wanted you to go to Lourdes.'

'Yes, but it would have been the wrong thing, Fergus. Lourdes doesn't mend broken spines. Nothing does. People would have been so disappointed and I would have felt I would have failed them somehow if they saw me in a wheelchair for the rest of my life.'

'I think it's a load of rubbish,' said Fergus.

'You can't mean that.' Kate was shocked. 'Why would Our Lord let people believe it and go there in millions if it wasn't true?'

'Have you ever considered that Our Lord mightn't be there?'

'No I have not, and neither have you. This is being said to shock me, like a schoolboy. Of course you believe in God.'

'Well if I do I don't like him much,' Fergus said. 'He's taken away my housekeeper weeping and wondering where her duty lies. She came to a tearful conclusion, Canon Moran and Father Hogan's need is greater than mine.'

'I'm delighted,' Kate said. 'Best thing for her, for them and for you.'

'Why for me?'

'You'll have to live like the real world lives now, instead of having everything done for you, being a peter pan with occasional flashes of bold atheism now and then. It will be the making of you.'

'What will I do?' shouted Fergus.

'Find a wife,' Kate said.

'No, seriously what will I do now? Miss Purcell's going.'

'I'll get you someone to come in and clean the house. That's all you need.'

'But the cooking, the washing.'

'I'll teach you to cook. I'm teaching Grace O'Neill so I might as well have two pupils, and until you find someone who takes in washing properly you can bring it here.'

Kate wrote to Dara about the lessons. She said they were priceless. She said that Grace hadn't known you could get rashers of bacon cut for you, she thought they started life in plastic wrappings. She said that Michael put half the dough in his hair and on the kitchen walls, and that Fergus was in grave danger of becoming a kitchen bore. He kept saying there was nothing to it, and when were they getting on to something a bit more elaborate?

The entire Vartin family had taken to saying *pogue mahone* as a greeting each day and Dara wished mightily that she could be around the first time one of them actually said it to anyone who understood Irish.

As an act of solidarity she decided to tell Madame Vartin what it meant. It was the only gift she could give her, a little superior knowledge. Laboriously she translated it: *Va baiser ma fesse.*

Madame's face was quite stunned when she heard it, and Dara wondered had she gone too far? But no. Madam Vartin thought this was a nugget of information and hugged it to herself with glee.

'Pogue mahone, Stéphanie,' she would say to her rival each morning, and she and Dara exchanged winks of delight when nobody was looking.

Rachel told Patrick that he might need to organize activities for the bad weather. She chose a particularly wet and gloomy day to tell him this so that he could see what she meant.

'Ah, the fishermen would be out on a day like this, and golfers never let a little rain get between them and their game,' Patrick said.

'Their wives?' said Rachel.

'They can get their hair fixed, their nails done.'

'Not every day they can't.'

'What do you think then?'

'Some activities, maybe cooking classes even. How to make traditional Irish fare.'

'Not a bad idea,' Patrick said. 'Who would we get to do it?'

'Let's think nearer the time. There could even be people around here?'

'Hey,' said Patrick suddenly. 'Kate Ryan's made a good job of teaching Grace, and Grace says she's very funny and has long stories about the ingredients and everything. Do you think she could do it?'

'I don't know where you get your ideas, Patrick,' Rachel said in admiration.

Jim Costello, the young manager, had not yet met Kerry, son of the house. Jim had been away finding staff and interviewing applicants when Kerry had come home.

He had not been in Mountfern for the tragedy. He knew the Dalys, of course, and remembered the little girl with the long hair and big eyes as a friend of Grace O'Neill's. He called to the dairy to sympathize on his return.

He was surprised to see an older girl there. 'I don't think we've met,' he said and offered his hand.

'Mountfern is really looking up now that I'm off nursing in Dublin,' Kitty Daly said, eyeing him up with unconcealed pleasure. 'You *and* Kerry O'Neill. I must say it's the place to be.'

'I haven't met him yet, I hear he's a matinée idol,' Jim said.

'He's all of that. He's like something from another world,' Kitty said.

'Ah well, no chance for the rest of us then.' Jim was courteous, admiring and yet distant. He had come to offer his sympathies, it would be crass to let it turn into flirting. And anyway Jim Costello was much too cautious a young man to become too involved with anyone in a small town. His career was of much greater importance than any dalliance with a local girl, even one as pretty as this tall willowy girl with the beautiful crinkly hair.

As he left he said again that he was so sorry about her sister.

'It's impossible to believe it happened,' Kitty said bleakly. 'This is the first time I've been home since, and three times I've gone upstairs to call her. And I keep expecting all those friends of hers to come traipsing in looking for her.'

'I didn't mean to upset you.'

'No, it's nice to talk a bit. My dad won't talk about her at all and my mam has more conversations with her in heaven than she ever had when poor Maggie was on earth.' She smiled gratefully as Jim Costello went out the door.

'Let's write to Dara,' Grace said.

'You always say that when you want to wriggle out of my arms,' Michael complained.

'Not true. Anyway I'm much better about remembering your poor sister stuck with all those awful screaming children than you are.'

'How can she be learning any French if she keeps writing to us and reading our letters?' Michael grumbled, annoyed to be distracted from his long embraces with the lovely Grace.

But Grace was sitting up and had got out the writing pad. 'Come on, Michael. Stop fooling around . . . I'll start. What will I tell her?'

'Don't tell her about Declan Morrissey getting drunk and asking Mary Donnelly why she was never married. I want to tell her that.'

'That's not fair, that's the best bit. I can remember nearly all the speech.'

'No, I thought of it, you say something boring about clothes or something first.'

'I don't write about clothes. Hey, I'll tell her Kerry's coming back for a weekend.'

'He'll probably have told her that himself.'

'I don't imagine Kerry writes, he's bad at letters.'

'Well, to Dara he would surely?' Michael thought that it would be very bad of Kerry to be so neglectful.

'Yes, maybe.' Grace was doubtful.

'And I'll write about Kitty Daly being back.'

'I don't know.' Grace was still more doubtful.

'Grace, for heaven's sake, you're the one who said let's write, now you don't want to say anything.'

Eddie Ryan went into Leonard's. Tommy looked left and right. His father was busy talking to Mr Williams. Swiftly Tommy handed Eddie three aniseed balls from a jar.

'Thanks,' Eddie said briefly.

'Don't eat them here,' Tommy hissed.

Tommy paid Eddie protection money of a sort. He fed him a small amount of sweets that would not be missed from giant jars in order to buy some peace and quiet from Eddie's gang. Eddie swaggered in most days and the arrangement was sweets of Tommy's choice, otherwise they all came in together and Tommy's father got into a temper, ordered them out and told Tommy that the young Ryan boy was an out and out hooligan. Tommy didn't want any guilt to attach to Dara by association.

He wished that she would write. All he had so far was a picture postcard of some château on the Loire with a list of complaints about the food, and the price of ice cream and the price of stamps.

'Any news of Dara?' he asked Eddie.

'You ask me that every time,' Eddie said.

'And you usually have a smart answer rather than saying yes or no,' Tommy snapped.

'There was a letter this morning, Mam read bits of it at breakfast. What would be in the bits she doesn't read, do you think?'

'Maybe about how great it is to escape from you, Eddie.'

'If you're going to be like everyone else then we will drop our deal?' Eddie said with menace.

The thought of Eddie's gang jostling and pushing and creating havoc in the newsagent's shop made Tommy Leonard feel faint.

'We'll go on the way we are,' he said.

'I thought that's what you'd like,' Eddie Ryan said cheerfully.

Tommy watched him go out of the shop and head for the shop that used to be Meagher's until Mr O'Neill had bought it. It was a sort of travel agency and tours office. Surely Eddie wasn't going to terrorize them and be paid off in excursions by coach to the Ring of Kerry?

Tommy found the days very long, and on his half day he found the hours very long. Twice he had headed off up the street to look for Maggie to come and talk to him. He didn't dare tell anyone that in case they thought he was going mad or that he hadn't cared about her death.

Tommy woke a lot with his heart beating thinking of Maggie's fall.

Jacinta and Liam had discovered that the cousin wasn't too bad after all. Her name was Amanda, which was a bit rich for Mountfern, and she loved horses. She had been very disappointed that they didn't ride, being in the country and everything. In desperation they asked their father if they could ask Miss Johnson to teach them.

Marian had two tame ponies she said, they were practically geriatric she admitted, nobody could come to any harm on them. She bit her lip when she had said that. The raw grief of the children in Mountfern was still in everyone's minds.

'Why don't they have the ponies and play with them up in the paddock?' she said to Dr White. 'There'll be no fees, no lessons, it will take their minds off things.'

'You're a decent woman, Marian,' Martin White said, and meant it. He used to think that she was a bit uppity and gave herself airs, but he didn't like her being publicly humiliated by O'Neill either. And it would stop his children from driving him into the asylum on the hill where he had sent so many patients over the years.

Grace saw the activity in the paddock behind the Grange. 'Would it be in the way if we joined in?' she asked.

Liam and Jacinta were delighted to see Grace again, at first they were ashamed of Amanda, but Amanda turned out to get on famously with Grace. Like everyone else.

When Marian saw that Patrick's daughter was interested she brought further and better horses, and a regular little riding school began.

'Come on, Michael. Get a hat, that's all. She insists we wear hard hats.'

'Don't be mad, where would I get something like that? It's like asking me to get a top hat or a bowler.'

'Please, Michael.'

'No. I can borrow yours if I'm going to have a go, which I may not, I haven't decided yet.' Michael was very disappointed at the turn things were taking.

He had seen a summer ahead of them where he and Grace would sit and talk and fish and hold each other and kiss. He would wander with her, telling her the secrets of his heart as he was starting to do already. He would tell her his plans and hopes for when they were older, and how he would study hard – at accountancy perhaps, he had heard her father say that a man who was trained as an accountant was trained for everything. He would tell her how they would travel together. But Grace wanted to play childish games and walk round in circles sitting on an aged pony.

'Grace, we don't have all that much time together, why are you wasting it?'

'It's not wasting it, we'll know how to ride horses,' she said unanswerably. 'Your way we just sit and talk and whatever.'

'But remember, before, they sort of split us up, didn't want us going off on our own. Do you remember, that's why we all went to the bridge.' He gave a shiver.

'I remember.' Grace patted his hand soothingly. 'But then isn't this all to the good? If they know we're all together with Jacinta and Liam and Amanda, they'll be pleased. They won't start breaking things up?' She looked at him with her big clear eyes as if it were the most obvious thing in the world and he was the only one not to see it.

'Don't you want to be with me?' he asked nakedly.

'Oh Michael, of course I do, but we have all the time in the world to be together. Can't you enjoy this? It's new, it's fun.'

Jim Costello took about five minutes to sum up Kerry O'Neill as trouble. And he spent a further five minutes working out how he was going to cope with him. This job at Fernscourt was the prize, it was up to him to make sure that nothing ruined it for him. If he made a success of Fernscourt then in five to seven years there wasn't a bank in the country that wouldn't advance him money for his own hotel. And in the meantime he would meet exactly the kind of tourists and have just the right way to entertain them as he could have dreamed. His last hotel had been a trifle stuffy, still concentrated on the business-lunch trade which was only a status thing. Jim Costello knew that you made nothing by serving unimaginative and underpriced set luncheons to the local solicitors and bank managers and insurance brokers, but in a small place that was what kept the image of a hotel high. Here in Fernscourt it was different.

He liked Patrick O'Neill and admired him. But the son. Jim Costello had been in the hotel business all his life. Since he could remember he had been in his father's small hotel, then in the Shannon training school and in France and Switzerland; he was twenty-four and he knew how to spot trouble. The man at the bar who was going to be troublesome, the customer who might not pay his bill. The respectable woman who was using a hotel foyer as a pick-up place. One of Jim's strengths was that he always saw it in time, just *before* the incident happened, and managed to head it off.

With Kerry he spotted it the very first time he met him. When he sauntered into the hotel with Tony McCann from Derry.

There was something about Tony McCann that seemed like a challenge. He greeted Jim as if he expected to be thrown out.

Kerry on the other hand was full of charm. 'My father tells me there's nothing you don't know about the hotel business,' he began.

'Let's hope he still says that when his hotel is open,' Jim laughed back easily.

'Bit of a backwater this for a hotshot like you,' said Tony McCann.

'I don't think so, it's a friendly place and we hope to be so busy that I won't have much time for the bright lights myself.'

Tony McCann looked at Jim Costello without much pleasure. 'One of these ambitious fellows, all work and up a ladder, I suppose.'

'That's me, the fellows at school used to hate me too – study study, creep, teacher's pet. Are you in the hotel business too, Mr McCann?'

'No.'

'You're in what?'

'This and that.'

Kerry stepped in smoothly. 'Tony's a friend of mine up in the far north, just brought him in to see the ancestral home rise again.'

'Are you pleased with it?' Jim spoke directly to Kerry.

He shrugged. 'It's my father's dream, I guess he's really got what he wanted. It's looking good.'

'But you'll be coming back . . .'

'Relax, Jim, there's going to be no fatted calf killed for me, not for a long time. No, you're safe here for a few years yet.'

Jim flushed with annoyance. He had to decide now how to handle Kerry. Did he remain poker-faced and remote, loyal entirely to his employer? This way he would build a wall of resentment between him and the boy, who was only a few years yonger. Or did he make Kerry an ally of sorts? Wouldn't that be easier? He decided to go the friendship way.

'I'd say there's plenty to keep us both occupied if you *do* come back. Your father has some very grand plans.'

'Do you think they'll work out?'

'Not all of them by any means, but enough of them will and I'd say he's a man who would learn by mistakes. Am I right?'

Kerry seemed amused to be consulted. 'Yes, that's true in most areas. He's extraordinarily practical, but this one I'm not sure. He wants so much for it to succeed it could blind him.'

'As I said, let's hope it will and the problem won't arise.' Jim had decided how to play it: friendly but not servile, discreet but not what the Americans called tight-assed. He would always repeat pleasantly to Patrick any conversation he had with the son. With Kerry you'd need to cover your back.

He hoped McCann would clear off out of the place too. He was pleased to see Kerry's car drive off to the big town with McCann and then come back without him. The fellow had obviously gone back north. What on earth had brought him down for such a flying visit? There was something watchful about him as if he hadn't believed Kerry O'Neill came from this kind of set-up and had come down to check.

He reminded Jim of a very tough Guard he had once known who came on Saturdays for a steak and a few whiskies to thank him for being lenient about closing time during the week. That Guard had a swagger when he came in to collect. Tony McCann had the same kind of swagger, as if he had come to Mountfern to collect.

It wasn't easy to find Kate alone. Patrick made three tries. Finally he hit a morning when Mary seemed occupied with deliveries in the yard, when John had driven to the town and the guard seemed to be relaxed.

Kate was sitting by her big French window, studying the typing manual from which she intended to teach Dara. He had tapped lightly on the door, and she hadn't looked up when he came in.

'I'd have thought you knew all about typing,' he said.

Kate looked up surprised. 'It's you Patrick, sit down won't you? I didn't know you were in the place at all.'

She smiled at him encouragingly but she got little response. He sighed deeply.

'Did you come in to draw big heavy breaths at me?' Kate asked.

'No. I'm just low, that's all.'

'What has you low?' She was sympathetic but not totally sure that he was serious.

'I *am* low, Kate. I feel everything's gone wrong. So many terrible things have happened. That child, that poor child dead and buried.'

'Ah sure, Patrick, that has us all low. There's neither rhyme nor reason in it.'

'It was never meant to be like this. Pointless tragedy, and confusion everywhere.'

Kate looked at him. It seemed out of character, this type of talk. She waited to hear what it was about.

'You see, I got everything I wanted – the land, the permission to build – and God knows how, I've actually built the thing.'

'So what's wrong?'

He went on with his catalogue of what was right first. 'The children like the place. That's not saying it as it is, they love it. This is a real bonus, I thought they would be pleading for brighter lights, but no. That's largely due to your children, by the way.'

'I know, my twins have formed a welcome-the-O'Neill-family movement, haven't they?' Kate was polite and almost hid her anxiety about just how warmly they were welcoming them.

'No, don't worry about that, Kate. Grace and Michael are a couple of kids still, and you got Dara well away out of Kerry's clutches.'

So he had realized! She laughed guiltily.

But he had moved on. 'I worry now all the time. About the way it all happened, it's as if it weren't the right thing to do somehow . . .'

'Coming back?'

'Yes, or coming back in this way. Nothing's gone right since . . .'

'That's not like you – not the Patrick we know.'

'Shit, Kate, can't you quit acting like someone's li'l old grandmother? Every time I look at you in that bloody chair, I think to myself that if I'd stayed where I was you'd be on your two feet. When I see all the signs being put up on the road, when I have to meet the people from the tourist board and talk about projections and over views and market share, I wonder what the hell it's all about. Why I'm not out on the freeway in New Jersey buying up a couple more neighbourhood bars. What am I *doing* changing every single thing I touch here, getting the priests and the parson to tidy up their graveyards? Christ, that wasn't what I wanted to do. I wanted to be welcomed here, but nobody remembered anyone belonging to me . . .'

'Oh, stop all this self-pity, for God's sake,' Kate interrupted. 'You knew that on day one, nobody remembered the O'Neills from a hole in the ground, so stop saying it's come as a surprise to you now. Four long years ago you knew that. You wanted a life here where you came from, and you've got it. Stop bellyaching about changing things and being remembered . . .' Her face was flushed with anger at him.

He reached over and took her hand. 'I suppose you don't believe me, but it's looking at you that gives me the worst feeling of regret. Honestly and truthfully if I could turn it all back I'd never have come if it meant doing this to you.'

'You *didn't* do it to me, you big loud-mouthed clown. I did it. I walked under the bloody digger. You had signs, I didn't see them. How many times do I have to say to you and to Fergus, to everyone. I'm *not* looking at you every day and saying "Why oh why didn't he stay in New Jersey and I'd be able to walk?"'

Her eyes blazed and she had flung his hand away.

'If I say I wish you had stayed in New Jersey – and I do, believe me, I do say it many times a day – it's not because of that . . . not because of my being in this chair . . . oh no.'

'Then what . . .?' Patrick was alarmed.

'I wish you had stayed in your precious America because if you had then there would have been a living for us here, for John who never really wanted it in the first place but who made such a fist of it for us, for his wife and children, and a living for the children themselves if they want to stay here. It's been in John's family for years, it's not easy to see it go up in smoke because of some Yank looking for his roots.'

Patrick's mouth was open.

'I mean it, I knew I shouldn't have started but since I have I won't suddenly clam up like you do, I'm not cunning and watching what I say. *That's* the reason I wish you hadn't come here, not because I had an accident. I have to think of this whole bloody business as an accident otherwise I'd go insane.'

Patrick was shocked. 'But we've been over this a dozen times, all of us. You're not going to lose trade, you're going to gain it. You'll have the custom from the hotel ... We've been through this.'

'Yes, we'll have them buying musical shillelaghs and leprechauns, that's what we'll have. They won't come in to drink here, neither will anyone with an ounce of sense in their head when they can have your Thatch Bar.'

'You never said ...'

'Why *should* I say anything to you? You never say anything real. You always work out where the advantage lies and then you speak. I was damned if I was going to tell you how I felt, specially since we didn't put in any objections in the beginning. Like Fergus said we should.'

'Please, please let me assure you, let me promise ...'

'I don't want any charity, I just want us to be able to make our own way as we always did. Surely you'd understand that.'

'I understand that better than anyone would. Jesus Christ, I know about dignity and having your place somewhere. I was raised by a man who was a wino, a bum, we had no place anywhere, I wanted to be called Mister O'Neill, I wanted to make my own way more than anything in the goddamn world ...'

'You never said that about your father before ...'

'Why *should* I tell you, or tell anyone? It's my business, and it's a part of my life I don't boast about.'

'Oh no, you wouldn't mention anything unless there was some purpose ...'

'What do you mean? What are you saying?'

'Nothing much, just showing how bad-tempered I can be, I expect.' Kate seemed to have run out of steam suddenly.

'There's enough for us both here, Kate.'

'I hope you're right.'

'Do I really only say things that are for my own gain?'

'I never said that,' Kate insisted. 'I said you didn't speak without thinking – like the rest of us do.'

'I suppose you're right, but you've got to cover your back in my world,' Patrick said. His tone changed.

'I came to say something to you, something quite serious.'

'What is it?' There was alarm in her eyes.

'No, serious, as opposed to brittle,' he reassured her. 'I wanted to warn you about the case.'

Her eyes narrowed. 'Fergus said it wasn't proper to talk about it at all, that we must remember not to speak of it even to the children because of ... well, because of Michael and Grace I suppose.'

'Yes, my lawyers said the same thing. Talk about covering their backs ...'

'So?'

'So, I wanted to say this, just between the two of us. You've had a terrible injury, nothing will make you walk again. You must get something, the *only* thing that can make life a bit better. You must get as much money as you can.'

Kate looked at him startled.

'This is just us. I've been three days trying to get you on your own, and then we nearly ballsed it up by having a barney . . . You only have one chance, Kate.'

'Why are you telling me this?'

'In order that you will get what is fair.'

'Still, it's not right of you to talk to me about it. Fergus said that if you did then I was to . . .'

'Fergus said, Fergus said, don't talk to me about Attorney Slattery, he gives me the sick, that fellow with his calf's face . . .'

'You will *not* say that about Fergus.' Kate flashed again.

'Sorry, sorry. Peace, peace.' Patrick spread out his hands. 'Look, I'm just trying so hard and I seem to fall every step of the way . . .'

'But Fergus said that if you came and offered . . .'

'And for once he was right, the attorney Slattery. If I *was* such a bastard as to come and offer you a deal then of course you should not talk to me. But I'm not, Kate, I'm offering you a warning: they will try to make you accept a low offer out of court. If it goes to court they'll try to trip you up, try to make you take less, try to prove to the jury, who are ordinary people without great wealth, that you live a fine life and that since your little pub would never have been a gold mine, and since you're a woman who should be bloody grateful to have a roof over your wheelchair, then the least compensation should have you on your poor broken knees with gratitude.'

'Why . . .?' she began.

'Why? Because I know you, I know your pride which is a great strength but also a weakness. The "I'm fine thank you" air you wear around you like a cape . . . nobody is to dare offer a word of sympathy to Kate Ryan or if they do they'll bear the consequences.'

'I cope the way that suits me,' Kate said.

'You cope brilliantly, and it's not just to suit *you*, it's to help your husband and your family and everyone. Nobody feels you're a cripple, but in three weeks' time if it goes to court you have to drop it, you have to lose this brave way of going on. You've *got* to tell them what it's really like, otherwise you'll get nothing.'

'You mean, lie? Act?'

'I do *not* mean lie and act, you stupid woman, I mean tell them the plans you had for this place and how you can't bloody see them happen now. The life you had with your husband, how you wanted another child and that's over.'

'Why do you want me to stand up and spin these self-pitying tales, make a public exhibition of myself, tell a tissue of lies just to get money in the bank? How little you understand anything.'

'Jesus Christ, how little *you* understand anything. I didn't break your bloody back, if I did I could pay for it. Sometimes I wish I *had* broken it, gone out with a cleaver and broken it. That way I could have gone to gaol.' His face was working and he was close to tears.

She looked at him wordlessly.

'What kind of pride is this that means you are denying your family what is rightfully theirs?'

'You sound just like Fergus,' she said.

Patrick stood up. He shrugged helplessly.

'I'll leave you, Kate, before we start again.' He smiled and his face was transformed as it always was. He looked at her sitting so still in the chair.

'It's no wonder half the town is in love with you,' he said. 'I could fall in love with you myself.'

'Oho, it's a well-known thing that, to say you could fall in love with the unattainable. That's very Irish, Patrick, you've inherited a lot of your forefathers' little ways of going on. That's the kind of thing all those mountainy old bachelors would say.'

'I'm a mountainy old bachelor too by nature, I guess.'

'That will certainly disappoint the gossips here.'

His eyes were cold. 'What do they say, the gossips?'

'That you intend to ask Rachel to marry you some day.'

He was startled. For Kate who was Rachel's close confidante to speak like this. 'Well,' he said.

'However it's not something Rachel and I talk about,' she said.

'You don't, heck.'

'You mustn't flatter yourself too much. We *used* to talk about you certainly, but not nowadays.'

There was an unsettling truth in the way she spoke. There was a little silence.

'I don't handle things very well sometimes,' he said eventually.

'There are some things that it isn't a matter of handling, or coping with or sorting out like business deals.'

'I know.'

They sat companionably for a few moments.

Kate was a much more still person than she had been before. There was a time when Kate Ryan could not have allowed a silence of longer than two seconds.

Patrick was not a man much given to sitting and musing either. But here he sat and looked ahead of him into the flower-filled garden where the big orange cat sunned herself and the soft cluck of the hens in the distance was soothing. There was no sign of the terrible dog, perhaps someone had been dispatched to take it on a far-distant walk so that its baying could upset another parish.

'I must go now,' he said.

'You were very good to come and see me. Thank you for what you said. No matter what happens I'll remember that and appreciate it.'

He leaned over lightly and kissed her on the forehead. He had never done that before.

'And you promise me you'll remember what I said? It doesn't make you weak, it makes you strong.'

'I'll remember,' she said.

And he left.

Kate sat still for a long while. She could understand why Rachel was so enmeshed with this man. He was alive and aware and reacting all the time.

It must have been a heady thing for Rachel to realize how essential she was to him and how much he needed her.

No wonder she felt bereft now that he most likely didn't need her any more. Kate's fists beat on her useless legs. The only point in living was to be needed, to be an inspiration, to be the power in something. Nobody understood that, nobody.

Fergus, with all his childish spite against the O'Neills didn't have the glimmerings of an understanding. He didn't know *why* she was a person who needed compensation. It didn't have all that much to do with paralysis. It had to do with having no role.

John Ryan in a million years would not understand. He would say she was being hysterical, and that of course she was important, more than important . . . but essential to all of them.

But Kate Ryan knew she wasn't essential any more. They didn't need her like they had once needed her. John was stronger and more his own man, he made decisions with certainty, he coped with the pub as she had once wished and prayed that he would. He still found time to write his poems. He was not as gullible as she had once thought him to be. He was firm with the children, he drove a car, their own car, around Mountfern. He was a slimmer, fitter man than the man of three years ago, more confident in every way.

But he didn't lean on Kate as he once had. He didn't need her at every turn of the day.

That was why she needed some goddamn compensation. Not that money was any good, but the reason she should get anything was because her husband didn't depend on her any more.

And the only man who had the faintest understanding of this was the man who was *meant* to be their great enemy. Patrick O'Neill.

'I can't like that young Costello,' Fergus said to Kate.

'You can't like anyone with hand, act or part in Fernscourt.'

'Wrong. There's a lot of decent people working for him. Don't make me out to be unreasonable.'

'Lord, you're the most reasonable man in the world usually; this is your only blind spot. What has poor Jim Costello done now?'

'I heard him talking to Canon Moran, meant to be a sort of private chat. But I could see what he was getting at.'

'You listened to his confession!'

'No, it was in the open air out in the church grounds. You know, beside the garden that O'Neill's workmen built up for them. He was telling the poor doddery old canon how great it would be if the bishop came to the opening.'

'Well the bishop *is* coming to the opening, surely?'

'Yes, but Jim wanted him to speak at the blessing bit and he was explaining this awful plamawsy way to the canon that Mr O'Neill wouldn't like to suggest it, and Mr O'Neill wanted it to be the canon who spoke, but wouldn't it be great if the bishop were to say a few words too. You know, a lot of devious bullshit.'

'And you're the one always giving out about Patrick's language!'

'The poor old canon thinks he's the one now who thought of asking the bishop, he's back up at the presbytery trying to word the letter.'

Kate changed the subject. Fergus was getting moody.

'And how is your Miss Purcell up there with the clergy?'

'As happy as anything.'

'Well it leaves you a bit freer, anyway. Whatever you want to do you don't have to take her future into consideration.'

'I don't want to do much, Kate. I just want things to stay the same.'

To his surprise she leaned across from the wheelchair and patted his hand. 'I know. I know just what you mean,' she said.

'Are you going to the hotel opening, Mary?' Fergus was civil.

'It's very kind of you to be so interested but the answer is no. Some one person should be here to keep the door open in case in the Republic of Ireland there happens to be one or two souls who are *not* going to the opening and think they might be served a drink in a wayside pub.'

Mary's face was flushed with anger and loyalty to her stance about the rightness of everything the Ryans did and the wrongness of the O'Neills.

Fergus blinked wearily. He had brought this attack upon himself and there were many ways that he supported her entirely. But she was a trying woman.

He had only broached the subject of the opening to her on instructions from Sheila Whelan.

'Say the odd kind word to Mary when you're passing,' Sheila had asked.

'Have you a suit of chain mail for me to put on when I'm talking to her?'

Fergus had been bitten too often to feel easy about saying anything to Mary Donnelly.

'She's a great woman when you get to know her. She has all the qualities of a good wife – loyalty, determination, everything.' Sheila sighed.

'Are you trying to make a match for her by any chance?'

'Oh, I think it would be a brave soul who would attempt to make a match for Mary these days.'

'Or for me?' Fergus teased.

'Oh, we're dying to marry *you* off, Fergus,' Sheila said.

'Who's we?'

'Kate and myself, we'd love to settle you down. But I'm only giving you a big head. Listen, when you see that cousin of mine, Mary, will you tell her she's to go to the opening of the hotel. It's only a false kind of loyalty to the Ryans saying she is going to boycott. Use your charms.'

'My charms haven't much of a track record,' Fergus had said gloomily.

And indeed he felt he was right, Mary Donnelly showed no reaction to his charming manner except to reject the notion of going near the new hotel. She sniffed and said that the Ryans were going not to show offence, and because they had a standard of manners much higher and more generous than the O'Neill family.

Fergus sighed again. Talking to Mary was like trying to climb up a waterfall.

'Can I talk to Kate? I have to get her to see Kevin Kennedy, that's the barrister. I want to fix up a proper consultation but Kate's always too busy making potato cakes, or hemming serviettes or some other nonsense. If the woman could only understand that she must give her whole heart and mind to Kevin Kennedy and the court case, then she won't *have* to hem all those table napkins.'

'Will you be able to get her a great compensation do you think?' Mary looked eager and excited. 'I'd love more than anything for her to take a fortune off that man. I'd really love it.'

'That's not the way it's going to be, he'll pay nothing, it's the insurance company. I don't know, I really don't. These cases are like throwing a dice. It could be any figure that comes up.'

'There must be some system.'

'There is a sort of system, but it depends what way it's presented. It's very practical you know, very matter of fact. What were her earnings, what could be said to have been lost in terms of money? There's something built in for pain and suffering, and then there's a category called mental distress. But it all depends on judges and juries in the end, and they're often cautious men, careful with other people's money even if it's insurance companies. Oh God, I wish I knew.'

'You sound very worried.' Mary's face looked quite pleasant when she wasn't making some strong point, she had a softness about her that wasn't in her normal style.

'I am worried, Mary, I'm worried that Kate and John are turning down their only chance of getting what they deserve and are owed. They don't seem to grasp that this is the one and only time they'll ever get any stake together for any kind of life.'

'And show that bastard what the courts of Ireland think of him.'

'Yes, but with respect, Mary, mightn't we do better if we played down that side of it?'

'I know what you mean, I'm as bright as the next man. I'll sing low on the revenge bit – is that what you mean?'

'That's what I mean.'

'I'll feel it in my heart though,' Mary said.

'So will I,' said Fergus.

'Oh bring him along, certainly,' Kate said when Fergus suggested a consultation with Kevin Kennedy.

'He's quite important, Kate, you won't just play along and joke and make eejity remarks about it being half your own fault?'

'I never make eejity remarks. Remember when I was your righthand woman in the office, don't say I make eejity remarks.'

'I remember. I remember well,' Fergus sighed.

'So, I'll be polite and use long words. But isn't he on our side, is he not our lawyer, why do I have to be impressing him and putting on an act for our own counsel? Isn't it the judge and the jury I have to do the tragic queen act for?'

'It's no act, Kate. You are badly injured in the name of Jesus, will you stop being the bravest girl in the school about this and start thinking of your future and your family's future?'

'You're cross with me.'

'I'm furious with you. You think it's not quite nice somehow to let anyone know how much your life was changed that day, how much your chances lessened. One day, one day when it's too late you'll wish you'd listened, you will be very sorry then. In three or four years' time when the pub might need a new roof, or when Dara might wonder why there was no money to send her to university or the kids might want to go on a school trip to Rome or John, God forbid, might get a virus pneumonia and be off work for four months and you'd have to pay someone to come in and run the pub . . . Won't it be a great consolation to yourself to say that way back in 1966 when you had your chance, your one chance to explain your case, you were too refined, too well-brought-up or some kind of bullshit to get the compensation you and your family deserved? Fine warm comfort these high and mighty principles will be to you and your family then.'

His eyes blazed with rage on her behalf.

Kate changed immediately. She sat upright in her chair and reached for a notebook.

'You are perfectly right as always,' she said without a trace of irony. 'Tell me what kind of things will we cover with Mr Kennedy when he comes.'

Kevin Kennedy wore an expensive suit but it was crumpled, and his shoes needed a good shine. Kate looked at him and decided that he was a bachelor whose housekeeper was lazy and indifferent. He had a big mane of greying hair, a rather theatrical bow tie and nicotine-stained fingers which groped restlessly for more cigarettes still. Kate judged him to be about fifty, and realized after a very short time that he was much sharper than he gave the impression of being. He seemed to shamble through explanations and accounts but yet he remembered everything that had been said and came back to points which she had been sure he had forgotten.

He was very good at drawing her out. Kate found herself responding easily to his questions about the limitations to her life caused by the accident. She agreed that their earnings were considerably diminished since she could no longer work for Fergus in the mornings and since they had to pay out a salary to Mary Donnelly. Kate told how her concentration had lessened, she found it very hard to read a book to its end, whereas once she always had her nose in some book from the library.

Fergus was startled to hear this, she had never said it to him. But that was often Kevin's gift, he managed to make people tell things. Very often when he was on the other side of a case cross-examining, his gentle persuasive voice made people tell things they wished to keep secret. But here in Kate's green room Kevin Kennedy was slowly drawing the picture he would need.

Fergus sighed with admiration as Kevin talked to the Ryan couple about how their life had changed, the pain, the huge incapacity, the lack of being able to act as a real mother to the children the way other mothers could, like going up to the school or joining in any outings and activities.

'And of course your normal married life, the life between the two of you that you would have expected to have?' Kevin Kennedy was gentle.

Fergus felt a hot flush coming up his neck.

Long ago, long before Kate's accident, he had put the thought of her sex life with John Ryan far from his mind. He knew it must exist but he never wanted to think about it, and yet it used to come back to him, the notion of the two of them entwined. He assumed that since the accident it had been out of the question. To his embarrassment John was beginning to stammer.

'Well, I wouldn't say that it was exactly over . . . you know, sort of . . .'

Fergus felt the bile rise in his throat. Surely John could never be so gross and unfeeling as to expect Kate . . . No, it wasn't possible. He felt unsteady for a moment.

'I'll slip out and get something from the bar . . .' he said.

'Thanks, Fergus.' Kate was cool. 'I asked Mary to get a tray ready, perhaps you could bring it to us . . .'

He went out, loosening his collar.

'Kate said she thought sandwiches and a bottle of the good Jameson,' Mary suggested. 'I have it here ready and all, I didn't want to go and disturb you.'

'That's good of you.'

'Are you all right, Fergus?' She looked genuinely concerned.

'Yes, I'm just tired. Give me a large one while I'm waiting.'

'What are you waiting for?' Mary obediently poured him a double measure from the optic and waved away the pound note he offered.

'I don't know really, just giving them a chance to talk, I suppose,' he said, wondering how long would Kevin Kennedy spend on lack of conjugal rights, and compensation for same. Wildly he wondered whether John was saying that really it wasn't fair to blame Patrick O'Neill in this area because he and Kate were able to have a very satisfactory coupling despite everything.

Fergus felt his hands shaking and he gripped the glass tightly with both of them.

'It must be very hard, this kind of thing, when you're a friend of the family as well.' Mary was sympathetic.

'Have a drink, Mary.'

'No thanks, Fergus, I don't think . . .'

'Have a bloody drink.'

'Very well, keep your hair on. I'll have a vodka and tonic, thank you very much.'

'Not at all. Good luck.'

Mary raised her glass solemnly. 'Good luck, really and truly good luck. They're relying on you.'

'No they're not, they think they're grand, they think it's lovely to be financially ruined and crippled.'

'Shush now.'

'I won't shush. And anyway nobody would rely on me, it's Kevin they should rely on.'

'Oh him?' Mary sniffed. 'From Dublin, and a man.'

'Yes, I suppose those are points against him. I wonder has it crossed your mind that I too am a man, Mary. Perhaps you should take that into consideration when you and I are having these little social drinks.'

'I know you're a man, Fergus,' Mary said.

'I'm glad someone does, I've almost forgotten myself.'

'But you're not a real man, not like ordinary men.' Mary was full of beaming approval. 'Here, will you take this tray in that you came out for or they'll think you fell into bad company.'

'You're not the worst, Mary,' Fergus said, picking up the tray and carrying it back into the room.

They seemed to have exhausted sexual dysfunction or the possibility of suing for removal of conjugal rights. They were on to the topic of what they could expect to be awarded.

The tray was left beside Kate on the big round table which Rachel had found and covered with a floor-length green cloth. Nowhere else in Ryan's pub had the elegance of this room.

They looked like four ordinary people having a drink, Fergus thought as Kate poured generous measures and added a splash of water from their only cut-glass crystal jug. No sign of their business together.

Sheila Whelan came back quietly by bus.

It should only be two hours and three-quarters, but the bus visited every townland on the way. It took mountainy routes and it went almost full circles into the countryside to pick up and drop farmers from crossroads that were off the beaten track. There was plenty of time to sit and think.

Think about Joe with his gaunt face and his sad tales clutching her from the hospital bed.

It hadn't turned out as he had hoped, he told her. He wanted to come home to Mountfern. To die.

'There's no question of dying, Joe,' she had soothed him, her words automatic, her expression effortlessly kind. Even to the man who had left her all those years ago, hurling abuse to justify himself as he went.

His life had not indeed turned out as he hoped. There were children, four – two sons and two daughters – children that Sheila was not able to bear, and he had scorned the idea of adopting and raising another man's sons.

The woman he had left everything for was a restless woman. The children had been reared wild, left to run wild. None of them would settle in anything, school or work. The eldest boy had gone to England a few hours ahead of the Guards, it turned out.

Joe had got to thinking about Mountfern in recent weeks. He thought of all the people he knew there, Jack Leonard and Tom Daly. He hadn't heard that Tom Daly's little girl had met with such a terrible accident. Sheila told him about Maggie, but his mind wandered away in the middle of the story. She stopped after a while when she saw he wasn't concentrating. It was too sad a tale anyway.

He remembered Jack Coyne and that nice dour Doctor White. Was old man Slattery around? No, well the son was a grand young fellow. And of course the canon. It would be good to wander down River Road to Ryan's like in the old days. He had heard of the new hotel across the river, there was a lot of talk about it in the papers. He hadn't known of Kate Ryan's accident but he was sure that they'd got great compensation.

And since there were no real ties with Dublin, no – for all that he had a home – it was a house really – and she would understand that he wanted to go home at the end. She'd probably be pleased for him. When all was said and done. So could he come back to Mountfern? Could he come home?

Sheila had talked to the nurse who recognized instantly that Sheila Whelan was someone to whom the truth was told. She heard that Joe had weeks and possibly only days to live. She had confirmed what she suspected – that he would never leave his hospital bed.

She told him he could come home.

She begged him not to worry what people would say and what people would think. Nowadays, she said, people were much too busy with their own business to worry about the middle-aged postmistress and her husband. She said that Dr White would be able to continue any treatment.

Joe's eyes had filled with tears at her goodness. He had never meant to hurt her in the past, he had never wanted to be cruel.

She said she understood. She sat and held his hand until he fell asleep. Three days she was there helping him make his plans, telling him where they would put his bed.

He said it would be good in a way for her to have a man around the house again, and that was the only time she had cried. The tears had come down her face and she wept at the useless lives most people led and how little anyone understood about anyone else.

She asked the nurse to make sure that nobody was kept away because of her visits but the nurse shook her head and said that poor Mr Whelan's wife wasn't in the best of health and wasn't able to come and see him. Sheila read this to mean that the woman who had borne Joe Whelan's four children suffered from her nerves or drink or both. She discovered that there were neighbours who would supervise the funeral, kind people in the small Dublin street who had known nothing of any previous existence in Mountfern.

When he fell into his coma and she was assured that he would not know anyone around him again, she left as quietly as she had come and took the bus back to Mountfern. She did not feel saintly or unselfish, she felt a weary tiredness. And for the first time in her life she felt something like anger. Anger about people who stood by and let things happen. At herself for wasting all those years thinking that Joe knew what he was doing and that there was some sort of plan. She might have been better not to have been so dignified and discreet. She could have gone after him and fought for him. And got him back.

Or she could have got a court order and got maintenance from him if she hadn't valued her good name so highly and been too proud to ask for it. That way she would have had strong shoes to wear instead of making do with patched soles and avoiding puddles. She would have had the money to go to Rome when the diocese was making the pilgrimage. She could have given Mary Donnelly something better than she had, some holiday or some outfit to get her over the worst days of the pain, the days when you need some distractions.

Instead she was coming back on the bus to Mountfern where nobody except Kate Ryan would know whether Joe Whelan was alive or dead. She would ask

Canon Moran to say a mass for his soul, but she would just say that it was for a friend. It wasn't that the canon would ever tell anyone but she had been so silent and secretive about this, she would keep it that way to the end.

But for the rest of her life she was not going to sit and take a back seat. She was going to take part in things, not just observe them.

CHAPTER TWENTY

Patrick finished the steak and kidney pie. 'That was quite excellent, Miss Hayes.'

'It's a pleasure to serve you, Mr O'Neill.'

He sat by himself at the table. Grace was having supper at the Ryans'. It was a night of a cookery lesson, she had explained. He knew it was just another chance to see young Michael but he pretended to take the cookery classes very seriously. Kerry was miles away in Donegal. When Olive Hayes had gone back to her kitchen he sat quite alone. As he sat many an evening.

It would be different when the hotel opened, he told himself. There would not be this stark realization that he found himself reading through his meals, and sitting idly after them, fiddling with the television, if he didn't get out more work. He had discouraged Marian from suggesting outings, and now she had ceased trying to interest him in little trumped-up schemes. He wished he could ask Rachel here.

He stood and stretched . . . the evening seemed to stretch as well.

He had put off so long and so firmly any thought about what would happen to Rachel when the hotel opened that he found himself doing it again automatically. But tonight somehow he felt able to think about it.

She *could* take instruction. And if she did, then there would be no problem about her previous marriage, since it wasn't a Catholic marriage. Hell, it wasn't even a Christian marriage.

And she *could* fit in here, there were ways where she seemed to have adapted better than he had.

Rachel got on so well with Kate Ryan, with Sheila Whelan, with Loretto Quinn. Brian Doyle said that she was the only person connected with the entire enterprise who might be considered sane. Mary Donnelly, that madwoman running a one-woman band for the annihilation of men, said that Rachel was one in a million.

Why did he hesitate to ask her even to something simple like supper in his own house?

He knew why, it was out of guilt.

He still felt that this woman was part of his past. He had gone willingly and excitedly to her arms while the children had stayed in a big white house in New Jersey with their always-ailing mother.

And Rachel wasn't Irish, or part of the great scheme. That's why he kept her at such a long arm's length.

Dara's postcard arrived at Hill's Hotel for Kerry. It sounded very casual with an attempt to be sardonic:

> 'I heard there was a bank strike at home, I didn't know there was a postal strike as well!! But then how does everyone else manage to write to me, I wonder? It's a puzzlement, as they say in *The King and I*.
> France is magnifique.

372

I'll be back in Mountfern on the last Thursday in August.
Love Dara.

Kerry read it and smiled. He would have taken a hotel postcard and written straight back, but he had a lot on his mind. He had lost a great deal on three consecutive nights.

It was time to call Father.

But if he won tonight, it would all be sorted out. No need to tell Father about anything.

Tony McCann was apologetic. If it were up to him there wouldn't be a problem in the world, Kerry knew that, didn't he? If it were only McCann himself or Charlie it would have been a no-problem area. But *these* fellows . . . McCann's voice trailed away a little. For the first time Kerry began to feel a little afraid.

'Do you not have any idea where he is, Miss Hayes?'

'No, Kerry, he doesn't tell me where he goes. He just said that he would be back late.'

'Whatever time he comes in, do you hear me, whatever time, can you get him to call me?'

'I'll leave a note, certainly. I don't want to intrude but is there anything wrong?'

'No no, heavens no.' His voice was falsely bright.

'It's just that you sound so urgent somehow. I wouldn't want Mr O'Neill to be alarmed.'

'No no, it's nothing.' He sounded impatient.

'I'll leave him a note then in case I'm gone to bed. I'll say you'd like him to ring back but it's not urgent.'

Kerry spoke very slowly and deliberately. 'Tell him it *is* urgent but there has been no accident or anything. It's very urgent.'

'Very well, Kerry, whatever you say.'

Patrick came in at eleven-thirty.

He had spent a very pleasant evening with Rachel. He called at Loretto's and asked whether she would like a drive. He wanted to look at the ruined abbey in case it would be a place they could take the guests on the barge that he was going to operate from the new landing stage.

'You're going to have night boat trips?' Rachel was surprised.

'No, but maybe it's not a bad idea. They could go through the trees and along the river, the only light . . . the fireflies in the darkness.'

'They don't have them here,' Rachel said.

'Fireflies? Of course they do.'

'No. Didn't you notice?'

'Anyway, will you come with me in the car and let's see if this abbey is worth our time?'

'It's been around since the fourteenth century, I think it might be worth a glance all right. Let me get sensible shoes.'

They had walked easily and companionably like the old days. Three times he was about to tell her that he wanted them to be more open and seen to be close friends. Three times he stopped himself.

After all he wasn't yet ready to offer her anything much, and he would clear it with his children before changing things even slightly. He left things as they were.

Next morning up at the hotel Jim Costello came to Patrick, there was an urgent call from his son in Donegal.

'Would you like a bit of peace and quiet to take it?'

'No thanks, Jim, it won't be long.'

Jim had sensed the tetchiness in Kerry O'Neill's voice. He moved away.

'Did she not leave you my message?'

'That's some greeting, Kerry. Yes, Miss Hayes did leave a message but it was late when I got in.'

'What time?'

'Eleven-thirty.' Patrick took a deep breath. 'I went for a walk with Rachel Fine up around the old ruined abbey . . . she thinks that we could . . .'

'I'll hear Mrs Fine's thoughts another time, Father. I'm in a bit of trouble. Financially.'

Patrick's voice was ice cold. 'Yes, Kerry?'

'And I would be grateful if you would bail me out.'

A silence.

'Are you still there, Father?'

'Yes. I'm still here.'

'What did you say?'

'Nothing yet.'

'Will you?'

'I don't think so.'

'You *said* you would.'

'No, I said I would discuss it, we are discussing it. How much?'

'A thousand pounds.'

Patrick was shocked. Literally shocked. 'You can't be serious.'

'I am.'

'Well find it then.'

'We made a deal.'

'We made no deal, I said I'd discuss it. I will not hand out a year's wages to an insolent young pup who rings up and demands it as of right.'

'Father, this is serious.'

'You bet your fucking life it's serious,' Patrick said.

'I thought you were going to . . .'

'I thought my father was going to do a lot of things for me too, like getting me enough to eat and shoes to wear. But it didn't happen. Learn the hard way, Kerry.'

'Aren't you going to discuss it?'

'Yes I will discuss it. When you come back.' Patrick's anger was ebbing a little.

'I could come back today.'

'No you could not. You can stay there and do the work you are meant to be doing. I will discuss it in a few weeks' time, when you're back here for the opening. Meanwhile get out of it the best you can, and if you steal from Hill like you stole from me, I'll have you in gaol.'

There was a silence.

'Life isn't easy, Kerry, it's a matter of finding ways round things; and if one thing doesn't work, try something else. You'll discover that.'

'Yes, I probably will,' Kerry said slowly.

Rachel Fine sat in her sitting room and watched the evening fall on Fernscourt.

She felt very tired. The game was too arduous. She blew cold, he ran after her – she showed some response, he ran away. It was so immature, so unsatisfying. Somehow tonight, for the very first time, Rachel was prepared to stop the struggle, the never-ending spiral of hope, the belief that things were going well.

He was a man who hadn't enough room in his heart for a full-time loving relationship. He never had time for it with his wife Kathleen either. Whether she had been frail or not he would still have wandered, and it was not without importance to note that he had wandered to a business colleague rather than find a sheerly social relationship.

She sighed, thinking of the years behind and the years ahead. The music on her record player was low so as not to disturb Loretto below. Chopin, soothing and familiar. Perhaps even at this late stage of her life she might even take up the piano again. When she was back in New York.

Would she be back in New York . . .?

Yes, sooner or later. Why not make it sooner, go at her own time? See the opening just because she had worked so hard for it. Give him one ultimatum so that he would never say he didn't know, and then go. But she had to be prepared to go, not to give herself nine lives like a cat, otherwise what was the point of giving ultimatums?

There was a soft knock on her door. Loretto would never have let him upstairs, and yet who else could it be?

She walked wearily over to the door and opened it.

There stood Kerry O'Neill, the boy she had always hoped would be her stepson one day.

He leaned against the jamb of the door. 'Hi Rachel.'

'Hallo Kerry.'

She made no move to ask him in.

'How you been?'

'Fine, and you?' They still stood there.

'Reasonably fine, I'd be better with a drink inside me, to be very frank.'

'Well you know me, Kerry, a non-drinking lady. But I'm sure if you were to go to Ryan's . . .'

'I don't want to go to Ryan's,' he said sharply.

She shrugged.

'Surely my pa keeps some drink here.'

'Your pa lives in the lodge, Kerry. I live here.'

'So you never see him?'

'At work.'
'I want to talk to you, not him.'
'I told you I don't have any drink.'
'I know. It doesn't matter, I have.' He waved a bottle of whiskey. 'Now can I come in?'

Mary thought she had seen the blond figure of young Kerry O'Neill slip quietly across the footbridge earlier, but since he hadn't come into the pub and there was nowhere else he could be heading, she must have been mistaken.

Rachel stood back and let Kerry come into her sitting room. He stood looking at it with his cool objective eye.
'Lovely,' he said at last.
'Thank you.'
'I mean it, you have wonderful ways, Rachel. Anyone else would have ruined this place and filled it with clutter.'
He sat in the chair by the window where Patrick always sat and looked across in the darkening evening at Fernscourt.
'I can provide a glass and water,' Rachel said.
'Great, this is far too elegant a place for a man to sit drinking a bottle by the neck.'
He was so engaging, just like his father. His compliments were not so frequent and lavish that they sounded automatic. Instead they made people feel very touched and grateful to be praised.
She brought a tray to the little low table – Irish crystal glasses and a jug. A pretty china bowl with ice in it, a tray of cheese biscuits and for herself an orange drink. She sat down opposite him. She had not invited him, but since he was here she would be gracious. Being a hostess was second nature to Rachel Fine, she had waited on Kerry's father for many years in the same elegant way.
'Your health,' she said politely, raising her glass of orange.
'And yours.' His eyes were bright, he raised the very large goblet of neat Irish whiskey and looked at the patterns of the glass admiringly.
Rachel was very good at not being the first to speak. She had learned that first from her mother, who said that the men in the family were the ones to be considered, and then from many many nights waiting to assess Patrick's mood before she spoke. She knew how to leave a perfectly agreeable silence that would encourage the other person to begin.
Kerry smiled as if he could see into her mind. It was a knowing smile full of confidence.
'And how long are you going to be with us?' he asked genially.
Rachel was shocked by the insolence of his tone. So shocked that it made her speak sharply.
'I was just going to ask *you* the same question. Are you with us for long or do you have to get back to Donegal?'
Kerry smiled even more broadly; he sensed a fight and he welcomed it.
'Oh, *I'm* here for the duration, Rachel, this is my home.'

She controlled herself with difficulty. 'Well of course, and has your father decided what part you will play in the hotel?' Polite interest, but letting him know that everyone realized it was Patrick who called the shots.

'I'm sure you're much more aware of what my father has decided or has not decided than anyone.'

She smiled coldly but made no reply. From years of training herself not to over-react, not to fly off the handle, Rachel had perfected a calm and measured response even to situations that were outside the bounds of any manners or fairness.

'My involvement is always in ideas for design, and sometimes it's an uphill job.' She forced a little laugh that she did not feel. 'I can tell you the designer is the one who always ends up carrying the can – it's too stark, it's too cold, it's not Irish enough – my, but you need extraordinary patience in this job. Lucky I have it!' Again her tinkle was very false and again she felt that Kerry recognized this.

'Perhaps you've been too patient.'

'How do you mean?'

'You know, hanging around too long, hoping that when this is over – when that is over – the world will settle down as *you* would like it, as *you* design it.'

She wondered how much more of this she could take, this pretence of deliberately misunderstanding his discourtesy.

'At least the day of the opening is in sight,' she said. 'We'll see then if it works.'

'And what will you do then? Go back to Brooklyn?'

'I live in Manhattan.'

'Sure, but you *do* live in New York, will you go directly back there? After the hotel opens?'

His question echoed so much her own bitter thoughts and decisions of earlier that evening that it brought a heavy, weary feeling to Rachel. It was as if she suddenly decided to give up the bright sunny response.

'I don't know,' she said simply. 'I'm not sure.'

'Rachel!' He was teasing. 'Not sure? Of course you are, you've every step planned out, haven't you?'

'No. Not every step.'

'Most of them then. You've been part of my father's life for a very long time. A lot of people didn't rate your chances very highly.'

'I don't know how you could know any of this. You were a child.'

'Sure I was a child, I didn't know really, not for certain, not until my mother's last illness. That's when I knew.'

Rachel looked at him impassively.

Kerry poured another large goblet of whiskey, his hand trembling slightly.

'Those nights when she was alone in the house, and he was with you – in Manhattan, as you remind me. Out until early hours of the morning. Sometimes I stood on the landing and watched him come in, go into the cloakroom and rinse his mouth, freshen himself up before he came up to her bedroom. She was always awake, always waiting for him to come back from you. From your apartment in Manhattan.'

Rachel looked at his white and angry face.

'He sat in a chair drinking whiskey, that's why he used a mouth rinse, it was not to hide traces of me. He sat talking about her illness, about you all. That's what I gave him in those months, just a chair, a whiskey, and an ear for his troubles.'

'He had plenty of ears at home if he had come there.'

'Sure he had, but you were so young, your mother was so frail, he couldn't . . .' Kerry's eyes blazed at her suddenly.

'Don't you dare to talk of my mother, don't bring her in casually like that . . . don't speak of her.'

'Kerry, this is absurd. *You* mentioned your mother, you mentioned something that has upset you in the past, I was merely telling you what it was really like . . .'

'I don't want your version of what things were really like. If it were a true version it would be fairly sordid.'

'You are unfair to your father and to everyone if you persist in believing all this . . .'

'Oh, it was all hand-holding and platonic. Don't be pathetic, Rachel.'

'I am *not* pathetic, I am telling you what is true. During the time of Kathleen's last . . .'

'I told you not to mention her name.'

Her eyes filled with sudden unexpected tears. She turned her head away in a vain attempt to hide them.

Kerry put his glass down on the table. 'I'm sorry.'

She didn't trust herself to speak.

'I mean it. I am sorry. I guess I'm upset. I shouldn't take it out on you.'

She stood up wordlessly as if to say that his visit was over. But Kerry decided that it was not over yet.

'Please, I said I spoke out of turn. Please?'

He had such a persuasive way, she noticed almost dispassionately. Kerry believed that if you were charming enough in sufficient doses it would open every door. And he had usually been right.

'I didn't intend to come here and harangue you, I intended . . .'

'What did you intend?'

'I guess I wanted to know what was happening. Is that so bad? Things are fairly unsettled. Father has me up at the other end of the country, he's so unapproachable, he tells me none of his plans, I hear from this side one set of things, from another side a different . . . It sure is a rumour factory here, isn't it?' He grinned companionably, the shouting put well behind.

'And what do they say on all these different sides?'

'Oh, some say that my father is the object of a hate campaign, vandalism, slogans, mysterious happenings; others say that since the prophet Elijah there hasn't been such a welcome appearance. Then they say that the hotel will be open on time and that it hasn't a chance of opening; that Father's going to marry Marian Johnson and she's going to change her hairstyle and get some new clothes, or that he's going to marry you and you're going to keep all your nice clothes the way they are but change your religion . . . And I hear that he has hundreds of bookings from the States and that he has no bookings . . . So do you see why I came to have a talk in case you could set me straight on some of these issues, anyway?'

She looked at him, and realized that he was making it all up, there was no way that people in Mountfern would confide such things to the son of Patrick O'Neill. But he was right in his summing up of the different viewpoints.

Kerry patted the chair beside him. 'Come on, Rachel, sit down and talk to me. I won't speak out of turn again. Promise.'

She sat down, knowing it was a very dangerous thing to do.

'There, that's better. And now have a drink. Come *on* Rachel, if you're going to be an honorary Irish person you'll have to learn to drink.'

It was easy and comforting to sit there with him instead of sitting on her own.

He had admitted his temper and his feelings. It was only natural that a boy should love his mother and want to keep his memories of her almost frozen in the viewpoint of the troubled teenager that he was at the time.

Rachel sipped the drink that he mixed for her, a whiskey and dry ginger. It tasted sweet and warming, not like the wine she sometimes sipped at functions, which was bitter and alien. Here in the sunset looking across the river with the handsome boy admitting his petulant temper and smiling at her like a conspirator it was easy to sit and talk and drink the sweet, fizzy, harmless liquor.

Kerry talked of the hotel in Donegal, how lonely he was up there and how the place seemed so remote. He often went to Derry across the border, it was exciting somehow to be in a place that was ruled by another country, to see other flags flying. Most of the people in Derry were basically Irish, he explained to Rachel, and they felt much more at home in the republic. He had met a few guys who were easy to rub along with there. Rough guys, not the kind who would be welcomed with open arms in the front doors of Fernscourt, he said scathingly. Still, they were alive all through, which was more than you could say for many of the people you met in this country, north or south. Rachel took this to mean that they were able to play cards with him or point him to some kind of game down town.

And Rachel found herself telling Kerry more than she intended to about some of the problems in getting deliveries in time and how she always tried to shield Patrick from the more troublesome side of things, partly because he had so much to think about he really could not be expected to give time to wondering why some weavers in Connemara had not been able to come up with the consignment they had promised months back. And partly because any grizzling or even mild criticism always seemed like a condemnation of his decision to come back to this land and build his dream castle.

Together they sighed amicably about the difficulties of dealing with the great Patrick O'Neill. There was none of the usual fencing between them and no hint of the flash of anger and the instructions not to speak his dead mother's name.

Rachel told of how Maurice, the Ryans' missing tortoise, had been discovered in the hen house where apparently he had been living for months in total contentment. And Kerry told how he had discovered that Jimbo Doyle really was making it big on the ballad-singing circuit, he was even booked for an appearance in Donegal, which had to be the Vegas of Ireland.

The sun sank behind the big house and the trees. The river took on its black rippling look where it seemed like a dark ribbon instead of a living, flowing thing.

Somewhere, possibly from down near the bridge, they heard the sound of a fiddle playing, an air that sounded sad and plaintive, but all Irish airs seemed sad to Rachel and Kerry. The boy reached across and patted her hand. There were tears in Rachel's eyes again but this time she wasn't hiding them, they fell down her face.

'I could have fitted in here, I could have stayed and been part of it,' she wept.

'But now you think you'll go back?' His voice was soft, like honey.

'I decided today I'll have to go back. He thinks he doesn't need me, he thinks he can manage on his own . . .' She let a sob come through her voice.

'I know, I know.'

'You can't know.'

'Well I do, he doesn't need me either. He never did.'

Rachel looked at him, tear-stained. He was so different tonight, vulnerable, understanding.

'I think he finds it hard to express himself to you . . .' she began, trying as usual to make bridges.

'I'm only his son, his flesh and blood. It shouldn't be so very hard to express himself.'

'He does care for you . . . I know.'

'And I know how fond of you he is too. I didn't always want to see it, I can tell you, but . . .'

He looked so straightforward. Rachel felt fuzzy and a little confused, but she could see that Kerry was being genuine towards her and she wanted to reassure him that he was important to his father.

And now Kerry was admitting that she, Rachel, was a part of Patrick too. She was certainly a little heady.

She placed her hand on Kerry's knee. He lifted it to admire her rings.

'These are very beautiful,' he said softly. 'Did you choose these yourself or were they a gift?'

She saw no guile in the words. It was a question. She held her hand away and admired the topaz and the emerald.

'Your father bought me the topaz a long long time ago. The emerald I bought myself. I have a little garnet too, but I don't wear them all at once.'

'No, no.' He was holding her hand and admiring the way the light caught the stones.

'It means fidelity, a topaz,' she said dreamily. 'I remember that very well.'

'Is it your birthstone?' Kerry asked interestedly.

He was so relaxed and easy to talk to tonight, Rachel wondered why she had ever thought him prickly and difficult.

'No, I'm Gemini – that's the emerald.' She turned her hand in his to examine the green stone.

'I got the emerald because of that and also because it means "success in love". I guess I wasn't so lucky there.'

Kerry said nothing, he fingered the tiepin he always wore these days. Even when he wasn't wearing a formal shirt and tie he seemed to have this pin on his lapel somehow.

'My, that's a topaz also,' Rachel realized for the first time.

'Yes. Topaz, that's right.' His voice seemed strained.

'And was *that* a gift or did you buy it, like I bought my emerald?' She was being giggly now.

'It was both, in a way. I paid for it to be made into a tiepin, but it was a gift, from my mother. Father gave her a topaz for fidelity also, you see. He never asked where it was when she died, I don't know if he realizes this is where it ended up.'

Rachel felt a sudden lurch in her stomach. 'I think I'm going to be sick,' she said, staggering to her feet.

Loretto Quinn was serving Jack Coyne next morning when Kerry appeared in the shop. He was in his stocking feet, walking lightly, and his clothes were crushed and rumpled.

'Hi Loretto. Well hi Jack, how are things?'

'Things are reasonable.' Jack wasn't able to reply as quickly as usual, he was so startled to see O'Neill's son come in casually through the back of the shop, meaning that he must have been upstairs.

Upstairs with O'Neill's woman.

'So they are with me, pretty reasonable. Loretto, can I have some oranges please, perhaps half a dozen . . . Sorry Jack, am I cutting in on you?'

'No, please.' Jack could hardly wait to see what else the young Kerry O'Neill was ordering.

Kerry said he'd take eggs, bread, four slices of that really great bacon – how could anyone in America *think* they had tasted bacon until they came to Ireland? And he'd better take a packet of those aspirin tablets too.

He smiled at them both, punched Jack playfully, and said that the little red sports car was a dream on wheels and he thought he'd either have to buy it so that it would be his own or possibly play Jack a game of poker for it.

Then light and cheerful he ran back up the stairs, leaving Loretto and Jack open-mouthed below.

Rachel woke painfully. Her head was pounding and she had a sense of unreality. What *could* have happened to make her feel so ill? Bits of it came back to her. The whiskey, the long chat with Kerry.

Then with such a shock that she sat bolt upright she remembered vomiting.

Her hand flew to her throat and she looked around her wildly. The bed was rumpled. Kerry's jacket was thrown on her chair. His shoes were lying on the floor where they had been kicked off. The other side of the bed had a little table and on the table was Kerry's watch, his cigarette case and his lighter.

With disbelief Rachel tried to take it in. She felt too frail to contemplate what could have happened. She wanted to lie down and pull the sheets and blankets over her poor hurt head. But she couldn't lie down. Not yet. Not until she knew.

As if on cue Kerry came into the room. He was wearing his shirt open, he was smiling.

'Hi there.'

'What . . . what?'

'It's orange juice,' he said delightedly, misunderstanding her. 'I squeezed six oranges so you'll love it. And if you feel strong enough I'm going to do you some eggs.'

'Not eggs,' Rachel said.

'Oh yes eggs, Rachel, they're known to be good for you. I got some bacon but I wasn't sure. I didn't know . . .'

'No bacon.' She struggled with the words.

'Sure sure. Well coffee anyway, after the juice.'

He sat on the bed familiarly, too close to her she thought in alarm, and pulled back.

She realized she was in her slip and that her brassiere was open. She realized that Kerry O'Neill was looking at her affectionately. The room seemed to swim and tilt a little.

'Kerry, how did . . . how did . . .'

'I got them in Loretto's,' he said sunnily. 'Oh, and I got you some aspirin too. Sip the juice first then I'll fix you some aspirin with the coffee.'

'You told Loretto . . .?'

'She's really come on in that little store, hasn't she? Jack Coyne was in there, he's an okay guy, I think. Father always says he's a gangster but these things are relative. To some people Father is something of a gangster. But enough about him, let's talk about you and me . . .'

Rachel gave a jump.

'. . . and what we're going to have for breakfast if it's too non kosher to fry a little bacon.' He smiled at her warmly and Rachel Fine with her drawn, lined face, her aching head and upset stomach looked up at him piteously. And knew she was somehow in his power.

It was the last Thursday in August and Dara Ryan had returned to Mountfern.

She felt quite different to the Dara who had left two months earlier. Older, wiser, more a woman of the world, she thought. After all she had lived in a household which had things going on under its roof that Dara would not have believed possible. She was going to look with new eyes on the clientele, male and nocturnal of the Rosemarie hair salon. She hoped she had become more sophisticated-looking. A girl she was talking to on the train told her that she could easily be eighteen, she looked *much* older than almost sixteen.

Dad thought she looked older, which was great. He held her at arm's length when he came to meet her at the station in the town. Grace and Michael had wanted to come too he said, but he had to refuse them, he needed the car for supplies.

Dara looked round and indeed the back of their old black car was filled with boxes. Things for the café, Dad said, every day now there was more stuff being brought in. They were ready to open it for business any time now.

'And what kind of form is Mam in? She doesn't get depressed too much now, does she?'

Dara kept looking lovingly at her father; she knew that in a changing world he would remain constant. It was hard to imagine Dad in bed with anyone, including Mam before the accident, but Dara knew that he wouldn't ever cheat on Mam like that appalling Monsieur Vartin.

'Your mother is a marvel,' he said simply. 'I don't know where and how she gets the ideas and the energy. She's an example to us who have the legs. She's so delighted that you're coming home. For ages now she's been saying only eight days more, only six days more . . .'

Dara was pleased. 'Isn't that nice, I was just the same, I hope we won't start to fight and ruin it.'

'Of course you will.' John was philosophic. 'But not immediately. We'll have a few days of a honeymoon period first.'

They drove down Bridge Street. Liam White was waving, and John slowed to a stop.

'You look different, did you have an illness?' he asked.

'Jesus, Mary and Joseph, Liam, that's lovely,' said Dara.

'No, you look foreign. Maybe it's the air, or the food.'

'I think she looks great altogether.' Dara's father was partisan and proud of his dark, handsome daughter.

'Oh, you look fine,' Liam said, as if that had never been in doubt. 'The question is, will it last?'

'Where's Jacinta?'

'Off somewhere with Tommy, she's the only one able to get him out of the shop. His father is afraid of Jacinta.'

'Aren't we all?' Dara said with some feeling.

Dara looked over at Daly's shop. It still looked the same. People came in to buy cakes and butter and groceries. Life went on. Dara swallowed hard. Everyone else had had two months to get used to Daly's Dairy without Maggie. Dara would too one day. Charlie was cleaning the windows, he waved his wet cleaning rag at her. The shop that used to be Meagher's seemed to have been all done up.

'What does Mountfern need a travel agency for?' she asked.

'Oh, there's amazing needs created in this place nowadays,' her father said almost ruefully.

Dara's eyes raked the town for Kerry

Perhaps he was back. Could he be running the travel agency? Would she ask Dad was he around? No, she was only minutes from home. And she had sent him a card giving the exact date of her return. There was bound to be some message from him when she got there.

The sign was up for Ryan's Shamrock Café. Nobody had told her it would look so big. There was a new door now in the front of the building that used to be the outhouse, the place where they had their party almost a year ago.

The old windows had been repainted and new glass fitted. On each window sill brightly coloured boxes of geraniums stood nodding in the sun.

Dara gasped. 'I never knew it was like this . . . like . . .'

'Like nothing on earth,' her father finished cheerfully. 'Still, it might keep a roof over our heads. Now here's your mother waiting for you.'

Kate sat in the door of the new café. She was all dressed up, one of Rachel's scarves draped around her, which was what designated the outfit as for an occasion. She stretched her arms out in welcome as Dara scampered from the car.

Dara's heart gave a little jump.

Mam's smile was wide and warm but she had big circles under her eyes and she was very pale.

Mam didn't look at all well.

There was huge excitement at Dara's return.

Grace and Michael came rushing in. Grace hugged her and said that she had become very French.

Michael said she had begun to lisp and speak broken English.

'What ees zat you say?' Dara punched him until he admitted it was all jealousy on his part.

Eddie wanted to know why she hadn't tried snails. He'd told all his friends that Dara was eating snails for her breakfast, dinner and tea and now he'd look like an eejit.

Declan asked could *he* go to France next summer, he wouldn't mind looking after children, it would be nice to have something younger than himself that he could boss around and give orders to.

Carrie asked if they ate everything raw – Jimbo told her he had heard that.

Mary Donnelly said she was pleased to hear that Frenchmen were not always making free with their attentions, as had often been reported.

Grace and Michael giggled at this and Kate and Dara exchanged glances. Mary had not been told about the discovery of Monsieur Vartin and Mademoiselle Stephanie.

It was marvellous to be back at home with everyone speaking English and everyone speaking at once.

But it was awful not to be able to ask about Kerry. Nobody had mentioned his name.

After supper Dara linked Grace out into the garden. They were meant to be doing a tour of the café.

'And what news of your big brother?' Dara tried to be light and joky.

'Oh, didn't he write to you? I *told* him you were coming home today. He was on the phone looking for Father.'

'How was he?'

'He was mainly sounding off about Miss Hayes. I had to keep the telephone very close to my ear in case she'd hear, he'd called the night before for Father, and a . . . oh, I don't know, she hadn't given the right message. But I did tell him you'd be back today.'

'Thanks, Grace.' Dara was bleak.

'Was it great, France?' Grace was eager. 'Did you go out at all to any parties or dances?'

'No, nothing like that.'

'What was the best bit?'

'We had a picnic . . . they call it peek neek, honestly. They had huge loaves of

French bread and cheese and peaches and wine . . . And we went to this place on a river, not the Loire itself but a smaller river like the Fern, and we went swimming, all of us. Even Madame. And we stayed there till quite late and it got dark, and they all seemed very happy . . .'

Grace looked at her, trying to see why this had been the high spot.

Dara went on. 'They seemed so safe, sort of. As if they'd always be together, and I understood all the conversation, which I usually didn't. I think it might have been the wine . . . And suddenly there were all these little pinpoints of light everywhere. Fireflies they were.'

'Oh yes, fireflies are lovely,' Grace said.

'I told them we didn't have any here, and Monsieur said I must look again when I got home. That was the best time, I think.'

Grace seemed pleased that Dara had a happy if unfathomable memory. She hugged her friend. 'It's great to have you home again,' she said.

And Dara felt a great ache.

It would have been great to come home if there had been a note from Kerry saying when he'd be back in Mountfern. If Maggie had been running up River Road after supper, hands clasped and eager to hear every detail. If Tommy had come in making jokes about the French.

And if Mam's face hadn't this tired look, and if she'd been able to eat her supper instead of moving the cold chicken and ham from one side of the plate to the other.

Loretto Quinn had to tell someone so she picked Sheila Whelan.

'It could be totally innocent,' Sheila said.

'It has to be,' Loretto said. 'Mother of God, you don't think that they'd have been sleeping together as man and wife would you?'

Sheila sighed a 'no'.

'But what was he doing back in town, let alone above in her room?' Loretto's open face was puzzled. 'Rachel told me herself that he wouldn't be coming back until the opening. And young Dara Ryan said that Mr O'Neill said he was still above in Donegal.'

'It's a mystery all right,' Sheila said. She had a feeling that something was very wrong here. If Kerry really had been sneaking into Mountfern and to Rachel for any purpose under the sun, not to mention the interpretation which would be put on it, then why had he advertised it so publicly?

People didn't die without orange juice and eggs. He could have waited until Jack Coyne had left the shop, he would have heard his voice before he came in. Kate Ryan had always been worried about Kerry, she had said there was something very strange about him, he didn't react like ordinary people.

Maybe Kate had been right.

Tommy Leonard was disappointed that he had missed Dara coming back. He had gone out with Jacinta to find good angles where Mountfern could be photographed.

Mr O'Neill was having a photographer next week who would take glossy pictures of the place and they would be turned into postcards. Some would be sold in the hotel, some in Leonard's. Privately Tommy thought that if the visitors could buy them at the information desk in the hotel they would be most unlikely to want to trek the whole way to Leonard's to buy the same thing. But his father had been very respectful and over-thanked Mr O'Neill.

Jack Coyne came in to buy a paper. He ignored Tommy and went instead to the older man. Jack lowered his voice so Tommy made an effort to hear. It seemed to be about Kerry O'Neill having breakfast with Loretto Quinn. Or was it Mrs Fine? In either case hadn't they little to talk about!

Tommy's thoughts went back to Dara. He wished he hadn't gone out with Jacinta, he felt sure no good would come of it. Liam White said that Dara had changed totally, got a smaller waist, a bigger chest and a sort of bold flashy look about her as if she had seen it all and done it all. Tommy knew that this couldn't be true, but he did wish that he had been able to see her himself and make these observations about her chest and her waist instead of hearing it all from Liam.

He stood there, legs aching, wishing that his father had not been so infected by Mr O'Neill's diligence that he now kept the shop open until nine o'clock in the evening.

Fergus went for a stroll which took him, as his strolls nearly always did, to the door of Ryan's.

'Can I have a look at the Parisienne?' he asked John.

'She's within, chattering to her mother, saying "oui" instead of yes half the time. The boys are giving her a desperate teasing over it. Take your pint and go in to see them.'

'Ah no, I'll let them talk. I'll see her plenty in the next few days.' Fergus knew how much Kate had been looking forward to the daughter's return.

'Wasn't it a great chance for her, Fergus?' John was very pleased with the way it had all turned out. 'We didn't know what we were sending the child to, really, it was just that . . .' He let the sentence trail away.

'Well, didn't it all work out very well when you consider . . .' Fergus Slattery didn't finish his sentence either.

He thought that this particular conversation was better left untold in this house. He hoped that the handsome young Dara Ryan had her head well turned by Frenchmen and that she would forget O'Neill's dangerous-looking son.

It was so good to have Dara home. Kate wondered how she had survived without her daughter. With Dara there was no need to pretend, with Dara there was a feeling of hope all around her. Kate knew that Dara could hear the true plans and the true worries about the Shamrock Café.

'It's not what we had planned, like, for our lives,' Dara had complained.

'A lot of things weren't what we had planned,' Kate said, touching the sides of the wheelchair.

Dara had noticed how much Kate hated the chair. Since the very first day she had been in it, it represented the prison bars to her. She could not make herself see it as a liberation, a way of getting about. Instead she regarded the chair as a hated object and put all her anger towards it, as if it were the cause of all her incapacity.

She wanted it out of her sight when she was in bed, no matter that she might need it in the night. She disguised it by draping rugs and scarves over it.

Dara seemed to understand. Once she had written a notice on it: 'I'm only a chair for God's sake, Mrs Ryan.' Kate had pealed with laughter when she woke and saw it.

They could talk easily now, the trip to France had been an inspired idea.

Dara gave her mind eagerly to the problems of survival when the new regime arrived.

'There's only one thing I don't like, Mam.'

'Tell it then.'

'I don't like you going up to the hotel to give cookery lessons.'

'Aha,' Kate said.

'What do you mean, aha?'

'I have a little plan about that, I can't tell you yet, but let's say it's not going to be a problem.'

'Tell me, I tell *you* everything.'

'I'll only go for a very very short time.'

'What's the point in it then?'

'This is the point, once I've got myself established, then Dr White will tell me, and indeed tell Patrick, that the strain is too much, and I can't do it any more, so . . . so I'll have to continue the lessons here. Do you understand?'

'Mam!'

Impulsively Kate opened her arms and Dara rushed to her.

'It's so good to have you home, child. I missed you so much. What do people do if they don't have a daughter? Tell me that.'

'Oh Mam, it's great to be back. They were nice in their way and they went to endless trouble over things but they'd have you starved half the time and they were riddled with sin.'

Kate laughed until she nearly cried; her pale face looked more colourful now.

Dara felt happier but she still resolved to ask Mrs Fine if Mam had been having any bad turns. She would ask her tomorrow. She half listened to Mam as she wondered whether Kerry might be home for the weekend. Grace was useless for any information. But of course he would come home this weekend. Now that he knew both from her postcard and from Grace on the phone that Dara was back.

Kate looked at Dara's face, lightly tanned from the hot French sunshine. She knew how Rachel would admire her, and indeed make further representations about getting Dara's ears pierced for her and giving her little gold studs.

It was odd that Rachel wasn't here. She hadn't been in all day.

Rachel Fine stayed in her room all day.

She crouched like an animal in the forest that is afraid to move because it doesn't know if it has been too badly injured. She heard the noises of Mountfern on a late summer morning. The carts that went by, the delivery vans, the sounds of hammering from across the river. She heard voices too in and out of Loretto's shop and children calling to each other as they chased along River Road.

Kerry had gone as light-heartedly as she had ever seen him. He had kissed her affectionately on the nose, he had been teasing and flirtatious. As he would have been after a night in bed with any woman.

They hadn't been together in that way. But she had no way of proving it.

A hundred times she told herself that no one would believe she could have opened her body to Kerry O'Neill, who was a boy, who had been a child when she first met and loved his father.

It would have been like an act of incest.

'So I'll head for the hills of Donegal now before anyone knows I've been here. And thanks, Rachel, thanks for everything,' he had said.

What was he thanking her for?

'But people do know, they'll think . . . You said you spoke to Loretto, to Jack Coyne . . .' she croaked.

'That's not what I mean. They don't count. I don't want to meet my father, I'm going to have to tell him about some money I owe, sooner or later. No point in getting him steamed up before I ask him.'

Rachel looked at Kerry and fought back waves of dizziness and nausea.

And when he was gone she felt a coldness through her bones that made a mockery of the sunny summer day outside.

She didn't answer when Loretto called up to know if she should bring up a parcel of materials that had just been delivered. So Loretto, more confused than ever, just left the parcel on the stairs and shook her head from side to side.

Rachel didn't go to see Dara, newly returned. She didn't call to collect mail at the post office, nor did she touch the parcel on the stairs.

When Brian Doyle sent round to know had some fabrics arrived, because young Costello was behaving like a pregnant cat over them, Loretto said there was no point in trying to get any answer from upstairs.

Brian said that he had always known it would happen, most people in the place had now gone clinically insane and the place for them all was the asylum on the hill.

He had been told that Kerry O'Neill was in Donegal and yet he had nearly been killed by the little bastard reversing his car at top speed this morning.

He had been told that Rachel Fine was waiting night and day for some swatches of material and now they had arrived she had apparently gone to ground like a broody hen.

O'Neill was like a lighting devil, and that leggy young Ryan child from the pub had snapped the head off him when he had addressed a civil word to her.

It was time to ring the asylum and tell them to come down with the straitjackets and take the people of Mountfern away.

As soon as he got to Fernscourt, Patrick was called to the phone in Brian Doyle's hut.

'Dennis Hill here, Patrick. I just rang to know if everything's all right?'

'That's good of you Dennis. It's crawling along, crawling, but we might have hot water to make them a cup of coffee at the opening. You will come, I take it?'

'I meant about your little girl.'

'Grace?' Patrick was alarmed.

'Is she recovering?'

'Recovering?'

'The accident. The accident on the bridge.'

'Grace didn't have an accident.' Patrick's heart was beating very fast. Could something have happened to Grace this morning that he didn't know about? He shouted to Costello. 'Was there any accident on the bridge this morning, did anything happen? Quickly, man.'

Costello was quick. 'Nothing at all,' he said crisply.

'And Grace, is she all right?'

'I saw her cycling by not five minutes ago with Michael Ryan.'

'Thanks, Costello.'

Patrick's breathing had changed its pace now.

'Sorry, Dennis. I was away from the phone for a moment. What did you hear?'

Mr Hill's voice was cold. 'I heard what your son told me yesterday, he had a call saying his sister had an accident in a fall from a bridge, she had been playing jumping and diving games with other children. He said that he had to go to Mountfern at once. Naturally I gave him permission.'

'There was no accident,' Patrick said dully.

'And I am delighted to hear it,' Dennis Hill said courteously. There was a pause. Mr Hill spoke again: 'He's a difficult lad, your son.'

'Speak to me straight, did he steal anything?'

'No, nothing like that!' Mr Hill was surprised.

'Well you'd better check before you fire him. You *are* going to fire him aren't you?'

Another pause.

'Yes, yes I think it's better to send him back to you. There's something there that attracts him.'

'Well I'm damned if I know what it is.' Patrick's voice was weary.

'Could be a girl. He's a handsome fellow.'

'The only one he seems to be with is an under-age schoolgirl. But that would figure. He's never done anything that you'd hope he would.'

'They don't, you know, children. I've got sons here in the business, and sons-in-law. They think I'm an old fool, they want me to clear out of it. That's the thanks you get for building up a business and handing it to them on a plate.'

'Thanks Dennis.'

'What for? I'm letting your boy go, that's not much to thank me for.'

'I mean for letting me know about your sons. It's less lonely somehow.'

'You'll survive. The girl's good, isn't she?'

'Ah yes, the best.'

'I've got one good fellow in my brood, wants nothing to do with the hotel, works out on a headland in a smallholding. Best of the lot of them, it's a pleasure to sit and talk to him for hours. You'll find that with the girl.'

'When I see Kerry will I tell him to call you?'

'Why prolong it all? Speeches, lies, excuses. Tell him to pick up his things when he wants to.'

389

As Patrick replaced the receiver he hoped he wouldn't see Kerry for a while. Like a day anyway. He might lose control completely. A boy who could use the circumstances of Maggie Daly's death, graft them on to his own sister. And all as an excuse to go to some gambling game or other. He might very possibly kill him.

Kerry looked across the Fern. His father's car wasn't outside the hotel. That meant he must be at home. He would set out for the lodge. Easier to talk to him there anyway. He would go by River Road – he would meet too many people on Bridge Street. This way he only had to pass Coyne's, Ryan's and the Rosemarie hair salon. Jack Coyne he had already met; Kerry smiled to think how the story would be reported. Jack would find a dozen excuses to talk to people that he would not normally have any business with.

He wondered would Rachel give any version of anything. Probably not. He would hear soon.

He turned on the car radio and they were playing 'Pretty Flamingo'. He turned the volume up high, pulled down the flap to keep the sun out of his eyes, and took a corner very fast.

The car that he pushed off the road was his father's. The sound of Manfred Mann was silenced by the screeching of brakes.

Kerry stopped the car and let out a sigh of relief. It had been close and it had of course been his fault. He ran his hand through his hair as he watched his father climb out of the car that was half in the ditch. His father walked towards him slowly and flung open the door.

'Get out of that fucking car,' he said in a voice that Kerry had never heard before. It was as if he were being held back by two strong men. Kerry could almost see them straining to pull him back.

While all the time his father wanted to tear him limb from limb.

He got out. 'I'm sorry, I was over too far . . .'

His father said nothing.

'And going a little fast, I guess.'

Silence.

'Still, no real harm's done. Can we get it out, do you think, or should we walk back for Jack Coyne?'

'What are you doing here?'

'I was coming to see you. I wanted to talk to you urgently and then I was going to head for Donegal. I said I'd be back at lunchtime.'

'You don't have to be back by lunch or at all.'

'But I said to Mr Hill that I'd do my best to get back today, he trusts me, and I think I should . . .'

'Hill doesn't trust you across the room, Kerry, he's just fired you.'

'He wouldn't do that.'

'He has done that. Just that.'

Kerry thought for a moment.

'He suddenly made up his mind and rang you to tell you, rather than tell me. That's unlikely.'

He was cool still, not blustering or defending himself with excuses with lies:

'Ah yes, you may think it unlikely because you forget that some people have human feelings, generous feelings. Dennis Hill didn't like to think of a girl falling off a bridge in a terrible accident, and her brother having to hotfoot it to her bedside. He called to know how she was.'

'I see.' Kerry's face was impassive.

'No you don't see. You'll never see how it would turn anyone's stomach, what you did.'

'I had to say something. I wanted to get away.'

'What a great thing to choose.'

'I needed to be out of there, I needed to be here.'

'Why?'

'I wanted to sort something out and see you.'

'You're seeing me, Kerry, by Jesus you are seeing me. Say what you have to say, and say it quickly.'

'Father, the money?'

'The money you called about yesterday, that ridiculous sum . . . You are not getting one penny of that from me.'

'I wanted to come and tell you personally the kind of people they are.'

'I don't care if they are cousins of the pope, they're still not going to find me coughing up their winnings at poker.'

'I'm not saying they're respectable people we don't want to offend. They're the reverse, they're very tough.'

'Good, then you've met it at last. People who are not going to give in to your every wish.'

'You wouldn't say good, Father, if you knew . . . Tony said that they're getting very annoyed with me.'

Patrick looked at his son.

'You are a spoiled selfish brat. It is my fault, it is not your mother's fault. I didn't see what was happening to you, I saw every other goddamn thing but I didn't see you for what you were. I was too busy, God forgive me.'

'I'm sure he will forgive you, Father, God always forgives people who talk nicely to him and turn up at mass, no matter what they've been up to.'

'Don't give me that.'

'And people who put stained-glass windows into churches, and new buildings into Catholic schools, God loves them mightily.'

Kerry's eyes were flashing. He would not be stopped.

'You can get away with it, Father, you always have, you can cut corners, you can break promises, you can give every tart in town a topaz, but as long as the Easter dues are generous God turns a blind eye.'

Patrick moved at him, his arm up as if to strike.

Kerry went on. 'And God understands a bit of battering too, if it's done in the right cause. Go ahead. Go on, I don't care. I don't bloody care.'

Patrick withdrew.

'You'll care when you're out working in a real job for the first time in your life in order to pay these hooligans, you'll care then when three-quarters of your wages will go to pay off a debt that not one of these farmers here would sleep a wink if he owed in a lifetime.'

'You don't think for a *moment* that they'll wait to be paid at fifteen pounds a week. That's well over a year. They want it now. On Monday at the very latest.'

'Give it up, you'll never get it. If you play for it you'll just end up paying twice as much. Work for a year, two years, regard it as your apprenticeship. They'll wait.'

'They can't wait, they're not ordinary people. They're in an . . . organization.'

'Cut that shit, they've organized themselves to smell a sucker and to rob a bank or a post office or two. Those fellows have no cause but themselves.'

'You don't understand . . .'

'I know that for a fact, Hill warned me about them a while back. There may be some fellows in a movement in Derry since the border campaign ended, but not your lot. They're for themselves.'

'Hill's an old fool, he knows nothing.'

'You're to collect your things from him, and he knows you're light-fingered, so there's no point in trying to make up any shortfall by dipping into the till before you leave.'

Kerry looked at him sharply. Things had gone very far if his father had warned an outsider against him.

'Can I stay at the lodge when I come back?' he asked.

'Yes.'

'Have you told Grace?'

'That she is meant to be lying like her friend Maggie under the bridge, but that in her case there's some hope she'll survive? No.'

'What *will* you say?'

'As little as possible. To you and about you.'

'That will be hard if we're living in the same house.'

'I'm moving into the hotel shortly, so is Grace. You can have the lodge until Christmas. We've paid for it until then.'

'Miss Hayes?'

'Will be going to her sister in New Zealand in a couple of weeks.'

'And my room in the hotel?'

'Will not exist, Kerry.'

'I'm not going to make a speech or plead, Father, this isn't about the future of the hotel or anything. It's about now. Could you give me just this stake? Then I'll never ask you again.'

'No.'

'Please. I've never said please before, maybe I should have. But I'm begging you.'

'No. If I do it now, then next month it will be fifteen hundred pounds. Go to them, tell them they have to wait a year or whatever it takes to make it.'

Kerry's eyes narrowed.

'On your own head then, Father. If you won't give it to me I'll have to get it elsewhere.'

'That won't be easy, you're running out of credibility.'

'I think I know where I can get it,' Kerry said and he almost smiled.

He got back into his car and drove away towards the main road. Patrick walked to Jack Coyne's and got three lads to come up and move his car. He didn't tell them how it had ended up in the ditch but he did not like the way Jack Coyne was looking at him.

There was something knowing and triumphant about the way the small rat-like man kept glancing at him.

'Have you been talking to Kerry?' Carrie asked Dara in a conspiratorial whisper.

'No, he's not home yet, but he might be back at the weekend. I keep hoping,' Dara said.

'But he *is* here. I saw him.'

'You never did!'

'Yes, last night. I said that's funny, Kerry home on a Thursday in the middle of the week. And then again this morning, he drove past here at a hundred miles an hour.'

'Had he anyone with him?' Dara was almost afraid to hear the answer.

'No, not at all. Why should he have anyone with him, isn't he your fellow?' Carrie saw things over-simply, Dara thought.

Dara sat on the window seat looking out at the moonlight. She couldn't believe that Kerry had been in Mountfern without even coming in to say hallo.

Grace could never have told her a lie. There could be no awful thing that they were keeping hidden from her, like that he was going out with Kitty Daly. No, Michael would never be a party to that.

Michael came to sit beside her.

'There's nothing you're keeping secret from me, is there?' she asked.

'How did you guess?'

'Oh God.' Dara's hand went to her throat.

'You see, Grace will soon be living across there,' he began.

'What is it?'

'I was wondering, I was wondering if I could . . . if we could show her the tunnel.'

'Is that all?'

'Well, I know it's quite a big thing to ask.'

Dara didn't seem to listen.

'Was Kerry home today?' she asked. 'Did he stay at the lodge last night? That's all I want to know. It's not very much to ask.'

'Of course he wasn't. If he was, he'd have talked to me, he talks to me quite a lot, as it happens.'

'He wasn't back then?'

'No. How many times do I have to say it?'

'Carrie must be going mad, that's all,' Dara said.

'And what do you say about . . .?'

Michael let his voice trail away. Dara was sitting happily on the window seat, her leg tucked underneath her, all the anxiety gone from her face. She didn't want to talk about tunnels or to talk about anything, she wanted to think about Kerry O'Neill.

Kerry said his goodbyes briefly in Hill's hotel. The staff were sorry to see him leave; some of the students who had been working as chambermaids for the summer were particularly sorry. He had been so sunny, so handsome, like summer lightning around the place.

He told McCann that he could get the money and have it on Saturday afternoon. McCann had said he would come with him to get it.

That was not what Kerry wanted.

'Look you've been in Mountfern, you know the set-up, it's a one-horse place. We're the kings of the castle there, if I say I'll get it I will, and then I'll get it to you.'

'No point in your driving all over the country,' McCann said laconically. 'I'll come with you. Then I'll get the bus back.'

It was a dispiriting drive. The back of the car was filled with Kerry's stuff, they couldn't give a lift to any of the girls they saw on the road even if they had wanted to. Which Kerry didn't.

They listened to music the whole way down. Tony McCann liked 'These Boots Are Made for Walking'. He said it was a great song, and sang it tunelessly with Nancy Sinatra.

Kerry said he liked 'Pretty Flamingo', he didn't know why but it reminded him of Dara Ryan, who was only a kid but very attractive.

'Is she pink and does she stand on one leg?' McCann had wanted to know with a laugh.

Several times Kerry O'Neill wondered why he found McCann such good company.

In Mountfern he told McCann there were three pubs he could drink in, and that he would be an hour at the most. Then he'd come with the money.

McCann had said that a cheque would be fine. His friends knew that Kerry wouldn't be foolish enough to give them a cheque that didn't work. That would be more stupid than not giving them anything at all.

Kerry had nodded fervently.

He settled McCann in Foley's, realizing that between taciturn old Mr Foley and the silent McCann little chat would be exchanged.

Then he drove down Bridge Street, looking neither right nor left of him. He realized that when he was back here full time it would be like living in one of those fish tanks that old Hill had in his hotel where people could look at the lobsters from every side. He averted his eyes from Fergus Slattery and turned right into River Road.

Loretto's eyes were like dinner plates as he walked past her and up the stairs to Rachel Fine.

Her face was as white as a sheet. She was sitting at a table with papers on it. A coffee cup sat beside her, full but cold.

She looked up in alarm as he came in softly.

'We have to talk, Rachel, you and I,' he said.

And he pulled up a chair beside her.

Friday afternoon. Could she really have been home only twenty-four hours? Dara felt she had been back for weeks.

She had gone to look for Jacinta and been told she was at her riding lesson with Marian Johnson.

Some time or other Dara would have to go into Daly's. It had better be now.

Mrs Daly smiled at her warmly and wanted to know all about France.

'Did you get to Lourdes at all while you were there?'

'No, Mrs Daly, but the lady I was staying with did. I asked her to say a prayer for Maggie. I wrote the name down for her on the back of a holy picture.'

Mrs Daly was pleased. She patted Dara's hand.

'You're a good child in spite of everything,' she said.

Dara repeated this to Tommy Leonard in a cross voice. 'In spite of what? What did she mean?' she asked.

Tommy couldn't take his eyes off Dara. She looked utterly lovely, he thought.

'In spite of being good-looking, she means. Mrs Daly hates good-looking people, she likes them with faces like ironing boards.'

Dara giggled. 'I don't suppose you can come off with me for a bit?'

'I can't. I used up all my time off going to hunt out sites and vantage points with Jacinta yesterday. You look just great, you know.'

'Thanks, Tommy. Well, if you've spent your free time with Jacinta I can but go in search of fun and games elsewhere. Sit out on the street and wait till King Kerry turns up for the weekend.'

'Oh, King Kerry as you call him is here already.' Tommy was pained to have to acknowledge it but at least it was good that Dara didn't seem to be tied up with him the moment she came back.

'He can't be!'

'Well then, he has a double. I saw him with a fellow from a horror movie going into Foley's, maybe they've taken to drinking in there.'

'Kerry doesn't drink,' Dara said.

'He could have started,' Tommy suggested.

'Today was it?'

'Oh, don't go up looking for them in Foley's, Dara, for heaven's sake.'

'I've no intention of going looking for them anywhere,' Dara flounced. 'Kerry will come and look for me when he's ready.'

Dara waited on the footbridge. She knew he would have to come and find her.

She saw the shadows getting a little longer. She leaned over and looked at her reflection in the water. She looked all right, she thought. Not a beauty, but all right.

Where *was* he?

She didn't hear the car stopping and his light step behind her. She felt his arms around her waist and as she looked into the river she saw him reflected there. He kissed her.

'In front of the pub, with them all looking out the window?' she protested.

'Right, let's go somewhere with no windows. Get in.' He opened the door of the little red car.

Dara walked towards it slowly. Was she being very cheap, very easy-to-get by going with him straight away? He hadn't written. Not once. Not even a card.

He hadn't got in touch when he got back. But for seeing her now, he might never have stopped.

He looked up at her from the car. 'You're so beautiful, Dara. I hope those Frenchmen didn't get what you wouldn't give me.'

He was talking out loud. Anyone could have heard him if they had been near the pub window.

She scrambled into the car at once.

'I'm only getting in to keep you quiet,' she said.

'Aren't I clever?' Kerry smiled at her and the car sped off up River Road and towards the stile in Coyne's wood.

In the wood he stood and looked at her.

'I can't take you in, I don't know what it is. In two months you've changed. I missed you,' he said, head on one side, smiling to charm her.

'No of course you didn't, you never thought of me at all. You never wrote, not once. You didn't even come to see me when I got back even though I sent you a card to tell you.'

'I wanted to but I couldn't, I just wasn't able to,' he said.

Dara looked hard at him. He was so handsome. But of course he was making excuses.

'They tied your hands?' she asked.

'No, of course I should have written but I'm hopeless. No, I meant to be there to welcome you, but I had problems. A lot of things to sort out.' His face was troubled.

'What were they?'

'Okay, I'll tell you. I was trying to get free from Donegal so that I could be here all the time. Here with you. It took a bit of organizing.'

'And have you organized it?' She sounded doubtful. She expected him to say it hadn't worked out.

'Yes,' he said surprisingly.

'By good timing, by the most spectacular good timing in the world, I'm free, just as you come back.'

'You're leaving Hill's Hotel?'

'Yes, mam.' He did a mock salute.

'How did you do it?'

'Not easy, a lot of aggravation I assure you. I'm still tidying up loose ends. I've got all my things in the car, see?'

'You mean you've just left *now*?'

'Just now. You're the first person I came to see.' He reached out for her.

He looked as if he didn't want to talk about it any more. Dara moved to what she thought were safer waters.

'I'm very pleased you're going to be around. Even if you *are* faithless and forgetful, I like you.'

'Why am I faithless and forgetful? I raced here to find you. Let me hold you.'

'Not for a moment.'

'Why? What is it?'

'I'm much older now and I understand more. I don't want to hold you and have you . . . um . . . touch me . . . and then for me to say no and you to get all upset.'

'Well it's very simple, you don't say no, and nobody gets upset.'

Dara looked at him with her big dark eyes. 'That's not what I want, and even though I like being with you, and like it a lot, when all is said and done it *is* my body, isn't it? And I can do what I like with it. Or not do what I like with it.'

He stood smiling at her, and admiring. 'Well, well, well,' he said.

'I thought I'd rather say it now. Sort of before anything got started so that you wouldn't storm off.'

'Very wise.' He nodded his head sagely, making fun of her.

'So, it's a bargain, then. You don't get all upset if I say I don't want to go any further.'

'Sure, and you don't get all upset, as you say, if I don't turn up all the time like a little lap dog. I'm going to be living here now and it will have its ups and downs. Give me some time and space to sort it out. Not asking a lot of questions all the time.'

'It's a deal,' she said. 'And I promise not to keep asking questions, if you'll tell me one thing. Is it true that you still don't love anyone but if you did love anyone it would probably be me?'

'Where did you hear that?' He smiled.

'You told me once. When we sat in your car. After I had come to look for you in that roadhouse.'

'It was true then and it's true now,' he said. 'If the situation changes in either direction, you will be the first to know.'

The weekend would be their last one before term began.

Grace said she hoped that she would be living in the hotel by the time school started.

'Kerry never said.' Dara was puzzled.

'Kerry's not coming to the hotel yet. I mean I'm sure he will later.' Grace seemed flustered.

'Why on earth isn't he going to the hotel? What happened?' Dara was astounded.

'Nothing, nothing at all.'

'I'm your best friend, for heaven's sake. I tell you everything, Grace, why don't you tell me?'

'I haven't even told Michael. I think there was some kind of row, I think Father didn't want him to leave the hotel in Donegal, but he insisted, he said he had to come back to Mountfern.'

He had to come back to Mountfern. Dara hugged this to herself with delight. He had indeed got into trouble over it but he had braved it all because he wanted to be back in Mountfern. With Dara.

CHAPTER TWENTY-ONE

By Sunday Kate was concerned about Rachel.

She hadn't called on Thursday to welcome Dara home. She hadn't been in on Friday, nor Saturday.

Sunday morning Loretto called to the pub to buy two bottles of stout.

'Going to have a bit of a batter?' Kate asked as she wrapped them in brown paper.

'No, I'm having Jack Coyne to his Sunday dinner, he was very helpful to me over a lot of heavy lifting and putting up shelves. I thought I'd cook him a meal for once.'

'Terrific. Where did Rachel go, by the way?'

'Rachel?' Loretto looked shifty.

'Yes, she must have told me but I've forgotten. She hasn't been in here for days, was it to Connemara this time or Dublin?'

'I don't . . . um . . . know.' Loretto wanted to leave. She had no intention of telling Kate what had been going on.

Later that evening Kate looked across the footbridge and saw a figure walking on the other side, along the towpath that led down from the bridge.

It was Rachel Fine, wearing a headscarf and sunglasses.

It wasn't cold enough for a headscarf.

It wasn't bright enough for sunglasses.

It was almost as if she didn't want to be seen.

On Monday morning Dara knew she would see Kerry. He had told her that the weekend would involve a massive reconciliation job with his father, so he wouldn't be around.

Dara did herself up to the nines. She was dying to see him again. She knew too that he didn't want her telling too many people that they met. That suited her very well, she was anxious to keep her own parents as much in the dark as possible.

'You're looking very flash, Dara.'

'Sophisticated is the word,' Dara said. She was alarmed if Jack Coyne thought she was flash. She must have gone too far with the lipstick.

'Like a dog's dinner, anyway.' He was admiring.

'Considering what Leo's dinners look like, that's not much of a compliment.'

'Leopold's not a dog, he's a freak,' Jack Coyne said. 'You should have let me drown him instead of having him there turning away custom.'

'Oh, don't be ridiculous. People love him.'

'Well, that's debatable. Any sign of Kerry O'Neill, by the way?'

'No, why do you ask *me*?' Dara was suspicious.

'I thought you might have heard from him. Specially seeing you're all dolled up.'

'Lord no.' She was over-casual. 'Kerry O'Neill isn't my type, nor me his, I'm certain.'

'Well, they say his tastes run to the maturer lady all right, but you'd never know.'

'Maturer?'

'Much maturer. Old even, some would say. Still if you *do* see him tell him I have that poker game in mind. He mentioned one the last time he was here a few days ago.'

'Then he *was* here the other night.'

'He was certainly here at breakfast time in the morning getting aspirins and orange juice for his lady love upstairs.'

'His what?'

'No, I'm saying nothing, but I'm surprised Loretto hasn't passed it on to your mother. Still, what with herself being your mother's friend and everything I suppose it's a bit complicated. Forget I said anything, will you.'

He was gone, leaving Dara fuming on River Road. She bent down and pulled up a handful of dried grass from the river bank to wipe off her lipstick.

Jack Coyne was always a pain and she knew that Mam and Dad didn't like Eddie and Declan hanging around his yard. But surely not even Jack Coyne could make up something like that about Kerry and Mrs Fine unless he had some reason.

Mrs Fine. She was older than Mam, surely. It was disgusting.

'Oh Patrick, this *is* a surprise!' Marian Johnson patted her hair with pleasure.

'Hardly a surprise,' Patrick growled. 'It is my office.'

'No, I heard you were going to Dublin.'

'No.' Patrick was unforthcoming. 'What can I do for you . . .?'

'Nothing really, I just came down to have a look around the place, to see the coach house and stables.'

'They're outside, Marian,' Patrick said dryly. 'They often are in houses like this.'

He realized he had been over-sharp.

'Come on, I'll take you out to have a tour,' he said good-naturedly. 'Not that there's anything to see of course, we're only playing at ponies and horses here, the guests will all be taken up to the Grange.'

'I know.' She patted his arm gratefully. 'I don't know what we'd do without you. You've changed the whole face of Mountfern.'

'That's not what I set out to do,' he sighed.

'All for the better, of course. You've improved the place out of all recognition. I mean, look at poor little Loretto's place across the river there . . .' Marian waved a dismissive arm at the bright shop frontage of Quinn's grocery and greengrocery. 'That used to be a real huckster's shop, and now it's grand enough for Kerry O'Neill to be seen coming and going at all hours of the day and night.' She smiled what she hoped was a mischievous smile.

Patrick looked at her almost pityingly. 'I know, Marian. I know. Don't wear yourself out trying to think up ways of telling me what half the town has told me already.'

'I don't know *what* you mean.' She flushed angrily.

As Dara passed Loretto Quinn's she saw Mrs Fine standing at the upper window. She was looking out over the river. She hadn't seen Dara.

For a moment Dara hesitated. Jack Coyne had been very definite. Then she shook herself. It was ludicrous. Mrs Fine looked a hundred.

On a sudden impulse Dara decided to go up and tell her that Mam was upset. It might do some good and it couldn't do any harm.

Loretto was out the back somewhere, so Dara ran straight upstairs.

'Mrs Fine?' She tapped lightly on the door and went in.

Rachel Fine turned round from the window. However badly she looked from down below she looked worse now. Dara could hardly hide her shock.

'Sorry, Dara. I wasn't expecting you. You look very nice.'

'Thanks Mrs Fine . . . um . . . Are you all right and everything?'

'I've had a bit of a cold, I think. Flu perhaps.'

'Oh, I see. Mam was wondering where you were.'

There was a silence.

'Well, I'll be off then, I suppose,' Dara said awkwardly.

'You enjoyed France? It . . . it must have made you grow up a lot.'

'Yes, I got lonely a bit of course, I didn't really expect that. I missed everyone here. All the time.'

Another silence.

'Mam's very fond of you, Mrs Fine, she wouldn't be afraid you'd give her an old cold.'

To Dara's fright, big tears came into Rachel Fine's eyes.

Rachel went to her bedroom and sat in front of the dressing table mirror. She looked old and tense, she looked lined and pathetic. Methodically she removed her make-up, cleansed her skin, applied a gel that was meant to restore the cells and carefully put on her make-up again.

As she did the feathery strokes around her eyes, Rachel Fine began to wonder was she going mad. First avoiding her friend for days and then making herself up like a call girl to go and see a kind woman in a wheelchair who wouldn't notice if she arrived dressed in a pillow case.

Kate was a little prickly at first.

'I must say it's nice to see you. Dara will be glad to know you called.'

'I've seen Dara. She told me you were wondering why I hadn't been in.'

'I didn't send her with that message.' Kate's eyes flashed.

'I know,' Rachel said wearily.

The first silence they had ever known fell between them. Eventually Rachel spoke.

'It's no use, Kate, I'm empty, drained, there's no me to talk to. I'll go away, you've nothing to say to me, nobody has.'

Kate's eyes blazed with anger. 'I have nothing to say to you! Don't give me that. Take offence if you bloody want to, sulk, imagine yourself wronged, insulted in some way but don't give me that about my having nothing to say, I have a million things to say, to ask, to tell, to share. I'm not the one who slides past the door, I'm not the one doing the avoiding. I can't avoid anybody for God's sake. I don't have that little luxury any more.'

'I didn't think you'd be upset.'

'No of course not, what right has a vegetable to be upset? Poor old Kate, she's lucky she had anyone come and visit her at all.'

'Kate, you know . . .'

'I know nothing. I'm scared sick about this café I've talked them all into doing. I don't want to make John into some kind of gligeen doing party pieces for Americans, the next thing we'll have his cap on the floor and ask them to throw dimes into it. I don't want the boys to be serving cakes and potato bread in case their friends call them sissies. I don't want Michael to be besotted by Grace with her honeyed words and smiles. I don't want that bloody Kerry O'Neill raising his little finger and taking the clothes off my daughter, my beautiful Dara, and then throwing her aside . . . So now tell me about the wonderful trouble-free family life I have.'

'What's the worst bit?' Rachel asked suddenly.

'I think it's Kerry. He's playing her like a fish on a line. He'll have her as soon as he wants to, he's the kind that gets everything he wants, and doesn't care about who he hurts on the way.'

'You're right.'

'I'm so frightened, and I wanted to talk to you, and now you've turned against me too. I'm sorry to be such a fool.' Kate groped round ineffectually for her handkerchief and cried salt tears down her newly powdered face.

Rachel's eyes were full of tears. 'I couldn't come near you because I didn't want you to know how stupid I've been. I've done something so stupid you wouldn't believe it, I was too ashamed . . .'

'You don't have to tell . . .'

'It's Kerry . . . I've done something so stupid . . . so terribly stupid . . .'

Hand in hand the two women sat in the darkening evening and Kate patted the beautifully ringed hands of Rachel Fine, who told how she had put herself in Kerry's power.

Tony McCann did not have a bank account. But he had been in and out of this particular branch so often to get change, to cash cheques made out to him by other people, that he always regarded it as his bank. He had missed it during the strike.

He handed over the cheque for a thousand pounds.

'In the money, I see?' the cashier had said to him pleasantly.

'If it were all mine I'd be hundreds of miles from here on a beach sipping rum and Coca Cola,' said Tony McCann.

The cashier sighed and thought about it for a moment. 'How do you want the money?'

'Ten-pound notes, a hundred of them,' McCann said. He looked idly round the bank as she went away to verify the cheque. How did people work here five days a week for forty years? Surely they must all have been tempted to take a carrier bag of wads of fivers and run. It was remarkable that so few of them did when you came to think of it.

'Mr McCann?' It was a man now, a senior man in a suit, with a pinched-looking face.
'Yes?'
'There seems to be a problem about the cheque.'
'That's not possible.'
'I'm afraid so. It has been cancelled and reported stolen.'

'It's me. McCann.'
'Yes?' Kerry O'Neill's voice was anxious suddenly.
'The cheque doesn't work.'
'I don't believe you.'
'You'd better believe me.'
'The bitch. The stupid bitch.'
'You'll sort it out then?'
'I'll sort it out.'

'Mr O'Neill?'
Brian Doyle was hesitant. Patrick O'Neill was like a devil these days, even the most mild request was met by a bout of bad temper.
'Doyle?' He was curt.
'Mrs Fine wants to have a word with you.'
Once Brian had called Rachel by her first name, and that had not found favour either with his boss.
'Good, then I'm sure she will,' Patrick said.
'On the telephone,' Brian explained, as if he were talking to a child.
It had been as much as Patrick could do to stay sane when faced with the Irish telephone system. He had been assured that it was a European thing, not just Irish, but that didn't make it any easier to bear. He said he would make a mental note not to open a chain of hotels on the continent of Europe, and people had smiled at him indulgently. The eager American, hustle bustle. He knew what they said.
But if Rachel was on the telephone for him that meant he had to leave his office and walk across to Brian Doyle's headquarters, that was where the only phone link so far had managed to be installed.
Patrick moved quickly. He would not let Doyle see how annoyed he was to be summoned by Rachel, whom they all knew to be his fancy woman, to walk across the courtyard, through the Thatch Bar and over to those excrescences that Doyle called his headquarters.
'Yes?' he said curtly, watching Brian pretend to busy himself elsewhere in the cramped space.
'Can we talk?'
'Here?' He couldn't believe it.
'No. Anywhere. It's important.'
'Why didn't you come up here in the first place instead of having me walk half way round the country to tell me you were coming?'
'I don't want to come there.'
'I haven't time to go over to Loretto's.'

'No, I don't want you to come here either.'

'Is this a game of hide and seek, by any chance?'

'Please.'

'Where then?'

'Coyne's wood. At the far end up by the old ruined church on the small back road that leads to the Grange. There's a stile.'

'Jesus,' Patrick said.

'I'll leave now, I'll wait. You get away when you can.'

He held the receiver in his hand for a while and out of the window of Doyle's headquarters, through the clutter of the ledge, he saw across the Fern in the distance a figure come out of the door of Loretto Quinn's shop and get into a small green car.

'Thanks, Brian,' he said as he replaced the receiver.

'Lovely day for a bit of a spin out into the country,' Brian said.

Patrick gave him a look that told Brian that the wise man addressed no words at all to the great O'Neill these days.

Canon Moran was picking flowers near the stile up in Coyne's wood. That was all Patrick needed.

The old man looked up with pleasure as the American approached. This was a bonus for him, he liked a good chat.

Patrick looked at him thoughtfully. It was a good life being a country priest in Ireland. Canon Moran had all the respect and none of the work in the parish. He had baptized and married and buried people from the place for as long as anyone could remember. There was no way he would be sent away nor his honours stripped from him.

He could wander in a second childhood, collecting summer flowers.

'You know what you were asking me, about marriage to those who had never been baptized?'

Patrick tried to keep the maddened irritation out of his face.

'Yes, Canon Moran. It was just something I wondered about in the abstract. Like I sometimes wonder about the angels. You know, thrones and dominations and seraphim. I wonder why they'd have a VIP system in heaven.'

Canon Moran had often wondered about angels too, and particularly about guardian angels. He couldn't ever see on what basis the poor angels were given mortals to look after. Some angels must have had a very easy time and others a desperate job altogether.

Patrick wondered was he going to spend the entire morning debating guardian angels with an almost senile cleric who held an armful of daisies and heathers and some prickly yellow gorse. Still it was better than discussing marriages to infidels. He looked round wildly for any trace of Rachel.

The canon's old eyes may have been sharper than Patrick thought.

'Well, I won't hold you up, you're a busy man, Mr O'Neill, a busy man, a good man and a generous man. It's very heartening to know that men like you with all your worldly wealth still keep the laws of God.'

Patrick was rarely at a loss. But now he had no idea what to say.

Canon Moran filled the gap for him. 'And if ever you should need any further talk – just in the abstract of course – about the marriage of unbaptized persons who convert to the Catholic faith, then I know just the man in Archbishop's House. We were in the seminary together. He didn't end up in a quiet place like Mountfern, he's a big expert in canon law and there's nothing he doesn't understand about previous marriages contracted outside the Church or any other church which would be recognized as solemnizing a Christian marriage according to their own lights . . .'

'Yes, yes.'

'They would be entirely null and void and wouldn't need to be taken into consideration,' Canon Moran finished triumphantly.

'Well yes, that's good. I'll remember that if I need to think about it,' Patrick said.

'It would be good if you needed to think about it, Mr O'Neill. Life can be lonely at times, and we're all very pleased here that you've come back to the land of your fathers. We wouldn't want you to feel . . . well to feel a bit alone back there in that big place.'

For a second time Patrick was without words. He was touched by the old man, he felt a lump in his throat.

Again Canon Moran filled the pause. 'So I expect you'll want to be off for a bit to wander down there by the trees with all the climbing roses on them. They look so beautiful at this time of year, someone should make them into a calendar, I always think.'

The old man walked back towards the road and Patrick went slowly down to the trees where the roses did indeed wind around the big heavy trunks and the branches, and where Rachel sat on a fallen tree.

'How's Jimbo's singing career these days?' Kate asked Carrie.

'He's doing very well, he's going to cut a record,' Carrie said proudly.

'Is that a single or an LP?' Kate was well up in records from hearing the children talk.

'It's going to be an EP, ma'am. You know, the middle kind of one.' Carrie's face was shining.

'And does he like all this travelling around? I hear he was as far afield as Donegal.'

'Oh he likes it all right, Mrs Ryan, it's grand for him. But I don't like it all that much, to tell you the truth.'

Kate was sympathetic. 'And does he not suggest you go along with him?'

'He's always suggesting it, but how can I?'

'It's hard all right.'

'Well it is. You see he's never suggesting I go along as Mrs Jimbo Doyle, if you know what I mean. Just as Carrie.' She looked very glum.

'Suppose he got work round here, wouldn't that keep him at home?'

'But that's the point, there's plenty of work round here, with the hotel he could be working seven days a week. But he has his heart set on being a star you see, so the work is only interfering with it.'

'But if he got singing work, I mean. When the hotel opened.'

Carrie's face lit up. 'Wouldn't that be the makings of us. But Mr O'Neill thinks of Jimbo as a handyman, he wouldn't employ him as a singer.'

'I could have a word, maybe.'

'Oh ma'am, and if you were to say it to Mrs Fine, maybe Mr O'Neill would listen to her, too.'

'We'll see what we can do,' Kate promised, and Carrie went out to the kitchen and made a big dinner for Leopold in order to have somebody to celebrate with.

'Wouldn't it be great if poor Jimbo got a chance to do a turn over in Fernscourt when it opens?' Kate said to John.

'Less of the poor Jimbo, there was a bit about him in the papers on Sunday. He's doing fine.'

'Well then, it shouldn't be hard to get him taken on now and then in the Thatch Bar.'

'I wouldn't say he'd have time for that,' John said.

'What do you mean?' Kate couldn't follow the reasoning.

'We'll offer him a job singing in Ryan's Shamrock Café. If he's good then let him sing here, not have him across the river.'

Kate got a sudden cold feeling. There was a time when she was the one who would have thought up that plan.

'That's a better idea altogether,' she said dully.

'Of course it is.' He patted her hand.

'Dara will you give me a hand with these table napkins?'

'*No*, Mammy, *no, no, no.*'

'That's lovely, I must say.'

'I'll do anything but that, I hate hemming bloody napkins.'

'Do you think I like it?'

'Well, you've got nothing . . .' She stopped.

'Nothing better to do. How right you are. Sit in a wheelchair, give her some napkins to hem, stop her hands from becoming paralysed as well as everything else . . .'

'Oh Mam, really . . .'

'What do you mean, really? Really nothing. That's what you were saying, wasn't it?'

'It's not like you to be so sorry for yourself.'

'It's not like you to be such a selfish little madam.'

A pause. 'I'm sorry, and that *wasn't* what I was going to say . . .'

'What were you going to say?'

'I stopped but I'll have to say it now because the way you finished it is worse.'

'Well what was it . . .'

'I was going to say you've got nothing more important to do like I have, I want to . . . well, I want to be around a bit . . .'

Kate looked at her blankly.

'Sort of outside, you know, not in here putting hems on squares.'

'I'd like to be outside a bit too.'

'I know, Mammy, I know, but you've sort of had your life. *Oh God*, I don't mean that. It's so easy to say the wrong thing. I mean you've had this bit, the bit of hunting and deciding and doing things that matter.'

'Yes.'

'You don't understand.'

'I do. I've had the bit that matters. You haven't. Off you go, find the bit that matters.'

'Sometimes there's no pleasing you, Mam, do you know that? You get annoyed if we don't tell you what's going on, you get more annoyed if we do tell you. It's not just that you have all this . . .' Dara waved at the chair. They never used words like cripple or paralysed or invalid in the house. Sometimes, not often they spoke of the 'accident'.

Kate looked thoughtful, not annoyed, and not so sad either.

'I will do a bit of hemming, Mam, but not now, I want to be around, if you could know what I mean at all.'

Kate seemed to have recovered her humour.

'No, I do see what you mean. You must be around. But Dara, he may not be back for fun and games this time, he may have other things on his mind.'

'Oh, him?' Dara flushed and flounced a bit. 'I wasn't thinking of him.'

'Of course not, and even if you were why should you listen to me about him? It's just that I think he's here for a purpose this time.'

'God, you're very dramatic at times.' Dara was gone, mascara and lipstick in the pocket of her white jacket ready to put on when well out of sight of Ryan's Licensed Premises.

Patrick sat down on the fallen tree beside Rachel.

For a moment neither of them said anything. The wood smelled fresh and flowery. Canon Moran had tottered away, there was nothing to disturb them. Butterflies went in and out of the trees, and sometimes a bird rustled in some kind of activity. It was a peaceful place.

'We should have spent more time here,' Patrick said.

She smiled at him. Perhaps this might be a bit easier than she had feared. He had sounded so forbidding on the phone.

She twisted her hands together. 'It's so difficult to tell you this.'

He moved his cuff slightly so that he could see his watch. 'But I am going to hear it. Right, Rachel?' he said.

He had the smile she had known for so many years. It was the smile when someone was going to waste his time. But he owed them. So he would listen.

It was to that smile that she would have to tell her tale.

'Give me a large brandy will you, John.'

'Things must be bad over there if you're at the large brandies before lunch,' John Ryan said mildly, putting the glass in front of Brian Doyle.

'I'll be hiding it in a tea flask, I tell you.'

'Any one thing or things in general?'

'Who knows? Nothing would please him. He went off to meet your one up in Coyne's wood as if they were a pair of kids. That didn't last long, he's back inside there now with a face on him that would stop a clock.'

'It can't have gone well, the outing,' John agreed. 'Did Rachel come back with him or what?'

'Did she come back with him? Indeed she did not. Those two are like the things you see – you know, kind of statues of a man and a woman. When one comes out the other goes in, one means sun, one means rain. I saw them once somewhere. Blackpool I think it was.'

John laughed. 'Are they as bad as that?'

'Oh, God, John, the older people are the worse it hits them, this love carry-on. I think I'm too old for it myself and I'm years younger than O'Neill.'

'You'd better hurry up and marry that girl of yours in the town before someone else does,' John advised him.

'I don't want to be tied down. Men are miserable when they're tied down, they're meant to roam free, wild like nature intended.'

'It's easy known Mary Donnelly's over in the post office today,' John said.

'She is too, I went in to send off some forms for O'Neill that had been lying on his desk for a month and he wouldn't look at, but today he took the face off me about them, and there was the hatchet face standing behind the grille, snapping and barking at poor Fergus Slattery because there was too much sealing wax or something on his parcels. God, wouldn't a man want to be free, not tied to a woman who'd yap the arse off him.'

John was mild. 'I don't know, look at the people round here who are not tied to women – Jack Coyne, Fergus Slattery, Papers Flynn, O'Neill himself . . . You can't say that makes a flight of free birds, now can you?'

'Go on out of that. You've one of the few happy marriages around, and look at the thanks you got for that. I'll have the other half of that brandy now, if you don't mind.'

'It's just as well you weren't laying into the booze like this when the structure was going up,' John commented. 'Nobody would dare go into the place at all for fear of it coming down on top of them.'

'You could do yourself a favour, Eddie,' Jack Coyne said.

'What's that, Mr Coyne?' Eddie was suspicious now. He saw in his mind the shadow of Sergeant Sheehan at every turn.

'You know where they're digging out the road for the new entrance up on the road beyond. Where all the vehicles are parked?'

'Yes, I know it.'

'I was just thinking that if someone was to let the brakes off a couple of those vehicles, well there'd be an unholy mess when they started to move them again in the morning, there'd be people skating into each other and falling over . . . It would be great sport altogether.'

Eddie looked at Jack Coyne and remembered what his father had said about him. 'There's been enough accidents up in that place,' he said in a voice more courageous than he felt.

This was unanswerable. Jack was taken aback, but he rallied.

'It wouldn't have anything to do with anything like that, and wouldn't that make you of all people anxious to make sure that O'Neill doesn't get away with everything and ride roughshod over the whole place?'

'I'm out of it now, Mr Coyne.'

Eddie spoke in a cloak and dagger voice.

'You are in your bottom,' Jack said. 'Wait till I tell your father, not to mention Sergeant Sheehan, what you've been up to with cans of distemper.'

'They'd want to know who gave us the distemper, Mr Coyne.'

'I suppose O'Neill's paying you more than I am. That's what it always is in the end.'

'You never paid us anything, Mr Coyne.' Eddie was stung.

'So you're looking for something now, you mean little git.'

Eddie walked away in what he was sure was exactly the way the good sheriff would turn his back on the bad guys in town.

'Don't turn on the light.'

Rachel turned on the light and saw him lounging in her chair.

'Why did you do that?' Kerry asked. 'I wanted us to sit and have another nice talk in the dark summer evening. Maybe we could give you another drink and get you all amorous again. Hey, that would be good.'

'If you don't leave I will,' she said.

'You're not surprised to see me.'

'I got your message. I knew you'd be here sooner or later.'

'It's sooner because there was some little misunderstanding about that cheque you gave me.'

'I changed my mind. I cancelled it.'

'That was a very foolish thing to do.'

'Are you going?' she asked him.

'No, and neither are you. This is Mountfern, Rachel; this is not an apartment, it's a couple of rooms over a wayside store. It's where you have to stay because you aren't good enough to stay in the Grange, and because you'll never stay in Fernscourt.'

She moved towards the door.

'Wait,' he ordered. 'Just see how hopeless it is for you, Rachel. Write this cheque out again, with a note saying that it was all a mistake. *Do it.* Tell them that you apologize for the embarrassment caused to Mr McCann.'

'*Mister* McCann.' Rachel gave a great shout of mirthless laughter. 'That guy's never been called Mister in his life, and never will be. You don't frighten me, Kerry. I'm going for Patrick.'

'You're going for my father.'

'Of course I am. If his son is behaving like this and harassing me then he will want to be told.'

'Rachel, Rachel.' Kerry was languid. 'You live in a world of romantic movies and women's journals. You see yourself as the lady who has been slighted and insulted. Grow up. Look at the reality. You're a has been, you're a passed-over, middle-aged woman . . .'

'You're not hurting me.'

'I'm glad, because that's not my intention. I just want you to see how ridiculous you are. Once people can see the absurdity of themselves they are better off for it.'

He walked over to her, a writing pad and a pen in his hands. 'Write it Rachel. It makes sense.'

'I will like hell write it.'

'I'll tell my father what fun and games we had.'

'You can, I've already told him.'

Kerry's face didn't change. Not a muscle moved.

'He knows nothing happened between us.'

'Does he?'

Kerry looked down at the cheque. He looked back at Rachel. Something about his smile alarmed her.

'So could *you* explain why you wrote the cheque in the first place?' he asked.

He knew by her face that he had hit home. That was the one bit of her unsatisfactory conversation with Patrick in Coyne's wood that had been worse than all the rest put together. He had listened impassively from his seat on the fallen tree. The drink, the dizziness, the passing out, the tears, the hangover, the arrogant behaviour of Kerry going down to the shop in the morning . . . all those things were capable of some kind of explanation. But why had she given in so readily to the demand for money? Unless she had hoped somehow to pay him off.

It had seemed a long day to Dara since she set out that morning all dressed up and had the upsetting meeting with Jack Coyne.

People were behaving strangely in Mountfern today. Jacinta said that there was some terrible row between Mrs Fine who was Mr O'Neill's mistress and Mr O'Neill, and he had ordered her back to America because of something unmentionable she had done.

Dara asked what it had been but Jacinta said her lips were sealed.

Liam White said he thought Mrs Fine had got drunk and made a pass at Kerry.

Tommy Leonard said there was some scandal about Kerry, he had had breakfast in the wrong place. But he, Tommy, knew nothing about it and wasn't going to start speculating.

Mary Donnelly admired Dara's dress and said that now that she was so grown up why didn't she find herself some nice new friends instead of just staying all the time in the same little circle.

'It isn't a circle, it's just whoever is here,' Dara cried out in confusion.

Nobody had ever talked about circles before in Mountfern.

She came home confused and somehow let down. She sat with her mother for a little. Even Mam looked odd, she thought.

Kate looked with love at her beautiful daughter. Please may something happen that would take this dangerous Kerry O'Neill away from their place.

410

His deliberate cruelty to Rachel, his blackmail, the cynical way he treated everyone around him made Kate shiver.

'Are you all right, Mam?' Dara had noticed the way her body had trembled suddenly all over.

'I'm fine. Can you pass me that light wool stole . . . the new one Rachel brought me.' Kate settled it round her shoulders.

Dara had a look as if she were going to say something and had thought better of it.

'What is it?'

'Well, I don't suppose it's possible that Mrs Fine could fancy Kerry. I know it sounds ridiculous, but do you think it could by any chance be true?'

When Dara saw the look of shock and embarrassment followed by anger come to her mother's face, she knew that there must indeed be something in what awful horrible Jack Coyne had said. She wished with all her heart that she had never asked.

It was about the most revolting thing she had ever heard in her life, and the worst thing was that her mother had known about it already.

'What are you going to wear?' Fergus asked Kate.

'To the hotel opening?'

'No, Kate, to your court case.'

'I thought you said it would be settled before we *got* to court.'

'I did, and that's what Kevin thinks too, but we have to be prepared to go into court. All of us.'

'I didn't think about it.'

'Well *do* think about it.'

'Do you want me to paint my cheeks white and draw circles under my eyes?'

'No, but I don't want you dripping in all Rachel Fine's silks and scarves and jewellery either.'

'Fergus, I'm weary of this. It's a sum. It's a sum no matter what I wear. It's going to be ten thousand pounds at most and two thousand pounds at least. Isn't that what we all agreed?'

'That's what you and John and I and Kevin Kennedy and about three others agreed. It's not what those hotshots across the river and their big faceless insurance companies agreed. It's not what a jury of pudding-faced farmers and shopkeepers agreed. Not yet.'

'What do you want me to wear? I'll wear it.' She sounded tired.

'It will be over soon.' Fergus sounded tired too.

Dara's bedroom door was open, she was standing by a picture of Our Lady Queen of the May.

'What are you thinking about?' Michael asked.

'Should we pray for a lot of money next week or would that be wrong?' Dara asked.

'I don't know.'

'I was just wondering what you thought. You say so little these days, I thought you might have *some* opinion.' Dara was annoyed.

Michael was even more annoyed. 'I say very little, I have no opinions, *you* are the one who says nothing, you've this awful shrug, this awful way of just putting anyone down.'

'Ha ha.' Dara was bitter. 'I've often heard of people accusing others of the very fault they have themselves. *You* haven't a word to throw to a dog these days, yes even Leopold doesn't bother to come and snuffle at you any more, you might as well snuffle at a block of wood.'

'I only have to come into a room for you to leave it,' Michael cried. 'Look at you now, standing up already, off again. I don't care. I don't care one tuppenny damn, just don't go round saying that it's *me* that's being difficult, you're the one like a bag of weasels.'

'I'm standing because I haven't sat down yet, you great clown. I only asked you a civil question, a reasonable question, like should we be saying the thirty days prayer or not. It's the kind of thing we used to talk about once. When you talked, that was.'

Dara's lip was trembling a little. Michael saw it.

'I don't think prayers work,' he said. 'I'm not sure but I don't think they do.'

'I'm not sure either, but suppose they did, would it be wrong?' She looked very near tears.

'Why the sudden interest in money?' Michael asked. 'We never needed it before.'

'I know, I just thought it might help to make things better, stop everyone from being so worried. Stop all the terrible things happening.'

Awkwardly he put his arm around her shoulder. 'It's not as bad as that.'

'Sometimes it is.'

'I know, for me too.'

'Oh you! Everything's fine for you.' She sounded envious.

'Not all the time. I'll tell you sometime.'

'We never talk these days,' she said.

'Remember when we got into such tempers because we couldn't sleep in the same room any more!' Michael said.

'I still think you got the better room.'

'Yeah, but I got Eddie and Declan.'

She smiled at him. This was better, more like old times.

'Let's go out,' she said. 'It's the last day of freedom. We'll go to the tunnel.'

'It's such a sunny day . . .' Michael began.

'Oh come on, it was always a sunny day when we went to the tunnel.' She looked eager.

With great misgivings Michael agreed. They walked along River Road past Loretto Quinn's at the very moment that Rachel came out, in her cream linen suit with its cream and brown blouse.

She stopped when she saw them. Uneasily.

Dara stopped too.

Rachel spoke first.

'Can I give you a ride?' she asked.

'No thanks, we're just going for a walk,' Michael answered.

412

Dara said nothing.

'Well, if you're sure . . . ?'

Michael looked at Dara, waiting for her to answer. There were no words so he had to speak again.

'Honestly, thanks. It's our last day of the holidays.'

'Yes, the last day of the holidays,' Rachel repeated. 'You will never forget this holiday . . .' Her eyes went towards the big bridge. 'Nobody knew it was going to turn out like this.'

She got into her green car and drove away.

'Why were you like that?' Michael asked.

'Like what?'

'You know.'

'I can't tell you. Not yet.'

'All right.' He looked disappointed, Dara noticed. Perhaps she would tell him in the tunnel.

Miss Hayes had gone to Dublin. There were a lot of things she had to do. There was the matter of her passport, and her traveller's cheques. There were formalities about her ticket with a travel agency, a meeting with some distant cousins, and she wanted to buy material to make a few nice suitable garments for the journey. Miss Fine had been very helpful about the need for pure cotton, and avoiding synthetic fabrics. Mr O'Neill got her a lift to the town and she would take the day excursion train from there.

Kerry came to the lodge to see Grace. He looked dishevelled and scruffy.

'I wish you didn't behave like this, Kerry, like someone on the run. So I know you and Father had some big row again, and nobody ever tells me. Grace isn't meant to know anything upsetting . . . but he hasn't thrown you out, it's you who are making the big drama out of it.'

'It's a bit complicated. I just have to sort things out and then it will all be fine. I don't want to be at home, not until things are settled.'

'Can you tell me about it?'

'No, Gracie. Not yet.'

'Kerry, where are you staying?'

'I'll tell you eventually, honestly.'

'You're so jumpy, you said you wanted to talk to me about something. What is it?'

'Gracie, you believe that everything's marvellous. Everyone's good and all things are going to end happy ever after.'

'I don't believe that, but I only concentrate on things that make me happy. You concentrate on things that make you miserable, like fighting with Father and only seeing the old fussy side of Miss Hayes. She'd be so pleased to do all your clothes for you . . .' Grace shook her head in wonder that Kerry couldn't see the easy route to everything.

'I have to go out, there's someone I have to meet, then I'll come back, and you and I will talk about plans and the future and you can lecture me to your heart's content.'

They were barely into the tunnel when Dara felt at peace. She had been happy here with Michael like they had been happy when they played in the ruins of Fernscourt.

'You know, there are plenty of these tunnels, we used to think this was the only one in the world,' she said.

'For us it was,' Michael said.

They walked along the narrow passage to their special room. Dara chattered away more easily than she had done for a long time.

'It looks different,' she said.

'Of course we haven't been here for ages,' said Michael.

They lit the candles in the old rusty candelabra they had found on a dump and polished.

The place was full of shadows and shapes, as it always was.

But Dara saw that there were bunches of grasses tied in a way that they never had them before. She saw there were cushions that they used to keep on the floor as seats all piled up on the broken couch. She knew instantly that this was not the way they had left it.

She knew that Michael had brought Grace to the tunnel. Her heart turned over at the betrayal.

She decided not to make an issue out of it. There had been too much drama. But she wouldn't tell him about Mrs Fine and the terrible story that she knew was true. She couldn't trust him any more.

So they talked lightly of other things. They talked about school tomorrow. And they talked a little about Mam's case next Thursday. When they would both be in their classrooms trying to concentrate on their work.

Dara fought down the feeling that her twin brother had been disloyal. She tried not to think of him in this tunnel with Grace. She thought he looked a bit edgy and worried, as if he had seen something that was upsetting him, but since he didn't say what it was, she didn't ask him.

Papers Flynn said to Sergeant Sheehan that it was going to be a cold winter, he had heard that as a fact.

'The winter is months away,' Sergeant Sheehan said, wondering what this was leading up to.

'There's a very nice kind of a shed behind the presbytery, a place where no wind would come whistling through at all, if a person was to want a bit of shelter.'

'The very thing for a bit of shelter,' the sergeant agreed. 'Unless of course you'd be lifted out of it by some housekeeper that isn't herself a person of the cloth at all.'

'That would be a hard thing if it were to happen. I just mentioned it in case anyone would think of making it their headquarters,' Papers explained.

The sergeant nodded sagely.

Papers was getting old. There was a time when he would take his chances in anyone's shed. His main priority in life was to avoid being organized. But now he found battles hard to fight. This was his way of asking Sergeant Sheehan to square it with Miss Purcell and the clergy that he could live there when the cold weather came.

Patrick said that he didn't mind if the rest of the hotel wasn't finished for another decade, he wanted his own suite completed and ready to move into this week.

'That wasn't on the schedule,' Brian Doyle was unwise enough to say.

'Your schedule, Doyle, should be published and bound and sold, it would be the comic best-seller of the year.'

It was totally impossible to insult Brian. 'That might well be right but we'll have to take men off other work to sort it out for you. It's not just getting it ready, it's making it so that we don't have to traipse through it all the time.'

'That would be very acceptable,' Patrick said with heavy irony. 'Not to have this army of craftsmen you employ traipsing through my quarters. Yes, that would be a great bonus.'

'When do you want to sleep here?' Brian was practical.

'Tomorrow night.'

He wanted to be resident in the hotel before the compensation case began. He wanted to be well out of his son's way. It was becoming increasingly obvious he should be in his own place. At once.

He walked around the unfinished set of rooms that were to be his new home. Three bedrooms, two bathrooms, a sitting room, a study and a small kitchen.

The main rooms faced the Fern and were on the first floor of the house. He hadn't wanted a kitchen but Rachel had insisted. He wouldn't always want hotel food. There might be times when Grace would want to cook for the family. It was good to have a place where they could close the door and leave the hotel to get on with itself.

His study was the biggest room. Two walls were lined with shelves. Rachel said they could get antique furniture later, visit auctions in big country houses maybe, but for now he should have space for his papers and his books.

Had she ever seen herself with him there, he wondered. There was no hint ever in her suggestions, that she might join him in this lifestyle. No room for her clothes was ever taken into consideration. Instead she had urged him to fit out rooms for both Kerry and Grace from the outset so that they would always consider it their home.

Grace had been busy throughout, deciding where she wanted her closet, her bureau. Kerry's room, though it existed, had not been furnished or discussed, it was now an official dressing room.

Brian accompanied Patrick on his tour of inspection.

'Tomorrow night,' he repeated in the tone that he would use to soothe a dangerous drunk or someone who was both soft in the head and violent.

'Good.' Patrick deliberately misunderstood the tone, and averted his eyes from the open floorboards, the electric wires and cables still loose from the wall.

The windows were smeared with squiggles to show that there was glass in them, and there were heaps of wood shavings where the carpentry was still in progress. Furniture in crates stood in the corridors.

Patrick smiled at it beatifically.

'As long as I have my own little place here, Doyle, I'll be fine,' he said.

'I often think, Mr O'Neill, God forgive me, that if you'd come home and built yourself a nice bungalow on this site you'd have saved yourself and everyone else a lot of trouble.'

'How unselfish you are, Doyle. Imagine thinking that you could have passed over the entirely disproportionate wealth I have put your way, not to mention all the extra you made on the side.'

He clasped Brian warmly by the hand and patted him on the back at the same time.

'Tomorrow around six o'clock I'll move in. Come and have a drink with me here to celebrate.'

'I will, Mr O'Neill, I look forward to that. I was always a great fan of *Alice in Wonderland* myself.'

Rachel's choking feeling in her throat returned as soon as she got into her car and drove away from the twins. Dara had been filled with scorn and hate.

And no wonder. A girl of barely sixteen, in love for the first time with a handsome boy who probably filled her head with lies and false assurances. And then the town is saying everywhere in whispers that he has slept with her mother's friend.

No wonder those dark eyes blazed with contempt and hurt.

Rachel remembered those days in June when she had got very close to the girls. She had loved the elder-sister role. That was all part of a celtic mist of fantasy now.

But it wasn't time for self-pity yet, she must get into the hotel, get her business done, and be on the road as soon as possible.

If she were to have any tatters of dignity left over the whole incident then she must keep calm and workmanlike until she was well out of sight of the cast of interested spectators.

She parked her car and walked purposefully up the hotel steps in search of Jim Costello.

They had run into a problem over some of the Irish-linen panels. It was proving difficult to get exactly the same shade of dye in each batch. Young Jim Costello had understood the matter at once. It was a question of deciding whether to attempt to get them all the same or to have deliberately different toning shades.

Together they had walked the public rooms, climbing ladders and dropping swathes of material.

Jim wanted this hotel opening to stagger his rivals and quite possibly his future employers or backers. Rachel knew that he was as eager and keen as anyone to get it right.

Eventually they agreed that it would be gradings of colour. They had to do this in case some wall panels were to fade in the sunlight and could never be replaced exactly.

It would mean another visit to the small linen mills.

The workmen saluted her on her way out to the car. They had respect for her since she never threw her weight around and had a quick smile, but didn't stop to bore them with woman's kind of chat.

Leaning against her small green car was Kerry.

'What are you doing?'

'Waiting for you.'

'You've waited in vain. I'm just leaving. Excuse me . . .'

She tried to get past him. He did not move.

She turned around and walked purposefully back up the steps. Kerry ran after her; it was as if he knew that she was heading straight for his father.

'I'm giving you one last chance,' he said.

She didn't stop. He was beside her now.

'Look at this house, Rachel, this is your one chance to have it all, it's what you gave your whole bloody life for, isn't it? Don't throw it away. Write that cheque out. This minute. Or I tell him everything.'

'Come with me and we'll tell him together.' She was heading for the staircase.

'I have to have the money. McCann's people are very angry with you and with me because of you. These guys aren't people you play around with.'

He stood in front of her barring her way up the stairs.

'*Will* you get out of my way?' She raised her voice so significantly that the workmen all stopped whatever they were doing and nudged each other. A barney between O'Neill's woman and his son in full view of everyone was worth watching.

At that very moment Patrick O'Neill appeared on the landing at the top of the stairway. He took in the scene in a second and saw the gawping faces looking at the unexpected floorshow.

He did the one thing guaranteed to end the excitement and to wound more seriously than any other action he could have taken. He looked at them both dismissively and walked past them without addressing a word to either of them.

Most of the journey to the weavers was on a good straight road, which was just as well. Rachel drove with minimum concentration. Her eyes blurred over sometimes and she had to blink hard to clear her vision.

For no reason at all she thought of a little old man who was in the garden of the Haddassah nursing home, a psychiatric home for elderly Jewish clientele. It was the home where Rachel's mother had died. The old man sat in the garden looking almost unbearably sad. Once Rachel felt compelled to ask him what was upsetting him so much.

'I'm not mad, you see,' he had said to her resignedly. 'I'm as sane as you or any other visitor. My nephew put me in here because he wants to steal all my inventions and pass them over as his own. But it *sounds* such a mad thing to say, that it only gives everybody further proof that I am indeed mad.'

She had been struck at the time by the logic of the old man's argument. But she had only shaken her head sadly and marvelled at how sane the very far from sane could sound.

Today, driving across Ireland in the late summer sun, pausing sometimes for a flock of sheep, a herd of cattle, or on one occasion for a great group of young laughing nuns who were going on some kind of outing, Rachel Fine remembered the old man and wished she had been more sympathetic to him.

Grace was startled to see Kerry looking so wild when he came back to the lodge.

'I've just seen myself reflected in the window and you are quite right, I do look a wreck. Listen, I'm going to clean up. Grace, can you put all these newfound cooking skills to advantage and fix me some eggs. Then we'll talk.'

She heard him singing in the bathroom and her face brightened as she went happily to the bright sunny kitchen of the lodge.

She would be sorry to leave this little house in the middle of all the trees. She would miss the pleasant company of Miss Hayes, and her bedroom where the small brown rabbits often hopped up on her window sill and snuffled their noses against the pane.

Still, it would be exciting in the hotel.

Jim Costello had told her that there was nothing as heady as a successful hotel, the place buzzed with activity and you got the feeling that it was alive twenty-four hours a day. She smiled at the memory.

He had added that every hotel needed a really beautiful woman to be at the centre of it, and now Fernscourt was going to have that as well as everything else.

Kerry came out, his hair damp, wearing clean white trousers and a white sweater.

'That's more like it,' he grinned at her. 'Now tell me all that you've been doing.'

Grace felt that it was he who should do the telling. She had been doing nothing, she said.

'Nothing? Every day, all day, off on a bicycle with young Ryan. Don't tell me you've been doing nothing.' His eyes were very bright.

'Well, you know, we've been fishing and talking and just fooling around.' She giggled apologetically.

His face looked hard somehow. 'What kind of fooling around?'

'Oh heavens, you know. Nothing too serious.'

'It had better not be serious, it had bloody better not be.'

'What do you mean?' She was frightened.

'You're not to be made cheap, you're not to throw yourself away on some kid from a pub who's wet behind the ears but who knows like any animal what he wants and will do all he can to take it.'

Grace jumped up, eyes blazing. 'Michael is *not* an animal. I will not have you speak of him like that.'

'Not until I know he has done you no harm, that he hasn't forced you to do anything you shouldn't have done.'

'I've done plenty of things I shouldn't have done, like you have as well,' Grace cried with spirit. 'Anything I do with Michael I do because I want to.'

'You must not want to, he must not make you *want* to. You're so young, you're my sister, you aren't to lie down for any country hick.'

'It's not like that.'

'It had better not be.'

'And what about you, you and Dara, why is nobody saying anything to you about all this?'

'That's different.' He was dismissive.

'But why is it different?'

'I'm a man, it's different for men.'

'Dara isn't a man.'

418

The phone rang sharply into the silence between them.

'That's Michael,' Grace said in relief. But it wasn't, it was a man with a Northern Ireland accent to speak to Kerry.

Kate sent Declan away when she heard that the doctor had arrived.

Martin White smiled at the youngest Ryan, who hadn't yet turned into a hooligan like his brother Eddie.

'Will you miss them when they go back tomorrow, or will it be a bit of peace for you?' he asked.

'I suppose I'll feel they can get up to less trouble inside the walls of the convent and the brothers' than roaming wild round this place,' Kate sighed.

'I know, my two have gone cracked on this riding nonsense, hard hats and crops and boots, and God knows what else, you're lucky you were spared that. You're pale, any pains and aches?'

'I've an upset stomach, I seem a bit nauseous somehow but I think that's only tasting all this food we're going to be offering in the café . . . if there's anyone to offer it to.'

'Do you need to take this on?'

'It's take this on or go under.'

'The compensation maybe?' he suggested tentatively.

'It won't keep a family, Martin. Oh Lord God how I'm dreading Thursday, the palms of my hands start to sweat at the thought.'

Dr White said that he would give Kate a mild tranquillizer on the day of the case.

'Will it make me dopey and stupid-sounding?' Kate wanted to know.

'Nothing could do that.' Dr White was amused.

'Maybe I don't need any tranquillizer. I'm slow enough already.' She seemed very down.

'It will take the sharp edge off the anxiety, that's all. It won't affect your powers to say yes or no to a million pounds.'

'I'm not the one saying yes or no, it'll be John, John and Fergus.'

He looked at her sharply. In the last few weeks she had seemed less alive to him. It was hard to pinpoint exactly what it was.

'I know I don't have a degree in psychiatry, but is there anything wrong, Kate? Anything you want to talk about?'

She gave him a brittle smile. 'Anything wrong apart from being paralysed, in a wheelchair for life, possibly losing all our trade to a bar across the river? No, not much.'

Dr White was often accused of having a poor bedside manner. He was unsparing of his time and energy to help a patient but he was never at hand with the coaxing and condolences that a lot of the parish felt they needed from time to time.

He stood up and prepared to leave. He didn't even acknowledge what Kate had said.

'See you on Thursday,' he said briefly and was almost out the door when Kate called out.

'Martin. I'm sorry.'

'Why should *you* be sorry?' He had his hand on the door.

'I mean for being a smart aleck. You were being kind. There *is* something wrong. But it's very hard to say it.'

Dr Martin White stood sympathetically waiting for her to find the words. He would have stood there all day and all night if necessary and Kate knew it.

'I'm not in charge any more. I'm not a person who decides things . . .' She fumbled with a lace-edged handkerchief. The doctor looked at her, trying to get her to say more.

'It's just that there's no *me* nowadays, as if I'd lost my personality or something.'

He was blank in his lack of comprehension. 'I don't know what to say to you except that you must be half cracked. Aren't you a legend for miles around, and as for being in charge, wouldn't you buy and sell the rest of us? They say it was you that thought up that café idea. Bound to be a gold mine.'

Kate knew when there was no more to be gained. She thanked the doctor, said that it must be just an attack of nerves over the court case, and told herself again that it was a strange irony that the only one in the whole place who understood what she felt was Patrick O'Neill. She had a very strange dream about Patrick that kept coming back to her because it was so vivid.

She dreamed that she was in Coyne's wood with him and he had taken out a huge shovel and started to dig a great hole.

It was a grave, he said, like one of the mass famine graves and it was for all the people in Mountfern. They should have died over a hundred years back at the time of the Famine but they had gone on living by mistake. That was why he had come back, to finish the job properly.

In the dream she asked him if anyone would be saved, and he had said only Kate herself could go free. She wasn't from this place to begin with and so if she ran now she could go back to where she came from. She had tried to run and had woken in terror with none of the usual joy that a dreamer would feel waking from a dream like that. Because asleep or awake Kate Ryan would never run through the wood, and she kept seeing Patrick's face smiling sympathetically at her. He seemed to be across a room as he smiled. A courtroom.

Michael and Dara walked quickly across the bridge.

They told each other they had better hurry to Leonard's to buy exercise books and pencils for tomorrow. They ran past the Presbytery and up Bridge Street. They weren't really hurrying to buy their stationery, they wanted to be over the bridge before the thoughts started to come as they always did.

And because in their different ways they wanted to think about the tunnel.

Dara thought that if Michael had taken Grace there, then she too could have used it. It made her furious to think that this was why she had lost Kerry O'Neill, because she wouldn't trust him, she wouldn't love him properly. And she had wanted to so very much. Why hadn't she told Michael ages ago that she would take Kerry to the tunnel?

There it would all have been safe and it would have been like a home.

Grace and Michael obviously thought so, she told herself bitterly, remembering the sofa piled with cushions.

Michael had thought they would never leave the tunnel. Everywhere he could see signs of Grace and he being there together. It was astonishing that Dara hadn't noticed. But what was alarming him much more was what he had seen. The cushions on the sofa like that, he and Grace hadn't put them there, and there was a rug that didn't belong to them. There were matches and some orange peel.

Somebody else had been in the tunnel.

He could not believe that Grace would have told anyone else. And it wasn't possible to believe that she might have been there with anyone else.

Jim Costello spoke briefly to Brian Doyle.

He said he knew O'Neill's demand to have the rooms ready was ridiculous, but for God's sake let Doyle not forget who was paying their salaries.

'He's more nervous about the bloody court case than he is about sinking his whole fortune in the hotel,' Jim said wonderingly.

'Wouldn't you think he'd have more sense?' Brian had little time for finer feelings.

'In a way I can see what he means. The whole place is waiting eagerly to know what will happen. If Kate Ryan doesn't get enough the mood will turn against him fast. It won't be easy for him to carry on here.'

'Ah, that's only a small problem compared to the troubles he has with his family life . . .'

Jim hadn't got where he was by being a gossip. 'I don't know much about that, I only see the work side of him.'

'You do in your arse. You know like the rest of us know that his son had a go at his woman, and if the place doesn't go up in fireworks over that, then it never will.'

'At least his daughter is no trouble to him,' Jim said primly.

Brian knew everything. 'I saw you had your eye peeled in that direction. Sound man,' he said approvingly.

'She's only a child, but are we going to see your fiancée Peggy at the opening?'

'Probably,' Brian muttered without any great enthusiasm.

'Good, make sure she's on the invitation list, they're posting them next week.'

'Isn't it a miracle that it's going to open at last?' Brian looked around him in surprise.

'Take that look off your face, Brian, people will think you're surprised it's staying up. That's not good for business.'

Kerry was listening carefully to the voice at the other end of the phone.

The lady had told the bank that after all she had made a mistake, the cheque had not been stolen.

Kerry let out a great sigh of relief. Rachel must have seen that it was pointless.

He had never felt so relieved in his whole life. But the voice on the phone told Kerry that his problems were far from over. They were only starting. There would be no criminal proceedings since the cheque was no longer deemed stolen. But it was still stopped. It could not be cashed.

Kerry was still to find his thousand pounds.

'It's impossible,' he said in a thin unnatural voice.

There was a silence.

Then he was given a proposition. He could do something for them instead. Repay his debt that way.

His whole body strained and his knuckles were white as he waited to hear what they wanted him to do.

It would involve storing some merchandise out of sight in a very safe place. A place that nobody knew about.

Kerry could feel his muscles relaxing. He knew the exact place.

Michael went to the lodge that evening.

Miss Hayes had come back on the excursion train from Dublin, she was showing her materials to Grace.

'I'd make you a dress for the opening, but you'll want something smarter from the shops,' Miss Hayes said.

'Why can't you wait till the opening?'

'The ship sails before.'

Michael seemed impatient and not anxious to join in the conversation. Grace eventually seemed to understand and went outside with him.

'Did you tell anybody? About the tunnel, did you tell anyone else?' His eyes looked wild.

'Why? What's wrong?'

'I went there today with Dara. She didn't notice we'd been there but it's all changed, someone else has been there, maybe even sleeping there.'

Suddenly it clicked in Grace's mind. Of course that was where Kerry had been spending the nights.

Michael had made her swear she would tell nobody, but she had told Kerry the last time he was home from Donegal. She hadn't thought it mattered. Not Kerry.

Looking at Michael's face she realized it did matter.

'No,' Grace said. 'Of course I didn't, you told me not to tell anyone, didn't you?'

Dara walked in Coyne's wood. She didn't expect to see him, and she didn't want to see him.

But he was there, as some part of her knew he would be. Because she didn't feel very surprised.

He looked happy and relaxed, not strained as he had been before.

Dara said nothing. She stood there in her yellow and white candy-striped dress with the big artificial yellow rose pinned to it. Mademoiselle Stephanie had given her that when she was leaving France, that and a wink of complicity.

Tomorrow she would go back to school, and this strange summer would be over. There was no birthday party planned for the twins this year. Their party room was a café now, and the date was almost coinciding with their mother's compensation case.

She looked at him levelly.

He put his head on one side and smiled.

Dara would not smile back.

'What is it? Tell me.'

'You know. The whole town knows.'

'I don't.' He was innocent and bewildered.

'Mrs Fine.'

'She's pathetic,' he said with scorn. 'She is quite pathetic. You know that she fancied my father for years, he got tired of her and now she made . . . Well, it's too much to talk about really.'

'No it isn't.'

'Well, she made some silly advances at me, she got all drunk and slobbery, and crying, and saying she loved it here in Mountfern and these are her type of people and why couldn't she stay . . .'

It sounded familiar and likely from Mrs Fine's conversations with Dara's mother. From what she had overheard and picked up in the past.

'And then she became silly. Well, it's gross, and I had to untangle myself, and put her to bed. I went back the next morning to see that she hadn't done herself in or anything, and I got her breakfast and because I did these uncharacteristically nice things the whole place says I'm leaping on her.'

Dara looked at him. Willing it to be true.

'I mean, Dara, look at me. Am I the kind of guy who would go for a woman of that age, a little tubby Brooklyn Jewess? It's ludicrous.'

He was so handsome, he was not the guy to go for a woman old enough to be his mother.

'Are you going to say anything to me or will you stand there all day just repeating accusations?'

'I don't know.'

He looked hurt and bewildered.

Dara spoke. 'When I was in France I saw these fireflies. I didn't know what they were, they were like little teeny weeny fires in the evening. I asked Madame what they were called. She said "mouche à feu". They used to make me pronounce words so that I'd get it right. I kept saying it, "mouche à feu, voici la mouche à feu". Firefly, firefly. And I thought of you. I thought of you every time.'

He took her in his arms, and she laid her head against his chest. She could hear his heart beating.

Dara spoke almost dreamily. 'I found out why we don't have them in Ireland, I asked and now I know. They're sort of exotic fireflies, and Ireland is too cold and wet and windy for them. They wouldn't survive here. They wouldn't survive at all.'

Grimly and with far less pleasure than he thought that he would feel, Patrick O'Neill moved into his hotel. He decided to do it without ceremony, without any marking of the occasion. He would reserve all the festivity for the grand opening.

He moved his own things in and slept a night in the place he had created. He did not sleep well.

All kinds of unwelcome thoughts came to him, dreams, and half dreams. He got up eventually and walked in the moonlight, as he had walked years and years ago it now seemed, when the place was a ruin.

The moon hadn't changed much, nor had the river that it shone down on. But everything else had.

CHAPTER TWENTY-TWO

Olive Hayes left Mountfern exactly the way she wanted to, in dignity and with style but with no razzamatazz.

For four years she had lived quietly in this family, kept their confidences and made no judgements about them. Now she would no longer be part of their lives.

Kerry barely acknowledged her departure.

She had known this would be the case. She was no longer of any use to him. There had been a time when he had been charming, but charm was a currency, no need to spend any of it on Miss Hayes.

She felt a great sense of peace and achievement, and no last-minute regrets about leaving. It was what she had always planned.

Mr O'Neill's generosity made it possible to come back if things did not work out. She was letting her little house in the town to a young couple with a baby. They paid a small rent and would continue to put that into Sheila Whelan's post office for her.

When Olive Hayes called quietly and decorously to say goodbye to the people in the pub, she had a quick moment with Kate. Unlike most of the place who would have wished her luck in the compensation case, Miss Hayes had a different wish.

'I spent a lot of time, Mrs Ryan, wondering what to say about this and perhaps I am just an interfering old busybody, but perhaps, being confined to the house, you mightn't realize that Kerry O'Neill is a very dangerous young man.'

'Oh Miss Hayes, don't I know it,' Kate sighed. 'I know only too well how unstable he is. I did my best by sending her to France, but I can't banish the child from her own town for ever.'

'With respect, it's not that he's unstable, he is very aware of what he is doing and what he wants. He is totally self-centred. Perhaps with the help of God your daughter will see through him.'

'Get out there fast to those nuns and start them praying.' Kate smiled wanly.

Olive Hayes took her seriously. 'When I heard that he would be living in the lodge on his own, I did ask Bernadette to get some prayers said for a special intention.'

Kate held her hand for a long moment before Olive Hayes left Mountfern.

It was, as Michael expected, not nearly as easy to see Grace once she was in the hotel. The excitement of the new life, the attention and the fuss kept her busy all the hours that she had free from school.

They had arranged to wave to each other at certain times at night and make mirror flashes across the river.

Michael had worked out 'I love you' in morse code, but Grace said it was endless, and you'd be exhausted working out all the short long short longs of it just for one sentence.

Tommy Leonard seemed to understand. 'Wasn't it easier before girls?' he said to Michael.

'Like when there was just Adam in the garden of Eden?' Michael laughed.

'No, you know what I mean.'

'But you don't have any problems with Jacinta, she's there all the time, living on the other side of the street and everything.' Michael was envious.

'It isn't Jacinta I want, you thick oaf.'

Grace told Michael that her father was giving her a new dress for the opening. She was to go to Dublin to buy it. She was going to ask for the day off from school. Could Michael come with her and help her choose?

School had reopened and the notion of giving Michael a day off to go shopping with a girl in Dublin was about as acceptable to the authorities as suggesting a trip on a flying saucer.

'Come on, Mike, think of something.'

'But it's not just Brother Keane, he'd have to explain to Mam and to Dad and if I went without saying anything to them Eddie would hear and tell, or Tommy Leonard would. Lord, Grace, we can't just waltz off to Dublin as if we were adults.'

'We are adults – in lots of ways.' Grace pouted at him.

'Yes, well.' Michael reddened thinking of their last visit to the tunnel. He felt it was official to go there now, now that Dara had given permission. So he was more adventurous in his approach to Grace as a celebration of this.

'Don't be such a mother's boy,' she taunted.

That hurt. Especially since it was really his mother he feared most. He had the feeling that she worried about his friendship with Grace. And that she would be astounded to think he would even suggest the shopping trip.

That morning Kate had spoken for the first time to Dara and Michael about the upcoming court case.

She had said that she wanted them to give her all the support they could. What she needed was to know that they wouldn't go around blabbing or being silly about it. That they would be the model of good behaviour for just these few days, since the eyes of Mountfern would be on the whole family for a short time. Some people wished them to get a fortune, some wished them not to get anything significant in case it would prejudice the hotel in any way. But the truth of the matter was that there would be a respectable sum of money which would be placed in a bank for the children's education.

It was all upsetting having to go to court, but what would make it worthwhile was the knowledge that the Ryan children were working hard and would deserve any benefit that might come to them.

She had been quite solemn, and for the first time for a very long while she had sounded sad.

She had said that in many ways her own life was over, and that this was not something to feel bitter about, people's lives ended in different ways. But it would all have a meaning if her children were to be strong and to have a bit of class when faced with the wagging tongues and over-excitement of a small parish.

Michael and Dara had promised that they would not let her down.

Going to Dublin mid week on a train, telling Brother Keane a pack of lies – that would be letting her down.

426

Michael said he couldn't go and help Grace choose a dress.

Grace said that was all right then, she might ask Jim Costello was he going to drive to Dublin any time soon, she could get a ride in his car. Michael wasn't to give it another thought.

The District Court sat every week in the town, and cases that were of a higher jurisdiction or that were appealed were heard when the Circuit Court came four times a year for a period of three weeks each time.

At one stage there was a judge who had been interested in fishing who had driven out to the Fern each evening after the summer sessions and sat on his little stool looking for all the world like an old tramp. He and Fergus Slattery's father had struck up a friendship without either ever knowing the other was involved in the law, so great was their interest in the fish that swam the Fern and the methods of taking them out of the river.

Nowadays with better roads and better train services the barristers and judges didn't spend long in the town. They rarely came as far as Mountfern.

Kate and John Ryan were surprised to see Kevin Kennedy come into the pub the night before the case.

'Fergus didn't say you were coming,' Kate said, flustered.

She moved the wheelchair in her quick agile way back over the ramp and they beckoned him into her big green room. How right it had been to make this room into a proper sitting place for her. Seeing that she was going to sit for the rest of her days it made it much more bearable to sit in pleasant surroundings and not to apologize for wherever you were.

John got Mary to take over his place pulling pints. Most of the clientele would know who Kevin Kennedy was anyway and what it was about.

'Good luck and get them a fortune,' said one man as Kevin squeezed his way past the counter.

'Luck is exactly what it's about,' he said, turning round, 'it has not a thing to do with what people deserve, or they would get a king's ransom.'

His serious voice startled the drinkers. They had expected some sort of joky answer.

'Fergus doesn't even know I'm here . . .' he began when they were in the room.

'Well, don't you think maybe . . .' John began.

'No no, I'm on my way to him, it's just that we've had an offer. A firm offer. Six thousand pounds. A yes or a no. That's what they say.'

'Yes,' said Kate.

'We must ask Fergus,' said John.

'What do *you* think?' Kate asked John.

'I don't know what to think. We could go into court and fight all day and come out with less but the fact they offer it at all twenty-four hours before the case means they think it might go further against them.'

Kevin Kennedy looked from one to another.

There weren't many consultations on his cases, usually it was a matter of working straight from the brief, from the case to advice. But when he had met the people involved in their houses, he had often felt his city prejudices against country people were confirmed. They were so often inarticulate, and often grasping. This time it was different. There was a gentle pace of life that he liked in Mountfern, there was a graciousness about this couple and their handsome dark-eyed children whom he had seen briefly.

There was a sense of repressed energy about the crippled Kate Ryan that gave her more life than most women who were able to walk and run. She was quick, opinionated and impatient, and she had had a long hard lesson in having to learn that she must lean on others. He liked the husband too. All very genial and easygoing on the outside, but he had a logical reasoning mind. Fergus Slattery had said the man was a poet too in a small way.

He felt involved with these people in a way he hadn't felt involved for a long time. He had been through every case reported: the factory worker who only this year had been awarded £3,000. The sum had been based on his earnings, and how much more he could have expected. He had been twenty-eight, he had lost an eye. Everyone had accepted that £3,000 was fair, he had been earning £14 a week.

There was an agricultural labourer in his mid forties. His injuries were terrible even to read about. He got £7,000. His case had included the plea that he would never be able to marry and have a family. The award was considered high. There was that woman who had spent four months in the special hospital in England. Her barristers had proved such mental anguish, the compensation was £7,000.

They were looking at him, as if he should know. And he didn't know. He couldn't tell them either what was fair or what would happen.

'It's very tempting to say that we'll take it,' Kate said. 'It's so tempting that I have to think it's the wrong decision.'

John had his hand on hers as he spoke. 'It would be such an easy way to finish it off. To say we'll take it and put it in the bank for the children to go to university maybe, or for rainy days which may well come this way.' He nodded his head across in the direction of Fernscourt, and Kevin Kennedy remembered the danger to their small business from the new hotel.

'So you'd like to refuse it . . .?'

'I think we shouldn't accept it too readily,' John said. 'I know that sounds like sitting on the fence . . . I'm not a gambling man and I'm not in the world of doing deals or bargaining, but I have this feeling you shouldn't accept the first offer. Am I right?'

Kevin was about to say there was no need to accept anything now as there would undoubtedly be time to do so tomorrow, but Kate spoke first.

'I'm sure you know how much more than just a mere solicitor Fergus has been to us. It's as if his own spine were broken.' She spoke clearly and without any sense of drama. She just wanted to be sure he understood how important the tall gangling country lawyer was in their lives.

'Yes of course, of course,' he murmured.

'So I suppose you will bring him in on this, won't you, and ask him what he thinks we should do. I don't think John and I should really make any decision without Fergus being here.'

'Of course. I just wanted to get a gut reaction. Sometimes a surplus of lawyers can confuse people rather than help.'

'Did you get a gut reaction?' Kate asked.

'Yes. You'd take anything, Mrs Ryan, anything not to have to face a court. It's your back, it's your legs, we should listen to you. Your husband is aware of all this but he's thinking about what you'll both feel years from now, and trying to take that into account. I'm with Mr Ryan, but then it didn't happen to me.'

Fergus said, as they knew he would say, that it was not enough.

Kevin Kennedy said that it was about what they could hope for from the jury.

Dr White said that was a lot of money, he had many patients with broken bodies after car accidents and they hadn't got a third of that.

Fergus said that they were dealing with multi-millionaires here, big foreign international companies with coffers of money which they guarded like misers and wouldn't give out to the people that were struck down and obviously deserving it.

John said that he knew he was a cautious man but wouldn't six thousand pounds go a very long way, and buy them everything they ever needed? And since no money would buy Kate the chance of walking again then maybe they should take this now and be done with it. But, then . . .

Kate sat very still as they talked.

They leaned over to make a point, they interrupted each other. Four men all wanting the best for her, and coming at it in their different ways. She felt curiously detached from it. As if up in the air looking down at them, the doctor, the solicitor, the barrister and the publican.

They talked themselves out at around the same time and they all looked at her.

'It's up to you in the end, Kate. Whatever you say, that's what we'll do.'

She looked slowly around the little group.

'Fight,' she said. 'I think we owe it to the children to do this for them. Let's fight to the finish.'

Kevin Kennedy said that he was going to spend the night in Mountfern. He had heard there was a delightful old-world place called the Grange. Everyone exchanged glances. What was wrong with it he wanted to know? Nothing, it was just that Patrick O'Neill stayed there.

'He's moved,' Kate said. 'He went into the hotel.'

This surprised the others, but then Kate always knew everything ahead of most people.

'That's fine then.' Kevin Kennedy was businesslike. 'I'll give them a call. If our friend Mr O'Neill has moved out, that's all right, then.'

It was a sunny morning.

'I don't know whether that makes it better or worse,' Kate said.

John had slept on the divan bed in her room. Not that either of them slept very much. He had got up to make tea twice. He pulled back the curtains over the glass doors to reveal Leopold sitting mournfully outside.

'If that animal lets as much as the smallest yowl out of him, I'll kill him with my own bare hands,' Kate said.

Leopold seemed to sense the danger. He raised his front paw hopefully as if someone might shake hands with him through the closed door.

She looked sleepy and anxious.

John stood beside her bed. 'Could you get another hour if I closed off the light again, and left you in peace?'

'No no. I'm too jumpy.'

'So am I. I can neither stand, sit nor lie.'

'What are you going to do?' She saw him pulling on a jumper over the shirt he had worn the previous day. He obviously wasn't going to get washed and ready for the court at this early hour.

'I don't know. I feel trapped in here, somehow.'

Something in her face made him realize how trapped Kate must feel all the time.

'Not that I'm going to go out or anything,' he said hastily.

'Take me out too.'

'It's only half six in the morning.'

'Come on, we'll go for a walk.'

He dressed her and she slid into her chair. Quietly they let themselves out the front door of the pub – they didn't go through the back yard for fear of waking Mary Donnelly.

The river was glorious in the September early morning. Leopold trotted with them, delighted with the chance of an early morning outing but staying at a respectful distance.

Up past the Rosemarie hair salon, its pink curtains drawn firmly.

'Do you think she's still at it?' John asked.

Kate laughed. 'Not at all, she's far too busy getting ready for American hairstyles, she even has books on how to do it so that they'd like it.'

'Oh, she always knew how to do it so that they'd like it,' John said. 'They tell me of course, I wouldn't know from any personal experience.'

And as they came back again to the footbridge and the day was about to begin for everyone else, they stopped and looked over at Fernscourt.

They could see Patrick O'Neill in his shirt sleeves at one of the windows on the first floor.

'It's a hard day for him too,' Kate said.

They looked across the river to the landing stage, up the path with its rockeries and shrubs leading to the great sweep where the drive came in. They looked at the steps up to the big house, the bedroom wings fanning back on either side, the workmen beginning to arrive in twos and threes.

And they saw Patrick standing still at his window.

He must have seen them too.

But because it was the day that it was, nobody waved at anyone else.

Rachel was coming to get Kate dressed.

They had been such friends for so long that nobody saw anything remotely odd about this merging of both sides of the case.

They had several differences of opinion about what she should wear with the simple grey and white dress which had been ironed by Carrie, and then done again by Dara and finally given a going over by Mary.

Rachel said no lady could be seen without gloves. Kate said only the gentry wore gloves round here.

Rachel said a little eye shadow made Kate look much more attractive. Kate said that a country jury would think eyeshadow meant she was the whore of Babylon.

'Stop making people into yokels, Kate, this is the sixties, they all move with the times here like everywhere else.'

Kate said she wasn't going to risk it. She had promised Fergus she would look demure.

They were ready far too early.

Rachel tried to distract her with tales that didn't have any bearing on what was about to happen.

That was harder to do than she had imagined. Almost all her conversation was related to Patrick or to his hotel.

'Grace is going to Dublin for the day,' she said, thinking this might be a fairly neutral road to go down.

'Don't I know!' Kate exclaimed. 'My poor Michael is distraught over it all. I told him that it was very vain of Grace to go miles and miles to buy *another* new dress when she has trunks of them, but that was the wrong thing to say. No criticism of the lady.'

'Princess Grace,' Rachel said.

'She *is* a bit of a madam, isn't she? But I'm prejudiced. Anyone who could lead Michael Ryan any kind of a dance should be in the darkest hob of hell in my view.'

'Perhaps she'll not get anywhere with the young hotel manager.' Rachel smiled at the wonderful partisan nature of Kate's reactions.

'I'd prefer if she tired of Michael really, and did it soon, so that both the twins could get over these glittering young O'Neills sooner rather than later.'

'Yes we'd all be better if we had got over the O'Neills early in life,' Rachel said bitterly.

Rachel looked very sad, and for the first time since Kate had known her she thought that her friend looked old. The life had gone out from her face. And when that vivacity wasn't there for all to see there were lines instead, lines that looked quite deep.

She took Rachel's hand in hers and stroked it silently for a moment. She hardly trusted herself to speak in case she said the wrong thing or that she started to cry.

'Stop it, quite enough self-pity,' Rachel said. 'It's your day of woe today, not mine. Do you feel all right?'

'Yes, Dr White gave me something to calm me down. I feel fine.'

'Have you been to the lavatory?'

'Yes, *and* I've hardly had food or drink pass my lips so I should be all right.'

They talked to each other through the mirror, each seeing the reflection of the other. It wasn't quite the same as talking face to face. You could be more indiscreet.

'Kate?'

'Yes?'

431

'He wants you to get a lot, you know that. He was delighted you refused the offer. He says . . .'

'No . . . please no.'

'You're my friend, you'll always be my friend, even when I'm an old lady in a home in Flatbush.'

'Of course I will.'

'When he's married to somebody with ten saints' names who had the good fortune to come from this one-horse town . . .'

'Rachel . . .'

'What loyalty do I owe him? He says you shouldn't take any less . . .'

The chair spun around. Kate's eyes were blazing.

'No, do you hear me, *no*. You must stop. If there's going to be any dignity, anything saved from this circus and farce that I'm heading off to, then the only way is to do it honestly . . .'

'I wasn't going to . . .'

'Yes you were, you were going to tell me what his side are prepared to go to. I can't know that, don't you see that? I must never know what they're willing to give.'

'It's just because you're my friend. I wanted the best for you,' Rachel cried, still bewildered by the intensity of it all.

Kate's voice lowered. 'I *know* you mean well, but can't you see, if I have any hope at all of living what passes as a normal life with this man as my neighbour across the river, with my son head over heels with his daughter . . . with us depending on him for our custom from his hotel . . . then how would I feel if I had seen his hand?'

'He's on your side, that's all I was saying.'

'I know, I know. Now please can I beg you to say no more than that. Now, Rachel Fine, can you kiss me goodbye and good luck?'

Rachel bent to kiss her in the chair. She put her arms around Kate and laid her cheek against Kate's thin cheek.

'May you always have the best of all possible things and even things that are impossible,' she said in a shaky voice.

'Haven't I you as a great good friend? That's worth a lot to me,' Kate said as she manoeuvred her chair to the door.

John and Dr White were waiting for her in the pub, Fergus and Kevin Kennedy would be already at the courthouse.

Rachel stood in the green room after Kate had gone. She didn't know if this was praying or not, but she went to the mournful picture of the Madonna, one she had chosen herself because there were a lot of green and blue hues in it and it went with the room.

She stood in front of it and looked into the big sad eyes of the picture.

'Please don't let them cheat her, don't let them talk her into a cheap deal. Go on, please. It's not much to ask. There are thousands of good things and bad things happening all over the place today. Let this be a good one for Kate Ryan. Please.

The morning was hot and heavy. Dara's mind would not stay on parsing.

'Come on, Dara, wake up. Subordinate adverbial clause modifying what?'

'What, Sister?'

'What is it modifying?'

'I'm not sure, Sister Laura.'

'You might be a lot surer if you looked at the book instead of outside the window, it isn't written in letters of fire on the Dublin Road. The clause, for your information, reads . . . Come *on* Dara, this is very simple if you just concentrate.'

'I know, Sister.' The girl's face looked wretched.

Sister Laura knew all about the case that was coming to court today.

'There's no better way of taming the language than this. You'll know for ever how sentences are constructed.' The nun's round face was eager to help the white-faced child.

'Who else knows . . . ?' Sister Laura decided to take the attention away from Dara Ryan.

'Sister! Sister!' A few of them waved their hands.

Sister Laura looked around the classroom to choose, and her eye fell on the empty seat where Grace O'Neill normally sat. The child had gone to Dublin for the day. Her father had asked permission.

'Grace will say she has to see the doctor. That's not true, she's going to buy a dress. But it's not as frivolous as it seems, Sister Laura. I want her to be out of Mountfern on the day of the compensation case, so I asked the young manager to invent an excuse to take her. It would be more diplomatic. More sensitive.'

He had been right, of course. He was a very good man. Not just because he had given them the money for the school hall or all that extra material for curtains that the Jewish lady had delivered. But he really was kind and out for people's good. Sister Laura couldn't bear it when she heard people speaking badly of him. It was only envy, envy of a man who had done so well and come home to spend his money where his father had been nobody. She knew that if the compensation had been up to him, he'd have given the Ryans all they ever needed. But of course it would have been very hard to live with for them, knowing that it was his charity.

Sister Laura's eyes turned to the holy picture which hung in the classroom, Our Lady of the Wayside. She looked into the sad eyes of Our Lady and made a quick prayer that she would ask her Son to give proper compensation to the Ryans. Then she said that she would parse the sentence herself and would like the entire class to give their undivided attention.

Brother Keane had warned them not to trifle with him today, he had a toothache. Nothing that was bad enough to mean he had to leave his charges and go into the town to the dentist, but certainly something that was bad enough to remind him of its existence every waking moment. He felt it was only fair to the boys to apprise them of this fact.

Michael wondered again and again where Grace and Jim Costello would be now. There had been no difficulty in her getting off school and she had said they were going to set out early.

Michael had cycled across the Grange early to wish her a good trip, she had come down the stairs all dressed up in a yellow flowery dress he had never seen before. She looked as fresh as a daisy . . .

'You look terrific,' he had said. 'You don't need a new frock at all, wouldn't that be lovely for the hotel opening?'

It had been the wrong thing to say. Still, she had been pleased he had cycled all that way to see her. She kissed him without his suggesting it. Just put both her arms around his neck and stood on tiptoe to kiss him, and at that moment Jim Costello's car had pulled up.

'I know we swore we wouldn't talk about the case,' she whispered to Michael.

'I know.' He swallowed.

'But whatever happens we'll still be as we are. And I hope your Mom gets a lot, I really do.'

Something in the way she said it made him feel put out. But perhaps it was the fact of that awful Jim Costello with his sickening smile sitting waiting for her. That must have been what it was.

The classroom was airless. A dying wasp beat uselessly against the window. Even if it got out it wouldn't last another hour. Michael wondered if he should finish it off now with his ruler.

Brother Keane was looking at him. Did he imagine it or was there some sympathy in the teacher's swollen face?

Today they were doing an exercise which the class hated more than anything. Brother Keane would ask them to speak on any topic for one minute. There were to be no ems or ahs. There was to be no trick-acting or imitating the speaker. The brothers hoped it would make the boys more articulate and able to express themselves. The boys hated it, and though never short of a word in the playground, they were struck dumb when asked to speak in front of the class.

'Michael Ryan. Give us the benefit of your knowledge and experience of the pike, a fish which abounds in our River Fern.'

There was a snort round the room. Either this was a trick question of Brother Keane's or else he was going soft. The pike was dead easy to talk about, they'd all been fishing for pike since they were old enough to be allowed near the water.

'What would you want to know about it, Brother?' Michael's face was anxious. 'Like there's so many kinds of ways to start.'

'Well, kindly choose one, and don't hold up the class any more.' Brother Keane's hand was on his face.

'Well, like any fish the pike needs oxygen, not for its lungs because they don't have human lungs or animal lungs even, they don't have any lungs so to speak of. Not lungs as we'd know them.'

'Could you tell us what they do have instead of what they don't, please. Start again.'

'Pike have to take in water through their mouths and in that water there's a bit of oxygen like there is in the air. And they let it out the gills. But that's what all fish do. So what's different about the pike? The pike has a bad reputation like a wolf has in the animal kingdom. They say he preys on the other fish, and lies in wait for them in the reeds on the river bank. But in a way that's all to the good because a pike is carrying out a function, he's making the river bed a cleaner better place. It's his nature to go for what he can. It's only ignorance, really, to condemn the pike, we'd all be pike if we could, and the world might be a better place if there were more pike in it ready to go out and scavenge for themselves.'

The boy's face was red and angry. Nobody had said a word against the pike. Not ever, to Brother Keane's knowledge.

Out in the yard earlier Brother Keane had heard voices raised about the court case which was being decided at this very moment.

The boy was said to be very friendly with the daughter of the house and it was probably a question of divided loyalties.

Brother Keane liked Michael Ryan. Compared to his younger brother Eddie he was like the Archangel Gabriel.

'That's very informative and well explained,' he said, to the mystification of the class. 'Now Tommy Leonard, may we have your discourse please on the benefits of the Rural Electrification Scheme.'

'Ah God, Brother, that's much harder than pike,' said Tommy Leonard, who had been discovering that life was very far from fair.

Mrs Daly asked Rita Walsh when would there be any news from the court house.

But Marian Johnson answered first, she said that it could be any time from eleven in the morning on. It might be settled outside without their having to go in. She knew this from the highest authority. A Mr Kennedy who was representing the Ryans had stayed in the Grange last night. A very pleasant man, from Dublin. He was going to spend a second night there no matter what the outcome. He said it was too far to drive back to Dublin, and the Grange was exactly the kind of place he had always wanted to stay in but never come across.

Marian patted her hair reflectively and Rita Walsh sensed another reason to bring Miss Johnson and her thin flyaway hair back on a regular basis to the Rosemarie hair salon.

Canon Moran and Father Hogan had been asked by several parishioners to pray for a special intention. And indeed to offer mass for that intention. Nowhere had the intention been defined.

The priests agreed that it must have to do with the court case, and that one side definitely wanted the Ryans to get a great deal of money and the others wanted them to get very little in case it would somehow offend O'Neill.

'It's a poser, isn't it?' young Father Hogan had said.

'Not at all, we will just pray that justice will be done in the courts today. That covers it all,' said Canon Moran, who had lived a very long time and understood almost everything.

'I'd better leave you and stop hiding here in this nice quiet place.' Sheila Whelan had drained the teapot.

'It *is* a nice quiet place. You were very good to settle me here.' Mary Donnelly spoke gruffly in her gratitude.

'Wasn't it lucky they got you, just when they needed someone? They'd never have survived without you.'

435

Mary hardly remembered that summer and its shock and sadness now. She rarely thought of the man who had let her down so badly. Even when she was condemning men in general the face of this one did not come easily to mind.

Sergeant Sheehan passed by as the women came out into the sunshine.

'Starting early, Sheila,' he said jokily.

'Lord, I've been discovered,' she laughed.

She looked thoughtful when he had gone.

'What is it?' Mary noticed her face.

'I don't know, I was tempted to talk to him there about something, but I can see I'm getting as bad as the rest of them.'

'What was it?'

'Probably nothing, but I saw a lot of activity over on the towpath. You know, beyond the bridge on the other side of the river. Lights in the middle of the night over there, and banging about.'

'What on earth were *you* doing on the towpath in the middle of the night?'

Sheila had been walking because she couldn't sleep.

She had heard that Joe had died. The nurse had let her know quietly, as she had asked.

She would go to no funeral in Dublin nor would she tell anyone but Kate Ryan of his death.

Still, it had been impossible to close her own eyes, knowing that Joe Whelan was lying in the mortuary of that Dublin hospital where they had all been so kind to him, and where presumably his woman would recover enough to go and pay her respects, and three of his four children would be with her. The fourth mightn't dare come back from England in case he faced charges.

It had been too hard to try to sleep, so she had walked instead.

'Oh, you know me, Mary, I'm as odd as two left shoes.'

'Maybe you imagined it,' Mary said.

'Maybe I did,' said Sheila.

Fergus felt his hands shaking when he started to shave so he had put down the razor immediately. He didn't need to come to the court spattered with blood. He wondered what would make them steadier. He thought absently of a small brandy and port, his father used to take that concoction sometimes when he had what was called a chill.

But Fergus rejected it. Warming and steadying it might be, but very soon he might need one every day before shaving, even before getting out of bed.

By the time he was ready to leave the house his hands had calmed down. He'd done a magnificent job on his face, he thought, not a nick anywhere, and he tied a firm knot on his dark grey tie.

He knew that Kevin Kennedy would barely comb his hair, and yet here was he – the poor country solicitor, an unimportant figure – titivating himself like a peacock. Like a medieval champion going to battle wearing his lady's favours.

God, let him be right, urging them to go on. Kevin Kennedy had said to him a dozen times that it was impossible to know with country juries, but then Kevin was a city man who always feared the country and was never at ease when milk didn't come from bottles and when land didn't mean small manicured gardens.

Fergus gave a wan wave across the street to Sheila Whelan before he climbed into his car and drove to the town. He knew she was the one person in Mountfern who would have the tact not to wish him luck as if it was all a bet on the two-thirty.

Please God let them get twelve thousand pounds. A sum that would see them right for the next fifteen years, until the 1980s. Let them get that. Let Kate know no more anxiety and fear.

Kate sat in the car looking out calmly left and right as they drove the straight road into the town. The September countryside was beautiful this year, it had been a good summer but not too dry. They passed through villages as small as Mountfern, but places with somehow more importance because they were on the main road. Of course that would all change soon. Already there were new signposts; they wouldn't be a little midlands outpost for much longer.

'I should come out driving with you more,' she said to John, who frowned furiously at the road. 'You went to all that trouble to learn to drive for me, and I hardly ever get into the car with you. From now on we're going to have grand drives together, the two of us.'

Martin White said gruffly that he hoped they'd be able to afford a better car than this one when the day's work was finished.

'I never thought of getting a new car, did you, John?' Kate was startled at the very idea.

'Lord, not at all, isn't this one fine for us and whatever we want to do in it?'

'Well, what will you do with the money?' Martin White had known them long enough and well enough to ask that question.

'The future, the children . . .'

'Shore the place up a bit . . .'

'Try to keep the business we have . . .'

'And maybe attract a few of the nobs that come to the place across the river.'

Suddenly they both laughed.

'We're like the twins,' Kate said, wiping her eyes.

They were driving up to the steps of the courthouse.

It was a big ugly building. Neither John nor Kate had ever been in it. Dr White said he had, a few times, and it was the most disappointing place you ever saw. From outside it was all pillars and steps and looked very imposing. But inside you wouldn't give it the time of day.

The Garda station was attached to one end, and the library to the other, so most people had some kind of knowledge of bits of the building anyway.

It was right slap in the middle of the town, otherwise they might have been able to pull it down and build something more suitable. Nobody would regret its passing, it was no national monument. It came from a time when justice was administered by the English anyway, so nobody would have any sentimental attachment to it.

But to take down the courthouse would mean dismantling the town. It would also mean losing the only landmark. 'I'll meet you on the courthouse steps' was as good a way of making sure you'd find someone in the crowded narrow streets as any other. The bus stop was opposite the courthouse. There were always a few people gathered on its steps, most of them having nothing at all to do with the business of law and justice.

But today they recognized a few people who had to do with their own case. Mike Coyne, a cousin of Jack, who worked on the local newspaper. Two of the hospital staff who would have been called as witnesses. And parked right at the bus stop where he was certain to be moved on was Fergus.

Fergus stood beside his car like a soldier on point duty. He could hardly believe it when John Ryan drove Kate and Dr White into his sights and all three of them were laughing aloud, as if they hadn't a care or a worry in the world.

People stood around in little clusters. Kate's wheelchair was taken without fuss from the back of the car and moved up to where she was sitting. Gracefully and without making any big production out of it, she slid from one seat to the other. She looked at ease in her chair.

She had been told that there were seventeen steps up to the courthouse door, and there were two choices: either two strong men lifted the chair with her in it – Dr White and John would do that – or else she could go in a back way through damp long corridors.

She said she preferred the back way. It would be too nerve racking for those carrying and those watching. And she said that somebody should write a letter to the local paper on the lack of facilities for wheelchairs.

They headed towards the back door.

But they didn't get there. Down the steps at a fast pace came two men, the Dublin solicitor and a local man; more men followed – one was in robes, a barrister – and behind him Kevin Kennedy, also in robes.

Fergus felt his heart turn over, and realized there had been a last-minute offer.

'Wait for a moment,' he called in a strangled voice to the little procession with the wheelchair.

'Is anything wrong?' Kate asked, turning round.

John narrowed his eyes. 'It's Mr Kennedy, he seems to want to talk to us.'

'Oh Jesus, let them not have an adjournment,' said Dr White, who had often made it known that he had little respect for lawyers.

Far far away, it seemed, Patrick O'Neill stood by himself at the other side of the wide steps.

Kate thought it was strange for him to be alone, she had so many people with her. Then who would have come? Grace was at school, Rachel was back in Ryan's pub, and Kerry? Who knew where he would be?

Patrick looked nervous and very much alone. She longed to call out to him. She wished she could send him a message saying his own words back to him, telling him that they would always be friends. It was as he had told her, a formality that was necessary to maintain their friendship.

But she couldn't speak. And anyway they were coming towards her, her side. Kevin Kennedy, and Fergus. Their faces were impassive. Neither of them spoke, they each looked at the other.

'You say it, Fergus,' Kevin Kennedy said, standing back a little to give the stage to Fergus Slattery.

'They have made a suggestion.' Fergus felt his voice was very thin.

'Yes, Fergus, and what do you think?' John asked.

'What do they say?' Kate was calm.

'They say eight thousand pounds,' Fergus said in a voice that came from a million miles away.

'Eight thousand pounds.' John said the words.

'Two thousand pounds more than they said yesterday,' Kevin Kennedy said, as a further explanation.

'My goodness,' said Kate.

There was a silence.

Behind Fergus and Kevin the other side stood in a little group. Patrick was still at a distance from them. He was not joining in.

Kevin Kennedy spoke then. 'As your counsel, I can only give you my opinion, you do not have to take it. You do understand that, Kate?'

He hadn't called her Mrs Ryan. Nobody noticed.

'Yes indeed, and what do you say?'

'I say that you should have a quiet moment with your husband, and ask each other do you believe that you can live with this as fair and reasonable compensation, and if you can, then I will accept it for you.'

There was a pause. Nobody moved.

'And if you think that you will always wonder and worry about what you would have got if you fought on, then we will fight on.'

Almost imperceptibly Fergus, Kevin and Martin moved away, and John and Kate were left looking at each other.

John bent down and looked into her eyes. They didn't say anything, neither of them said a word nor did they nod a head. Then after the long look John stood up.

'We'd like to take it,' he said simply, his hand in his wife's cold hand.

Fergus let out his breath like a whistle. 'You're doing the right thing, I'm sure of it. I'm sure of it,' he said happily.

Kevin Kennedy was smiling too. And Martin White.

The little circle was almost unwilling to break up, but Fergus was the one to do it.

'Come on, Kevin, let's go and tell them,' he said like a schoolboy.

Kate held John's hand to her cheek. She didn't need to say anything and neither did he. Dr White was the only one to speak.

'Look, they're coming over,' he said, and there, moving first with halting steps, came Patrick O'Neill. But as he got near them he broke into a run.

In the small dark public house behind the courthouse they went to drink a toast. They drank to insurance companies and to justice being done. Kevin had to go back into court as he was in other cases, cases that had not been settled so amicably on the steps.

He shook their hands and said he hoped to meet them again socially, as he was going to spend the rest of the week in the Grange. In fact it was so infinitely better than the Grand, the Commercial or the Central. It was fortunate for him that through this case he had discovered the ideal place to come when he was on circuit. He was delighted that everybody was satisfied. That's what barristers actually wanted, despite their reputation as loving the sound of their own voices.

And Fergus told himself that £8,000 was almost what he had wanted for them, so near that it made no difference. It was worth so much not to have poor Kate go through all that ordeal which she had been dreading.

And Dr White was quite forthcoming for him, and told stories of cases way back where he had been called as an expert witness.

John noted that this pub would not survive if it hadn't been lucky enough to be so well positioned right behind the courts, the library, the county council offices and the barracks. It had shabby scored tables, and torn dirty lino, but it was in the right place. He found his mind straying and hoping that Ryan's Licensed Premises was really in the right place, that it would really get all this extra business that had been promised. He didn't want to worry Kate with it, not now, not for a long time until she had got over the trauma of all this.

He looked at her sitting there with them all. Nobody who came in would know she was in a wheelchair, she looked a handsome lively woman, her head thrown back laughing at some silly tale the doctor was telling. They were all half hysterical with the relief that it was over.

Patrick was in high good form too. He resisted the urge to keep buying drinks for everyone, and waited instead while the doctor went to the counter or Slattery threw a ten-pound note on the tray of the boy in the dirty apron who was serving them. They were all so happy, so relieved that it was over. He knew he had to go along with the good will and the delight. Because it could do nothing but harm and destruction if he were to let them know that Kate Ryan hadn't got half enough for her compensation. The insurance companies were prepared to go to £12,000 outside the court, and even to £14,000 as soon as the case began.

At £8,000 they thought they had got away very lightly indeed. But Patrick knew that if this were ever known it would destroy everything he had tried so hard to build.

And of course it wasn't known. It wasn't the kind of thing that the insurance companies would ever reveal. Instead it was reported with excitement in Mountfern. It was quite possibly the exact sum of money that pleased everyone. It was large enough to seem like a sum you look at in the bank and consider yourself a family of substance, which the Ryans would never have been able to do under any other circumstances. But it was not so large it sounded like a punishment. As the news filtered through Mountfern, the heads nodded with satisfaction. Even the Dalys, who had always said that anyone could be hit at any time by a digger and that it was a scandal to go suing that good man who was such a benefactor, could find no reason to condemn the settlement. Even Jack Coyne, who said O'Neill should be hounded to the ends of the earth to prove he couldn't go round throwing his weight and machinery into the citizens of this place, had to stop his tirade.

By anyone's standards, including Jack Coyne's, £8,000 was a lot of money.

Sheila Whelan was one of the first to visit Kate.

'You must be so glad it's all over,' she said. As always she had said exactly the right thing and struck the note that Kate wanted to hear. There were no congratulations offered, nor curious questions on how the huge sum of money was going to be spent. Kate was grateful to sit and talk to her.

'There'll be a procession through shortly, I'll leave you alone,' Sheila said. 'You'll want to talk to everyone else.'

'No I will not. I feel like issuing a bulletin and sticking it up outside over the fuchsias there, saying Mrs Ryan would like to thank all the inquirers . . .'

'Sit out in the pub, I'd advise, then you won't have to have heart-to-hearts with people, and if anyone you really want to talk to comes, you can come back in here.' There was a look of strain around the postmistress's eyes.

'Did anything happen?' Kate asked.

'Not now, I'll tell you all about it again.'

'Is it bad?'

'No, it's all over now.'

'Oh Sheila.' They sat in silence. The sympathy was so great there were no words for it. A man who walked out and who only wanted to come back when he was on his deathbed. Such things couldn't be mourned in formal ways. They had to remain unsaid.

Sheila had been right; the procession did go on all day. Rita Walsh was in, delighted at the news, overjoyed that it was all over, wondering should they invest it in something that a gentleman friend of hers had told her about. It was like a syndicate and you all put in so much and there was hardly any risk, and people had been known to double their investment in a year, Rita could get the details. Kate told her that she herself would like nothing better but unfortunately John was an old stick in the mud. Rita sympathized over the dullness of husbands in general and said that the offer of advice was always there if Kate needed it. A woman has to look to herself, Rita advised sagely. Kate couldn't meet John's eye as he pretended not to be listening, she was terrified they would break out laughing.

Canon Moran and Father Hogan came in together. They said they were out taking a little constitutional and good news of the happy outcome had reached them. They wanted to say how very pleased they were that God's justice had been done, and it was a wonderful example of how patience and resignation to the will of the Lord was often rewarded, even on this earth.

At least, Canon Moran did all the speaking. Father Hogan looked in disbelief at the trays of currant bread and scones that he saw on the counter. The rehearsals for the Shamrock Café were well under way. There were tables and chairs already in position, and any day now it would be ready to go. John had decided on no big opening ceremony, just let it creep on people.

Father Hogan's pink round face was alight with excitement. 'We'll be able to come by here regularly on our constitutional, Canon,' he said, as Kate was murmuring that out of their very generous compensation she and John were most anxious to make a small contribution to the needs of the parish. It had been a highly satisfactory visit for the clergy.

Dara heard on the way out of the convent. Jacinta White told her.
 'Eight *thousand* pounds. You'll be the quality now.' Jacinta sniffed.
 'Don't makes jokes like that.' Dara could hardly take in the amount.
 'It's not really a joke, you'll be as good as anyone.'
 'We were always as good as anyone already.'

Jimbo Doyle rang Carrie to tell her.
 'I know already, they're all here celebrating,' she said.
 'Will I come and bring my guitar?' asked Jimbo.
 'I don't think they're celebrating *that* much,' Carrie said firmly.

Miss Purcell, who was now happily installed in the presbytery looking after the canon and Father Hogan, dropped a note into her old employer Fergus Slattery. She said that she was delighted that he had been able to get so much money for Mrs Ryan and her family, and that his late father would have been proud of him. Miss Purcell added primly that money wasn't everything, but she was sure that the Ryans would use what they got wisely, and perhaps Fergus could tell them about the damp that was seeping through at the Sacred Heart Altar since good people to whom much had been given were often anxious to give some of it back to God at the earliest opportunity.

Michael and Tommy were walking out of the schoolyard when they heard. Tommy was still complaining about the unfairness of teachers. Brother Keane had now in fact succumbed and been taken to the town to visit the dentist by a delivery man who thought he had been bringing boxes of copy books, pens and other stationery supplies to the brothers, not taking one of the brothers with a swollen face off to a dentist.
 One of the younger lads came running up.
 'Your Ma got a fortune,' he shouted.
 Michael felt his stomach constrict.
 'Eight thousand pounds,' shouted the young fellow, delighted to be the one who brought the news.
 'That's all right,' Tommy said. 'That's about what they said would be fair – in our house.'

Patrick had told the Ryans that he would come in later for a drink, he had a few things to attend to in the hotel first. He had clasped their hands warmly and any reserve that might have been between them was now gone.
 Back in his office, he sat with a curiously empty feeling at his desk. For once there were no interruptions; most times he had never been able to have a full five minutes without some crisis. But today nobody came near him. Brian Doyle had said that he heard it was a fair settlement and Patrick had agreed.

The sour taste in his mouth just wouldn't go. Last night he had wanted to offer £12,000 and had been told very sharply that it wasn't up to him to offer anything.

'Let me add to it, secretly,' he had asked.

They wouldn't hear of it. A claim had to be settled and be seen to be settled. It was not fair on other insurers if Patrick was going to play Father Christmas with awards.

If the Ryans were known to have received something way above what they would expect and were about to accept, then would not all other claimants have similar expectations?

There was nothing to stop Patrick O'Neill making any ex gratia payments himself, out of his own funds. But it must not come with the name of the insurance company.

But Patrick knew that if it came from him it would be charity.

He sat at his desk and wished that his daughter was back from Dublin and that she would walk in the grounds with him talking to him as she once had, before she had become coquettish and head-turning.

He wished that Kerry was different. That was it, just different. Like another person. He could see hardly any way now that he and his son would have any warmth and understanding between them. A gambler, a liar, a callous boy caring nothing for anyone. And quite possibly Kerry had been with Rachel. The thought of his son in an intimate embrace with Rachel was a thought he had tried to keep far from his mind.

Rachel lying back on the bed, confused with unaccustomed drink, laughing maybe, in a silly way. Her thick hair spread out on the pillow and Kerry, his own son, leaning over her. It was *not* believable. He hit his desk with his fist. He would not believe it.

He had always been able to cope before, or if there was something that he couldn't deal with he had put it out of his mind. He had decided not to think about Kathleen's illness when he was not with her, and so never in his long drives to work or in his business day had he let it come into his mind. After he had beaten and fired his first dishonest manager he had allowed no thoughts of the man, no regrets to come back to him at any stage. Kerry's expulsion from school, his stealing the silver, these he had managed to banish. But the image of his son and Rachel was too horrifying to get rid of.

Everything was turning out like a nightmare, just a few short weeks before the day he had dreamed about since he was a boy. The day he would open his own huge palace on the spot where the landlords had once driven his grandfather to an emigrant ship.

Fergus Slattery sat alone in his office too. Deirdre Dunne with her usual discreet face, pursed lips and habit of looking left and right before she delivered any utterance had said that it was an excellent result and he must be very satisfied.

Now as he sat by himself and tried to give time to the other files that were on his desk Fergus let his mind go back over it all.

He still wished that O'Neill had never come to Mountfern. There was nothing the man could do which made Fergus glad that he had invested the savings of a life's work and investment into changing the face of the village his grandfather left.

Why couldn't he have just come back for holidays, like these people he was hoping to find to fill his hotel? He could have worn a shirt with shamrocks on it, bought a fake shillelagh, had his picture taken beside the tinkers with their donkeys, or at a cottage where he might conceivably have roots.

But O'Neill had to do it his way, no matter who got hurt. And to Fergus's mind a lot of people had. Not just Kate Ryan.

People had changed and become greedy. Everyone semed to be doing things for the wrong reason. Look at his own poor Miss Purcell for instance, talking about having to do up the Sacred Heart Altar in the church and get rid of all the damp to smarten the place up for the visitors. If it was important to spend all that money getting rid of damp around the small side altar, and Fergus didn't think it was one of life's essentials, then it should be done for God surely, or for the people who were going to pray in the church, Mountfern people, so they wouldn't have to see weeping walls and fungus around the statue of the Sacred Heart and drips coming down to endanger the altar lamp. The visitors in Fernscourt might not even be Catholics, and if they were they would probably go off to mass at the old abbey fourteen miles away and take in a bit of history as well. And the vicar was busy getting his graveyard weeded and cleared up before the visitors came. This *had* to be the wrong approach too, Fergus thought. If old Protestant graves and tombstones were to be honoured then why wait till some Americans, possibly of Episcopalian stock, came to see them?

But Fergus wasn't going to get anyone to agree with him. Kate had often warned him against becoming an old eccentric before his time. He was thirty-one. Could his time have come now, by any chance?

Loretto Quinn heard the news from Rita Walsh. She was dying to run up and say a few words of congratulation to Kate but she couldn't leave the shop. At that moment Jack Coyne came in.

'Would you mind the place for me, just ten minutes? I'll be back by then.'

'God, what am I, a messenger boy?'

The man who owned Coyne's Motor Works and thought of himself as a substantial businessman did not like being thought suitable to fill in behind the counter in what he would always think of as a huckster's shop.

Loretto was struggling out of her shop coat, one of the smart coats that Rachel had got her months back. Rachel had said it was always a good idea to have something to wear to show you were working and to take it off when work was over. Loretto had agreed eagerly and also it happened that everyone said how smart she looked in the shop coats anyway, so it had been a great suggestion.

Jack Coyne grumbled but agreed to hold the fort for ten minutes.

'One minute later now and I'll leave and pull the door after me.'

Loretto was gone flying up to Ryan's to add her good wishes.

'Who's minding the shop?' Mary Donnelly wanted to know. Mary was beaming like a sunrise and couldn't do enough for people.

'Jack Coyne said he'd keep an eye on it,' Loretto said.

'He has his eye on you,' Mary said in a doomed voice.

'Never in a million years. He hasn't said a word of it.' Loretto tossed her head. She *had* wondered why Jack Coyne came so often to call. And perhaps in his narrow mean face there were the traces of interest.

'Oh certainly he has,' Mary said. 'Wouldn't it be a nice tidy little business to add to his own?'

'Yes. Well.' Loretto seemed a bit put out. And yet again Kate and John Ryan exchanged glances across their pub.

Happy to be on the same wave length and happy that the ordeal was over and their future was secure.

Jim Costello was glad the court case was out of the way because now his boss could give undivided attention to the hotel opening. It had all been full of problems, and there was a pressing need for Patrick to call everything to order. Jim suggested a meeting with an agenda.

Patrick was scornful. This was ninnies' work – agendas, and 'it was agreed' and 'it was decided' – that was the stuff for nobodies. He hadn't made his fortune by sitting on his butt attending meetings.

'There are areas which have to be sorted out in the presence of other people,' Jim said, rather prissily Patrick thought.

'Like what and like which people?'

'Like line authority and what position you want your son to hold in the hotel, and that must be discussed in his presence. That's one thing.

'Like what penalty clauses you have arranged with Brian Doyle about what he calls the last little finishing touches and I regard as work still left undone. Like whether Mrs Fine is or is not in charge of the decor and the arrangements for the presentation on the opening day.'

Patrick felt stopped in his tracks. These were three punches he hadn't expected to be hit with. He took the easiest one first.

'There's never any problem with Rachel,' he said. 'Give her complete charge. She's had years of knowing how to get on with people, she doesn't stand on their feet like I do. What's the fuss anyway? Who's objecting?'

'No, that's not the point. Mrs Fine says that you don't want her to make the arrangements for the opening. She says that she won't be here for it, and you want the public relations people from Dublin to make the arrangements. They've been on the phone twice wanting to know the brief. Mrs Fine just smiles at me and says she won't be here, *you* just say "Rachel will sort it out". I'm sorry, Mr O'Neill, I know it sounds like whingeing and whining and running to you with every little problem. But can you see how hard it is to decide what is and what is not my responsibility? They're all quite major things and rather sensitive areas.'

Patrick looked at him. Costello was unflinching, he didn't sound like a moaner. The man had right on his side.

'I take your point. First tell Doyle that I'll kick his ass from here to Galway tomorrow morning and then from Galway right across to Dublin unless he has all those shithouses or whatever they are moved tonight. Do you hear me? Tonight.'

'The things he calls offices or store rooms.'

'I don't care if he calls them the *Pro-Cathedral*, they're shithouses and they are not to be here tomorrow morning. But he is, and eight a.m.'

'Yes. Will I arrange . . .?'

'Just tell him I'll see him here at eight a.m. And Costello?'

'Mr O'Neill?'

'If you see my son tell him to fuck off. If he cares to turn up properly attired on the day of the opening then I shall of course be pleased to see him. Not otherwise.'

Jim Costello's eyes flashed. 'No, I'm afraid I can't give any message like that for you. That is family business. I will *not* be put in the position of delivering one kind of ultimatum and then delivering back the news of another kind of shrug. I'm sorry, but no.'

Patrick looked at him with admiration. 'I was right to pick you. Right, I'll deal with Kerry, but your side of it is clear. He has no position in this hotel.'

'And the other . . .?'

'I'm going to find Rachel myself. Do you have any idea where she might be?'

Jim shook his head and seemed about to say it wasn't any of his business. But Patrick forestalled him with a laugh.

'Hey, relax. If you're not going to do my dirty work for me with my son then I don't suppose I have any hope of getting you to patch up a lovers' quarrel for me, do I?'

He punched his manager genially on the arm and went out the door of his hotel to stand on his steps and glare at the offending prefab huts that Brian Doyle would be asked to remove the next instant. He noted that Jim Costello had had the good sense not to acknowledge even by a glance that Patrick had just let slip to him that the dispute with Rachel Fine was a lovers' tiff. Jim Costello had been a very good choice indeed.

Where was Rachel?

Kate had expected her at any moment, but she knew now that she need not doubt her friend. Rachel would be here, at some time, it didn't matter when. She would be so glad to share the good news, and to know that a whole day and even more did not have to be spent arguing in open court.

She would be delighted too that Patrick was so pleased and thought it was a fair sum.

Kate looked at the door more than once. She was anxious to go back into her cool green room and talk to Rachel alone.

Rachel walked alone along the river bank. She walked from the landing stage upriver, on a path that was overgrown still but not as covered with briars and brambles as the stretch from Fernscourt downriver to the bridge.

It was quiet here and she would meet nobody. She walked, a small woman in her flat-heeled stylish brogues. Rachel had hardly walked without high heels since she was seventeen years of age, but in Mountfern she had learned to change so many of her ways that changing her footwear seemed minor. She had her hands in the pockets of her suede jacket, her Hermès scarf tied jauntily around her neck.

To anyone watching she looked an elegant woman enjoying a stroll by the river. Over the years she had learned to keep her feelings well away from the public view. Her face was in a pleasant half smile. But her thoughts were very different from the gentle expression on her face.

Patrick O'Neill had said that Kate would get at least £12,000 and the insurance company was quite prepared to pay £14,000 without any great quibble. How had it come out at so little in comparison to that? And why had Patrick said or done nothing to show that he thought it had not been adequate?

From what she had heard, and Rachel had heard plenty of accounts, there had been roistering and celebrating, and banging each other on the back and everyone was now everyone else's best friend.

She felt sick to the bottom of her stomach that he could be so hypocritical. And even more sick that she had not had the guts and courage to shout down her friend and tell her what the bottom line had been.

If, a few short hours ago, Rachel Fine had been brave enough to resist this girl-guide mentality of having to fight fair that Kate had been babbling about, the Ryan family could have had £14,000 in their bank account. Enough to make them secure for ever. No matter what happened to their business as a result of the building of Fernscourt.

Rachel turned and looked back at the hotel. She knew very surely that she would not now wait for the opening, she would go back to New York as soon as she could manage it without upsetting innocent people.

She would go back home.

There were a lot of people in the bar when she came in. She went straight to Kate and kissed her on each cheek.

Kate's eyes were full of tears. 'Isn't it wonderful? It's like a dream,' she said.

Rachel swallowed.

'Have you been talking to Patrick?' Kate asked.

'No. No, not since.'

'He's delighted, he thinks it's fair.'

'I'm sure he is.' Rachel was pulling away.

'Oh, do you have to go, really? I wanted to talk to you more than anyone.'

Rachel had rarely been so moved. She couldn't say anything.

'And Rachel, I wanted to thank you for trying to do what you did. But it wouldn't have been fair, you do see that don't you? It couldn't have worked. As it is, it all worked out just as we wanted. That's what he said they were going to give, and that's what we took.' Kate's eyes shone. Her face was tired but her eyes were dancing with light.

'He said that?' There was no incredulity in Rachel's voice, just a flat tone.

'Well yes, we asked him you see, afterwards. In the pub.'

'Yes of course. Kate, I'll be back, later or tomorrow, and we'll talk for all the hours that are in the day, but this is something I can't put off.'

'All right, I won't hold you, and thank you again for all the support. I'm going to sleep well tonight, for the first time for a long while.'

Rachel laid her hand against Kate's face in a way she had never done before.

447

It was as if she were trying to say something through the palm of her hand that she couldn't say in any other way.

Then she hurried out of Ryan's and walked down River Road. She didn't cross the footbridge to Fernscourt, nor did she stop at Loretto Quinn's. Rachel Fine walked the whole way to the bridge and turned left. Then she walked up the steps and knocked at the door of the ivy-covered house where Fergus Slattery lived and had his office.

It was short and it was clear.

Rachel found herself giving no complicated explanations, she did not stop to go into her motives, nor did she twist her hands and her handkerchief as she had when she was trying to explain to Patrick that she had got drunk with his son but had not made love with him.

Fergus was a different kind of listener. There was no stony impassive face, he reacted angrily and loudly to every sentence.

She gave him all the details of the various meetings, the strategy, the decision to offer six but to expect a strenuous refusal, the decision to go to ten the moment that eight had been refused and to settle at anything up to fourteen even as the case was about to begin. Then it was over and they sat in silence for a full minute.

'I suppose you wonder why I'm telling you all this.'

'No, it's very natural that you should tell me, you're Kate's friend, you are hurt on her behalf.' He was gentle.

'But I'm also Patrick's friend. You must know that.'

'Yes of course I know that.'

'It's not just because it's over, and because Patrick doesn't want me here any more . . .' She saw him raise his eyebrows in surprise, and went on hurriedly. 'No, it has nothing to do with that, surprisingly.'

'Of course,' he said, but she wondered whether he believed her.

'It's because it's not fair. Patrick has always been fair. And recently some madness has entered into him, and he's not being fair at all.'

She looked very troubled. He saw what a very beautiful woman she was in this afternoon light, huge dark eyes moving restlessly about her.

'You do know that nothing can be done now?' Fergus said. 'We have taken their offer and accepted it willingly. I thought it was enough, and so did Kennedy the barrister. But more important than that, Kate and John were perfectly satisfied.'

'I know.' Rachel's voice was small.

'And everyone in this place thinks it was enough, so they have their pride, and people don't say it was too much, so the Ryans won't become objects of hate and envy.'

She looked at the tall gangling young man with the white face and the hair that would never sit in any order or style. Rachel could see that he had always loved Kate Ryan in a hopeless, ineffectual sort of way. His face was stricken to think how poorly he must have represented her on this the only occasion he had ever had a chance to ride out to battle for her. Perhaps he was trying to justify the small award by saying that it was what the village would tolerate.

'She could have got so much more if she would only listen to me this morning. I tried to tell her but she wouldn't hear.'

'No, that's Kate for you,' he sighed.

'But we were friends. It couldn't have been unethical between friends.'

'What do you want me to do, Rachel?'

She looked at him, surprised.

'No, I mean it. What should I do now? My own instinct is to put it out of my mind, pretend we never had this conversation. Do you think I should do anything different?'

'Are you mad at me?'

'Most certainly not.' He leaned across his desk and took her hand to reassure her on this. 'You have always been a great friend to Kate, I have to say that sometimes I thought she spent too much time with you, seeing that you were so close to O'Neill, and that O'Neill is in many ways her adversary.'

'He *is* her adversary, even though he doesn't intend to be,' Rachel said. 'He will close their business and eight thousand pounds is not enough to compensate them for that.' She was agitated and distressed.

Fergus let a little silence fall between them.

'Fergus, would *you* have listened if I had told you, instead of trying to tell Kate?'

Again a little silence, but eventually he spoke.

'Truthfully, yes. I think I would have listened. It would be unethical and if anyone heard me saying this I would be in danger of being struck off the rolls, but I would have listened.'

Rachel warmed to his honesty. 'I don't think it's unethical to help a friend.'

'The Incorporated Law Society might not see it that way.' He smiled ruefully. 'They mightn't be so understanding about how fond I am of Kate.'

'You sort of love her, don't you?'

'Yes, that's it, sort of.' He spoke without embarrassment but he looked out the window on to Bridge Street not at Rachel as he spoke.

'She has everything, you know, life and common sense, and a quick lively mind which I don't, and . . . oh, a lot of things. But you're right, it's only a sort of love, not real love. I don't want to take her away from John, I don't want to go to bed with her. I suppose in ways I avoid getting involved with people, and this type of feeling I have for Kate does as a substitute. Very silly really.'

'I had to tell you, Fergus. It's up to you what you do now that you know. If you want to go along with this charade that it was the greatest award since Lord knows when, then do. I won't be here. I'm going home.'

'Isn't this your home?'

'I thought it was, but it's not.'

'We'll miss you. I wish you were not going away.'

Eddie Ryan avoided Jack Coyne very deliberately. But Eddie couldn't avoid trouble. He had been so used to playing around Coyne's Motor Works that vehicles of every sort fascinated him now.

Mr Williams had an old battered station wagon. He left it outside the graveyard where he was busy tending the graves. Eddie couldn't see anyone around. The grass in the graveyard was high. Mr Williams was bent low.

Eddie looked left and right and slipped into the driving seat. He would drive the car to the end of the road where there was a farmhouse with two gates. He could drive in one and out the other, and back to where the car was now.

He had reckoned without the herd of cows which were coming out one entrance on their way back to the fields after milking. They seemed to be coming in the windows and his grasp of driving was not as sound as he would like to have thought.

The cows were delighted with a break in the normal milking routine and were prepared to stand chewing the cud and dribbling until the last day dawned. At that moment a tractor came round the corner. Eddie knew the explanations of what he was doing in the vicar's station wagon would be difficult, not to say impossible. He left the car rapidly and slipped past the staring cows. He heard the tractor hit the car, and kept running until he got to Bridge Street.

His face was innocent when the story got to Ryan's pub, the tale of poor Mr Williams's car, and poor Brigid Kenny's cows, and Brigid Kenny's poor son on the tractor, who was somehow held to blame for it all.

To his shock and outrage he heard Mrs Whelan from the post office coming in and telling his father and mother that Brigid Kenny had seen young Eddie running away from the farm. Mrs Whelan of all people. She had always been so nice.

Eddie's father was furious.

Eddie was asked to come out to the back yard.

That could only mean one thing.

Kate was furious too. The danger, the stupidity, the downright disregard for human life.

'You'd think that in this house of all houses there would be some attention paid to what can happen when people get hit by vehicles,' she stormed at him as Eddie had slunk back into the house with his hands, legs and bottom aching from the hiding he had been given in the back yard. He looked miserable and wretched and a tiny grain of sympathy stirred in her.

'Why are you so awful?' she asked him, interested genuinely. And he could detect the change in her tone.

'I don't feel awful inside,' he said, his tears not far away. Tears that had not come during the beating.

'What do you feel inside?'

'I feel it's all very boring,' he said truthfully. 'I'd love to be somewhere else, somewhere that I'd be important, and that people would talk about me.'

'They're talking about you tonight.'

She tried not to let her voice sound as if he had been forgiven in any way. Terrible things lay ahead, like the apology to Mr Williams, like asking Jack Coyne to give an estimate on how much it would cost to repair the damage to the station wagon, like trying to explain to Brigid Kenny (a sour woman at the best of times) and to her son (who was slow by any standards even amongst the Kenny family), what exactly Eddie Ryan had been doing on their property running amok.

'I suppose I'd like to be important to someone,' Eddie said simply.

Kate looked at him and to his amazement she had tears in her eyes. 'You're very important to me.'

'Only to be giving out to and telling people you're sorry about me.' He wasn't complaining, that's just the way he saw things.

'Why do you think that?'

'Well, when I asked was I getting anything to wear at the opening, they all laughed. Nobody even thought I'd be *at* that opening. That's not being very important.'

He was totally unprepared for her to lean forward from her wheelchair and take him in her arms.

'I know what you mean, Eddie. It's hard not being important enough to go to Dublin to get an outfit. I'd like to go too. I'd love to go in and out of the shops, in Grafton Street, and down Wicklow Street. Not to buy there, it would be too dear. Then I'd go to George's Street, and I'd buy something there, and a bit of other shopping – oh, stuff that would bore you, household things. And maybe into a bookshop, get a present for your dad, and then give myself plenty of time and walk down the quays with all my parcels and get the train home. And your father would meet us in the town and drive us home, and I'd try on whatever I'd got, and turn around on my own two good legs and show it off, and you'd all say what you thought, and people would take notice of me, and I'd be important again.'

She was still holding him to her as she spoke. When she released him and held him away from her she saw that the boy was biting his lip.

'I never knew, Mam . . . I never knew,' he said.

'It's all right, Eddie,' she said. 'We'll survive.'

'If I had the money, Mam, I'd take you to Dublin for the day,' he said.

'I know you would.'

She was silent now, so Eddie crept away.

Things were very odd at the moment, there were no two ways about it. Mrs Whelan shopping him, Dad belting the life out of him, and Mam throwing her arms around him and saying she'd love to have two proper legs again.

And there were more peculiar things happening at every turn. Mr Coyne, who was a hundred if he was a day, had brought a bunch of flowers to Mrs Quinn, who was nearly a hundred, and the two of them were carrying on like something out of a musical. And Kerry O'Neill had told him to fuck off out of the way when he had asked him what was he doing with a boat going up and down between the bridge and the landing stage. Marty Leonard, who was Tommy's younger brother, said that Tommy had four pictures of Dara stuck up in his room and he kissed each one goodnight before he went to bed. And Father Hogan had asked him what were the opening hours going to be in the Shamrock Café when it opened and was there any chance that he could buy some of the potato cakes to eat walking along the road.

Eddie thought that everyone in Mountfern was going mad.

Dara found that her mother seemed withdrawn and somehow wistful these days. She sat and looked out into her garden where the summer flowers were coming to an end.

'Will I bring you the trowel and fork?' Dara asked.

'No. Let's leave it for a while. Who sees it?'

'You do, we do.'

'That's what I mean.'

'Well, we were always the ones who saw it, it hasn't been on Telefis Eireann or anything,' Dara replied with some spirit.

'Are you happy with your linen dress for the opening?' Kate asked suddenly.

'Happy isn't the right word, it looks what it is, a boring linen dress that gets a huge balloony bottom in it if you sit down. It's a nice blue colour, and Mrs Fine gave me that necklace. I suppose it's all right, and for all that will be looking at me over there, it's fine. Why?'

'You can have a new dress if you like,' Kate said.

'What kind of dress, Mam?'

'Whatever you like.'

This had never been said in the history of their lives together. Dara's mouth was open. There had been a long lecture on thinking that they were millionaires because of the compensation. They had been warned against false expectations and a change of lifestyle. Now out of the blue she was being offered any kind of dress she liked.

'Do you mean something from a shop in Dublin?' she said in disbelief.

'Certainly.'

'But why, Mam? We're meant to be saving the money for the day we might need to expand the Shamrock Café. And the fees for university.'

'It's my money, it's mine, I got it by breaking *my* back. If I say you can have a new dress you can have one. Do you hear me?'

Kate's eyes were full of tears. Dara rushed to her and threw her arms around the woman in the chair.

'Mam, I'm sorry, of course I want a dress, I just didn't want you to be spending all your money on me. That's all.'

She could feel Kate's body heaving.

'I'd *love* a dress. I'll go to Dublin on the excursion train on Saturday, I'd *love* it.'

'And Michael, he can go and get a jacket. Will you go with him and see he doesn't buy an old rag or anything?'

'I will, Mam.'

'You're going to be dressed like the finest in the land. I'll get you both off school midweek one day. If Princess Grace can go to Dublin for her clothes so can the Ryans take time off from their studies to do the same thing.'

Sergeant Sheehan was tired. It had been a day when nothing that could have been straightforward was straightforward, everything had more turns in it than a corkscrew. Even the relatively simple business of organizing extra guards for the hotel opening had turned out to be a minefield of petty politics. Was there nobody who would talk straight left in the town? His face creased into a smile when he saw Sheila coming out of the church.

'What were you praying for? Let me guess. You were praying not to have to walk into one more person asking you eejity questions like I do.'

She looked at him affectionately. She had known Seamus and Mary Sheehan for years, she had been with Mary sometimes to see their unfortunate son in the home over on the hill. Seamus was usually too upset to go with his wife, and it was a long lonely journey for the woman to go on her own.

'No, Seamus, I wasn't praying at all.'

'Well God, you've enough to do. I hope that mad Miss Purcell hasn't roped you in to clean the church and take the damp out of the Sacred Heart Altar.'

Sheila laughed. 'Oh, I get roped in like everyone, but I was in there for a different purpose entirely, and you were the very man I was hoping to meet as a result of it. In fact I was going to come over to the barracks.'

'Anything wrong?'

'I'm not sure. I think something may be very wrong. Will you come in and I'll tell you about it?'

'What'll you be doing in Dublin?'

'Shut up, Eddie,' said Dara. 'You know it's meant to be a secret, we don't want half the place to know we're going. Mam's saying it's a special favour and not saying that we're going on the train. Sister Laura and Brother Keane only think we're going in to the town with Daddy.'

'But what'll you be *doing*, will you be going to George's Street?'

'God, he's heard of George's Street, is there any end to his sophistication?' mocked Dara.

'I just want to know.'

'You're not coming with us, you're not.' Michael was vehement. 'You'd ruin every single minute of the day, not just for us but for everyone on the train, and everyone in Dublin as well.'

'I couldn't ruin the day for them *all*,' Eddie protested.

'You could, they'd be the worse off for your being there. Go *away*, Eddie.' Dara was impatient.

'I just thought maybe you'd take Mam,' he said.

'What?' They looked at him in amazement. Eddie had never suggested anything remotely unselfish in his life.

'Yeah, she might like an outing, and get something to wear herself.'

'She doesn't need anything to wear, Mrs Fine gets her things,' Dara said.

'She might like to get her own.'

'She'd hate all the fuss and the noise and how could she manage in the chair?'

'You could push it down the quays. Down to O'Connell Bridge,' Eddie said.

'Is this some trick?' Dara asked.

'What's behind it?' Michael wanted to know.

'I was just being nice,' Eddie said.

They didn't believe him, but they did tell their father.

John Ryan thought it was well worth putting to Kate. He came into her room to suggest it.

'How about if the children were to take you with them tomorrow?'

She was flustered and pleased. But no, she couldn't think of it, it would be too much of a drag. It would slow the twins down too much, it would spoil their day.

'Nonsense, I've talked to them, they think it's a terrific idea, they'd love you to go. And if they want to wander off and leave you for a bit, they can, and come back to you, can't they? It'd be just like here or going into the town, or the time we went to the abbey on the lake, people came and went from you and you had a grand time.'

'I did.' She smiled happily. 'Thank you for thinking of it, John.' Her voice was small, and full of emotion.

'Oh, I didn't think of it,' he said airily. 'Credit where it's due. It was Eddie apparently, gangster Eddie who thought you'd like the trip.'

He grinned at her, expecting her to think it as unlikely and funny as he had. He was surprised to see some of the pleasure go out of her face. Kate had thought that this was all John's idea to give her a treat. But it hadn't been his idea at all.

Fergus had known that he had to face the Ryans fairly soon. He would never tell them about his conversation with Rachel, and he knew that no matter how bitter and resentful on their behalf she might feel, she too would keep her counsel to herself.

But he had to go soon, otherwise it would grow to become a huge secret and it would get out of all proportion.

He had hated having to go there knowing what he did, but after the first time it was easy. Nobody else knew that O'Neill's side had got away so lightly. Fergus believed that O'Neill must accept a great deal of the blame in this regard. It was not, he thought, just his natural and long-standing dislike of the man, it was just the way things had to be.

To try to take some of the fire from Rachel's anger he had pretended to think O'Neill might have been an innocent party. He knew that this is what she had wanted to believe. But in his heart there was nothing that would take away his belief that O'Neill was a villain and would remain one until the end, whatever the end might be.

Fergus was astounded that he had defined his feelings for Kate Ryan so openly to O'Neill's woman. He had hardly defined them to himself before this. But the very act of articulating that he half loved Kate, and that it was not the kind of emotion that would destroy him or make him destroy anyone else, was a liberating thing.

When he sat in Ryan's and joked about the potato cakes for the café, and planned outrageous stage Irish jokes to be played on the visitors to the hotel when they arrived, Fergus felt a kind of freedom. It was as if some burden had been lifted. As if he knew that he could leave this place if he wanted to, he wasn't tied by any cords. He knew he would stay here for ever. But now it would be because he wanted to, not because of anything unsettling that would never be said.

Grace was in Fernscourt examining her room without much pleasure. Not long ago it had been great fun here. Mrs Fine was pointing out where the light was best to put her bureau, Father had taken her in his arms and hugged her on almost every occasion, saying how wonderful it was that the dream was coming true, and Jim Costello had been around smiling and admiring.

It was all very different now. Father was distant and distracted, there was no sign of Mrs Fine, and Jim had been so prissy. Yes, that was the only word for it.

'Grace, I'm going to have to ask you not to throw yourself at me, the situation is quite impractical.'

Impractical. How *dare* he come on like this, using words like impractical, and suggesting that she had thrown herself at him. She had merely told him she was a big girl now and ready for anything.

Jim Costello had told her that she was the most beautiful girl he had ever seen in his whole life. *That* bit at least was something. But he had said that it would be playing with dynamite to get involved with her at this stage, under the eyes of her father and brother.

And then he had gone and more or less said this aloud in front of them. Grace hadn't known where to put herself.

She wished she hadn't been so harsh to Michael about the trip to Dublin. It had turned out that Father had wanted her out of Mountfern on the day of the court case and Father might have been able to arrange for Michael and Dara to have gone too.

Grace sat on her bed and felt that it had all been handled very badly. She was even having second thoughts about the very expensive dress she had bought.

Mrs Fine would have chosen something better for her.

Dara and Michael sat on the window seat. It was nearly like old times.

'What are you reading?' Michael asked.

'It's a letter from Madame Vartin. It's quite hard to read, she's got awfully squiggly writing.'

Michael grinned. 'And an awful squiggly habit of writing in French.'

'Oh, I can read the French easily enough,' Dara said loftily if not very truthfully.

'What's she writing about then? Here, let's see.' Michael reached for the letter.

'No, there might be things in it you shouldn't read.'

'From Madame Vartin? You said she was a religious maniac.'

'Yes, but she might be writing about sex.'

'Oh, I know all about sex,' Michael said.

'Do you?' Dara was eager and begging. 'Do you really know all about it? Is it great?'

'Well not *all*, not . . . well not everything. But it's pretty great as far as it goes.'

'I often wondered did you . . .'

'Sort of, not completely . . .'

'How nearly . . .?'

'Give us the letter.'

The confidences were over, Dara realized. She read a paragraph from the letter.

'This is the bit I don't understand, it's got something to do with Monsieur leaving his job, or begin sacked I think. I hope. Anyway she says he is too young to make a retreat. What in the name of God would he make a retreat for anyway? He's full of mortal sin all the time and glories in it.'

'Where does it say about him going on a retreat?' Michael read the paragraph and began to laugh. 'Fine use of money it was sending *you* off to France, even I know that and we're all desperate up in the brothers'. It's retiring, you eejit, "faire sa retraite" means retire.'

'He'll be jumping on Mademoiselle Stephanie all day,' Dara said gloomily, and then brightened up. 'Oh no he won't, she's getting married, isn't that great?'

'They all sound cracked to me,' Michael said.

'There's Grace going down the towpath,' Dara said suddenly.

Michael jumped up on the seat to look. True, Grace was walking purposefully along towards the bridge. She wore her blue jeans and those funny little red lace-up shoes she had, and a blue and red stripy shirt, and there were red ribbons in her hair.

She looked as pretty as a picture.

Michael was pale and unhappy. Dara decided she would break their code of not offering advice.

'Do you know what I would do if I were you?'

'No,' said Michael gruffly.

'I'd ask Grace straight out. I'd say, "Is anything wrong, things seem to have changed?" At least that way you'd know.'

'She'll just smile and say nothing's changed,' Michael grumbled.

'She might actually tell you if there is something wrong.'

'I don't want to hear it if there is,' Michael said. He feared that Grace was greatly smitten by the handsome young hotel manager, and because Jim Costello had the sense to play hard to get Grace fancied him all the more.

'Do girls like being asked direct questions like that?' he asked doubtfully.

'I do,' Dara said. 'If anyone asked me a direct question like that I'd respect them, and that's the truth.'

'Dara, I was just passing,' Tommy Leonard said.

'Oh Tommy, how could you be just passing? The brothers' is at the other side of the town to the convent.'

'I know, I heard they built them that way on purpose, so that we couldn't all get at each other.'

Dara giggled. 'Not at all, it never crossed their minds.'

'Listen, I hear you're one of the few people in the world who likes direct questions rather than beating around the bush . . .'

In her head Dara heard a warning bell. She didn't want to lose Tommy Leonard as a friend.

'I used to be like that, it's true, but I've gone off it again,' she said hastily. 'I hate direct questions now and I snap the head off anyone who would ask me one.'

'Phew, I'm glad we sorted that one out,' said Tommy Leonard in a mixture of disappointment and relief.

Grace told Michael that she couldn't imagine what he was talking about. Of *course* she loved being with him. But there was so much school work to do, and she had a little table fixed up for herself in one of the residents' lounges where she could work in the evenings. And she couldn't be going out all the time. And sometimes when she did get through with homework there were things about the hotel she had to learn. After all she would be living there and working there always.

'But not immediately,' Michael cried. 'We're going to go to the university aren't we? And get degrees and travel, before we come back to work in Mountfern.'

'Oh yes, of *course* we are,' Grace said.

But she didn't sound convinced.

'Then why are you learning about the reception desk now from Jim Costello?' Poor Michael let it all slip out.

Grace gave him a long look.

'I'm sure you wouldn't want me to be discourteous to anyone on my father's staff,' she said, and Michael heard a ring of the boss's daughter in her voice that he had never heard before.

Since the day Kerry had told her about Mrs Fine and the awful scenes, Dara felt as if a huge boulder had been lifted out of her rib cage. She had known always, of course, that Kerry couldn't possibly . . . not of his own free choice . . . but people had been so definite.

And of course that was the interpretation that would be put on it. As Kerry had said, he had been uncharacteristically nice, and look at the thanks he had got for it. If he had fled, which is what you'd expect him to do from a drunk boring woman who was telling him her life story and looking for consolation of every sort . . . then things would have been better by far.

She didn't get to see him often. He had told her that because of this very bad row with his father he was doing a very ordinary menial kind of a job, he was keeping quiet about it, and in a few weeks it would all be over and they could see each other as much as they liked. He had made her promise to cut school one day and he would drive her to Galway. They would walk along the beach in Salthill in the autumn sunshine, they would buy bag after bag of lovely crisp chips, they would eat those ice-cream cones with big bars of milk flake chocolate stuck in the middle of them. And best, they could wander around hand in hand and kiss each other in the main streets of Galway city if they wanted to.

'I know a place we could go, Kerry,' she said suddenly. 'It's a tunnel. It used to be a secret place for Michael and me when we were younger but nobody uses it now.' She looked at him eagerly.

To her shock his face changed completely.

'No,' he said sharply. 'No tunnel, that's out of the question.'

He stood up. It reminded her of that time he had walked away before when she had refused his embraces. The sense of loss was sharp in her memory. She looked at him longingly.

'Will you promise without any whys. Just for me?'

'Yes, I promise,' Dara said, feeling slightly ashamed of herself as she did so.

Martin White wasn't surprised to hear that Kate Ryan wanted him to call. She said it was for a check-up before she committed herself to the big journey to Dublin.

'It's about more than that isn't it?' the doctor said.

'How did you know?'

'I thought it was possible one day there not long ago.'

'I couldn't be . . .' Kate looked horrified.

'Why couldn't you? You know the way it's done, and I'm delighted you're able to do it.' Martin beamed uncharacteristically.

'But not with me like this.'

457

'Of course it could, and will.'

She leaned forward and clutched his hand. 'I'm very strong, you'll admit that, and a lot of my strength came from you giving me things straight. Be straight now. Will it be dangerous?'

Martin took her thin hand in both of his. 'Not only will it not be dangerous, it will be wonderful. I couldn't be more pleased for you.'

'Do you think you'll go to gaol?' Declan asked Eddie when they were both in bed.
'No. Not this time.'
'Will you next time?'
'I might. Why?'
'Then I could have your bed.'
'You'd be just as bad as I am if you were brave enough.'
'I am brave.'
'No you're not, you think there's a ghost in the press.'
'I don't really think there is, I think there might be.'
'There is, a big one, but *I'm* not afraid of it. Goodnight.'

Eddie turned over and went to sleep knowing that Declan would be awake for hours looking at the door of the big cupboard in the corner of the bedroom, fearful over what might come out of it.

The river had never looked so lovely as that night. There was a flutter of birds in the trees, and they heard the cry of a fox in the still night. For two city people to recognize a fox at a distance wasn't bad. Rachel was wearing her flat shoes as if she had known they were going to walk, and he helped her over the fallen branch of a tree or through the complicated little gates that the local people called stiles.

They had driven there separately. Rachel insisted. They had parked both cars on the river bank. Behind them Coyne's wood rose dark and mysterious and further over were the hills around the Grange.

The sound of their footsteps was soft and rustling in the leaves. They came to an old wall, a good vantage point to look up at Fernscourt. Until now they had talked not at all, yet there was no air of expectancy. No tension or waiting for one of them to bring up the subject.

It came up very naturally. Patrick laid his hand over hers.

'I wish it had been different,' he said.

'Oh, so do I,' she sighed. But not with accusation; more like people sighed when it was no longer spring or when the heat went out of the day.

'It isn't anything to do with the not being Irish bit . . . believe me.'

'I do believe you. You see, you've always had a different feeling about being an American to other people I've met in my life. They all loved being American, *and* being whatever else they were, but to you being American meant losing being Irish, so you had to come back and recapture it.'

She walked apparently contentedly beside him and they came to the footbridge opposite Ryan's.

She led the way across into Fernscourt. He had been hesitant in case on this, her last night, she might not want to go into the place that had taken all his money, his time and his heart. They walked to a seat which she had arranged a long time ago when the garden plans were being discussed.

They sat and looked across the Fern at the lights in Ryan's pub where there were still a dozen or so in the bar. And at Loretto Quinn's where the rooms were being held in case Rachel might change her mind. In the soft dark night dogs were barking, they could hear an owl hooting far away and the moths flew around them gently. There was the permanent sound of the river but they had grown so used to it they didn't hear it any more.

'I'll be very lonely here.'

'No no, you'll have far too much to do,' she said. 'Your days will be filled from morning to night. I'll think of you sometimes at this time, and I'm sure you will be in your office there or with Jim Costello in the front-of-house role. You won't be sitting idly here watching the stars over Mountfern.'

'And what will you do in New York?' He was gentle too, and wistful.

'I don't know yet. I'll work hard, I can come to anyone with great references now . . .' She waved her hand at the hotel behind them. 'I've kept a portfolio of all my work. I must have known I'd need it.'

'Do you think we will be friends, you and I?'

'Some time, not for a while.'

'Nobody has shared as much of me as you have. I'm not good at giving bits of myself.' He looked at the ground.

She wanted to shout at him and say she was the most betrayed woman in the land. She had worked ceaselessly for his dream and to keep his relationship with his family good. She had bought presents for his children's birthdays for as long as she could remember, she had advised and cajoled and succeeded in keeping some kind of family love alive between them all. What was her reward? She was assumed to have slept with the son and then to have paid him to keep quiet about it.

'And because we *are* being so civilized can I say just one thing . . . and you won't get up and walk away?' she said.

'Certainly.' He was ultra formal.

'And you won't put on that formal mask with me.'

'Very well, say it, Rachel.' He smiled at her, that familiar smile with the starry lines going out from the sides of his eyes.

There was a catch in her voice which she hadn't intended. She had forgotten how much she loved his smile.

'About that night that Kerry came to my rooms.'

'Yes.' He sighed as if he had known it would be this.

'He came for a purpose, a very specific purpose.'

'Yes, so he said,' Patrick agreed.

'Don't be absurd, Patrick, don't be utterly ridiculous. There is really something lacking in you if you could believe that he could have wanted to . . . to be with me in that way.'

Her voice sounded confident and dismissive. This was not the woman who had wrung her hands in Coyne's wood and explained and contradicted and apologized. Rachel was firm and decisive now, she was dismissive of Kerry and all his tales.

'So what purpose?'

459

'He came to warn me off, to send me home. And he has achieved that purpose.' Her eyes were angry but her voice was calm.

'What was he saying . . .?'

'He was mainly saying that if I had any hopes of replacing his mother, I should forget them, that I was not worthy to mention her name, that our affair was sordid and disgusting and that her memory would never be . . . sullied, I think, by the insult of your marrying me. It was very bitter. Very violent.'

'I think this all very exaggerated. Kerry has no feelings for me . . . whether I marry or not, it hardly concerns him.'

'You may be right in that he has no feelings for you, but he has very strong feelings about his mother.'

'He doesn't give any sign of them to me.'

'How would he to you? To you of all people. He doesn't tell you that he has Kathleen's topaz made into a tiepin, that he has her picture in a watch chain, in his billfold, and in a plastic folder just loose in his pocket.'

Patrick started to speak but Rachel went on. 'And I don't say this just because he told you a pack of lies about me, in itself that's not the worst thing.'

'What *is* the worst thing?'

'The worst thing is that you believed him. That he was able to make you believe him. That Kerry with his record of deceit, gambling, theft, lies and utter selfishness was able to make you, an intelligent loving sensitive man, believe him rather than me . . . the woman who has loved you, worked with you and for you all these years. That's the worst thing, how he was able to convince you so easily . . .'

'And is that the reason you're going?'

'That and one or two other things. I think you've changed, I think the effort of making this place changed you a lot.'

'How has it changed me?'

'You were always so straight. Back in New York when there was a fight you fought fair. If another guy won the contract you shook him by the hand, you said it was only money, only work, you wished him well. If a guy lost you shook him by the hand too. You were straight.'

'I haven't cheated anyone here.' Patrick was bewildered.

'You cheated Kate Ryan.'

'I had to, Rachel. What else could I say? "You were robbed, madam, but please accept my personal cheque for the balance"?'

'You celebrated with them that justice was done. Justice was *not* done.'

'Do you really believe I am at fault over this?'

'Yes,' Rachel said simply.

He picked up her hand and stroked it. 'We have grown apart, you and I. There was a time when we could have talked it out all night, and you would have agreed that I did the only possible thing, give them their dignity if I couldn't give them an adequate settlement.'

'Even if we had been able to talk it out all night, if we still had that kind of life, I don't think I would have agreed.'

'But you would have understood why I did what I did,' he sighed.

'Yes, I'd have understood.'

Together they sat and looked across at Ryan's, where the lights had gone out finally and stragglers walked or cycled home along River Road.

'Will you not stay for the opening? Please, Rachel.'

'No, no, you can call me when it's all over and tell me how it went.'

'It will be good to talk to you on the telephone anyway. There are so many day-to-day things I'll want to tell you about.'

'No, Patrick. No calls. Only on the day of the opening.'

'No calls?'

'If we're going to live our own lives, it's childish to keep calling each other.'

'But as friends even?' He was begging her.

'No, we're not friends yet, we will be some time.'

There was a long silence.

'I feel very empty. I let you down, didn't I?'

'Let's be the only couple in the history of the world who said goodbye without any recriminations,' she said, standing up to go.

She bent down and kissed him on the forehead.

He put his arms around her waist and held her to him.

Gently she released herself and walked away. Down the path to the footbridge and across the Fern.

Patrick sat in the grounds of his hotel and watched Rachel walk without turning back all along the river bank, past the old wall and the funny stiles.

He heard her car start and drive away towards the town.

CHAPTER TWENTY-THREE

The weather forecast had said sunny with scattered showers.

'I hope they'll be scattered over the rest of Ireland and not all concentrated in this direction,' Miss Purcell said sternly.

The canon had a chest cold that would not go away. Dr White had said that a man the canon's age was to expect chest colds and not to stay in a draught.

Miss Purcell would have liked more concern and a preciser prescription. The canon would have to be in a considerable draught during the blessing ceremony. She had been very insistent about woollen underwear, and the wearing of a scarf while not actually involved in the religious offices.

Father Hogan was reassuring. Most of the time Canon Moran would stay well away from draughts. The huge marquee built by the landing stage was meant to be utterly windproof. And then there would be plenty of activities inside the house proper. Miss Purcell was to have no further worries.

Father Hogan also described at great length what he heard was going to be served to eat. There was an amount of salmon being delivered to the hotel that would frighten you, and there would be plates of it all afternoon if people wanted it, they could come back for helping after helping. There would be potato salad, and all other kinds of salads, and buttered brown scones.

Father Hogan said that there had been considerable discussion about whether or not to have a hot lunch, but the salmon faction had prevailed. There would be soup first, of course, served in cups so that it would be easy for people to manage it. There were two huge tureens of soup on their own little heaters and you could come back for second cups or even a third cup here too.

By the time Father Hogan had begun to weigh up the merits of the fresh fruit salad and lashing of cream as opposed to the hot apple tart with ice cream, Miss Purcell began to wonder if the young priest could possibly be becoming *too* interested in food. She had let out his soutane once already and it needed a further easing at the seams.

But she dismissed the thought as unworthy. And almost blasphemous. What was better than to see a healthy young priest enjoy his food? She thought back on the days that Fergus Slattery wouldn't notice what she served so long as there was a bottle of tomato ketchup on the table.

Papers Flynn stirred in the outhouse where he had slept well all night. There was something happening today. What was it? He remembered that it was the hotel opening.

A barge had been brought from a Dublin canal, and painted in bright colours. There were going to be tours up and down the river to the old abbey near the lake. It would be great sport to watch it. Papers would find himself a good vantage point on the bank to see the comings and goings.

He was pleased to think of a day filled with such activity. He had all the details from Carrie. Papers had called there about his usual business and Mrs Ryan had invited him into the kitchen for a plate of dinner.

Mrs Ryan was a lady he liked a lot. She never asked him to clean himself up. She wouldn't give him any old guff about finding himself a roof over his head. Mrs Ryan knew that Papers didn't want to be tied down. She gave him useful things like a pair of big hessian bags with strong handles on them: she thought they might come in handy for transporting his belongings, and they were the very thing.

Mrs Ryan had taken Papers aside and said that he may have heard that recently they had been given a very substantial sum of money as compensation for her accident. Papers had heard it, certainly. Up in Matt Foley's at the top of the town they had said that the Ryans were going to spend it all on a carpeted lounge bar with music playing in the background. In Conway's pub they had said that the lot had gone into a building society and there wasn't going to be a penny of it spent ever. It was to be their nest egg, their insurance policy for years to come. He had travelled on further to Paddy Dunne's pub, where the story was that the money had been set aside to send Mrs Ryan to a hospital outside Boston where they were able to do miracles with what other places had said were incurables. It cost five thousand pounds before they would look at you, and there would be the fare and everything, but she'd be walking again by the springtime. Paddy Dunne had read an article about the place in a Sunday paper.

Papers would never dream of asking Mrs Ryan which if any of these stories were true. He was surprised when she suddenly volunteered the information.

'We've been very lucky, Papers, and I was wondering if you'd join us in celebrating our good fortune.'

'Well now, ma'am.' Papers was cautious.

'I mean, I wouldn't normally dream of offering anyone money, but seeing as how we got so much ourselves. It's mainly in a savings account and it's going to be used for the children's education, in case any of them are bright enough to be able to use it. But we kept a few pounds aside for ourselves, and for people we know.'

She handed him three pound notes folded over.

'It's not a great deal but I don't know whether you'd like a cap, I was going to get you a cap, but John said that a man should choose his own cap for himself.'

'He's right there,' Papers agreed sagely.

'Or it might not be a cap at all that you'd like, so will you get yourself something, and regard it as sharing part of our good fortune?'

Papers had been very pleased indeed to have had his wishes considered and discussed so carefully without anyone making mention of the county home, which usually came up when people had his welfare at heart.

In an uncharacteristic burst of speech he had told Mrs Ryan that he might buy himself a little spirit stove that he had seen in a shop. He had been debating if it was worth the investment, but it would give him more freedom, he'd be able to go farther afield if he had his own way of being able to make a cup of tea.

He had thanked Mrs Ryan very formally and assured her that he would report progress on the spirit stove. If he bought it, he promised that he would be very careful with it. And ended his speech by saying that she was a great woman to be celebrating good fortune when there were many in the land who would say that it was no good fortune to have the two legs struck from under you, but was glad that Mrs Ryan was able to rise above that.

He had been surprised to see tears in her eyes. And she had said that oddly she didn't worry about her legs being useless, she had got over that part of it, she just felt that she herself had lost her personality and was useless as a person. Papers hadn't understood that and he told her it was a bit deep for him. She cheered up then and agreed and told him to have a good plate of stew before he left, and to come and watch any of the activities on the day of the opening from Ryan's bar.

'You know you're invited like everyone else in the place to the Thatch Bar in the evening, he wants the whole of Mountfern to come.'

'Well . . .' Papers was doubtful.

'He's not issuing personal invitations, just wants everyone to turn up for a drink and to wish the place luck. Of course there are some who would prefer to inspect it at their own time rather than being herded together. Some people of the more independent kind, private people will take up his invitation at a later date.'

Papers had been relieved to hear that, he thought at first that he might be expected to go, but Mrs Ryan had set his mind at rest on that point. Papers could join the private sort of people, the people of independent mind who didn't want to go as part of the herd.

Rita Walsh woke with a start. Why had she set her alarm clock for seven o'clock? Then she remembered.

It was the day of the opening. She had two young girls from the convent coming at eight o'clock to start shampooing. The schools had the day off and Rita had picked two of the more reliable Sixth Years to help her. She had trained them in the art of washing hair without drowning the client.

All the towels and capes were clean and ready in little heaps in the salon.

She would get milk and biscuits from Loretto, she had tea and coffee there already, and in honour of the occasion she had bought a dozen nice blue and white teacups.

There would be a steady procession all morning. And since everyone would want to be finished and out by twelve-thirty, she had decided to open very early and accommodate everyone.

It was only regulars today. Mrs Daly, Miss Johnson, Miss Bryne the physiotherapist, Dr White's wife. Loretto Quinn was coming in to have her hair combed out, she had the set yesterday. She also had the ring. She told Rita Walsh that in your life you found one Barney. It would be too good to be true to imagine you'd find another. But Jack Coyne was a man often very much misunderstood, and he had told Loretto that it was lonely to be in business in a big way and have no company in the evening when he came in after a long day's work. Loretto had understood this too.

Rita had been very pleased for Loretto and agreed that it was often easy to get the wrong end of the stick with Jack until you knew him. She had done Loretto's hair free as a celebration and said she must come in for a lot of back-combing and lacquer since this was a special day, the day that people would hear about their engagement. Loretto must look her best.

Jack Coyne was going to the opening under sufferance. One of the terms of their very unromantic and highly practical contract had been that Jack would end his vendetta with Mr O'Neill and that Loretto would smarten herself up and learn to drive. The new Mrs Jack Coyne must be not only a successful shopkeeper in her right but a well-turned-out woman driver.

John Ryan woke at seven. He had slept badly. Twice during the night he had got up to get a drink of water, his throat felt dry and he couldn't seem to get comfortable in the bed.

If Kate had been lying beside him in the old days, she would have woken too and gone to make them a cup of tea. They might have sat during the dark night and talked about the hotel that was finally going to open, and all the fears that they shared as well as the totally different fears that one had and the other had not. It would have looked less shadowy, that big house across the river, and less full of terror.

But Kate had not been in the room for over three years. Sometimes John slept on the divan in her green room below. He was always aware of how much she hated it when she needed to use the lavatory, whether she dragged herself into the chair and wheeled herself to the bathroom, or used the bedpan. Either way it distressed her so much that he often felt he was more of a hindrance to her than a companion. It was more sensible for him to sleep upstairs, though it was lonely.

And sometimes he felt it was selfish, particularly after they had made love. But then, making love itself was a selfish activity these days. There was no trace of the pleasure and excitement for Kate that had delighted him before.

John looked across at Fernscourt as the morning light fell on the great marquee. Normally he never let his mind go down this particular train of thought but today he didn't pull himself up. He stood holding the bedroom curtain in his hand and looked at the landing stage, the brightly painted barge, and the first signs of activity in the big cultivated grounds, and wondered what things would have been like if Patrick O'Neill's grandfather had been thrown out of a cottage in Cork or Galway or Clare instead of in this small bend on the road in the midlands.

How different everything would have been then.

Grace O'Neill woke with a jump because there was a noise in her bedroom. But it was only her new dress and its heavy coat hanger falling from the door of her closet where she had hung it last night. She wanted to see it first thing so that she could make an instant judgement. Now it was in a crumbled ball on the floor.

She leaped out of bed to rescue it and held it up against the light. It *was* beautiful. She had been silly to think it was baby dollish, it would look classy and striking.

Grace hoped that Michael would be cheerful today. She hated to see that hangdog look about him, as if someone had taken away his favourite toy.

She went to the window and leaned out. The huge marquee blocked the view across the river. She could not see Ryan's pub properly.

She felt sorry for Michael having to share a room with that terrible Eddie. Declan was harmless enough but Eddie was too much.

Michael had explained that there was a partition. He had begged for one, and Jimbo had been instructed to build a plywood wall dividing the room.

She compared it to Jim Costello's room. Well, it was more a suite really. He had a study, a bathroom and kitchenette, with a big bedroom that faced the river. She had seen it when he was taking her on a grand tour.

Jim had explained that the big sofa turned into a bed at night. By day the room looked expensive and impersonal. As if it were a genuine hotel bedroom, and Jim was just passing through. There were no photographs or personal things around his room.

Grace liked to think of the frank admiring looks he gave her, and the promise that when the day was over and there was time to think, he would be able to sit down and talk to her properly.

Loretto Quinn woke and examined her hair to see how much of the set remained. Rita was going to brush it up for her and lacquer it like a board later in the morning.

There were several things she wanted to do before she opened the shop. She wanted to finish her letter to Mrs Fine, telling her that there had been a dozen requests to rent the rooms, and that Loretto was going to give them to a young chef who said that he never lived on the premises, it always led to hassle, and he had wanted something nearby. He had been very impressed with the little kitchen, and said that the cooker was a very good make and one of the most expensive on the market.

Loretto wanted to thank Rachel for that as well, she had never appreciated it at the time. She wanted Rachel's advice on what she should wear for her wedding next spring. Would a lemon-coloured suit be nice or would it take the colour from her?

Loretto also wanted to leave a note in to Fergus Slattery. Jack Coyne had said to her that the country had never been the same since the Married Women's Property Act. It was a joke, but she was going to ask Fergus just to make it clear to her in words she would understand that if she and Jack had a bust-up in the years to come, that Jack couldn't take her little shop from her. And Loretto had to iron her dress, and once she had sorted through the potatoes and shaken the earth off them, she would paint her nails pink, as people would be admiring the ring.

And she had to decide about the picture of Barney that hung over the mantelpiece in her kitchen.

She took it down and looked at his face. It wasn't a very big picture, nor a very good one. His hair was sticking out in a spiky way that wasn't really like the way Barney was. The years in between made it hard to remember exactly the way he was.

As she looked at the picture Loretto noticed that the big old frame was coming apart, it was old and cracked. It would be dangerous to leave it hanging in that position in case it fell on anyone. Loretto's decision was made for her. She couldn't put the picture up again the way it was.

She took out the photograph of Barney Quinn and put it in a smaller frame, a stand-up type which you could put on a shelf. In front of the potted plant. But in time it could be moved over beside the plant or towards the back of the shelf.

Eddie Ryan woke and looked out the window.

He had promised his mother that he would do nothing today that would bring any disgrace on the family.

'It's an important day, and I'm in a bit of a fuss and bother about it already, so it would be the living end, Eddie, if you were to be a worry to me, if I had to be looking round asking people where is that boy and what's he up to now.'

'Maybe I'd better stay in bed all day,' Eddie had said quite seriously. It seemed to be the only way he could guarantee being no trouble at all.

'No, I'd be afraid you'd fall out of the window or hang yourself or something. I wouldn't be able to take my eyes off the house while we're over there,' Kate had grumbled.

Mam had bought him a great jacket that day in Dublin, it was full of pockets and zips and wasn't at all the kind of thing he thought Mam would buy. He'd been sure it would be something like a blazer or a suit jacket when he was unwrapping it.

'How did you know this is what I'd want?' His eyes were shining.

'I guessed,' Mam had said.

She told him it was in the nature of a bribe, a promise of peace on the day of the opening.

Declan stirred and rubbed his eyes. 'Is it morning?' he asked. Declan sometimes behaved as if he were retarded.

'No,' said Eddie. 'It's the middle of the night and all those ghosts you're so afraid of have been at it again. They've bitten the head off Jaffa. Oh God, it's lying on the ground all covered with dried blood.'

Declan let out a screech that could be heard on the Dublin road and leaped out to see if this was true.

Carrie, who had been getting sick in the bathroom for the fourth morning running and was beginning to work out that there might be a very unsettling reason for this, got such a fright at Declan's screams that she knocked over the entire contents of a tray that was perched dangerously on a white chest of drawers. The tray held – or had held – talcum powder, Dettol, dried-up calamine lotion, milk of magnesia, a glass eye dropper, and a bottle shaped like a crinoline lady full of blue bath salts.

The recriminations were lengthy. The court of inquiry into why all those particular things were on a tray was endless. Kate said that it was a great thing for a woman in a wheelchair to be told that the bathroom she could never go up the stairs to see had now turned into some kind of boxroom or rubbish dump, filled with old chests of drawers and trays and the Lord knew what else.

Dara was accused of having weighted it down too much with the crinoline lady. Dara, woken from sleep with what she considered monstrously unfair charges, said that the crinoline lady was, if anyone would care to remember, a gift from Marian Johnson to say thank you when Dara had gone to help in the Grange at a function. Dara had thought she was being paid, which was the only reason she had gone, and had been outraged by the blue crinoline.

Mam had said then to put it up in the bathroom somewhere out of people's sight, and now she, Dara, was being blamed for it.

Eddie said he would stick a compass in Declan's heart if he told anyone why he had cried out, and that this was no joking matter.

Poor Declan tried to say that he had been having a nightmare, he had dreamed that a ghost had bitten off the head of the cat, and that the side yard was awash with blood.

John said that it was too much for a human to bear. One of his sons was a hardened criminal, the other a certifiable lunatic.

Jack Coyne woke with a feeling of wellbeing that surprised him. What was he feeling so good about?

He remembered that despite all the trials and tribulations, a few of them aided and abetted by Jack himself, Fernscourt was going to open today.

Well, he was going to the festivities of course, no point in making any lone point, over something that was happening anyway, and passing up a free dinner.

Anyway there would be lots of fellows there from the Tourist Board and from Aer Lingus and the American airlines. And there would be journalists and local councillors, two bishops no less, a rake of priests, four TDs at the last count, not to mention the high and the mighty for miles around. If he couldn't get a bit of business out of today he'd be in a poor way.

Then he remembered Loretto, and how she had agreed to everything. It had been well worth getting her those flowers back a bit, and saying that he would be happy to go dancing of a weekend. Women really and truly liked those kinds of things. It was the way they were. And Loretto had been very practical too and agreeable to some of his suggestions. She had been adamant about maintaining her own little shop rather than considering its possible sale as a site for some other business once the hotel got going. She had been equally firm about not learning anything whatsoever about maintenance work. She didn't want to spend her life in greasy overalls lying under some lorry. She had agreed to learn how to drive, however, which would be very useful for car delivery or collection or going for spare parts.

She had a nice smile, Loretto had. He had never noticed her at all until recently, thought she was a streelish little one in a shabby boxeen of a shop.

It was extraordinary how she had livened up when O'Neill's foreign woman came to live there. And would anyone be able to explain what had happened to send *her* packing so suddenly?

Fergus Slattery heard the telephone ring at seven-fifteen. That had to be some crisis.

He dragged himself unwillingly from a dream where he was advising the Rolling Stones about their grammar, and telling them that the song 'I Can't Get No Satisfaction' actually and literally meant that they *could* get satisfaction, which was fine if this is what they wanted to say.

The Rolling Stones had been delighted with Fergus, and had asked him to get on the payroll. He wouldn't have to leave Mountfern, but could advise by phone or letter on anything that needed revision. They promised to come and see him when next they were passing that way, and Fergus had told them they'd get a great bed and breakfast in Ryan's. Dara had been so grateful to him and had apologized for ever thinking he should be put down like an old horse.

Loath to leave such entertainment, he went in his bare feet to the phone.

'It's Rosemary.'

'*Who?*'

'I know we haven't seen each other a great deal over the past while, Fergus, but I am your only sister.'

'My God, Rosemary, is anything wrong? It's the middle of the night. Did something happen?'

'Of course something happened. I'm hardly ringing you for a chat out of the blue.'

'What is it? The boys . . . was there an accident . . . ?'

'The boys are fine wherever they are. They don't bother to let me know.'

He waited.

'It's James. He had me out of the house, changed the locks. He can't do this to me. He can't throw me out of my own home.' She was near to tears.

'When did this happen?'

'The locks were changed last night, I stayed in a guest house. I was waiting until I could ring you to know what to do.'

A wave of pity came over him for this tall shruggy woman, with no warmth and no charm. He remembered her visit at the time of their father's funeral, her lack of any kindness, her cruel taunting remarks.

And now at this ungodly hour of the morning she had finally been locked out of the family home in Manchester.

'Wait until nine-thirty, Rosemary,' he said.

'What will you do then?'

'I will do nothing, but you'll go to a solicitor – a solicitor in Manchester, mind, not in Mountfern. And you'll tell him what happened, and the circumstances leading up to it, and he will tell you what to do.'

'I don't know any solicitors in Manchester, for heaven's sake. If I did have any legal contacts do you think I'd be ringing you?'

'No, I know that. I know that very clearly.'

'So what's the point in saying find a solicitor, find a solicitor? I could have looked one up in a phone book myself.'

'I think that's probably the best thing to do.' He kept his tone even.

'Are you serious?'

'Yes, Rosemary. It sounds distant and may even sound harsh, but I can't give you any advice whatsoever. You must see that.'

There was a silence.

'I'm sorry about it all. Do you think it can be sorted out, the difficulties with James?'

'Difficulties.' She gave a snort of laughter and said the word again, mimicking his accent. 'Difficulties! No, I don't think they can be sorted out, as you say.' Her tone was scornful.

'Well then, the best I can wish you is that you are able to work out adequate provisions and settlement and that it is done with as little hurt and animosity as possible.'

'Jesus, but you're a pompous bore, Fergus.'

He had been going to say that if she wanted a holiday she could come to the house where she had grown up in Mountfern. He would not say this now.

He thought of the night that he had been going to give her the old Victorian sewing table belonging to his mother and had changed his mind over some insult that she had slung at him. Perhaps her whole life was a series of such non happenings.

'I hope I'm not as bad as you make me out, but I'm sure like all of us I must have my faults.' He put on a mad simper as he said this. He tried to look at himself in the hall mirror but the light was bad and he could only see his tousled hair and his crumpled pyjamas.

He did a little dance while holding the phone and leering at his reflection. It pleased him to know that Rosemary could have no idea of his manner.

There was no more to say now, so Rosemary had rung off. Fergus was well into his capering dance now so he continued it, round and round the hall, pretending to hold up a ball gown and curtseying at himself every time he came to the mirror.

As he passed the hall door in a spectacular twirl he saw two eyes looking at him through the letter box.

Fergus stopped in his tracks. 'Who's that?' he asked fearfully.

'I'm sorry, Fergus.' A thin voice came apologetically through the slit in the door.

He threw open the hall door and there was Loretto Quinn, a letter in her hand.

'I was just about to put this through the door but I heard these swishing sounds so I looked in in case something was wrong.'

Loretto had never looked so alarmed in all the years he had known her.

'But you were pleased to see that everything was as normal.' Fergus beamed at Loretto as he took the letter. 'I always have a little dance like this to start the day. They advised us years ago in the Four Courts, they said there was nothing like it for settling the mind into a good legal way of thinking.'

Loretto's mouth was still open as Fergus bowed to her theatrically and closed the door.

Jim Costello woke with a toothache.

He gave himself five minutes to decide whether he could bear it for the day or whether it would incapacitate him for the day. He decided it would render him speechless.

He rang Dr White and asked the name of the dentist in the town. Then he rang the dentist.

The dentist was sorry, but he had limited surgery hours today, he was actually going to the official celebrations at the opening of a big new hotel.

'I'm the manager of that bloody hotel, and there won't *be* an opening unless you do something with my tooth,' Jim said, maddened with pain and the man's slow obstinate voice at the other end of the phone.

'Well well well.'

'Can you do it or can you not?' As he spoke Jim Costello realized how like Patrick O'Neill he was becoming in his speech. It sat better on a middle-aged American tycoon than on a young Irish hotelier.

He changed his approach.

'As you can see I am utterly relying on you. Just a temporary dressing, anything. You've been highly recommended in these parts.'

'I don't really . . .'

Jim played his final card. 'And if you knew the whole story about the problems we've been having and all the celebrities who are expected today . . . Well, you'll meet them yourself. If it ever gets going at all.'

That did it. The man said Jim was to get into a car and drive like the clappers, he'd open his surgery early for him. A chance to hear the inside story about Fernscourt was too much to pass by.

Mary Donnelly woke and spoke to Leopold, who had been waiting patiently for her to stir.

Leopold was a more intelligent dog than many people gave him credit for. He knew the way to stay in Mary's good books was by not waking her or snuffling round for anything interesting and certainly not by offering any of his paws in the form of a handshake. Mary was of the opinion that there was far too much insincerity and over-greeting going on in the world. She liked silent ruminative thoughtful encounters. Leopold had adapted to her ways.

He was surprised that she seemed to be making a speech to him, it was not her usual way of greeting the day. He held his head on one side and tried to understand what she was telling him.

It had nothing to do with a walk. But there was no abuse in it either. He couldn't fathom it at all.

'Leopold, this is a black day for this house. But apparently none of us are allowed to mention it. The new way of going on is to pretend a problem doesn't exist. That way we can all go on drinking and slapping each other on the back.

'Listen to me well, Leopold. This is the beginning of the end. You and I could be walking the roads of Ireland with packs on our backs. There's going to be nothing in the profits of this establishment to put a dinner on the table for either of us once this hotel gets going. But to be fair, Leopold, they never put your dinner on the table. More the floor.'

The dog looked at her trustingly.

'Don't mind me, Leopold,' she said, scratching his ear. 'I am totally mad. Not a little mad. Totally and completely mad.'

Brian Doyle woke with a thick head. They had been celebrating until a late hour. O'Neill had said that as far as could be seen to the naked eye the structure seemed sound, and more or less approximated to the plans that had been given to Brian Doyle. He had bought Brian several drinks on the strength of this. Then back in the town Brian had decided to finalize the arrangements for taking Peggy, his girlfriend of many years, to the opening. He would call for her at noon, his brother Paudie would drive them so that they need not worry if there were a few drinks taken during the day.

He had been neglectful of Peggy, particularly during these last weeks. He had wanted to explain to her that this was all over. He had not been prepared to meet her mother, a battle axe if ever there was one. The mother had said that Peggy would be going to no opening or closing of any hotel whether built by Brian Doyle or built by the Emperor of China.

Peggy had, according to her mother, belatedly come to her senses over Brian Doyle, she realized that having her name up with him for so many years had brought her nothing but heartbreak and humiliation and, what was more distressing still, had cut her off from any other avenue and future. So that was all in the past now, thanks to the good Lord who had opened her eyes, and she had instructed her mother to pass the burden of the message on to Brian if he ever made an appearance in the next year or so.

This was the heavy artillery.

Brian sat in Peggy's mother's kitchen letting the words wash over him and trying to work out where Peggy might be.

'Don't start it all up again,' said the woman in front of him who had not ceased to speak since he entered the house. 'You're a bachelor, Brian, stay one. For God's sake, will you go back out to that hotel and pat it and stroke it and be with it morning, noon and night? That's what you want.'

'I can't go to bed with the hotel,' Brian said eventually.

'And as sure as your name is Brian Doyle you can't go to bed with my daughter either. Sweet talk or no sweet talk. Ring or no ring.'

It hadn't crossed Brian's mind that a ring should form part of the proceedings. There was plenty of time for that.

He had left the house disconsolately and on the street run into Seamus Sheehan, the sergeant from Mountfern.

Since Seamus was off duty they went to a pub and Brian explained that he was not a knave or a philanderer at heart, it was just that he was too young to settle down.

Sergeant Sheehan said that basically all men were too young to settle down, his long life in the Guards had taught him that. He cross-questioned Brian about the tunnel behind the bedroom wing, and whether there was any entrance in it under the brambles and briars.

Brian said that he couldn't bear to think of any more entrances or exits to that hotel than there were already. There had been an unmerciful carry-on about where the drive was going to be at the start, most people thought that it was never going to get off the ground at all.

But Sergeant Sheehan went on and on. Any entrances to old shafts or tunnels or anything they had come across?

Brian Doyle had said that when it was a question of a fairy fort some of the men he had working for him were as superstitious as old shawlies who would go and tie things to a May tree. They had just avoided going anywhere near it and in the end the best thing had been to build a trellis and drape these creepers over it. Made a kind of wall of sorts.

No, he had no idea if there was anything in it. He didn't give much thought to the fairy world himself, there was too much happening in the so-called real world. If they were there, which seemed highly unlikely, then leave them to get on with it, that was Brian's philosophy. Oh, the sergeant meant non fairies? No, he could not imagine that anyone with a marble left in their head would want to be burrowing around under all those blackberries and old thorns. But then Brian was always the last to be told anything. The whole Pioneer Total Abstinence Association could be having their annual general meeting in those bushes before anyone would think of telling the poor builder.

But wasn't it a bloody miracle that the place was finished and none of them were in gaol or up in the asylum on the hill?

Too late Brian Doyle remembered the youngest Sheehan boy was in that very asylum. He looked glumly into his pint. There were some things you could never backtrack your way out of, and it was wiser not to try.

Sergeant Seamus Sheehan woke and made his wife a cup of tea.

'This is your big day,' she said sleepily. 'Is the weather good for it?'

He opened the curtains a little and peered out.

'It's bright,' he said. 'It'll be sunny with scattered showers, they said.'

'Ah well, that's grand, and they'll have a tent set up so you won't notice the showers.'

She was pleased that her husband would be on show and a man of importance today. There were very senior men from Phoenix Park, the Garda headquarters, coming to the reception, and there were local guards from around coming in to help with the traffic and because there would be VIPs coming to the reception. Seamus would have more responsibility than he ever had before.

Seamus Sheehan was glad he hadn't told his wife about the plan to close in on the tunnel that morning. He had been in the town last night setting it all up with the force there.

He had been praised for the excellent surveillance he had kept, and the superintendent said that he was a model of what an efficient rural sergeant could do by knowing the people of his place and being able to spot anything untoward.

McCann, Byrne and Red Molloy were no mean prize to get in one net.

The plan was to take them early *and* have it wrapped up before the guests started arriving.

Whatever they were up to, that crowd, it must have something to do with the opening. A possible kidnapping.

Guaranteed, of course, to get the worst publicity for Ireland if it took place when a load of American journalists were actually on the spot feeding their faces with salmon and brown bread. They would get them into different cars and take them by different routes to the Garda station in the big town.

Charlie Byrne was the thicko, he'd certainly tell them what was going on.

Sergeant Sheehan was glad that it would all be over well before his wife had put on the new suit that was hanging up outside the wardrobe so that it wouldn't get crushed, together with the frilly white blouse and a handbag so new that it was still in the paper bag from the shop and had tissue paper inside it to make it keep its shape.

Kate felt that the day had started poorly. All that shouting and the upset in the bathroom.

But these were as nothing compared to the fact that Carrie was now almost certainly pregnant. That was the first thing to be coped with.

She called the girl into her room and asked her to close the door.

'Have a plain marietta biscuit, Carrie, take one there from the tin on the window.'

Carrie's eyes were huge. 'I was just going to have a drink of bitter lemon or something, ma'am . . .'

'No, the biscuit is best. I remember myself.'

Carrie's eyes were full of tears. 'It must be definite, ma'am,' she said. 'I'm very sorry.'

'Why are you saying you're sorry to *me*?'

'Well, you've been very nice to me, I don't want to go bringing disgrace on you. That's the last thing I'd want.'

'You won't do that. It's all a matter of what way we look at it.'

'What do you mean?'

'Mrs Fine used to say to me that life was all about how you looked at things. If you saw the sunny side then things were sunny . . . You know, the Americans have some book about it.'

Carrie looked at her, bewildered.

'So what I mean is this, there's going to be no tears, no apologies, no shame. No saying to Jimbo that you're sorry. It's not *your* fault any more than it is his.'

'But he could say I'd been with anyone. Jimbo's going to be a known singer. There's going to be people here today who will have heard of him.' Carrie was full of awe.

'Yes, but he's your Jimbo, he's not going to walk out on you?'

'If I gave in to him, let him have his way, what's to stop him thinking I let other fellows have their way?'

Kate's face was very impatient.

'Loretto Quinn and Jack Coyne are going to announce their engagement today, I wouldn't be surprised if Brian Doyle might even stir himself to propose to that long-suffering Peggy. What more natural than you and Jimbo too?'

'But ma'am, he mightn't want to . . .'

Kate wasn't listening. 'Yes, a big occasion like this, a very good place, we could even get a bit in the newspapers about it. Singer to wed, it's a good time of year to think of an Easter wedding.'

'*Easter?*'

'Yes, well that's for Loretto and Jack. But you and Jimbo might find that to fit in with his career you might suddenly get married straight away, before Christmas.'

'Oh ma'am, wouldn't it be great if he'd agree?'

'Of course he'll agree. He'll be delighted,' said Kate with much more confidence than she felt.

Sheila Whelan woke with a heavy heart.

Patrick O'Neill had been in last night, anxious to talk.

'You're about the only one I can really sit down and talk to.' He looked tired and lonely.

'Haven't you half the country to talk to?' She smiled.

'Not really.' He gave a heavy sigh.

'You'll miss Rachel tomorrow?' Sheila was one of the few people who could speak like this without causing him offence.

'I'll miss her, that's very true. She put so goddamn much into it, I wanted her to see the opening, even if afterwards . . . well . . .' His voice trailed away.

'Probably better for her to go at once if she was going to go at all,' Sheila said.

'Yes, women see it that way. I'm going to call her tomorrow night. At midnight our time it will only be early evening in New York. She agreed that we would talk on the telephone tomorrow.'

He looked boyish and eager. Not the great O'Neill opening the most talked-of hotel in Ireland, who kept his lady friend in doubt about his intentions all the time she was here. Sheila Whelan thought that men were impossible to understand and that perhaps the less time and effort spent trying to understand them the better.

'What are you doing tonight? Getting a good sleep for tomorrow, I hope. You'll have a long day.'

'I can't sleep at all these nights. I walk the grounds a lot. I had a few drinks with Doyle. I don't know which of us is more surprised that he hasn't ended up in one gaol for fraud and I haven't ended up in another for attempted murder!'

'Go on, you'd be lost without Brian to give out about. You'll miss him, I promise you.'

'Sheila, you're very discreet . . .' Patrick began.

'Not any longer,' she interrupted him.

'What on earth do you mean?'

'Just that. I'm *not* discreet any more. If I see something I don't like then these days I say it. It's hard to get used to, I keep hoping I'm doing the right thing.'

She had told him no more despite his concern.

Sheila knew that if anyone was going to be hurt by what she had done it would be Patrick. She had discovered that Kerry O'Neill was taking boxes and packages into a disused tunnel which led to Fernscourt.

He was involved with a gang of hoodlums, probably thought they were freedom fighters instead of bank robbers, which was what they were. Sheila knew that on the morning of the hotel opening the tunnel would be closed off, the gang taken into custody and as a courtesy to Patrick O'Neill and to all the employment he was bringing to the area his son would not be questioned until the following day.

There was a belief that Kerry O'Neill, though most certainly some kind of an accomplice, was not involved in the criminal side of things. Or not yet. Sergeant Sheehan said that it was all being done to pay his gambling debts.

She thought of Seamus Sheehan's son in the home, of Patrick's son running with bank robbers, of her own husband's son who couldn't come back from England for his father's funeral.

Many times Sheila had wished that she had given birth to a boy. A child of her own who would grow up under her eyes. This morning as she dressed for the day

475

and all it would bring Sheila felt glad that she had no son. She was better off today only worrying about herself.

Dara's hopes of a long leisurely time to get ready had been dashed. First there was all the work clearing up the bathroom, then Mam wanted to be helped.

Mam looked very pale and even unwell. There was a light sweat on her forehead and she had that distraught look she sometimes got.

'It's going to be fine,' Dara said soothingly.

'What is?'

'The opening. The day!'

'Oh yes. Yes of course.'

Dara looked at her, concerned. Mam hadn't been at all well of late. Look at the way she had felt after the trip to Dublin. Don't say it was going to be the same now. Dara held up the navy and white outfit. It had been chosen by Rachel Fine, of course. Hadn't everything? It was smart, but Dara would have dressed Mam in something less severe. It had a lot of small buttons down the back which would need to be fastened.

Mam smelled of good soap and talcum powder. More gifts from Mrs Fine. Perhaps as the years went by Mrs Fine's gifts would wear out, and her influence would die away. Mam had said very firmly and very briefly that she would not be coming back again to Mountfern.

Dara sat by the dressing table part of the green room. She looked long at Mam's face to see any signs of illness.

'Would you tell me if there was anything wrong, if you felt badly?' she asked her mother.

'Yes and no. Yes if we could do anything about it.'

'Then there *is* something wrong!'

'No, I feel jittery today, that's all, a bit like going to the compensation case. You know the feeling.'

Dara knew the feeling, she *had* the feeling. She wasn't at all sure that Kerry would like her dress. She had spent such hours choosing it in Dublin, and spent so much money on it. It looked a simple red silk. In the hand it looked only like a crumpled scarf, but when Dara put it on she looked great! Or she hoped she did. But you'd know with Kerry.

She had fastened the tiny buttons and Mam looked very well, smart and stylish. The dress had a full skirt. Mam never wore clothes that let you see her legs properly, even though they looked perfectly all right.

Dara felt the overpowering sympathy that she sometimes did for her mother, who could not stand up and who knew that she would never be able to stand again.

'Dara, one little thing about today.'

Dara sighed. It was going to be about not smearing on too much make-up, not disappearing with Kerry, about being understanding to Michael, or keeping an eye on Declan or trying to stop Eddie from alienating the whole parish.

'Yes Mam,' she said dutifully.

'If I were your age, and I were as lovely as you . . . I would not want to listen to someone saying what I'm going to say now, but it's only very short and then we don't have to talk about it again today. All right?'

Dara nodded. What alternative had she?

Kate took her hand. 'I just want you to know how sad I am that Rachel isn't here today. She worked on every stone of this place as much as any of Brian Doyle's men, as much as Patrick ever did. And at this moment she's in New York City, probably crying her eyes out and thinking of it all.'

Dara had taken her hand away and was moving restively.

'And the reason that she's not here is Kerry. She did nothing wrong, nothing bad, nothing that she couldn't stand up in the pulpit and talk about. She got a little drunk, and she's not used to drink, that's all.'

'Mam, please . . .'

'I said it's short. Kerry drove her out, Dara, for these reasons: he didn't want her to marry his father. He has always been much more fond of his mother than of Patrick, he thought that Rachel should not replace her.

'Then he got into great debt at a card game and he asked Rachel for money . . . It's very complicated but he didn't get it finally, so he let everyone think that he and Rachel were together. You've heard that, I know. I just wanted to set it straight in your mind.'

'Oh Mam, I heard the real story from Kerry,' Dara said.

'You heard a story from Kerry. I doubt if it was the real one.'

Kate's eyes were far away. 'You're a grown girl, Dara, you are sixteen – although I think that's young, I'll still think you're young when you're twenty-six . . . I am not poisoning you, I'm warning you. That's all. Of course you'll be with Kerry today, and he will be charming and lovely and make you feel good. But I felt you had to know that he is dangerous.'

Michael wondered for the fiftieth time was his jacket a bit sissyish. It had looked fine in Dublin. But hadn't everything? Tommy had said it was great, you'd expect Michael to break into a waltz as soon as he put it on. Grace had been non-committal. She had been slightly annoyed that he had found the time and possibility of going to Dublin with Dara when he hadn't gone with her.

For no reason Michael kept remembering Maggie talking about the hotel opening. She said there would be television personalities coming to it and that maybe they would all be introduced to them on account of knowing the O'Neills so well. They had laughed at Maggie for her enthusiasm. And she was dead for over three months when the hotel did open.

Something had gone out of their summer, something more than Maggie. They stopped being a group somehow. They hardly saw Jacinta and Liam now, and as he had feared Grace was a million miles further away now that she was just across the river.

Tommy Leonard wished that he had a new jacket like Michael's. He wished that he didn't have skin that looked as if it had been treated with Harpic lavatory cleaner and he wished that he had smooth blond hair that looked good whatever way it fell, instead of spiky awful hair not unlike Eddie Ryan's.

He had heard there was going to be dancing in the Thatch Bar. His mind went back a year to when the Ryans had that great party in the outhouse that was now the café. He remembered not being quick enough or interesting enough to keep Dara's attention when Kerry came into the room. He wondered could anyone ever be quick or interesting enough. It wasn't *only* looks. Dara wasn't so shallow that she would go for appearances only. But Kerry was so sharp and clever. He knew when to say nothing and when to smile. He seemed to know what people were thinking, and say it first.

Suppose Kerry was to get a job somewhere else. Would that make everything all right? Or would the whole place still be watching out for him, looking up the road, almost waiting for him to come back?

Whatever Tommy wore Kerry would wear the opposite and he was sure Kerry would look just right today. If Tommy wore his best suit you could be sure that Kerry would be in some pale blue sweater and jeans, and if Tommy wore his corduroys and Aran sweater, Kerry would be in a formal suit and tie. Wouldn't it be wonderful to see what he was picking out to wear?

Kerry was up very early.

Everything had been neatly stored in the tunnel. They knew to keep well away today of all days.

It all had been simple. Just provide a depot they said, the tunnel was a fine idea. Better than a warehouse, a lock-up shed.

The boxes had been stacked. There were crates of drink, and big boxes with cartons of cigarettes.

Kerry understood about the weapons. He wasn't so clear about the drink and cigarettes. McCann had been laconic. These things are sold, they make money, money is needed for supplies.

From time to time he wondered what kind of movement they were in. At times he even suspected basely that they might well be in no movement except a gang of their own. But it didn't concern him now. He had stored their goods, he had wiped out his debt.

The day was starting. He felt that tingle of excitement he knew when something new was about to start. Kerry felt good. There was nothing he couldn't do. Look at what he had done already.

He had shipped Rachel Fine back where she belonged.

He had paid his poker debt.

He would sort out the situation with his father. Father wanted a son around here, for Christ's sake. He wouldn't make a lot of waves.

There would be speeches, and no doubt Father would say something about how sad it was that his wife Kathleen hadn't lived to see this day.

Kerry knew his mother would not have wanted to live here in this town. But if she were to see what was happening she would be proud of him. That her son had not forgotten her. He fingered his tiepin. That he had not let anyone else take her place.

Papers Flynn liked Kerry O'Neill.

478

He never understood that Kerry could be laughing at him. Kerry often complimented him on his clothes, and said that he thought it was a great idea to tie so much string around the waist – it could be the in thing if the fashion writers got a hold of it.

Papers didn't rightly know what Kerry was saying half the time. But the boy always seemed to be smiling, which was good. And of course Kerry sometimes slept rough too. Papers knew that he slept in that tunnel.

He had been in to investigate it for himself a few times. In theory it should have been a great place to stay, but Papers thought it was a bit closed in, he preferred somewhere less restricting.

Papers never asked himself why someone with Kerry O'Neill's wealth slept out. There didn't have to be a reason. He would greet him nowadays as a fellow knight of the road.

On the morning of the opening he was pleased to see Kerry on the river bank. 'All spruce and ready for the great occasion, I see,' Kerry said to him.

Papers grinned, pleased. 'It's going to be a nice day for it,' he said, looking at the sky.

'Well, Papers, just so long as it won't interfere with your enjoyment of the salmon,' Kerry laughed.

Papers felt he was being invited to more than a drink in the Thatch Bar. He didn't know how to cope. He decided to change the subject and trade information instead.

'If you've still got your place in the tunnel you'd want to keep an eye on it,' he said confidingly. 'I saw Sergeant Sheehan and Mrs Whelan looking at it last night, and the sergeant was there again this morning.'

Kerry's heart turned into a lump of lead. It was one thing losing a thousand pounds at a poker game. It was another thing altogether losing the contents of those boxes in the tunnel.

If they were discovered and seized Kerry's chances with the crowd he had been dealing with were very poor indeed.

He left Papers abruptly and walked to a point between Loretto Quinn's and Jack Coyne's establishments, where he could see the towpath properly. Sergeant Sheehan was walking back towards the bridge.

The staff could hardly believe that Mr Costello was not there to direct everything in his quick light voice that brooked no argument. Instead there was a series of conflicting orders. Nobody could say whose job it was to set out the glasses and whether they should get their final polish before they left the hotel for the marquee or when they were in place on the tables.

The drink which had been kept in cold rooms . . . should it be moved out early or left to the last minute? The temporary staff hired for the day, who was in charge of their arrangements?

Please God let it be true that it was only a quick visit to the dentist, they told each other. Otherwise there was going to be the most appalling confusion and nobody liked to think of Mr O'Neill's face, and the humiliation in front of all the people who were going to be arriving.

MAEVE BINCHY

If Jim Costello were here the staff wouldn't be making ten trips back and forth when two would do. Jim would have a timetable, a schedule, and a calm manner that would snuff out any crisis before it had time to develop.

If Jim Costello had been here he would have seen the red sweating face of Kerry O'Neill as the boy ploughed back and forth through all those brambles and briars around the fairy fort. As he got the last lot through, there was a groan and the sound of falling earth. The pit posts had collapsed, barring the way behind him.

Kerry laughed aloud with relief. His laugh could be free while he was underground. When he came to the surface he controlled it. From now it was simple.

Kerry was in his shirt sleeves, struggling with boxes and crates. To the staff who had been hired for the day he was just one more worker bringing just one more load to join the general store of food and drink.

To the regular staff he was O'Neill's troublesome son who had decided to do a bit of work for a change because Mr Costello had been struck with the toothache.

Nobody found it the slightest bit odd to see boxes being stored in the huge glass conservatory at the back of the main house. After all this was a gala, there were probably going to be drinks in every room, not only the official bars, the marquee and the Thatch Bar.

There were more boxes than Kerry would have believed possible. His heart pounded with the fear of discovery, and his arms and back ached with having to carry the weight of so many loads.

The conservatory had been an inspired idea. It was one of the few rooms that would not be in use, and the chance of them being accidentally investigated by an eager barman would be unlikely.

It had been decided that there was too much glass in this room, too many panes and too many plants to make it a suitable place for a party. Jim Costello had been at enough functions to know that it was not wise to mix euphoria, free liquor and plates of glass.

Kerry's carefully stacked boxes would be safe here. Until they could be collected tomorrow. One phone call saying what he had done. And then he was clear.

'I can either take the tooth out now, which will guarantee you have no pain, or I can give you a temporary filling and we'll try to save the tooth later.'

Jim Costello did not need a moment's thought. 'Give me a mirror,' he asked.

He looked. The missing tooth would show – only a little, but it would be seen.

'I'll have the filling, if you will,' he said. He lay back in the chair.

He knew there was nothing to be gained by fussing and looking at his watch, the man was going to take his own time doing the job no matter how agitated the patient was. Better relax and realize that the world can if necessary go on without you.

Grace was surprised to see Kerry.

'You look terrible,' she said.

'Can I use your bathroom?'

480

'Yes, but what happened?'

'I want to clean up. I have to go back to the lodge and get changed, and I don't want anyone to see me like this and ask questions. God, how I hate questions.'

'Sorry,' Grace said sulkily.

In a few minutes he looked more presentable. Now no one would comment.

'Well, are you looking forward to the day?' he asked.

'Yes and no. Michael is still very down. I hate people not to be good-tempered.'

'What's wrong with him?'

'Oh, he's being silly, he'll get over it. When can we go back into the tunnel?'

Kerry laughed suddenly. 'Any time you like,' he said, then he stopped, 'Hey wait don't go back there, there's been a subsidence. It's dangerous now, some of those old posts have given way.'

'They couldn't have . . .'

'They have,' he said curtly. 'And anyway, no fooling around, you hear. You're not to be just anyone's. You're Grace O'Neill, you're very important.'

She hugged him. 'Oh, Kerry, it's nice that you're all cheerful again. Maybe today . . . maybe Father . . .'

'Yes, it could happen. Why not?' Kerry left her room and ran lightly down the stairs, through the hall filled with sprays and blooms and people from the florist's. As he was going down the steps of the hotel to his car, he saw Jim Costello coming up.

'Your big day,' Kerry said pleasantly.

'Yes, great beginning with a butcher in a dentist's chair,' Jim said ruefully.

'I heard. Is it okay?'

'Look at it this way, I don't think he loosened too many of the others, and I've wiped away most of the blood.'

Kerry laughed. He used to think Costello an arrogant little guy. But he did have a sense of humour. And a great sense of command. Kerry stood and watched while he managed to restore order to the huge hall in moments.

Jim Costello looked back at Kerry too. The fellow seemed high or excited. He laughed too readily, like people do when they are in the middle of something dangerous.

Kate had sought the moment to tell John their news. She had not been able to find it.

She had thought that last night when the bar closed they might sit in the garden and she would tell him then.

But the bar just wouldn't close. The sense of excitement about the opening was everywhere.

Mary Donnelly had worked like an automaton. She said it might be the last good night's business they ever had. Keep serving, keep pouring, keep clanging the till.

There was no danger of a raid. Sergeant Sheehan wouldn't be so discourteous. And even if some of his superiors would be here for the official opening of Fernscourt, none of them would arrive the night before, so a little after-hours drinking would not be anything to come down on too heavily.

There was no time last night. They were both too tired. She had been going to tell him this morning, until all the drama in the bathroom and Carrie's predicament had intervened. It almost seemed like a surfeit of pregnancy to tell John about hers!

Perhaps this evening, in the peace and quiet. Perhaps that would be a good time.

She settled herself in her finery, and waited for him to come and wheel her across the footbridge and to the party.

The music was marvellous. *Tales from the Vienna Woods*, a selection from *The Gondoliers* and some rousing Sousa marches. Jim Costello had known the right band to hire, and the right repertoire for it to play.

On all sides of Mountfern they smiled when it struck up. The gala opening was under way.

For ages Dara sat on the window seat looking at the crowds gathering.

She could see cars coming down the big drive that led from the main road to Fernscourt. Local people walked up River Road and were crossing by the footbridge.

She saw Dad wheel the chair across, and a little lump came in her throat. Mam would so much have liked to have walked. Poor Mam, missing Mrs Fine in spite of everything.

Dara had not been upset by her mother's remarks. That was what Mrs Fine *would* have said, after all. All that about Kerry being dangerous.

She stood up and smoothed the red dress. It did look very very good. And nobody had said anything about the make-up which meant that she didn't have quite enough on. She would put on more lipstick and go across. Kerry would be waiting for her.

Mary Sheehan couldn't understand it. Her husband had said that he had to do one simple job which would put him in great standing with the lads and the superiors today. He had brought guards in early from the big town, saying that there was a cache of stolen goods in some hole or tunnel over on the towpath.

The guards arrived early in order to have it all cleared by the time any festivities began. They had gone in and found nothing but children's playing things.

Seamus Sheehan had looked in disbelief at the clay and the splintered wood. This hadn't been heaped like that last night. The tunnel had stretched further. Surely it had?

But then he hadn't followed it. He hadn't needed to. The boxes and crates had been here in this room. This room now with nothing but children's tables, chairs, and a broken sofa.

Sergeant Sheehan stared in front of him as he sat stupefied in his chair. It was no use that Sheila Whelan backed him up. What did people from the big town make of Sheila except to think she was the local postmistress? They weren't to know that she was the soundest person in the place.

He had been a fool not to have gone in straight after McCann had left last night. He had thought it would be better to do the thing by the light of the day.

He had been wrong.

One of the men from the tourist board stood near Patrick and told him who the people were. This was the Protestant bishop arriving now, a very big gesture, people would talk of this for a long time. There were TDs from all political parties and one cabinet minister. There were other hoteliers there, and the man from the tourist board said that their faces were forty shades of green. They muttered from one vista to the next about the size of the grant O'Neill must have got, the money he must have sunk in it, the hopelessness of trying to compete with anything like this, the folly of believing that there could ever be a return on such expenditure.

Patrick loved it. Every moment of it.

And he loved it when Mr Williams the vicar introduced him to the Walters and the Harrises. People of substance, who had estates near Mountfern. Mr Walters said his father used to come here a lot in the old days, and Colonel Harris said that he had old pictures of the place in its previous existence. It was wonderful to see it rise again.

They spoke as if a mere half century of being a ruin had been a slight inconvenience and that it had been no trouble for Patrick to get the place started again.

Patrick gave several grateful looks at Jim Costello. The man was a wonder. He managed to be everywhere and yet unobtrusive. Small, handsome and efficient, courteous and determined. What he would give to have had a son like that!

His own son was behaving well for once. His face looked flushed and excited. He was the centre of attention as he moved easily among the crowd.

But while Costello moved about seeing that people were all right, that no one was left alone or feeling outside things, Kerry moved like a glorious light that has no purpose except to be looked at and admired.

The twins crossed the footbridge together, as they had done so many times.

In the days when their lives were full of fantasy and imagination they could not have dreamed up anything as splendid as this.

'You look terrific, Dara.'

'Thanks, Michael. So do you. Very very smart.'

Dara wanted to hold his hand for some reason, to reassure him. They walked up through the laurels. The marquee for lunch was by the landing stage and the barge. But the drinks and welcoming party were around the steps and the main hall.

They came into the crowded forecourt and Dara saw him. There stood Kerry in his new white jacket that he had told her about, his pink and white shirt. He looked like a hero, not a man. She saw him laughing and bending a little to listen, then he threw back his head and laughed again.

He was with Kitty Daly, who looked stunning. Her long hair hung loose like a huge halo around her, almost like a cape over her magnificent dress.

Kitty was wearing the copper-coloured dress that had been made for Maggie. On Maggie it had been a big flowing dress. On Kitty, who was tall and leggy, the copper dress was a mini-dress.

She looked at Kerry O'Neill with all the confidence of a beauty who doesn't need to wonder if other people are looking at her.

She would expect them to be looking. And liking what they saw.

'Are you all right?' Jim Costello spoke to Dara Ryan, who was holding on to one of the huge urns near the steps.

'Yes. Yes, why?'

'I thought you looked dizzy for a moment.'

'No. No, I'm fine. Thank you very much.'

Jim looked at her appreciatively. 'You look very well, I must say, Dara, really very smart.'

'Thanks, Mr Costello.'

He wondered why her voice was so dead. She really did look well in that red silk. Unlike Grace, who looked like a meringue in all that pink linen and broderie anglaise.

But Dara Ryan had no life in her eyes, she had hardly heard the compliment.

Michael came back with two glasses of orange. They had sugar around the edge and a slice of real orange cut so that it was fixed to the glass.

'Have this,' he said.

Dara took it silently.

'She can't know, she wasn't here for the dress and everything.'

'I know, I remembered that.'

'She must have just found it at home.' He was trying to take the pain out of Dara's eyes.

'Yes. Yes, that must have been it.'

'And I'm sure he doesn't like her *really*, it's only with all that hair and everything . . .' His voice trailed away.

Papers Flynn and Mary Donnelly raised their glasses to each other as they sat in the warm autumn sunshine outside Ryan's pub.

Mary produced soda bread and slices of ham.

'Much better fare here than we'd get across there,' she said.

'It's that all right.' Papers ate happily.

'I never go for salmon all that much,' Mary said.

'Full of bones, it would have your throat in ribbons,' said Papers, who had never tasted salmon in his life.

Eddie saw Leopold crossing the footbridge.

He remembered his mother's advice: do nothing, nothing at all without careful thought. He stood there and tried to think carefully. What would a normal person do? Would they ignore Leopold? Or would they take him home? Would they offer him a plate of salmon? The more he thought, the more Eddie realized that careful thinking helped him not at all.

He watched the dog go round the hotel and out towards the back.

The action moved down towards the marquee. Luncheon was being served. The band had started to play lunchtime numbers like songs from *The Student Prince* and *The Merry Widow*.

Dara watched as Kerry's arm guided Kitty towards the huge lunch tent. He had never even looked for her.

She stood high on the steps of Fernscourt and watched them. Why had he not looked for her? Why had he said he loved her only short days ago, why did he hold her and say she was precious and beautiful beyond all imagining, if he was going to be with Kitty Daly? Did he know all the time that Kitty was coming, that she had turned out to be so beautiful?

Dara didn't believe that he could have held her in his arms and thought of Kitty. It was impossible. Kerry was so good, so true, and he wanted the best for her. For everyone.

Suddenly it made sense to her. He did want the best. And up to now she had been the best in Mountfern. She had been young and not bad-looking, and she had loved him. But now there was a better best. There was Kitty, and he had to have her. The way he had to have that jacket which had cost a fortune. And he had to have the car. And money for gambling.

With a shock she realized that he might have had to get Rachel Fine out of Mountfern. He hadn't liked her and she might have married his father and become a person of importance. She shook her head. All this and seeing Maggie's dress. It made her feel dizzy, as if she were going to fall.

She sat down on the steps and to her astonishment Leopold came and laid his head on her lap.

'What in the name of God are you doing here, Leopold?' she asked him and he looked up at her from an awkward angle, trying to explain that he thought there might have been a bit of fun and he had come because everyone else was there.

Eddie appeared at that moment, looking anxiously round from behind an urn.

'Can I take it that you'll be responsible for him now, could we say that I handed him over to you?' Eddie said.

'Wouldn't you know that you'd have to let us down by bringing Leopold?' Dara said.

'I didn't, he came across all by himself.'

'Yeah, carrying his invitation in his teeth.'

'What'll we do, Dara?'

'We'll take him home. Come on,' she said.

'But it's not over. There's lots more to go.' He was disappointed.

'Wouldn't it be safer to go, Eddie, before you do anything dreadful that'll be remembered for years, like the confession box?'

Eddie was philosophical. 'I suppose it would be best,' he said.

They made a funny little threesome, Eddie with his spiky hair, Dara in her magnificent red silk dress, and Leopold, happy now that he had seen all there was to see.

Kerry O'Neill was coming out to look for Dara and he saw them reach the footbridge. She had probably been sent to take that awful brother and awful dog home. She would be back later. He would see her then.

Michael found Grace with Tommy and Jacinta and Liam.

'She didn't know,' he said, 'that it was a special dress for Maggie.'

They agreed. Grudgingly. Kitty couldn't have known.

'It looks quite different on her anyway,' Grace said. Grace was very disappointed with her own outfit, she wished that Mrs Fine was still here, she was great at advising people. Mrs Fine had been so nice to them that time, that short time at the beginning of the summer.

Marian Johnson could look wonderful, Mrs Fine had said, if she wore tailored clothes. She needed well-cut almost mannish garments, not the soft fly-away things she usually wore.

Today Marian looked very smart in a dark blue and white suit and a blouse with a cameo brooch like Mrs Whelan wore. She was with a very shabby big untidy man that people said was a barrister. Grace heard them say that he was Marian's escort. Imagine having escorts at that age.

She went over to her father who was standing momentarily alone.

'Do you miss Mrs Fine, Father?' she asked unexpectedly.

Patrick put his arm around his daughter. 'It's funny you should say that, I was thinking of her this very moment. She's going to call tonight. Or I'm to call her. Anyway when it's over, we'll talk.'

'So you're still good friends with her?' Grace looked pleased.

'No, sadly not. But tonight is special, she and I will talk tonight and then not again for a long while.'

Jim Costello toured ceaselessly. He found smears on some glasses. They were dealt with effortlessly, not by any shouts and roars but by a quick quiet word with someone and the use of the phrase 'this minute, please' on almost every occasion.

He ensured that the rooms where valuable antiques were kept had people watching them, and he checked that the revellers had not got into the conservatory. He frowned slightly at the boxes which had been stored there. He looked at the top one. Whiskey.

It was probably some fail-safe idea of O'Neill's. He was determined that nobody in the county would go dry. He must have ordered a few more crates put in this morning.

At least they were out of the way, nobody would think they were meant to come and carouse in here.

'Where's Dara?' Grace asked Michael.

'I don't know. I've been looking for her.'

Michael was afraid that Dara might be crying somewhere.

'Do you think she's upset about Kitty being with Kerry?' Grace asked.

'I don't know. Do you think he really likes Kitty, or what?'

'I expect he just wants to have fun with everybody,' Grace said.

'Isn't that what everyone wants?'

Michael saw Grace look around as Jim Costello passed by. A feeling of sadness came over him. Having fun with everybody. Yes, that probably was what everybody wanted. It was what the O'Neills wanted anyway.

Everyone was in the marquee now listening to the speeches. The band was silent and respectful as the dignitaries spoke. All of them praised the courage and foresight of Patrick O'Neill, to come back to this spot and build his monument. They said that faith like his was needed more and more. They looked forward to the day when Americans who came to stay in his hotel would themselves come to build in Ireland and put stone on stone in friendship as their ancestors had done. There was hardly anyone in the main house to see the curtains move in the breeze that came in the open window. And there was nobody there to see when the curtains flapped against the ashtray and knocked it over. The cigarette smouldered on the carpet for a long time before the breeze fanned it into a flame and the flame caught the curtains. The long blue drapes that Rachel Fine had worked on so long to get the right texture, the right shade and the right look for Fernscourt.

The kitchen staff were far away from it, Jim Costello was hearing himself praised in the marquee, the staff who would serve in the Thatch Bar were busy setting up the place for the onslaught they would have descending on them as soon as the speeches were finished. There wasn't a man in Mountfern who wouldn't prefer a pint to the glasses of champagne which were on offer in the big tent.

There was nobody to see the way the singeing became a flame and the way a breeze carried the flame to the pelmet. The residents' lounge burned discreetly and thoroughly behind the closed doors.

By the time the door burned down the blaze was out of control.

'Did you see Dara?' Kerry asked Tommy Leonard. 'I've been looking for her all day.'

'Yeah, I can see you have.' Tommy's eyes were fixed pointedly on Kitty Daly's arm, which Kerry still held.

'Well, if you see her tell her I've been trying to find her.'

'Certainly,' Tommy said. 'I'll tell her your sight was taken from your eyes and you're going round with a white stick bumping into things, desperate to find her.'

Segeant Sheehan saw the fire first.

In years to come he would always remember that. The disappointments of the morning, the shame and the laughter were as nothing when compared to being the hero who discovered the fire and arranged the fire-fighting force.

He wasted no time, when he saw the smoke. He yanked Jim Costello from the marquee and together they ran towards it.

Then to the kitchen with shouts about telephoning for further help. By this stage the carefully placed fire extinguishers would be useless. A hose was in place within minutes and the sergeant got Jimbo Doyle, who had the loudest voice in the county to give the alarm through the main house in case there was anyone in any of the bathrooms or in any other part of the building.

The Thatch Bar was emptied of its staff, who were marshalled into a line of water carriers.

Chauffeurs of cars, three bus drivers and five taxi men from the big town were roped in.

A serious fire-fighting effort had begun before they saw any need to alert the people in the marquee. There was no danger to life, and even if the fire could not be contained there was very easy emergency escape for everyone across the footbridge and over the River Fern.

Sergeant Sheehan had been the first to see the fire. The first in Fernscourt that is.

Papers Flynn had seen the smoke much earlier.

A lifetime of never getting involved leaves its mark. Papers never brought up any subject first, he was a person who responded rather than initiated. You only got into trouble by paying attention to anyone else's business.

He sat in the sun outside Ryan's and saw the smoke coming out of a side window. Papers looked at it silently for a long time.

Mary Donnelly had gone into the house with Mrs Ryan's daughter. That boy who was always in trouble had come back too, and the nice dog. Papers had always admired Leopold and thought him a fine animal.

He wondered should he say anything about the smoke, but the habits of a lifetime held him back.

Eddie came out and joined him on the seat.

'I could go back if I wanted to,' Eddie said.

'Oh you could right enough.'

'I wasn't sent away or anything.'

'No no, you wouldn't be.'

'Well I usually would be, but not this time.'

Papers nodded in agreement.

'I'll have to make that clear to Mam, I came back of my own free will. I wouldn't want Mam sitting in the chair there thinking maybe I'd been ordered to leave.'

The mention of Mrs Ryan in her wheelchair galvanized Papers. Suppose there was a fire and Mrs Ryan wasn't able to get out.

'Would you think that's smoke over there?' he said to Eddie.

Eddie squinted at it. 'It is, it is all right.'

He ran back into the pub. Mary and Dara were just coming out.

'I'm going back, Eddie, it's up to you but maybe you'd prefer to stay here,' Dara said. She looked very serious but not as if she were fighting or giving out to him.

'There's smoke,' Eddie shouted.

Dara took no notice of him.

'Mary has pointed out rightly that Mam and Dad paid a fortune for this dress, and I must go back and get value out of it for them. Even if I don't feel like it.'

It was as if she were talking to herself.

'I think the hotel's on fire,' Eddie said.

This time he managed to get their attention.

And by now the figures of Sergeant Sheehan and Jim Costello could be seen, running as fast as they could. Eddie was right, the hotel was very definitely on fire.

Patrick's speech was almost over. He had thanked everybody who should have been thanked but it wasn't tedious. The officials who had helped him all felt included in his generous tribute to the authorities, and the people of Mountfern felt individually acknowledged as he looked around the crowd and his eyes seemed to rest on them. Each and every person knew how much they meant to him, he said. He explained that a homecoming would be nothing if it weren't for the people. Buildings were symbols but the people were the heart of it all.

He said his family meant a great deal to him, but in a sense he had found a greater and wider family of friends.

He was about to end by wishing that this new family of friends should join him in the Thatch Bar when the cry went up. It was a terrible sound, the cry that told them that Fernscourt was on fire and it was going to burn to the ground unless something was done quickly.

They started to move the people from the marquee.

'Over the bridge' was the cry but nobody wanted to go. They stood in groups watching with horrified fascination as the flames leaped from the windows of the residents' lounge and appeared too in the narrow windows of the piano bar. The line of people passing the buckets was slow. The hose seemed a trickle.

Men ran up, throwing off their coats, to join the fire fighting. Orders were given and countermanded. The guards arranged for buckets to come from the river, everyone told everyone else that the fire brigade was coming.

'Ring them again someone, and tell them to send everything they've got,' Martin White said.

Then he moved over to Kate Ryan's side. 'Back home with you now, that's an order.'

'The children,' she said.

'They'll follow. Come on, Kate. I'm taking you home.' John had moved the chair on and wheeled it rapidly towards the bridge.

Mrs Daly blocked their way. 'We should get people to pray,' she said. 'That's what we have to do now. It's about time we realized it.'

'You've realized it for years, Mrs Daly,' John said. 'Now could I get past you there, I'm a bit anxious to move Kate across so that I can go back and fight the fire.'

She stood aside, hands still clasped.

'God, she's worse than I thought,' John muttered as he wheeled Kate swiftly across the bridge.

'She might be right,' Kate said grimly as they came to the pub.

Dara thought they looked very formal somehow, like a picture. A man standing, a woman sitting, both staring at something. Something impossible to believe.

Kate put her hand up on her shoulder to cover John's hand which was resting there.

'How in the name of God did it start?' Kate asked.

'It'll be all right,' he soothed. 'Look, it's less than before, it's much less. They've got it under control.'

Dara came to stand beside them.

'Where's Eddie?' Kate asked.

'He's here, and there's Declan coming across the bridge now.'

Eddie came up to his mother. 'I was over here when it happened, talking to Dara and Mary and Papers. I had nothing to do with it, Mam,' he began.

Kate drew him close to her. 'Of course you didn't Eddie, darling Eddie,' she said into his hair.

Eddie pulled away and looked at her. Nobody had ever called him darling Eddie in his life.

'In fact I was the first to spot it,' he said.

'Of course you were.' She held his hand very tight and her eyes were full of tears.

Michael caught up with Declan on the bridge.

'Come on, Mam will want to make sure we're all safe,' he said.

'Now we're all here I'm going back across,' John said.

'You're going in that door behind the counter,' said Mary.

'I can't sell a drink while the place is burning down across the way, I have to help.'

'Aren't there plenty of big strong men huffing and puffing and playing fire engines over there? People want to buy drinks to calm their nerves. You're a publican, it's your duty to sell them.'

The Ryan family smiled, all together. The same smile. John went back into his pub.

Patrick O'Neill had been quick to organize as well.

No standing dumbstruck at the awful and unexpected happening. Like Jim Costello he was quick to see the frail and the feeble and get them organized.

'Colonel Harris, I wonder if I can ask you to help the canon out that way, that's very good of you. Liam, it would be a great help if you could get a chair for Mrs Daly, she wants to do a bit of praying but I think she should do it sitting down. Jimbo, get the drivers to get back into their cars and move them way down the drive.'

And all the time with his dream burning before his very eyes he kept assuring people it was under control, and that the brigades were coming and there would be order restored in no time.

Carrie stood with a tear-stained face in a straw hat which had got very crushed by people trampling on it, but she had put it back on for some kind of comfort.

'Don't worry now, Carrie,' he said. 'We'll all be in the Thatch Bar this evening laughing over this.'

It was then he saw that part of the roof on the Thatch Bar had caught.

Kerry worked with the rest on the fire line. Beside him Tommy Leonard and Jack Coyne passed buckets.

The hose was taken to deal with the straw roof on the bar. So they were relying on the human chain to keep the first fire under control.

'Well at least it's only a hotel,' Jack Coyne said, panting. 'Think what it would be like if it was an army barracks or something with all those guns and explosives in it. Everyone here would be blown sky high.'

'Jesus Christ,' said Kerry, dropping his bucket.

'Kerry?' The people near him looked at him in alarm.

'Oh my God!' Kerry shouted. 'Get back. Costello, get them back, get everyone away from it, get them away from it. Get back.'

They thought he was hysterical. They pushed him out of the way in their efforts to fight the fire.

They would pause to wipe their foreheads and look to the main road, hoping for the comforting sound of many fire engines.

But it was a long way from the town.

Jim Costello didn't like Kerry's manner.

'Will somebody get O'Neill's son away from here?' he called in his cool voice, the voice that was used to being obeyed.

But Kerry had run on to the steps.

'There's guns,' he shouted, 'guns and gelignite. The whole place is going to blow up.'

'Don't mind him.'

'It's under control, we're winning, we've beaten it.'

All around him were the soothing sounds of people who thought it was a brainstorm.

'I beg you, Costello.' Kerry was grabbing wildly at Jim's coat. 'They're in the conservatory.'

Jim remembered the boxes. The boxes and crates.

'They're whiskey, you madman,' he said.

'The top ones are. The others are ammunition.'

At the pub they couldn't understand it. Why everyone had started to run down to the river.

At first people protested, what was it about, they were winning, the fire was beaten. When they heard what it was about they ran too, helping others, and looking over their shoulders in the panic of disbelief.

Grace had been looking for Michael when the cry went up that everyone was to abandon the fire fighting. There was something in the hotel that was about to explode.

She looked round wildly for Michael but there was no sign of him.

'Get Grace back over the river,' Patrick shouted to Jim Costello as he rounded others towards the footbridge.

'Come on, Grace.' Jim ran with her for a few yards, then he left her at the laurels. 'Go on!' he shouted as she paused.

'I don't want to be on my own . . .'

'You're not on your own, stupid. Look, there are all your friends up by the pub.'

'Did Michael go without me?' Grace's lip trembled.

'Go on, please, Grace. That's my job, to get you over the river. Please, just go.'

'And you?'

'I'll see you later on. I'll come and look for you.'

'Promise?'

'I promise,' he shouted over his shoulder and ran back to the crowd trying to hold Kerry O'Neill back from the flames.

The boy's face was wild.

'I put it there, I have to take it out.'

Jim Costello felt Patrick O'Neill standing beside him.

'What's in it, Kerry?' Patrick asked.

'I don't know. Guns, ammunition of some kind.'

'Of what kind?'

'I don't know, I tell you.'

'Was it set to explode?' Jim looked at Patrick with new respect.

'No, Father, it wasn't meant to be here, it was McCann's friends.'

'What were they trying to do with it?'

'I was storing it for them in the tunnel until they collected it.'

Seamus Sheehan was beside them, and Dr White.

The sergeant spoke. 'Is it gelignite?'

'I don't *know*, I tell you. How do I know what gelignite looks like?'

'Were there detonators with it?' The sergeant was quiet.

No tempers, no lack of control, and here they were, five men standing beside a possible inferno.

'What do they look like?' Kerry was piteous now.

'Were there separate containers, boxes?'

'Yes. Yes, I think so.'

'And you've put them all together. In there?' The sergeant indicated the burning building.

'Yes, I didn't look, I didn't have the time.'

'We'd better not risk it,' said Sergeant Sheehan, and they turned to leave.

'I'll go down the driveway to tell the fire brigade.' Jim Costello was a quick thinker.

'Get any drivers, anyone in the buses far away down the drive,' Patrick called.

He looked at neither his son nor the doctor, neither his hotel manager nor the local sergeant as he began to walk away towards the footbridge.

'Father . . . Father, they're in the conservatory, the fire hasn't got there yet, we could get them out,' Kerry cried.

Seamus Sheehan shook his head. 'It's too hot, they could go any minute, flames or no flames.'

Kerry broke away and ran towards the house.

The sergeant made a move to run after him. Jim Costello was already half way down the drive towards the main garages of the hotel.

'Don't die saving him, Sheehan,' called Martin White. 'Let him go, he put the stuff there, let him go up with it.'

They heard the sound of the fire engines about five seconds before the explosion.

It wasn't as huge as they had thought it would be. But it was huge enough to blow the back out of Fernscourt, and the fire now raged so that they knew it would never stop even if the fire engines dared come near it.

Nobody knew if there would be another explosion. To go anywhere nearer than they were would be suicide. And as it was they weren't sure what had happened to Kerry.

It seemed like slow motion as they watched it from the bridge. Hands to their mouths, stifling cries, and the sound of Mrs Daly's prayers as a low drone in the background.

Then they saw the figure of Patrick O'Neill walk slowly up the steps of Fernscourt.

It could only have been seconds, but time stood still before he came out dragging Kerry with him.

Kerry was walking, his face was in his hands.

The crowd saw Martin White take off his jacket and put it around Kerry's shoulders. They couldn't see what had happened when the doctor took Kerry's hands away from his face but they did see Patrick and Sergeant Sheehan turn away in pain from Kerry O'Neill's burns.

They had to let some of it burn itself out. It looked stark and terrifying, the Thatch Bar naked apart from a scattering of scratchy burned straw.

Patrick had been handed a brandy of a size that nobody had ever drunk and survived. He stood in the very spot where the entrance to his hotel might have been.

If things had been different.

If Kate Ryan had not had her accident that day.

If things had all been quite different.

The son who had been sharp enough to see where the entrance to their hotel should be had not been sharp enough for anything else. He was heading into the hospital in the big town in the back of an ambulance.

All around him Patrick heard the consolations and the encouragements. It would rise again.

The insurance would pay for everything, wasn't it a miracle that nobody got killed or seriously injured?

They clutched at his arm, he even felt himself being hugged by people too full of emotion to trust themselves to speak.

All around him he saw people finding each other, exclaiming they thought the other was lost.

He saw Jimbo wiping big tears out of Carrie's eyes with a green table napkin that said 'Ryan's Shamrock Café'.

He saw the lawyer Slattery who had always hated him and the O'Neills taking off his coat to put it around the shivering Grace. The coat looked enormous on her and it hid her silly pink and white dress.

Slattery had got her a cup of coffee, and was speaking to her soothingly.

Sheila Whelan was of course beside Patrick. Knowing that he wanted to say something rather than platitudes.

'My God, Sheila, look at the misery I brought to people,' he said. 'Look at the sheer waste and misery.'

'You didn't bring it, Patrick. It came all on its own.'

'Jesus, who brought it if I didn't bring it?'

'You could say I did. I told Seamus Sheehan about the tunnel.'

'What in the name of God took him in with that gang?' Patrick asked.

'Seamus heard it was because he owed them money.' Sheila spoke gently.

'Yes. I wouldn't give it to him.' Patrick's heart lurched and he looked at his ruined hotel. 'I expect he had to get it somewhere. My God, if I had known the price we'd have to pay.'

'You'd have had to call a halt somewhere,' she consoled him. 'You couldn't have gone on paying for everything all his life, that would have been worse than your father paying for nothing all of his.'

'Oh God, how am I going to tell Rachel?'

The sun shone down as mockery on the smouldering ruins of Ireland's finest hotel. Its light played on the remains of what had been described as the dream of international cooperation come true.

In groups they stood and ran it over in their minds, the causes and the possible outcomes.

As usual, because it was Mountfern there were as many theories as there were people speaking.

The electricity was faulty, the chimneys had never been right. It was a cigarette, it was an attempt to assassinate some of the VIPs. It was a bottled-gas cooker, it was a bonfire to get rid of the rubbish.

They said that he would rebuild it right away, it would open in the spring. That he would take over the Grange and put his guests there, that he would walk out tonight and never come back. And then the roof went in.

It went with a series of cracks and groans as the timber fell and knocked down further stonework, and the shower of slates fell on top.

There was something very final about the way it fell.

The people of Mountfern raised a great roar as it went in. It was a startling sound. A roar went up from all the throats at the same time.

It was neither a shout of triumph nor a great wail of regret.

It was just a roar.

Patrick's eyes suddenly filled with tears. He didn't understand these people at all.

He saw Jack Leonard and Tom Daly, who had cheered when they had burned this house down in 1922; they had cheered as the ruins fell, Brian Doyle had told him. Today they cheered again.

How had he thought that this was his place and these were his people? He didn't even begin to understand why they had made that sound.

The twins stood together. Very close.

They weren't exactly touching but you could hardly have put a piece of paper between them. Tommy Leonard envied them their closeness. He had nobody like that. Nobody who would always be there no matter what.

For as long as he could remember they had been like that. Not so much this summer perhaps, but way way back. When they were both his best friends. Before he started to love Dara. He was right beside them but he couldn't think of anything to say that wouldn't sound appalling. He really was getting more and more like Eddie Ryan, he thought to himself grimly. It was an awful fate.

If he had been Kerry O'Neill he would have known the right thing to say. The word or the gesture that would have been what they needed.

He said, 'At least we have each other. Everything else has changed and gone, but we'll always be together in one way or another, won't we?'

Dara's eyes filled with tears.

'I don't mean love or anything, but as great friends. Won't we?'

Tommy looked from one to the other, anxious that there should be no misunderstanding. Anxious that he wasn't being seen to presume.

Dara laid her hand against his face. She didn't even try to wipe away her tears.

'I don't know what I'd do without you, Tommy Leonard,' she said.

Although he could hardly believe it, Tommy knew, when he went over it again in his mind, that Dara meant it.

Mary served, and Sheila had gone behind the bar to help her.

Carrie, face aglow with Jimbo's delight and pride, ran back and forth with sandwiches and soda bread that they would never be serving now to American visitors.

Brian Doyle said he was glad that Peggy had got on her high horse and not come to the opening in the end, because a) she was highly strung and b) she might get very put out by all these weddings in the air – Jimbo Doyle's and Jack Coyne's, two of nature's bachelors.

Brian said that it would be like a sacrilege to discuss who'd get the job of building the place up again, but he wanted it known that it was a heart scald and an agony from day one and he wouldn't wish it on his worst enemy.

Kate sat with John in the side yard.

There were no words between them.

She had told him the news in the most natural way.

John had sat with his head in his hands, bemoaning all that had happened.

'I'm weary, Kate, weary and sad. There has been nothing but destruction and death since that place was begun. There's never any hope, no beginnings.'

'I'll tell you something about new life and new hope, that you'll hardly believe,' Kate said.

They sat together in the yard that was filled with flowers. He held her very close, he pressed her to him.

He would take such care of her, he would make sure that it would all be all right.

A new life. Another person. Another Ryan.

They called Patrick to the phone. Again. He had taken so many calls that Jim Costello had eventually monitored them, standing in Kate's green room and dealing with whoever called.

But this time he called Patrick. It was long distance. From New York.

'Rachel, Rachel.' His voice choked and he couldn't speak.

But at last he found the words. The words to tell her about the end of the dream. Then he put down the receiver and walked through the glass doors into the yard filled with flowers where Kate and John Ryan sat in a world of their own.

They looked up at him as he stood there, a big man always filling their place, dominating their lives.

'I came to tell you. I'll be going home,' he said.

Echoes

For dearest Gordon with all my love

PROLOGUE

People seemed to know without being told. They came out of their houses and began to run down the main street. The murmur became louder, and almost without knowing they were doing it they started to check where their own families were. It was still just a figure, face down in the water. They didn't know for sure whether it was a man or a woman.

'Perhaps it's a sailor from a ship,' they said. But they knew it wasn't anyone who had gone overboard. No nice anonymous death of someone they didn't know. No informing the authorities and saying a few prayers for the deceased unknown sailor. This was someone from Castlebay.

They stood in silent groups on the cliff top and watched the first people getting to the water's edge: the boy who had first seen the waves leaving something frightening on the shore; other men too; people from the shops nearby and young men who were quick to run down the path. Then they saw the figures coming down the other path near the doctor's house, kneeling by the body in case, just in case there was something in a black bag that could bring it back to life.

By the time Father O'Dwyer arrived with his soutane flapping in the wind the murmur had turned into a unified sound. The people of Castlebay were saying a decade of the rosary for the repose of the soul which had left the body that lay face down on their beach.

Part One
1950–1952

It was sometimes called Brigid's Cave, the echo cave, and if you shouted your question loud enough in the right direction you got an answer instead of an echo. In the summer it was full of girls calling out questions, girls who had come for the summer to Castlebay. Girls who wanted to know would they get a fellow, or if Gerry Doyle would have eyes for them this summer. Clare thought they were mad to tell the cave their secrets. Specially since people like her sister Chrissie and that crowd would go and listen for private things being asked and then they'd scream with laughter about them and tell everyone. Clare said she'd never ask the echo anything no matter how desperate she was, because it wouldn't be a secret any more. But she did go in to ask about the history prize. That was different.

It was different because it was winter anyway, and there was hardly anyone except themselves in Castlebay in winter; and it was different because it had nothing to do with love. And it was a nice way to come home from school that way down the cliff road; you didn't have to talk to everyone in the town, you could look at the sea instead. And suppose she did go down that crooked path with all the Danger notices on it, then she could go into the cave for a quick word, walk along the beach and up the real steps and be home in the same time as if she had come down the street talking to this person and that. In winter there was hardly any business so people waved you into shops and gave you a biscuit or asked you to do a message for them. She'd be just as quick going by Brigid's Cave and the beach.

It had been dry, so the Danger bits weren't so dangerous. Clare slid easily down the cliff on to the sand. It was firm and hard, the tide had not long gone out. The mouth of the cave looked black and a bit frightening. But she squared her shoulders; it looked just the same in summer yet people went in there in droves. She shifted her schoolbag to her back so that she could have both hands free to guide herself and once she got used to the light there was no difficulty seeing the little ridge where you were meant to stand.

Clare took a deep breath: 'Will I win the history prize?' she called.

'Ize ize ize ize,' called the echo.

'It's saying yes,' said a voice just beside her. Clare jumped with the fright. It was David Power.

'You shouldn't listen to anyone else, it's like listening in to confession,' Clare said crossly.

'I thought you saw me,' David said simply. 'I wasn't hiding.'

'How could I see you, didn't I come in out of the light, you were lurking in here.' She was full of indignation.

'It's not a private cave, you don't have to keep shouting Cave Occupied,' David retorted loudly.

'Pied pied pied pied,' said the cave.

They both laughed.

He was nice, really, David Power, he was the same age as her brother Ned

– fifteen. They had been in Mixed Infants together, she remembered Ned telling someone proudly, wanting to share some experience with the doctor's son.

He wore a tie and suit when he came home from school, all the time, not just when he went to Mass on Sundays. He was tall and he had freckles on his nose. His hair was a bit spiky and used to stick up in funny directions, one big bit of it fell over his forehead. He had a nice smile and he always looked as if he were ready to talk except that something was dragging him away. Sometimes he wore a blazer with a badge on it, and he looked very smart in that. He used to wrinkle his nose and tell people that it only looked smart when you didn't see a hundred and eighty blazers like that every day at his school. He'd been at a boarding school for over a year but now it was closed because of scarlet fever. Only the Dillon girls from the hotel went to boarding school and of course the Wests and the Greens, but they were Protestants and they had to go to a boarding school because there wasn't one of their own.

'I didn't think it would answer really, I only tried it as a joke,' she said.

'I know, I tried it once as a joke too,' he confessed.

'What did you ask it as a joke?' she inquired.

'I forget now,' he said.

'That's not fair – you heard mine.'

'I didn't, I only heard eyes eyes eyes.' He shouted it and it called back the three words to him over and over.

Clare was satisfied. 'Well I'd best be off now, I have homework. I don't suppose you've had homework for weeks.' She was envious and inquiring.

'I do. Miss O'Hara comes every day to give me lessons. She's coming . . . oh soon now.' They walked out on to the wet hard sand.

'Lessons all by yourself with Miss O'Hara – isn't that great?'

'It is, she's great at explaining things, isn't she, for a woman teacher I mean.'

'Yes, well we only have women teachers and nuns,' Clare explained.

'I forgot,' David said sympathetically. 'Still she's terrific, and she's very easy to talk to, like a real person.'

Clare agreed. They walked companionably along to the main steps up from the beach. It would have been quicker for David to climb the path with Danger written on it, it led almost into his own garden, but he said he wanted to buy some sweets at Clare's shop anyway. They talked about things the other had never heard of. David told her about the sanitorium being fumigated after the two pupils got scarlet fever; but all the time she thought that he was talking about the big hospital on the hill where people went when they had TB. She didn't know it was a room in his school. She told him a long and complicated tale about Mother Immaculata asking one of the girls to leave the exercise books in one place and she thought that it was somewhere else and the girl went by accident into the nuns' side of the convent. This was all lost on David, who didn't know that you never under pain of *terrible* things went to the nuns' side of the convent. It didn't really matter to either of them, they were no strain on each other, and life in Castlebay could be full of strains so this was a nice change. He came into the shop and, as there was nobody serving, she took off her coat, hung it up and found the jar of Clove Rock. She counted out the six for a penny that he was buying and before she put the lid on the jar she offered him one courteously and took one herself.

He looked at her enviously. It was great power to be able to stand up on a chair in a sweetshop, take down a jar and be free to offer one to a customer. David sighed as he went home. He'd have loved to live in a shop like Clare O'Brien, he'd have loved brothers and sisters, and to be allowed to go up to the yard and collect milk in a can when the cows were being milked, or gather seaweed to sell to the hot sea baths in bundles. It was very dull going back to his own house now to his mother saying he should really have some sense of what was what. It was the most irritating thing he had ever heard, especially since it seemed to mean anything and everything and never the same thing twice. Still, Miss O'Hara was coming tonight, and Miss O'Hara made lessons much more interesting than at school, he had once been unwise enough to explain to his mother. He thought she would be pleased but she said that Miss O'Hara was fine for a country primary school but did not compare with the Jesuits who were on a different level entirely.

Clare was sighing too, she thought it must be great altogether to go back to a house like David Power's where there were bookcases of books in the house, and a fire on in that front room whether there was anyone sitting in it or not. And there was no wireless on, and nobody making noise. You could do your homework there for hours without anyone coming in and telling you to move. She remembered the inside of the house from when she had been up to Dr Power for the stitches the time she had caught her leg on the rusty bit of machinery. To distract her Dr Power had asked her to count the volumes of the encyclopedia up on the shelf and Clare had been so startled to see all those books in one house for one family that she had forgotten about the stitches and Dr Power had told her mother she was as brave as a lion. They had walked home after the stitches with Clare leaning on her mother. They stopped at the church to thank St Anne that there hadn't been any infection in the leg and as Clare saw her mother bent in prayer and gratitude in front of the St Anne grotto she let her mind wander on how great it would be to have a big peaceful house full of books like that instead of being on top of each other and no room for anything – no time for anything either. She thought about it again tonight as David Power went up the street home to that house where the carpet went right into the window, not stopping in a square like ordinary carpets. There would be a fire and there'd be peace. His mother might be in the kitchen and Dr Power would be curing people and later Miss O'Hara would be coming to give him lessons all on his own without the rest of a class to distract her. What could be better than that? She wished for a moment that she had been his sister, but then she felt guilty. To wish that would be to want to lose Mammy and Daddy and Tommy and Ned and Ben and Jimmy. Oh and Chrissie. But she didn't care how wrong it was, she wouldn't mind losing Chrissie any day of the week.

The calm of the shop was only temporary. Daddy had been painting out in the back and he came in holding his hands up in front of him and asking someone to reach out a bottle of white spirit and open it up this minute. There was an awful lot of painting going on in the wintertime in Castlebay, the sea air just ripped the coats off again and the place looked very shabby unless it was touched up all the time. Mammy came in at the same moment; she had been up to the post office and she had discovered terrible things. Chrissie and her two tinkers of friends had climbed on the roof of Miss O'Flaherty's shop and poked a long wet piece of seaweed through to frighten Miss O'Flaherty. They could have given the unfortunate woman a heart attack; she could, God save us all, have dropped stone dead on the floor of her own shop and then Chrissie O'Brien and her two fine friends would have the sin of murder on their souls until the Last Day and after. Chrissie had been dragged home by the shoulder, the plait and the ear. She was red-faced and annoyed. Clare thought that it was a good thing to have frightened Miss O'Flaherty who was horrible, and sold copy books and school supplies but hated schoolchildren. Clare thought it was real bad luck that Mammy happened to be passing. She smiled sympathetically at Chrissie but it was not well received.

'Stop looking so superior,' Chrissie cried out. 'Look at Clare gloating at it all. Goody-goody Clare, stupid boring Clare.'

She got a cuff on the side of her head for this performance and it made her madder still.

'Look, she's delighted,' Chrissie went on, 'delighted to see anyone in trouble. That's all that ever makes Clare happy, to see others brought down.'

'There'll be no tea for you, Chrissie O'Brien, and that's not the end of it either. Get up to your room this minute, do you hear. This *minute*.' Agnes O'Brien's thin voice was like a whistle with anger, as she banished the bold Chrissie, wiped the worst paint off her husband's hands with a rag that she had wet with white spirit, and managed at the same time to point to Clare's coat on the hook.

'This isn't a hand-me-down shop,' she said. 'Take that coat and put it where it's meant to be.'

The unfairness of this stung Clare deeply. 'We always leave our coats there. That *is* where it's meant to be.'

'Do you hear her?' Agnes looked in appeal to her husband, did not wait for an answer but headed for the stairs. Chrissie up there was for it.

'Can't you stop tormenting your mother and move your coat?' he asked. 'Is it too much to ask for a bit of peace?'

Clare took her coat down from the hook. She couldn't go up to the bedroom she shared with Chrissie because that would be like stepping straight into the battlefield. She stayed idling in the shop.

Her father's face was weary. It was so *wrong* of him to say she was tormenting Mammy, she wasn't, but you couldn't explain that to him. He was bent over in a kind of a stoop and he looked very old, like someone's grandfather, not a father. Daddy was all grey, his face and his hair and his cardigan. Only his hands were white from the paint. Daddy had grown more stooped since her First Communion three years ago, Clare thought; then he had seemed very tall. His face had grown hairy too – there were bits of hair in his nose and his ears. He always looked a bit harassed as if there wasn't enough time or space or money. And, indeed, there usually wasn't enough of any of these things. The O'Brien household lived on the profits of the summer season which was short and unpredictable. It could be killed by rain, by the popularity of some new resort, by people overcharging for houses along the cliff road. There was no steady living to be gained over the winter months, it was merely a matter of keeping afloat.

The shop was oddly-shaped when you came in: there were corners and nooks in it which should have been shelved or walled off but nobody had ever got round to it, the ceiling was low and even with three customers the place looked crowded. Nobody could see any order on the shelves but the O'Briens knew where everything was. They didn't change it for fear they wouldn't find things, even though there were many more logical ways of stocking the small grocery-confectioner's. It all looked cramped and awkward and though the customers couldn't see behind the door into the living quarters it was exactly the same in there. The kitchen had a range, with a clothes line over it, and the table took up most of the space in the room. A small scullery at the back was so poky and dark that it was almost impossible to see the dishes you washed. There was one light in the middle of the room with a yellow light shade which had a crack in it. Recently Tom O'Brien had been holding his paper up nearer to the light in order to read it.

Agnes came downstairs with the air of someone who has just finished an unpleasant task satisfactorily. 'That girl will end on the gallows,' she said.

She was a thin small woman, who used to smile a lot once; but now she seemed set in the face of the cold Castlebay wind, and even when she was indoors she seemed to be grimacing against the icy blast, eyes narrow and mouth in a hard line. In the shop she wore a yellow overall to protect her clothes, she said, but in fact there were hardly any clothes to protect. She had four outfits for going to Mass, and otherwise it had been the same old cardigans and frocks and skirts for years. There were always medals and relics pinned inside the cardigan; they had to be taken off before it was washed. Once she had forgotten, and a relic of the Little Flower which had been in a red satin covering had become all pink and the pale blue cardigan was tinged pink too. Agnes O'Brien had her hair in a bun which was made by pulling it through a thing that looked like a doughnut, a squashy round device, and then the hair was clipped in. They never saw her doing this, but once they had seen the bun by itself and it had alarmed Clare greatly because she hadn't known what it was.

The dark and very angry eyes of her mother landed on her. 'Have you decided that you would like to belong to this family and do what's required of you? Would it be too much to ask you to take that coat out of my way before I open the range and burn it down to its buttons?'

She would never do that, Clare knew. She had hoped her mother might have forgotten it during the sojourn upstairs. But the coat was still going to be a cause of war.

'I told her, Agnes, my God I told her, but children nowadays . . .' Tom sounded defeated and apologetic.

Clare stuffed her school coat into a crowded cupboard under the stairs and took a few potatoes out of the big sack on the floor. Each evening she and Chrissie had to get the potatoes ready for tea, and tonight, thanks to Chrissie's disgrace, it looked as if Clare was going to have to do it on her own. In the kitchen sat her younger brothers Ben and Jim; they were reading a comic. The older boys Tommy and Ned would be in from the Brothers shortly, but none of this would be any help. Boys didn't help with the food or the washing up. Everyone knew that.

Clare had a lot to do after tea. She wanted to iron her yellow ribbons for tomorrow. Just in case she won the history essay she'd better be looking smart. She would polish her indoor shoes, she had brought them home specially, and she would make another attempt to get the two stains off her tunic. Mother Immaculata might make a comment about smartening yourself up for the good name of the school. She must be sure not to let them down. Miss O'Hara had said that she had never been so pleased in all her years teaching as when she read Clare's essay, it gave her the strength to go on. Those were her very words. She would never have stopped Clare in the corridor and said that, if she hadn't won the prize. Imagine beating all the ones of fifteen. All those Bernie Conways and Anna Murphys. They'd look at Clare with new interest from now on. And indeed they'd have to think a bit differently at home too. She longed to tell them tonight, but decided it was better to wait. Tonight they were all like weasels and anyway it might look worse for Chrissie; after all she was two years and a half older. Chrissie would murder her too if she chose to reveal it tonight. She took upstairs a big thick sandwich of cheese, a bit of cold cooked bacon and a cup of cocoa.

Chrissie was sitting on her bed, examining her face in a mirror. She had two very thick plaits in her hair; the bits at the ends after the rubber bands were bushy and didn't just hang there like other people's, they looked as if they were trying to escape. She had a fringe which she cut herself so badly that she had to be taken to the hairdresser to get a proper job done on it, and at night she put pipe cleaners into the fringe so that it would curl properly.

She was fatter than Clare, much, and she had a real bust that you could see even in her school tunic.

Chrissie was very interested in her nose, Clare couldn't understand why but she was always examining it. Even now in all the disgrace and no meal and the sheer fury over what she had done to Miss O'Flaherty she was still peering at it looking for spots to squeeze. She had a round face and always looked surprised. Not happily surprised, not even when someone was delivering her an unexpected supper.

'I don't want it,' she said.

'Don't eat it then,' Clare returned with some spirit.

She went back downstairs and tried to find a corner where she could learn the poem for tomorrow; and she had to do four sums. She often asked herself how was it that with six people living in that house who were all going to school, why was she the only one who ever needed to do any homework?

Gerry Doyle came in as she was ironing her yellow ribbons.

'Where's Chrissie?' he asked Clare in a whisper.

'She's upstairs, there was murder here, she gave Miss O'Flaherty some desperate fright with seaweed. Don't ask for her, they'll all go mad if you even mention her name.'

'Listen, would you tell her . . .' He stopped, deciding against it. 'No, you're too young.'

'I'm not too young,' Clare said, stung by the unfairness of it. 'But young or old, I don't care, I'm not giving your soppy messages to Chrissie, she'll only be annoyed with me, and you'll be annoyed with me, and Mammy will beat the legs off me, so

I'd much prefer you kept them to yourself.' She went back to the ribbons with vigour. They were flat gleaming bands now, they would fluff up gorgeously tomorrow. She couldn't get herself up to the neck in Chrissie's doings because there would be trouble at every turn. She must keep nice and quiet and get ready for tomorrow, for the look of surprise on Mother Immaculata's face, and the horror on Bernie Conway's and Anna Murphy's.

Gerry Doyle laughed good-naturedly. 'You're quite right, let people do their own dirty work,' he said.

The words 'dirty work' somehow cut through all the rest of the noise in the O'Brien kitchen and reached Agnes O'Brien as she pulled the entire contents of the dresser's bottom cupboard on to the floor. Tom had said that she must have thrown out the length of flex he was going to use to put up a light outside the back door. She was sure she had seen it somewhere and was determined that the project should not be postponed.

Tommy and Ned were going through the paper for jobs as they did every week, marking things with a stubby purple pencil; Ben and Jimmy were playing a game that began quietly every few minutes until it became a slapping match and one of them would start to cry. Tom was busy mending the wireless which crackled over all the activity.

'What dirty work?' Agnes called: a grand fellow, that Gerry Doyle, but you had to watch him like a hawk. Whatever devilment was planned he had a hand in it.

'I was saying to Clare that I'm no good at any housework, or anything that needs a lot of care. I'm only good at dirty work.' He smiled across, and the woman on her knees in front of a pile of tins, boxes, paper bags, knitting wool, toasting forks and rusted baking trays, smiled back.

Clare looked up at him with surprise. Imagine being able to tell a lie as quickly and as well as that. And over nothing.

Gerry had gone over to the job consultation, saying he heard there was going to be a man from a big employment agency in England coming round and holding interviews in the hotel.

'Wouldn't that be for big kind of jobs, for people with qualifications?' Ned asked, unwilling to think anyone would come to Castlebay to seek out him or his like.

'Have sense Ned, who is there in this place with any qualifications? Won't it save you shoe leather and the cost of writing off to these places if you wait till this fellow arrives and he'll tell all there's to be told?'

'It's easy on you to say that.' Tommy, the eldest, was troubled. '*You* don't have to go away for a job. You've got your business.'

'So have you,' Gerry pointed to the shop.

But it wasn't the same. Gerry's father was the photographer; during the winter he survived on dances, and the odd function that was held. In summer, he walked the length of the beach three times a day taking family groups and then out again at night into the dance hall where the holiday business was brisk and where there would be a great demand to buy prints of the romantic twosomes that he would snap. Girls were his biggest customers, they loved to bring back holiday memories in the form of something that they could pass around the office and sigh over when

511

the dance was long over. Gerry's mother and sister did the developing and printing, or they helped with it, which was the way it was described. Gerry's father expected the only son to take an active part, and since he had been a youngster, Gerry had tagged along learning the psychology as well as the mechanics of the camera.

You must never annoy people, his father had taught him, be polite and a little distant even, click the camera when they aren't at all posed or prepared and then if they show interest and start to pose take a proper snap. The first plate was only a blank to get their attention. Remind them gently that there's no need to buy, the proofs will be available for inspection in twenty-four hours. Move on and don't waste any time chatting when the picture is taken, have a pleasant smile but not a greasy sort of a one. Never plead with people to pose, and when gaggles of girls want six or seven shots taken of them remember they're only going to buy one at the most so pretend to take the snap more often than taking it.

Gerry's beautiful sister Fiona had long dark ringlets; when she wasn't working in the darkroom in their house during the summer she sat in the wooden shack up over the beach selling the snaps. Gerry's father had said that a town like Castlebay was so small you could never have a business if you tried to get big and expand and hire people. But keep it small and run it just with the family and there would be a great inheritance for Gerard Anthony Doyle.

But Gerry never had the air of a boy about to step into a secure future. He examined the paper with the O'Brien boys as eagerly as if he would be having to take the emigrant ship with them.

How did he know whether there'd be a living for him here? His father was always saying that all it needed was a smart-alec firm to come in for the summer and they'd be ruined. Who knew what the future would bring? Maybe people would want coloured photography, there could be newfangled cameras, it was living on a cliff edge his father always said. At least in O'Brien's they could be sure that people would always want bread and butter and milk. They'd want groceries until the end of the world and as long as the trippers kept coming wouldn't they be selling ice creams and sweets and oranges until the last day as well?

Gerry always made everything sound more exciting than it was. He saw a future for Tommy and Ned where they'd work in England and then, just when all the English would be wondering what to do and where to go for the summer holidays, Ned and Tommy would come back home to Castlebay, get behind the counter, help out with the shop and have a great holiday as well. And they'd be fine fellows at the dance because they'd be so well up in everything after being in England. Tommy complained that it wouldn't be much of a holiday coming home to work like dogs in the really tough part of the year when O'Brien's was open from eight o'clock in the morning until midnight. But Gerry just laughed and said that would be their investment, that was the only time of the year that there'd be work for all hands. The rest of the year they'd be falling over each other with no one to serve, but in the summer the whole family should be there to make sure that everyone got a bit of sleep anyway and to keep the thing going. It was like that in all seaside towns. Gerry was very convincing. Tommy and Ned saw it all very rosily, and really and truly Gerry was right, shouldn't they wait till the man came and had a list of jobs for them instead of scanning all the ads which told them nothing when all was said and done?

Clare had turned the iron on its end by the range; she was folding the blanket and the scorch sheet and wondering where to replace them since everything from the dresser seemed to be on the floor. Gerry Doyle was sitting on the table swinging his legs and she got a sudden feeling that he was giving her brothers wrong advice. They weren't capable and sure like he was, they were the kind of people who agreed with everyone else.

'Would this man who came offering jobs in the hotel, would he be offering the kind of jobs where you could get on or jobs you'd just have to work hard at?'

They were surprised that she spoke. Her father took his head out of the shell of the wireless.

'It's the same thing, Clare girl, if you work hard you get on. If you don't, you don't.'

'But trained like, that's what I mean,' Clare said. 'You remember when that Order came and the girls were all going to be taken off to do their Leaving Certificate and learn a skill if they became postulant nuns.'

Ned roared with scorn. 'A postulant nun! Is that what you'd like us to be, wouldn't we look fine in the habit and the veil?'

'No that's not what I meant . . .' she began.

'I don't think the Reverend Mother would take us,' Tommy said.

'Sister Thomas, I really think we're going to have to do something about your voice in the choir,' Ned said in mincing tones.

'Oh I'm doing my best, Sister Edward, but what about your hobnailed boots?'

'Sister Thomas, you can talk, what about your hairy legs?'

Benny and Jimmy were interested now.

'And you've got to give up kicking football round the convent,' said Ben.

'Nuns kicking football,' screamed Jimmy with enthusiasm. Even Mammy on her knees and having triumphantly found the bit of flex was laughing and Dad was smiling too. Clare was rescued unexpectedly.

'Very funny, ha ha,' Gerry Doyle said. 'Very funny Mother Edward and Mother Thomas, but Clare's right. What's the point of getting a job on a building site without any training as a brickie or a carpenter? No, the real thing to ask this fellow is nothing to do with how much, but what kind of a job.'

Clare flushed with pleasure. They were all nodding now.

'I nearly forgot why I came,' Gerry said. 'The father asked me to have a look at the view from different places, he's half thinking of making a postcard of Castlebay, and he wondered where's the best angle to take the picture from. He wondered would there be a good view from your upstairs. Do you mind if I run up and have a look?'

'At night?' Clare's father asked.

'You'd get a good idea of the outlines at night,' Gerry said, his foot on the stairs.

'Go on up lad.'

They were all back at their activities and nobody except Clare had the slightest idea that Gerry Doyle aged fifteen and a half had gone upstairs to see Chrissie O'Brien aged thirteen.

Nellie was on her knees with the bellows when David came in. 'I'm building up a nice fire for your lessons,' she told him.

Her face was red with the exertion and her hair was escaping from the cap she wore. She never seemed comfortable in the cap, it was always at the wrong angle somehow on her hair and her head seemed to be full of hairpins. Nellie was old, not as old as Mummy but about thirty, and she was fat and cheerful and she had been there always. She had a lot of married brothers and an old father. When David was a young fellow she used to tell him that she was better off than any of them, in a nice clean house and great comfort and all the food she could eat. David used to think it was lonely for her in the kitchen when they were all inside but Nellie's round face would crack into a smile and she assured him that she was as well off as if she'd married a Guard, or even better off. Her money was her own, she had the best of everything and every Thursday afternoon and every second Sunday afternoon off.

David started to help with the fire but Nellie stood up, creaking, and said it was going fine and wasn't that his teacher coming in the gate.

Angela O'Hara's red bicycle was indeed coming up the gravel path. She was tall and slim, and she always wore belts on her coats as if it were the only way they'd stay on. Other people had buttons, but of course other people didn't fly around on the bike so much. She had red-brown hair that was sort of tied back but with such a loose ribbon or piece of cord that it might as well not be tied back at all. She had big greenish eyes and she used to throw her head back when she laughed.

Miss O'Hara wasn't at all like other grown-ups. She wanted to know did they all get a refund of fees because the school had to close for the scarlet fever. David didn't know, he said he'd ask, but Miss O'Hara said it didn't matter, and not to ask because it might seem as if she was looking for more money, which she wasn't. David had forgotten that she was being paid to teach him, it wasn't the kind of thing you'd think about, he sort of believed that Miss O'Hara did it for interest. She had found that very funny. She said in many ways she would well do it for interest but the labourer was worthy of his hire as it said somewhere in the gospels, and if she were to do it for free what about the fancy order of priests he was with – they certainly didn't do it for free. David said he thought the main cost was the food and the beds in the dormitories, he couldn't imagine that the actual lessons would cost anything.

She came for an hour every evening, after she had finished up at the school and called in on her mother. Mrs O'Hara was all crooked from arthritis and David thought that she looked like an illustration of an old tree in one of the children's books he used to read. A book probably tidied away neatly by his mother for when it would be needed again. Miss O'Hara had two sisters married in England and a brother, a priest, in the Far East. She was the only one who had never travelled, she told him. He asked what would have happened if she had travelled and her mother had got all crippled living by herself.

'Then I'd have come back,' Miss O'Hara had said cheerfully. Since her sisters were married and her brother was a priest she would have been the one to look after her mother anyway.

The O'Hara house was out a bit on the road towards the golf course, and Miss O'Hara cycled everywhere on her big red bicycle with the basket of exercise books in the front. There were always copy books and when it rained she had them covered with a waterproof sheet. She wore a long scarf wound round her in winter and if there was a wind sometimes her long hair stood out behind her in a straight line. David's mother once said she looked like a witch heading for the cliff road and you'd expect her and the bicycle to take flight over the seas. But his father had refused to let a word of criticism be spoken of her. He said that nobody knew how much she did for that crippled mother of hers, morning noon and night, and wasn't it proof to note that when poor Angela O'Hara went on her two weeks holiday a year somewhere they had to have three people in and out of that house to mind the mother and it was never done satisfactorily even then. His mother didn't like Miss O'Hara, it had something to do with her not admiring things or not being excited enough about his mother going to Dublin for outings. It had never been said, it was just a feeling he had.

The table with his books on it was near the fire and Nellie would bring in a pot of tea and a slice of cake or apple tart.

Miss O'Hara always talked to Nellie more than she talked to his mother, she'd ask about Nellie's old father out in the country and the row with the brothers and had they heard from the sister in Canada. She'd giggle with Nellie about something new that Father O'Dwyer's housekeeper had said. The woman's name was Miss McCormack, but everyone called her Sergeant McCormack because she tried to run not only Father O'Dwyer and the church but the whole of Castlebay too.

Miss O'Hara came in now, her hands cold from clenching the handlebars in the wind, and she held them out to the fire.

'God, Nellie, isn't it a sin having a great fire like this banked up just for David and myself. We could work in the kitchen, you know, beside the range.'

'Oh, that wouldn't do at all!' Nellie was horrified.

'You wouldn't mind, David?' she began . . . and then suddenly changed her mind. 'No, don't take any notice of me, I always want to change the world, that's my problem. Aren't we lucky to have this grand place in here, let's make the most of it. Nellie, tell me what are they building on the side of Dillon's? It looks like an aerodrome.'

'Oh, that's going to be a sun lounge, I hear,' Nellie said, full of importance. 'They're going to have chairs and card tables maybe in the summer, and tea served there too.'

'They'd need to have rugs and hot-water bottles if it turns out anything like last summer. Come on, college boy, get out your geography book, we're going to make you a world expert on trade winds, you're going to make them green and yellow striped with jealousy when you get back to that palace of a school of yours. We'll show them what a real scholar is, the way we breed them in Castlebay.'

Paddy Power was tall and thick-set, with a weather-beaten face. His face was beaten by weather of all kinds, but mainly the sharp wind that came in from the sea as he walked up lanes to people's houses, lanes where his big battered car wouldn't go. He had a shock of hair that grew in all directions as if he had three crowns on his head; it had been brown and then it was speckled but now it was mainly grey. Because of his bulk and his alarming hair he sometimes looked fierce, but that was before people got to know him. He had a great way of talking, a kind of good-natured bantering until he could see what was wrong; his talk was merely to relax the patient until he could see where the piece of grit in the eyes was, or the splinter in the hand, the glass in the sole of the foot or feel for the pain in the base of the stomach without too much tensing and alarm.

He was a burly man who never found clothes to fit him and never cared about them either. Life was far too short, he said, to spend time in a tailor's talking rubbish about lines and cuts and lapels. But for all his bulk and his haphazard attitude to his appearance, he was a healthy man and he was able to go down the path from his own garden to the sea and swim for nearly six months of the year and to get a game of golf a week as well. But Paddy Power was tired today; it had been a very long day and he had driven seventeen miles out to see a young woman who would be dead by Christmas but who talked cheerfully of how she knew she'd be better when the fine weather came. Her five children had played noisily and unconcerned around the feet of the doctor and the pale young husband just sat looking emptily into the fire. He had also had to have an unpleasing chat with one of the Dillon brothers from the hotel and speak seriously about liver damage. No matter how carefully he tried to phrase it, he had ended up with a blank wall and a great deal of resentment. Today it had ended with Dick Dillon telling him to mind his own bloody business, and that Paddy Power was a fine one to talk, half the country could tell you that he was drunk as a lord three years ago at the races, so he was in a poor position to cast stones. There were two bad cases of flu in old people, where it was settling in on chests that were never strong, he could see both of them turning into pneumonia before long. People talked about the *good seaside air*, and the *bracing breezes*. They should be here in a doctor's surgery in winter, Paddy Power thought gloomily, there'd be less of the folksy chat then.

Molly said that David was getting on like a house on fire with his lessons, and that he did two hours on his own each morning.

'She's a fine scholar Angela, isn't it a pity that she never got the recognition for it,' Paddy said, wearily taking off his boots and putting on his slippers.

'Never got any recognition? Isn't she a teacher above in the school with a big salary, hasn't she all her qualifications, that's not bad for Dinny O'Hara's daughter.' Molly sniffed.

'You miss the point, Moll. That's a bright girl and she's stuck here in Castlebay teaching children to be waitresses and to serve their time in shops. And what kind of a life does she have in that house? I mean the Little Sisters wouldn't do as much for their flock as Angela does for her mother.'

'Oh I know, I know.' Molly was anxious to leave it now.

'Still, a man on a white horse may ride into town one day for her yet.' He smiled at the thought.

'I'd say she's a bit past that now,' Molly said.

'She's only twenty-eight years of age, a year older than you were when we got married, that's what she is.'

Molly hated when he spoke about things like that in front of Nellie. Molly hadn't grown up here, she came from a big town and she had been at school in Dublin. She didn't like anyone knowing her business nor indeed her age.

She looked at herself in the mirror, no longer young but not too bad. She had made a friend of the buyer in that shop in Dublin and now there was no problem in getting clothes. Nice wool two-pieces, loose enough so that you could wear a warm vest and maybe even a thin jumper under them. You needed a lot of layers in Castlebay. And Paddy had given her nice brooches over the years so that she always looked smart. No matter who came to the house, Molly Power looked well-dressed and ready to receive them, her hair was always neat and well-groomed (she had a perm every three months in the town) and she always used a little make-up.

She examined her face. She had been afraid that the climate in this place might have made her lined or leathery like a lot of the women, but then they probably didn't use any face cream even.

She smiled at herself, turning her head slightly so that she'd see the nice clip-on earrings she had got recently to match the green brooch on her green and grey wool two-piece. Paddy saw her smiling and came and stood behind her with his hands on her shoulders.

'You're right about yourself, you're gorgeous,' he said.

'I wasn't thinking that,' she said indignantly.

'Well, you should have been,' he said. 'A glamorous thing, not like a mother and wife.'

She thought about being a mother for a moment. She had believed it would be impossible. So many false alarms. The weeks of delight followed by the miscarriages at three months. Three times. Then two babies born dead. And then when she hardly dared to believe it, David. Exactly the child she wanted. Exactly.

Angela thought David was a grand little fellow. He looked like an illustration from those Just William books, with his hair sticking up, his shoelaces undone and his tie crooked. When he worked he sort of came apart.

Wouldn't it be lovely to teach bright children all the time without having to pause for ever for the others to catch up. She looked at him as he worked out a chart of the winds and gave it to her triumphantly.

'Why are you smiling?' he asked suspiciously.

'I don't know. I could be losing my mind. I've noticed myself smiling nowadays whenever any child gets anything right, it's such a shock you see.'

He laughed. 'Are they all hopeless at the school here?'

'No, not all, some are as smart as paint. But what's the point? Where will it get them?'

'Won't it get them their exams?'

'Yes, yes it will.' She stood up a bit like a grown-up who wasn't going to follow the conversation on with him. He was disappointed.

Angela cycled home from Dr Power's house into the wind. Her face was whipped by it and the salt of the sea stung her eyes. Any journey in winter seemed like a voyage to the South Pole, and she wondered for the millionth time would they be better if she moved her mother to a town. Surely this wet wind coming in through every crack in the cottage must be hard on her, surely it couldn't be healthy living in a place that was only right for seals and gulls for three quarters of the year. But then she mustn't fool herself: if they moved to a town it would be for herself, so that

517

she could have some life. Let's not pretend it would be for her mother's poor old misshapen bones. And anyway what more life would there be for her in a town? She'd come in as a schoolmarm with an ailing mother, that's if she were to get a job at all. A schoolmarm who was freewheeling down to thirty. Not something that was going to light many fireworks. Stop dreaming, Angela, head down, foot down, pedal on, only a few more minutes now, the worst bit is over, you're past the blasts of wind from the gap in the cliff. You can see the light in the window.

People called it a cottage because it looked small from the front but in fact there was an upstairs. It was whitewashed and had the formal little garden with its boxed hedge and tiny path up to the door.

She wondered how they had all fitted there when her father was alive, when they were children, they must have been crowded. But then her parents had slept in one room upstairs, the three girls in another and Sean, the only boy, in the third. And downstairs the room which she had now made into a bedroom for her mother had been a kind of sitting room she supposed. There had been no books in it in those days, there had been no shining brass ornaments, no little bunches of flowers or bowls of heather and gorse like she had nowadays. But of course in those times the small house had been home for a drunk, an overworked and weary mother and four youngsters all determined to get away from it as soon as possible. How could there have been time for the luxury of books and flowers?

Her mother was sitting on the commode where Angela had put her before going up to the Powers'. She had dropped her stick and the other chair was too far away so she had nothing to support her and couldn't get up. She was uncomplaining, and apologetic. Angela emptied the chamberpot and put Dettol in it, she got a basin of soapy water and a cloth for her mother and helped her to wash herself and put on powder. Then she slipped the flannel nightdress that had been warming on the fireguard over her mother's small bent head and helped her to the bed in the room adjoining the kitchen. She handed her the rosary beads, her glass of water and put the clock where she could see it. She didn't kiss her mother, they weren't a kissing family. She patted her on the folded hands instead. Then Angela O'Hara went back into the kitchen and took out the essays which would be handed back next day. There was no doubt about the winner, that had been obvious all along, but she wanted to write a little paragraph on the end of all the others. They had done the essay in their free time to enter for the prize that she had provided. She wanted to give them some encouragement, some visible proof that she had read them, even the illiterate ones.

She wet a pot of tea and settled down with the wind howling outside and very shortly the sound of her mother's gentle snores about ten feet away.

Clare O'Brien had arrived early at school. The back of her neck was almost washed away, such a scrubbing had it got. The stain on her school tunic was almost impossible to see now, it had been attacked severely with a nail brush. Her indoor shoes were gleaming, she had even polished the soles, and the yellow ribbons were beautiful. She turned her head a few times to see them reflected in the school window, she looked as smart as any of the others, as good as the farmers' daughters who had plenty of money and got new uniforms when they grew too big for their old ones, instead of all the letting down and letting out and false hems that Clare and Chrissie had to put up with.

She thought the day would never start. It was going to be such an excitement going up there in front of the whole school. And there would be gasps because she was so young. Years and years younger than some of them who had entered.

Chrissie would be furious of course, but that didn't matter, Chrissie was furious about everything, she'd get over it.

Clare walked to the end of the corridor to read the notice board. There was nothing new on it, maybe after this morning there might be a notice about the history prize. There was the timetable, the list of holidays of obligation during the year, the details of the educational tour to Dublin and also the price of it, which made it outside Clare's hopes. There was the letter from Father O'Hara, Miss O'Hara's brother who was a missionary. He was thanking the school for the silver paper and stamp collecting. He said he was very proud that the girls in his own home town had done so much to aid the great work of spreading Our Lord's word to all the poor people who had never heard of Him.

Clare couldn't remember Father O'Hara, but everyone said he was marvellous. He was very tall, taller than Miss O'Hara, and very handsome. Clare's mother had said that it would do your heart good to see him when he came back to say Mass in the church, and he was a wonderful son too, she said. He wrote to his mother from the missions, she often showed his letters to people – well, when she had been able to get out a bit she had.

Father O'Hara made the missions sound great fun altogether. Clare wished he would write a letter every week. She wondered what did Miss O'Hara write to him. Would she tell him about the history prize this week?

There was Miss O'Hara now, coming in the gate on her bicycle. Mother Immaculata had a face like the nib of a pen.

'Could I have a word, Miss O'Hara, a little word please. That's if you can spare the time.'

One day, Angela promised herself, she would tell Mother Immaculata that she couldn't spare the time, she was too busy helping the seniors to run the potin still and preparing the third years for the white-slave traffic. But not yet. Not while she still had to work here. She put her bicycle in the shed and swept up the armful of essays wrapped in their sheet against the elements.

'Certainly Mother,' she said with a false smile.

Mother Immaculata didn't speak until they were in her office. She closed the door and sat down at her desk; the only other chair in the room was covered in books so Angela had to stand.

She decided she would fight back. If the nun was going to treat her as a disobedient child over some trivial thing as yet unknown, and let her stand there worrying, Angela was going to draw herself up so high that Mother Immaculata would get a crick in her neck looking up. Angela raised herself unobtrusively on to her toes, and stretched her neck upwards like a giraffe. It worked. Mother Immaculata had to stand up too.

'What is all this about a money prize for an essay competition, Miss O'Hara? Can you explain to me how it came up and when it was discussed with me?'

'Oh, I've given them an essay to do and I'm awarding a prize for the best one.' Angela smiled like a simpleton.

'But when was this discussed?' The thin pointed face quivered at the lack of respect, or anxiety at discovery.

'Sure, there'd be no need to discuss every single thing we did in class Mother, would there? I mean, would you ever get anything done if we came to you over what homework we were going to give them and all?'

'I do *not* mean that. I mean I need an explanation. Since when have we been paying the children to study?'

Angela felt a sudden weariness. It was going to be like this for ever. Any bit of enthusiasm and excitement sat on immediately. Fight for every single thing including the privilege of putting your hand into your own very meagre salary and giving some of it as a heady excitement which had even the dullards reading the history books.

It was like a slow and ponderous dance. A series of steps had to be gone through, a fake bewilderment. Angela would now say that she was terribly sorry, she had thought Mother Immaculata would be delighted, which was lies of course since she knew well that Immaculata would have stopped it had she got wind of it earlier. Then a fake display of helplessness, what should they do now, she had all the essays corrected, look here they were, and the children were expecting the results today. Then the fake supplication, could Mother Immaculata ever be kind enough to present the prize? Angela had it here in an envelope. It was twenty-one shillings, a whole guinea. Oh and there was a subsidiary prize for another child who had done well, a book all wrapped up. And finally the fake gratitude and the even more fake promise that it would *never* happen again.

Mother Immaculata was being gracious now, which was even more sickening than when she was being hostile.

'And who has won this ill-advised competition?' she asked.

'Bernie Conway,' said Angela. 'It was the best, there's no doubt about that. But you know young Clare O'Brien, she did a terrific one altogether, the poor child must have slaved over it. I would like to have given her the guinea but I thought the others would pick on her, she's too young. So that's why I got her a book, could you perhaps say something Mother about her being . . .'

Mother Immaculata would agree to nothing of the sort. Clare O'Brien from the little shop down by the steps, wasn't she only one of the youngest to enter for it? Not at all, it would be highly unsuitable. Imagine putting her in the same league as Bernie Conway from the post office, to think of singling out Chrissie O'Brien's younger sister. Not at all.

'But she's nothing like Chrissie, she's totally different,' wailed Angela. But she had lost. The children were filing into the school hall for their prayers and hymn. Mother Immaculata had put her hand out and taken the envelope containing the guinea and the card saying that Bernadette Mary Conway had been awarded the Prize for Best History Essay. Mother Immaculata left on her desk the neatly wrapped copy of Palgreave's *Golden Treasury* for Clare O'Brien for Excellence in History Essay Writing.

Angela picked it up and reminded herself that it was childish to believe that you could win everything.

Mother Immaculata made the announcements after prayers. Clare thought the words were never going to come out of the nun's thin mouth.

There were announcements about how the school was going to learn to answer Mass with Father O'Dwyer, not serve it of course, only boys could do that, but to answer it, and there must be great attention paid so that it would be done beautifully. And there was a complaint that those girls in charge of school altars were very lacking in diligence about putting clean water in the vases. What hope was there for a child who couldn't manage to prepare a clean vase for Our Lady? It was a very simple thing surely to do for the Mother of God. Then there was the business about outdoor shoes being worn in the classroom. Finally she came to it. Mother Immaculata's voice changed slightly. Clare couldn't quite understand – it was as if she didn't *want* to give the history prize.

'It has come to my notice, only this morning, that there is some kind of history competition. I am glad of course to see industry in the school. However, that being said, it gives me great pleasure to present the prize on behalf of the school.'

She paused and her eyes went up and down the rows of girls who stood in front of her. Clare smoothed the sides of her tunic nervously. She must remember to walk slowly and not to run, she could easily fall on the steps leading up to the stage where Mother Immaculata, the other nuns and lay teachers stood. She would be very calm and she would thank Miss O'Hara and remember to thank Mother Immaculata as well.

'So I won't keep you in any further suspense . . .' Mother Immaculata managed to draw another few seconds out of it.

'The prize is awarded to Bernadette Mary Conway. Congratulations Bernadette. Come up here, child, and receive your prize.'

Clare told herself she must keep smiling. She must not let her face change. Just think about that and nothing else and she'd be all right. She concentrated fiercely on the smile; it sort of pushed her eyes up a bit and if there were any tears in them people wouldn't notice.

She kept the smile on as stupid Bernie Conway put her hand to her mouth over and over, and then put her hand on her chest. Her friends had to nudge her to get her to her feet. As she gasped and said it couldn't be true, Clare clenched her top teeth firmly on top of her lower teeth and smiled on. She saw Miss O'Hara looking round at the school and even looking hard at her. She smiled back hard. Very hard. She would never let Miss O'Hara know how much she hated her. She must be the meanest and most horrible teacher in the world – much meaner than Mother Immaculata – to tell Clare that she had won the prize, to say all those lies about it being the best thing she had read in all her years teaching. Clare kept the smile up until it was time to file out of the hall and into their classrooms. Then she dropped it; it didn't matter now. She felt one of her ribbons falling off; that didn't matter now either.

The girls brought sandwiches to eat in the classroom at lunch, and they had to be very careful about crumbs for fear of mice. Clare had made big doorsteps for herself and Chrissie since her big sister was still in disgrace. But she hadn't the appetite for anything at all. She unwrapped the paper, looked at them and just wrapped them up again. Josie Dillon, who sat beside her, looked at them enviously.

'If you're sure?' she said as Clare passed them over wordlessly.

'I'm sure,' Clare said.

It was raining, so they couldn't go out in the yard. Lunchtimes indoors were awful, the windows were all steamed up and there was the smell of food everywhere. The nuns and teachers prowled from classroom to classroom seeing that the high jinks were not too high; the level of noise fell dramatically as soon as a figure of authority appeared and then rose slowly to a crescendo once more when the figure moved on.

Josie was the youngest of the Dillons, the others were away at a boarding school but it was said that they wouldn't bother sending Josie, she wasn't too bright. A big pasty girl with a discontented face – only when someone suggested food was there any animation at all.

'These are lovely,' she said with a full mouth to Clare. 'You're cracked not to want them yourself.'

Clare smiled a watery smile.

'Are you feeling all right?' Josie showed concern. 'You look a bit green.'

'No, I'm fine,' Clare said. 'I'm fine.' She was saying it to herself rather than to Josie Dillon who was busy opening up the second sandwich and looking into it with pleasure.

Miss O'Hara came into the classroom and the noise receded. She gave a few orders: pick up those crusts at once, open the window to let in some fresh air, no it didn't matter how cold and wet it was, open it. How many times did she have to say put the books away *before* you start to eat. And suddenly, 'Clare, can you come out here to me a minute.'

Clare didn't want to go, she didn't want to talk to her ever again. She hated Miss O'Hara for making such a fool of her, telling her that she'd won the prize and building up her hopes. But Miss O'Hara had said it again. 'Clare. Now, please.'

Unwillingly she went out into the corridor which was full of people going to and from the cloakrooms getting ready for afternoon classes. The bell would ring any moment now.

Miss O'Hara put her books on a window sill right on top of the Sacred Heart altar. There were altars on nearly every window sill and each class was responsible for one of them.

'I got you another prize, because yours was so good. It was really good and if you had been competing with people nearer your own age you'd have won hands down. So anyway I got this for you.' Miss O'Hara handed her a small parcel. She was smiling and eager for Clare to open it. But Clare would not be bought off with a secret prize.

'Thank you very much, Miss O'Hara,' she said and made no attempt to untie the string.

'Well, aren't you going to look at it?'

'I'll open it later,' she said. It was as near to being rude as she dared to go, and in case it had been just that bit too much she added. 'Thank you very much.'

'Stop sulking, Clare, and open it.' Miss O'Hara's voice was firm.

'I'm not sulking.'

'Of course you are, and it's a horrible habit. Stop it this minute and open up the present I bought you so generously out of my own money.' It was an order. It also made Clare feel mean. Whatever it was she would be very polite.

It was a book of poetry, a book with a soft leather cover that had fancy flowers painted on it with gold-leaf paint. It was called *The Golden Treasury of Verse*. It was beautiful.

Some of the sparkle had come back into the small face with the big eyes. 'Open the book now and see what I wrote.' Angela was still very teacherish.

Clare read the inscription aloud.

'That's the first book for your library. One day when you have a big library of books you'll remember this one, and you'll take it out and show it to someone, and you'll say it was your first book, and you won it when you were ten.'

'Will I have a library?' Clare asked excitedly.

'You will if you want to. You can have anything if you want to.'

'Is that true?' Clare felt Miss O'Hara was being a bit jokey, her voice had a tinny ring to it.

'No, not really. I wanted to give you this in front of the whole school, I wanted Immaculata to give it to you, but she wouldn't. Make you too uppity or something. No, there's a lot of things I want and don't get, but that's not the point, the point is you must go out and try for it, if you don't try you can't get anything.'

'It's beautiful.' Clare stroked the book.

'It's a grand collection, much nicer than your poetry book in class.'

Clare felt very grown up: Miss O'Hara saying 'Immaculata' without 'Mother' before it. Miss O'Hara saying their poetry text-book wasn't great! 'I'd have bought a book anyway if I'd won the guinea,' she said forgivingly.

'I know you would, and that eejit of a Bernie Conway will probably buy a handbag or a whole lot of hairbands. What happened to those nice yellow ribbons you were wearing this morning?'

'I took them off, and put them in my schoolbag. They seemed wrong.'

'Yes, well maybe they'll seem right later on, you know.'

'Oh they will, Miss O'Hara. Thank you for the beautiful book. Thank you, *really*.'

Miss O'Hara seemed to understand. Then she said suddenly, 'You *could* get anywhere you wanted, Clare, you know, if you didn't give up and say it's all hopeless. You don't have to turn out like the rest of them.'

'I'd love to . . . well, to get on you know,' Clare admitted. It was out, this thing that had been inside for so long and never said in case it would be laughed at. 'But it would be very hard, wouldn't it?'

'Of course it would, but that's what makes it worth doing, if it were easy then every divil and dirt could do it. It's because it's hard it's special.'

'Like being a saint,' Clare said, eyes shining.

'Yes, but that's a different road to go down. Let's see if you can get you an education first. Be a mature saint not a child saint, will you?'

The bell rang, deafening them for a moment.

'I'd prefer not to be a child saint all right, they're usually martyred for their faith, aren't they?'

'Almost invariably,' Miss O'Hara said, nearly sweeping the statue of the Sacred Heart with her as she gathered her books for class.

Chrissie and her two desperate friends Peggy and Kath had planned a visit to Miss O'Flaherty's to apologize. Gerry Doyle had apparently told Chrissie last night that this was the best thing to do by far. After all, she knew it was them, they'd all been caught and punished by their parents, why not go in and say sorry, then Miss O'Flaherty would have to forgive them or else everyone would say she was a mean old bag who held a grudge. Chrissie hadn't gone along with this in the beginning but Gerry had been very persuasive. What could they lose, he argued? They didn't need to *mean* they were sorry, they only needed to say it, and then it would take the heat off them all so that they could get on with the plans for the party in the cave, otherwise they would all be under house arrest. Do it soon, and put your heart and soul into it, had been Gerry's advice. Grown-ups loved what they thought were reformed characters. Lay it on good and thick.

Clare was surprised to see the threesome stop outside Miss O'Flaherty's shop. She was sure they'd have scurried past but they were marching in bold as brass. She pretended to be looking at the flyblown window display that had never changed as long as she knew it, but she wanted to hear what was coming from inside the shop.

The bits that she heard were astonishing. Chrissie was saying something about not being able to sleep last night on account of it all, Peg was hanging her head and saying she thought it was a joke at the time but the more she thought of it, it wasn't a bit funny to frighten anyone. And Kath said that she'd be happy to do any messages for Miss O'Flaherty to make up for it.

Miss O'Flaherty was a big confused woman with hair like a bird's nest. She was flabbergasted by the apology and had no idea how to cope.

'So anyway, there it is,' Chrissie had said, trying to finish it up. 'We're all as sorry as can be.'

'And of course we're well punished at home,' added Kath. 'But that's no help to you, Miss O'Flaherty.'

'And maybe if our mothers come in you might say that we . . .'

Miss O'Flaherty had a jar of biscuits out. There would be no more said about it. They were harmless skitters of girls when all was said and done, and they had the good grace to come and admit their wrongdoing. They were totally forgiven. She would tell all their mothers. They skipped out of the shop free souls again. Clare was disgusted with them. Miss O'Flaherty was horrible and she deserved to be terrified with bits of seaweed. Why were they saying sorry now at this late stage? It was a mystery.

She didn't get much enlightenment from Chrissie, who was annoyed to see her.

'I'm sorry, Peg and Kath, but my boring sister seems to be following us around.'

'I'm not following you, I'm coming home from school,' Clare said. 'I have to come home this way, it's too windy to walk on the cliff road.'

'Huh,' said Kath.

'Listening,' said Peg.

'You're so *lucky* that you don't have any sisters younger than you,' Chrissie said. 'It's like having a knife stuck into you to have a younger sister.'

'I don't see why. We don't think Ben and Jimmy are like knives,' Clare argued.

'They're normal,' Chrissie said. 'Not following you round with whinges and whines day in day out.' The other two nodded sympathetically.

Clare dawdled and looked into the drapery. She knew everything off by heart in that window too. The green cardigan on the bust had been there for ever, and the boxes of hankies slightly faded from the summer sun were still on show. Clare waited there until the others had rounded the corner. Then she walked slowly on down the street towards the big gap in the cliffs where the steps went down to the beach, back home to O'Brien's shop which everyone said should be a little gold mine since it was perched on the road going down to the sea. It was the last shop you saw before you got to the beach so people bought their oranges and sweets there, it was the first shop you met on the way back with your tongue hanging out for an ice cream or a fizzy drink. It was the nearest place if you sent a child back up the cliff for reinforcements on a sunny day. Tom O'Brien should be making a small fortune there people said, nodding their heads. Clare wondered why people thought that. The summer was the same length for the O'Briens as for everyone else. Eleven weeks. And the winter was even longer and colder because they were so exposed to the wind and weren't as sheltered as people all along Church Street.

Molly Power said that it was lonely for David having no friends of his own and perhaps they should let him ask a friend to stay. The doctor thought that there were plenty of young lads in the town, boys he had played with before he went off to boarding school. But Molly said it wasn't the same at all, and shouldn't they let him ring his friend James Nolan in Dublin and invite him for a few days. His family could put him on the train and they could meet him. David was delighted, it would be great to have Nolan to stay, Nolan had sounded very pleased on the phone. He said it would be good to get away from home, he hadn't realized how mad his relations were. They must have got worse since he'd gone to boarding school and he hadn't noticed. David told him it would be very quiet after the bright lights of Dublin. Nolan said the lights of Dublin weren't as bright as that, and his mother wouldn't let him go to the pictures in case he got fleas. He couldn't wait to get to the seaside.

'And will my class increase by a hundred per cent?' Angela O'Hara asked him when she heard that Nolan was coming to stay.

David hadn't thought of that. He didn't know. It was something he hadn't given any thought to.

'Never mind.' Angela had been brisk. 'I'll sort it out with your parents. But we had a plan for twenty days' work to cover the time you were at home, if Mr Nolan arrives that will cut six days out of it. What are you going to do? Abandon it or try to do the work anyway?'

He was awkward and she rescued him.

'I think you'd rather not have Nolan seeing you taught lessons by a woman. It's a bit like a governess, a country schoolteacher coming to the house.'

'Oh no, heavens, nothing like that.' David's open face was distressed. 'Honestly, if you knew how much I've learned since working with you, I'd be afraid to let on in case they'd never send me back to the school again, they'd put me into the convent here.'

He was a mixture of charm and awkwardness. It was very appealing. The image of his bluff kind father and yet with a bit of polish that must have come from his mother thrown in.

'Why don't I set out a bit of work for you and Mr Nolan to do each day. Say an hour and a half or two hours. I'll correct it, without coming in on top of you at all, and that way there's no embarrassment.'

The relief flooded his face.

'Is Mr Nolan as bad at Latin as you are?' she asked.

'A bit better, I think. He's going to need it too you see, he's going to do Law.'

'Is his father a barrister?'

'A solicitor,' David said.

'That makes it nice and easy,' she said with a bitter little laugh.

David was puzzled, but she changed the subject. It wasn't David Power's fault that the system was the way it was. A system that made it natural that David Power should be a doctor like his father, and James Nolan of Dublin a solicitor like *his* father, but made it very hard for Clare O'Brien to be anything at all. Angela squared her shoulders: hard, but not impossible. Hadn't Clare the best example in the land sitting teaching her? Angela, youngest daughter of Dinny O'Hara, the drunk, the ne'er-do-well, the man looking for every handout in Castlebay. And she had got the Call to Training, and higher marks in the college than any other student, and they had scrimped to send her brother to the missions, and she had nieces and nephews in comfortable homes in England. Nobody in the town could pity them when they walked behind her father's coffin five years ago. If Angela could do it with a drunken father and a crippled mother, then Clare could do it. If she cared enough, and today it looked as if she cared almost too much.

'So, College Boy,' she said to David, 'let's get on with the hedge school before the gentry come down from Dublin and catch us with our love for books!'

'You're great, Miss O'Hara,' David said admiringly. 'Wasn't it a pity you weren't a man, you could have been a priest and taught us properly.'

Molly Power was very anxious that things should be done right for David's young friend, and there were endless instructions to Nellie about breakfast on trays and getting out the best silverware until David begged that they just come downstairs as usual. Then they'd have to do their homework for Miss O'Hara before they felt free, but what a long day stretched ahead. Nolan loved the beach being so near, it was almost like having your own private swimming place, he said enviously, to be able to climb over a stile at the end of the garden and have a path going down to the sand and the caves. A path with *Danger* written all over it. Nolan tried out the Echo Cave and the other smaller caves. He wore wellington boots and slid and scrambled over the rock pools, he picked up unusual shells, he walked out to the end of the cliff road to see if the Puffing Hole was blowing. He walked the course on the golf links and planned that he and David should take lessons next summer. He couldn't believe they were allowed to go to the cinema at night. In Dublin he had only been to matinees and that was before his mother had heard of all the fleas.

Nolan was very popular in Castlebay. He was so handsome for one thing, small, with pointed features and hair that didn't stick out in angles like David's but fell in a sort of wave across the front of his forehead. He had very sharp eyes which seemed to see everything, and he wore his clothes with style, turning up his collars and striding round with his hands buried deep in his pockets. He used to joke about being short and said that he suffered from a small-man complex like Napoleon and Hitler.

He was polite to Mrs Power and insatiable for medical details from Dr Power. He praised Nellie's cooking and he said that he thought Castlebay was the most beautiful place in Ireland. In no time he was an honoured guest. Even Angela O'Hara liked him. He wrote out his preparation dutifully in small neat writing, and Angela had immediately sent him a note on the first batch of corrected work: 'Kindly make your writing much less fancy and much more clear. I have no idea whether or not you have written the correct ending on the cases of the nouns. I will not be mocked.'

'She must be quite a character, why don't we meet her?' he asked David.

David wasn't really sure, but he knew that it somehow reflected discredit on him. 'She's shy,' he lied, and felt worse.

Next day they saw a figure like a dervish flying past on a red bicycle. The machine did a dangerous turn and an envelope of papers was thrown from the basket to David.

'Here you are, College Boy, save me facing the winds over your way.'

David caught them neatly.

'This is the man who doesn't know the neuter plural from a hole in the ground,' she shouted cheerfully. 'You've got to make the adjectives plural too, my friend. No use just throwing them there and hoping they'll decline themselves.'

'Can't you come and teach us up at the house?' Nolan called out flirtatiously.

'Ah, too much to do, but aren't we doing fine by correspondence course?' Her hair stretched out behind her in the wind, blowing like someone in an open car in a film. She wore a grey coat and a grey and white scarf.

'She's gorgeous,' breathed Nolan.

'Miss O'Hara?' David said in disbelief. 'She's as old as the hills.'

They were still laughing over what age Miss O'Hara would be when Nolan was twenty-five, the age he thought he might take a bride, when they met Gerry Doyle. He had wellingtons and a fisherman's jersey and somehow he seemed much more suitable for the place than they were. Gerry was about the only one who would ever ask him what his boarding school was like, and what they had to eat and what kind of cars fellows' parents had.

'I was thinking they might burn that school of yours down if it has the plague,' Gerry said agreeably. He thought it was all more serious than they were being told, plague and pestilence and scarlet fever, otherwise why would they close down a big important school? He suggested too that they should look out for germs when they got back, in stagnant pools or in the curtains.

David made a mental note to talk to his father about it when he got home.

'Do you want to come to a midnight feast, isn't that the kind of thing you have in your place all the time, before the plague and all?'

'I was at one and we were caught,' David said sadly.

'I was at that and another, the other wasn't caught,' Nolan said as a matter of record.

'Yes well, tomorrow night in the Seal Cave starting at eleven-thirty. If you could bring a few sausages and your own bottle of orange or even beer.'

'Can we?' Nolan's eyes were shining.

'Why not? This is Castlebay, this isn't a backwater like Dublin,' David said bravely, and Gerry Doyle told them that there'd be girls and tins of beans and sausages . . .

Gerry Doyle had told Chrissie not to say a word to Tommy and Ned about the party in the cave. It wasn't that he had anything against them but they were the kind who could accidentally let something slip. He wasn't even telling his own sister, he said, because she was the same. Chrissie was pleased that Fiona wasn't coming and so were Peggy and Kath. Fiona looked a bit too attractive for their taste; she was fourteen of course, which would make her look a lot better, just automatically, than the rest of them but still they all felt a bit second best when Fiona was there. And of course Chrissie wouldn't think for a moment that Tommy and Ned should be invited, they were far too uncertain – they'd wonder aloud for days and in the end they'd all be found out and the picnic in the cave would be stopped. Gerry had said that there'd be about a dozen of them or so, no point in alerting the whole town. They were to meet there at eleven-thirty, and everyone was to try to make their own way in twos and threes at most. So as not to be noticed.

Clare stirred in her bed when she saw Chrissie's legs swing to the floor on the other side of the room. To her surprise, Chrissie was fully dressed. She was moving very quietly and feeling round for her shoes. The light of the Sacred Heart lamp fell on her as she was picking up what looked like a great lump of sausages and rashers from the shop! Chrissie was actually wrapping these stealthily in white paper and darting nervous glances at Clare's bed.

In a flash Clare understood she was running away. In a way this was great. She would have a bedroom to herself, she wouldn't be tortured by Chrissie morning noon and night any more. There would be less rows at home. But in another way it wasn't great. Mammy and Daddy were going to be very upset and the Guards would be here in the morning and Father O'Dwyer and people would walk along the cliffs when the tide came in looking for a body as they always did whenever anything happened in Castlebay. And there would be prayers for her and Mammy would cry and cry and wonder where she was and how she was faring. No, Clare sighed reluctantly, better not to let her run away, it was going to be more trouble than it was worth.

Chrissie looked at her suspiciously when she heard the sigh.

'Are you running away?' Clare asked casually.

'Oh God in heaven, what a sorrow it is to have such a stupid sister. I'm going to the toilet, you thick turnip you.' But there was fear in her voice.

'Why are you dressed up in your clothes and taking sausages and bacon if you're just going to the toilet?' Clare asked mildly.

Chrissie sat down on the bed, defeated. 'Oh, there's an awful lot of things I'd like to do to you, you're a spy, you were born a spy, it was written on you plainly, you'll never do anything else except follow people round and make their lives a misery. You hate me and so you destroy everything I do.'

'I don't hate you, not really hate,' Clare said. 'If I hated you properly wouldn't I let you run away.'

Chrissie was silent.

'But Mammy would be desperately upset and Dad too, I mean they're going to be crying and everything. It's not that I'm spying, I just thought I'd ask where you were going in case they think you're dead or something.'

'I'm not running away. I'm going out for a walk,' Chrissie said.

Clare sat up in her small iron bed. 'A *walk?*' she said.

'Shush. Yes, a walk, and we're going to have a bit of a meal on it.'

Clare raised herself up and looked out the window behind the Sacred Heart statue and the little red lamp. It was pitch dark outside. Not a thing stirred in Castlebay. 'Are Peggy and Kath going too?'

'Shush. Yes. And Clare . . .'

'Is it a picnic?'

'Yes, but you're not coming, you're not going to spoil every single thing I'm doing, you're not going to ruin it for me.'

'Oh, that's all right if it's only a picnic.' Clare had snuggled down under the blankets again. 'I just didn't want the fuss if you ran away. That's all.'

There was a small red travelling clock on the kitchen mantelpiece. David took it to bed with him. Nolan said that he'd wake all right in the spare room but David didn't want to take any chances. The clock was under David's pillow and its alarm was muted but it woke him from a deep sleep. For a while he couldn't think what was happening, and then he remembered. He had the bottle of cider and the sausages packed neatly in his school gym and games bag. Nolan had bought four bottles of stout and two packets of marshmallow biscuits which he said were great if you toasted them over a fire. Gerry Doyle had said there would be a bonfire in the back of the Seal Cave and that they knew it would work because they had tried it out already. There was a part of the cave which was perfect for it.

The only problem was Bones, the dog. David's father said that Bones would go up and lick the paws of any intruder or assassin but he'd bark the house down if you went in or out yourself. He was more of a liability than a watchdog. David and Nolan had decided to bring Bones with them to the midnight feast. It was either that or drug him and though Nolan preferred the notion of knocking him out for a few hours David had been too strictly brought up, in a house where even aspirins were locked away, to think that this was remotely possible.

He crept into the spare room and Nolan was indeed dead asleep but woke eagerly.

'I was only thinking with my eyes shut,' he said.

'Sure, and snoring with them shut too,' David said.

They shushed each other and crept down the stairs. Bones jumped up in delight and David closed his hand around the dog's jaw while stroking his ear at the same time. This usually reduced Bones to a state of foolish happiness and by the time Nolan had eased open the door they were safe. Bones trotted down the garden to the back wall ahead of them, finding nothing unusual in the hour. David and Nolan with their torches in their pockets stumbled. They couldn't shine a light until they were over the stile, it would surely be the one moment that David's mother was going to the bathroom and would look out the window and then waken the neighbourhood.

But down the path which said Danger they used their torches, and slipped and slid more than they walked. It was dry now but it had been raining earlier and the twisty path had a lot of mud.

'This is fantastic,' Nolan said, and David swelled with pride. When they got back to school Nolan would tell everyone of the terrific time he had in Power's place and the others would look at him with respect. He had always been slow to tell people about Castlebay, it sounded like such a backwater compared to the great places they all came from, but looking at it through Nolan's eyes he realized there was much more to it than he had thought.

Down on the beach Bones ran round like a mad thing, up to the edge of the sea and back again, barking excitedly, but he could bark for ever down here, the sound of the waves crashing and the wind whistling would carry it far away. Dr and Mrs Power wouldn't even hear it in their dreams.

The Seal Cave was dark and mysterious-looking. David was quite glad he wasn't on his own. There was a big fire at the back; Gerry was right, there *was* a part of it that was dry and not dripping with slime. They had begun the cooking and rashers dangled dangerously on long sticks and a couple of toasting forks. There were at least a dozen people around the fire. There were giggling girls nudging each other and breaking into loud laughter. That was Peg and Kath, he knew them to see; and Chrissie O'Brien from the shop. David looked around for Clare but she was too young probably. Chrissie couldn't be more different to Clare, he thought. Screeching with laughter and knocking the food off other people's forks. Clare was solemn and much gentler somehow.

David had never had stout before, but the others were drinking it. It almost made him throw up, it didn't taste like a drink should taste. Manfully he finished one bottle and began another. Nolan seemed to like it and he didn't want to look a sissy. Gerry Doyle seemed to notice though.

'You could have some champagne cider if you liked, it's a different taste, nice sort of drink,' he suggested.

David sipped some: now this was more like it. Sweet and fizzy, very nice indeed.

Gerry, small and eager, was hunched up over the fire. He looked very knowledgeable.

David held his glass up to the light. 'It's good stuff this,' he said appreciatively.

Later when he was getting nowhere after the groping had begun, Gerry marked his card again. No use trying anything with that one, she just laughed all the time. There was the one who would be more co-operative. A manly wink which David returned unsteadily. Gerry Doyle was a good friend to steer you in the right direction.

There were mystery ailments all over Castlebay next day, but against all the odds nobody broke ranks and the midnight feast was never discovered. Chrissie O'Brien had come back home covered in mud with cuts all down her legs where she had fallen coming up the steps from the strand, and she was sick twice into a chamberpot in the bedroom. Clare said grumpily she hoped that these midnight feasts weren't going to be going on all the time. Chrissie was too busy plotting the morrow and how she would explain her ripped and mud-covered coat, to answer Clare. In the end she decided she would go out early before anyone saw the state she was in and then she could fall again and be considered too sick to go to school. It worked too, nobody noticed that half the mud had dried and the scabs on her legs had started to heal. Chrissie's friend Peggy managed to get to school and stick the day but Kath had been sick in the classroom and had to be sent home.

Up in Power's house there seemed to be no explanation for the burn that had appeared as if by magic on James Nolan's mouth. In fact it had come from his eating a sausage directly from the long bit of skewer it was cooked on, but it was announced as being something that had come upon him unexpectedly during the night. Molly Power worried endlessly what his parents would say when he got back and fussed interminably about it when she wasn't fussing about David who was as white as a sheet and had to go to the bathroom every few minutes. The third peculiar thing in the house was Bones. He had apparently let himself out in the night and was found asleep in the garage with a cooked sausage in his paws. Dr Power told her that in the long run it was often better not to think too hard and try too earnestly to solve all problems. Sometimes it was better for the brain to let things pass.

Gerry Doyle's father told him at breakfast that there had been terrible caterwauling in the middle of the night and did he know anything about it? It sounded like a whole lot of women or girls crying on the doorstep. Gerry looked at him across the table and said that he thought he had heard that mad dog of the doctor's wailing and baying around the town during the night – could that have been it? It could, his father thought doubtfully and sniffed around him. 'This place smells like Craig's Bar,' he said to his wife and stamped off to what they all called his office, the front room beside the main bedroom. Gerry's mother got annoyed and started to slam out the breakfast dishes in a temper.

'Brush your teeth for heaven's sake, Gerry, and eat an orange or something before you go to school.' Fiona was not only kind she was practical.

Gerry looked at her gratefully. 'I had a feeling there might be a bit of a trace,' he grinned.

'Trace?' said Fiona. 'You nearly knocked us all out. Was it great fun?'

'It was in a way.'

'I wish you'd have let me . . .'

'No.' He was very firm.

'But I'm older even than some of them who were there.'

'That's not the point. You're not that type. No one must ever say that anyone was messing around with *you*. You are all I've got, I've to look after you.'

He was serious. Fiona looked taken aback.

'You've got all of us . . . like we all have . . .' she said uncertainly.

'What have we got? We've got Dad, who lives in his own world. When did Dad say anything that wasn't about the business?'

'He just mentioned Craig's Bar, didn't he?' Fiona laughed.

'Yes.' Absent-mindedly he took a peppermint out of his pocket and unwrapped it.

'What's wrong?' she asked, her big dark eyes troubled.

'I don't know. It's just he's so dull and unadventurous. How are we ever going to get on if we stay as timid as he is? And Mam . . . Well, honestly.'

'She's a bit better, I think,' Fiona said softly. They had not talked about this before.

'She's not. You say that because she went out to the garden and hung out the clothes. You think that's some kind of success. She hasn't been out of the house for six months. Six months. Tell me if that's normal or not normal.'

'I know. But what can we do? They don't want to tell Dr Power.'

'It's all his fault, he thinks that if we tell Dr Power there's going to be some kind of trouble.'

At that moment, Mr Doyle reappeared, small and dark like his son, with the same quick smile and almost elfin face. 'I'm only wondering does anyone in this house intend to go to school or have we all graduated without my knowing about it?'

'I'm just off. Dad, I may be going past David Power's house, will I ask his father to come and have a word with . . . ?'

'If anyone needs a doctor they'll go and see Dr Power and if they're not able to go, Dr Power will be brought to them,' said his father sternly. That was that. Gerry went to brush his teeth as had been suggested, and met his mother creeping along by the wall, alarmed by the word 'doctor'.

'Don't worry, Mary, go back into the kitchen, there's no need for a doctor,' his father said.

He called at the surgery that evening.

'Well, Gerry?'

'I don't know, Dr Power.'

'It can't be too serious an ailment if you've forgotten it already.' The old doctor was cheerful.

'It wasn't an ailment at all.'

'Good, good. Was it something wrong with someone else?' The man's eyes were sharp.

Gerry seemed to hesitate. 'No, I suppose people have to look after their own illnesses, don't they?'

'It depends. If you saw a wounded man lying on the road you wouldn't say he'd better look after his own illness.'

'No, it's not like that.'

'Would you like to tell me what it is like?'

Gerry made up his mind. 'No, no. Not now. I came to know if David and James Nolan would like to go out this evening? For a bit of a laugh like?'

Dr Power was thoughtful. 'I think there's been enough laughs for the moment. I think it's time the laughing died down for those two and they got a bit of work done.'

Gerry looked him in the eye. 'Does that mean they can't come out? Is that what you're saying?'

'You're as bright as the next man, Gerry, you know what I'm saying, and not saying.'

'Right. Tell them I called and was sorry they weren't allowed out.'

'No, I won't, because that's not the message. Tell them yourself if you want to.'

Gerry Doyle's great skill was knowing when not to push it any further. 'You're a hard man, Dr Power,' he said with a grin, and he was off.

Paddy Power wondered whether he had been going to ask about his anxiety-ridden father or his withdrawn, possibly phobic mother. Maybe the boy hadn't noticed anything wrong with either of them. He was a funny lad.

A parcel arrived for Angela, a small flat box. It was a beautiful headscarf from the parents of James Nolan. 'Thank you so very much for all the help with tuition, your pupils in Castlebay must be very lucky to have such a gifted teacher.' It was a square with a very rich-looking pattern on it, the kind of thing a much classier woman would wear. Angela was delighted with it. She showed it and the letter to her mother but it was a bad day and the old woman's joints were aching all over.

'Why shouldn't they be grateful to you, why shouldn't they send you something? It's money they should have sent. Doesn't the postman get paid for delivering letters?'

Angela sighed. She told David about it that evening. 'Wasn't it very thoughtful of them?' she said.

'They have great polite ways up in Dublin,' David said wistfully. 'We'd never have thought of giving you a thing like that, and we should have.'

'Don't be silly, College Boy. I was only telling you so that you'd know your friend appreciated the lessons and all that.'

'He thought you were very good-looking,' David said suddenly.

'I thought he wasn't bad himself, but a bit small for me. How old is he, about fifteen?'

'Yes, just.'

'Oh well, that's no difference at all, tell him I'll see him when he's about twenty-five, I'll be coming into my prime about then.'

'I think that would suit him fine,' David laughed.

It was shortly before the school re-opened that David met Gerry Doyle again.

'Have you had any good drinking nights since the cave?' Gerry asked.

'I think I'm going to be a Pioneer. I was never so sick. I was sick eleven times the next day,' David said truthfully.

'Well at least you held on to it until you got home,' Gerry said. 'Which was more than some people managed. Still, it was a bit of a laugh.'

'Great altogether. Nolan said he'd never had such a night.'

'He was telling me you've got a record player of your own, a radiogram in your own bedroom, is that right?'

'Not a radiogram with doors on it, but a record player yes, you plug it in.'

'How much would they be?' Gerry was envious.

'I'm afraid I don't know, it was a present, but I could ask.'

'I'd love to see it,' Gerry Doyle said.

David's hesitation was only for a second. His mother had never *said* he wasn't to have Gerry Doyle into the house but he knew she wouldn't approve. 'Come on, I'll show you,' he said.

Any other lad in Castlebay might have held back but not Gerry Doyle. He swung along the cliff road companionably with David as if he had been a lifetime calling on the doctor's house socially.

The summer houses looked dead, as they passed, like ghost houses and it was hard to imagine them full of families with children racing in and out carrying buckets and spades, and people putting deckchairs up in the front gardens.

'Wouldn't you need to be cracked to rent one of those for the summer?' Gerry nodded his head at the higgledy-piggledy line of homes.

'I don't know. Suppose you didn't live beside the sea?' David was being more tolerant.

'But if you had the money to rent one of those for a couple of months what would you spend it on that for, why wouldn't you go abroad to Spain or to far places like Greece even?' Gerry was beyond believing that anyone could pay good money for a place in his own Castlebay.

'But if you were married with children you wouldn't be able to take all of them abroad,' David argued reasonably.

'Ah well, I wouldn't be married, so I suppose that's the difference.'

'Not now, but later.'

'Not ever. Do you want to?'

'I thought I would,' David said.

'You're off your head, David Power,' said Gerry Doyle agreeably.

Mrs Power was in the hall arranging some winter branches in a vase.

'Hallo,' she said when the hall door opened. 'Oh hallo, Gerry, do you want to see the doctor?' She looked slightly quizzical. Her head had inclined towards the surgery entrance. Patients didn't come in the front door, they went in by the porch on the side.

'No thanks, Mrs Power, I'm coming to look at David's record player,' he said confidently.

'I beg your pardon?' She was polite, but frosty.

'Oh, I'm going to show Gerry the record player . . . how much was it, by the way?' David didn't feel as brave as he sounded.

'It was a present, David dear,' his mother said with a smile that wasn't in her eyes. 'We don't ask how much a present cost.'

'No, but maybe you could tell Gerry then, he was wondering if he might buy one.'

'I think it's a little beyond Gerry,' said David's mother in that tone he really hated. But Gerry didn't seem to notice in the slightest.

'You might well be right,' he said cheerfully. 'It wouldn't be until the end of the summer anyway, I work for pocket money but there's nothing really for me to do that's useful until the trippers come. Still it'll be nice to see it anyway.' He smiled straight into the disapproving face of David's mother and with his arm on the banisters and his foot on the first step he called to David. 'Is it up here?'

David followed him without looking back to see the grim expression that he knew had settled on his mother's face.

At lunch Mrs Power waited until Nellie had left the room. 'Paddy, could you ask David not to bring Gerry Doyle back here to the house.'

Dr Power looked up mildly from his newspaper. 'Well, he's sitting beside you, Molly, can't you ask him yourself?' he said.

'You know what I mean.'

'Is this some kind of row?' The doctor looked from his wife to his son.

'Not on my part,' David said.

'See what I mean,' said Molly Power.

'Well, it seems you are being off-hand with your mother. Don't be like that.' Dr Power went back into the paper.

'*Paddy*. Please. Explain to David that Gerry Doyle's perfectly all right but he is not a guest in this house.'

Wearily he put down the paper. 'What's it about?' he said, looking from one to another.

There was no reply.

'Well, what did young Doyle do that caused the upset?' Again he looked from his wife's flushed face to his son's mutinous one.

'Nothing,' David shrugged. 'He came upstairs. I showed him my record player. He admired it. He went home.'

'Molly?'

'That's not the point, as you know very well. You're not an infant David, you know well what I'm talking about.'

David looked blank.

'Your mother is saying that she goes to a lot of trouble to keep this house nice and she doesn't want people tramping all over it. That's a reasonable request, isn't it?'

David paused, deciding whether or not to buy this explanation. Then he saw its flaws. 'Oh sure, sorry Mummy, I didn't know that was what it was about. I thought you had something against Gerry Doyle himself. You know, like Nolan's mother went through that bit of thinking everyone had fleas. No, that's fine, of course I won't ask people back without asking you first.'

Molly smiled uneasily. She wasn't at all sure that she had won.

'And I'll be going down to his house later on today, he said he'd show me the darkroom and let me help to develop some of the pictures his father took at a wedding.'

He smiled brightly from one parent to the other and helped himself to a glass of orange squash.

Gerry Doyle's sister was gorgeous-looking. She wore an overall, which was like an artist's smock, and she looked like an illustration in a book. She seemed a bit shy and answered yes and no when David asked her about anything. But she was very polite and helpful. She offered to go and make cocoa and said she'd run over to O'Brien's for a quarter of a pound of broken biscuits as well.

535

'Why didn't you ask her to the Seal Cave?' David wanted to know.

'Oh, you couldn't ask your *sister* to a thing like that. It's all right for Chrissie and Kath and Peggy and those, they're the kind of girls you'd expect to have at a thing like that, but not Fiona.'

David felt he had overstepped some limit he didn't know about. He felt awkward. He felt too that it was hard on the girls who had been there. They had all had great fun and played spin the bottle; and the boys had given them cider and beer and encouraged them like mad. Then the girls had got a bit silly and one or two of them were crying and Kath had been sick and they had fallen and everything. But it was all part of the night. It was a bit cruel somehow to think that Fiona was a different type of girl, one you wouldn't bring to a party like that, but it was true. When she came back with the tray of cocoa and biscuits David knew that he would not like Fiona to have been to a party like that either.

He would have liked to ask her to write to him at school. Nolan had a girl who wrote him long letters. But he thought it was too complicated to set it all up. Firstly if Fiona had said yes he would have had to explain the whole system where the letters were read by the priests and so the girl who was writing had to pretend to be another boy. Nolan's friend who was called Alice used to sign her name Anthony. She had to remember not to talk about hockey matches but say rugby instead, in fact the letter was in so heavy a code or disguise none of them could really work out what it meant. Still it was nice for Nolan to be able to get the letter and tell everyone how good-looking Alice was. It would be nice to do the same with Fiona. But if Gerry wouldn't let her come to a party in a cave down the road he would almost certainly be very much against her writing letters in code to a boy in a boarding school. That would be fast, and Fiona Doyle was not going to be thought of as fast. David noticed that he kept thinking of them as orphans even though they lived with their mother and father. That was odd.

'Your parents don't take much part in things, do they?' he said enviously.

'They work too hard,' Gerry said. 'It was always like that. It's a dog's life, and Mam hates the work but what else is there?'

'What would she prefer to be doing?'

'Arranging flowers on a hall table in a house like yours,' Gerry laughed. 'But isn't that what every woman would want?'

The roof didn't fall in and the skies didn't flash with lightning when David got back home that evening. He sensed that his parents had had a little chat. His mother was sewing the Cash's name tapes on some new socks and pyjamas for him. She seemed to have forgotten the row at lunchtime totally.

'I suppose in a way it will be hard to settle into all that studying again,' she said.

David was determined to be equally pleasant. 'Yes, but I'm very glad that I had Miss O'Hara, very glad. Nolan said we were dead lucky down here to be able to get someone like that, up in Dublin teachers are sharks, he said, they ask for a fortune for grinds and they smell of drink.'

David's father laughed from the other side of the fire. 'Your friend James is full of nonsense. You can't make generalizations about any job no more than you can about mine or his father's. Dear dear.'

'You know the way Nolan goes on,' David said.

'Of course I do, he's a very bright young fellow, we liked him, your mother and I did. Ask him down any time, or any of your other friends, the house is big and there's plenty of room. And it's nice to hear a bit of noise around the place.'

That's a different tune to the one they were playing at lunch, David thought to himself. Then I was invading the privacy of the house. He heard himself saying that he'd love to ask Nolan again, and he was very grateful to be allowed to invite people home. Nolan's mother was still fussing apparently and when she wasn't worrying about fleas she was worrying about ceilings falling down. Nolan said she was having a tonic for her nerves but it didn't seem to be doing much good.

On the last evening before he went back he said he'd like to go and say a proper thank you to Miss O'Hara, and maybe give her a small present. David's mother said that Angela O'Hara wouldn't like that at all, she had been paid adequately, but Dr Power said no, David was right, why not give her a book of some kind from the shelf, she always admired the books when she came to the house.

'You don't need to go up to Dinny O'Hara's cottage,' Molly Power said.

'Dinny O'Hara has been in the churchyard for five years, he's unlikely to come out and corrupt the boy now,' said Paddy Power, and David saw his mother's face get that tight-lipped look again.

Nellie helped him to wrap up a book about Irish place names. They took the torn paper cover off it and it was lovely underneath. Nellie looked at the small print in admiration.

'Imagine Angela O'Hara being able to read all this and understand it. Ah well, that's what comes of keeping to your books.' She had been at school up at the convent with Angela herself, and had been there the day the news came of Angela's scholarship to the big town. In those days the nuns had been so proud that one of their girls had won the scholarship they used to make the uniform themselves with their own hands. They had kitted out the young Angela for her secondary school because they knew that anything Dinny O'Hara would get into his hand went straight across a bar counter and he wouldn't do much to help his little girl get on.

'She deserved to do well,' Nellie said unexpectedly, as she was making a nice neat corner on the parcel and tying the string tightly. 'She never crowed about all her successes and her high marks and all. Nobody could say that it all went to her head.'

David didn't think that Miss O'Hara had all that much to crow about. To be teaching in that awful convent, to be here in Castlebay with her old mother – when she must have wanted to get far away. Why else did she go in for all those scholarships? He didn't think she had the huge success that Nellie seemed to think. But of course compared to Nellie it must be fine, she didn't have to clear out grates and ranges and scrub floors and make beds and cook meals and wash up and wash clothes and go out in the cold and see they weren't bashed down by the wind. Being a teacher must seem like a nice cushy job to Nellie.

He turned left outside the gate and went along the road towards the golf course. It was longer than he remembered, no wonder Miss O'Hara always flew round the place on her bicycle. There was a light downstairs in the O'Hara cottage: he hoped that her old mother wouldn't answer the door bent over the two sticks.

But the door was opened by Clare O'Brien. Clare was thin and alert, big brown eyes and fair hair tied in bunches. She always looked as if she was about to ask a question. He remembered meeting her in the Echo Cave and she had said that it would be like heaven on earth to have lessons from Miss O'Hara without the rest of the class. Maybe that's what she was doing now.

Clare seemed pleased to see him. 'She's putting her mother to bed, she's got awful pains altogether today, she can neither sit nor stand. Miss O'Hara said she'd be back in a few minutes. Will you come in and sit down?'

David was a bit put out that she was there; he had wanted to make a flowery speech to Miss O'Hara without an audience. But he could hardly order the O'Brien girl to go home or say that his conversation was private. He looked around the kitchen.

'Isn't it like Aladdin's Cave?' whispered Clare in awe.

It was a typical kitchen for a cottage in this area. The fire had been replaced by a small range. That must have come from Angela O'Hara's salary – it never came when Dinny O'Hara was alive nor from the widow's pension that the arthritic old woman got every week. Perhaps the brother and sisters abroad sent money, David wouldn't know. Miss O'Hara was very private, she never told you all about herself and her family like everyone else in Castlebay did all the time, that's why you were interested to know more. David looked up at the walls. Everywhere there were shelves. Each alcove had shelves from ceiling to floor, and there were ornaments and books and biscuit boxes and more books and sewing baskets and statues. Clare was right. Almost like a toyshop on a Christmas card. There was no inch of wall without a shelf, and no inch of shelf without an object. Most of the objects were books.

'She knows where every single thing is, would you credit that?' Clare's big brown eyes looked larger than ever in the semi dark of the room. There was a table with writing paper and a bottle of Quink ink and blotting paper. Miss O'Hara must have been writing letters with Clare when her mother took a turn.

'Are you getting lessons?' he asked. There was a touch of envy in his voice. He would have preferred to learn in this funny enclosed place where everything had a story and every item was known in its little place. It was a much better place to study than his mother's sitting room with the copies of *Tatler and Sketch*, and *Social and Personal* laid out beside *The Housewife* which came every month by post from England. When the copies were a couple of months old they went to the surgery, and of course there were all the encyclopedias and big leather-bound books. But they weren't read and touched and loved like things were here.

'Oh no, I wish I could, no I'd like that more ·than anything. I'd be a genius if I had Miss O'Hara to teach me on her own.' She spoke with no intention of making him laugh. She was utterly serious.

He was sorry for her. It must be desperate not to have enough money for education. You always felt that came automatically.

'Maybe you could do things for her, you know, do the messages or cook or something in exchange.'

'I thought of that,' Clare said solemnly. 'But I think it's a bit unfair, she'd have to be looking round for things for me to do. It would be like asking for charity.'

'I see.' He did see.

'But I came up tonight because Miss O'Hara *is* going to help me, I'm to write to the convent in the town, a kind of letter that would make them think well of me, and inquiring about their scholarships in two years' time.' Her eyes were shining over the very thought of it.

'Miss O'Hara got a scholarship there herself, years and years ago. She says you have to be dead cunning, and look on it as a war.'

Angela O'Hara came into the room then. 'Don't give away all our secrets, Clare, maybe College Boy here might be disguising himself and trying to get into the convent ahead of you.'

Nolan would have made a witty remark. David couldn't think of one, he just laughed. 'I'm in your way, you're writing letters,' he said awkwardly.

'Don't worry about that, David, Clare's writing her own letter actually, and I am meant to be writing one to my brother. I find it so hard to know what will interest him about here. You know: got up, went to school, did not strangle Immaculata . . . every day it becomes a bit repetitive.'

'What does he write? I suppose his days are a bit samey too,' David said.

Angela took out an airmail envelope with the stamp neatly removed for the school collection. 'I was just thinking that very thing . . . My mother keeps all Sean's letters, every single one of them – look at the boxes of them – and he does seem to be saying the same thing over and over. But it's nice to hear.'

'When you get older I expect there's not much to write about,' Clare said helpfully.

'Or more when you don't really share the same kind of life,' David said. 'That's why I never had a penfriend in India or anything, once you'd described your life and he'd described his that would be it.'

'It is a bit like that,' Angela agreed. She picked up a thin piece of airmail paper and read to them:

Dear Mother and dear Angela,

Thank you so much for your letter which arrived here yesterday.

We are in the middle of a rainy season which makes things very difficult but still it is thanks to all the great and good support that we get from home that God's work can be done.

I wish you could see the little Japanese children, they are really beautiful. I suppose I didn't have all that much to do with children before I came out here, on the missions. Perhaps little Irish children are even more beautiful . . .

Angela broke off and said it was easy known that he never had to pass one day of his lifetime teaching little Irish children in a convent or he would think otherwise.

'It's a bit like the letter he wrote to the school, isn't it?' Clare said.

'It's a bit like every letter he writes,' Angela said, putting it back in the envelope. 'There's nothing for him to say, I suppose, that we'd understand. I do ask him things myself sometimes, like do they ordain many Japanese priests out there, and what happened to all the Chinese they had converted before they left China, did they go back to their old religion or what. But he never answers those kind of things.'

She was silent in thought for a while. David coughed.

'I came to say goodbye and thank you,' he said. 'And to give you this book to tell you how grateful I am.'

Angela sat down and reached for her cigarettes without saying anything. When she spoke it was with a softer voice than either Clare or David had ever heard her use. 'That's very good of you,' she said and bent her head over the twine, fiddling with the knots.

'It's only old twine, you can cut it if you like,' David said helpfully and Clare found a knife. Miss O'Hara sawed through the string, and they all bent over the book. Time passed easily as they read why places they knew were called what they were called, and they were all enraged that Castlebay wasn't in it and said that the man who wrote the book hadn't travelled at all if he couldn't include a fine place like this. From the other room there were sounds of moaning but Miss O'Hara said not to take any notice, it was her mother trying to get into a comfortable position to settle for the night, it wasn't really sharp pain. They had a cup of tea and a bit of soda bread and eventually Miss O'Hara shooed them out into the night lest people think they had been kidnapped.

Angela told herself not to be so sentimental over David's present. It was very thoughtful of the boy certainly, but he came from a nice peaceful home where there was time to be thoughtful and there was ease and comfort. And his father was one of the most generous men that ever walked. It was in the boy's nature to be bright and generous. But it was so different to what she could expect from the children she taught up in the convent. Half of them would never do any kind of an exam, almost none of them would ever open a book again after they left her, except a novel or a magazine.

Not Clare of course. She was the one that would keep you going. Imagine teaching a class full of Clare O'Briens or of David Powers for that matter. She sighed. It was a pity as David had said that she hadn't been born a man. She could have become a priest and taught bright boys in a school where the principal would not go into shock if she asked for a globe.

She wondered did Sean ever regret his choice in teaching the children of Chinese and Japanese workers in pidgin English. Would he have liked the days spent in an ivy-covered college like the one that David and young Nolan went to? Would Sean have liked the evenings in study and chapel and walking reading a breviary in cloisters or discussing philosophy in a dining hall? It was a question that couldn't really make sense, since her brother Sean had never shown interest in any other life except the missions. He had followed the road that got him there without pausing to think or to wonder did people miss him. She missed him from time to time, his letters were no way of knowing him, and recently they had become very static.

You couldn't even hint at that to her mother. Every letter was kept in a box with the date it was received written laboriously on the envelope. As if someone was going to check them some time. The stamps were neatly cut off to add to the school stamp collection, they were never re-read but Mrs O'Hara knew almost by heart the names of the villages and the settlements and the places up country and down country. She knew them better than she knew the countryside around Castlebay, for it had been a long time since she could walk and see it. Angela wondered sometimes what her mother would think about all day if she hadn't a fine son who was a missionary priest to fill her mind.

Back at school Nolan told everyone that Power was a dark horse. They should see the great place he lived in, a big house on a cliff with its own private way down to the sea. They had a maid and a labrador and every single person in the place knew them by name and saluted them. David felt it was going a bit far to call Bones a labrador, but he agreed that the rest was mainly true. He also found himself the centre of attention because of having taken Nolan to a party where real sex games were played. This was the cause of a lot of questioning and David wished he knew how much Nolan had elaborated on the innocent kissing games they had played by the firelight before the drink had taken over and everyone had been too dizzy and confused to play any games at all. But it was good to be a hero, and he laughed knowingly about it all.

He was pleased too when Father Kelly said that he was an exemplary pupil and had kept up meticulously with the suggested course of study which had been handed out to all pupils on the day the school had closed because of the scarlet fever. The essays had been written, the poems had been learned, history questions had been written out and illustrated with neat maps and family trees, the maths and geography were completed, and the Irish and Latin exercises done in full.

'You got private tuition? Well, he was a good man whoever he was,' Father Kelly said in one of his rare moments of approval.

'It was a she actually, Father,' David said apologetically.

Father Kelly's brow darkened: he had been too swift with his praise. 'Ah, some of them are competent enough I suppose,' he said, struggling to be fair, but losing interest.

David told Nolan that Gerry Doyle had a smashing-looking sister, really beautiful, but that he wouldn't take her to the cave that night.

Nolan was very positive about this, as he was about everything. 'Of course he couldn't bring his *sister*,' he said as if it were obvious to a blind fool, 'I mean I wouldn't have let *my* sister go. We couldn't have taken Caroline to a party like *that*, where people would be . . . well you couldn't take Caroline there. Gerry Doyle was quite right. Is she going to write to you?'

'I didn't ask her.'

'Right, Power, you've got the technique, don't be too easy to get, don't be a pushover. Leave them wondering, that's what I always do.'

'Will Alice be writing again this term?'

'No, I think I've grown out of Alice,' said Nolan in a voice which revealed that Alice had grown out of him.

Nolan said his mother had got a bit better about things and that she had agreed to go away next summer for a holiday by the sea. Nolan's whole family had been wanting to do this for ages but his mother had always said the seaside was full of rats and beetles and sea snakes. St Patrick had only got rid of the land snakes according to Nolan's mother, but he had no power over the huge snakes calling themselves eels which came in on beaches all over the country. But now the tablets she was taking had made her forget, and they were going to inquire about renting one of those cliff houses in Castlebay. Because Nolan had come home with such glowing reports they were going to try there first. David was delighted: the summer would be full of adventure if Nolan and his family came to Castlebay.

Angela said that Clare must write the letter herself, it was no use putting grown-up words into a ten-year-old head. But she would monitor it for spelling, and style. She found Clare a writing pad that had no lines on it, but with a heavily-lined sheet you put under the page you were writing on. Clare should ask the convent whether there was any particular course of study she should concentrate on, since she was very anxious to prepare herself as diligently as possible for the open scholarship in 1952. Clare tried to remember the words diligent, concentrate, but Angela said no, she must use her own words, and she must sound like a real person, someone they would remember when the time came. She said to tell the nuns that her parents were business people. Clare wondered was that true; but Angela said, years ago she had told them her father was a substantial farmer who had fallen on hard times because of the Troubles, and since that was way back in 1932 it sounded reasonable. It would have done her no good to say she was the daughter of the town drunk and she was burning to get herself on in the world.

'Do you think there's any hope I might get it? You see I don't want to get myself all excited like I did . . . well . . .'

'Over the history essay.' Miss O'Hara nodded. 'No, I think you have a chance, a good chance if you work like the hammers of hell. Oh and don't tell anyone, it's easier somehow if you don't.'

'But David Power knows.'

That didn't matter, Miss O'Hara thought, he'd have it long forgotten. But Clare shouldn't mention it at school, or at home, it only got people into a state. Clare had thought there was too much going on at home without letting them get into another state over a scholarship in the distant future.

Tommy and Ned had been for interviews and they couldn't wait to go to England. They had heard that there was massive reconstruction being done over there since the war, the place was full of bombed sites only waiting to be built up again, and roads from one place to another planned for, and housing for all those who lost their places during the raids.

The man who had come to Dillon's Hotel for two hours had taken their names and addresses. He had asked them very little but said they should report to him when they got there; they should wait till the fine weather until they came over. There'd be no trouble at all finding digs; the roads around Kilburn and Cricklewood were filled with Irish households only delighted to have lads from home in to stay. They'd be like mothers to them, they wouldn't need to go near English strangers at all. The man said he was a businessman who could get a good deal for his own countrymen; he didn't like to see Irish lads being made fools of, he'd see them right when they came over.

Clare's father wondered could the man be a chancer. Why would he be doing all this for love? Why wasn't he an agency like any other agency that took fees? That way made sense, a person could understand that, but this way was hard to fathom. A man with an open shirt coming to Dillon's Hotel and giving them all a piece of paper with his name on it and saying he could be found any Friday night in one of two pubs in Kilburn – it sounded a bit suspicious.

But Tommy and Ned would have none of it. What had they to lose? If, after one week, he turned out not to be getting them their full wages, they could leave him and go on to one of these agencies that Da was talking about. They weren't bound to him. He had said he wanted nothing in writing, no complications of any sort. They should be delighted to have his name, and have him as a friendly contact over there instead of making such a fuss about everything.

Tommy had left school. He had no exams, no certificates and, after all his years in the Brothers, he could barely read and write. Clare thought wistfully of David Power that night up in Miss O'Hara's kitchen and the book he had given to her as a present. Tommy would have thrown it aside. He couldn't even read what was written on a packet in the shop, if someone asked him. He didn't read the paper and he never opened a book of any sort now that he had been released from the classroom. He was meant to be helping his father get the shop to rights before he went off to London to seek his fortune. A lot of the time he spent just hanging around.

Clare's father was rearranging the shop, and that was hard to do while people were still being served. It meant that a lot of it was done in the evening when they were meant to be closed. Of course a place like O'Brien's could never close properly: if Mrs Conway came for a pound of sugar, or Miss O'Flaherty decided that she wanted some biscuits with her late night tea, there was no refusing them.

But there was less of a flow after six o'clock, less of the sound of the ping when the door opened and a figure stood letting in the cold sea winds until the door swung closed.

Last summer it had been so crowded trying to sell ice-cream in the middle of everything else, that this year he was going to move the ice-cream cabinet down to one side of the little shop. Chocolate and sweets would be high up over it, and fruit beside it, so the beach people could be served all in one area; while the people who had rented houses on the cliff road could ponder and deliberate and finally settle for cooked ham and tomatoes as they always did, on a less cluttered side of the shop. It was all fine in theory but it was hard to do and still keep track of where everything was. Each evening they scrubbed shelves and tacked on new oilcloth. The floor was a constant disappointment to them; the lino needed to be replaced but of course there wouldn't be funds for that, so instead new bits were nailed down near the door where the wear and tear was most obvious. Boxes that only contained a few things were emptied out and stored neatly in the storeroom. In the summer, visitors were mad for boxes and lots of the suppliers didn't leave any behind. It was best to have a pile of them ready.

It was worthy work but it ate into homework time. Miss O'Hara had drawn everyone in the class a map of Ireland, a blank map. They were to trace it or copy it and reproduce it every fourth page of their history exercise book. Then, when they learned of the battles and the treaties and the marches and the plantations, they could fill them in on their own maps and they would know what happened where. Clare was lost in the Battle of Kinsale, drawing little Spanish ships and Red Hugh's army on its way down from the north when she heard the voice calling. Perhaps if she pretended she didn't hear . . . This was the wrong thing to do. The door was thrown open and her mother stood quivering with annoyance.

'Aren't you a fine lady thrown on the bed when you're needed?'

'I'm not thrown, I'm filling in this map, look.'

'I've looked at enough of that childish nonsense, you're a grown girl, get downstairs and help your father at once. We've been calling and calling and not a word out of you.'

'It's my homework.'

'Don't be ridiculous, nobody has homework drawing ships and little men, stop that act and come down *at once*. Your father wants a hand to clean those top shelves before we put things up there.'

'But how will we reach them – what's the point of putting things up there?'

'Are you going to debate this from up here or come down like you're told!'

'Where are you off to, Chrissie? We'll be taking down all those old notices stuck to the windows this evening . . .'

'Oh, I can't stay, Mam, I'm going up to Peggy . . . she's going to teach me how to make a frock.'

'A frock?'

'Yes, she's got a pattern, she says it's easy to cut around it. Soon we'll be able to make all our own clothes.'

'Well, all right, but don't be late home.'

'No, I won't. Bye Mam.'

'Clare, what are you doing?'

'The trade winds. We've got to know all about where they come from and why they blew the fleets of . . .'

'Right, get a bowl of hot soapy water, will you, and come with me. These windows are a disgrace, you can't see through them in or out.'

'Clare, child, I know you work hard at your books but couldn't you give your mother a hand with the washing? She's got very thin on us altogether.'

'The washing, Dad?'

'Washing the clothes. I asked her to sit down and have a cup of tea and she said she couldn't, there was a pile of washing to do. You'll have to do washing when you have a home of your own, why don't you take a turn now and learn how to do it properly? There's a good girl.'

'What about Chrissie, Dad, could she do it tonight, and I'll do it the next time, I've this legend to learn. There's all kinds of desperate names in it.'

'Chrissie's gone to do her homework with Kath.'

'Uh,' Clare said.

'You could go on saying the names to yourself as you did the washing,' her father said.

'No, the book would get wet. Do I *have* to, Dad?'

'You don't *have* to. I thought you'd be glad to help your mother.'

'Tommy or Ned?' She asked without much hope.

'Well, if that's the kind of thing you're going to be saying . . .' he turned away in disgust. To suggest that *boys* would do the washing! Clare was being very difficult altogether.

'Oh, all *right!*' Clare slammed closed the story of Jason and the Golden Fleece. She only knew Jason, his father, his two wicked step-uncles and the name of the ship. There was a huge cast still to master, so it would mean waking up early . . . again.

'Clare, come here till I teach you to darn.'

'No, Mammy, I don't want to learn to darn.'

'You that wants to learn everything? Look, it's very simple. Do you see this hole, what we have to do is to make a criss cross . . .'

'No, Mam, I'd like not to know how to do it. Ever.'

'Why, child? When you have a home of your own you'll want to know.'

'But if I know now, I'll be darning Tommy's socks, and Ned's, and Dad's, and Jim's, and Ben's, and maybe even Chrissie's.'

Agnes put her arm round the thin little figure, and smiled. 'Aren't you the funny little thing.'

'No, Mammy, I'm the sensible little thing. I'll never learn to darn, never.'

Agnes was annoyed to see her affection rejected. 'Have it your own way, and you can go and do the washing up if you're not going to take advantage of the lessons I was going to give you.'

'But . . .'

'Chrissie won't be in, their class have a special extra class today.'

'That's right,' Clare said glumly. 'Of course they do.'

'Have you a cold, Clare?'

'No, it's just a cough, Mam. Dust or something in my throat, I think.'

'Have a drink of water then.'

'Right.'

'Clare, don't spend all day in the kitchen, come back and help me with these boxes, and put a scarf or something round your mouth if you're breathing in all the dust.'

'Mam, when we've finished this lot, can I go and do . . .'

'Do your homework, do your homework. Why is it that you're the only one in this family who has to make the excuse of doing your homework? Look at the rest of them.'

'I know. Look at them, Mam.'

'What's that supposed to mean?'

'Nothing.'

Often Clare had to do her homework in bed, there was literally no other place and no other time. This made Chrissie very cross. She grumbled loudly if Clare turned on the torch.

'You're spoiling my sleep and ruining your own eyes. You'll be blind soon and we'll have to take you round by the hand and you'll have a white stick,' Chrissie said with satisfaction.

'Shut up, Chrissie, I'm learning something. I can't get it into my head if you keep distracting me.'

Chrissie was surprised at the strength of the reply. 'I'll tell on you, if you don't stop that mumbling and learning and having a light on, I'll tell. *That* will put a stop to it.'

There was no reply. With her hands in her ears and eyes closed Clare was repeating under her breath the words, '*Do Ghealadh mo chroi nuair chinn Loch Greinne,*' over and over.

'You're as thick as the wall,' said Chrissie. 'You mean you don't even know one line after all that saying of it?'

'I don't know what *Ghealadh* means. It's hard to learn when you don't know what something means.'

'Ah will you come on out of that, you don't know what *any* of it means. How would people know what Irish poetry meant? It's just words.'

'It means something happened to my heart when I saw Loch Greinne, but I don't know what happened. *Ghealadh,* what would that mean?'

'It might mean Stop. My heart stopped dead when I saw Loch Greinne.' Chrissie laughed at her own wit.

'Didn't you learn it when you were in our class?'

Chrissie shrugged. 'We might have, I forget, I forget all of it. What's the point?'

Clare had gone back to her book.

'I mean it, I'll tell, and you'll be in right trouble then. I'll say you kept me awake with your caterwauling of poetry pretending you understand it. Wait and see. You'll suffer for it.'

'No I won't,' Clare said. 'I won't suffer from it at all, *you* are the one who'll suffer. It will be wondered why you do no homework, why you don't know anything. It might even be wondered what you and Kath and Peggy get up to. You're not going to say anything, and you know it so will you shut up and let me get this learned so that I can go to sleep.'

Angela waited in the surgery. There was only one other patient, old Mrs Dillon from the hotel. Angela would have thought that the doctor would have visited her privately, but Mrs Dillon whispered that she had come to see him secretly. She had pretended to her family that she was going to say the thirty days prayer in the church, but in fact she had come to explain that her daughter-in-law was poisoning her. Angela sighed. Poor Dr Power. He probably got as much of this as Father O'Dwyer did in the confessional. Angela settled down with an old copy of *Tatler and Sketch* and began to read about the happenings up in Dublin. She was in for a long wait. But in a few moments, Dr Power was ushering old Mrs Dillon out the door, and the woman was smiling ear to ear.

'You'll have time for the thirty days prayer after all, and say a few Hail Marys for me,' he called out after her.

'Sure you don't need them, Doctor, aren't you a walking saint,' called Mrs Dillon.
'She's only saying what's true.' Angela stood up and walked across the corridor with him.
'No. I'm a walking liar, that's all.'
'What did you tell her?'
'I told her I was in there during the week inspecting the place for hygiene and I have instruments that could detect poison a mile off. But there wasn't a trace of it in Dillon's Hotel. I said that the cold weather often made people think the taste of food had changed, that it was a common belief, then I gave her a bottle of rose-hip syrup and she's delighted with herself.'
Angela laughed: he looked like a bold boy who'd been found out telling a fib.

'And who's poisoning *you*, Angela, Mother Immaculata up at the convent, maybe?'
'Not a bad guess, I think she'd like to a lot of the time. No, it's not poison. It's sleep.'
'Too much of it or too little of it?'
'Hardly any of it.'
'Since when?'
'Three weeks, now.'
'Do you know what's causing it? A worry, a problem?'
'Yes, I do.'
'And is there anything that can be done about it?'
She shook her head wordlessly.
He waited, but nothing came. He reached for a prescription pad, shaking his head. 'I won't have you lying awake at night, of course you can have something. But Angela, child, it's no use just knocking yourself out with these.'
'I know. Thank you, Doctor.'
'And I'm not always such a blabbermouth, like I was there about old Mrs Dillon. If it would help to talk about it at all, I *could* keep it to myself. In fact I usually do.'
'You don't have to tell me that, Dr Power. Don't I remember always how good you were about my father.' But she was resolute. She thanked him and said she would go straight to the chemist now before they closed. She smiled a tired smile at him and he noticed she did indeed have the dark circles of sleeplessness under her eyes. As far as he knew it wasn't a man, he'd have heard in a small place like this. It was even more unlikely to be a casual sexual encounter resulting in a pregnancy – and anyway, Angela O'Hara wouldn't lie awake sleepless over something like that. She had been a Trojan in all that business of the child up in the convent who was pregnant: she had been so practical and down-to-earth when everyone else had been flying about in the air. It was Angela who thought of explaining to the girl how the infant would be born, and it was Angela who suggested that the girl's uncle should be shipped off to England with a warning delivered from enough tough people to make him believe that his life would not be safe if he were ever to return to Castlebay. That had been about four years ago; surely Angela herself couldn't have brought such a disaster on herself? He sighed and went in to the sitting room. Molly was reading by the fire.

'Nothing changes, nothing gets much better,' he sighed.

She looked up surprised. Usually he was an optimistic man, seeing hope where there was any kind of life. 'Is anybody dying?' she asked.

'No, nothing like that. Wasn't it a pity I wasn't a ship's doctor.'

'Paddy, don't be ridiculous, you can't dance well enough to be a ship's doctor. That's all they do. They don't have anything to do with sickness or curing people.'

She looked nice, he thought, when she was being enthusiastic and cheering him up, she looked young herself. It was when her face was discontented that she developed the pouting, double-chinned look of her mother – a woman who had been born disagreeable and lived to make life disagreeable for everyone round her until last year when she got a coronary right in the middle of complaining that she hadn't got enough presents for her seventieth birthday.

'I'm very ignorant all right,' he said and went over to the drinks cupboard. His hand hovered for a moment over the sherry but settled round the bottle of Irish. What could be so bad that Angela O'Hara couldn't tell him?

Angela got the sleeping tablets in the chemist and didn't correct Mr Murphy there who thought the pills were for her mother.

'It's a terrible curse, that arthritis, and you know there's no cure for it. Years ago people didn't know what it was; now they know what it is but they can't cure it. Not a great advance, when you come to think of it. These will give her a good night's sleep, anyway,' he said.

'Oh yes,' Angela said.

'You're not looking all that well yourself, Angela, you want to get a bit of rest too you know. Up in that school all day with the voices of those children, I don't know how you stick it. When we come up to see Anna and Nan in the concert we're nearly deaf from the shrieking of them all round the school, and then you have the poor mother . . .'

'I'm as strong as a horse, Mr Murphy,' said Angela and she dragged herself out of the chemist and into the post office. She had her foot on the doorstep when she realized she couldn't take Mrs Conway this evening – the bright artificial voice, the inquiries about how well Bernie was doing, the mention once more of the history prize. Angela would never get an answer to the question she wanted to ask, and today she wasn't strong enough to take Mrs Conway head on. Some days she'd be able to deal with ten Mrs Conways before breakfast. But that was all before she had got the letter.

The letter had arrived three weeks ago, with all the beautiful stamps which she usually cut off and put in the envelope on the mantelpiece at once. They saved stamps for the missions, foreign ones in one section and Irish ones in another. Once a year they got a letter at the school thanking them for their great Missionary Effort. Angela would always pin this up on the wall, knowing that somehow it annoyed Immaculata but there was no way she could fault it. She hadn't noticed that this letter was different to the others, that it had been addressed to her alone and not to her mother. She hadn't seen the word *Confidential* all over it. She could easily have opened it as she sat beside her mother.

The letter began: 'Angela, I beg you read this alone. I was going to send it to the school but I thought that would cause more fuss. You'll think of some reason why I put confidential on it. You'll think of something, Angela. Please.'

And it went on to tell her how Sean had left the religious house three years ago; how he was married to a Japanese girl; and how Father Sean had one child of fourteen months and another on the way.

Sean O'Hara had told the Brothers from an early age that he was going to be a missionary priest. They were pleased with this: it was far preferable to the other ambitions in the school, which seemed to be to drive the Dublin train or to own a sweetshop. Occasionally the Brothers tried to divert Sean to their own order; but firmly he said that what he wanted was not the job of teaching schoolboys who were already Catholics in Castlebay, he wanted to go out and meet savages and convert them to Christianity.

He was never a holy kind of boy, and none of his schoolmates thought that there was anything remotely pious in his vocation. They were slightly envious in fact to think that Sean would go off to all these exotic places. It was never firmly decided whether it would be Africa, or India or China. The Brother who taught geography was quite grateful to young Sean, as the boy was always sending off to Missionary Orders asking for details of their work; and in return for magazines and pamphlets Sean organized the silver-paper collection for them too.

He had even managed to get a missionary priest to come and give a talk at their school when he was around thirteen. The priest told him to slave hard at his books and maybe he would be taken into a seminary; but for everything in this life it was essential to be good at the books.

Sean was three years older than Angela but he found her a willing ally. She borrowed books for him from the convent; she shared the task of going round to look for their father each evening and finding a neighbour willing to help carry him home. It was she who insisted that a corner of their kitchen be made into a sort of study for them, and had the oil lamp fixed firmly to a shelf so that it couldn't be taken away from them. Their two sisters, Geraldine and Maire, were already planning to leave the nest. Geraldine had been in touch with a hospital in Wales where she could train as a nurse, and Maire had a friend who worked in a very nice store in London which was so smart that it wasn't like being a shop girl at all. Fifteen and sixteen, and their futures were certain. Within months they were gone. Holidays at home very rarely, letters from time to time, pictures of grandchildren never seen, never known, growing up with English accents and a promise to come home some day.

Geraldine and Maire had come home for their father's funeral. Grown-up, distant, wearing black coats and hats, startled that everyone else wore raincoats and headscarves. They had borrowed the black outfits specially. They had looked around with restless eyes at the wet cold churchyard, and at the entire population of Castlebay standing with bent heads against the wind. It was so unfamiliar to them after thirteen years in another country. They had looked pityingly at the small house that had been their home for over half their lives and shaken their heads sadly. Angela had been enraged. *They* didn't know how hard she had worked during her father's last illness to try to make the place look respectable, so that her mother would have some dignity at the end. So that she could give the neighbours tea and cake and whiskey without feeling ashamed of their home.

But of course the best consolation at the funeral had been Father Sean. He had been due back later in the spring but when Angela wrote to him and to the Superior of the Order – a measured letter explaining that her father would not be alive in spring, the liver damage was irreversible – the Order had acted swiftly and humanely. Of course young Father O'Hara could be spared from the mission fields a little earlier.

And home he came, stepping from the bus to a buzz of excitement; children ran ahead up to O'Hara's cottage to give the news that he had arrived. The long skirts of his habits he raised slightly to avoid the mud of Castlebay, the way they were used to avoiding the swamps of the Far East. Father O'Hara, home to give his father Extreme Unction and to say his Funeral Mass.

Father Sean had a word for everyone in Castlebay. His eyes didn't cloud with pity for the people, he didn't look sadly at his old home, his bent mother, nor did he close his ears from the life his father had lived. 'He was an unhappy man in this world, let us pray he finds that happiness he was always seeking in the next.' It was generous and forgiving and loving, people said. He had been away for most of his father's spectacular unhappiness, away in the seminary in the novitiate and eventually in the mission fields. But still, the principle was the same, and if he was able to forgive his father for all that neglect and trouble, people thought it was big-hearted of him in the extreme.

Angela's mother's bones ached less when Father Sean was around, and on the very last morning, before he went away again for five years, he said a little Mass at a side altar in the church just for the two of them. They didn't even have an altar boy; Angela answered the responses in Latin from her missal. Geraldine and Maire had gone back to their families in England with promises to return regularly.

When the Mass was over, Mrs O'Hara pressed eighty pounds into her son's hands for the missions; she had been saving it and hiding it for years waiting for his visit.

He had gone that day. The tears of goodbye were in the house, and the brave faces were at the bus stop opposite Conway's post office; there was a waving of handkerchiefs, and the pride of the widow that everyone in the town should see how her fine tall son had turned out.

And the letters never failed: thanks for the cuttings from the local paper, or for the news that their stamp collection had been the biggest in the county; sympathy to the Dillons when old Mr Dillon died, a holy picture to be given to the family with a few words of blessing written by Father O'Hara himself; less and less about what he did himself and more and more in response to their own tittle-tattle in the fortnightly letter which Angela now wrote for her mother since the arthritis had reached the old woman's hands.

Not long ago, Angela had written on her own behalf a little request: 'Sean, you're so good to be interested in all our petty goings-on here, but tell us more about you. In the beginning you used to tell us about the House and the various fathers who lived there, and the schools you all started. And I remember the day a bishop came to confirm everyone and there was a monsoon and they all ran off into their huts and no one got confirmed that year. It's *interesting* to us to know what it's like for you every day, and what you do all the time. If you were a priest here with Father O'Dwyer we'd know, but it's so different out there we find it hard to visualize . . .'

Why had she written that? If she had said nothing maybe she would never have had the letter that burned a hole through her handbag; the letter that told of the end of the vocation for Father Sean but would spell the end of any kind of life at all for his mother.

Sean had written that he couldn't bear the deception any more, he said that Shuya and he found the letters from home unbearable now; they referred to a life long past. And when money arrived for Masses, it was spent on rent and food. Sean taught English in Tokyo. There had never been a religious house of his order there at all; the address on letters from Castlebay was in fact the house of Shuya's brother. Sean collected any mail from him.

The family spoke English, and were puzzled to know why he was still addressed as 'Father' on the envelope, and why their house was described as a religious foundation.

The other fellows had been terrific about it all, even his Superior. They had tried to change his mind at first and said that, even though Shuya was pregnant, surely Sean could come back to the House, and a provision be made for the child. They didn't understand that he loved her and wanted to have a family with her, and that long before he had met her, the conversion of the Far East had lost all sense for him. He could only see that they were fine with their own beliefs and he didn't think the Lord wanted them changed at all.

Eventually, when everything got more settled, he was going to send his plea to Rome to be laicized and released from his priestly vows. It happened much more than people thought. Then he would be free to remarry Shuya in a Catholic church, and their children could be baptized. Shuya said she had no objection to the children being Catholics.

There was a finality about it that was chilling. The letter left no hope that Shuya was a dalliance, a shameful thing which you often heard whispered about when priests went abroad – something like that or two bottles of the local liquor a day. This woman was in his mind his wife. His fellow priests *knew* about her, they had been kind and supportive. His Superior knew. And Sean found the letters from home 'unbearable'. He couldn't 'bear' to read them now because they referred to a life that no longer existed. *To hell with him*, she thought in fury. He can bloody bear to read them for as long as we send them. I shall never tell that woman about the Japanese Shuya, I shall *never* tell her about the half-Jap grandson, called Denis after his grandfather. How could poor Mammy take it in and cope with it, if even Angela who was young and meant to be modern and intelligent couldn't take it in herself? And then there were other moods: poor, poor Sean, how desperate, with only one life to lead, and finding it empty. Led on and seduced by this Japanese woman with no religion and no morals. To her, a priest was the same as anyone else; she would have no idea what a sin it was, and what a terrible decision Sean had to make. At other times still she had moments of calm: it's not so bad, we'll say nothing, Mammy doesn't read my letters, I'll write him ordinary letters referring to his new life, and ask him to write the old-style letters referring to his old life. That way nobody will be hurt.

But in the night, when she had been asleep for about an hour and would wake with that start which she knew meant no more sleep for the rest of the dark hours, Angela knew that she was fooling herself. A lot of people had been hurt already. And in her moments of real self-pity she got up and lit a cigarette and looked out of the window: *she* had been hurt most of all. Struggling all that time, scrimping to send him money, even during her teacher-training when she was penniless from start to finish and wore away her legs walking because she had neither bicycle nor bus fares. She had come back for a one-year appointment to the convent here, the year her father was dying. She had decided that she owed her mother that support and that the woman should have at least one of her children around for the bad months that lay ahead. She had been loath to leave the big, cheerful school in Dublin; but the Reverend Mother there had said she would certainly keep her job open for a year – Miss O'Hara was too good a prize to lose. She had walked the cliffs with her brother Sean when he was back for the death and the funeral. They had talked as naturally as they always had, the bond hadn't been shaken in the slightest. They had stopped at stiles and leaned on grassy banks looking out to sea where the gulls swooped and cried; and Sean had talked gently about ties, and duty, and doing what you felt you had to do. And she knew then that she wasn't going back to her job in Dublin, she was going to stay and look after her mother. She felt no resentment, then or later. She didn't hate Geraldine for not shipping her English husband and children over to Castlebay, nor Maire. How could they do anything of the sort? Sean was a missionary priest who had already given up his life to good, and anyway what use would a boy be around the house, even suppose he had been able to come home?

But somehow, now, in the dark sleepless hours where her heart was caught with a permanent sense of alarm and dread, she felt little love for him. How dare he talk to her about duty? How *dare* he? Where was his duty, she might ask. The first temptation and he leaves his priesthood, he closes his ears to what he had known since he was old enough to learn his catechism: that once a priest always a priest. He had slept with a Japanese woman, over and over, she was about to have his second child. Angela had never slept with anybody, and she was more entitled to try it than was a priest of God.

In his letter he said that he had told Shuya all about Angela, and Shuya had said it sounded as if she were strong enough to sort out the whole thing. Thank you very much Shuya, Angela thought in the night. Nice, helpful, Japanese sister, thank you. Shovel it all on to Angela, as usual. Oh, you're becoming an O'Hara all right, Shuya, don't doubt it.

Clare received a letter from the nun in the secondary school enclosing the syllabus for the 1950 open scholarship. It arrived with the usual crop of bills, receipts and advertisements from suppliers which made up the O'Brien family post.

Agnes was sitting near the range so that she could supervise the lifting over of the big teapot and the spooning out of the porridge. The older boys and Chrissie sat on one side of the big kitchen table with its torn oilcloth; Clare and the two younger boys had their backs to the door. In winter, breakfast was one meal where they were unlikely to be disturbed. The ping of the shop bell never went before the family was off to school.

The kitchen was warm and not really uncomfortable, but it was so cluttered that it was almost impossible to move once any of them stood up from the table. There were clothes and schoolbooks scattered around on the dilapidated couch, there were bags that hadn't yet been sorted for the shop heaped up against the wall. The washing hung perilously from the ceiling and the dresser bulged with so many things that had been 'just put there for the moment' that it was impossible to see the plates and dishes.

Tom O'Brien groaned and sighed as usual over the brown envelopes, the ones with windows in them and the ones without. Then he gave a start. 'Well now, Clare, there's a letter here for *you*!'

Clare had never had a letter before, so it created a lot of interest in the O'Brien household.

'I suppose she's got some awful, ugly, scabby lover,' Chrissie said.

'Don't talk like that, don't be such a loud-mouth always,' said Agnes O'Brien crossly to her troublesome daughter.

'Well who is it from? Why don't you ask her? You always ask me everything, where I was, who I talked to. Why can't Saint Clare be asked anything?'

'Don't speak to your mother like that,' said Tom O'Brien, who was already in a bad humour. 'Come on, Clare. Tell us who the letter is from and stop all this mystery.'

'It's a list of books for exams,' Clare said simply, producing the roneoed sheet of paper that the nun had sent. She left the letter in the envelope.

'What do you want that for?' Chrissie scoffed.

'So there won't be any mistakes in what I have to study.'

Chrissie looked at the list. 'We did all those last year,' she said.

'Good.' Clare was calm. 'Then maybe you'd have the books for me to use later.' She knew that Chrissie's books were long torn up, or scribbled on, or lost. It was not a subject her sister would discuss for much longer.

Agnes O'Brien had more on her mind than book lists. She was preparing to send her two first-born sons to England, where they were going to live in a strange woman's house and go out to work with grown men of every nationality each day. It was a terrible worry. But what was there for them here in Castlebay? If they only had a few fields of land it would have been different, but a small shop like this one, there was hardly a living in it at all.

Clare decided to show the letter to Miss O'Hara after school, but she was careful not to be seen hobnobbing with the teacher in case anyone should suspect that she was favoured, getting extra help and advice all the way. She would go to the O'Hara cottage instead. Miss O'Hara never seemed to mind her dropping in, and surely she would be interested in the letter.

Mrs O'Hara answered the door slowly and painfully. Clare had been tempted to run off again when she heard the scraping of the chair that meant the old woman was beginning her long, aching journey to the door, but that would be worse.

'I'm sorry for getting you up.'

'That's nothing,' the old woman said. 'I may have to be getting up to answer the door myself in a short time, that's the way things look.'

'Are you getting better?' Clare was pleased.

'No. But I may be on my own, that's the way the wind is blowing.'

'Miss O'Hara going to move out of the house?' It was incredible.

'And out of Castlebay, by the looks of things.'

'She can't!' Clare was stung with the unfairness of it. Miss O'Hara *had* to stay, until she got her scholarship. She *couldn't* leave now.

'Is she getting married or something?' she asked, full of hostility to the whole notion of it.

'Married? Who'd have that big long string of misery? Of course she's not getting married. Restless, that's what she's getting, restless. Her own words. She's up pacing the house all night long, you couldn't get a wink of sleep with her. What's wrong you ask her. Restless, she says. Ah well, nobody has any time for you when you're old. Remember that, Clare.'

Miss O'Hara returned just then. She looked very tired. She had been short-tempered at school too for some time, though not with Clare. So Clare didn't expect sharp words.

'*God Almighty*, am I to get no peace, at school, on the street and now at home?' Clare was shocked.

'You give people an inch and they take a bloody mile. What is it tonight, Clare, is it the long division or is it the Long Catechism? Tell me quickly and let's be done with it.'

Clare stood up and placed the letter from the distant convent on the O'Hara kitchen table. 'I thought you'd like to see the reply they sent me, since you helped me write the letter.' She was at the door now, her face red and furious. 'Goodnight, Mrs O'Hara,' she called, and was gone.

She marched down the long golf-course road, where more and more people were doing bed and breakfast in the season. Down towards the top of Church Street and straight into the town. She didn't even see Chrissie and Kath sitting on a wall swinging their legs and talking to Gerry Doyle and two of his friends. She didn't notice all the excitement in Dwyers' the butchers, when the mad dog belonging to Dr Power had run off down the street with a leg of mutton.

At home two suitcases were being packed even though the boys wouldn't leave for a few days yet. It was a rare thing to go on a journey; the packing was always taken very seriously.

Clare's father had found a good leather strap that would hold one case together – the locks had long rusted and wouldn't catch any more. They would probably use several layers of thick cord to hold the other.

Mam could hardly be seen in the kitchen behind the lines of washing. There were five bars – long wooden slats, and they went up and down over the range on a dangerous pulley system that only Mam could work, everyone else reached up by standing on a chair. But today there seemed to be a crisis of enormous proportions. The range was out. And Mam was standing on it at the back fixing what must have been a row of washing that had fallen, judging by the rage and the pile of ash-covered clothes in the corner of the kitchen.

Mam looked as if nothing would please her, and indeed nothing did.

'Can I do anything to help?' Clare asked after a moment, thinking that was a better approach than asking what had happened.

'It would be nice if *someone* did something to help,' Mam cried. 'It would be very nice if *anyone* in this house did something to help. That would be very nice. And very surprising.'

'Well, tell me what you want, and I'll do it, do you want me to make the tea?' Clare asked.

'How can you make the tea for eight people, don't be stupid, child.'

'Well, what do you want me to do?' Clare's voice was becoming querulous. What was the point of being nice to Mam if she was going to be so bad-tempered? Clare wished she hadn't come into the kitchen at all but just gone upstairs to the bedroom.

'Why don't you go and stick your nose in a book, isn't that all you ever want to do?' Mam shouted and at that moment the rest of the clothes from the line, all of them damp and some of them almost dripping, fell on top of Clare's head.

There was a silence and then Mam was down ripping the shirts and sheets off Clare and flinging them regardless to the floor. 'Are you all right, child, are you hurt?' Mam was near to tears with the shock. Her hands tore at the clothes until she could see Clare's face. When she found it, it was laughing, from shock more than anything. Mam hugged her, with the damp clothes between them. Then she hugged her again. Normally any thought of pressing wet clothes would make Mam start talking fearfully about rheumatic fever. But not now.

'You poor little thing, are you all right, are you all right? That was God punishing me for being cross with you over nothing.'

Clare was bewildered and delighted. The accident seemed to have put Mam into a great temper for some reason.

'Now let me get you out of all this wet swaddling clothes . . . or we'll both have rheumatic fever. And I'll put on the kettle and you and I'll have a cup of tea, just the two of us with some biscuits, then we'll throw the whole bloody lot of this into the bath, it'll all have to be done again anyway. And we'll get one of those useless men of ours to mend the line.'

Mam looked happier than she had done for a long time.

David Power was in great trouble, and because of him so were the rest of the school. Father Kelly had read the letter out to Assembly not once but three times as a living example of how deceitful boys could be.

The letter was from a girl who was called Angela O'Hara and who apparently came from Power's home town. The letter was now almost known by heart throughout the school:

Dear David,

I have no objection to sending you the family tree of the Tudor monarchs with notes on how each one treated Ireland. I would have thought after all the money you pay in that great ugly castle up there, one of those priests who doesn't even have to make his own bed or cook his own breakfast could find time to do it for you, however. But I do not intend to join in your silly games of calling myself 'Andrew' when I write to you and filling the letter up with details of fictitious rugby matches. If that is the kind of hot-house nonsense that is encouraged in your school I am sorry for you, and for the men who are supposed to be in charge of you.

I wish you continued success and also to your friend James Nolan.
Regards Angela O'Hara

The grossness of this letter had never been equalled in the memory of every single member of the Order. Imagine a boy writing to *anyone* else for a teaching aid, when it was known that this was the best school in Ireland and one of the best in the whole of Europe. Imagine describing it as, letting it be believed to be, 'a great ugly castle'.

To allow, nay encourage, such slurs on men who were the anointed priests of God, to make remarks about these priests not cooking their own breakfast – as if this is what they had been ordained to do! Worse still, to encourage deception, to ask this girl whoever she was to pretend to be a boy, to sign herself with a false name, to invent details of rugby matches to deceive the innocent guardians in whose care they had been placed. And more, to suggest that this was a common practice. That this had been going on undiscovered in the school before this sickening letter had been exposed. There would be thorough investigations and in the meantime those boys who knew anything were expected to come forward.

David apologized to everyone as best he could. He couldn't have known she would do a thing like this. She had been great altogether before, he appealed to Nolan, who in all honesty had to admit that this was so.

'She must have gone mad, that's the only explanation,' David said.

'Yes, that must be it,' said Nolan who was familiar with madness, if extremely annoyed to have been mentioned by name in the letter that shook the school.

The sleeping tablets were very odd. You could feel your legs getting heavy first, then your arms, and your head wouldn't lift from the pillow and suddenly it was eight o'clock in the morning. Angela felt that it took her until noon to wake up properly. Then she felt fine for the afternoon. So at least they bought her some good hours, hours when she could correct exercises, mark tests and try to undo some of the harm she appeared to have done during the first weeks after the letter from Sean, the weeks when she had hardly ever closed her eyes.

Mother Immaculata had said she was looking her old self again, which was irritating beyond words, and Sergeant McCormack, the priest's housekeeper, said she was glad that Angela seemed to have got over whatever it was that had made her so disagreeable. Mrs Conway asked was there anything in particular that Angela wanted – she kept coming into the post office and leaving again without making any purchase at all. And her mother said she was glad the pacing had stopped and added mysteriously that whenever Angela had any definite plans the fair thing to do was to tell them immediately.

But Clare O'Brien was not won back so easily, not in those alert hours of the afternoon. Angela looked at the small white face and the large dark eyes. It was only a few months ago that there had been those bright yellow ribbons and the big bright hope that she had won a history prize. Now there was nothing of that. There was the watchful look of a dog that has been struck once and won't let it happen again.

Angela had tried to put it right.

'Here's that letter back from Sister Consuelo. It's very encouraging really, isn't it?'

Clare took it with thanks.

'I was a bit hasty that day you came to the house, I had a lot on my mind.'

'Yes, Miss O'Hara.'

'So I'm sorry if I appeared a bit short-tempered, it had nothing to do with you, you know that.'

'Yes, yes indeed.'

'So why won't you come on back again, and we'll get a bit of work done, any evening you like.'

'No thank you, Miss O'Hara.'

'*God dammit*, Clare O'Brien, what do you want me to do, go down on my bended knees?' There was a silence. 'I'm going to tell you something now for your own good. You're a bright child. I would *love* to see you get the bloody scholarship. I don't mind working till midnight every night to help you get it. What better way could I spend my time? But you have a really *sickening* habit of sulking. Oh yes, you have. I remember you were just the same when you didn't win the history prize. *Nobody* likes a sulker, Clare, it's a form of blackmail. I didn't get what I wanted so I'm not going to speak to people. It's about the most objectionable vice anyone could have, so my advice is to get rid of it if you want to have any friends.'

'I haven't many friends,' Clare said.

'Think about it. That might be why.'

'Anyway, you're leaving, so why tell me you'll help me?' She was still mutinous.

'I'm leaving, am I? That's the first I heard of it. Where am I going?'

'Your mother said . . .'

'My mother doesn't know what time of day it is.'

'She said you paced round the house all night planning to leave.'

'Oh, Christ Almighty, is that what she's on about?'

'So you're not?' Clare had brightened a little.

'I'm not, but unless I see a marked change in your attitude, I might as well have left as far as you're concerned. Come up to me this evening and we'll make a start. I need a bit of distraction to tell you the truth.'

'It'll soon be the bright weather and the long nights will be over.'

'Why do you say that?' Angela sounded startled.

'My mother always says it to cheer people up. I thought it was a nice thing to say.'

'I think it is.'

She decided not to send him a telegram, and it took her five weeks from the day she got the letter before she was able to reply. Only the thought of him waiting and watching for a Japanese postman to bring a letter made her put pen to paper at all. She began the letter a dozen times. The words didn't ring true. She couldn't say she was glad he had confided in her, she would prefer never to have known a thing about it. She couldn't say she sympathized with him because she didn't. She could find no words of welcome for her sister-in-law Shuya, her new nephew Denis, nor any enthusiasm about the arrival of the next child. Instead, her mind was full of snakes and worries slithering around. Would her mother have a stroke if she heard the news? Was there a possibility that the family might have to pay back some of the money spent educating Sean to be a priest, now that he had abandoned it all? Was it something that he might be excommunicated for, and the excommunication made public? Would all the priests in Ireland hear about it? Would Father O'Dwyer get to know through some clerical bulletin? She knew she should think kinder thoughts and treat him as a lonely frail human being; those were the words he used about himself, but then in the next sentence he said that he now knew perfect happiness, and understood for the first time why man and woman were put on this earth.

Several times she had her foot on the doorstep of Mrs Conway's post office prepared to send the wire telling him that his news had been received and urging him to communicate no further. But what would the town make of *that* piece of intelligence. The houses and shops up and down Church Street and up the golf-course road and across on the far cliff road would buzz happily with speculation. If Angela wanted to send a telegram like that it would have to be sent from the next town. And it might provoke Sean into doing something really foolish. After all he had talked fondly, and insanely, in his letter of the day when he could come back to Castlebay and show it to his wife and children. *Father* Sean O'Hara show Castlebay to his wife and children! He must be raving mad! Not just *mad*, but sheer raving *lunatic* mad!

She tried to imagine what she would advise if it were somebody else. Her friend Emer back in Dublin, whom she had taught with and prowled the likely places with looking for husbands. Suppose it were Emer's brother. What would she say? She would probably urge a noncommittal kind of letter to tide things over. Fine. But once you started to write to your own brother about something like this you couldn't remain uncommitted. It was ridiculous to expect that you could behave like an outsider. So eventually she wrote from the heart.

She wrote that she was shocked that he had given up his vocation, and that he must realize everyone in Ireland would be shocked too, no matter how good and supportive his fellow priests in the mission field had been. She said that if he was absolutely certain that this was not a temporary loss of faith, then she was glad that he had found happiness in his relationship with his Japanese friend, and pleased that the birth of their son had given them both so much pleasure. She begged him to realize that Castlebay in 1950 was a place where understanding and casual attitudes towards married priests simply did not exist. She wrote that, as she sat in the dark room with the rain outside the window, and with her mother poking at the open door of the range with a rough old poker that she held in two hands, it became more and more obvious that their mother should never know. After her time, then they might all think again; but it would destroy the woman's life, and they had all agreed that when lives were being handed out Mam had had a very poor one given to her. She said she knew it was hard; but could he as a higher kindness write letters that assumed he was still in the Order. And because Mrs Conway looked at every envelope that went through her post office, Angela had decided she was going to address hers in the way she always had done. Could he imagine the excitement if she were to drop the Father bit? She said she knew this was not the warm, all-embracing letter he had hoped for, but at least it was honest and it was practical and for the moment that was the best he could have.

It was on the dresser for two days before she could put it in the postbox. It was sealed and there was no fear that her mother would open it – the old woman thought that it contained the usual letter and the four folded pound notes for Masses. She half hoped it would blow away or fall down and be lost so it would never be sent.

Clare O'Brien, looking around her with wonder as she always did, spotted it. 'Can I post that to Father O'Hara?' she asked eagerly. 'It would make me feel very important posting a letter to Japan.'

'Yes, you post it,' Miss O'Hara said in a strange voice.

'Will we look at the globe to see how many countries it will go over before it gets to him?' Clare asked. She loved getting out the old globe which creaked when it spun round.

'Yes.' Miss O'Hara made no move to pass the globe which was near her.

'Will I get it?' Clare was hesitant.

'What? Oh yes. Let's see.' Angela lifted the globe on to the table. But she didn't start to move it yet.

'Well, it will leave Castlebay . . .' Clare prompted.

Angela O'Hara shook herself. 'That's the hardest part of its journey,' she said, like her old self again. 'If it gets out of Mrs Conway's sticky hands without being steamed open for Madam in there to read it, then the worst's over.'

Clare was delighted to be made party to such outrageous accusations about awful Mrs Conway, the awful mother of really awful Bernie Conway. She decided to take the letter to Japan by the westward route and brought it over the Atlantic to Nova Scotia where they said all Irish planes stopped first, and then she took it slowly across all the United States, going to Hawaii and then on to Japan. That's probably the way they'd take it, Clare thought, less land, less places to stop in. Could you choose whether it went one way or the other? Miss O'Hara shook her head. Clare supposed it depended on which way the planes were going first; she looked at Miss O'Hara for confirmation and to her surprise she thought she saw tears in her eyes.

'Will he be home soon at all?' she asked sympathetically. She realized that poor Miss O'Hara must miss her brother and maybe she shouldn't go on and on about how far away he was and how huge the world was. Maybe it wasn't tactful.

Chrissie said that Clare wasn't normal because her big toe was bigger than her second toe. This was discovered when Chrissie was painting her toenails and the bedroom smelled so much of lacquer that Clare had wanted to open the door.

'You can't do that,' Chrissie hissed. 'Everyone will smell it.'

'But nobody can *see* it under your socks. What's the point of it?' Clare had wanted to know.

'It's the difference between grown-up and being a stupid eejit like you are,' Chrissie had explained.

Clare had shrugged. There was no use in trying to talk to Chrissie about anything, it always ended up with an explanation that Clare was *boring* and that seemed to be the root cause of everything. Chrissie taunted her about every aspect of her life.

'Your hair is awful. It's like a paper bag, it's so flat.'

'I don't put pipe cleaners in mine like you do,' Clare said.

'Well, that's it. You're so stupid you can't even put curlers in.' And then on another tack: 'You've no friends at all at school. I see you in the playground on your own, you walk to and from school all by yourself – even your awful stupid class must have sense, they know not to be friends with you.'

'I *do* have friends,' Clare cried.

'Who? Name me one friend. Whose house do you go to in the evening, who comes here? Answer me that! Nobody!'

Clare wished devoutly that Kath and Peggy didn't come so often – it meant that she couldn't go to the bedroom, and downstairs she was always being asked to do something.

'I've lots of friends, different friends for different things you know, like I'm friendly with Marian in domestic science because we're at the same table and then I'm friendly with Josie Dillon because I sit beside her in class.'

'Ugh, Josie Dillon, she's so fat, she's disgusting.'

'That's not her fault.'

'It is too, she's never without something in her fat hand eating it.'

Clare didn't like Josie all that much: she was very dull, she couldn't seem to get enthusiastic about anything. But she was harmless and kind and she was lonely. Clare didn't like all the faces that Chrissie was making.

'Ugh, Josie Dillon, well if you had to have a friend I might have guessed that it would be someone like that big white slug.'

'She's not a slug, and anyway your friend Kath had nits in her hair, everyone in the school knows that.'

'Aren't you *horrible!*' screamed Chrissie. 'What a desperate thing to say about anyone. When I think how nice Kath always is about you.'

'She was never nice about me, all she said ever was shut up and go away, like *you* say.'

Chrissie was looking at Clare's feet. 'Put your foot out.'

'Why? I won't,' Clare said.

'Go on, just for a moment.'

'You'll put that awful red paint on it.'

'No I won't, I wouldn't waste it. Go on, let's see.'

Suspiciously Clare put her leg out of her bed and Chrissie examined her foot.

'Show me the other one,' she said after a while. Nervously it was produced. Then Chrissie pronounced that Clare was deformed. Her second toe should be longer than the big toe, Kath's was, Peggy's was, Chrissie's was, anyone you saw on the beach had feet like that. Clare fought back. Why was it called the big toe if it wasn't the biggest one?

Chrissie shook her head. 'Oh well,' she said.

Clare was frightened now. 'I think I'll go and ask Mam,' she said scrambling off the bed. A hand thrust her back.

'You'll do nothing of the sort, Mam will want to know why we were talking about toes, she'll want to see mine maybe, keep your awful complaints to yourself, and don't be seen in your bare feet.'

Clare crawled back on to her bed.

Chrissie looked at her and decided to be sympathetic. That was worse than anything else that Chrissie had ever done.

'Listen, nobody'll notice, and I tell you, I won't give you away.'

Clare looked miserable still.

'And Josie Dillon's not *too* bad. It's better than having no friend, isn't it?'

'Did you have a friend at school, Miss O'Hara?' Clare wanted to know.

'Yes, several. Why?'

'I just wondered, what happened to them?'

'Well, Nellie Burke is working up in Dr Power's house, she was a friend when I was about your age, and Margaret Rooney, she went to England and got married, she lives near my sister. And Cissy O'Connor became a nun God bless her, she's praying for all of us in a convent up in the North.'

'They weren't working like a demon like you were, like I am?'

'Oh no, they weren't working like demons at all, they thought I was mad.'

Clare was pleased with this, it made her path seem less odd.

'But when I got to the big convent, to the secondary school, it was different because there were lots of people there with the same interests, you didn't have to hide your work or anything. And when I went to the training college I had great friends altogether, still have in a way, but of course it's not the same now that I'm away, most of them teach in Dublin you see. But there'll be plenty of time for you to make friends, don't worry.'

Angela was being reassuring. Someone must have been getting at the child. Wouldn't you think they'd be delighted to see someone try to get on? Give some encouragement and support. But it had never been the way.

'I do worry a bit, I don't want to be abnormal.' Clare was solemn.

'Well, I hope you're not big-headed enough to think that you're something special. That would be a sin of Pride you know.'

'I suppose so.'

'You can *know* it, not suppose it. It's there in black and white in the catechism. The two great sins against Hope are Pride and Despair. You mustn't get drawn towards either of them.'

'Were you ever tempted a bit to either of them?' Clare was an odd mixture. She could be quite familiar and probing sometimes as if she were the equal of the teacher sitting opposite her, yet she could also be totally respectful, and up at the convent she never gave a glimmer of the intimacy they shared in the O'Hara cottage.

'If I was, I suppose it was a bit more towards Despair,' Angela said. 'Sometimes I used to think I'd never make it and what was it all for anyway. But I did and here I am, and I'm teaching the second great genius to come out of Castlebay, so will

561

you open your books and not have us here all night talking about sins against Hope and friendships long gone.'

Clare giggled and got out the special copy books she had bought in Miss O'Flaherty's shop, a different colour to the school ones so that she would never get confused. They both knew that nobody at school would be pleased if they knew that Miss O'Hara was giving hours and hours of private tuition free to a ten-year-old. It was never mentioned. And at home Mam thought that Clare was getting help because she had fallen behind a bit. It was a devious business studying your books in Castlebay.

When the summer came David began to wish heartily that Nolan's family had never decided to rent the house on the cliff. First there had been the letters, they wanted the Very Best house, and could the Powers send them a list of accommodation. Castlebay wasn't like that, there were twenty houses on the Cliff Road that people let for the summer, usually a month at a time. And up towards the golf course there were other kinds of houses, smaller maybe but great for people who played golf all day. And then at the other side of the bay there was a jumble of houses, some owned by people who lived twenty miles away but who came out to stay there for the summer. People just knew the houses and knew what they wanted, it was very hard to explain all this to the Nolans. Molly Power was worn out from trying to explain.

She settled on Crest View and arranged the letting with Mrs Conway's sister who owned the house. She spoke of the professional people from Dublin, who would arrive with the three children and their maid and she insulted the Conways and all their relatives by suggesting that a coat of paint be put on the porch which was peeling somewhat under the constant wind and spray. But huffed though they were the Conways arranged that the porch be painted. They weren't going to have any professional family from Dublin casting aspersions on the house they were renting by the sea.

David was worn out inspecting Crest View with his mother and being forced to face unanswerable questions about where the Nolan parents would sleep, in this front room or that. And would Caroline Nolan share a room with the friend she was inviting? And did David think the room on the stairs was big enough for the maid? Dublin maids might have notions about themselves.

Nearer the time Mrs Power arranged to have a box of groceries delivered from the town to the kitchen of Crest View to welcome them. David had watched his mother while she dithered over the list.

'I don't think she'll notice really what you order,' he had said helpfully. 'Nolan says his mother is mad most of the time.'

'David will you *stop* that silly kind of talk!' his mother had cried out in rage. 'Here am I wearing my fingers to the bone trying to see that you have nice friends for the summer, and that they are comfortable when they get here and all the help I get from you is to say that some poor woman you've never met is mad. Honestly.'

'I did meet her when she came to see Nolan at half term,' David said.

'And . . . ?'

'And it was one of her good days apparently.' He was unconcerned.

O'Brien's shop looked well, he thought, it had a new sign over it, and one of the ice-cream firms had put up a big tin sign as well so it looked much more modern than last year. He supposed they'd all be working in the shop: all the O'Brien family, cutting ice-creams, counting out sweets, putting oranges in white paper bags, giving change, getting greaseproof paper for the slices of cooked ham or the half-pounds of rashers. Wasn't it nice for Tommy and Ned to have that to do as a way of getting pocket money in the summer.

There was no sign of either of them. He asked Chrissie where they were and heard they had gone to England months ago. What for? To work on the buildings of course. It gave him a start.

Chrissie didn't know if they liked it or not. They only wrote very little on a Friday. They wrote every Friday? Well they sent something home of course. Of course. He'd forgotten. Mrs O'Brien was serving another family, young Clare was cutting ice-creams carefully and watched equally carefully by those who were buying them. It would be a disaster if a twopenny ice-cream were ever the teeniest bit smaller than the allotted ridge. Only Chrissie had time to talk.

'James Nolan and his family are coming to stay up in Crest View.'

'Oh, the fellow who burned his mouth.' Chrissie giggled.

'The very one.'

'Well he's in great time, Gerry's going to be organizing a picnic way down the sandhills of the golf links soon, he'll tell you all about it,' she hissed conspiratorially.

That was good news. David had been wondering whether this visit would live up to the last. A secret picnic in the sand dunes – that would be great.

'Does he have any sisters or anything? Gerry was saying there aren't enough girls. Though *I* think there are,' Chrissie said.

'He has a sister, Caroline, and she's bringing a friend but I don't think . . .' He stopped suddenly. It mightn't be polite to say that he didn't think *they* were the kind of girls you invited to somewhere that there was going to be messing.

Molly hadn't been so excited for a long time. To think that a Dublin family who were quite well known were coming to stay in Castlebay just on the word of a boy who had been a visitor in her house. She was very flattered. She hoped that young James Nolan hadn't exaggerated the style of their living.

The letters from Sheila Nolan had been courteous and warm, but alarmingly had given the impression that Castlebay was a little like Monte Carlo. She had said she so looked forward to going to the Spa each day with Molly. The Spa? She must mean the seaweed baths, but they were old and shabby and rusty, and only priests or cranky sorts of people went to bathe there. Molly could hardly have them transformed with a coat of paint as she had done with the house.

But wouldn't it be great to talk with Dublin people again, and laugh over Robert's at the top of Grafton Street, and wonder was that nice Miss so-and-so still in Switzer's and had Brown Thomas changed their displays. It was such a pity that there were so few people she could ask to meet the Nolans. The Dillons at the hotel were a very mixed bunch, and it was hard to think who else they could ask. The Nolans would think them very dull sticks.

Paddy had told her to relax, but men never understood anything. He said that he had seen the high and mighty of the land coming on holidays to Castlebay over the years and it was funny but they never seemed to want the comfort and style of home, there was something in the big bay, the cliffs and the sunshine that made up for everything else. He was certain it would be the same with the Nolans.

Yes maybe, but Molly wished they had the kind of life where friends dropped in for a sherry or they had a group of people to meet in the hotel. The danger of going out with Paddy was that every drunk and hopeless poor creature in the place would attach themselves with details of their symptoms. Molly also wished they had a conservatory. Wouldn't it be lovely to say to the Nolans, 'Do come into our conservatory with your coffee, we always sit here in the evenings.' Why hadn't she pushed Paddy more about it? Bumper Byrne who did most of the building in the town said that it wouldn't be hard to do but Molly had wanted someone with a little more style than Bumper. Now she had no conservatory at all.

Her heart fell when she remembered Sheila Nolan writing about where to shop. Shop? In Castlebay? Imagine a woman from Dublin who was used to going to places like Smith's on the Green having to stand in O'Brien's little shop and wait while those children laughed and skittered. That coarse Chrissie with the frizzy hair, and the thin worried-looking one, Clare, who often had a book in her hand if the shop was quiet. And they had nothing nice, nothing at all.

As she thought of O'Brien's with no pleasure she remembered that she hadn't put any flour or indeed any baking things at all on the list. The Nolans were bringing a maid after all, she might want to make scones or bread the first evening, they wouldn't know where to shop. Molly should have thought of a pack of brown flour, white flour, bread soda, it would show she understood that they didn't need to live off shop food all the time like people who knew no better.

Better do it now, she'd have so much on her mind tomorrow when they arrived and anyway she'd be getting her hair done and making the last-minute arrangements. A walk would do her good, it was a lovely day. She set off down the Cliff Road trying to look at Crest View quickly as if she were a stranger who hadn't seen it before. It certainly looked the smartest of the houses with its newly painted look. And Molly had seen to it that the grass was cut too, unlike some of the other places along the road. Down on the beach there was already great sign of activity, the season had begun, Paddy was surely right, the Nolans would love it.

She had hit a quiet time in O'Brien's, only Clare was serving, and she was deep in a book.

'Whenever you're ready,' Molly said.

Clare looked up, unaware that she should be paying attention to the customer. 'Did you do clouds at school, Mrs Power?' she asked.

'Clouds?'

'Clouds. Mam and Dad didn't and I was wondering about the cumulus. There seem to be lots of different kinds of them, I thought it was one name for one cloud.'

'I haven't time to talk about clouds now, I want to buy some flour, that's if you are serving. Perhaps I should wait for your mother . . .'

'No, no.' Clare put down the book guiltily. 'What did you want, Mrs Power?'

The child got the flour and the bread soda, she even suggested lard and then she added the items up carefully on the back of a white paper bag. She looked so intense that Molly felt a pang of guilt about having put her down so strongly. She was very young and after all it was good to see a child trying to study. But she looked so streelish in that faded dress which was much too short for her and too wide around the shoulders. Why couldn't Agnes O'Brien dress the child properly when she was on show for the summer, it gave such a bad impression of Castlebay. Molly's irritation returned.

'It's one pound four shillings altogether, Mrs Power.' Clare proffered the list but Molly waved it away and rooted for notes in her handbag.

At that moment a group of English visitors came in to be served and Tom O'Brien, hearing the ping of the door and the voices, came out to serve them. They were nicely spoken people staying at Dillon's Hotel and Molly looked at them with interest in case they might be possible company when the Nolans arrived.

Tom O'Brien stood like a landlord in an inn, pleased to see the civilized chat between Mrs Power and the visitors. It was only when the door pinged again to admit further customers that he thought he should speed up the process and serve someone.

'Well I hope I'll see you while you're here,' Molly said, pleased to discover that the two English couples had brought a car and a dog each on their vacation. This alone made them into people of standing.

She turned to Clare. 'I'll take my change now and rush along home,' she said.

'It's twenty-four shillings, Mrs Power.'

'I know, I gave you five pounds.' Molly was impatient.

'Hurry up, Clare, give Mrs Power her change. Come on now.'

Clare hesitated. 'You haven't . . . um given . . . me the money yet,' she said despairingly.

'*Clare!* Mrs Power said she gave you a five-pound note.' Tom O'Brien was horrified. 'Give her the change this minute. What did it come to? Twenty-four shillings. Give Mrs Power three pounds sixteen shillings and stop dreaming.'

'Mrs Power, you put the five pounds back in your handbag,' Clare said.

'I'm very sorry, Mrs Power.' Tom pushed his daughter away from the drawer where they kept the money. He started rummaging for notes and coins.

'Look, Daddy, there isn't a five-pound note there. Mrs Power took it out but she put it back in her bag when she was talking to those people . . .'

Everyone in the shop was looking on with interest.

Two spots of red appeared on Molly's face. 'In all my life . . .' she began.

'Please forgive this, Mrs Power . . .' Tom O'Brien was mortified, he kicked the door into the back open so that Agnes could come out and help with the ever-growing group of spectators.

Molly had opened her bag and there on top of it for anyone to see was a five-pound note, hastily stuffed back there. She wouldn't have hidden it anyway, she told herself, but now there was no opportunity to do so. It was far too obvious to everyone. The flush deepened on her face.

'It's *perfectly* all right, Mr O'Brien, your daughter is totally correct, I did indeed put it back into my bag in error. How good that you have such a watchdog.' Graciously she handed over the note, waving Tom away and giving it deliberately to Clare.

Clare took it calmly and gave the change. She joined in none of the mumblings of her father, nor the assurances of how it could happen to anyone.

'Thank you, Mrs Power,' Clare said.

'Thank you, Clare,' said Molly Power.

The door pinged behind her.

'She'll never shop here again,' Tom O'Brien said to his wife.

It was a long day. Clare never got back to the chapter on clouds in her geography book. There was never a moment for her parents to speak alone with her or for her to explain the misunderstanding with Mrs Power. As the hours went by she became less repentant and more angry with Mrs Power. It was *her* fault after all, and she hadn't apologized, not in the smallest way. Clare hated her father for having humbled himself, she could have killed him for being all upset and sorry over something which was that woman's fault, not hers, not his.

The shop was empty for a couple of lovely minutes. Clare reached her hand out to her geography book and took it back. She looked across at her mother.

'It's all right, he'll forget it, it will all be forgiven and forgotten by tomorrow,' Agnes said soothingly.

'There's nothing to forgive! She didn't give me the money. Was I meant to give her three pounds sixteen shillings *and* her shopping? Was I?'

'Hush Clare, don't be difficult.'

'I'm not being difficult. I just want to know. If I am meant to do that, then tell me and I'll do it. I just didn't know.'

Agnes looked at her affectionately. 'I don't know where we got you, you're brighter than the lot of us put together.'

Clare still looked mutinous.

'There are some things that are neither right nor wrong, you can't have rules laid down for. Would you understand that?'

'Yes,' Clare said immediately, 'I would. Like the Holy Ghost.'

'Like what?'

'Like the Holy Ghost, we have to believe in Him without understanding Him, He's not a bird and He's not a great wind. He's something though, and that should be enough without understanding it.'

'I don't think that's the same at all,' said Agnes, troubled. 'But if it helps you to understand the problems of trade in a small town then for heaven's sake use it.'

It was eleven o'clock before they closed the door in O'Brien's. Tom O'Brien had a pain across his back from bending and stretching and lifting. He had forgotten the summer pain and the constant tiredness. This was just the first week: there would be another ten like it, please God, if they were to make a living at all. He was behind in paying one of the creameries and the bacon factory always allowed people a bit of credit until the summer pickings were in. He sighed deeply, it was so hard to know about things. Last year everyone had wanted those shop cakes with the hard icing, this year he had only sold two of them and the rest were growing stale under his eyes.

Everything was so precarious nowadays, and a man with a wife and six children had nothing but worries morning noon and night.

He worried about the two lads gone to England; particularly Tommy, he was so easily led, so slow to work things out. How would he survive at all in England where people were so smart and knew everything? And Ned, though he was a brighter boy, he was still very young, not sixteen until the summer. Tom O'Brien wished that he had a big business, one where his boys could have come in to work with him, gone to other towns and served their time in big groceries and then come home to Castlebay. But it was only a dream. This was an outpost and it wouldn't be here at all, the community would have broken up and scattered long ago if it weren't for the yearly influx of visitors that began in the first week of June and ended sharply on September first. Eleven weeks to make sense of the other forty-one weeks in the year. He called out to Agnes, wanting to know if there was any hot water.

'What do you want with hot water at this time of night?'

'There's these bath salts we sell and there's a picture of a man with an aching back on the front and it says he gets great relief by putting these in his bath,' he said simply.

Agnes read the packet too. 'We'll boil up some. Clare child, before you go to bed will you fill a couple of saucepans, and Chrissie. Chrissie?'

'I think she was doing some holiday work with Kath and Peggy,' Clare said automatically. She knew that the amusements had started for the summer and the three were dolled up to the nines with their painted toenails freed from summer socks.

'That one should be running the country with all the homework and holiday work she does,' grumbled Tom O'Brien. 'Why is it that she gets these bad reports every term, I might ask.'

'They're fierce strict up in the convent now, it's not like the Brothers. They say awful things about everyone.' Clare was struggling with the saucepans. One way to buy an easy life was to keep Chrissie's cover, that way she got to stay out later and she tortured Clare a bit less.

Clare's mother was opening the packet of bath salts. 'It's hard to think that it would work,' she said doubtfully. 'Go on into the bathroom, Tom, and we'll see if it's any good.'

Clare was still there; the youngsters were asleep a long time; Chrissie would come home when the amusements had closed down, when she had won something on the roll a halfpenny table and maybe had a ride on the bumpers. Tommy and Ned were asleep in their digs in Kilburn.

'Go on up to bed, Clare child. You've been a great help today,' her mother said. 'I've got to fire a bit of energy into your father, we can't have him getting pains and aches in the first week of the summer season.'

Clare heard them laughing in the bathroom and it sounded comforting to Clare as she got ready for bed. She looked out the window and saw Gerry Doyle walking down towards the beach with a very pretty girl, a visitor. *That* would annoy Chrissie if she were to hear of it. She saw a crowd who had been in Craig's Bar carrying brown bags of bottles with them, they were heading off the Far Cliff Road on the other side of the bay; they had probably rented a house there. In the distance the

567

music of the dance could be heard. That's where everyone was. Chrissie was dying to go, but not until she was sixteen; it was two years and five months away. The moon made a pointed path out over the sea, Castlebay was coming alive for the summer.

The Nolans arrived on the train from Dublin and the Powers had driven to the station in the town twenty miles from Castlebay to meet them. Dr Power called a porter immediately when he saw the amount of luggage that was assembling beside them. There would be two cars, the Powers' own Ford and a taxi. Sheila and Jim Nolan looked around them with interest and then spotted David running towards them. There were a lot of handshakes and much giggling from Caroline Nolan and her schoolfriend Hilary.

Mrs Nolan wore a very flowing sort of dress with huge red and green flowers on it as if she were going to a garden party of some type. She glanced around, sniffing the air as if suspecting it might be germ laden.

Dr Power took both of her hands in his and his face was wide with welcome, then he shook the hands of Jim and said what a pleasure it had been having their son to stay, and how everyone in Castlebay was waiting to welcome the whole family; he said his wife was organizing tea in the rented house for them, otherwise she would be here too.

Jim Nolan was a thin, fair-haired man of a slightly distracted appearance. He also had a role in watching out for the eccentricities of his wife. Sheila had a face which must have been that of a beauty when she was younger. Even now approaching her late forties she was handsome, with pale eyes and a disconcerting stare. She looked long and hard at Paddy Power.

'You are a good man, you are a man we could trust,' she said after a pause.

Dr Power was well used to intense stares like this. In his line of work he came across them regularly.

'I very much hope so, because you'll need to rely on me, on us for a bit until you get used to the ways of our strange country parts.'

With that he shooed them gently into his car with most of the luggage. David was to organize the taxi for the young people and Breeda, the Nolans' maid. There was a lot of waving and goodbyeing, until they would meet again in twenty miles' time in Castlebay.

It seemed to David that Caroline and Hilary seemed a bit scornful of everything they saw. They wanted to know where was the nearest big town to Castlebay, and giggled when they were told that they were in it. They asked when would they be on the main road and giggled even more when they learned they had been on it for three miles. They asked about tennis and were very disappointed to know that there wasn't a proper club, but they could play at the hotel. How did you meet people if there wasn't a club they wondered, and David found himself apologizing almost. Eventually, the taxi driver who also drove a hearse and had a half share in a pub, took over from him and explained Castlebay in much more attractive terms, talking about the quality who came every year and how the place was much sought after. English couples came too, often middle-aged people with a car and a dog and golf clubs. Fancy them coming all the way to Castlebay when they had the whole of their own country and Scotland and Wales to choose from. David realized that this was a much better way to go than his own style of excusing things. He brightened up and told them about the golf club and how this year he and Nolan were thinking of learning. You could hire clubs there.

Caroline and Hilary giggled and thought this was great, they might learn too.

You didn't really get a good view of the sea until you came over Bennett's Hill and David looked at them eagerly to see if it pleased them. Their faces seemed to say it all, so he sat back happily and exchanged conspiratorial winks with the taxi driver.

The girls were silenced for once as the whole coast spread before them . . . the tide was out so the beach spread out like a huge silver carpet, the headlands at each end looked a sharp purple and as they came to where the roads divided there was no need to explain any more, Castlebay explained itself. They drove down the main street – Church Street – with the big church on the right, past all the shops, well-painted and decorated for the summer, some of them with low whitewashed walls where holidaymakers sat and chatted in the sun. People were eating ice-creams and carrying beach balls and children had rubber rings and fishing nets. You could smell the sea. It was like paradise.

The taxi driver drove slowly down Church Street so that they could savour it all; the girls looked excitedly from the front of the big dance hall, to the entrance of Dillon's Hotel. They saw Dwyer's the butchers with a big notice saying 'Get your holiday meat here'. Everyone seemed to be talking to each other or waving or calling, it was as if all the people on the street going down to the sea knew each other.

Majestically the taxi turned right at the Cliff Road so that they could have a good view of the beach.

'There's Gerry Doyle!' cried Nolan, delighted to recognize him. 'Who is that he's with?'

'That's his sister, I told you about her, Fiona,' David said.

The Doyles waved and James Nolan let out all his breath in a great rush. 'She's *gorgeous*,' he said.

The girls in the back were annoyed. They didn't have to say anything, you could just sense it in the way they rustled.

'How are we going to become great golfers if you're going to sigh like that over the first girl you see in Castlebay?' David said.

'Quite right.' Caroline was approving. 'We don't want the holiday spoiled by silliness and falling in love.'

'No indeed,' said Hilary very vehemently.

It was totally unconvincing but there wasn't time to debate it because everyone was getting out of the taxi and there was a joyous reunion on the lawn. David noticed that his mother had had her hair done, and was wearing her best dress. Bones was not there; he must be tied up at home on the very accurate assumption that he would not lend any tone to the gathering. The sun was shining down on the garden and Molly had brought Nellie with her in order to help serve a welcoming tea. There were canvas chairs and stools out in the garden, the cups were arranged on a tray in the porch and there were sandwiches and bridge rolls cut in half with egg on some and ham on others. There was apple tart too, on two large plates. Nellie had a small white hat on as well as her apron. James introduced her to Breeda who immediately took off her hat and coat and went into the kitchen to help.

Mrs Nolan was sitting back in her chair, eyes closed with pleasure. 'What a *wonderful* welcome,' she said. 'What a beautiful place. James, we are lucky that you have marvellous friends like these to make it all possible.' Molly Power reddened with pleasure.

'Heavens it's very small and simple after Dublin,' she said in a tinkly voice that David didn't often hear.

'It's heavenly,' said Mrs Nolan. 'And the flies are going to be quite manageable I do believe.'

'The flies?' Molly was startled.

'Yes, but one has to expect them, I've been watching, you get about one bluebottle to eight flies, that's not too bad is it?'

'No, I suppose not.' Molly was puzzled.

'We brought quite a lot of muslin with us of course, but in the end we have to realize this is holidays, this is the great outdoors and . . . well they can't kill us?'

'Er . . . no?'

'The flies. They can't *kill* us. And I think this place is heavenly.'

And that put the seal on the summer. Dr Power had told her that it was one of the healthiest places in the world because of the sea and the ozone and the gulf stream, and goodness knows what else he had added for good measure; so now Nolan's mother need have no fear of fleas or damp or anyone catching anything. Mrs Conway's sister had come down to inspect the professional people from Dublin and had been slightly overawed to see eight people on the lawn of Crest View being served tea by two maids. But her curiosity got the better of her so she came in. She was given a chair, a cup of tea and fulsome thanks from Mrs Nolan as having provided the best house in Castlebay. Mrs Conway's sister took everything in, asked about eight searching questions and left to go to the post office and fill them in on the new arrivals. Dr Power had given his lecture about drowning. Every year he said for the past fourteen years there had been a death in the summer. All except one of them had been people who had just arrived; the accident had happened in the first few days, before they got used to the terrible undercurrent that pulled you out and sideways after a big wave. There were notices all round the beach but people didn't believe them. There was a lifeguard – but there was only so much he could do and if a bather was swept out by huge waves, the call often didn't go up until it was too late. Dr Power was very grave. Caroline was enraged by the warning; she pointed out that she had had swimming lessons in the baths in Dunlaoghaire. Dr Power said that some of the people whose purple bodies he had seen had been swimming in other places for thirty years. Castlebay had a very very strong undertow and he would be a poor man to welcome them to the place if he didn't tell them that. He was solemn and they all fell quiet for a moment. It was enough to make it sink in. Dr Power turned his attention to the golf club then, and the chance of a game with Mr Nolan and whether they should make the boys junior members for the summer and get them lessons from Jimmy the Pro. Mrs Nolan wondered was there a nice hairdresser in the place, since Mrs Power looked so elegant there must be. Nellie and Breeda were in the kitchen having a chat about the dance, the amusements and the pictures.

Caroline stretched and said she felt filthy after the journey, would anyone mind if she changed? She and Hilary dragged cases upstairs and settled into their room. They came down not long after; Caroline had her hair loose now, not tied back behind her neck. It was curly a bit like Fiona Doyle's, but not as luxuriant. She wore a yellow shirt and white shorts. She looked really smashing.

'Will you show me the town of Castlebay?' she asked David.

It would be very nice to be seen with this lovely thing in white shorts and yellow shoes to match her shirt. He would love people to look as he took her for a tour. But it would have been bad manners.

'Sure I will,' he said, deliberately misunderstanding her. 'Let's all get our swimming things and meet here in ten minutes and I'll take the conducted tour to the beach.'

David thought that Caroline was a little put out. Great, he thought, she fancies me.

It *must* have rained some days. There had to be clouds and a wind would definitely have come up at high tide. But none of them remembered it. Hilary said it was the best holiday she ever had in her life and since she and Caroline had a fight the following term and were not best friends any more, it was her first and last time in Castlebay. Mrs Nolan grew stronger and got browner every day; she and Molly Power became firm friends and even took tennis lessons at the hotel in the early mornings when there weren't many people about. It was something they both wished they had done in their youth, but it didn't matter, they were catching up now. Nolan's father stayed for two weeks, then had to go back to work, but he came down every weekend.

They had their lunch outside almost every day and David usually ate with them. On Sundays they came to lunch at the Powers', a proper lunch with roast beef or two chickens, and soup first and pudding afterwards. And when the trippers had to eat oranges or try to boil cups of tea for themselves on the beach, the Powers and the Nolans could just walk up the cliff either to the doctor's house or to Crest View, and Nellie or Breeda would serve a real tea with sandwiches and biscuits and apple tart. It was heaven.

They went for picnics too, and because the Nolans had a primus stove they often cooked sausages which tasted much better in the open air. Mrs Nolan couldn't be told that they fried sausages on their own – she was afraid of conflagrations – but they kept the primus in the Powers' garage so that there was never any fuss.

It was the first summer for a long time that nobody drowned in Castlebay. One child did get into difficulties but Dr Power made him vomit up all the sea water and in an hour the incident was almost forgotten. A woman fell and broke her hip on the path going down to the beach and Dr Power went out in his shirtsleeves and hammered in a board nailed to a stick saying *Very very dangerous path*. The Committee didn't like it at all, and wanted it removed. Dr Power said he was the one who had to pick up the pieces when people got injured and that if anyone removed his sign he would call the Guards. Eventually the Committee arranged a neater sign, properly painted and agreed to spend some money next year in making the path and steps less perilous.

Clare watched it all from the shop. It was like a different world to her, these carefree people with different clothes every day. Caroline Nolan, who had brown legs and white shorts, must have had seven different-coloured blouses. She was like a rainbow, and her friend Hilary was the same, and they were always laughing and the boys all stood round and laughed too when they were there. There were the Dillon boys from the hotel, and Bernie Conway's brother Frank, and David Power and James Nolan, and of course Gerry Doyle. Normally Gerry didn't join anyone's crowd, but he often seemed to be passing by, or perched on his bike leaning against the wall chatting to them.

They seemed to have endless money too, Clare noticed. Hilary bought ice-creams three or four times a day, and that Caroline thought nothing of buying a bottle of shampoo one day and Nivea Creme the next and three fancy hair slides the day after. Imagine having so much pocket money that you didn't even have to think before you bought things like that.

David Power was the nicest of them all, but then he always had been nice and he was from here. He didn't change because of his new crowd.

'Can you do me a favour?' he asked one day.

'Sure.'

'Nolan and I want to buy some things, but we . . . um don't . . . want to bring them home with us, can we pay for them and leave them here?'

'Do you want them delivered?' she said eagerly. Her father had been right – Mrs Power did not visit the shop any more. This might be the breakthrough.

'Oh heavens, no,' David said. 'You see we don't want them to know at home or at Nolan's, if you know what I mean.'

Clare made up the order for sausages, and bottles of orange and red lemonade, for bread and butter and biscuits. She even suggested tomato ketchup and when David wondered about a cake with hard icing on it, she said she'd put one of their own knives in the bag as well so that they could cut it.

'Is it a picnic in a cave again?' she whispered, eyes round with excitement.

'No, not a cave, down the sandhills,' David whispered.

'Oh great. When will you be collecting the food?'

'That's what I was wondering, could you sort of hide it outside somewhere, where nobody could find it except us? We'll be going about two o'clock in the morning.'

They debated putting it in the doorway behind the big potted palm. But suppose a dog got at it? Or if they put it anywhere too near the shop, Clare's father might think it was burglars coming to rob the place and raise an alarm.

'Is Chrissie going to the picnic?' Clare asked.

'Well yes, yes she is.'

'Then that's fine, I'll tell her it's in the press under the stairs and she can bring it with her.' Clare was satisfied she had sorted it out so well. She took David's money and gave him the change. Also a list of what he had bought so that he knew how the money had been spent.

'I'm sorry that you . . . I mean, I think it would be a bit . . .'

'I'm too young for picnics,' Clare said simply. 'Too young and too boring. In a few years I'll be old enough, I hope.'

David seemed relieved that she was being so philosophical.

'You will, definitely. Definitely,' he said, full of encouragement.

At that moment the floating, flowery prints of Mrs Nolan appeared at the door of O'Brien's.

'Do let's have an ice-cream Molly, in Dublin you couldn't be seen dead licking a fourpenny wafer. So full of *germs*, too. Isn't it marvellous to be here?'

There was no way that Molly could refuse to come in now. Clare acted quickly. 'I'm sorry, we don't have any of those Scots Clan left,' she said to David in a clear voice. 'We'll be getting deliveries this afternoon.' She turned politely to the two ladies. 'Can I get you an ice-cream?' she asked.

'Is it all kept nice and *fresh*?' Mrs Nolan wanted to know.

'Oh yes, indeed. Look inside if you like, but why don't I open a fresh pack just in front of you?'

Mrs Nolan was pleased. David scurried out, unnoticed. Clare went to the kitchen and got a clean jug of hot water, and a clean sharp knife. She dipped the knife in the water and slit open the carton of ice-cream. She made the indentations on it firmly and cut two fourpenny wafers which she handed over gravely.

'This *is* a nice shop, Molly,' said Mrs Nolan.

'Oh yes, yes indeed,' said Mrs Power uneasily.

'I think it's a better place than where you told us to shop.'

'It's very good, all right,' Molly agreed, looking at the ceiling.

Clare prayed her father wouldn't come in and start fawning. She bade them farewell.

'Nice little girl,' she heard Mrs Nolan say. 'Very undernourished looking, but a bright little thing.'

Chrissie said that Clare had a horrible gloating smirk on her that was terrible to look at, and that Clare would be unbearable now she knew about the picnic in the sandhills.

Clare sighed. She said that David's bag was in the press behind the coats, and there was one knife of theirs as well.

'Did he say whether Caroline and Hilary were coming or not?'

He hadn't, but Clare presumed they would be. Weren't they old enough?

'Oh they're old enough, but Gerry Doyle seemed to think they weren't.'

Chrissie was *hoping* they weren't. Gerry Doyle had too many eyes for Caroline Nolan altogether. She had seen him laughing too much with her – over nothing. She didn't explain this to Clare but Clare seemed to understand somehow.

'They'll all be gone back at the end of the summer, and you'll still be here,' she said comfortingly.

'I know that, stupid,' Chrissie said, examining her face in the mirror. 'That's both good and bad.'

Nolan was very disappointed that Fiona Doyle wasn't in the number that giggled their way up the sandhills in the moonlight. He had decided that Caroline and

Hilary could come – thereby making it respectable – and he was very annoyed with Gerry for putting it out of bounds to *his* sister.

'It's not as if there was going to be all that messing like we had in the cave,' he said to Gerry.

'I know, but she's just not going to come with us, not at night. Not in the sandhills.'

'You sound like as if you're talking about a nun, not about Fiona,' James Nolan grumbled.

Gerry gave him a smile that took all the harm out of it. 'Listen, I know what you mean, but Fiona *lives* here, you know. It's not just a holiday night out like it is for your sister, and for Hilary. If you live in a place, it's different. There's places in Dublin you wouldn't want Caroline to go, even though there might be nothing wrong with them in themselves.'

Nolan was impressed.

They had a wind-up gramophone and they had walked so far that nobody, not even the seagulls, could hear it.

They lit the primus and cooked the supper; and David had his arm round Caroline for a while, and Chrissie was snuggling up to Gerry Doyle – but he had to disengage himself a lot to open cans or to see to the stove and turn the sausages. Nolan found himself with Kath, who had improved a lot since last winter, he thought. Nobody paired off and disappeared, but as the light from the primus flickered and died and people didn't bother to wind up the gramophone it became obvious that it had all worked out nice and neatly.

It was Gerry Doyle not Chrissie who decided when the party was over, and with a little laugh managed to get them all on their feet again, blouses being hastily rearranged and a few little giggles here and there. They walked back along the beach which was silvery and magic, stopped chattering when they reached the foot of the steps and then whispered and giggled their way home.

They weren't drunk this time, Kath and Chrissie giggled, but more experienced. Hilary and Caroline raced along the beach in the moonlight, putting their fingers to their lips and giggling. Hilary had been heavily romanced by one of the Dillon boys who had buck teeth but wasn't bad.

James and David walked at a more leisurely pace, James telling David he had put his tongue in Kath's mouth and it had been *horrible*. It was all full of spit. There *must* be some other way of doing it. David nodded with interest and said there must; he didn't reveal that Caroline Nolan's mouth had not been full of spit at all, but had been very nice indeed.

Caroline and Hilary were lying on the cliff top when Gerry passed by the next day.

'You didn't get caught?'

'Not a bit of it. Mummy takes so many sleeping pills she wouldn't know if we had had the picnic in the garden,' Caroline said.

'So does my mother, and pills to keep her awake and pills to calm her down.'

'Like Smarties,' Caroline giggled.

'It was a nice night,' Hilary said.

'Yeah, could have been better though.' Gerry seemed to be looking directly at Caroline.

'Yes. Well,' she said, flustered.

'I came to take your pictures for my wall,' he said,

'Oh we've lots of pictures already, nearly an album,' Caroline said.

'No, I don't mean the ones you bought, these are for me, as souvenirs of the most gorgeous girls to come to Castlebay. Ever.'

They protested. They hadn't the right clothes, no make-up, nothing. He soothed them and they agreed. Hilary first, joking at first, making faces, then posing in silly ways then smiling, then looking straight at the camera. 'You must have a hundred there,' she said.

'At least. Now Caroline.'

There was less joking this time. Caroline seemed to relax immediately. 'I feel very foolish,' she said once. 'This isn't the kind of thing I do.'

'You're not doing anything,' Gerry said. 'You're just being yourself, you're fine. I think you look lovely through this, very nice indeed.'

She basked in his approval and smiled and leaned towards the camera. Without even realizing that she was doing it she ran her tongue across her lower lip and opened her eyes wider. It seemed quite natural to look at the camera as if hypnotized while Gerry clicked and clicked and talked on naturally too. He spoke about her skin and how it was very soft and tanned and he hoped that somehow by light and shade this would show up on a black and white film. She didn't feel embarrassed at these compliments in front of Hilary, and Hilary didn't giggle or feel embarrassed either. In fact she just wished she had put more into the whole thing the way Caroline was doing, then Gerry Doyle might have said something nice about her skin and her hair too.

He put his camera away.

'That's what I love, taking pictures of beautiful women. That's what I'd love to do all day, not sweating couples at the dance and hopeless family groups on the beach.' His voice sounded bitter. That was unusual for Gerry Doyle who was always so carefree.

'Why don't you do that then? You always seem to do what you want.' Caroline's eyes met his and she was saying more than the actual words.

'I do usually,' he grinned.

It seemed to Angela that more people than ever asked her about Sean that summer. People who had never asked about him before. Mother Immaculata wondered was he going to Rome for the Holy Year, so many fathers from all over the world were going to go to the Holy City. Angela thought he couldn't be spared from the mission fields. Young Mrs Dillon from the hotel told her excitedly that there were two guests who were actually going to Japan in September. Maybe they could take something to Father Sean for her, or go to see him. Angela said that by ill chance she thought September was the very month he had said he would be away touring the Philippines.

Sometimes she surprised herself with the way she could talk about vocations and missions, when she knew all that she did. What was the Lord thinking of all those years ago when he hovered over O'Hara's cottage and picked Sean? Didn't God *know* what was going to happen in the future? Why did He let Himself be mocked and bring such unhappiness on everyone? She was leaning the bicycle up against the wall of O'Brien's when she realized with a sudden shock that *everyone* had not been made unhappy, in fact very few people had. There was a possibility that only she was unhappy about it all. Her brother was totally content, learning as he said for the first time the meaning of true content. Her sisters Geraldine and Maire were quite content about it too. They sent him letters at Christmas and on his birthday and their children added bits in round unformed writing. And back up in the O'Hara house her mother who was sitting out in a chair watching the people walk up and down to the golf course, saluting and smiling and nodding at everyone who passed, she was happy too. Secure in the knowledge that she had a son a priest, interceding for her directly to God, making ready her place in heaven.

Angela didn't know whether to be pleased or outraged that she was the only one who suffered over Sean's predicament. She should be pleased, she supposed, that it meant that the sum of human misery was less. But the sheer *unfairness* of it all seemed huge when you began to think of it like that. Mouth set hard she marched in, and saw young Clare working away. Her face wasn't tanned golden like the girls who sat on the wall up in Cliff Road. She didn't wear a bright pink blouse that would have given her life and definition. Instead she looked shabby and wan, in a dress with faded yellow and pink flowers that must have been Chrissie's. She was furrowed with concentration, getting somebody change.

'I'm quite quick at change usually,' Angela heard her telling the woman. 'But when the shop is crowded and we are all at the drawer of money together it's easy to get flustered, that's why I'm being a bit slow.'

The woman smiled at the earnest child who didn't even have time to see Angela at the other side of the shop. Mrs O'Brien asked about Angela's mother, whether the weather was good for her bones, if there was any word of Geraldine or Maire coming home this summer, and how soon would his Reverence be back – wasn't it a pity he hadn't been able to come this year, he could have gone to Rome for the Holy Year. The Dillons were going to go there in October when the season was well over. Imagine going to Rome and being able to see the Holy Father. There had been talk of making a collection to send Father O'Dwyer, but nothing had come of it, the idea had come too late and everyone was working so hard now there'd be little time for meeting about it. Angela responded with a series of automatic grunts and replies. Often she felt that if you had been born dumb and never known the gift of speech you could converse quite happily with most of Castlebay. All you had to do was to listen and nod and smile and shake your head and make a sound. She knew she was right when she was packing her shopping in the basket of her bicycle and she overheard Mrs O'Brien saying to Miss O'Flaherty that Angela O'Hara was a very nice girl and it was no wonder the children were all mad about her. Angela smiled with pleasure at this and was only slightly taken down when Miss O'Flaherty's complaining tone which saw very little right with the world said that was all very fine but when was Angela O'Hara going to get a husband for herself.

That was indeed the question, Angela said to herself wryly. Suppose, just suppose she did herself up and went to the dance and found a nice fellow here for the summer holidays, he'd live in Dublin or Cork or Limerick, or Dagenham like the fellow she met three years ago did. What then? There was no point in thinking about it. If she had stayed with her mother this long she was going to have to stay the distance. There was a time five years ago when she might have left, but she couldn't leave now. She couldn't trust her brother not to blow the whole thing apart. Miss O'Flaherty, who was in a poor position to throw stones, would have to wait a long time before she saw Angela O'Hara getting a husband for herself.

Weeks later she met Dr Power. He slowed down his car to drive beside her along the golf-course road.

'I was thinking of dropping in to have a look at your mother.'

'Do that but for God's sake let me get in five minutes before you and put a clean blouse on her otherwise she'll be complaining all night that you saw her shabby.'

'I have to go up and see someone in the club first. I'll call on my way back.'

Wouldn't *he* be a lovely person to be married to, Angela thought. Old as the hills of course, but so calm and kind. That fusspot towny wife of his was very lucky; Angela wondered did she know how lucky she was or did she sit there restlessly examining her rings and her lightly painted nails and wish for a life of more sophistication. Was she grateful for that bright son of hers, did she love the big white house that looked straight out to sea on two sides and was she pleased every morning when she woke up to hear Nellie cleaning out the fires and making the breakfast? Nice laughing Nellie Burke who had wanted to be a film star when they were at school. Dr Power wasn't a saint exactly. Sometimes he was bad-tempered and impatient with people, But he was very kind and Mr Murphy in the chemist said that you'd travel far to find such a good doctor. If he was above in Dublin with a brass plate on the door of somewhere in Fitzwilliam Square he would be called a consultant physician and people would pay him a fortune. Angela hoped that Mrs Molly Power was never given this piece of information, for deep down Paddy Power was like herself, he wouldn't leave. He had been born on a big farm outside Castlebay and it had been his life since he could remember. He wasn't going to any square for any plaque on his door or any fees in his bank account.

She smartened her mother up, giving her a quick wash and a dusting of talcum powder. A clean slip in case Dr Power decided to feel her poor knee joints, and clean stockings of course.

She looked well when she was smartened up, Angela thought, the fine handsome face of Father Sean O'Hara got its good cheek-bones from the mother's side, and her hair was curly and soft. Everyone looked a bit better when they were smartened up, Angela said to herself firmly, and changed her own dress and put on a little lipstick.

'Now we're like two tarts on a night out,' she said to her mother.

Mrs O'Hara looked round the room nervously in case anyone might have heard. 'You say terribly stupid things sometimes, I'm sure people get the wrong idea of you.'

'I bet they do, mother dear,' Angela said, as the doctor arrived.

It had been some visitor who played too much golf, no exercise at all, at home fifty weeks of the year, and then thirty-six holes of golf over a hilly course here, five days in succession. No wonder he had collapsed. There should be Danger notices on the golf course as well as on the beach.

'Will he be all right?' Angela asked.

'Oh, the worst he has to recover from is all the abuse from me. He'll be fine. I might have done him a good turn even, warned him about his way of life. He may live to a hundred and thank me every day. Enough about him, how are you, Mrs O'Hara?'

Angela watched him as he felt the swollen joints of her mother's legs. And then he took the twisted lumpy hands in his own.

'It hasn't got much worse to the outside eye,' he said cheerfully, 'but I know that's not much help inside where it's all aches and pains.' He made it easy for them to complain a bit; Dr Power's patients didn't have to bite back their fears and their telling the tale of their illness. He had all the time in the world.

She walked him back to the car.

'Mind you, I think you put on a clean blouse and a clean face for me yourself,' he said, teasing her. 'Did you want to consult me too?'

'No, I'm fine,' she laughed.

'If you were fine you'd sleep at night,' he said.

'I nearly do now. I only take half one, not a whole tablet like I did in the beginning.'

'Is it any better whatever it is that's worrying you?' He was on one side of his car. She leaned over with her elbows on the roof of the car.

'It is a bit better, I suppose. It hasn't gone away but I've got used to it.'

'It's not any kind of sickness or health worry. You needn't tell me: I could tell you the name of a very nice doctor, someone strange to you?'

'No. It's not that, thank you all the same.'

'And if it's a man, we're not worth it. Not one of us is worth a woman staying awake one hour over us.'

'Stop fishing.' She laughed. 'You're fishing for information, *and* for compliments, half the town is sleepless over you Dr Power. I was only thinking that this evening in the house there, wasn't it an awful pity I wasn't around ten years earlier and I might have caught you.'

'Oh, you'd have had to be around long before that, I'm an old dog. A dull old dog.'

He got into the car and wound down the window. 'If you find a fellow you want to go off with, go now. Do you hear me, don't be thinking you have to grow old in that house there. I'll sort your mother out, I'll see she gets looked after. You live your life.'

'No, it's not that, honestly.' She smiled at him affectionately.

'Or a nun or anything,' he said suddenly.

'Oh it's *definitely* not that.' She pealed with laughter.

'No, well I suppose one in the family's enough,' he said and he was gone.

One was more than enough, Angela thought as she went back into the house.

Gerry Doyle had taken two smashing photographs during the summer. One was of David and Caroline playing with a beach ball and the big waves rolling in behind them. David thought it looked great, like an advertisement for Come to Sunny Somewhere, like you saw for English seaside resorts. The other picture was of Nolan sitting eating an ice-cream on the wall outside O'Brien's shop. He was surrounded by girls: Hilary was sitting on one side, and Gerry's own sister Fiona on the other, and at his feet sat Chrissie O'Brien and her two henchwomen Kath and Peggy. He looked like a sultan, tanned and powerful and surrounded by women, all he needed was the headgear. These pictures did Nolan and Power a great deal of good at school. In fact David began to wonder if half the pupils and their parents might turn up there next summer. The Seal Cave had become a legend for night adventures, the sand dunes for even more excitement, Brigid's Cave where you shouted a question and the echo answered. The tennis in the hotel and up on high stools at the bar afterwards for a lemonade, the lessons up at the golf club and the junior tournaments. Not only did they have the stories, they had the proof in these photographs. David kept the picture of Caroline under a piece of paper in the back of his atlas. It was awkward being in love with your friend's sister because you couldn't talk to him about it freely. You couldn't say that you had kissed her at the pictures and she hadn't asked you to stop. He couldn't tell Nolan that he had kissed Caroline in the sea and in the Echo Cave. He did tell Nolan that Caroline was going to write to him at school and call herself Charles, but Nolan was only mildly interested. Fiona Doyle, Gerry's sister, was going to write to Nolan calling herself Fred and Hilary was going to sign herself Henry. If Chrissie O'Brien could write she would probably have written too and signed herself Christopher, but it was deeply suspected however, that Chrissie was illiterate and so the question didn't arise. David Power and James Nolan decided that since she had Gerry Doyle right there in Castlebay she would be too occupied even to consider writing to people in boarding school. Gerry Doyle seemed to win all the girls without ever making the slightest effort.

They didn't know that Chrissie was growing more sure every day that Gerry Doyle didn't fancy her as much as he had at one time. She discussed it at length with Kath and Peggy, but they reached no conclusion. She had gone as far as she could go without going the whole way, or without even doing things that would embarrass them seriously in the broad daylight when they remembered it. What else were you supposed to do? Her spots had gone, her hair had got blonder, and, thanks to the pipe cleaners, was much curlier. She had a big bust and a tight red belt around her waist. She never plagued Gerry or bothered him or asked him to go steady. And still he seemed to have gone off her. It was a mystery. Kath and Peggy agreed, all fellows were a mystery.

'We must take up photography seriously, it seems to make you very popular,' Nolan suggested to David one day.

'I've a feeling it's more than that,' David said. He liked Gerry but he wished that Caroline didn't think he was so great. It was irritating to be in the middle of saying something to her and then to see her face light up and her hand go up waving. He knew that could only mean Gerry Doyle had been spotted again. And Gerry would just wave back with a friendly smile, he never came panting up eagerly like Bones did, shaking with enthusiasm and pleasure to be noticed. Less like Bones, more like Gerry Doyle, that seemed to be the motto as far as success with women was concerned.

Success at school was easier. David came first in the class at the Christmas tests and Nolan came second. Nolan hated being second and the following Easter it was Nolan first and Power second. They made a pact not to work hard during the summer term and to spend all the time getting really good at tennis. Tennis was about the only game that Gerry Doyle didn't play and excel at. And that's because it was the only one he hadn't tried.

Chrissie said she wanted to leave school and learn something useful. Like what, they had asked her. She shrugged, anything, anything except boring school lessons. Nobody knew how time was wasted up in that convent she assured them, the nuns had no control and the children just sat there doing nothing all day. It was pointed out that Clare seemed to get on all right, but Chrissie said that proved nothing, Clare was distinctly odd, she had no friends, she was driven to study her books out of sheer despair that the rest of her life was so awful. This line of argument did not go down as well as Chrissie had hoped, there was no question of her leaving school at fourteen she was told, she would stay on another year and mind her manners too. Anyway it was wrong to say Clare hadn't a friend, hadn't she Josie Dillon?

Miss O'Hara had been very pleased with Clare's work over the months, she said that by any standards she would have to win the scholarship. She'd nearly get it this year while she was eleven, so next year she should have no problems at all.

'Sometimes I feel guilty teaching you, Clare,' Miss O'Hara had said one evening. 'You are able to read on your own now, and you actually enjoy it, all I'm really doing is sitting here praising you.'

'You won't stop?' Clare was terrified.

'No, of course not, I just meant that people like Josie Dillon or the young Murphy girl might benefit more, at least they might leave school knowing how to read. That would be nice for them.'

'Josie *can* read,' Clare said. 'Of course she can.'

'But she doesn't, does she? I can't ask her to read aloud from the history book in class or the English book, she can't take any part in the plays we read aloud or we'd be all day and all night in the classroom. You know that.'

'She's not very interested, that's all.'

'What *is* she interested in? Her sisters were all right you know, not genius standard but reasonable. Josie'll never get a chance to go away to school like they did, it just won't be worth it.'

'Yes, she knows that.'

'Is it settled? I was only guessing. Does she mind?'

'No, I think she's quite glad, you know she doesn't really want to leave home, she's nervous, she doesn't want things to change.'

'You should give her a hand if you're a friend of hers, why don't you help her to get on a bit? And it would be good practice for you too.'

'Practice for what?'

'Practice for being a teacher. Hey, have you forgotten that's what all this is about? We're making a teacher out of you, Clare O'Brien.'

'Oh yes, yes of course.'

She hadn't realized that this is what Miss O'Hara saw as the end of the road. Being a teacher in a convent, either here in Castlebay and cycling home every afternoon, or somewhere else somewhere like this. She didn't know that Clare wanted to see the world, she wanted to be an ambassador or the head of a big company or an interpreter, not just a teacher. But of course it would be very tactless to say anything like that. It would be saying that Miss O'Hara hadn't done well enough for herself.

'So? Are you going to give her a bit of help? Not doing it *for* her, you know, explaining it a bit.'

'She'd wonder what was the point?'

'Well if she likes staying here, why not tell her that she should work hard enough to get herself into some kind of commercial college, then she could learn book keeping and typing and shorthand and she could work in the office of the hotel when that old dragon of a grandmother of hers dies and lets any of them into the office.'

Clare was never so happy as when she was allowed in on grown-up viciousness like this. It made her feel very important. 'I'll see what I can do,' she said.

'It's better coming from you,' Miss O'Hara said. 'Most people think that any advice given by a teacher is bound to work out to their doom in the end.'

Josie had her twelfth birthday when all her sisters and brothers were away at school. Her mother, who was always called Young Mrs Dillon, said that they should put off the celebrations until the rest of the family came home on their holidays. Surprisingly Josie didn't agree, that's what had been said when she was ten and when she was eleven she said, it was not happening this year. This year she would like to invite Clare O'Brien to tea and then for them both to go to the pictures.

The pictures! At night, and during the week. It was unheard of.

Clare O'Brien said that her mother said it would be all right if Josie's mother said it was all right. Young Mrs Dillon looked at the large pasty face of her youngest daughter and was moved. It would be all right, she said. At least from what she could see the young Clare wasn't as much of a tinker as her sister Chrissie was, and perhaps it was good that poor Josie should have some friend even if it was a child from a huckster's shop.

While they were waiting for the picture to start Clare told Josie that she was so lucky to have a bedroom of her own and that was something Clare would like almost more than anything in the world.

'It's all right for you,' Josie said. 'You *like* studying.'

'I don't really *like* it, nobody could like learning things off by heart and nobody could like long division and fractions and problems. I just do them so that I'll get what I want afterwards.'

'What do you want?' Josie looked at her with a dull face.

Clare wondered whether to risk it. 'Well, I sort of hoped that since we don't have any money or anything, not for secondary school, I wondered if I worked hard maybe they'd take me on free like, to encourage other people to work hard.'

'Who would?'

'Some secondary school.'

'I don't see why not, they should be glad to have hard-working people like you instead of lazy people who pay.'

Clare was heartened. 'So that's why I do it, you should too.'

'But we have money to send me to a school, there's no point. I don't want to go to one.'

'What *do* you want to do?'

'Stay here.'

'In the hotel?'

'Of course, where else would I go?'

'But you'd better learn to do something Josie, otherwise you'll be making beds and serving on tables there. The boys will all serve the time as hoteliers, won't they?'

'I suppose so.' Josie had never thought about it.

'And Rose and Emily, they'll do something I bet like a hotel management course or something.'

'Yes, well they might.'

'So to make sure they don't push you out of it, *you* should do something.'

'What could I do, Clare?' Josie looked at her pathetically.

Clare didn't want to come up with a solution too quickly. 'You could get trained for something they haven't done, so that you'd always be needed.'

'Like what?'

'Well suppose you did a commercial course, would you have anyone to stay with in the town so that you could live with them and come back home at weekends?' She knew that the Dillons had at least three sets of cousins in the town.

Josie remembered that slowly too. Yes, it was possible. 'But I'd be all on my own there.'

'Isn't it attached to the convent, the secondary school?'

It turned out that it was, and after all if Clare's plans went right she would be in the secondary school herself. They could barely concentrate on the film when it came on, real-life plans were more exciting.

'They'd only laugh at me. I'm no good at spelling and everything, I'd never learn all that stuff.'

'I could give you a hand if you like.'

'Why would you do that?' Josie was almost ungracious in her disbelief.

'Because you're my friend,' said Clare awkwardly, and Josie smiled from ear to ear.

It began then: the working in Dillon's Hotel rather than at home. It was much easier, and nobody seemed to mind. Clare wasn't one to be up to any devilment, not like Chrissie. If you passed the hotel you could even see the two of them working at an upper window with their books out. Clare helped her with the spellings first and Josie thought that it was a marvellous coincidence that Miss O'Hara announced a spelling bee at the very same time. The handwriting became neater, the exercise books were clean and orderly, and Josie even stooped less and seemed more alert.

She once asked a question in class and Mother Brendan had nearly fainted. Clare frowned across at Josie, they had agreed the improvement must be gradual, and that she mustn't look so smart that they would decide to send her off to her boarding school and spoil everything.

The nuns had a rule that they never walked anywhere outside the convent alone, so it was common practice for a nun to ask a lay teacher or an older girl to accompany her to the post office, to Miss O'Flaherty's stationery shop or whatever errand it was. So Angela was not surprised when Mother Immaculata asked if she would accompany her down the town.

Together they walked out the convent gates and down the hill. It was never easy to find idle chat for Mother Immaculata at the best of times, and this was not the best of times for Angela. She had slept very badly despite the half pill taken with warm milk. She had a letter from Emer in Dublin with the great news for Emer that the engagement ring was being bought on the following Saturday. She wanted to know if Angela would come to Dublin and be her bridesmaid. Angela's mother had been very very stiff this morning and dressing her had been like bending painful wood to pull on stockings and to twist aching arms into garments. The children's voices had been shrill all morning, a child had been sick during religious instruction in First Year and despite open windows and Dettol the smell seemed to permeate the school. Now when she had been hoping for a cigarette and a look at the paper she had to waltz this ridiculous nun down town to buy a postcard or whatever it was she wanted.

'Why don't they allow you out on your own, Mother? I'm delighted to accompany you of course, but I've often wondered.'

'It's part of our Rule,' Immaculata said smugly. Angela felt like punching her in the face.

'Are they afraid you'll make a run for it?' she asked.

'*Hardly*, Miss O'Hara.'

'Well there must be some reason but I suppose we'll never know.'

'We rarely question the Rule.'

'No, I suppose you don't, that's where you have my wholehearted admiration. I'd question it from morning to night.'

The nun gave a tinny little laugh. 'Oh, I'm sure you would, Miss O'Hara.'

Angela wondered again how old she was – possibly only ten years older than herself. This white-faced, superior woman was quite likely to be below forty. Wasn't it extraordinary. The children probably thought she was ninety, but on the other hand the children thought every teacher was ninety, so that was no guideline.

'I wanted to talk to you actually – that's why I seized this opportunity.'

'Oh yes?' Angela was wary. What was so urgent it couldn't be discussed within the confines of school? Could Immaculata possibly have heard Angela talking about the stink of the school being quite bad enough without having the children puking all over the place?

'It's about your brother, Father O'Hara.'

Hot bile in her throat and a feeling like a hen's wing of feathers in her chest.

'Oh yes?' She said it again, willing her face to look normal, reminding herself that this stupid, mannered nun paused for effect after every single phrase she uttered. There was nothing sinister in the way she waited.

'There's a sort of mystery, you see,' Mother Immaculata said.

'Mystery, Mother?' Angela played the game by the rules: the more quickly she spoke the quicker would be the response.

'Yes. I was wondering is he . . . well is he all right, you know? If everything is all right.'

'Well I sincerely hope so. It was when I last heard. How do you mean?' Angela could hear her own voice speaking briskly and marvelled at it. How great of it to come out with just the right responses when her brain had frozen solid and seemed to be unable to control it.

'You see there's this sister in our Community, she is not in this house but she was staying with us last year. You may not have met her – she was hardly ever in the school, she was mainly in the nuns' quarters. It was more or less a holiday that brought her to us.'

Angela kept a bright interested face in the monotone and swallowed the cry urging the nun to get on with it.

'And Sister has a brother who is in a seminary and he is about to go to their foundation house, and he hopes to go to the foreign missions, and you see this is why Sister came to me.'

She paused. The smile from Miss O'Hara was as polite as that of any child who thought that favours were to be bought by courtesy.

'And Sister is in this predicament, because alas her family, far from being delighted that a second child had been called by God are standing in this boy's way. They say they want to know what kind of life it is out there and can they talk to any of the priests who have come back from the missions so that they can know what their son will be doing in his new life.' Mother Immaculata paused to tinkle an unsatisfactory little laugh. 'As if any of us could know what our lives in Religion were going to be like.'

Angela swallowed and nodded.

'So I told Sister about our Father O'Hara here from Castlebay, and I gave her the address. And Sister got this very strange letter back from him. Very strange.'

'She was writing so that he could tell her parents about the daily life out there, was that it?' Surprisingly strong and unfussed.

'Yes indeed, and Sister says that *her* letter was very clear, which I am sure it was, because she does express herself very well. Of course it's not easy to explain to an ordained priest that your family is not totally committed to the vocation of your brother, but I told Sister that she could write in freedom on that score. I told her that although I wasn't here at the time, I felt that Father O'Hara's own path to the ordination was not entirely spread with roses, that he had his own difficulties.' She smiled at Angela.

Bitch, Angela thought with a ferocity that frightened her, she told this blithering Sister all about drunken Dinny O'Hara and his outbursts.

'No indeed,' said the voice of Angela O'Hara, 'far from being spread with roses I can tell you.'

'Anyway, Sister had this very strange letter.'

'He couldn't help her?'

'Not that exactly, he *did* give a very detailed account of the daily life, and how they had to regroup after the expulsion from China, and he wrote about Christianity in Formosa and in Macao and the Philippines, and of how they hope local people will train as priests and help in all this work.'

'So?'

'But it was strange, two things were strange, he said nothing at all about Japan, where he is himself, he said nothing of the work that the Foundation does there, and he also said . . . I think these were his very words, "I feel sure my sister will have told the community of some of my own problems here, so I am hardly the man to write to your parents on your brother's behalf". That was more or less it. I think those were his exact words.'

Oh, Angela thought, we can be sure those were his exact words. Immaculata, you must have them by heart now and the rest of the letter, but there's no mileage in quoting the bits that don't sound strange, that don't sound as if there might be the trace of scandal or trouble in them. No no, don't learn by heart and remember his words where he was helpful to this garrulous fool of a nun and her indecisive brother. Just the bit that might yield some gossip.

'Well well, what could he mean?'

'That's what we wondered, Miss O'Hara?'

'Oh, does Sister's family want him to explain himself more?' She was just within the bounds of manners but only just.

'Of course not, it's just that it's worrying.'

'What is?'

'The problems he has, his own problems, that he told you about that he expected you had told the community about. All that. And why he is hardly the man to help in this matter.'

'Because he's such a rotten letter writer.' Angela was amazed that Mother Immaculata didn't see it too.

'But the rest of his letter was very clear.'

'That's it, he can be marvellous describing the climate and the soil, I told him we should have him in the geography class. But he's useless about describing what he feels, and thinks. I think it's not just him, really. I believe that all men are hopeless at telling you what you want to know. My mother and I are always criticizing him for not giving us his feelings about it all . . .'

'But there must be more to it.'

'Exactly, Mother, that's what I always say, and what Mam says. There *must* be more to it. What's it like when he finishes a day in Tokyo, does he walk home through the crowded streets and look at the people's faces and think that he and the other fathers made progress today, that the Lord's word was spread among the people? Do the young Japanese children understand what it was like in Bethlehem, it's hard enough for us but what about them?' Angela was burning with indignation at this brother of hers who couldn't describe the everyday business of being a missionary to everyone's satisfaction.

In the end Immaculata gave up. They were at the top of Church Street.

'Where did you want to go?' Angela asked innocently.

'Nowhere.' Immaculata's mouth snapped like a mousetrap. 'I just wanted to talk to you about all this.'

Angela was sunny-tempered about it. 'Well never mind Mother, I wanted to get some cigs anyway so you can accompany me into a shop for them. I'd go down to the end of the street to O'Brien's to give them the turn, but we might be late for class.'

She smiled like an angel, wrapped the scarf round her neck flamboyantly and went into a shop which was half a pub and stank of stout, so that Immaculata had to hover in a fury at the door.

She wrote to him that night as she had never been able to write before. She said that he had broken the agreement and broken it shabbily. How else might he have done this in ways that she didn't know? Must she live a tormented life wondering where would be the next weak link, the next confession of something wrong, something irregular? She said that she would prefer that he came home and asked Father O'Dwyer to allow him to announce it from the altar rails, rather than have any more of this. They had been through it a dozen times by letter and reluctantly he had agreed; now he was going behind their backs and allowing the worst, the most powerful thing that a place like Castlebay could ever know to run riot. Rumour, speculation, suspicion. She must have his word that this would happen no more. Why couldn't he have ended his letter to the mad nun where any normal person would have ended it? What was the need for this confused breast-beating, and to a community of nuns of all people on the face of the earth?

She added that she *knew* it must be hard, she did realize that. She knew he was trying to keep faith with people and she had managed to stop silver paper and sales of work for him, saying that the money was coming in different ways from the mother house. She really and truly *did* know that he was so transparently honest and generous that he hated hypocrisy, but surely he must know how everyone's hearts would crack in two if any of this were known. Since he must remember his home town it was only fair that he should keep faith with it and not hurt the people he claimed to love so much.

She put extra stamps on it, and for the first time she left out the word 'Father' on the envelope. She laughed at her silliness when she was buying the stamp from Mrs Conway.

'Heavens above, I forgot to put Father. Still I'll leave it rather than write it in a different ink. It's so hard to remember when it's your own brother.'

It was the right line to take. Mrs Conway laughed too, and said imagine what it must be like being the Pope's sister, you'd probably forget to call him your Holiness as well. Mrs Conway wondered when he'd be home and Angela said that she hoped soon.

She got a letter from him three weeks later. He had read what she said but none of it was important now. He had wonderful news. He had sent all the details of his situation to Rome, and he and Shuya were going to go to Rome themselves, together with Denis and little Laki, who was such a beautiful girl and so like her mother. They were all going to Rome.

He was going to plead his case; there was every belief that he would be heard favourably, that he would be released from his vows, that he would be laicized. Then everything would be perfect. He could come home to Castlebay and bring his family.

The mills of Rome grind slowly. Another summer came and went and Angela learned to sleep at night without the tablets. Sometimes during that summer she took herself with a book out far to the rocks, but she rarely read. She stared at the sea.

At the beginning of term Fiona Doyle shyly presented her with an envelope: it was a picture of Angela, sitting on a rock looking at the sea. Taken completely unawares.

'Gerry's very pleased with it, he says it's a bit artistic,' Fiona said.

'Tell him it's very artistic and I'm very grateful, I'll put it on my wall at home,' Angela said. She looked at it again; it looked like a picture to illustrate The Lonely or The Mad or The Outcast.

That was the summer when Father O'Dwyer went out on a sick call one night and unfortunately passed a lot of parked cars on the Far Cliff Road over the other side of town. He was surprised to notice that there seemed to be people in all of them. Precisely two people, one male and one female. Father O'Dwyer was horrified by what he saw, and he wished he could think it had only been the trippers, the people from big towns whose morals might already have been in danger, but there was ample evidence to convince him that some of his own flock might have been involved.

At the beginning of September when the visitors had gone home he preached his horror and warnings and his threats about what would happen if any of this was noticed in winter time. Parents and guardians were urged to be for ever vigilant, young people were teetering on the edge of an abyss, and alas the world we lived in had lowered its standards and debased its values. Next year there might be a radical change in the leisure pursuits, the whole ethos of the Dance would have to be looked at again. Father O'Dwyer was purple in the face about it for three weeks and his housekeeper the Sergeant McCormack went round with her mouth in a thin line of disapproval that His Reverence should have been vexed so severely.

That was the summer when Josie Dillon and Clare O'Brien learned to play tennis at the hotel. They used to go to the courts early in the morning when Mrs Power and Mrs Nolan were having lessons; they would act as ball boys, and then afterwards because of their help and because Josie was a daughter of the house they got a short lesson as well. Chrissie was disgusted with this, especially since she and Kath and Peggy had been asked formally by Young Mrs Dillon not to come into the bar again. Barred from the hotel at the age of fourteen. It was so unfair, and there was goody goody Clare who was only eleven and the awful white slug Josie playing tennis as if they were somebodies. Clare had a pair of white shorts that Miss O'Hara had found at home, and she unearthed an old pair of Ned's games shoes which she whitened up with Blanco every night. Josie had got her an old racquet from the hotel, and with her white school blouse she was the equal of any of them. Angela saw her one morning as she ran earnestly up to the net to return a difficult shot and she paused, pleased that she had bought the child a pair of shorts in the Misses Duffy's shop. Angela had washed them once or twice and turned up the hem on the

587

legs in order that Clare wouldn't think they were new. It was well worth it to see the child looking so confident, and was it her imagination or had Josie Dillon lost some weight? Certainly she was able to move around the court better than Angela would have expected.

That was the summer when David Power seemed very disconsolate. Angela had met him once or twice on his own, mooching around hands in pockets. Nolan was with Fiona Doyle morning noon and night, and Nolan's sister? Oh she seemed to have developed an interest in photography. Ha Ha. David laughed bitterly at the poor joke and the poorer situation. Maybe they could all have a double wedding, you saw that sometimes, didn't you, brother and sister marrying sister and brother. Angela said you didn't see it all that much actually; and that the Doyles were like summer lightning; they were different to everyone else. They weren't *real* like everyone else, they didn't get involved in anything, they just floated around on the outside. David didn't understand, the Doyles had got pretty involved with the Nolans as far as he could see. No, Angela insisted, Fiona just goes her way and James follows along carrying the milk can, carrying the shopping, paying for the bumpers rides or whatever. Gerry goes around the beach with the camera, and Caroline trots behind him. Their father Johnny Doyle was the same years ago, everyone was fascinated with him, he was like a gypsy. David said he didn't think Angela understood, Angela said she was willing to have a bet with him, but it was unfair to take money off minors.

That was the summer Tommy and Ned O'Brien stopped sending home money from England. Mrs Conway noticed of course, almost before Agnes and Tom O'Brien did.

'Not helping out are they nowadays?' she asked with a show of great concern.

'Oh, we told them to keep that, they had to set themselves up a bit better over there, give themselves a bit of comfort, a start you know,' said Agnes O'Brien with a big smile that didn't manage to cover the hurt and worry.

It was also the summer when Angela got a letter from her friend Emer every week. Emer would just about forgive Angela for saying that she was too old to be a bridesmaid at the age of twenty-nine, she would overlook the insensitivity that was involved. After all didn't that make Emer a little bit old to be a bride at thirty? But what Emer would not forgive, or even countenance, was for Angela not to be at the wedding. They would be getting married next Easter; since Kevin and she were both teachers this was a very suitable time for them. The problem was that everyone seemed to be taking over the wedding on them. Emer's mother hadn't spoken to her for four weeks, her two married sisters were in and out of the house at all hours with advice that nobody wanted. Her father had said more than once in Kevin's hearing that he wasn't going to finance a great extravagant do for a third time. He had thought that all that was behind him now and since Emer wasn't exactly in the first flush of youth, he had thought it should be done quietly. Kevin's family were all religious maniacs; there were old nuns who were getting permission to leave convents for the ceremony, and war to the knife among various priestly cousins as to who was going to do the marrying. Emer said it was like a three-ring circus with a Greek tragedy going on in the wings. Angela was to miss it at her peril.

The letters were light relief compared to everything else. Angela said that she would be there, of course. Nothing would stop her. She had to force herself to remember that these were indeed all real disasters and crises for Emer; the letters were so funny and full of ridicule they hid the hurt and the humiliation. Well so did Angela's own letters, perhaps. Wry accounts of life in a one-horse town with the demon Immaculata and the horrific Mrs Conway of the post office. Not a word about what it felt like to be trapped here for ever with the shadow of a mad brother – who had left the priesthood, taken up with a Japanese woman and produced two children – hovering on the horizon.

Dunne was to be Head Boy in their last year. David and James had agreed not to compete for the honour because they had been too busy keeping up their postal romances and working for their exams. They explained this to Dunne at the beginning of term so that he wouldn't get any notions about himself. Dunne however had become very authoritarian. He said they were talking nonsense and the Community wouldn't have dreamed of appointing either Nolan or Power to any position of trust since they were both unreliable and dishonest, and were known to carry on illicit relationships with the opposite sex. Nolan said that Dunne was showing all the signs of becoming a roaring homosexual. People who got all steamed up and purple in the face over other people's relationships, illicit or licit with the opposite sex, were queers, and that was widely known. David said that he heard Dunne had been called Daisy as a child and maybe they should revive the name. Dunne waged a war on them and saw to it that their every activity was monitored, their letters scrutinized, and even if they were going for a quick cigarette they were sure to be caught and reported.

In a way it was no harm, it gave them time to study, for what else was there to do? And for Nolan it was particularly helpful because it took his mind off the faithlessness of Fiona. David was mightily pleased to hear that Caroline was suffering the same kind of deprivation at her school. She had been expecting to hear from Gerry Doyle but a similar lack of communication seemed to be occurring there also. Nolan said that Caroline had been pretty annoyed when they had been home at half term. He had been in a very poor temper indeed on his return; he had telephoned the Doyles in Castlebay and spoken to Gerry. When he had asked to speak to Fiona, he was told that she was studying. Where? Upstairs. Well could she come down-stairs? No, not during term time, she had to work. As cool as a cucumber. The rat, and not a word about Caroline either, Nolan had mentioned that she was home for half term, and Gerry Doyle had just said that was nice.

A few weeks later David got a letter signed Charles. The letter in its heavy code seemed to be saying that she was sorry the summer had been a bit complicated and she saw things more clearly now. He read it several times and the message definitely was one of reconciliation. He wrote back a short letter, saying he was too busy to get into correspondence at the moment, with the Leaving and Matric coming up, but he looked forward to seeing her next summer. A distant letter, and he signed himself David not Deirdre, just so that she'd get into trouble in her convent. She needed a little punishment for all she had done to him.

Gerry and Fiona Doyle's father was taken off to hospital in the town, and it became known that he would not come back. For a while there was a lot of talk that Mrs Doyle didn't go in to see him like you'd think she would have done. Then Dr Power let it be known that the poor woman had a kind of temporary condition, something to do with blood pressure, which meant that she found it very oppressive to go out of the house at all. Dr Power also suggested that poor Johnny Doyle was better not to be troubled with too many visitors since he found it hard to speak. Gerry drove his father's van everywhere now, and acted as an unofficial taxi service for anyone wanting to go into the town. The nurses said Gerry was an extraordinary visitor. He calmed not only his father but the three other men in the ward.

The screens were put around while Johnny Doyle hissed with what was left of his voice that Gerry mustn't expand, he must listen to nobody telling him that Castlebay was a boom town, there was a living, a small living, nothing more. It wasn't something like a dance hall or a hotel or even like an ice-cream shop that you could make bigger. There were just so many people and so many snaps of themselves they would buy. Gerry agreed, he nodded, he promised.

The old man died more peacefully because Gerry was there easing away his worries. Gerry told him that the business was doing fine, which it was, that Gerry would never expand it, which he would, and that Mam was getting much better, which she was not. Her agoraphobia was so bad now that she didn't even go to answer the door. Gerry had eased her guilt about not going to see her husband by saying that Dad was too tired to talk. He only took Fiona three times because it was too distressing.

Gerry was there when they closed his father's eyes. He didn't cry, he asked the nun was it always as peaceful as this, and the nun said no, Mr Doyle had been lucky, he had died with few worries, his son was reliable, his wife was cured and his business was in good hands. Not everyone had such peace at the end.

One of the old men in the ward asked Gerry Doyle to come and see them even though his father was gone. Gerry said he would come every week or so, but not regularly because he didn't want the men waiting on him. One of the young nurses who thought that Gerry Doyle was an extraordinarily attractive young fellow told him that he was quite right, and she congratulated him even more when another old man wanted to know if Gerry would take his picture. Gerry looked at the wasted face and the thin neck coming up out of the pyjamas and decided against it, but he explained that it was very hard to take pictures indoors with these white walls and he would wait till the weather was better. The weather became better but there were no old men left to take pictures of.

Gerry put all his efforts into his work, his mother got a bit better sometimes and at other times she got worse. He never let Fiona come home from the pictures in the dark by herself, and he helped her to do the housework, especially cleaning the windows and polishing the brass knocker on the door so that the place looked well on the outside. Since nobody much came in, the inside wasn't so important.

But if you saw Fiona Doyle with her shiny ringlets and her well-ironed dresses, or Gerry Doyle with his elfin smile and easy ways, you would never know that there was a thing wrong in that house; or that their father had died from cancer, their mother was in the grip of her nerves and that the bank manager had offered to give them a big loan to expand the business. Gerry told his mother that Dad had told him to go ahead with any plans and his mother fretted and worried about that, but since she worried about everything it didn't make any difference to him.

Fiona must have understood that his father's wishes did not include any kind of expanding, but she said nothing. She was quiet and smiled gently but said very little. That's the way Gerry thought it was best to be for a girl. Otherwise you got your name up with people and you got talked about, and people misunderstood. He didn't want any of that for Fiona.

The letter from Sean had an Italian stamp. He had been five weeks in Rome, he said, and had wanted to get settled in before he wrote. Things were progressing but very slowly. He had no idea that there would be such an endless form-filling and waiting about and answering the same questions twenty times for some underling and trying forty times to see the person one step up but not being able to. Still the process was underway. He and Shuya had got here pretty exhausted after such a long journey and he was working now as a tutor to a very ancient family, real nobility. They had a house in Ostia which was at the mouth of the river Tiber and on the sea. It was a huge villa, and Sean taught the boys for three hours a day, which gave him time to go up to the Vatican to see how things were getting on. Shuya helped in the linen room because she was a wonderful seamstress. The children loved the place, they had a little lodge of their own to live in, they were well established there. It was torturing to be so near and yet so far. Last week he had seen a group of Irish pilgrims; they had all carried Aer Lingus bags with the name of the travel agency added to it. He had been dying to talk to them, but he was keeping his word. If Angela said it was so desperately important that nobody must know until after the laicization then she must have her reasons, he had held himself back from chatting to his compatriots. Sometimes when little Denis said the sea was beautiful Sean got an urge to carry him in his arms right back to the beach at Castlebay. He was longing to hear from her, and of course letters would travel much quicker to Italy than to Japan.

They would. Angela addressed the envelope to Mr and Mrs S. O'Hara and she changed her writing so that Mrs Conway wouldn't guess. Lord Almighty, was she becoming paranoid? There *must* be other O'Haras in the world, mustn't there?

Clare said that there was a typewriter in the hotel and Josie had got a book called *Teach Yourself Typewriting*. It didn't look too hard, but the bits with your little finger were crucifying, you had to keep typing Qs and As and Zs with your little finger so that you could do it without looking. Josie was full of confidence now. She had gone on a diet too, and she had her hair cut. She had also begun the process of convincing her parents that it would be a good idea to take this course. Angela had managed to manoeuvre Immaculata into a position where the nun had thought she had dreamed up the whole idea of Josie's future career herself, so they would be able to rely on her for support. Now the only real thing was Clare's scholarship. It would be held in the Easter holidays. Angela would be in Dublin at Emer's wedding, but that didn't matter. Clare could cope on her own now. In February she had asked Mother Immaculata if she thought she should enter, and once Immaculata began to think of it as her own project all was well. Nothing had changed, Angela had noticed, in nearly twenty years. The nuns were still enthusiastic that one of their pupils might win a place, they offered extra tuition here and there, all of which Clare accepted gratefully. She surprised them all with how much she knew already.

Funny little dark horse, they said in the Community room, you wouldn't believe she was Chrissie O'Brien's sister; remarkable little face with those big dark eyes and fair hair, you didn't usually get that mixture. The nuns were kind. They made her gifts – a lace handkerchief to bring with her, numerous holy pictures all mounted on bits of satin with sequins and decorations. One old nun gave her a fountain pen which had been sent for a feast day and another gave her a bright-coloured carved pencil box. Immaculata bathed in the glory of it and Angela O'Hara watched entertained from the sidelines.

'What have they said at home?' Angela asked her.

'I haven't said. You said not to say.'

'You'd better say now, otherwise they'll think you're holding out on them.'

'Right,' said Clare, 'I'll tell them this evening.'

Agnes O'Brien was looking into the big saucepan with no pleasure. 'This thing about getting cheap meat because Chrissie works in Dwyers' is a mixed blessing,' she said. 'This is a pile of bones when all's said and done.'

'It'll make soup,' Tom O'Brien said, peering in at it.

'Yes. Again!' Agnes said. 'Still there's few enough mercies to be thankful for these days, I suppose I mustn't turn up my nose at meat got for half nothing.'

Clare took her books out of her schoolbag and covered them immediately with a paper bag. Any schoolbook left casually round that kitchen could well be covered in soup, spattered fat, dust from the range or a variety of stains.

'Something nice happened at school,' she said. She rarely spoke of school now. It had raised such scant interest. The very fact she announced it like that claimed their attention.

'What was that?' Agnes asked, transferring her glance from the big saucepan.

'Mother Immaculata and the other nuns think I should enter for the scholarship to the secondary school. In the Easter holidays.'

'Secondary school?' Tom O'Brien was astounded.

'I know Dad, I mightn't get it, there'll be people from all over going in for it. But isn't it great that the school think I should try?'

'A scholarship. That means they'd take you without paying, as a boarder and everything?' Agnes said.

'Yes, if I won it.'

'How do you win it, is it a competition?' Ben was interested.

'Sort of,' Clare said. 'Well yes, really. A lot of girls come and sit an exam, on one day, and the best one gets to go to the school.'

'For ever?' Jim wanted to know.

'Well for ever until school's finished, you know, sixteen or seventeen.'

'Would you stay at school that long?' Ben's eyes were round with interest.

'That's very good,' Agnes said slowly. 'Tom, what do you think of that, Clare going to the secondary school?'

'With the daughters of everybody,' Tom said happily.

'I haven't won it yet,' Clare said.

'Ah, but they wouldn't be putting you up for it if they didn't think you were in with a chance.' Tom O'Brien rubbed his hands delightedly. 'Mother Immaculata is a very intelligent woman, she knows what she's doing.'

Clare smiled to herself: it had all been kept from intelligent Mother Immaculata for nearly two years.

'I'll need to study very hard for the next few weeks. I'm not saying that to get out of things, you know that?' She looked from one to another.

'We know that, child, weren't we always anxious that you should be at your books?' Clare's mother really seemed to believe that she had been.

'Wait till everyone hears that,' Tom O'Brien said happily. 'There'll be very few who'll look at us crooked then.'

'Only if I get it.'

'You'll get it. Agnes, see to it that this child doesn't do one hand's turn of housework, do you hear me?'

'I was just going to tell you, don't have her out there lining shelves and running messages for you.'

They argued happily over the saucepan of mutton bones while Jim and Ben looked on.

The door opened and Chrissie arrived in her blood-spattered apron. 'God it's freezing out, and in the shop too with the door open. I nearly cut off my arm to give to Miss McCormack with the chops for the parish priest.'

'Clare's going to the secondary school,' shouted Jim.

'For years and years and it's all free,' said Ben.

'I'm *not* going,' Clare cried. 'I'm only entering a competition to go, you wouldn't say you'd won the crossword in the paper if you just did it, would you?'

But she was unheard.

'What do you think of that, your young sister has been chosen to go and enter for a scholarship in the school in the town,' Agnes said triumphantly.

'Look at that now,' said Tom O'Brien.

It was too much for Chrissie. A long hard day's work in a cold shop, home for her tea and they're all praising Clare, horrible sneaky little Clare, going behind everyone's backs.

'Will you be a boarder?' Chrissie asked.

'*If* I win it, but I mightn't have a chance, I might never get there.'

'Oh, you'll get there, you get everything you want,' Chrissie said bitterly.

'I don't, I don't!' Clare cried. 'I hardly ever do.'

'Oho no, it's Saint Clare this and Saint Clare that. Well I hope you *do* get to your boarding school, then I'd have my room to myself for a bit without Saint Clare spying on me and making my life a misery.'

'Chrissie, stop that.' Her mother looked at the angry girl with the red face in the filthy butcher's coat. 'You should be delighted that Clare's doing so well.'

'They'll think all the more of you up in Dwyers' if your sister's in secondary school,' said Tom excitedly.

'Oh they wouldn't care there if she was in the county gaol,' Chrissie scoffed.

'But I'm glad all right, I really am, a bit of peace in this house at last.' She slammed out and upstairs, so Clare's hopes of taking her homework there vanished.

'Don't mind her,' said her mother, 'she's delighted really.'

Chrissie went upstairs and threw herself on the bed. It was too much, coming today of all days, today when Gerry had come in for a half-pound of minced meat. Chrissie had joked with him like she always did, how was it that he was doing the shopping, a man in a house with two women? He had said nothing, just smiled. Then she had asked, out of politeness, out of *niceness*, how was his mother, did she still feel she couldn't leave the house? Gerry had turned on her. In a low voice that the others couldn't hear he had called her a big-mouth. He had said the word several times. Big-mouth Chrissie, can never leave well alone, never knows when to say things and when not to. Big-mouth. She had stammered, what had she said wrong, wasn't she only inquiring after his mother? But Gerry hadn't smiled. Chrissie should not use her big mouth to air other people's business in public, he had said.

Frightened, she had asked him would she see him at the pictures that night, a crowd of them usually went on a Friday evening.

'You may see me, you may not,' Gerry had said. His anger was over. He was distant now. She knew that just from a civil inquiry about his stupid old mother, whom she hadn't seen for months come to think of it, she was going to see no more of Gerry Doyle.

And now there was going to be a God Almighty fuss about Clare. Wasn't it desperate the way things never come singly. There was all that fuss about Tommy and Ned having left their digs in London, and when Mam wrote to the landlady to know why they weren't replying, the landlady wrote back this real snotty letter saying they had disappeared, owing her three weeks' rent. Dad had been very upset and nearly cried. They sent a postal order to the woman in England and their apologies.

The O'Brien boys had left their jobs: they were working with a different gang now. The landlady, who had become more friendly since the sudden and unexpected appearance of three weeks' rent, which she had said goodbye to a long time ago, told the O'Briens that the fellows their sons had joined were rough and not what they'd want. She said that everyone was paid on a Friday night in this pub so if they wrote a letter there it would reach them. And then of course there was a letter. Ned was sorry they hadn't written, but times were hard. They had changed jobs and changed where they lived; there wasn't much to spare at the moment and he hoped that Mam and Dad understood. Mam and Dad wanted no money – only please keep in touch. So the odd postcard arrived. Nobody in Castlebay liked getting postcards: it gave Mrs Conway a perfect right to comment on all your business. Agnes O'Brien sent Ned a pound note in an envelope addressed to the pub, asking him to buy proper envelopes and stamps: she didn't want the whole of Castlebay to know their business. And why was there never a word from Tommy?

Well, Tommy wasn't much for writing as they all knew but he was fine, getting on great.

Tom O'Brien wondered would the scholarship cover everything, supposing Clare did win it. Everything, Clare said firmly. She didn't know but she wasn't going to have it all debated now. Miss O'Hara had said that she should assume she was going to win and that when she won she was going to go, otherwise she would waste precious time worrying about things over which she had no control.

Dr Power said that he would drive her into the town on the day of the scholarship. He said he had to go once a month anyway so it might as well be that day. No, of course it wasn't too early. Angela had asked him this favour since the bus would have the child too late. He would pick her up in the evening, he said, and it would be a privilege. He hoped that he would have some part in bringing honours to Castlebay. When he said that Clare's parents were almost overcome, they hadn't realized that it would be an actual honour, they thought it might be just one more problem.

There were still six weeks to go. Clare came steadily to Miss O'Hara's house twice a week. Sometimes Miss O'Hara just gave her an essay title while she busied herself making her mother's meal or setting the place to rights. Then she would go over the essay, praising and correcting, discussing and debating. Clare never felt she wrote a bad essay, but she learned how to write one that would win her even more praise. She was to consider this day as an audition, her one chance. There would be no other.

She was writing an essay on the 'Rural Life versus the Urban Life' which had been one of the topics a few years ago on the scholarship paper, when Miss O'Hara gave a sudden start. Clare looked up and saw that the teacher was reading a letter. Old Mrs O'Hara looked up too, and they waited for some explanation.

'It's Emer,' Angela cried. 'She and Kevin are so sick of the whole fuss about the wedding, do you know what they're going to do? They're going to get married in Rome. They have it all arranged, they're going to get married in a side chapel in St Peter's basilica in Rome on Easter Monday. A friend of Kevin's is a priest who's doing some postgraduate work . . .' Angela was reading from the letter now ' ". . . He has said there is no problem, we've sent all the documents and we will be married in the Holy City. Now nobody can object to that, can they? Even Kevin's awful cousins are struck dumb because they can't fault us, it would be like criticizing the Pope or something. And it's too dear for anyone to come, and it's too far. And I can wear what I like not what my sisters say, and we can have a honeymoon there as well. I can't think *why* we didn't think of it sooner." ' Angela hugged herself with pleasure. 'Isn't that magnificent?' she said to the old woman and the young girl who looked at her, dumbfounded.

'But that means you can't go,' her mother said.

'It does not. I was going to Dublin, now I'll go to Rome instead.' Angela threw herself into a chair and spoke to the ceiling. 'Now I do believe in miracles,' she said, smiling up at it.

Emer couldn't believe it. 'And you'll be my bridesmaid?'

'Why not? They've seen lions eating Christians in Rome, they must have seen ageing bridesmaids as well.' Angela was phoning from Dillon's Hotel – that way Mrs Conway would have had to tune in deliberately to hear her.

'We'll have a great time, and you can be round for the honeymoon bit too, can't you? You don't have to rush off home the next day.'

'No, I'll bring my best nighties and a frilly dressing gown and I'll get into the bed with yourself and Kevin. It'll be great.'

'Oh Angela, it's the very best news in the world that you're going to be there. Imagine you coming all the way to Rome. What a friend you are. I'll never be able to thank you.'

'When I get married I'll have the ceremony in Jerusalem, then we'll put you to the test.'

Emer laughed. 'I don't think there's much chance of a romance between you and the best man, but you never know.'

'Oh you never know, Italian music and wine, it could be highly romantic.'

'Angela, isn't it *marvellous*. I feel like a young girl again.'

'So do I, truly,' Angela said.

Everyone seemed to know she was going to Rome. Dick Dillon – who had given up drink and was as bad-tempered as a weasel – called her into the hotel one day and showed her a lot of brochures. Apparently, because of the pilgrimages, the best way to go to Rome would be on an all-inclusive tour. That way she'd have a hotel booked already, and she'd be with people while she needed them. Angela was very grateful to him: she had feared the plane would be too expensive, but of course Dick Dillon was right. It turned out too that all Emer's party were going on a similar kind of arrangement.

Dick Dillon said he had been in Rome once and he had thrown coins into the fountain which meant you would come back again but he never had. He shook his head gloomily.

Angela said there was nothing stopping him going back any time he wanted to. He said that she didn't understand: now that he had given up the jar there was no point in going anywhere. Being in Italy and not being able to drink that wine? And the grappa, oh God, the grappa gave a fierce kick to the back of the throat, it was marvellous stuff. No, there would be neither rhyme nor reason going somewhere like Rome and drinking milk.

They got on to less heartbreaking subjects: Angela said she was glad that Josie was going to the commercial college next year, and hadn't she come on a lot lately? Dick Dillon agreed – she had been a terrible pudding of a poor thing but she seemed to have brightened up all right. Good for her anyway, *she* wouldn't be left on the side while the bright brothers and sisters got the pickings of the hotel; she wouldn't be left in a corner with no position, no status, just drinking her liver to bits like he was.

'But you're all right now, Dick,' said Angela a bit impatiently. 'Why can't you wrest your share back for yourself, or take control, or get in there and fight, or whatever you want to do?'

'I suppose I don't know *what* I want to do. That's the problem.' Dick Dillon was morose.

'Come to Rome with me as my escort,' she said.

'I could, I suppose, but I'd be no company and we wouldn't be able to go on anywhere they served drink,' he said, taking her seriously.

'You'd better stay where you are then, I'll send you a postcard of your fountain.'

David Power was furious that she was going to Rome.

'I was going to bribe you to go over my whole history course with me. You make it all sound so reasonable, as if they were normal people.'

'Then I must be getting it wrong, because most of them weren't.'

He was wrapped up in himself, his worries, his future.

'You'll be fine, David, you're very bright, you've worked hard, it's only nerves now after all the years. Anyway you've got weeks yet to cover the things you aren't sure of. Look at Clare O'Brien – she's really the one to pity, one shot, only one chance for a proper education. Your father's a very kind man, he's going out of his way to drive her to that scholarship next week. If she doesn't get it, that's it. And she's mad to learn.'

'I bet she's a bit fed up with you going off to Rome when she needs you.' He was still mutinous: it had never occurred to him that Miss O'Hara would be doing anything except waiting for chances to teach.

'No, oddly enough, she's very pleased for me, but then of course females are much more considerate than males, and generous, it's known.'

David smiled, his good humour restored.

'I hope she gets it.'

'I hope she gets it too. I remember this time seventeen years ago, it must have been the year you were born, I went over to the town to do the scholarship too, and I had no idea how many farmers' daughters there might be up against me. To be the brightest in Castlebay wasn't much, it was the rest of the county all around.'

'And when you got it, was it great?'

'No. Not really. My father was very drunk that day and very abusive. It had nothing to do with the scholarship. Well, not at first. Then he got upset about that and said that people were giving Dinny O'Hara's child their charity. No, the day wasn't great.' She brightened up. 'But it was great afterwards . . . How's James Nolan?'

'Languishing over Fiona Doyle – not over his revision I'm afraid.'

'And his sister? Languishing too?'

'She's got over her miseries. Much more fickle females are than males.'

'Has she transferred her attentions back to you?' Angela ignored his barb.

'There was a tentative move in that direction, but I discouraged it, until my exams were over.' He was as proud as punch. 'I'll play a bit hard to get.'

'Oh, I'm glad I'm not your age, you'd have my heart broken in bits.'

'Will you pray for me in Rome, Miss O'Hara?'

'Of course I will, Clare, in St Peter's itself on Easter Sunday, and again at the wedding on the Monday, and I'll go to Mass somewhere specially for you on the Tuesday, on the day.'

'That should work.' Clare was adding it up in her mind. 'Nobody will have that many prayers for them. I wish you were going to be here.'

'No, in a way it might be worse for you, might make you too anxious. You're probably better on your own.'

She was doubtful. 'There'll be no one to tell.'

'Yes there will, there'll be Dr Power in the car coming back; there'll be Josie, she'll be dying to know. And your mother and father. Now be sure to tell them all about it, they mightn't *sound* as interested as you hope, but in their own way they are.' Angela sought more people that Clare could talk to. It wasn't easy to find them, she would be wise to keep away from the convent: Mother Immaculata would depress her into the ground, with the Answers She Should Have Given and the Things She Ought To Have Said.

'You could always talk about it to David Power?'

'I wouldn't tell him about it, Miss O'Hara. He's a bit snobby.'

'No, he's not. His mother is, but he isn't, not at all. But suit yourself. Hold on till I get back. I'll be back on the Saturday night late, too late for you, but leave a note up in the house about how you got on, and come round after early Mass. We'll have breakfast together and you'll tell me step by step how you went in there, flags waving for Castlebay.'

Suddenly Clare threw her arms round Miss O'Hara, on the side of the road where it divided in three to go to the golf club, to the Cliff Road or down Church Street. There was nobody but a man on a bicycle and his dog passing by to see.

'You're so kind, you're the best help anyone in the world could have. I'll never be able to thank you.'

Angela was embarrassed but she hugged her back quickly and released her. 'That's all right, child, wait for the long weeks until we know, that's going to be the hard bit.'

Kevin was a lovely fellow, Angela thought. He was waiting with Emer at Kingsbridge station to meet her the night she arrived in Dublin. He ran up to take her suitcase and welcome her. He had freckles and reddish hair and he was as delighted with Emer as if she were a present that had been handed down to him from a Christmas tree.

Emer hadn't changed at all in the seven years since they had met. She had a brown corduroy pinafore dress and a white blouse; with her shoulderbag she could have been a student still. Angela touched her own face in some kind of reflex, she wondered had the years of living in wind, rain and sea spray with an invalid woman and teaching in a very narrow school taken their toll? She must look much, much older than Emer, when she was in fact over a year younger. And her clothes. They were drab and old. Though she had ironed them all and folded them with care in Castlebay now she wished she could lose the suitcase that Kevin was carrying as they swung along the platform to the bus. Emer had her arm linked and the years rolled away.

'I'll never be able to thank you for this, you know,' Emer said, looking at her with a shining face. 'It makes it all more normal, less odd if you know what I mean.'

Kevin was nodding too, eagerly: 'You're a very good friend, Angela, I can't tell you how pleased we both were, Emer danced round the room when you rang that day. It was terrific of you.'

'I couldn't wait for the post,' said Angela.

'My mother is pleased too, and Lord God nothing has pleased her since I don't know when. She remembers you coming to the house and she thinks you're much more reliable than any other friend I have.'

'Why on earth does she think I'm reliable, I'd hate to be reliable,' Angela said indignantly.

'Well you went and looked after your mother, didn't you? I mean how more reliable could another mother think one could be? You get all the points in the world for that.'

They laughed as if they had never been separated, and as if they had both known Kevin always. As they climbed on the bus and ran lightly upstairs so that they could smoke, Angela felt the first pang of envy for Emer. Wouldn't it be great to be on the verge of spending your life with this easygoing, happy man. They talked on the bus about the house they had bought, and how it needed a lot of doing up but it would be terrific in the end. They took her to the kind of a restaurant that hadn't existed when she was in Dublin. It had candles in wine bottles, and a foreign man serving them – it was like being abroad already.

Mrs Kelly was at the door waiting for them.

'Here you are at last, Angela,' she said crossly.

'What has she been up to, keeping you out till this hour? Why on earth were you not brought back here straight from the station, there were sandwiches made and all.'

'Isn't it wonderful news about the wedding! Imagine being married in Rome! Could you ever have believed it?' Angela was an expert at changing subjects and getting old women to talk about more cheerful things. And you didn't always do it in one step either.

'Well yes it is of course, but it's so far away, and the family . . . and I'm not altogether sure whether . . .'

Angela clapped her hands like a gleeful schoolgirl. 'I think you're all marvellous, Mrs Kelly, but I'd do the same if it were my daughter, if there were a chance of her seeing the Holy Father and having all the Easter ceremonies in Rome. *Anyone* can get married in Dublin but if it were my choice I'd much prefer to think a child of mine was able to have all this experience and there'll be the photos and everything.'

It was the right thing to say. An element that had not yet been introduced, that it was one up on everyone else. Mrs Kelly liked it. She liked it so much that she offered them both a sherry as a nightcap.

Emer was about to refuse and Angela hissed, 'Last night under this roof.'

So they all sat down and talked about how impressed people would be when they saw the pictures. Mrs Kelly asked Angela what kind of a hat she was going to wear. Angela had never worn a hat in her life and was momentarily stuck.

'We're going to choose it tomorrow morning,' Emer said.

On the way upstairs Emer said that it would be a great excuse to get out of the house for an hour or two, before the family came to wave goodbye and annoy them all.

There was a divan bed in Emer's room which was used as a settee when she was on her own but could be made into a spare bed. That was where Angela was to sleep, but they both sat on it and talked for two hours. In the end they remembered that they would still have days and days in Rome, and that from now on Angela was to come to Dublin every year and stay with Kevin and Emer in a house where nobody would interrogate you the moment you came in the door.

'I never spoke to you about money,' Emer said as she got into bed. 'Kevin asked me to say that the groom gives the bridesmaid a present, and he wanted me to find out tactfully if you'd like some of the money towards the fare instead of a gift. He said I wasn't to say it straight out but I can't think of how else to say it.'

'Isn't he very kind. You are so lucky, Emer.'

'I know.' She hugged her knees in bed, a schoolgirlish gesture. 'I can hardly believe how lucky I am. Well, what will I tell him?'

'Tell him I was touched to the heart but I'd prefer a present. I don't spend much in Castlebay you know, I live at home. I don't go anywhere much, I save a bit each week in the post office and I save that much again at home like a mad old lady in a box under my bed.'

'Why on earth do you not put it all in the post office?' Emer was amused.

'Because I wouldn't give it to that demon Mrs Conway to know how much I *have* managed to put by over the years. No honestly, Emer, I really do have the money, thank you and Kevin very much, and I don't spend much on clothes so I'm fine. I was always hoping that I'd have a great opportunity like this.'

Emer blinked away tears. Angela looked so sad lying on her elbow in the divan bed, her long brown hair brushed and tied loosely back with a rubber band, her face pale and worried looking. Emer felt guilty that her friend had such a sad life and was now spending her savings coming to Rome. Yet Angela seemed absolutely determined to be there, from the very first moment too. It was almost as if she had been looking for an excuse to go there and this was it. It was marvellous to have such enthusiasm as that, compared to everyone else moping and complaining. Emer drifted off to sleep happily, and didn't know that Angela smoked five cigarettes hoping that sleep would come, and when it didn't she took half a sleeping tablet with a sip of water.

They were meeting the best man in Rome, and so the party that set out on the plane were Kevin's cousin Marie who worked for Aer Lingus and could get a reduction, and Emer's Uncle David who was an artist of some kind and who went to the continent once a year to paint. It had all been balanced with great care. One relative from each side but no mothers or fathers, no clerics or nuns from either side and no sisters or brothers. Emer provided a bridesmaid and the best man who was working his way there by train was a friend of Kevin's and a teacher in the same school.

There had been a full day of discussion about whether the parents should come, but Kevin and Emer while pretending a certain enthusiasm had marshalled every possible argument against their making the journey. It worked. They were through the barrier at Colinstown airport in Dublin, with Angela, Uncle David and Kevin's cousin Marie. The wedding had begun.

He was waiting outside her hotel. She had *told* him not to come in person – it was a hotel where Irish pilgrims stayed, but he should leave a note for her saying where they should meet.

The taxi that Father Flynn had organized for Uncle David, Cousin Marie and Angela stopped outside the door. Sean jumped eagerly but Angela motioned him angrily away. Her first shock was that he was wearing a blue suit with a pale blue shirt open at the neck. It had never occurred to her that he didn't dress like a priest any more.

David and Marie spent ages being assured that she was fine, that she had her passport which she would need, that they knew of her at the desk, and then they all repeated to each other where they were going to meet for lunch the next day. At the foot of the Spanish Steps, on the bottom step, that way nobody could get lost.

Angela stiffened as she was aware of Sean listening eagerly to the arrangements. She wanted to keep him out of it, she wanted the two lives separate. She *hated* him for standing there mute and dying to join in. She hated herself too for keeping him at such a distance with a wave of her hand. Eventually, finally they went, back into the taxi and on to the hotel where Father Flynn and the happy couple had gone. Where the best man should be arriving tonight if all went well. Emer had been upset that Angela couldn't change her arrangements and stay at their hotel too, and that she wouldn't even try. But Angela had insisted that the booking remain the way it was. They would see plenty of each other, the hotels were only ten minutes' walk apart.

She was given the key to her room and pointed towards a very dangerous-looking lift. Sean came towards her.

'Are they gone?' he asked fearfully.

'Yes.'

'Oh Angela. *Angela.* Thank you, bless you for coming, bless you, and thank you from the bottom of my heart, Shuya says I must begin by giving you her thanks, she wants you to know that very specially.' He had his hands on her shoulders and his face was working uncontrollably.

'Don't . . .' she began.

'If you had any idea what this means to me.' He shook his head from side to side. There *were* tears in his eyes, she hadn't been mistaken.

'Please . . . I'll just go and . . .' She wanted to give him time to pull himself together, to stop this fawning tearful act, so unlike her confident brother the priest who was always so right and who knew what people should do and what they shouldn't do, and who knew about duty and staying with one's mother in Castlebay for all of one's life.

'I'll come with you.' He lifted the suitcase.

'No, you can't, what would they think?' She hissed this furiously at him.

In easy Italian he explained to the small fat man behind the desk. The man nodded, si si. Father Sean could still charm them, Angela thought bitterly.

There was barely room to breathe in the perilous lift. Angela held her breath as it groaned up the flights. Sean opened the door of the small room. There was a single bed, a dressing table and a chair. On the wall were five hooks with hangers on them. Single rooms didn't have luxuries like wardrobes or washbasins. They had passed rooms called *Il Bagno* and *Il Gabinetto* on the corridor. Angela looked around her, this wasn't how she had wanted to meet her brother. She had wanted to come in and lie down and gather her thoughts. She had wanted to have a bath and change her clothes, hanging up her wedding finery and the new hat bought in Clery's this morning. Was it only *this* morning they had been in O'Connell Street with all those crowds? She had wanted Sean to leave her a letter suggesting a nearby café. She could have strolled there in the cool of the evening and they could have talked at a quiet table. Talked for hours if need be. She hated this hot, emotional, awkward meeting.

He had put her case on the floor and laid the big bag carrying her wedding hat carefully on the dressing table beside the big room key. And as she stood not knowing what was going to happen now, totally out of control on her first time staying in a hotel, her first time out of Ireland and her first time meeting her only brother since he had left the priesthood, Sean put his arms around her and with his head on her shoulder he cried like a baby. She stood there dry-eyed, wondering how could anything be as bad as this. He wasn't stammering how sorry he was that it had all happened, he wasn't saying that he had made a mess of everyone's lives. No, he was stumbling out words about the laicization and how long it was taking, and how glad he was to see Angela because he had been so afraid from her letters that she meant he was never to come back to Castlebay again.

They all found the Spanish Steps with no problem. Marie, the girl who worked in Aer Lingus, had been in Rome several times, and David the middle-aged artist had been there years ago. Emer and Kevin would have found the planet Mars if that had been the rendezvous point, so excited and full of energy did they seem. Father Flynn was excited too – this was *his* show, his town now, and he loved every minute of the role of organizer. Angela was the last to arrive but she was only minutes after the others. She had paused to buy dark glasses and had found herself always in the kind of shop where these glasses cost a fortune. In the end she paid a fortune, and the woman in the shop admired them and said that now she had a *bella figura*.

The others laughed when they saw the new Angela. They told her that it had not taken her long to go native and they joked about overindulgence in wine the night before. As they debated where to eat Emer asked Angela in some concern what she *had* done the night before.

'Wandered,' Angela said. 'You know me, wander and only half absorb where I am and what I'm doing. It's a beautiful place, isn't it?' Emer was satisfied. Years and years ago in Dublin Angela used to wander like that, for ages along the canal, or in the Dublin mountains, walking around for miles. It figured she would do the same in Rome. Emer went back to the argument about lunch, they dismissed the very notion of Babbington's Tea Rooms, an English-style place just beside them. They hadn't been in Rome for a full day yet, it wasn't long enough for them to start hankering over good old tea and scones.

They walked companionably to a place that Father Flynn knew. 'I haven't completely wasted my time here praying and studying,' he said happily. 'I've done some useful things like discovering where to eat and drink.'

A man in a cream-coloured jacket and a very showy handkerchief in his pocket made a play for Angela in the restaurant, jumping up from his table to ensure she had an ashtray and trying out his few lamentable words of English on her.

'I think these glasses suit me, I might wear them all the time,' Angela said when the man had backed out of the restaurant bowing and smiling and ogling. She hadn't seen that much attention in years.

Then they left her alone. Once she had made a little joke they thought she was all right, she could opt out for a while and run the whole night over for herself as if it were a film. She had got Sean out of her room eventually, and he had written down the name of a café. She said she only needed an hour to calm herself and unpack; but as it turned out she did neither, her clothes remained in their suitcase and her anxiety grew ever more. She kept looking at the travelling clock and wondering why she had sent her brother, red-eyed, away. She was going to have to talk to him anyway, why hadn't she left the oppressive bedroom with him and gone to one of those picturesque squares?

They did walk to a square, the Piazza Navona. There were restaurants all around and the centre was full of people selling things and doing tricks as if it was a carnival. Not a person seemed to have a care except the O'Haras, she thought. They sat and ordered tiny coffees.

He had recovered himself fully. 'Let me tell you all about my family,' he began. She listened. She heard of Shuya and how he had met her almost immediately after they had gone to Japan to regroup after the expulsion from China; she heard of Denis who was three and the brightest child that had ever been known. And of Laki who was a baby of eighteen months, so beautiful it would make your eyes prickle when you saw her. And of the life they lived in Japan in Shuya's brother's house, and what they did here in the strange villa in Ostia, and how they would get married here in Rome as soon as the laicization came through. He talked like someone possessed: he had always been a great one to hold the floor, but that was because he was the only one who could, at home. He had been away to seminary and then on the missions, he was a priest of God who had more right to tell tales and get a hearing, who had better tales to tell. She listened. Nothing had changed much except the content. He was sure of his audience, sure that she was glad to know details of Laki's birth which had been a complicated one, sure that she was as absorbed as he was in the minutiae of the laicization process and his dealings with the Congregation for the Clergy.

Once or twice she tried to interject, but he raised his hand slightly in that clerical gesture which was only slightly a courteous request for permission to speak further – it was mainly a statement that he was *going* to speak further.

He wasn't going to go back tonight: it was too far, it would be too late. He would stay in Rome. Shuya had insisted, said it would be less tiring because surely he would want to talk to his sister again in the morning. As the monologue went on Angela became grateful that he was going to stay in Rome. Since she was obviously not going to get any innings at all, she would *need* the morning to try to explain to him some of the things that stood in the way of his sunny view of the future. But where would he stay? Much of his chat had included how short of money they were and how even fares were a big consideration. But he was fine for a bed. A friend of his, an English priest who was staying at the English College, said there would always be a bed there for Sean. It was nearby.

He talked of the priests he had met and the ex-priests, and of the spirit of change and questioning in the Church. He was prepared to talk for ever about such things. Angela nodded and made the necessary sounds as he spoke but all the time her mind was racing. It was just like getting his letters; he ignored every point she

..ad made in her own letters, and had written as if Angela had addressed no thoughts, pleas or words to him at all. She had written to say that she was coming to meet him to explain to him face to face how impossible it would be – laicization or not – to return to Castlebay with a Japanese or any wife and two children. He seemed to have ignored the main part of her letter, and acknowledged only the first sentence, that she was coming to Rome to see him.

She hoped that a change of venue might change the tack of the conversation, so she suggested they have a meal. He hesitated. Angela said she would be glad to pay. He agreed. It was just that he felt so guilty spending anything on himself instead of on Shuya and the children. But nothing changed, he ordered for them in perfect Italian, bottles of mineral water as well as wine; told her he could make spaghetti thirty-four different ways now, and he made a salad every evening at home, often with leaves they plucked from the garden. You can actually eat *all* kinds of things like the leaves of flowers. Did Angela know that?

She didn't, but by the end of the evening she knew a lot of things like that. She could have gone into Radio Eireann at home and asked to be a panelist on *Information Please* after all she learned in the Piazza Navona, as the lights came on and the musicians played, and other people had beautiful Roman evenings. From her handbag she took a piece of paper and wrote down four words. Then she handed the list to him.

'What's this?' he asked, surprised and even a little amused.

'It's our agenda for tomorrow morning. When we meet in the daylight. I want to discuss the subjects written down there and nothing else.' She smiled pleasantly; she took a sheaf of huge Italian notes in almighty denominations and signalled for the bill.

Sean was reading aloud. 'Hypocrisy and Betrayal. Family and Community. What *is* this Angela? It looks very like the title of some sermon or a pamphlet in the Catholic Truth Society.'

She was still easy and relaxed. 'Let's leave it till tomorrow, will we? It's been a lovely evening and it's too late to start on these things now.'

He was genuinely bewildered; he wasn't acting. He sought to placate her. 'Right, sure, whatever you like. And we'll arrange for you to come to Ostia.'

She shuddered at that. She felt a slow sweat form on her shoulders and back at the thought of meeting this Japanese woman who shared a bed with her brother the priest, and a dread of meeting these two children.

'Not until after Emer's wedding, not until next Tuesday.'

She was firm: he was disappointed.

'But we were *sure* you'd come for Easter itself.'

'I'm going to go to the Holy Week Ceremonies tomorrow and all of the weekend with my friends. When that's all over I'll come to Ostia.' If it's too awful to face, she thought, I can always pretend to be sick. To have a fever or something.

Sean was downcast. 'I had thought that . . .'

'It's all fixed.'

'No, I mean I thought that maybe you were going to ask us to the wedding. To Emer's wedding.'

She looked at him, stunned.

'I've met Emer, remember, I met her when you were in Dublin, and she came to Daddy's funeral.'

'Yes, she knows you as a priest.'

'But surely you've told her?' He was amazed.

A headache was beginning right across her eyes. 'Don't be ridiculous, Sean, of course I haven't told her, I haven't told *anyone.*'

'This is much more complicated than I thought,' Sean said, shaking his head. 'I thought it was only Mam you were keeping it from until the time was right. I didn't know that you had such old-fashioned views, and hard attitudes. I'm still a Catholic for God's sake, I haven't given up my Faith or anything. I still go to Mass and Communion.'

It was far too late to debate it now. The bill was paid and they walked amicably back to her hotel. All the time he pointed out places to her as if she were an ordinary tourist and he were her ordinary brother. He kissed her on each cheek and walked away into the night to his friend who was still a priest and who would not lie awake all night anguishing about what had happened to Father Sean O'Hara, and what course his life would take now.

She was businesslike in the morning. She said that she would prefer him to listen to her and only speak when she asked his view: otherwise her visit would have been wasted. He was startled but agreed. She examined the possibility of his coming back to Castlebay once more, once only and pretending to be still a priest. He was so horrified, he leaped up from the table. But she persisted. Examine it: technically, what would be the flaws, did he still have any clerical clothes, could he get away with it or would someone from the Mother House hear of it? No, don't ask *why* was this necessary at the moment, just see could it be done? According to Sean, even if he wanted to do an insane thing like this he couldn't do it. He would be found out in days, and as he wouldn't say Mass in Father O'Dwyer's church, he would be an object of suspicion at once.

Could he say that since the Order had left China there had been a change in the Rule and priests had become workers and teachers and were working among the community more? Could he imply that *all* priests had been downgraded, not only Father Sean? No that was ludicrous too. You only had to read the papers to know that this was untrue, it wouldn't hold good for five minutes.

Could they pretend that he had died, been kidnapped? Sean looked at Angela as if she weren't all there. Why on earth should anyone begin such a tissue of hypocritical lies and bungling?

Angela's eyes flashed. She would tell him why, because if he told their mother the truth it would break her, literally *break* her. The only thing of value she had done was produce a priest for God, it was the only constant and hope in her soul and it was her only standing in the community. That's what Angela meant about Betrayal. To tell the old woman with the enlarged joints and crooked limbs that her priest wasn't a priest – that would be betrayal of a high order. Angela had come to Rome to beg her brother not to do this.

He was patient with her, he began to explain that once the process of making him a layman was completed, he had as much right before God to marry as anyone had, so he had anticipated it but it would then be regularized, post hoc. Angela silenced him with a word, this was *her* time: last night had been his. He was to decide between hypocrisy and betrayal. She would listen to no more speeches about breaths of fresh air blowing through the dusty corridors of the Vatican and new thinking and the Congregation of the Clergy. There was no fresh air blowing through Father O'Dwyer's church in Castlebay except what came in the windows on the day of the east wind. There was no radical rethinking in the O'Hara cottage, there was no spirit of brotherly love and understanding among people like Sergeant McCormack. Sean must decide between *hypocrisy* and *betrayal*. He must decide on the old principle of the greatest happiness of the greatest number. Which way would less people get hurt.

But, Sean protested, there could be no question of that, the truth was the truth, it was absolute. It couldn't be tinkered with and played with like plasticine, deciding who should believe what.

Their coffee cups were refilled over and over. Angela banged on the table to get him to stop talking and listen to her account of daily life in Castlebay. She didn't intend it to be humorous, but sometimes she said things that made him smile and she smiled herself to acknowledge that she did exaggerate in some areas. But not in the general picture.

She swore that it wouldn't matter all that much for her; to be frank she would prefer not to have the pitying and patronizing stance of Immaculata for the rest of her working life, and she would like not to have the knowledge that they had just stopped talking about it all every time she appeared. But she could live with it, she had lived with her father's reputation after all. She'd survive, but she was going to fight with every breath in her body for her mother not to have to try to survive it.

'When Mam dies, Sean, then I'll walk with you down Church Street in Castlebay. Don't come to her funeral, but six months later you can come back and I'll stand beside you.'

'That's the wrong way to do things,' Sean said. 'To wait till someone dies before you can bring your children home. How do you tell your son and daughter that you have to wait until their grandmother has been buried before they can come home, come home to where they belong?'

Angela's heart lurched again. He really and truly thought that these half-Japanese children and their mother *belonged* in Castlebay. She looked at her watch, and stood up to call for the bill again. It was time to go to lunch with the wedding party. He looked confused and unsettled.

'You will come, you will still come and see us?'

'Yes,' she promised.

'On Tuesday, and you'll stay a few days.'

'No, I won't stay the night, I might come again, but I'll just come for the day. Thank you all the same.'

'But why not? There's a bed there.'

'There's a bed in the hotel too, I'd prefer to come back.'

'Shuya will want to know do you send her a greeting.'

'Yes, yes of course.'

'What is it? What is the greeting?'

'Say I am happy to meet her.'

'It's not very warm,' he grumbled.

'It's all I've got. And you think about what I've said, because we have to sort it out. Will you discuss it with Shuya?'

'Yes, I suppose so, but it's hard, her family were so good, so welcoming, I don't want her to think mine are like a row of stones.'

'No. I understand.'

'Thanks anyway Angela. You're doing your best,' he said.

That's what did it, that's when the tears started, she threw some money on the table and stumbled away. *Doing her best!* God, wasn't she doing her bloody best! The ingratitude and lack of understanding were no longer possible to take. She ran almost blindly away. She heard him calling that he would collect her at the hotel on Tuesday and she nodded, not able to look back. She ran until she was well away, then she began asking directions and from the concerned looks people gave her she realized she needed dark glasses if not a full veil to cover her red-blotched face.

Father Flynn was a treasure, there was nothing he didn't know the answer to. He said it was going to be as dull as ditchwater when he got back to Dublin after all this, and the place was so gorgeous too. Dublin was so grey and gritty. Kevin's Uncle David, considered a little eccentric by the rest of Kevin's very straight-laced family, didn't usually go a bundle on priests: he said that normally they gave him a pain in the top of the stomach. But this little Druid was an exception. He wore a soutane which didn't at all suit his small round figure. Once when they were passing a lingerie shop which sold frilly waspie-waist corsets he asked Emer and Angela should he get something like that for himself to wear so that he would look good in wedding photographs. Father Flynn was full of stories about everyone and everything, all very ridiculous but not hurtful. And best of all, he could laugh at himself. He seemed to be well known everywhere they went. Italian shopkeepers setting out their cheeses on display would shout greetings to Fazzer Fleen.

But he had his serious side too and he told them that it was an honour to be married in St Peter's, and that obviously they would remember it all their lives. Nobody was so forgetful as not to recall where they got married, but this was something special. He took them down to the crypt chapel and they looked at it in awe on Holy Thursday afternoon just as the huge basilica was getting ready for its Holy Week ceremonies. Emer and Kevin were to be married here – it was almost too much to take in.

And the man seemed to know about clothes. He was fascinated by what they should wear at the wedding and thought that they would look absolutely great – apart from the shoes. There was something about Irish shoes that didn't look quite *right* in Rome. Late on Thursday evening the strange party wandered along the Via Condotti, and Angela and Emer tried on different footwear and paraded them for Father Flynn, Kevin, Marie and David. Marie became so excited that she started trying them on too, and Father Flynn said if his soutane didn't hide them he would be sorely tempted by those grey suede ones. Everyone in the shop was nearly hysterical, and when they settled on the fiercely elegant ones that all three had decided to buy, Father Flynn began to haggle like a fishwife about the price and brought the cost down enormously.

He stopped them at a flower stall where he was well known too. He did great gesticulations and explanations about the colour of dresses, Emer's white with a blue trim, her hat blue with a white ribbon. Angela's dress was beige and her hat was white with beige and brown flowers. The family who ran the flower stall became highly excited over the wedding and fought amongst each other about what the bouquets should be. Soon they were all shouting at each other while the Irish group looked on amazed. Flowers were being held up to Emer first, then to Angela, heads were shaking, arms were waving and in the end a satisfactory combination of flowers and timings and delivery to the hotel and prices was arrived at. The family gave everyone a buttonhole there and then as a gift. There was hand-kissing and good wishes, and they seemed as pleased as if it were one of their own family.

'Could you imagine my mother being as pleased as that over anyone's wedding?' Emer said wistfully. 'Is it any wonder people would love to come here to get married, total strangers are delighted with us and at home there's been nothing but fuss.'

'My family would have half the geriatric priests and nuns on the move by now, all of them complaining,' Kevin said.

'Less of that attitude,' Father Flynn demanded. 'I'll be a geriatric priest some day, and when your children are getting married in about thirty or thirty-five years from now, I want someone to come for *me* in a wheelchair and take me to the party.'

He was *so* nice, Angela thought with a rush of affection. Despite all his joky going on he was one of the kindest people she had ever met. What a sensitive little man he was; wouldn't he be a great priest to have in a parish instead of dull old Father O'Dwyer; instead of people who couldn't even stay *in* the priesthood. *Stop.* She was not going to think about Sean until Tuesday: that was her little treat to herself. She hoped she would be able to keep to that promise and enjoy herself.

There had been a bit of a problem about the best man. He hadn't turned up. But Father Flynn had that sorted out too. If the best man wasn't there, couldn't David stand in? David was doubtful, he wasn't actually in the State of Grace, he said, he wasn't what you would call a conventional person to take part in the ceremony, as one of the performers, that was. Father Flynn seemed to regard a public announcement of being in a state of sin as the most normal thing in the world.

'There's no question of being a performer,' he said. 'You're only a witness, you could be alive with mortal sin, reserved sins and all, it wouldn't make a whit of difference to the ceremony. Of course, now that you're here in Rome, if you wanted someone to hammer a good confession job on you, I know plenty that would see you right.'

'Well, now I don't think . . .'

'No need at all, just letting you know it's there if you want it. I know a priest who's almost stone deaf, there's a queue a mile long outside his box but I could get you up to the top of the line by shameless pull and influence.'

It was hard to know if Father Flynn was joking or not. But in any event by the time they got back to the hotel after the wonderful warm afternoon wandering around Rome, the best man was there. His name was Martin Walsh. He was about six foot two tall and forty years old. He was painfully shy and he had got on the wrong train. He looked as if he was about to burst into tears. Father Flynn had it under control in minutes.

He couldn't have arrived at a better time the little priest said, because they were all going to split up now and meet again at nine o'clock. Martin would have *hours* to get over the shock of it all, and have a bath and a few cold beers and a chat with Kevin. Everyone else was perfectly capable of looking after himself or herself. He said this because Martin had kept babbling his apologies about not being there to organize the flowers and the bridesmaids. He had bought a handbook on the best man's duties and he seemed to have fallen down.

Father Flynn told him to throw away the book on the role of the best man. Everything was much simpler in Rome. Martin's big sad face started to look human. Up to now he had looked like a thin wretched bloodhound.

The little wedding party walked with faltering steps into the huge basilica which they had visited every day since they came to Rome. Today it was different. There was a mixture of formality and casualness. People shouted good luck in different languages and a group of Germans took their picture. The walk seemed endless, but then they were in and down the marble stairs to the little chapels beneath. Father Flynn disappeared to robe himself, and the others knelt silently, heads down.

Angela prayed hard. She forced words to come into her head and she mouthed them to herself. She asked God to be kind to Emer and Kevin, and to make it a nice life. She explained to God that Emer had kept the rules and that it would be a good idea to reward her. Emer deserved to be happy. With her gloved hand she squeezed the white-gloved hand beside her and Emer grinned gratefully.

Father Flynn shone in his gold and white vestments. He was smiling at them all. The words began and Angela felt her eyes water when she heard Kevin's and Emer's uncertain voices. Then it was done. They were man and wife. They pecked at each other chastely and went to sign the huge register. The photographer was anxious to get them outside and grouped – on the steps first, then down to the centre of the square beside the big column, a great place to stand because you got a view of St Peter's in the background.

Sean was in the foyer when she came downstairs.
'Tell them you mightn't be coming back tonight, just in case, and in case they worry about you.'
'I'm coming back here tonight,' she said.
'It's so dear going up and down on the train,' he pleaded.
'Shall we go now?'
He shrugged; but soon he was in high good humour. Young Denis knew his Aunt Angela was coming. Angela shuddered and hoped he hadn't noticed the revulsion she felt coursing through her. She asked what language he spoke. Apparently he spoke Japanese and English and now because they were in Italy they were using a lot of that. *Mia Zia*, Sean said dotingly.
'What?'
'*Zia*, the Italian for aunt. *Zio* is uncle. *Mia Zia*, my aunt.'

Angela wondered could this possibly be happening? Was she really having a language lesson as they walked? It had all the qualities of a dream where the wrong people are in the wrong places saying idiotic things. But this had been going on too long for it to be a dream. She wasn't going to wake up and find Father Sean still sending for stamps and silver paper from the Far East. That was long gone now.

She tried to tell him about the wedding – anything, rather than fall into the normality of his life with him. She didn't want to hear that this was the platform he normally sat on to wait for the cheaper train, she didn't want to become part of his ridiculous pattern of commuting from this new home and family to try to get audiences and hearings and advance his documents further with the Congregation of the Clergy. She wanted this *over*. She looked at the station, at the monument to Mussolini, who made the trains run on time for the first and only period in Italy's history. By the time she came back here tonight she would have met them. Sean's family. It wouldn't make her feel any different, she knew that.

'What would you like best to happen now?' he asked her suddenly as they sat on the train opposite each other.

'I don't know.'

'What would be the very best thing that could happen as far as you are concerned? Best for everybody.'

She looked out the window at the buildings with all the washing hanging from sticks and poles that jutted through windows.

'I don't know, Sean, I really don't. I suppose I'd like you to reconsider and to ask to go back to your Order, for Shuya to see that this is your vocation, and for her to return to Japan with the children. I know it's not possible and it's not going to happen, but you did ask me what I would like.'

'Shuya must be a mind-reader,' he said happily. 'She said this is what you want.'

'I'm coming to see them, I'm doing that much – stop getting at me!'

'I know, and I'm so happy, soon you'll know them. A normal way of life is beginning for all of us.' He was like a child who thinks he's getting a bike for his birthday. Angela closed her eyes and kept them closed to discourage further conversation.

They waited in a hot noisy line of people for a bus and they didn't get a seat. Sean was smiling, blinking into the sunlight and bending down to look out, squinting for landmarks to point out to her.

After the bus ride, they walked for ten minutes. The gates of the villa were huge and wide, like the big gates of ruined Castlebay House at home. But the villa couldn't be more different: it was yellow-coloured with white shutters and there were flowers tumbling all over the walls. Sean looked through the gates with pride. Wasn't it beautiful? The Italians knew how to do things with style. The Signor and Signora didn't spend a great deal of time here of course, but they kept it up fairly well didn't they, when you considered everything. Angela wondered why they weren't going in. Maybe at this last moment he was getting some nerves, beginning to doubt the sense of the mad enterprise. It was only eleven o'clock in the morning and she felt she had put a whole day over her.

They moved away, to her surprise. It must have shown in her face.

'Our entrance is round here,' Sean explained easily. They went in a much narrower entrance a few hundred yards down the wall. It didn't need to say 'servants' entrance', that was so obviously what it was. Here the flowerbeds were overgrown and the walls of the out-houses were peeling in the sun. But there were flowers too, and as Angela walked beside Sean, she saw some small, dark-eyed Italian children playing in and out of the open doors. It would be a good place for a child to grow up in some ways, a bit in the shadow of the Big House of course but it was safe and friendly and there would be plenty of other children to play with. She was walking warily now: she must keep her wits about her.

'There they are . . . we're home . . . Shuya! Shuya, she's here! Denis, come here . . . !'

The little boy had his hand up to his face, shy, not wanting to be the first to make the move, hanging back. Behind him came waddling a small fat baby with nappies hanging down underneath its knitted knickers. And leaning against the door was Shuya. Not in Japanese clothes as Angela had thought she would be, not wearing a bun with two sticks coming out of it, no big wide belt with a rose attached to it, no tiny pointed feet.

Shuya looked like an old, old woman. She had an Eastern face, like the face of a poor Chinese or Filipino woman holding out a begging bowl, the kind of face you saw in the missionary annals. Her skin was muddy grey, her hair was lank and tied back like Angela's own. She wore a shapeless dress and over it a long, faded cardigan. This could not be Shuya. Shuya must be inside waiting to come out, this was somebody else minding the children for her, an older friend. The thin tired figure smiled at them both. 'Welcome An-jay-la . . . wel-come. It is so good of you to come all this way to meet your family.'

Shuya's smile moved from brother to sister as she walked out of the shadow into the sunlight. Her smile was bright and it made her old thin face look less beaten, less resigned. Sean was staring at her with delight. In a flash Angela thought she understood it all. He was *lonely*. The poor stupid fool was *lonely* out there and she was kind to him, she was the first person to be kind and warm. That's what it's all about. It didn't make it any better, but it was some explanation.

'Hallo Shuya,' she said. Every word seemed leaden, but she forced them out. 'I'm very glad to meet you. Will you introduce me to the children?'

There was a pause. She must say something a bit warmer, Sean had probably built her up to the skies, described her as beautiful and generous and brilliant, just as he had built this sad creature up when he had spoken of her to Angela.

'This is Laki,' Shuya said. The toddler was whirling her two fat little arms round like a windmill in the effort to keep upright.

'Hallo Laki O'Hara.'

When the limelight was off Denis he realized it was safe to approach. 'I am Denis,' he said.

'I knew you were, I knew it the minute I saw you.'

There was no sending this lot back. Better banish the dream of Father Sean

611

rediscovering his vocation, and his instant family being absorbed somewhere back in Japan. These were here to stay.

She went back on the train every day. Sean had been right, it would have been much easier to have stayed the night, but she had to stay true to her earlier words, and not let it appear that her first visit had been an inspection, and that she would stay if they passed the test. She brought them toys, she bought ridiculous over-decorated boxes of sweets. Laki sat on her lap and Denis wanted to know why she couldn't speak Japanese or even Italian. Shuya said little.

On Thursday, Sean had to see two priests who knew better routes than the ones he had been following. There was great hope they would steer him in the right direction. Angela said she would still come to Ostia, as usual. This was only her third visit but already it seemed natural. In fact she was glad that Sean would be away. Perhaps Shuya might talk more, might say the things that Sean reported her as saying. The woman was so quiet that Angela could hardly believe that she was the author of such philosophical announcements as Sean had always claimed. Shuya said little or nothing in her presence, and served the simple salads and pasta as if she were a maid, sitting a little away from the others as they ate. But when Sean wasn't there she would have to speak.

At first she was content to let young Denis talk to his aunt, but Angela put a stop to that. She asked Denis to go and collect her ten different kinds of leaves, each one different, from the grounds, and lay them all out on a sheet of paper; then they would try to put names on them. Denis went off happily; Laki was playing with a fat Italian baby about her own age. The women were on their own. Shuya seemed to recognize it too: she sat with her hands folded, waiting for Angela to begin.

It was hard because Angela had to be in the role of questioner for such a long time. Shuya replied dutifully. She had three brothers, and two sisters. Her mother was dead and her father had married again. Yes, they did like his new wife, but now he lived with his new wife's people and they did not see much of him. Her family liked Sean. No, they didn't really think anything about his having been a priest. Or being a priest still, as Angela said. No, you see it was just a job to them – he had been teaching when he was a priest, he was still teaching. He had not been married before, now he was married to Shuya. It was so simple.

On close questioning Shuya proved to see some complications. She said that it was a very big thing, it was like being married to the Church and the Church would release you if you found a higher happiness. But there were a lot of formalities. That is why they were here, that is why Sean had gone to the Vatican again this day as he did so many days.

No, of course it didn't matter to her, not even a little bit, about whether this laicization happened or not. But since it mattered so much to Sean it had become important to her too. She wished it to happen to please him. Then they could get on with their lives.

This was a minefield. Angela had to tread carefully. Where did they see the rest of their lives? Shuya didn't really know. They did love Italy of course, and anyone with children would love to be here, the people adored all children. But after? Sean would want to teach in a school, possibly. He was so clever, and he could teach so well. He would want to teach and live in a school at the same time. Then Denis could go to the same school and there would be a school nearby for Laki.

And where would this school be? In Italy or Japan or where? Shuya didn't know exactly where, but it would be somewhere in Ireland. She wasn't sure if Sean knew himself, but of course it would be Ireland.

She began to explain to Shuya about Ireland, and about Castlebay. She was never interrupted as she had been by Sean. Shuya came out with no roaring denials and assurances that things had changed now. Shuya listened as if she were being told a tale from a far country. She listened as if Angela knew what it was like because that was her land. She was passive during the recounting of the struggle to get the money for Sean's ordination, and the moment of glory at his first Mass and then his first Mass in Castlebay, and even his return seven years ago for his father's funeral. So passive that Angela wondered if she understood any of it. Angela tried to explain that despite what all the clergy in Rome said to each other, it made not a bit of difference back home, whether a priest had been laicized or not. Even if his marriage was as white as the driven snow in the eyes of God and state, in the eyes of the community it could never be accepted.

She begged Shuya to ask her questions, to challenge what she said. Shuya said there was no reason to challenge anything. Obviously Angela must be telling the truth, but did this mean that Sean should never go back to Ireland? Was this what Angela was trying to explain?

Yes. That was it. That's what she had been trying to say to Sean in her letters, and again when she had met him in Rome. Had he not told her this? Oh he had told her, but then when Angela had agreed to come to see the family on Tuesday, and come back again Wednesday and today, he realized that he had been forgiven and that it would all be all right. He had hoped that this would happen and now it had.

Denis came back with his leaves. He was about to lay them out for discussion and identification. Angela passed a hand wearily over her forehead, she was in deeper than ever now. Her visit had been the positive green light that Sean had been waiting for. Was she ever going to get out of this mire of misunderstanding or was she walking everybody further into it?

For the first time Shuya seemed to take some action of her own. She suggested that Denis and Laki have their lunch and siesta in the house across the courtyard. Denis felt short-changed.

'Your Aunt Angela will be here when you come back,' Shuya soothed, marching them over the cobblestones, bringing some of Angela's sweets as a bribe. It was the house of a gardener and his wife, who also helped with the sewing in the linen room. When the gardener went to market his wife had a young lover in and on those occasions Shuya took her children: so it was a fair exchange. Angela was taken aback by the racy life in the servants' quarters and the casual way that Shuya had accepted it. But it worked in her favour and she was not going to criticize.

She seemed younger, stronger, when she came back and sat down. It was as if her listening had a different quality. She scented a problem where she had thought there was none, she wanted to hear, to learn and to see what could be done. This

613

time she talked back, she asked questions, mainly unanswerable ones. Like why, if these people were very religious, would they not recognize and believe in a document signed by the Pope saying that Sean was released from his vows? Or why would people who say they follow a rule which is based on love for each other not give that love? Angela was helpless. But because she didn't bluster, because she didn't defend and make excuses, the conversation never became angry. In the end Angela asked about Japan: wasn't there some code of honour that they had too, some kind of thing that an outsider might think was odd? Shuya paused. They had *ko* which was a sort of filial piety, but it wasn't the same as what was being asked for here. With *ko* you had to be docile to your parents and for a woman in particular docile to your mother-in-law. But they didn't have anything which meant hiding the truth, and no notion that hiding the truth could ever be a good thing in itself.

The sun came in through the slats in the shutters and Angela felt a great sadness and tiredness. In Rome, Sean was bent over still more documents with still more clerics. In Castlebay the neighbours would have cleared away her mother's lunch things. It would still be cold and windy. Up at the convent Mother Immaculata would be getting the timetable ready for the summer term. In Amalfi, Kevin and Emer would possibly be holding hands after lunch in a restaurant by the harbour or be on a boat to Capri. In O'Brien's shop Clare would have told them about the scholarship exam and how she couldn't wait until Miss O'Hara got back to hear the details. And here she was with this woman discussing *honesty* and *truth* and *hypocrisy*. She felt as if she would like to curl up and go to sleep for a month, waking up only when everything else was sorted out. She was thinking about this so wistfully that she almost missed Shuya's words.

'I suppose then that the best thing is for us not to go to Ireland at this time. It is best for Sean to alter some parts of his dream?'

'What?'

'For him to change his hopes about going to Ireland at this time.'

'Do you think he will? He's so set in his belief that it will be all right. I wore myself out and he didn't change an inch, not an inch.'

'Well, I will explain to him.'

'Shuya, how can you explain, he will only think that I tried to browbeat you or go behind his back or something.'

'But that is not so.'

'I know it's not so. I'd have said every word in front of him, but he'd have interrupted me a thousand times, I don't understand *this*, I haven't understood the *other*, Moral Law, Canon Law . . .'

'I know.'

She didn't dare to hope that this strange ugly woman with the lined face and the clothes of a begger should be able to convince her big handsome brother of anything. 'Could you . . . ? I think it would make everyone happier. Not just my mother, Sean's mother. But other people as well. They would be happier not to have to face it. I find that hard to say, especially since I know you and I know the children. I don't think it's fair or it's right, but I do think it's the way it is.'

Shuya nodded. 'I think it's the way it is,' she said.

There was a silence.

Could it be possible?

'What would you do if you didn't come to Ireland?' It was tentative.

'Stay here I suppose until the laicization, and after that . . .' she shrugged. 'I feel that may be a long time anyway, if it ever happens.'

'I suppose he'll keep trying.'

'He says it was like an official contract with his God. It was made formally, it must be ended formally. Like a business deal. His God wouldn't wriggle out of it, neither must he.'

'But in a way God *did* wriggle out of it, if He took Sean's vocation away.' Angela was trying desperately to be fair.

'The hardest bit is going to be the letters from your mother.'

'I know. I know. What should I do? Should I not post them, should I not write them? Will I just write a sort of account of her instead?'

'It's hard,' Shuya said. 'And on you it is most hard of all.'

Angela looked up, surprised and touched at this sympathy. Her brother had not sounded so soft and so understanding.

'I manage,' she said with a weak grin.

'Yes, but you manage alone, you manage without your sisters in England. Nobody has mentioned them because obviously there is nothing they can or will do to help. You manage without the help of anyone in your town, your priest or your friends. And you do not complain, you spend your teacher's salary to come to see us even though you think that we should not be here, and that Sean should still be a priest.'

Angela couldn't find words, she stammered. 'It's not . . . it's not that easy on you, you have nothing either.'

Shuya's plain face smiled, a smile of disbelief. 'But I have everything, I have everything in the world,' she said. And on cue two figures started staggering across the yard, Denis weighed down under still more leaves and Laki, her face a red rim of pleasure from the tomato sauce she had eaten on her spaghetti lunch.

She came again on the Friday. Sean was still high with hope – the two priests he had met yesterday were really helpful. They had shown him how things could be simplified. Go for the direct route always, they had said. Don't be misled, don't go up side alleys. Angela's heart fell when she listened to him. She had been foolish to get buoyed up with hope that Shuya would change his mind. Then he said, 'Shuya and I were talking last night. She was saying something very interesting. She has the most extraordinary insights, you know.'

Shuya was up in the Signora's linen room at the time having insights about hemming frayed pillowcases and darning perfect small darns in white silk.

'What did she say?'

'It was about the difference between country and town. It's the same in Japan, it's the same here. In the country people are slower to see what's happening in the world, they resist change. It takes so much longer to persuade people in the country of anything. It's not their fault of course.'

She listened with a new patience. Perhaps she even looked like Shuya now, her hands folded, waiting for him to get to the point.

'Things will change of course, but in their own time. You can't rush people and expect them to go at your pace. In terms of absolutes you might be wise to hold off until the growth of acceptance is sufficient . . . until the ground swell of opinion has become so strong that there will be no doubt and no confusion. That way the hurt is lessened, the debate is less sharp and the lines of love rather than the letter of the law would mould people's attitudes . . .'

. She closed her eyes with relief. In his convoluted way he was telling her that he wasn't going back to Castlebay.

They were all sad to be leaving Rome on the Saturday, and Father Flynn was at the airport to wave them off as he had welcomed them ten days before.

'It worked out all right, did it?' he said to Angela when there was no one else around – the others were all dealing with luggage.

'What?'

'What you had to do, sort out?'

She looked at him hard. Another Irish priest in Rome. Sean talking his head off everywhere he went about it all. It was only too possible that Father Flynn knew, and had known from the start. But she was going to admit nothing.

'Oh, I sorted myself out a great few days. I really love Italy. I'm heartbroken to leave, like they all are.'

'You might come back?'

'It would cost a fortune.'

'I'm sure it would be appreciated,' he said and let it drop. He was laughing and smiling and wondering what he would do next Tuesday when he had no big important wedding to officiate at.

The journey home was something she forgot. She must have talked to people, she must have said her goodbyes and gone to the station to get the train home. She caught the bus to Castlebay: Clare was waiting at the stop. At a hundred yards away Angela knew she had won the scholarship and she started to cry.

She was crying as she got off the bus, but Clare put a finger to her lips.

'Don't say anything, Miss O'Hara, don't say anything, only you and I know. Not Mother Immaculata yet, not Mam or Dad. I wanted to tell you first.'

'I can't tell you how happy I am, I can't tell you how glad.'

Clare picked up the teacher's bag. 'I'll walk you home. We can talk when there aren't people looking at us.'

She was right. It would only take half an hour for it to be known everywhere that the two of them were crying and embracing.

They walked up the golf-course road, Clare bubbling about how the nun, the very nice nun in the town convent, had asked her to telephone the day before the official results, just in case there was any news. And Clare had telephoned this morning and yes, the nun had said it was definite, her Mother Superior was going to ring Mother Immaculata tomorrow. It was absolutely definite.

They had got to the O'Hara house and Angela let herself in.

'Do you want to be on your own . . . a bit?' Clare held back.

'Of course I don't. Mother! Mother, I'm back.'

The old woman was sitting in the chair and her face lit up. 'I was hoping you'd get the bus, was the plane very frightening? Did you have holy water with you?'

'I was laden down with it. Mother, I've got great news for you. The best, the best.' She had both her hands on her mother's shoulders as she spoke, and suddenly she remembered that for her mother the best news might be the imminent return of Father Sean from the mission fields. Hastily she jumped in. 'Clare's done it, Mother, she's won it. Isn't that bloody marvellous!'

Angela threw herself down at the table and sobbed as if her heart would break. The tears that had never come in Rome came in a torrent. Her shoulders shook.

Clare and Mrs O'Hara looked at each other in alarm. Nothing could be heard but the heavy sobs from the table. Mrs O'Hara reached out but was too far away to comfort Angela. Clare didn't know whether she should move towards the teacher or not. Tentatively she touched her on the arm and patted it awkwardly.

'Don't cry,' she said. 'Please.'

From the chair came support. 'Oh Angela, please stop that crying, we should be delighted for Clare, there was no crying in this house when *you* got the scholarship.'

Angela raised her head and saw the two stricken faces. Her own face was blotched and stained. But she found what they were both looking for, her good humour and her strength.

'It's the journey, and the shock and the pleasure, the sheer sheer pleasure of it. Well done, Clare, well done, may this be the first of many triumphs for you.' Her smile blazed out through the tears and suddenly Clare wanted to cry. But that would be ridiculous. Instead she did something much more ridiculous, she ran into Miss O'Hara's arms and together they swung around the room shouting with excitement. Mrs O'Hara clapped her hands in her chair and they laughed like people who had long forgotten what they were laughing at.

Part Two
1957–1960

Clare hated sharing the room with Chrissie when she came home from school during the holidays. Chrissie's clothes smelled of sweat, she always had stockings rolled up and stuffed into shoes, the dressing table was covered with spilled powder and hair clips and combs with tufts of Chrissie's curly hair caught in the teeth. She used Clare's bed as a place to store her clothes and only very grudgingly removed them when the occupant returned from boarding school at the end of term.

Clare thought almost nostalgically of her small clean white bed in the dormitory, of the chair where her uniform lay neatly waiting for the morrow, with the stockings folded on top like a cross. It was always nice and airy in the dormitory, freezing sometimes, actually, but there was never that close smell of bodies that you had sharing a room with Chrissie. Worst of all were the blood-spattered white coats. It had never been defined who was to wash these coats and where the washing was to be done, but while it was in dispute two or more of them often festered on the floor. Clare would hide them under other garments so that she didn't have to speculate what part of what dead animal had bled over Chrissie's middle. She looked around her in disgust.

She *should* feel sorry for Chrissie, she knew this, but it didn't make it any easier. It was a desperate life standing up in Dwyers' butcher's shop and having to hack great bits of carcasses of dead sheep and cows. It wasn't a glamorous job, and it couldn't do her any good at the dance when fellows asked where she worked. Clare had suggested more than once that she try to work somewhere else. The chemist maybe? And be with that old bore Mr Murphy, Mr Murphy, a daily communicant who kept his own daughters under lock and key? No thank you very much. Or the hotel even? And be a skivvy passing round dinner plates or washing up for Young Mrs Dillon and her mad old mother-in-law, no thank you, not even if Clare was friendly with them. Thank you, Chrissie would prefer to earn her own wages and be done with the place as soon as she left it in the evening.

There had been a hope that she could have used the room they had called the Boys' Room, the downstairs room where Tommy and Ned used to sleep all those years ago when they lived at home. But Mam and Dad said that room had to be used as a storeroom now, and since the business was far better than ever before a storeroom was needed. The new caravan park up on the Far Cliff Road meant a great deal of trade. People in caravans had to buy everything; they didn't do much cooking so it was mainly cold ham and tins of things. When they trekked across from the caravan field O'Brien's was the first shop they met, perched as it was at the top of the steps going down to the sea. Very few of them went any further, and then the caravan people came back again to stock up for the day on the beach, and on the way home they would buy things for their tea. It was all great but it did mean that the Boys' Room was gone as a possible place to sleep, and Clare felt she must keep the rows to a minimum, only fight over things that are really important.

Miss O'Hara and Clare had another secret, another scholarship, another over-ambitious project. Clare O'Brien was going to go for the county scholarship.

621

One student in the entire county would be offered a place in University College, Dublin, to study Arts, to do a B.A. degree. It was called the Murray Prize. A Mr Murray long dead had left his money for this, and the competition was fierce. Usually a bright boy from one of the seminaries won it, but three years ago it had been a girl, a very brainy girl whose father was professor already. Clare and Miss O'Hara had decided to take it on.

The prize was awarded on the strength of marks received in the leaving certificate together with a personal interview. Those candidates with a sizeable number of Honours Papers and who had already announced their participation would be called to appear before a committee. Even to be called to interview by the Murray committee was an honour. But it was an honour that wouldn't happen until the end of August. The examination results had to come in first. Miss O'Hara had begged Clare to enjoy the summer, it might be her last summer of freedom. If she *did* get to university there would always be the need to study, and she would have to work for extra money – the Murray scholarship was not princely. If she did *not* get to university then she would be working during the rest of her summers, so there was even more reason to enjoy this last one. Have a bit of a fling, Miss O'Hara had advised her, and Miss O'Hara had said embarrassingly that Clare was turning into a fine-looking girl and she should make the most of it.

Clare looked at herself in the mirror. She wanted to lighten the colour of her hair: she used Sta-Blonde shampoo, which claimed to bring out the blonde highlights, but it didn't or else there were no highlights to bring out. She would have used some peroxide in the rinsing water like some of the girls at school did but, really, one look at Chrissie's peroxided fuzz would be enough to turn you against the stuff even if the smell of it didn't. Clare had grown tall, all of a sudden, when she was fourteen. Nobody had expected it, least of all Clare, and it was highly irritating. School uniforms had to have false hems and be let down to the last possible thread. She wore her hair in a pony tail with one of those nice plastic clips. Chrissie had said it made her look like a horse, but Clare had taken no notice. The great thing about going away to school was meeting so many other people and being able to compare Chrissie with them. Now she no longer believed her elder sister and didn't feel put down by the scathing insults heaped on her all the time.

Clare would like to have had blue eyes. Brown eyes were wrong in her face she thought, her complexion wasn't right for them. If she were like Ava Gardner, or had a dark smouldering face, then big brown eyes would be good; but she thought they looked out of place with her light hair and fair skin. Still. There was nothing she could do about them. Josie told her they were fine, and what's more they were unusual, so there. She should be delighted with them and stop complaining.

Josie was going from strength to strength these days. She was already in the office of the hotel, wearing a frilly white blouse and a cameo brooch. She had lost a great deal of weight in the two years she spent living in her aunt's house while she went to the commercial college. Her aunt was the meanest woman in Ireland and the meals that were served were extremely sparse. But it was all to the good and Josie's two sisters looked at her with shock each time they came home from their boarding school, and, eventually, the Hotel and Catering College. Slow, fat Josie could type letters like the wind, had understood book keeping and simple accountancy. She was helping Father and Uncle Dick and Mother with far more confidence than they seemed to be able to drum up. In fact Rose and Emily were quite jealous of the sister they used to call poor Josie. They even complained when they saw her change into whites and play tennis with that Clare O'Brien from the shop. But Josie was calm. She and Clare played tennis every morning from eight to nine; then they went to work, Josie in her family business, Clare in hers. They played again at seven in the evening. Rose and Emily had all day to play if they wanted to. It was unanswerable. Which was why Rose and Emily hated it; it was even further irritating to see that Josie and Clare played well and often played a mixed doubles with guests from the hotel.

Clare and Josie had more fun at the dance than Rose and Emily who thought, wrongly, that they would be exotic and a treat coming home as they had from Dublin. But the visitors didn't know where they had come from and the locals all knew the two girls who were around all the time; they were never without a partner.

Leaning over the balcony and watching Josie rocking enthusiastically to 'See You Later Alligator', Emily complained loudly one evening that the young ones had it very easy, didn't they? Nice cushy job ready made for them in the hotel, no studying hotel management, all plain sailing and life one long holiday. Chrissie O'Brien, another wallflower, watched her younger sister with equal rage and said that there was no justice in life. Rose and Emily had to disassociate themselves. Annoyed they might be, but they weren't going to ally themselves with terrible Chrissie O'Brien.

The Nolans still came to Castlebay, they were part and parcel of the place now. At least, Mr and Mrs Nolan did. Of James, there was no sign, Josie sighed.

'Maybe he'll come down this summer, and you'll dazzle him,' Clare said.

'No, I interrogated his mother, he's in France picking grapes with David Power. Can you imagine anything more stupid, those two picking grapes? They don't need the money, why aren't they here where they *are* needed?'

'It's a funny time of year to be picking grapes,' Clare said thoughtfully. 'I thought all that was much later on.'

'Maybe they're up to no good. They could have French mistresses.' Josie was deliberately making herself miserable.

'They should be working for their exams,' Clare said primly. David Power was about Fourth Med by now; and James Nolan had a B.A. in economics, but he still had to do his Bar Final. Josie was right; they were much too grown-up and sophisticated to pick grapes or whatever in France, but they were much too grown-up and sophisticated to come to Castlebay as well.

Molly Power was delighted with the letter. It said she was to let the Nolans know too. David and James would be arriving next Thursday week. Things hadn't worked out exactly as they had hoped in France, long explanations later, but meanwhile they thought they would come back to Castlebay. Waving the letter Molly ran out on to the drive as she heard her husband's car on the gravel.

'Great news, David's coming home next week.'

His face lit up with pleasure. 'David's coming back, Bones,' he said and the animal did three circuits of the car, barking delightedly.

Paddy Power took his wife's arm and they sat on the garden seat, looking straight out to sea. On a day like this it was paradise.

Nellie called from the kitchen window. 'You look very comfortable out there, stay as you are. I'll bring out your dinner.'

A polite protest.

'Sure why don't you act like the quality,' Nellie said and closed the window.

They smiled at each other, pleased greatly that their son was coming home.

'I arranged for old Mrs O'Hara to go into the County Hospital for a couple of weeks today. Observation, I call it.'

'And what is it? What has she got?'

'Nothing, as far as I can see. Nothing she hasn't had for years. But I want to give Angela a holiday, that's what it's really about. Angela hardly ever gets a break. I want her to enjoy a bit of this summer. Lord, she's living in a place that half of Ireland and indeed half of England as well seems to be descending on . . . but she never gets out to enjoy it.'

'You're very thoughtful.' Molly touched his knee affectionately.

'I've always liked her, always, she's got such pluck, I know it's a funny word, it's not a word for people like us, but that's it. Pluck. Do you know I often think young Clare O'Brien from the shop has it too. I always see her as sort of an echo of Angela O'Hara.'

'Do you?' Molly frowned.

'Same way of sticking their chins up and getting on with things, no matter what.' Dr Power smiled at the thought.

'I don't think so.' Molly was shaking her head. 'Angela had spirit certainly, and it's wonderful she got so far, considering . . .' She left unsaid the ripples of disapproval over Dinny O'Hara's behaviour, and her own remoteness towards the life looking after an old woman.

Dr Power hid his impatience. He hated Molly in that *grande dame* mood. 'Well the child Clare O'Brien has nobody to be apologizing for, just the fact that she was born poor and triumphed over it.'

'She was born sneaky, Paddy, you're too kind, you don't see these things. A woman would notice. She has deceitful eyes.'

'*Molly.*'

'Well, you say what you think, I say what I think.'

'But it's silly. Silly, to say such a thing about a child.'

'To me some of the things *you* do and say are silly. I don't pass remarks about them.'

'All right, Moll, all right. Life's short, let's leave it.' The day seemed less shiny somehow for him.

Gerry Doyle arrived at the O'Haras' cottage later in the afternoon. He was to give them a lift to the hospital. 'Take as much time as you like,' he told them. 'I'm in no hurry, so don't be rushing.'

But they were ready: Mrs O'Hara tremulous and afraid of a bumpy journey in that young tearaway's van, Angela pale and anxious. The little suitcase had been packed.

'Well will we head off then?' Gerry was a great person to drive them. He didn't care enough about Mrs O'Hara to be making inquiries about how she felt, and he had plenty of good casual chat to keep Angela distracted. Dr Power had said that since he went into the town every Tuesday to get equipment and supplies, he'd be the very man to give them a lift. Dr Power had even gone and called on Doyle's Photographics himself to save Angela the business of asking him for a lift.

He was kind and practical about getting the old woman into his van. 'Tell me first what movements hurt you most, and I won't drag you the wrong way,' he said.

Mrs O'Hara had to pause and think. The worst bit was having to bend her legs. Right, that was easily organized, Gerry got a box for her to stand on then she sat into the front seat of his van and Angela eased her legs in as straight as it was possible to do. Mrs O'Hara settled in fairly cheerfully. Angela climbed into the back.

'You're very agile for a woman of your age,' Gerry said, smiling at her in the driver's mirror.

'Will you stop that nonsense, I could run rings round you. Your generation have no stamina.' She grinned back at him through the mirror. He was a handsome lad. She had always liked him. Much more than his sister, and she had often asked herself why she didn't take to Fiona Doyle, without ever coming to a satisfactory conclusion.

They were good youngsters both of them. Since their father's death, they had not only kept the business going, they had made it boom. The big increase in visitors had meant a huge demand for snaps. During the summer the Doyles hired another photographer to help out. They had smartened up their little booth on the cliff with bright paint, and they had been doing great business calling to the houses along the Cliff Road and the Far Cliff Road taking family pictures, which they enlarged and presented in a little cardboard frame. Nearly every family wanted to have a souvenir like that, something to show at home, the family in their own place. Messages used to be sent urgently to get young Jimmy back from the amusements, or call young Eddie up from the beach; Mother would change into her best dress and the milk bottle would be hidden away while the picture was being taken.

'I see your star pupil is home from school,' Gerry said.

'She is a star pupil,' Angela said proudly. 'I have great hopes for her, I really do.'

'So do I,' said Gerry, smiling roguishly. 'Great hopes altogether.'

'Stop sounding like the villain in a pantomime,' Angela said crossly. *Please*, she thought, don't let Gerry Doyle distract Clare before the interview. Don't let him get his hands on her until she's won the Murray Prize.

They were very nice to Mrs O'Hara in the hospital, and the change suited her. Everything was new and interesting: the Little Flower ward with the big statue of St Theresa and the roses falling around the crucifix in her arms. Mrs O'Hara had always had a great devotion to the Little Flower. The woman in the next bed was some distant relative by marriage so they spent hours tracing people long dead and lowering their voices about people whose careers had not been too glorious. Angela felt nothing but relief that her mother was being well looked after. Dr Power had been right: the change would do Mam good. She spent the first few days after her mother left doing a kind of spring-clean. She never liked to paint the place while the housebound woman was there; the smell would be hard to bear. She pulled all the furniture into the middle of the floor, and began to take down the books and ornaments. It was a much longer job than she would have believed but it was a very peaceful one. She sat on a ladder dusting books and reading them at the same time, polishing ornaments and remembering who had given them or where they had come from. It was days before she actually began to paint. She had gone in twice and been reassured that her mother was happy and well looked after. This was a good break for her, housepainting in the morning, a stroll down to the hotel, a sandwich sometimes with Dick Dillon, still mourning the fact that he had been put off drink and pushed sideways in the chain of command in the hotel. Then she would go down to the beach, and swim. She would know at least twenty people that she passed, pupils present and past, people from Castlebay sunning themselves. But usually she took a book and sat on the grassy cliff base. Then when it got very hot she would run down into the sea and battle with the breakers. Once she came across a small child who was being constantly buffeted by the waves and knocked down every time she got to her feet. Angela swooped her up and carried her out of the water. She was just the kind of child who could be one of Dr Power's casualties. The kind of thing he was always worrying about, visitors who didn't know the pull of the current, the strength of the waves. She found herself telling the family tearfully that they must pay more attention to a child of that age or she would be swept out to sea. The child's parents were grateful and startled, and she overheard them saying as she left that possibly she had a child that was drowned herself and that's what had unsettled her so much. Angela didn't *feel* unsettled. She felt fine. But she realized that it was the first summer she had ever got a tan, been to the pictures regularly and gone to the dance.

She hadn't intended going to the dance. She thought women of thirty-five were pathetic in their summer dresses, their white cardigans and their newly lacquered hair queueing up at the ticket desk with the hope of a starry and glittery night ahead. Even when she heard that the Castlebay Committee were having a special dance to raise funds she didn't think of going. The Committee was going to charge a big price for the ticket, but there were going to be enormous spot prizes. Every business in the place was giving something. Gerry Doyle was going to take a family or group portrait free, Mrs Conway in the post office was offering a set of a dozen views of Castlebay on postcards with a small frame as well. Dwyers' were giving a leg of lamb. Miss O'Flaherty was offering a writing case with pad and envelopes. The O'Briens were giving two big tins of Afternoon Tea assortment, the best biscuits there were. The money they raised would go to make the place look more attractive, to build a proper car park possibly and prevent the road being cluttered with cars making it impossible to get in or out of Castlebay. Or maybe plant a big flowerbed on the way into town where the three roads met. Some people wanted to put up fairy lights down Church Street, and others wanted to have public lavatories built on the beach. It would all be debated long and excitedly during the winter, and the money raised would sit in Mrs Conway's post office for ages. Angela, as a teacher and respected member of the community, had been on the Castlebay Committee but it never occurred to her that she was expected to go to the dance. Dick Dillon said that this is what always happened when you had a bunch of old meddlers and busybodies running things, now they were all nicely stuck and had to go to the wretched dance or their lives wouldn't be worth living.

'Will you come as my partner?' he asked Angela in a voice filled with such doom he might as well have been asking her to leap off the cliff with him in a suicide mission.

'Certainly,' Angela said.

He looked at her suspiciously. 'You can collect me at the hotel then,' he said.

'No Dick, a gentleman collects a lady at *her* house,' Angela said in a parody of every Doris Day film she had seen. If Dick had seen the films he didn't recognize the parody.

'Very well,' he said. 'Seeing as how I don't drink any more I might as well get value out of the car by driving it.'

She hardly thought about the dance again, she was so busy painting the house. She decided that the only way to do it was to divide the big downstairs room into two halves, and when the first half was painted she would put back the books and knick-knacks before starting the other side. It did look much brighter and more awake. She was standing in a paint-spattered smock and her hair in an old scarf admiring it, when a car stopped at the door. James Nolan and David Power had come to call. Better than that, they had brought a bottle of champagne cider.

She was delighted to see them. She had followed their careers with delight and when nobody else remembered what exams they were doing, Miss O'Hara always did. She used to know the names of their professors too and she never asked embarrassing questions like did they have girlfriends, did they spend much money on drink, and what exactly were they doing in France?

They picked chairs and stools out of the heap of furniture and sat happily telling her about everything. David was tall and fair-haired with a peeling nose, and James small and dark-looking like a little Italian, so tanned was he after whatever they had been up to in France. They were full of plans for the summer. It was going to be two hours' work every morning and then free as the air all day and all night. They wanted to know was there any talent in town. Any gorgeous blondes or redheads with tiny waists and huge bosoms. Angela said she wouldn't have noticed if the town was full of them, but they'd have to look sharp before Gerry Doyle grabbed everything that was going.

'That fellow, is he still at it?' James Nolan said. 'I know I'm a small runt of a thing myself, but he's a dwarf. What *do* they see in him?'

'I can't believe he's *still* the Romeo,' David complained. 'He was always getting the girls without having to lift a finger. I'd have thought they'd have seen through him by now.'

'Different crop every year of course,' Angela said.

'But seriously, Miss O'Hara, seriously.' David looked lovely when he was trying to be serious. He pushed the long lick of hair on his forehead back so that it stood up like a fan. 'Now would you as a *woman* . . . well, as a *female* – would you tell us what's so attractive about him.'

'As a *female*, I would find it very hard to explain. He's good company, he has a nice smile, he smiles a lot. He doesn't try too hard to please, but he does seem to *like* women, without exactly flirting with them. Is that any help?'

She looked from one handsome student to the other as they sat in her upside-down house. They were both thoughtful.

'That's a great help, actually,' David said earnestly. 'Not trying too hard to please. I think that's where I fall down.'

'I don't think I *like* women like he does. I think I like the idea of women more than I like them as people,' said James Nolan.

'I'm sorry I don't have a couch free,' Angela laughed. 'You could lie down one by one and I could psychoanalyse you, maybe I could psychoanalyse half of Castlebay, and I'd make a fortune. Your father could send me a few patients, David, and maybe Father O'Dwyer could too. Oh and anyone left roaring and bawling after the dance could always come here for a midnight session, I'd straighten them out.'

She was great at knocking down their pomposity. David had been glad to hear from his father that the old woman was in hospital for the summer, he didn't like calling to see Miss O'Hara when her mother was there, you felt you should talk to both of them. He remembered why he had come.

'I really wanted to know if you'd like to come with us to the Castlebay Committee dance next week. Mummy and Daddy are going too and the Nolans and we were all going to have a drink in our house first and go together.'

Angela was flattered to have been asked; but she regretted that she had a date already.

They were excited when they learned it was Dick Dillon. A romance? A local love affair possibly? A slow-flowering friendship blossoming into a late romance? Would there be wedding bells pealing out from the church before long?

She said they shouldn't be so cruel and heartless and tease an old maid, a poor spinster of the parish. David said it was just because she wasn't an old maid they could tease her. It was the best compliment she had ever got, even though anyone else hearing it might have thought it inexplicable.

Clare came twice a week to rehearse the interview for the Murray Prize. They had found out who sat on the board: an uncle of Josie Dillon on her mother's side was one of them. He was a bank manager and the Murray money was in his bank so that gave him some kind of right to be there when it was being handed out. According to Josie he was mad and snobbish, and thought that Dillon's Hotel in Castlebay was rather beneath him. Angela and Clare were still working on their strategy for him. Clare arrived shortly after the boys had gone.

'The place stinks of drink,' she said accusingly.

'It's my age, at the change of life we women become all funny, we start shifting the furniture around and drinking on our own.'

Clare laughed. 'You're never at the change of life yet, Miss O'Hara?'

'*Of course I'm not!* God, remind me never to make jokes talking to children. Please Lord, let me never be ironic again. The drink was a gift from two young gentlemen callers. They came and brought champagne cider and invited me to the Castlebay Committee dance. How about that for a poor, old, decrepit, barren geriatric?'

'Who was it?'

'David Power and James Nolan.'

'And are you going?'

'No, I thought I'd leave the field free for younger, plainer women. I'm going with Josie's uncle. He did ask me first. Are you going?'

'I suppose I will, Josie and I'll go together. You don't need a partner. I think she'd rather like it if James Nolan was around, she fancies him a lot.'

'Tell her to pretend she doesn't even notice him, that will work. Come on now, do something to help me, lift one end of this contraption with me, I'm going to paint it out in the back. If I paint it here I'll stick to it every time I pass by. It's not going to rain they say on the wireless, so that should mean we'll have a nice fine evening ...'

She broke off suddenly. Clare hadn't moved, she was sitting troubled and hadn't even been listening.

'What is it?' she said. 'You surely haven't got the results yet?'

The only thing that could make Clare's face so downcast must have to do with the Leaving Certificate results, but they weren't due for two more weeks.

'Tommy's in gaol,' Clare said simply.

'Tommy. Tommy?' It was so long since she had seen the O'Brien boys she had forgotten their names. It came to her a couple of seconds later. 'In gaol? In England? What did he do?'

'Housebreaking.'

Angela sat down. 'When did you hear? Who told you?'

'Just now. The afternoon post. I'm afraid I came up to you straight away. I couldn't bear to stand in the shop thinking about it. Mam will be furious. Still. I'll cope with that.'

'God Almighty, isn't that desperate? How do you know?'

'A letter from Ned. So as not to worry Mam and Dad immediately, but so as I could forewarn them in case it gets back to them. What *does* he want me to do? Tell them or not to tell them? It might appear in a paper he said, then again it might not. Thomas O'Brien is a very ordinary name he says, but Thomas O'Brien from Castlebay would place him pretty clearly. Here, you can read the letter ... see if you know what he wants. See if you know what I'm meant to do.'

Angela didn't reach out to take the ill-written pages on their lined paper. She sat with her elbows on her knees and her head in her hands. There was a silence for a while. 'I don't need to read the letter, I know what he wants,' Angela said eventually. 'He wants *you* to make the decisions. He wants *you* to take on the responsibility.'

Clare was surprised. 'Why?'

'Because you're not Chrissie who wouldn't know what day it was, and you're not your mother who would cry her eyes out, and you're not your father who would get into a temper and you're not Ben and Jim who are too young to be taken into account. And because you're bright and got a scholarship, that's going to fit you and make you ready for any burden from now on.'

Clare was very startled at her tone. 'Miss O'Hara ...' she began.

'What sentence did he get?' Angela asked crisply.

'Ned says two years.'

'That was more than ordinary housebreaking. He must have had a weapon. The great thick fool.'

'No wonder he never wrote home.'

'Tommy was hardly able to write if I remember rightly. What do you think you'll do?'

'I don't know. I've no information. If I thought it was going to get into the papers here I'd tell Ma and Da, but if not what's the point in hurting them?'

'I know, what we need is information as you say.'

'But I've no way of finding out . . .'

'I have. See can you find a writing pad under those newspapers there, I'll write it now and you can get it into the six o'clock post.'

'Who? What will you say?'

'I have a friend in London. He's a priest – but not like Father O'Dwyer here or anything. He'd find out for us.'

'But could you ask him? Wouldn't he . . . ?'

'No, he wouldn't be shocked, and he's one of the best men in the world to keep a secret. Have you the paper? I'll start straight away.'

Clare's eyes filled quickly with tears of gratitude as Miss O'Hara wrote her address across the top of the paper and then wrote: 'Dear Father Flynn, I wonder can you help me. Yet again . . .'

Father Flynn was magnificent. There was a reply in eight days. He had been to see Ned, who was working in a pub now, washing up. It was a rough sort of place, Father Flynn had got him a new job where he was better off – he could live in and the landlord would keep an eye on him. He had heard the details. Tommy had been in with a gang. They had done several jobs and six months ago, Tommy had got probation for his part in the theft of building supplies from a site. This time it had been a smash and grab raid on a small jeweller's shop. What they hadn't realized was that the jeweller was still in his shop when the windows were broken with crowbars and the goods seized. The jeweller's mistake had been to stand up. He had been hit on the side of the head by one of the gang – he could not identify it as being Tommy. But the rest of them escaped and were gone well to ground when the police came looking. Only Tommy was there still with some of the jewellery.

Tommy had said he didn't know who the others were, and couldn't give descriptions. He insisted that he had only met them that night and they didn't give their names. So, according to Ned, the gang were pleased with him and they would make sure he got his share when he came out. He would be out in eighteen months. Father Flynn had visited him in Wormwood Scrubs and reported that he was very pleased to have some contact with home. Since he had been asked to be totally frank, Father Flynn had to report Tommy O'Brien in poor shape, he was missing most of his teeth; he asked for nothing but comics to read from the prison library and he had all the appearance of a loser. Since it was hardly helpful to make such comments without offering anything more positive as well, Father Flynn wondered was there a way Tommy could be brought back to Castlebay when he was released. He did not seem a strong enough character to survive on either side of the tracks in the life he had found for himself in London. If Castlebay was not a realistic solution Father Flynn would try to keep an eye on him, but it would be hard. As soon as Tommy was released he would be given money to show approval that he hadn't squealed; and within three months he would be inside again, for he would loyally go along with the next job suggested to him, and be the patsy there as well. As regards publicity there would be none. The name T. O'Brien had appeared in a local evening paper in London; it would not be taken up by the Irish newspapers. Unfortunately, the arrest and imprisonment of people with Irish names was only too commonplace now. It didn't rate as news.

Angela and Clare read this glumly. He had certainly been as frank as they had asked him to be. But he had been exactly the right person to go and see what was happening. He made no judgements and expressed no shock or disapproval.

'I wonder how Tommy lost his teeth. A fight maybe?' Angela said.

'Maybe they just rotted away,' Clare said. 'He was very nervous of everything, Tommy. He wouldn't ever go to the dentist. I can't think how he was brave enough to get in with a gang of robbers, I'd have thought he would have run a hundred miles in the opposite direction.'

Her face was sad even though her voice was calm. She hadn't cried or shown any great shock when she read the priest's letter. She sat very still with her elbows on the table and her chin in her hands. Clare had the ability to be very still, Angela had noticed. When she was reading only the turning of the pages showed she was awake. When she listened it was the same. Now she heard of her brother's disgrace without expostulating, or making excuses.

'I don't suppose he had to be very brave to get in with a gang. Probably need to be brave *not* to get in with one. Will you write to him in gaol?'

Clare hadn't thought of this. 'Is there any point if he can't read the letters? Would we be better to pretend we didn't know he was there at all? I think that's what he'd like best,' she said without conviction.

'Too late for that. Ned wrote to you, remember? You can't pretend you don't know. You can keep it from your parents and the rest of them but you can't go back on what you know.'

'Yes.'

'So, will you write to him?'

'He never wrote to me, not in six years, nor to any of us, it would only be hypocritical, wouldn't it? And maybe even boasting. Look at me, how well I'm doing, I even have my sights on being a college girl, a graduate, and where are you? You're a gaol bird.'

'I don't suppose you'd write a letter like that.'

Her immobility had gone, her eyes flashed. 'You think I ought to, don't you? If it were you, you'd be sunny and forgiving and like a saint, the way you are about everything. But the world isn't full of saints, it's full of ordinary selfish people like Tommy who go stealing, and me who doesn't want to write him pious letters.'

Angela said nothing.

'I know I shouldn't say it's all right for you, I *know* you had your share of awful things years ago when your father was ... but that's all long past you, people have

631

forgotten that, you've no shames and no secrets now. You're where you want to be, and you're nice and safe as a teacher here, and your family are all respectable, and you've got a brother, a priest, for God's sake. I've got a brother with no teeth who can't read and who's in Wormwood Scrubs.'

'Clare,' Angela said sharply.

She looked up.

Angela paused. No, not now. It wasn't bad enough, it was only a fit of annoyance and self-pity. She wouldn't tell her.

'Nothing.'

Clare was surprised.

'If you don't get the Murray Prize remind me that I was going to tell you something this afternoon and I changed my mind.'

'Why won't you tell me?'

'I won't, that's all. Now are we going to waste any more time listening to how sorry you are for yourself? You asked me to find out about Tommy, I have. He's your brother, write to him if you want to, don't if you don't want to. I'm not spending one more minute discussing it. If you haven't the generosity to give some bit of hope and optimism to that poor eejit in there, then you haven't. I'm not involved in making you a nice person, nobody can do that for you. I'm only helping you to get on academically. Let's see, where were we?' She took out a notebook and checked the items they'd covered last time. 'Now we've been over a lot of current affairs and you're fine on Eisenhower and the Middle East and the end of Anthony Eden, and King Hussein of Jordan, but there's a good chance that none of the committee will have ever heard of them. Maybe we should concentrate on what they really know about, the Pope and de Valera. When was Pius XII consecrated as Pope . . . ?'

'I'm sorry. Of course I'll write to him.'

'Write to who you like. Pius XII. And what was his name?'

'Pacelli, Eugenio Pacelli, he's eighty-one, he was elected in 1939, the year the war started, he was Papal representative in Germany.'

'*Nuncio, nuncio*, say it.'

'Nuncio.'

'And don't come out with it too cocky. Try not to sound as if you know everything. They won't like that.'

They laughed. Clare wanted to say more about Tommy, but she was headed off.

'De Valera . . . now this is a tricky one, they'll be bound to love him or hate him, but you're not expected to have any views . . . just facts. Born?'

'In New York in 1882, of a Spanish father and Irish mother, brought up in Bruree, County Limerick . . . but I do have views . . .'

'Of course you do, but when you are being tested for the Murray Prize is not the time to express them. If any of this lot are in their fifties or over they'll remember the Civil War. Not just remember hearing about it, they'll bloody remember it themselves, so will you go carefully and don't throw the whole thing away. We could concentrate on what Dev did in the last war, that shouldn't offend many of them, but if there's anyone with an Anglo-Irish accent there watch it, the English never forgave Dev over our staying neutral. No point in waving a red rag to a bull.'

'Thank you, Miss O'Hara.'

'Stop simpering and keep learning. Talking of simpering, did Gerry Doyle ask you to the Castlebay Committee dance?'

'Yes he did. I said no, Josie and I were going on our own, we'd see him in there.'

'It's you who should be teaching me,' sighed Angela.

Dick Dillon looked very cross when he came to collect Angela. She invited him in and offered him a cup of tea or a glass of orange. He looked around in surprise.

'You have it very nice, considering.'

'Considering *what*?'

'I don't know, just considering,' he said. Angela wondered why couldn't she have said to Dick Dillon that she'd see him inside? Why did she have to put up with this groaning and grousing?

'I painted it recently, while mother's in hospital. Dr Power said she should go in for observation. She'll be back soon.'

She heard her own voice, boring, talking trivia to this old man. What did young Clare mean the other day when she said that Angela had got all she wanted? She did not want to be talking to a reformed alcoholic sitting there patronizing her little house. In as grouchy a manner as his own she flung his orange squash in front of him and very deliberately took a bottle of gin out of the press.

'Since I haven't been put off it yet, I am going to have a drink to get us through this night, Dick Dillon. So will almost everyone around you, so you might as well get used to it now.'

A slow smile of admiration came over his face. 'That's the first time anyone has treated me as a normal human being for seven years,' and he raised his own glass to her. 'Good luck,' he said beaming all over his face.

Molly Power had laid out little plates of biscuits with cheese on some and mashed-up eggs on others. The eggs ones had been a mistake. She had forgotten how quickly they would go soggy. She had nuts in little bowls and that afternoon she had gone and collected masses of gorse, which looked gorgeous in bowls and jugs all around the room. Their sitting room had yellow curtains and the chintz covers had a lot of yellow in them too. One day Nellie had brought in gorse and Molly had been about to throw it out – but Mrs Nolan had admired it. So now Molly had adopted it as her own idea.

David was rubbing Nivea Creme into his nose. 'I think all the peeling's gone now,' he said, looking at himself in the mirror over the mantelpiece.

'I told you to stop pulling at it and picking at it, it would have gone much sooner if you'd left it alone,' his mother said.

David sighed. There was never anything that Mother didn't know or wasn't right about.

'I know, I know,' he said wearily.

'Well it stands to reason. You're fair-skinned. You get burned. You must wait until the dead skin falls off. Don't pull at it.'

'I won't,' David said, exasperated.

'I don't know why you're getting into a mood.' Molly was annoyed. 'Here we are, having a party for all your friends before you go to the dance. You will have a marvellous evening and all you can do is snap at anyone who tries to help you.' She sounded aggrieved.

David said nothing.

'It's not as if your father and I ever interfere in your life or ask you what you get up to. When the dance is over, do we ever say you must come straight home? No we don't. We let you live your own life.'

'Ah, come on now,' David, trying to hide his anger without much success, laughed insincerely. 'Come on, Mother, I'm a grown-up man, not a little boy with a fishing net. I live my own life in Dublin – naturally I live my own life here too.'

'*Naturally*,' she said in her pouting voice.

He chose not to hear the sulk.

'Good, then we're both saying the same thing.' He squared his shoulders in his new jacket and gave himself one last look.

'Well, that will have to do. If I don't get the lovely Caroline away from Gerry Doyle tonight, I never will.'

'Gerry Doyle? Don't be ridiculous. He'll be there taking snaps.'

'Oh no he won't, he'll have a minion doing that. Gerry will be there on his own terms, making no effort and they'll all come crawling to him.'

'That's disgusting and all in your mind.'

'See for yourself tonight. Caroline's only one of a queue.'

'I never heard such nonsense . . . oh there you are Paddy, don't you look nice and clean?'

'Clean?' Dr Power roared. 'Is that all you have to say to me?'

'I meant dressed up and smart,' Molly laughed.

'Clean,' he snorted. 'What were you saying was nonsense, when I came in?'

'This belief that Gerry Doyle is some kind of ladykiller. Even Caroline Nolan. Caroline, with the whole of the university to choose from . . .'

'Caroline's here,' Dr Power said. 'There was a great tooting of cars and I saw her arriving up at the crossroads. She has a Morris Minor all of her own now. Anyway, she said she took it into her head to come to Castlebay, and I told her she picked a good night and that she was to come up here for a drink first. She got into a great fluster and said she'd have to wash her hair. I don't know why women go on so much about their hair. They're always washing it or having it done at the hairdresser's, and complaining if you don't know every rib of it that's been changed.'

'Well now we'll see if she's interested in that Gerry Doyle,' Molly said to David. 'And stop eating the cheese ones. If you want to eat anything, eat the ones with egg on them.'

Chrissie had given the dance a lot of thought. At one stage she was fully prepared to abandon it. A snobs' dance, an old people's dance. Catch Chrissie O'Brien dead at that? Then she saw that the feeling of the town was not the same as her own. In Dwyers' they discussed endlessly whether they should give mutton, beef or pork as a spot prize, and Kath and Peggy had even bought new dresses. Chrissie decided that she didn't want to be humbled watching Gerry Doyle ignore her. He only gave her the coolest of nods these days. She couldn't bear him to see her standing there as he whirled by with whatever new glamorous piece who had come to town. Even if he danced with her once or twice like he used to, that would be fine, but he had lost all interest. He didn't need Chrissie.

She sighed a lot when people asked her was she going to the Committee dance. 'Only if someone asks me,' she said. 'I'm too old to go to a dance without a partner.'

Kath and Peggy couldn't understand it. The *point* was to go without a partner and find a partner there. But Chrissie was adamant. Bumper Byrne the builder was buying meat and heard Chrissie O'Brien talking like this. He told his younger brother Maurice, or Mogsy as he had been called ever since anyone could remember. Mogsy came down to the shop.

'Will you be my partner for the Committee dance please?' he said across the counter. Mr Dwyer the butcher sighed with relief.

'What do you mean by being a partner exactly?'

'I mean I'll pay for you, I'll dance with you when you're not asked up by other people. I won't stand in your way if some fellow you want a spin around the floor with comes along, and I'll buy you minerals at the bar,' said Mogsy who wore his hat back to front and wasn't too bright.

Chrissie considered it. 'And what would *you* get out of it?' she asked ungraciously.

'I don't know.' Mogsy hadn't thought of it like that. 'I suppose I'd get the right to dance with you and put my arm around you and say you were my date for the night. Aren't you the best-looking girl in Castlebay?'

Chrissie smiled across the marble counter. 'Thank you very much, Mogsy, I'd be glad to come to the dance as your partner,' she said.

Best-looking girl in Castlebay. Well now. Not that anyone was saying Mogsy Byrne was bright or anything, but he wasn't *too* bad, and she would never be left standing, and she'd go in on his arm. That would show Gerry Doyle not everyone had to sit around and wait for him.

'Good, that's fixed then.' Mogsy was off.

'Have you a suit and everything?' she asked.

'I've a gorgeous suit,' he said.

'We'll show them, Mogsy,' she said.

Josie and Clare were putting on their make-up.

'It must be something to do with the colour of your lips to start with,' Josie said. 'Sari Peach looks quite a different colour on you than on me.'

They had bought one lipstick between them in Murphy's chemist. Mrs Murphy had said it was very unhygienic to share a lipstick, it could pass on germs. They had laughed the whole way home remembering how the whole school would share one lipstick at times and nobody had come out in a rash.

Clare wore a red corduroy skirt and a white frilly blouse: she had a red velvet ribbon on her hair. She dressed up in Josie's room because Chrissie had the bedroom at home commandeered. Josie had a lemon-coloured dress with a square neck back and front, trimmed with white broderie anglaise.

'Are you sure I don't look like a tank?' she asked for the tenth time.

'What am I going to do with you?' Clare wailed. 'You *don't* look like a tank, you haven't looked like a tank since you were twelve and you're nearly eighteen now. That's a third of your life you haven't looked like a tank and you still think you do!'

Josie laughed. 'I'm thinner than Emily and Rose. They hate it.'

'They hate everything. They're like posh versions of Chrissie. She says that I'm thin because of all the badness in me, it eats up the food from within, and you're thin because you've got worms.'

They fell about the room laughing. Which was worse, to have worms or inner badness?

'I don't think he has anyone else this summer, anyone serious that is,' Josie said, pouting at herself in the mirror.

'James?'

'Who else?'

'Not a sign of it. He and David have been playing golf a lot. Miss O'Hara told me. They call into her sometimes on the way there or back. No sign of women at all. His sister's arrived. Lady Caroline. I saw her rushing into reception downstairs asking for a loan of a hairdryer.'

'Did they give her one?' Josie wanted to befriend the beloved's sister.

'I think so, there was a great fuss – you know the way Lady Caroline talks, she expects things done.'

'I hope they got her one.'

'I don't, I'd like her to have rats' tails for once instead of looking like an advertisement.'

'I think she fancies Gerry Doyle.'

'Tell her to join the queue,' Clare said, applying more Vaseline to her eyelashes to get them to curl.

'I was just thinking,' Josie said. 'Suppose I won the spot prize we gave, you know the one the hotel gave.'

'Well, what would be so funny?'

'It's a weekend, all expenses paid, staying here. I could have a room with a sea view and have Emily bring me my breakfast in bed.'

Chrissie was just ahead of them at the ticket box. She was arm in arm with Mogsy Byrne who was in charge of the churns when the farmers brought the milk in. Tonight, he wore a suit. He looked a bit drunk already.

'I would have thought that the elegant Miss Clare O'Brien and her friend Miss Josie Dillon wouldn't be seen paying for their own tickets to the dance,' Chrissie said loudly.

She looked awful, Clare thought. After all that work and all that flinging of clothes and make-up around the bedroom. The pink satin dress was much too tight, the white cardigan was grubby and the glittery diamante jewellery looked flashy, like the bright red lipstick and heavy white powder. Still, other fellows were giving her admiring glances. Maybe she was more suitably dressed than Clare, perhaps the blouse and skirt were a bit dowdy, a bit schoolgirlish.

They were playing 'The Yellow Rose of Texas'; the ballroom was festive, with balloons and decorations all around, and a big banner saying that the Castlebay Committee welcomed everyone and thanked them for their support. There was a

636

huge table, groaning with gifts, on the stage near the band, and a spotlight going around picking out lucky couples who would then be given a gift. The instructions were that not too many should be given early, and only the inferior ones. As Clare and Josie came in they saw a couple in the spotlight being presented with a small talcum powder and bath cubes in a presentation box. There were much greater things to come. They were heading across to a corner which they thought was a good vantage point when they were both asked to dance at once. This was a good omen, they thought, as they were whirled out on to the floor.

Dick Dillon said he was great at the waltz but he wasn't going to make a public display of himself over this jiving, and rock and roll.

Angela said the waltz was her forte too, just so long as they didn't twirl too fast. As luck would have it the band had announced 'Tales from the Vienna Woods' just as they came in.

'I suppose you'll want to go to the ladies' cloakroom,' Dick grumbled.

'Why would I?' Angela asked and they were off, round and round, bending and swooping, Dick looking over his left shoulder and Angela looking to her left. He held her firmly in the small of the back and didn't slip, even though the floor had been treated to make it shine. Angela's beige silk dress, the one she had bought for Emer's wedding, swirled round. If Emer could see this! It is *ridiculous*, she thought, I am a ludicrous figure. And she smiled to herself as she saw admiring glances, not laughter. She saw Dr Power pointing her out to Mr Nolan. That would have been her party if she hadn't agreed to come with this madman.

The madman in question spoke out of the side of his mouth. 'I think we're showing them a thing or two,' he hissed.

'I'd say they'll clear the floor any minute for the two of us to do a demonstration,' Angela said, and at that moment the spotlight landed on them and the band leader announced that they had won a leg of lamb kindly presented by Messrs Dwyer, the premier butcher in Castlebay.

Everybody was in good humour, and suntanned and cheerful. Simon, the handsome lifeguard, who wore a pullover tied casually round his shoulders, was talking to Frank Conway who was a guard, and very tall with a back like a ramrod. A lot of the girls were eyeing them with interest. Frank Conway kept glancing at the door. 'I was watching to see if I could see Fiona Doyle coming in,' he explained.

Simon smiled. 'I bet a lot of people are. But I wouldn't be surprised if the guard dog hasn't let her out.'

'The what?'

'Her brother. He is like a guard dog. He barks if anyone comes near. It's fine for him to do what he likes, but she can have no fun.'

Frank was disappointed but he wanted to stand up for Fiona. 'In a way, Gerry's right, you can't have *girls* doing what they like – it wouldn't be right.'

'You're not like that with your sister Bernie. She's a free agent.' Simon glanced at Bernie Conway, smooching with one of the visitors.

'Yes, well.' Frank was irritated now on every score. When the dance was over he went up to Bernie and invited her for the next waltz.

'This *is* a surprise,' she said, not altogether pleased. --

'I think you should behave in a more ladylike way in public.'

'I think you should go and stick your fat head in a bucket,' said Bernie, and walked off the floor. Simon saw her free, and asked her back to dance.

'My brother is mad. Stark staring mad,' she said.

'Let's not talk about your brother,' said Simon, holding her very close to him and running his hand up and down her back.

Gerry Doyle never *asked* anyone to dance. He always seemed to be beside the girl that he wanted when the music started, and he would smile and hold out his hand. He asked Josie Dillon first, and she was glad to be seen out on the floor by James Nolan, who had just come in. Josie had noticed that Caroline's dark hair looked nicely set, so the hotel must have been able to find her a hair dryer all right. Gerry was a terrific dancer of course, and she was glad that she and Clare had spent some time learning the Twist at the beginning of the summer. The world was divided between those who could and couldn't do it. Gerry had probably been *born* knowing how to do it.

He admired her dress, he said it was a lovely sunny colour, that she and Clare O'Brien looked the classiest girls in the whole ballroom. She asked would Fiona be here, but he said she had a summer flu. They both agreed that Uncle Dick had turned out to be a demon dancer. He hadn't been off the floor since he came in and insisted on doing formal quicksteps to the rock and roll numbers.

James and Caroline Nolan had arrived, and Gerry had seen them. He escorted Josie back to where he had found her with a big smile. 'I wish they all danced like you, Josie Dillon, the Ginger Rogers of Castlebay.' Josie was pink with delight. She was about to tell Clare, but at that moment Clare was whisked off by Uncle Dick. Josie could have died of mortification. Why couldn't Uncle Dick just sit down like other old people, or venture gently into a foxtrot or something? Why did he have to make a fool of her by asking her friend to dance? The band announced a series of Latin American numbers beginning with the 'Blue Tango'.

'I'm not great at it, not a semi-professional like yourself,' Clare had confessed.

'Listen to me once, you're meant to be a bright girl. It's one step rock back, two steps rock back, three steps rock back. Repeat that.'

They hadn't started to dance yet. Clare repeated it.

'Right, hold on tight and follow me, none of this independent doing fandangos on your own.'

He stood beside her but facing in a different direction, he stretched their arms out as if they were pretending to be scarecrows in a field. He waited for the beat and they were off. The man was a wizard. She began to enjoy it and relaxed when it came to the turns. She noticed other people admiring them too, and saw from one part of the room Miss O'Hara, doing a very amateurish version of the same thing with Dr Power, smiling proudly towards her . . . Gerry Doyle – dancing with Bernie Conway – was looking at her in delight. David Power, dancing with Caroline Nolan, called her attention to the spectacular couple. Clare would have preferred it to have been a younger and more dashing man but she forgot about that after a while. Especially when they went into the cha cha '. . . rock forward, rock backward, side close side . . .' he said and after a few bars she had all the confidence in the world. They won a spot prize too. A bottle of Jameson Ten Year Old.

'You can have that, my drinking days are over,' Dick Dillon said.

'Your dancing days sure aren't,' Clare said and went, flushed with success, to leave the bottle in the ladies' cloakroom and get a ticket for it.

The Committee were very pleased. They had charged a slightly higher price for admission, which was justified by the many gifts which would be given away, but it also kept out some of the riff-raff. Not *all* the riff-raff, they noticed, as they saw Mogsy Byrne throwing Chrissie O'Brien around in the way most calculated to show her knickers to the crowd. Still.

There was a brisk trade at the mineral bar. Oranges and lemons and ginger beers were passing with speed across the counter, and there was a percentage on all that for the Committee, too. No real drink could be served in the dance hall, on this night any more than any other. Dancers wanting a break to visit a pub applied for a pass-out card, and a good few had small bottles in hip pockets.

The band, which was there for the season, had dressed itself up to mark the special nature of the night. The men wore rosettes in their buttonholes, and Lovely Helena, the vocalist, wore a big rose at the waist of her tulle and net dress.

Out in the street, youngsters who were considered well below the age tried to peer in and every time the inner door swung open they caught a glimpse of the glitter inside. Through the ventilators the sound of the singing and the clapping of the announcement of yet another prize being delivered were heard, and then blasts from the band again. During the summer people became used to the sound of the dance hall. It was as familiar as the waves crashing on the shore, background music.

Sometimes people shook their heads with amazement and said wasn't it extraordinary that Lionel Donelly of all people would have had the foresight to build a dance hall, to borrow the money and build a big monstrosity that everyone said would be a white elephant. Now there were people driving to it from far and wide. Lionel, who never passed an exam in his life, had gone to England to learn the building trade and learned that people were building dance halls.

Clare went back to the dance floor. She thought she saw David Power coming towards her, but before he was near enough Gerry Doyle reached out his hand for her. It was a slow smoochy dance and he didn't bother holding her at arm's length for a few bars, he put his arms around her at once and she laid her cheek against his. They were the same height. She had worn her flat shoes.

The lights were dimmer for this number, the sparkles of the glittering globe cast a thousand little shines on people. 'Once I had a secret love,' sang the girl in the miles of net dress at the microphone. People sang the words softly to each other, oddly assorted people like David Power who sang them into Josie's ear because he hadn't got to Clare O'Brien before Romeo. James Nolan sang them into Bernie Conway's ear, because when he saw Gerry Doyle dancing with her, he thought she must be something special. Dick Dillon and Angela didn't sing them at all because they were concentrating on the curly bits and side chassis. Gerry didn't sing them because he didn't need to, and Clare had her eyes tightly closed.

At the last dance Josie was happy because finally James had seen her and flung her into a spirited version of 'California Here I Come'; and a great many other people were happy too. The Committee had made a great deal of money, the dance had

639

been a social success, and all the people who had given spot prizes were pleased with the advertising.

'I have a caravan,' Gerry Doyle told Clare. They had danced together three times, almost enough to be considered a lifetime commitment for Gerry.

'A what?'

'A caravan. All of my own. I'm looking after it for people. They only come at the weekend.'

'Really, that's nice,' Clare said innocently.

'So?'

'So what?'

'Will we go there? You and me?'

'Now?' she asked, her heart beginning to beat faster.

'Sure.'

There was a pause. He was looking straight at her. She must say yes or no. She was not going to make any blustering excuses.

'No,' she said. 'Thanks all the same.'

His eyes showed nothing, there wasn't a hint of persuading her to change her mind.

'Right,' he said. 'Goodnight sweetheart.'

Before her eyes, he went over to Caroline Nolan. She heard him sound surprised to see her, as if he hadn't known she was in the dance hall all night.

Clare watched Caroline smiling delightedly as Gerry suggested something. It was too far away to hear, but when he put his arm around Caroline's shoulder and they walked off together, she knew it had to do with his having a caravan.

Dr Power said he would give Angela a lift in to collect her mother. He never made that journey into the town without driving people in one direction or the other; he was the kindest man that ever lived.

'I saw you leaping about in great style with Dick Dillon,' he teased her.

'Well would you have believed it? The man could have medals for it. I never got such a surprise.'

'He's a very nice fellow, Dick. Never got a proper chance in that hotel. The old mother always preferred his brother. Still, he consoled himself fairly spectacularly during his day.'

Angela smiled, that was one way of describing a man who had been as heavy a drinker as her own father. Of course, Dick Dillon had been able to have the money to do it in comfort, and the trips to Dublin to be dried out, and now he had stopped. He had seen her home and come in after the dance; she had made tea and bacon sandwiches, and they had talked long into the night.

'What he needs is a steadying hand, Angela,' Dr Power said.

'Am I going to be hearing this for the rest of my life?'

'Probably. They'll say you could do worse. He's not a bad catch, sensible too nowadays, all the wild oats sown. Oh, they'll say that.'

'But it's not a question of catching, sure it's not? I always thought that if it happened it would be two people suddenly discovering they were more interested in each other than anything else. Not a *catch*.'

'It *should* be like that,' Dr Power said, negotiating a herd of cows and the boy who was halfheartedly moving them along the road.

'How about you?' She felt impertinent, but he could always laugh it off if he didn't want to answer.

'I met Molly at a dance in Dublin on my twenty-fifth birthday. She had a red dress on and she had her head back laughing and I thought to myself that I'd love her to be laughing like that at things I said. And that was it, I suppose. I went after her relentlessly. It was nothing to do with her being a catch, or me being one.'

'And she did go on laughing, didn't she?'

'Yes, mainly. Sometimes it's a bit quiet and dull here in the winter, and I wish she had more people to meet that would entertain her. Or that we had more children. If you have only one you concentrate on him too much. I'm always thinking about his medical studies and Molly's always wondering about his meals and damp clothes and what he does with himself in Dublin. If we had half a dozen it would be more spread out.'

'But David's sensible, isn't he, and he's as bright as paint.'

'He is, and we've managed to move very successfully from the notion of you and Dick Dillon.'

'He's an old man, with nothing on his mind except his long-lost days of drinking and sometimes the thought of an olde tyme waltz.'

'He's not ten years older than you. He's a fine man and he's lonely. Don't throw the idea aside too easily, Angela, girl.'

He was being serious. She decided not to make any more jokes.

'It was funny Fiona Doyle going off to London in the middle of the busy season to do that photography course.'

'It was bad timing, but I suppose she had to go when the opportunity came up.' Dr Power looked straight ahead of him at the road and the small white houses which broke the monotony of the hedges as they went along. Sometimes it was hard to be a country doctor and to hold the heartbeats and consciences of everyone in the parish. He knew only too well what bad timing it was for Fiona Doyle to have to go to London.

There had been a haze over the sea when Clare got up at six-thirty. It would be another hot day. A scorcher. Well, that's what they all wanted: eighty hot days with a little rain at night just to keep the farmers happy. Clare picked up all the litter from the corner of the shop which they had cleared for people to stand around having lemonades and fizzy orange, ham sandwiches and chocolate biscuits after the dance. It was good business: there was nowhere else to go except the chip van. But it was wearying clearing up in the morning. She put the returnable bottles all together in a crate, and stuffed the others into the rubbish bin. She opened the doors to let the fresh air in and glanced up the street with its white and coloured houses all still asleep. The winter painting done in Castlebay always looked at its best on an early summer morning; the town looked so clean, like sugared almonds. The pink of Conway's post office and the lime-green walls of Miss O'Flaherty's looked just right.

Clare went back to put on the kettle; her mother would be up soon, and not long after that her father would be down moving boxes, worrying over supplies and only just remembering to pause and shave before the early morning caravan people came in looking for their breakfast materials.

The kettle was boiling as Agnes came downstairs. Before she could reach for her shop coat which hung on the back of the kitchen door, Clare saw with a start how thin she had grown, and how tired.

'Why don't you have a bit of a rest today? I can cope with it.'

'*Rest?* On a day like today – it's going to be one of the busiest yet. Are you mad?' her mother wanted to know.

'You look very tired, that's all.'

'Of course I look tired, and Tommy Craig looks tired up in the bar and Young Mrs Dillon looks tired. Lord God, Clare, when would we not look tired if not in the middle of the season?'

'Shush shush, I'm not attacking you, Mam, I wanted to know if you could have a couple of hours more rest that's all.'

Agnes softened. 'No, I'll be all right when I've had a cup of tea, nobody looks anything until they've had a cup of tea.' Her thin face smiled a bit, but she wouldn't even sit down to drink it. She was hurrying into the shop and sure enough as soon as she was behind the counter the door pinged and the first customer arrived.

It was non-stop all day. A lot of people seemed to take advantage of the clear blue skies to plan picnics, and Clare was busy cutting sandwiches and wrapping up ice creams in several layers of newspapers.

Caroline Nolan was early. She ran in from her little Morris Minor, which spluttered and made noises outside.

'Picnic things,' she said to Clare, barely politely.

'For how many?' Clare asked.

'I don't know. Can I take things and if we don't need them bring them back?'

'No,' Clare said.

'What?'

'I said you can't. Suppose you brought back tomatoes or bananas that had been out in the sun all day – who else would want them?'

'I meant tins, or things that wouldn't spoil.'

'Why don't you just work out how many might be going?' Clare was impatient with this glowing girl, all fresh and summery in a white dress with big red spots; she looked so clean and awake and lively compared to Clare in her faded dress and her tired thin mother in the yellow shop coat.

'Maybe you can help me?' Caroline had decided to be charming. 'You see, a friend suggested we take a drive out to this place where you see seals, and I'm to provide a picnic. He, my friend, would bring a bottle of wine. And I'm not sure whether he meant us plural, like my brother and David, or whether he meant us singular, just me. You see my problem?'

'No,' said Clare. 'Ask him. Ask him did he mean you singular or you plural, then you'll know.'

Caroline left the shop.

Half an hour later she was back. 'He said he meant you plural,' she announced.

'Bad luck,' Clare said, and without being asked made a selection of the freshly made ham sandwiches and cheese sandwiches, apples, bananas, oranges, a packet of chocolate biscuits and four bottles of fizzy orange.

Caroline took it in silence and packed it into the boot of her car.

Gerry came in for cigarettes a bit later.

'I thought you'd be off on your picnic,' Clare said.

'I'm going to join them later, I gave them directions to get to the seals. Why don't you come with us?'

'How can I? I have to work here. Anyway, I'm not asked.'

'You are, I'm asking you.'

Clare laughed. 'No thanks. How can any of us take a day like today off? How can *you* take today off, come to think of it?'

'Why do I pay someone to take pictures for me, if it's not to give me a day off. Come on, be a devil.'

'Stop it, you know I can't.' She was annoyed now, she wished he'd go.

'One day out of the summer? One sunny day?' He wasn't joking.

'Go away Gerry, go away.' Clare was laughing but her voice had a steely ring. 'We are going to take care of our business, even if others we wouldn't mention are letting theirs go down the plug-hole.' And anyway, Clare told herself, there was no point in going out with that gang without the proper ammunition. Clare had no crisp cotton dress with big red dots on it, Clare had no golden suntan, she had a faded mauve dress and long white legs in old-fashioned sandals. Hell, she wasn't going to compete with Caroline unless she had a chance of winning, and if she wanted the attentions of Gerry Doyle she wouldn't look for them now.

The good spell was set to last. In the days after the picnic, Clare decided that she hated sunshine. For other people it meant that the holiday dream was coming true, it meant a healthy out-of-doors life. For the young couples in their tents it was pure magic, for the Nolans and their friends just more long days lost in sandhills on seal beaches, on golf courses, and racing in and out of the waves. For children it meant rushing into the shop asking for a bottle of fizzy orange, open please and with three straws. But for Clare the sun just meant it was time to take the cakes and things that might melt from the window, and to make sure the stocks of ice cream were ready for Jim and Ben to cope with.

Gerry came in. 'I've a message for you, come on, up to the post office, now! Old Ma Conway said there was a phone message, they're going to ring again in fifteen minutes, well ten now, come on.'

Clare's heart was thumping as she ran up Church Street with Gerry. The hotel and the chemist and the dance-hall and the hardware shop passed in a blur. And then they were in Conway's.

'Oh you found her?' Mrs Conway looked disapprovingly over her glasses.

Please may it not be about Tommy. Oh please God, I'll say the thirty days prayer, please Our Lady, I'll begin the thirty days prayer *today* if it's not some awful thing about Tommy.

'You must be very nervous,' Gerry said sympathetically.

Her heart gave another jump. 'How do you know, I mean what do you mean?'

'Your results,' he said simply. 'That's what it is, isn't it?'

It was. It was the convent, incoherent with delight – in all their years they had never been so proud. Clare had done nine subjects on her Leaving Certificate and she had got honours in *all* of them except mathematics; but of course she had passed that safely. And now wasn't there every chance that she would be called for the Murray Prize interview? Three of the sisters were starting a special novena today and Clare could be assured that the whole Community would remember her every day at Mass. She could hardly see Mrs Conway's pinched face, forcing itself to be congratulatory, having heard every word. Gerry lifted her off her feet and swung her round three times.

'Eight honours, eight honours, hell's bells and spiders' ankles!' he shouted.

'*Eight honours!*' Clare screamed. '*Eight!*'

'Well I must say I think congratulations are in order . . .' Mrs Conway said, her face pursed at the horseplay.

'I must tell Miss O'Hara, now,' Clare said. 'Now, this minute.'

'I'll drive you up in the van.'

She hesitated for a moment.

'I won't come in, I know you want to tell her on your own.'

Angela was out in front of the cottage, watering the scarlet geraniums. The sun shone in her eyes and she had to put up her hand to shield them as the van screeched to a halt. Clare tumbled out the door before it had properly stopped.

'Eight, Miss O'Hara, *eight!*' she shouted excitedly, and Angela put down the water jug and ran towards her. She clutched the thin body – trembling with excitement – to her in a big awkward hug of delight.

They had both forgotten Gerry, who sat motionless in his van watching them with his dark handsome eyes.

The whole town knew by evening. Josie had been so excited when she heard that she put the lid on her typewriter and said she was taking some time off to celebrate. Agnes and Tom O'Brien were bewildered with pleasure and worn out shaking people's hands across the counter and taking praise on behalf of their bright, hard-working daughter. Dr Power was going past on his way to the caravan site and stopped to pay his respects. Sergeant McCormack had got wind of it, and it wasn't long before Father O'Dwyer's little car stopped outside O'Brien's as well. It was a miracle that anything was bought or sold, or money taken or change given in that shop all day with the comings and goings.

'Will you come to the dance to celebrate tonight?' Gerry said.

'Ah, there'd be too much of a crowd there, all the Caroline Nolans and all,' she said, smiling at him.

'We could go somewhere where there wouldn't be,' he grinned back.

'I don't think so, don't change any of your own plans.'

'There are eighty nights in the summer,' Gerry said. 'If you don't come tonight you'll come another night.'

She had a lovely night. She had a drink with Dick Dillon who taught her how to make a drink called a Pussyfoot which had no alcohol in it but sort of fooled you into thinking it had. Josie gave her a yellow blouse and a yellow ribbon to match it for her hair – she had been saving it as a surprise. Josie had a date with James Nolan and was in seventh heaven herself: they were going to the pictures and he had said he would meet her in the queue. She swore to tell Clare everything that happened and had worn a dress with a high collar in case he might start to fumble and she would have to decide whether to let him or not.

Clare walked down the Cliff Road. It was sunset and people could be seen indoors, finishing their supper or just sitting around with the dishes still on the table before heading off for the night's entertainment. It had been so long in arriving, this day. She was going to savour every minute of it.

It was getting dark now and she shivered a little in her new yellow blouse. Josie and James Nolan were well into the Main Feature and who knew what else at the cinema. Chrissie and Mogsy Byrne had gone down the sandhills, she knew that because she had seen Chrissie changing her slip and getting out her good knickers, the ones with lace on them. Gerry Doyle was in his caravan. No, she was *not* going to the caravan park. She would go up to the amusements and have two rides on the bumpers and then if she didn't meet anyone she would come home and pitch Chrissie's things to the other side of the room and go to bed. She would *not* go to the caravan park tonight.

There was never a greater demand for space than this summer. Somehow the word had spread that there was fun galore in Castlebay. Not all the visitors were desirable of course: this would be discussed by the Castlebay Committee during the winter. There had been a very noisy element with tents, and the dirt of the caravan people had to be seen to be believed. Dr Power said they weren't to be blamed until somebody put up lavatories and washbasins for them, and arranged proper bins and a rubbish collection.

There was hardly a day that Angela and her mother weren't approached by passing visitors asking for a night's lodging.

To her surprise her mother had said they should do it. Everyone else in the town made a profit out of the summer, why shouldn't they?

Angela washed sheets and tidied up the back room. Why not? It would be a few quid, and people were so grateful. She would point out that she had a mother who wasn't well and couldn't have anyone noisy. But it had been fine. First a couple of girls who had crept in like mice after the dance, stayed four days and had both said that Gerry Doyle was the most gorgeous thing they had ever seen in real life. Up to now they had only seen his likes on the cinema screen. Then there had been a married couple, a quiet pair in their forties, dull, nothing to say to anyone or each other, Angela pitied them, and was puzzled when they said it had been a lovely visit and they would come back next year. Then two lads from Dublin, with accents you could cut, roaring laughing at nothing and saying it was the best fun they'd had in years. The night they had got very drunk they had the decency to sleep in the shed rather than trying to find their room. Angela told them they were marvellous and refused to charge them for the night's accommodation.

'You won't suffer for that, Missus,' one of them said. 'We'll send you our mates.'

And indeed there was a never-ending supply of Dubliners, lads from building sites, from factories, and then the two housepainters, Paddy and Con. God, they'd never seen the like of the place, they were going to have a swim immediately, they were sticking to themselves with the sweat after the train and the bus, and the sea looked a treat.

'Be careful,' Angela called automatically. 'There's a very high tide, it's treacherous at the end of August. They call it a spring tide.'

'Oh, you couldn't drown us,' called Paddy and Con.

She heard the cry about half an hour later. It was like a wail growing and fading, louder and softer. And she knew there was someone drowning down on the strand. She had been buying the bacon and eggs for their tea in O'Brien's. She had her bicycle with its carrier basket parked outside. Automatically she found her feet heading for the cliff top and there saw everyone clustered and pointing out beyond the caves and the fishing rocks. The waves were enormous.

On the edge of the water there was a commotion. Five or six men were trying to hold back the struggling figure of Simon. Ropes and lifebelts had been thrown, to no avail. Angela's stomach lurched when she saw a hand raised desperately, far, far out, and beside it the head of someone else. There were two of them. She dropped the bacon out of her hands, and she knew that it was her lodgers, Paddy and Con.

They were shouting at Simon on the beach. 'You've been out twice, you've been battered, you can't do any more, it's suicide. You've done all you can. Simon, have sense.'

Simon's side was bleeding from where he had been scratched against the rocks.

'Let me go! Let me go!' His face was working and his eyes were full of tears. Gerry Doyle was gripping him, holding his arm behind him in a lock.

'What's the point in getting you killed? Look at your back, you've been thrown on the rocks twice. What are you trying to prove? You've done all you can, for Christ's sake, you warned them – you went out after them once and brought them back in.'

'They're new, they were all white,' Simon wailed, 'let me go.'

There was a great cry from the people who could see the figures.

'One's holding onto a rock, he'll be all right. Look! Look!'

But in seconds a huge wave pulled the small figure, its white arms flailing, down into the sea.

Helplessly the crowd watched. There was no boat, no swimmer, no throw of a lifebelt that would reach Paddy and Con. They would die in front of a thousand people.

Father O'Dwyer had been sent for, and as if by reflex, the people standing near him went down on their knees.

Father O'Dwyer called out the rosary and the swell of Holy Marys increased. Simon stopped struggling eventually and sat with his head in his hands, sobbing. Gerry Doyle sat beside him with an arm protectively around his shoulder.

There was no sign of the figures now, the waves kept crashing as if they were unaware of what they had done. Men went for strong drinks, women gathered up their children and issued useless, angry warnings about the need to stay in shallow waters.

Clare had come out too. She felt a hand reaching for hers and to her surprise, it was David Power.

'Would it have been quick do you think?' she asked.

David shook his head.

'Oh,' she said in a small voice.

'I don't know. Not the first bit, not the being swept out, they'd have known what was going to happen.'

'I suppose so.'

'I have to go down there,' he said. 'With my father.'

'When?'

'When the tide comes in tonight, they'll be washed up.'

She was full of pity, and warmth, and she squeezed his hand.

'I don't *have* to, but I will. He just said that he'd like me to, and anyway I'll be a doctor soon myself. I'll have to then. It's just . . . it's just . . .'

'I know, it's just when it's your own beach.'

He smiled at her gratefully. 'They might come in sooner.' He was full of dread.

'Would that mean they'd get battered up more?'

'I don't know.'

There was a great sound from the beach again and people were shouting and pointing. On the side of the beach near the caves, where it seemed calm, there was something that looked like a person. And near it was something similar. There was no movement, no waving or swimming. Then you could see they were face down. Bobbing on the water like the airbeds that they sold up at the top of Church Street. They didn't look like people: they looked like a bad joke.

Clare turned away, suddenly feeling a bit faint. This is what being dead looked like. She had almost forgotten she was still holding David Power's hand and when she turned it was towards him. She put her head on his chest. He put his arm round her shoulder. Then she pulled away a little.

'You've got to go down,' she said.

Gerry Doyle and two other fellows passed, helping Simon up the steps. The lifeguard's side had been examined on the beach by Dr Power, who had asked Gerry to get him away as soon as possible. Dr Power didn't want Simon there when the bodies came in. They would float in with the last minutes of the incoming tide.

Gerry Doyle looked at Clare evenly. 'If you've finished canoodling, you might go to your friend, Miss O'Hara – she's the one who's going to have to cope with it all and go through their things.'

'Why?' Clare cried, shocked. 'Why on earth will she have to do that?'

'Because they were staying with her, they're from her house, that's why.' Gerry put his arm under Simon's and continued to shove and push him along the street.

Clare saw Angela, standing by herself with her hands over her mouth in disbelief. Her hair blowing loose behind her, she was looking down on the beach while the crowds stepped into the shallow water and pulled the bodies of Paddy and Con on to the sand. Father O'Dwyer was there with his holy water, and his soutane, his long black skirt flapping in the breeze. Dr Power was urging people to keep the children well away and leaning on the chests of the dead men in the futile hope that there would be any life left in them. And in a minute beside him was his tall fair-haired son, helping too, looking calm and in control; not the trembling boy who had been standing moments earlier with his hand in Clare's.

Clare turned away from the scene on the beach. Gerry was quite right. If she was to do anything to help it should be for Miss O'Hara.

They talked about nothing else for days. The dance was cancelled that night as a mark of respect, and so was the cinema. They didn't know what to do at the amusements so they compromised by not playing the juke box. Clare and Angela had found an address amongst the few shabby belongings of Paddy and Con, and the Guards in Dublin were asked to go around and inform the families.

It had been strangely unreal for everyone and the greatest sympathy in the place was given to Simon. Nobody knew the families of Paddy and Con, any more than anyone had really met the lads in the short couple of hours they had spent in Castlebay between getting off the bus and being taken out of the sea. Simon's easy laughter had disappeared now. He was a very serious young man. He didn't go to the dance in the evenings and he had little time for high jinks on the beach. He sat nervously on a high stool that he had made himself from boxes, and he shouted angrily at children who played ball in his line of vision. One night in Craig's Bar he lost his temper and said that the Castlebay Committee were totally irresponsible encouraging people to come there with their plans for fairy lights and big car parks. They should build a pier and breakwater, they should enclose a swimming pool and only permit people who were known to be strong swimmers to venture beyond it. You wouldn't let people play with matches and jump through bonfires would you, he had said in a high nervous voice. They forgave him over and over, they told him of the children he had saved, of the cramp victim he had rescued, of the artificial respiration to the girl who swallowed so much water. They praised him for the countless others he had made safe by his daily parades up and down the beach edge. But his eyes got darker and they knew they would never see him again when the summer was over.

Angela and Clare didn't talk about it, not after the first night when they had found the address and folded all the clothes neatly into the two shabby grip bags. Talking about it only made things worse. Instead they rehearsed feverishly the kind of questions that Clare might face on the first Thursday in September when she had to meet the Murray Prize Committee.

They planned her appearance down to the last detail. She must look in need of their gift but not too needy. She must look quiet enough to be studious but not so quiet that she looked dull. Neat enough to be thought respectable but not so drab as to be thought dreary. Her good marks would impress them automatically, her grasp of current affairs was masterly, her simple direct explanation about coming from a family which was anxious for her success but not in itself academic was so patently honest it would have to convince them. She was not a fly-by-night either, she had always been ambitious, hadn't she got the scholarship to secondary school at the age of twelve?

In the end Angela said she was satisfied. There was literally no more they could do to prepare for this event. They would end up making her so nervous that she would not be able to speak at all.

Angela lent her a navy jumper and the good silk scarf that James Nolan's mother had given her all those years ago. It had lain idly in a drawer and this was an ideal opportunity to give it an outing. She wore her good blue skirt and a pair of Josie's shoes. Her hair was to be shining and in a pony tail, only the barest hint of make-up, like a trace of Sari Peach lipstick, rubbed on and rubbed off again.

If school hadn't started, Angela said, she would have gone into the town and waited nearby until Clare came out. It would have made it better for both of them.

But term would have started. Angela's twelfth year in the convent. For a woman who was going to stay twelve months, things had escalated. She felt no bitterness towards Sean about that now. It had been her own decision for a long, long time. She didn't even rebel at the thought of his unctuously clerical tones when he gave that advice. She had no more hate for Sean and the differences between what he preached and what he did. It had been a long time, teaching beside Mother Immaculata, certainly. But it had been a longer time for Sean in waiting for a laicization that never came.

Gerry Doyle called to the O'Brien house the night before.

'I have a job tomorrow, so I'll be going to town. I can give you a lift.'

'That's very nice, but I was getting the bus. The timing's all right for once and even if it's a bit late I'll be fine.'

'I'm going to the door,' he said. 'The Committee have asked me to photograph them and the shortlist of candidates. So go on the bus if you like but the lift is there.'

There were two girls and five boys. Gerry arranged them according to height and took several shots. He was able to relax them without having to clown around. It was a gift, Clare thought as she watched him. He never called her by her name. He was professional. It mightn't look good for her to know him, he was making sure she had nothing special about her one way or the other. He left her free to examine the competition. The girl was taller than Clare; she looked older and very studious. She had bushy, badly-combed hair and glasses. She could have been quite nice-looking but she had made no effort at all. There was a tear in her tunic – she wore a school uniform, for heaven's sake – and her shoes were down at heel. Anxiously Clare looked down at Josie's smart shoes and the neat cuffs of Miss O'Hara's good cardigan. Maybe she looked cheap and superficial?

'Makes us feel a bit like cattle,' said a small boy, who didn't look old enough to have done his Intermediate Certificate let alone his Leaving. But Clare was not deceived: this was the most dangerous one, she felt sure. Two of the others were clerical students: they wore black jerseys and were more reserved. There was a nervy boy who would irritate the committee and one who spoke after such a long pause each time, the interview would surely be over by the time he had answered anything.

The girl was nice. She had been at a convent about fifty miles away. She asked Clare how many honours she had got in her Leaving. Angela had prepared her for that and told her not to boast, and if at all possible to keep her great score to herself.

'I don't think they go on that any more,' she said. 'That's what I've heard, anyway. Nowadays it's not the number you have it's what they think of you.'

The boy who kept drumming his fingers looked up startled at this. 'Is that right?

Then I'll be lost. I got six honours, I thought that was what was going to sail me through.' He laughed nervously, showing some broken teeth.

Clare thanked Miss O'Hara again and again in her mind. Miss O'Hara had beaten this nervous laugh out of her long ago.

They talked easily enough until the lady chairman came to address them. She was a self-important woman in a tweed suit; she had a huge chest and looked so like a pigeon, Clare was not afraid of her resounding voice. They were to be taken in alphabetical order. Clare was second last; the nervy boy was O'Sullivan, and he would be last.

She kept her mind calm. She refused to get up and go to the lavatory even when the others did suddenly. She knew she had eaten or drunk nothing that would make her need to go; she had eaten barley sugar sweets just as she had done when she was twelve and Miss O'Hara had been training her to get the scholarship to school. That had not been terrifying neither would this. She had eight honours in her Leaving Certificate. She was the equal of any child in Ireland.

Gerry Doyle was told he would be needed in two hours. They would have come to their decision then. That surprised him. He'd thought they wouldn't decide there and then on the day. But it was better that she knew today. He didn't think she'd make it. Just from looking at them he thought the big untidy girl or the small boy who looked like a child prodigy were the most likely. Those were the kind of faces you saw in a newspaper with a paragraph underneath saying what they had won.

He came back in good time and sat in his van reading the local paper. There were three of his pictures in it this week: a wedding, a sand-castle competition and the foundation stone for the new wing of the Brothers' school in Castlebay.

The awful bossy woman with the big chest rapped on the window for him as if he were the gardener and called him in to photograph the winner of the Murray Scholarship to University College, Dublin, Clare O'Brien.

Angela O'Hara asked Dr Power if she could have a word with him in his car. He was practically home and suggested she come into the surgery. She didn't want to. The house then, and have a sherry? No. It was something a bit unethical she wanted to ask, better to ask him on neutral ground. Unethical? His big bushy eyebrows rose. Angela? Nothing desperately unethical, she assured him, a fake doctor's cert, that was all.

'Get into the car,' he said. 'This is serious. If I'm going to be struck off we'd better make sure it's worth while.'

She laughed at his kind, worried face and told him what she wanted. She'd like to go to Dublin for a few days. Her best friend Emer had just had a baby, and now they wanted her to be godmother to the baby. Young Clare was going up to Dublin to start life at university, and it was a great opportunity to show her round a bit – not be a mother hen but just show her a few things so that she wasn't a total gobdaw when term started. It would be lovely to have a few days off school, but she couldn't ask for it. It was unheard of. Immaculata would have a blue fit. Was it possible that Dr Power could say she had something which meant going to Dublin?

He looked at her over his glasses, doubtfully.

'I never asked you before. I never in all my years up in that place asked for one day off.'

'You misunderstand me. Of course I'll do it. I think you should have a fortnight in Dublin . . . I'm only trying to think what you might have.'

She gave him a look full of gratitude. 'Would we say it was in my womb? That should embarrass Immaculata so much she'd shut up about it.'

'Yes, but there's no reason why you wouldn't go into the County Hospital if it were just a D and C,' he objected. 'It would have to be something that needed going to a specialist for or some kind of specialist hospital. A skin disease?' he suggested brightly.

Angela was doubtful. 'She might keep moving away from me and telling people not to use the same cups at our tea break.'

'Blood tests, you're a bit anaemic and I want it checked further.'

'You're a great sport,' she said. 'I was hoping I could rely on you.'

'I'm not doing it because I'm a sport. I'm doing it because you *do* need a break. I'd feel quite justified signing a certificate saying you are under great pressure and you need a change and a rest, but of course, if you wrote that to any of that lot of beauties up in the convent, they'd think you were having a nervous breakdown and they wouldn't let you back again. Blood tests it will have to be.'

Emer and Kevin were delighted to see them.

They had to fight the nuns and nurses off to get baby Daniel home from the nursing home without having him baptized. They explained that the godmother had to come from the country but there had been terror that the baby's immortal soul would be lost during the delay. Anyway it was all settled now. Martin, the shy best man, was going to be the godfather, and best surprise of all, Father Flynn was going to perform the baptism. Wasn't that something! To gather the cast of the wedding in another city five years later!

They hadn't noticed the colour go from Clare's face when the priest's name was mentioned. She sat silently. She had been pleased to be invited to this warm, friendly house, to meet the laughing, undemanding friends of Miss O'Hara's. She had been delighted to be included in the christening party the next day, but she didn't want to meet this priest who knew all about her family and had been to see Tommy in prison. She would ask Miss O'Hara could she get out of it.

As they got the house ready on the evening before the christening Angela felt wistful as she often did in the presence of Emer and Kevin, they were so utterly complete as a pair, they hardly needed the rest of the world at all. And their delight in this funny, creased, red-faced baby was so touching it would bring tears to your eyes. When they peered at him in his cot Angela thought she had never seen anything so happy.

She wished them so well that she didn't like the little feelings of envy that came to her unwillingly when she was with them. Nowhere else did she wish so strongly that *she* had found a Kevin of her own, someone she could share everything with. Someone she could laugh with about Dr Power and his kindness. Someone she could talk to at night about Sean and Shuya. She remembered, returning from her last visit to her brother's family: she had longed to take off her shoes and sit down by the fire and tell Emer and Kevin all about it. But it wasn't the same telling a story to a couple. When the evening was over they would go to bed, she in the neat guest bedroom with the gingham curtains and bedspread, they in their big double bed where they would lie in each other's arms and whisper low how terrible it was for Angela. She didn't want that sympathy, however loving and generous. She wanted a sharing. It was lonely holding Sean's secret for seven years.

She looked over at Clare, who was on a chair helping to put up the silver and white decorations they had organized for the sitting room. She had been rather short with the child there earlier on. She had no business being short with her; after all, she refused to talk to Father Flynn about Sean even though it was Father Flynn who had found the school in England for Sean to teach in.

She was just as much an ostrich as Clare, burying her head in the sand, refusing to accept someone's help and thank them for it in a simple straightforward way. It was uncanny how alike their lives had been. Scholarships, first to the convent and then to college; neither of them came from scholarly families, and both of them had brothers in trouble. And Father Flynn was being a lifeline to both brothers – one despairing in an English school and waiting for a voice from Rome that would never come, the other reading comics in an English gaol.

The day was winding down, and Clare found herself near Father Flynn. 'Thank you very much for all you do for my brother, Tommy,' she said, forcing the words out. 'And for Ned too, getting him a job and seeing that he writes home. It's very good of you.'

Father Flynn looked at her. 'Oh, then you're Clare O'Brien, of course, that writes the letters to Tommy. He looks forward to them, and sometimes I read them to him – so don't say anything bad about me in the next one or I might find myself reading it aloud!'

Clare warmed to him. He hadn't shaken his head sadly and said it was a Dreadful Situation; Miss O'Hara was right.

'There's not really anything for him in Castlebay, you know, Father. I was thinking about it, he'd only be hanging around.'

'There's plenty of time to think yet, maybe he'd be better hanging round there than where he was hanging around.'

'Yes, that's probably true. Maybe I was just trying to keep him away, out of sight, out of mind.'

'But that's not true of you,' he smiled. 'He's not out of your mind. You're a generous girl. I hope you have a very successful career at university and that you meet a lot of people and read a great deal and have years that you'll always remember.'

Nobody had wished her well in such terms. Nobody had spoken aloud all her own hopes and dreams. She did want to read a great deal, and have time to read, and she wanted people to talk to, people who would talk about the things they read. This funny, fat little priest with the beady eyes knew just what she wanted.

She went to see Miss O'Hara off at the station. They had inspected the hostel where she was going to live, and Angela had said it wouldn't be bad at all because in a week it would be filled with girls from all over the country, united in their hatred of the nuns who ran the place and all as nervous as Clare, but none of them as clever. Miss O'Hara had walked the legs off her round the city, and they now knew which side of Stephen's Green was which, and where the Physics Theatre was, which oddly was where a lot of the first Arts lectures would be held. She had registered and got her student's card.

Clare felt very experienced, catching a bus back from the station to O'Connell Bridge, she looked out eagerly at the city which was to be her home for three years. It was so bright – that was what she was going to find most hard to get used to. In Castlebay in winter there were hardly any lights on Church Street, none at all on Cliff Road or the golf-course road, but in Dublin even side streets, even lanes were lit up. And shops had their lights on in windows all night so that you could go and look at what they had for sale any hour at all. As the bus went up the Quays to the centre of Dublin the buildings were reflected in the river Liffey: the Four Courts, the big churches and the rows of tall buildings shimmered in the dark water. It was all so enormous, after home.

She had walked through the grand stores with Angela O'Hara, and looked at the rings and bracelets in the windows of jewellers'. She had been to the second-hand bookshops and bought all her texts for the first year. Angela had even climbed up on ladders in order to get better or cheaper editions for her. She had made herself known at the big red-brick hostel where she would stay. Angela had come with her and informed the nuns that this was no ordinary pupil, it was a Murray Prizewinner, and that her fees would be paid by the committee. The nuns were impressed. It reminded Clare a little of her secondary school, and she was disappointed that it had no garden or cloisters. It was part of a big terrace of Georgian houses, and the convent was in fact four of them all joined together. Angela had said she wouldn't have time for gardens. There was always Stephen's Green in the summer, and the fact that the hostel was so near the university meant it was worth its weight in gold. She could get out of bed literally minutes before lectures while other students had to cross the city.

Clare got off the bus at O'Connell Bridge and leaned across the parapet looking below to where two swans went by. They looked confident, even arrogant. They felt no unease about being swans in a place where everyone else seemed to be human beings. Clare smiled at the thought. She owed Miss O'Hara so much – or Angela as she must now call her. She owed her everything, including these last days, this great preparation.

She knew which bus would take her back to the hostel but she decided to walk. She would walk almost everywhere anyway, why not start now? She went up Grafton Street, pausing to look at fur coats, at household equipment, at pictures and frames, at a chemist's window full of perfumes and soaps and talcum powders. She saw books on display and furniture, big deep leather chairs in shops. She read the tariffs in hairdressers', she saw the sign to the little church in Clarendon Street. At the top of Grafton Street she wouldn't need to pause like so many new students, she knew to walk on along a side of Stephen's Green and on to her hostel. She had left her luggage there earlier, and they said that the young ladies would be arriving after six p.m. She had discovered that there wouldn't be supper, so she was that much ahead of all the rest who thought that there would. She looked up at its slightly forbidding outside, took a deep breath and walked into her new home.

There were going to be three in a room. She was the first so she could choose her bed. It was unlikely that there would be much study done here: it was too small, there wasn't much light, and anyway the libraries were meant for study. Clare took the bed by the window. It was the one where she would get most fresh air and she had checked, there didn't seem to be draughts. She thought of Chrissie alone in the bedroom at home, puzzling out her relationship with Mogsy Byrne.

The first room mate arrived. Mary Catherine was American, her father wanted her to have an Irish education, she had never been so cold in her whole life, she couldn't believe that they didn't have a bathroom attached to the room, she couldn't understand why there hadn't been a reception down there to welcome them, she was going to study English, she had majored in English Literature at her college, she was very confused, and where were the closets? Clare sat on the bed wondering how she was going to live with this voice for a year, when the door opened and in came a girl with short curly hair and tears streaming down her face.

'Isn't it *awful*,' she sobbed. 'It smells just like school, there's no supper or dinner or anything tonight, there's a list of rules as long as your arm, *how* are we going to survive it?'

She threw herself on the empty bed and sobbed into her pillow. Her luggage had the name Valerie painted on the end of each case.

Clare decided to take control. 'Of course it's awful Valerie – if that's your name – it smells even worse than school. I'm Clare and this is Mary Catherine and she's from America and she hates it because it's cold and it's not got a bath each and no closets, whatever they are. And of course there's no supper and no welcoming party because they don't know we're all expecting a bit of a fuss of it, but for God Almighty's sake let's not start moaning and groaning before we even start. Why don't we go out and have some chips and think what could make the place better?'

She could hardly believe that it was Clare O'Brien, the scholarship girl from Castlebay, speaking. She'd never really shouted at two totally strange girls, had she? But it had worked like magic.

The chips cheered them up so much they had apple pie and ice cream. Clare told them about the Murray scholarship. Mary Catherine said that her father was a mailman in the States, but he had told her to tell everyone in Ireland he was in government work – which in a sense was vaguely true. She was the only child. He had dreams of her marrying someone who owned a castle in Ireland. Valerie said her parents were separated. Her father lived in England with a fancy woman, and he had to pay for her education. Valerie didn't want to go to university but her mother said she must, and she must stay there for years in order to get as much out of that rat as possible.

They were immensely cheered by each other's life stories, and they learned what they would have expected: that none of them had any experience with men. Mary Catherine knew a girl in the States who went the whole way with four boys before she left school. No, amazingly, she didn't have a baby, but she didn't have a friend either. A girl in Valerie's school left hurriedly in the middle of Fifth Year but it had been a great mystery because she didn't have a boyfriend. There was a whisper round the school that it was someone in her family, her father or her brother. Clare offered some tales from Castlebay of things that had happened down the sandhills, but they were all second-hand and third-hand. She was going to say that she had her doubts about Chrissie and Mogsy at times; but Mogsy and Chrissie were such non-glamorous people she decided she wouldn't embark on it.

Full of food and confidences and friendship they stood up to go back to the room they were going to transform. They were going to buy a second-hand book-shelf on the Quays, they were going to buy coat hooks and screw them into the wall so that there would be more space for their clothes. They were going to price cheap reading lamps and buy one between them.

Just as they were leaving the restaurant, someone called from a crowded table. 'Hey it's Clare, Clare O'Brien!'

She was startled. All she could see was a sea of young men in duffle coats and scarves. One was waving. It was James Nolan. He stood up and came over to them.

'Well, well, well,' he said.

It seemed to be very little to say after coming all the way across the restaurant. She introduced him to Mary Catherine and Valerie, smiling at him politely as if to assure him that she wasn't claiming any friendship.

'Well, well,' he said again. 'Is the rest of Castlebay up in Dublin too?' His eyes roamed over Mary Catherine and Valerie, assessing them.

'Josie Dillon might be coming up for a few days,' Clare said eagerly.

Josie had begged her to find out James Nolan's haunts, and said that she would love to come to Dublin if Clare could track him down. Imagine meeting him on the very first night!

'Josie?' He looked blank.

'Josie Dillon from the hotel.'

James Nolan shook his head absently.

'You must remember her, you were often with her in the summer,' Clare blurted out, and could have kicked herself.

'I don't think I do.' James was polite but bored by the subject. Clare would have liked to hit him hard.

'It's my mistake. I'm sure she doesn't remember you either.' Her eyes flashed a bit and he looked at her with surprise.

'No. Well. Listen, it's nice to see you girls. Oh, and there's a party on Saturday. All three of you of course. Here, I'll write it down.' He scribbled an address and time on a piece of paper.

'Ten o'clock! We have to be *back* at that place we're staying by eleven o'clock,' Valerie said, disappointed.

'Late pass, ask them for a late pass, cousin invited all three of you to twenty-first. The nuns love cousins, they think they're safe, sign of a big united family. They love twenty-firsts, it gives them a sense of continuity.'

They promised to be there and they linked arms, giggling as they went down the dark unfamiliar streets, and said that they'd all be lost if it had not been for Clare to guide them and tell them where they were and get them invited to a party on their very very first night in Dublin.

It was a great alliance. When other girls were lonely and self-conscious, they often looked with envy at the three girls; the tall fair one from the back of beyond with the dark brown eyes, the American with her outlandish clothes, and Valerie, the curly-headed terror. It was Valerie who made friends with a workman doing some building work on the outside of the hostel wall. She pointed out that if he were to put three very sturdy bars jutting at intervals they could climb back into their room at night.

He was very nervous about it. 'You might get fellas climbing in to attack you,' he had protested. Nonsense; Valerie explained that there were three of them in the room, and any fellow climbing in uninvited would meet his match. She supervised the placing of the rungs carefully, and also their disguise. No passing nun could see them and realize what they were, a stairway to freedom. Valerie very cunningly asked that one or two extra rungs leading nowhere be hammered in as well. That way the purpose would never be discovered. And indeed it wasn't. They allowed very good friends to know the route, and regularly the light step of a girl was heard to fall into their room and someone, shoes in hand, would creep through, whispering a sorry or a thank you, but giving no explanations.

Clare and Mary Catherine didn't really use their escape route all that often but it kept them sane just knowing it was there. Only Valerie got real value from the contraption. She went dancing and to parties, and needed the footholds she had so cleverly organized at least three or four times a week. Valerie usually lay with her curls barely peeping from above the sheets when Clare and Mary Catherine were heading off to lectures. It was always kept as a polite fiction in front of nuns and other girls that Valerie was very lucky to have late lectures. Valerie rarely attended any of them anyway, no matter what time of the day they were held. As she told Clare and Mary Catherine, her mother had said nothing about passing any exams, only about using up the money for fees at university.

At Christmas, Valerie went home to her mother who was going to sit and curse her father all the time; Mary Catherine went to stay with American friends. Clare caught the train home. Her mother had asked Gerry Doyle to pick her up; he sent her a postcard, saying, 'Passion waggon will be parked in darkest side of yard outside station. See you then. Love, Gerry.' The other girls were intrigued. Even more when they heard that he was the heartbreaker of the country who had twice invited Clare to his caravan.

She felt cheerful going home. There was no guilt – she had written to her mother every single Friday, and to Tommy as well. She had written less to Angela. She had thought she would write more to her than anyone but it was very hard to describe it all: the National Library every afternoon, where it was peaceful and studious – you felt that everyone there was a real scholar, not just learning things with their hands in their ears for exams. She had read a great deal around the courses and everything on the course. She could meet every member of the Murray Committee, look each one in the eye and say truthfully that their money had not been wasted. Funny that she couldn't seem to write this to Angela.

She saw David Power on the train, and put her head back into her book so that he wouldn't notice her as he came along the corridor. It wasn't that she didn't want to talk to him, but it was silly, there she had been three months in the same city and never laid eyes on him, only to meet on the way home – it would be very forced.

He saw her only as they were getting out of the train and his face broke into a great smile. He thought she looked very nice, in her navy duffle coat, knitted navy and white scarf and her hair in a jaunty pony tail with a white bow on it. It was only the other day that she had been a kid. But then, his mother kept saying it was only the twinkling of an eye since he was in rompers.

He saw his father waving from the other side of the gate. 'Can we drive you home?' he said. 'I'm delighted I saw you in time.'

'I have a lift actually, but thank you very much,' and as they came to the barrier he saw Gerry Doyle leaning casually against the machine that wrote your name in metal.

Gerry wasn't bothering to move and wave and position himself as everyone else was doing, as David's own father was doing. Gerry knew he would be seen when the time came. Clare raised her hand in salute.

'Second fiddle to Gerry Doyle, winter and summer, it's the story of our lives,' David said and went over to his father.

'Your mother's in the car, it's very cold. I didn't want her waiting in the draught.'

'Quite right,' David said. For some reason he couldn't explain to himself he was glad Clare hadn't accepted the lift. His mother didn't really get along with her. All right in her place of course, but David felt that his mother thought her place was behind the counter in O'Brien's, not as a university student and certainly not as a passenger in the doctor's car.

She had forgotten it would be so quiet, that it had always been so quiet at this time of year. There were no lights or Christmas trees in the windows, there was no traffic bustling up and down the street. She had forgotten how few people there were there, and how the wet spray stung your face when you went outside the door.

She had forgotten too how handsome Gerry Doyle was. He wore a leather jacket and his hair was long and shiny. In the station he had looked like a film star. He had brought a rug for her to wrap around her knees.

'Is there anything wrong?' Clare asked suddenly.

'Your mother had a fall. But she's fine. Fine,' he said.

'How fine?' Her voice was clipped.

'She nearly came to meet you with me, that's how fine.'

'Why didn't they tell me? Why did no one tell me? Where did she fall?'

'She fell on the cliff path. She broke her ankle. She wasn't even kept in hospital more than one night.'

Clare's eyes filled with tears.

'No, it's not bad, honestly, she hobbles a bit and that's all. Your dad's being very nice to her and he brings her tea in the morning.'

'She must be bad then. When did it happen?'

'About three weeks ago. Listen Clare, will you stop, I was going to tell you just as we came into Castlebay so that you'd have no time to be going through all this

657

useless kind of nonsense. So as you'd see her in five minutes and know she was all right.'

'She could have been killed.'

'She couldn't. Don't make it so dramatic. She's been through all that now, it will only make it worse if you start attacking them for not telling you and saying what could have happened.'

He was right. She admitted it grudgingly.

'Very well, tell me about other things. I'll see Mam soon enough.'

He told her that business was changing, as he had always suspected it would. More and more people were bringing their own cheap cameras to the beach, Murphy's chemist was demented with visitors wanting their holiday snaps developed. The demand for beach photographs was growing less.

But then he had always known it would, so the thing to do was to change direction, to expand. He was in portrait photography now, and doing special commissions for hotels and new buildings which wanted prestige pictures of their premises. It meant of course that he would have to improve his own premises. Big important places only came to you if they thought you looked big and important too.

Wasn't that risky, Clare had wondered. No, it was business, Gerry assured her.

He told her that Josie Dillon had managed to get a whole lot of people to come to the hotel for a bridge weekend, and it was such a success that bridge people from all over were going to come there regularly. Josie's Uncle Dick had learned to play bridge when he'd been ordered off the drink apparently, and he had been saying for years that they should do this but he'd done nothing about it. Now he and Josie were as pleased as punch. Josie's sisters were hopping mad and her grandmother claimed that it was all *her* idea in the first place.

She told Gerry about the size of the university and about the Annexe where they had coffee every morning and how there were hundreds and hundreds of nuns and priests studying too, which she had never expected.

Was Fiona back yet for Christmas, she wanted to know. It would be interesting to compare notes with her about what her polytechnic was like.

No, she wasn't coming home apparently, in fact Gerry thought he might go over and see her.

'Not coming home for *Christmas*?' It was unheard of.

Gerry kept looking at the road.

'But what's she doing that she's not coming home?'

He sighed, almost his whole body went into the sigh. 'Jesus, Clare, you're not an old biddy, why do you sound so amazed? She wants to stay there, that's all. Do I have to build up a story for you too, an explanation? Will everyone in Castlebay want a full account of what everyone else from Castlebay is doing for the rest of their lives?'

'I'm sorry, you're quite right,' she said contritely. 'I don't talk like this in Dublin, it must be coming home that makes me do it.'

'Yeah, well some of us never left home, don't forget that, but we grow up too in our own way.'

She wasn't sure what he meant but it sounded like a criticism. She nodded apologetically. They drove on in silence for a while.

'I'm going tomorrow in fact,' he said. 'I haven't told anyone else, I'll just go.'

'Sure,' she said, 'that's a good idea.'

'I might go to see Tommy and Ned while I'm in London,' he said unexpectedly. 'I haven't laid eyes on them in years.'

She jumped a little but he couldn't have noticed.

'Do you have their address to give me?'

'No,' she said. 'No, I don't.'

'Would your mother . . .'

'I think not.' Her mouth closed like a trap. She too stared ahead of her.

'Right,' he said eventually. 'As we were saying there's no reason why being brought up in Castlebay means you've got to be at everyone's beck and call the whole time.'

She smiled, biting her lip. She had as good as told him now, hadn't she? She might as well have said the whole thing. It would have been easier in the long run.

Chrissie had got the ring for Christmas, she and Mogsy – whom she would now like to be referred to as Maurice – would be married next June. Mogsy – or Maurice – was building a house for them, a small place up near the creamery. Dwyers' had said Chrissie could go on working until there was a sign of a little Byrne coming along. They couldn't do fairer than that.

Clare's mother looked tired. 'Aren't you going to hare up and see your friend Miss O'Hara before you even sit down to talk to us?' she said the first night.

'Don't be giving out to me. I'm only just home.'

'Home! It's not much we'll see of you. Up there with the books, hardly a word to your own flesh and blood.'

'Mammy, why are you saying all this?' I'm only in the door! I'm not going up to Miss O'Hara's, I'll go and see her tomorrow or the day after maybe, but you never minded that, you were always grateful to her too.'

'I know, don't mind me, I'm cranky these days.'

'What is it?' They were on their own.

'A bit of everything.'

'It's not Chrissie's wedding, you're not upset about that?'

'Not at all, for every shoe God made a stocking. I tell you those two were matched in heaven.'

'Well what then?'

'I suppose I get to thinking, I wonder about Tommy.' Clare's heart jumped. 'You'll know this yourself in years to come, there's something about the eldest one, I don't know what it is. But he never writes, he never comes back. Wouldn't it be great if he walked in this Christmas, that's what I was thinking I suppose.'

'Tommy never wrote more than his name in his life, you know that.'

'Yes, but I'm not settled about Ned's letters, he's hiding something. I'm going to ask Gerry Doyle when he comes in here will he go and see him, he's going to England tomorrow.'

'When did he tell you that? He said he was going to tell no one.'

'I asked him if he'd pick up some supplies for us before Christmas and he said he wouldn't be around, he just told me now, a few minutes ago when you were getting your stuff out of his van and being surprised at the sound of the sea all over again.'

'Gerry'd not have time to go finding Tommy and Ned.'

'Ah he will, he's a good boy for all that they give him a bad name around here. I'll have a word with him tomorrow.'

Clare left a note into Gerry Doyle's house that night. She said she wanted to stroll out to see the cliffs, her mother said she was stark raving mad but you might as well talk to a stone wall as to any of her children.

Gerry was sitting on the wall next morning as she had asked him. It was dark grey and threatening but it wasn't raining. They were both wrapped up well.

'There's a bit of a problem about Tommy,' she said.

'I thought there was from the sound of you.' He didn't sound triumphant or curious.

'Wormwood Scrubs to be exact,' she said.

'That's a bit of a problem all right.' He grinned at her comfortingly. 'And your ma doesn't know?'

'Nobody knows except Ned and me.'

'That's hard.'

'No, it's worse on him in the gaol, and the old man they beat up doing the robbery, those are the people it's hard on.'

'Sure, well what will I do, say I can't find him?'

'No, could you just ring Ned, I've his phone number here written out, and talk away to him and then tell Ma that Tommy's fine. Would that be all right?' She looked very young and very anxious in the cold morning air.

'That's fine, I'll look after it.'

'Thanks Gerry.'

She hadn't asked him to keep it to himself, she didn't need to.

'About Fiona,' he said.

'It's none of my business,' she said suddenly.

'No, but anyway, she's having a baby this week. A Christmas baby of all bloody things.'

Clare nearly fell off the wall with shock. But for Gerry's sake she hid it. 'She's lucky to have you,' she said.

'We're a great pair,' he said and leaped lightly off the wall. He helped her down.

'Happy Christmas anyway,' he said.

She looked at him gratefully. His small pointed face was cold in the chilly dawn. He had said as little as could possibly be said, offered little sympathy when there was nothing to say. He had told Fiona's secret just so that she would have something in return, so that the pain and shame of her telling could be written off in a balance on some kind of scales.

'Happy Christmas, Gerry,' she said. 'You're very very nice.'

'I've always been telling you that, you're the one that didn't realize it,' he joked.

'I don't mean *that* sort of nice,' Clare said, but she wondered as she said it was she being truthful. He was so handsome and kind, he had this great sense of being in charge, nothing could go really wrong if you told Gerry. Fiona had been very lucky to have a brother like that. Fine help poor Tommy or Ned would have been in such a predicament. She felt sorry that he wouldn't be around for the Christmas holidays. She felt this odd kind of wish to hold on to him. Not to let him go.

'I'd better head for foreign parts,' he said. He was still holding her hands since he had helped her down from the wall.

'Safe journey. I hope . . . I hope Fiona'll be all right.'

'I'm sure she will, she's going to give the baby for adoption, and then I suppose I'll have to teach her something about photography.'

'About *what?*'

'Photography.' He gave his familiar crooked grin. 'That's what the whole place thinks she's been studying for the past six months.'

Angela was delighted to see her, no of course she wasn't too early, come on in and have breakfast like the old days.

'When I'm properly grown up and have my own place, I'll have exactly the same breakfast as you do,' Clare said, tucking in.

'What do I have that's special?'

'You have white shop bread and you have nice thin shop marmalade and you don't have thick homemade bread and awful homemade marmalade like people buy at sales of work.'

'Is this all your university education has done for you, made you whinge and whine about shop bread? Tell me about it all there, tell me about Emer and Kevin. Why don't you write to me, great long letters like you did when you were at school?'

'I don't know, I really don't know.'

'That's very honest of you.' Angela smiled, not at all put out. 'Anyway you're very busy up there.'

'It's not that.' Clare struggled to be honest. 'I write to my Mam, and to Josie and to Tommy. I *do* have time.'

'It might be easier in a while,' Angela seemed untroubled by it. 'Let me tell you about the place above. You won't credit this. Immaculata has gone totally and completely mad this term, the men with white coats will be stepping out of a van for her before Easter, mark my words.'

Mrs O'Hara frowned. 'You're very foolish and wrong, Angela, to say such things in front of a child. For all Clare's great marks she's only a child.'

'It's all right, Mrs O'Hara,' Clare said. 'I've heard it all, I say nothing, I keep my mouth closed.'

'You're the only one in this county who does then,' grumbled Angela's mother.

There was a long and insane story about Mother Immaculata having a Christmas pageant where everyone had to bring a toy for a poor child, they would all be gathered by the crib. Then one child had asked where they would go.

'To the *poor*,' Mother Immaculata had shrilled.

'But aren't we the poor?' the child had asked. 'There isn't anyone poorer than us.'

Clare laughed and while more tea was being poured she wrote Angela a note. 'I want to talk to you about Tommy, but not in front of your mother.'

Angela suggested that Clare come upstairs to see some new books that she had bought, and Clare sat for the first time in her teacher's bedroom. She was surprised at how sparse it was, with the very very white bedspread and the crucifix hanging over the bed head. There was a small press, Mary Catherine would have wept over the lack of closets. And a white chair. No carpet but a nice rug on the floor. Somehow it was a bit sad.

'I had to tell Gerry Doyle about Tommy,' she explained. She told everything except Gerry's secret.

'I had to tell him,' she said eventually when she saw Angela's troubled face. 'What else could I have done?'

'I suppose you could have let him find out and hoped he wouldn't tell your mother.'

'But it would have been so devious, such a long way round.'

'You might be right. I'm sure you are, it's just that now you've told him you're sort of in his power.'

'That's very dramatic.' Clare tried to laugh.

'He's a very dramatic young man. I've always thought that. Far too handsome and smart for Castlebay, he's dangerous almost.'

'I won't be in his power, honestly.' She looked straight into Angela's eyes. 'As much as I know anything, I know that. I'll never be in his control.'

David came into O'Brien's shop on Christmas Eve. Bones sat obediently outside the door.

'You can bring him in, everyone else brings their hounds in,' Clare's father said. 'In fact Mogsy Byrne brought in two cows a month ago.'

'I'd thank you to remember his name is Maurice, Dad, and he did *not* bring them in, they came in because the young fellow who was meant to be minding them wasn't.'

'Congratulations Chrissie, I heard you are engaged.' David was polite.

Chrissie simpered and showed him the ring. David said it looked terrific.

'No sign of you making a move in that direction yourself?' she said, arch woman of the world now, trying to encourage those who were hanging back.

'Oh, I think I'd better wait till I'm qualified. It's bad enough asking someone to take on a doctor but a medical student would be a fate worse than death, and we'd have nothing to live on.'

'Have you lost your heart up in Dublin?' Chrissie wondered.

'Chrissie, stop it, you're very forward,' Agnes said.

'No, I've been working too hard really to have any time for romance.' He smiled easily at them all. 'Is Clare here?'

'No, no sign of Clare – where would she be but up in Miss O'Hara's or in the hotel with Josie Dillon, there's no sign of her round here, I can assure you that.' Chrissie's voice was resentful. 'Sorry your visit was in vain,' she said spitefully.

'Not at all, I came for cigarettes,' he said easily. 'And for a tin of those nice biscuits as well for Nellie, and some black pudding.'

'Your mother got black pudding this morning,' Tom O'Brien said – it would be no use alienating a customer by selling the same thing twice.

'I'm sure she did but I bet she didn't get enough, I want six bits on my plate when we come back from Mass tomorrow morning. You've no idea how I miss black pudding in Dublin, they only have mean little slivers of it, and it doesn't taste the same at all.'

He wished them happy Christmas and they found a piece off the end of some cooked ham for Bones, and Bones gobbled it up and raised his paw in the air even though nobody had been offering to shake hands with him at all.

Clare was lying on Josie's bed telling her all about the hostel and the rungs up the wall and the laughs with Mary Catherine and Valerie. She told her about the lectures and the debating society on Saturday nights, and the hops, and how each Society had dances which were meant to make money.

Josie was disappointed that she had only met James Nolan on two occasions – in the café and at the very hot crowded party in somebody's flat. Clare revealed that he had danced with Mary Catherine twice, if you could call it dancing in those dark rooms; but he hadn't asked Mary Catherine out on a date or anything. Clare *didn't* tell her that James Nolan had forgotten her, she didn't think that was useful information; instead she said that she got the impression he was a bit fickle and faithless. But Josie said that was only when you didn't know him well.

Josie was thrilled about how she was building up the winter business in the hotel; and Uncle Dick had become really nice, not mad and grouchy like he used to be. Granny was totally gaga now; she had told Josie that Josie's mother had been putting arsenic in all their food for years now, and had even poisoned some of the guests, which was why they hadn't come back since. Her sisters Rose and Emily were home for Christmas and weren't a bit pleased about the bridge weekends; and they had almost told her to her face not to interfere. Clare didn't know how awfully quiet the place was in winter. When they were young they hadn't noticed it so much, but it was really so quiet you wouldn't believe it. She had learned to play bridge herself with Uncle Dick and sometimes the two of them went up to the Powers' and played a few rubbers with Mrs Power and Mr Harris, that auctioneer man who lived in a big house halfway between the town and Castlebay. He was *eligible*, Uncle Dick said, but he was also a hundred and ten. Well he was thirty-seven, eighteen and a half years older than Josie, twice their age. Uncle Dick must be mad. Clare agreed and told Josie not to dream of trapping the eligible Mr Harris.

They speculated about Chrissie and Mogsy and wondered what either of them could see in the other. Would their children be as awful as both of them, or twice as awful?

Father O'Dwyer went round to the houses of the sick on the night of Christmas Eve and brought them Holy Communion. He came to the O'Hara cottage as his last visit. Angela had prepared the place for his visit and had a little candle-lighting in front of the crib.

She had gone upstairs while the old woman's confession was heard and then when the Priest called her she came down to kneel while her mother received Communion. They were all silent for a few minutes, but after that Father O'Dwyer had a cup of tea and a tomato sandwich from which the crusts had been cut off.

'Isn't it a pity that Father Sean didn't make it over to see you this Christmas?' he said conversationally.

'Oh well, you know the way it is,' Angela said meaninglessly.

'You see he's in a part now where they don't even have proper postal services,' Mrs O'Hara said. 'That's why we have to write to their house in England in order that priests there can forward them or deliver them when they're going out.'

'Yes, yes,' Father O'Dwyer was soothing the way he listened to all old people, not taking in very deeply what they were saying.

'But maybe he'll come back next year,' he said.

'Please God, Father, please God. Still the way I look at it is that it's better that he's there doing the Lord's work with savages and people who never heard of God than here coming to see me.'

Her face was radiant in the firelight and the aftermath of receiving Communion. Angela bit her lip hard.

Father O'Dwyer patted Mrs O'Hara on the hand and said, 'That's right, that's right, that's the spirit that sends the labourers into the vineyard.'

Dr Power had asked Nellie would she like to go home for Christmas.

'You ask me that every year and the answer's always no sir, thank you very much, I have a nicer time in this house, and a better meal and more peace. And I can go down to see them all in the evening.'

'If you're sure . . .' he said.

'Anyway sir, the mistress wouldn't like you playing fast and loose with the arrangements. I'd like to see her face, if I said I wouldn't be here for Christmas Day.'

'Stop trying to stir up a row, Nellie,' he said affectionately. 'This is a happy house now, do you hear me?'

'It is and all sir,' said Nellie goodnaturedly. 'I've been here since I was sixteen, that will be twenty years next year, and there's hardly a cross word ever said under this roof.'

'You've been here too long, Nellie. Why don't you go and marry someone?'

'And have a lout asking me to cook his dinner and polish his shoes for nothing for him, aren't I like a king here, with my own wireless that I can take upstairs and plug in the bedroom if I want to, and a big chair beside the range. What would I want with marriage?'

'Will you sit with us and have your Christmas dinner at our table tomorrow?'

'God love you sir, you ask me that every year too, and I won't. The mistress would be annoyed for one thing, and for another I'd be dropping the food off my fork.'

'You're a very obstinate woman.'

'I've no brains but I'm not a fool, that's all.'

Clare had bought bright Christmas decorations while she was in Dublin. It had been marvellous going down Moore Street and Henry Street with Mary Catherine and Valerie listening to the women shouting their wares, and the last of this and the last of that in order to whip people up into a frenzy thinking things were running out. Clare had bought the last of the shiny chains, only to see dozens more coming from under the stall. She had also bought the last of the Christmas sparklers which were like low-key fireworks giving off little tinselly sparks. Jim and Ben had loved them and they were a treat in Castlebay so she felt it was a good buy. She had gone without lunches for three weeks in order to buy the gifts, and had stocked up on bread and butter from breakfast to keep her going through the day.

It was bright and cold on Christmas morning. The O'Briens went to early Mass from habit. There was no need to be back in case anyone would call to the shop. Nobody would admit that they had forgotten anything for Christmas, the family would be able to eat their meal undisturbed.

Clare had wrapped up all her presents and Chrissie eyed this pile of gifts with some suspicion.

'I hope you realize that being engaged and everything we have to put all our savings towards our future,' she said to Clare. 'We can't be wasting everything on silly gifts.'

'Sure,' Clare had said and resisted the temptation to pull out every hair of Chrissie's permed, frizzy head.

After their breakfast there was an endless amount of preparation for the main meal. Agnes, still frail and unable to move about, sat with her leg on a stool and gave instructions, lift the ham carefully from the water where it had been soaking. Carefully, don't drown the whole kitchen. Set the table properly. Properly, Chrissie, it *was* Christmas Day, take that dirty cloth off and find a cleaner one. And peel the potatoes Ben, not with your finger, with a knife, and move that holly Jim, before it sticks into people.

Tom O'Brien sat beside her, repeated her orders with increasing impatience, and added little asides of his own about how you'd think people would be glad to help when their unfortunate mother had been injured in a fall.

Clare did most of the work and when the meal was ready she was nearly exhausted. She couldn't understand why a lot of this work hadn't been divided up and done the night before, but a word of criticism would open the floodgates, and she kept her thoughts to herself.

After the plum pudding, she distributed her gifts. Mam thought the scarf was very nice, a bit light for this kind of weather, but very nice for warmer weather, that is of course if you would wear a scarf at all in warmer weather. Her father looked with interest at the map of the county she had found with such trouble in a second-hand shop in Dublin, and then framed. It was very generous he thought; of course it would be a poor man who didn't know his own county, but maybe strangers might look at it. Jim and Ben genuinely *were* pleased with the puzzles and games she had got them. Chrissie looked at the manicure set with dulled eyes.

Clare had been so sure that Chrissie would love a manicure set, for as far back as she could remember Chrissie had been filing and painting her nails, her fingernails and her toenails, surely the set in the little red case would be exactly what she would like. But Clare must have been remembering a time too far back. Chrissie opened the parcel with her stubby fingers and Clare noticed that her hands were calloused and her nails were bitten short. Still, she thought hopefully, maybe.

Chrissie turned it over and said it was very nice, especially of course if you were a student and had time to be doing your nails. She put it aside and never looked at it again during the day.

665

Clare got a box of sweets taken from one of the shelves from her mother, and a tinsel card from Jim and Ben. Her father gave her £1 peeled from the notes in his pocket. She fought the stinging of the tears in her eyes. They were her family for heaven's sake, they didn't need to be going on with too much ritual. It was silly to get upset because of the lack of trappings.

Angela had warned her long ago that one of the dangers of going away to be educated was that you expected too much when you came back, and you built up a whole wall of disappointment that was unnecessary. It had been a bit like that when she came home from the scrupulously clean convent boarding school and had to share a room with Chrissie, it was the same now. After knowing people like Emer and Kevin with their politeness and consideration towards each other and everyone they came in contact with . . . this seemed a dull, leaden sort of day.

She remembered Mary Catherine reading somewhere that more people wanted to commit suicide on Christmas Day than any other day. She would not join them. Putting her elbows on the table full of dirty dishes and the wrappings of the presents that only she had given, Clare managed a big smile.

'Will we tell a ghost story?' she said.

'Who knows one?' asked her father.

'We could make one up as we went along, each person adding a bit. You start, Chrissie.'

'I don't know how to make up ghost stories.' Chrissie was not going to join in.

'Yes you do. Just start.'

The others looked eager.

'Once upon a time there was a ghost that had this desperate sister,' Chrissie began. 'It had four brothers who were all right but it had a really terrible sister . . .'

There was always a Christmas tree in the window of Dr Power's house. On the side where it could be seen from the road. There were presents which had arrived by post from the Nolans in Dublin and from cousins and friends all over the place. David placed his own gifts there on Christmas Eve night, wrapped in red crêpe paper and each one with a cut-out Santa Claus.

David looked at all the neatly labelled parcels. He glanced through at the dining room already set with gleaming glass and shining silver, decorated with holly and criss-crossed crackers. Why did it feel so empty and hollow? He hated Nellie being in the kitchen, although he knew she would never come and join them; he hated the games-playing, where he and his mother and father would pull crackers and read jokes and exclaim over gifts. If they only knew about some of the homes he visited in Dublin when he had been doing his practical work, then they'd find this kind of playing at Christmas very shabby. But his father must know.

They walked across in the cold Christmas air to Mass; everyone was good-humoured and cheerful despite the wind. Dr Power dealt with a young woman who had fainted, and reassured her it was just the result of a three-mile walk fasting on a cold morning. 'But I'd have to fast and go to Holy Communion on Christmas morning, wouldn't I?' the woman said, detecting some criticism in the doctor's voice as he bent her head down.

'Of course you would, that's just what the Lord likes on His birthday – people nearly killing themselves,' Dr Power muttered.

All through the day, David felt as if he were under some kind of spotlight. They were all anxious to know what David thought, what David wanted. Did David think they should eat now? Have a sherry? Would David like to open the presents? Was he sure he liked the sweater? If it wasn't big enough, if it wasn't the right colour it could be changed.

They had soup first, and little fingers of toast; and then the turkey was carved – was David sure he wanted the leg? There was plenty of breast.

They clapped when the flame lit on the plum pudding, and they raised their glasses to another good year and to the year that lay ahead. Molly Power wondered whether the Nolans were at this moment having their Christmas lunch in Dublin, and they drank a toast to them too.

'James' mother gets very odd at Christmas,' David said, to make conversation. 'Apparently last year she had a handkerchief on her head all through the meal.'

Dr Power burst out laughing. 'Did she say why?' he asked.

'Well, she did when Caroline asked her, she said you never knew with ceilings – then I don't think they asked any more.' David grinned back, thinking of the story.

'I don't like you telling stories like that about Sheila, she's different, she's unusual, that's all, you make her sound batty when you talk like that.'

'She is a *bit* batty, I think,' David said apologetically. 'You know, not dangerous or anything but definitely not firing on all cylinders.'

Dr Power frowned slightly and David understood.

'Sorry, I was just joking – unusual is more the word for it.'

Molly smiled, pleased. She didn't like her friend being defined as insane. She passed round the liqueur chocolates, exclaiming with delight as each centre was read out. Would she have kirsch or would she try cherry brandy? Which was more alcoholic? David fought down his wish to say that since there was less than half an eggspoonful of alcohol in each it was immaterial.

'*Do* you see a lot of Caroline?' Molly's voice was over-casual.

'A fair bit, but I'm working hard, very hard. People never believe this of students. We went to a party just before I came down here, she sent you both her love.'

'I think she likes it here, I think she's a Castlebay person at heart, she wrote a very nice note in her Christmas card saying it must be lovely in the winter.' Mrs Power was still fishing.

'Oh, I think just for holidays,' David said.

'You'd never know. A lot of people thought they'd come here for holidays and changed their minds, ended up staying here altogether.' Dr Power patted his wife's hand as he said this. David felt a sense of overpowering claustrophobia. Not only were they wrapping him in cotton wool while he was here; they were planning the day when he came back full time as a doctor to help his father; and they were now planning his wife for him.

'I think I'll go for a bit of a walk . . . all that food . . .' he stammered.

He stood up, anxious to be out of the warm room, the smell of mince pies and the beam of their attention.

But it was no use. They both thought that would be a great idea: Dr Power went to get his stick and Molly ran upstairs for her coat and gloves. David carried the tray of coffee cups out to the kitchen Nellie was nodding off to sleep beside the big range with the wireless on, and Bones was fast asleep due to a surfeit of turkey.

He left the tray quietly on the kitchen table and wrapped his scarf round his neck.

He knew he was a selfish, selfish ungrateful so and so, but he wished that he had fourteen brothers and sisters to share the responsibility with him; or that he had no parents at all like one of the students in his year, who was going to spend the festive season with a lot of English people in Belgium. Everyone knew that English girls were outrageous and this fellow was going to have a really great time.

'Ready, David,' called Molly and everyone in the house woke up in confusion: David from his dream of permissive coach travellers, and Nellie and Bones from their kitchen sleeps.

The family walk was underway and soon it would be the family tea, and then tomorrow it would be the family Stephen's Day. David sighed heavily and hated himself for the sigh.

On New Year's Day Clare went for a walk on the beach to collect shells and make New Year's resolutions.

'I will not expect too much of my family.

'I will work out a better revision system, not just big pencil marks saying *must revise later.*

'I will get a job in a café one night a week in Dublin.

'I will have my hair cut in an interesting style.

'I will find a person to take me out on a date.

'I will write a proper letter to Angela O'Hara every single week.'

She found some nice cowries and put them in the box she had in her pocket. She heard a shout and there was David.

'I hoped I'd find you here. You and I are the only people who use the amenities out of season.'

'Or in season, they're all too busy to come down on the beach, my father can't even swim.'

'Anyway, here you are.' He looked pleased to see her, she felt suddenly a little embarrassed.

'Where's Bones, you don't look fully dressed without him.'

'Poor Bones, he has a cough. Believe it or not, he's coughing like an old man. My father has him dosed better than if he were the president but Bones is whooping and hacking away. Nellie has an old jumper tied round his neck, you never saw the cut of him.'

Clare laughed at the idea of it but said it was rotten to think of Bones not being well.

'Will you do me a favour?' he asked.

'Sure.'

'I want to go back the day after tomorrow . . .'

'But term doesn't start until . . .'

'Exactly. That's the point. I have to say it does, will you back me up?'

'Certainly, but I can't go back the day after tomorrow.'

His face fell. 'No, I suppose you can't.'

'No, I don't mean leaving here or anything, they wouldn't mind. It's just I've nowhere to stay. The hostel doesn't open for us till the first day of term.'

'Oh.'

'We could say medical school opens earlier, I could say that to anyone, but anyway what does it matter what I say? I don't meet your parents.'

'No, but if you'd gone back they'd know, everyone knows everything here, every single thing.' He sounded annoyed.

'I'm sorry,' Clare said. 'I know what you feel, and I wouldn't mind at all going back myself, but you do see . . .'

'You could always stay in our flat, my flat,' he said.

'No I could *not*.'

'I don't mean any funny business, you'd have your own room, one of the fellows won't be back until term starts.'

'We'd be killed if I was caught, and I'm damn well not going to risk getting caught for something I haven't done, or putting myself in danger unless I'm getting value out of it.' She was full of conviction and quite unaware how vehement she looked.

'All right, calm down. I see your point of view.'

'Did you have a nice Christmas?' she asked suddenly.

'Not very. Did you?'

'Not very.'

'Are you missing lover boy Gerry Doyle? I hear he went off to the bright lights of London.'

'No, I'm not missing him. I don't suppose I gave him a thought. I must be the only woman in the western hemisphere that isn't.'

'Aha then he'll go after you all the more,' David said.

'Have *you* a lover girl in Dublin that you want to be back to meet?' she asked.

'Yes and no. Yes there is a girl, but it's not only that. I feel a bit too *important* in the house. I'm all they've got. Do you know what I mean? I think they pay too much attention to me.'

'It's the reverse in my house. They don't pay enough attention to me. I'm not nearly important enough.'

He laughed. 'Nobody ever gets what they want, do they? Will I see you at all in Dublin? I could ring you in the hostel some evening.'

'Great,' she said.

He never rang, but that was no surprise.

Clare thought about it, and decided that David had never meant it, it was just the way the Powers had of saying goodbye. They couldn't actually say the word, it seemed too final, so they said something insincere instead, like promising to ring you at the hostel.

Perhaps it was just as well, she thought, making the best of it. There were thousands and thousands of men in UCD; she shouldn't try to get a date with someone from Castlebay who was on the other side of the cliffs so to speak.

Valerie had had a fairly uneventful Christmas, all things considered. She had nearly come to blows with her mother when they were playing Scrabble: her mother said Quorn was a word, and Valerie had claimed it was a proper noun and the name of a hunt somewhere. Her mother had flung things on the ground and said she wouldn't be patronized. They had an adventurous time with a cook book, each taking it in turns to make a dish, one more exotic than the other; apparently Valerie's father in England had refused to pay any actual money but would pay bills in the local grocery so they only chose dishes with very highly priced ingredients.

Mary Catherine had an adventurous Christmas too; James Nolan invited her to his house three times. She had thought Caroline was a *pain*. Caroline was finishing her thesis for her M.A. about Spencer and Ireland and thought almost everyone in the world was illiterate and that Americans were more illiterate than most. James Nolan showed a very unhealthy desire to go the States in the summer: he said he would be sure to look up Mary Catherine and her family, and perhaps he could come to stay? She had agreed, and made sure not to give him her home address. Her mailman father told her when she married a man who owned a castle to keep her American side of things under wraps until the deal was done. James Nolan wasn't exactly a castle owner but he was an attorney almost, and that couldn't be bad. No, of course she didn't love him. But she wasn't going to pitch him overboard yet. Clare thought of Josie back home typing away in the hotel, organizing bridge conferences with Uncle Dick, fighting off her two jealous sisters Rosie and Emily. She sighed. It wouldn't be reasonable to tell Mary Catherine to hold her horses, because James Nolan couldn't remember Josie Dillon from a hole in the ground.

Mary Catherine came running up the stairs two at a time. 'There is a *dee-vine* young man downstairs asking for you, Clare. I said I would see if I could find you.'

'You mean thing! Why didn't you say I'd be down in two ticks?'

'Because I'm your friend. I wanted you to put on something good and to comb your hair and put on some make-up. I'm *too* good a friend, that's what I am.'

'Oh, it must be Gerry Doyle, he's the one who always gets that reaction.' Still, she did put on a little lipstick.

She picked up her duffle coat.

'Very confident he's going to ask you out,' Mary Catherine said.

'You should play hard to get,' Valerie suggested. 'He'll think it's too eager if you go down ready for the off.'

'That fellow only knows people who are too eager, that's the style he's used to. Anyway, we'll just go out for coffee, I imagine.'

'I think we should leave the window unlocked. You may need to climb the rungs tonight from the sound of it.' Valerie was pleased.

'He's not strictly good-looking. He's got an *aura*,' said Mary Catherine.

'You and your auras, you learned that word a week ago, everything has an *aura*.' Clare was gone before they could retaliate. She ran lightly down the stairs. Gerry was standing in the hall as relaxed as if he had been a regular visitor.

'This is a great surprise,' she said with genuine and unaffected pleasure. 'I didn't know you were in Dublin.'

'I'm not. I mean not in Dublin itself if you know what I mean, I'm passing through, on my way back from London. I got a longing to talk to you.'

She was going to say something joky – but his face looked tired.

'Great,' she said simply. 'Let me take you away from here before they devour you.' She tucked her arm companionably in his and they went out of the hostel and down the steps. 'Coffee or a drink?'

'A drink would be very nice. Do you know a pub?'

'There's two here, just round the corner. Shows you my virtuous life, though, I don't know what they're like. Have a look into the first one and tell me what you think.'

He came back in seconds, grinning. 'How many people are there in Dublin – half a million maybe?'

'More, much more, I think. Why?'

'In that pub, who do I see but David Power and Caroline Nolan looking into each other's eyes.'

'Go on. Well, we could have a Castlebay reunion, if you'd like that.'

'No. I wouldn't like that. I'd like to talk to you, that's why I came to find you.'

They went into the second pub. There was a mixed collection of drinkers: students in college scarves, workmen from a building site nearby, a few red-nosed old regulars.

'This is Paradise,' Gerry said. 'No one from home. Is it still bitter lemon or have you got more adventurous?'

'Still bitter lemon,' she said, pleased that he had remembered.

He told her about Fiona. The baby was a boy, born the day after Christmas. She called him Stephen. The old nuns had been very kind – disapproving of course, and thought Fiona was a great sinner – but kind in the end; and they had arranged the adoption when the baby was three weeks old. Fiona had a sort of depression apparently. That's why he had gone over again, to cheer her up, to reassure her that she had done the right thing. There was no other course open to her if she wanted to live her life in Castlebay. She had to pretend it had never happened. She *had* to keep it a secret.

Clare didn't want to hear about the baby's father, but Gerry wanted to tell her. He was a married man. Wouldn't you know? One of the crowd that came down golfing last year. He had told Fiona he was single; he had also told her when she wrote to him about the pregnancy that there was no question of his becoming involved; and that if she made any trouble all his friends had agreed to say that *they* had had her too. What options did she have? If this were known at home she would be a slut *and* a fool – what a combination . . .

He talked on about the business. Times were hard and getting harder. It hadn't been as easy as he had thought: there were all the expenses. If Clare could only see what he had to lash out on equipment – the new modern machines were so expensive, and of course they would eventually pay for themselves, but the trouble was *when*.

Even doing the place up had cost a lot of money. There had been some good commissions, but not enough.

'What are you going to do?' she asked sympathetically.

'Survive. Isn't that the only thing to do? What you and I have always been doing.'

He looked as if it might be quite an effort to survive. Shadows under his eyes, and his face pale. She felt very protective towards him suddenly, almost as if she would like to put her arm round his shoulder and draw him towards her soothingly. She had never felt like that about Gerry Doyle before, and had been rather relieved. It was as if she were the only girl in town who hadn't caught the measles. But this was different. This wasn't being keen on him like Chrissie and everyone else. This was wanting to look after him, he seemed defenceless and vulnerable sitting there in front of his pint glass.

She reached out and took his hand.

'So I thought I'd come and tell you about it. If there's anyone who'd understand, it's you.'

Pleased and surprised she asked, 'Why me?'

'Lord, it hasn't been easy for you to get where you've got. No one to help you on, just Clare do this do that, iron that shirt Clare, sort those potatoes Clare, when they should be so proud of you and helping you to study.'

He had noticed, all those years. He understood.

She was trying to lessen the intensity of his stare: he was looking at her as if his eyes were boring through her.

'You're different, Clare. I've always said that to you. You and I are the same type. We're the only two they produced in Castlebay. We belong together.'

She was startled now and not quite sure how to handle it.

'Look at that couple over there,' she said suddenly as a girl student, somewhat the worse for drink, started climbing on the lap of her companion. 'That's *belonging together* in a rather public way. How long before they're thrown out?'

She turned her bright smile back to him but his glance hadn't changed.

He grasped her hand. 'Stop talking about things that don't matter. It's true. We *are* the same. And I know every thought you have, as you know mine.'

'I don't know yours, Gerry. Really I don't.'

'Well you will.'

'When will I? I have so much work to do here in this university I'll never have time to get round to reading people's thoughts?'

'Not *people's* thoughts. *Mine*. I'll wait for you.'

'It will be a long wait. I'm going to get a list of letters after my name, you know.'

'Stop trying to avoid it. I'll wait for you, no matter how long I have to wait. In your heart you know that.'

She looked at his troubled face, never so handsome as now, and wondered what he meant by all this. It had a very solemn air about it. Like a vow.

She met David Power not at all during the term, and got over her pique that he had promised to ring her. She went on one date to the Abbey Theatre. The serious history student who had asked her said he hoped she didn't mind being in the gods. By the time they got there they were nearly ready for a hospital bed. He told her that he didn't believe in spending money foolishly; and when they had a cup of coffee afterwards and he said, 'You *don't* want anything to eat, do you?' Clare agreed in her mind that indeed he was *not* someone to spend money foolishly. Or even at all. He asked her to go to the National Gallery with him on the following Saturday afternoon. But she didn't like him enough; and she preferred going there on her own anyway. And it was honestly *too* mean to ask someone on a date to a place that was free. She wrote about it to Josie, deliberately making it worse than it was. She didn't want Josie to know how much fun it was in Dublin. She didn't want Josie to know that she had met James Nolan either.

James always looked deliberately well-dressed, as if he were posing as a very elegant man at the races.

'Is your nice American friend Mary Catherine loaded?' James had asked her unexpectedly in the Annexe one morning when she was having coffee and reading an article in *History Today* at the same time.

'Loaded?' She pretended she hadn't understood.

'Loaded with money, weighed down with wealth.'

'I have no idea,' Clare said, looking at him with her big dark eyes opened wide in innocence. 'What a strange thing to ask.'

'Well I can hardly ask *her*,' he complained.

'But why not? If you want to know, isn't she the one you should ask?'

'It looks odd. And anyway women are so apt to take things the wrong way.'

'I know,' Clare said sympathetically. 'Isn't it sickening?'

'You're laughing at me.' .

'I am not. I'm horrified by you if you must know.'

'It's just that I was half thinking of going to the States this summer – see how American I've become? I don't say "going to America" I say "going to the States" – and if I could stay with Mary Catherine's family for a bit it would cut down the cost.'

'Sure, but why would it matter if they were loaded or not? Couldn't you stay with them, if she asked you, even if they were just ordinary, and not wealthy? Wouldn't it be a bed wherever it was?'

James looked down into his coffee cup. 'Yes, but it is my last summer holiday before I settle down to work. I'd like to go somewhere where they have a bit of *style*. A swimming pool, a ranch or a big apartment on Fifth Avenue . . . She's very secretive about where she lives. That's why I asked you.'

'Why don't you just come back to Castlebay as usual? I think the complications about America are wearing you out.'

'You don't understand anything Clare, that's your problem.'

'I know,' Clare grinned at him. 'It's always been my problem. I'm as thick as the wall.'

They parted friends, and yet Clare felt guilty. This pompous man was being a real heel towards two of her friends. It was disloyal sitting in the Annexe and giggling with him.

Emer and Kevin said they would be delighted if Clare came to stay for Easter. She had offered them a deal: she would babysit, wash up every single thing that went into the sink and do two hours a day digging the garden. In return could she have a place to stay and a little food? She had written to Angela and said she couldn't bear to go back to Castlebay: this was just the period when she had to revise and prepare for her First Arts. She'd try to square David Power too. She left a note for him at the medical faculty. He rang her that night at the hostel.

'Why should I help you?' he asked in a mock temper. 'You never helped me at Christmas.'

'Your romance didn't suffer as a result of it,' she said sharply.

'Do you have a fleet of detectives?' he inquired.

'Please, David, it's just that I really do have to work, I'm the scholarship girl don't forget, I don't get chances to repeat things. And I don't get any time at home. It's not like your house.'

'OK. *I'll* go along with *your* lies.'

It annoyed her. 'Thanks very much, David. I'll see you in the summer, I'm sure,' she said curtly.

'Oh, I'm sure you'll have thought up something else by then,' he said.

She hung up immediately before she could lose her temper with him. *Spoiled, self-important pig.*

'They *don't* resent it.'

'They do, Clare. They mightn't even realize it, but you've grown in ways that they never will. You speak better than they do, than you used to. You look better. It's not just the book learning.'

Clare twisted her glass in her hand. She and Angela were having a drink in the corner of Dillon's Hotel lounge. There was a beautiful view of the beach. Shortly, Josie would be putting her cover on the typewriter and would come for the game of tennis. Some things hadn't changed over the years. But Clare realized that Angela was right. She did have much more confidence. Her own mother would never dream of coming into the hotel and sitting down in the cushioned chair looking out over Castlebay. That wasn't for the likes of them, she would say. Her father wouldn't stand at the bar and drink his pint in the hotel either, it would be Craig's or nowhere. Jim and Ben would be tongue-tied and shoving at each other. And as for Chrissie! She and Mogsy wouldn't be caught dead inside a stuffy place like that, she had said on more than one occasion. Clare sighed. Lord knew that Dillon's Hotel was hardly the sophisticated capital of the world, but wasn't it maddening to think that she was the only member of her family who would feel comfortable there having a glass of shandy.

'I'll be very nice at the wedding. All day,' she smiled at Angela.

'Good, I don't want to sound like a sermon on charity but you have had so much more than Chrissie and you always will have. Make it as nice a day for her as possible.'

'All I'll get for my pains is Chrissie giving out to me all day, and if I'm *nice*, that will be further cause for complaint.'

'You promised.'

'Yes. What about your brother, when he was being ordained? Was that a hard sort of day?'

'No.' Angela's voice seemed distant. She was looking out to sea. 'My father didn't have a drop to drink. Dr Power gave him some tablets and told him it was dangerous to drink with them. I don't know whether it was or not. And my poor mother had a hat with a veil. I'll never forget it – and gloves. No, that day was no trouble at all.'

'You don't talk about him much nowadays.'

'I'll tell you some time.'

'Sure. I'm sorry.'

'Here's Josie and Dick.' Angela looked up brightly. 'You're looking very well, Josie. Very pretty.'

'Thank you. I've been on another diet. The summer visitors will be here at the end of the week. I'm trying to ensnare one of them.'

'One in particular, or just anyone?'

'Well, I have my eye on one. But he's a bit hard to get.'

Clare didn't catch Angela's eye. She had told her about Josie, and James Nolan going to the States for the summer; and debated whether or not she should tell Josie this.

Angela had said she should have let it fall casually ages ago, but Clare said it was very hard to let things *fall casually* when Josie sat up on her bed and hugged her knees and made plans for the summer.

'This is the last night we'll sleep together,' Clare said to Chrissie.

'I'm sure neither of us are sorry about that,' Chrissie sniffed. She was examining her face in the mirror with dissatisfaction. There was a definite spot on her chin.

'Well, it's the end of one part of your life. It must be exciting,' Clare soldiered on.

'Well, I'm twenty-one. It's time I was married.' Chrissie was defensive.

'It'll be a grand day.'

'Yes, it will. It'll be grand without any pats on the head from you, either.'

'I'm not patting you on the head. I'm just trying to say I'm pleased. That it's great. That it's the first wedding in the family. That's all.'

Her face was angry. Chrissie softened.

'Yes, well. All right. Sorry. I suppose I'm a bit jumpy and everything.'

'You're going to look terrific. The dress is fabulous.'

It was hanging on their wardrobe with an old sheet draped over it to keep it clean.

Chrissie looked at it mournfully.

'And your hair, it's super. I've never seen it so nice.'

'Yes, well. Peg's coming round in the morning to give it a comb out. You know, get it right for the veil.'

'Maurice will be delighted with you.'

'I don't know. Look at this spot. It's going to be desperate in the morning.'

'Listen. I tell you what to do. I'll dab a bit of Dettol on it. And don't touch it, do you hear? The Dettol won't work if you touch it, and then in the morning if it's not gone we can put some extra make-up on it. But it will have flattened a bit if you don't touch it.'

'Why were you never like this before?' Chrissie asked suspiciously.

'Like what?'

'Interested in spots, and ordinary things.'

'I always was, but you used to say I was mad, remember?'

Fiona Doyle said she'd be happy to look after the shop for them while they went to the wedding. She asked how thick she should cut the bacon and was there anyone she should or should not give credit to. Tom said she was a model shop girl and that if ever the photographic business folded, there'd be a job for her in O'Brien's ten minutes later. Agnes said that Fiona was a brick to come down so early because it gave them time to get ready themselves without rushing out into the shop every time the door opened.

There had been a pink card with 'All Good Wishes on Your Wedding Day' from Tommy, and a nicely wrapped tablecloth from Ned with a small greetings card wishing them every happiness, and regretting that he wasn't able to be there. Clare saw the fine hand of Father Flynn in both of these gestures.

Chrissie had been pleased. It hadn't struck her as remotely odd that neither of her brothers would return for her big day. Agnes was pleased too. She had somehow resigned herself to the thought that the boys weren't coming home again. Gerry Doyle had assured her they were well settled there, and wasn't it better in this day and age, when half the country were down taking the mailboat to England looking for jobs, that her two sons had got there first and got themselves established. In fact Agnes O'Brien was more cheerful than she had been for a long time. Her ankle had recovered now, everyone said that it was her accident which had finally been responsible for the Committee putting up the new steps and railings, so she was regarded as a bit of a heroine.

She dabbed unaccustomed powder on her nose and looked affectionately at Tom as he struggled into the new suit he had bought. He had needed one anyway, and this was the perfect opportunity. He struggled with the unfamiliar fabric which seemed hard and full of pointy bits and corners.

'I'm just so relieved,' said Agnes. 'Glad that she's settling down.'

'Mogsy Byrne isn't the worst, I suppose,' Tom O'Brien said reluctantly.

'No, when you think the way Chrissie *could* have gone.' They'd never spoken of it before, but they had been through their worries. Was Chrissie getting a name as being fast? Did she hang round with the girls who were known to be up to no good in the caravan park? They were lucky that poor Mogsy, not the brightest man in Castlebay, but the brother of Bumper Byrne who was certainly the sharpest, was going to take Chrissie on for life.

There had been a time when Chrissie had held out for Dillon's Hotel; but after a look at the menus, the rates and whole set-up she listened more carefully to her future brother-in-law's advice. Bumper and his wife Bid had advised Chrissie not to throw away her money just making the Dillons rich. Why pour out all that money so that Young Mrs Dillon could have a new fur coat? Chrissie had wanted the day to be very splendid, but she and Mogsy listened obediently and heard that it could still be splendid without paying out a fortune. And this way they could invite more people; which was always good for business, and it didn't insult people and cause grievances.

In fact Chrissie and her Mogsy had come round to the view that Dillon's Hotel would be a very stuffy place to have a wedding anyway.

So they were having it in the big room behind Father O'Dwyer's house. It had been a storeroom once, but Dr Power and Miss O'Hara had somehow managed to persuade Miss McCormack that it should be used for the parish. Father O'Dwyer took very careful note of what she said. Now it was used for fêtes, and sales of work. They had the Irish dancing competitions there too, and recently it had been used for weddings or christening parties. There were long trestle tables covered with cloths, and there was a big tea urn. There would be plates of sandwiches, and bridge rolls, and sausage rolls. There would be jelly and cream as well as the wedding cake. Gerry Doyle was going to take the photographs, and cousins were coming from three separate towns for the occasion.

Chrissie and Mogsy had said they were keeping it small, but that still meant forty-five people. Just enough, Agnes thought, pleased for it to look respectable. There was no question of a rushed job. Nobody could say it was a hole-in-the-corner affair.

Clare was being very good over all the arrangements, Agnes noticed with surprise. And she was keeping Chrissie calm this morning; she had even bought some bath oil at Murphy's chemist and said that Chrissie should be allowed to have the bathroom to herself for half an hour so everyone else should wash quickly or else wash at the kitchen sink. Agnes hadn't expected Clare to be so helpful. Usually she and Chrissie had nothing but harsh words.

The young couple were going on a week's honeymoon to Bray: which was just another seaside resort, but still it would be miles away from Castlebay and that was the main thing. Then they would be back, a married couple living in the new house, and Mogsy would be organizing the churns and the milk collection; and Chrissie would be back in the butcher's shop, but with a new respect now. There would be two rings on her finger, she would be 'Mrs Byrne', and she could talk about 'my husband'. Agnes felt a great surge of sympathy for her large, brassy, argumentative daughter.

She could hear laughter coming from the bathroom. Clare was scrubbing the bride's back.

'You'll be next, Fiona,' she said to the beautiful dark-haired girl standing quietly in the shop.

'Oh, I don't know, Mrs O'Brien, who'd have me?'

'Tut tut child, aren't you the most beautiful girl in Castlebay?'

'I haven't got much life in me though. Fellows like someone with life in them. I'm like that advertisement up there on the wall: *Do you wake tired?* I seem to wake tired all the time.'

Agnes O'Brien had never heard the young Doyle girl utter a sentence as long as that in her whole life. She wasn't at all sure what to do. She wished Fiona had chosen a better time to confide in her.

'If I were you I'd go and have a chat with Dr Power, it might be tablets you need. Dr Power has great iron tonics in bottles too, they'd make you feel strong. Maybe it's a lack of iron.'

The thin, kind face of Agnes O'Brien under her unaccustomed hat and dotted with unfamiliar powder was concerned. Fiona shook herself.

'That's what I'll do, Mrs O'Brien. I'll go up to him the next chance I have. It could well be lack of iron.'

Agnes beamed; and then decided to hurry on the bride and her sister.

Peggy had now arrived dressed in her bridesmaid's gear and carrying a hair-brush and a can of lacquer. She pounded up the stairs.

'Your room looks different,' Peggy said, looking around. Clare said nothing. She didn't mention that she had put all Chrissie's clothes in the wash, everything that she wasn't taking on the honeymoon. Clare would personally transfer these to the new home. Chrissie had an alarming habit of saying that she'd 'leave this here' or 'leave that here for the moment'. She couldn't grasp the fact that she was actually moving residence. Clare had taken all the old shoes and put them in a box marked 'Chrissie's Shoes'. For the first time in years there was actually room to move.

Peggy began the back-combing and the teasing of the hair, expertly and with great intensity.

'Are you sure you're not in a huff because I asked Peggy to be the bridesmaid instead of you?' Chrissie asked for the twentieth time.

'No. I think you're quite right. I told you,' Clare said.

Chrissie examined her miraculously cured spot. 'It was just that we didn't know if you'd come or not. You see?'

Clare bit back her rage. There had never been any question of her not coming. 'I know,' she said sympathetically. 'I'll try not to be *too* jealous of Peg,' she added cheerfully, and Chrissie laughed.

Peggy shrugged her shoulders. Chrissie *hated* Clare! What on earth were they laughing like old friends for? Oh well. It was her wedding day. She was entitled to laugh if she wanted to. Not that marrying Mogsy Byrne was anything much to laugh about, Peggy thought sourly. She'd prefer to be a spinster of twenty-two than marry Mogsy.

Father O'Dwyer was waiting at the gate of the church when the wedding party arrived. The Byrne family were all installed. The O'Briens arrived together – it was only a five-minute walk from their shop up Church Street and this was the triumphal journey. Chrissie walked on her father's arm. She wore a white dress, which the dressmaker had said was far more suitable as a dance dress. Chrissie had giggled, and said why not, one day it would be a dance dress. Her veil was short and held in place by a headdress of wax flowers.

It was a sunny Saturday morning in June. The season hadn't really begun; the people would start arriving in the next few days. But the whole town saw Chrissie O'Brien go to her wedding. They waved and shouted from shops and houses. Josie Dillon waved out from the hotel. Miss O'Flaherty at her stationery shop; the Murphys were in the street in front of the chemist's shop. Dwyers' had a big sheet of paper with *Good Luck Chrissie* written on it. She was very excited when she saw it, and kept drawing people's attention to it.

Behind Tom O'Brien and his daughter walked Peggy in a very bright yellow which didn't suit her.

Clare and her mother walked next, with Jim and Ben. Clare wondered would she ever walk like this with her father, as she had seen so many other girls walk to the church. It was nice because everyone had a chance to see the wedding party without having to go up to the church uninvited and peer. But Clare couldn't imagine it. She could not see herself going through this kind of parade for anyone. It would have to be somebody quite extraordinary waiting up there in the church if she could endure this pantomime for him.

Just as she was wondering what kind of person it could be, Gerry Doyle appeared at her elbow.

'Stop dreaming about me and listen,' he said.

'You arrogant thing!' she laughed.

'I'll run on ahead. Make sure Chrissie stops yapping enough for me to get a proper picture of you all coming into the church. Do you hear me?'

'Just her and Daddy? Or all of us?'

'I'll want both, but she's so excited now she'll have half the town in the picture. I'm relying on you to calm her down.'

Clare smiled at him affectionately. Gerry Doyle understood how this album would be treasured for years, when Chrissie and Mogsy had few ceremonies to entertain them.

Yes, she'd calm Chrissie down for him. Even if it meant being bossy, superior Clare again.

Chrissie became very quiet in the church, and you could hardly hear her responses. Maurice Byrne resplendent in a blue suit, was almost as mute. Only the firm unchanging voice of Father O'Dwyer could be heard properly. Then it was over and it was into the room that was too small to call a hall.

There were photos cutting the cake; and then the going away photograph of Chrissie with one foot on the ground and one foot in the car, the big Cortina that her brother-in-law was letting them drive to the station. There was confetti too – the understanding being that the family would clear it up before nightfall. Then Mr and Mrs Maurice Byrne had gone.

Nobody worked hard in Second Arts. It was a year off in a way because there was no serious examination at the end of it.

Valerie had had an eventful summer; her father had gone to hospital in England and had written from his hospital bed a long apology for his life. What had her mother done? Instead of laughing hysterically and opening another bottle to give her further fluency to curse him, didn't she up and off to England? Her father had got better; and promised to abandon the fancy woman and come home. But not immediately. These things needed time, he had said. Valerie's mother, however, had become a different person. No more morning cocktails. In fact, no cocktails at all. There was now no question of wasting as much money as possible and making-that-bastard-pay-up. Now it was different. Valerie must work hard in UCD, and make full use of the generous fees her father paid for her; she must remember that money didn't grow on trees; and what's more, they had to spend the whole summer doing up their house and getting it in order for the return of the Prodigal Father. Since Valerie had only scraped First Arts this was going to be a hard year. She was full of gloom.

Mary Catherine had been very off-putting when James had asked if he could come and call. She had said that the family would be moving around a lot during the summer; and, really, it wouldn't be a good idea, because they were sure to be vacationing with friends whenever he arrived. James had tried to pin her down by giving her definite dates; but she had been adamant. James seemed much more interested in her this year; he had asked her to a dress dance. Mary Catherine had spent the entire summer working in a soda fountain making milkshakes. It was very wearying trying to explain Ireland to people – they thought it was full of cottages and leprechauns. Her mother worked in the garment district and her two younger brothers did paper deliveries all summer. She hardly saw any of them until the big Labor Day picnic that the parish organized. Mary Catherine said it was nearly as difficult to explain America to the Irish as it was the other way round. She said she was hopeless at being an ambassador and that is exactly what her father thought that she was going to be when she graduated. Why else should she be so highly educated if it weren't to get herself a big job like that? Obviously he had decided that she wasn't going to marry an Irish nobleman with a castle if she hadn't nabbed one the first year and he was pinning his hopes on her becoming a career woman instead.

Clare said she hated anyone being secretive but she had very little to tell. It was a summer like any other in Castlebay. Chrissie's wedding had been exciting, and the weather had been good. Which was smashing, because that meant business was good and everyone was happy. Yes, she had met Gerry Doyle a bit. But he had been followed around by a very glamorous piece who had been meant to stay for three weeks. Her name was Sandra. And when the three weeks were up, Sandra decided that there was plenty to keep her in Castlebay, so she stayed the whole summer. Gerry Doyle had found her a caravan that wasn't being used. They were the talk of the town, but Gerry didn't take the blindest bit of notice. Apparently she was a student in Queen's University up in Belfast, and she had a red bathing suit which she wore all summer long, with open shirts of pink and purple and orange, all the colours that are meant to clash with red. She had a big mane of hair and she used to wash it in public with a shampoo, using the new shower that Dr Power had got the Committee to put up near the bottom of the steps to the beach. Valerie and Mary Catherine were rather sorry to think that the handsome Gerry had been so spoken for during the whole summer.

'Didn't you have any adventures and romances at the dance or anything?' Valerie asked interestedly.

'No. I hardly went to dances. I went to the Committee dance, because I had to, like everyone else, but I had no romances. I worked in the shop from morn to night, it was bloody exhausting. Do you know I find myself apologizing to Josie that I don't have romances in Dublin and to you that I don't have romances in Castlebay.'

It wasn't a light year for David. This was the year of his finals. He told James that he was going to put his head down and study, and he must be counted out of any socializing. James was affronted: it was his final year too, he insisted, and the Law was every bit as sacred as medicine. Wouldn't David come to this dance and make up a party? He had invited the American heiress who had played so hard to get during the summer.

David was resolute. He was going to work.

He found Caroline less than understanding these days. She had been very moody down in Castlebay, and had fought with her mother on every possible occasion. She had been obsessed with a rather trampish-looking girl called Sandra from Northern Ireland who seemed to be Gerry Doyle's choice for parading around the town. Caroline had even worn her own shirts loose over her bathing suit and had bitten the head off her mother when Mrs Nolan had complained mildly that Caroline seemed to have forgotten her skirt.

'Do you *still* find Gerry attractive?' David had asked her in exasperation. 'I thought you got over all that as a child.'

'Oh, don't be so patronizing,' she had snapped. '*Nobody* gets over Gerry Doyle. He's just there driving everyone mad all the time, isn't he?' She said it as if it were as obvious as night following day. He felt very irritated.

Or maybe he had just lost his way with girls. That could be it. He had taken Bones for long walks down the Far Cliff Road. Bones was nice and simple. He just wanted walks and for people to throw things which he would bring back. Bones imagined rabbits for himself and went happily in useless pursuit of them. It would be easier to have been a dog. Bones felt no guilt, no uncertainties. If he didn't get what he wanted he sat panting and smiling with his foolish face, and sooner or later, someone took him for a walk, threw him a stick or gave him a bone. Bones didn't sit smoking in his kennel at night and wondering what to do. Like David did. Well, his bedroom, but the principle was the same.

For the first time in his life he had not enjoyed the summer in Castlebay. He had grown away from Caroline so much that there was hardly any pleasure in being with her. She seemed to find him plodding, and yet she didn't really know what she wanted either. She was restless and impatient, she wouldn't talk about her career and her future. It was all too silly, she said, there she was with an M.A. degree and no chance of a job, she had to learn shorthand and typing like that patronizing halfwit Josie Dillon in the hotel who kept hanging on to her and giving her advice for some reason. *A nice commercial course* indeed! She had mocked Josie's accent. David had always liked Josie: she was far more pleasant than her two older sisters. And she had been such an ugly duckling when she was young – but Caroline wouldn't have known any of that. Anyway, David knew Josie was trying to cultivate Caroline from a deep interest in Caroline's brother. It was very transparent; and futile.

But that hadn't been the main problem of the summer: the main problem had been at home.

His mother had talked happily about his coming back to Castlebay to help his father in the practice. The way she put it reminded him of the times he used to help Nellie make shortbread, or help old Martin in the garden. She didn't understand that he was almost a fully qualified doctor. You didn't go round *helping* people if you were qualified, you practised medicine. He had his intern year to do first in a hospital before he was even allowed to practise; then he was going to do a year in paediatrics and a year of obstetrics and . . . but his mother had said in that really *irritating* voice, that it really wasn't necessary to do all that extra work. The best training was on the ground. His father needed all the help he could get. He even employed a young doctor to come and help in the surgery as a locum during the summer season – there was always something happening to the visitors. He had a heavy enough caseload with the people of Castlebay themselves . . .

David knew from Nellie all about the miscarriages and the two stillbirths that had gone before. He knew from unasked-for confidences from people like Mrs Conway or Miss McCormack, what a precious child he had been. 'To have come the full term, to have survived birth, to grow up strong and handsome.' To be nearly a doctor. It was a dream come true, people said. In his disgruntled moments, David had wondered how you got out of someone else's dream and started dreaming your own.

Clare had a very satisfactory second year. She set herself a very disciplined plan of work, and kept to it. Since nobody else seemed to be doing any work at all her efforts brought her to the attention of the tutors, and this is what she needed. Her plan was to do an M.A. thesis in history, and she would need the enthusiasm and support of the various members of the History faculty, she would also need their advice about how to get money to survive. The Murray Prize was for a primary degree. Once she got her B.A., that was it, she would be on her own.

But she was determined to have a social life as well. Every Friday was late pass night and Clare made the most of it.

Living in such cramped discomfort – three in a bedroom that should really only have housed one – Mary Catherine and Valerie were also involved by necessity in everything she did. They were all more or less the same size; which was both good and bad. Good, because it meant that in dire need one good blouse could be worn by any of them. And they had even bought a black polo-necked jumper between them and insisted that anyone who wore it had to use dress shields, and it had to be washed after the third wear.

But it was *bad* when they were looking for a favourite garment and realized that it must already be on the body of one of the other two. They learned to dress for their dances and their hops and their social outings of various sorts, each sitting on her own bed: if they all stood up it was like the bear cage in the zoo.

The dressing table was an area of war. Valerie didn't buy make-up. She claimed she didn't *use* make-up, but she wore a great deal of heavy black eyeliner (Mary Catherine's); she made heavy inroads into the Sari Peach lipstick (Clare's); she was loud in complaint about spilled face powder but her own nose was suspiciously unshiny so she must have used it fairly regularly. Mary Catherine had a habit of leaving bits of cotton wool all over the room. Wool that had removed eye make-up, lipstick or the painted pancake which she sometimes spread on face, throat and shoulders.

Clare was accused of leaving combs filled with hair around the place. Just because she had long hair, they said, this was no reason why most of it should be distributed round the room.

But despite this, they never had a tiff that lasted longer than a few minutes – except the time that Mary Catherine discovered Clare had gone out wearing Mary Catherine's only smart shoes, and that Valerie had not only broken her mascara box but what was left of it was swimming in water and was a revolting grey puddle. *That* argument lasted a long time, and included three threats on Mary Catherine's part that she would go back to the United States where people were normal.

They would go to Bective, or Palmerston, or Belvedere or Landsdowne; they were the names of rugby clubs which held dances every weekend. It was funny to go to a rugby club; nobody in Castlebay knew anyone who played rugby. Possibly David Power's school had, but even the school the Dillon boys had gone to played proper football and hurling; and anyone from Castlebay who ever came to Dublin to see a match would come for the All-Ireland finals at Croke Park; they wouldn't dream of coming for rugby international at Landsdowne Road.

Clare went to a rugby match at Landsdowne Road, one cold afternoon, to cheer on UCD. It was called the Colours Match, played every year between Trinity College and University College. The Trinity students were very upper class; and in order to pinpoint the difference even more all the UCD supporters would chant, 'Come on COLLIDGE, C-O-L-L-I-D-G-E, college.' It got a laugh no matter how often they did it.

Clare had a date for the match, a law student called Ian. She had met him at one of her Friday outings; and he had taken her to the pictures twice, and once out to a *bona fide*, which was a pub three miles outside the city. If you were a *bona fide* traveller you could go there and drink late. Clare didn't really like Ian – he seemed a bit pompous and superior. He didn't talk about normal things, it was all 'making an impression' and 'how things sounded', or 'how they looked'. But she had been having discussions with the girls; both Valerie and Mary Catherine united against her saying that Clare was becoming the devil to please, and you'd expect a law student to go on a bit and show off. That's what they were studying, for heaven's sake, that's what they'd be doing for the rest of their life in courtroom.

Ian had borrowed his parents' car and they went to a pub after the Colours Match. Then he took her for bacon and eggs in one of the big cinemas and to the film. They did a bit of necking during the film, but Clare kept lifting her head away from him, which annoyed him greatly.

'Later then?' he asked.

'Later,' she said staring at the screen.

They drove back to the hostel an odd way, through a lot of back streets. And then there was a bit of waste ground, where cars sometime parked during the day. Ian stopped the car.

It was all very embarrassing. Clare wept later, in the bedroom, while Valerie produced some vermouth to calm them all down. It wasn't a bit like the films, where people were able to say no without offending. It was *awful*. It was like the rugby tackles they'd been looking at during the match. And worse it was all *her* fault. She had *said* later, according to Ian. He called her all kinds of names. He had said she was a tease, and that it was physically bad for a male to be put into this state of excitement without being able to relieve it. That had worried her too. It was all her own silly fault. That's why everyone said you shouldn't go in for necking and groping and all. It just encouraged boys and made them sick if they couldn't go the whole way.

Valerie said it was ludicrous that you couldn't say yes or no, as you felt like it, like having sugar in your tea or not. But Mary Catherine said it was much more important than having sugar in your tea, and that it was so complicated because there were these limits. You were allowed to go so far, and it was all fine, you were a warm sweet responsive person; and then there was some line which, if you crossed it, meant you were going the whole way, and if you didn't boys got this awful thing about being in distress.

Though they discussed it in great technical detail, they couldn't agree from their limited experience where this line was, and how you crossed it. It had been different for all three of them. Maybe it was different for everyone, which was why there was always such an almighty fuss about the whole thing.

Clare said it had been a lesson to her. She was a scholarship girl, and the Murray committee had meant her to study, not to go round in people's parents' cars groping them and being groped and then being driven home in a black fury with accusations coming at her thick and fast. From now on, there was going to be no messing with men.

She had it all planned out. She would get her B.A. in Autumn 1960, then she would study for two years for her M.A. That would bring her up to 1962. Yes, fine. Then she would go to Oxford or Cambridge to do a doctorate, her Ph.D. She would tutor, of course, while she was there. That would get her to 1964. Then she would go to America, to Vassar or Bryn Mawr, for three years as a visiting fellow. In 1967, she would return and she would take a position as Professor of Modern History in either Trinity College or UCD – wherever the History professor died first. To make her mark on the place she should serve a seven-year term, writing, of course, all the time. Then, at the age of thirty-four, she would marry. It would be just in time for her to have two children, and no more. She would marry a don in some other field, and they would have a small unpretentious house covered with ivy, and lined with books. They would live near a café and they would eat out most evenings, all of them, including the babies as soon as they were old enough to get their hands around chips.

Valerie and Mary Catherine rocked with laughter at the long-term plan, it was so detailed – the names of the most prestigious universities in the world, the age at which everything would happen, and the need for chips nearby.

'It's not a joke,' Clare said, her brown eyes full of determination. 'I will *not* teach children in a school. I'm not going to have all this open to me and end up teaching rotten, stupid children who don't want to learn. I will not teach. And I will not get married until I'm good and ready. If I wanted to get married, I could have stayed at home in Castlebay and picked my nose like Chrissie.'

'She feels very strongly about it.' Valerie spoke as if Clare weren't in the room.

'I tell you, when she's settled down with a nice job, and a nice engagement to a nice young man, she'll remember this and laugh,' Mary Catherine said.

'You're nearly as stupid as boys, the pair of you,' Clare said, and drank some more vermouth.

Clare had a phone call from Dr Power next morning. She caught her throat in alarm, but he came quickly to the point.

'Mrs O'Hara died, Lord rest her, and since you and Angela were such friends, I thought you'd like to know.'

'When is the funeral, Doctor?'

'On Sunday, but don't you go spending all your money coming back now, it was just in case you wanted to send a Mass card.'

She rang Emer, who said she would send a telegram at once. Then Clare walked up to University Church.

The priest wrote Mrs O'Hara's name down in his notebook so that he would remember to include it in his prayers at Mass. Clare had two half-crowns in her hand. He shook his head.

'Isn't it five shillings, Father? I thought that's what it was for students?'

'It's nothing, child. I'll be glad to say a Mass for the repose of the woman's soul. Was she a friend of yours? A relation?'

'No, she wasn't really a friend. She was my teacher's mother, she used to sit there while this teacher used to give me extra lessons. She has a son a priest, and that used to give her a lot of happiness even though she was a sort of cripple.'

The priest was pleased to hear that. 'Well, she'll have a lot of Masses said for her soul by her own son, but don't you worry, I'll say a Mass for her as well.' He wrote his name on a Mass card, on the dotted line beside the word 'celebrant', and Clare thanked him for his generosity. She wouldn't have minded paying five shillings for Angela's mother's Mass, but it did make things a lot easier now that she didn't have to. Guiltily she bought a stamp, and stood in the post office, writing a letter of sympathy. She wondered what would Angela do now.

It took a long time to answer all the letters of sympathy and to send notes of thanks for the Mass cards and the flowers. Angela did it methodically each night. She changed the position of the furniture in the cottage and put her mother's chair upstairs so that she wouldn't find herself looking over at it.

People had been so generous – even Immaculata had been human and offered her more days off than she was entitled to. Angela had said no, thank you, she would prefer to take a couple of days at the end of term. Immaculata hadn't liked that. Christmas, and the concert, and everything. That was it, Angela said. She would find it hard to put her soul into the Christmas concert this year. So Immaculata had to agree.

Geraldine and Maire had been more helpful than she could have hoped during the whole time of the funeral. And they distracted people, in their black coats and their English accents, and their innocent and transparently honest concern that Father Sean hadn't been able to come home for his mother's funeral. Guiltily they admitted to each other that they hadn't written to him much and that they never got more than a Christmas card from him these times. Geraldine even went so far as to wonder was he happy in the priesthood; he had been so full of it all in the early days.

But Angela was never in the position where she had to answer a direct question about him, only mumble a regret that he wasn't there to say the Mass.

There was so much to organize: food for the people who would call, beds for Geraldine and Maire, dividing Mother's things so as to give the girls something to remember her by. They even had to talk about the cottage itself. It had been very hard to sit down with her two sisters who were almost foreign to her with their talk of shops and towns and seaside resorts she had never heard of in England. But it had to be done, they were entitled to a share of what small amount their mother left.

She showed them their mother's post office book: there was just over £100. She also had a burial policy so her funeral was paid for. Angela said they would divide the £100 into four. Maire wondered should they send it all to Sean for the missions: that was what their mother was most concerned about always.

For a short minute Angela was tempted to tell them. It was late: there would be no more callers to interrupt them. It would take it from her shoulders a little if she could lay it on theirs too. They lived in England, for God's sake, they could go to see him, decide for themselves about his plight and what their attitude should be. But something about Sean and Shuya seemed too vulnerable to let them be exposed to Maire and Geraldine and their strange, enclosed worlds. She wouldn't tell them yet.

Would her mother's soul think she was right to have told Sean nothing about the death? Was that the right thing to have done in terms of real and genuine acting for the best? She was very much afraid that a lot of her protestations to Sean had been hypocritical. Why did she not let him come home now and declare himself? His mother was no longer there to feel the shame and the hurt. Was there a possibility that Angela was becoming a settled schoolteacher who didn't want things upset for herself?

Angela wondered why she had never told Clare about Sean. In ways she had been closer to Clare than to anyone. Clare had her own secret and disgrace with poor Tommy in gaol over in London. But there had never been the right time. And now it was almost too late.

Angela looked at Clare's letter of sympathy, and the Mass Card signed by a priest at University Church. The girl was very good to have written so soon and to have spent what little pocket money she had on having a Mass said. Angela knew what a sacrifice that would have been. Clare had written that Angela must have some consolation in knowing that she had always been there to provide a safe and happy background for her mother to live in; and that she had done it with no sense of grudging, but with humour and happiness; that it was a great gift to give a parent. And Clare said that she would never be able to do anything as positive herself. It was possibly the only letter that didn't say what a great consolation it must be to have Father Sean praying at this time and how sad it was that he hadn't been able to get back for the funeral.

Angela went to England during the last week of term. She told the children that she would like no Christmas cards this year and that she might stay away for Christmas with her sisters or with friends in Dublin. Everyone seemed to think this was a very sensible thing to do. No point in trying to celebrate Christmas in an empty house, although there were plenty of people who would ask her for the day.

It was cold and wet on the mailboat; and stuffy and uncomfortable on the train journey to London. She was puffy-eyed from lack of sleep as she got on yet another train to take her to Sean's school.

She walked a mile from the station, and remembered the day she had come with Sean to see the big house in Ostia where his wife and babies were tucked away in the courtyard. She recalled the sense of dread she had felt then at meeting them, and how it had been replaced by sadness.

She had been here to this school before, when Father Flynn had arranged the job, in the days when the cause at Rome had not been deemed lost. Sean had still been enthusiastic, and as busy in his letters to the Vatican as he had once been in his visits.

There had been little mention of it recently in his letters. He had written that Shuya had taken in a lot of work; and that Denis was doing very well in the Junior School; Laki was getting on famously at the nearby convent, and they both had lots of friends. It wasn't really permanent or anything, but it was a very good, expensive education for Denis that they wouldn't have been able to afford.

Angela wondered what kind of work Shuya was doing: surely in a school like this they wouldn't go along with her doing mending and sewing as she had been doing in Rome? But perhaps they were less hidebound in England: maybe a Latin master's wife might well take in sewing or even washing.

Angela arrived at the small gate lodge. The garden was much more cared for than when she was last here, even though it was midwinter. There were nice silver trees and golden bushes giving colour. The door was painted a bright, sunny yellow. It was a much more cheerful house than when she had seen it first.

She knew that Sean would be at school and she intended to meet him as he left his classes and came home for lunch. He had said that one of his greatest joys was to walk across the playing fields just for half an hour's peace in the cottage with Shuya, and then walk back. Angela understood only too well how welcome that break from the shrill little voices would be. She didn't have such luxury herself: Immaculata saw to that.

She tapped on the yellow door. Shuya. A smiling, delighted Shuya, arms outstretched.

'I saw you from upstairs. I ran down. Welcome, welcome. I can hardly believe it. I am so very happy. We are all so happy. And you have a suitcase, this time you will stay with us.'

'This time I'll stay with you, Shuya.'

They had tea, and Angela looked around. Shuya was *different* somehow. Younger-looking, smarter. She had her hair up in a chignon; she wore a light-green jumper and skirt, and a big white collar pinned with a brooch of Connemara marble.

Angela had brought it the last time she came to visit, and her heart was touched to think that this might be the only piece of jewellery that Shuya had. Shuya talked about the work she took in. It was far from washing and sewing. It was typing for theses; it was translations for Japanese businesses in London; it was roneoing and duplicating for anyone that needed it – one of her biggest customers was the school itself. They found it far better to pay Mrs O'Hara for neatly done examination papers, or notices, or leaflets, than to work a machine themselves and ruin reams of paper. She had quite a cottage industry going, she told Angela proudly; and she even employed a girl to come three afternoons a week to help her.

On the piano there were pictures of the children; grown now so much that Angela realized she would hardly know them. Denis, over ten years old and Laki eight. In another frame was a picture of her mother, the only nice one that had ever been taken. Young David Power and James Nolan had taken it years ago when they got a camera first and were busy snapping everyone in the town, to try to set up as some kind of rivals to Gerry Doyle. It had been a rare thing to catch her mother smiling, without the lines of pain on her face.

Her eyes rested on it. And Shuya noticed.

Very quietly she said, 'Have you come to tell Sean about his mother?'

'Yes,' Angela whispered.

'Is she very ill? Does she ask for him?'

'No. It's not that.'

'Because if it helps, he must go, go alone, dressed as a priest. If it is best. I will persuade him, if it is best.'

'No Shuya, no. She's dead. She died a month ago.'

'One month ago?'

'I know. I know. I had to make up my mind on my own. It seemed best.'

There was a silence.

'Please Shuya, wasn't it best? It took the decision away from him. Sean didn't have to decide.'

'Maybe he should have decided. Maybe he can't be protected all the time from having to make a decision.'

'I don't know anything any more,' Angela said sadly.

'Forgive me. Please, what am I thinking about? Your mother has died, and I give you no sympathy. I must be so cruel and thoughtless. Tell me about her death. Was it sudden?'

'Yes. Yes, she had a heart attack, you see. If it had been something slow then I would have let Sean know. But it would have been too late for him and I didn't want . . .'

'Please. Please. I think you did what was going to be the most painless for Sean. As always you acted for his good.'

Shuya stood up and put her arm around Angela's shoulders. 'You did what was best. I thank you for not having to go through all that with him. All the agonies. I thank you for giving us all this peace. He will become resigned to his mother's death. She has only been a dream to him, for thirteen years, since he last saw her. It is not a real person he will mourn. It is an idea.'

'You are wise, Shuya.'

'I think I shall be a teacher. I am doing examinations that will qualify me to teach typewriting and shorthand. I suppose they will recognize these examinations in Ireland.'

'Well, yes. But are you going to Ireland?'

'Sean talks of little else.'

Shuya pointed out the path she should walk to meet Sean. She said she would leave them alone in the house to talk. The lunch was all ready.

He wore a heavy overcoat with the collar turned up and his hands were in his pockets. He looked younger than a man of almost forty. His face split open into a big foolish smile . . . he started to run towards her and then stopped.

'Is it bad news?' he asked suddenly.

'Mam died very peacefully. She died without fear. It's all over.'

He blessed himself. 'The Lord have mercy on her soul.'

'I came when it was all over to tell you.'

'You're very very good to us.' He took her and hugged her to him.

'I hope I did right. It was all so quick and so sudden. I could have telephoned you. I rang people to tell Geraldine and Maire. But I just didn't, Sean. I thought that if Mam can see you she'll understand everything and it would have been too much on you, and, to be honest, on us.'

She felt better having admitted her own selfishness. He had his arm around her shoulder as she walked back to the gate lodge with him.

'Does Shuya know? Have you told her?'

'Yes.'

'What does she think? Does she think it was for the best that Mam is dead and buried without my being there?'

In a flash Angela understood what Shuya had meant. People *protected* Sean. They kept the world away from him. If she were to say now that Shuya gave her approval there would be the quick smile of relief and everything would be fine.

'Yes. Shuya said it was the right thing. She thanked me for giving you all a gift of peace, that was the way she put it.'

Sean smiled as she knew he would. 'I would like to have been there to hold my mother's hand. But if it all happened so suddenly, then thank you again for shouldering everything, Angela.' His arm was around her companionably still. 'Was it all very sad, very harrowing?'

'No. You know the way people say it was a blessing. It was, Sean. She was in *such* pain, all the time. Every movement was an ache or a stab to her. She couldn't dress herself, or move without help.'

His face was pained. He wouldn't want this to be part of his idea of his mother.

'Dr Power said that she had the worst arthritis he had ever known. And she was incontinent too, not because she really was, but because she couldn't get up in time.'

He closed his eyes with distress.

'It wasn't much of a life. She wasn't really happy from the time she woke up in the morning. It *is* peace for her. I look at the corner of the room where she used to sit and I think that all the time.'

'How long ago?'

'A month. I couldn't come any sooner, because of school. You know the way it is.' She smiled at him the resigned conspiratorial smile of one teacher to another.

They had reached the house. He looked anxious that Shuya wasn't there when they went in.

'She's gone into town. She said she'd leave us to talk, I told her there was no need.'

Angela found herself pouring the soup for her brother, even though this was not her house. She put on a kettle to make tea afterwards. She cut the bread. She had been in the door only a minute and already she was mothering him.

'I wish the children had seen their grandmother. They have no grandmother,' he said.

'Well neither did we, Sean, not to speak of. Dad's mother was dead before we were born, and Mam's mother died when I was a baby. You don't remember her, do you?'

'No. But Denis and Laki will have a better life than we did, things are different now. And they know that one day they'll go to Ireland. I have books, look, here . . . Lots of books about Ireland, so that they'll know. And we have books about Japan too. They're not going to grow up confused, and not knowing who they are like we did.'

'You want very much to come to Ireland, then?'

'But I've always said that.'

'I know. I know.'

Sean thought about his mother being dead and put his head in his hands. It didn't seem real to him, he said, he thought of her cheerful and full of chat and bursting with information about things and the centre of everything. She *had* been a bit like that perhaps in 1945, when Sean had last been home, when the glory of the priest – son in full regalia very largely compensated for the loss of the drunken troublesome husband who had been a heart scald to her for her whole married life. Yes, Mother was bright in her spirit then, even if she had pains in her joints. And Sean hadn't seen her since. He could be excused for thinking that she had been a woman with as clear a glance and a smile as she had in the photograph frame on the piano.

She played with her cheese salad while he talked about times gone by.

'We'll say the rosary for her tonight, all of us,' he said. 'That will make it important for the children.'

She wished she could get it out of her head that her brother was living in mortal sin and that it was quite incongruous for him to be organizing rosaries. And yet he seemed to see nothing out of character in it.

'Will the new Pope make any difference do you think?' she asked suddenly, reaching out and touching his hand. 'He looks kind.'

'It hasn't got anything to do with kindness. It's just as complicated and tedious as the civil service,' Sean said sadly. 'If I could *get* the papers to John XXIII then it would be a matter of days – but if I could have got them to Pius XII it would have been the same.'

'Does the fact that it's gone on so long mean there's more hope or less?'

'I don't honestly know. It means that there's more red tape, I suppose. If something has already been looked at by one person then other people are slow to take the file themselves.'

'Do they know here?' She nodded her head up to the school.

'At the very top yes. Otherwise no. I was very lucky to get in here.'

He was much less confident than he was before. There was a time when he would never admit that he was lucky to have got anywhere. It was all open to him, the whole world, whatever life he wanted. This whole business with Rome had changed his thinking.

But before they had the children with them, before they were all kneeling and saying a rosary for the dead grandmother the children didn't know and wouldn't have understood, she had to go back to his plans for Ireland.

'So you think you'd like to come back to Castlebay.'

'You wouldn't mind?'

'No. Of course not,' she lied.

'Well I know you said that, long ago in Rome. You did say that the only reason for me to stay away was because it would break Mam's heart.'

'That's what I said. I'm not going back on it.' She couldn't be any warmer. It just wouldn't come out as more welcoming. It would be lunacy. It would upset everyone, the enormity of the deception for all those years. Denis, a big boy of ten. How could he not see it?

'No, no, I know you're not going back on it. You've always been straight as a die, Angela. No one could have a better sister or friend.'

She made the tea, and poured a cup for herself. Her hand was shaking.

'It's been awful for you, all of it. What will you do now, will you live on in the house on your own?' His voice was full of concern.

'I don't know yet. I will for the moment.'

'Yes, yes.'

'Maybe you'll want the house? If you come back that is?'

Now she had said it, brought it right out in the open. This nonsensical idea of the priest going back to live in his native town with his Japanese wife and grown-up children.

To her relief he didn't seem to think that this was automatically the way things would go.

'Oh, I don't think we'd want to *live* in Castlebay. Where would I work? Where would they go to school?'

Angela fumed inside for a quick moment. What was so wrong with the convent where she taught? Or the Brothers, which had been good enough to educate Sean O'Hara. Still, this was all to the good.

'True, I suppose. But you do want to go back do you, and meet everyone – talk to Mrs Conway in the post office, Sergeant McCormack, the Murphys, the Dillons.' She had deliberately chosen awful ones to mix in with ordinary people. She had to tread carefully.

'Well, it's my home. It's where I came from.' He was defensive. She didn't want that at any cost.

'Don't I know it's your home – I'm offering you Mam's house to live in. Of course it's your home. I just asked what sort of way you'll be coming home. Will it be in the summer? Do you want me to let people know you're coming, or will you explain it all when you get there?'

'I thought that you'd ... I don't know. That's something that can all be arranged later.'

'Of course it can.'

She went to see Father Flynn on her way back through London. He said they must go out and have dinner.

'I know now why people become priests. It's a licence to eat dinners out in restaurants for the rest of your life. I never ate in so many restaurants before or since as when we were in Rome.'

'Ah, those were the days all right. But this is half-work. Young Ned O'Brien asked me to the place he's working in. The landlord's just opened a dining room off the pub, and the bold Ned no less is running it. Wait till I turn up with his ex-school marm.'

'I don't think he'll be a bit delighted. Not that I ever taught him anything. I don't think we can lay his educational deficiencies at my door. And Tommy, he's out isn't he?'

'For the moment. That was something I was going to ask tonight.'

'I'll make myself scarce.'

'You don't need to. He knows you're in on it.'

'You're grand and easy about things, Father Flynn. Is it something that goes with the job, like deafness goes with teaching?'

They saw Ned, important and nervous at the same time. Father Flynn pretending ignorance of everything so that Ned could put him at ease. In the midst of doing this Ned lost a lot of his own nerves. He explained that there were three things you could have: steak, chicken or fish. And you got soup before and ice cream after, no matter what you chose. But the price depended on the main course. He could have Father Flynn as his guest but, to be honest, he wasn't sure about Miss O'Hara. Angela said that there was no question of her being a guest, she was going to have steak, the dearest, and was going to love it.

'I'm very sorry to hear about your mother, Miss O'Hara,' said the head waiter of the new dining area in which they were, as yet, the only guests.

'How did you know about it?'

'Clare writes to Tommy every week, regular as anything. She told him. I sort · of . . . well, I read the letters to him. I'm very sorry.'

'Thanks Ned. She was old and in awful pain, it was for the best.'

'I don't think Tommy'll stay long with your friends, Father,' Ned hissed out of the side of his mouth.

'A pity. Why?'

'He keeps thinking these other lads will be looking for him. I don't think they want to see hair nor hide of him, but he has had a message that they're leaving him some money next week, his share like.'

'But if they don't want him in on whatever they're doing, then maybe he *might* stay with the Carrolls?' Father Flynn had got Tommy a live-in job with an Irish family who owned a small greengrocery. Tommy would be sweeping and helping at first, but they'd keep an eye on him; and if he was any way helpful at all, they'd give him a shop coat and let him serve the public.

'You know Tommy, Father. He's just a big baby.'

Angela sighed and wondered were all brothers big babies.

'What will I do, if Sean comes back to Castlebay?' she asked, later.

'You'll survive it, like you've survived everything else,' said Father Flynn.

She went back to Dublin in time to spend Christmas with Emer and Kevin. The boat was filled with returning emigrants, singing and happy to be on the way back to small villages or towns all over Ireland.

The house was full of holly and ivy and long paper chains across the hall. Emer hoped they weren't too cheerful. After all Angela had been recently bereaved. No, she assured her, they were exactly what she wanted to see. Clare would be dropping by that evening on her way to the station. She had a Christmas present for Daniel and Emer had invited her to supper.

Clare looked thin and tired, Angela thought, but was very cheerful. She told them she was hopeless with men and that once she felt her academic work was under control she was going to take lessons from someone who knew. It was apparently like bridge and driving a car: even stupid people could be good at it if they learned the technique.

Clare wished that she could stay here in this pleasant, easygoing household for Christmas, but shook the idea away. She was looking forward to seeing home again. There would be no Chrissie, and she had painted her bedroom before the summer ended. There was good news about Ned from London and no bad news about Tommy. Angela had been full of detail, and had even written a letter to Clare's mother to describe the elegance of Ned in his new job. Compared to everyone else's Christmas hers would be fine.

Valerie was going to have to face the return of the long-lost father, and *Mary Catherine* had been invited to the Nolans and was wishing every minute of the day that she had refused. Clare thought about them both as she stood on the cold platform of Kingsbridge station waiting for the train.

On an impulse she went to the phone box and rang Val, who was still at the hostel.

'I'm in a great hurry. The train's nearly going. Tell him what you think, don't go along with all your mother's lovey-dovey bits. *You're* not in love with him. He's your father and he walked out on you. Tell him that you were greatly upset and that it might take a bit of time to be sure he's back for good.'

'What?' Val was stunned.

'There's no need to pretend that nothing happened. That's pretending that he's a madman. He left when you were thirteen and needed him. Don't just gloss over that, or he'll think it was a perfectly reasonable thing to do.'

'Then we'll spend the whole of Christmas fighting, and my mother'll come after me with a cleaver,' Val said.

'Nonsense, you can do it without a fight. Happy Christmas.'

She looked the Nolans up in the book and rang. James was surprised to hear her on the phone. 'Nothing wrong is there?' he asked.

'Heavens no, James. You're far too young to think a telephone call means bad news.'

He was annoyed – as she meant him to be – and went to find Mary Catherine.

'Tell them your father's a postman. Immediately,' Clare said.

'What?'

'The only reason you're not going to enjoy Christmas is because you're going to be up to your ears in pretence. Tell them, for heaven's sake, the moment they ask, or *before*. They're not going to throw you out in the street.'

Mary Catherine started to laugh.

'Well will you?' Clare said impatiently. 'I have to go for my train in a minute.'

'I guess I will,' Mary Catherine said. 'When you put it that way, there's no sense in not.'

The porters started shouting excitedly that the train was now backing into the platform and would be ready for boarding.

Clare wondered what would someone say to her if they were to give her good advice for Christmas just as she had been dispensing to others. She decided that Angela's age-old advice had always been the best. She must be *positive* and *cheerful*, and never let them think her education and her hopes were a threat to them.

She did all of that as if it were a Christmas homework she had been set to do. She helped her mother make a last-minute Christmas cake. She called to see her married sister's new house. She went with Jim and Ben on the back of a cart to a farm where they had a lot of holly and ivy and were glad to see people thinning it out. They decorated the shop and the house.

She went for long walks with her father down the Far Cliff Road, and discussed with him seriously the possibility of buying a soft ice-cream machine. There was little to discuss, really, except whether her father had the courage to borrow the money to buy one or not. It would obviously be a huge draw; sooner or later someone else in Castlebay would get one and a lot of trade would move to the place where the delicious whipped-cream cones were on offer. But Clare's father hunched his back and worried over and over about the wisdom of getting into debt for something that would only be used eleven weeks of the year. Clare said that people bought those soft ice-creams in Dublin even in the winter. You often saw people eating them in cinema queues. But her father puzzled and wondered . . .

Dad looked old and tired; and though he said he liked to get out in the fresh air to walk with her the wind seemed to hurt his eyes and make him seem frail. She debated telling him about Tommy; but the debate with herself did not take long. A man who couldn't decide whether or not to get an ice-cream machine couldn't possibly cope with having a criminal son.

Josie was cheerful, but busy. She had decided all on her own to inquire whether there might be a demand for a Christmas programme, as it was called in hotels. And there was; they were going to have twenty-nine guests over Christmas and everyone was in a fever of excitement. There was bad blood between the family about it, and her sister Rose, who was meant to be coming into the hotel full time, said that since *Josie* seemed to make all the decisions nowadays, what was the point, and she was going to go to another hotel.

David Power came into the hotel that night for a drink and to wish them well in the Christmas programme. The guests were assembling and the Dillons were at their wits' end. They had never thought of finding someone who could play the piano. In the summer they always gave bed and breakfast free to any student who would play the piano in the lounge in the evenings.

Josie's mother looked at David appealingly. 'Just for about an hour, David? You would be helping us better than you could ever believe.'

'But I'm no good,' David protested. 'Clare, can't you play?' he beseeched.

694

'No. In my education, there was never time for it. But a renaissance man like yourself now. Every social skill . . .'

'I *hate* you, Clare O'Brien,' he said good-naturedly.

Josie thanked him profusely and led him to the piano. Haltingly, he got into a version of 'There Is a Tavern in the Town'. Dick Dillon, who was planted amongst the guests, began to sing and in no time they were all joining in. It was obvious after about three songs that he would be there all night. Dick got him a pint and left it on the piano. Bones, who had been sitting patiently in the hall, hoping that the music would stop soon, was taken into the kitchen and given a plate of soup. He fell asleep beside the Aga and dreamed of sandhills full of rabbits and big firm beaches when the tide was out, where people would throw sticks for him hour after hour.

In the summer of 1959 some people said that the world was going to end: it was the hottest weather ever known. Tom O'Brien cursed his cowardice as he saw people troop past his door to go to Fergus Murphy's soft ice-cream machine. Fergus built up a lot of business because people bought sweets and magazines and groceries while they waited for the ice cream queue to file by. The Castlebay Committee congratulated themselves on their foresight in organizing a booking register so that visitors could be directed to the available rooms in the resort rather than having to knock on doors. There were two full-time lifeguards and when the tides were high people had to bathe between two flags. Nobody drowned that summer in Castlebay, and nobody fell and hurt themselves on the paths up the cliffs because they were all finally built properly with rails to hold on to. People still went into the Echo Cave and asked it questions. The Dillons were very distressed to hear of plans for a new and huge hotel but were subsequently overjoyed to discover that two of the five businessmen who were going to start it were undisclosed bankrupts at the time, so that plan never got off the ground. Dr Power said he was getting old and slow and he was so proud that his big handsome son had passed Final Med with flying colours. He would do an intern year in Dublin and then who knew what would happen.

James Nolan was called to the Bar and did his first case in court. He said he thought he was never going to get another brief but he carried a great many papers tied with pink tape.

Fiona Doyle announced her engagement to Frank Conway, the pride and joy of Mrs Conway. Mrs Conway had never been anxious for her Frank to marry anyone, and she had her doubts about the Doyles in general. Gerry was as wild as anything and should be kept in a zoo if half of what you heard about him was true. And the mother was odd – some kind of phobia they said. She hardly ever went out. But you couldn't say a word against Fiona – a good-looking girl, great self-respect. She'd never let a man near her, even in the days when a girl was silly and could have her head turned. Mrs Conway sighed. Frank could have done a lot worse, she supposed. She gave them her blessing. And then that pup Gerry Doyle had the impudence to say he'd like a *talk* with Frank, since Fiona had no father. Mrs Conway never found out what the chat was about, but it had impressed Frank no end.

Chrissie Byrne discovered on her second visit to Dr Power that she was indeed pregnant, and bought a maternity smock on the way back from the surgery to the butcher's shop. Ned O'Hara came back for a flying visit to Castlebay with his fiancée, Dorothy. Dorothy thought everything in Castlebay was terrif. When she and her Neddy got old, like about thirty, they would come back here and start a restaurant. Dorothy thought the O'Briens' house was terrif. Dorothy's mother was Irish, and she wished that her mum had taken her to Ireland before – it was simply gorgeous.

That summer, a registered envelope arrived for Agnes O'Brien. There were twenty-five ten-pound notes in it and an ill-written note from Tommy saying he had been saving for years to get a present for his ma, and now he had.

Tom said immediately that they must tell nobody outside the house about it. They discussed long and secretly that summer what Mammy would do with the money. Chrissie was left out of the discussion because she was a Byrne now and if Bumper, Bid and Mogsy knew about it they'd be down like a flash.

In the end it was spent on a new coat for Agnes and the long and often discussed extension on the side of the shop. It was Tom O'Brien's one concession to the magnificent site of his business: he wanted a Perspex roof on an extra room where they could put a couple of tables and chairs. This way they could serve those who wanted to sit down for their Club Orange or their tub of ice-cream. And they were even going to add sandwiches and tea next summer. Tommy's gift made it possible.

In the summer of 1959, Mother Immaculata asked Angela O'Hara whether she intended to stay on in the school or, now that she was free to see the world, if she planned to travel. Angela, seeing that Immaculata would love Miss O'Hara to roam off around the world, said firmly that she was going to stay in Castlebay. It was also the summer that Dick Dillon asked Angela O'Hara to marry him and she said very gently that she thought they would drive each other mad within months, and the ambulance would be arriving from the town and they'd both be locked up in the asylum on the hill. Dick had smiled bravely and she had patted his knee and invited him to the Committee dance so that he would know she liked him greatly.

Clare's professors said she would get a First: they were all in agreement. *Clare O'Brien to get a First* – she said it to herself, not caring to believe it. Any student with a First was worth looking at. From then on she would never have to apologize again. Clare went off into one of her rare little daydreams in the National Library. Imagine it. Never would she have to tell people she was only a scholarship girl or she had to do this because of some Committee or other, she would be her own person. And a scholar. She tore a page from her ring file and decided to write to Angela O'Hara there and then. She wrote as she hadn't been able to write before, she said that somehow for the very first time she believed that it was actually happening. Only now did she feel it had worked, all that praying up in the church, and all the shouting in the Echo Cave and all the learning and learning, the disciplines that Angela had taught her.

Angela replied by return of post. She said that it was the most wonderful letter she had ever received in her life. It made everything – and everything included the seagull-faced Immaculata – all worth while. She said it was a letter written on the crest of happiness, and from that heady standpoint the world was there for the taking. She hoped that that would last for ever.

It was a warm and generous letter. Clare folded it in four and put it in the little flap at the back of her big, black leather notebook. The book, which she carried everywhere, had been a gift from the nuns in the secondary school when she won the Murray Prize. Immaculata had sent her a picture of Maria Goretti, with a big padded frame of coral-pink velvet. Fortunately her mother had liked it, and it hung in the back of the shop getting grimier and dirtier as the years went by. Gerry Doyle had given her a fountain pen. He had insisted. He had only been asked to do the pictures he said because there was a candidate from Castlebay. She knew this wasn't true but it was nice of him to say it. She still had the pen. She never lent it to anyone and she always put the cap on very carefully, clipped it to her notebook and then put a rubber band around the whole thing. She had so few possessions that she valued them all. She thought about Gerry. She could never write to him like she did to Angela but somehow she did want to talk to him. It would be nice if he came to Dublin again and they could walk by the canal maybe, or she could show him off to the girls. She sighed. She'd never get any kind of degree if she spend time daydreaming like this.

Still, she bought a postcard of O'Connell Street and sent it to him; a cheerful card saying it would be nice to see him if ever he passed through Dublin.

She heard nothing for ages.

She was annoyed.

Thank God she wasn't in love with him.

It was neither one thing nor another, being an intern; David discovered that very early on. Some people thought he was a fully-fledged doctor, who knew *everything*; others thought he was a schoolboy dressing up in a white coat and wouldn't ask him the time of day in case he got it wrong. And the hours! There was the solidarity of a prisoner-of-war camp in the Res, where bewildered young doctors coped with the unfamiliar and the frightening without any sustained sleep. They told each other that they would never sleep again. That their metabolisms would never recover from the strange hours and speeds at which they had to grab food. And even more immediate and urgent – their social lives were now finished for ever.

James Nolan, handsome, well-dressed young barrister, carrying his black bag that contained wig and gown casually slung over his shoulder, said he despaired ever of seeing David any more.

David was paged urgently, and rushed to the phone. 'Dr Power speaking.'

'Dr Power, this is Mr Nolan, barrister at law. I wondered if you would like to come and have a long boozy lunch with me. I got a cheque for seven guineas.'

'A lunch?' said David in disbelief.

'You *know*. You've heard of them. They're what people have in the middle of the day. Food and wine. You sit at tables.'

'You bloody don't do that here,' David said.

'Well, can you come? It's a gorgeous autumn day, walk a bit towards me and I'll walk a bit towards you.'

A wave of impatience came over David. How could James be so insensitive? He had no idea of what David's life was like. He had been up all through the night – but that made no difference to today's schedule. The ward round went ahead as usual. Blood tests here, a drip there, organizing an X-ray for another. The ward Sister – a poisonous woman – never gave him any information about the patients: she confided all that only to the consultants. The housemen were made to look fools as a result.

This morning a difficult patient had pulled the drip out three times, and so three times it had to be set up again. Then there was the teaching round with the consultant. And now he was in outpatients. He had been examining a man's swollen foot when James had rung.

As politely as he could, David told James that he would have to find someone else to celebrate the seven guineas and to lunch with. David's own lunch would be something very quick and not very nice. If he ate at all. Then it would be dealing with admissions, seeing the patients, getting the preliminaries sorted out before greater men came to deal with them. And he was on call after that. Barristers? Lunches? Guineas? Bloody parasites.

He returned to the man with the swollen foot. 'I don't know,' he said honestly. 'I'd like to see the other foot. Can you take off your shoe and sock?'

The man was hesitant.

'So that I'll be able to compare,' David explained.

Reluctantly the man took off the other shoe and sock. The foot that he knew would be examined was nice and clean. The foot that he hadn't expected to be asked to bare was filthy. It was a foot that had not been washed in a long time. David stood slightly back from it to see if there was a similar swelling. His eyes met the eyes of the foot's owner.

'I didn't think, you see . . .' the man said.

'I know,' David said sadly. 'That's the trouble. We hardly ever do.'

He was on his own. He had never felt that Dublin was lonely when he was in the medical school, but now, isolated in hospital, it was different. That was your life. You didn't escape from it – or if you could you found nobody to escape with.

Full of self-pity in the darkening evening air, he walked up Kildare Street. People were going in and out of the National Library and the College of Art. The Dail had its guards at the gate, and that seemed to be bustling too. Everyone except David Power had something to do.

Suddenly he saw Clare leaving the library with her bunch of books. She looked lovely in the evening light.

'Clare! Clare, I was hoping to catch you,' he lied.

She was pleased to see him. He tucked his arm into hers. 'Will we go and have a coffee?'

'Sure. What were you hoping to see me for?'

'To ask you if you'd come out tonight. I know it's ridiculous short notice and everything but we never know in the hospital when we'll be on or off.'

She didn't seem put out by the shortness of notice. She'd love to. But first she had to go back to the hostel and see was there a message. Someone had said he was going to be in Dublin, possibly tonight, and if so she and her two friends were going to go out with him. If not then she'd go with David.

'I can't say fairer than that,' she said.

He grumbled as they walked towards the hostel: why three girls and one man? What kind of superman was this?

'It's Gerry Doyle,' she said simply, as if that explained everything.

A great and unexpected surge of annoyance swept over David. Gerry was so *cheap*. His line was so *obvious*. When he was a kid he had thought Gerry was good company, there was always a touch of the dangerous, the daredevil about him. But not now. Gerry was too slick. And too *much*.

'I thought you'd have outgrown him,' he said in a very superior voice.

Clare was surprised. David Power didn't usually talk like this. 'Nobody outgrows Gerry,' she said. It was an echo of what Caroline Nolan had said to him. A flash of anger came over him.

'What's so great about him? Has he some new technique as a lover or something?'

'I wouldn't know.' Clare was cool.

'Well, what *is* it then? It's not his intellectual conversation is it? Surely Gerry Doyle isn't a rough diamond concealing a poetic soul?' His face was twisted in a way she had never seen before.

'Why are you so cross?'

'I'm not cross. I'm just disappointed with you for making yourself so cheap. You've always been different. Why be so bloody predictable? Following as soon as Gerry Doyle raises his little finger. Gerry's a nobody, Clare. He's just *trashy*, you deserve better.'

She was unaware of the crowds moving up and down the street and even the people who had to move off the footpath because they couldn't get past the angry young couple.

'You keep your disappointment to yourself, David Power. Don't come bleating it out to me. You can take yourself off with your insults and your jeers. *You're* the one that's cheap, not me. I've been working here all day, and now I've finished. I'm going back to my friends and if Gerry's around he'll cheer us all up and make us laugh. He'll make no comments about whether we're predictable or not. He'll be nice to us. That's what you'll never understand in a million years. Gerry is *nice* to people. He's *glad* to see them. He smiles and he asks them questions and he listens. He *likes* people. And I'm *glad* he's coming to Dublin tonight, and Val will be glad, and Mary Catherine will be glad.'

'I didn't mean . . .'

'Oh, go away and leave me alone. I'm tired.'

'I'm tired too. I've been on duty since I don't know how long. I'm cross-eyed with tiredness.'

'Yes,' she said briefly. 'I see that.'

'Can I still come along with you, if he's there, or . . .'

'No. You cannot. I'm not going on an outing with you both knowing that you've said he's cheap and flashy and what was it . . . trashy. I'm not going to sit in a pub with you and know that you mocked at him and his lack of education, and made

699

fun of his intellectual conversation. You can find your own company tonight. And whoever it is, she has my sympathy.'

Clare turned away. David watched her as she walked in a rage along Stephen's Green.

Clare had a letter from David a week later.

> People often make jokes about medics being illiterate and now I see why. It's so long since I wrote anything that wasn't an examination answer, a report on a case, or notes at a lecture, I'm not sure how to begin. But I want to say I was in an extremely bad mood the other day when we met and I am very sorry indeed for taking it out on you. I really do apologize. You were minding your own business, you were loyal to a friend. I just behaved like a boor. I don't know why I said all those things about Gerry Doyle. Reluctantly, I have to put it down to simple, unattractive jealousy. I've always envied him his easy charm. I envied his reputation as a ladies' man. And that night in particular I envied him because he was going to go out with you when I wanted to. It's hard to say all this, and I'm sure I'm saying it very badly but I want you to know I regret it all very much. There's a Halloween dance in the hospital. I'd love you to come as my partner . . .

Clare sent him a postcard. David turned up at the hostel, in James Nolan's car, to collect her. She wore the same yellow and red dress that Mary Catherine had worn to the dance with James.

'Same dress, same car, only the cast has changed,' Mary Catherine said as she looked out the window.

'Don't they breed them handsome in Castlebay,' said Valerie watching David in his dark overcoat and white silk scarf, tucking Clare into the car.

They had decorated the Res up with funny faces cut into turnips and little nightlights burning inside. There were pictures of witches on the wall, and the lights were covered in red or black paper. They had apples hanging from a string and you had to bob for apples too. Everywhere there were basins and baths and the fronts of shirts were wet as heads were pushed far into the water. The hilarity was more important than the actual trapping of the apple. They had a big selection of records; and a lively nurse with her leg in a plaster cast was responsible for playing them three at a time, saying after the third, 'Thank you very much, end of dance, thank you.'

David was very popular, and much in demand for the Ladies' Choice. Clare was nearly knocked down in the rush of nurses towards Dr Power. It was funny to hear him called that. She kept expecting to see his father.

He introduced her to other doctors, interns and even registrars.

'Who's looking after the sick tonight?' she asked.

There was a system of call, and about a third of the people there couldn't drink in case they were needed.

'Those are the ones to watch out for,' a bearded doctor told Clare. 'If they can't drink, their minds are very definitely set in other directions.'

'I'd better stay with the winos then, if I want to keep my virtue,' she laughed. David seemed proud of her, and she saw him with new eyes. In this world he was relaxed and funny. She never thought of David Power as someone you laughed with. In fact, when his face came to her mind, she used to think of him as being a bit solemn. Either with his parents when he was young, or walking with Bones along the beach in winter.

Of course when the Nolans had come to Castlebay he had been fairly excited and laughing during those summers when she had been stuck behind the counter in the shop . . .

'What are you thinking about?' He was dancing close to her.

'About you,' she said truthfully.

'Good. Were they happy positive thoughts?'

'Yes, I suppose they were. I was thinking how well you fit in here, how happy you seem.'

'I think that about you too. You always disapproved of me in Castlebay.' He was half teasing.

'Jealous, I suppose. You had more freedom. You could have such a good time.'

David smiled. 'I used to envy all of you. A sweetshop, you could come and go as you liked, they weren't sitting waiting for you to come in, hanging on your every word . . .'

'No one's ever satisfied with what they have. I told you that. Do you remember?'

'I remember. I didn't think you would,' he said. 'I remember it because I thought it was a sad sort of thing to say and to mean.' His smile said he wanted her to cheer up.

She laughed at him, and at that point the music changed to a faster beat, and Mary Catherine's red and yellow dress was swung into a very energetic version of 'Down by the Riverside'. It was actually a Ladies' Choice but David and Clare hadn't noticed. Several nurses retreated in defeat.

The supper was magnificent. Real Halloween food: colcannon, mounds of mashed potatoes with chopped-up onion and kale in it as well as threepences and rings. There were plates of sausages, and afterwards huge amounts of toasted barm brack, with extra rings pushed in so that there could be a lot of happy screaming at the thought of a marriage within a year.

Clare got a ring, which she nearly swallowed. 'Lord above, how frightening,' she said.

'Did you nearly choke?' David asked.

'No, the thought that I'd be married in a year.'

They were sitting in an alcove of the big room, a window seat away from the crowd. They had brought their glasses of red wine, and the noise was away in the background.

'Would that be the end of the world?' he asked.

'Yes. It would. The end of *my* world.' She explained her plans, the M.A. the Ph.D. the terms in the United States, in Oxford or Cambridge and finally the history professorship. She felt he was smiling inside.

'I will, you know. I really will. If I got this far I can get to the moon.'

'I know.' He was gentle.

'You don't know, David. You really don't. For all that you were brought up beside me, you don't know how hard it was to get here. I don't want to go on and on about it. But, you see, it's not just like saying I want to be a film star, or I want to be the Pope, for me to say I want to be a professor of history. When I was ten I wanted to be an Honours university student. And who would have believed then that I could?'

'You give me very little credit. I do know. Of course I do. It's you knows nothing about me. What do you think I want for my career? Tell me. Go on.'

She paused. 'I suppose you'll go home and be a doctor with your father,' she said.

'See, you don't know a thing. I'm not going back to Castlebay for ages. If at all. Being a doctor like that in a small place . . . You choose it. You can't have it chosen for you.'

'But everyone thinks . . .'

'Everyone thought when you were a small girl in the convent that you'd leave school and marry someone from up the road. Like Chrissie. But you didn't.'

'It's not the same. If you didn't want to be a doctor why did you become one?'

'I do want to be a doctor. But I haven't become one yet. I have years more to do, at least four or five in different hospitals learning under specialists, seeing the new developments . . . There's much more to being a doctor than saying tut-tut-poor-thing and knowing when to call the ambulance.'

'So will you be a specialist?'

'I don't know. I think I would like to be a GP, like my father. But not yet. And not in Castlebay. Can you see anything so stupid as sitting down with my mummy and daddy, like I did when I was a young boy, coming home from school, and describing How I Spent My Day?'

She giggled. 'I know, it does sound silly. But perhaps you'll marry someone and then it won't be like that. It will be more normal.'

'Not yet. And if I'm going to wait for you to be thirty-four, I'll be nearly forty.'

'Oh, I wouldn't go back to Castlebay even when I'm thirty-four. You'd better not marry me,' Clare said, anxious that there should be no misunderstandings. 'I just said I'd be ready to marry then, not give anything up like my Chair of History.'

'I think you'd be too complicated for me. I think I'd better marry someone else all right.'

'Caroline Nolan? Would she be suitable?'

'Not really.'

'Why not?'

'I don't know. My mother thinks she'd be suitable. Her mother thinks she'd be suitable. Her brother thinks it too. That's probably why.'

'Does *she* think she'd be suitable?'

'I don't know,' David laughed. 'Let's dance.'

A red-haired doctor with a Cork accent asked David if he would lend him the lovely lady in the red and yellow dress for one dance. He was called Bar. He said most people in Cork were called some form of the name Finbarr, with his being the patron saint. Bar said that he was a registrar and very important in the hospital and that David's whole career would depend on Clare being nice and willing and co-operative and giving herself in every way to Bar. Clare pealed with laughter at this and asked whether this line of chat ever worked.

'Sometimes,' Bar said gloomily. 'But less often than you'd hope. Women seem to be brighter these days. They have minds and things.' Was she David's girlfriend? No. Good. Just a girl next door from Castlebay, that was nice. Clare said it wasn't exactly next door, but this was never a concept you could explain to anyone in Dublin; they all thought that you were rewriting Cinderella if you explained the gulf of difference between the O'Brien and Power families.

Bar was holding her very tight and saying that he was on call so he couldn't have a drink, which made the party a bit of a bore – but on the other hand it did sharpen his awareness of who were the best-looking girls.

Diplomatically, Clare released herself in order to help him choose the best-looking girls. Bar found this irritating but he couldn't fault her. They were discussing the attributes of a group of girls in the corner when David rescued her.

'Thank God,' she said as she danced with David again. 'That fellow's like an octopus.'

'I'm disappointed that groping is out,' he said.

'David! You'd never grope. You'd make sophisticated gestures when you knew the feelings were returned. Aren't I right?'

'You are. God you are,' David said, holding her close to him but not allowing his hands to roam like those of Registrar Bar, the octopus as he would be known for evermore.

On the way home he parked the car. Clare looked up in alarm.

'It's all right. I haven't turned into an octopus. I just wanted to talk for a bit. It's one of the few nights I'm not crashing to the ground with sleep. James says I'm the most boring friend to have. I have no time off, and I can't stay awake when I do.'

They talked on easily, happily, like old friends.

'We should go out together, sometimes . . . you know, the pictures or a coffee. What do you think?' He looked enthusiastic and casual at the same time. He didn't sound as if he were asking her for a date, or a commitment, just friendship.

'I'd like that, certainly. Of course I would,' she said.

'There'd be nobody to bother us here,' David said. He didn't need to mention that there would be plenty of people to bother them in Castlebay. He gave her a kiss on the cheek to settle it and drove her back to the hostel. He watched in alarm as she climbed up the iron rungs and disappeared through a window.

'Was he nice?' Mary Catherine asked sleepily as Clare climbed in the window.

'Very.'

'Did he jump on you?'

'No, no. Nothing like that.'

'But it's desperately late, what else were you doing?'

'Talking. Just talking.'

'God, that's serious,' Mary Catherine said, waking up.

'Don't be silly, go back to sleep, I've hung up your dress, it's not too sweaty.'

703

'What is it?' Valerie was awake now.

'Clare's back. She *talked* to him all night. They're in love.'

'Great,' Valerie snorted and settled down again.

'I'm *not* in love. Even if I wanted to be in love with David Power I couldn't. So there.'

'Why? Is he in fact your long-lost brother? Why not?'

'Because his mother would throw a cordon of Guards around the big house on the cliff if she thought that any of the O'Briens from the huckster's shop had notions about her son. That's why.'

Clare had snuggled down in her bed and pulled the sheets to her chin. Mary Catherine was wide awake and concerned. 'You can't let that kind of crap stand in your way! You're not going to tell me that . . .'

'I'm not going to tell you anything till tomorrow. *Goodnight* Mary Catherine.'

Ned's letter was short. Tommy had left Mr Carroll's greengrocery shop on a Friday. He had said that he wouldn't take his week's wages. He had got another job and it wasn't fair to ask to be paid for the last week. The Carrolls had telephoned Father Flynn, but no one could find Tommy. Until the following Wednesday, when the police found him. In a stolen car which had crashed during a police chase. The car was being chased because it was seen leaving the scene of a robbery with violence. Tommy had ended up with a dislocated shoulder, a broken jaw and a nine-year sentence. Ned just wanted to ask Clare whether someone should tell Mam and Dad now or was the pretence to go on for ever.

Poor, stupid, *stupid* Tommy. She couldn't think of him as bad Tommy, dangerous Tommy, in with a gang of thugs and joining in their violence. She could hardly remember him, but he had seemed nice like Ned was last summer when he came home.

She would tell them. But not by letter. And not making a special visit.

She would tell them when she went home for Christmas.

It was hard to choose the moment to begin. There never seemed to be any time when they were all together. Mam was thin and tired, but she was always on the move, from range to table, from kitchen out to shop, from shop to storeroom. Dad was always fiddling with things, and Jim and Ben were coming in one door and out another.

After tea, the first night home, she thought she had them all in one room, at least.

'I have some bad news about Tommy,' she said loudly, to get their attention. 'He's not injured, or sick, or anything. But it *is* bad news.'

They all stopped what they were doing. She certainly had their attention.

'So will you sit down, and I'll tell you,' she said.

'Stop acting like a judge and jury. What is it? If you've something to say, say it.' Her father was annoyed.

'I wanted to tell it to you from the start. Jim, why don't you put the sign up on the door?'

'How long is this going to take, for God's sake?' Tom O'Brien was now worried.

'Tommy . . . Tommy . . .' The tears were already starting to form in Mam's eyes. One by one, they sat down round the table and she could hedge no more.

'I had a letter from Ned. Tommy's in gaol. He's going to be there for . . . for a long time.'

'How long?' Mam's voice was almost steady. She didn't ask what he had done, or why he was there. Just how long.

'This is hard, Mam. Very long. Nine years.'

She looked at the table. She couldn't bear to see the shock round her. They had all thought that Tommy was living an ordinary life until twenty seconds ago. Now they had to try to understand all this at one go. She *should* have told them ages ago.

'You can't mean nine *years*,' Agnes said. 'You can't mean *years*.'

Clare told them what Tommy had done. She told them what he had done before. It seemed like a story about somebody else's brother as she was telling it. She looked at her mother's face, and realized that it certainly sounded like the story of someone else's son.

Gerry Doyle came in while she was telling them.

Mam was crying. Dad was throwing back his head and saying what would you expect. Jim and Ben were round-eyed, and teetering between a grudging admiration of their brother for doing something as brave as running with a gang and a sense of horror about the disgrace that was going to fall on the family.

'I didn't think *Closed* meant me,' Gerry smiled around the kitchen door.

'It does tonight.' Clare gave him a smile that wasn't a smile, and to her relief he understood.

'Sure. It was only a packet of fags. I'll take one and run. Pay you tomorrow. All right?'

He was gone. Clare settled down again for the abuse. How dare she play God and decide to hold the first bit of news back from them? What did she and Ned think they were playing at, telling packs of lies? How could anyone know now if *this* was the whole truth? And who was this priest that none of them knew, fiddling in their affairs? And did Ned's fiancée know all about it too? Was she in on the whole deception?

Clare soldiered on. Already it was getting easier. The more they knew, the less frightening it became. She wished that she had told them ages ago, she admitted this to them, but she said truthfully that since she had hoped that Tommy might have just had that one phase, it would be a pity to damn him in their eyes for ever.

Mam wondered did anyone else in Castlebay know. And Clare looked her straight in the eye and said that nobody knew. She decided that she could trust Angela and Gerry. They had kept it to themselves so far; there was no reason for them to speak now.

The news made them look older. All of them. Clare wondered had it done that to her too when she got the first letter from Ned. Mam's thin shoulders stooped more under the navy cardigan she wore, and Dad's face looked grey and set while he painted the new extension that would never bring him a day's happiness now that he knew it was built with stolen money. Jim and Ben lost a bit of their good spirits.

Clare saw that they stayed in the house more than usual, rather than roaming the town looking for divilment with their friends from school.

Chrissie arrived on visits, the size of a mountain now, and said that it was like going to visit a graveyard instead of your own family at Christmas time. If this was the cheer that Clare brought home with her she might as well have stayed in Dublin.

Clare said she was going to spend a day with Angela. They were going to go over a lot of work Clare had to do for her finals.

'Don't be telling her our business now,' Agnes warned.

'Why would I tell her anything of the sort?' asked Clare. She had planned to spend hours discussing it, if Angela had the time.

She lost the sense of time there. They must have had tea, or a meal. There was certainly drink, a bottle of port wine was on the table.

At one stage Dick called, and Angela asked him to go away.

It wasn't all Clare's tale.

The story of Father Sean O'Hara was told too. Not only had he left the priesthood years and years ago, but he had a grown-up family nearly. And they were all coming to Castlebay for the summer. They had booked a caravan. Father Sean O'Hara was coming back to show his home to his Japanese lady friend, and to show his children their roots.

In Dublin Clare could meet David anywhere she liked. He could come to the hostel to collect her, she could take a bus up to his hospital and they could have coffee in the canteen. They could go to the pictures or to have a drink. Nobody took any notice. In Castlebay it was almost impossible to do any such thing. Without even saying it they knew they were going to be further apart for the two weeks they spent in Castlebay than if they were on different sides of the Atlantic. They didn't have to tell each other that it would be awkward to invite the other home. They knew. Like they knew about spring tides, and about Father O'Dwyer's sermons. Clare would not be invited to the Powers' for supper. David could chat easily with the O'Briens across the counter, but they wouldn't let him in to see their kitchen with its old rusty range, its torn lino and its boxes of supplies all round the place, an inelegant overflowing storeroom for the shop which had never been properly organized.

They couldn't go and sit in Dillon's Hotel for hours on end, or the whole town would know about it. Clare didn't play golf, and Castlebay would have mocked her if she had learned. It wasn't for the likes of Clare O'Brien. That meant the golf course and its rolling dunes were out. If they went to the pictures together there would be talk.

And they didn't want talk. It wasn't worth it. They weren't in love with each other. They were friends. They were great friends. But such a concept didn't exist in Castlebay, and if it were going to exist it was very unlikely it would develop between the handsome, eligible son of the doctor and the bright perky little girl from the store.

They went for a long walk with Bones. David had had a bad row with his mother that morning and was not going to apologize in order to keep the peace. He had said he was going to the pictures that night and he was thinking of asking Clare. Molly had said very sweetly that it wouldn't *do* at all. It would be unfair on the girl. It would give her ideas. Raise her hopes. Furious, he had said this was rubbish, that he often met Clare in Dublin and neither of them had any hopes, just a good friendship. Molly had raised her eyebrows very high and said she thought David could have done better for himself, a professional man, than to be going out with the sister of Mogsy Byrne and Chrissie O'Brien. He had laughed in his mother's face and said that since she couldn't find anything to blame Tom and Agnes for, she had to draw in the least respectable member of the family and her eejit of a husband to complain about. Molly Power, with two bright spots of red on her face, had stormed out of the room and upstairs. His father had already gone out on his rounds but the whole thing would be aired again this evening. He almost told Clare but stopped. She might take it as a slight, even though she was always making jokes herself about confusing the rank and file of Castlebay.

Clare nearly told David about Tommy. He was so nice and understanding, so solid and unshockable, he might well reveal that both his mother's and father's parents had been in gaol for years. But she didn't want him to have more things to apologize for when he met her. Nellie had told Chrissie that there had been an almighty row this morning already about David meeting Clare at all. Better not let him know she was the sister of a criminal in an English prison as well as being one of the poor O'Briens, God help us.

There were New Year's Eve celebrations in Dillon's Hotel but Clare didn't feel any heart for going. She suggested to her mother that they ask Angela O'Hara for supper.

'We're not the kind of people that have people to supper,' her mother said.

'Maybe we should be,' Clare said. Her father said he didn't mind, it was no concern of his what the women did or didn't do.

The evening was a surprising success. Angela taught them to play rummy and even Agnes began to enjoy it. She had been hesitant at the start and wanted to stay out of it. Angela said more than once that it was very nice to spend New Year's Eve with a family.

'Oh, you wouldn't call this much of a family,' Tom said disparagingly.

'Why ever not? One daughter married and going to give a grandchild this spring. Another, the town genius. Two lads in England making their own way, two here, and please God there'll be work for them when they leave school. A good business . . . what more of a family could you want than that?'

Agnes said when you looked at it like that it was true, they had a lot to be thankful for. But she sighed a sigh that went down to her feet almost as she said it.

'Everything isn't as it seems,' Tom O'Brien said darkly, shaking his head.

Angela nodded enthusiastically at him. He was absolutely right, nothing *was* as it seemed, there wasn't a family in Castlebay without its own sadnesses and worries and confusions. She often thought that at Mass on a Sunday, people kneeling there so calm-looking and only the Lord knew what was in their hearts. Every one of them had a worry. She had hit it just right. This gloomy-sounding old soothsaying cheered up the O'Brien family greatly. They weren't alone in their cross. In fact Clare's father was so cheered that he thought it was time for everyone to have a glass of something to see the sixties in. They wished each other Happy New Year and shortly afterwards Angela left: she had promised Dick Dillon to look in on him in the hotel and wish him the compliments of the season.

Clare walked her up the road. She felt very wide awake and restless. She went to the seat that the Committee had put up last summer, the big green seat just at the top of the steps. A perfect vantage point for surveying the beach on a crowded summer day. Tonight you could just sit and look at the stars and the bright clear night. The sea looked navy somehow, and the cliffs like cardboard cut-outs.

Gerry arrived, silently, and sat beside her.

'You pad around like a leopard or a cat,' she said. 'You frightened the life out of me.'

'Happy New Year,' he said taking a half bottle of brandy and two little metal cups out of the pocket of his leather jacket.

Clare clapped her hands in delight.

'Aren't you one of the wonders of the world. Do you go round with mobile picnics and parties in your pocket all the time, or is it only on festivals?'

'It's only when I see you on your own. I was coming out of the hotel. I saw you coming down here, and raced home for the supplies.'

They toasted each other and looked out to sea.

'This is *the* year, isn't it? The finals, the big degree?'

'Yes, Lord I'll have to work when I get back, I'm doing nothing here. I thought I was going to get lots of reading done, but I haven't opened a book.'

'I'm sorry for intruding the other night. Was it a family conference?'

'It was about Tommy.'

'Don't tell me. It's not my business.'

'Oh no, it's all right. You know anyway. But he did it again, and this time they wounded a man so badly he'll be in a wheelchair and Tommy's gone to gaol for nine years.'

Gerry let out his breath like a whistle. 'Nine years. Lord.'

'So this time I decided I would tell them at home. They have a right to know. They were very low as you can imagine. Angela cheered them up a lot tonight. But they think nobody knows, so I swore that nobody did.'

'Sure.'

He was easy and her restless feeling was fading fast. Or maybe it was the brandy. He had put his jacket around both of them. It kept out the wind, and it was companionable. He kissed her, a long gentle kiss. She didn't pull away. He put his arms inside her duffle coat and held her to him as he kissed her again.

She felt something touch her leg and jumped.

It was Bones looking at her eagerly, waiting for her to disentangle herself from Gerry. Behind Bones, a dozen yards away, was David.

'I was just going to say Happy New Year,' he said. 'I'm sorry. I didn't mean to disturb you.'

He turned very quickly and walked along the Cliff Road home.

Bones looked hopefully at Gerry and Clare, in case there was going to be any fun and games for him. But deciding there wasn't, he cantered off after David who was walking unnaturally quickly through the bright starry night.

His parents were still at the hotel. Nellie had gone to her family. The house was empty. David nearly took the door from its hinges with the bang he gave it.

He was going to sit down in the sitting room where the fire was still warm and have a drink to calm him down but the fear that his parents would come back and that he would have to talk to them civilly was too great. He poured himself a large whiskey and went up to his bedroom. He pulled back the curtains and looked out at the sea. Years ago, when Gerry Doyle had first seen this room, he had said in admiration that it was like a ship. You could see no land unless you turned your head or leaned out to see the garden beneath.

There were two big rooms with bay windows upstairs, and his parents slept in the one next door. David had a window seat running round the three windows of the bay. His toys had been kept inside it when he was young. He looked to see were they still there and indeed, there was a small cricket set, a blackboard and easel, there were boxes of soldiers and boxes of playing bricks. His Meccano set was still there and there was a box which said David's Colouring Things.

It annoyed him to see them still there. And yet what should his mother have done with them? Given them away? They were his after all, and one day he might want them for his children . . .

But anything would annoy him tonight.

It had been a very boring evening. He had made a very tactless mistake with Josie Dillon. Apparently Clare had never mentioned that Mary Catherine had been an off-and-on girlfriend of James Nolan since the Lord knew when. Josie had been distressed by the news but even more by the fact that Clare hadn't told her. She had become quite weepy and had gone off to bed before the singing of 'Auld Lang Syne', so that would have to be sorted out.

But nothing had prepared him for the strength of his feelings when he saw Clare in Gerry Doyle's arms like that. He felt sick all over until he was nearly shaking to think of it again. Him, with his arms around her, inside her coat, fondling her, and kissing her, there on the bench in the dark, with a cheap half-bottle of brandy at their feet. David had walked up to them because he recognized Clare's duffle coat, and the moonlight was shining on her fair hair. It was quite obvious who she was. He hadn't really seen Gerry; it was dark that side of the bench, and they weren't kissing when he started to walk over. If only Bones hadn't rushed across he might have been able to escape without speaking to them.

But even so it was churning his stomach to think of Gerry Doyle's mean, small, dark face pressed on Clare's. To think of *him* giving her brandy and forcing himself on her. And to imagine that bright Clare, lovely, bright, sunny Clare, could be so stupid as to fall for it. Why was she letting him crawl all over her?

David felt so sick he couldn't finish his whiskey. He poured it down the wash basin, and lay back on his bed.

He was pale at breakfast and his mother asked him whether he might be getting flu.

'There are two doctors in this house, Mother. Leave the diagnosis to us,' he snapped.

Dr Power looked up in alarm. 'I heard a kind courteous inquiry after your health from your mother who is concerned about you,' he said quietly.

'Yes. I'm very sorry. That's what I heard too. I apologize, Mother.'

'That's all right.' Molly was gracious. At least he was able to say sorry now, a few days ago when she had said something perfectly harmless about the young O'Brien girl he had leaped down her throat and he had *not* apologized on that occasion.

'I'm in surgery all day, David. Do you want to take the car and drive off somewhere? It might be a nice break for you.'

'That's very nice, Dad.' He paused. He'd better make the offer. 'Would you like to go for a drive, Mother?'

Fortunately it was a bridge afternoon and she had to get ready for it. But it was nice of him to ask her. Honour had been satisfied.

New Year's Day or not, people would have their ailments and Dr Power shuffled off into the other side of the house. Nellie made David a big turkey sandwich with lots of stuffing in it and a flask of tea. He didn't even notice where he was driving until he came to a wild rocky place he had only seen from the road before. He parked the car and got out.

It must have been the same for centuries, he thought. Bleak and unwelcoming, the sea washing on it endlessly, as remote in the summer as in winter. Who would walk for forty minutes as he had through thickets and briars and down stony crumbling paths to get to a place that didn't even have a sandy beach? He threw stones into the water mechanically, one after another in a kind of rhythm. He couldn't be so obsessed with Clare that he shivered at the thought of Gerry touching her. He was only awake last night because he had drunk too much, because he had a stupid quarrel with Josie Dillon, because he was worried, as he was always worried, about this business of coming home to live like a child again in the house with a mummy and a daddy and a doctor's coat.

But her face was there, and her shoulders, and her hair. And her bright smile, and the way she was always so interested in everything and had so many views on any subject. He remembered the day he had felt so annoyed with her outside the National Library in Dublin when she was running back to her hostel to know if Gerry had rung. He remembered the relief that she didn't seem to be at all interested in the amorous Mr Doyle. Her work plans were daunting and over-ambitious, but she was certainly destined for a first-class B.A. and acceptance as an M.A. student. So why was she behaving like a cheap tramp last night? That's what it was. The cheapest way to go on, with a bottle of spirits and right in public. And with Gerry, who had felt up and touched every girl who was any way attractive and quite a few who were not.

His hand throwing the stones into the sea paused and he dropped the stone and clenched his fists. Gerry Doyle would never touch her again. Never. He would keep his hands to himself. He would not go near Clare O'Brien, he wouldn't dare. Last night had just been silly, a New Year silliness, to be excused but never to be repeated.

He would explain this to Clare, and she would understand. They would even laugh about it.

But what would he explain?

He wished he had taken Bones with him. Just looking into the dog's foolish face helped; but he hadn't known where he was going to go and the dog could have been a liability.

What would he say to Clare?

The wise man would say nothing. The wise man would make a little joke and forget the scene on the cliff top.

But David began to think he was not a wise man. He could not forget the tableau and he couldn't stop a feeling of light sweat forming on the back of his neck at the memory.

He couldn't want Clare that badly for himself. He couldn't. It must be pure bloody jealousy that Gerry struck lucky on New Year's Eve in the cold, while he, David, had a boring evening listening to old-timers singing 'Darling, You Are Growing Old' – which was too painfully true – having a totally ludicrous conversation with a tearful Josie Dillon, and then coming across Love's Young Dream on the bench.

No. It was more. He wanted to see Clare. Now.

He wanted to tell her that she was special. And to ask her to give him a chance to prove himself her lover as well as her friend.

It was highly awkward, but as sure as he knew anything he knew he loved her.

Clare didn't know why she felt so furious all next day. There was no way she could fault David. He hadn't been rude. Under the circumstances he had been polite. His voice hadn't dripped with sarcasm, as it had that time he had unleashed a tirade about Gerry in Dublin when he called him trashy.

But she wished he hadn't come along. It had been nothing, it had only been a couple of kisses, and she didn't think it would have gone any further. It was too public a place for one thing; and she *wouldn't*, for another.

But she had this feeling that David was always on the verge of going on to another level in their friendship. She had never admitted this to the girls. She kept telling them how unsuitable the liaison would be, and they made jokes about the security forces Mrs Power would need to employ and where she should station them around Castlebay. But Clare knew it wasn't just a joke.

She felt they talked as she never could with anyone. They didn't just talk gossip or plans. She was always interested to know what he thought about things. He never bored her. And she had the feeling that he was delighted with her. But he had never touched her or kissed her. So she was a bit in the dark about what he really felt. She would like to have been close to him, closer than she was, but she didn't want to push it because she had no idea at all how he felt.

Anyway it might be just hero worship. When she'd been the poor little girl in the shabby cotton dress in the shop, David and James Nolan had been swaggering round Castlebay like gods. Now she was their equal in a way. He sought her out and didn't meet other people at all.

It was all such bad timing. If only she had stayed at home. Or gone straight home. Or said no to Gerry Doyle. Or if only that big idiot of a dog hadn't spotted them and come like a detective to find them out.

She'd never know now what David Power had felt about her, if anything. It would have vanished on that cliff top last night. *Damn* Gerry Doyle, to the pit of hell.

Very few people came in on New Year's Day. It was a holiday of obligation and they had all been to early Mass. Clare hadn't looked round to see if David was in the church. She thought she saw his father, but she didn't want to meet any of them. She hurried home afterwards, down the quiet cold street.

Clare decided that she would invite Josie to supper, too. If only her mother would get out of this servile approach things would be much better. There was no reason why Josie Dillon shouldn't have sausages and beans, and brown bread-and-butter in their kitchen. She would enjoy it.

Clare had tried to catch Josie's eye in the church, but Josie looked away every time. Possibly she hadn't seen her.

The shop doorbell went. Her father was cleaning the paintbrush out in the back. Ben and Jim were reading the funnies in a paper. Chrissie had arrived for a woman-to-woman chat with Mam and was sitting on a hardbacked chair while Mam ironed. Clare had been half reading a very dense account of the differences between common law, equity and statute law, for what she had been hoping would give her a better understanding of the history of the English courts.

'I'll go.' Chrissie quite enjoyed meeting the public and serving them now that she was such an important person in the town. Mrs Maurice Byrne, and seven months pregnant too.

'It's young Dr Power, for Miss O'Brien,' she said scathingly on her return.

Clare went out and pulled the kitchen door a little closed behind her.

'Please come out with me now. Please,' he said as if preparing for a long debate about it.

'Right,' she said and took down her duffle coat from the hook.

She was surprised to see the car outside the door.

He held open the car door for her, and then ran round the other side. 'I wanted us to go for a drive,' he said. His eyes looked very bright but he didn't look upset.

'Yes, of course.'

They drove to that strange rocky place, bleak and dangerous. They got out of the car and looked down at it. Apart from the seagulls, there wasn't a soul around.

'I was down there this morning,' he said.

Clare said nothing.

'I was down there for a long time. Throwing stones in the sea. And I realized something.'

She looked at him.

'I realized I love you,' he said.

'I love you too.'

She didn't know why she was crying, it was ridiculous to cry when this happened. This was the best thing in the whole world that could happen. Why did the tears come down out of the corners of her eyes? She could taste them mixed with the spray, the salty spray which came up and whirled lightly around them as they kissed each other and held on to each other on the cold New Year's Day of 1960.

Part Three
1960–

David's father and mother drove him to the train; Dick Dillon and Angela drove Clare.

'There's David,' Angela said, pleased, as they stood on the platform.

Clare was casual. She had a book in her hand already. Everyone knew she was going to study all the way to Dublin. David waved cheerily, and his mother nodded, a kind of bow as if she had hurt her neck. Dr Power had gone to the newsagent's stall to buy David a magazine for his long journey.

When the train was half a mile from the town they were in each other's arms in the corridor, each whispering the other's name over and over. They were going back to Dublin. City of freedom. So Clare was in a hostel run by nuns and David was a resident doctor in a big city hospital. Compared to where they came from this was licence and freedom.

The book on the history of law and the magazine just bought at the news stand lay beside each other on the seat of the train unread. The train was not crowded. They had a compartment to themselves for most of the journey, and when they were joined it was by an elderly American who said it was the coldest country he had ever visited in his life and he had visited a few. David encouraged him to wrap something round his feet – it was the extremities that often felt most cold. The American had a huge muffler and they tied it loosely around his ankles. He was asleep in no time and they kissed and held hands and snuggled up to each other happily in the corner without interruption.

They had two whole days in Dublin before anyone knew they were back. Clare's hostel didn't open till Sunday; and David wasn't expected in the hospital until eight a.m. on the Monday morning. It was only Friday night. They had made no plans, almost as if they both felt it might be unlucky.

Now in the winter evening outside Kingsbridge they walked past the line of taxis and to the bus. Clare had one small case, David two huge ones. She accused him of having brought all his washing home for Nellie to do and he opened his eyes wide. Didn't everyone do that?

She wanted to ask him what they were to do now. Or better, she wanted to tell him all her options: she could stay with Kevin and Emer, if he wanted to go and stay with James for example. She could go to the hostel and throw herself on the mercy of the nuns. They thought she was one of the most reliable girls they ever had, so they would grumble only a bit and let her into her room – even though it hadn't been aired for her and no hot-water bottles had been put in the small iron beds.

She had £18 in her wallet. They could stay in a guest house: there were lots of them in Glasnevin, she knew lots of students who had cheap digs out that way.

But she thought she should wait and see what David had in mind. Her throat closed over once or twice in case he suggested that they sleep together. She hoped and prayed he wouldn't ask her to. Not yet. She had to think. It was all too sudden.

As they got on the bus to O'Connell Bridge, David said easily, 'You know the flat I used to stay in before they locked me up in the hospital?'

'Yes.'

'I still have the key. And I can go there always. There'll be nobody back until Monday. And there's lots of rooms. You could go in the one I used to have, it's one of the nicest. And I could go . . . well anywhere. Far away from you, I think, so that I won't come and break down the door and get at you.'

She smiled at him, relieved that she hadn't spoken, pleased that he felt the need to break down the door, and very grateful that he wasn't going to. He had said absolutely the right thing.

They had a honeymoon without sex. They held hands and she took him on tours of her Dublin. He had never been inside the Bank of Ireland to look from within at what had once been the Irish Parliament. He said he must have known that but somehow he had forgotten. She promised to take him on a weekday.

She crossed the road with him and showed him the book of Kells in Trinity College. He said he had known it was there and he had been going to see it one day.

They climbed Nelson's Pillar to look out over the city. It had a long, dark, windy staircase. There was a lot of pausing to catch breath and to kiss. David embarked on a long tale of a doctor who was married but having an illicit romance with another married lady. They couldn't go anywhere to make love because they were too well known, so they used to meet twice a week inside Nelson's Pillar and make love on the stairway. If any tourist climbing up or down was troublesome enough to interrupt them they just flattened themselves against the wall.

'That's why I brought you here of course.' She laughed and jumped lightly ahead of him so that he'd know she wasn't contemplating it for a moment. She took him down the Quays to St Michan's, an old Protestant Church where they had a totally preserved mummy in the vaults.

In the evenings they made themselves meals. David was rather better at preparing them than Clare.

'I thought you'd be very domesticated, big family, all those brothers to cook for,' he teased.

'I'd be fine throwing a big dinner for eight on the table, lump of bacon, half a ton of spuds. But I've never cooked just for one or two. We get the food handed to us up in the hostel.' She sounded apologetic.

'It's not the end of the world, Clare. Stop looking so mournful!'

'What will we have tonight? Will we go out and get something or what?' She hoped he'd say that they'd get chips from the place down the road.

'Oh, there's lots of eggs there – why don't you just make an omelette?' He was talking absently, concentrating on clearing out the grate.

Clare looked stricken.

'There's a bit of cheese there, isn't there? We could have a cheese omelette,' he called.

'I'll do the fire, *you* do the omelette.'

'Don't tell me you can't make an . . .' David stopped when he saw her face.

'We never had them at home. If you show me, I'll know then.'

'Listen, it doesn't matter, scrambled eggs, anything . . .'

'Show me how to make an omelette. I want to know.' Her face was set and determined.

'All right then.' David was good-natured. 'It doesn't matter a damn, you know, you *do* know that, don't you?'

They kissed over the frying pan. It didn't matter a damn.

On Sunday night, he asked her. 'What are we going to do?'

'I don't know.'

They sat for a long time on the floor with a bottle of wine between them.

'It's too soon isn't it? We met too soon.'

'We met when we were babies, David.'

'You know what I mean. Now. It's too early.'

'I love you. The other seems unimportant. I wouldn't want to be a history don somewhere without you.'

'I don't want to be anywhere without you.'

'Maybe we can go round the world only taking universities that will have research facilities for both of us.' She smiled nervously.

'But in real life . . .' he said.

'Yes. Real life. Which begins tomorrow.' She looked stricken.

He kissed her and rocked her in his arms. 'Nothing bad can happen now, I was never more sure in my life. I'll love you for ever. I half loved you always and didn't know it.'

'No, nothing bad can happen now,' said Clare.

They knew immediately of course. Mary Catherine and Val. There was no point in denying it.

'Do you mind if I don't talk about it,' she said.

'Yes we bloody do,' Valerie said indignantly. 'What kind of nonsense is that? We've told you everything, every pant and groan.'

'It's very unfair to hold out on us now. It's secretive and it's not like you at all. I can't understand it.' Mary Catherine was upset.

'But there's nothing to tell. I beg you, there's no new panting and groaning in it, in fact there's a lot less than there was with Ian that night in the car. So now, will that satisfy you?'

'It will not. How did it happen? Did he say he loved you, did a thousand violins start to play? I *must* know.' Valerie was sitting on her bed, legs crossed like an old-fashioned tailor. She looked very young, Clare thought. They were all young, nobody was twenty, she was too young to feel the way she did. The realization swept over her.

'You see I'm too young,' she said stupidly.

'For what? God Clare, you're very irritating when you put on this dramatic bit. Does he think you're too young for him or what?'

'No, but it's all right for him. He's old, he's twenty-five. His life's nearly over. In terms of studying I mean.'

'This is very tedious,' complained Valerie.

717

'I *told* you it was tedious,' Clare said defensively.

'It may pass over. Seriously, if you've known the guy all your life and never thought about him in that way until ten days ago, it's bound to blow over.'

'It won't. That's what really is going to be tedious for you. I can't think of any better way to put it than this and it's going to make you vomit.'

'Say it,' said Valerie grimly.

'I feel as if I'd been looking and looking for something I'd lost and now I've found it. It's like going home, except much nicer than going home, it's like you think going home should be.'

'It's a bit soppy,' Val said objectively.

'I'm afraid it is.'

'Will you be any fun do you think, ever again?' Mary Catherine asked.

'Oh I hope so, but do you see what I mean, it's no good my talking about it, I can only use these awful, sickening words.' She looked from one to another.

'It's going to be very hard,' said Val. 'In the middle of a perfectly normal conversation about sex or about who we're going to set our sights on at a party we'll remember that you've had this coming home feeling about the boy next door.'

'Will you do me one favour, will you get it into your heads that he is not the boy next door. Whatever he is, he's not that.'

He was hungry for every detail of her, he told her that he used to envy the O'Briens as children going off with their jam jars picking blackberries, or with the same jam jars on strings trying to catch pinkeens. There were always children running in and out of the shop and calling to each other winter and summer while his own house was very big and you could hear the clock ticking in the hall.

She told him about how terrible Chrissie had been and somehow they made her into a comic character. All her cruelty, and pulling Clare's hair, and trying to persuade her she was abnormal didn't matter any more.

He told her about his father and how he tried hard not to drag David back to the practice but he really wanted him there. Tomorrow. David admitted that his mother sometimes drove him mad. She was full of childish nonsenses; but years ago in a man-to-man talk his father had urged him not to be impatient, and said that Molly had given up a lot of bright lights and fun to come to a backwater as a country doctor's wife. It irritated David greatly that his father should be somehow grateful to his mother for this. It was her choice after all. And there was the history of miscarriages and stillbirths so she had to be forgiven her little silliness from time to time.

He told her that his mother came to Dublin every year to spend a few days with the Nolans; and he used to be ashamed of her carry-on, sitting in the lounge of the Shelbourne, or the Ibernian or the Gresham having afternoon tea. Far too dressed up, and asking at the top of her voice who all the other people were, then trilling with affected laughter when David hissed that he didn't know and saying that really he was quite a recluse. Clare was sympathetic. It was probably because Mrs Power wanted to feel important just for a couple of days; she could go home and remember that so and so had saluted her and so and so had made a fuss of her. It was like a child really. David's father indulged her just like a child. Some people always got that kind of treatment.

After a while she told him about Tommy. She wasn't going to. He didn't need to know and it seemed disloyal to them all at home with this sad secret they hugged to themselves. It seemed somehow indulgent to confess it in the great heat of love. Maybe David shouldn't have to hear it either. But she told him suddenly, when he had been talking so honestly about his own life and hiding nothing. She told him quickly and unemotionally. He reached across the table and held both her hands tight. He was upset but not shocked. If Tommy were such an eejit as to get in with this kind of a crowd, maybe the safest place for him was in gaol. And since he'd always been such a nice fellow he wouldn't get beaten up by the other prisoners or the warders or anything.

'When you and I go to London some time . . . we'll go to see him,' David said expansively. 'And that'll show him that he's not cut off or anything.'

Go to see Tommy? In a *prison*, on *visiting day*? She nodded at him, unable to speak.

He reached out and stroked her face. 'I don't think you have any idea of how much I love you, you are part of my soul. I would do anything for you. Going to see Tommy would make me happy if it were to give you some ease and pleasure. I'd go tonight on the mail boat.'

She closed her eyes and held his hand to her face. 'I don't deserve you. I'm so narrow and one-track and self-obsessed. Why do you love me so much?'

'I've no idea. It's just there. Filling all those empty spaces I used to have. There's no more doubt now. I just want you and what's good for you.'

He sat opposite her in the little café, his face tired from lack of sleep, his shirt collar open at the neck, his smile enormous and all over his face, lighting it up.

'You look like a man that's won the Sweep,' she said admiringly.

'Now you're just feeding me lines so I'll say that I *have* won the Sweep when I've won you,' he said.

As they left the café he asked whether anyone else knew where Tommy was.

'Angela. She was the one who insisted I write to him every week. Oh, and Gerry Doyle,' she said.

He frowned. Why had she told Gerry? He tried to keep his voice casual but she knew he hated Gerry knowing the family secret before he did.

'It was a long time ago. Gerry was going to London and my Mam asked him to go and find Tommy. I had to tell him what was happening. I couldn't have him going around investigating it and turning it up for himself, and then not knowing what to say. It was easier to tell him straight out. He never said a word, naturally.'

'Naturally.'

'Why are you studying in bed?' Valerie complained.

'Because I did nothing today. I met David for two hours, I went back to the library and I wrote him a letter. That was another hour. Then I spent an hour thinking about how nice it would be to go to London with him. Then I spent about half an hour working out how he should tell his father he can't possibly go back to Castlebay until he's done three years at least in Dublin hospitals. Then I went to this place where they do your hair cheaply in the afternoons, then I went out to the hospital with my new hairdo and had a cup of tea in the canteen with him, and gave him the letter. Then I came home. That's the work I did today, that's the amount of work the Murray scholar has put in towards getting her first-class honours degree.'

'All right, all right.' Valerie hadn't intended to bring on such an onslaught.

'No. It's not all right. I didn't know this would happen.' Clare looked mournful.

'Christ, you're only having a bit of fun. One day, one day, Clare O'Brien, with this fellow – it's not as if it were something stupid, like me making eyes like a sheep at that fellow who doesn't even know that I am alive, or Mary Catherine going out with James. You've got the real thing, what we all want. Stop *bellyaching*.'

'I know it must *sound* like bellyaching . . .'

'It does.' Valerie was grumpy.

'But if you knew how annoyed I am for doing nothing today. If you knew.'

'I'm *beginning* to know. For God's sake will you get out of bed, put on your coat, sit at the dressing table and work properly. Stop hanging out of the bed and trying to read with the light on the floor. Do it properly. I'll get to sleep. Don't mind me.'

'Valerie, stop making yourself into a tragedy queen,' Clare said.

Val laughed at the scorn; but she said that it was no harm to take Professor Clare O'Brien down a bit. She talked about her studies as if they were a sacred ritual. Clare had to smile as she climbed out of bed and put on clothes so that she wouldn't freeze.

A girl they didn't know tapped on the window, having climbed up the rungs. Clare let her in and she thanked them profusely.

'You three are a legend in this place,' she said breathlessly. 'I mean you're so old, and so settled, and make all your own rules.'

'We're also mad,' Val said from the bed. 'We take it in turns to get up and get fully dressed in the night to keep guard over the others.'

The girl was startled and said she should be off.

'You have to make a cup of tea for us as your payment for going through the room,' Clare said, as a joke – but ten minutes later the girl crept back with two cups of tea.

'I presume your friend is still out,' she said, nervously looking at Mary Catherine's bed.

'Of course she is,' said Val. 'It's only three o'clock in the morning.'

Clare said that Valerie was giving them all a reputation for being stone mad. Val said that she wondered what on earth Mary Catherine and James Nolan could be doing until after three in the morning if they weren't in bed together.

About ten minutes later, Mary Catherine came through the window. She and James Nolan *had* been in bed together, and it had been all right. Not *great*, but *all right*, and she would like them to start a novena this minute because her period was due in exactly nine days' time, so if ever a novena was called for it was now.

Dick Dillon told Angela that he hadn't changed his mind. That he wasn't much of a catch for her, and he wasn't as well read, but at least she knew that he'd never turn into a drunk on her. Then he remembered that a drunk is exactly what Angela's father had been and he apologized so much for the remark that she had to tell him to shut up or she would beat him to death with her bicycle.

But *seriously*, he said. Wouldn't it be a good idea? Angela was lonely in that cottage, he was lonely in a little corner of the hotel, his bedroom and sitting room. He would be agreeable to whatever she wanted – live in her cottage, build a new place, he could get a site easily. Angela could go on teaching if she liked. The ban on married teachers had been lifted now. Or she could take a rest from it. He so enjoyed her company. He was never one for the flowery words, but genuinely he had flowery thoughts in his heart.

Angela was thoughtful. She said that in her heart she still felt it would be the single most foolish act since the partition of the country but she wouldn't think of it now. There was something else to the forefront of her mind. But the thing that was in her mind would be out of it one way or another at the end of the summer.

Then she would sit down with him seriously and discuss his suggestion, without any jokes or smart-alec remarks.

'It's not so much a *suggestion*, it's more a *proposal*,' he said, affronted. 'This . . . thing, this worry in the summer. Is there anything I could do to make it easier for you?' he asked.

She looked at him. He had a very kind face. 'No, Dick. Thank you all the same.'

'It isn't another man?' he asked anxiously. 'You're not making up your mind about another person or anything like that?'

'No. There's no other man in that sense at all.'

'You're not thinking of entering the convent?' He was fearful of all the rival possibilities.

'Immaculata would have the place closed down rather than let me into the community,' she said.

'Well, sure one religious in any family is enough,' said Dick Dillon, unerringly putting his finger on the one thing that was guaranteed to set every nerve end jangling. Father Sean O'Hara. Who still wrote excited letters about how much they were all looking forward to the summer.

Paddy Power said it was a very clear day altogether, you could see cliffs and headlands miles and miles away. Nellie had told him he was back early: it would be half an hour before the lunch was ready, the potatoes were still like bullets. Molly said she'd walk a bit along the cliff with him since it was so bright and fresh out.

'Will you go up to see Sheila? You like going there in January.'

'Yes. I was thinking of it. David was a bit offhand on the phone when I suggested it.'

'Offhand?'

'He said he might find it very hard to get any time off to meet me, he just said that he'd like to warn me in advance.'

'Well that's fair enough. I remember it was like that in my time as well, you don't have a minute of your own.'

'Oh, he has minutes of his own all right.'

'What do you mean?'

'He said to me that he heard the Guards had to be called to Dillon's Hotel, I asked how he heard that – we hadn't told him – and he said that he had met Clare O'Brien and she'd told him. Josie Dillon had written to her all about it, apparently.'

'Well?' Dr Power couldn't see where all this was leading.

'Well it shows he gets enough minutes off to meet that Clare O'Brien.'

'Molly, don't be giving out about that child. You've always had a down on her.'

'I've had nothing of the sort. I just mentioned to you in passing that it's odd our son has time to meet her when he's not going to be able to have any time to meet his own mother.'

'Now, now, now. He ran into her – what more natural than they talk about Castlebay?'

'No, he didn't say he ran into her, he said when he met her, as if they met all the time. And stop sounding exasperated with me like that. I *know*, I tell you.'

'If he *is* meeting her, would that be the end of the world?'

Molly looked triumphant. 'A minute ago I was drawing conclusions, I was imagining things. Now all of a sudden I'm right.'

'Yes, Molly . . .'

Valerie said you couldn't do a novena for something like that. God just wouldn't listen. Clare said that if anything had happened it had happened now and no amount of prayers could change it. Mary Catherine said that neither of them had understood the nature of prayer. In her parish back in the States it had been very clearly explained. God knew in advance that you were going to pray later. It was foreknowledge, not predestination. They had endless debates about it, but fortunately events overtook them and on the appointed day the news was good, so there was a great sigh of relief from the bedroom of the three ageing eccentrics.

Mary Catherine said she wouldn't run the risk again, although James had said that he would Look After Things. She said she didn't really want to either. She couldn't think why she had in the first place except that she was so sick of him pestering her about it, and saying no, and finding excuses, and thinking up reasons why not. She said he had nearly dropped dead when she said she would go back with him to this flat. The same one that David had lived in . . . They all brought their girls there, it seemed.

But Mary Catherine said they probably talked much more than they actually seduced. James said he was fairly experienced, but without being too technical Mary Catherine thought he wasn't. No honestly it would be too detailed, she couldn't say any more. And she had asked him very casually if he thought that David Power was a ladies' man, and he had said that David was being terribly secretive and the belief was that he was having it off with a fast nurse up in the hospital otherwise why wouldn't he come out to play with the rest of them?

Mary Catherine said she couldn't see the need for secrecy but if it was so desperately important to Clare and David, she'd go along with it. She didn't care much one way or the other she said, she had a far bigger worry of her own. How to brush off James politely. Far from casting her aside once he had his way with her, he was on the phone morning noon and night, presumably hoping to have his way with her over and over again. She didn't want to turn him down too brusquely and she certainly didn't want him to tell everyone that she was a good thing.

In the safety of daylight and public places Clare and David talked about sex. David told her that he never had it with anyone, he had implied to the lads that he was at it all the time, but he actually never had. There was a sort of a near miss on one occasion but he needn't detain her with that. Anyway that had all to do with drink and nothing to do with love.

They discussed almost abstractly what they would do if they had the opportunity presented to them. Suppose now for example that Clare had her own flat where nobody would bother them. Suppose David had his own place. Would their resolution be so strong?

Clare said that she could never go through the anxiety. She didn't like to tell tales on Mary Catherine, but it turned out that David knew anyway. This was a bit alarming, but they couldn't fault James really since Valerie and Clare knew all about it as well.

David said that there were probably ways round the anxiety bit, and what with being a doctor and everything he'd have more access to the ways round it than anyone else. Anyway people went to the North of Ireland where you could get contraceptives legally, so there should be no problem there.

'That's *if* we were thinking of it seriously,' Clare said.

'Yes, that's if we were,' David agreed.

Emer rang Clare at the hostel and asked her would she do her a great favour. Kevin had been asked to go and find out about new educational aids in London. For three whole days. And would you believe it, she was going too. Her mother was looking after Daniel. And what she'd really like is if someone were to stay in the house, to keep an eye on it. Would Clare like to? Clare said she'd like to very much.

She contemplated not telling him. For two whole hours.

Then she told him. He asked for his three days' leave at that time.

'I hope we won't have to be doing any more novenas,' Valerie grumbled.

'Suppose I never want to see you again afterwards?' she said as they went to the bedroom.

'Why wouldn't you want to see me again afterwards?'

'Mary Catherine didn't with James.'

'They don't love each other. They're only just pretending to.'

'So being in love would make all the difference?'

'That's what I've always heard.'

David stroked her long fair hair on the pillow afterwards. He kept moving his hand from the top of her head to the end of the hair. He was afraid to speak in case she was hurt or unhappy.

Her eyes were open as she lay there beside him but he couldn't read her face. Was she frightened? Or disappointed? Had she felt anything like the pleasure that he had, or the peace he felt now?

'David,' she said. Her voice was very small.

He gave a great cry of delight and gathered her up in his arms and held her to him. He couldn't believe that it was possible to be so happy.

James Nolan tracked David down eventually.

'I thought you'd been murdered and the body buried,' he said. 'Nobody knew where you were.'

'Is anything wrong?' David asked quickly.

'Depends how you view it. Your mother's coming to stay with mine tomorrow. Both maternals are a bit shirty that you couldn't be found. I think you'd better ring your own to pat down ruffled feathers. Where were you anyway?'

'Wouldn't it *have* to be this weekend she was looking for me? Wouldn't you bloody know.'

James shrugged. 'I did my best. I thought maybe you'd gone off with a bird. I said there was a match on and that you might have gone to that.'

'A match for three days!'

'I said it was in Northern Ireland.'

'OK, that'll do. Thanks, James.'

'Don't hang up, where *were* you?'

'As you said. At a match.'

'I'll deal with you. You're meant to be coming to lunch with us on Sunday.'

Molly Power was martyred, on the phone.

'Please don't think I'm checking up on you. I don't mind where you go on your time off. Your father's always saying you're a grown man. I agree entirely.'

'I'm glad to know you're coming up to Dublin,' he said, gritting his teeth.

'It's just that the Nolans thought it was so *odd* that you couldn't be found. I mean, David, nobody wants to keep checking up on you, I've told you that, it's just that if anything happened to your father – God forbid that it should – and we were looking for you . . .'

He held the receiver at arm's length. He would like to have smashed it against the wall.

'. . . do you think you'll be able to *tear* yourself away from *whatever* is occupying you so much to come and meet us when I'm in Dublin?'

'I'm really looking forward to Sunday lunch,' he said, willing an eagerness into his voice.

'Am I not going to see you *until* Sunday?'

'No . . . I meant that, in particular . . . of course I'll see you before then.'

He leaned his head against the wall when the three minutes were up. 'Clare,' he whispered to himself. 'Clare, Clare.'

'Are you all right Doctor?' A young nurse with freckles was looking at him. A lot of the young housemen went a bit loopy, she had been told, and she thought it could well be true.

Angela read the letter with great surprise. If Clare had got into a political group, or become very active in a cause, she would not have been so surprised, but David, lovely big nice David Power who was coming back to Castlebay next year to share the work with his father? How had it happened? And what would Clare do if she married him? She would marry him, it seemed, reading between the lines. Clare had said how they both felt as strongly as each other and they couldn't bear to be apart. She said he had it as badly as she did. Angela was bewildered, reading the outpourings. Bewildered because there seemed only one thing to say. So she said it:

I suppose you must work as hard as you possibly can, get your First as you know you can, then relax, and do your Higher Diploma. And then, who knows? I might be put out to grass here and you'd be over-qualified, but I'm sure they'd take you in the school. But as Mrs Power, young Mrs Power, would you *want* to work? Would you want to teach all day . . . ?

Clare read the letter in dismay. She had been *stupid, stupid, stupid*, to tell Angela. The woman understood *nothing*. There was *no* question of going back to Castlebay. That was what all the *agonizing* was about. David didn't want to, she didn't want to. The *root* of the problem was how to explain this to David's father without breaking his heart. In a million *years* Angela wouldn't understand. She had been too long in Castlebay, that was her trouble.

'I'm going to meet your mother-in-law and your intended on Sunday,' Mary Catherine said.
'How on earth . . . ?'
'James has asked me to lunch. He said Mrs Power was coming and that David would be there too. Didn't he tell you?'
'Yes. It slipped my mind.' David hadn't told her. She was furious.

'I didn't want to talk about anything bad, that's all.'
'Your mother coming to Dublin isn't bad.'
'Yes it is. It makes it all more real, it brings that side of things into our life here.'
'She comes every year. You don't have to announce to her at lunch in the Nolans' house that your plans for the future have changed.'
'No. But I'd prefer to be with you on Sunday. Not there.'
'Mary Catherine's going. They must be having a big do.'
'*That's* an idea. Why don't I get James to ask you too?'
'Are you stark staring mad?' she asked.

The ideal thing would have been to find somewhere near the hospital, but the roads were too posh and the prices of flats were too high. If they went far out of the city they could afford somewhere nice but then it would be pointless, David would hardly ever be able to escape to somewhere so far away. They read the small ads in the evening papers and couldn't believe how quickly any reasonable-sounding bed-sitter was snapped up. Sometimes they found long queues on the doorstep of a place that had only been advertised that very day. They got to know other young people and exchanged information. Rathmines wasn't too bad, people said. It was about twenty minutes' walk from UCD. Lots of people had bed-sitters there. They went on an expedition, just knocking on every door: that was meant to be as good a way as any. Clare looked around at the area. There was a big main street and a lot of tall houses which had once been family homes but now housed several families. Some were very well kept with well-painted halls, nice half-moon tables where the post for each flat dweller was laid out in neat rows. Others had torn lino, walls badly in need of papering and a faintly unpleasant smell about them. These were the ones they were going to be able to afford.

It was a nice area, they decided. A bit like a village or a place all on its own rather than part of the Dublin they knew. But there were buses constantly back and forth, it was near the canal for walks and, because this was where a lot of young people had flats, the shops stayed open later. There was also a chip shop nearby. Clare looked at it gratefully. This might be very useful indeed.

They looked at the small grimy room up three flights of stairs, in the big house with the uncared-for garden and the peeling paint-work. They looked at each other and said yes. They handed over the first month's rent and moved in on Saturday. The landlord said he hated students usually but seeing that this was a young married couple, that was quite different. He did hope that there was no question of a child yet because they would understand he had to run a quiet house. They shook their heads. No, there would be no question of that and they quite understood.

David had given her a plain ring which cost fifteen shillings; one day it would be a proper one. Like one day it would be a proper place to live. They had an oil stove, and the place smelled of paraffin; the bed was a bit lumpy and the little cooking ring was very dirty after the last tenants. The bathroom was down two floors. But it was their own. And apart from Valerie and Mary Catherine who had to know everything, nobody else in the world knew where they were.

They went out to buy bacon and sausages and a bottle of red vermouth for their first supper. They bought a bookcase at a second-hand shop because the landlord said he didn't like his walls being mutilated. The walls were so rough and uneven, and had such shaky plaster, they would have been hard put to take a nail let alone a shelf. Clare felt settled when the books were in place.

He kissed her hands and looked up at her face. 'Look, it's all going to be all right. You'll study and I'll come to you every minute I can. You'll get your First and I'll finish my year and start somewhere else, just as if it were the most natural thing in the world. I won't be an intern, we can live together like this, only better. I'll be getting real money.'

'So will I,' Clare said excitedly, 'if I'm tutoring.'

'We haven't a worry in the world. If we can do this . . .' he waved his hand expansively around the small shabby room '. . . if we can do this in a few days, can't we do anything?'

It was a lonely Sunday, but all Sundays could be a bit down in Dublin.

Clare scraped at the cooking ring for a while, then she went out to buy a Sunday paper. A bell was ringing and great crowds were going into the big church in the main street of Rathmines. She hurried past. There had been five Sundays since she was in mortal sin. She had gone to Mass as usual the first Sunday, but it was ridiculous, she couldn't say any prayers, it was hypocritical to kneel there knowing that she was going to commit further mortal sin. For all her brave words to David, it *was* a sin, and that was that. There was no point in acting the part of a person who was praying. If Clare were the Lord she'd prefer those kind of people not to come to church at all.

Val had gone to a lunch where six people were going to make a curry. It sounded awful, yet Clare would like to have been there. She didn't feel she could ask Emer and Kevin if she could call, it seemed like using them, and anyway she did feel slightly embarrassed going back to their place even though they had no idea why she should be. Mary Catherine was at this Nolan lunch and so was David. Perhaps she should have said yes, and agreed when, in his innocence, he had suggested she should be invited too. It would have been hard to take: Mrs Power's rage and scorn would have communicated itself to everyone there and Clare didn't really like James or Caroline Nolan enough to think they might have supported her. But still this was very hard too, this hanging around and waiting.

It was like being in love with a married man, like that girl who was so depressed in the hostel last year. She had been having a romance with one of the lecturers; she was suicidal at weekends.

'Don't be so silly,' Clare told herself aloud. 'There is no comparison. We have a flat together of our own. He'll be coming back here. It's his *mother* he's seeing, for God's sake, not a wife. Why feel so chilly? Why this awful sense of doom?'

There were five cars parked in the drive in front of the Nolans' house: Mr Nolan's, his wife's, Caroline's and James's. David didn't know who the last one belonged to. He ran lightly up the steps. Breeda opened the door. She took his coat, and put it in the breakfast room, where a lot of other coats were already hanging and draped.

He went up the stairs to the first-floor drawing room. His mother was standing by the fireplace, leaning on the mantelpiece. She looked very made-up and a bit fussy, David thought. Too many frills at her neck and her cuffs. He didn't have time to see who else was there, since Molly gave a scream of welcome.

'The *prodigal*! He's torn himself away!'

He wished she hadn't. It made such a commotion. He should have gone in quietly and greeted James's mother and father. But now because she had called such attention to him, he had to go straight to her.

'You're looking marvellous, Mother,' he said, kissing her on the cheek.

'Oh, you're a worse flatterer than your father,' she said, still in this high silly voice that he hated.

He looked around. Mrs Nolan looked vague and sort of fluttery as usual. David wondered yet again why his mother didn't see how strange Sheila Nolan was, how dotty, for want of a more technical word.

'Lovely to be here, Mrs Nolan,' he said dutifully.

'Oh, David.' She looked at him as if she had never seen him before but as if she had learned his name to make him feel welcome. 'How good of you to come to see us. Your mother is here too you know.' Sheila Nolan looked around vaguely.

'Yes, yes. I've just seen her.' David was beginning to feel trapped, to experience the hunted sensation that Mrs Nolan managed to create all around her.

'David – they tell me you love sherry. Sweet or dry?' the woman stared into his eyes as if waiting for the Meaning of Life in his answer.

'Dry would be very nice, Mrs Nolan.' He *hated* sherry of any kind.

He saw James had managed to get a gin and tonic, but it was too late, the sherry glass was in his hand. Caroline was talking to Mary Catherine by the window. Two priests were talking to Mr Nolan. One of them looked familiar, yet David hadn't met him before. Breeda came in and passed round cheese straws and little bits of celery filled with cheese.

The voices of his mother and Mrs Nolan talking archly at him receded, and David wanted Clare and their little room and a tin of tomato soup. He wanted to be miles from this overheated room and babble of chat. He answered the questions automatically: yes, it was pretty hard work, no, he didn't know that specialist, but of course he knew him by name, and how nice of the Nolans to say they'd have a word. He asked his mother about home, and about his father, and had Bones recovered from the terrible paint incident. Molly Power said that Bones had never looked beautiful but nowadays he would actually frighten you to look at him. They had cut off so much of his coat where the spilled paint had all hardened and matted. He looked very odd but had no idea that his appearance had changed. Old as he was, he still ran round in circles barking happily. Molly said you couldn't take him for a walk anywhere because the explanations were so lengthy when you met anyone, and the memory of finding him lying on his back on the kitchen floor in a pool of red paint was not one you wanted to relive.

'Will you be down before Easter to see him? And us indeed,' she asked.

'Not a chance . . . oh and about Easter . . .' he began, but Sheila Nolan had clapped her hands. Lunch was ready.

They moved to another very overheated room with nine places set around a table, two bottles of wine already open and a huge joint of beef on the carving table.

'Isn't this the life,' said Molly Power wistfully as they went into the room with its heavy dark furniture and thick curtains. Her voice was envious for a life which could assemble people around a table like this, far from Castlebay.

David took his mind from the dingy bed-sitter not two miles away, and forced himself to feel some sympathy for his mother. Dad had always said that she needed very little to make her happy. And it was true, there she was, revelling in the showy lunch that Sheila Nolan had organized in her honour. He was not going to be rude to her. He wasn't going to spoil her visit. He'd tell her about Easter later.

David was sitting between Caroline and one of the priests. Caroline was in high form and full of confidences and whispered questions.

'Do you think James is serious about the Yankee lady? Oh go on, he must tell you. I don't believe this strong silent act. Men do tell. I know they do.'

'But you are so wrong, Caroline, men are much too gentle and sensitive to discuss their emotions, would that we had the strength of women, able to bring anything out in the open, air it, examine it and dust it down.'

She laughed. 'Do you think they're *involved*, if you know what I mean? Once upon a time he used to be only interested whether she had money, now he's a bit lovesick, I think.'

They both looked at Mary Catherine, who was battling with interrogation from Mrs Power and glances of fluttery hostility from Mrs Nolan.

'Why don't you ask her? She'd tell all, the way women do.'

'No, she's like a tin of sardines that one, I wouldn't get to first base, to use her own kind of language.'

'And how about your own romances. Are you the toast of the Incorporated Law Society?'

'You only ask me that to break my heart. You know I think of no other man.' Caroline waved her eyelashes up and down at him jokily.

'What chance would a humble country hick like myself have with a sophisticated girl like you?' David smiled. He had always liked Caroline. He had fancied her of course when he was very young, and in phases ever since, she was so easy to talk to, so joky, and she took nothing too seriously. He remembered with a start that his mother had always regarded them as a likely match, and with some alarm noticed that Mrs Power and Mrs Nolan were looking at them fondly.

Caroline was unaware of it. 'I never tried seriously to capture you, David, I hate failure, I feel that with you I have to bide my time, wait till you're ready for me, and fall into my arms like a ripe plum. Maybe on the rebound from some other female.'

She threw back her head of dark hair and laughed. Clare had once said that Caroline Nolan had too many good, white, even teeth, it was a sign of great money and breeding, rich people didn't rot their children's teeth with sticky things, and rich people took their children to the dentist regularly.

Caroline did look very healthy.

She looked very attractive too: she had a lemon-coloured jumper and a green and gold sort of tartan-type skirt. She wore a big amber necklace. She said that she must have been mad to listen to the nuns who said that a degree was the answer. It wasn't the answer, it was the question. You had to ask yourself what to do then. Fortunately now that she had done the boring secretarial bit she was nicely installed in her father's office as a solicitor's apprentice where she should have been years ago. Before she became old and grey.

She turned to pass the vegetables in their heavy tureens and David found himself talking to the priest with the small buttons of eyes.

'I know your face from somewhere, Father. Would there have been a picture of you in the paper or anything?'

'I hope not. I'm in bad enough books with the archbishop already. No, I don't think I've come across you – I know you're from Castlebay. Your mother was telling me before you arrived.'

'I'm not such a genius as she makes out,' he said.

'She didn't make you out to be a genius at all,' the priest said.

'I don't know if that's good or bad.'

'We do have a mutual friend though. Angela O'Hara. She and I met at a wedding in Rome, oh it must be eight years ago now. A long time. But somehow we all remained great friends. A couple called Quinn got married . . .'

David remembered why the priest was familiar. He was the Father Flynn whose round face shone out of the wedding photos in Kevin and Emer Quinn's bedroom.

The photo that he had looked at for a long time as Clare slept in his arms in the big bed that belonged to Kevin and Emer.

Mary Catherine didn't like David's mother one bit. She thought that Clare was going to have a hard time of it with this one.

'Tell me about Castlebay,' she said brightly, smiling her perfect smile and pretending an interest she didn't feel. 'I hear it's one lively town.'

'You hear wrong,' Mrs Power said definitely. 'It's a small community, very, very small, swollen to about twenty times its size in the summer. A lot of *riff-raff* have been coming recently, and *loud* people. It used to be a wonderful family resort. Remember, Sheila, when you all came down . . . ?'

Molly caught David's eye and realized that she mustn't run down the place she was trying to get him to come home to. '. . . But I think that's just my age, really. For young people, for young *professional* people, *working* there, for the *doctor* or the young *solicitor*, or the people in the hotel, it's a wonderful life. And a lot of very nice people a few miles back from the coast. Very nice indeed. Wonderful big estates and everything.' She nodded owlishly.

David raged within. She had never been invited to any of the big estates nor did she even know anyone who had. Why did she try to impress people with a line of chat which was just making her pathetic?

'I was thinking of spending a few days there this summer. When I do my degree I'll have to go back to the States, so best see a bit of Ireland while I can.'

Molly was a little nonplussed. On the one hand the girl had been talking about her father being a postman and her mother working in a clothes factory of some sort, hanging garments on rails. On the other hand, the Nolans seemed to think that James was serious about her. Who knew what way to jump?

'Well, that would be very nice, dear,' she said noncommittally. 'Be sure to let us know when you arrive, and come to see us.'

'Thank you, Mrs Power.'

'Will you stay in Dillon's Hotel?'

Mary Catherine spoke without thinking. 'I guess Clare will find me a bed . . .'

'Clare?'

It was too late. Clare had asked her not to bring up her name at all, but it was done now.

'Clare O'Brien, I share a room, I've been sharing a room with her.'

Molly Power sniffed. 'I doubt if there's going to be any room for you with the poor O'Briens – but maybe Clare didn't describe it to you properly. It's not a place that anyone could *stay* in.'

David's face flushed a dark red.

Mary Catherine spoke quickly. 'I explained it badly, I meant to say that Clare said she would book me in somewhere. But heavens, who knows if I'll ever get there, there's so much work to do . . . Was your last year full of frights and horrors, Caroline?'

'Dreadful. I didn't know you shared a room with Clare O'Brien.'

'You never asked,' Mary Catherine said with spirit.

'I know Clare O'Brien,' said the small priest. 'A very bright girl. She won that scholarship for three years from your county, didn't she? I always think it must be the most terrible pressure on young people when they get that kind of bursary . . .' He chattered on lightly, knowing there was some tension in the air but not knowing where it came from.

'So you know Clare O'Brien too, Father? My goodness, doesn't she get about?' She turned to Sheila Nolan. 'Remember them, Sheila? Big, straggling family, not a penny to bless themselves with?'

'I don't think so.' Sheila Nolan's vacant blue eyes were vaguer than ever.

'Oh you *must* remember them, we used to go in to buy ice creams there. Though I never particularly liked dealing there. Not terribly *clean.*'

'Why did we buy ice creams there, then?' Mrs Nolan was bewildered.

'It was near the beach, that's why, I think.'

'I would never have bought ice creams there had I known it wasn't clean.' Mrs Nolan's thin hand went to her throat as if regretting the possible germs that might still lurk there.

'No, no. That's not the point. I was just telling you who the family were. One of them put her mind to her books and she's come a long way. Everyone here is on calling terms with her except you and me . . .' Molly Power looked fussed and annoyed. Sheila Nolan looked confused and worried about possibly unhygienic ice creams eaten in the past.

Father Flynn thought he saw the lie of the land. He asked his colleague, Father Kennedy who was the new curate in the Nolans' parish, to tell them all the story of the archbishop's garden. It was a harmless little tale but it distracted them.

Father Flynn looked at David levelly. 'People often sound much more cruel than they are. In their hearts they're probably very kind.'

'Yes,' David mumbled.

'Eat up. That's lovely beef. I bet you don't get food like that in the hospital.'

David didn't respond.

'And there's nothing for concentrating the mind like eating.'

David had to smile. 'I knew the clergy were dangerous,' he laughed.

'That's better. Give Clare my love.'

'Were you the priest who was so helpful about her brother?'

'You must be a *good* friend if she told you all that. Yes. Not that I was all that much help as it turned out.'

'Clare said you were great.'

'Is she going to get a First? She was very eager about that.'

'I think so. I'll keep her at it.'

They spoke low and stopped when Caroline turned to join the conversation.

At the other end of the table Molly whispered behind her hand to Sheila. 'I can't explain it, but I *never* liked that girl. She didn't ever do anything against me, but I don't *trust* her. Do you know the feeling?'

'I do.' Sheila was equally conspiratorial. Her glance rested on Mary Catherine. 'That American girl is going back where she belongs,' she said.

'The pity of it is, that it's hard to say where Clare O'Brien belongs now and where she should go back to,' Molly whispered.

She was lying on the bed reading the verses in the Memoriam column. 'Listen David, listen to this one: "Now every year upon this day/We ask just why you went away." '

Clare pealed with laughter. 'They couldn't could they? Each year on her anniversary, they sit down and say, "What *could* have happened to her?" '

He sat beside her. 'Why aren't you studying? You said you'd have a full day without me, what are you doing reading this rubbish? Where are your books?' He looked around, there was no sign of study.

'Don't give out to me. What was it like?'

'Oh, very Nolanish, you know.'

'I don't know.'

'Men are hopeless at describing things, you're always saying that. There was too much to eat.'

'I know. You smell of food.' She nuzzled him.

'Oh, and your friend Father Flynn was there. He's over for a few days' holiday.'

Her face was bright at the thought of him; then it looked puzzled. 'How did he know you knew me?'

'Castlebay and everything.'

'Yes.' She looked at him. 'David. Was there any more?'

'I nearly lost my temper with my mother and walked out . . .'

'Tell me the whole thing.'

It wasn't *so* bad. Nothing they hadn't known already: that David's mother did not think the sun and moon and stars shone from Clare. That was all. Why was David so upset?

'I didn't want to be there. I wanted to be here.'

'You're here now.'

Much later they did the boldest thing they had ever done. They ate a tin of pears, with spoons, straight from the tin, and bits of the juice kept falling on their bodies and they had to lick it off their shoulders – or wherever it fell. Towards the end of the tin they were covered in the sweet pear syrup and so was the bed. They laughed until they both ached. They dropped the pear tin down on the floor, and put their sticky arms around each other again.

'Is this squalor? Is this what we live in?' Clare asked.

'It's lovely, whatever it is,' David said.

Father Flynn decided to go to Castlebay to see it for himself. He booked himself into Dillon's Hotel, made a courtesy call on Father O'Dwyer, and told Sergeant McCormack that he had heard her highly spoken of, which inspired her to make scones for his tea. Choosing his time well, he went to O'Brien's shop and told them that Tommy was getting on well, with a prison visitor who was bringing him picture books of wild flowers and he sometimes drew them. They marvelled at some English woman who would take the time to go to visit an Irish boy with no teeth in gaol for robbery with violence. Father Flynn said he knew it was hard, but the odd letter, with no criticism or abuse but just descriptions of what life at home was like, would work wonders. Clare had been unfailing in her letters. Agnes was proud to hear that. Clare had never got uppity despite her great success and advances, she told Father Flynn.

'You must be hoping she'll find a good man and marry him and settle down,' the little priest said.

'That one? Marry and settle down? She's going to be a professor, no less. She never had much of an interest in boys when she was young, and I used to think that was a mercy. Chrissie had far too great an interest in them. But not Clare. I suppose in a few years she might meet a professor somewhere, but she'll be gone from us in Castlebay, I knew that the day she got into the secondary school.'

'Suppose she were to marry and come back here?'

'But who would she marry here, father? Hasn't she more book-learning than anyone in the parish?'

He called on the Powers too, because deep in his heart he was a man filled with curiosity. A big, square house, built to withstand the gales and spray from the sea. Father Flynn noted that it must have to be painted every year. There was a large garden, part of it obviously leading to a cliff path down to the sea. It wasn't an elegant house; but it was sturdy and substantial.

Inside too it was comfortable. No antiques, nothing very old, but nice furniture and good carpets, big arrangements of flowers and greenery on window sills and surfaces. A pleasant maid with wispy hair and a broad smile showed him into the drawing room while she went to get the mistress. Molly was delighted to meet him again, and flattered that he should have come to call.

Father Flynn liked David's father enormously: a bluff, kind man who was an old-style adviser to his patients. Probably does a lot of the work that dry stick Father O'Dwyer should be doing, Father Flynn thought ruefully. Over a drink, a lot of admiration for their magnificent view of the sea and some words of sympathy to an elderly mad dog, half-shaved, half-particles of red paint, he talked to the big warm man. He told him about the work with the emigrants in Britain, some of its lighter side as well as its gloomy overtones; that it was often the weakest and the least prepared who were the ones who had to emigrate.

Dr Power told him of the good and bad things in Castlebay. People would never die of loneliness, as they might in a big English city; but attitudes could be cruel, and tolerance was low. In nearly forty years of practice here he had seen a lot of intolerance: families couldn't cope with what they called 'shame and disgrace'. He was sure Father Flynn knew well what he meant. You didn't stamp out young love and young desire by refusing to face up to the consequences.

Dr Power said it was great to have lived through the years that saw TB being wiped out. When he started off, people still hid the fact that they had tuberculosis in the family. It was denied, and if anyone had a spot on the lung it was considered a disgrace and something that would prevent other members of the family being able to marry well.

Father Flynn said he had had the pleasure of meeting Dr Power's son, a fine boy, in Dublin. What were his plans?

Dr Power didn't know, precisely. If the boy were going to work back home then the sooner he came back the better. He would want to find a wife for himself; and it would be wiser for him to be installed here, and choose from here, rather than starting off a life with some girl in a big place with lots of life in it and then asking the poor woman to come back here with him. There was a slight sadness which Father Flynn thought must be hearking back to his own situation.

'And do you think he's met anyone that suits him yet?' he asked.

'Divil a fear of it. He's having too good a time with all those nurses up in the hospital,' said Dr Power with a laugh.

Father Flynn talked about it with Angela too.

'Aren't you a terrible old woman?' she teased him.

'Terrible. That's why I'm so good in confession. I'm never bored and I like to meddle in other people's lives.'

'Are you meddling with David Power and Clare O'Brien?' she asked.

'It worries me a bit, and I only know the fringes of it,' he said. 'I don't know why I feel that it's so doomed. But that's the word that keeps coming to me.'

'It could just be First Love.'

'It could.' He was doubtful. 'But I must get over this tendency to play God. Are you going to let this brother of yours come here and upset everyone?'

'I promised him in Rome. Those were my words. That's how I bought him off from doing it years ago. I can't go back on that now. He's like a child, you can't go back on a promise to a child.'

'Children can do dangerous things. Sometimes promises needn't be kept.'

'Is it dangerous for him to come home? He's had his heart set on it. I don't have children, you don't. We don't know all this about showing them their roots. I mean, I don't think it matters, and you don't. But suppose it's everything? Then he should do it. I'll survive it if I have to.'

There was a silence. He drank his tea, and looked admiringly around the book-lined room. When he spoke, it was with the voice of one introducing an entirely new subject.

'That's a very civilized fellow in the hotel, Dick Dillon, brother of the man running it, I think. Very pleasant sort of a man altogether. Someone you could always rely on, I'd imagine, if there was a crisis.'

'I'm sure you imagine right, Father Flynn. Such a pity that you got over this tendency to play God, isn't it? You could have had a field day there.'

Before he left Castlebay Father Flynn decided to buy a few postcards of the place: not the garish ones which looked like everywhere else, but those nice black and white ones full of outlines which Angela often used to send him.

He asked Josie Dillon where they were on sale.

'We haven't had them for ages. I used to put them up just to please Gerry Doyle – that's the photographer – he took them, you see. But visitors mainly preferred the coloured ones. But now you mention it, he never brought any replacements. You could ask in Doyle's, it's the place with the big bright sign, Doyle's Photographics. You can't miss it.'

You couldn't miss it. Josie Dillon was right.

There was a small, dark-haired man inside.

'Father? What can I do for you?'

He was a likeable fellow, with an easy smile.

'This is a very grand place.' Father Flynn looked round in admiration. 'I'd not have thought Castlebay would have something so fine as this.'

'Don't let my mother hear you, or my sister, or, Lord rest him, my father. They would all agree with you.'

'Well I'm not a businessman – what would I know? Is it too small an order to ask do you have those nice pictures of the place, the black and white ones. They were very good. I kept the ones people sent me.'

Gerry flushed with pleasure. 'Go on, is that a fact?'

'I can't find them in the shops.'

'I didn't bother. Hold on till I see where they are.' He pulled out drawers here and there, and called to an assistant. There was difficulty in finding them.

'It doesn't look as though I'm much of a businessman either,' Gerry grinned.

'If it's too much trouble . . .' Father Flynn began.

'No. It's a matter of honour now.' He found them. 'Here they are.'

'Could I have . . . er a dozen, please, assorted views.' Father Flynn had been going to buy three cards, but after all this trouble on his behalf he felt it would seem piffling.

Gerry had made a bundle and thrust them at him.

'There's more than twelve there.'

'Nobody else ever praised them before. I'd like you to have them. As a present.'

'That's extraordinarily kind of you . . . Mr Doyle,' Father Flynn said in some embarrassment.

'Not at all. You keep sending them to bishops and priests and tell them to get their ordinations and enthronements recorded by me.'

'You're a very fine photographer. I'd be delighted to put any work in your way. But I'm sure you hardly need it.'

Father Flynn looked around again at the big counter, the carpeted floor, the large framed photographs on the wall. It had all the appearances of a studio in a large city. He recognized a picture of Clare on the wall – taken a few years ago, but very recognizable as the same face.

'Is that Clare?' he asked.

'Do you know Clare?' Gerry was pleased. 'That was when she got the Murray Prize, a scholarship to UCD. They sent me to take the winner. I never believed it was going to be Clare. I hadn't enough faith. Fortunately she did.'

'She works very hard, certainly. I met her with friends in Dublin.' Something made him uneasy about the way Gerry was looking at the picture.

'She's very unusual. For Castlebay that is. I don't think she's from here at all. I think she's a changeling. I've always thought that. Like myself.' He laughed to take the oddness away from the statement. 'That's why I'll marry her. When she's ready. When she's got all this studying out of her system.'

'And bring her back here?' Father Flynn sounded politely doubtful: inside he felt a slight tremor of anxiety.

'Oh, no. Clare's grown well beyond Castlebay. And as soon as I get this business organized, so will I.'

'Tell me about Gerry Doyle. The photographer,' Father Flynn asked Dick Dillon.

'Trouble from way back,' said Dick. 'But the women won't hear a word against him. Even a sensible woman like Angela O'Hara says he's got a nice way with him.' Dick Dillon snorted, and Father Flynn shivered a little in the sunshine.

Sometimes they finished at about ten o'clock, and everyone else in the Res went for a few drinks before closing time. But David never joined them. These days, he would hare out of the hospital down to the bus stop.

'I don't know why you even call it the Residence,' one of the other doctors said to him. 'You barely reside here at all.'

David grinned. 'I had no idea we were going to be on call so much, I thought we'd have far more freedom.'

'No, you didn't. You knew you'd be cooped up here, you just didn't think you'd meet such an available girl.' The red-headed registrar laughed at his own perception.

David Power's face was cold and hard. 'I beg your pardon?' he said.

'It was only a joke . . .'

'I didn't think it was a bit funny.'

'No . . . Well, I'm sorry. I mean I don't know anything about it, I know nothing.'

'That's right, you know nothing, which gives you licence to say everything. That about sums you up.'

He marched, white with anger, out of the Res sitting room, having thrown his white coat over the back of a chair.

'What did I say?' Bar pleaded to the empty room.

It was cold and wet. The bus took for ever to arrive and even longer to get to Rathmines. He burned with rage still. A nice, *available* girl. *Available. Clare.* How dare he?

David was tired and very much on edge when he climbed the stairs. Clare was at the makeshift desk they had rigged up for her with planks of wood and builder's bricks. She was wearing mittens on her hands which made her look so endearing he stopped and stared at her with pleasure.

Her eyes were tired and had circles under them. 'Lord, are you home already? Is that the time?'

He was pleased she called it home, but a little disappointed that she hadn't been waiting for him, looking out for him.

'Did you get a lot done today?'

'I'm back into it again, thank heavens. I didn't notice the time or anything. I heard a man selling oil so I rushed downstairs with the can and got some.' She looked proudly at the glowing little oil heater.

'It's lovely and cosy. What are we having to eat?'

She looked stricken. 'There's nothing. I meant to get something.'

'There must be something. Toast even?'

'No. There's nothing.' She opened the little press. 'Look, real Mother Hubbard stuff. Bare. We'll go out and get chips,' she added when she saw how disappointed he was.

'I only just got in,' he said. 'I'm dog tired.'

Clare got up and reached for her coat. 'Stay here, I'll go out for chips and bring them home.'

'Then I'll be here all on my own,' he grumbled.

She looked at him startled. This wasn't his way of talking.

'Darling Clare, I'm sorry. I'm just desperately overtired, I hardly know what I'm saying.'

She was full of concern. 'What are you apologizing for? Sit there. Rest for ten minutes. I'll be back and we'll have a feast.' She wouldn't hear of him moving.

She took his shoes off and pulled the two pillows into a bundle behind him. She said no to money, she had some. Dinner would be her treat. She was gone down the stairs, and he felt guilty.

What a way to come home. Like a typical husband shouting, 'Where's my tea?' This was a hopeless way to go on. Both of them so tired they could hardly talk. No money, no comfort. If they had more money Clare could have lived in a flat near the hospital: they wouldn't have this smelly stove, and this filthy house with bicycles, and the smell of urine downstairs in the hall.

He felt restless, got up and walked over to her desk. In her big, firm writing with the funny old-fashioned fountain pen and ink, not a ballpoint like everyone else, she had pages of notes.

She had been concentrating on economic history lately. The works of John Maynard Keynes were this week's project . . . she had taken notes in the library, now she had been sorting them out and fitting them into her scheme. She was so bright and hungry to know. He wondered had he lost some of that himself, he used to feel a bit that way at school, and so did James Nolan then. Nowadays James was so languid it was hard to know what he felt, and David was so tired and so used to sleeping with an ear ready to be called to a ward that he would have thought that hunger for information was a luxury.

There was a letter to Clare on the desk in a brown business envelope. The odd thing was that it was addressed here, to this flat. Nobody knew they lived there, *nobody*. And even worse, it was addressed to her as Clare O'Brien. They had told the landlord they were married. It had a Castlebay postmark.

David had never read anyone else's letter in his life. This time he justified it. He wanted to know. If he asked her she would tell him, and there would be an explanation; but he had already been so testy and crotchety tonight he didn't trust himself. He would just have a quick look and then nothing need be said. He pulled the short letter out of the envelope. It was on headed paper which said 'Doyle's Photographics' and it was signed Love Gerry.

Clare had bought them a choc-ice each as a treat. The man in the shop said they must be supermen to eat ice cream in weather like this. She unwrapped the chips and found plates. There was an awful plastic flower in a pot which they always put on their table for meals and made jokes about Doing the Flowers. They had tomato sauce and salt as well as the vinegar that the shop had provided. Clare chattered happily about the advantages of living in bed-sitter land where you could go out any hour of the day and night and get food.

David said nothing.

'Lord, you really are tired. Maybe you should just go to bed a couple of the really bad nights there, so you don't have to drag yourself up here.'

'Maybe,' he said.

'Did anything happen?'

'No.'

'Is anything worrying you, then?'

'That letter.' He pointed to the desk.

'What letter?' She stood up. There were two letters: one was from her mother addressed to The Ladies' Reading Room at UCD. She had said that this was a quicker way of getting your post and her mother hadn't questioned it.

'This one?' she held up the brown envelope.

'Yes.'

'If you read it, why are you worried?' Her voice was cold now.

'I didn't read it. I swear to you. But I know who it's from. And I was wondering why you gave him our address and told him you lived here. This is our secret. And we're meant to be man and wife. Why the hell is Gerry-bloody-Doyle allowed into anything and everything? And don't tell me what everyone says when his name is mentioned, that *it doesn't count telling Gerry*, or *Gerry knows everything*, or *everyone loves Gerry*, because I find that sickening.'

She had taken the letter out of the envelope and was reading:

Dear Clare,
I did what you asked me, I hope to hell it doesn't get lost in the post or I'll look a nice criminal.
　　The place is full of activity here, your Chrissie getting ready to produce your nephew or niece, our Fiona getting ready to marry Frank Conway, Josie walking out with a very suitable older man. I suppose you know all the details. Only you and I left around from the old guard.
　　Send a card or something so that I know it arrived OK.
Love Gerry.

She read this, brushing aside his protestations that he didn't want to hear it. She threw the letter on the bed at him, she reached into a drawer and took out a post office book and threw that too.

'I asked him to get my post office book for me from my room at home in Castlebay. I didn't want Mam asking what I needed my savings for. I need my savings, you bloody, suspicious, mean-minded pig, because now that I live here I have to buy things that I didn't have to buy when I lived in the hostel. Like milk, and bread, and tea, and sugar, and packets of soup and Vim. And I pay a share of the rent here. And it all costs money. And I don't have a penny left. In fact I owe Valerie three pounds. So in order not to appear a kept woman or a hanger-on, or to define even *more* the fact that I am poor Clare O'Brien and you are rich David Power, I sent for my savings account.'

Her eyes blazed with rage. 'I asked him to send it here because I didn't want a valuable thing like a post office book with sixty-three pounds in it, money I've been saving for three years, to get lost in college or get mislaid at the hostel. And Gerry Doyle doesn't give a tuppenny damn if I live here or on the top of the Dublin mountains, so I gave him this address. *And* I was not going to tell him that I am pretending to be your wife, so I gave him my name. *And* the landlord no more thinks we're married than he thinks that he's charging us a fair rent.'

Her hair had fallen over her face as she spoke. She lifted her plate of chips and poured them roughly onto David's plate.

'I have no appetite now, I'd do anything rather than share a meal with such a mean-minded human being.'

'Come back . . . come back!' he called.

'I'll *not* come back. Not tonight. I'll come back tomorrow when you've gone.'

She had grabbed up a few papers and put them into her duffle bag, she had pulled the nighty from under the pillow.

'Clare, you can't go out in that rain . . .'

'I went out once, to get *your* supper, didn't I? To give *you* time to poke around and make accusations. Go to *hell*!'

She ran faster than he did and jumped on the last bus going towards the city. She got off and slipped round behind the hostel looking left and right. She climbed the rungs, praying that Valerie and Mary Catherine might be out. But it was not a night for prayers to be answered.

They were reading magazines and listening to Chris Barber on their small portable record player. When she came through the window, furious and dripping, they were convulsed with laughter. They laughed as they got one of the younger and more frightened occupants of the hostel to go for tea, and they laughed as they gave her a big bath towel and ran a bath for her in the big old bathroom at the end of the corridor.

They felt that it called for even more than tea, so the brandy was taken out from the drawer. And eventually she laughed too. She laughed as she dried her hair and sipped the tea with brandy in it and told them the outline of the story. And then eventually she went to bed in the third bed.

Valerie and Mary Catherine had fought like tigers not to have a third girl. They said that since Clare had paid until Easter anyway it would be double letting, and the nuns couldn't do anything as dishonest as that, could they? Secretly Mary Catherine had been certain that Clare would be back: she felt that the romance with David was not going to get beyond first base. But she said none of this as Clare sighed happily and settled back into her old familiar place. Neither did Valerie.

'I'm really sorry. It makes me such an eeejit,' Clare said.

'Nonsense, it makes you much nicer,' said Valerie. 'Now we know you're still normal, and not all this awful sickening peace and calm of true love. That was the distressing bit.'

Bar apologized to him formally as they were having coffee the next morning.

'I'm afraid I spoke out of order last night. I meant no disrespect.'

'That's fine. Sure. Thanks,' David mumbled.

'You look a bit rough. I don't want to say anything that you'll take amiss, but are you all right?'

'Sure, I'm fine.' David swallowed his coffee and went back on the wards. He had spent about three hours tidying the flat. He had removed all the rubbish, including the uneaten chips. This morning he had gone out and bought supplies of tea, coffee, milk, sugar, cornflakes, sardines and oranges. He had arranged them as well as he could, and he had bought a vase too. He left the vase on the desk with a note:

This is for the flowers I would like to bring you tonight. I'll understand if you don't want me. But I will be heartbroken. You are all I ever dreamed of and hoped for. You are much, much more. Please know that I didn't think I was mean-minded. But I realize I am. I don't want you to put your arms around me and say it's all right, that you forgive me. I want you to be *sure* that you do, and to know that my love for you will last as long as I live. I can see no lightness, no humour, no joke to make. I just hope that we will be able to go back to when we had laughter, and the world was coloured, not black and white and grey. I am so sorry for hurting you. I could inflict all kinds of pain on myself, but it would not take back any I gave to you.

He had written it over and over to try to take out the phrases that sounded tired. He tried to make it just himself. But he was in such unaccustomed low form, it didn't end up sounding like him. Perhaps he should have just left a card with a heart on it, or should he have gone round to the hostel after her last night? He had telephoned from a phone box and asked to speak to Mary Catherine. The nun on duty had asked did he know the time, all the young ladies were in bed, he could leave a message in an emergency. He had hung up. Perhaps he should have feigned illness at the hospital and taken a day off. He could have waited at the bottom of those rungs, Clare would have had to come down that way, she wasn't meant to be a resident. Perhaps he should have stood in the hall up at UCD and waited till she came in for lectures.

Most of the morning was spent speculating between beds.

The secretary at the front desk handed him a note as he passed. 'This just came for you, Dr Power.'

In her big firm handwriting she had written:

It was just our First Row. That's *all* it was. Of course I love you. I'm hot-headed and impatient and I'm very sorry for that too. I am ashamed I ran out and left you there, tired and depressed. I love you and I'm greatly looking forward to those flowers and whatever else you might think of as a way to spend the evening.

They were often too tired to talk, too tired to make love when they went to their bed, but not irritably tired. They looked forward to David's proper leave days with excitement and planned them down to the last detail. They went to the zoo, which was lovely in the winter because it wasn't crowded, and they went out to Bray on the train one day and climbed Bray Head to look all over County Wicklow and County Dublin.

Sometimes they ate out, and they had gone to the pictures with Mary Catherine and Valerie one night. But they didn't mix much with David's hospital set, and they didn't look up old friends. James had given up on Mary Catherine and he seemed to be in a very social set. David and Clare didn't need James Nolan, they didn't need anyone but each other.

They had decided not to think about the future yet. David was going round doing interviews for hospitals where he would do his Post Intern year once he finished his present post in July. Clare had her mind fixed firmly on her degree.

By next September they would both be earning money, they would afford a better place, they would not get married yet, they just skated over that bit, but neither of them wanted to bring on the storm. Up here in Dublin in their own little world, nothing mattered, nobody bothered them.

They would be all right unless something happened.

Coming up to Easter two things happened.

Dr Power had a mild stroke.

And Clare discovered she was pregnant.

It was Angela who found him when he passed out. He was just getting into his car, which he had parked a quarter of a mile from the golf club in order to give himself a little walk. He had bandaged the finger of the barman, delivered a strong lecture on the danger of sharp knives, and explained that it didn't matter whether a lemon was finely sliced for drinks but it did matter if dangerous knives were left where people could cut their hands on them.

He walked cheerfully down to the car and then felt everything go dark. He realized that he must be about to faint and lowered himself to the ground beside his car. He tried to call out but he could hear a rushing sound and knew that he was losing consciousness.

Angela was hanging up some clothes on the washing line. She saw the car, and just as she was about to turn back into her house, she saw his black bag thrown on the ground. She ran quickly and was at his side when he was recovering consciousness.

'Did you have a fall?' she said.

'No, Jhangelgha,' he said. 'Shmore a vainting . . .' His voice sounded very odd. As if he were drunk. She was practical as he would have expected.

'Tell me what to do in yeses or nos. Can you stand up if I help you?'

'Yesh.'

'Will I open the door and put you sitting in the car?'

'Yesh.'

He started to speak again, she had the door open and the big man seated in the passenger seat.

'Now, do you want me to get your wife, or to go to a phone and call the hospital in the town? Sorry you have to answer yes or no. Will I get Mrs Power?'

'No.'

'Will I phone the hospital?'

'No. Drive.'

'No, Dr Power. I could curse myself to the pit of hell but I can't drive. Let me get someone to drive you . . . is it safe to leave you here?'

'Yesh. Shafe.'

'Very well, I'll get my bike, I'll be back in five minutes . . .'

'Anjheala.' He seemed agitated.

'Trust me, trust me. I'll get the right person. Are you better here or would you like me to help you back to my house?'

'Alrigth.'

She was a blur of bicycle wheels and then he heard a car coming. Dick Dillon and Gerry Doyle stepped out. The two men he would have picked himself in the whole of Castlebay.

They had been marvellous to him in the hospital, masking their shock that it was the man himself who needed a bed, not one of his patients.

One of his oldest friends Tim Daly was with him in no time. 'That's a light one, Paddy, take more than that to put you in a wheelchair,' he said.

That was what Paddy Power wanted, no fancy chat, no pretending nothing had happened. He knew a stroke when he saw one, and even more so when he had just been through one.

He pointed at his mouth. 'Shpeesh,' he said.

'Sure, that can go on for a day or two even in the slightest of strokes, you know that.'

'Shide,' he said indicating the side of his body.

'Same thing, it's not paralysed in any strict sense, it's just a bit numb.'

'Yesh.' Power's face was sad.

'Will I drive out to Molly myself, and tell her we're keeping you here for a few days, bring her in with me maybe?'

'Itsh far.'

'No it's not. It's no trouble. And would you like me to tell David? There's no need, as you well know. You could stay here and come out and he need never be any the wiser. Is that what you'd like?'

'Yesh.'

'Sleep a bit, Paddy. It's hard I know, but it's what will do you good . . .'

'Tim . . . Tim . . . locum.' He was straining.

'I have it in hand. I've told him three weeks, you're not to get frightened. I said that, so that you can have a real rest, maybe a week away somewhere with Molly.'

Dr Power closed his eyes, secure at last that everything was under control.

Tim Daly was right. It was a very light one. So light that it was never even referred to as a stroke. Dr Power said that it wouldn't give a young mother confidence if she thought that the doctor attending the birth of her first baby might keel over paralysed. It was described as a little turn and it caused hardly any comment in Castlebay. The locum doctor was a nice man too and not a bit put out by people saying that if he didn't mind they'd wait until Dr Power was ready before they'd have their stitches out or go for those blood tests.

Dr Mackey had lived for a long time in the North of England in industrial towns. He thought the peace of Castlebay was something that should be bottled and put on prescription for those who were tense or anxious all over the world.

'Faith and there's a fair few very tense and anxious here all the same,' Paddy Power said to him. He, Dr Mackey, and Dr Tim Daly were all having a progress discussion. Paddy had been out of hospital for a week: Dr Mackey was still booked for another ten days. The speech had fully returned to normal and there was no more trace of numbness. But Paddy agreed that it was a warning, and agreed further that his own advice to anyone in similar circumstances would be cut down drastically. He knew there should be no more night calls. He would in fact have to cut out a lot of his long drives over bad roads on home calls. He needed someone else to help him. Since there would not be a living for two doctors, he would need a younger man as an assistant. That man should be the one who intended to follow him. David.

'I have written to him. It was easier to write than to say.'

'You're not asking him much,' sniffed Dr Mackey. 'To come back to a ready-made practice. You can teach him all he doesn't know already. You won't be a dog in the manger trying to keep the good will – an *ideal* set-up for any young doctor.'

Dr Power sighed. 'Ah yes, but this young doctor was all set to do his paediatrics and then obstetrics and then the Lord knows what . . . he hadn't it in his mind to come back now. That's what I said to him, I said I knew it was bad timing. He's coming home tomorrow. The hospital gave him compassionate leave. He had to tell them I was at death's doors but he'll be here tomorrow.'

Molly came in with Nellie and a tea tray. Molly had surprised them all by being so calm. They had expected hysterics and they had got a very practical woman. She had even agreed that David should not be alerted until they knew the extent of the trouble.

Tim Daly thought that he must have misjudged her. He had often said to his own wife that Paddy Power had deserved someone less feathery and citified than Molly; but maybe he had been wrong. Anyway there was never any doubt about that son of his, a big, square, handsome, bright lad. Tim Daly sighed again thinking of the strange hand of fate that had dealt him five daughters in succession and no boy anywhere along the line.

David knew about his father before he got the letter. He had heard from Angela almost immediately after it happened. She wrote that she was becoming increasingly unable to mind her own business as she grew older and unable to avoid meddling in other people's affairs, but just in case he would need more time to think about it than he would get, his father planned to write to him in a few days and tell him of a mild stroke which was genuinely believed to have been slight and no threat to his life, but which would mean that he might need David much sooner than expected. Angela said that he mustn't acknowledge the letter or anything, it was just sometimes nicer to be forewarned.

She had written to him at his hospital, and without her having to put it in writing he knew she hadn't written to Clare. It was to give him time to think. It was all bad news but he thanked her deep in his heart.

He thought. Three times he was pulled up for not paying attention, and on one occasion a patient said to him that he looked as if he was on another planet.

He went into a cubicle in casualty and sat on the bed. Suppose he did go home? In July, when he finished this intern year? Suppose Clare studied on, back and forth from Castlebay to Dublin? Suppose she took her degree and was accepted for M.A.? It was by thesis. You could write a thesis anywhere, couldn't you? He was desperately vague. Could you do it from Castlebay?

He rang the admissions office of the university, and the voice kept saying he would have to come in and discuss it.

'*God damn it!*' David cried. 'There must be a *rule*. Can people do their M.A. without being in the university or not? *Yes* or *No*? Is that too much to ask?'

It was, or the tone in which he asked was too much to reply to.

He couldn't go back to hide in the cubicle, it was time to go back to work.

He had hidden nothing from Clare up to now and there was no point in pussyfooting around and trying to get non-existent information about her degree. Anyway, their futures were together. She deserved to know anything that he knew.

He would do no special pleading.

He wouldn't try to sell her on the idea of going home. He wouldn't apologize for his father's ill health.

He would tell her no flowery tales about how much she would love his mother once David and Clare were married.

He would gloss over nothing.

But he must tell her.

There was no bus coming so he decided to walk. He saw he coming up the road towards him, hands in pockets, thoughtful.

'You came to meet me,' he cried.

'Yes, I wondered if we could go somewhere just to have a drink maybe?'

'That's great.' He tucked her arm into his. It would be easier to tell her in a pub that their life in Dublin, their freedom, their study, was going to be cut short.

He carried the drinks to the corner table. He would tell her at once.

'David. You're not going to like this. But it's no use putting it off. I'm pregnant.'

There was a long silence.

'I'm very sorry. But it's confirmed. I sent a sample to Holles Street. It's positive, and I . . . well, I know . . .'

'But you *can't* be . . . we took such care.'

'Not enough, it seems.' She looked very small and young and frightened.

'Oh Clare, Clare,' he said. 'What will we do?'

'I don't know. I've had two weeks to wonder and worry. And I still don't know.'

'You should have told me.'

'What was the point? Silly, frightening both of us to death unless it was definite.'

'And it's *definitely* definite?'

'It is David. It is.'

He put his head in his hands. 'Oh *Christ*,' he said. '*Christ, God*, isn't that so unfair. Isn't that *all* we need.'

His drink was untouched and so was hers. Nobody was near enough to hear them or have any idea what they were talking about.

She sat icy and withdrawn. She had hoped he would touch her, put his arms around her. Now she felt she would kill him if he tried.

He took his head out of his hands, hair tousled, face flushed. 'I'm sorry,' he said.

'What for?'

'For it happening. I'm meant to be a doctor. Some medical knowledge I have.'

'Don't worry about *that*. It's not an exam. Nobody's going to give you marks or take them away for it.'

'Clare!'

'Well? What else is there to say?'

'I don't know. I suppose we should think what we'll do . . .'

She was silent.

'Make plans . . . It's just, just such a shock, and such a bloody shame. Now of all times.'

'Yes,' she said.

Her face looked small, white and hurt. He remembered suddenly that he hadn't told her about his father. She didn't even know that side of it. He remembered too that she was in the most feared condition of any girl from any small town and maybe any big town in Ireland. She was In Trouble.

He reached out for her hand. 'We'll sort it out,' he said.

She pulled her hand away.

'You haven't touched your drink,' he said awkwardly.

'Neither have you.' The pint looked too big and too sour.

'I think I'll have a brandy,' David said. 'Would you like that, for the shock? Doctor's orders.' He tried a watery smile.

'No. Thank you,' Clare said.

When he came back, she leaned across the table. 'I'm terribly, terribly sorry. I can't say any more. I know how frightening this must be for you, David. I'm trying to keep calm and think what on earth we're going to do. But you probably don't know what you feel yet. It's probably still unreal to you.'

'Yes. That's right,' he said, grateful that she understood that much.

There was another silence.

He drained his brandy. 'Will we go home?' he said.

They stood up and left, each afraid to touch the other and walking several paces apart.

Out in the street the yellow light shone down and made their faces look even more strained. They walked in silence towards the bus stop where David had been heading less than an hour before. They sat silent on the bus, too. Once or twice they looked at each other as if to say something but the words didn't come.

About two stops before their own David stood up. 'Will we get out here?' he asked her diffidently.

'Yes. Of course.' She was very polite. Under normal circumstances she would have questioned him and joked and argued.

They were beside the canal. 'Let's walk a little here,' he said.

They walked in silence and both stopped when two swans glided up to them.

'I only have a bit of chewing gum,' Clare said in almost her ordinary voice. 'Do you think they'd like it, or would it stick their beaks together?'

'Will you marry me?' David said.

'What?'

'Will you marry me. Please.'

'David?' her voice was low and unsure.

'*Please*,' he said again.

'David, you don't have to say anything yet. Don't say anything now. I don't expect you to . . . you don't have to. Honestly. We'll talk, we'll make plans, it's not the end of the world.'

'I know. I love you,' he said.

'And I love you. That's never changed, that never will.'

'So,' he said, eyes shining. 'We'll get married. Now rather than later. Won't we? Say yes. Say, "Yes David." '

'You know I'd love to, but there are other things, other possibilities which we should discuss. You know that.'

'Not with *our* baby, our own child. No other possibilities.'

She stared at him, her eyes filling with tears.

'You haven't given me your answer, like they do in stories.' He was eager and still not sure what she would say.

She paused and took his face in her hands. 'If you mean it . . .' she began.

'That's not an answer, that's a conditional clause,' he said.

'I would love to marry you. Yes. Yes, *please*.'

They walked home and bought chips, and wine, and a chocolate cake. They sat down by their oil stove to make plans and to think about the future.

'Can we get married here? In Dublin? I couldn't bear it at home.'

'That's not the way my wife is going to talk about our big day!'

'You know what I mean.'

'Yes. Of course we'll get married here. Wherever you like. London. Paris. Rome.'

'And then we'll come back and get ourselves a bigger flat, and wait till the exam and the baby. There's a month between them. The finals are over at the end of September and the baby arrives in October, the third week.'

He held her hand between his. 'Isn't it marvellous,' he said again.

'I'm so glad you're pleased. I was afraid that when you get your job in the hospital, you wouldn't like coming home at night to a baby.' She smiled at him. He said nothing.

'I mean it's not what a young doctor, a junior hospital doctor wants to come back to, a flat of nappies and a wife at her studies . . .' She was worried by his sudden silence. 'But the great thing is that I *will* be able to do a lot of work at home, I was discussing it with one of the postgrad students. She said that as long as they know your circumstances and can see that you're in there and doing the work and consulting every week or so, you don't have to present yourself every day or anything.'

'Oh.'

'What is it?'

Then he told her about his father's stroke, and that they would have to go back to Castlebay.

Because of Angela's letter, they had five days. Five terrible days. Sometimes they raged at each other, sometimes they just clung together. There were times when they were calm and worked out the alternatives. There were no alternatives. Sometimes Clare taunted him and said he was a Mummy's Boy. No other man would throw his whole career away. Sometimes he wounded her and said that her love was meaningless and shallow if it could change because of place. True love survived wherever it lived. They knew of a doctor that Clare could go to – he had been struck off the medical register, but he did a steady practice in terminations. Because he was a doctor, it wouldn't be dangerous. Then they could think again. But they never talked of that seriously. The miracle of a child of their own seemed about the only cheerful thing in the middle of all the tears and confusion. They would solve none of the dilemma if the baby were taken out of the picture. The pregnancy, and having to tell both families, was not the biggest thing.

The biggest thing was going back.

Neither of them wanted to.

David was going to.

That's where it stood when David got the letter from his father.

Clare cried and cried when she read the letter. It was so generous, so understanding. The old man had put down on paper all the things they had been talking about during the week. He said he regretted so much asking this of David that he barely had the strength to write it. He set out clearly the impossibility of asking another doctor to hold the fort for three or four years until David might feel ready to return. He sympathized almost dispassionately with David.

> What is very hard, for both of us, is this emotional blackmail. I hate to ask you back: you hate to give up your plans. But I have to ask and you have to say yes or no. If I had died, then your decision would be much more clear cut. If you had not wanted to take over this practice then it would have been far easier for you not to have done so. Your mother might have moved to Dublin and nobody would have been greatly hurt or let down. This, I am afraid, is the hardest way and I am well aware of it.
>
> All I can do is try to make it as attractive for you as I can. This house is yours, as you know, but you might feel more independent if you had a place of your own. We could do up the Lodge for you so that you could have a private life of your own and not feel like a little boy again. But the other thing of course, David, is that a doctor in a small community like this can't have much excitement in his private life, if you know what I mean. It's all very hard on you, boy, it's a letter I hate having to write to you . . .

The Lodge. It was a small house just within the half-acre garden of the Powers' residence. It needed a new roof. It had about four rooms, David thought. No kitchen, and only an outside lavatory. They had always been intending to get it done up. At the moment it just housed extra furniture.

It would be their new home.

They travelled back on the train together.

This time they were quiet. They looked out as the fields and telephone wires flashed by. At one place where the train slowed down there were children at a gate waving excitedly at the passengers. A six-year-old held up a fat baby who waved like mad with his two fat arms and his face split into a grin showing one tooth. David and Clare automatically reached for each other's hand. By Christmas they would have something like that. Not as big, not with a tooth, but a bit like that. They gave each other encouraging smiles. They weren't silent out of pique, or despair. It was just that they had been over the plans so often they didn't even want to mention them again.

The plans were complicated. Clare was going to stay on the train while David left as one of the first passengers. His mother would meet him and he would hasten her out of the car park as quickly as possible. Clare had asked Angela to arrange for someone to meet her. She had telephoned Angela at school, and could almost see the disapproving face of Immaculata.

Clare had said that for reasons she would explain later she didn't want to be met by Gerry Doyle, but anyone else, and for reasons which she would also explain she would be the last person to leave the train, well after Mrs Power had cleared the car park. Angela said she understood perfectly.

She felt sick when he went through the ticket barrier without a backward glance, as they had arranged.

She waited till a porter walked through the train picking up newspapers before she got out.

The ticket checker was surprised. 'Well, now! I was off to my tea. Fall asleep on the train, did you?'

Clare smiled at him. Lucky man. Just his tea to worry about.

In the car park Dick stood, waving enthusiastically and coming forward to carry her bag.

Molly Power wore driving gloves. She had been told that they gave you a better grip on the wheel. She looked very well, David thought, her hair freshly done, a nice wool two-piece in a soft green – not the fussy, insecure over made-up woman he had met a few short months ago at the Nolans' house.

She was calm and practical about his father too. She understood the nature of his attack and the need not to exert himself. There was no evidence of panic or anxiety. She spoke pleasantly of Dr Mackey the locum, of the great delight that David had returned home so quickly to discuss things, of the conversation she had held with Bumper Byrne about getting the Lodge fixed up.

David raked her face for clues of how she would react in a couple of hours when she knew she was going to have Clare O'Brien as a daughter-in-law.

Dick Dillon was easy to talk to. He talked about things, not people. She asked was it easy to learn to drive, and he said it was very easy. He showed her the pedals at his feet and said he'd have the theory of it taught to her by the time they got back to Castlebay. And indeed he had. A was accelerator, B was brakes and C was clutch.

She studied his big feet in their neatly-laced, shiny brown shoes as he told her what he was doing each time. 'I see, you have your foot heavy on C and lightly on A and as you release C you press A. I have it,' she said excitedly. 'And now you're pressing B because you want to slow down at the crossroads,' she said.

'I want to *Stop* at this crossroads, Madam. Because I see a big sign saying *Stop*.'

'That's great. I have the hang of it. I'll get a licence as soon as I can.' She would need to know how to drive, and to drive far, if she were going to be living in Molly Power's garden.

His father listened attentively. David said they had hoped to marry in a couple of years' time and he had hoped to get further experience in Dublin hospitals. But now, since circumstances said otherwise, they were happy to come back and start both married life and practice all at the same time.

His father looked thoughtful. Weren't they very, very young to settle down? Clare wasn't twenty yet, well, only barely twenty. Still very young.

No. David was firm. Circumstances had changed so they would marry now. In a few weeks' time in Dublin.

'So Clare is pregnant.'

'We're very very pleased,' David said defiantly.

'You may well be. But is it the best start for a marriage, for a young girl like Clare, for the baby?'

'Dad, whether it is or not, it *has* started. We never thought for a moment of trying to unstart it.'

'No. No. I'm glad of that.'

'So, I suppose what I'm trying to say is, that once we've told Mum and once Clare has told her family, we'll just get on with it.'

'Is Clare home?'

'Yes.'

'You didn't say . . . Molly didn't say she was with you.'

'We thought it best to come separately from the station.'

Dr Power gave a very deep sigh.

'I'm sorry to have to break it to you like this, Dad.'

'You're very irresponsible, really, you know.'

'Well we didn't mean it to happen, obviously. But then, as you know, I'm sure only too well from all your years here, it just does happen.'

'I didn't expect it to happen to my own *son*. You shouldn't have taken advantage of her. It's not *fair*. Just because you knew her from home, because you knew she was going to be timid.'

'There was no taking advantage of her. You don't understand. In Dublin nobody thinks of Clare as poor little Clare O'Brien from the shop. That's only here. And not everyone here. It's mother, and a few people. I didn't think *you'd* be like that.'

'I'm not being like anything, boy. I realize you're upset. I'm just saying it was a pity that this had to happen to you. You, with your whole life ahead of you.'

'Ahead of us now, Dad. That's what I'm trying to tell you.'

'She's only a child, a child herself. She doesn't know what she wants.'

'Oh she does, she very much does. She's going to finish her degree, you know. Her finals are a month before the baby is born. So we want to get married as soon as possible.'

'It won't be soon enough for Castlebay.'

'Well to hell with what they think.'

Dr Power poured himself a very small brandy.

'It's medicinal. I prescribe it for myself now and then.'

'Are you going to drink my health? *Our* health?' David asked.

'Not immediately.'

'You're not shocked, Dad.'

'Not in that sense. I don't know. You're very young, David. You've only got one life. You don't have to marry Clare if you don't want to. You can be very honourable and just without marrying her. You can acknowledge the child and give her maintenance. But there's no shotgun at your head. Not today, not in 1960.'

'You've got it all out of proportion. The fact that Clare is pregnant is only part of a much bigger thing, which is that I love her. I love her desperately, Dad. I'll never want anyone else in the world. I couldn't contemplate anyone else marrying Clare. I didn't explain that properly.'

'I think I'll let you explain that to your mother. You'll have to do a fair bit of explaining there, so there's no point in doing it twice.'

'Do you think I could have a medicinal brandy?'

'No. I don't. I think you can make your explanations without any stimulant.'

'If I'm to be your partner in this practice, then I can prescribe too. I prescribe myself a brandy twice the size of yours.'

Dr Power laughed and poured it for him. 'Go to it, son,' he said.

'Aren't you coming with me?'

'No, I'm a man who mustn't have too much excitement. I'm going into my study.'

Agnes O'Brien had noticed that the tourist trade was beginning to have a bit of a surge at Easter. More and more people who owned their own caravans up in the site thought they should get value from them by coming more than once a year. She wasn't surprised to hear a ping on the door. She was very surprised to see Clare.

'What brings you back? You never said you were coming?'

'I got a chance, suddenly. So I came,' Clare said.

'You never wrote or anything.' Her mother was full of wonder. In her world people wrote letters announcing what they were going to do; *then* they did it.

'No. As I said, I just got the chance.' She must hide her impatience with her mother. 'Will we have a cup of tea or anything?'

'What am I thinking of, I didn't expect you, you see, come on in, give me your bag.'

'You look much better, Mam, how's your leg?'

'Oh, that's long forgotten, now haven't I enough to be worrying about without thinking of old ailments? No, thank God, I walk fine now, not even a bit of a limp.'

'That's great, Mam.'

'Well come on in, and don't stand there staring around as if you'd never seen the place before.'

'Where's everybody?'

'Your father's gone with Ben to get him a job, or we hope he will. There's a new garage opening out at the crossroads. They want two young fellows to work there. They'll have them trained by the summer, when the business will be great. Your father's gone up there with Ben. Ben's not great to give an account of himself.'

750

'When did they go?'

'They were to meet the man up there at six. Why?'

'I want to talk to you.'

Clare had put the Closed sign on the shop door. Agnes laid down the kettle without filling it.

'Mother of God, you're pregnant,' she said.

It took time for her mother to stop crying. Clare had time to fill the kettle, boil it, make the tea, cut them two slices of fruit cake and find two paper table napkins for her mother to use as a handkerchief.

'How you can sit there, as bold as brass, and tell me this? How you can do it? It's beyond belief!' her mother wept.

'Mam, I've told you nothing. I just nodded when you asked me was I pregnant. Then you started to cry. Now let me tell you what I really came home to tell you . . .'

'Oh! You weren't going to *bother* with this then, were you? This isn't *news* at all. This is something we were meant to expect, along with your high and mighty ways.'

'*Please*, Mam. Let me tell you. I'm getting married.'

'A bit late in the day for that isn't it?'

'No. Listen. I was going to get married anyway, and this just means we get married a bit sooner, that's all. Honestly, that's all. But it was the getting married bit I wanted to tell you about.'

'I'm not stopping you, tell me about it.' Agnes's eyes were red, she hadn't touched her tea and cake.

'It's David, David Power. We're getting married in a few weeks' time in Dublin, and then he's coming back here – I mean we're both coming back here. His father hasn't been well and . . .'

Agnes stood up. 'David Power! You let *David Power*, the doctor's son, make little of you, and get you into trouble? I don't believe it. I can't believe my own ears.'

She knew this was her mother's vocabulary. In advance she had warned herself of words like *disgrace* and *get into trouble*. But it still didn't make them easy to hear.

'I wish you wouldn't put it that way. At this moment he's up in his house telling his parents too. And whether this had happened or not we were going to get married anyway. So don't talk about people *making little* of other people, or of him *disgracing* me. I was just as eager, all the time, as he was.'

'Don't boast of it, you little tramp. Don't stand there like a slut in my kitchen and tell me what you were eager for and what you weren't. You've ruined us all in this family. We'll be the laughing stock of the place – marrying into the Powers no less. Do you think that Mrs Power is going to let the likes of *you* cross her doorstep? Do you think that woman is going to let her son, with the fine education he has, marry a girl from a shop in Castlebay? A girl who is no better than she should be?' Agnes was laughing now, a twisted, ugly laugh. 'Now, *I* never did even my Primary Certificate. *I'm* not college educated like you. And yet *I* can see with the two eyes in my head that there'll be no marriage. There'll be an *explanation*. David almighty Power will have to go abroad to finish his education – or some such excuse. Don't be fooling yourself, girl. There's going to be no wedding for you. Only *disgrace* and a child to bring up. And there's going to be nothing for us but jeers.' Agnes started to cry again.

Clare found herself pitying the thin woman with the rolled-up table napkins crying at her kitchen table.

She spoke very gently. 'Mam, listen to me. I know this is hard to believe. But it's true. David is twenty-five years of age. He's a grown man. He doesn't have to ask their permission for anything. We've arranged the marriage, and the priest. It *will* happen. If his mother turns against him, let her turn. She'll turn back eventually. You know the Lodge up in their garden near the cliff edge, well, Bumper Byrne is going to get it done up and that's where we're going to live. *Mam.* And when Chrissie's baby is born, she'll wheel hers down to see you, Mam, and I'll wheel mine along the Cliff Road. And there's no disgrace. No jeers. It's all *grand.* Don't you understand?'

Her mother looked up with tear-stained face. 'It's all very simple for you, Clare. But life isn't like that.'

'It is, Mam. I'm as good as David. In every way. He knows that. And so do I.'

'If you think that you'll be the only two in Castlebay who do,' her mother sniffed.

'Mam, drink your tea. Please, Mam.'

'When is it going to be born?' She looked at Clare's stomach.

'End of October. Just after my exams.'

'You're never going to go on with your exams.'

'But I have to. That's what it was all about, the three years. I've got weeks in hand. They may have to cut a hole in the desk for me to fit into it, but still I'll manage.'

'Don't say things like that.' Her mother had sipped the tea; she was getting back to normal.

'So what I was going to suggest was this: that we say David and I are getting married in Dublin, not having a big fussy wedding because we're both still studying, and then as soon as the house is done we'll be back. No need to mention anything else at all, is there?'

'But people aren't fools, Clare. They can count to nine like the rest of us. If someone gets married in April and has a baby in October, they'll know.'

'But what will they know that matters?' Clare's impatience was beginning to show.

Her mother sighed deeply. 'You'll never understand. And, Clare, child, if you believe they'll let you be happy here you'll believe anything.'

David decided to say it quickly.

'Mother, I've just had a long chat with Dad and it's all sorted out. I finish my internship, and come back here at the beginning of July.'

Her face brightened. 'I knew there'd be no problems. Paddy kept saying it was a pity to call you home before your time, but I said you'd be happy to come.'

'You were right. And I love the idea of the Lodge. I'll talk to Bumper Byrne myself tomorrow.'

'There's no real hurry with the Lodge, is there? Your room is there ...'

'Well . . . you see . . . I've other plans too, Mother. This is my big news. I'm getting married.'

'*David!* You can't be *serious*. You've never told us a word . . . we didn't even know you were courting. Paddy, Paddy . . .'

'He's gone to the study. I wanted to tell you myself.'

'But haven't you told him . . . ?'

'Yes. He knows.'

She suspected trouble.

'I just thought I'd tell you myself, in my own way. I'm going to marry Clare O'Brien. Very soon. In four weeks' time. In Dublin. And as soon as she has finished her degree she will come back here and we will live in the Lodge.'

The colour had gone from Molly's face. She was standing, she had jumped up in her first excitement. Now she swayed slightly, and held on to the back of the chair.

'We intended to get married later on, and live in Dublin. But, of course, now, with Dad needing me back at home that's all changed.'

'*Clare O'Brien.*'

'So we're not having any big wedding, or any fuss. But Father Flynn, do you remember him, he's going to be over again, he's going to be based in Dublin now and he's going to marry us . . .'

'I don't believe it.'

He deliberately misunderstood her. 'Oh, but he is. And he's been very helpful about it all.'

'You know what I mean. I cannot believe that you are being forced to marry that girl. No matter what you may have done.'

'Not forced. We want to. I've explained that. We've planned this for a long time.'

'When you discovered she was up the pole.'

David swallowed. He had rehearsed with Clare how they would behave when their parents said the unforgivable things, when the accusations started. Somehow he hadn't thought his mother would use such a coarse expression. 'That's a vulgar way of describing it.'

'She's a *vulgar* girl.'

He was very calm. 'No, that's not true. Clare isn't in the least vulgar. She is gentle and sensitive, she is bright and well educated and considerate. I would never think of her as vulgar. Never. But she is poor. And her family are poor and uneducated. And her sister Chrissie is most definitely vulgar.' He spoke without any anger.

'David. You *mustn't* do this.'

'I'm going to say this very carefully. So please listen to me. Just listen, and then talk later. It's very important. Nothing you say, *nothing*, will make me change my mind. I love Clare. I *will* marry her. And we *will* be happy. And we will have a child in October. And any harsh words you say now will only make things difficult between us, always, so I'm going to beg you not to say anything until you've had some time to think . . .'

She was without words. Looking at him.

He moved towards her. She stiffened as if forbidding him to touch her.

'I don't know what to do, Mummy,' he said, using the form of address he hadn't used for years. 'I really don't. You see I want to talk to you about it all now, and tell you about how happy I am and how much Clare means to me. But I'm afraid . . . I'm afraid you'll say something so hurtful that I'd find it hard to forgive.'

She nodded mutely.

'So I'm going to go out with Bones for a bit. I'll come back in at half-past eight. And then I'm going to meet Clare at nine in the hotel. She will have told her family then too.'

'*David* . . .' It was a sad cry.

He left the room and, pretending he didn't see his father hovering at the study door, called for Bones. He looked back at the end of the drive, and he saw the two silhouettes in the window. He saw his father put his arms around his mother, who was obviously crying on his shoulder.

Ben had been taken on at the garage, so Tom O'Brien returned in a fine good humour.

'What's all this? The Closed sign on the door?' he asked. 'Ben's not going to be able to keep the lot of us with the job he's got. Why are we closed, will you tell me?'

'Clare's home. She came unexpectedly. We were having a chat.'

'Clare's back?'

'She's engaged, Tom. Engaged to be married.'

'Clare? Never! To some college fellow, is it?'

'To David Power.'

'Our David Power? But I thought she hardly knew him in Dublin?'

'That's not the way it would appear.'

'Well that would beat the divil.' He scratched his head, not sure what to make of it, looking at his wife's face for guidance. Agnes's eyes looked a bit too bright, but she showed no signs of crying.

'Isn't that a bit odd?' he searched her expression, but got nothing. 'Isn't the whole thing odd?'

Clare came down the stairs. 'Have you heard my news?'

'You have me stunned,' he said.

'Is that all I get? Where's the congratulations? And the delight? Where's the looking at my ring . . .' She held out a small diamond for admiration. It had been bought with the remains of her savings and the money the pawnbroker gave David for his good sheepskin coat.

She approached her father to give him an unaccustomed hug. He looked at Agnes and, seeing what he considered approval, gave her the hug. Then she hugged her mother.

'Mam says it won't be easy. But nothing's easy, is it?'

'I suppose it isn't, child. But I'd say you've taken on the World Champion when you're taking on Molly Power.'

She didn't mention the baby to her father, and though his eyes seemed to ask many a time, neither she nor her mother took him up on the unspoken questions.

Clare looked at the clock. There was still half an hour before she met David in the hotel.

She had a sudden feeling of fear. Suppose they had talked him out of it? Suppose she had come all this way to meet him, and to agree to going back cheerfully to Castlebay, suppose she had made all those concessions and somehow that mother of his had talked him out of it? Suppose he was at the hotel gate, and said with fallen face that he had agreed to wait until the baby was born before they married? Then she really would feel *cheap*, and *betrayed*.

They were both in the hotel lounge by five to nine. They entered by two different doors. Bones was with David, refusing the polite request to sit in the corridor outside.

They nodded at each other.

The worst was over.

'What will I get you to drink, Mrs Power?' he asked gently.

She smiled at him.

Rose Dillon was behind the counter. She had always tried to include David in her parties and picnics without success. She smiled at him coquettishly still. 'To what do we owe this honour? We don't see nearly enough of you in Castlebay.'

Clare watched fascinated: Rose Dillon didn't even acknowledge that she existed, sitting in the chair by the window. She only had eyes for David.

'I'll be coming home for good soon.'

'Oh, that will cause a flurry – they'll be dying to marry you off,' she twinkled.

'I'll be married off sooner than you think,' David said.

Rose frowned. She looked over at Clare O'Brien and shook her head. *No*. That would be *ridiculous*.

They walked up to Angela's cottage to tell her. She was the one person they hoped would be totally delighted. She could see that from their faces. She was touched.

'Will you come to the wedding? Please? It's going to be a bit tense.'

'I'm great at tense weddings,' Angela said.

'Father Flynn will be marrying us.'

'He and I could nearly set up a company, awkward weddings catered for. A speciality in fact.'

'Will you though?'

'If Immaculata lets me. I don't want to anger her too much – after all, the big guns will be out in the summer when the prodigal returns.'

'What's that?' David asked.

'You didn't tell him about Sean? That was good of you, Clare, but in love and marriage you can tell all. It's allowed.'

David looked bewildered.

'Listen, David. Your marriage, which is going to raise a few eyebrows and the imminent birth of your child – which has not been announced to me but I am sure is a likelihood – will raise a few more. But let me assure you that those eyebrows will have you long forgotten when the other excitement hits the streets of Castlebay. When Father Sean O'Hara, much respected missionary priest, returns to stay in a caravan with his Japanese wife and his two children.' She laughed when she saw David's face. 'I hate to take the limelight away from the pair of you, but prepare to live in obscurity . . .'

Dr Mackey delivered a nine-pound baby to Chrissie Byrne. It was a boy, and Chrissie and Mogsy said he was going to be called John Fitzgerald after the President of America. Clare went to see her. And got little thanks for her visit.

'You were always one to steal someone else's thunder, Clare. You must have announced your engagement just to spite me as soon as you heard that John Fitzgerald had arrived.'

'Don't be a goon.'

'Always the same,' grumbled Chrissie.

'Here, let's see him.' Clare was eager.

'Don't touch him. You'd drop him.'

'I just want to look at him.' Clare peered in at the little bundle in her sister's arms – a red face and lots of black hair.

'He's beautiful,' she breathed, with such admiration that Chrissie was slightly mollified.

Clare decided she had better ask her. Life would be intolerable if she didn't.

'David and I are having a very small wedding, as you know. Just his family and ours, and a couple of friends. Will you and . . . er Maurice . . . be able to come?'

Chrissie looked doubtful. 'It's very soon, altogether. I'd have John Fitzgerald with me. Maurice and I have been discussing it. I think with regret we will have to refuse.'

Clare looked just disappointed enough, but not too upset. Nothing that would make Chrissie go back on her decision. 'I'll keep you some of the wedding cake,' she said.

'Imagine you marrying the gentry,' Chrissie said. 'What I can't understand is why you're going back to college. Haven't you done it now? Haven't you got what you were out to get? A rich husband?'

It wasn't at all as she would have expected. Mrs Conway had been pleased. She made a point of crossing the road to tell Clare that she wished them well. 'I always thought my Frank could have done worse than marry you,' she said – which was a high accolade.

Josie, oddly, did not seem as pleased as Clare would have thought. She was very formal about the news and only offered the most distant of congratulations.

Josie had been walking out with Mr Martin Harris, the auctioneer. Martin was *mature*, which meant old; and *responsible* which meant dull. Josie, who had never been jealous of anything Clare had done, was now very envious of Clare coming back to Castlebay and snatching the only attractive man, and the only *catch*, from under their noses.

Father O'Dwyer wrote out her letter of freedom. It was an odd thing not to get married in your own parish, but this Father Flynn had been a very decent person and he was sure he would do it right.

Angela had begged her to call on Immaculata. There was great false excitement in the convent over the ring, which was admired by the whole community. There was genuine excitement about how Molly Power would take the new daughter-in-law.

They kept the meetings with the families as brief as possible.

David shook Tom's hand and thanked him for letting him marry Clare.

'Divil much a say I had in it one way or the other,' Clare's father said.

'I know you'll be pleased to have her back in Castlebay,' he said manfully to Clare's mother.

'I suppose it *may* turn out all right,' Agnes O'Brien said.

Up in the big house, Molly waited nervously at her fireplace; she had re-arranged everything in the room a dozen times, and shouted at Nellie who was sulking in the kitchen. She had changed her dress twice.

She saw them walking up the drive. Laughing. The girl was *laughing*, instead of shaking in her shoes.

David had his own key.

'Mother, we're here,' he called.

Clare was tall. Molly had forgotten that. She was tall and thin, and her face seemed pale.

'Well.' Molly looked her up and down. It was just on the right side of being a calculated insult. But only just.

'Hallo, Mrs Power,' Clare said. Her voice was steady.

'So,' Mrs Power said.

I won't let her annoy me. I will not rise to her bait, Clare told herself, fists clenched by her sides.

David wasn't saying anything, which was what they agreed.

'David has told you our news, and our plans, Mrs Power.'

'Oh yes.'

'So I just wanted to add that I hope very much that I will make him happy, and that eventually I will make you and Dr Power pleased that we married.' Not too confident. It angered Molly more than anything had ever done in her life.

'I doubt if that will ever be the case,' she said holding back the temper that was threatening to spill out. 'I am here to greet you. Would you like me to ring for tea?'

'Thank you, but no, Mrs Power. If I may, I'll just go and pay my respects to your husband. I have a lot of things to do before going back tomorrow. Thank you for welcoming me to the house, and I'll look forward to seeing you at the wedding.'

I could kill her, Molly thought. *I wish she were dead.* The feeling swept over her and was gone. She felt shock and guilt. It confused her and she didn't make her farewells as she intended to.

'What . . . oh . . . yes. Yes, the wedding day. Yes.'

Clare had smiled and was out of the door.

'Thank you, Mother,' David said. His face was in a pleasant smile but his eyes were cold.

It was much later when she saw him. Sitting on the wall, by the hotel.

'You were going to run out of town without telling me.' He was cold and unsmiling.

'Don't be ridiculous.' She forced a light laugh that she didn't mean. 'Of course I was going to tell you. If I hadn't seen you tonight I'd have left a note for you.'

'You're a liar.'

'Now stop that,' she said, her anger rising. He was not going to upset her, she would not let him, but *hell*, he wasn't going to call her a liar. Especially since he was right.

'You had no intention of telling me,' Gerry said.

'Why wouldn't I tell you? Don't *dramatize* everything so much. I've been telling all my friends that I'm getting married. Why wouldn't I tell you?'

'Because you knew what I'd say.' There was no answering smile on his lips.

'And what would you say? What will you say?'

'That you're mad. You mustn't do it.'

One more attempt, thought Clare. Just one more, to get this on to some kind of normal plane and then I abandon it.

'Well, listen to me, just because you and I were the only people left, everyone else getting hitched, that's no reason why I'm going to stay single just to keep you company. I'm delighted with it all. And I won't put up with any nonsense from you.'

'Don't do it. *Clare*.'

'Stop it. Can't you wish me well? Like ordinary people?'

'I do wish you well. But not married to David Power. And you're not ordinary people, I've always told you that. Neither am I.'

'You're certainly not like generous people or mannerly people,' she said.

'You can't marry him. You have to marry me. You always knew that.'

She looked anxiously at his pointed face for the lopsided smile, the grin that made anybody else grin too. There was none of it there. She stared at him, shocked.

'Well, I don't suppose there's anything more to say.' Clare moved towards the entrance gate.

Lithe as a cat, Gerry leapt to the ground. 'Don't go yet.'

'Of course I'm going. I'm not talking to you for one more minute. How dare you upset me and say all these things? How *dare* you? If it were you that had got engaged, I'd be so pleased and wish you well.'

'Got engaged? Got engaged? You and David haven't *got engaged*. You're getting *married* in three weeks. What does that mean? Well? What does it mean?'

'Go to hell.' She turned and ran past him.

He ran beside her, half jumping, half running. 'It's the wrong thing to do. Girls like you, like Fiona, you shouldn't be just forced to make fools of yourselves. *You're* not tramps. You're too trusting. If something goes wrong then you should work it out properly . . .'

She stopped and looked at him levelly. 'In my case, *nothing* went wrong. *Nothing*. Do you hear me? Everything is fine, as right as can be. Our marriage is a bit sooner than we intended but it's exactly what we wanted. It's going to be perfect.'

Gerry had stopped opposite her. He looked straight into her eyes. 'Your marriage to David Power is not going to be perfect. You foolish, *foolish* girl. Your marriage is doomed.'

The girls had been magnificent. They had been through the entire hostel in search of clothes, and since everyone was so much in awe of Valerie and Mary Catherine, clothes were forthcoming. They had a huge selection for Clare to choose from.

There was a nice pink suit which fitted Clare very well. They took a wine-coloured hat from another girl, and a very expensive black bag. Now all she needed were wine-coloured gloves and good black shoes.

They bought her the gloves between them, and she bought the shoes herself. She was kitted out.

Mary Catherine was to be bridesmaid, and James Nolan the best man. David seemed a little cool with James. Clare didn't know why. Anyway they were all in such a frenzy with study and getting clothes ready and dismantling their flat in Rathmines and finding a better one, that there was little time to speculate.

Clare had received a note from Caroline Nolan wishing her well, expressing surprise at the suddenness of it all, and regret that the Nolan family offer of hosting the wedding hadn't been taken up.

Clare had been adamant about that. It was not going to be on Nolan territory. It was to be on neutral ground, the hotel near the church. Father Flynn had discussed the menu and suggested one that seemed not too ambitious. David and Clare had opened a bank account: the manager loved young doctors and David, without actually saying it, implied that he was well on the way to being a consultant in Fitzwilliam Square. They had a small overdraft. It would pay for the wedding. There was no way the Nolans could get their hands on Clare's day.

They went through the list. There were the *relaxed* and the *tense*. The relaxed seem to outweigh the tense. David's father, Angela, Father Flynn, Emer and Kevin, Mary Catherine and Valerie. And James and Caroline would be all right, wouldn't they. Snobby, Clare thought, but all right. And what about Ben and Jim? *Tense*, Clare said, and if by any unlucky chance they did become relaxed it would mean that they had become hooligans.

Well, that was a fair number of easy people. On the other side of the scales would be David's mother, who would look like an avenging angel all day long; both Clare's parents, who would be so timid and fearful of doing the wrong thing they would have everyone's teeth on edge; and there would be the Nolan parents, who seemed to regard this marriage as in the same class as the loss of the *Titanic*.

'It's great that we're able to laugh about it,' Clare said.

'That's the only thing that makes me feel it's not doomed,' David agreed.

Clare didn't like the use of that word. It made her shiver.

The O'Briens came up by train the night before. Jim had never been in Dublin before; Ben had been once on a school trip. Clare met them at the station. She was taking them by taxi to the hotel where they would all stay the night. Mr Ryan, the owner, had arranged a very good rate. There were three rooms booked: one for Clare's parents, one for her brothers; and one for herself, where the girls would come tomorrow to help her dress.

Her heart filled with pity for them, for all she was putting them through, as she saw them getting out of the train. Blinking after the long journey, tired and nervous about what lay ahead . . . Their suitcase was enormous and very shabby – surely there were a couple of *small* bags at home? But then, they rarely went anywhere.

Ben and Jim were chastened by the hugeness of Kingsbridge station. The boys were squeezed into the front of the taxi. Clare's parents looked nervously out of the car on each side. She chattered: there would be tea and sandwiches in the hotel,

Mr Ryan was going to have it ready. There wasn't a bar as such, but he said that he could get a few bottles of stout for them. Clare's father brightened; and so did Ben, but Ben was told that there was no question of a bottle of stout for him. There wasn't much need for conversation. They were all so tired that the tea and stout were enough to close their eyes.

Ten times Clare's mother asked what time they had to leave. Ten times, without complaining, Clare told her that they would walk across to the church – a distance of fifty yards – at eleven o'clock.

It was a beautiful sunny day. Mary Catherine and Valerie arrived giggling in their finery. They had the hat and the good black bag with them. Those were only borrowed for the day: the owners were so terrified to let them out of their sight, they had promised to return them before nightfall.

'I brought some brandy. In case,' Val said.

'Not now,' Mary Catherine said. 'We have to dress the bride.'

Clare looked pale so they rouged her up. She also looked extremely smart. The outfit was a work of genius and Clare blessed the anonymous donors. She felt that it was taking the Something Borrowed superstition a little too seriously, and they were all laughing at that, when Clare's father arrived beating on the door nervously and saying they had only twenty minutes – should they be on their way?

Clare didn't know there would be music. She was surprised to hear the burbling sounds of a church organ. Her father's arm stiffened in fright.

The altar did seem a mile away, but soon she was near enough to see them turning round. She saw the admiration in Angela's face first, and it was warming. She saw Angela clutch Emer, and they were both nodding with delight at her. Her unnaturally clean brothers seemed surprised too at how well she looked and this made her hold her head high. She saw Caroline's eyebrows go up, and that was pleasing too, as was the big smile from Dr Power. But best of all was the way Mrs Power's face changed just a fraction. The superior look which seemed to be built into it as she was whispering to Mrs Nolan left it for a moment. And because Clare felt so exhilarated, her smile was sparkling.

By the time David turned round she was glowing with confidence and happiness; transformed, almost, from when she had started to walk up the aisle. He had never known she could look so beautiful. He looked at James standing beside him and smiled. James smiled back encouragingly. The coldness, the tactless words James had spoken, were forgotten. David was stepping out of the pew to take his beautiful, beautiful bride to the altar.

The Powers were not taking any photographs. If the Nolans had brought a camera it was not produced. Kevin Quinn had a camera though; and when Father Flynn saw the sparsity of picture-taking he gave Jim O'Brien some money and sent him off to a nearby chemist to get three more films.

'Keep snapping,' Father Flynn hissed to Kevin. 'You're the official photographer.'

They walked cheerfully enough across to the hotel. Mrs Power looked at it as though it were some kind of museum piece. She was annoyed to hear the Nolans saying they hadn't known it was there, and what nice antiques in the hall. Mr Ryan had taken the decision to serve the drinks out in the conservatory, which opened on to a garden. There were flowers and plants and rays of sun coming through coloured glass.

'It's not bad at all,' hissed Valerie through clenched teeth. 'The way Clare was going on, I thought we were in for a place smelling of cabbage, with sauce bottles on the table.'

'There's nothing wrong with the place,' Mary Catherine said. 'But isn't the mother-in-law a *bitch*.'

'She'll soon see she's outnumbered,' Angela said. They jumped. They had not intended anyone else to hear. 'I agree, she's behaving like a bitch, but she's got no confidence, herself. When she sees the rest of us thinking it's marvellous, she'll come round.'

'I'll go and talk at her for a while,' Val said. 'Blind her with tales of my background.'

Mr Ryan called them in to lunch. There was cream in everyone's tomato soup, and a little chopped parsley on top.

Mrs O'Brien wondered whether it was just a decoration; Father Flynn solved that by spooning his own down noisily the moment grace had been said. Agnes saw what to do, and her family followed her. The rolls were slightly warm; and there were little clusters of bottles on the table: red wine, white wine, orange squash, and stout bottles artistically arranged at intervals.

The seating plan was a miracle of diplomacy. No O'Brien was left without a friendly neighbour. Clare and David felt the breath they had been holding all day begin to slip out naturally. It was too big a number for general conversation, but there was a nice buzz; and by the time Mr Ryan and his two waitresses had cleared the chicken à la crème away and dusted the table for the bringing on of the ice cream and cake, it was far more friendly than anyone could have believed possible.

Molly Power was flanked by Kevin Quinn on one side and Father Flynn on the other. Without being deliberately rude, there was nothing she could do but respond.

Agnes O'Brien was on the other side of Father Flynn, and then there was Valerie. They had dispensed with the traditional order of seating since that would have been a *certain* recipe for disaster.

Father Flynn had instructed James in some of his duties: he asked him to call upon Miss O'Hara to speak, and to ask David's father to say a few words too.

'It's not *traditional*, Father,' James complained.

'Whose side are you on, boy?' Father Flynn had replied sharply.

It worked. Tom O'Brien's bumbling words, the studying of his piece of paper, went almost unnoticed. If it had just been Tom, and the fluent young barrister James Nolan, the difference would have been very marked.

Dr Power was warm and cheerful. Doctors were often apt to say at weddings that they brought the bride or the groom into the world, as if that gave them special standing in the community. In this case he had brought both of them into the world, and had considerable responsibility for the existence of the groom. He wished them long, happy years in Castlebay – which as everyone knew was the centre of the Universe, and would those people who had not yet been to Castlebay please hurry up and go there.

Angela, more hesitant than she ever had been at school, spoke about how sentimental teachers always became once the pupils were out of their hands.

James was flowery. It was very nearly over. David stood up to speak last.

Clare had to fix her eyes firmly on the heap of telegrams so that she would not cry at his words. He was speaking simply and directly about his happiness and his hopes for both of them. He was thanking everyone there by name for all they had done. Nobody could be more happy than he was at this moment.

They all clapped. Molly's gloved hands; Agnes's thin bony hands; Jim's and Ben's scrubbed clean hands – examined before they were allowed out; Father Flynn's plump little white hands and Angela's long artistic hands.

Clare went up to change, to remove the pink suit – on which not a crumb or drop had been spilled – to place the hat and the handbag back in tissue paper. She wore Valerie's good grey dress and a set of cheap wine-coloured glass beads, which matched her gloves. She grabbed up her own shabby bag. She was ready for Going Away. James had said he would give them a proper present later when they were settled into their new home. In the meantime perhaps the car might be useful. David thanked him again warmly as he took the car keys in his hand.

'It's good of you, James. And thanks for all the marvellous support. At the meal. You know.'

They stood awkwardly waiting for Clare to come downstairs. 'It was all great,' James said.

'Yes. Yes, of course.'

'And it will all turn out marvellously well.'

'Yes,' David said.

They were both thinking of the days when they could say anything to each other. A long time ago.

For the three-day honeymoon they had said they were going to a quiet hotel in Wicklow and everyone had nodded sagely. They were in fact going back to their new flat, which was in total chaos. They wanted nobody else. They wanted no gaiety or candlelit dinners, they just wanted each other and the knowledge that the day they had dreaded was over.

James Nolan had left champagne cooling, and when they got back to the Nolan house, Breeda was ready with a tray of glasses.

'This is more like it,' Caroline said.

'It was very nicely done, very nice,' her father said.

Dr Power took his glass of champagne and walked out into the well-kept garden. A man was mowing the lawn. For other people it was an ordinary working day.

Molly saw him standing by himself and went out to him. She stood beside him wordlessly.

'You were very good, Moll,' he said.

'Good?'

'You didn't want it, but you didn't let that spoil their day. Even though your heart wasn't in it.'

'Clare . . .' she paused.

He said nothing.

'She looked very well, I thought. The outfit was smart.'

Inside, the champagne was flowing. Caroline wanted to know why Clare hadn't carried that super handbag away with her when she was leaving. 'There was a fearful coldness between James and David, did you hear? James was nearly not going to be the best man?' She was giggly and conspiratorial.

'I *didn't* know,' Valerie said, giving her the cue to go on.

'*Apparently*, when David told James about the marriage, and the *hurry* and the *dramas* and all, James said, very reasonably I think, but anyway he said *bad luck* or something, and David said what do you mean, and James said that *really* David didn't *have* to marry a *scrubber*, and David poured his glass over James – it was in a hotel bar all this – and walked out, and James had to run after him. Gosh, it was *awful.*'

'Wasn't it?' Valerie said fervently. 'Wasn't it about as *awful* a thing to say as anyone could think of.'

'No, what I mean is . . .' Caroline saw she had put her foot in it.

'Isn't it *quite* extraordinary how James ever managed to make it to being an attorney with a mind like that,' Mary Catherine said in amazement.

June had always been a stifling month, waiting for the end of term.

Angela had written to Sean and Shuya in reply to their excited letter. Yes, indeed, she would be here, she would be in the cottage as always, and once they had decided what they were going to do, they could come and tell her, she would be happy to see them all, as she was always happy to see them.

Sean had said no, he hadn't written to anyone in Castlebay about his changed life, who would he write to? But Angela had been very firm on that one: it was Sean's story to tell, not hers. He must be the one to decide who to talk to and what to say.

No letter with any change of plans came. There was no reprieve.

They would be here on Saturday.

On Saturday morning, panic came over her as she was buying meat in Dwyers'. Chrissie, back at work, wanted to know if Miss O'Hara was going to have a party.

'No. Why?' Angela said, alarmed.

'Well you're just after buying enough meat to feed an army.'

Angela looked in horror at the huge lumps of meat. Without thinking she had bought dinner for Sean and his family. She felt dizzy and leaned against the wall.

'Are you all right?' Chrissie asked, frightened. 'Jimmy! Give Miss O'Hara a hand.'

She had steadied herself again.

'I'm very sorry. I've got a bit of summer 'flu, I think.' She paid for the meat, put it in her bicycle basket, and wheeled it home. She didn't dare to get on the bike for fear she might faint. Though in a way it wouldn't be a bad time, if she had to die, to die now. She sat at home glumly all day. Why had she not had the courage to tell people after her mother died? Why had she lied to them, and gone along with their messages of sympathy, their requests for prayers? She had never taken a penny of their money: she had said that it should all be sent to the missionary headquarters. But they wouldn't remember that.

She thought of the nice, honest people who always asked after him, the people she had fooled, rather than the awful people who would crow with horror. She didn't care all that much about the Sergeant McCormacks and the Mother Immaculatas. She thought about Dick Dillon, and her heart went down to her feet.

It was a beautiful day, the kind that they would sigh over, the trippers in for the day, the visitors down for the month, the shop-keepers who had been hoping for weather like this all year.

Shuya and Sean would sigh with pleasure too, and Denis and Laki would be as delighted with the long golden beach and the bright blue sea. She never remembered feeling so sad.

She had shown herself she was a person of no courage. She hadn't the courage to beg them not to come, nor the courage to go to the station and welcome them with open arms. What a useless, spineless friend and sister she had turned out to be.

They would have been here three hours at least now. They had taken the overnight boat from England, the morning train to the town, and since there was no one to meet them to take them to Castlebay, they would wait for the bus. They would have been in their caravan for an hour.

Had they taken the children for a swim? Had they gone to O'Brien's shop to buy provisions? Had Sean leaned eagerly across the counter and shaken Tom O'Brien's hand?

'Don't you remember me, Mr O'Brien? I'm Dinny O'Hara's son Sean. And this is my wife, and these are my children. Say hallo to Mr O'Brien, Denis . . .'

Were they on their way up the street now? Had they reached the corner? Were they turning down the golf-course road?

She had said she would be in her cottage. She wanted to run away.

She never remembered the clock ticking so loudly or her heart moving so oddly in her chest.

She sat and waited.

And waited.

By the time the children should be well in bed, there was a knock on the door. She steeled herself and went to it slowly. There was no sound of voices on the step. Perhaps they were upset that she hadn't come to meet them.

She opened the door.

It was Dick Dillon.

'Hallo,' she said faintly. She stood leaning against the door. She made no move to ask him in.

'I was wondering if I might come in at all? Or would that be out of the question? I do come to call here occasionally, you know.'

'Dick, I'm sorry. Come in.'

'I know you said you didn't want to come up this week, and that you'd explain it all later.'

'Well it didn't do much good my telling you that, did it?'

'I knew it was all right to come.'

'That was very arrogant of you.' Her voice was weary.

'No. It wasn't arrogant. I knew I could come. I knew they weren't here.'

'What?'

'I knew I wouldn't be blundering in on top of them. They're sitting down on the seat at the end of the town looking at the sea.'

He had discovered them by complete accident. He had seen them getting off the bus, he had looked because of the foreign woman, and the children being half foreign-looking.

'He didn't recognize me. I was in my drinking mode when he was here last. I'd only have been a blur to him or indeed he to me.'

'So how did you know?'

'The boy said when were they going to see Aunt Angela, and the woman said they were going to their caravan first, and Aunt Angela would be waiting up in her cottage for them later when they got settled in, today or tomorrow.'

'I'm sorry, Dick. I'm very, very sorry.' Angela wept. 'I'm such a coward, I'm so bloody weak, I couldn't tell you.' She put her head on his shoulder and sobbed like a child. His arms went around her, and he patted her comfortingly.

'It's going to be all right,' he said, as if to a very small, very upset toddler. 'Dick is here, he'll look after things.'

They sat in the sunset and watched the red ball disappear down behind a big navy line of horizon. Behind them, the music of the amusements and the cries of laughter, and around them the chitter-chatter of holidaymakers.

Denis and Laki were both fast asleep, exhausted. Already he had pointed out the Brothers' School where he had gone every day, he had shown them the big rock pools where he used to play, and he had taken them into the Echo Cave to shout their questions.

Sean had remembered O'Brien's shop. But it had been much smaller then; he didn't know the boy serving there – it must be one of the young sons. He saw Mrs O'Brien in the background; but he was shy suddenly. It wasn't the place to catch her eye and begin the great comeback. He had bought a colouring book and pencils in Miss O'Flaherty's shop, but she was busy serving someone else and he didn't know the young woman who served them.

On the street, a child of about eight looked at Laki with interest. 'What land do you come from?' she asked.

'I was born in Japan, I am half-Irish, half-Japanese,' Laki said proudly.

'I had a Japanese doll when I was young. It didn't look a bit like you,' the girl said curiously.

They had eaten their meal and made plans for the next day; there would be swimming and a picnic lunch on the beach. But first they would call on Aunt Angela. The children had thought this perfectly satisfactory.

'This is a good place to have as another home,' Laki said. Sean had been talking about Castlebay as their 'other home' for as long as the children could remember. But this time he said nothing.

'I'll show you the town,' he had suggested to Shuya. But when they came to the bottom of the street, he hung back; he didn't want to go to the dance, he was too old to take her to the amusements. A middle-aged couple on the bumpers? It would be idiotic. Then, in the hotel, sitting drinking, and seeing other groups: would he go up to them? If so, would he give his name? He remembered the Dillons vaguely, but he hadn't known any of them well.

He had hesitated as they approached Church Street. It was Shuya who pointed out the nice bench.

'That wasn't here, years ago,' Sean said. 'Probably afraid that people might sit here and cuddle or do something outrageous like that.'

She put her arm around him. She sensed his unease, the flatness about everything.

'It's changed a lot, of course. Everything,' he said.

'It must have. Was that big amusement centre always there?'

'Much smaller, much shabbier. And I don't think the dance hall was like that. Of course, in those days I wasn't likely to be going into it, so I hardly noticed it.'

'It's funny,' Shuya said. 'Most people, when they go back, find that things have grown smaller. Here you find they have all grown much bigger.'

'You wouldn't know the place in ways,' he said. 'It's very painted and bright and the shops have all got things hanging outside them, buckets, and water wings and sunhats. There was none of that in my day.'

There was a silence.

'Would you like us to walk up to your home, to see it, even if you don't want to go in?'

She was trying hard. It worked.

'Yes, that would be an idea. I don't think we'll go up Church Street, we can go up the Cliff Road, it's longer but it's very nice.'

'Let's go by the Cliff Road,' said Shuya.

They walked on to the golf-course road. Late golfers were coming back from their drinks after the last hole.

It was a warm, balmy evening. They walked on till they saw the house. The curtains were drawn and there was a light in the main room. Angela must be waiting there for them.

'Is it cheating to walk past it, and not go in?' he asked.

'Angela said come any time we were ready. I don't think you're ready now,' Shuya said gently.

'No. I'm not, somehow.'

'Well then, it's not cheating.'

He pointed out where his room had been, and which had been the window he used to climb out of if he wanted to race out and have an early-morning swim. They marvelled at the energy of a boy who could have raced down a half mile to the sea and a half mile back . . . he would run on the road, and there would be cows going for milking . . . he would be back in his room and studying again before anyone in the family got up.

He showed her the little geraniums that his mother had planted in the window boxes and said that it was wonderful they had survived so well. He pointed out the chimney where the birds had made a nest, and the porch where they had to scrape off the snow in winter in case it became too heavy and broke the glass.

Shuya whispered that now she had a very perfect picture of the way he used to live.

They walked together back down the road, arm in arm, to the caravan park; again by the quiet cliff road, not the bustling Church Street with all its lights and the fun of the season getting underway.

Dick Dillon came downstairs; he had been peeping through the dark bedroom window.

'They've gone,' he said.

They had heard whispering outside and he had crept upstairs to have a look. Angela had remained at her post. If they knocked she was to let them in and Dick was to leave the back way. He would not stay and greet them – otherwise they would get the impression that the whole of Castlebay would accept him as willingly. They had to make their decisions according to the facts, not just from meeting Dick.

'What do you think they were at?' she asked.

'We'll probably never know that,' he said.

'Would you stay the night, Dick?' she asked suddenly.

'What?'

'I don't mean in the bed with me, I'm not inflicting that on you. Just in the house.'

'I'd love to stay with you, and since you're on the subject, it would be no infliction at all if you weren't to bother to go to all the trouble of making up another bed.'

'Ah, it's no trouble, Dick,' she laughed.

'I was hoping maybe you might have no bedclothes aired.'

'They're aired, and it's the middle of summer. Will there be a hue and cry for you if you don't go back to the hotel?'

'Angela, my girl, they don't know whether I'm there or gone, whether I live or die in that place.'

'Stop playing on my sympathies, you'll have your own bed here, I'll go and make it for you now.'

'I'd be no trouble to you, that's a grand big bed you have up there. I was just looking at it and speculating.'

'Speculate away. Dick?'

'Yes.'

'Thank you *very* much.'

She thought they would go to late Mass, so she was surprised to see the four of them at First.

When she saw Sean and the two children go to the altar to receive Communion she closed her eyes. Castlebay would forgive a lot but it would never forgive that.

She left before the Last Gospel. She was buying her Sunday paper from Mickey Mack outside the gates when she heard a farmer say to his wife, 'Did you see the Chinese woman at Mass, and the two half-caste children, going to the rails and all?'

'Isn't China full of Catholics?' said Mickey Mack: he wasn't an ignoramus just because he couldn't read the papers he sold.

She had plenty of soda bread, and cornflakes for the children. Dick had gone back to the hotel and he wouldn't come to the house until she sent for him. She could always phone from the golf club if there was an emergency.

She sat down to read the paper, calmer now. Nobody had recognized them.

They must have been having some kind of second thoughts if they had come to look last night but had not come in.

She waited for them with a dread that was much less sharp around the edges. And she didn't feel too bad about herself either. Last night Dick had assured her that she had behaved most honourably. She felt less of a coward today.

Today she could take them.

They arrived excitedly, chattering like starlings. There were hugs and a present for Aunt Angela and delight at the breakfast.

Shuya wandered round the room entranced by the books and objects. 'You never told me it was like this, Sean.'

'It wasn't, when I was here.' He seemed sad. Shuya was praising the one thing that didn't date from his time.

Casually, very casually, Angela asked him had he met any friends to introduce to Shuya.

'No.' He seemed troubled. 'Not yet.'

'Of course, a lot of Sean's friends would have been made through his mother, and through you, Angela. When he came home, she would gather people round and because of his status as priest, people would call.'

Shuya understood.

'I don't seem to know anyone from school.'

Angela clenched her fists. *Know anyone from school?* The man was mad! Thirty years ago, little fellows running in and out of the Brothers? Who in the name of God would he know?

'No, I suppose you've grown away, and they have,' she said cautiously.

'You know, it's very changed, Angela. Do you not find that?' he said.

This was it. If she moved carefully, this might be the lifeline that was being thrown. There would be no point in coming back to a *changed* Castlebay.

'Oh I do,' she sighed. 'I think what it used to be like in the old days, room to walk on the footpaths, only a few families on the beach . . . You knew everyone to say hallo to.'

Shuya was playing the game too. 'Sean told me last night that it has changed too much, become big and what was the word you used . . . ?'

'A bit *brash*. Hasn't it? To be honest, Angela, it's getting a bit like those places in England, that used to be so nice, but very noisy and full of trippers.'

'What can you do?' Angela cried. 'I often think of leaving it myself, getting a better job in a bigger school. I don't know why I hang on, but like you, I suppose it's roots.'

Shuya said levelly, 'If *you* left, Angela, you could always come back. To see people. After all, you do have friends here. Sean doesn't have many.'

'I wouldn't say that . . .' He didn't want to appear friendless.

'No, you'd know a lot of people, of course, Sean. But Shuya's right. They're Mam's friends, not our own. Really, the best of ours went away. It's the same in a lot of small places.'

He repeated it. 'The best of ours went away. It's true for you, Angela. True.'

The children came in from the garden: it was scorching, could they go for a swim? Of course they could. Would Angela join them on the beach? No. If they didn't mind. But she'd be here tonight. She had bought a lot of meat, would they come and have a big supper?

'Which is a nice, quiet part of the beach . . . um . . . for the picnic?' Shuya called.

Angela told her the part where there was least chance of Sean O'Hara being unmasked.

'We were thinking, Angela, that it would be a pity not to see a bit of the rest of the countryside around here, now that we're this far.'

Her breathing was short – it was going to happen. 'I think that's a good idea. Take day trips, is it?'

'No. Go on and see a few other places, places they can remember, write about in their projects and scrapbooks.'

Shuya said, 'And I want to see Dublin. I was promised Dublin.'

'Well, of course, that would be nice. But the caravan?'

'There's people queuing up to get into caravans, they'll even let us have the balance back, which is very fair.'

'But you'll come back again? To Castlebay? Before you leave Ireland?'

'No. It wouldn't make sense. We'd be retracing our steps.'

'I see. Yes. You're right, of course.'

Shuya said, 'So we thought we might start out tomorrow. They can let the caravan from lunchtime.'

Angela said nothing. Her heart was too full.

Sean mistook the silence for disappointment. 'I don't want you to think we're running out on you. I'll never be able to thank you for the welcome. It's just . . . it's just . . .'

'I think I understand. Some things have changed a lot.'

'And some things haven't changed at all.'

'The bus leaves early. We must rise very early . . .' Shuya said.

'I have a friend – you won't remember him – Dick Dillon. He could give you a lift to the town, and you could start out from there . . .'

'Would he mind?'

'Not at all. I'll tell him tonight.'

'Angela . . . there's just one thing . . . about this Dillon man.'

'What's that?'

'You won't tell him who I am? You see I'd prefer in a way if people thought . . .'

'I won't tell him who you are – didn't I say I'd leave it to you to tell who you want.'

She came down the Cliff Road with them all and kissed them goodbye at the corner by the seat that looked out to sea. They walked on up to the caravan park. She told them Dick Dillon would pick them up at the caravan site at a nice civilized time, like ten o'clock.

When she went home she prayed on her knees, long sobbing prayers of thanks to a Lord that she had thought recently had been hard-hearted.

The days fell into a hypnotic routine. They got up early. There was no one on their part of the beach so they went down the steps beside the Lodge to the beach for an early swim. Bones knew about this, and even though he was so old he had to be helped back up the steps again, he always came with them. There was no one to see the swelling of Clare's stomach except David, who patted it lovingly as they went out into the early-morning waves.

Then they ate bacon and tomato, which they loved. David joined his father, and Clare walked down the Cliff Road to her old home. She had a cup of tea in the kitchen, did any shopping that was needed. Then, while it was still early, she would walk back the Cliff Road watching the families getting ready for the day on the beach, and she would let herself into the Lodge. The day would pass in studying. David usually found time to come in at least twice before he was home for the evening. They rarely went out to the hotel, and apart from the Committee dance they had no social outing. It was peaceful in the evenings, the sunset looking like an exaggerated picture from their own window. And sometimes they did a little desultory painting of the upstairs rooms. Bumper Byrne's contract had only gone so far as to get the place habitable and have the downstairs part decorated. 'After all, who'll be looking at the upstairs except the pair of you?' he had said cheerfully. David and Clare were so happy to be into the place they didn't argue.

There were three rooms upstairs: their bedroom, the room they would make into a nursery and the storeroom. Clare had thought of having that made into a study. Wouldn't it be great to have a place you could spread your books and papers and never have to take them up when a meal was needed or when you had to tidy the place up? But, David had said, what was the point of having a study upstairs? Wouldn't it be a bit antisocial, locking herself away there, and when the baby arrived . . .

Clare agreed. She would leave it till later.

They painted the nursery a sunny yellow colour, and as soon as they started murmuring quietly about hoping to start a family around Christmas, Nellie became very excited and made curtains for them with all kinds of nursery-rhyme figures on the fabric.

David took his toys from the window seat of his old bedroom, slowly bit by bit, and always when his mother was out. He wasn't stealing them, he just did not want to have to mention the child. Her face froze over in a mask when the subject was hinted at. David dreaded thinking about how she would react when the baby was born.

'I think she'll come round. Not to me, but to the baby.'

'We should make sure she has some time with him herself. Or her, of course.'

They were convinced that it would be a boy. He was to be christened Patrick Thomas.

As the days went on it seemed impossible they had lived any other kind of life. The hectic, rushed meetings in Dublin, the dirty flat with the smelly hall and the unpainted, uncarpeted stairway in Rathmines seemed from a different life lived by different people. David said he could hardly remember the name of the registrar with the carroty head who was always fighting with everyone in the Res. Clare said that if she were on a torture rack she wouldn't be able to remember anything at all that she and Mary Catherine and Valerie talked about for two and a half years.

Now they talked about David's patients. He delivered three babies that summer. But, actually, Mrs Brennan had done most of the work, she was a marvellous midwife he said, reassuring and practical. The women loved her. That interested Clare, she had always thought Mrs Brennan was an almighty bossy boots but this cast a new light on her. David told Clare the secrets of the town, knowing that she wasn't going to speak of them to anyone. Josie Dillon's grandmother had senile dementia and was in the county home; very quietly, the whole thing was done, but that was where she was. Mrs Conway was going to the town shortly to have a hysterectomy. Father O'Dwyer had such a bad chest David's father had told him that it was an act of suicide to continue smoking and the Lord would look on it very poorly indeed. Father O'Dwyer had told Dr Power to keep his religious pronouncements to himself and concentrate on medicine. 'I am concentrating on medicine, you stupid man,' Dr Power had roared at him, and there had been a slow process of reconciliation in which David had to be the middle man.

She learned that her own brother, Jim, was very hard of hearing – not just slow, and stupid, as they had all thought. He was going to have a hearing aid, and David said that there could well be total hearing loss.

'Maybe you could teach him lip-reading, after finals.'

'Teach him what?' Clare laughed. 'I don't know how to lip-read.'

'But you could learn, couldn't you? It could make all the difference. Otherwise he'll just end up like Mickey Mack or someone.'

Clare was shocked. Yes, of course she could learn. There must be books on the subject, and diagrams. Yes, of course, she would.

David was becoming like his father already, concerned and involved in everything that happened. In a few weeks people had stopped thinking of him as a boy helping his father and holding the fort until the real doctor arrived. The day came when a woman said to David's father that she had begun with young Dr Power and she thought she would continue with him if that was all right, he had been so helpful.

David's father took out a bottle of sherry at lunch that day, and Molly had laughed with pride and told Nellie about it as the meal was being put on the table. And as they smiled about how well David was settling into the practice, no mention was made of his wife sitting fifty yards away, bent over her studies with a cup of soup.

There was no phone in the Lodge yet but there was a buzzer from the house, so that David could be woken for night calls. It was awkward, because it meant he had

771

to go up to his parents' to hear the details before setting out. Still, they had been promised a phone soon, and were at the top of the priority list.

Clare heard the buzzer with surprise one morning; David had long gone on house calls, they must have known she was on her own. Resignedly she walked to the house. Molly was in the hall.

'There's a call from Dublin for you,' she said and held the receiver out as if it might contaminate her.

'I'm sorry for disturbing you,' Clare said.

It was Mary Catherine. She and Val had the most marvellous flat, they were installed now and they would keep it for a year. Val was going to do a Higher Diploma in education and Mary Catherine was going to do a Diploma to be a librarian. Any time Clare wanted to come and stay, there was plenty of room.

A longing so great came over Clare, it almost made her faint.

Miles and miles away from Dracula, who was sighing as if the phone were needed urgently. Molly was just in earshot, fiddling with some flowers that didn't need adjustment.

Clare sighed too.

'Well? Can you come up? Will you?'

'I'll write to you about it.'

'Can't you talk?'

'That's right.'

'Do your best. We'd love you to come. David, too, of course, if he can get away. We've got a big double bed in the spare room.'

'Sounds great.'

'So you'll try?'

'As I said, I'll write.'

She told Mrs Power pleasantly that her friends were inviting David and herself to visit.

Mrs Power gave a tinkling laugh. 'That's *very* nice of them, Clare dear. But David's never been short of a place to stay in Dublin. Heavens *no*. We've *lots* of friends there, and the Nolans' house has always been a second home to him.'

Clare smiled. And before her face cracked with the effort, she returned to the Lodge and started to bang things, hard, with a ruler. She was so angry she was shaking. She tried to concentrate on her work but *that woman*'s superior voice rang in her ears. She was going out.

She left a note on the table in case David called in, and marched out nearly taking the door from its hinges. She walked first to Bumper Byrne's lean-to shed that he called his office, and spoke to him sharply about their gate. It was meant to be a proper entrance, with a gate, and tarmacadamed path. What was it but a hole in the hedge? No. It was *not* perfectly adequate for the moment. She would like it done. This week. Could he tell her which day? No? Well then, she'd wait here till he *could* tell her which day. No. She didn't mind waiting at all. In desperation Bumper said he'd have someone up there on Thursday, and she thanked him warmly.

Then she went to Peter O'Connor who had a saw and used to cut down trees.

He'd be about the only person in Castlebay who could advise her on how to build a hedge.

'I want to plant a hedge that looks small and harmless now but will grow up like a flash and make a big forest,' she said to him.

He knew why she wanted the hedge.

'I'm not great on the pronunciation but I think it's called Cupressors that you want.'

'That's the Latin for a cypress tree, is that what you mean?'

'The very thing. I could get you a set of nice young plants . . .'

'Not *too* young, Mr O'Connor.'

'When do you want them in?'

'This afternoon. And I'd like them to grow twenty feet tall by next week.'

'Come on, now. She's not as bad as all that?'

Clare laughed. 'Of course not. Just as long as it's grown fairly soon.'

She called to see her mother. The shop was full.

'Do you want me to get behind the counter and give you a hand?'

'Are you out of your mind? The doctor's wife? Serving? Have some sense.'

She went into the hotel.

'Will you have lunch with me Josie? A real lunch in the dining room? I'll pay . . .'

'I can't, Clare, not in the middle of the season. Mummy'd go mad and Rose would make another scene. We're meant to leave those tables for the paying customers.'

'I would be a paying customer,' Clare said crossly.

'No, real people. Not us. It's ages since I've seen you. How are you, anyway?'

'Like a weasel,' said Clare and left with a wave.

She thought she would go up to Angela's cottage. She bought a bottle of sherry in Costello's, and snapped the head off Teddy Costello who called her Mrs Power.

'God Almighty, Teddy, we were in mixed infants together – you called me Clare until a few months ago. Am I to start calling you Mr Costello?'

He stammered, he thought it was what she'd like, what Mrs Power senior would like. He was sorry.

'You know what they say in the films: "You're beautiful when you're angry, Miss Jones." ' It was Gerry. He had been behind her, and she hadn't noticed.

She laughed, in spite of herself. 'No, *really*, Gerry, this Mrs bit is the last straw.'

'Fiona likes it. She says it makes her feel grown-up.'

'It doesn't do that for me. It makes me feel we're all in some school play or other.'

'You see, I told you,' he sighed. 'You should never have married him. Go off and abuse the rest of the town. You've demolished Teddy fairly successfully,' he added good-naturedly, and disappeared.

Just as she was leaving the shop she saw Angela carrying fruit and a big bottle of orange over to the back of Dick Dillon's car.

773

'Are you going on a picnic?' she asked enviously.
'Just a few miles down the coast. Dick has a day off, we thought we'd explore a bit.'
'Great.'
'Why aren't *you* at your work by the way?'
'I came out for a bit of air.'
'And a something to keep you going?' Angela eyed the bottle-shaped parcel.
'Yes. Well.'
'I hope it helps the studying,' Angela said cheerfully and waved goodbye.

Disconsolately Clare walked back to the Lodge. Her anger with her mother-in-law was gone. But so was a lot of her good spirits. She hoped that David had been in and out while she was on her travels. She didn't feel like talking to him now, she wouldn't be able to get the despondent note out of her voice. There was a note on the table beside her books.

Glad you went out, it's the best day of summer. Why don't we take a day off together and go down the coast a bit? I was in seeing Peter O'Connor's child who got burned and he told me you'd ordered little saplings for the garden. That's a great idea, he's going to look them out for us and bring them tomorrow which is very speedy for Castlebay!

I love you my darling, and I'll see you this evening.

He wrote his name with a heart round it.

She sat down at her table and cried till the tears showered down on her big handwriting in all the files of notes.

He was the most generous and loving man in the whole world and here she was marching around the town trying to build a drawbridge and moat between him and his family. She felt wretched and shabby: maybe some of the things that Dracula believed about her were right? She just wasn't good enough for David.

They had their picnic down the coast. There were gulls and two small seals, and a school of porpoises too. They lay in the sun, happy and rested; they ran in and out of the sea; they drank their bottle of wine and their flask of coffee and ate their hard-boiled eggs and brown bread and butter. And the ice cream, which hadn't melted, wrapped up in six newspapers.

They kissed and laughed, and David accused her of having given Peter O'Connor unmentionable favours in order to make him do the hedge so quickly, and even more favours to Bumper Byrne and his gang, who had suddenly produced a very presentable entrance, having promised it since last April.

Clare said all his female patients were in love with him and that Rose Dillon at the hotel was definitely out to get him, married man or not. They wished they had taken old Bones with them; he would have loved this beach but he was getting a bit creaky now and he might have found the walk down and back too much for him.

They were as happy as they ever had been.

On September first she went to Dublin on the train. She had fourteen days before her exams began. David was going to come up for two weekends, and then to collect her and take her home when the exams were finished. She said it would be a waste for him to come with her now.

'I wish you all the luck in the world, my girl,' Dr Power had said, 'but you've never done anything except come in the top league in every examination you ever did. Do you remember my driving you into the town all those years ago, to do your scholarship? I remember it as if it were yesterday . . .' Dr Power beamed at her, and sighed at the way the years had flashed by.

Molly had decided to be charming. 'I hope you get all the questions you're looking for,' she said. 'Maybe that's not a very intellectual way of putting it but you know what I mean . . .'

They drove round by O'Brien's and she went in to kiss her mother good-bye.

'Lord, child, it's not the ends of the earth you're going to,' Agnes said.

'I know, Mam, but this is *it*, this is the B.A., the degree.'

'Well I know, Clare, and we all hope you'll do very well, but that's all behind you now, isn't it?'

Her mother came to the door and waved, puzzled at the exasperation that had come into Clare's face. After all, she had only said what was true. A lot of people didn't think that Clare should have bothered to go back to college to do that exam after getting married.

It was somehow like showing off.

'Will we have to learn first aid?' Val asked fearfully as Clare took off her shoes and eased her back with a cushion.

'What do you mean?'

'In case your man gets born here, what do we do? I know you need a watch to time things.'

'Not a chance. Week beginning October fifteenth. David's father hopes it's going to be the eighteenth, that's the feast of St Luke apparently, and Luke was a doctor in his time. What is it?' she asked suddenly as she saw Mary Catherine looking at a diary.

'Oh dear. You'll miss Conferring,' she said.

'I will *not* miss Conferring. I will bloody not. If Patrick Thomas is three days old, I'd be well enough to travel, wouldn't I? I *can't* miss Conferring. Maybe he'll come early . . .' Clare addressed her stomach. 'Be a good boy now and please your Mammy . . . arrive around the end of September, maybe the twenty-ninth, so that Mammy will be ready to come back up to Dublin and get Conferred.'

Mary Catherine was still looking at her diary. 'That would be quite a good day, actually. Feast of St Michael and all the angels.'

Clare clapped her hands. 'Right! Did you hear that? Be here on September twenty-ninth and we'll add Michael to your names.'

'I thought this yucky mumsy stuff only started *after* they were born,' said Valerie.

It was just as she had dreamed it would be. Plenty of room, books all around the place, cups of coffee being made all day and all night, friends dropping in. Down to the National Library where people noticed her condition and smiled congratulations. In to

UCD where people noticed her condition and were surprised. She had been a quiet student, and only the people in her own group knew her well.

She paid her examination fee, and got her number. It made it seem very close when she had the card with her own number.

She went to see Emer and Kevin and she noticed from their faces they were surprised to see how pregnant she now looked. Perhaps she had been holding herself in at home: everyone here seemed more aware of it.

Clare discussed the work she had done with her tutor.

'I didn't think we'd ever hear from you again,' he said.

'Why on *earth* did you think that?' Clare asked furiously.

'Well, married bliss, and a summer in Castlebay, a *summer* there, mind, not a week. I thought you wouldn't open a book again.'

'*My* only worry is the B.A.' Clare smiled at him. 'I suppose I sound a bit intense, and off my rocker to a lot of people. But when it's so hard, you get a kind of Holy Grail thing about it.'

'I know, I wish they all found it as important as you do.'

'Wish me luck then.'

'You don't need luck, Clare O'Brien . . . or whatever your name is now. You're the grade, everyone in the department knows it.'

They knew. Now all she had to do was prove it to them. She smiled as she went to sleep that night.

She had phoned David. He had just returned home after his second visit to Dublin. The Lodge was lonely without her, but in under ten days she would be back and they would wait. Together.

He wished her courage and energy and confidence. He couldn't say he loved her because he was standing in the hall, but he did say, 'And everything,' which was their code word.

She turned over and went to sleep happily.

Mary Catherine woke up in alarm.

'Come quickly! She's groaning, and shouting!'

'What? Who?'

'Clare. She's doubled over. Jesus, Mary and Joseph, I think she's having the baby. After all our joking about it.'

'Don't be ridiculous. It couldn't be. It's not for weeks yet.'

'Shut up. It could be a miscarriage. No, it couldn't, it's much too late . . . I don't know. Get an ambulance.'

'She keeps saying no.'

Clare was white-faced, with sweat coming down her forehead. 'It's all right,' she gasped. 'I couldn't be having it. I couldn't. These aren't those pains you have. No downward pull or whatever they said.'

'We don't know any doctors here, we're not on anyone's list, we're calling an ambulance, Valerie's phoning it this minute.' Mary Catherine was trying to be calm.

'Please don't. I can't go to hospital. The exam . . . There's nothing wrong.'

'Please, Clare. Just go in and be a false alarm, will you? Just for us? Please. Then you can come out twenty minutes later, and we'll all laugh at it. Please.'

She kicked the door closed with her foot so that Clare couldn't hear Valerie explaining down the phone how bad the patient was. 'Then we'll all go in and do the exams calmly.'

'I don't want you to be up half the night,' Clare cried.

Valerie came in, looking pale. 'We'll get dressed. We'll go with her.'

'*No!*' screamed Clare.

The ambulance was there in ten minutes. The girls had packed Clare's things quietly, and out of her line of vision.

The ambulance men were reassurance itself.

'It's all a false alarm,' Clare said with a tear-stained face. 'I'm so sorry and you see we're all starting our exams tomorrow. Our finals.'

She bent over with pain.

The ambulance men exchanged glances, and the driver leaped smartly into the driving seat and switched on the siren.

The pain was beyond anything she could possibly have imagined; nothing helped; not panting like a dog as they had taught her, nor reciting poetry very fast in an undertone, nor writhing and wriggling into different positions. A lugubrious student midwife kept telling her to relax. Clare wanted to kill her.

She was in labour for two hours before they told her that something was wrong. The midwife, listening for the third time to the foetal heartbeat, straightened up with more than usual gloom.

'The baby's in some distress.'

'Oh my God,' cried Clare wildly. 'What's wrong? Can you tell what's wrong?'

'The heart's not standing up to the contractions.'

'But will it be all right? The baby, I mean?'

'I can't say,' said the midwife, 'I shall have to report it.'

It seemed like hours. Clare felt pure terror; and the most intense longing for David. It had never occurred to her that the birth would be anything but straightforward; now it appeared that the baby was being killed by something uncontrollable inside her own body. Before she had held it, kissed it or even looked upon its face, her baby would die; and there was nothing she could do about it.

She was holding her breath as though that might ease the baby's distress when the door swung open to admit Bar, the red-headed doctor whom David disliked so much. The examination took seconds.

'Cord's dropped,' he said. 'I'm very sorry. I know how disappointed you will be. We shall have to do a Caesarean. We'll also have to ask you to sign a piece of paper giving your consent.'

'A Caesarean,' said Clare, high-voiced with joy. 'Oh thank God. Thank God. I'd forgotten all about Caesareans.'

Later she knew that a dropped cord was the worst emergency after a haemorrhage. Then she was only aware of Bar, now in a white mask and a green overall, giving clipped instructions. His face, which before had seemed rather heartless, now looked blessedly confident and know-it-all. Sister McClusky, summoned because she was an 'expert at cords', was an enormous, jovial woman who stuck her hand inside and gave Clare a running commentary on how well the baby was coping, all the way to the operating theatre.

'I love you,' she said, then they put her under. She felt the first violent pain of the knife, heard someone say it was a beautiful baby girl, before the anaesthetic took effect and she knew no more.

She woke up in the recovery room where the first person she saw was David holding their baby in his arms.

'She grinned,' he said. 'I've been holding her for an hour, waiting for you to come round, and she gave me the biggest grin you've ever seen.'

'She's not normal, is she?' said Clare.

'Darling, she's *perfect*.'

'You're lying to me, she's a mongol.'

'Here, see for yourself, she's beautiful.'

'Babies don't grin until they're six weeks old.'

At this point the baby began to cry, steadily angrily; and Clare, taking her in her arms for the first time, made two extraordinary discoveries. The first was that on contact with her mother the baby instantly stopped crying; and the second was that she was indeed utterly, perfectly, beautiful. True, the nose was a bit squashed, but her eyes were big and clear, and she had masses of hair. Her fingers looked as if they'd been soaked too long in washing-up liquid, but they were slender and graceful with long, pointed nails – almost as if they'd been specially manicured for her debut. Round one minute wrist and one ankle were plastic bands stating that she was Girl Power, and the date and time of birth.

With a flash of insight, Clare suddenly wished that they could all stay here forever, the baby safely cradled in her arms, protected by the hospital staff. For with this new love came also a new and terrible vulnerability, from which there would never be an escape. How shall I endure chicken pox, and tree climbing, and reading about children dying in fires? she thought. Life stretched away in an infinity of dangers and she felt afraid.

Part Four
1960 –1962

There were all the explanations: nobody got their arithmetic wrong, but it was the strain and the stress of the exam that brought the baby on; or she was genuinely a baby that was kicking and screaming to be born and would not wait the time; or Clare had been eating all the wrong food and not taking enough rest.

She had a very small face, but it wasn't nearly as red as the faces of other babies in the hospital; and her eyelashes were longer than any they had ever seen. She was so delicate and fine, that suddenly John Fitzgerald Byrne became a huge, hulking monster in comparison, and any other baby was crabbed and ugly.

Clare and David looked at each other and back at this magnificent person they had created. They kept saying over and over that they couldn't believe it. They said it so often in front of Father Flynn that he said he thought that's what they wanted her christened.

They decided they would give her a name that nobody else had, nobody else they knew. She wouldn't be Molly or Agnes; nor would she be Chrissie or Caroline or Angela or Emer or Valerie or Mary Catherine. She would not be a Fiona or a Josie or a Bernie. She would be a name that nobody had used before and put a shape into like wearing a jumper.

They didn't know any Victorias, and neither of them knew anyone called Martha; so those two were considered. Then David thought of Olivia, and the more he said it the more the tiny baby seemed to suit it; and the more they liked it. Olivia Power. It was a name that sounded made for her.

'You'll have to have a saint's name as well,' said the nurse who knew everything.

'I don't mind, any saint,' Clare said cheerfully.

'Mary's always nice,' said the nurse.

'What's your mother's name?' Clare asked David suddenly.

'It's Molly, you know that.'

'Yes, but what's it short for?'

'Margaret.'

'Right. We'll call her Olivia Mary. I just didn't want to let poor Saint Agnes feel left out. Da was put out enough about John Fitzgerald Byrne, I'll tell you that . . .'

Olivia Mary Power was ten days old when she left the hospital. Her mother was still pale, and rather shaken-looking. Olivia would need more bottles than a baby which had gone the full nine months, but she was perfectly well and healthy. She had a small christening, with champagne, in the private room which had been found for Clare when they realized she was a doctor's wife and not the hysterical student they had taken her for when she was admitted. There were flowers and cards, and a great deal of admiration.

At no time did anyone say that it was a pity that this of all babies had to be premature since they were going to pretend in Castlebay anyway that it was a premature birth even if it were six weeks late.

And at no time did anyone mention to anyone in the room that it was a pity that Olivia Mary Power could not have delayed her arrival for ten days so that her mother could have sat the examination for the degree she had so much wanted.

There was so much delight about the new baby, it would sound unwelcoming to say anything about bad timing.

'Do you think she minds desperately and isn't saying?' Valerie asked Mary Catherine.

'I have no idea. I know I was about to show her the examination papers and something stopped me. And I never mentioned them again.'

'It's funny, I've never been afraid to ask her anything, and even when I was on my own with her and the baby the other day, I couldn't ask.'

'Neither could I. That plausible attorney called me to ask me out, and in the midst of my saying no, he suddenly cut in and asked was she going funny in the head about the exams. He said that since he met her as a kid she's been talking about getting a degree, and now she doesn't mention it.'

'I don't *think* she minds. I think she's so goddamned pleased about the baby.'

'There's a bit in the New Testament about a woman getting all pleased about a man being born into the world.'

'Spare me your interpretations of the Bible, Val. Nobody in Ireland has ever read the book as far as I can see.'

'Wasn't that the worst luck ever? Poor Clare.'

Dick and Angela were learning to cook from a book, and each week they made something new in Angela's kitchen.

Angela agreed. 'I thought it would be the end of the world, and that we'd hear the tears of her the whole way from Dublin. But it seems she's not taking it badly at all.'

'I suppose, now she has the baby . . .' Dick broke off and frowned into the bowl. 'Is this the pale and light in texture that I should beat it until?'

'The people who write these books should be hanged. It looks pale and light in texture to me, but how would you know? This one says cook till ready. If we knew when "ready" was, we wouldn't need their stupid books.' She banged round the kitchen a bit.

'I suppose she could always sit it again next year.'

'She could. But people don't. It's like that. And with a small child she won't keep up her studies. How could she?'

'You're worried about her.'

'I am, but don't mind me. I worry about everything.'

Agnes read the letter out to Tom: the way the child's hair came forward and sideways from the crown like a little star. How the tiny toes each had a perfect little pink nail on them. How David had to bring all the things for the baby when he came up in such a rush, and he couldn't find half of them so he had packed table cloths and sheets and teatowels instead of the little matinee coats and vests.

'She seems to be delighted with the child,' Agnes said, pleased.

'Didn't it arrive a bit early? Isn't that what people will think?' Tom O'Brien looked at her over his glasses, waiting to see what reaction he would get.

'Wasn't it *miles* too early? Isn't that why she missed her exam?' Agnes said. 'But even if . . .'

'Tom, will you stop that, doesn't everyone know that the child wasn't expected for an age. Clare thought she was going to be doing her B.A., and everything.'

'Yes. Yes.' He saw there was going to be no scolding and complaining on the home side, which was a great blessing. 'Queer sort of name they gave it,' he grumbled.

'Oh you can be sure that's the Powers' doing. Some fancy choice of Molly's. That's what it will turn out to be. But saying nothing, that's always the best.'

Nellie wanted to know when they'd be home. She had been down to the Lodge on her day off in order to have it right for them. She hadn't liked Clare coming in there at first, she was sure there would be airs and graces. But as the months went on Nellie had felt sorry for the girl, stuck in there at her books all day. If ever you passed the window she wouldn't even look up, reading and studying and learning.

Nellie had known from the word go that there was a child on the way, and she knew better than anyone how enraged it had made the Mistress. The trouble was that the Mistress had no real friends she could talk to, and was sore to the bottom of her heart about it. She woke bad-tempered and she went to bed bad-tempered.

Nellie pitied her. She wasn't a bad woman – full of nonsense, of course, but everyone had something a bit wrong with them. Of course she'd have liked David to have got a finer girl than one of the O'Briens from the shop. David Power was the equal of anyone, but if he *had* got the little O'Brien girl into trouble and if he *did* seem happy to marry her, then Nellie thought that the best should be made of it all. There was no point in conducting a war across fifty yards of garden. Maybe it would be better when the baby came back, but you didn't need to be a genius to see that the Mistress was even more livid that the child had arrived so early. Now there was *no* way of covering up.

Molly said that they'd be arriving on Saturday.

'Will I set the tea for all of you in the dining room?' she asked.

Molly was about to say no, then she thought again. 'Yes, that's right, set it for all of us.'

Nellie smiled to herself, at least she had done that much for the young couple, they wouldn't have to be banished to their own little place and wait till the Mistress buzzed for them.

Dr Power was waiting on the platform, eager as a child.

They were in the front of the train, so they passed him, blinking happily into the carriages. Clare felt the tears come to her eyes, and David leaped up to wave out the window. 'Father, father.'

They didn't like Dr Power to drive on his own now, so he had brought Mrs Brennan with him. She had wanted to do a few things in town. She was waiting now in the car. Molly had said she'd prefer to meet them at home and because she had arranged a welcome-home supper, Paddy hadn't argued with her.

He hurried until his steps were a run down the platform and he peered into the white bundle. He took off his glasses and wiped them and put them on again.

'Isn't she perfect, God bless her, perfect little girl,' he said.

Clare was very nervous of anyone else touching the baby; but there she was thrusting it into her father-in-law's arms. He joggled her around expertly. He was so sweet that other people started to look at them.

'We're making a circus of ourselves,' he said. 'Come on, Clare, girl, let's go home.'

They walked to the ticket gate and Dr Power showed off his grandchild. Mrs Brennan in the car admired the baby with all the right words.

'Am I holding her right, do you think, Mrs Brennan?' Clare asked.

It was very much the thing to have asked. Mrs Brennan's face softened to the girl she had thought of as a bit of a madam up to now. All the way back to Castlebay they had lessons on supporting the head, and keeping the spine firm and the way to tilt the bottle. Dr Power hid his smile of pleasure when he saw how genuinely interested Clare and David were in what the woman was saying.

Six months ago they would both have crossed the road to avoid talking to Mrs Brennan. Now they hung on her every word.

Dr Power drove to the door of the big house.

'Molly has supper for you all here. Will we go straight in and show her the baby or would you like to go to your own house first?'

There was no doubting which he wanted.

David looked at Clare quickly.

'We'd love to come in and show off the baby,' she said.

Molly had been to the hairdresser, and she was wearing her best knitted two-piece. She was standing in the sitting room as if the gentry were coming.

David ran in and kissed her, and then stood back.

Clare put the baby straight into Molly's arms, which startled her. She had expected to bend over Clare and admire the child that way. Now she was holding her grandchild all on her own.

They couldn't stop admiring the baby. Clare looked at Molly occasionally, when she wasn't looking; Dracula was absorbed in the baby.

Nobody was going to be forgiven for anything, like blighting David's young life, forcing him to marry a girl from the lower classes, a shotgun wedding and an early baby. But given all that, at least Molly liked her granddaughter. At least she wasn't going to reject the child. Things were looking up.

At Mass next morning they met Gerry. He was full of congratulations.

'Olivia, that's a fine posh name for Castlebay,' he said approvingly.

'Ah, they're sick of these Davids and Clares and Gerrys, the dull old names,' Clare laughed.

'I hope they won't call her Olly,' David said.

'Make your own nickname then,' Gerry said.

'Livy?' Clare suggested.

'Liffey even?' Gerry said: David was buying the papers from Mickey Mack.

'I'm sorry about the exam,' Gerry said in a low voice.

'It doesn't matter,' she said brightly.

'Of course it does.'

'No, really. It sort of faded away. I didn't think it would.'

'You can't fool me. I know that's what you wanted so much, so don't throw my sympathy back at me as if it was worth nothing.' He stamped off.

They insisted that Angela come back to the Lodge where Nellie was minding Olivia.

They had coffee and toast, and Angela said she was going to give the baby a book, not a matinee coat, because she couldn't knit for one thing and everyone else gave matinee coats.

'You gave me my first book, remember,' Clare said. 'To console me for not getting the Prize.'

'*A Golden Treasury*. And it turned out better in the end.'

Clare cradled the new infant to her, and her thin white face looked misty remembering all that struggle ten years ago.

Angela wondered, as she saw Clare plant a kiss on the baby's forehead, did she regard this child as a consolation prize for not having got a history degree? And did she think it had all turned out better in the end?

Chrissie was the only one who mentioned that they had only been married five months when the baby was born. 'I'm disgraced in front of the Byrne family,' she said.

Clare sighed. 'Weren't you able to tell them the baby came early?' she asked.

'No baby comes *that* early.'

'Is there a chance that you'd like to look at her at all? I brought her to see her cousin. John Fitzgerald seems in great form.' Clare struggled as she felt she had been struggling for years just to get some kind of normal reaction from her sister.

'Oh I have nothing against the child, poor creature, it's none of her doing.'

'Good, then here she is to have a look at.' Clare handed her over. She had found that this was a sure-fire way of making people enthusiastic about the baby, once it was in their arms they felt different.

'She's grand, isn't she?' Chrissie said. 'A bit small of course.'

'That's to do with being born prematurely, I told you,' Clare said.

Chrissie had to laugh then.

'Come here to your Auntie Clare.' Clare picked up John Fitzgerald and gave him a cuddle.

'Well now, you're a big fellow. Six months old. You're a fine big fellow.'

'If you knew all the trouble I had with him being born,' Chrissie said.

'Well I do a bit. It's not a bundle of laughs, is it?'

'What are you talking about? You didn't have to give birth to this little thing at all! Wasn't she lifted out of you?'

'It's a way of describing it, I suppose.' Clare gritted her teeth.

'Sure there'd be no problem, we'd all have a half dozen if that's all there was to it. You wait, Clare, you wait for the next one, and see what it's like. I was in labour for fourteen hours. *Fourteen hours!* But of course that wouldn't be right for the wife of a doctor. They wouldn't leave her pushing and shoving for a whole day and into the night.'

'It must have been desperate all right.' She would have been happy to push Olivia into the world too. But useless to say that to Chrissie.

'Well it was, it wasn't something you forget in a hurry. Still it's more natural, in a way more normal. Imagine, you're only the same as me now, after all the grand plans, all the studying.'

'I know, isn't it strange?' Clare said without rancour.

Chrissie felt guilty. 'Well, you'd done enough anyway, hadn't you?'

'Oh definitely.'

All the patients seemed pleased that David was a father. It was nice to have a family man, they said. They sent soft toys for the new baby, they embroidered little dresses. Often the people who had little or no money to pay a doctor were able to give gifts, and they loved an excuse.

A man gave him a pair of hares that had been shot that day. 'Tell your wife to make a nice jugged hare, very good for a baby that is.' Another gave him potin to wet the baby's head and a woman whose house was always thought to be of the illest fame sent a miraculous medal to the little girl and said that this medal would protect her all her life.

Clare became more deft at giving the bottle but it still took a long time. In fact everything about Olivia took a long time. Clare looked with awe at the women trailing six or seven youngsters around with them. How had they managed? Maybe it was only the first that was such a problem, after that you had a team to help you. Now that she came to think of it she remembered giving a bottle to Jim and to Ben, while Mam was in the shop.

Olivia was so sweet you could play with her for hours. Just poking her gently in the tummy made her wave her arms and legs a bit. And she smiled, long before babies smile Olivia was smiling.

'I'm sure everyone must feel a bit like that, but they don't have the time to say it and think about it,' Clare said, looking at the small white bundle in the cradle.

'I don't have all that much more time to say it and think about it, I'm off again.' David finished his cup of tea as he pulled on his coat. 'I don't know how Dad looked after a quarter of this, I really don't, and yet he must have, you don't hear any complaints about him.'

He kissed his wife and daughter and ran through the rain to the car. He was becoming more and more involved in the work and all the patients; he said you'd learn as much in a month in Castlebay as in a year up in the hospital.

In the first few weeks there was no question of doing any studying, and Clare had no intention of beginning it until after Christmas. Everyone said a baby needed your full attention for the first three months. What nobody had said was that a baby took every ounce of your energy for the first three months too. But maybe you were meant to know that.

Olivia was a good baby they said, people who knew, people who had had babies like Mam, and Molly Power and Chrissie and Young Mrs Dillon and Anna Murphy and a dozen more. And the amount she slept was good. But sometimes she cried for long long times. Clare was despairing one morning and just before she took her child up to its grandfather in the surgery she discovered that a nappy pin was open and sticking into the tiny leg.

'How could I have done that to you? How?' Clare wept and held the small baby so close that the howls started again as the child began to feel suffocated.

The bath took a long time. You had to be very careful to hold her properly, she was so slippy, and you had to keep the soap from her eyes and yet make sure she didn't get cold.

And then the bottle. This was a slow day, she kept pushing it away. Finally it was almost finished and she was laid down. But she wouldn't settle. Over and over Clare took her up. It seemed an age before she agreed to sleep, even though her eyes were fighting to stay open.

Then there was the washing. Nellie had offered to help, but unfortunately she had offered when Molly Power was there, raising her eyebrows. So Clare thanked Nellie profusely, and said not at all. It was quite impossible to imagine that a tiny baby like that could provide such a mound of washing. Not to mention David's shirts. At home nobody changed their shirt every day. Dad would wear his shirt for four days maybe. And the boys . . . Lord knew when they changed theirs. But David had a fresh shirt every single day. It took seventeen minutes to iron each bloody shirt in the beginning. Now it took eleven. It was still far too long. Eleven minutes. That was a whole hour on five shirts one morning, and it was easier to do five at a time because otherwise he used to seem disappointed that he hadn't a choice.

'If you hate it so much I'll do it, it might be quite restful,' he had said once when she protested.

'No you damn well won't, the very first day you do one your mother will call and see you, and I might as well throw my hat at it after that.'

Today she had decided to iron three. But in the middle of the first one Olivia woke up again, and since it was nearly time for her bottle that was the end of the shirts. Then David was home for lunch. Then she had to tidy herself up. This was the day she had been invited for a cup of tea in the big house. Molly talked almost entirely to Olivia, in baby talk, and twice asked the baby, who was not yet three months old, whether she thought that matinee coat was a little bit too tight.

Clare answered, as the baby didn't. It was a fine fit.

'Why then, Olivia, do you have these little red marks on your arm, little sore marks? *Poor* Olivia.'

Clare wanted to hit Molly with one of the big hard uncomfortable cushions on the sofa. Instead she sat back and swallowed her thin tomato sandwich.

David rang her later in the afternoon.

'What's wrong,' she asked, alarmed.

'Nothing's wrong, I'm just celebrating that we have the phone that's all.'

'Yes, it's marvellous. No more buzzing from the Great House.'

'Now, Clare!' he laughed.

'Sorry. Sorry. Will you bring home some chops from Dwyers'?'

'It might be closed when I'm coming back. Why don't you ring them and ask them to deliver?'

'And have Chrissie calling me Lady Muck for a month.'

'Oh well, do what you can. I have to go. I thought I'd just ring.'

'There was nothing you wanted to say?'

'Only that I loved you.'

She hung up, and realized she should have said she loved him too.

She asked Nellie to look after the baby in the kitchen and walked down to Church Street and a confrontation with Chrissie.

Her mother-in-law moved the curtain in the sitting room and watched her go.

She wrote to Valerie that evening but tore up the letter. It was a list of complaints and moans and grouses. It was the kind of letter you would hate to read. Then she put the pieces in the range in case anyone ever found them torn up in the bin and pieced them together. She wondered was she going mad to imagine anyone piecing together one of her letters to Valerie.

David was called out twice in the night.

When the phone went the second time Olivia woke too. Clare went to pick her up. David was putting on his socks and shoes as he talked to the woman on the phone.

'It's no life this, is it?' she said jiggling the crying baby up and down in her arms.

'It's not for that woman.' David nodded at the phone which he had just put down. 'Those bloody dogs they have out there have just eaten the face off her baby.'

'*No!*'

David had his clothes on by now.

'What will you do?' Clare asked, stricken.

'Hope the baby's dead, properly dead. Hope we can get its mother to agree to go into the hospital. For a couple of days, anyway. She'll need more than just a sedative after that lot.'

He was down the stairs and into the car. It was three hours, and dawn, before he came back. Olivia was asleep again. Clare was in the kitchen, she had a kettle ready and made some tea. He took the mug gratefully.

'Was the baby dead?' she asked.

'Not quite,' he said.

She waited. He said nothing.

'And Mrs Walsh? Is she all right?'

David still said nothing. His shoulders were shaking. He was crying, but he didn't want her near, he went to the window and looked out at the dark sea and the shapes of the cliff heads only becoming visible now. He stood there for a long time and she found no words or gesture to help him.

She went over to the big house to take the paper back. She had read it from cover to cover. There was a voice in the kitchen, talking to Olivia. She thought David must be back, but she didn't see his car. It was Gerry. He was dangling a little woollen ball, a brightly coloured pompom, in front of the baby who was looking at him eagerly.

'Gerry?' She was not pleased. He had given her a fright, and anyway, how dare he come in uninvited?

'I don't remember asking you in,' she said.

'I don't remember a time when friends in Castlebay had to wait to be invited in. Maybe it's different here in the . . . um . . . in the Lodge.' He made the name of the house sound laughable.

'What do you want?'

'I came to see your daughter and ask her would she like her photograph taken. That's all.'

'Don't be childish, Gerry. What do you want?'

'What I said. Would you like a picture of the baby . . . as a wedding present?'

'No,' she said quickly.

'What nice manners they teach up at the Lodge.'

'No thank you. I'm sorry. No thank you very much.'

'Why not? I take nice pictures of babies. They like me.'

Olivia was indeed gurgling up at him and the red, black and yellow ball of wool.

'I'd prefer not, if you don't mind. Thanks, though. Sorry about my manners.' She smiled, hoping he'd go.

He stood up. 'She's beautiful,' he said. 'I sometimes think *I'd* like one.'

'Well, nothing's stopping you.' She tried to be light. 'You know how to set about it.'

'Ah, but it would be no use if it weren't yours too.'

She flinched.

He put up both his hands in peace. 'I'm off, I'm off. Take that look off your face.'

He did have his camera with him, in its shabby black bag that he had always used. 'Whenever you think she's old enough, I'd love to.'

'Sure. I'll talk about it with David,' she said.

'Do that.' He smiled and was gone.

She felt very uneasy and didn't know why. He only wanted to take a photograph. He had only made those sort of flattering remarks that he made to everyone. Why did she feel so bothered?

She invited her mother-in-law to see the baby being bathed. She spent the whole day tidying the place up first.

Molly came to watch the ritual.

Clare tested the heat of the water with her elbow, feeling very experienced.

'Do you do that? How strange,' Molly said. 'How very strange, with all the thermometers and everything. Ah well.' She sighed as if her granddaughter was being brought up by a thick, ignorant peasant who knew nothing.

One grey morning she heard a timid tapping on the door. It was her mother.

'You haven't been down for a bit. I called to see you.'

'That's great. Come on in.'

Agnes O'Brien looked around as if fearful someone might ask her what she was doing there. 'Have you done up the parlour yet?' she asked.

'You're always asking me that. What would we need a parlour for or a sitting room or drawing room or whatever we'd call it? This is where we live.'

Agnes jerked her head up towards the big house. 'But wouldn't they expect . . . ?'

'Let them expect what they like. David and I want to make this a nice bright room that we can live in. Armchairs and bookshelves and the advantage of it being the kitchen as well.'

'And when are you going to start?' her mother asked innocently.

'Will we have a cup of tea?' Wearily she emptied the tealeaves from the pot and put it on the range.

'Are you not using a kettle?'

'There's just the two of us, Mam.'

She was wrong.

Molly Power was at the door.

'I thought you might want something from town, I'm going in with Mrs Dillon this afternoon. Hallo, Mrs O'Brien.'

'Good morning, Mrs Power. Good morning.' Agnes stammered a little.

'Come to admire the baby?'

'Yes, well, Clare hasn't shown her to me yet.'

'Clare dear, do show the baby to your mother.'

Clare fumed. Her mother had made it seem that she had never seen her granddaughter at all. Mrs Power made Clare feel like a very unsatisfactory hired help.

She went upstairs for Liffey. She was not only wet, her nappy was filthy. The clean nappies were downstairs.

She went down to get them.

'Oh, don't bother dressing her up specially.'

'I'm not,' Clare hissed.

She did a rapid change job and Liffey, alarmed by the speed and lack of gentleness, cried in fright. Clare handed her first to her mother.

'I don't know whether I should . . .'

Why did Mam have to be so humble?

'You had six of your own, I'm sure you won't drop her.' Her voice was sharp. The teapot was hissing. Trying to shield her actions from her mother-in-law, Clare put four spoons of tea into the boiling water and pulled it aside.

'What a funny way to make tea,' Mrs Power said clearly.

'I've told Clare a dozen times not to do that,' Agnes said. Awkwardly she passed the baby over to Mrs Power. For a few minutes Molly Power cooed at her grandchild, and by magic the child stopped crying.

'There you are,' said Molly triumphantly, as if she alone knew the secret.

She refused a cup of tea without actually shuddering, and left.

Clare and her mother were full of gloom.

'You shouldn't let her see the house like this, Clare, really.' Agnes looked at the heap of dirty clothes in a corner, the unwashed saucepans on the draining board.

'It's my house. I'll have it look exactly the way I want to.'

'Oh all right.' Her mother was about to take offence and leave.

'Not you, Mam, sit down. I mean her. Why should we bow down before her? I'm damned if I'll do everything the way Lady Molly wants.'

'No, but you could do a bit of cleaning and cooking, that's not bowing down before her,' Agnes said coldly.

Clare knew that she wouldn't drop in again casually; she would have to go and invite her from now on.

She had been very entertained by Angela's attempts to learn to cook; and decided it wasn't a bad idea. She might well do the same herself. She made shortbread biscuits one morning and took a plate of them up to the house for Molly.

'Won't you come in and have coffee with me?' Molly said.

'I left her there on her own,' Clare said.

'Oh well. Another time then.'

The woman could have said, go back for her, couldn't she?

She lay on her bed resting one morning, and her mind just drifted off. She wasn't asleep for more than a moment. David came in.

'Hey, you worried me. I thought you weren't here.'

'What is it? What's wrong?'

'Clare, what *are* you doing? Olivia's crying her head off downstairs, Bones is sitting looking at her, and there's no lunch.'

'It's not lunchtime.'

'It's half past one, I thought I'd be late.'

'Christ, I'm sorry, David. I must have fallen asleep.' She leaped from the bed and raced down the stairs. With Olivia in one arm she grabbed a saucepan and broke three eggs into it, she reached for some butter.

'What are you doing?'

'David my love, I'm making you a scrambled egg. I'm sorry, I'll make a proper dinner this evening, I tell you I must have drifted off to sleep. I feel so tired sometimes.'

'I know. I know. It's all right.'

'It's not all right, I'm dreadfully sorry.'

'Look, will I make toast or something?'

'No, hold your daughter, I'm quicker.'

She swept the breakfast things away and into the sink.

'I don't want you to feel you have to cook a lunch for me every day, don't think that . . .'

'Darling David – will you stop it. One day, just *one* day I fell asleep. Every other day I love to have lunch with you. I love it. I used to be very lonely when you were up with your mother and father and I was there at the window working.'

They both looked over at the window as she spoke. No books there now, just a big arrangement of dried flowers.

'Aren't you going to start studying again?'

'What for?'

'Clare, please. Don't be like that. For your degree of course.'

'I studied for it once, why should I do it again?'

'Because you didn't take it, you clown. You were happy studying.'

'Not all the time I wasn't. A lot of the time I was worried and anxious.'

'Will we go to the pictures tonight?'
'Are you trying to entertain me by any chance?'
'A bit I suppose.' He looked troubled.

Clare asked Angela was there any kind of Christmas present you could make for
people, by cooking, something that would look as if you'd gone to a lot of trouble
over it.

'I suppose you could make fudge,' Angela said doubtfully, 'and put it in nice
coloured boxes. But why do you want to make things? You're worse than me. And
I think they'd expect a bit more than fudge from you.'

'Who'd expect? I don't care what they expect, I'm so tired, I tell you Angela I
can't stay awake these days. It's such an effort to go into town, and there's nothing
here . . .'

'Well stay awake long enough to go into town just one day. Make a list of what
you want. Come in with Dick and me on Saturday afternoon.'

'Yes, I could do that. I'll ask her Ladyship would she mind Liffey.'

'Liffey. Isn't *that* a name, now. How did you think of it?'

'I just made it up,' Clare said. She didn't want to tell anyone that it was Gerry
Doyle's idea.

'Am I going to teach you to drive, Clare? Remember we set it all up. You learned
the theory all at once.'

There was a silence at the back of the car.

'I think she's asleep, Dick,' Angela said.

'No, sorry, what was it?'

'Will I give you driving lessons after Christmas?'

'I don't know if I'd have the time. It's very kind of you. If I have the time . . .'

Molly and David were sitting by the fire in the big house when she came back.

'You look exhausted,' David said.

'David, you must get Clare some nice clothes, it's terrible to have her dragging
round in all that studenty-type thing. No wonder the girl looks so dawney.'

Clare let them talk about her.

'Why don't we all have a sherry, you've provided the excuse.' David leaped up.

'A really nice coat in a good bright colour, something that would put some
colour in her face.' Molly was thoughtful. 'A cherry red maybe.'

David handed them both a sherry.

'Thank you, my dear,' Molly said.

Clare said nothing.

'Was it exhausting?'

'It was very tiring all right,' Clare said.

'Did you leave your parcels in at the Lodge?'

'No. This is all I got.' She had a small shopping bag with a few little things in it.

She sat on a stool looking into the fire and eventually David and his mother
went back to talking as they had been before she came in. They didn't even try to
bring her into the conversation.

David bought all the Christmas presents in the end. He even wrapped them and wrote the cards. He put the Christmas cards she was to send to Mary Catherine and Valerie in front of her and she wrote Love from Clare on each of them.

When David opened his Christmas present from Clare he said he was delighted with the shirt. It was just what he wanted. You couldn't have enough shirts. He said this one was particularly nice, and he put it away hastily before his mother could see it had been bought in the shop in Castlebay and was exactly the same as half a dozen which he had already.

David had bought Christmas tree decorations when he was in town: he couldn't bear anyone in Castlebay to see him buying them locally. He brought a tree home from one of his country calls, the man whose child had been sick was delighted to give the young doctor a fine green tree.

'Your wife will enjoy decorating that, Doctor,' the man beamed as they fitted the tree into the back of the car.

'Oh, she's going to love it,' David said with a smile he didn't feel.

He looked carefully at his mother's tree that evening and did something a bit similar to their own; Clare looked up at him gratefully as he stood on a chair.

'That's terrific, David, it looks really lovely. I'd do it myself but I'm just worn out.'

It was cold clear weather, from the window David saw his parents warmly dressed and in their comfortable walking shoes setting out with the dog. He knew they would head far along the cliff away from Castlebay and they would point things out to each other, and see the birds swooping low and hares running through the fields. They would come back to a hot lunch. They would sit on either side of a big well made-up fire and read. He looked over at Clare to know if she too would like a walk. She was sitting at the kitchen table. She had been reading, but in fact she had dropped off over her book.

There was a call for the doctor to come quickly. A child. Come quickly. They rang off. A five-year-old had fallen over rusty farm machinery and opened his eye.

David remembered Clare saying that she had cut her leg years ago on the rusty spikes of half-hidden machinery. He felt a surge of anger about people raising children so casually among all these dangers.

Soothing, reassuring, and speaking confident words he didn't mean, David wiped the drying blood from the child's face. It wasn't too bad. Calming and chatting to distract their attention he said it wasn't bad at all, it would all be fine, now now, could someone start to make some tea. Then he took out his bag and put five quick stitches into the small face. He examined it critically. It wasn't bad. The child looked at him trustingly.

'Isn't that fine,' David said.

'I'm Matthew.'

'Of course you are, and you're better now.' David gave him a hug just as the tea tray was being brought in.

'Aren't you the cut of your father, and the same grand ways with you.' Matthew's mother was holding one of his hands between both her own.

'Thank you.'

'We were all delighted when you married a local girl, not getting yourself a fancy wife from Dublin.'

'I'm glad.'

'And how's your own little girl, Doctor?'

'Oh she's beautiful, thank you. Simply beautiful.'

'I'm glad to hear that, you give so much to other people's children, it would be very sad if you didn't find happiness in your own.'

Liffey was crying when he got in. She was wet. Her little legs were red and chapped, and the napkin soaked. As it was cold, she had obviously been lying like that for some time.

Clare was lying in bed reading a recipe book.

'I thought I'd make drop scones, they don't look too hard,' she smiled at him.

'Sure, that would be fine, Liffey's very wet.'

'I'll see to her in a minute.'

'She's been wet for ages, Clare.'

'Oh all right.'

David spoke sharply. 'No, I'll do it, it'll be quicker.'

'Oh good.' She went back to studying the recipe book.

Clare went back to bed early, so she should have had a fair bank of sleep when Liffey woke. But the child cried and cried and Clare never turned over in bed.

David got up. He fed and changed her again, but she still wouldn't settle. He walked her up and down. Eventually, she slept.

About ten minutes before he intended to get up Liffey began again. He poked Clare gently.

'You get her this time, love, will you, I want to grab a few minutes' sleep.'

Clare swung her legs out of bed and put her woolly dressing gown on over her long nighty. She picked up Liffey with a few words of comfort and carried her downstairs.

When David had washed and shaved and come down for his breakfast, Clare was sitting at the table, asleep. The kettle was on the range, hissing and spitting; Liffey was screaming from her cradle.

That was the morning David told his father in halting, broken sentences that he thought Clare was suffering from post-natal depression.

His father said that these things were too easily defined and put into categories. Clare was a bit low. Life was very different and less demanding than it had been last year, and it should never be forgotten that the child had missed her degree. That would be hard enough on any girl but on a little girl who had fought like a tiger to get there it must have been harder still.

David said it was more than that. If it was only that they could talk about it and sort it out, but she was so physically tired, she was drowsy all the time, and without losing any love for Liffey she seemed to have lost interest in her.

David's face was white and his eyes were dark and sleepless-looking. His father was full of pity for him.

'I think you should still try other ways before you say that we should treat it, or send her to someone.'

'I don't want to send her to anyone, but couldn't she be put on Tofranil? Wouldn't that sort her out in a month or two? Dad, that's what we'd say for anyone else. Why can't we say it for Clare?'

'Because it could be a lot of other things, she could be lonely, she could be unsure of herself, Molly might be making her feel inadequate. Talk to her. Talk, and tell her things and maybe you'll see. It's not a question of her being some unfortunate woman who has no one to understand her. She's got a fine husband, a great husband.'

'I can't be all that great if she's changed so much.'

'Do you still love me?' he asked her.

'David, what can you mean? I love you more than ever.'

'That's the third time you've been too tired to make love.'

'I'm sorry, I just felt a bit weary. OK. I don't mind, now I'm awake.'

'It's too late now.'

'Oh David, stop sulking.'

He swung his legs out of bed and plugged in the electric fire. He wanted to talk and he didn't want them to freeze.

'I promise you on my oath I'm not sulking. But when I think the way we were jumping on each other this time last year, it seems as if we were two different people.'

'This time last year we were in Dublin and we hadn't all the responsibilities we have now,' she said.

'This time last year, you were working fourteen hours a day for your exams, I was working fourteen hours a day in that hospital, we had to get round the city on buses, we were up to here in anxiety. Now we have our own house, our own child, our freedom to jump on each other morning, noon and night if we wish to do so, I have a gentle and satisfying amount of work to do rather than the mayhem as an intern, you have no official things to do and we're still too tired.'

'You're not, I am,' she said, correcting the facts.

'But why, Clare, *why*? I'm not just being a raging beast like all men trying to demand my rights, or more rights, or anything. Why are you so tired?'

'There's so much to do,' she said.

'Are you sure you love me, and you know I'm not picking a fight?'

'Yes, of course.'

'Then let me tell you what you did today. You got up and *I* got breakfast. And *I* changed Liffey. And I said I'd get a leg of lamb in Dwyers' on the way home and you said no, *you* would. Before I went out I brought in some potatoes from the bag outside. *I* peeled a few, *you* said leave them. I came home for lunch. You had been asleep all morning. Liffey was wet and bawling . . . you were upset because there was no lunch. Clare . . . this is terrible. This isn't meant to be a row, do you understand, I'm just trying to find out why you could be tired? I made us a tin of soup and we had some of Nellie's bread while you got the bottle for Liffey. This time I insisted on getting the meat. I left it back in the house at three o'clock. You were asleep in the chair. Clare, *I* put the bloody meat into the oven, and that's how we had dinner. I thought we'd go to the pictures but *you* said *you* were too tired. You've been asleep all morning, all afternoon and now you're weary, you say, when you come to bed. I'm your doctor as well as your husband. Of course I'm worried about you.'

'I'm very sorry. When you put it like that, it's indefensible.'

'Darling heart, I'm not blaming you, I'm only asking you as my best and dearest friend, can you tell me what's wrong?'

'I don't know. I didn't think anything was.'

'But we can't live like this. I mean, you can't go on like this – if I weren't a doctor I'd bring you to a doctor.' He smiled and put both his hands on her face.

'What do you think?' She looked like a worried child.

'I think it's a depression.'

'I'm not sad.'

'No, a clinical depression.'

'But I swear I'm not depressed.'

'And your exams?'

'Yes, but I've got over that. Honestly I have. I had harder things to fight against ten years ago. Now I'm a nice middle-class married lady, no worry about the fees. If I haven't the guts to do it again it's my own fault, not anybody else's. Not Liffey's fault, not yours, only mine.'

'And will you have the guts to do it again?'

'I think I'm too tired. There, I've said it again.'

'I'd like to give you an anti-depressant.'

'More energy, like?'

'No, I'm not going to talk to you as if you were an ignoramus, they've got nothing to do with iron or energy, they work on the chemicals, on amino acid in the brain, and on the nerve endings. It would take about three weeks to make any difference.'

'What does your dad think?'

'I'll ask him.'

'I'm sure you have asked him, it doesn't matter, you have to ask him things.'

'He thinks you're just lonely and unsure of yourself here.'

'And you think it's a post-natal depression, and I think it's just tiredness.'

'It could be a bit of all of them,' David said.

'Well feed me the medicine, Doctor, and let's hope we see a miracle cure.' She smiled at him, a smile from the old days, and he went to sleep feeling a little better than he had felt for some weeks.

Next day he suggested that they take Liffey to see Mr Kenny, and Clare said that was a great idea: the nice old solicitor had sent them a lovely silver spoon for the baby. But when David got home expecting Liffey and Clare to be ready, the baby hadn't been changed or dressed, and Clare said she felt very tired today.

David said fine, they'd go another day and without making any big drama out of it he started her on a course of Tofranil.

'I was up this way and I wondered if there was a cup of tea going.'

'Nobody's up this way, but you can have a cup of tea,' she said.

'You never come down town any more,' Gerry said.

'And how would you know whether I do or not?'

'Your mother mentioned it to me, as it happens.'

'Oh Lord. I meant to go to see her this week.'

'This week? Clare, she's only ten *minutes* away. She thinks you've joined the gentry.'

Clare felt very guilty. The days ran into each other, yes, it was a whole week since she had brought the baby over to her mother, it must be three days at least since she had seen her mother-in-law.

'Do you feel all right, Clare?' Gerry asked gently. He was sitting at the kitchen table.

She was pouring the kettle of water into a teapot.

'Thank you very much for all this interest, Dr Doyle. Have you become a medical consultant now as well as a home counsellor, bearing me advice from my family?'

'I'm serious, Clare.'

She brought the tea to the table.

'I'm tired, that's all. It's very exhausting looking after a baby.'

'That one doesn't seem to need much looking after. She's fast asleep.'

'Ah, but they wake up, Gerry, that's a little trick they have.'

They drank their tea.

'And is the handsome young doctor giving you anything for your tiredness?'

'Yes of course he is . . . a course of tablets.'

'Good. I'm glad he noticed.'

'Please don't speak badly of David, Gerry, it makes me very upset.'

'I'm not speaking badly of him. I'm just saying he's wrong for you.'

'Now you really must go.' She stood up, coldly. 'Friend or no friend, Gerry, you are not coming into my house when David is not here and saying that. No you bloody can't.'

'You're only getting upset because it's true.'

'Oh don't be ridiculous. You can win any argument if you say things like that. The truth is I am upset to hear any bad reference made to David at all, and if you ever knew what it was like to love someone rather than just . . . well . . . use them . . . then you'd understand.'

'I love you,' he said.

There was a silence.

Then she threw her head back. 'Don't be idiotic. You only say that because you once or twice made a pass at me and I didn't give in. You feel it's broken the track record for you, it's not one hundred per cent. Bingo! Isn't that it? That's what it's all about. I pity any girl you really say that you love because you don't know what the word means.'

He sipped his tea. 'In this case I suppose it means that I'd do anything to have you, anything.'

She felt frightened.

'Please . . .' she began.

'I saw David one day last week kneeling in the middle of the road. I thought of putting my foot on the accelerator. Nobody would have blamed me. He was in the middle of the street, any court would have let me off. Then I saw he was looking after a puppy someone had run over. I couldn't do it.'

Clare stood up. 'You aren't serious, you're just saying these things to make yourself sound like a villain.'

'No, it's quite true. Quite true.' His voice was calm.

'But *why?*'

'Who knows? Who knows anything about why people love other people? Anyway I decided that it could never be done that way, and even if David had an accident, a genuine accident, and you were a grieving widow, that mightn't work. It might take years for you to get over him. So it has to be a different way entirely.'

'This is a game, is it?'

There was another silence.

Clare didn't like him sitting there looking at her. 'I'll tell you something, maybe it's foolish but I'll tell you anyway. I don't feel all that well, I think I have a sort of depression, and honestly I can't take any more upset. I would be sitting here day and night in a panic if I thought that anything you were saying, *any* of it, were true. Can you reassure me that it's not? Please?'

'I thought you had a depression,' he said sympathetically. 'Remember Fiona did too, in England that time. But she got over it, and so will you. Is he giving you proper tablets for it?'

'Yes.'

'You'll be fine, and you'll be back at your books, and madam there will grow up to be a pride and joy to you.'

It was as if he hadn't said any of the other terrible things. Clare felt dizzy.

'So put everything out of your head. I'll just love you quietly from a distance. For ever. You know?'

'Or until summer,' she said.

'No, for ever. But you're right, there's no point in getting you upset, you're to get yourself better now.'

He got up to leave.

'Yes. Yes I will, I'll be fine.'

'And go to see your Mam, eh? And Josie, right?'

'Right. Goodbye, Gerry.'

The baby woke just then and began a little cry.

'Aren't you going to pick her up?'

'Yes, in a minute. I was just seeing you off. Hush, Liffey, I'm just coming.'

'Liffey?' he smiled from the door. 'You call her the name I gave her.'

'I think we're going to have to come to terms with pastry,' Angela said.

'I came to terms with it years ago, I love it.'

'No, I think we should make it. We've been avoiding all these recipes that begin telling you to roll out the crust. Let's make the damn thing tonight.'

'Right,' he said. 'Will I get the ingredients?'

'No, I'll call into O'Brien's on the way back from school, I think it's only flour and lard or something, but I might be wrong.'

'I can't think of any other woman of your age who doesn't know how to make pastry,' he said, teasing her.

'Less of that, you got yourself an intellectual as a girlfriend, you should be delighted with yourself and counting your blessings all the time.'

'Are you my girlfriend?' he said, pleased.

'Of course I am. I didn't mean to be but I am,' she said.

The following night they made the pastry. It was nightmarish. The book had said you could use lard *or* butter *or* margarine.

'Why doesn't it tell us what ordinary people use?' Angela fumed.

It had told them to Rub The Fat Into The Flour.

'That actually is not English, you rub something out, or you rub something, you don't *rub in. God*, these people.' They made it look like breadcrumbs which is what it said, but it also said use a Light Hand.

'That's the most stupid thing I ever heard. How can you be light with all this rubbing?' Dick had an apron on over his good suit. Angela had insisted.

'I don't know what you wore a good suit like this for, just to do cooking,' she scolded. But she knew well . . .

It was the same reason that she had worn a smart blouse and washed her hair.

The question had to wait until they worked out what Bake Blind meant. By process of elimination they discovered it meant that you put the pastry into the oven and you cooked it by itself first. Angela wrote a short note to the book's publishers saying that it should be withdrawn for its general misinformation.

Then they sat down and poured themselves a drink. Dick stood up again and said he would like Angela to marry him.

'Dick, are you sure? You've been asking me a long time you know.'

He put his glass of orange squash down on the table and took her hands. 'I thought that maybe when you let slip that you were my girlfriend that we had made a bit of progress,' he said.

'I'm very difficult,' she said.

'I know,' he said.

'And you're set in your ways of course,' she added.

'I am *not* set in my ways. When I got to know you, which is not today or yesterday, I was set in my ways. Now I do all kinds of things I'd never have done before. I read long books, I cook great meals. I'm cheerful instead of miserable. What do you mean, set in my ways?'

'Yes, please.'

'What?'

'I said yes please, I'd love to marry you.'

Angela tried the beautiful ruby ring on, the ring that Dick Dillon had bought long ago hoping for the day it would be needed. It was perfect.

'I'll make you a good wife – not a peaceable one mind, but I'll be good to you, and love you and look after you.'

'The love bit is the most important one,' he said shyly.

'It is for me too, I just felt awkward saying it.'

'We don't need to feel awkward any more,' he said, and they sat in the firelight, as the pastry burned black in the oven and the red ruby glittered and shone.

'Do you have this funny feeling that it's all over? It's all happened? Like everything went into the past tense instead of the future tense?' asked Clare.

David looked at her. He had no feeling like that at all. 'I know, I know,' he said, his heart heavy.

'Oh good. I was afraid it was just me. I suppose we'll get used to it, and adapt.'

'I think that's what happens to people,' he said.

'It's not regrets or anything. You know that?'

'Of course.'

'But you must find that too. I mean you don't regret coming back here, but the kind of work you do, the life we lead, it sort of happened a bit soon, didn't it?'

He patted her hand. She *was* much brighter than before, she was far more aware of Liffey and spent hours playing with her. She had taken driving lessons from Dick Dillon. David had even seen some of her history textbooks out by the window again.

Perhaps Clare was just too young and unprepared to settle down so quickly. Perhaps she would never settle down. It made it all the harder to tell her that he *loved* this life. He liked caring for sick, frightened people, and curing them with medicines from his black bag; or sewing up their wounds; delivering their children sometimes or closing the eyes of their dead. A couple of years ago he might have been mildly tolerant of his father's brand of medicine, preferring instead to think of a more scientific approach. Now he couldn't see anything that would be better for the patients than to see a face they trusted, an old face and his son a newer face. This gave them some confidence and very often that was three-quarters of the battle.

It all made him feel unsettled. He didn't worry about Clare's health any more but he felt that the great closeness they had grown used to, and accepted as if it was their natural right, had disappeared. The words were the same, the interest was there, she was eager to hear about his cases and discuss them. But it was as if she believed that somehow they had been shunted into a siding and forgotten about, and they were trapped in this middle-aged world, so they had better play the role of old people as cheerfully as possible.

Dick and Angela were married in Dublin. There had never been the slightest discussion about it. They knew they wanted nobody from Castlebay, not one of Dick's hotel relations, and Angela said that she certainly didn't want to draw sisters and brothers and the whole of Japan on her either. It was arranged with no fuss, Father Flynn again, of course, and Emer and Kevin.

Just the five of them at a small side altar early one morning.

'It's not festive enough for you,' Father Flynn complained.

'Our life is festive enough, Father, we don't need it on a wedding day. Honest.' He gave in grudgingly.

They went back to Emer's and Kevin's house and they had scrambled eggs and bacon and a cake that Angela and Dick had made themselves from the section called 'Simple Cake Making' which they said was another example of lies in cookery books.

Reluctantly they allowed Father Flynn to take one photograph of the occasion which, when it came out, was so ludicrous that Angela said it could illustrate an article called Christmas Day in the Asylum.

They took the picture out occasionally if they wanted a good laugh, but they didn't need anything to remind them of the best day of their lives. That's just what it was, Dick said, pure and simple. The best day ever. And for once even Father Flynn found himself without a word to say.

It came as a great surprise to hear that the Nolans were going to take a house on the Cliff Road again. Mr Nolan hadn't been well: he had been told to take things easy and get a bit of sea air. Caroline had finished her apprenticeship and was in the throes of looking for a job. She thought she would have a break. James said that he could prepare his few briefs just as well in Castlebay as anywhere else.

That was the way the news was broken to David by letter. He read it to them all with suitable James gestures and Clare was surprised to see how pleased they all were.

Even Nellie was delighted. 'It puts the Mistress into great good humour when that lot comes down, and their Breeda's a very nice girl, I'll be glad to see her again myself.'

Mrs Power started in a mad rush to get the garden done up. There was a nice corner with lupins and she wanted to be able to have afternoon tea served there. She had all the deckchairs of course but they looked a bit shabby.

'I'll paint the deckchairs blue for you, and we'll look like an ocean-going liner. What do you think?' Clare looked at her mother-in-law.

'I don't think so . . .'

'Oh go on, you've got blue and white china, you could get blue paper serviettes. It would be terrific.'

Mrs Power seemed to regret having shown how flustered she was to Clare, she wished she hadn't admitted her wishes to impress the Nolans, she began to take it all back.

'Well, thank you, dear, for the idea anyway,' she said dismissively.

'Are we going to do it?' Clare cried, 'because if we are I'll ring Bumper and ask him to get some cans of paint round here right away.'

'I think not, Clare. Thank you, no.'

Two red spots burned in Clare's cheeks. 'A bit flashy, might it be?'

'Since you say the word, that's just what it might look like, you know, a little . . . well, a little overdone.'

'Common?' Clare asked.

'No, no, heavens what a thing to say about your idea, but you know . . .'

'I know,' Clare said grimly and walked back to the Lodge.

'You've got a common flashy mother,' she said to Liffey, 'a mother who is a little . . . what's the word again . . . overdone.'

Liffey seemed pleased with the attention and the tone of Clare's voice.

'And Liffey, you also have an almighty bitch of a grandmother, I never want you to forget that. She is in the major league of bitchiness as your godmother Mary Catherine would say, she is a Class A bitch.'

Clare felt better when she had defined everything. Liffey was a good listener.

Caroline looked very elegant. Clare remembered when she had come to Castlebay first, and she had been so jealous of all the fun Caroline and her friend Hilary had been having with David, James and Gerry Doyle.

How strangely it had all turned out. She felt uneasy when she thought of Gerry and his strangeness.

She was surprised when Caroline, languidly reclining in a deckchair with Liffey on her lap, said, 'Is Gerry Doyle still the Main Attraction?'

'I think so,' Clare said carefully. 'I'm not as in touch as I used to be. Possibly the younger ones have other heroes, but I think he does very well.'

'Well, I think I'll stroll down later and have a look at him,' Caroline said. 'Now that you've taken the most gorgeous man in Castlebay, I'll have to start looking round at the second bests.'

She laughed, and they all laughed. David too.

Clare was furious. The *bitch* – why did she say that in front of Molly? Clare had seen the look of regret come over Molly's face. Suppose David and Caroline had married, now wouldn't that have been something special? Suppose she and Sheila Nolan had been cooing over Liffey. Molly would have much preferred that than have Liffey also the granddaughter of O'Brien's shop.

Valerie came to stay in the Lodge for a week.

'I can't stand Caroline Nolan,' she said. 'Stop being so nice to her, Clare.'

'I'm only being civil. Not nice. She'll be gone in a couple of weeks.'

'I wouldn't bet on that, she's asking that old man the solicitor friend of David's father . . .'

'Mr Kenny.'

'Yes, she's asking him are there any openings for a solicitor round here, a country practice would be so much more interesting than a city one, you'd see all sides of the law.'

'But she couldn't be a solicitor in Castlebay, there isn't any need for anyone apart from poor old Mr Kenny and most people go to the town.'

'Aha, that's what he told her, she's going into the town today to investigate possibilities. Gerry Doyle's giving her a lift.'

'That's all baloney, as Mary Catherine would say, she's just gone to get a quick feel from Gerry Doyle, she fancies him rotten, she always has. She pretends it was David, but I remember all those years. It was Gerry this and Gerry that.'

'I hope you're right,' Val said.

'I wish you didn't have to go, you make me feel safe,' Clare said.

'You are safe, stupid.'

'Well, normal, then.'

'Come to the dance tonight,' Valerie said suddenly.

'No, I'm too old, too dull. David's going to be out all night, nearly, he rang. Mrs Brennan says there are complications in a confinement.'

'You come anyway, David would like that, I know he would.'

'I don't want to, I feel wrong, somehow.'

'I won't go either and I was so looking forward to it.'

'Damn you, Valerie, now I have to go. I have to wash my hair and go.'

'Yes you do,' said Valerie, pleased.

They all had a drink at the hotel first, Caroline, James, Josie and Martin, Valerie and Clare, then they crossed the road and headed for the dance hall. The sound of the band hit them as soon as the swing doors opened.

'I feel that old excitement, just like when we were young,' Caroline said.

'So do I,' James Nolan said, eyeing Josie Dillon speculatively.

Martin said nothing.

Inside, the familiar smell of sweat and perfume and suntan oil came to them, and the band struck up a Paul Jones.

Clare remembered the excitement of the Paul Jones years ago when you could stop opposite literally anyone, and half the girls in the ballroom wanted to stop in front of Gerry Doyle. She forced herself to relive that sense of excitement.

'Come on girls, get into the ring,' she called.

'Good to see the grass widow enjoying herself for a change,' Caroline said.

Clare refused to wonder what that meant. It probably meant nothing. It was a clever-clever thing that Caroline *would* say.

She stopped opposite a boy of about sixteen, red faced and sweating with nerves. It might even be his first dance.

'Hallo,' she smiled. 'I'm yours, I think, for the dance.'

'Um, thank you, I'm not a great dancer,' he said.

'You couldn't be any worse than I am,' Clare said cheerfully and she made him feel so confident in their gallop around the room that she knew he would come back and claim her over and over, unless she told him.

'That was lovely,' she said. 'I'm married to the local doctor here. We have a little girl. It makes me feel nice and young again to dance like that.'

He was gone like a bow from an arrow. A married woman! Heavens!

Valerie seemed to be happy, Clare thought later as she looked down on it all from the balcony, a freckled man in a check suit had asked her to dance several times over, he looked nice and they were chatting away too. James Nolan, the smooth, two-faced rat, was dancing cheek to cheek with Josie Dillon who was admittedly very foolish indeed to allow and encourage such a thing. Clare didn't approve, but she could have foretold it. She could also have foretold that Caroline and Gerry Doyle would have found each other out too.

She leaned with her elbows on the balcony looking at them. Caroline was taller than Gerry, but who wasn't? Saying not much but smiling a lot, not groping but dancing very close. Very sure of each other. Clare wished that Valerie would leave the check-suited man and come up here for a moment. Then she would get over this silly idea that Caroline Nolan was a troublemaker with eyes for David. Anyone could see that Caroline had eyes only for Gerry Doyle.

Clare remembered the days when she and Josie would come to the dance and be rushed off their feet. Not so for Josie tonight, she never left James Nolan's side. Not so for Mrs Clare Power, the doctor's wife, and mother of the doctor's daughter. None of the boys who used to ask her to dance would approach her now, and it wasn't the Castlebay Committee dance where she would have found older people to dance with. She didn't mind being a wallflower, she didn't really wish David was here, she felt she had grown away from the dance. Not too old for it, just away from it.

Three little things happened before they played the national anthem and the night was over. Martin told Josie in a shaking voice that he was leaving now and would she like to come with him or not. He put a lot into the question, and Josie answered head on. No, she would not, she would like to stay. Thank you.

Then Bernie Conway came up to Clare and said it was marvellous to see her again, she had been such a recluse in the beginning.

'I suppose it was the shock of the baby coming so early.'

'It must have been,' Clare agreed.

'And who's looking after her tonight? David?'

'No, no, if he were free he'd be here, Nellie Burke loves to have her from time to time.'

'Oh, the resident domestic. Nice,' Bernie said.

There was a pause.

'I'd never have expected to see you here on your own ... after ... after everything,' Bernie said.

Clare wanted to push her out the window on to Church Street but decided against it. 'I'm not really on my own, I came with about five or six other people, I'm just not being danced with at the moment,' she smiled sweetly. 'Like you.'

And the third thing was that Gerry Doyle and Caroline waved casually and went off into the night towards the caravan park.

Caroline's father said she was very sensible to get experience in a country town, there was nothing as useful as learning the business on the ground at every level. They were all congratulating her on having got a position in the town twenty miles from Castlebay.

James said he hoped she would get the firm to send all the cases to advise to him, he needed a good country contact. Sheila Nolan said she would come down and help to settle Caroline in, and then she could come across to Castlebay and see Molly for a winter weekend. Dr Power said that she'd find it a real change from the summer, in fact some of the Castlebay Committee didn't agree with Josie Dillon that visitors should be allowed in the place in winter at all, let them think it was the land of eternal summer.

Clare was silent. She remembered how she had laughed when Valerie said that Caroline was a schemer and that she was plotting to be down in this part of the country. Was Caroline really a bit keen on David as Valerie had all but said? It couldn't be. Hadn't she taken up her romance with Gerry Doyle exactly as she was planning? Perhaps she was scheming to be near Gerry Doyle. Surely not. Caroline had too much intelligence for that.

They often had tea in the garden at Crest View, Caroline seemed to be able to summon it up with a wave of the hand, while Molly Power would fuss for three days about any entertaining, Sheila Nolan never seemed to think of it, and Clare never suggested it in the Lodge since she thought none of them would want to come there.

But Caroline just knew automatically that what people loved around five o'clock was a huge pot of tea, and plates of nice thin tomato sandwiches. Even Dr Power loved dropping in, for half an hour or so. Caroline had painted all the deckchairs bright red.

'Do they belong to us, strictly?' James asked.

'Of course not, but they were so tatty. The old bat who owns the place will be delighted with us.'

Molly said it was a *very* clever idea. And very *tasteful*.

She took Liffey sometimes but not always. A ten-month-old baby was lively and needed attention, Caroline had limited time for babies. And this summer it seemed as if Caroline was calling the shots. After all she was planning to become a native. Almost.

David did seem to find her good company, but then he always had. They had been friends, and now he seemed to laugh and relax more with Caroline than he did even with James.

She sat with her hand on the pram, rocking the sleeping Liffey. Mrs Nolan was describing some dream in elaborate detail; Molly Power listened enthralled. Dr Power and James Nolan were discussing the business of calling doctors as expert witnesses in court cases. Breeda was refilling the teapot and setting out further plates of sandwiches. David and Caroline were sitting on the whitewashed wall of Crest View watching the beach below.

What am I doing here? Clare thought. This isn't *my* place. I'm not meant to *be* here with these people.

It was like an echo of what Gerry Doyle had said.

'I always hated saying goodbye to this place,' Caroline said. 'Now it's not goodbye at all. I *am* glad about the job.'

'So are we,' David said eagerly. 'But won't it be very dull? Honestly, Caroline, you've no idea how quiet it can be in this area. I know the town is bigger but it's still small after Dublin.'

'How could a town with Gerry Doyle be dull? Answer me that.' Caroline was being light and joky but she saw immediately she had said the wrong thing.

'Oh, him,' David said.

'I was only teasing you, I don't think he'll form part of my winter social life, hardly the suitable escort for the legal profession.'

'You must choose your own friends, I'm only a stick in the mud.'

That *wasn't* so, and anyway she'd find it hard to make friends at first. 'I'll be relying on you and Clare to introduce me round.'

'We hardly know anyone.' He wasn't apologetic, he was stating a fact.

'We'll have to take up golf again, will we do that, have a game every now and then?'

'I'd *love* that,' David said. 'Yes, that's something I really would like. I'm meant to have an afternoon off in the middle of the week, I hardly ever take it.'

'Well now.' Caroline smiled at the marvellous notion. 'There we'll be, old country doctor, old country solicitor, out for an afternoon's golf.' Her laugh pealed out like a bell. 'Who would have thought it, David, that we'd come to this?'

Clare listened to them from her red-painted deckchair. Old country doctor, old country solicitor, and there was Clare – old country nothing.

The wasps were dying, the seaweed was coming in on the tide, the visitors were packing up. Angela was getting her books and charts ready for school.

Clare came to the door, wheeling Liffey in a push-chair.

'She must be nearly a year.'

'Next week. Is Dick here, Angela?'

'No . . . oh hell he is, he said to say he was out if anyone came. But for you. Come on in.'

Dick was at the table with plans spread out all over it. He jumped guiltily.

'It's only Clare, love,' Angela said.

'We were going to tell her anyway.'

They were going to make their cottage into a small hotel. Dick was getting his share out of Dillon's, which would suit everyone there, and they were going to open a small twelve-bedroom hotel of their own. Angela owned the field behind the cottage: they would build a hotel just for golfers, with places to leave their clubs, with early breakfasts if they wanted it, with late suppers. They might not get a licence to serve alcohol; but people could order a bottle of whiskey or whatever and it would be supplied in their room. Their plan was to open it next June, Angela was going to leave the school.

'Is that why you've been doing the cooking?' Clare asked eagerly.

'The one thing we *proved* is that we have to hire a cook before anything else, we'll make the beds and wash up but *not* cook!'

They had tea and looked at the plans. 'That should cost a fair bit of money,' Clare said.

'I'll be owed a fair bit of money out of Dillon's,' Dick said.

'Will your brother be pleased or furious?'

'He'll be delighted I'm out of his hair, but he'll be furious about this, that's why it's a secret you see, the money bit goes through this week. A firm in the town are handling it, in fact that girl – what's her name? – was here.'

'Caroline Nolan?'

'The very one. Nice girl for a Dubliner, very straightforward.'

'Um,' said Angela.

'Um indeed,' said Clare.

'What did you want Dick for, by the way?' Angela remembered why Clare had called.

'I was wondering would you give me a few secret golf lessons when Angela went back to school, I thought you'd have some time on your hands, but now I see you won't.'

'I'm not the one to give you lessons, I'm very bad.'

'I don't mind only learning a little.'

'No Clare, you don't understand, I'd teach you the wrong grip, the wrong stance, you'd have to unlearn it all over again.'

'Why don't you go up to Jimmy the Pro?' Angela wanted to know.

'I wanted to learn secretly, without anyone else knowing.'

'That's why you can't ask David,' Angela said.

'Right.'

'What about Gerry Doyle, he's a good golfer?' Dick suggested.

'No, I'd probably spend most of the lesson on the flat of my back in the sand dunes,' Clare laughed.

'I'll tell you – that girl Caroline, *she* loves golf, she says she's going to come over here and play as much as she can. *She* might be the one.'

Dick Dillon's face shone with pleasure at having solved a problem.

'I'm sorry, Clare,' Angela said, 'some men are as thick as the wall. But you mustn't worry.'

'I don't know what you're complaining about, you've come up with no suggestions. I've given two, and they've been laughed out of court,' Dick grumbled.

'I'll solve it for you,' Angela said, 'why don't I book lessons with Jimmy and you could so-called come along and watch, and join in, it wouldn't look like you learning.'

'It would really, and anyway you don't want to learn.'

'If I'm to be the genial co-proprietor of a golfing hotel I'd better know how to play the damn game,' Angela said. 'I'll talk to Jimmy, and you come up casually like around Lesson Two or Three.'

'You're always helping me,' Clare said. 'It's probably very silly.'

'No, I think you're quite right,' Angela said seriously, in a way that let a shiver of cold go through Clare.

Josie was in tears at the Lodge that evening. Martin never wanted to see her again. He said she had made a fool of him over James Nolan. Oh how stupid she had been, Josie could kick herself from here to Dublin and back, she was so annoyed. What should she do? Clare was so good with men.

'I am not good with men, what makes you think that?'

Well hadn't Clare got David Power as her husband, and the town Romeo Gerry Doyle was saying only the other night in the hotel that he wished he had moved in before the young doctor.

'Gerry was saying that. In front of people?'

'Yes, yes.' Josie was much more interested in her own disasters. Should she write to Martin? Did James have any *real* interest in her? What did Clare think . . .

'I can't tell you what I think until I know what you want,' Clare said, exasperated. 'If you tell me straight out what you want, I'll tell you what I think you should do.'

'I want James Nolan, but I don't think he wants me, so if I'm sure of that and that there's no hope there, I want Martin. Now is that honest and truthful enough for you?'

'You wouldn't just like to be on your own for a bit and let life go by, and eventually meet someone else?'

'No thank you.' Josie was firm.

'That's what I think you should do.'

'I told you what I wanted, it's easy for you to say that, and all this bit about being independent, you have a husband, a child, and Gerry Doyle ogling you as well.'

'Right. I'll drive you out to his house, you can put a letter under his door: "Dear Martin, I behaved stupidly, I suppose I wanted to see did you really care about me . . ." that sort of thing. Not too cringeing, not too apologetic, but don't be defensive either, we'll write it now if you like . . .'

'I don't think James Nolan will ever . . .'

'I agree. I don't think James Nolan ever will either . . .'

Two weeks later Josie and Martin bought the ring. Three diamonds in a cluster. 'You're a genius, Clare,' Josie breathed to her a few days after the announcement.

'That's what I am,' Clare agreed.

But Clare couldn't be a genius for herself.

She despised women who were coquettish to men, and during those heady days when she and David had been so in love that Dublin just seemed like the backdrop on a stage for them, he and she used to laugh at the posturings of women who thought flirtatiousness was attractive, and the men who were fools enough to be taken in. They had sworn then that they would always be able to tell each other how they felt and say it straight out, the other was allowed ten minutes to be upset but after that he or she was to remember that this was the Love of the Century and that any plain speaking was a part of the very special relationship they had.

Clare wondered would it work if they went back to Dublin and raced round in duffle coats in the rain. In the winter and spring of 1960 it had been easy to talk, in the winter and spring of 1962 they had lost it.

She wrote him a letter one day. A long letter trying to recapture how it had been. But she re-read it and it sounded like a list of complaints so she tore it up.

She even tried to talk to his father about it. Very obliquely. But she realized soon that the old man thought that everything was fine between them. He acknowledged that Clare had been a little low after the birth of the baby, perfectly normal under all the circumstances, he saw no yawning gaps or wide distances now. It would have been cruel as well as pointless to try to tell him about them.

She found it very hard to study again. Almost impossible.

She wrote to the cheerful tutor who had said he had never expected to hear from her again. She said that he might have heard what had happened on the day she was ready to sit her finals, but that the baby was now almost a year and a half, and that Clare would like to get back to work again. He wrote back saying that she had to apply formally of course, but he knew there would be no trouble once people knew the facts, the very dramatic facts. He admired her courage for starting again, because in eighteen months she must have got out of practice. He said to be sure to contact him if she were in Dublin.

And that was it. No other way of getting back into the frame of mind she had been in once. She looked at her notes. How had she been so intelligent? How could she have written those paragraphs on the left-hand side of each double page, paragraphs headed 'essentials' and then on the other side quotes, references, details. Was there a possibility that she once knew all this? Did other people up in Dublin know this kind of thing now?

Should she go to Dublin for a few days? Would that make it more real?

She discussed it with David. He said he thought she should go.

She planned to stay with Emer and Kevin and the now monstrous Daniel. They were dying to see Liffey, having met her only at the christening. Would David come too? Just for a couple of days?

No, he said. It was the worst time to leave. Old people got pneumonia at this time of year. But he'd love her to go, really and truly.

'Have you gone off me, David?' she asked him that night without rancour.

'Well really, what nonsense,' he said. 'Are you sulking because I can't get away?'

'Of course not, I meant it much more generally.'

'I haven't gone off you, sweetheart, why should I?'

'I don't know, who knows why people love and they don't?' She was standing in the same spot of the kitchen as she had been when she had heard Gerry Doyle say those words from the kitchen table. She had echoed them unconsciously.

She shivered a little.

'Well I know. I know I love you and I haven't gone off you. So there.'

'Are you happy, David?'

'What's happy?' he asked, shrugging his shoulders.

'This room is beginning to be like the Echo Cave,' Clare said. 'You asked me a year ago was I happy, when you were telling me that I wasn't loopy. You asked me then was I happy.'

'This is very intense. What did you say?'

'Don't you remember?'

'No, and love, don't pick a fight because I can't remember every word of every conversation we have had in two years. If I were to quiz you, there must be many things you've forgotten.'

'That's fair. I'll tell you what I said. I said I was happy. And you said "But . . ." asking a question and I said, well, "But . . . we'd sort of got a bit settled down hadn't we" and you said yes you felt that too.'

'Well, what's the production?'

'The production is that we've changed a lot, you were the one who was beseeching *me* and wanting to know how *I* was, now I'm the one.'

'I've had a hard day, a really hard day. A woman of forty-four died today. Down the coast. She'd been fine, not a thing wrong with her. Cancer all over her in two months. She had six children and a big stupid husband and I had to stand there and talk about the good side of it. Clare, there was no good side to it, believe you me there was no good side.

'I came back and sewed up the eye of a child of five whose father hit her with a chair, the father is in a worse state than the child. I have to write a report of it all for Frank Conway. Frank Conway asked me how his mother was and I had to tell him she won't come out of hospital.

'Then Dad asked me if I'd mind looking after everything on my own for a week in about a month's time, he's feeling very tired he says, he wakes at night with his heart racing, he'd like a little rest.

'Rest? He's hardly doing a quarter of the load, so if he wants a rest at this level of work the man is really bad. Then I come back here and I'm met with pleas and beggings to come to Dublin which I can *not* do much as I might like to. And now the whole fabric of life has to be analysed.'

There was a silence.

'I'm sorry,' she said.

'There's no reason why you should be. These are the joys and horrors of my day, not yours.'

'What *would* you like from me? What would have been best tonight? Tell me.'

'I suppose a bit of peace, chat about other things, not about us and where we were going and who loved whom more.'

He stood up and put his arm around her. 'It's all right, Clare, it's not magic all the time, but people in jobs like ours, well like mine and when you were studying feverishly you were the same, you understood . . . in the time off you need just to relax, not to have to think of what love is and what it isn't.'

'I see. I do,' she said.

The telephone rang. David answered it.

'Oh hallo.' His face broke into a smile. She knew it was Caroline Nolan, who understood what people wanted in their time off. They didn't want *concepts*, they wanted a nice effortless exchange of words and an arrangement to play golf.

She wrote to Emer and said she wouldn't come just yet, she wanted to stay at home to sort out a few things. Emer said there was no bother, the bed was always there. Mention of the beds in Emer's house always caused Clare to feel a little guilty.

Angela was a very good golfer, Jimmy the Pro said. She had a swing like a man. Angela did not regard this as the high praise which Jimmy intended it to be.

'Your little friend here now isn't too bad either.' Clare made a face at him. 'Try to keep your head still and you wouldn't be a disgrace at all.'

'Great,' Clare said.

'Why don't you come out and play with that husband of yours sometimes? When the solicitor lady isn't around. I bet David would love a good game of a Saturday.'

'I must, but I'd be no match for him.'

'Oh, you'd give him a game, you did quite well there at the second, you were on the green in three and you only took two putts.'

'But it's a par three.'

'It's very respectable, I tell you.'

'Was it good, the golf today?' she asked him when he came home next time.

'No. I couldn't hit a ball out of my way.'

'What did you get on the second?' she asked innocently.

'Don't talk to me about the second, it's a par three, I took seven,' he wailed.

'Never mind, there are days and days, aren't there?'

He looked at her gratefully.

In women's magazines they told you to smarten up your appearance, lose weight and turn back into the girl he married. She tried wearing make-up but rubbed most of it off again, it looked heavy on her and unnatural in this part of the world. Her clothes were all right, she had a few nice jumpers and skirts and she wore smart blouses as well. She didn't need to lose weight. She was almost too thin if anything, and she was better-looking than the girl he had married. So there was no joy there. The women's magazines had never met a wife who was so tense and irritating that she had driven her husband into the arms of a country solicitor. That wasn't one the agony aunts could handle.

But still she would try. She followed every bit of an article in *Woman's Own* about how to do a perfect evening make-up.

She used the shadow and the eyeliner exactly as they directed.

She put on the taffeta skirt she had worn only once at the dance. And a nice top. She got her hair set in big loose ringlets.

Chrissie came over to the hairdresser's and stood in her dirty overall.

'I saw you coming in here, where are you going tonight?'

'Nowhere,' Clare hissed from under the dryer.

'You must be going *some*where, why else are you getting your hair done?'

'Oh go away, Chrissie,' she said.

'This is a public place, you can't order me around here.'

Clare knew that everyone would hear of the pleasant sisterly exchange between the young doctor's wife and the assistant in Dwyers' butchers.

She called in to her mother.

'Are you all right, Clare? You look as if you've been crying.'

'It's make-up, Mum.'

'Where's Liffey?'

'Nellie's minding her, I was getting my hair done.'

'Waste of money in this wind, it will be blown out before you get home.'

Jim came into the shop. Clare turned around and spoke to him, moving her lips deliberately.

'I wish you wouldn't speak to Jim like that,' her mother said. 'You make it sound as if he's a halfwit. Jim's not a halfwit, he's only idle, aren't you, Jim?' Her tone was affectionate but she got no reply. Jim hadn't seen her lips move and he hadn't realized that anyone had spoken to him.

She had slaved over a good dinner for David, he was tired and distracted, he didn't notice her hair, her eyes, the food or the way she had made everything look nice.

He said he was exhausted, they went to bed early, and David fell asleep as she was about to move towards his side of the bed.

'Caroline?'

'Oh David, don't tell me you're going to cancel the golf. I've been looking forward to it all morning.'

'So have I, no, of course I'm not cancelling it. Look I was thinking, it's such a long drive back for you after the game, why don't we have a meal before you head off?'

'Oh, that's very nice, but I don't want to put Clare to too much . . .'

'No, I thought we'd go out somewhere, you know.'

A pause.

'Yes, that would be super. Where did you think?'

'Well, I don't know why I said somewhere, there only is one place, the hotel. We can get a nice enough meal there.'

'Great, that's very nice. Give me the strength to drive back here again.'

'Good, good. I'll book us a table then. I'll ring them and reserve a table for the two of us.'

At first it was just a game of golf with Caroline, then it was golf and a couple of drinks at the club. Now it was golf, drinks and dinner. Josie was on the phone next day. Just for a chat.

'I hope the food wasn't too good last night, you'll be setting me impossible standards,' Clare laughed.

'What do you mean?'

'Well, I'm going to ask the golfers to come *here* next week, would you and Martin join us as well?'

Josie thought that would be great. She was relieved to know that Clare was in the picture about David playing golf and being seen with Caroline. Her sister Rose had come in all excited from the dining room last night to say that David Power and Caroline Nolan were holding hands under the table. But that mightn't be true. Rose had always had a soft spot for David, and Rose had been very bitter and odd since Josie had announced her engagement.

Clare asked Molly if she'd like to come to dinner next Thursday.

'It's a bit far in advance to be planning that isn't it?' Molly said. 'But that would be very nice. Do you think you could manage it?'

Angela said that under any other circumstances she would drop everything and come, but the Mother Provincial of the order was visiting the school and the nuns were having a sort of feast for her. In all the years she had worked in that school since 1945 they had never offered them a bit of food and now it was happening. 'It will be horrific, I'll take notes in a jotter and tell you later.'

'In all the years you've known *me* this is the first time I've ever offered you a bite of food, and it would be the same night,' Clare sighed.

'Is it for anything special?'

'Survival or something,' Clare said.

'Oh, you're inviting your mother-in-law?'

'And my husband's golf partner.'

'That's ambitious, what are you giving them to eat?'

'I haven't thought yet.'

'Let me give you a hint, give them something cold to start, like hard-boiled eggs with stuffing in them. Emer said that she went out to a house to dinner in Dublin and they had a whole lot of tins of sardines and lemon juice mashed up and served in a china bowl and people helped themselves and spread it on bread and it was lovely.'

'That might be fine in Dublin, but if you didn't give them soup here they'd have you taken to the county home.'

'Soup's hard to concentrate on and serve if you've got to think of the next bit.'
'Keep your fingers crossed for me, will you?'
'You'll be fine,' said Angela with no confidence in her voice.

Old Mr Kenny said that it was very nice of the young people to think of inviting him to dinner, he was very touched. And that made up her eight.

She asked Nellie to help her bring two chairs from the big house and she went through all her dishes and cutlery to make sure she had enough. She did all her preparations secretly when David wasn't there. Any time he came home she dropped the fussing. He was pleased about the dinner, that meant that he couldn't really have a great deal to hide, she thought. If he and Caroline had been up to anything more than these long relaxed conversations, the quick peck on the cheek as they said goodbye, surely he couldn't bring her into the house and act as if nothing was going on. She had phoned Caroline at work, and she too had been pleased at the idea of dinner after golf.

'What a lovely thing to suggest, Clare. Will you be able to manage?'
'Manage what?' Clare asked pleasantly, seething with rage.
'Oh, dinner and everything.'
'Gosh I hope so,' Clare said and went back to the kitchen in a fury.

She took Liffey out of the pram and spoke to her seriously. 'Listen to me, kid, this world is full of bullshit, as my friend Mary Catherine, who is your Godmother, used to say in her less refined moments. Now you and I aren't going to put up with that, we are not going to be walked on, Liffey Power. And I make you a solemn promise. If you are a good baby on Thursday, if you don't wet anyone or get sick over them or cry, I will give you a great life full of freedom and adventure, and if you want to go up in a Sputnik and your father says no, I'll fight that you can go up in a Sputnik.'

Liffey clapped her hands, pleased with all the concentration.
'So that's it, a deal. Good.'
Bones came into the kitchen.

'And you too, friend, no scratching your bum when they're here, no huge unexpected howls because you've seen a bluebottle or the lighthouse or anything. Just look like a sweet affectionate hound who loves the young mistress. Of course you could take a bite out of Miss Nolan's rear end but make it look as if she attacked you first. What will I give you? I'll tell you, I'll save you from the knacker's yard. David said you might have to be put down, I won't hear of that.'

Bones smiled at her and she went back to the cookery book.

It would have been so easy if she could have had Nellie, and Nellie would love to have helped, but the whole point of it was that she couldn't. She *had* to do it on her own. She couldn't even let Nellie know how nervous she was. Nellie's first loyalty was to her own household, she could well tell Molly that there was pandemonium out in the Lodge. That would defeat the whole thing. She had phoned Valerie for tips, and Val had said keep it simple and give them so much to drink they won't remember what they had to eat, which might have been fine for Val's people but was not much help here. Val said that she should warm the bread rolls and put cream in the soup, and to have mashed potatoes or roast potatoes because they couldn't let you down.

Chrissie said wasn't it great to be able to afford huge lumps of beef like this.

'Why didn't you ring up and we'd have sent it over to you?'

'I hoped if I came you might give me a nice cut and show me what direction to carve it in,' Clare said humbly.

'Carve it? Just cut a lump off for each person like you always do,' said Chrissie, helpful and sensitive butcher-sister who could be relied on to put your nerves at ease before an occasion.

Thursday was early closing day in the town twenty miles away. It was David's golf day, and it was the day of the dinner.

Clare thought the women's magazines would be proud of her and the way she said to David that he must bring Caroline back to the house whenever he liked, she would want to change for dinner. The others were coming about seven, so after they had a few drinks in the club . . .

'Won't we be in your way?'

'Not at all,' Clare trilled.

He kissed her goodbye on the nose and then kissed Liffey.

'Bones is creaking a lot, isn't he, I wonder is he in pain? The problem is he always seems to be smiling, you wouldn't know.'

'Oh, Bones has plenty of life in him.' She patted the dog's head. A promise is a promise and Bones wasn't going to be sent to sweet dreams while Clare was around.

Liffey deposited all her carrots and mashed potato on her best hand-smocked dress. Clare snatched it off and washed it. It might just be dry enough to put back on her again. That was the dress Molly had made such a fuss about. It was being worn in her honour. Then when she was cleaning the spoon, the beautiful silver spoon that Mr Kenny had given the baby, Bones thought it was a toy and galloped off with it.

He took it round the garden three times and then buried it in a flowerbed.

The cream was off, of all days in the year, and two of the table napkins had tears in them. In her haste rushing past the table she knocked over a jug of water so she had to put pillow cases under the corner and pray it would dry out in time.

Because Caroline would change in their bedroom Clare deliberately made it look a much more cosy and loving place than it actually was. She bunched the pillows right up close as if this was the way they normally slept, and she took out her black nighty, the one that actually looked awful on, but exotic if draped around the place. She put a bunch of flowers in the room, and a soft romantic lamp.

She had also tidied up the cupboards and drawers in case Caroline would poke around. Any shabby old shoes or things that were not meant to be seen were hidden firmly in the spare room, and she removed the bulb so that no light could be thrown on that confusion, should somebody open the door in error.

They all arrived at once.

David poured sherries and everyone said wasn't this all nice at least three times each.

Caroline looked glowing with health. Her hair looked shiny and smart. Clare had *hoped* it would have become matted and windblown. She said she'd simply *love* a quick wash, and came down in a commendably quick time wearing a long red wool skirt and white lace blouse.

'It was simply marvellous out there today,' she said. 'You really should learn, Clare.'

'Did somebody tell me you were taking lessons, Clare?' Josie asked.

Clare could have smashed her face. 'No no, but they may have seen me once with Angela up there, she's learning.'

'Oh yes.' Angela Dillon was a sore subject in Dillon's Hotel. There was great fear that Uncle Dick and the schoolteacher might well have lifted the entire golfing trade from the old hotel.

'James plays a lot in Dublin, in fact some think that he spends far too much time on the course,' Caroline said. *That* wasn't a tactful subject either. Martin's hand tightened round his glass at the mention of the perfidious James Nolan.

Clare decided the meal should be served.

Damn the magazines to the very blackest spot of hell.

The rolls had burned black in the oven. Black.

She sliced some of Nellie's soda bread and put it on a plate. Molly said that Nellie had one of the lightest hands with pastry and bread in the country.

'This bread is very nice too,' Mr Kenny said.

'This *is* Nellie's bread,' Clare said in despair.

The beef was tough; the mashed potatoes were dry; the sprouts were soft and the gravy was lumpy.

Clare could see a series of plates with food left and eventually had to admit that no one was having more and that knives and forks had been left together. Burning with embarrassment she cleared the table.

There was no cream for the chocolate pudding. It had been too late to go and get any more. She had cursed her mother and father for not having a phone, because they could have sent someone over with cream or even ice cream. She should have gone herself, she should have put Liffey into the back of the car and raced down, but at the time she had thought it was better to stay at her post, it seemed less flurried.

They waded through the pudding. Nobody had the cheese she had laid out so carefully with biscuits in lines.

She went to make coffee and discovered that the full coffee jar she had seen in the press was not full of coffee, it was the jar she used to keep cowrie shells in, until she found a place to display them.

She said she had to go to Liffey for a moment and crept out of the house in the dark to see could she find coffee in her mother-in-law's kitchen. It was Thursday, Nellie's evening off. She wouldn't be there. She fell over Bones and landed flat on her face. Bones barked joyfully and so loudly that Dr Power came out to see what was happening.

'My God, Molly,' he called, 'there's somebody in our kitchen!'

David was masterful. He picked up a golf club and insisted that his father stand back.

As Clare crept out of the Powers' kitchen with grazed hands, a bruised forehead and a suspicion of a loosened tooth, Bones was baying at the moon with excitement.

'I'll kill you,' she said to the dog. 'You'll go for the chop and I won't lift a finger to help you.'

Suddenly she saw the entire party framed in the light of the Lodge waiting for her, and David advancing slowly with a golf club.

In the distance she heard the familiar sound of Liffey waking and starting a crying jag that was going to last two hours.

Angela laughed till she cried.

Clare *was* crying as she told the story.

'No I *can't* see the funny side. *Stop* all that laughing. I'm so bloody fed up. I made a *fool* of myself. I might as well have got up and danced on the table in my knickers. It was *dreadful*. They pitied me, all of them, even Josie.'

'It's your own fault,' Angela said. 'You were always the one who was great with the advice to Mary Catherine . . . tell them your father's a postman, see do they care. Why couldn't you have told them you had a coffee jar of cowrie shells?'

'Not on top of the burned rolls, the lumpy gravy, the tough meat. I bet Chrissie did it on purpose, gave me some old hindquarters of a donkey.'

'What about David?'

'He patted me down afterwards, he said first dinners are always a trial. *First!* First and last more likely. How was Mother Provincial?'

'Like a hamster, wrinkling her nose, pointed little teeth.'

'What did they talk about?'

'The decline in faith and morals. And we had egg sandwiches and tea, that was the feast.'

'I'd have loved it,' Clare said feelingly. 'Compared to what went on in my house last night it sounds like paradise.'

Gerry Doyle called in on a wet Thursday.

'I'm a bit busy, Gerry.'

'I can see that,' he said, looking at the open newspaper on the kitchen table.

'Well,' she said awkwardly.

'Well, it took some time. But it's happened.'

'What has?' Her heart was full of fear.

'David.' He stood there smiling.

Her hand went to her throat. 'What's happened to him?'

'I think he's found true love, Clare. In a caravan.'

'*What?*'

'Well, it's much too wet to play golf isn't it? Look at that, they'd be soaked through.' He had been sitting down uninvited, but when he had given her the news, he stood up.

'See you,' he said, and left.

David came home quite dry.

'Did you get a game or was it too wet?'

'No, we battled on, quite exhilarating you know in the wind and the rain.'

'I'm sure.'

'Horrible night for Caroline to have to drive all that way back,' he said.

'Isn't it. Should we have asked her to stay or anything do you think?'

'No, no, but I'll tell you she *is* thinking of getting a caravan here, just in case she wants to stay over. Makes a lot of sense, doesn't it?'

'Gerry Doyle is in a lot of trouble,' Clare's mother said.

'What way?'

'Well he has a big bill here for one thing, you know three months. All his groceries and cigarettes, it mounts up.'

'I'm sure it does.'

'Your father said I should ask him about it, what with my always getting on well with him.'

'And?'

'And he said he was a bit pushed. And Chrissie says he has a bill as long as your arm in Dwyers' too, and he can't get credit in Costello's any more. He over-extended himself with that place, they don't get enough orders for that size of a set-up. They were fine when they had the little hut and the developing in the house. Dick says he'll have to sell up.'

'Gerry's a survivor.'

'That's what I've said always but when I asked him about his bill here and he said he was broke, I said it was all right, pay a little off it here and there to keep Tom happy . . . and he said I wasn't to be nice to him, he wasn't going out with a whimper, when he went it would be with a bang that would be heard all over the county. What can he have meant?'

'I'll take Liffey to Dublin in a week or two, show her the other Liffey, the river.'

'That's a good idea.'

'Will you go and have your dinner with your parents when I'm gone?'

'Yes, some of the time. I'll cook here a bit maybe if I feel up to it. Oh and Caroline will be in her caravan. I'll probably have a meal or two with her to settle her in.'

Gerry came again.

'I have pictures this time,' he said.

'What kind of pictures?' She was feeding Liffey and needed her full concentration.

'Can I have a cup of tea?'

'No, Gerry, you know I don't like you coming here.'

'Here, you're making an awful mess of that. I'll feed her. You put on the kettle.'

'Will you go then?'

He fed Liffey expertly, holding the spoon just long enough in her mouth for her to have to swallow what was on it.

Clare poured the tea. She had no sense of alarm. He looked vulnerable as he sat feeding Liffey and gurgling at her.

'Oh, the pictures. These ones.' He emptied an envelope on the table. About a dozen black and white prints of David and Caroline making love on the cramped bed of a caravan.

She put her hand over her mouth and went to the sink. She vomited and retched.

He moved her away and turned on the tap. He cleaned the sink and gave her a glass of water.

'Drink that,' he said.

She threw it at him. It missed and shattered all over the floor. She was shaking.

Calmly he took a towel and wet it under the tap, he went up close and wiped her face, as you would wipe a child's face. She was powerless to stop him.

She poured herself another glass of water and drank it.

'What are you going to do?'

'Nothing,' she said.

'OK.' He put his hand on the door.

'Take these.' She gathered them up with a shaking hand.

'Sure,' he said.

She sat for a long time staring into space.

She told David she felt a sort of 'flu coming on, if he didn't mind she'd sleep downstairs.

He was concerned, and felt her forehead. She did seem a bit feverish.

They made up a bed for her. In the kitchen near the fire.

'It looks very cosy,' he said. 'Maybe we should move down here altogether.'

'Remember when we lived in Rathmines? It was so tiny, and the bed, the stove, the dining table were all on top of each other.'

'That's right,' he said, and sighed.

She got into bed and pulled up the sheets like an obedient child.

He kissed her forehead.

'David?'

'Yes?' He looked alarmed.

'Nothing, thanks for everything, sleep well.'

She heard him go upstairs, the lavatory flush, and eventually his shoes fall. He was in bed.

She saw the reflection of the bedroom light go off. He was asleep.

She got out of bed, wide awake. What on God's earth was she going to do? She made a pot of coffee.

She sat up all night and only when she heard the bed creak did she get back into her own.

He tiptoed down and made a pot of tea.

He brought it to her bedside triumphantly.

'Who's a good husband?' he said.

'David's a good husband,' she said mechanically.

She looked very fluey, David thought as he went up to the big house. Funny that she hadn't a temperature – he had taken it automatically. But her eyes were bright, her forehead hot and she was white as a sheet. Or maybe it was just that he felt he could hardly look at her these days without guilt and confusion.

It was so easy to believe when he was with Caroline. Nobody would be hurt, nobody was going to make any demands, there would be no public scenes and at no time would Clare ever be humiliated. It would be discreet and it would be between them. Nobody would know. They would be the first lovers in the history of Castlebay who would get away with it.

Caroline was so relaxed about everything, she never demanded to know what he thought or what he felt. She wanted no promises, no reassurances and certainly no discussion of the future.

After a session with Clare about where they would be in ten years' time and did he really love her and would they ever have got married if it hadn't been for Liffey, it was like a warm bath to come to Caroline.

Caroline said that he must of course make love to Clare, why ever not? She wanted no stories about separate beds or lack of relations. David was taking nothing from what he and she had if he and Clare made love any more than she was stealing anything from Clare by having him come to her in the caravan.

Sometimes he asked her what was going to happen. Would they have a great fight and hurt each other or would they just drift apart? She would laugh and say it was nonsensical to think of the future. It was very restful and it took all the guilt away.

Clare was still lying in her made-up kitchen bed when she heard David's car drive off on his rounds.

A minute later Gerry Doyle came in. 'Quite right too,' he said when he saw the bed.

'*Get out!*' she cried.

'Shush shush.'

'Gerry, I'm going to call Mrs Power. *Help!*'

He put his hand over her mouth gently, and his arm around her. Her thin body in the pink brushed-nylon nightdress with its long sleeves trembled. Her eyes were wild.

'What do you owe him? You saw what he's done to you. Clare?'

She wrenched herself free. And out of his grasp. On her way to the door she picked up the carving knife.

'Don't be silly.' He wasn't a bit afraid. 'Put it down, Clare, I won't touch you, put it down, you'll hurt yourself.'

She laid it down.

'I'll go now, I'll come back for you later.'

'Come back for me?'

'I think we should go away, you and I and Liffey, far away.'

'You're mad.'

'No, not at all. We leave the pictures on the table so they know why. And off we go.'

'I know you're in trouble, Gerry, I know you have money problems, could I lend you some or get you some or something?'

'We'll get plenty in time. You and I, we'll go to London maybe. I can work there, we'll have a home.'

'This is fantasy . . . you must stop.'

'You're not to use big words like that to me, those are for the Powers. I'll come back tonight.'

'No you mustn't, I'll tell David, I'll tell Dr Power, you can't.'

'You won't tell any of them, I know. You want to come away with me.'

'Stop, don't go, let me explain!'

'Make up your mind, one minute you're telling me to go, with a carving knife – the next you're calling me back.'

'Don't come back tonight. Don't. I won't be here. Or I'll have the Guards here and David and his father and everyone, you must understand now I do *not* want to come away with you, whatever David's done, I am going nowhere with you.'

'See you.'

He was gone.

She sat frightened, teeth chattering.

David phoned about six o'clock. His last call had left him near town, it made more sense to have a meal there than driving home through all this storm. How was her 'flu?

'David, can you *please* come home?'

'What is it?'

'In all the time we've been here I've never asked you to come home, I've never been a clinging person. Isn't that true?'

'Darling, of course it is, of course. But it's awkward now. I met Caroline, I just made arrangements to have a meal with her, as it happens.'

'You can have three hundred and sixty-five meals a year with Caroline if you just come home *tonight*.'

'I *am* coming home.'

'No, *now*. I'm frightened.'

'I'll make it an early meal,' he said. 'I'll be home then, and you can tell me what's worrying you.'

'I see,' she said, and hung up.

She left a note on the kitchen table which said, 'I feel very edgy and unwell tonight, so I've gone to the main house where there will be a lot of people to keep me company.'

That would do either for Gerry if he came, or for David.

At six-thirty she knocked on her mother-in-law's door.

'You don't have to knock, Clare,' Dr Power said. He was just about to listen to the news.

'Come on in and sit down.'

Molly was darning by the fire, they had finished their supper.

'I hope you don't mind. I've not been feeling well all day, and David's been delayed. He won't be back until about nine or ten. Do you mind if I stay here?'

They exchanged looks.

'Of course not,' Molly said.

'I think it's in bed you should be, David said you have a touch of 'flu.'

'It's not 'flu, it's just jitters, I have this awful sense of something going to happen.'

'Nonsense, it's the storm. You're even nearer the sea than we are. Don't give in to it, child. Stay with us for a bit, then I'll walk back and tuck you up. And tuck her ladyship up too.' Liffey chortled in the basket. She could only make it stretch to an hour and a half. By eight o'clock she was back in the Lodge.

Dr Power glanced at the note. 'Well, you can tear that up now, he'll find you asleep in bed when he gets back.'

He fussed and filled a hot-water bottle for her, then he went up the stairs. She was ashamed that she hadn't made the bed since last night, since David had slept in it.

Dr Power didn't make any comment.

As soon as he was gone she locked the door and put a chair against it, then she made sure the windows were fastened.

She would stay up by the fire. David could only be an hour, couldn't he? There was no way Gerry could get in.

There was a movement behind her. And there he was, in his leather jacket, smiling at her easily.

'Oh my God.'

'I was in the dining room. It's all right, it's all right.'

'You don't *understand*. You've read it all *wrong*. I'm *not* coming away with you.'

'You've always wanted me, we're the same type, Clare, I said that to you years ago. We're greedy and we want everything. Well we're going to have it. David's different, he's gentler, born into a gentle life.'

'If I did anything in my whole life that would make you think I was in love with you I swear I can't remember.'

She wasn't frightened, now, that he'd hurt her. She just couldn't bear the great fight when David came in, the producing of the pictures – and David had always thought that she liked Gerry. It was so unjust, so terribly unjust. David was the one who was unfaithful, and here was she locked into the house with Gerry Doyle.

'Will you pack your things? I have the car up the lane.'

'You are talking like a madman. There's no question of it.' Gentler, now. 'I've admired you and liked you, like everyone, but that's all.'

'Very well.'

'What?'

'You know what you are saying. I presume you mean it.'

'I do.'

He went to the door, her body was relaxing by the moment with relief.

'You'll be sorry of course. Sorry you didn't come with me tonight. You'll always be sorry. You'll wake in the bed beside your cheating husband, or in a bed downstairs, and you'll be sorry you didn't leave tonight with me.'

'No, Gerry. I won't. We'll always be able to talk you and I . . . always.'

'No,' he said.

She waited, when he was gone, hoping to hear the sound of the van starting up in the lane. There was no sound. Or the crashing of the sea and the wind drowned it if there was.

David cursed himself for having rung home. It was just that he had wanted to know how her 'flu was. *Now* look what he had brought on himself. This was exactly what he knew would happen despite all Caroline's fine words. Now he was pleasing neither of them. Clare would be fretting at home over whatever was worrying her, and Caroline would be annoyed that he had to leave early, and slightly scornful. She had been like that once or twice recently. More or less taunting him, saying, *of course* he must go home to *poor Clare* if she needed him. Caroline had said more than once that there were no chains around his legs tying him to *her* apron strings. It had been very humiliating and oddly he had also felt like defending Clare. He would feel that way tonight too. The girl had 'flu, he would say, and how defensive and idiotic it would sound.

He parked his car in the little yard of the small house that Caroline rented. He had been looking forward to the evening. Perhaps he would say nothing about his promise to be home early, perhaps he could ring and say that something had happened . . .

Caroline was not in the kitchen. He had let himself in the back door. A saucepan with water was hissing on the back burner of the gas stove. He reached out automatically and pulled it away. The bottom had just begun to burn.

'Caroline,' he called. There was no answer.

That was odd. She must be at home. She still had the city habit of locking the doors when she went out.

'Caroline,' he called again. Perhaps she was in the bathroom upstairs. He didn't want her to get a fright if she came out and saw him unexpectedly. 'I'm here,' he called again.

There was a sound from upstairs.

'Are you all right,' he called, alarmed suddenly and taking the stairs two by two.

Caroline was sitting grey-faced on the bed. Both of her hands were held to her mouth.

'What is it?' Could she have been attacked? Raped even? Why didn't she speak?

'Oh my God, my God,' she said over and over.

David told himself that he was trained to deal with people in shock, but it was no use, he had forgotten what to do if he had ever known. He knelt down opposite Caroline. He stroked her bent head, he unclenched her hands, he tried to get her to look into his eyes. That was the hardest bit. She wouldn't meet his glance.

'Tell me, darling Caroline, tell me.'

'I can't.'

'Did anyone hurt you, touch you?'

She shook her head.

'Please, please, I have to help you. Have you had bad news from home? Your father, mother?'

'No, nothing like that.'

'Did you see something, an accident, what is it Caroline? Tell me and I'll help you.' He went on stroking her hair and looking up as she sat on the bed, her face stricken and her eyes wild.

'David,' she said.

'Has it anything to do with me?'

'He's mad, he's mad enough for a mad home, to be locked away for ever . . .'

'Who? Who are you talking about? *Tell* me.'

'Gerry Doyle.'

'What has he done now?' David stood up in impatience.

He followed Caroline's glance to the dressing table and saw what had made her the way she was.

One by one he looked at the dozen pictures, bile rising in his throat at what had been private turning into this. 'It wasn't like that,' he said eventually. 'It was special. You know.'

That cheered her somehow, she reached out a cold hand for his.

'Why did he do this?' David looked through the pictures once more and turned them face down on the dressing table.

'Because he's mad,' Caroline said simply.

David pulled the bedroom chair up beside her and held her hands. 'Did he give them to you?' he asked gently.

'No, they were here when I came home.'

'Did he leave a note or anything?'

Caroline reached down and picked up a piece of paper, it had *Doyle's Photographics* on it. In small writing it said:

Delivery three sets of pictures only.
a) Miss Caroline Nolan.
b) Doctor David Power. The surgery, Castlebay.
c) Mrs Clare Power. The Lodge, Castlebay.

'My God.' David stood up. 'That's what Clare wanted. That's why she rang.'

'She's seen those?' Caroline's hand was to her mouth again.

'I don't know. She rang me, very hysterical, I mean I rang her to say I was coming here, she said she wanted me home. I said I'd be home fairly early.'

'She couldn't have, she *couldn't* have seen these?'

'No.' David was slowly going over the conversation. 'No, she couldn't have. She said I could have dinner with you three hundred and sixty-five days a year or something . . .'

'What?'

'She said I *must* come home tonight, I said I was meeting you for dinner, she said you can have dinner every other night of the year but please come back now.'

They looked at each other wildly.

'He couldn't have given them to her, she wouldn't say that if she'd seen them.'

'But why did she want me home?'

'Do you want to go back?' She sounded frightened.

'I can't leave you.'

'But suppose, just suppose he *has*.'

823

'He couldn't have. I'd have known by her voice.' David stood up and paced the room. 'I'll ring her, that's what I'll do.'

He telephoned the Lodge, there was no reply. They looked at each other: was that good or bad?

'She might have gone in to your mother and father,' Caroline suggested.

'No, however bad she felt she wouldn't do that.' He looked tormented.

'Where could he have been, just at the window of the caravan?' she glanced over at the dressing table.

'That's what he must have done. But why? I mean is it for money? His business is meant to be in a bad way, but he couldn't expect us to pay him.'

'We would, wouldn't we?' Caroline said simply.

'Yes I suppose we would. But he doesn't *ask* for money. Do you think it's because he disapproves, because he wants you and he's jealous?'

She shook her head. 'I don't think that would explain it.'

'But *why*? Why would someone do that, it's so perverted. To peer through a window . . . my God. He must be obsessed with you, it's the only explanation, he can't have you himself so he does what he can to ruin the chances of anyone else having you.'

'Oh, he's *had me* himself, many, many times. That's not likely to be the reason. He's actually lost his mind and become a lunatic.'

She had her head in both hands and didn't see the look of shock and pain on David's face. She went on talking.

'The trouble is we can't really tell the Guards or they'll want to know why, but he should be locked up, shouldn't he?' She looked up for confirmation.

'He didn't sleep with you,' David said.

'David, that's neither here nor there. You sleep with Clare, do I mind that, did I ever mind it? Once?' Her voice was getting shrill and hysterical. 'Christ, this isn't the time to do the Victorian Husband bit, everyone in the county has been with Gerry Doyle in some form or another, the point is what do we do?'

She looked young and frightened and alone.

'I know this is the most unhelpful thing in the world, but I think I should go back to Castlebay. Under the circumstances I don't think you should come with me . . .'

'No.'

'I'll ring you when I get there, I'll ring to know are you all right.'

'Sure.'

'I'll come to see you first thing tomorrow morning, when we're calmer, we'll decide what to do.'

'Great.'

'Is there anyone, have you any friends, anyone who could come in, or someone you could go to?' He looked around, willing himself to find her some support, hating to leave her.

'No.'

He swallowed and couldn't speak.

She turned her head towards the dressing table and the pictures that were turned upside down.

The wind and rain lashed the car, the road was strewn with bits of branches.

A steady drumming beat in David's heart. May Clare be all right, may Clare be all right. May he not have shown her the pictures, may he not have shown her the pictures . . .

Clare stood at the window for a long time. She hadn't heard the car starting up. Perhaps he would come back again. But then he had been very final when he had left.

Please God he had been lying when he said he showed the pictures to David, and to Caroline. Please may David not know about them. It made everything so definite if he knew, if he had seen. She would deny she had ever seen them if David asked her. She couldn't bear to hold any discussion based on what she had seen. It didn't make her retch now, it made her sad. But she had known for months, hadn't she? All Gerry Doyle had done was to make her admit it to herself.

Please may Gerry go away from Castlebay, for ever and ever. Please, please.

Gerry closed the door gently behind him. He had never slammed a door in his life. He would like to have taken it from its hinges.

Clare had looked at him as if he were mad. As if *he* were mad! It was Clare who was mad. To have hoped that she would be accepted in that family for one thing, to have looked at the evidence in black and white and *then* to decide to stay . . . That wasn't the Clare O'Brien he used to know, the Clare he had the plans for. He had been so *forgiving* towards her, so *understanding*. He had said so little when she behaved like a common *tramp* and got into trouble with the boy from the big house. No accusations had come from him. And there she stood tonight, *frightened* of him and *doubting* him.

He hit violently at some gorse that jutted out of the hedge between the Lodge and the cliff. He remembered telling a hundred girls, maybe more, about the old saying, 'When the gorse is out of bloom then the kissing's out of fashion.' They had always been surprised that gorse seemed to bloom all year round, and Gerry would laugh. He hit again and scraped his hand on the prickly branches.

How dare Clare talk to him in that frightened, teeth-chattering way? How *dare* she look up at him as if she were afraid he might strike her? She had more to fear from her big unfaithful husband than from him . . . from Gerry, who had always wanted her, *waited* for her.

He moved angrily to the cliff top and looked out at the sea.

Everything had gone now. *Everything*. Not just the business, he had seen that coming for many a month, but Clare's face tonight . . . He had not foreseen that. She was frightened of him as if he were a stranger who would do her harm, not her soul's other half. Her one true friend and love who would make a home for her and her baby, and accuse her of nothing except bad luck, as he had had.

His breath came in short bursts.

She *would not* do this to him . . . She *would not* back out now . . . Now, after *everything* . . . After all he had planned . . .

Clare! It was too much to take, too much for her to do now at this stage.

She would regret it for the rest of her life.

There would be no drive to England in the van tonight for her.

There would be no new life for her.

What did she mean by throwing back all he offered her?

She would want him in a little while, when it was too late. When he had gone. When nobody knew where he was. She would stand on the cliff and wish she had left with him tonight.

He found that he was trembling, shaking with anger. He had never known such a sensation – it was as if a great wind had taken hold of him and borne him up in the air...

He was shaking too much to drive. He would walk on the beach. It would clear his head.

He slipped and climbed down the path. The beach looked dark and dangerous, but the bigger waves were dying down; the tide must be going out now. It was on the turn anyway. He walked, his head wet from the salt spray and the rain; but he didn't care.

He had really blown it now.

The business was a shambles. He couldn't meet even one of the bills that were piled neatly on the desk under a paperweight for whoever would have to go through them. He hoped it wouldn't be Fiona but he couldn't think who else it might be. When the staff couldn't get in tomorrow, there would be a hue and cry but he had left no note to say that he was going to England. There would be no Guards looking for him for bounced cheques. He could always get by on credit; that's what he had always done.

There were very few lights up in Castlebay. He looked up at the outlines of the houses clustered together and the dark spire of the church. He would never look at them again from here, or at all. Once he got to London it would be a new life. It would be *exciting*. It would not be exciting to stay to see their sympathy, to work for someone else, to see Clare, lovely, *lovely* Clare put up with that *sod*. He was *glad* he had done it. He was near the rock pools. Since he was a child he had loved walking over them, balancing, teetering on the edge. It was only inches of water if you did trip over and fall in. Tonight the waves were crashing over them... but still, it was a temptation.

He walked around them, playing games with himself, his feet and legs wet to the knee. He cried out with hysterical excitement. It was ludicrous, but it was exciting.

The wave knocked him down and he cut his cheek on the jagged rock.

It wasn't funny any more. Here came another one. Then the drag, he felt his leg being scraped across the rocks. Desperately he reached out with his hands.

But the drag was too great.

When the third wave had reared up at him, he knew he was going to drown or be battered to death on the rock pools where he had played since he was old enough to walk.

'Clare.' He rattled the door. It was locked.

'Clare? Are you all right?' She came to the door pale but calm.

He reached out his arms for her but she stepped out of his way.

'I'm very sorry. I was frightened. It's the storm, I'm all right now. I'm sorry I called you home.' She spoke like a stranger.

'I rang, I rang twice about seven, and again at a quarter to eight.'

'I was in your parents' house.'

'Are you all right?'

'Yes I am now, I think. But I don't feel like talking. Do you want tea or food? Were you able to have your dinner?'

'No, no it doesn't matter.' He wasn't concentrating.

'Was the road bad?' Again like a person making conversation.

'Yes, branches, and in one place a tree down, you'd have to drive right up on the ditch to get past.'

'Imagine.'

'Clare.'

'You know I said I'd like to go to Dublin for a few days and you said that would be fine, because you could get looked after . . . ?'

'Yes?' His voice was hollow.

'I'd like to go very soon. Tomorrow maybe.'

'You're not all that well, wait a few days.'

'I don't want to wait.'

'It's silly to take Liffey off the whole way across the country when you're not well.'

'It's sillier to stay here on my own hour after hour listening to the sea when I'm not well.'

'You don't have to be on your own here.'

'No. David, will you do me a great favour? Will you not make a scene? I've had as much drama as I can take, and I'm sure you've had a bad day too. But I want to go up to Angela and Dick tonight. Please.'

She must know.

He must have shown her the pictures. David's heart was like a stone.

'Why? What brought this on?'

'I think if I stayed here tonight it might be bad for us. We might say things that would hurt each other.'

He tried a little laugh. 'Heavens, isn't that very fanciful?'

'No,' she said. 'It's not.'

'Do you want to take Liffey with you?'

'Please.'

'I could try to explain . . .' he began.

'And so could I. But we know too well how easily people say things that are unforgivable when they're hurt or annoyed. We've done very little hurting and wounding. Don't let's risk it tonight.'

'Have you packed?' he asked.

'Yes, just things for tonight. I'll come back tomorrow when you've gone out and I'll sort out what we'll need in Dublin.'

'I'm saying yes, not because I'm weak but because I think you're very sure what you want, and I'm not, so we should go along with the one who is sure.'

He grinned at her and she almost took a step towards him.

'Thank you,' she said formally.

'Is Angela expecting you?'
'Yes.'
'Well.' His shoulders drooped.
'She doesn't ask, you know Angela, she doesn't ever ask.'
'I wasn't thinking of that.'
'It's better.'
'I suppose it is.'

So many times they had wished Liffey would sleep rather than struggle and chatter and try to escape. Tonight when they could have done with a bit of distraction she lay in Clare's arms breathing evenly, her long eyelashes making shadows on her cheeks.

David held his daughter tight in his arms and two tears came down his face. 'I'm sorry, Liffey,' he said.

'Why are you sorry?' Clare said gently. 'I have much more to apologize to her for. But it's only like talking to ourselves until she can understand.'

'Goodbye, Clare.'
'Goodbye, David. For a while.'
They didn't touch.

Angela had seen the car drawing up outside the cottage; she had sent Dick scurrying off to bed in case Clare wanted to talk.

Clare stood with Liffey in her arms and watched the car turning and going back down the golf-course road. She gave a little wave but David was looking straight in front of him and didn't see.

'Come in,' Angela said.
'It's very hard to explain.'
'Most things are quite incapable of being explained. I've always thought that,' said Angela.

She showed Clare her bed and made a cup of tea from a kettle which had been boiling in readiness.

'That's to take to bed on your own,' she said. Clare blinked her gratitude at the teacher who knew by magic when people wanted to talk and when there was nothing left to say.

Jim O'Brien ran back into the shop looking frightened.
'Dad, Dad, where are you, where are you?'
'Where would I be but getting out of my bed?' Tom O'Brien grumbled.
'Dad, come here will you.'
The boy looked frightened.
'Dad, come out with me . . . now, come quickly.'

Tom O'Brien pulled his coat over his pyjama top. He had his day trousers on and his shoes and socks, he had been dressing on the side of the bed when he heard the shouts.

They ran on to the top of the cliff and Jim pointed down on the beach. 'I think it's a person, Dad, it's a body.'

There was wind and spray. Tom O'Brien took off his glasses and wiped them. 'It's a shape, but it couldn't be a body, who'd be in the water in this weather?'

'It is, Dad. It *is*. I'm going down, will you get the Guards and Dr Power?'

Jim O'Brien, almost totally deaf, didn't hear his father warning him to take care. He started down the steps to the big treacherous beach at Castlebay where somebody drowned nearly every summer but where they had never seen a body washed in by a winter tide.

People seemed to know without being told. They came out of their houses and began to run down the main street. The murmur became louder, and almost without knowing they were doing it they started to check where their own families were. It was still just a figure, face down in the water. They didn't know for sure whether it was a man or a woman.

'Perhaps it's a sailor from a ship,' they said. But they knew it wasn't anyone who had gone overboard. No nice anonymous death of someone they didn't know. No informing the authorities and saying a few prayers for the deceased Unknown Sailor. This was someone from Castlebay.

They stood in silent groups on the cliff top and watched the first people getting to the water's edge; the boy who had first seen the waves leaving something frightening on the shore; other men too; people from the shops nearby and young men who were quick to run down the path. Then they saw the figures coming down the other path near the doctor's house, kneeling by the body in case, just in case, there was something in a black bag that could bring it back to life.

By the time Father O'Dwyer arrived with his soutane flapping in the wind the murmur had turned into a unified sound. The people of Castlebay were saying a decade of the rosary for the repose of the soul which had left the body that lay face down on their beach.

David had only had two hours' sleep when he heard the shouting. He thought it was still part of his dream, but it was real. He sat up in bed – Clare wasn't there. He remembered the scene last night, taking her up to Angela's house, and he remembered coming back and taking the house apart looking for any trace of the photographs. He knew Clare hadn't taken them with her – he had looked in her small bag. She had only some things for the baby and a nightdress for herself.

He had put off ringing Caroline until it was too late to ring her. Then he told himself it would be cruel to wake her when he had nothing helpful to say.

He had been dreaming that people were coming after him, waving papers or big envelopes at him, all running down Church Street calling at him in anger. In his dream he didn't know why they were so against him but he was frightened and trying to run away.

Then he realized the shouts were real. It was Bumper Byrne's voice and Mogsy's, and then his father's.

'Come quickly, there's someone on the beach, there's been a drowning.'

His heart nearly burst in fear.

He ran down the stairs in his crumpled shirt and trousers, he hadn't undressed last night.

He caught the unfortunate Mogsy Byrne who was at the doorway by his arms. 'Who is it? God damn you who *is* it?'

'I don't know . . . I don't. I don't . . .' Mogsy was stammering at the wild-eyed look of David Power who was always so calm and capable.

'*Tell* me,' David roared at him. 'Tell me or I'll break your neck.'

'He's got his face down, David,' Mogsy managed to get out. 'I left the cliff before they knew, they said to come quickly.'

He had said 'he'. It was a man, it was a man thank God, it was a man. Oh God, thank you for letting it be a man.

David's eyes had cleared. He grabbed a coat and ran to the surgery for his bag, his father was already there.

'Don't come down the steps. Please, Dad. I'll do it. Come down the other way.'

'I've been coming down those steps to take bodies out of the water since before you were born.'

'Who is it, is he dead?'

'They don't know, they think it's Gerry Doyle.'

David put out his hand to steady himself on a desk. Just beside a big brown envelope printed with the words Doyle's Photographics.

His father was already out of the surgery and heading towards the cliff. David steadied himself, put the envelope in a drawer of his own things, down at the bottom of it. And with shaking legs he followed his father to the cliff path.

They saw the group around the body and realized even at this distance that their work would not be needed. Father O'Dwyer had been sent for, he was the only one who might be any help to that body which lay spreadeagled on the beach. Even through the wind and rain and from far away David knew it was Gerry Doyle's lifeless body. He held his arm out to steady his father.

'Young fool,' Dr Power said. 'Bloody young lunatic, his whole life before him. What did he want to do that for? Bloody criminal fool to throw away the one life God gave him.'

David's heart was like stone when they turned the body over and he saw all the lacerations and tears down the side of the face of Gerry Doyle. As if in deference to his father he stood back and let the older man pronounce what everyone knew, that life was extinct.

'Where's Clare, will the pair of you come in and have breakfast with us?'

'She's not here, Dad, she spent the night up at Angela Dillon's.'

'She *what*?'

'Dad, please. You asked me where she was, I told you.'

'Yes, yes you did. Well, will you come in and have a bit of breakfast? You could do with one after all that.'

'No. No thanks, I'll make a cup of tea, that's all I want.'

'And has my grandchild gone to live up with Mr and Mrs Dillon or am I not to ask about that either?'

There was a bit of a smile on his face to take the harm out of the question. But it didn't hide the worry.

'It was only last night, Dad. It'll sort itself out.'

'Clare has some kind of 'flu, she was shivery and very jumpy last night, I'm not interfering, I'm just telling you.'

'Did she say what was wrong?'

'That she was frightened, she had a cup of tea with us, I brought her back. You weren't home.'

'Yes.' Dr Power narrowed his eyes. 'Lord God, is that Gerry's van parked in the lane over there? It *is*. What on earth is it doing up here? Lord have mercy on him, poor fool. And he could be one of the nicest fellows you'd ever talk to.'

Clare slept, to her great surprise. She slept well in the strange white bed with its clean hard sheets and its hot-water bottle. Liffey slept in a cot. Clare had been surprised when Angela said there was a cot, she had forgotten that Angela kept summer visitors, and had thought it wise to invest in two cots years ago when her mother was still alive.

Liffey too had slept. Maybe it was being away from the roar and crash of the sea, or from all the anxiety.

Clare only woke because Angela had come in with a cup of tea. To her surprise, Angela had drawn up a chair beside the bed and sat down. Surely she wasn't going to give a lecture or want a heart to heart chat at this time in the morning.

Certainly Angela's face looked drawn and strained.

Clare thanked her for the tea and waited.

'Take a big sip.'

This was different, there was bad news of some kind. She put down the cup and looked almost on reflex at Liffey as if to make sure that she was all right. 'What is it?'

'There's been an accident. Gerry Doyle was drowned. They've just carried his body up from the beach.'

Total silence. Only the sounds from Liffey's cot where she played happily with the red satin rabbit whose ears had been torn off long ago.

'Clare?'

'He's dead. Is he dead?'

'Yes, it doesn't seem possible. Gerry of all people.' There was no one as full of life.'

Angela broke off as she looked at Clare's face. It was expressionless. She just sat in the white bed with her long hair tied loosely behind her pale face, staring straight ahead of her. Her hands were clasped around her knees.

It wasn't natural to react like that. Angela was alarmed.

Clare *had* been friendly with Gerry of course, very friendly maybe. Perhaps even now when Clare's marriage seemed to be going so disastrously wrong, Gerry had been on hand to give consolation. Could that be the explanation of this sense of shock and disbelief? Angela reached out her hand, hoping that if she patted Clare's arm or did something warm the girl might come out of this trance.

She was totally unprepared for Clare to throw herself into Angela's arms, sobbing and shaking. And the only words she could distinguish over and over were, 'He's really dead, thank God, thank God.'

They said it was accidental death, that had to be said, otherwise he couldn't be buried in consecrated ground. And things were bad enough for the poor Doyles without that.

They said he must have been out for a walk and slipped, his face and side had been very lacerated so he could have been walking on the rock pools, everyone knew that Gerry Doyle loved to balance there. That's what they said but nobody believed it, not for a moment. They knew it was suicide.

It had to be suicide, his business was in ruins, it was a matter of weeks before it would have been taken from him, there was a farmer out in the country who had been making very open threats to come after Gerry on account of the farmer's daughter being pregnant and Gerry Doyle taking no interest in this state of affairs. Fiona Conway, pregnant and heartbroken, told how he had said he wouldn't be in Castlebay for much longer, but she had thought he meant he was going to England. Mary Doyle his mother said that only two days previously he had sent her £20 in an envelope with no explanation, just the words 'From Gerry'. Agnes O'Brien said that she had been saying for months that the boy was in trouble of some kind but nobody had ever listened to her. Josie Dillon said he had cashed two cheques at the hotel which had bounced but they had kept it quiet, and Gerry had thanked her and said when he went to another land and made his fortune he would think of her. She had thought he was going to emigrate, *how* could anyone have thought he would do something like this?

As quickly as they could the formalities were organized and the body was released for burial.

Gerry Doyle would be laid to rest after ten o'clock Mass on Thursday, Father O'Dwyer announced from the pulpit, and blew his nose loudly because he still couldn't take it in.

David went through his work automatically, everywhere he went they talked about the tragedy. A woman with chest pains pointed to the pictures on the walls, framed photographs of the First Communions and Confirmations. He was a lovely boy, always a laugh, never took anything too seriously. In the next house the old man who had hardening of the arteries was more interested in what could have happened to poor young Doyle than he was about his own imminent departure to the county home which David was trying to introduce.

'He was practically born in the water that young lad, which is unusual in these parts, half of Castlebay never takes to the sea at all, but the young Doyle fellow, he swam like a fish.'

In the room of a ten-year-old girl with jaundice they talked as much of Gerry Doyle as of the patient. He told them not to be worried by the colour of her urine, it was quite natural that it would turn the colour of port wine. They nodded and said that they had heard Gerry Doyle's business was in a bad way but surely he wouldn't drown himself over a thing like that? There had to be more to it than that.

'If people drowned themselves when their businesses went wrong, wouldn't the sea be full of bodies?' asked the child's father.

David agreed absently and looked at the little girl's eyes. They were yellow and he told her that her skin would go a little bit yellow like a Chinese.

'Are the Chinese yellow?' the girl asked. 'Really yellow?'

'Come to think of it they're not, any I saw aren't yellow at all.'

'Have you *seen* a Chinese?' The girl was very excited.

'In Dublin, yes, there were Chinese students at University and there was a Chinese restaurant we went to.'

She could have talked to him for ever about it. He wondered would Liffey want to know things like that too. His heart sank again when he thought of Liffey. And Clare.

The day ended somehow and he went back to the surgery. Quickly David retrieved the envelope and brought it back to the Lodge. He saw his mother pretending not to look through the curtains at him, but he went on as if he hadn't seen.

The kitchen was tidy. He looked around hopefully for a note. Clare had been in during the day, he could see that. The dishes and cups he had left after his breakfast were washed up and put away. He noticed that she had done some shopping: a packet of tea, a pound of butter, a loaf of bread and some sliced rashers of bacon were placed on the table near the range. The bed upstairs was made and although some of her clothes were hanging in the wardrobe she must have taken others. Most of Liffey's things seemed to have gone, and one of their two suitcases had disappeared. He looked around to see if she had taken all her books. It would be good in a way if she had, that would mean she had gone through with her plan of going to Dublin for a while.

Please may she have gone to Dublin. Let her not be here for the funeral. Please.

He sat down in the kitchen, having locked the door first, and he took out the pictures. He looked at them again. Exactly the same as he had seen last night at Caroline's. Last night? Is that all it was? There was the same list in the small handwriting naming the three people to whom they were being sent. He must have given them to Clare. He must have come to this house, that's why his car was there, his big ugly van with the name of the business, parked in the lane beside their house. David's father had phoned the Guards to report it being there, they had come to collect it but it had told them nothing. But it told David everything, he must have called on Clare. That was what had frightened her so much, that was why she had wanted him to come home. But had he come in and spoken to her, shown the pictures to her personally? Or had he just pushed them through the door and said he would be back?

David opened the front of the range and one by one he put them in. There was nothing exciting about these pictures taken through a caravan window. They were not the kind of pictures that would do anything except destroy the three people they were sent to. That was what Gerry Doyle had done before he destroyed himself.

Why? David allowed his brain to start on that again. All day he had pushed the thought out of sight while he attended to his work. But now as the flames burned up the record of his time with Caroline, time that he had convinced himself was not evil because nobody was losing and nobody was being hurt . . . he wondered again why Gerry had bothered. It couldn't have been blackmail. Caroline and David didn't have the kind of money it turned out that was needed by Doyle's

Photographics, they would only have been able to pay a few pounds a week at the very most. He didn't hate David, in fact they always got on very well when they were children, and of late, well David had been a bit scathing about how easily women fell for Gerry but he would never have known that. Or if he had, he couldn't have cared enough to hound David in this way.

David had assumed that it must have been Caroline, but she had been adamant, she had said with an unattractive honesty that had revolted him that she was Gerry Doyle's for the asking, and had been – and, no doubt, would be again – so it could not have been unrequited passion that made him take the pictures.

What did that leave?

It only left Clare.

Clare.

He remembered the time he had come across them kissing on the bench over the beach, and how annoyed he had been. He remembered Clare running up from the National Library back to her hostel to see if Gerry Doyle had rung. He remembered the easy way Gerry Doyle danced with Clare in the ballroom with the glittery revolving light sparkling over them as they smiled at each other.

It was Gerry Doyle she had asked to get her post office savings book that time. Then, only weeks ago, he remembered Gerry complaining that Clare wouldn't let him come and photograph Liffey. 'She's afraid that if I take the picture, I somehow steal the child,' he had laughed. And Clare had said nothing.

The photographs were all burned. He poked around and the ashes were gone, mixed into the other ashes of the range. He closed the little gate and looked around. The clock was ticking and below the sea was crashing. Those were the only sounds. Those were the sounds that gifted bright Clare O'Brien heard all day, and all evening. That was the life he had given her.

She was too smart now for Chrissie and her mother to feel easy with her. She wasn't smart enough for her mother-in-law to make her welcome. And Gerry Doyle had loved her and wanted her to come away. He had taken the pictures to prove that there was nothing to keep her any more. He had wanted Liffey as well, she must have sensed that at the time he wanted to photograph the child.

Had he come to the house and asked her to go away?

Did he drown himself because she wouldn't go.

After all, as the father of that sick child had said this afternoon, if everyone whose business was in a bad way swam out to sea then the beach would be littered with bodies. Gerry Doyle didn't kill himself over cheques that bounced and bills that would not be paid. But if he was prepared to go to such lengths and take such photographs to incriminate her husband then he really must have wanted Clare, and wanted her enough to end his life if she wouldn't come with him.

The clock ticked on and the waves crashed on. He walked around the small house restlessly. There was no sign of Clare in this house. No pictures she had chosen on the wall. No books. There were some in the spare room but they had always looked as if they were in transit, not as if they had come to stay. On the window sill was a cookery book and inside in Clare's big bold writing were the instructions for the dinner party that had been such a disaster. That was the only evidence that this woman had lived here.

David Power put his head in his hands at the kitchen table and cried.

For *all* that had happened.

Tuesday evening. It was only twenty-four hours ago that he had come to the house sure that she would pack her things and leave in his van. Would he have killed them all? Would he have driven Liffey and Clare into the sea? Clare didn't know. He *might* have been sane, and really meant them to go to England as he said. But that in itself wasn't sane. She had been over it a thousand times, there was no way she had led him on. A few kisses years ago, a few dances holding him close. But Gerry Doyle had that and much much more from every girl he met. He couldn't have seen it as some kind of attraction or involvement. So, he knew that she wasn't very happy with David, that her life had not turned out to be the dream she once thought . . . but still.

Angela and Dick had been wonderful, but to say that, to think that was just to let the record go into a groove where it said the same thing over and over. They had always been wonderful. For as long as she could remember.

'Take the car,' Dick had said. 'I don't need it just now. If you want to go and collect anything.'

She took his car, and went back to the Lodge, she knew that both Molly and Nellie were looking out of different windows trying to see what she was up to. She didn't care. She didn't even know what she was up to herself.

Methodically she went through the house tidying it for David, she made the bed and put all the washing together in a pillowcase, none of her own things, only his. She left the place so that it wouldn't offend anyone if Molly and Nellie came in to look after poor David. She even cleaned out a particularly grubby corner of the food press she had been meaning to do for ages, and lined it with fresh paper.

She made a big rubbish bag out of one of the pillowcases, and into that she threw all the torn stockings, almost-empty marmalade jars. She sat in the unusually tidy kitchen for fifteen minutes trying to think of something to say to David in a note, and then decided there was nothing to say.

He had left her no note, after all. He had been here all night, and then they said he had been called down to the beach when Gerry had been found. Perhaps there had been no time.

With her head in her hands she sat there. Could Gerry really have sent those pictures to David? Could he have left them in the van? No, the Guards had said there was nothing in the van, Angela had told her that, no photographic things even. It had been empty as if he had been clearing out.

Suppose Gerry had dropped the pictures into the surgery. Suppose Dr Power had opened them. Her heart gave a jump thinking of that nice old man seeing such indecent evidence of his son's adultery with a family friend. Then she hardened her feelings. Why should she care now? The pictures were not of Clare. She had been here minding the child and the house while all this was going on. She was not going to let herself feel sympathetic when she was the one who deserved a great great deal of sympathy.

She stood up, arranged the things she had bought for his supper where he could see them, and then loaded the car with the suitcase she had packed. She put the pillowcase of rubbish in the back, she shook more anthracite into the range, and pulled the door behind her.

'I won't stay here for ever,' Clare said to Angela.

'You haven't been here two days yet, stop being so dramatic. Aren't you company for us?'

'Not really. Not at the moment.'

Liffey asked to get up on Clare's lap and then she wanted to get down again. She waddled over to Angela with the same request.

'It's a pity Gerry didn't see Fiona's child born.'

'What?'

'Fiona's having a child any time now, you know that.'

'Oh of course, I was thinking of . . . Why do you say that?'

'He loved children. He was very good with them too. He often talked about Liffey here. Did you know that?'

'No.' Clare shivered.

Angela decided to change the subject. 'I was talking to Fiona on my way back from school, I went down Church Street. She was going in to Doyle's Photographics to sort things out . . . Clare? What is it?'

'Oh my God, my God I forgot that entirely. Can I take the car again Angela, please, five minutes.'

'Of course you can but what . . .'

Clare was out the door and into the front seat. The keys were always left in the ignition. Dick Dillon looked out the window upstairs to know who was driving his car off crashing the gears like that.

Fiona wore a grey smock with a big white collar attached to it. She hadn't any mourning clothes in maternity wear. They probably didn't make them, Clare thought.

Fiona was sorting through the brown envelopes with their codes and dates.

'I'm very sorry,' Clare said.

'I know.' Fiona went on sorting. 'It sort of helps to do this, it makes things more normal in a way.'

'Yes.'

There was a silence.

Clare had acted on such an impulse when she remembered the photographs that she hadn't paused to think how she would ask for them. Now she was here and she must speak. She couldn't let anyone discover them, nobody should open an envelope and see what she had seen on Sunday night. Nobody should be allowed to look at what she had to look at.

'Fiona?' she began hesitantly.

The perfect oval face, pale with dark circles under the big dark eyes, looked at her inquiringly.

Clare swallowed and began to speak. 'Do you know the way just when you think there's no way out of something . . . you know there's no way out and when somebody helps you. It can change your life.'

Fiona looked at her, confused.

'Surely in your life, ages ago there must have been some problem, some big worry, and maybe Gerry helped you, just said nothing, asked nothing, but gave help.'

Fiona looked at Clare, trying to read in her face whether she could have known about that first pregnancy, and how Gerry had come to England to look after her. Clare felt she was walking on very thin ice.

'I suppose all of us have something like that in our lives, and if someone agrees to sort it out then it *can* be solved.'

'Yes.' Fiona was still doubtful.

'Well I know Gerry did a lot of that for people, you probably don't know how he helped a lot of people when they were in trouble, and I'd like to help him now.'

'How can you help him now?' Fiona cried.

Clare spoke quickly. 'There are some pictures, here somewhere or in a private file or somewhere, that I don't think he'd want people to see.'

'What sort of pictures?'

'Does it matter what kind of pictures if you believe me? If you believe that Gerry wouldn't have wanted them found.'

'Is it very important?'

'I think it is.'

'But why wouldn't Gerry have sorted it out before he . . . before he . . .'

'He didn't drown himself, Fiona.'

Fiona looked left and right. Nobody had said this aloud in front of her but everyone had thought it.

'But . . .'

'He couldn't have Fiona, he wasn't that kind of a person, *you* know that.'

'I didn't think he would but how else . . . ?'

'Because he was upset, he must have been upset and just went climbing around the rocks. He was always doing that.' Of course it wasn't possible but it would be good for Fiona to think this, and she was beginning to believe it.

'I suppose . . .'

'And it would give a lot of people a better chance if the pictures weren't seen. I just know this, like I know I got a second chance and you probably did too . . .'

Fiona's big troubled eyes filled with tears. 'Gerry did give me a second chance years ago. I wanted to do one thing and he wanted me to do another, he was quite right as it turned out.' Almost unconsciously she stroked her stomach as if thinking of the other child Stephen, now in somebody else's family.

'Well this is what I mean.' Clare didn't want her to confess. 'If I could just . . .'

Fiona handed her a key. 'If they're anywhere they'll be in his room in that steel cabinet. By the window.'

'Thank you Fiona.'

She found them at once. There was hardly anything else there except the cheerful postcard she had sent him once from Dublin, the letter asking him to find her post office savings book and another note thanking him when he had.

It was the same brown envelope that he had showed her on the kitchen table back in her house. But there was an invoice note on it saying that there were copies being sent to Miss Caroline Nolan and David Power as well. So she was too late after all. With leaden movements she placed the contents of the drawer into her big briefcase, the letters she had written him, harmless little notes. Why had he kept them? She put it in and left the drawer open.

She leaned her head against the window.

Should she tell Fiona there was nothing, or should she say that she had found them? Which would cause less worry?

As it happened she needn't have worried, there was no decision to make. Fiona knocked on the door.

'Can I come in?'

'Yes.' Clare was still looking out the window at Church Street, at the people going about their lives in an ordinary way.

'I'm glad you came,' Fiona said.

'Why?'

'Because now I do believe for the first time that it *was* an accident. If Gerry was going to end it himself, he'd have left nothing to get him into trouble . . . or you, Clare. He worshipped you. Now I think it must have been an accident.'

'Yes, it must have been.' Clare's gaze was still on the road.

'And so he'll not have gone to hell. I couldn't bear Gerry to go to hell for taking his own life, that's what I've been thinking since Monday morning.'

Clare put her arms awkwardly around Fiona and looked over her shoulder, out of the window at the view that Gerry Doyle must have seen every day as he sat in this ridiculous, over-decorated office and ran his father's steady little business into the ground.

David was looking at an X-ray with his father.

'That poor hip's worn away a lot on her, hasn't it?' Dr Paddy Power was full of sympathy for an elderly woman out on the Far Cliff Road. 'She must be in great pain with that all right.'

'She doesn't complain very much, but she's limping a lot.'

'Ah well, nothing for it, it's terrible to have to tell them it'll just get worse.'

'But you don't tell them that, do you Dad?'

'No, I tell them they're lucky it isn't malignant or anything, try to look on all the positive side of it, no point in being negative and saying it's arthritis and it just gets worse and worse . . . David? What is it?'

David had jumped up as if he were shot.

'I've just remembered something. I have to go.'

'Hey . . . come back here, leave me the notes, you've got poor Mrs Connolly's whole life story with you.'

'What? Yes. Sorry.'

'Are you all right, son?'

'I have to go out for a bit. I'll be back shortly.'

The *negatives*. Why hadn't he remembered them? They were probably in a drawer in Doyle's Photographics, unless of course the little bastard had sent them to someone else like the solicitor's firm where Caroline worked, or to Clare's parents.

He walked around clenching and unclenching his hands in the dark afternoon. He would have to do it. He walked determinedly down Church Street.

Fiona was by herself in the shop. She looked very young and innocent. Too young for the great curve under her grey smock with its white collar.

'Oh David,' she said. 'Aren't you nice to call.'

He swallowed a bit. 'I don't have the right words to say. My father seems to know exactly what to say that helps people. I don't. Maybe when I'm older and have seen a lot of awful things I will.'

'At least you came in, that was very kind of you,' she said.

Now it was more difficult than ever.

'I'm sure a lot of people have been to say how shocked they are, how upset.'

'No. It's a bit awkward, you see.'

'Why?'

'I think a lot of them think he may have . . . that he may have meant to do it.'

It was impossible to stand talking to this beautiful serene girl who thought her little monster of a brother might have been swept away by some tide.

'Well I don't suppose we'll ever know . . .' he began.

'But I do know. I know he couldn't have meant to do it, take his own life. I *know* that.'

'No, no.' He was soothing.

'I just know.'

'Of course.'

He couldn't broach it, he couldn't say that he had really come not to express sympathy but to know if he could rummage through her dead brother's private files.

'What are you doing here? You should be at home resting,' he said in his professional voice.

Fiona looked at him gratefully. 'No, I'm better to keep busy.'

What an end to the Doyles. The bright glittery Doyles of long ago.

'That's good,' he said uselessly.

This was going to be the last time he would talk to Fiona normally. She was going through the picture orders methodically, she would come across prints or negatives, she would scream when she saw them possibly, or feel faint. She might be so revolted she would show them to someone in authority like Father O'Dwyer and ask him what she should do. She was a simple girl, simple and inexperienced, she would be so shocked by all it would mean, for Gerry as well as for him and Caroline. Could he dare?

'Fiona. I was wondering,' he began.

She raised her eyes and he saw the dark shadows underneath for the first time.

'I was wondering . . .' he began. But he couldn't do it. There weren't the words.

'Nothing,' he said, turning to go.

'Clare left her scarf here earlier, can you give it to her?'

'Clare was here?'

'Yes. About an hour ago.'

'What on earth for?' He said it without thinking.

Fiona looked at him thoughtfully. 'Nothing in particular. She just came in.'

'Of course.'

He left with a stooping walk.

Clare had come for the photographs, she hadn't come just to sympathize. If she had, Fiona would have said so.

David didn't notice anyone who spoke to him as he walked back up Church Street and turned left to go home.

Chrissie shouted something at him out of Dwyers' but he didn't hear it. He didn't notice Rose Dillon from the hotel hooting the horn of her scooter at him. Nor did he see Ben O'Brien his brother-in-law waving at him from a pick-up truck.

He turned up his collar and paused at the crossroads. Should he go up to see her now? Should he ask Angela and Dick for a few minutes to talk? What would he say? 'I believe you've got the pictures. I'm sorry.'

No, there was nothing to say. He turned and went back to the big house. He walked past it and on to the Lodge. How had he never noticed how silent the place was? And sad.

Clare sat in the car, motionless. She must burn them. Now. But it was much easier said than done to burn something if you hadn't a house of your own. And at the moment she didn't feel she had a house. She could hardly go to the shop: 'Oh. Hallo Mam, Dad, excuse me, I'm just going in to the range to burn a few things, I like a nice fire . . .'

And she had behaved quite madly enough with Dick Dillon and Angela already to ask them did they mind if she burned a few papers in their range.

What about Josie? Would she be able to accept Clare coming in and saying that she'd like a few moments on her own poking around at the Aga in the hotel kitchen? It was nonsensical. Her mind churned. But she would *not* leave them somewhere where they could be found. They were so awful, those pictures and their negatives, she wanted the satisfaction of seeing them burn in flames. Only that way could she begin to get them out of her mind.

There should be a public burning place, somewhere that people could go and get rid of the things that depressed them or frightened them. A public burning place in the middle of every town.

She remembered suddenly that Dr Power had made a great fuss once about there being no incinerator up at the caravan park. How were the unfortunate campers meant to keep the place hygienic he had thundered unless there were proper rubbish collections and somewhere for them to burn things? The proper rubbish collections had never been set up but the brick incinerator had. It used to burn during the summer getting rid of the worst of the campers' litter.

The caravan park. That would be a nice bit of irony, go up and burn the evidence at the scene of the crime. There wouldn't be a fire in the incinerator now, but she could make one. She had her matches in her handbag, there was a can of petrol in the back of Dick Dillon's car. The more she thought of it the more she liked the idea. She drove slowly down Church Street, past O'Brien's shop, past the bench that looked out over the cliff to the sea, and turned left down the Far Cliff Road to the caravan park.

David rang Caroline again. He had been so relieved the first time when the woman with the bad cold at the solicitor's office had said she was not there. No other explanation. She wasn't at her house either. Now he had rung her office and her house three times and had found her at neither of them. He was no longer relieved, he was worried. He hadn't wanted to talk to her, and presumably she had felt the same at the beginning. But now it was Wednesday evening – two days after the discovery of the pictures. They should talk.

'If Miss Nolan isn't in do you know when and where I could find her?' he asked the woman with the streaming cold.

'In Dublin,' the voice said.

'Has she gone on holiday?' David asked.

'No, she's gone and left. All of a sudden. Gone for good.' The sniff was full of disapproval for the flashy irresponsible ways of a young solicitor from Dublin who didn't know how things were done.

David didn't know whether he was relieved or upset. Relieved, he thought. At least in Dublin Caroline would have people to look after her, people to talk to. In the town here she had nobody. He clenched the kitchen table as he thought of it.

He seemed to spend a lot of time at this table. Sitting here while the time passed. They had thought it would be nice to have a kitchen which was also a living room, that had been the plan, but they had never really done it up or chosen any furniture for it properly. It must have been a kind of prison for Clare.

He thought of Caroline going back to Dublin, her chin raised with that determined look, driving through rain and fog in her little car. He thought of Caroline saying that Gerry Doyle couldn't have had any hopeless unrequited love for her. 'He had me.' Those were her words. Did Gerry Doyle have Caroline in the caravan park, did he share all the same things? God, God. At least David had been spared pictures of it. He only had his imagination.

It was windy and exposed up in the caravan park. It was impossible to see why so many people headed from all over Ireland and England to come here in the summer. It seemed like a different planet.

Clare knew which was Caroline's caravan. She had listened wordlessly when David had said what a good idea it was to get one, she could always spend the summertime in it fully, or in the winter it provided a place to have a change of clothes or an overnight stop when it was too late to drive back to the town. She had forced it out of her mind then. She had refused to think of it.

The same way that she had refused to think of David and Caroline making love. She had blocked it from her mind. Even on the nights that she knew with every instinct that they had she did not acknowledge it. It made things safer, like not stepping on cracks in the pavement. She had never admitted it to herself until she saw those pictures. God, but Gerry Doyle was clever. In a few more days she might well have thought he was a possible alternative to such a cheating husband. It wasn't likely but she hadn't known just how bitter and resentful she would feel. Those pictures that she had in her hand, had gone a great way towards doing what Gerry, mad insane Gerry, had wanted them to do. She must burn them. Now.

Maybe she would feel a bit better.

The wind whipped her hair as she took the can of petrol out of the boot. You couldn't light a fire on a day like this without a rag soaked in something that would leap up in flames.

The grey anonymous caravan that Caroline Nolan had rented for six months stood like a big menacing shape, not far from where Clare was standing. This was where her husband came when he was meant to be playing golf. Those pictures had been taken on a bright afternoon; Gerry must have followed them, on his light little feet. They hadn't bothered to draw the curtains. Who would look in at them? The caravan looked out to sea . . .

She was drawn to see it. Looking left and right as if anyone else would be in this wild place, she tiptoed up to it. It was stripped bare of any possessions, there were no lamps, rugs, little ornaments in it. She remembered her mother-in-law giving Caroline some cushions, two rather nice ones. They were still there, oddly. But none of the tartan rugs that had figured in the pictures, nothing at all.

Perhaps she had gone. Caroline. Perhaps when she saw the pictures she had run for it. Perhaps she was just trying to hide the evidence. She was so clever that one, you'd never know what she was up to.

She took the big envelope out and laid it down on the cold iron bars of the incinerator, she shook some petrol over a cleaning rag and watched the pictures and the negatives and the letters she had written to Gerry Doyle burn. It was a small fire. She poked and poked, they were gone, there was no way that anyone, not a fleet of detectives, could know what they were.

She breathed in the salty air. She still felt restless and jumpy, somehow she had thought that burning the pictures would help but it hadn't. It was all still here, the memory, the caravan. The knowledge of what they had done and might still do, the caravan. The loneliness, the lies he had told her. The caravan.

Almost without realizing it she was walking towards it. It was set far away from the others. She still had the petrol in her hand, the matches were in her pocket.

She paused for one long moment and acknowledged what she was doing. 'Yes,' Clare said aloud. 'Yes, I bloody will.'

The petrol soaked the bed, she put most of it there, and then more near the door. She lit the rag, threw it in and ran as fast as she could away. By the time she reached Dick Dillon's car, parked on the road outside, the flames were coming from the windows.

She drove excitedly back towards town, and stopped the car not far from her parents' shop. She could see the blaze in the winter evening . . .

She felt better than she had for a long time. She called in to her mother.

'What are you driving Dick's car for?'

'God, you were always great with the greeting Mam, I'll say that for you.'

'I've never been able to understand you Clare, never.'

'You didn't do too badly, Mam. Do you think I might have a cup of tea or is it only abuse I'm going to get?'

'Make it for yourself then. Some of us have work to do.'

'Are you cross over something in particular or what, Mam?'

'I don't know what you're up to, that's all.' Agnes had her mouth in a hard line.

'I don't really know myself, Mam, I'm meant to be going up to Dublin to see about sitting this exam again. I'm sort of on the way there – Liffey and I.'

'You're never taking that baby up to Dublin, away from her home.'

'Not for ever Mam, just to give her a taste of city life, look what it did for me.' Clare's eyes were bright, too bright.

She was still sitting on the counter sipping a mug of tea when the shouts went up that there was a fire in the caravan park.

'What's all the fuss and excitement?' Clare asked giddily.

'Lord God, child, someone might be burned to death.' Agnes was white with anxiety.

'Who'd be up there in the middle of winter?' Clare said.

'How could a caravan catch fire unless some poor unfortunate turned over a stove or an oil lamp on themselves?'

They came for David but he wasn't able to move.

'Ask Dad, take him in your car,' he stammered out to Brian Dillon who had come with the alarm.

David's limbs had stopped co-ordinating, it took him five whole minutes to pick up the phone.

The post office took what seemed like an hour to connect him to Dublin.

James Nolan answered the phone. He made a pretence that David was a long-lost traveller who had just returned to civilization. 'We never thought we'd hear your voice again.'

'Cut that out,' David said roughly.

'What?'

'Is Caroline there? Quickly.'

'Well quickly or slowly I can't tell you. Isn't she meant to live in your neck of the woods?'

'James please. I beg you.'

'Have you two had a lovers' tiff?'

'I said I beg you.'

'Very well, since you beg me so nicely, she is here but I'm not to tell you.'

'Are you sure, have you seen her, is she in your house?'

'I don't know where she is this minute but I spoke to her at breakfast and she rang me at the Law Library to arrange something for this evening. But shush, I didn't tell you.'

'No.'

'David? Are you all right?'

He had hung up.

The burning of the caravan was a mystery. It must have been youngsters playing with petrol, everything had been soaked in it. Poor Caroline Nolan.

The Guard had rung her in the big town but they couldn't find her. Still wasn't it a mercy that nobody had been hurt?

Clare drove in to the garage where her brother Ben worked. She got Dick Dillon's car filled up and also the petrol can he kept at the back. She drove back to the O'Hara house.

'You said only a minute. I was worried,' Angela said.

'Stop sounding like my mother.'

'Are you all right? You look very flushed.' Angela was concerned.

'No. I'm much better now. There was something I had to do.'

Mrs Corrigan from the other side of the road came in with the news that there had been a big fire over on the Far Cliff Road, and a caravan burned to a shell.

Angela wanted to know was anyone hurt.

'Who would be there in the middle of winter?' Clare had said, her eyes still too bright.

'People are sometimes,' Angela said cautiously.

'Well, they're up to no good then.'

Angela looked so frightened then, that Clare took pity on her.

'It's all right, Angela, it's all right, there was nobody in it. I did check.'

Clare picked up Liffey and held her tight, she was so big now it was quite a weight.

'Well Liffey, in a day or two you and I are heading off to the great unknown to seek our fortune – well, to seek Mummy's degree for one thing.'

'I'll never say. You won't, either, I hope.'

'No, of course not, but you're different, you can know everything. The good and the bad.'

'It wasn't all that *very* bad, considering,' Angela said with a smile.

'No it wasn't was it?' Clare seemed recovered now.

'Did you know that Clare's up in Angela Dillon's house?' Agnes asked Tom O'Brien that night.

'Sure hasn't she been living up there since she was ten years of age, what's strange about that?' he asked.

'No that's just it, she *is* living up there, she's been there three days.'

'Nonsense, Agnes, you must have got the wrong end of the stick. Hasn't she a perfectly good house of her own?'

'I know, but that's what I heard, so I asked her straight out.'

'And?'

'You never get a straight answer from Clare, she said she was on her way to Dublin to inquire about exams or some such nonsense.'

'Better say nothing, say nothing at all, you'll get little thanks for what you say.'

Agnes thought that for once he might be right. This could be one occasion when it might pay to take no notice.

People said that Gerry Doyle's poor mother had to take so many tablets now for her nerves that she would hardly realize what was happening at the funeral. Fiona had tried to get her a black coat and she said no, she always hated black, it reminded her of funerals. Gently Fiona had tried to persuade her that this actually was a funeral, and didn't know whether to be pleased or upset that her mother hadn't taken in the fact that Gerry was dead.

Nellie Burke's family asked her was it true that David Power and Clare were living apart. Nellie, stubborn and loyal, said she knew nothing of the sort. Her brother's wives, who were spectacular gossips, were disappointed. They thought she would be the source of all information. So they had to make do with saying that a marriage like that could never work. They had known it from the start. She had been a silly little girl to think that a bit of education made her the equal of the doctor's son.

'Did David tell you that Caroline Nolan's packed up her job and gone back to Dublin?' Paddy Power asked Molly.
    'I don't believe you.'
    'So Mr Kenny says, remember he got her the job in the first place, very upset he is about it all. Just told them she wasn't suited to country life, worked all day and all night to get her work finished and left. Same in her house. Wrote them a cheque for the rest of the quarter and vanished.'
    'I must ring Sheila.'
    'Maybe not, Moll. Maybe not. Let it settle down a bit yet.'
    'Why do you say that?' She looked anxious.
    'We don't know half of what goes on, we might be making it worse.'
    'How could we make things worse, we're their friends, we haven't done anything to upset Caroline, to make her run off from here.'
    'No Moll, you haven't and I haven't,' he said levelly.
    She looked at him in alarm and realized he wasn't going to say any more.

'There'll be so many there they won't miss me. I'm not going,' Clare said.
    They could hear the bell tolling on the cold, wet morning.
    'You shouldn't hurt the living. Fiona, his mother.'
    'I can't stand there and pray for the repose of his soul. It's a mockery.'
    'It's what people do, it's a custom, think of it like that.'
    'You don't know . . . you don't know . . .'
    'Clare, stop it this minute. Of course I don't know, you didn't tell me, and you are not going to tell me now when we have to be in the church in ten minutes' time. I've arranged for us to put Liffey in Mrs Corrigan's, she'll not be going, she's got five babies in that house already.'
    'No. I have to stay here and mind Liffey.'
    'Clare, stop being a child. Put your coat on. Now.'

'Would you like to walk up to the church with me, son?'
    'Dad, I was half thinking I wouldn't go. You know, stay here in case anyone needs one of us.'

'If they need us won't they know where to find us, where would anyone find anyone on the day the bell is ringing for a young man?'

'I know but . . .'

'There's going to be talk if you don't go.'

'That's nonsense, the church will be full, the whole of Castlebay will be there.'

'And you should be there.'

'But there are a lot of things I can't explain . . .'

'And there's no need why you *should* explain, just come up to the church with me now, come on David, it's a small thing to do, but it's a big thing if you don't do it.'

'If you think . . .'

'I do think. Come on now, the bell's ringing, your mother's gone already in the car.'

With cold hands they blessed themselves. Almost all of Castlebay went into the familiar church. The only thing that was unfamiliar was the coffin up near the altar rails. It was covered with Mass cards and there were two wreaths, one from his mother arranged by Frank Conway, and one from Fiona and Frank also arranged by Frank Conway. For some odd reason other people hadn't sent flowers. You didn't associate Gerry Doyle with flowers for the dead.

The church always seemed colder at a funeral. In the front row Mrs Mary Doyle knelt in the black coat that had been borrowed for her, her eyes vacant and her hands clasped. Beside her Fiona sat. Face paler than ever, wearing a loose black coat and a mantilla. She looked like a Spanish widow, she had never looked really Irish at all.

David and his father arrived just at the same moment as Angela, Dick and Clare. They exchanged the funeral words people spoke at such times – terrible tragedy, young man, makes you wonder at the sense of anything.

David and Clare let the others go in before them.

'Did you burn the caravan?' he asked.

'Yes. And the pictures. And the negatives.'

'It doesn't matter I suppose,' he said eventually.

'No.'

As if they were a million miles from each other they walked into the church side by side. Angela and Dr Power sat beside each other deliberately. David and Clare joined them. So Castlebay was not treated to the sight of the young doctor and his wife having a public coldness right in the middle of a funeral. They genuflected and knelt down, where they had been manoeuvred to be. Beside each other.

There had never been a Mass as long as this.

When she was certain it must be the communion it was only the offertory. When she was sure it was the last Gospel it was only the post-communion.

Sitting, and standing, and kneeling, beside David; looking at his cold hands clasped in front of him; noticing that he needed a haircut; seeing that his shoes were well-polished and wondering had Nellie done that for him.

And then every time she lifted her glance seeing that coffin which they said held Gerry Doyle.

Where would she go back to? If she could go back . . . ?

Before she got pregnant? No, that would mean no Liffey, and the only good thing that had come out of all this was Liffey.

After Liffey was born, had she been really terrible then? It was odd, she couldn't remember much about all that winter and spring. She must have been a poor companion. As drugged and vacant-looking as Gerry's unfortunate mother looked now.

Was that where she would start again?

David wished that she wasn't kneeling beside him, but there was nothing else they could do. She had her elbows on the back of the seat in front and her forehead resting on her clenched hands. He noticed how thin her wrist was, with the watch he had given her hanging slightly loosely on it. When he glanced at her he saw her eyes were open and distant. She wasn't praying, obviously.

There was plenty to think about. He felt a great weariness come over him. He was too tired to make her promises, to beg her to come back to the Lodge, to tell her it would all be all right. It might not be all right, and they had never lied directly to each other, they had lied by omission. He had never denied that he was with Caroline, because she had never asked him what way he was with Caroline. If it hadn't been for those pictures, they would have had a chance. Those pictures. If he could only go back to before the pictures . . .

Had she really burned them? Is that what she had been doing when she went to burn the caravan? He shivered to think of it. Suppose the wind blew the wrong way and had swept the flames towards her? But why should she have gone up to the caravan park to burn the pictures, for God's sake? Couldr.'. she have burned them anywhere? He turned his head and looked at her, head still leaning on one hand, her dark eyes looking ahead, her shoulders tense and full of hurt. Had he been right when he said that nothing made any difference now? Was it too late?

The priest had walked around the coffin with the thurible and the sickly sweet smell of incense filled the church as Father O'Dwyer made his circle of the box that contained Gerry Doyle. Then four men, men who had been boys with Gerry and who had watched helplessly while he had taken their girlfriends away, picked up the coffin as if it were no weight at all. They walked out of the church followed by the whole congregation.

They walked, heads bent in the wind, the quarter of a mile to the graveyard which stood high on a hill. There the grave had been dug and the two gravediggers removed their caps as the funeral procession arrived.

Visitors often looked at this little graveyard and said it would be a beautiful place to come to rest. Surrounded by a stone wall, filled with the celtic crosses of years, its own little ruined church covered with ivy in the corner.

Because it was on a hill you could see the whole beach below, the white flecks of the waves coming in ceaselessly. The sand and stones being pulled out in their wake. Hardly anyone could have looked back down at the beach without remembering that this is why they were here.

The only people who didn't look were Gerry's mother and sister. Mrs Mary Doyle looked vaguely around. It was like a bad dream, everyone seemed to be looking at her she thought, but her sister held one of her arms and her daughter held the other. There was no sign of Gerry but he must be away working somewhere, he'd be here soon.

Fiona's tears were mixed with the salt wind and rain, but she felt much more at peace now, now that she realized Gerry couldn't have done it on purpose. Whatever those pictures were, Gerry would never have left anything behind him, deliberately . . . not anything that would hurt someone or ruin their life.

She listened to Father O'Dwyer, she didn't understand the Latin words, but she knew that they were necessary to set Gerry's soul at peace.

Angela looked at Dick. His face always looked very cross when he was upset, and he was greatly upset by all this. Last night he had whispered to her that there was a lot of violence in Castlebay, a sort of passion that was very destructive.

'It might cease now. Now that poor Gerry Doyle is dead,' Angela had said.

'No, it seems to be starting, what could have possessed that young fellow to do a thing like that. What could have been so bad that made him do it? And look at the caravan being burned out. I know that may not have anything to do with it, but it all seems very violent. All of a sudden.'

Angela said nothing. Some day she would know what it was all about.

Molly Power looked across at the O'Briens as they stood together. Agnes thin and frail always, her two sons beside her, Tom standing a bit back. That's all she had now, after rearing that huge family, two boys in England, that Chrissie married into the Byrne family. And Clare. Who knew what to make of Clare? Certainly her parents didn't; and Molly didn't. She looked over to where the girl was standing stiffly, her long hair blowing in the wind. A good dark coat, not that terrible duffle coat she used to live in at one time. She was a strange girl. No wonder David found it so hard to deal with her.

Father O'Dwyer knew how to bury the dead of his parish. He had been doing it for years. But the dead were never like this. The dead were old men and women who hadn't been able to survive a winter. Or someone who died tragically young leaving a family of small children. Occasionally the dead might be children – that was very hard, but there was something to say, about God taking innocent little souls to himself.

Paddy Power wondered what would Father O'Dwyer say to a congregation who knew what a life Gerry Doyle had lived, and that he had ended up by taking that life himself.

Dr Power had reminded himself only that morning that God was merciful: and if God was, then Father O'Dwyer must be also.

The priest looked around at the cold faces all spattered by the sea spray and whipped by the wind. He would not keep them long but he must keep them long enough to do honour to the dead man. Otherwise why have the ceremony at all?

'You all knew Gerry Doyle, and as we stand here around his grave and pray that his soul is in heaven with the angels we will all remember his love of life, and how he was involved in everything that went on in Castlebay . . .

'I think it's true that since this young man personified life, and youth and energy, his sudden death will make us realize once more what a very slight hold we have on our mortal lives, how easily they can be whipped away. While we pray for Gerry this morning, let us think of the briefness of our own lives. This time next year, not all of us who stand here now may be here, and in ten years' time, many more will have gone to their Maker. But it's not only the old and those who are ready to go, it's the young who are totally unprepared to face the kingdom of heaven, and who still have so much to say to each other and to their families and their friends.

'If Gerry Doyle had been given one more day there might have been many things he would wish to have said, things to put straight, people to reassure. But the Lord doesn't let us know the time He calls us. Everyone here has a cheerful memory of Gerry. Let us keep those memories in our hearts and pray that his soul is in heaven today, and will rise again on the Last Day.'

There were the last three hail marys and the glory be to the father and then Fiona leaned forward to raise the shovel of earth, the first one to fall on the coffin that had been lowered into the ground. She looked down into the big open grave.

'Thank you Gerry,' she said unexpectedly.

People were almost embarrassed, nobody ever spoke at a time like this, certainly nobody expected the quiet dignified Fiona to say anything so emotional. One by one the men shovelled on earth, filling up the dark hollow space.

This was the bleakest part of a funeral. The finishing touches. People huddled closer together almost unconsciously as if they were looking for some warmth from just being in a crowd.

Clare and David moved together. Partly because they were jostled, partly because they wanted to.

It was David's turn to take the spade in his hand. He paused and looked at Clare. Her glance was steady. She didn't turn away.

David dug into the heap of clay that lay beside the grave and heard it fall on to the earth that was already on top of Gerry's coffin. He took three steps back towards Clare, she had her hand out in its little knitted glove.

He took it and they both watched the gravediggers finish off the work that the parish had begun. Two tall bony men, they had it finished in no time. The two wreaths were put on the little mound. In a year they would put up a tombstone to Gerry Doyle, Born 1935, Died 1962, and passersby would shake their heads and say he died very young.

The people began to trickle down the hill, towards Craig's Bar some of them, some to Dillon's Hotel, others to open up their businesses which had been closed to honour Gerry Doyle.

A long time ago, back in Dublin when there had been a simple sort of life,

David used to take Clare's hand in its knitted glove and put it into his pocket for further warmth. He wondered did he dare do that now. Very gently he drew her hand towards him and she placed it in his pocket without him having to do anything.

They walked down the twisty road with the loose stones. Down the hill to Castlebay.